THE YEAR'S BEST
SCIENCE FICTION

ALSO BY GARDNER DOZOIS

ANTHOLOGIES

A Day in the Life
Another World
Best Science Fiction Stories of the Year, #6–10
The Best of Isaac Asimov's Science Fiction Magazine
Time-Travelers from Isaac Asimov's Science Fiction Magazine
Transcendental Tales from Isaac Asimov's Science Fiction Magazine
Isaac Asimov's Aliens
Isaac Asimov's Mars
Isaac Asimov's SF Lite
Isaac Asimov's War
Roads Not Taken (with Stanley Schmidt)
The Year's Best Science Fiction, #1–21
Future Earths: Under African Skies (with Mike Resnick)
Future Earths: Under South American Skies (with Mike Resnick)
Ripper! (with Susan Casper)
Modern Classic Short Novels of Science Fiction
Modern Classics of Fantasy
Killing Me Softly
Dying For It
The Good Old Stuff
The Good New Stuff
Explorers
The Furthest Horizon
Worldmakers
Supermen

COEDITED WITH SHEILA WILLIAMS

Isaac Asimov's Planet Earth
Isaac Asimov's Robots
Isaac Asimov's Valentines
Isaac Asimov's Skin Deep
Isaac Asimov's Ghosts
Isaac Asimov's Vampires
Isaac Asimov's Moons
Isaac Asimov's Christmas
Isaac Asimov's Camelot
Isaac Asimov's Werewolves
Isaac Asimov's Solar System
Isaac Asimov's Detectives
Isaac Asimov's Cyberdreams

COEDITED WITH JACK DANN

Aliens!
Unicorns!
Magicats!
Magicats 2!
Bestiary!
Mermaids!
Sorcerers!
Demons!
Dogtales!
Seaserpents!
Dinosaurs!
Little People!
Dragons!
Horses!
Unicorns 2
Invaders!
Angels!
Dinosaurs II
Hackers
Timegates
Clones
Nanotech
Immortals

FICTION

Strangers
The Visible Man (collection)
Nightmare Blue (with George Alec Effinger)
Slow Dancing Through Time (with Jack Dann, Michael Swanwick, Susan Casper, and Jack C. Haldeman II)
The Peacemaker
Geodesic Dreams (collection)

NONFICTION

The Fiction of James Tiptree Jr.

THE YEAR'S BEST
SCIENCE FICTION

twenty-second annual collection

edited by Gardner Dozois

st. martin's griffin ✦ new york

www.stmartins.com

ISBN 0-312-33659-4 (hc)
EAN 978-0-312-33659-2 (hc)
ISBN 0-312-33660-8 (pbk)
EAN 978-0-312-33660-8 (pbk)

FIRST EDITION: JULY 2005

10 9 8 7 6 5 4 3 2 1

acknowledgment is made for permission to reprint the following materials:

"Inappropriate Behavior," by Pat Murphy. Copyright © 2004 by SCIFI.COM. First published electronically on *SCI FICTION*, February 11, 2004. Reprinted by permission of the author.

"Start the Clock," by Benjamin Rosenbaum. Copyright © 2004 by Spilogale, Inc. First published in *The Magazine of Fantasy & Science Fiction*, August 2004. Reprinted by permission of the author.

"The Third Party," by David Moles. Copyright © 2004 by Dell Magazines. First published in *Asimov's Science Fiction*, September 2004. Reprinted by permission of the author.

"The Voluntary State," by Christopher Rowe. Copyright © 2004 by SCIFI.COM. First published electronically on *SCI FICTION*, May 5, 2004. Reprinted by permission of the author.

"Shiva in Shadow," by Nancy Kress. Copyright © 2004 by Nancy Kress. First published in *Between Worlds* (Science Fiction Book Club), edited by Robert Silverberg. Reprinted by permission of the author.

"The People of Sand and Slag," by Paolo Bacigalupi. Copyright © 2004 by Spilogale, Inc. First published in *The Magazine of Fantasy & Science Fiction*, February 2003. Reprinted by permission of the author.

"The Clapping Hands of God," by Michael F. Flynn. Copyright © 2004 by Dell Magazines. First published in *Analog Science Fiction and Fact*, July/August 2004. Reprinted by permission of the author.

"Tourism," by M. John Harrison. Copyright © 2004 by M. John Harrison. First published electronically on *Amazon.com*, August 2004. Reprinted by permission of the author.

"Scout's Honor," by Terry Bisson. Copyright © 2004 by SCIFI.COM. First published electronically on *SCI FICTION*, January 28, 2004. Reprinted by permission of the author.

"Men Are Trouble," by James Patrick Kelly. Copyright © 2004 by Dell Magazines. First published in *Asimov's Science Fiction*, June 2004. Reprinted by permission of the author.

"Mother Aegypt," by Kage Baker. Copyright © 2004 by Kage Baker. First published in *Mother Aegypt and Other Stories* (Night Shade). Reprinted by permission of the author.

"Synthetic Serendipity," by Vernor Vinge. Copyright © 2004 by Vernor Vinge. First published electronically on *IEEESpectrumonline*, July 31, 2004.

"Skin Deep," by Mary Rosenblum. Copyright © 2004 by Dell Magazines. First published in *Asimov's Science Fiction*, October/November 2004. Reprinted by permission of the author.

"Delhi," by Vandana Singh. Copyright © 2004 by Vandana Singh. First published in *So Long Been Dreaming: Postcolonial Science Fiction & Fantasy* (Arsenal Pulp Press), edited by Nalo Hopkinson and Uppinder Mehan. Reprinted by permission of the author.

contents

acknowledgments

The editor would like to thank the following people for their help and support: Susan Casper, Ellen Datlow, Gordon Van Gelder, Peter Crowther, Nicolas Gevers, David Pringle, Andy Cox, Marty Halpern, Gary Turner, Lou Anders, Eileen Gunn, Nisi Shawl, Mike Resnick, Cory Doctorow, Vernor Vinge, M. John Harrison, Robert E. Howe, Darrell Schweitzer, Susan Marie Groppi, Karen Meisner, Jed Hartman, Richard Freeburn, Patrick Swenson, Bridget McKenna, Marti McKenna, Jay Lake, Deborah Layne, Edward J. McFadden, Sheila Williams, Brian Bieniowski, Trevor Quachri, Jayme Lynn Blascke, Lou Antonelli, Paul Melko, Mark Rudolph, Tehani Croft, Zara Baxter, Allan Price, Andrew Finch, Stuart Barrow, Robbie Matthews, David Hartwell, Warren Lapin, Roelf Goudriaan, Bob Neilson, David Murphy, John O'Neill, Kelly Link, Gavin Grant, Gordon Lilnzer, Gerard Houarner, Guy Hasson, David Lee Summers, Diane L. Walton, Linn Prentis, Vaughne Lee Hansen, Shawna McCarthy, Rich Horton, Mark R. Kelly, Jonathan Strahan, Mark Watson, Michael Swanwick, and special thanks to my own editor, Marc Resnick.

Thanks are also due to Charles N. Brown, whose magazine *Locus* (Locus Publications, P.O. Box 13305, Oakland, CA 94661. $52 for a one-year subscription [twelve issues] via second class; credit card orders call 510-339-9198) was used as an invaluable reference source throughout the Summation; *Locus Online* (www.locusmag.com), edited by Mark R. Kelly, has also become a key reference source. Thanks are also due to John Douglas and Warren Lapine of *Science Fiction Chronicle* (DNA Publications, Inc., P.O. Box 2988, Radford, VA 24143-2988, $45 for a one-year/twelve-issue subscription via second class), which was also used as a reference source throughout.

summation: 2004

In spite of the fact that some people have been sitting by the graveside impatiently waiting for SF to "die" for the entire twenty-first century, to date the genre actually seems to be in pretty good shape, both commercially and artistically, with the total number of books published going up, not down. Many SF titles are selling well, new SF lines are coming into existence, and the old established ones are looking pretty solid (only the troubled magazine market seems to be really hurting).

If anything, the market is *expanding*, not contracting, at least at the small-press level. Lou Anders, former editor of *Argosy*, is starting an ambitious new SF line for Prometheus Publishing, called Pyr Books. Mike Resnick has been named executive editor of BenBella Books and is starting new lines there of SF and SF–related nonfiction. Red Deer Press of Calgary launched a new SF imprint called Robert J. Sawyer Books, edited by Sawyer himself. Newly named editor in chief of Phobos Books, John J. Ordover, is expanding the SF line there as well. MonkeyBrain Press is also bringing out a new line of genre-related nonfiction titles.

Young Adult fantasy and SF lines also keep proliferating. Wizards of the Coast is launching a new YA fantasy line called Mirrorstone; Penguin is launching Razorbill; Abram's Books for Young Readers is bringing us Amulet; Bloomsbury USA is launching Bloomsbury Paperbacks; and Houghton Mifflin is starting Graphia.

(In other editorial news, Jennifer Hershey has moved to Random House, where she's become editorial director, and Sharyn November has been promoted to editorial director of Firebird Books, although she will still continue as senior editor of Viking Children's/Puffin Books.)

The year 2004 also saw the opening of the Science Fiction Museum and Hall of Fame in Seattle, Washington, the first major museum devoted to science fiction in the entire world.

The major, wide-sweeping changes in the nature of publishing itself that have been hanging over the horizon for quite a while now seemed to inch a bit closer to reality this year as well. For a number of years, the more wide-eyed and enthusiastic cyberoptimists have been predicting industrywide changes driven by such technological innovations as "smart paper," better and cheaper e-books, and instant "print on demand" printing of books in bookstores. In fact, these changes have been predicted for so long that they have become a joke to some Luddite critics. But that doesn't mean they're not still coming, although everything takes a lot longer to actually come into widespread social use than the visionaries initially predicted. Not too many years back, when Amazon.com had yet to run into the black, critics were laughing at it and other online booksellers, saying they were a fad that would never last, but today the online booksellers are an established and rapidly expanding part of the book industry. Penguin Group USA has even started selling all of its titles directly to customers via its own Web sites. The commercial potential of e-books was widely dismissed after the dot.com bubble burst, but there are signs that this industry may be reviving as well; certainly the e-book-selling site *Fictionwise*, which the more cynical industry insiders were predicting wouldn't last a year, still seems to be going strong. Sales of electronic subscriptions and downloads for PDA through sites like *PeanutPress* are increasing as well.

The future may take longer to arrive than you think that it will, but sooner or later it gets here, notwithstanding.

In 2004 circulation continued declining slowly for most in the ailing magazine market—throughout the entire magazine industry, in fact, way outside of genre boundaries—but at least, as of press time, we hadn't lost any major markets, knock wood (although it looked for a minute, however, as if we were going to; see below). Some new magazines were even started, although many of them immediately ran into difficulties of their own. (See the summations for the *Twenty-First, Twentieth, Nineteenth*, and *Eighteenth* annual collections for more about the technical reasons behind the decline in circulation and how it has affected nearly every magazine in the country, not just genre titles; I get tired of rehashing the same material, especially as, judging by the questions I get asked at conventions and online forums, nobody is listening anyway.)

Asimov's Science Fiction registered an 8.9 percent loss in overall circulation in 2004, gaining 995 in new subscriptions, from 22,933 to 23,933 (miniscule, but a gain nevertheless), but losing 3,732 in newsstand sales, dropping from 7,668 to 3,936, and sell-through dropped from 60 percent to 34 percent. *Analog Science Fiction & Fact* registered an 18 percent loss in overall circulation in 2004, losing 3,899 in subscriptions, from 31,715 to 27,816, while newsstand sales declined by 3,427, falling from 8,883 to 5,456, and sell-through dropped from a record 61 percent to 50 percent. *The Magazine of Fantasy & Science Fiction* registered a 11.8 percent loss in overall circulation, losing 1,529 in subscriptions, from 16,562 to 15,033, while newsstand sales declined by 995, from 4,881 to 3,886, and sell-through fell from 44 percent to 40 percent. No current circulation figures were available for *Realms of Fantasy* by press time, but their 2003 figures shows them dropping from 20,541 in 2002 to 18,337 in 2003 in subscriptions, but rising from 5,472 to 8,995 in newsstand sales for an overall gain of 5.1 percent.

Nobody likes to see these kinds of figures, but they don't necessarily, mean that the genre magazines are doomed; there's a lot of built-in margin, including the fact that digest-sized magazines are so cheap to produce that you don't have to sell many of them to break even. Nevertheless, these kinds of losses can't go on indefinitely without leading sooner or later to disaster. The next couple of years will be critical for the genre magazines, which must somehow not only stop their slow decline but also turn it around and rebuild circulation if they are to survive. That's why I'm urging all readers to take the time to *subscribe* to one of the genre magazines if they like having a lot of short SF and fantasy out there to read every year. It's never been easier to subscribe to most of the genre magazines because you can now do it electronically online with the click of a few buttons, without even a trip to the mailbox. Don't procrastinate—just put this book down right now and go to your computer and *do* it!

In the Internet age, you can subscribe from overseas just as easily as you can from the United States, something formerly difficult to impossible. Internet sites such as

Peanut Press (www.peanutpress.com) and Fictionwise (www.fictionwise.com), sell electronic downloadable versions of the magazines to be read on your PDA or home computer, which is becoming increasingly popular with the computer-savvy set. Therefore, I'm going to list the URLs for those magazines that have Web sites: *Asimov's* site is at www.asimovs.com. *Analog*'s site is at www.analogsf.com. *The Magazine of Fantasy & Science Fiction*'s site is at www.sfsite.com/fsf.

There were some other big changes in the magazine market this year. The longtime editor of *Asimov's Science Fiction*, Gardner Dozois, stepped back from his full-time role to take a consulting editor job with the magazine instead, freeing up time to pursue other interests. The new editor is Sheila Williams, moving up from her longtime role as executive editor; the changeover is official as of the January 2005 issue, when Dozois's name came off the masthead and Williams' name went on. The British magazine *Interzone* has been going through chaotic times as well, missing issues and demonstrating all the signs of being a magazine in trouble; at last, in the spring of 2004, longtime editor David Pringle, who'd run *Interzone* for twenty-two years, stepped down to deal with personal difficulties. For a while it looked like the magazine might die, but Andy Cox, editor and publisher of *The Third Alternative*, came to the rescue, buying the magazine, which will continue under the TTA Press umbrella as a sister magazine to *The Third Alternative*. The new *Interzone* is trying for a slicker, more contemporary look, more like the graphics and design in *The Third Alternative* than those of the old magazine, and has also grown slightly in size to match its new sister. The first TTA issue of *Interzone* was something of a mess, with interior design and layout that made it almost impossible to read the text in some places, but this problem has been straightened out to some extent in subsequent issues. I didn't like the first two TTA covers, which struck me as murky and bland, generic cyberpunk, but the cover of the most recent issue, featuring a giant woman in a skin-tight spacesuit striding across the landscape, is probably a lot more effective in "popping" from the newsstand. Andy Cox is to be congratulated for saving this grand old lady, long the flagship of British science fiction, but I hope that he doesn't entirely lose the old *Interzone* regulars such as Alastair Reynolds, Dominic Green, Eric Brown, and Greg Egan in the transition; to date, most of the Cox *Interzones* have featured largely the same crew that sells to *The Third Alternative*. The magazine was a little weaker than usual this year, but there was good stuff in both the final Pringle issues and the new Cox issues from Alastair Reynolds, Dominic Green, Liz Williams, Jay Lake (so prolific that he seemed to be *everywhere* in the semiprozine market this year), Karen Fishler, Michael T. Jasper, and others.

Amazing Stories came back to life yet again in 2004, a Lazarus trick it's performed a number of times in the past, reincarnating itself this time as a slick, glossy, large-format magazine with media images on the cover. There was too much emphasis on media and gaming for my old-fashioned tastes, and too much of what fiction they did run was short *Twilight Zone*–ish twist-ending stuff. But they did feature some good work, especially a story by James Van Pelt, as well as stories by Paul Di Filippo and Bruce Sterling, and there were interesting interviews with George R. R. Martin, Frederick Pohl, and others. *Amazing Stories* started out being edited by David Gross, but in midyear he stepped down to be replaced as editor by Jeff Berkwitz. A couple of 2005–dated issues appeared, and then the publishers announced, rather mysteriously, that the magazine was going "on hiatus" because it had been "too successful." No one is quite sure what this actually means, but, in my experience, magazines that go on hiatus seldom return from it, so this may well be a very bad sign.

(Subscription addresses for the professional magazines follow: ***The Magazine of Fantasy & Science Fiction***, Spilogale, Inc., P.O. Box 3447, Hoboken, NJ 07030, annual subscription—$44.89 in the U.S.; ***Asimov's Science Fiction***, Dell Magazines, 6 Prowitt Street, Norwalk, CT 06855—$43.90 for annual subscription in U.S. ***Analog Science Fiction and Fact***, Dell Magazines, 6 Prowitt Street, Norwalk, CT 06855—$43.90 for annual subscription in the U.S.; ***Interzone***, 217 Preston Drove, Brighton BN1 6FL, UK, $65 for an airmail one-year [twelve issues] subscription; ***Realms of Fantasy***, Sovereign Media Co. Inc., P.O. Box 1623, Williamsport, PA 17703—$16.95 for an annual subscription in the U.S.; ***Amazing Stories***, www.paizo.com/amazing.)

Turning to the increasingly important Internet scene, it shouldn't come as a surprise to anyone by this point that some of the best stories of the year appeared on Ellen Datlow's *SCI FICTION* (www.scifi.com/scifiction) page on the Internet, including stories by Pat Murphy, Christopher Rowe, Terry Bisson, Robert Reed, George R. R. Martin, Daniel Abraham, Michaela Roessner, Walter Jon Williams, Mary Rosenblum, Alex Irvine, Howard Waldrop, and others. This is still the best place on the Internet to find good professional-level science fiction, although they also publish a lot of horror, fantasy, and hard-to-classify slipstreamish stuff. Eileen Gunn's *The Infinite Matrix* (www.infinitematrix.net) hung on for another year, although in a somewhat diminished state due to budget problems, but there was still a lot of interesting, quirky stuff to read there, including columns by Howard Waldrop, David Langford, and John Clute, stories by Karen D. Fishler, Leslie What, and others, and a whole archive of good stuff from previous years. *Strange Horizons* (www.strangehorizons.com) continues to "publish" (we really do need a new term for this!) a lot of good professional-level stuff, although very little of it is science fiction. The majority of it is fantasy, slipstream, and soft horror, including, this year, worthwhile work by Vandana Singh, Liz Williams, Brenda Cooper, Ellen Klages, Daniel Starr, Kate Bachus, Bill Kte'pi, and others. I'd sure like to see them publish more science fiction, though, especially rigorous hard SF, which isn't a description that can really be applied even to the few SF stories that do appear on the site. On the other hand, *Oceans of the Mind* (www.trantorpublications.com/oceans.htm), which is available by electronic subscription, publishes mostly core science fiction, with only the occasional slip into something else. Overall quality here seemed a bit lower than last year, but they still featured interesting stuff by Russell Blackford, Mark W. Tiedeman, Paul Marlowe, K. D. Wentworth, and others. New electronic magazines continue to proliferate like (what's a polite metaphor? Like flies? Like maggots?) like quickly proliferating things on the Internet, and many of them won't last out the year ahead. One new electronic magazine that is already operating on a reliable professional level of quality, though, and that seems quite promising, is *Aeon*, whose first issue this year featured an almost novel-length story by Walter Jon Williams, plus strong work by John Meaney, Jay Lake, Lori Ann White, and others.

And SF stories continued to spread across the Internet, appearing in places where it wouldn't seem intuitively logical to look for them. *Salon* (www.salon.com), for instance, now features several SF stories per year, including, this year, strong stories by Cory Doctorow, D. William Shunn, Alex Irvine, and others. Stories, including a few of the year's best, also showed up in such peculiar places as the Web site of an organization of electrical engineers (Vernor Vinge's "Synthetic Serendipity") and as, of all things, an *advertisement* for a novel being sold on Amazon.com (M. John Harrison's "Tourism")!

There are *also* lots of sites that feature mostly slipstream and soft horror, among the best of which are *Revolution SF* (www.revolutionsf.com), which, although not always of reliable professional quality, did feature interesting stuff this year from Steven Utley, Lou Antonelli, Danith McPherson, and others; *Fortean Bureau—A Magazine of Speculative Fiction* (www.forteanbureau.com/index.html), which featured quirky stuff this year from Greg Beatty, Bill Kte'pi, Paul Melko, Jay Lake, Tobias S. Buckell, and others; *Abyss and Apex: A Magazine of Speculative Fiction* (www.klio.net/abyssandapex); *Ideomancer Speculative Fiction* (www.ideomancer.com); *Futurismic* (www.futurismic.com/fiction/index.html), and *Bewildering Stories* (www.bewilderingstories.com).

After this point, although good original SF and fantasy becomes somewhat scarce, there's still a lot of good *reprint* SF and fantasy stories out there to be found. Most of the sites that are associated with existent print magazines, such as *Asimov's*, *Analog*, *The Magazine of Fantasy & Science Fiction*, *Aurealis*, and others, have extensive archives of material, both fiction and nonfiction, previously published by the print versions of the magazines, and some of them regularly run teaser excerpts from stories coming up in forthcoming issues; *SCI FICTION* also has a substantial archive of "classic reprints," as do *The Infinite Matrix* and *Strange Horizons*. The British *Infinity Plus* (www.users.zetnet.co.uk/iplus), also has a wide selection of good-quality reprint stories, in addition to biographical and bibliographical information, book reviews, interviews, and critical essays. As long as you're willing to read it on a computer screen, all of this stuff is available to be read for free.

An even greater range of reprint stories becomes available for a small fee, though. One of the best such sites is *Fictionwise* (www.fictionwise.com), a place where you can buy downloadable e-books and stories to read on your PDA or home computer. In addition to individual stories, you can also buy "fiction bundles" here, which amount to electronic collections, as well as a selection of novels in several different genres; more important to *me*, you can also subscribe to downloadable versions of several of the SF magazines here—including *Asimov's Science Fiction*—in a number of different formats (as you can at the Peanut Press site). *ElectricStory* (www.electricstory.com) is a similar site, but here, in addition to the downloadable stuff (both stories and novels) that you can buy, you can also access free movie reviews by Lucius Shepard, articles by Howard Waldrop, and other critical material. Access for a small fee to both original and reprint SF stories is also offered by sites such as *Mind's Eye Fiction* (tale.com/genres.htm), and *Alexandria Digital Literature* (alexlit.com) as well.

Reading fiction is not the only reason to go online, though. There's also a large cluster of general-interest sites that publish lots of interviews, critical articles, reviews, and genre-oriented news of various kinds. Perhaps the most valuable genre-oriented sites on the entire Internet, and one I check nearly every day, is *Locus Online* (www.locusmag.com), the online version of the news magazine *Locus*; not only do you get fast-breaking news here (in fact, this is often the first place in the entire genre where important stories break), but you can also access an incredible amount of information, including book reviews, critical lists, obituary lists, links to reviews and essays appearing outside the genre, and links to extensive and invaluable database archives such as the Locus Index to Science Fiction and the Locus Index to Science Fiction Awards. Other essential sites include: *Science Fiction Weekly* (www.scifi.com/sfw), more media-and-gaming oriented than *Locus Online*, but still featuring news and book reviews, as well as regular columns by John Clute, Michael Cassut, and Wil McCarthy; *Tangent Online* (www.tangentonline.com), which changed editors again in late 2004 and looked like it was going to die for a while, but which has recovered under a new editor, and still is publishing a lot of short-fiction reviews; *Best SF* (www.bestsf.net/), another great review site, and one of the few places, along with *Tangent Online*, that makes any attempt to regularly review online fiction as well as print fiction; *SFRevu* (www.sfsite.com/sfrevu), a review site that specializes in media and novel reviews; the *Sci-Fi Channel* (www.scifi.com), which provides a home for Ellen Datlow's *SCI FICTION* and for *Science Fiction Weekly*, and to the bimonthly SF–oriented chats hosted by *Asimov's* and *Analog*, as well as vast amounts of material about SF movies and TV shows; the *SF Site* (www.sfsite.com), which not only features an extensive selection of reviews of books, games, and magazines, interviews, critical retrospective articles, letters, and so forth, plus a huge archive of past reviews; but also serves as host site for the Web pages of *The Magazine of Fantasy & Science Fiction* and *Interzone*; SFF NET (www.sff.net), which features dozens of home pages and "newsgroups" for SF writers, plus sites for genre-oriented "live chats"; the *Science Fiction Writers of America* page (www.sfwa.org), where news, obituaries, award information, and recommended reading lists can be accessed; and *Audible* (www.audible.com) and *Beyond 2000* (www.beyond2000.com), where SF–oriented radio plays can be accessed. New review sites include *The Internet Review of Science Fiction* (www.irosf.com), which features L. Blunt Jackson's short-fiction reviews as well as critical articles, and *Lost Pages* (lostpagesindex.html), which features some fiction as well as the critical stuff. Multiple-Hugo-winner David Langford's online version of his funny and iconoclastic fanzine *Ansible* is available at www.dcs.gla.ac.uk/Ansible, and *Speculations* (www.speculations.com) is a long-running site that dispenses writing advice, writing-oriented news, and gossip (although to access most of it, you'll have to subscribe to the site).

Things change *fast* in the Internet world, though, so a lot of this information may already be obsolete by the time you read it. The only way to be sure what sites of genre interest are out there is to fire up your computer and go look for yourself.

It wasn't a particularly good year in the semiprozine market, with even many long-established magazines only managing to produce one issue, although some promising new magazines were born and joined their older brethren in struggling to survive.

Absolute Magnitude, The Magazine of Science Fiction Adventures, Fantastic Stories of the Imagination, Weird Tales, the newszine *Chronicle* (formerly *Science Fiction Chronicle*), and the all-vampire-fiction magazine *Dreams of Decadence*, with titles consolidated under the umbrella of Warren Lapine's DNA Publications, suffered another year of being unable to keep anywhere near to their announced publishing schedules this year, with the exception of *Chronicle*; *Absolute Magnitude, The Magazine of Science Fiction Adventures*, and *Fantastic Stories of the Imagination* only managed one issue apiece, and even *Weird Tales*, which until now had been pretty reliable in meeting its schedule, only managed three issues out of a scheduled four. Circulation figures are not available for the DNA magazines, so it's impossible to say how well or how poorly they're doing.

I saw no issues this year of *Century*, *Eidolon*, *Orb*, *Altair*, *Terra Incognita*, or *Spectrum SF*, which are all probably dead. I also saw no issues of *Artemis Magazine: Science and Fiction for a Space-Faring Society*, *Neo-Opsis*, and *Jupiter*, although whether these magazines were still active was unclear. There was only one issue of the Irish fiction semiprozine *Albedo One* this year, one of *Tales of the Unanticipated*, one of the Sword & Sorcery magazine *Black Gate*, one of the fantasy magazine *Alchemy*, one of the long-running *Space and Time*, one of the flagship of the slipstream movement, *Lady Churchill's Rosebud Wristlet*, and one of the similarly slipstreamish *Say . . .* (here each issue has a different title, such as this year's *Say . . . why aren't we crying?*). *Electric Velocipede*, *Flytrap*, *Full-Unit Hookup: A Magazine of Exceptional Literature*, *Talebones: The Magazine of Science Fiction and Dark Fantasy*, *Hadrosaur Tales*, the new "Alternate History" magazine *Paradox*, and the long-running Australian semiprozine *Aurealis* all brought out two issues apiece this year (although the most recent *Aurealis* arrived here after the end of the year, so we'll consider it for next time). Of these, some of the best stuff was to be found in *Talebones*, which featured good stories this year by Paul Melko, David D. Levine, Devon Monk, and others, and in *Electric Velocipede*, which featured good work by William Shunn, Jay Lake, Chris Roberson, Christopher Rowe, Liz Williams, and others.

The most vigorous of the fiction semiprozines, judging by how well they meet their production schedules, anyway, seem to be *The Third Alternative*, the leading British semiprozine, long-running Canadian semiprozine *On Spec*, and the cheeky new Australian semiprozine, *Andromeda Spaceways Inflight Magazine*. Of these, by far the best in terms of literary quality is *The Third Alternative*; although the stories, which run to slipstream and dark, surreal, understated horror, are not always to my taste, they're almost always extremely well written line by line, and the magazine attracts some of the best talent in the business; good stuff appeared here this year by Tim Lees, John Grant, Karen Fishler, Jay Lake, Susan Fry, Tim Pratt, Vandana Singh, and others. A superficial description of *On Spec*—little science fiction, lots of slipstream and soft horror—makes it sound very similar to *The Third Alternative*, but somehow there's a discernible difference in tone; the stuff in *The Third Alternative* is more sophisticated and more elegant, and somehow *On Spec* comes across as "gloomy" rather than "dark." This gray gloominess seems to be something that a lot of Canadian publications take pride in—the subscription ad for *On Spec* even boasts that "Nobody does dark like Canadians!", although I'm not sure they really ought to be boasting about that—and I think it might be good for them to lighten up a bit. The covers here were great, as usual, but often more evocative than the fiction, although interesting stuff by Karen Traviss, A. M. Dellamonica, Jack Skillingstead, E. I. Chin, and others. *Andromeda Spaceways Inflight Magazine* runs mostly science fiction, but often not stuff at a terribly high level of professionalism, and there's an (I feel) misguided emphasis on "humorous" pieces here, something that's hard to do well; the fact that the magazine is edited by someone different every issue, one of a group of rotating editors, also makes it difficult to maintain a level of quality from issue to issue. The best stuff here this year, in my opinion, was the more "serious" and less jokey stories by Stephen Dedman, Mark W. Tiedmann, Liz Williams, Colin P. Davies, and others (unlike *On Spec*, they could *darken* a shade or two, or at least become more substantial).

Two very promising new fiction semiprozines debuted in 2004, one American and one British, *Argosy* and *Postscripts* respectively. *Argosy*, one of the handsomest and most expensive-looking semiprozines ever published—with a gorgeous cover by the Dillons, perhaps the most prestigious artists ever to produce a semiprozine cover—came out in a package of two shrink-wrapped volumes in a slipcase, each package containing a "regular" issue of the magazine and a separately bound novella. The buzz about *Argosy* was immediate, widespread, and intense, probably the most buzz any semiprozine launch had garnered in the industry since the launch of *Century*, and it seemed clearly headed for success—but then it hit a roadblock. The chain bookstores objected to its unusual format, supposedly because they didn't know how to shelve it (the same thing that killed the Tor Doubles in the eighties), and refused to carry it. Intense warfare broke out behind the scenes between *Argosy*'s publisher and the chains. By the time the second edition came out (in two different versions, a "connoisseur edition" with the slipcase and the novella, and a "proletariat" edition consisting of just the "regular" magazine), editor Lou Anders had left *Argosy* to launch the new Pyr SF line for Prometheus Books, and the third issue did not come out as scheduled; as months went by without it, the future of the magazine began to look questionable. Toward the end of the year, an announcement was made that the third issue of *Argosy* was about to ship—although by press time we hadn't seen it yet. The announcement was also unclear about whether *Argosy* would be continuing after that, or who the editor would be if it did (Anders presumably bought the stuff for the third issue). In the two issues it managed in 2004, *Argosy* published good work by Caitlin R. Kiernan, Jeffery Ford, Charles Stross, Cory Doctorow, Benjamin Rosenbaum, Mike Resnick, and others. The British *Postscripts*, although still a good-looking magazine, is nowhere nearly as upscale or ambitious in its packaging as *Argosy*, which is probably a good thing, as it may increase its chances of survival. It publishes a mix of SF, slipstream, soft horror, and even some mystery, and in the two issues it produced this year produced good stuff by Peter F. Hamilton, Brian Stableford, Eric Brown, Jack Dann, Jay Lake, Jeff VanderMeer, and others. Let's hope that *Postscripts* can stay afloat in the treacherous seas of the semiprozine market, because, produced as it is by two of the sharpest people in the business, Peter Crowther and Nick Gevers, its potential is enormous.

I don't follow the horror semiprozine market anymore, so I'll limit myself to saying that among the most prominent magazines there, as far as I can tell at a distance, seems to be the highly respected *Cemetery Dance*, *Weird Tales*, and *Talebones*, and that a new horror magazine edited by Marvin Kaye, *H. P. Lovecraft's Magazine of Horror*, was launched this year and managed two issues, publishing interesting stories by Holly Phillips, Tim Pratt, and Michael Jasper; *Weird Tales* provided intriguing stories by Tanith Lee, Charles Harness, and Ian Watson.

There are only a few survivors left in the critical magazine market (most new critical magazines that start up these days do so in e-magazine form, not in print formats, a trend I expect to see continue), but those still left standing are solid and reliable. If you can only afford one magazine in this category, then the one to get, as always, is *Locus: The Magazine of the Science Fiction and Fantasy Field*, an indispensable source of information, news, and reviews for anyone interested in science fiction, particularly valuable for writers and would-be writers; new editor Jennifer A. Hall left this year, with former editor Charles N. Brown coming out of semi-retirement to replace her. After a couple of shaky years, when it was missing issues, new(ish) editor

John Douglas has returned *Chronicle* (formerly *Science Fiction Chronicle*) to being a solid, interesting, reliably published newsmagazine again. Another reliably published magazine, one that has reliably kept its publication schedule for more than a decade now (something of a miracle in the semiprozine world!) is David G. Hartwell's eclectic critical magazine, *The New York Review of Science Fiction*, probably the most accessible and entertaining to read of the critical magazines, some of which can get formidably abstract and scholarly. The people who put out *The Third Alternative* were publishing a short-fiction review magazine called *The Fix*, but I didn't see any issues this year (which, of course, considering it's published on the other side of the Atlantic, doesn't necessarily mean that they aren't still doing it).

I suspect that the destiny of most print semiprozines is to eventually become online e-magazines, just as print fanzines have largely been replaced by the blog. That doesn't mean you can't enjoy them while they're here, though!

(***Locus, The Magazine of the Science Fiction & Fantasy Field***, Locus Publications, Inc., P.O. Box 13305, Oakland, CA 94661, $60 for a one-year first-class subscription, 12 issues; ***The New York Review of Science Fiction***, Dragon Press, P.O. Box 78, Pleasantville, NY, 10570, $36 per year, make checks payable to "Dragon Press," 12 issues; ***Postscripts***, PS Publishing, Hamilton House, 4 Park Avenue, Harrogate HG2 9BQ, England, UK, published quarterly, £30 to £50, outside the UK; ***Argosy Magazine***, Coppervale International, P.O. Box 1421, Taylor, AZ, 85939, $49.95 for a six-issue subscription; ***Interzone***, TTA Press, 5 Martins Lane, Witcham, Ely, Cambs CB6 2LB, England, UK, $36 for a six-issue subscription, make checks payable to "TTA Press"; ***The Third Alternative***, TTA Press, 5 Martins Lane, Witcham, Ely, Cambs. CB6 2LB, England, UK, $36 for a six-issue subscription, checks made payable to "TTA Press"; ***The Fix: The Review of Short Fiction***, 5 Martins Lane, Witcham, Ely, Cambs. CB6 2LB, England, UK, $36 for a six-issue subscription, checks made payable to "TTA Press"; ***Talebones, A Magazine of Science Fiction & Dark Fantasy***, 5203 Quincy Ave SE, Auburn, WA 98092, $20 for four issues; ***On Spec, The Canadian Magazine of the Fantastic***, P.O. Box 4727, Edmonton, AB, Canada T6E 5G6, $22 for a one-year (four-issue) subscription; ***Neo-Opsis Science Fiction Magazine***, 4129 Carey Rd., Victoria, BC, V8Z 4G5, $24.00 Canadian for a four-issue subscription; ***Jupiter***, Ian Redman, 23 College Green, Yeovil, Somerset, BA21 4JR, UK, £9 for a four-issue subscription; ***Aurealis, the Australian Magazine of Fantasy and Science Fiction***, Chimaera Publications, P.O. Box 2164, Mt. Waverley, Victoria 3149, Australia, $50 for a four-issue overseas airmail subscription, "all cheques and money orders must be made out to Chimarea Publications in Australian dollars"; ***Albedo***, Albedo One Productions, 2 Post Road, Lusk, Co., Dublin, Ireland; $25 for a four-issue airmail subscription, make checks payable to "Albedo One"; ***Pirate Writings, Tales of Fantasy, Mystery & Science Fiction***, ***Absolute Magnitude. The Magazine of Science Fiction Adventures***, ***Aboriginal Science Fiction***, ***Weird Tales***, ***Dreams of Decadence***, ***Chronicle***—all available from DNA Publications, P.O. Box 2988, Radford, VA 24142-2988, all available for $16 for a one-year subscription, although you can get a group subscription to four DNA fiction magazines for $60 a year, with ***Chronicle*** $45 a year (12 issues), all checks payable to "D.N.A. Publications"; ***Tales of the Unanticipated***, Box 8036, Lake Street Station, Minneapolis, MN 55408, $15 for a four-issue subscription; ***Artemis Magazine: Science and Fiction for a Space-Faring Society***, LRC Publications, 1380 E. 17th St., Suite 201, Brooklyn New York 11230-6011, $15 for a four-issue subscription, checks payable to LRC Publications; ***Lady***

Churchill's Rosebud Wristlet, Small Beer Press, 176 Prospect Avenue, Northampton, Massachusetts 01060, $16 for four issues; ***Say . . .***, The Fortress of Worlds, P.O. Box 1304, Lexington, KY 40588-1304. $10 for two issues in the U.S and Canada; ***Alchemy***, Edgewood Press, P.O. Box 380264, Cambridge, MA 02238, $7 for an issue; ***Full Unit Hookup: A Magazine of Exceptional Literature***, Conical Hats Press, 622 West Cottom Avenue, New Albany, IN 47150-5011, $12 for a three-issue subscription; ***Flytrap***, Tropism Press, P.O. Box 13322, Berkeley, CA 94712-4222, $16 for four issues, checks to Heather Shaw; ***Andromeda Spaceways Inflight Magazine***, P.O. Box 127, Belmont, Western Australia, 6984, $35 for a one-year subscription; ***Hadrosaur Tales***, P.O. Box 2194, Mesilla Park, NM 88047-2194, $16.50 for a three-issue subscription, make checks payable to "Hadrosaur Productions"; ***Electric Velocipede***, $15 for a four-issue subscription—it seems like you can only order this online, so for more subscription information, check their website at www.members.aol.com/evzine/index.html; ***Space and Time: The Magazine of Fantasy, Horror, and Science Fiction*** Space and Time, 138 West 70th Street (4B), New York, NY 10023-4468, $10 for a one-year (two-issue) subscription; ***Black Gate***, New Epoch Press, 815 Oak Street, St. Charles, IL 60174, $29.95 for a one-year (four issue) subscription; ***Paradox***, Paradox Publications, P.O. Box 22897, Brooklyn, New York 11202-2897, $15 for a one-year (four-issue) subscription, ***Cemetery Dance***, CD Publications, 132-B Industry Lane, Unit #7, Forest Hill, MD 21050, $27 for six issues; ***H.P. Lovecraft's Magazine of Horror***, Wildside Press LLC, P.O. Box 301, Holicong, PA 18928-0301, four issues for $19.95.)

It wasn't a bad year overall for original anthologies, with one major SF and one major fantasy anthology; as for the rest of year's anthologies, most of them may have contained only a few really good stories apiece, but there were a *lot* of them published, especially in SF, an encouraging sign.

The best original SF anthology of the year was undoubtedly *Between Planets* (SFBC), edited by Robert Silverberg, a collection of six original novellas, only available as a selection of the Science Fiction Book Club. The best stories here are those by Nancy Kress, Walter Jon Williams, and James Patrick Kelly, but nothing in the anthology is less than good, and I would expect to see most of these novellas (the others are by Stephen Baxter, Mike Resnick, and Silverberg himself) turn up on one Best Stories of the Year list or another. (As an old dinosaur, solidly retro and uncool in his tastes, it struck me as a nice change to see an anthology that featured nothing *but* solid, center-core SF instead of the trendy genre-bending and mixing that many of the year's other anthologies attempted to one extent or another.)

It's harder to come up with a clear follow-up candidate for best original SF anthology, although all the anthologies I'm about to mention are worth reading. *Synergy SF: New Science Fiction* (Five Star), edited by George Zebrowski, and *Microcosms* (DAW), edited by Gregory Benford, are both anthologies that have spent several years on the shelf in publishing limbo before finally being published (since 1996 in *Synergy's* case!), and it shows to some extent. Still, *Synergy SF* features an excellent novelette by Eleanor Arnason and good work by Charles L. Harness, Damien Broderick, Jan Lars Jensen, and others, and *Microcosms* features a first-rate novelette by Pamela Sargent, as well as good work by Tom Purdom, Stephen Baxter, Jack McDevitt, and others. The best story in *Space Stations* (DAW), edited by Martin H. Greenberg and John Helfers, is by newcomer Brendan DuBois, but the anthology also features strong work by James Cobb, Pamela Sargent, Jean Rabe, Julie E. Czerneda, Jack Williamson, Gregory Benford, and others, and at mass-market prices is a good value for your money. Much the same could be said, although it's not quite as strong overall, for *Cosmic Tales: Adventures in Sol Space* (Baen), edited by TKF Weisskopf, which featured good work by Allen M. Steele, Jack McDevitt, James P. Hogan, Wes Spencer, Gregory Benford, and others, as well as a posthumous story by Charles Sheffield. A mixed fantasy and SF (mostly fantasy) anthology about dogs, *Sirius, The Dog Star* (DAW), edited by Martin H. Greenberg and Alexander Potter, was weaker than either of the last two books named, but still had interesting work by Tanya Huff, Kristine Kathryn Rusch, Michelle West, and others. *Visions of Liberty* (Baen), edited by Mark Tier and Martin H. Greenberg, was a bit too didactically libertarian for my taste, although your mileage may vary. A few years back, I criticized the "black SF" anthology *Dark Matter* for not having much actual *science fiction* in it, but that's a charge that can't be laid against *So Long Been Dreaming: Postcolonial Science Fiction & Fantasy* (Arsenal Pulp Press), edited by Nalo Hopkinson and Uppinder Mehan; although it contains some fantasy and some fabulism (mostly flavored with Caribbean folklore), *So Long Been Dreaming* also features some strong science fiction, just as promised, and, what's more, SF infused with a cultural perspective rarer than it should be in the genre. The standout story here is by Vandana Singh, but there's also powerful work by Nisi Shawl, Andrea Hairston, Karin Lowachee, Greg van Eekhout, devorah major, Tobias S. Buckell, and others.

Some of the most interesting anthologies of the year were Alternate History anthologies, most of which mixed Alternate History with fantasy (in fact, Alternate History Fantasy seems to be emerging as a sub-subgenre of late) and/or fabulism/slipstream/Magic Realism/whatever we're calling it this year. *The First Heroes: New Tales of the Bronze Age* (Tor), edited by Harry Turtledove and Noreen Doyle, features one SF story (appropriately enough, a time-travel story by the late Poul Anderson; I've seen the Gene Wolfe story here listed as an SF story too, but although it's true that it's also a time-travel story, it *also* features the literal physical existence of gods and man-eating giants, which stretches the definition a bit), and one nearly impossible-to-categorize story (by Gregory Feeley), with the rest falling pretty solidly into the Alternate History Fantasy camp. Overall, it's a strong anthology, with the best stories being the aforementioned stories by Anderson, Wolfe, and Feeley, although the book also has good work by Lois Tilton, Brenda Clough, Judith Tarr, and Turtledove himself. A similar mix of Alternate History, fantasy, and hard-to-classify stuff characterizes *Conqueror Fantastic* (DAW), edited by Pamela Sargent; the best work here is probably by Sargent herself (one of the fantasies) and James Morrow (one of the unclassifiables), but the anthology also features good work by Kij Johnson, Jack Dann, Stephen Dedman, the late George Alec Effinger, and others. *ReVisions* (DAW), edited by Julie E. Czerneda and Isaac Szpindel, sticks a little more closely to core Alternate History; although some of the Alternate History scenarios featured are pretty unlikely, none stretch as far as giants or centaurs or ghosts. Best stuff here is by Geoffrey A. Landis and Kage Baker, along with entertaining stories by Laura Anne Gilman, John G. McDaid, Cory Doctorow, and Charles Stross, the editors themselves, and others. *All-Star Zeppelin Adventure Stories* (Wheatland Press), edited by Jay Lake and David Moles, is not so much a sober Alternate History anthology (the cover makes this clear, if the title doesn't) as an attempt to create a collection of stories infused with a sort of playful retropulp sensibility in worlds where zeppelins continued to fulfill a major role in international affairs after World War II. Some of the authors included play this fairly straight, speculating on social/economic factors that might have helped the zeppelin endure, while others push it well beyond "plausible" to a heightened deliberate absurdity, including tales of zeppelin-borne civilizations that must remain forever aloft and stories that feature living mile-long zeppelins that darken the skies in great herds over the American plains. Fortunately, few of the stories take themselves too seriously, and the anthology is a lot of fun in a sly, sardonic way; the best stories here are by David D. Levine and Benjamin Rosenbaum, but there's also good work by James L. Cambias, James Van Pelt, Paul Berger, Tobias S. Buckell, and others, plus a classic reprint by Howard Waldrop. (There were several other zeppelin stories published here and there this year, including a long one in *SCI FICTION* by Gary W. Shockley, although whether they were originally intended for *All-Star Zeppelin Adventure Stories* and were rejected or missed the deadline or whether it's just "zeppelin time" this year, as last year seemed to be "dragon time," is difficult to say.)

There was a long-delayed "regional" anthology finally published this year, after having changed publishers several times. *Crossroads: Tales of the Southern Literary Fantastic* (Tor/Forge), edited by F. Brett Cox and Andy Duncan, is a mixed reprint and original anthology that features a mixture of SF, fantasy, slipstream/fabulism, and what more or less amounts to straight mainstream stories. My biggest complaint about *Crossroads*, oddly, is that it's not regional *enough*; quite a few of the stories here don't feature much in the way of Southern local color, a flavor you'd have thought would be strong in the stew, and might just as well take place anywhere as in the South. Still, although some of the contents are disappointing, there is also a lot of strong stuff here; the best story is by Jack McDevitt, but the anthology also has good original work by Michael Swanwick, James L. Camibias, Don Webb, Scott Edelman, and others, plus good reprints by Gene Wolfe, John Kessel, Ian McDowell, Kelly Link, Andy Duncan himself, and others. Another "regional" anthology of sorts, if you can consider Australia a region (and why not, I suppose, if "The South" can be a region?) was *Agog! Smashing Stories* (Agog! Press), edited by Cat Sparks, which was interesting but failed to live up to its overheated title. Another Australian anthology, which we missed, and will have to save for next year, was *Encounters: An Anthology of Australian Speculative Fiction* (CSFG Publishing), edited by Maxine McArthur and Donna Maree Hanson. I caught up with two regional anthologies I missed last year: *Open Space: New Canadian Fiction* (Red Deer Press) and *Island Dreams: Montreal Writers of the Fantastic* (Véhicule Press), both edited by Claude Lalumière. Both anthologies suffer from the usual drawback of stuff in Canadian short-fiction markets in that many of the stories are gray and gloomy, set in dystopias or brutal after-civilization-collapses postapocalyptic societies, but there is good work in *Open Space* by Melissa Yuan-Innes, Derryl Murphy, Collen Anderson, Ahmed A. Khan, and others, and in *Island Dreams* by Glenn Grant, Mark Shainblum, Yves Meynard, Dora Knez, and others.

Good novellas in individual chapbook form continued to be published. PS Publishing brought out *Mayflower II* by Stephen Baxter; *No Traveller Returns* by Paul Park; and *My Death* by Lisa Tuttle; Golden Gryphon Press brought out *Mere* by Robert Reed; Night Shade brought out *Viator* by Lucius Shepard; and Subterranean

Press brought out *Liar's House* by Lucius Shepard, and *The Dry Salvages* by Caitlin R. Kiernan.

It was another good year in 2004 for original fantasy anthologies; there were a *lot* of them published, although only a few really stood out. Annoying as the overheated editorial copy is (almost as annoying as in 2001's *Redshift*, which was going to be the *Dangerous Visions* of science fiction, just as *Flights* is supposed to be the *Dangerous Visions* of fantasy), the best overall fantasy anthology of the year is probably *Flights: Extreme Visions of Fantasy* (Roc), edited by Al Sarrantonio. There's nothing either particularly "dangerous" or "extreme" here (Neal Barrett Jr.'s story may be the most dangerous, and it contains nothing that wasn't in Dante hundreds of years ago, while any issue of *Lady Churchill's Rosebud Wristlet* or *Polyphony*—or *The Year's Best Fantasy & Horror*, for that matter—will contain experiments with the fantasy form considerably more extreme than anything in this anthology), the book contains too much horror for my taste (just as *Redshift* did), and too many of the stories are minor or weak. But it's such a *huge* anthology, that, all being said, the good stories left behind once you toss the others out *still* make up into a large anthology of first-rate fantasy stories by Gene Wolfe, Elizabeth Hand, Tim Powers, Thomas M. Disch, Patricia A. McKillip, Neil Gaiman, Orson Scott Card, Elizabeth A. Lynn, Jeffery Ford, the beforementioned Barrett, and a number of others. Another good original was a YA fantasy anthology called *The Faery Reel: Tales from the Twilight Realm* (Viking), edited by Ellen Datlow and Terry Windling, which had good work by Tanith Lee, Gregory Frost, Jeffery Ford, Patricia A. McKillip, Kelly Link, Katherine Vas, and others. *Emerald Magic: Great Tales of Irish Fantasy* (Tor), edited by Andrew M. Greeley, was a mixed reprint and original anthology (mostly original) that featured good work by Charles De Lint, Tanith Lee, Diane Duane, and others. Other original fantasy anthologies, not operating on the level of these first three but still worthwhile at relatively cheap mass-market paperback prices, included *Masters of Fantasy* (DAW), edited by Bill Fawcett, *The Magic Shop* (DAW), edited by Denise Little, *Rotten Relations* (DAW), edited by Denise Little, *Little Red Riding Hood in the Big Bad City* (DAW), edited by Martin H. Greenberg and John Helfers, and *Faerie Tales*, edited by Martin H. Greenberg and Russell Davis. There was also a new volume in a long-running sword-and-sorcery anthology series, *Marion Zimmer Bradley's Sword and Sorceress XXI* (DAW), edited by Diana L. Paxson, this the first one not edited by the late Bradley herself, and a new volume in a longrunning comic fantasy series, *Turn the Other Chick* (Baen), edited by Esther M. Friesner, although it's overpriced as a hardcover and should have been a mass-market instead. (Plus, as indicated, good fantasy stories could be found this year in ostensible SF anthologies such as *The First Heroes* and *Conqueror Fantastic*.)

As the newly emerging slipstream/fabulism/New Wired/interstitialist/postransformationist subgenre continues to precipitate out from the parent body of genre SF/fantasy, further individual subvarieties are already beginning to differentiate themselves, so that although one may not be able to define the differences precisely, it's pretty easy to discern a difference in *flavor* between, say, the *Polyphony* camp and the *Lady Churchill's Rosebud Wristlet* camp or *The Third Alternative* camp, and a difference between all of them and what China Mieville seems to mean when he talks about the "New Weird." I think at this point I tend to prefer the more robust and muscular "interstitialism" of the *Polyphony* books and *All-Star Zeppelin Adventure Stories*, with its mixing of tropes from various genres (which usually means that the stories at least *have* plots and action), to the more abstract and surreal stuff you usually find in *Lady Churchill's* and some of its imitators—but it's early days yet for this whole area, and I've heard readers argue it exactly the other way around, for reasons exactly opposite the reasons for my own preferences. At any rate, my favorite anthology this year among those that dance on the edge of genre (considering it to be a slipstream/fabulism anthology rather than an Alternate History anthology, which in some ways is a better fit for it anyway) was the beforementioned *All-Star Zeppelin Adventure Stories*, followed by *Polyphony, Volume 4* (Wheatland), edited by Deborah Layne and Jay Lake, which features strong and quirky work by Lucius Shepard, Alex Irvine, Tim Pratt, Theodora Goss, Jeff VanderMeer, Greg van Eekout, and others. *Leviathan, Volume Four: Cities* (Night Shade Books/Ministry of Whimsy), edited by Forrest Aquirre, is a good deal more surreal and self-consciously "decadent," but still features interesting if sometimes somewhat abstract work by Jay Lake, Stephen Chapman, Ursula Pflug, and others. *McSweeney's Enchanted Chamber of Astonishing Stories* (Vintage), edited by Michael Chabon, a follow-up to last year's *McSweeney's Mammoth Treasury of Thrilling Tales*, again promises to deliver a kind of retropulp sensibility that most of the stories don't really manage to deliver (*All-Star Zeppelin Adventure Stories* comes a good deal closer), but any anthology with stories by Stephen King, Peter Straub, and China Mieville in it is probably going to be worth reading, and this one is too, especially at trade paperback prices.

There were also several cross-genre anthologies this year: *Irresistible Forces* (Penguin/NAL), edited by Catherine Asaro, which mixed SF with romance, and *To Weave a Web of Magic* (Berkley), editor anonymous, that mixed fantasy with romance; and *Murder by Magic* (Warner Aspect), edited by Rosemary Edghill; and *Powers of Detection: Stories of Mystery and Fantasy* (Ace), edited by Dana Stabenow, both of which mixed fantasy with the mystery story.

As usual, novice work by beginning writers, some of whom may (or may not) later turn out to be important talents, was featured in *L. Ron Hubbard Presents Writers of the Future Volume XX* (Bridge), edited by Algis Budrys, and two new anthologies from the Annual Phobos Fiction Contest for new writers, *Absolutely Brilliant in Chrome* (Phobos Books), edited by Keith Olexa, and *All the Rage This Year: The Phobos Science Fiction Anthology 3* (Phobos Books), edited by Keith Olexa.

I don't follow horror anymore, but several anthologies that I noted in passing included: *Dark Dreams: A Collection of Horror and Suspense by Black Writers* (Dafina Books), edited by Brandon Massey; *Gothic! Ten Original Dark Tales* (Candlewick Press), edited by Deborah Noyes; *A Walk on the Darkside: Visions of Horror* (Roc), edited by John Pelan; *Tales of Van Helsing* (Ace), edited by Jeanne Cavalos; and *Haunted Holidays* (DAW), edited by Martin H. Greenberg and Russel Davis.

(Finding individual pricings for all of the items from small presses mentioned in the summation has become too time-intensive, and since several of the same small presses publish anthologies, novels, *and* short-story collections, it seems silly to repeat addresses for them in section after section. Therefore, I'm going to attempt to list here, in one place, all the addresses for small presses that have books mentioned here or there in the summation, whether from the anthologies section, the novel section, or the short-story collection section, and, where known, their Web site addresses. That should make it easy enough for the reader to look up the individual price of any book mentioned that isn't from a regular trade publisher; such books are less likely to be found in your average bookstore, or even in a chain superstore, and so will probably have to be mail ordered. Addresses: ***PS Publishing,*** 98 High Ash Drive, Leeds L517 8RE, England, UK, www.pspublishing.co.uk; **Golden Gryphon Press,** 3002 Perkins Road, Urbana, IL 61802, www.goldengryphon.com; **NESFA Press,** P.O. Box 809, Framinghan, MA 01701-0809, www.nesfa.org; **Subterranean Press,** P.O. Box 190106, Burton, MI 48519, www.subterraneanpress.com; **Old Earth Books,** P.O. Box 19951, Baltimore, MD 21211-0951, www.oldearthbooks.com; **Tachyon Press,** 1459 18th St. #139, San Francisco, CA 94107, www.tachyonpublications.com; **Night Shade Books,** 3623 SW Baird St., Portland, OR 97219, www.nightshadebooks.com; **Five Star Books,** 295 Kennedy Memorial Drive, Waterville, ME 04901, www.galegroup.com/fivestar; **Wheatland Press,** P.O. Box 1818, Wilsonville, OR, 97070, www.wheatlandpress.com, **Small Beer Press,** 176 Prospect Ave., Northampton, MA 01060, www.smallbeerpress.com; **Wildside Press/Cosmos Books/Borgo Press,** P.O. Box 301, Holicong, PA 18928-0301, or go to www.wildsidepress.com for pricing and ordering; **Thunder's Mouth,** 245 West 17th St., 11th Flr., New York, NY 10011-5300, www.thundersmouth.com; **Rose Press,** 22 West End Lane, Pinner, Middlesex, HA5 1AQ, England, UK, therosepress@groups.msn.com; **Agog! Press,** P.O. Box U302, University of Wollongong, NSW 2522, Australia, www.uow.ed.au/~rhood/agogpress; **Aqueduct Press,** P.O. Box 95787, Seattle, WA 98145-2787, www.aqueductpress.com; **Phobos Books,** 200 Park Avenue South, New York, NY 10003, www.phobosweb.com; **Fairwood Press,** 5203 Quincy Ave. SE, Auburn, WA 98092, www.fairwoodpress.com; **BenBella Books,** 6440 N. Central Expressway, Suite 508, Dallas, TX 75206, www.benbellabooks.com; **Red Deer Press/Robert J. Sawyer Books,** 813 MacKimmie Library Tower, 2500 University Drive NW, Calgary, Alberta, Canada T2N 1N4, www.reddeerpress.com; **Darkside Press,** 4128 Woodland Park Ave., N. Seattle, WA, 98103; **MirrorDanse Books,** P.O. Box 3542, Parramatta NSW 2124 Australia, www.tabula-rasa.info/MirrorDanse; **Haffner Press,** 5005 Crooks Rd., Suite 35, Royal Oak, MI 48073-1239, www.haffnerpress.com; **Meshia Merlin,** P.O. Box 7, Decatur, GA 30031, www.meishamerlin.com; **North Atlantic Press,** P.O. Box 12327, Berkeley, CA, 94701; **Prime,** P.O. Box 36503, Canton, OH, 44735, www.primebooks.net; **Arsenal Pulp Press,** 103-1014 Homer Street, Vancouver, BC, Canada V6B 2W9, www.arsenalpress.com; **Fairwood Press,** 5203 Quincy Ave SE, Auburn, WA 98092, www.fairwoodpress.com; **MonkeyBrain Books,** 11204 Crossland Drive, Austin, TX 78726, www.monkeybrainbooks.com; **Cambrian Publications,** P.O. Box 41220, San Jose, CA 95160-1220, www.cambrianpubs.com; **Shambhala Publications,** Horticultural Hall, 300 Massachusetts Ave., Boston, MA 02115, www.shambhala.com; **Red Jacket Press,** 3099 Maqua Place, Hohegan Lake, NY 10547, www.redjacketpress.com; **Black Inc.,** Level 5, 289 Flanders Lane, Melbourne, Victoria 3000, Australia, www.blackincbooks.com; **Willowgate Press,** P.O. Box 6529, Holliston, MA 01746, www.willowgatepress.com; **Wesleyan University Press,** University Press of New England, Order Dept., 37 Lafayette St., Lebanon, NH 03766-1405, www.wesleyan.edu/wespress; **Underwood Books,** P.O. Box 1919, Nevada City, CA 95959, www.underwoodbooks.com; **Overlook Press** www.overlookconnection.com; **Bloomsbury Publishing,** 38 Soho Square, London W1D 3HB, UK, www.bloomsbury.com; **CSFG Publishing,** P.O. Box 89, Latham Act 2615, Australia, www.astspeculativefiction.com.av; **Véhicule Press,** Independent Publishers Group, Order Department, 814 North Franklin Street, Chicago IL 60610, www.vehiculepress.com.

It was another strong year for novels—and although some of the biggest sellers were out on the ambiguous fringes of genre, and yes, there were more fantasy books published than SF (the "SF-is-dying" crowd perk up their ears and sit forward eagerly), there's *still* a huge number of SF novels being published every year, more than there were twenty years ago, and *far* more than any one individual reader could possibly *read*, even if one spent all of one's time during the year doing nothing else.

According to the newsmagazine *Locus*, there were 2,550 books "of interest to the SF field," published in 2004 both original and reprint (but not counting "media tie-in novels," gaming novels, novelizations of movies, or novels drawn from other TV shows; for the most part, these totals don't reflect print-on-demand novels either, or novels offered as downloads on the Internet). This sets a new record, up by 5 percent from 2003's total of 2,429, the fourth year in a row that the total has increased. Original books were up by 8 percent to 1,417 from last year's total of 1,375, itself an increase of 8 percent over the 2002 total of 1,271; reprint books were up by 7 percent to 1,133 over last year's total of 1,054 titles, itself an increase of 9 percent from the 2002 total of 970. The number of new SF novels was up by 7 percent to 253 titles as opposed to last year's 236. The number of new fantasy novels was up by 14 percent to 389 titles as opposed to last year's 340. Horror was also up, but only slightly, rising to 172 titles as opposed to last year's 171 (in 2002, though, it only had 112—which itself was the highest total since 1995; horror seems to be making something of a recovery from the Big Horror Bust of the late nineties).

Busy with all the reading I have to do at shorter lengths, I didn't have time to read many novels this year, so, as usual, I'll limit myself to mentioning novels that received a lot of attention and acclaim in 2004. They include: *Camouflage* (Ace), by Joe Haldeman; *River of Gods* (Simon & Schuster UK), by Ian McDonald; *Crucible* (Tor), by Nancy Kress; *Light* (Bantam Spectra), by M. John Harrison; *Lurulu* (Tor), by Jack Vance; *Air (or Have Not Have)* (St. Martin's Griffin), by Geoff Ryman; *Exultant* (Del Rey), by Stephen Baxter; *Forty Signs of Rain* (Bantam), by Kim Stanley Robinson; *Iron Sunrise* (Ace), by Charles Stross; *The Life of the World to Come* (Tor), by Kage Baker; *Superluminal* (Eos), by Tony Daniel; *The Zenith Angle* (Del Rey), by Bruce Sterling; *The Wizard* (Tor), by Gene Wolfe; *Iron Council* (Del Rey), by China Mieville; *The Algebraist* (Orbit), by Iain M. Banks; *White Devils* (Tor), by Paul McAuley; *Century Rain* (Gollancz), by Alastair Reynolds; *The Last Garden of Everness* (Tor), by John Wright; *Beyond Infinity* (Warner Aspect), by Gregory Benford; *Newton's Wake* (Tor), by Ken MacLeod; *Banner of Souls* (Bantam Spectra), by Liz Williams; *Consequences* (Roc), by Kristine Kathryn Rusch; *Dead Lines* (Ballantine), by Greg Bear; *Forge of Heaven* (Eos), by C. J. Cherryh; *Crux* (Tor), by Albert E. Cowdrey; *Time's Eye: A Time Odyssey* (Del Rey), by Arthur C. Clarke and Stephen Baxter; *Affairs at Hampden Ferrers* (Little Brown UK), by Brian Aldiss; *The Runes of the Earth* (Putnam), by Stephen R. Donaldson; *The Skinner* (Tor), by Neal Asher; *Coyote Rising* (Ace), by Allen Steele; *Pandora's Star* (Del Rey), by Peter F. Hamilton; *The Ordinary* (Tor), by Jim Grimsley; *One King, One Soldier* (Del Rey), by Alexander C. Irvine; *Eastern Standard Tribe* (Tor), by Cory Doctorow; *Stamping Butterflies* (Gollancz), by Jon Courtenay Grimwood; *Black Brillion* (Tor), by Matthew Hughes; *Mortal Love* (Morrow), by Elizabeth Hand; *The Dark Tower VI: Song of Susannah* (Scribner) and *The Dark Tower VII: The Dark Tower* (Scribner), by Stephen King; *Polaris (Ace)*, by Jack McDevitt; *The Family Tree* (Tor), by Charles Stross; *The Labyrinth Key* (Del Rey), by Howard V. Hendrix; *Alphabet of Thorn* (Ace), by Patricia McKillip; *Ringworld's Children* (Tor), by Larry Niven; *Shadowmarch* (DAW), by Tad Williams; *Broken Angels* (Del Rey), by Richard A. Morgan; *Crossing the Line* (HarperCollins), by Karen Traviss; *Lost in Transmission* (Bantam Spectra), by Wil McCarthy; *Cowl* (Tor), by Neal Asher; *The Boy Who Would Live Forever* (Tor), by Frederik Pohl; *Crache* (Bantam Spectra), by Mark Budz; *Gaudeamus* (Tor), by John Barnes; *Very Bad Deaths* (Baen), by Spider Robinson; *In the Night Room* (Random House), by Peter Straub; and *Going Postal* (HarperCollins), by Terry Pratchett.

Without doubt, the first novel that drew the most attention this year, by a large margin, was *Jonathan Strange and Mr. Norrell* (Bloomsbury) by Susanna Clarke, which was not only a huge best-seller, but which drew rave reviews everywhere, including sources from well outside the genre. Other first novels that received a fair amount of attention this year (although nothing came even close to the Clarke) were: *City of Pearl* (Eos), by Karen Traviss; *Crux*, by Albert E. Cowdrey; *The Year of Our War* (Gollancz), by Steph Swainston; *The Holy Machine* (Wildside), by Chris Beckett; *The Coyote Kings of the Space-Age Bachelor Pad* (Del Rey), by Minister Faust; and *Olympic Games* (Tachyon), by Leslie What. Other first novels included: *Trash Sex Magic* (Small Beer), by Jennifer Stevenson; *Orphanage* (Warner Aspect), by Robert Boettner; *Weapons of Choice* (Del Rey), by John Birmingham; *Fitzpatrick's War* (DAW), by Theodore Judson; *The Gods and Their Machines* (Tor), by Oisin McGann; *The Labyrinth* (Prime), by Catherynenne M. Valente; *Through Violet Eyes* (Dell), by Stephen Woodworth; *Move Under Ground* (Night Shade), by Nick Mamatas; *Firethorn* (Scribner), by Sarah Mickelm; *The Arcanum* (Bantam), by Thomas Wheeler; and *Ghosts in the Snow* (Bantam Spectra), by Tamara Siler Jones.

There were a number of hard-to-classify novels out on the edge of genre this year, as well as associational novels by genre authors, and ventures *into* genre by well-known mainstream authors, including: *The Jane Austen Book Club* (Putnam), by Karen Joy Fowler; *The Zenith Angle* (Del Rey), by Bruce Sterling; *The Confusion* (Morrow), and *The System of the World* (Morrow), by Neal Stephenson; *The Rebel: An Imagined Life of James Dean* (Morrow), by Jack Dann; *A Handbook of American Prayer* (Thunder's Mouth), by Lucius Shepard; *Cloud Atlas* (Random House), by David Mitchell; *The Plot Against America* (Houghton Mifflin), by Philip Roth; *Adventures of the Artificial Woman* (Simon & Schuster), by Thomas Berger; *Stone Cribs* (St. Martin's Minotaur), a mystery novel by Kristine Kathryn Rusch writing as "Kris Nelscott"; and historical novel *Owls to Athens* (Tor/Forge), by H. N. Turteltaub (a pseudonym for Harry Turtledove). Some of these, especially the Stephenson and Fowler novels, were among the best-selling titles of the year.

Small presses of varying sizes of "small," including some that until recently had mostly concentrated on short-story collections, also published a fair number of novels this year, among them: *The Scarlet Fig, or, Slowly Through a Land of Stone* (Rose Press), by Avram Davidson; *Perfect Circle* (Small Beer), by Sean Stewart; *Life* (Aqueduct Press), by Gwyneth Jones; *The Course of the Heart* (Night Shade Books), by M. John Harrison; *Harp, Pipe and Symphony* (Prime Books), and *Spondulix* (Cambrian Publications), by Paul Di Filippo; *Letters from the Flesh* (Red Deer Press), by Marcos Donnelly; *Medicine Road* (Subterranean Press), by Charles de

Lint; *The Prince of Christler-Coke* (Golden Gryphon Press), by Neal Barrett Jr.; *Getting Near the End* (Red Deer Press), by Andrew Weiner; *Bengal Station* (Five Star), by Eric Brown; *The Holy Machine* (Wildside Press), by Chris Beckett; and *Kiss the Goat* (Prime Books/Wildside), by Brian Stableford.

Although there are a good number of fantasy novels and borderline genre-mixing things on these lists, there are also a lot of pure-quill center-core SF novels here that would clearly and unambiguously be science fiction by almost anybody's definition, including those by Haldeman, McDonald, Harrison, Ryman, Kress, Stross, Baxter, Vance, Baker, Reynolds, Banks, MacLeod, Doctorow, Benford, Hamilton, Robinson, McAuley, Asher, Cowdrey, Brown, McCarthy, Morgan, Pohl, Traviss, and lots of others. So center-core science fiction *still* hasn't been driven off the bookstore shelves, although gloomy prognosticators ensure us every year that this is just about to happen.

This is the best time in decades to pick up reissued editions of formerly long-out-of-print novels. So many such novels are coming back into print these days, from both small presses and regular trade publishers (to say nothing of print-on-demand books from places such as Wildside Press, and the availability of out-of-print books as electronic downloads on Internet sources such as Fictionwise, and through reprints issued by The Science Fiction Book Club) that it's become difficult to produce an exhaustive list of such titles; therefore I'll just list some of the more prominent reprints that caught my eye. Old Earth Books reissued: *Davy* and *A Mirror for Observers*, by Edgar Pangborn; *City* and *Way Station*, by Clifford D. Simak. Reissued by ibooks: *The World Inside*, by Robert Silverberg; *The Languages of Pao* and *To Live Forever*, by Jack Vance; *This Immortal* and *Damnation Alley*, by Roger Zelazny; *Bill, the Galactic Hero*, by Harry Harrison; *Flandry of Terra* and *Agent of the Terran Empire*, by Poul Anderson; *Watchtower*, by Elizabeth Lynn; and *I, Robot: The Illustrated Screenplay*, by Isaac Asimov and Harlan Ellison. Eos reissued: *Lord of Light*, by Roger Zelazny; *Beggars in Spain*, by Nancy Kress, and *Forge of Heaven*, by C. J. Cherryh. Bantam and Bantam Spectra reissued: *Dying of the Light* and *Fevre Dream*, by George R. R. Martin; *A Wizard of Earthsea*, by Ursula K. Le Guin; *Thomas the Rhymer*, by Ellen Kushner; and *Foundation*, *Foundation and Earth*, *Second Foundation*, *Prelude to Foundation*, and *Forward the Foundation*, all by Isaac Asimov. Ace reissued: *Neuromancer*, by William Gibson, *A Talent for War*, by Jack McDevitt, *Rocket Ship Galileo*, by Robert A. Heinlein, and *The Golden Globe*, by John Varley. BenBella reissued: *The Sheep Look Up*, by John Brunner; *The Shore of Women*, by Pamela Sargent, and *The Listeners*, by James Gunn. Tor reissued: *Glory Road*, by Robert A. Heinlein, *The Beginning Place*, by Ursula K. Le Guin, and *Marooned in Realtime*, by Vernor Vinge. Orb reissued: *The Boat of a Million Years*, by Poul Anderson; *Sleeping in Flame*, by Jonathan Carroll; and *Lavondyss*, by Robert Holdstock. Baen reissued: *The Witches of Karres*, by James H. Schmitz, and *Kaspar's Box*, by Jack L. Chalker. Del Rey reissued: *Gateway*, by Frederik Pohl and *Lord Foul's Bane*, *The Illearth War*, and *The Power That Preserves*, by Stephen R. Donaldson. Vintage reissued three books by Philip K. Dick: *Vulcan's Hammer*, *Lies, Inc.*, and *The Penultimate Truth*. Warner Aspect reissued: *Glorianna*, by Michael Moorcock, and *Tides of Light*, *Great Sky River*, *Across the Sea of Suns*, and *In the Ocean of Night*, by Gregory Benford. Wesleyan University Press reissued: *Stars in My Pocket like Grains of Sand*, by Samuel R. Delany and *Star Maker*, by Olaf Stapledon. NESFA Press reissued: *Silverlock*, by John Myers Myers. Red Jacket Press reissued *Judgement Night*, by C. L. Moore. Beacon Press reissued: *Kindred*, by Octavia E. Butler. Plume reissued: *Sarah Canary*, by Karen Joy Fowler.

Omnibus collections of reissued novels included: *Legions of Space* (Baen), by Keith Laumer; *The Fall of the Towers* (Vintage), by Samuel R. Delany; *3XT* (Baen), by Harry Turtledove; *Death and Thraxas* (Baen), by Scott Martin; *Powers of Two* (NESFA Press), by Tim Powers; *To Die in Italbar* (ibooks), by Roger Zelazny; *Eternal Frontier* (Baen), by James H. Schmitz; *The House on the Borderland and Other Mysterious Places* (Night Shade Books), by William Hope Hodgson; *Yaleen* (BenBella Books), by Ian Watson; *The Complete Roderick* (Overlook Press), by John Sladek; *The Cobra Trilogy* (Baen), by Timothy Zahn; *The Solar Queen* (Tor), *Lost Worlds of Witch World* (Tor), and *Gods and Androids* (Baen), by Andre Norton; *redemolished* (ibooks), by Alfred Bester; and *A World Divided* (DAW), by Marian Zimmer Bradley. Also, many omnibuses of novels—and many individual novels—are reissued each year by The Science Fiction Book Club, too numerous to individually list here.

Many of these titles have been unavailable for years, if not decades, and they include some of the classics of modern science fiction, so don't miss your chance to get them while you can.

What's going to win the major novel awards is anybody's guess. The Preliminary Nebula Ballot this year pits three novels from 2003 against three novels from 2004; I think that Gene Wolfe's *The Knight* might have a slight edge, but it's hard to call. It's impossible to predict what's going to win the Hugo at this point, because we don't even know what's going to be on the ballot yet, but *Jonathan Strange and Mr. Norrell* sold so enormously that I wonder if it's going to be a contender.

This was another strong year for short-story collections, with some especially good retrospective collections that give overviews of an author's entire career. The year's best collections included: *Breathmoss* (Golden Gryphon), by Ian R. MacLeod; *Mother Aegypt and Other Stories* (Night Shade Books), by Kage Baker; *Hunters of Pangaea* (NESFA Press), by Stephen Baxter; *Stable Strategies and Others* (Tachyon), by Eileen Gunn; *Designer Genes: Tales of the Biotech Revolution* (Five Star), by Brian Stableford; *The Banquet of the Lords of Night and Other Stories* (Night Shade), by Liz Williams; *The Atrocity Archives* (Golden Gryphon), by Charles Stross; *Trujillo* (PS Publilshing), by Lucius Shepard; *Innocents Abroad* (Tor), by Gene Wolfe; and several big retrospective collections: *Phases of the Moon: Six Decades of Masterpieces by the SFWA Grand Master* (Subterranean Press), by Robert Silverberg; *The John Varley Reader* (Ace), by John Varley; *Novelties and Souvenirs: Collected Short Fiction* (Perennial), by John Crowley; *Lord Darcy* (Baen), by Randall Garrett; *The State of the Art* (Night Shade Books), by Iain M. Banks; *The Collected Short Fiction of C. J. Cherryh* (DAW), by C. J. Cherryh; *Dancing Naked: The Unexpurgated William Tenn* (NESFA Press), by William Tenn (which doubles as a collection of essays); and *Seventy-Five: The Diamond Anniversary of a Science Fiction Pioneer* (Haffner), by Jack Williamson.

Other good collections this year included: *Thumbprints* (Golden Gryphon), by Pamela Sargent; *Neutrino Drag* (Four Walls Eight Windows), by Paul Di Filippo; *Two Trains Running* (Golden Gryphon), by Lucius Shepard; *American Sorrows* (Wheatland Press), by Jay Lake; *Stagestruck Vampires and Other Phantasms*

(Tachyon), by Suzy McKee Charnas; *Heat of Fusion and Other Stories* (Tor), by John M. Ford; *Sleepside: The Collected Fantasies of Greg Bear* (ibooks), by Greg Bear; *Men and Cartoons* (Doubleday), by Jonathan Lethem; *Tales of the Grand Tour* (Tor), by Ben Bova; *Secret Life* (Golden Gryphon), by Jeff VanderMeer; *Love's Body, Dancing in Time* (Aqueduct), by L. Timmel Duchamp; *Cartomancy* (Gollancz), by Mary Gentle; *The Cat's Pajamas* (Tachyon), by James Morrow; *The Cat's Pajamas: New Stories* (Morrow), by Ray Bradbury; *Dogs in the Moonlight* (Wildside) and *Green Grow the Rushes-Oh* (Fairwood Press), by Jay Lake; *He Do the Time Police in Different Voices* (Wildside), by David Langford; *Quicksilver and Shadow* (Subterranean Press), by Charles de Lint; *Songs of Leaving* (Subterranean Press), by Peter Crowther; *Take No Prisoners* (Willowgate Press), by John Grant; *Salome and other Decadent Fantasies* (Wildside), by Brian Stableford; *Different Kinds of Darkness* (Cosmos), by David Langford; *Bumper Crop* (Golden Gryphon), by Joe Lansdale; *The Rose in Twelve Petals and Other Stories* (Small Beer), by Theodora Goss; *Horses Blow Up Dog City and Other Stories* (Small Beer), by Richard Butner; and *Mountain Men* (Baen), a collection of Henry Kuttner's little-known "Hogben" stories, accompanied by similar comic work by David Drake, Eric Flint, Ryke Speer, and Henry Kuttner.

(Noted without comment: *Morning Child and Other Stories* (ibooks), by Gardner Dozois.)

Reissued collections this year included: *I, Robot* (Bantam Spectra) and *Robot Dreams* (Ace), by Isaac Asimov; *Distant Stars* (ibooks), by Samuel R. Delany; *The Doors of His Face, The Lamps of His Mouth* (ibooks), by Roger Zelazny; *Swords in the Mist* (ibooks), by Fritz Leiber; *Sailing to Byzantium* (ibooks), by Robert Silverberg; *Daughter of Regals and Other Tales* (Del Rey), by Stephen R. Donaldson; and *The Notebooks of Lazarus Long* (Baen), by Robert A. Heinlein.

And, as usual, "electronic collections" continue to be available for downloading online as well, at sites such as *Fictionwise* and *ElectricStory*.

It's worth noting that many of these collections—including Baker's *Mother Aegypt and Other Stories*, Stross's *The Atrocity Archieve*, Sargent's *Thumbprints*, Baxter's *Hunters of Pangaea*, Williams' *The Banquet of the Lords of Night*, Shepard's *Two Trains Running*, Gunn's *Stable Strategies and Others*, Lethem's *Men and Cartoons*, and Duchamp's *Love's Body, Dancing in Time*—feature original, never-before-published work.

Although a few regular trade publishers such as Tor, Baen, Ace, and DAW feature on these lists, they're dominated to an even larger extent than usual this year by small-press publishers, with Golden Gryphon Press especially prominent, although Subterraean Press, Tachyon, Night Shade Press, and others were also very active; in fact, between them, small presses were responsible for the bulk of the short-story collections published this year.

It was a decent year in the reprint anthology market, with some big retrospective anthologies giving you good value for your money, in addition to the usual "Best of the Year" and award anthologies. There will be six best-of-the-year anthologies out in 2005. Science fiction will be covered by four anthologies: the one you are holding in your hand, *The Year's Best Science Fiction* series from St. Martin's Press, now up to its twenty second annual collection; the *Year's Best SF* series (Eos), edited by

David G. Hartwell and Kathryn Cramer, now up to its tenth annual volume, *Science Fiction: The Best of 2004* (ibooks), edited by Jonathan Strahan and Karen Haber, and *Best Short Novels* (Science Fiction Book Club), edited by Johanthan Strahan. There'll be two best-of-the-year anthologies covering horror: the latest edition in the British series *The Mammoth Book of Best New Horror* (Robinson, Caroll & Graff), edited by Stephen Jones, now up to volume fifteen, and the Ellen Datlow half of a huge volume covering both horror and fantasy, *The Year's Best Fantasy & Horror* (St. Martin's Press), this year up to its seventeenth annual collection, edited by Datlow and Kelly Link and Gavin Grant. Fantasy will be covered by three anthologies: the Kelly Link and Gavin Grant half of the Datlow/Link and Grant anthology, by *Year's Best Fantasy* (Eos), edited by David G. Hartwell and Katherine Cramer, now up to its fifth annual volume; and a revived fantasy best-anthology series from ibooks, edited by Jonathan Strahan and Karen Harber. The most recent Nebula Awards anthology is *Nebula Awards Showcase 2004* (Roc), edited by Vonda N. McIntyre.

Of the stand-alone retrospective anthologies, the best was probably *The Locus Awards* (Roc), edited by Charles N. Brown and Jonathan Strahan, which featured classic stories such as Gene Wolfe's "The Death of Doctor Island," Ursula K. Le Guin's "The Day Before the Revolution," George R. R. Martin's "The Way of Cross and Dragon," and Joanna Russ's "Souls," as well as excellent stuff by Pat Murphy, Harlan Ellison, Connie Willis, John Varley, and others. *The James Tiptree Award Anthology 1: Sex, the Future and Chocolate Chip Cookies*, edited by Karen Joy Fowler, Pat Murphy, Debbie Notkin, and Jeffrey D. Smith, also provided an interesting overview of recent work in the field as well, including good stuff by Greg Egan, Ruth Nestvold, Karen Joy Fowler, Kelly Link, Carol Emshwiller, and others. An overview of a tradition of SF writing from a different culture is provided by *The Best Australian Science Fiction Writing* (Black Inc.), edited by Rob Gerrand, and offers fine stories by Greg Egan, George Turner, Terry Dowling, A. Bertram Chandler, and others.

(Noted without comment is: *A.I.s* (Ace), edited by Jack Dann and Gardner Dozois.)

The best fantasy reprint anthology of the year was probably *In Lands That Never Were: Tales of Sword and Sorcery from the Magazine of Fantasy & Science Fiction* (Thunder's Mouth Press), edited by Gordon Van Gelder, which featured work by Fritz Leiber, Ellen Kushner, Pat Murphy, Ursula K. Le Guin, Charles Coleman Finlay, Jeffrey Ford, and others, although another contender would be *New Magics: An Anthology of Today's Fantasy*, a YA fantasy anthology edited by Patrick Nielsen Hayden, featuring work by Neil Gaiman, Charles de Lint, Ursula K. Le Guin, and others. Also of interest was a mixed reprint and original (but mostly reprint) anthology called *The Mammoth Book of Sorcerers' Tales* (Carroll & Graf), edited by Mike Ashley.

There never seem to be many horror reprint anthologies, but I noticed *Great Ghost Stories* (Carrol & Graf), edited by R. Chetwynd-Hayes and Stephen Jones, and *The Mammoth Book of Vampires* (Carroll & Graf), edited by Stephen Jones.

Reissued reprint anthologies of note this year included: *The Science Fiction Hall of Fame, Volume 2A* (Tor), edited by Ben Bova; *Masterpieces: The Best Science Fiction of the Twentieth Century* (Ace), edited by Orson Scott Card; *New Worlds: An Anthology* (Thunder's Mouth), by Michael Moorcock (contents assembled from several previous *New Worlds* anthologies); *The Houses of the Kzinti* (Baen), edited by Larry Niven (assembled from previous *Man/Kzin War* anthologies); *Christmas Stars* (Orb), edited by David G. Hartwell; and a slew of reissued reprint anthologies from ibooks: *Time Wars*, edited by Charles Waugh and Martin H. Greenberg; *Dragon Fantastic*, edited by Rosalind M. Greenberg and Martin H. Greenberg; *What Might Have Been, Volume 1: Alternate Empires* and *What Might Have Been, Volume 2: Alternate Heroes*, both edited by Gregory Benford and Martin H. Greenberg; *The Ultimate Cyberpunk*, edited by Pat Cadigan; *My Favorite Fantasy Story* and *Merlin*, edited by Martin H. Greenberg; *Vamps*, edited by Martin H. Greenberg and Charles Waugh; *Wild Cards II: Aces High* and *Wild Cards III: Jokers Wild* edited by George R. R. Martin; *Jack the Ripper*, edited by Martin H. Greenberg, Charles Waugh, and Frank D. McSherry Jr. and *The Best Time-Travel Stories of All Time*, edited by Barry N. Malzberg.

The year 2004 was again fairly weak overall in the SF-and-fantasy-oriented nonfiction and reference book field. The most useful of the year's reference books was probably *Historical Dictionary of Science Fiction Literature* (Scarecrow Press), by Brian Stableford, but there were a number of other books that scrutinized one period or another of genre history, including a study of the early years of science fiction, *The Gernsback Days: A Study of the Evolution of Modern Science Fiction from 1911 to 1936* (Wildside), by Mike Ashley and Robert A. W. Lowndes; a critical look at more recent SF; *X, Y, Z, T: Dimensions of Science Fiction* (Borgo/Wildside), by Damien Broderick; a historical perspective on South American SF, *Brazilian Science Fiction* (Bucknell University); and an analysis of *The Evolution of the Weird Tale* (Hippocampus), by S. T. Joshi.

As has become usual, there were a number of studies of the works of individual authors, including: the inevitable study of Philip K. Dick, *I Am Alive and You Are Dead: A Journey into the Mind of Philip K. Dick* (Metropolitan Books), by Emmanuel Carrere; *Solar Labyrinth: Exploring Gene Wolfe's Book of the New Sun* (iUniverse), by Robert Borski; *Ray Bradbury: The Life of Fiction* (Kent State University Press), by Jonathan R. Eller and William F. Touponce; *There and Back Again: In the Footsteps of J. R. R. Tolkien* (Cadogan Publishing), by Mathew Lyons; *The Cherryh Odyssey* (Borgo/Wildside), edited by Edward Carmien; *A Sense of Wonder: Samuel R. Delany, Race, Identity, and Difference* (Wesleyan University Press), by Jeffrey A. Tucker; and *The Road to the Dark Tower: Exploring Stephen King's Magnum Opus* (NAL), by Bev Vincent. There were also volumes of essays *by* writers as opposed to about them, including *The Wave in the Mind: Talks and Essays on the Writer, the Reader, and the Imagination* (Shambhala), by Ursula K. Le Guin; *Dancing Naked: The Unexpurgated William Tenn* (NESFA Press), by William Tenn, which also doubles as a short-story collection; *The Crazy Years: Reflections of a Science Fiction Original* (BenBella Books), by Spider Robinson; *Why Should I Cut Your Throat?: Excursions into the Worlds of Science Fiction, Fantasy and Horror* (MonkeyBrain Books), by Jeff VanderMeer; *The Grand Conversation* (Aqueduct Press); and *Kicking the Sacred Cow* (Baen), by James P. Hogan. There were also books of interviews *with* SF and fantasy writers, including *Speaking of the Fantastic II* (Wildside), by Darrell Schweitzer; and *Hanging Out with the Dream King: Conversations with Neil Gaiman and his Collaborators* (Fantagraphics), by Joe McCade. Probably more entertaining and more accessible for most readers were *Projections: Science Fiction in*

Literature and Film (MonkeyBrain Books), edited by Lou Anders, a collection of essays, some original, mostly reprint, discussing either print SF or its adaptation to film (being who I am, I found the essays dealing with print SF more interesting—although Lucius Shepard's film reviews are enjoyably vitrolic—particularly the two essays by Michael Swanwick, John Cult, Mike Resnick, Sean McMullen, Michael Moorcock, and others; there's some "SF-is-dying" stuff, particularly by Robert J. Sawyer, but it's balanced by more optimistic views by other commentators) and a reissue of *Wizardry and Wild Romance: A Study of Epic Fantasy* (MonkeyBrain Books), by Michael Moorcock (Moorcock clearly knows his subject, and provides some fascinating insights into it, although the relentless Tolkien-bashing gets tiresome after a while).

Media fans will probably like *Five Seasons of Angel: Science Fiction and Fantasy Authors Discuss Their Favorite Vampire* (BenBella Books), edited by Glenn Yeffeth.

In the art book field, your best bets were probably the latest edition in a Best of the Year–like retrospective of the year in fantastic art, *Spectrum 11: The Best in Contemporary Fantastic Art* (Underwood Books), by Cathy Fenner and Arnie Fenner; and a retrospective of fantastic art of years gone by provided by *Worlds of Tomorrow: The Amazing Universe of Science Fiction Art* (Collectors Press), by Forrest J. Ackerman (although it would have been nice if he'd provided artist credits). There were also a number of strong retrospective overviews of the work of individual artists, including *Futures: 50 Years in Space: The Challenge of the Stars* (Harper Design International), by David A. Hardy and Patrick Moore, which doubles as a nonfiction text about space exploration; *Kingsgate: The Art of Keith Parkinson* (SQP/Fanfare), by Keith Parkinson; *The Paint in my Blood* (IFD Publishing), by Alan M. Clarke; *The Deceiving Eye: The Art of Richard Hescox* (Paper Tiger), by Richard Hescox; *Paintings, Drawings, Perceptions* (Underwood Books), by Ilene Meyer; and *The Art of Discworld* (Gollancz) by Paul Kidby and Terry Pratchett. Cartoon fans will want to have *The Best of Gahan Wilson* (Underwood Books), one of the best of all the cartoonists of the fantastic.

Turning to general genre-related nonfiction books of interest, the ones that'll probably be of the most interest to SF readers this year were *Chased by Sea Monsters: Prehistoric Predators of the Deep* (Dorling Kindersley), by Nigel Marven and Jasper James, the companion volume to the television show that pretended to take scientists back in time to explore ancient oceans, and a fascinating work of what might be called "speculative biology," *The Future Is Wild* (Firefly Books Ltd.), by Dougal Dixon and John Adams, an ingenious and gorgeously illustrated look at the strange creatures that might evolve to replace the familiar creatures of today millions of years from now (this actually came out a couple of years back, but I missed it; a mention of the new trade paperback edition is justified, though, I think), and *Ages in Chaos: James Hutton and the Discovery of Deep Time* (Tor/Forge), by Stephen Baxter. It's much harder to come up with a genre connection to justify mentioning *Conquest: Hernando de Soto and the Indians: 1539–1543* (Wildside), but I'm going to give it a try anyway. For one thing, it's by William Sanders (yes, *that* William Sanders), the SF writer, and as such at the very least deserves a mention as an associational item: for another thing, it deals with such a little-known period in history that many readers may also find that it delivers much of the same kind of kick that they get out of Alternate History. (How's that?) Sanders makes no attempt to disguise his dislike of de Soto and his conquistadors from the beginning, but they're a bunch that it's hard to find any good reason to like, even for somebody who was bending over backward to be "fair" and "unbiased"; basically all they did on their "expedition" was blunder around the South searching futilely for gold, taking slaves by the hundreds and working them to death, slaughtering Indians (including every man, woman, and child in at least one village), stealing everything they could find (including the food that kept them alive), and burning towns and villages to the ground. (De Soto also managed to get most of his *own* men killed in the process as well.) This, alas, is what First Contact with a technologically superior race could *really* be like, rather than the more benign scenarios we sometimes see in science fiction. Despite *Conquest's* horrific content, it's an enjoyable read; Sanders' style is clear and colloquial, always entertaining, sometimes wryly funny, and he's marshaled an enormous amount of facts about a little-known period in history (the expedition journals are the only descriptions we have of some of the Indian civilizations that existed on this continent before the fateful coming of the Europeans), one as different from the present-day world as many another author's alien planet. Nor is there much genre-related justification for mentioning *Terry Jones' Medieval Lives* (BBC Books), by Terry Jones and Alan Ereira, other than the fact that it might be worthwhile for fantasy fans to see just how complex, contradictory, and multifaceted medieval times actually *were*, as opposed to the watered-down, simplified, and bland version of them you get in all-too-many generic genre-fantasy novels.

The Hollywood machine continued to flail and judder and fart, emitting a loud, discordant grinding noise and puffs of black smoke, in its attempt to churn out successful genre movies, but many of them didn't go over even at the box office, let alone with the critics. Critically, the best-received movies of the year, especially in science fiction, were mostly products from smaller studios and production companies—not surprisingly, I suppose.

The best science fiction movie of the year, and one of the best in a number of years, was *Eternal Sunshine of the Spotless Mind*; it was not without flaws (it's slow in places, and rumor has it that the somewhat out-of-left-field happy ending was tagged on at the studio's insistence), but the performances were all excellent (Jim Carrey proving once again that he *can* act without mugging if the director sits on him), and it's refreshing to see an intelligent SF movie being aimed at an audience of intelligent adults who are expected to actually *think* about the ideas being presented, instead of a vehicle jammed with the standard action movie tropes and big special effects as a *substitute* for idea content. The best fantasy movie of the year was undoubtedly *Harry Potter and the Prisoner of Azkaban*, by far the best directed to date of all the *Harry Potter* movies, and the only one, in my opinion, that the adults are likely to enjoy as much as the kids. Another of the year's best movies, although it's hard to know where to categorize it (it's not exactly a comic-book movie, since it wasn't based on a existent comic book, but is more of an ironic postmodern comment on comic-book heroes in general), was *The Incredibles*, which received almost unbelievably respectful reviews for an animated film about superheroes, even from intellectual critics, and which many people felt should have been on the Oscar shortlist for year's best movie, period, instead of being relegated to the Best Animated Feature category. It's perhaps a stretch to categorize *Finding Neverland*, a partial biopic of *Peter Pan* creator J. M. Barrie, as a genre movie, although many critics seem to be doing so (perhaps because of the internal fantasy/dream sequences), but although it's nowhere near as historically accurate as it pretends to be, it deserves its slot on the Oscar ballot, and a mention here, if only for Johnny Depp's wonderfully nuanced performance—and because the *Peter Pan* connection does make it of at least marginal genre interest.

Below this point, though, things go downhill fast.

Nobody will ever know for sure, unless we consult the lady from the new TV show *Medium*, but I suspect that Isaac Asimov would have hated the big-budget movie "version" of his famous short-story collection *I, Robot* (I hesitate to call it a version, as it really has little to do with the book other than a shared title and a few character names). Isaac was a pacifist, after all, and (rightly or wrongly) felt that violence never really settled anything and was the last resort of the incompetent—so I doubt that he would have been happy with his robot stories being turned into a standard Will Smith adventure, with all the gun battles, explosions, car chases, and physically impossible action scenes that seem to be required by law to be put into a movie these days once the budget climbs past a certain point, especially if it's a sci-fi movie. For all the thud and blunder, *I, Robot* only performed lukewarmly at the box office, although it wasn't a complete dog. Another case of more being less was *The Chronicles of Riddick*, the sequel to an actually pretty good small movie called *Pitch Black*, which was good because it *was* small, and cleverly exploited the virtues of being so. Given a lot more money to work with, though, due to the success of *Pitch Black*, the producers threw out of the window everything that had made the earlier movie worthwhile, and produced a bloated and overblown standard action movie that threw everything it could into the mix, *including* the kitchen sink, and which sank out of sight at the box office. *The Day After Tomorrow* was another big special-effects movie, but it did extremely good business, one of the few such movies that did this year; I must admit that the special effects were extremely well done, especially the gigantic storm surge that drowns Manhattan, but the movie had little else to recommend it, being silly in the extreme. *Van Helsing* was almost as bad as last year's *The League of Extraordinary Gentlemen*, which puts it in the running for the exclusive title "worst movie ever made," and was a box-office bomb, as was *Alien vs. Predator*, although I suspect that the later movie (and perhaps even *Van Helsing*, alas) will make it up later in video rentals. *The Village* featured a "surprise" ending that most experienced genre fans had figured out within the first ten minutes of the movie, and struck most as a long way to go for very little result; movie after movie, director M. Night Shyamalan has been steadily losing (with me, anyway) all the credit he'd earned with *The Sixth Sense*, until now I'm at the point where I'm reluctant to watch his movies at all. *Lemony Snicket's A Series of Unfortunate Events* (with Jim Carrey back in his mugging mode) did well enough, although I get the feeling that it didn't perform quite up to expectations.

Comic-book movies had an uneven year as well. *Spider-Man 2* was pretty successful, both critically and commercially, as was, to a lesser degree, *Hellboy*, but in spite of featuring Halle Berry in a skintight leather cat suit (which you would have thought would have been enough to insure a lot of ticket sales right there), *Catwoman* was one of the biggest bombs (notice the restraint I demonstrate by refusing to say that *Catwoman* "dogged-out") of the year, and perhaps the most critically savaged movie of the year as well. Segueing into animated movies, *Shrek 2*, the year's other big sequel, seemed to do pretty well (although the critics didn't handle it as respectfully as they had *Shrek*) and is enjoyable enough, but it's nowhere near as good as the first movie had been. *Shark Tale* also made money, but it wasn't as good as its obvious model, last year's *Finding Nemo*, or *Shrek 2*, let alone *The Incredibles. The SpongeBob SquarePants Movie* did okay. *Team America: World Police* and *Thunderbirds*, two movies using a deliberately retro and campy style of puppet animation, did less well.

Two movies this year stretched the limits of moviemaking technology, with mixed results. Everything in *Sky Captain and the World of Tomorrow* was computer-generated except the actors—sets, backgrounds, props, *everything*—with the actors performing before blue screens on bare stages (which was all too evident in a couple of places, especially when they were looking the wrong way). It looked great, kind of a big-screen version of an old Fleischer *Superman* cartoon with live actors plunked into it, and if they had just managed to add a script that made sense and generated some suspense, and found an actor a bit more capable of charismatic swashbuckling than the cold and affectless Jude Law, it might have been a success. As it was, though, it tanked big-time, probably especially painful considering how much it cost to make in the first place. *The Polar Express* was an all-computer-animated movie, even the actors, using the motion-capture technology that had been developed for Gollum in the Lord of the Rings movies; at first, it looked like it was going to tank, too, but it eventually recovered and did pretty well. One widespread criticism, though, was that the computer animation made the characters look "creepy" or "scary," probably not the effect they were aiming for in a warmhearted children's movie, but which means that this technology might have a lot of future applications for horror movies.

There were a lot of ill-advised "remakes" of old movies, most of which failed at the box office, including *The Stepford Wives*, *The Manchurian Candidate*, *Around the World in 80 Days*, and *The Flight of the Phoenix*. Hollywood has been trying to duplicate the success of *Gladiator* for some time now, but it was a disastrous year for big-budget "historical" epics, what used to be called "Sword and Sandal" movies, with *Alexander the Great* (featuring a ludicrously miscast Colin Farrell), *Troy*, and *Arthur* all performing well "under expectations," to put it politely.

Coming up next year: the new *Star Wars* movie (some devoted fan is already camping out—literally—in line to wait for tickets, in spite of the movie's release date being months away, but let's just say that I won't be camping out next to him), a new *Harry Potter* movie (unfortunately not with the same director as the last one), a Tim Burton remake of *Willy Wonka and the Chocolate Factory*, supposedly taking it back closer to the original Dahl book, *Charlie and the Chocolate Factory*, lots more comic-book movies, and no doubt other unexpected delights (I suppose I really should add a glyph of irony here, shouldn't I?). Also coming up is a new animated movie by Hayao Miyazaki, who did *Spirited Away*, something I actually *am* looking forward to. (The film version of *The Hitchhiker's Guide to the Galaxy* looks promising, too.)

With the disappearance of many of the most popular SF-and-fantasy television shows in recent years—*Buffy, the Vampire Slayer*, *Angel*, *Babylon 5*, *Farscape*—and with other shows like *Enterprise* and *Smallville* visibly tottering on the brink throughout the year, there seems to be a feeling in some circles that the golden age of genre TV is behind us and receding fast. On the other hand, new shows such as *Lost* and *Stargate Atlantis* are pulling in big new audiences, even as older shows falter and die.

As Kathy Huddleston and other commentators have pointed out (including me in this space last year), genre shows on television have clearly been hurt by the current rage for "reality TV." Most of the older, now vanished genre shows, especially the SF shows, were special-effects-heavy, which made them expensive to produce; why pay huge amounts of money producing a genre show that will draw only a relatively small audience, when you can pay comparatively next to nothing to produce a reality show that will draw *immense* audiences, many times higher than the genre shows *ever* drew on their best days? This was probably a factor in the death of *Angel*, *Farscape*, and a number of other shows. On the other hand, there *are* new effects-heavy shows, such as *Stargate Atlantis* and *Battlestar Galactica*—none on network television, though, you'll notice. The tendency on network seems to be to run genre shows that have only minimal or tangential fantastic elements, such as *Joan of Arcadia* or *Desperate Housewives*, which don't demand big-effects budgets to do.

The big news in genre TV this year, announced just at press time, was the cancellation of the last surviving original-run Star Trek series, *Enterprise*, something that came as a surprise to few, since it has been obviously struggling and sinking in the ratings for the last couple of seasons. With the cancellation of *Enterprise*, and persistent rumors that there's not going to be another Star Trek theatrical movie, this may be the end of the once-mighty Star Trek franchise—as far as movies and TV are concerned, anyway; oddly, Star Trek novelizations and computer games, which are doing fine, may continue marching on long after there's no longer a first-run Star Trek series to be found on the air (old Star Trek shows will still be available in reruns for years—if not decades—to come, of course; your *grandchildren* may still be watching them). Another genre show that was once a heavy-hitter in the ratings, *Smallville*, is also making distressed wobbling noises, as if its wheels are about to come off, and probably will be cancelled soon. *Charmed*, once also a ratings powerhouse, is also suspected to be almost at the end of its rope, and will probably be cancelled either this season, or, at best, the season after that. Already dead are last year's "lawyers in the future" show, *Century City*, plus *Father of the Pride*, *Futurama*, *Wonderwalls*, and *Tru Calling*, which seemed set to make it into its sophomore season before suddenly having the plug pulled on it. (Reputedly killed by the success of a similar "I see dead people" show, *Medium*, introduced early this year; I guess the suits figured, why have two of them?)

Not all genre shows are going under, though. *Stargate SG-1* is still going strong, and launched a successful spin-off, *Stargate Atlantis*. *Andromeda* and *Joan of Arcadia* still seem to be doing well, as is the other "psychic" show, *The Dead Zone*. And *The Simpsons* and *South Park*, if you consider them to be genre shows in the first place, keep on truckin' on, as always (joined this year by *Drawn Together*, the first "animated reality show," a mind-boggling concept if there ever was one).

Some of the new shows have done well also. We've already mentioned *Medium* and *Stargate Atlantis*; ABC scored big with *Lost* and *Desperate Housewives*, two of the first successful *network* genre shows for a long time. Calling *Desperate Housewives* a genre show is a stretch (although it's narrated by a dead woman), but *Lost* fits solidly into a long genre tradition of "lost world" stories, coming across as a mix between *Survivor* and a much-more-adult *Fantasy Island* (or perhaps *Lord of the Flies*), with what I suspect will turn out to be a *Forbidden Planet*–style monster from the id roaming around and eating somebody every so often to add a pinch of danger and suspense. (That monster seems to be the key to the show's success to date, with everybody dying to know what it is, and everybody and their brother having a theory, but I wonder if *Lost* hasn't painted itself into a corner here—once they *tell* you what the monster is, many in the audience are going to lose interest in the show . . . but at the same time, if they stretch things out too long *without* telling you what it is, people are going to get frustrated and stop watching. It'll be interesting to see how long they can continue to walk this tightrope without falling off.) The new version of *Battlestar Galactica* (I'm still not at all sure *why* we needed a new one, but Lord knows, they don't ask *me* about these things) seems to be going over with the fans pretty well to date. And as a sop thrown to inconsolable *Farscape* fans, there was even a new *Farscape* miniseries this year, *Farscape: The Peacekeeper Wars*.

The Sci-Fi Channel is turning into a big producer of original shows, and one of the year's other big events, which unfortunately didn't live up to the anticipation it had generated, was a miniseries adaptation of Ursula K. Le Guin's famous fantasy novel *A Wizard of Earthsea* (mixed with bits of one of its sequels, *The Tombs of Atuan*). Hopes had been high for this show, but most Le Guin fans were disappointed in it. It seemed more like an attempt to generate a generic fantasy movie, with bits clearly influenced by Harry Potter and the Lord of the Rings movies, than a sincere attempt to translate the style and substance of Le Guin's work to the screen, and Le Guin herself scathingly denounced it in a series of essays on the Internet. In spite of the disenchantment of most Le Guin readers, the miniseries was a big ratings success for the Sci-Fi Channel, so they were probably happy enough with it. Let's hope they do a better job, though, with upcoming miniseries versions of Kim Stanley Robinson's *Red Mars* and Joe Haldeman's *The Forever War*.

A case could probably be made for listing some of The Discovery Channel specials such as *Chased By Sea Monsters*—whose deadpan conceit is that this is just another nature documentary, following scientists who have gone back in time to study the swarming CGI dinosaurs of various prehistoric oceans—as science fiction shows, because the gimmick is played perfectly straight, with little or no breaking of the fourth wall. And considered as science fiction shows, the now rather fake-looking CGI dinosaurs would have been considered to be amazing special effects even as recently as ten or fifteen years ago, which shows you just how fast the whole area of computer-generated animation is evolving.

The 62nd World Science Fiction Convention, Noreascon 4, was held in Boston, Massachusetts from September 2 to September 6, 2004, and drew an estimated attendance of 5,600. The 2004 Hugo Awards, presented at Noreascon 4, were: Best Novel, *Paladin of Souls*, by Lois McMaster Bujold; Best Novella, "The Cookie Monster," by Vernor Vinge; Best Novelette, "Legions in Time," by Michael Swanwick; Best Short Story, "A Study in Emerald," by Neil Gaiman; Best Related Book, *The Chesley Awards for Science Fiction and Fantasy Art: A Retrospective*, edited by John Grant and Elizabeth L. Humphrey with Pamela D. Scoville; Best Professional Editor, Gardner Dozois; Best Professional Artist, Bob Eggleton; Best Dramatic Presentation (short form), Gollum's acceptance speech at the *2003 MTV Movie Awards*; Best Dramatic Presentation (long form) *The Lord of the Rings: The Return of the King*; Best Semiprozine, *Locus*, edited by Charles N. Brown, Jennifer A. Hall, and Kirsten Gong-Wong; Best Fanzine, *Emerald City*, edited by Cheryl Morgan; Best Fan Writer, David Langford; Best Fan Artist, Frank Wu; plus the John W.

Campbell Award for Best New Writer to Jay Lake; and the Cordwainer Smith Rediscovery Award to C. L. Moore.

The 2003 Nebula Awards, presented at a banquet at the Westin Seattle Hotel in Seattle, Washington, April 17, 2004, were: Best Novel, *The Speed of Dark*, by Elizabeth Moon; Best Novella, *Coraline*, by Neil Gaiman; Best Novelette, "The Empire of Ice Cream," by Jeffrey Ford; Best Short Story, "What I Didn't See," by Karen Joy Fowler; Best Script, *The Lord of the Rings: The Two Towers*, by Fran Walsh, Philippa Boyens, and Peter Jackson; plus the Grandmaster Award to Robert Silverberg.

The 2004 World Fantasy Awards, presented at the Thirtieth Annual World Fantasy Convention in Tempe, Arizona, on October 31, 2004, were: Best Novel, *Tooth and Claw*, by Jo Walton; Best Novella, "A Crowd of Bone," by Greer Gilman; Best Short Fiction, "Don Ysidro," by Bruce Holland Rogers; Best Collection, *Bibliomancy*, by Elizabeth Hand; Best Anthology, *Strange Tales*, edited by Rosalie Parker; Best Artist, Donato Giancola and Jason Van Hollander (tie); Special Award (Professional), to Peter Crowther for *PS Publishing*; Special Award (Nonprofessional), to Ray Russell and Rosalie Parker, for *Tartarus Press*, plus Life Achievement Awards to Stephen King and Gahan Wilson.

The 2004 Bram Stoker Awards, presented by the Horror Writers of America during a banquet at the Embassy Suites in Phoenix, Arizona, on June 5, 2004, were: Best Novel, *lost boy lost girl*, by Peter Straub; Best First Novel, *The Rising*, by Brian Keene; Best Long Fiction, "Closing Time," by Jack Ketchum; Best Short Fiction, "Duty," by Gary A. Braunbeck; Best Collection, *Peaceable Kingdom*, by Jack Ketchum; Best Anthology, *Borderlands 5*, edited by Elizabeth and Thomas Monteleone; Nonfiction, *The Mothers and Fathers Italian Association*, by Thomas F. Monteleone; Best Illustrated Narrative, *The Sandman: Endless Nights*, by Neil Gaiman; Best Screenplay, *Bubba Ho-Tep*, by Don Coscarelli; Best Work for Younger Readers, *Harry Potter and the Order of the Phoenix*, by J. K. Rowling; Best Poetry Collection, *Pitchblende*, by Bruce Boston; Best Alternative Forms, *The Goreletter*, by Michael Arnzen; the Specialty Press Award, to Earthling Publications; plus the Lifetime Achievement Award to Anne Rice and Martin H. Greenberg.

The 2003 John W. Campbell Memorial Award was won by *Omega*, by Jack McDevott.

The 2003 Theodore Sturgeon Memorial Award for Best Short Story was won by "The Empress of Mars," by Kage Baker.

The 2003 Philip K. Dick Memorial Award went to *Altered Carbon*, by Richard K. Morgan.

The 2003 Arthur C. Clarke award was won by *Quicksilver*, by Neal Stephenson.

The 2003 James Tiptree Jr. Memorial Award was won by *Set This House in Order: A Romance of Souls*, by Matt Ruff.

Dead in 2004 or early 2005 were: **HUGH B. CAVE**, 94, veteran horror writer, author of over forty-five books, including the World Fantasy Award–winning collection *Murgunstrumm and Others*, winner of both the World Fantasy Convention's Life Achievement Award and the Bram Stoker Life Achievement Award; **FRANK KELLY FREAS**, 83, ten-time Hugo Winner as Best Professional Artist, and one of the most famous SF artists in history; **WILL EISNER**, 87, pioneering comic-book artist and graphic novelist, creator of the famous comic *The Spirit*; **JACK**

CHALKER, 61, well-known SF author of more than sixty novels, also a long-time fan, convention organizer, bibliographer, and small-press publisher; **F. M. BUSBY**, 83, well-known SF writer and Hugo-winning Fannie editor, author of *Cage a Man* and the Rissa Kerguelen series; **SONYA DORMAN (HESS)**, 80, SF short-story writer of the sixties and seventies, perhaps best known for her story "When I Was Miss Dow"; **ROGER D. ALCOCK**, 89, who wrote more than fifty SF stories under the name of Roger Dee; **ALFRED COPPEL**, 83, author of YA novels such as *The Rebel of Rhada* and of the Goldenwing trilogy; **TETSU YANO**, 81, Japanese writer and translator, who wrote many SF novels in his native language, but who is probably best known in the West for having translated works by Robert Heinlein and Frank Herbert into Japanese, and for his story, "The Legend of the Paper Spaceship"; **ROBERT MERLE**, 96, French SF writer, cowinner of the John W. Campbell Memorial Award; **JOHAN SPRINGBORG**, 58, Danish SF writer; **FRED WHIPPLE**, 97, scientist and author, coauthor of the early nonfiction book about space exploration, *The Conquest of the Moon*, with Wernher von Braun and Willy Ley; **BASIL WELLS**, 91, veteran SF writer; **DILIP M. SALWI**, 52, Indian SF writer; **ROXANNE HUTTON**, 50, SF writer; **KATHERINE LAWRENCE**, 50, author of SF short fiction, nonfiction, computer games, and TV scripts; **ROBYN HERRINGTON**, 43, SF writer; **BRIAN McNAUGHTON**, 68, horror writer; **REX MILLER**, 65, horror writer; **PAULA DANZIGER**, 59, author of YA novels; **MONIQUE LEBAILLY**, 75, French translator, writer, and editor; **MICHAEL ELDER**, 73, British writer and actor; **JACQUES DERRIDA**, 74, famous French philosopher and critic, founder of the critical school of deconstructionism that was influential on critical writing worldwide; Australian small-press editor and publisher **PETER McNAMARA**, 57, founder of Aphelion Publishing; **RAYMOND BAYLESS**, 84, fantasy artist and Lovecraft enthusiast; **FAY WRAY**, 96, actress best known to genre audiences for her role as the continuously screaming blonde beauty in the original *King Kong*; **JANET LEIGH**, 77, another scream queen, best known for the shower scene in *Psycho*; **ED KEMMER**, 84, star of the fifties television show *Space Patrol*; **CHRISTOPHER REEVE**, 52, film actor, best known to genre audiences for his portrayal of Superman in four *Superman* movies in the late seventies through the mid-eighties; **PETER USTINOV**, 82, well-known actor whose connection to the genre is tenuous, but whose face must certainly be known to anyone who's ever watched old movies on television like *Spartacus* or *Quo Vadis* or his sequence of films about detective Hercule Poirot; **JERRY ORBACH**, 69, Broadway performer and film and television actor whose connection to the genre is also tenuous, except for a role voicing an animate candelabra in Disney's *Beauty and the Beast*, but whose long-running role on television's *Law and Order* probably made him familiar to almost everybody reading these words; **HOWARD KEEL**, 85, veteran Broadway performer and film star, whose only real connection to the genre was his role in *The Day of the Triffids*; **PETER GRAHAM**, 65, long-time fan and fanzine fan, credited with coining the phrase "the golden age of science fiction is twelve"; **ALLAN ROTHSTEIN**, SF fan and convention-goer; **GEORGE FLYNN**, 68, scientist and long-time SF fan; **ANTHONY STERLING RODGERS**, six-month-old son of SF writers Alan Rodgers and Amy Sterling Casil.

Inappropriate Behavior

PAT MURPHY

As the story that follows demonstrates, that old movie line "What we have here is a failure to communicate" is likely to be just as true in the future, in spite of all our high-tech communications equipment—in fact, maybe even *because* of it.

Pat Murphy lives in San Francisco, where she works for a science museum, the Exploratorium, and edits the *Exploratorium Quarterly*. Her elegant and incisive stories have appeared throughout the eighties and the nineties (and on into the Oughts) in *Asimov's Science Fiction, The Magazine of Fantasy & Science Fiction, SCI FICTION, Elsewhere, Amazing, Universe, Shadows, Lethal Kisses, Event Horizon, Full Spectrum*, and other places. Her story "Rachel in Love," one of the best-known stories of the eighties, won her the Nebula Award, the Theodore Sturgeon Memorial Award, and the Asimov's Readers Award in 1988; her novel *The Falling Woman* won her a second Nebula Award in the same year. Her novella "Bones" later won her a World Fantasy Award, and her collection *Points of Departure* won her a Philip K. Dick Award. Her stories have appeared in our First, Fifth, Eighth, and Ninth Annual Collections. Her other books include *The Shadow Hunter; The City, Not Long After; Nadya: The Wolf Chronicles;* and *There and Back Again: by Max Merriwell*. Her most recent book is a new novel, *Wild Angel, by Mary Maxwell*. She writes a science column, with Paul Doherty, for *The Magazine of Fantasy & Science Fiction*.

THE MECHANO

There was a man asleep on the sand.

He should not be here. It was my island. I had just returned to my mechano and it was time for me to go to work. He should not be here.

I studied the man through the eyes of my mechano. They were good eyes. They worked very well beneath the water, at depths down to fifteen hundred meters. I had adjusted them for maximum acuity at distances ranging from two inches to five feet. Beyond that, the world was a blur of tropical sunshine and brilliant color. I liked it that way.

There had been a big storm the night before. One of the coconut palms had blown down, and the beach was littered with driftwood, coconuts, and palm fronds.

The man didn't look good. He had a bloody scrape on his cheek, other scrapes on his arms and legs, a smear of blood in his short brown hair. His right leg was marked with bruises colored deep purple and green. He wore an orange life vest, a t-shirt, a pair of shorts, and canvas boat shoes.

He stirred in his sleep, sighing softly. Startled, I sent the mechano scuttling backward. I stopped a few feet away from him.

My mechano had a speaker. I tested it and it made a staticky sound. I wondered what I should say to this man.

The man moved, lifting a hand to rub his eyes. Slowly, he rolled over.

"Bonjour," I said through the mechano's speakers. Maybe he had come from one of the islands of French Polynesia.

THE MAN

A sound awakened him—a sort of mechanical squawking.

Evan Collins could feel the tropical sun beating down on his face, the warm beach sand beneath his hands. His head ached and his mouth was dry. His right leg throbbed with a dull, persistent pain.

Evan raised a hand to rub his eyes and winced when he brushed against a sand-encrusted scrape on his cheek. When he rolled over onto his back, the throbbing in his leg became a sudden, stabbing pain.

Wiping away the tears that blurred his vision, he lifted his head and blinked down at his leg. His calf was marked with bloody coral scrapes. Beneath the scrapes were vivid bruises: dark purple telling of injuries beneath the surface of the skin. When he tried to move his leg again, he gasped as the stabbing pain returned.

He heard the sound again: a mechanical rasping like a radio tuned to static. He turned in the direction of the sound, head aching, eyes dazzled by the sun. A gigantic cockroach was examining him with multifaceted eyes.

The creature was at least three feet long, with nasty looking mandibles. Its carapace glittered in the sunlight as it stood motionless, staring in his direction.

Again, the mechanical squawk, coming from the cockroach. This time, the sound was followed by a scratchy voice. "Bonjour," the cockroach said.

He had taken two years of French in high school, but he could remember none of it. This must be a dream, he thought, closing his eyes against the glare.

"Do you speak English?" the scratchy voice asked.

He opened his eyes. The roach was still there. "Yes," he rasped through a dry throat.

"You shouldn't be here," the scratchy voice said. "What are you doing here?"

He looked past the monster, struggling to make sense of his situation. The beach sand was the pure white of pulverized coral. On one side of the beach was a tangle of mangroves. On the inland side, palm trees rose from scrubby undergrowth. The water of the lagoon was pure tropical blue—paler where the coral reef was near the water's surface; darker where the water was deep. Some hundred yards offshore, he could see the mast of a boat sticking up out of the water. His boat.

He remembered: he had been heading west toward the Cook Islands when the storm came up. He ran before the wind toward an island that was an unnamed speck on the nautical chart. He had made it over the reef into the lagoon before the surge smashed the boat against a coral head, cracking the hull, swamping the boat, sending him flying overboard to smash into the reef. He didn't remember breaking his leg and struggling through the surf to the beach.

"Thirsty," he rasped through dry lips. "Very thirsty. Please help me."

He closed his eyes against the dazzling sunlight and heard the sound of metal sliding against metal as the roach walked away. He wondered if the monster was leaving him to die.

A few minutes later, he heard the sound of the roach returning. He opened his eyes. The cockroach stood beside him, holding a coconut in its mandibles. As he watched, the roach squeezed, and the point of each mandible pierced the outer husk, neatly puncturing the nut in two places.

Still gripping the coconut, the cockroach took a step toward him, opened its mandibles, and dropped the nut beside him. A thin trickle of coconut milk wet the sand.

"You can drink," said the cockroach.

He picked up the coconut, pressed his lips to the hole in the shaggy husk, and tipped it back. The coconut milk was warm and sweet and wet. He drank greedily.

By the time he had finished the milk, the roach was back with another coconut. It pierced the shell before dropping the nut.

The roach brought him two more coconuts, piercing each one neatly and dropping it beside Evan. It stood and watched him drink.

"I think my leg is broken," Evan murmured.

The roach said nothing.

He closed his eyes against the glare of the sun. Many years before, as an undergraduate, he had taken a psychology course on the psychosocial aspects of emergencies and disasters. A guest speaker, a member of a search-and-rescue team, had talked about how people had managed to stay alive in terrible situations—and had described the mental attitude that helped those people survive. The search-and-rescue expert had said that survivors just kept on trying, doing whatever they could. "Step by step," he had said. "That's the approach to take. Don't try to find the answer to everything at once. Remember, life by the yard is hard, but by the inch, it's a cinch."

Evan thought about what he could do right away to help increase his chances of survival. "I need to get out of the sun," he muttered. "I need food, water, medical supplies."

There were so many things he needed to do. He had to find something that he could use to splint his leg. He had to figure out a way to signal for help. He needed to find water. So many things he had to do.

He fell asleep.

THE MECHANO

It was restful under the ocean. The light that filtered down from above was dim and blue. The world around me was all shades of blue—dark and light. I liked it on the ocean floor.

I had left the man asleep on the sand. But first, I was helpful. I always try hard to be helpful.

He had said he had to get out of the sun. So I had gathered palm fronds from the beach and stuck them in the sand where they would shade him. He had said he needed food and water and medical supplies. So I went to his sailboat and found some cans of food and a can opener and bottles of water and a first-aid kit. I carried all that stuff up from the sunken boat and left it on the beach beside him.

Then I headed for deep water. I had work to do.

I lifted my legs high as I walked, moving slowly to avoid stirring up the loose silt that covered the ocean bottom. My temperature sensors tested the currents—warm where they welled up from volcanic cracks below. My chemical sensors tested the water; it tasted of sulfides, a familiar musty flavor.

I picked my way through the silt to reach my favorite spot. There was no silt here: a rocky portion of the ocean bottom had pushed up. There was a great tall chimney, where a hydrothermal vent brought up hot water from deep in the earth. Over the centuries, the hot water had deposited sulfides of copper, zinc, lead, gold, silver, and other metals, forming the chimney.

The mining company had mined for gold not far from here. They had followed a rich vein of ore until it gave out. Then they gave up. I had sniffed around their tailings, but then I had found a spot near the chimney that was much more promising. I had spent my last few visits to this spot gnawing on the chimney and breaking loose big chunks of rock. Now I could do what I liked best—sort through those rocks. I tasted each one with my chemical sensors to find the rocks that were richest in gold and silver. Those I stacked up in a neat pile.

It was wonderful work. I liked to sort things. I was very good at it. At home, I liked to sort all my books by color: putting the red ones on one shelf, the blue ones on another, the black ones on another.

I worked until the light began growing dimmer, a sign that the sun was sinking low in the sky. I choose the best of the rocks and picked it up in the mechano's mandibles. Then I headed back to the island.

I made my way up a long slope to reach the shallow waters where the coral reef grew. There, the bottom was sandy and I could walk quickly without stirring up silt. Schools of brightly colored fish swam above me. The fish darted here and there, fleeing from me. They moved too quickly, I thought. I liked it better in the deep blue waters. I passed the man's sailboat, wedged between two coral heads.

I came out of the water on the side of the beach near the mangroves. As I emerged from the water, the crabs hurried back into their holes in the sand.

I placed the rock beside one of the burrows. On my first day on the island, I had noticed that the crabs all seemed to want the burrow that one crab had dug beside a rock. So I started bringing rocks for the other crabs.

There were now rocks beside thirty-two crab burrows. I had been on the island for thirty-two days and I had brought the crabs one rock each day. I was very helpful. I thought it was appropriate to bring rocks for the crabs.

If the man hadn't been on the island, I would have stayed and watched until the crabs came out again. I liked to watch the crabs. But I wanted to find out what the man was doing, so I didn't wait for the crabs.

I headed up the beach to where I had left the man. He was no longer in his spot on the sand. I could see a track in the sand where he dragged his leg.

I followed the track and trudged through the sand. The man was asleep in the shade of a palm tree. He was using his life jacket as a pillow. He had wrapped the water bottles and the cans of food and the first-aid kit in his t-shirt and dragged them along with him.

He moved in his sleep, shifting restlessly. Then he opened his eyes and looked at me with wide, wild eyes.

THE MAN

When Evan Collins woke up, he found four plastic bottles of water, six cans of tuna fish, a can opener, and the first-aid kit from his boat on the sand beside him. He had splinted his leg with the velcro splint from the first-aid kit. He had eaten a can of tuna fish and drunk a one-quart bottle of water. Then he had dragged himself into the shade and taken two of the painkillers, which helped with the pain but left him groggy and disoriented.

He had fallen asleep in the shade. When he woke, the giant roach was back.

Evan drank from one of the bottles of water and blinked at the creature. It was a machine, he realized now. Its carapace was burnished steel. He could see the neat mechanical joints of its legs. On its burnished steel carapace, he could see the stenciled words: "Atlantis Mining and Salvage."

Of course: It made sense now. It was a robot designed for work underwater. A human being was operating the mechanical roach by remote control. He'd seen descriptions of such systems at the engineering department's annual open house.

"You work for Atlantis Mining," he said. "You've told them that I'm here."

The roach didn't say anything. Evan pictured the man operating the mechano: a gruff, no-nonsense, working-class guy, like the kind of guy who works on oil rigs. Matter of fact.

"When is the rescue party coming?" Evan asked.

"I don't know," said the roach. "Do you want a coconut?"

Evan blinked at the roach. "A coconut? Yes, but . . ."

The roach turned away and walked deeper into the grove of coconut palms. It picked up a coconut, returned to Evan's side, pierced the nut, and dropped it beside Evan.

"Thank you." Evan took a long drink of coconut milk.

"You're welcome," said the roach.

Evan studied the roach, wishing he could see the face of the man behind the mechanism. This man was his only link to the outside world. He still hadn't said anything about Atlantis Mining and their reaction to Evan's predicament. "What did your supervisor say when you told him I was here?" Evan asked.

"I don't have a supervisor," said the roach.

"Okay," Evan said slowly. He felt dizzy and a little feverish, and the conversation wasn't helping. "But you did tell someone that I'm here, didn't you?"

"No," said the roach. Then, after a pause. "I'm going to talk to Dr. Rhodes. Do you want me to tell him?"

The flat, mechanical voice provided no clue about the feelings of the person behind it. "Yes." Evan struggled not to raise his voice. "When will you talk with him?"

"Tonight."

"That's good," Evan said. "Will you tell him that my leg is broken and that I need medical help?" He looked at the bottles of water and cans of food. One and a half bottles of water and five cans of tuna remained. They wouldn't last long.

"Yes. Do you want another coconut?" asked the roach.

Evan stared at the expressionless metal face, the multifaceted eyes. Evan Collins was an anthropologist on sabbatical, studying ritual welcoming orations of Oceania and determining how they varied among the various island groups—a fine excuse to spend a year sailing across the South Pacific. As an anthropologist, he prided himself on his ability to read people. But there was no way to read this person. Another coconut? No, what he needed was a rescue party. To get this person to provide that, he needed more information. "You know," he said slowly, "I never introduced myself. My name is Evan. Evan Collins. What's your name?"

"Annie," said the roach.

That stopped Evan. He revised his mental image of the person running the mechano. Not a working-class guy. A woman.

"Annie," Evan said. "That's a nice name. How long have you worked for Atlantis Mining?"

"Thirty-two days," the roach said.

Again, Evan Collins revised his assessment of the person behind the roach. A new employee, a woman—someone in a position of powerlessness. "So tell me," Evan said. "Who is Dr. Rhodes?"

The roach took a step back. "I don't want to answer questions," the roach said.

"Then I won't ask questions," Evan said quickly. Annie was his only contact with the world. He didn't want to drive her away. "You can ask me questions if you want."

"I don't want to ask questions," said the roach. "I want you to tell me a story."

THE MECHANO

Evan Collins had so many questions. He kept asking and asking and asking.

My mother used to tell me bedtime stories. Whenever my mother bothered me with too many questions or requests, I'd ask her to tell me a story. I collect stories, just like I collect rocks.

"What kind of story?" Evan Collins asked me.

I thought about stories that my mother liked to tell. "Cinderella," I said.

"You want me to tell you the story of Cinderella?"

"Yes."

He hesitated, and I wondered if he knew the story. Then he started. "Once upon a time," he said.

Once upon a time . . . yes, that was how fairy tales began. Once upon a time, Cinderella's mother died and her father married again. Cinderella had a wicked stepmother and two stepsisters.

In my mind, I pictured a chart that showed me all the people in the story as the man mentioned them. The father and mother and Cinderella formed a triangle, all connected by solid lines. The stepmother and her two daughters formed another triangle. The stepmother was connected to the father by a solid line. Mental pictures like this helped me sort out relationships that otherwise didn't make sense.

Cinderella's stepmother and stepsisters made her do all the work around the house—and at night she slept on a cot in the kitchen. The man said that this made Cinderella very sad.

I thought about Cinderella on her cot in the kitchen, and I wasn't so sure he was right. During the day, the house would be noisy and confusing with all those people talking and laughing. At night, it would be dark and lonely in the kitchen—very nice. If being called Cinderella was the price of being left alone, it seemed like a small one.

Then the prince decided to have a party and invite all noblewomen of the kingdom. The people in fairy tales were always having parties. The people in fairy tales were neurotypical, that was for sure. NTs were so social—always getting together and talking. NTs seemed to spend most of their time worrying about and establishing their social hierarchy.

That was what elementary school had been all about. It had taken me a while to figure it out, but all those games in the playground were really about who was boss.

I didn't care who was boss, and I didn't want to play those games. So I sat by myself and looked at the rocks that made up the wall at the edge of the playground. It was an old wall filled with interesting rocks of many different colors. Some had flecks of mica in them. I had started a rock collection, and I liked thinking about how the rocks in the wall would fit in my collection.

So I thought that Cinderella wouldn't want to go to the party—but the man said she did. She couldn't go because she didn't have the right clothes to wear.

I didn't see why she couldn't go to the party because of her clothes. It was one of those NT rules that didn't make any sense. NTs wanted everyone to look and act the same.

In school, the teacher kept trying to make me go play with the others, even when I explained that I wanted to examine the rocks. She wanted me to act like the rest of the kids and play their games. NTs thought that everyone should act the same way, everyone should fit in.

I was relieved when a doctor finally figured out that I was not neurotypical. All the doctors put their own names on my condition. High-functioning autism, one doctor called it. Asperger's syndrome, said another. Another one said I was PDD, which stands for Pervasive Developmental Disorders. The first doctor said that wasn't really a diagnosis, it was just a label.

Whatever the doctors called it, they agreed I was not normal; I was not NT. They explained to my mother and father that my brain was different from the brains of most people. My behavior was not the result of a mental condition. It was a neurological difference.

My tendency to focus on certain things—like the rocks in my collection—was one result of this condition. The doctors said I was perseverative—tending to fixate on one thing to the exclusion of all else.

NTs thought paying close attention to rocks was perseverative. But paying close attention to other people all the time, the way they did, was just fine. That didn't make sense to me. I didn't see what was wrong with paying attention to rocks. But I was glad that the doctors recognized what I had known for a long time. I was different. My mother cried when the doctors told her about all this. I don't know why.

So Cinderella's stepmother and stepsisters went to the party, leaving her at home. Then Cinderella's fairy godmother showed up. I put her on my mental chart with a line that connected her to Cinderella.

The fairy godmother was definitely NT. She waved a magic wand, and Cinderella was dressed in a golden gown with glass slippers. The fairy godmother wanted to make sure Cinderella fit in—and at the same time that she was better than everyone else. The fairy godmother was concerned about Cinderella's position in the social hierarchy, and that's very NT.

The fairy godmother told Cinderella that she had to leave the party before midnight—a simple enough rule. So much more direct than most of the rules that NTs followed. It was good that the fairy godmother told Cinderella the rule. NTs usually didn't talk about the rules they all followed. They just did certain things and then told me I was wrong when I did something else.

So Cinderella went to the party, then ran away at midnight and lost one of her glass slippers. Then the prince found Cinderella and put the glass slipper on her foot and said he would marry her. And the man said that Cinderella was happy. I remembered my mother had said the same thing when she told me the story of Cinderella. But I thought about the quiet kitchen, about Cinderella's cot where she could be alone, and I didn't think Evan Collins was right about that.

"Why is she happy?" I asked.

"Because the prince loves her. Because she is going to be a princess."

Those were NT answers. She was happy because of a relationship with another person and a new position in a hierarchy. If Cinderella were NT, she would be happy. But I didn't think she was NT. And if she weren't NT, she wouldn't be happy there. The prince would want her to go to parties and wear fancy clothes. She would rather stay in the quiet kitchen. That was what I thought.

"I don't think she is happy," I said. Then I turned away. I had to go talk to Dr. Rhodes.

I hurried away, crossing the sand to the recharging hut, a low-lying metal structure just large enough to shelter the mechano. Solar cells on the roof of the hut converted sunlight to electrical energy, which is stored in batteries inside the hut. Each night, I returned to my meat body and let the mechano recharge.

I backed the mechano into the hut, maneuvering it carefully so that two prongs of the charging unit slid into the sockets on the mechano's body. Then, reluctantly, I returned to my meat body, asleep in its sensory deprivation tank.

I did not like my meat body. When I was in the mechano, I could filter my sensory inputs. When the light was too bright, I could decrease the sensitivity of my visual receptors and decrease its intensity. When a sound was too loud, I could temporarily disable the audio receptors.

My meat body was so much more limited. As I let my consciousness return to the meat, I heard the steady hum of the pump that circulated the fluid in my tank. Dr. Rhodes told me that it was the quietest pump on the market, but it sounded so loud, so very loud I could feel its vibrations in my bones.

I floated in a tiny sea. The water that supported my body was saturated with magnesium sulfate—it was five times denser than seawater, and its temperature was exactly the same as my body. An intravenous drip provided my body with the nutrition it needed; a catheter drained away the urine.

Each night, I slept here while the mechano recharged. I could, if I wanted, leave the sensory tank and go to the exercise room or the cafeteria, but I usually stayed in my tank.

I thought about the man on the beach. I remembered that Evan Collins wanted me to tell Dr. Rhodes that he was on the beach. I sometimes had problems remembering things. Dr. Rhodes said I had a poor short-term working memory. But I remembered that I should tell Dr. Rhodes about Evan Collins and his broken leg.

I moved my hand to push the button that summoned an attendant. The water swirled against my skin, an unwelcome sensation. I heard a rattle and clank as the hatch in the side of the tank opened, letting in the light. I blinked against the glare as the attendant removed the electrodes from my head.

The attendant was a round-faced woman with dark hair. She talked to me as she removed the electrodes. "Do you remember me, Annie? My name is Kiri," she said. She smiled at me, and I nodded, but I didn't smile back. Already I was feeling overwhelmed.

I didn't say anything as she helped me out of the tank and gave me a towel and a robe. I knew that she wanted me to wrap my meat body in the robe, but I did so reluctantly. The touch of the cloth against my skin was irritating. The cement floor was cold against my bare feet.

I came back to my meat body to talk to Dr. Rhodes, and it always felt strange. My body was heavy and awkward; my hands were clumsy as I pulled on the robe. Kiri gave me a glass of water. I was always thirsty when I came out of the tank.

On the island, I was strong. My mechano could crack coconuts in its mandibles. My mechano could walk beneath the waves.

In my meat body, I was a little girl—twelve years old and skinny. My mother was a librarian; my father was a computer programmer. He called me "the Little Professor." I was part of an experimental program that Dr. Rhodes called a "therapeutic intervention."

I would rather be in my mechano.

I could hear voices from the corridor: people laughing and talking, the sound of sneakered feet walking down the hall. People were going to the cafeteria, to the exercise room, to dorms where they would sleep in beds. The other people here worked for Atlantis Mining. They were not part of the experimental program. They were NT.

Kiri led me down the hall.

"We are going the wrong way," I told her when we turned left down a corridor. Dr. Rhodes' office was to the right.

"We are going to a different room today," she told me.

In the different room, the fluorescent lights were humming overhead. I could see them flickering. My father once told me that fluorescent lights flickered sixty times every second because the electric current changed directions sixty times a second. He said most people didn't notice it. He could see the flicker, but it didn't really bother him.

It bothered me.

I closed my eyes against the flickering of the lights, but I couldn't shut out their noise. It filled the air like buzzing bees, like the school of bright fish that swam overhead when I was walking up from the depths to the beach.

I heard the sound of the doorknob turning and I opened my eyes to see Dr. Rhodes. He was a tall man with brown hair, and he always wears a white lab coat. "Hello, Annie," he said. "It's good to see you."

"It's good to see you, Dr. Rhodes," I said. Dr. Rhodes had told me that it was appropriate to greet someone in the way that they greeted you. He smiled.

I closed my eyes. "I have something to tell you," I said with my eyes closed. "On the beach, there's . . ."

"Hold on there, Annie," he said. "Why are your eyes closed?"

"The lights are bothering me," I said. "They're flickering and making a lot of noise."

"Is there something you could do about that other than close your eyes?" he asked.

I nodded. I began to rock, a comforting activity that absorbed some of the energy from the sound of the lights. My right hand gripped my left arm. I squeezed my arm in time with my rocking, and that helped, too.

"Do you want me to turn off the lights, Annie?" he asked. And suddenly the horrible buzzing sound was gone. The room was quiet except for the persistent whispering of the air conditioner. It sounded like tiny claws scratching against stone. "Open your eyes, Annie," Dr. Rhodes said.

I opened my eyes. The only light in the room was light from the hall, spilling in through the open door and the window. That light flickered too, but it was dimmer, so it wasn't as bad.

"Good girl," he said. "Now, what did you want to tell me?"

The whisper of the air conditioner shifted, getting louder. More claws, skittering over stone. It sounded the way the terrycloth robe felt against my skin. Scratching, scratching, scratching. For a moment, I forgot about what I had to tell him, distracted by the robe against my skin, by the noise of the air conditioner.

But I knew it was important to remember. As I rocked, I sorted through the details that I could tell Dr. Rhodes. It was difficult to choose the right one—they all seemed so important, and the air conditioner's whispering made it hard to think. I pictured the man's boat and the crack in its hull. I pictured the man on the beach, telling me about Cinderella. "Do you know the story of Cinderella?" I asked Dr. Rhodes. I was looking at my hands, concentrating on what I had to say.

"Yes, Annie, I know that story."

"Well, on my island . . ."

"Can you look at me when you talk to me, Annie?" Dr. Rhodes said.

His voice was just loud enough to cut through the scratching of the air conditioner.

"I wanted to tell you that on my island . . ." I raised my voice to be sure he'd hear me over the noise. I did not look at him. I was concentrating on remembering.

"Look at me, Annie. Remember, we're working on appropriate behavior."

I looked at him.

"That's good," he said. "Making eye contact is appropriate behavior."

I was looking at him and his lips were moving and that was so distracting that I couldn't think of what to say. I looked down at my hands—then remembered I had to make eye contact so I looked back at him.

"You're doing fine, Annie," he said, his lips flapping. His own eyes did not remain steadily on mine—they kept moving, shifting, looking at me and then looking away and then looking down and then looking back at me. His eyebrows were moving too, and it was confusing to watch, but I knew that he wanted me to watch. So I did, even though I couldn't think and watch at the same time. I wished I were in my mechano so that I could turn down my visual acuity. I tried to let my eyes go out of focus, but I kept seeing his eyes move.

That was how it was when NTs talked with each other. They looked at each other and they looked away. If I looked too much, Dr. Rhodes would tell me I was staring. NTs didn't stare, but they looked. It was all very complicated, like an intricate dance. Look up, look away, smile, blink, and it all meant something if you were NT.

I didn't understand that dance. I asked my mother what all that looking at each other and looking away meant exactly, and she couldn't tell me. She couldn't tell me how to perform the intricate eye dance that NTs did. But Dr. Rhodes wanted me to make eye contact.

"What did you want to tell me, Annie?" Dr. Rhodes asked.

I couldn't remember. I was watching his lips move, watching his eyes move.

"Last time we talked, you told me about the crabs on the beach," he said. "Are there still crabs on the beach?"

"Yes," I said, rocking and thinking about eye contact.

"Can you tell me about the crabs and look at me as you talk?" Dr. Rhodes asked.

I tried. I managed to tell him that some crabs had one big red claw, which they waved around.

Dr. Rhodes told me that they were fiddler crabs, that the male crabs had a big red claw that they used to signal to the female crabs and to scare away other male crabs. He said that he had studied crabs when he was an undergraduate student in biology, before he became a pediatric neurologist.

He asked me questions about the crabs and I answered as well as I could, through the haze of air-conditioner noise and the confusion of watching his mouth move.

Finally he said that it was time for me to go to the exercise room and our session was over. I walked on the treadmill for forty-five minutes, swam in the pool for forty-five minutes, and then went back to my tank, where I slept through the night.

DR. RHODES

The overhead lights were a distraction. He had forgotten about that. Usually, he met with Annie in his office, where his assistant had replaced the overhead fluorescent lights with incandescent floor lamps to give the place a warmer feel. But a technician had been working on the air-conditioning in his office, so he had moved his meeting with Annie to one of Atlantis Mining's regular conference rooms.

Still, he felt that his oversight had provided an excellent learning opportunity. He had given Annie an incentive to communicate her needs clearly, rather than assuming that he knew them.

The project was going very well, he thought. Over the next month, he would be evaluating how Annie's time alone in the mechano affected her ability to interact in her own body. He was pleased that Eric Westerman, the president of Atlantis Mining, had allowed him this opportunity to evaluate the potential of the telepresence experience as a therapeutic tool.

It was a pity that the storm had knocked out the cameras that ordinarily provided him with the opportunity to monitor Annie's daily activity on the island. He had put in two requests for repair to the supervisor of operations responsible for equipment on Annie's island and had received no word back. But the gap in the data was a minor matter. Tracking changes in Annie's behavior during therapy sessions was much more significant. All in all, he felt that the day's session had been quite successful.

THE MECHANO

I was back in my mechano, happy to be there. I opened my eyes to the first light of the tropical dawn and left the charging hut. It wasn't until I saw Evan Collins on the beach that I realized I had not told Dr. Rhodes about him. I had tried to tell Dr. Rhodes, but I had not succeeded.

The man was sleeping, his head pillowed on his orange life jacket. He didn't look good. The scrape on his cheek looked puffy and red. His skin was marked with red spots—bites of sand fleas. He had scratched some of them until they bled. He had wrapped his arms around himself, as if for warmth, but he was shivering a little in his sleep.

The bottles of water that I had carried from the boat were all empty. They lay beside him in the sand. I brought him a coconut, piercing it with the mechano's mandibles so that he could drink.

Then I went to work and sorted rocks. But I kept thinking about the man. I thought so much about him that I forgot to bring a rock for the crabs when I returned to the island.

When I got back, he was sitting up under the palm tree, and his eyes were open. There were dark circles under his eyes.

"Annie," he said. His voice was hoarse. "I'm very thirsty. I need water."

I looked at the empty bottles on the sand. "I brought all the water I found on the boat," I told him.

"Is there any fresh water on the island?" he asked in his rasping voice.

"No." The mechano did not need fresh water. "Do you want a coconut?"

"Okay. A coconut."

I had to search for a while to find a coconut. I had already brought him the ones that were nearby. But I found one, brought it back, and pierced it for him. He drank thirstily.

"What did Dr. Rhodes say?" he asked after he finished the coconut milk.

"He said that making eye contact is appropriate behavior."

"Did he say anything about rescuing me?"

"No," I said. Dr. Rhodes has worked with me on learning to read expressions. Evan Collins' mouth was turned down. His eyes were squeezed half closed. He did not look happy. "Do you want another coconut?" I asked.

THE MAN

Evan Collins watched the roach trundle off through the palms to find him a coconut. It had been all he could do not to scream at the roach, but he had managed it.

The painkillers left him groggy. He felt nauseous and thirsty, very thirsty. He knew he had to keep drinking. He had not had to urinate since he woke up on the beach the day before, an indication that he was not taking in enough fluid. Dehydration would kill him quicker than anything.

Life by the yard is hard, he told himself, but by the inch, it's a cinch. To stay alive, he had to keep drinking, and he had to get help. And to get help, he needed to understand Annie the roach and Dr. Rhodes.

The roach dropped a coconut beside him, neatly pierced.

"Thank you," Evan said carefully. The drink of coconut milk was helping, but he was still very thirsty. "It is good of you to bring me coconuts."

"My mother says it is good to be helpful," the roach said.

"I am very thirsty," Evan told Annie. "I will die if I don't have water to drink, if I don't get a doctor for my leg."

The roach watched him with its glittering eyes but said nothing.

"I wish I could meet you in person," Evan said. If he could see her expression, he would have a hope of figuring her out.

The roach took a step back. A tiny bit of body language for him to interpret.

"You don't want to meet me in person," he said. "Okay, I understand. That's perfectly normal."

"I am not normal," the roach told him.

The roach's voice was mechanical and flat, as always. Without nuances of tone, he could not tell how she felt about this perception of abnormality. He had to plunge ahead blindly. He risked a question. "How is it that you are different?"

The roach was silent.

"I think you might be smarter than other people." Never a bad idea to suggest a compliment, he figured.

"My father calls me the Little Professor."

"It's good to be smart," he said.

"It's inappropriate to be smart all the time," the roach said.

Earlier, she had said that eye contact was appropriate. Annie was very concerned about what was appropriate and what was inappropriate. Maybe rescue parties were inappropriate.

"How do you know that it's inappropriate to be smart?" he asked her.

"Dr. Rhodes told me," the roach said. "It's inappropriate."

He felt a little dizzy, a little feverish. "Is it wrong to be inappropriate?" he asked.

"Yes," said the roach.

"Is it always wrong?"

"Tell me a story," said the roach.

Too many questions, he thought. He had gotten carried away. She didn't like questions. "All right," he said. "Could I have another coconut first?"

The roach trudged off through the sand to get a coconut. It was a long time before it returned. He sipped the milk. He couldn't drink it all right away. He needed to save some.

"Did you tell Dr. Rhodes that my leg is broken?" he asked the roach.

The roach took a step back. "Tell me a story."

He closed his eyes for a moment. No more questions, he thought. Time for a story.

"Once upon a time, there was a boy named Jack who lived with his widowed mother. They were so poor that Jack's mother sent Jack to the market to trade their milk cow for food."

THE MECHANO

He was telling a story and that was good. I could pay attention to the story and not think about all his questions.

"Once upon a time . . ." The story was a fairy tale. A boy named Jack had traded a cow for a handful of beans, and his mother wasn't happy, even though the old man had said that the beans were magic. Jack's mother didn't listen to Jack—she threw the beans out the window.

Jack's mother was NT, I think—but Jack wasn't. There must be some NT rule that Jack didn't know about that said you shouldn't trade a cow for beans. I filed that thought away—if I ever had a cow, it would be inappropriate to trade it for beans.

The next day, when a giant beanstalk grew up from the magic beans, Jack climbed it right away, without asking his mother if he could. That was inappropriate behavior. Dr. Rhodes says I should always ask my mother's permission.

Jack found a castle that belonged to a giant. An old woman who lived in the castle hid Jack in an oven when the giant showed up.

I didn't understand why the old woman hid Jack, but there's so much about NT stories that I don't understand. Maybe the old woman just wanted to be helpful.

Anyway, the giant came home and got out a big bag of gold. The giant fell asleep, and Jack stole the gold. That was inappropriate. Dr. Rhodes says that it is appropriate to share, but it is inappropriate to take all of something even when someone offers to share. And the giant hadn't even offered to share.

Jack climbed down the beanstalk and got home with the gold. Then he climbed the beanstalk again and stole the giant's goose that laid golden eggs. Then he went back for a third time and stole the giant's harp.

I was sure that Jack was not NT. He kept doing inappropriate things and he kept going back to the giant's castle, a sign that he was perseverative.

The harp shouted when Jack was running away with it. When the giant chased Jack down the beanstalk, Jack chopped down the beanstalk and the giant fell to his death. I don't know if that was appropriate behavior or not. The giant was trying to kill Jack, but I don't know if Jack should have cut down the beanstalk.

Then the story was over. The man said he was thirsty, so I found him another coconut. It took a long time to find one, but I did. I brought it to him. Then I said, "Jack's behavior was not appropriate. He shouldn't have done those things." I knew Dr. Rhodes would not like the things Jack did.

"I like Jack," the man said. "He does very well for himself and his mother."

I thought about it. I liked this story better than Cinderella. Cinderella was very good and very helpful, but the fairy godmother made her go to the party and then she had to marry the prince, rather than staying in the quiet kitchen alone. She was punished for following the NT rules. Well, if she was NT, maybe it wasn't a punishment, but if she was like me, it sure was.

Jack broke lots of NT rules. He traded a cow for beans; he didn't ask his mother if he could climb the beanstalk; he stole stuff from the giant. But he got to go home to his little room in the cottage. He didn't have to go to a party or marry anyone.

I turned away, still thinking. It was time to talk to Dr. Rhodes.

"Annie," said the man. "Tell Dr. Rhodes about me. Tell him I need help."

DR. RHODES

"There is a man on my beach," Annie said.

"A man," Dr. Rhodes said. "That's great." He smiled. He had sent three e-mails to the man in charge of the Cook Islands mining operation, asking that he repair the cameras on Annie's island. He had yet to receive a reply, but Annie's mention of a man on the island meant that someone had been dispatched to repair the cameras at last. "He's going to fix the cameras," Dr. Rhodes said.

He knew that Annie did not respond well to change. Having a stranger on her island would be disruptive, and he needed to reassure her. "He will only be there for a short time," he said.

"He needs help," Annie said. "I tried to be helpful."

"That's all right," Dr. Rhodes said in a reassuring tone. "He'll fix the cameras and be on his way. You don't need to help."

"He says he needs help," Annie said. "His name is Evan Collins and he needs help." She was blinking rapidly. Clearly, the presence of this repairman on her island had upset her.

Dr. Rhodes was annoyed that the workman had engaged Annie in conversation, had told her that he needed help. Dr. Rhodes imagined the man—a semiskilled laborer, struggling with the cameras. Lazy, Dr. Rhodes suspected.

"Don't worry about him," Dr. Rhodes said firmly. "He's not your concern."

"He needs help," she insisted in a loud voice. "He says he needs help."

"I said that you don't need to worry about him."

"But the man . . ."

"Annie," Dr. Rhodes said firmly, "you know that it is not appropriate to shout, don't you?"

Annie did not say anything.

"Remember the deal we made when you signed up for this project? You will listen to me and do as I say. If you can't do as I say, you won't be able to continue with the project. Do you remember that?"

"I remember." Her voice was low.

"The man is not your concern. He'll fix the cameras, and he'll be on his way. We have our own work to do. Today, we're going to work on recognizing facial expressions."

THE MECHANO

I returned to my tank. I slept through the night. I returned to my island and my mechano just before dawn on the island. I went to the beach, where the man named Evan Collins slept.

He was not my concern. That was what Dr. Rhodes said.

The water bottles were empty. There were no more coconuts—I knew that. I had looked for an hour the day before to find the last coconut.

The man's breathing was shallow and uneven. Dark circles surrounded his eyes. He was covered with sand flea bites. Some of them were red and infected. The black scabs that covered the scrape on his legs were cracked, and flies had settled on them, feeding on the liquid that oozed from the cracks.

"Evan Collins," I said.

He did not open his eyes.

"Dr. Rhodes says you are going to fix the cameras," I said. "And then you'll be on your way."

Evan Collins did not move.

He was not my concern. I headed for the ocean. I had work to do.

But I stopped at the edge of the water. I circled back to stand beside Evan Collins. "Will you tell me a story?" I asked.

He did not move.

I went back to the recharging hut. I entered the hut. I shut down the mechano and I opened my eyes in my tank. I pushed the button to call the attendant, and I waited. Eventually, I heard the rattle and clank of the hatch. The hatch opened and I blinked in the glare.

I sat up when the hatch opened, staring at Kiri. "Is there a problem?" she asked. "Are you all right, Annie?"

"There is a problem," I said, speaking loudly to be heard over the hum of the pumps. "There is a man on my beach. It is not good. His face is red and his face is black and the fleas are biting him. It is not good. He is on my beach and his leg is broken. He needs a doctor. It is not good."

"A man on the beach," Kiri repeated. She was frowning. According to Dr. Rhodes' facial expression cards, that meant she was not happy. That was okay. I was not happy either.

"A man on my beach," I said again. "It is not good. I try to be helpful. I help the crabs. But I can't find any more coconuts. The man says he needs help. He says he needs medical help. He says he needs water." I closed my eyes against the lights and begin to rock.

I was thinking about the man. I pictured a chart that listed all the people involved in this. There was Evan Collins, Dr. Rhodes, and me. There were lines drawn between the three of us, making a triangle. Then I added Kiri's name to the chart and redrew the lines. There was a triangle with the man, Kiri, and me. Dr. Rhodes was off to one side.

"How did the man get to your beach?" Kiri asked.

"He has a boat that is underwater," I said. "The fish swim past it." I remember the boat, wedged between the coral heads. "It is cracked. It is not good."

"I will call Dr. Rhodes," Kiri said.

"No," I said. "Dr. Rhodes does not . . ." I stopped, not knowing what to say. "You need to tell someone else," I said. I was talking louder than I needed to.

I did not care. I was twelve years old and I cracked coconuts in my mandibles. I crawled on the ocean bottom and found gold in the rocks.

Dr. Rhodes would tell me that it was not appropriate to shout. I thought it was appropriate. There was a man named Evan Collins on my beach and it was appropriate to shout.

"There is a man," I shouted. "His name is Evan Collins. He is on my beach. I have no more coconuts for Evan Collins. He needs water. He needs help."

"Evan Collins," Kiri repeated. "I understand."

"He told me the story of Cinderella. He told me the story of Jack and the beanstalk. His name is Evan Collins and he has sixteen flea bites on his left cheek. He has a broken leg. His boat is underwater."

I felt Kiri's hand on my shoulder. "I will tell my uncle," she said. "I'll tell Uncle Mars."

I didn't like the touch of Kiri's hand on my shoulder. I didn't like the glare of the lights. I lay back down in my tank. "You will tell Uncle Mars," I said. "I will go back to my mechano."

Back on the island, the sun was up. I left the charging hut and headed for the beach. The only tactile sensation was the pressure of the ground against the feet of the mechano. Just enough pressure to let me know that I was standing on solid ground. Just enough to be comfortable, no more.

Evan Collins lay on the sand, still asleep. He was still breathing.

Kiri would tell Uncle Mars now about Evan Collins. I pictured the chart of relationships, where Kiri and Evan Collins and I were connected by lines, making a triangle. I put Uncle Mars' name on the chart and drew lines connecting him to Kiri and Evan Collins. It made another triangle. Together, the first triangle and the second triangle made a diamond. That was a good pattern, I thought. A diamond was a rock and I liked rocks.

I left Evan Collins on the beach. I walked into the water, happy when it closed over my head. I spent all day collecting rocks by the hydrothermal vent.

MATAREKA WARADI

Kiri's uncle was Matareka Waradi, but everyone called him Mars. Supervisor of remote mining operations for the Cook Islands division of Atlantis Mining and Salvage, he was a man with influence—a large man with a large personality. He knew everyone, and everyone knew him.

He had arranged for Kiri to work in the California headquarters of Atlantis Mining. Kiri was a good girl. She had worked hard to get a degree in nursing, and she had wanted very much to go to the United States for a time. At about the time that Kiri had mentioned this desire to Mars, the California office requested that he leave one of the mechanos at an exhausted mining site as part of an experimental program. The office wanted to put an unqualified operator in charge of this mechano. It was crazy what they wanted—Mars had asked around and found out that it was a pet project of Eric Westerman, the company president. Westerman was the son of the man who founded Atlantis Mining, and old hands in the company generally regarded him as a bit of a fool.

If Eric Westerman wanted to risk an expensive mechano in some crackpot experiment, Mars certainly couldn't stop him. But Mars learned (through a cousin who worked in the company's Human Resources Department) that this crazy project needed a nurse to care for the unqualified operator back in California.

So Mars made a deal. If Human Resources would hire Kiri to be the nurse, Mars would allow the unqualified operator to use the mechano. Mars insisted, of course, that he would not take responsibility for any damage to the mechano or other Atlantis Mining equipment resulting from operator error. And all had been well—until Mars received an e-mail from Kiri.

Kiri was, Mars knew, a levelheaded girl, a smart girl. And so he paid attention when he received an urgent e-mail from her. Kiri said that the unqualified operator—Annie, Kiri called her—had told Kiri that there was a man on the remote island, that the man's name was Evan Collins, and that he needed medical attention. Kiri was quite concerned.

It was a beautiful day with clear blue skies. Mars needed to check on operations on an unnamed atoll not far from the island where Kiri's operator was working. Besides, he needed to fix the cameras on that island—he'd received three emails from central headquarters about that. The man in charge of the experimental program, a fellow named Dr. Rhodes, had complained several times that he could no longer monitor the island. Mars had been ignoring the maintenance request on basic principles. He didn't know Dr. Rhodes. Kiri had mentioned in an earlier e-mail that the man was unfriendly. So Mars saw no need to extend himself on behalf of Dr. Rhodes.

But Kiri was worried. And it was a nice day for a flight in the company's Bush Hawk-XP floatplane. Piloting that was one of the benefits of Mars' position with Atlantis Mining.

Mars called his assistants and told them they were going out to the island to replace the cameras and check on how the experimental operator was doing.

From the air above the island, Mars spotted the sunken sailboat in the water. He swore beneath his breath and landed in the lee of the island. His assistants inflated the Zodiac, and they took the rubber dinghy in. They found Evan Collins in the shade of the palms, surrounded by empty water bottles and broken coconuts. He was delirious with thirst, but when they shook him, he returned to consciousness enough to drink. By the look of him, he'd been there for a few days.

They draped his head and wrists with wet cloths, mixed a packet of electrolyte powder with a bottle of water, and supported him while he drank, checked the splinting on his leg. His pulse was weak and fast, and he drifted in and out of consciousness.

Mars' assistants were carrying the man to the Zodiac when the mechano emerged from the water, carrying a rock. The mechano came toward Mars, its eyes focused on Evan Collins.

"Why didn't you tell someone about this man immediately?" Mars asked the mechano. "He's been here for days."

The mechano dropped the rock at Mars' feet. "I told Dr. Rhodes. He said the man was here to fix the cameras."

"Dr. Rhodes is an idiot," Mars said. "A fool and an incompetent."

"I told Kiri," the mechano said. "She told Uncle Mars."

"I'm Uncle Mars. Mars Waradi." Mars studied the mechano, wondering about the person who operated it.

THE MECHANO

Evan Collins lay in the bottom of the rubber dinghy. Soon he would be gone and I would be able to watch the crabs again.

The two other men were dragging the Zodiac into the water while Uncle Mars stood studying me. He leaned down and picked up the rock that I had dropped. "What's this?" he said. "A man is dying of thirst, and you bring him a rock?"

"It's for the crabs," I said. "I brought coconuts for Evan Collins, but I ran out of coconuts. I brought him all the water bottles from the boat. I was very helpful."

Uncle Mars was looking closely at the rock in his hands. "Where did you find this?" he asked.

"By the vent," I said.

The other men were shouting for Mars to come and join them. He looked at me, looked at the rock, then said, "I'll be back to talk to you about this." Then he turned away and joined the men at the boat.

I watched the plane take off, then I tidied up the area where the man had been, placing all the coconut shells in a pile, all the water bottles in another pile. It looked better when I was done. I felt better when I was done.

MATAREKA WARADI

Mars landed on the lee side of Annie's island and took the Zodiac in. He had received an e-mail from Kiri that morning, saying that Dr. Rhodes' experimental program was being canceled. Evan Collins had survived. But after his rescue, the researcher had had to explain exactly why he had failed to let anyone know that a man was stranded on the island. Upper management had reviewed the videotapes of Dr. Rhodes' sessions with Annie, and Annie's attempts to tell Dr. Rhodes about the stranded man had been noted.

"I feel bad for Annie," Kiri had written. "She's a strange little girl, but she has a good heart. Dr. Rhodes will be telling her today that he's wrapping up the program by the end of the week. I don't think she'll take it well."

Mars pulled the Zodiac up on the beach, out of reach of the waves. He spotted the mechano over by the mangroves. As he approached, Mars noted the rocks that had been placed on the sand by many of the crab burrows. All of them were similar to the rock that he had taken with him when he rescued Evan Collins.

"Hello, Annie," he said.

"Hello, Uncle Mars," the mechano said in its flat voice.

Mars sat in the sand beside the mechano. "You know, I analyzed that rock you brought back," he said. "Very high concentration of gold ore."

"Yes," the mechano said.

"Looks like you've collected a fair number of rocks like that one," Mars observed.

"Yes," said the mechano. "I brought them for the crabs. I am very helpful."

"Can you show me where you found them?" Mars asked.

"Yes," said the mechano.

"We thought the mining was tapped out around this island," Mars said. "My best operators had followed a rich vein of ore. They'd explored the nearby seabed, searching for other possibilities, and they'd come up empty. But you've found what looks like a promising source. How do you explain that?"

"I like rocks," the mechano said.

"Yes, I guess you do," Mars agreed. "I'm wondering if you'd like to work for me."

"Will I be able to look for rocks?" the mechano asked.

"That would be your job," Mars said.

"Will this be my mechano?" the mechano asked.

"It certainly could be."

"Yes," said the mechano. "I'd like that."

It took some doing, of course. Kiri spoke with Annie's parents, explaining at length what had happened, explaining what Mars saw as Annie's potential. Kiri had to find a therapist who was willing to continue meeting with Annie every other day. Mars had to make many arrangements—with child welfare authorities, with labor organizers, with company officials. But Mars was a man with many resources. He had many friends, a cousin in the Human Resources Department, and a niece Annie trusted, as much as she trusted anyone she met in her meat body. Eventually, he worked it all out.

THE MECHANO

The tide was beginning to come in. I stood motionless and watched the crabs.

A big crab sidled out of his burrow, eyes goggling in my direction. He had shiny black legs and a bright red carapace. He had a small black claw and a very big red claw, which he held up in front of his face and waved in my direction. When I didn't move, the crab turned to look seaward.

Other crabs were coming out of their burrows. Each one stared at me, then checked out the other crabs, waving his oversized red claw at the other male crabs around him. One crab sidled toward another crab's burrow, and they both waved their claws until the first retreated.

As I watched, a female crab approached, and the activity among the males increased. They were all waving their claws, while the female watched. She stared at one male and he ran toward her and then ran back to his burrow, toward her and back to his burrow, always waving his claw.

The female followed him, hesitated at the entrance to the burrow for a moment, then went into the burrow. The male crab rushed in after her. I watched as the mouth of the burrow filled with mud, pushed up from below. The male crab was closing the door.

The other crabs were waving their claws as other females approached, all of them communicating with each other and behaving according to rules that they all seem to know.

I liked watching the crabs. I didn't understand them, but I was happy to help them with rocks.

I thought about Uncle Mars and Kiri and my mother and my father and Dr. Rhodes, Kiri had explained to me what was happening—and when she explained, I had drawn a chart in my mind. Kiri talked to my parents (that was a triangle with Kiri and my mother and my father—I was off to one side, connected to Kiri by a line). Uncle Mars talked to me and talked to Kiri. Another triangle. Dr. Rhodes was off by himself, connected to no one. The crabs were connected to me. And Evan Collins was connected to me by a line.

I thought about the story of Cinderella. I thought I might be like the fairy godmother. I sent Evan Collins to the party with the other NTs. Now he would live happily ever after.

I liked fairy tales. I liked rocks. I would collect rocks for Atlantis Mining and Uncle Mars. I would bring rocks to the crabs, who would communicate with each other using gestures I could not understand. And I would live happily ever after, alone on my island.

start the clock

BENJAMIN ROSENBAUM

Americans are known for watching the clock, but, as the ingenious story that follows suggests, you may not have seen *anything* yet . . .

New writer Benjamin Rosenbaum has made sales to *The Magazine of Fantasy & Science Fiction, Asimov's Science Fiction, Argosy, The Infinite Matrix, Strange Horizons, Harper's, McSweeney's, Lady Churchill's Rosebud Wristlet*, and elsewhere. Recently returned from a long stay in Switzerland, he now lives with his family in Falls Church, Virginia. He has a Web site at: http://home.datacomm.ch/benrose.

The real estate agent for Pirateland was old. Nasty old. It's harder to tell with Geezers, but she looked to be somewhere in her Thirties. They don't have our suppleness of skin, but with the right oils and powders they can avoid most of the wrinkles. This one hadn't taken much care. There were furrows around her eyes and eyebrows.

She had that Mommystyle thing going on: blue housedress, frilly apron, Betty Crocker white gloves. If you're going to be running around this part of Montana sporting those gigantic, wobbly breasts and hips, I guess it's a necessary form of obeisance.

She said something to someone in the back of her van, then hurried up the walk toward us. "It's a lovely place," she called. "And a very nice area."

"Look, Suze, it's your mom," Tommy whispered in my ear. His breath tickled. I pushed him.

It was deluxe, I'll give her that. We were standing under the fifty-foot prow of the galleon we'd come to see. All around us a flotilla of men-of-war, sloops, frigates, and cutters rode the manicured lawns and steel-gray streets. Most of the properties were closed up, the lawns pristine. Only a few looked inhabited—lawns strewn with gadgets, excavations begun with small bulldozers and abandoned, Pack or Swarm or Family flags flying from the mainmasts. Water cannons menacing passersby.

I put my hands in my pants pockets and picked at the lint. "So this is pretty much all Nines?"

The Thirtysomething Lady frowned. "Ma'am, I'm afraid the Anti-Redlining Act of 2035—"

"Uh-huh, race, gender, aetial age, chronological age, stimulative preference or national origin—I know the law. But who else wants to live in Pirateland, right?"

Thirtysomething Lady opened her mouth and didn't say anything.

"Or can afford it," Shiri called. She had gone straight for the ropeladder and was halfway up. Her cherry-red sneakers felt over the side for the gunnel running around the house. Thirtysomething Lady's hands twitched in a kind of helpless half-grasping motion. Geezers always do that when we climb.

"Are you poor?" Tommy asked. "Is that why you dress like that?"

"Quit taunting the Lady," Max growled. Max is our token Eight, and he takes aetial discrimination more seriously than the rest of us. Plus, he's just nicer than we are. He's also Pumped Up: he's only four feet tall, but he has bioengineered muscles like grapefruit. He has to eat a pound or two of medicated soysteak a day just to keep his bulk on.

Thirtysomething Lady put her hand up to her eyes and blinked ferociously, as if she were going to cry. Now that would be something! They almost never cry. We'd hardly been mean to her at all. I felt sorry for her, so I walked over and put my hand in hers. She flinched and pulled her hand away. So much for cross-aetial understanding and forgiveness.

"Let's just look at the house," I said, putting my hands in my pockets.

"Galleon," she said tightly.

"Galleon then."

Her fingers twitched out a passkey mudra and the galleon lowered a boarding plank. Nice touch.

Frankly, we were excited. This move was what our Pack needed—the four of us, at least, were sure of it. We were all tired of living in the ghetto—we were in three twentieth-century townhouses in Billings, in an "age-mixed" area full of marauding Thirteens and Fourteens and Fifteens. Talk about a people damned by CDAS—when the virus hit them, it had stuck their pituitaries and thyroids like throttles jammed open. It wasn't just the giantism and health problems caused by a thirty-year overdose on growth hormones, testosterone, estrogen, and androgen. They suffered more from their social problems—criminality, violence, orgies, jealousy—and their endless self-pity.

Okay, Max liked them. And most of the rest of us had been at least entertained by living in the ghetto. At birthday parties, we could always shock the other Packs with our address. But that was when all eight of us were there, before Katrina and Ogbu went south. With eight of us, we'd felt like a full Pack—invincible, strong enough to laugh at anyone.

I followed the others into the galleon's foyer. Video game consoles on the walls, swimming pool under a retractable transparent superceramic floor. The ceiling—or upper deck, I guess—was thirty feet up, accessible by rope ladders and swing ropes. A parrot fluttered onto a roost—it looked real, but probably wasn't. I walked through a couple of bulk-heads. Lots of sleeping nooks; lockers, shelves; workstations, both flatscreen and retinal-projection. I logged onto one as guest. Plenty of bandwidth.

That's good for me. I may dress like a male twentieth-century stockbroker, double-breasted suit and suspenders, but I'm actually a found footage editor. (Not a lot of Nines are artists—our obsessive problem solving and intense competitiveness makes us good market speculators, gamblers, programmers, and biotechs. That's where we've made our money and our reputation. Not many of us have the patience or interest for art.)

I logged out. Max had stripped and dived into the pool—or maybe it was meant as a giant bathtub. Tommy and Shiri were bouncing on the trampoline, making smart-aleck remarks. The real estate agent had given up on getting anyone to listen to her pitch. She was sitting in a floppy gel chair, massaging the sole of one foot with her hands. I walked into the kitchen. Huge table, lots of chairs and sitballs, enormous programmable foodcenter.

I walked out, back to the Lady. "No stove."

"Stove?" she said, blinking.

I ran one hand down a suspender. "I cook," I said.

"You cook?"

I felt my jaw and shoulders tense—I'm sick of being told Nines don't cook—but then I saw her eyes. They were sparkling with delight. Indulgent delight. It reminded me of my own mother, oohing and aahing over brick-hard cookies I'd baked her one winter morning in the slums of Maryland, back when my aetial age was still tied to Nature's clock. My mother holding up the wedding dress she'd planned to give me away in, its lacy waist brushing my chin. One evening in college, when I'd looked up at the dinner table, halfway through a sentence—I'd been telling her about *The Hat on the Cat*, my distributed documentary (a firebrand polemic for Under-Five Emancipation; how cybernetics would liberate the Toddlers from lives of dependence)—and saw in her eyes how long ago she'd stopped listening. Saw that I wasn't Nine to her, but nine. Saw that she wasn't looking at me, but through me, a long way off—toward another now, another me: a Woman. Big globes of fatty breasts dangling from that other-me's chest; tall as a doorway, man-crazy, marriageable; a great sexualized monster like herself, a walking womb, a proto-Mommy. She was waiting for that Susan, Woman-Susan, who would never show up.

"I cook," I said, looking away from the Lady's eyes. Putting my hands in my pants pockets. I could have used a hug, but Max was underwater and Tommy and Shiri were trying to knock each other off the trampoline. I went outside.

"We could bring in a stove module," the Lady called.

Outside, a pigeon was poking through the lawn. It was mangy and nervous enough to be real. I stood for a while watching it, then my earring buzzed. I made the Accept mudra.

"Suze?" Travis said.

"Why are you asking, Travis? Who do you think is wearing my earring?"

"Suze, Abby's gone."

"What do you mean, gone?"

"She's not picking up. Her locator's off. I can't find her anywhere." When Travis was nervous, his voice squeaked. Now he sounded like a mouse caught in a trap.

I looked at the active tattoo readout on my left palm. Travis was home. I made the mudra for Abby. No location listed. "Stay there, Travis. We're on our way."

I ran up the plank. Max was dressed again, rubbing his dreadlocks with a towel from the poolside toweltree. Tommy and Shiri were sitting at a table with the Real Estate Lady, looking over paperwork in the tabletop display.

"We've got to go. A personal emergency has come up," I said. Max was at my side instantly.

"Listen, we want this place," Shiri said.

"Shiri, we all have to talk about it," I said.

"What's to talk about?" Tommy said. "It's *awesome*."

"This is the first place we've looked at," I said.

"So?"

The Real Estate Lady was watching us with a guarded expression. I didn't want to say that Abby was missing. Not in front of her. Not in front of that can-you-really-be-trusted-to-look-after-yourselves-all-on-your-own-without-any-grownups attitude that came off her like a stink. I took my hands out of my pockets and balled them into fists. "You're being totally stupid!" I said.

"What's the emergency?" Max said quietly.

"I know what Travis and Abby would say," Tommy said. "They totally want a place like this. Let's just get it and we'll have the rest of the day free."

"We can go windgliding," Shiri said.

"Travis and Abby didn't even agree to getting a house yet, never mind this house," I said. I felt Max's hand on my shoulder.

"That's because they haven't seen it," Tommy said.

"What's the emergency?" Max said.

"There's probably been a train wreck and Suze has to make sure she's the first ghoul at her flatscreen," Shiri said.

"Screw you," I said and walked out of the house. I was shaking a little with adrenaline. I got in our clowncar and clicked on the engine. Max hurried out the door behind me. I slid over to the passenger seat and he got in to drive.

"We can pick them up later," he said. "Or they can take a cab. What's up?"

I made the Abby mudra and showed him my palm. "Abby's missing. Travis hasn't seen her, and she's not picking up."

Max pulled out into the street. "She left the house this morning early, with that old black-and-white camera you got her. She was going to shoot some pictures."

I flipped open the flatscreen in the passenger-side dash and logged in. "That's no reason for her to turn off her locator. I hope she didn't stay near the house—a Nine walking around alone in the ghetto, taking photographs—imagine how that looks."

We hummed and whooshed out of Pirateland, up a ramp onto I-90. "Abby wouldn't be that dumb," Max said. But he didn't sound too sure. Abby's impetuous, and she'd been melancholy lately. "Police?" he asked, after a moment.

I shot him a sharp look. The police are Geezers—height requirements keep Under Twelves out of their ranks, and the Teens are mostly too uneducated and unruly. I didn't have any strings to pull with them, and neither did Max. "We wait until we have more data," I said. "Now shut up and let me work. Head home."

Most people have the notion that the public footage is this permanent, universal, easily searchable archive of everything that ever happens, clearly shot, from any angle. It's the job of people in my profession to help perpetuate that illusion. Actually, the networks are surprisingly spotty. There are millions of swarmcams wandering around in any major urban area, but they have a high failure and bug rate, and their pictures are grainy and indistinct—only a lot of imaginative algorithmic reconstruction makes them viewable. There are plenty of larger cameras linked to the net, but often hidden in a byzantine maze of permissions and protocols. And there are billions of motion sensors, audio pickups, locator tags, and data traffic monitors added to the mix, but they're not well correlated with each other. In a few hours on a Sunday morning, one square mile of downtown Billings generates enough data to fill all the computers of the twentieth century, plus all the paper libraries of the centuries before. It's hell to search.

But I'm good. I had enough footage of Abby on file to construct a good bloodhound, and then I spawned a dozen of them and seeded them well. Pretty soon the hits started coming back. Abby had crossed the street in front of our house at 09:06, and turned her locator tag off—on purpose, I imagined, since there was no error log. She'd stopped for bagels and udon in a deli on Avenue C at 09:22; shot pictures in the park until 09:56. She'd talked to a couple of Fifteens there and taken something from them. I couldn't see what, in the grainy gray swarmcam pictures, but it made the hair on the back of my neck rise.

From 10:03 I lost her; she'd gone up an elevator in a bank and disappeared. There's a network of private walkways and an aerial tram in that part of Billings that are poorly monitored. I had a cold feeling in my gut; that was a great way to lose me, if you were trying to.

I searched all the exits to those walkways and the tramway for Abby, buying a bunch of extra processing power on the exchange to run it faster. Nothing.

Max had entered among the spires and alleys of Billings. Dappled shadows of metal and translucent plastics and ceramics rippled over the clowncar. I looked out at the people walking through the corridors around us, all ages and sizes and colors. An old woman was walking slowly on a slidewalk just above us—she must have been an aetial Ninety, which made her a hundred and twenty or so. Walking, slowly, under her own steam. You don't see that every day.

I went back to some old footage I had of a birthday party and grabbed a sequence of Abby walking. I built an ergodynamic profile of her and fed that to my bloodhounds.

Bingo. At 10:42, Abby had left the aerial tramway in disguise. Platform shoes, trenchcoat, false breasts and hips and shoulders—she was impersonating a Fourteen or so. It looked ridiculous, like Halloween. She'd consulted a piece of paper from her pocket.

By 10:54 she was in a bad area. "Head for 30th and Locust," I told Max.

"Shit," he said. "No police?"

"I don't have anything yet that would warrant their attention. Nothing that proves she was coerced."

"So we need other backup," Max said grimly.

"Yeah." I looked up. "Can you get it?"

"I think so," he said. He made some Call mudras with one hand and started talking. "Hey, Dave, how you doing? Listen, man—" I tuned him out as he made his calls.

My last shot of Abby was at 11:06. She was being hustled into a doorway by a gargantuan Fifteen. His hand was on her elbow. Biodynamic readouts from a few stray hospital swarmcams confirmed that her pulse was elevated. Should I send this to the police? Would it prove Abby was coerced? But what was she doing with the weird disguise and the sneaking around? Just slumming? Or would I get her in trouble?

Was Abby buying drugs?

"Parkhill and 32nd," I said to Max. My fingers were still and I was just looking at that last picture, Abby and the giant, him pulling her into darkness.

"Can you meet us at Parkhill and 32nd?" Max was saying. "Damn, I know, man—that's why we need you."

When we got there, five of Max's friends were waiting. Four were clearly from his gym. Two of them were probably Nines or Tens (one swarthy, one red-haired and freckled) and they were even musclier than Max, their heads perched like small walnuts on their blockbuster bodies. The other two were Pumped Up Teens—maybe Fifteen or Sixteen. Their blond, Slavic-boned faces sat on bodies like overstuffed family room sofas or industrial refrigerators: fingers the size of my forearm, thighs the size of my entire body. I wasn't sure how we were going to get them in the building.

And then there was the fifth—an Augmented Three. She stood a little apart from the others, her tiny arms at her sides. They were clearly afraid of her. One soft brown eye scanned the clouds, and she had a beatific smile on her face. Her other eye was the glistening jewel of a laserlight connector, and there were other plugs and ports glistening in her brown scalp among her cornrows.

Max stopped the car.

"Who's the Three?" I asked.

Max turned to me. He looked nervous, like he thought I was going to make fun of him. "That's my sister, Carla."

"Cool," I said quickly. He got out before I could say anything yet stupider, like, "How nice that you've stayed close."

I opened my door and froze—Carla was running toward us. "Max!" she warbled, and flung her arms around his waist, burying her face in his stomach.

"Hi, honey-girl," he said, hugging her back.

I glanced at my palm readout. It had gone blank. So had the flatscreen in the car. It was a safe bet nothing near Carla would be recorded. You could sometimes tell where Augmented Threes and Twos were in the public footage by tracking the blank areas, the little blobs of inexplicable malfunction that followed them around. I once did an experimental documentary on Under-Five Augmentation using that blanked-out foot-age. It was called *Be Careful What You Wish For*—kind of a rueful, years-later followup to *The Hat on the Cat*.

"Carry me!" Carla said, and Max dutifully swung her tiny body onto his shoulders.

"Carla, this is Suze," Max said.

"I don't like her," Carla announced. Max's face went slack with fear, and my heart lurched. I grabbed the car door so hard my fingernails sank into the frame.

Carla exploded in giggles, then started to hiccup. "Just—*kidding!*" she choked out between hiccups. "You guys are so *silly!*"

I tried to smile. Max turned, slowly, toward the door. It was a formidable steel monstrosity, the kind with a biodynamic access plate governing its security system. Those things are supposed to be off-net, more or less invulnerable to cybernetic hacking. Carla waved at it and it popped open. The four muscleboys crowded their way inside—eager to get to Abby, and away from Carla—and the three of us brought up the rear, Carla still perched on Max's shoulders.

The stairway was dark and rank—it smelled like Teenagers, all their glands and excretions, smeared and sour. Most of the wallglow was dead, and one malfunctioning patch at the top of the stairs was flashing green and red, so that the bodies of the muscleboys ascended the stairs in strobed staccato.

The freckled gymrat was first to the doorway at the top. As he reached for the doorknob, we heard a long moan, and then a series of grunts. Almost snarls. And then, softer, a whimper—a high, female whimper—like the sound of someone tortured, someone in despair.

Carla started to cry. "I don't like it!"

"What is it, honey-baby?" Max said, his voice afraid. "*What's behind that door?*"

"Don't ask her that!" I barked. "Distract her, you idiot!"

"Max, should I make it go away?" Carla wailed. "Should I make them stop, Max?"

"No!" Max and I shouted at the same time.

"Max," I said as pleasantly as I could manage, "why don't you and Carla go play a nice game in the car?"

"But maybe I should—" Max said, looking at me from between Carla's tiny, shaking knees.

"Now!" I barked, and pushed past them.

Panting came from under the door, panting and groans. The muscleboys looked at me nervously. I heard Max's shoes clumping down the stairs behind me, and he started singing "The Itsy-Bitsy Spider."

"In!" I hissed, pointing at the door. The two overmuscled Nines threw their shoulders against it. It strained and buckled, but held. From inside the door came a strangled scream. The two Pumped-Up Teens braced themselves against the wall and each other, bent their knees, and crouched down with their shoulders under the Nines' butts. "Ready—now!" called the biggest, and all four of them pushed. The door shot open, and the muscleboys tumbled and collapsed through it. I sprinted over their bodies, springing from a buttock to a shoulder to a back to another shoulder, and I was through.

On a tiger-skin throwrug in the midst of a pile of trash, two huge naked Fifteens looked up. The male's skin was a mass of pimples and grease; shaggy hair fell over his shoulders and muscles. The female was pinned under him, her gigantic breasts flopping to either side of her thin ribcage, her knees pinioned around his hips. Between the wiry forests of their pubic hair, a portion of the male's penis ran like a swollen purple bridge.

"Ewww!" I shouted, as they flopped down, pulling the tigerskin over themselves. "Where's Abby??"

"Hi, Suze," said Abby dryly from an overstuffed chair to my left. She was wearing a white jumpsuit, and holding a pen and a paper notebook.

"What the hell are you doing?" I shouted.

"I might ask you the same." She motioned to the pile of muscleboys, who were struggling to their feet with dazed expressions.

"Abby! You disappeared!" I was waving my arms around like a Macromuppet. "Locator—bad area—disguise—scary—aargh!"

"Are you going to follow me around with a small army every time I turn off my locator?"

"Yes!!"

She sighed and put down her pencil and paper. "I'm really sorry," she called to the Fifteens. "My time was almost up anyway. Um, do you mind if we talk in here for a few minutes?"

"Yes!" gurgled the female.

"Abby, come on," I said. "They can't just stop in the middle. They have to, you know, finish what they were—doing. Until it's finished their brains won't work properly."

"Okay," Abby said. "All right, ah—thanks."

In the stairway, I said, "You couldn't just watch a porn channel?"

"It's not the same," she said. "That's all packaged and commercial. I wanted to interview them before and after. I have to know—what it's like."

"Why?"

She paused on the stairs, and I stopped too. The muscleboys, muttering, went out onto the street, and we were alone in the flashing green and red light.

"Suze, I'm going to start the clock."

Like she'd poured a bucket of ice water down my spine. "You're what?"

"I'm going to take the treatments." She spoke quickly, as if afraid I'd interrupt her. "They've gotten much better in the past couple of years; there are basically no side effects. They're even making headway with infants. In five years, it looks like most babies won't have any arrestation effects at all, and—"

Tears had sprung to my eyes. "What are you talking about?" I cried. "Why are you talking like *them?* Why are you talking like being like us is something to be *cured?*" I punched the wall, which hurt my hand. I sat down on the step and cried.

"Suze," Abby said. She sat down next to me and put her hand on my shoulder. "I love being like us—but I want—"

"That?" I shouted, pointing up to the top of the stairs, where they were grunting again. "That's what you want? You'd rather have that than us?"

"I want everything, Suze. I want every stage of life—"

"Oh, every stupid *stage*, as designed by stupid God, who also gave us death and cancer, and—"

She grabbed my shoulders. "Suze, listen. I want to know what *that* up there is like. Maybe I won't like it, and then I won't do it. But Suze, I want to have babies."

"Babies? Abby, your eggs are forty years old—"

"Exactly! Exactly, my eggs are only forty years old, and most of them are still good. Who do you want to have the babies, Suze? The Geezers? The world is starting again, Suze, and I—"

"The world was fine!" I pulled away from her. "The world was just fine!" Snot and tears were running down my nose into my mouth, salty and gooey. I wiped my face on the sleeve of my stockbroker's suit, leaving a slick trail like a slug. "We were fine—"

"This isn't about us—"

"Oh baloney!!" I lurched to my feet, grabbing the railing for balance. "As if you're going to live with us in a galleon and firewater cannons and go to birthday parties! You're just not, Abby, don't kid yourself! You're going to be *that!*" I pointed up the stairs. "Sexual jealousy and sexual exchange economy and cheating and mutual-exploitation-and-ownership and serial monogamy and divorce and the whole stupid crazy boring . . ."

"Suze—" she said in a small voice.

"Just don't!" I said. "Don't drag it out! If you want to do it, do it, but then leave us alone! Okay? You're not welcome." I turned and headed down the stairs. "Get the hell out."

Max was standing at the bottom of the stairs. I didn't like the way he was looking at me. I brushed past.

The boys from the gym were in the car, eating yard-long submarine sandwiches with great gusto. Carla sat on the front steps, talking to a rag doll. She looked up, and her red jewel of an eye flashed—for a moment it was as bright as looking into the Sun at noon. Then she looked past me, into the sky.

"What are you afraid of?" she asked.

I leaned against the doorframe and said nothing. A wind came down the street and crumpled sheets of paper danced along it.

"I'm afraid of cows," she volunteered. "And Millie"—she held up the rag doll—"is afraid of, um, um, you know the thing where if you take all the money people spend and the way they looked at each other that day and you put it inside what the weather's going to do and then you can sing to cats and stuff? She's afraid of that."

I wiped my eyes on my sleeve. "Can you see the future, Carla?"

She giggled, and then she looked serious. "You guys are all wrong about that. It's just a game you made up. There isn't any future."

"Do you like being Augmented?" I asked.

"I like it but Millie doesn't like it. Millie thinks it's scary but she's just silly. Millie wishes we were like people and trees and we didn't have to make things okay all the time. But then we couldn't play with bolshoiye-gemeinschaft-episteme-mekhashvei-ibura."

"Okay," I said.

"Max is coming out with Abby four thousand five hundred and sixty-two milliseconds after I finish talking right now and projected group cohesion rises by thirty-six percent if you don't have a fight now so you should take the clowncar and I'll give them a ride and I'd love to live with you but I know I'm too scary but it's okay but can I visit on Max's birthday?"

"Yes," I said. "You can visit on my birthday too."

"I can? I can?" She jumped up and hugged me, flinging her arms around my waist, pressing her cheek into my chest. "Wow, I didn't even know you'd say that!" She pulled away, beaming at me, then pointed to the car. "Okay, quick, go! Bye!"

I got in the car and clicked on the engine. Carla waved and she held Millie's arm and waved it too. The door behind her opened, I saw Max's shoe, and I drove off.

A quarter mile away from Carla, the flatscreen blinked on again, and my earring started buzzing like crazy. I told it to let Travis through.

"Abby's fine," I said. "She's with Max. They'll be coming home."

"Cool," Travis said. "Whew! That's a relief!"

"Yeah."

"So Tommy and Shiri sent me video of the house. It looks *awesome*. Do you love it too?"

"Yeah, I love it." I was on I-90 now. Beyond the spires and aerial trams of Billings, I could see the funhouse suburbs spreading out before me—windmills, castles, ships, domes, faerie forests.

"Cool, because I think they signed some papers or something."

"What? Travis, we all have to agree!" As I said it, it occurred to me that the only one who hadn't seen the place was Abby. I gripped the wheel and burst out crying.

"What? What?" Travis said.

"Travis!" I wailed. "Abby wants to start the clock!"

"I know," Travis muttered.

"What? You *know?*"

"She told me this morning."

"Why didn't you say anything?"

"She made me promise not to."

"Travis!"

"I was hoping you'd talk her out of it."

I took the exit for Pirateland, swooshing through an orange plastic tunnel festooned with animated skeletons climbing out of Davy Jones's lockers. "You can't talk Abby out of anything."

"But we've got to, Suze, we've got to. C'mon, we can't just fall apart like this. Katrina and Ogbu—" he was doing his panic-stricken ratsqueak again, and suddenly I was very sick of it.

"Just shut up and stop whining, Travis!" I shouted. "Either she'll change her mind or she won't, but she won't, so you'll just have to deal with it."

Travis didn't say anything. I told my earring to drop the connection and block all calls.

I pulled up outside the galleon and got out. I found a handkerchief in the glove compartment and cleaned my face thoroughly. My suit, like the quality piece of work it was, had already eaten and digested all the snot I'd smeared on it—the protein would probably do it good. I checked myself in the mirror—I didn't want the Real Estate Lady to see me weepy. Then I got out and stood looking at the house. If I knew Tommy and Shiri, they were still inside, having discovered a roller-skating rink or rodeo room.

Parked at the side of the house was the Real Estate Lady's old-fashioned van—a real classic, probably gasoline-burning. I walked over to it. The side door was slid open. I looked in.

Inside, reading a book, was a Nine. She was tricked out in total Kidgear—pony tails, barrettes t-shirt with a horse on it, socks with flashy dangly things. Together with the Lady's Mommystyle getup, it made perfect, if twisted, sense. Personally I find that particular game of Let's-Pretend sort of depressing and pitiful, but to each her own kink.

"Hey," I said. She looked up.

"Um, hi," she said.

"You live around here?"

She wrinkled her nose. "My mom, um, kinda doesn't really want me to tell that to strangers."

I rolled my eyes. "Give the role-playing a rest, would you? I just asked a simple question."

She glared at me. "You shouldn't make so many assumptions about people," she said, and pointedly lifted her book up in front of her face.

The clop-clop of the Lady's shoes came down the drive. My scalp was prickling. Something was not altogether kosher in this sausage.

"Oh, hello," the Lady said brightly, if awkwardly. "I see you've met my daughter."

"Is that your actual daughter, or can the two of you just not get out of character?"

The Lady crossed her arms and fixed me with her green-eyed stare. "Corintha contracted Communicative Developmental Arrestation Syndrome when she was two years old. She started the treatments seven years ago."

I realized my mouth was hanging open. "She's a clock-started Two? She spent twenty-five years as an unaugmented two-year-old?"

The Lady leaned past me into the van. "You okay in here, honey?"

"Great," said Corintha from behind her book. "Other than the occasional ignoramus making assumptions."

"Corintha, please don't be rude," the Lady said.

"Sorry," she said.

The Lady turned to me. I think my eyes must have been bugging out of my head. She laughed. "I've seen your documentaries, you know."

"You *have?*"

"Yes." She leaned up against the van. "They're technically very well done, and I think some of what you have to say is very compelling. That one with all the blanked-out footage—that gave me a real feeling for what it's like for those children who are wired up into the Internet."

An odd and wrongheaded way of putting it, but I limited myself to saying, "Uh—thanks."

"But I think you're very unfair to those of us who didn't Augment our children. To watch your work, you'd think every parent who didn't Augment succumbed to Parenting Fatigue and sent their toddlers off to the government daycare farms, visiting only at Christmas. Or that they lived some kind of barbaric, abusive, incestuous existence." She looked over at her daughter. "Corintha has been a joy to me every day of her life—"

"Oh, Mom!" Corintha said from behind her book.

"—but I never wanted to stand in the way of her growing up. I just didn't think Augmentation was the answer. Not for her."

"And you thought you had the right to decide," I said.

"Yes." She nodded vigorously. "I thought I had the obligation to decide."

The Suze everyone who knows me knows would have made some sharp rejoinder. None came. I watched Corintha peek out from behind her book.

There was silence for a while. Corintha went back to reading.

"My friends still inside?" I asked.

"Yes," the Lady said. "They want the place. I think it fits six very comfortably, and—"

"Five," I said huskily. "I think it's going to be five."

"Oh," the Lady looked nonplussed. "I'm—sorry to hear that."

Corintha put her book down. "How come?"

The Lady and I looked at her.

"Oh, is that a rude question?" Corintha said.

"It's a bit prying, dear," the Lady said.

"Ah—" I said. I looked at Corintha. "One of us wants to—start the clock. Start the conventional biological aging process."

"So?" Corintha said.

"Honey," said the Lady. "Sometimes if people–change–they don't want to live together anymore."

"That's really dumb," said Corintha. "If you didn't even have a fight or anything. If it's just that somebody wants to grow up. I would never get rid of my friends over that."

"Corintha!"

"Would you let her talk? I'm trying to respect your archaic ideas of parent-child relationships here, Lady, but you're not making it easy."

The lady cleared her throat. "Sorry," she said after a moment.

I looked out at the mainmast and the cannons of our galleon. The rolling lawn. This place had everything. The trampolines and the pools, the swingropes and the games. I could just imagine the birthday parties we'd have here, singing and cake and presents and dares, everyone getting wet, foamguns and crazy mixed-up artificial animals. We could hire clowns and acrobats, storytellers and magicians. At night we'd sleep in hammocks on deck or on blankets on the lawn, under the stars, or all together in a pile, in the big pillowspace in the bow.

And I couldn't see Abby here. Not a growing-upward Abby, getting taller, sprouting breasts, wanting sex with some huge apes of men or women or both. Wanting privacy, wanting to bring her clock-started friends over to whisper and laugh about menstruation and courtship rituals. Abby with a mate. Abby with children.

"There's a place over by Rimrock Road," the Lady said slowly. "It's an old historic mansion. It's not quite as deluxe or as—thematic as this. But the main building has been fitted out for recreation-centered group living. And there are two outbuildings that allow some privacy and—different styles of life."

I stood up. I brushed off my pants. I put my hands in my pockets.

"I want us to go see that one," I said.

—for Jeff and Terri

The Third Party

DAVID MOLES

New writer David Moles has sold fiction to *Asimov's Science Fiction, Polyphony 2, Strange Horizons,* and elsewhere. Here he unravels a suspenseful tangle of intrigue, espionage, and cultural conflict on a troubled distant planet—a tangle where it helps to know who all the players *are.*

It was closer to dawn than midnight when Cicero pushed aside the bar's canvas half-curtain. He brought a gust of wind and rain in with him, the wind blood-warm, the rain with the green taste of a stagnant pond.

There were three stools in front of the plywood counter, and the middle one was occupied. Cicero chose the one on the left and sat down heavily.

"Where have you been?" demanded the man on the middle stool. The language he used had no more than fifty speakers in the world.

Cicero ignored him. The bartender set a wooden cup in front of him and poured in three fingers of cloudy spirit. While it settled, the old man dished out a bowl of soup and set it down next to the cup. Cicero dipped a hand into his algae-stained rain cape and pushed a handful of zinc coins across the bar.

The other man sighed.

Cicero reached past him for the bottle of hot sauce and poured a generous dollop into the soup bowl. "Faculty reception," he said. "Couldn't get away." He stirred the soup with his long spoon. "You had to pick the first night of storm season, didn't you? It's pissing down out there." He took a noisy slurp from the short spoon and followed it with a gulp from the cup.

"Damn it, Cicero—"

"I'm joking," Cicero said. He balanced a fishball on the long spoon and eyed it critically before popping it in his mouth. "I was followed," he said around the mouthful. "Took me a bit to lose them."

The other man tensed. "Dealers?"

"What?" Cicero swallowed and put down his spoon. "Of course it wasn't the dealers! Do you think they'd use people? They'd use, I don't know, drones or something."

"Right," the other man said, relaxing.

"Marius," Cicero said, "what's gotten into you? It was the Specials or it was the Secret Empire, and either way I left them behind before I was out of the District. Strictly local."

Marius sighed and rapped on the bar to signal the bartender. Now it was Cicero's turn to wait impatiently while the bartender set down another bowl and refilled both cups.

Finally Cicero shrugged, and turned his attention back to his soup. "There *was* a reception," he volunteered, around another mouthful of fish. "At the Chancellor's. For the new Semard Professor of Inapplicable Optics. Had a nice chat with him about luminiferous ether."

"That's brilliant, Cicero. You're supposed to be teaching political economy, not physics."

"I'll teach what I damn well please," Cicero said mildly.

He was quiet for a moment, sipping his drink. After a little while he looked up. "Talking of dealers," he said. "They were at the University today. Two of them. Nosing around the library."

"What were they looking for?" Marius said.

"I don't know," said Cicero, "but I didn't like it. They weren't even in local clothes. I don't know who the librarians thought they were."

"Listen, Cicero," Marius said. "Galen's thinking about going home."

"And leaving Salomé to the dealers?" Cicero said. "Pull the other one."

"I'm serious," Marius said. "The consensus in Outreach is that it would be the safest thing."

Cicero put his drink down.

"Fuck the consensus," he said.

He waited for Marius to say something, and when the other man remained silent, said:

"What are you going to do?"

Marius sighed. "I don't know. Wait till they make a decision, I suppose."

Cicero looked down, toying with his cup. They were both silent for a little while.

"Marius," Cicero said eventually. "If we do go back—is there anyone you're going to regret leaving behind?"

"Plenty of people," said Marius. "The whole workers' movement, for a start." He looked at Cicero, and saw the expression on his face.

"Oh," he said. He shook his head. "No. Not like that."

Cicero sighed.

"You're in a tight spot, aren't you?" said Marius.

"I suppose I am," Cicero said.

He caught the first eastbound train back to the University District. It was nearly empty; the only passengers in Cicero's car were a couple of comatose, second-shift City clerks, slinking back to their families in the suburbs after drinking away the week's wage packet.

He felt very alone, all of a sudden. He was not supposed to be alone. Somewhere overhead were the two Community Outreach ships, *Equity* and *Solidarity*; there were analysts and computers, there was the QT network linking them to the Outreach offices at Urizen and Zoa, and through them to the rest of Outreach and to the Community at large. Some small but perceptible fraction of the Community undoubtedly was, right now, focusing its attention on this world, this continent, this city; perhaps even on Cicero himself.

The train passed the dockside shantytowns and the skeletal, rust-streaked shapes of waterfront cranes, and came out onto the long high span of Old Republic Bridge. For a moment the clouds parted; on the left was the great sparkling gray-green bay, with the darker green of the inland sea beyond, and on the right was Basia, bright and dirty and beautiful, wrapped in tropical foliage from the wooden houses of the poor to the gilded, steel-framed spires of the City.

A million people in Basia. A hundred million more scattered over the surface of Salomé. Working. Sleeping. Praying. Stealing. Killing one another, with knives, and bullets, and poor sanitation, and bad fiscal policy. Making love.

"Fuck it," Cicero said aloud, making one of the sleeping clerks snort and look up.

He wondered how many of the researchers and experts and self-styled authorities really understood what they were doing. Very few, he suspected. It was all very well for them to talk about the weight of history, about emergent complexity and long-term consequences, about gradual change in due course—when they never had to face the people whose lives were being turned upside-down by their decisions, face them and look them in the eye.

It was all very well for them to suggest that Outreach abandon Salomé to the dealers.

To suggest that he abandon Thalia.

The train reached the end of the bridge and started the long climb up to the green-topped cliffs on the opposite side of the bay, and the rain closed in again.

Cicero took a quick, deep breath, and let it out slowly.

"Fuck it," he repeated. "I'm staying."

He waited in the shadows of the barred gate of Palmer College as the University proctor made his way along the lane, pausing every few yards to rustle with his long staff among the stalks of climbing bamboo that overgrew the red walls of Graces, Palmer's ancient rival. The walls had stood against fire and riot and war in their time, but generations of peace had left them untested by anything more violent than the annual brawl with Palmer. And now that Graces was a women's college, there was not even that; any insults Palmer's undergraduates offered to the student body of Graces were on a purely individual basis.

When the proctor was out of sight, Cicero looked up and down the lane, tied back his hood and sleeves, and scrambled into the wet greenery. As generations of truant undergraduates had discovered—and the proctors knew full well—the bamboo was more than strong enough to support a climbing body, and its leaves more than deep enough to hide one.

Five years in Salomé's low gravity had done nothing for Cicero's muscle tone, but he made it to the top, and then along the tiled roofs to Labriola House, where he swung down into the open quad and onto the third-floor balcony. He unslung his satchel, paused for a moment to arrange his gown and brush the wet leaves from his hair, and knocked on the first door he came to.

After a little while, a sleepy maid opened it.

"Good morning, Leah," said Cicero. "Is Miss Touray receiving visitors?"

The maid bobbed up and down. "She'll receive you, sure, I'm sure," she said. "She's been up all night at her books. It'd be an act of charity, sir, if you'd convince her at least to close her eyes for a few minutes before chapel."

"I shall see what I can do," Cicero said.

Graces' star student was, in fact, at her books. The table that Thalia Xanthè Touray-Laurion bent over was stacked with books, four and five high, and there was paper everywhere the books were not. As Cicero entered the room she kicked her chair back and pushed her hair out of her eyes.

"Cicero!" she said. "What time is it?"

"Thursday," he said, kissing her. "The sixty-eighth of summer, though storm season seems to have come early this year." He opened his satchel and took out a small paper-wrapped package. "These are for you," he said, setting it down on the table. "The fruit filling, I'm afraid; with the dockworkers on strike there's no chocolate to be had."

She gave him a look, and he amended his answer.

"Six o'clock," he said.

"Six o'clock!" she said, looking back at her books and papers. "I need a window." She stood, and stretched. "Oh, Cicero!" she said, turning suddenly. "Did you know that the real numbers can't be counted?"

Cicero's brow furrowed. "I don't know," he said. "Did I?" He found the coffee press and upended it over the wastebasket to empty the filter. "Is that what you've been working on all night?"

"Yes!" Thalia said. "It's true! And I can prove it!"

Cicero filled the press from Thalia's bedside pitcher and set it on the burner. "What about that statistics thing for Bolte?" he said, trying to light the gas.

"Oh, that," Thalia said. She fished around among the books and papers and came up with a canary-yellow essay booklet. "Done. Yesterday afternoon." She picked up a pastry. "God, I'm starving."

The gas caught. Cicero turned from the burner and picked up the booklet. *Explicit quantification of subjectivity effects on prior distributions: an alternative to maximum likelihood estimation*. Thalia's handwriting was spare and direct, betraying an abundance of calligraphy lessons but also a distinct lack of patience.

"It's very good," he said as he turned the pages. "It's too advanced for Bolte, though."

And not just for Bolte, he thought. He'd had something like it back on Ahania, in History of Mathematics, or it would have been too advanced for him as well. He flipped through to the conclusion.

"Of course the real numbers aren't countable," he said absently, as he read, though Thalia's overnight project had nothing to do with the essay. "For any countable sequence of them, you can construct a series of nested intervals converging to a number that's not in the sequence."

He turned a few more pages, and looked up to see Thalia staring at him.

"Cicero," she said. "I spent all night proving that. I don't think anyone else ever has. You're an *economics* professor. Where did that come from?"

Cicero shrugged. "I don't know," he said. "I must have read it somewhere. Eat your pastry; it'll go stale." He took one for himself.

"I mean it, Cicero," Thalia said. "You're very bright, and I love you dearly, but you're not a genius."

"It's all right," he said. "You are." He kissed her again. "Did you know that the new Semard Professor says that the speed of light in a vacuum is constant, regardless of the relative velocity of the source and the observer?"

"Yes," she said. "I read his paper. I meant to write him about it; distance and time would have to vary with the observer's motion for it to work. Stop trying to distract me."

Cicero sighed. It wasn't Thalia that he was trying to distract; it was himself.

He stood back, looking around the room for a place to sit, and finally settled on the edge of the bed. The mattress was the martially virtuous kind the upper classes of Travalle and Thyatira favored, no more than a little thin cotton stuffing over hard wood, but at that moment it seemed infinitely inviting.

All he wanted to do was take Thalia's hand and pull her down onto it with him, to curl around her with the blankets drawn over their heads, to sleep there forever like enchanted lovers in some fairy tale, caring nothing for professors and colleges, revolutionaries and merchant adventurers. Nothing for orbiting starships overhead, invisible and threatening.

"Thalia," he said instead. "If I had to go away—would you come with me?"

She looked at him. "Go away where?" she said. "The islands? Port-St.-Paul?"

Port-St.-Paul was the capital of one of Travalle's island colonies; it was supposed to be Cicero's home. Six thousand kilometers of stormy ocean separated the islands from Basia: enough to make it nearly impossible for the University to check his forged credentials, enough to paper over any number of cracks in his cover story.

He'd spent the three subjective years of the voyage from Zoa in a constant mild fever, as specialized medical nano rebuilt him into a Roka islander from the DNA up, blood type and skin color and the shape of his cheekbones and the texture of his hair. The face he saw in the mirror was still mostly his own, and by now he had grown accustomed to the differences—the flatter nose, the hair in ringlets rather than curls, the skin no longer blue-black but a richer, more complex brown that could show a blanch or a blush; all so that to the Travallese, he would appear not alien, but merely exotic. It was still enough to make Cicero an object of curiosity, and occasionally, of abuse, but he rarely minded that.

No, what he minded was what it made of his affair with Thalia. Not just a scandal but, in some circles, a lynching offense.

He shook his head. "Never mind," he said.

His resolve had wavered for a moment. But his choice was already made, a long time ago. If he ever made it back to the world where he'd been born, it would still not be the home he had left. His family, his childhood friends—apart from a few who had made similar voyages—all of them had lived and died while he was traveling between the stars, and there was little chance he would ever see those few that had made the voyages again. That was the choice he had made; for Thalia and her people, though he hadn't known them yet. He couldn't ask her to make the same choice for him.

Thalia came and sat down at his side. "I'll take you back to Thyatira," she said, "as soon as I graduate. We'll get my father to endow chairs for both of us at Scetis Imperial."

Cicero smiled. "What will your mother say?"

"She'll be livid," Thalia said. "But that's nothing new. My father will love you."

He did take her hand then, and drew her to him.

"We'll change the world," she murmured. "You'll see."

When Thalia had gone off to chapel, Cicero left Graces College the way he had come in. He attended chapel himself, at Palmer. He held office hours, and was either too lenient with the students who came to him, or too severe, or both. He wrote a scathing letter to the editor of the leading City financial newspaper, and a more conciliatory one to Thyatira's leading economic journal.

He even went to the main library and lurked for a while in the Round Reading Room, listening to the rain on the leaded roof, the clanking of the clockwork elevators and the pneumatic hiss of the order tubes. He had some vague idea of confronting the dealers, but either their business with the University was done or they were occupied elsewhere, because they never showed.

Cicero left frustrated but also, on some level, relieved; he had no idea what he would have said to them. He went back to his rooms, then, and sat for a while, watching the rainwater well up in the crevices between the ill-fitting windowpanes.

What am I going to do? he thought.

Cicero's ship, *Equity*, had been the second to reach Salomé from the Community. *Solidarity* had arrived first to lay the groundwork for the mission, gathering and recording and transmitting data back by QT so that Outreach could plan how best to bring the lost colony back into human civilization. *Equity*, trailing the other ship by twenty years, brought the real missionaries: specialists like Cicero, trained to move among the people of Salomé like fish in water.

Equity had been in the Jokanaan system less than two years when the mission's telescopes first spotted the dealers' ship, half a light-year away, decelerating out of the unknown beyond. From Golden Age records and vague radio whispers, the Community knew that humanity had once spread much farther than the space they had explored; like any Outreach mission, the mission to Salomé had known there was a chance they would meet a counterpart coming the other way. They hadn't expected it, though. And if they had, they would have expected to meet a civilization not unlike the Community itself.

The truth took some time to dawn on them. While Cicero was immersing himself in his adopted culture, paying the inbound ship no more mind than if it had turned up on the other side of the Community, Outreach linguists were trading dead languages with the newcomers, trying to make sense of paradoxical phrases like *intellectual property* and *exploitation rights*. The newcomers' ship had the nonsensical name *Elastic Demand*; the organization it represented apparently was called something like *Marginal, Limited.* For their civilization as a whole the newcomers used the word *association*, which sounded like *community* but had troubling differences in nuance.

Even when the newcomers' quaint obsession with commerce had earned them the nickname *dealers*, and some of Cicero's counterparts back in the Community—experts in development economics—had begun to voice concerns, neither the Outreach offices nor the Salomé mission took those concerns very seriously. It simply did not seem possible for the principles that applied to orphaned, poverty-stricken planets like Salomé, with their joint-stock companies and steam-powered colonial empires, to apply to an interstellar civilization.

And then Marginal's sales force landed in Basia, the capital of the largest of those empires, and announced its presence to the Travallese state.

And Outreach—and the Salomé mission, in particular—suddenly had to take those concerns seriously after all.

Cicero had been taking it for granted that, having come to save the people of Salomé from themselves, Outreach would as a matter of course save them from the dealers as well. Abandoning an entire planet, to be swallowed up by a civilization so dysfunctional that it carried the idea of property across interstellar space, was not to be thought of.

It had never occurred to Cicero that Outreach might decide that the problem was just too big to handle.

And if it's too big for Outreach to handle, he thought, where does that leave *me?* What can I do, alone?

He picked up Thalia's essay booklet and leafed slowly through the pages, not so much reading as simply tracing the shapes of the words.

With the Outreach mission gone, Thalia and the rest of Salomé's people would be helpless. Cicero had to do something; there was no one else.

A knock at the door interrupted his thoughts. It came again; and then, as he stood, he heard the rattle of keys.

He went to answer it, and found the college porter with his master key already out. Old Professor Alier was with him, the Rector of Palmer himself. Next to Alier was a stocky, middle-aged man in a round hat and a black raincoat that was at least ten years out of style, followed by two uniformed City policemen.

"Professor Alier," Cicero said pleasantly, as the rector and the man in the round hat came inside. "To what do I owe the pleasure?"

"This is a damned unpleasant business, Cicero," Alier said. "The College has placed a great deal of trust in you, and you've chosen a fine way of repaying it." He turned to the man in the round hat. "You will keep the name of the College out of it, won't you?" he said.

Cicero's mind raced. It couldn't be that the College had discovered his affair with Thalia; that would be a matter for University discipline—or, at worst, the masked "knights" of the Secret Empire—not the official police. And while his teachings were certainly subversive, he doubted that even his enemies on the economics faculty would take them so seriously as to have him arrested. Marius' work, of course, was quite openly subversive, and if the authorities had somehow been aware of Cicero's connection to it, they would most certainly want to talk to him. But he didn't think that was possible.

No, the dealers were making their move, and using the Travallese state to do it; that was the only plausible explanation.

Cicero was rarely in contact with *Equity* and *Solidarity* and the rest of the Outreach mission. For emergencies, he had a simple voice phone, implanted behind his right ear. Hopefully it still worked; he hadn't used it since training.

He worked his jaw to activate the phone. There was an answering buzz along his jaw.

—Trouble, he subvocalized.

The man in the round hat had a lower-middle-class, City accent. "We'll do our best, sir," he was saying to Alier. In a reassuring tone, he added: "I don't mind telling *you* that in most of these cases, we avoid the inconvenience of a trial."

"Trial?" Cicero said. "What the Devil are you talking about?" He turned to the Rector. "Professor, who are these people?"

"Don't pretend to be thick, Cicero," Alier said. "This gentleman here, Mr.—?" He looked at the man, and, when no name was forthcoming, cleared his throat and started over. "This gentleman here is with the Special Police. They seem to think you can help them with their inquiries."

"Actually," the Special told Cicero cheerfully, "we think you're guilty of espionage, sedition, subversion . . ." He leaned close, and his tone became confiding. ". . . And several other charges that we expect to enumerate before the day is out."

A murmur in Cicero's ear distracted him.

—Is it the dealers?

He'd expected one of the communications people, but it was Livia, *Equity*'s captain and the Outreach mission's nominal second in command.

—Must be, he told her.—All local so far, though, he added. He tried to cover it with a cough.

—Look, Livia said.—We've got our own troubles up here.

"There must be some mistake," Cicero said aloud.

To Livia, he added:—I'm about to be arrested.

—String them along, Livia said.—When we know where you're being taken, we'll find a way to get you out.

Right, Cicero thought. String them along. How am I supposed to do *that?*

The Special shook his head. "I'm afraid we don't make mistakes of that sort, sir," he said. He nodded to one of the uniformed policemen, who produced a pair of manacles, and turned back to Cicero. "I'll just take that, if you don't mind," he said.

Cicero looked down and saw that he was still holding *Explicit quantification*.

"*I* mind," came a voice from the balcony. Cicero looked and saw Thalia coming up the stairs, and his heart sank.

She came up and addressed herself to Alier. "That's my essay for Professor Bolte, sir. I asked Dr. Cicero to give me some advice on a few points."

The Rector blinked. "Miss—Touray, is it?" he said. Cicero watched the conflicting emotions that passed over Alier's face: irritation, embarrassment, and an evident fear of upsetting one of the University's richest and most well-connected students. Alier turned to the man from the Special Police. "Surely there's no need for Miss Touray's essay to be taken in evidence," he said.

"Here," Cicero said, handing Thalia the essay. Their eyes met, and as their fingers touched briefly, Cicero's composure faltered.

His fingers tingling from the moment of contact, he slowly released the booklet. Cleared his throat, he said: "I'm sure this—" with a nod toward the policemen "—will all be cleared up shortly. I'll see you Friday at the usual time."

"Right," the Rector said. "Run along now, child."

Thalia nodded, and, with a backward glance at Cicero, turned to go.

"Just a moment, please—Miss Touray," the Special said, reaching out to bar the way. "That wouldn't happen to be—" he fished a piece of paper from his pocket and glanced at it "—Miss Thalia *Xanthè* Touray, Touray-Laurion, would it?" His pronunciation of the Thyatiran names was much better than Cicero would have expected.

Thalia nodded wordlessly.

The Special smiled. "Well, that's a bit of luck," he said. "Two birds with one stone, as you might say." He handed the Rector the piece of paper, and said to Thalia: "I've a warrant for your arrest as well, you see."

Fuck, Cicero thought.

And he turned to the policeman with the manacles, and with the heel of his right palm hit the bridge of the man's nose so hard that his neck snapped.

The other policeman swore and rushed in, knocking the Rector aside. Cicero kicked him in the stomach and sent him reeling back into the porter's arms.

"Run—" he started to say, turning toward Thalia.

And something hit him very hard in the back of the head.

Thalia watched Cicero crumple to the ground. She'd hardly seen the man in the round hat move. He stood over Cicero and exhaled slowly through pursed lips.

"That was a close one," he said, to no one in particular. He rubbed his knuckles.

The surviving policeman was throwing up in the doorway.

"Constable," the man said sharply. "If you're sufficiently well rested, you'll oblige me by taking the young lady into custody." He turned to the Rector, who was still pressed up against the wall, eyes wide with shock. "A cup of tea's what you'll be wanting, sir," he said. "Sorts you out a treat. We've things well in hand here."

"Yes," Alier said, rather unsteadily. "Yes, I'll just—" He trailed off, looking from Cicero's still-breathing body to the dead policeman and back again.

As the other policeman picked up the fallen manacles and went to put them around Thalia's wrists, the man in the round hat took Alier's arm and propelled him gently toward the doorway.

"On second thought, perhaps a small whisky," he said. Nodding to the porter, he added: "See that he gets one."

"Right you are, sir," the porter said.

The man watched them go down the stairs. When the sound of their footsteps had died away, he turned and knelt down between the bodies, feeling behind Cicero's left ear as if looking for a pulse. He seemed not to find it, and turned Cicero's head to check the other ear; but then, as Thalia watched in growing horror, he reached inside his coat and drew out a small penknife.

"What are you *doing?*" she said, as the man slipped the narrow blade under the skin, and the dark blood welled up. She struggled in the policeman's grip, and the man in the round hat looked up, fixing her with a cold glare.

"Quiet, now, miss," he said. "Right now you're a material witness. You don't want to become a suspect." He went back to what he was doing, fishing around in what was becoming a small pool of red, and came up with a teardrop of gold, no larger than the nail of Thalia's little finger. "There we go," he said. He tugged a handkerchief from Cicero's pocket and used it to clean the knife, which he folded and put away. Then he pressed the handkerchief against the wound. "That ought to do it."

He stood, holding the golden drop up to the light.

"What—" Thalia began.

"Hush," the man said, holding up a hand.

Thalia became aware of a tiny buzzing noise, like a faint and distant wireless voice caught by chance in between stations. It sounded angry—and worried.

"There's some as would give a king's ransom to have this under their microscopes," the man told Thalia. He let the thing fall to the tiles. "But the price of letting some others listen in would be much higher than that."

And he crushed the golden teardrop under his heel.

"Assault on an officer, resisting arrest, and willful murder," the Special announced as he came into the room. "I knew we'd find some way to lengthen your charge sheet, professor, but I didn't expect you to help us do it."

"I'm not a professor," Cicero said. There was a maddening trickle of blood beneath the bandage over his right ear.

Murder. He felt it again, the crack of bone, traveling up his arm with the shock of impact. Willful murder.

They were in the old wing of the Alicata Prison, he thought: stone walls and floor, and a steel door with a window of thick safety glass, so the guard outside could see and assist if Cicero became violent. There was little danger of that. Thick chains ran from his wrists through eye-bolts in the floor to his ankles, crossing under the heavy wooden chair on which he sat; he could shift a little in his seat, but that was all.

"Well, I can't very well call you *spy*, can I?" the Special said. He was standing; at the moment, he was looking out the tiny window into the hall. "And I very much doubt that Alexander Cicero is your real name."

"I'm not a spy, either," Cicero said. "I'm an assistant lecturer in economics."

The Special turned to face him. "What you are, professor, is something we have yet to determine." He leaned forward and put his fists on the table. "Don't try to convince us you're innocent. You gave up any pretense of that when you killed a constable."

"Shoot me for that, then," Cicero said. "Why should I give you anything else?"

The Special smiled and stood up. "Oh, we won't shoot you. You're far too valuable for that. No, I expect we'll keep you alive." He walked around behind Cicero and leaned forward. "Possibly for weeks," he said softly, into Cicero's good ear. "Some of our specialists are quite good at that."

Cicero twisted around until he could just see the Special out of the corner of his eye.

"Why don't you just tell me what you want?" he said.

"What I want?" the Special asked. He came around to the other side of the table and leaned over it to look Cicero in the eye. "What I *want*, professor, since you're kind enough to ask, is for you, and the rest of your kind, to go back where you came from."

"You mean Port-St.-Paul?" Cicero said. "Because—"

He never saw the blow coming. It struck him just below his wounded ear and snapped his head sideways. The pain was blinding, but, through it, he heard the Special's voice, leaning close:

"See here, professor. I've worn a mask before now. I've ridden with the Secret Empire. I've seen an islander hanged just for complimenting a fishmonger's wife on her dress, and I've held the rope that did it." He grasped Cicero's hair and pulled his head back, and his face, twisted with anger, swam into focus. "But I'd let that leering sodomitical beach-monkey have my *own* dear daughter before I'd let *your* lot have my country." He let go. "At least the islander was human."

The blow had made Cicero bite his tongue. He turned his head to the side and spit blood.

"I'm as human as you are," he said, and instantly regretted it.

The Special gave a short, humorless laugh. "The imitation's clever; I'll give you people that." He pulled out the other chair and sat down, studying Cicero's face. "I see that the accusation doesn't surprise you," he said with a thin smile.

Cicero closed his eyes. Yes, that had been stupid; it would have been better to keep quiet.

Still, he thought, better the state than the dealers. No way out now but forward. He took a deep breath and expelled it.

Opening his eyes, he said:

"We're human. And we're here to help."

The Special snorted. "Are you, now?" he said. "And your friends?" He took out a file folder and opened it. " 'Philip Marius,' " he read. "Profession, machinist. Charges, unlawful assembly, industrial combination, and sabotage.' " He turned the page. " 'David Solon. Profession, journalist. Charges, treason, subversion, incitement and libel. Jeanne Megaera, nurse: espionage, licentious behavior, *vitriolage*, solicitation, and attempted murder. Cyrus Mus . . .' "

The Special read another half-dozen names. It sounded like the state had a complete catalog of the Outreach missionaries in Travalle and its colonies. Cicero supposed the dealers had given it to them. He hoped at least some of the others had managed to evade capture.

"And then there's you, professor," the Special concluded. "I don't pretend to understand what, exactly, the Council of Economic Advisors thinks you're guilty of. But since you've signed your own death warrant two or three times already this afternoon, I think the question is—pardon the expression—academic."

He closed the folder. "It's an interesting idea of *help* you people have, professor," he said.

"I didn't say we were here to help *you,*" Cicero said.

The Special gave him an appraising look. "Point taken," he said. "Who, then? The islanders? The criminal classes?"

"Your grandchildren," Cicero said. "And your grandchildren's grandchildren."

The Special snorted. "Out of the goodness of your hearts, I suppose."

"Call it that if you like," Cicero said.

"How noble of you," the Special said. "My grandchildren didn't ask for your help, professor. And they don't need it."

"It's our help or the dealers'," Cicero said.

"'Dealers'?"

"Marginal," said Cicero. "You know who I mean."

"Oh, yes," the Special said. "The illustrious Marginal Limited Liability Corporation. Your competition. Now that they've arrived, you're offering to play fair with us, is that it?"

Cicero opened his mouth to speak, but the Special cut him off. In the accent of the dockside slums, he said:

"'Give me one last chance, sir, I swear I'll reform.'" He shook his head. In his own accent, he said: "How often do you think a copper hears that, professor? A good try, but much too late." He stood up and knocked on the glass. The guard outside peered in and then opened the door. "My coat," the Special said. "And my hat."

"Yes, sir."

As the guard fetched the Special's things, Cicero raised his voice. "Do you think *Marginal* will play fair?" he said. "They'll eat you alive!"

The Special took his coat and hat from the guard. Draping the coat over his arm, he turned to Cicero and said:

"Odd, professor; that's just what they said about *you!*"

The door closed, and Cicero slumped down in his chair. His mouth was full of the taste of blood, and the taste of failure, too.

At least it's not Thalia sitting here, he thought. They wouldn't treat her like this. She'll be safely on her way home by now.

"I am a citizen of Thyatira," she said, before the man even had time to sit down. "I demand to speak to the High Commissioner."

The Special reached out casually and slapped her across the face. Thalia froze, too shocked even to raise her hand to her cheek.

The man took off his hat. "None of that, now, miss," he said, his voice mild. "We know very well who you are; we even know that you're the High Commissioner's cousin. He'll hear about this in due course." The man leaned forward. "The question, miss, is: what *else* will he hear about?"

He raised an eyebrow, waiting for her to speak. When she said nothing, he smiled faintly, and sat down. He took out a folder and was quiet for a moment, leafing through it.

"Will he hear—for instance—that you're an islander's whore?" he suggested, looking up at her.

Thalia kept her face impassive. They couldn't blackmail her by threatening to tell her family. Cousin Milos already knew, from Embassy Intelligence. It was Thalia's mother who was going to be the problem, and for *that* confrontation, she had long been prepared.

The Special seemed to see that his shot had gone wide. "Well," he said. "I suppose that would be a manageable scandal. A few tongues will wag . . . probably set the cause of women's education back twenty years, if it gets in the papers. . . ." He shook his head sadly. "Oh, and your professor-boy will hang for it, of course. But one aristo's daughter having a little what-you-fancy behind closed doors, that's hardly the end of the world, is it?"

Thalia didn't answer.

"But what if it *was* the end of the world?" the Special said. He waited, studying her with unblinking eyes.

"What do you mean?" she eventually said.

The Special smiled. "I'm a reading man, miss," he said, "though I expect I don't look it, not to the likes of you. Magazines, mostly. Penny dreadfuls. A bit beneath you, I dare say. But they tell me you're interested in science, so perhaps you know the sort of thing I'm talking about. *Airship Stories. Wireless Stories. Astonishing.*"

Thalia had been reading *Airship Stories* since she was eleven years old. One of the chauffeurs had used to buy it in town, and sneak Thalia his copies when he was done with them.

"They ran a serial in *Astonishing* last year," the Special continued. "I don't know if you read it. 'Mask People of Naaman,' it was called."

"Shape-changing monsters from other planets," Thalia said. "Sensationalist trash."

The Special gave her half a smile. "Where's your professor-boy from?" he said.

Thalia looked at him. "You don't need me to tell you that," she said.

"Oh, I know where he *says* he's from, miss," the Special said. He referred to the folder and read out: " 'Port-St.-Paul, East Chatrang, Roka Archipelago.' I was hoping he might have been more honest with you."

She couldn't help laughing. "If you're expecting to tell you he's a Naamanite 'Mask Person,' you're more stupid than you look!"

"I'm not so smart as you, miss," the Special said, "but I'm not stupid, either. I know he's not from Naaman." He smiled. "He's from somewhere much farther away than *that*."

Thalia started to laugh again, and stopped, seeing the Special's face. His expression of faint amusement hadn't changed.

"You're serious!" she said.

The Special opened up the folder. He took out a grainy photograph, pushing it across the table for Thalia to examine.

"I expect you recognize Dr. Rosmer and Senator Oradour-Monatte," the Special said. "But these two; have you seen either of them before?"

The photograph showed the steps outside the Round Reading Room of the University Library. There were four men on the steps: one she recognized as a senior librarian, another as a Travallese politician. But the other two—

Their features were odd, foreign. They were short and stocky, more so even than Cicero. Both of them had strangely pale hair; the color was impossible to tell from the photograph, but Thalia didn't think it was the gray of old age. One of them, Thalia realized after a moment, was a woman; she hadn't seen it before because the two were dressed almost identically, in dark, close-fitting trousers and coats buttoned to the throat, cut like nothing she had ever seen before. Neither wore a hat, and the woman's hair was even shorter than the man's.

Thalia shook her head mutely.

"No?" the Special said. "That's reassuring. The one on the left—" he leaned forward, and tapped the picture "—calls himself Allen Macleane. The woman's called Bernadette Parker." He pronounced the foreign syllables carefully.

"And who are they?" Thalia said.

The Special sat back. "It's not who they are, miss, it's how far they've come. Since their last port of call—twenty light-years."

Thalia's bewilderment must have been plain.

"A light-year is—" the Special started to say.

"I know what a light-year is," Thalia said. "That's absolutely mad."

The Special shrugged. "I don't claim to know how they did it, miss," he said. "But they're here."

"Why?" Thalia said. "What do they want?"

"That's also a matter of some debate," the Special said. "They say they want trade. Not in gold or cloth or salt fish, which as I'm sure you've worked out wouldn't be worth the cost of shipping. In *knowledge*, Art, music, scholarship, literature."

"That still wouldn't be worth the cost of shipping," Thalia said.

"Right again, miss," said the Special. "What Mr. Macleane and Miss Parker and their friends—they call themselves 'Marginal,' Marginal Limited Liability Corporation—propose to do, is to set up a sort of interstellar semaphore or radiotelephone, connecting Salomé with—with the stars, I suppose, or at any rate the ones they know." He smiled. "We send them scratchy recordings of the Reunion Philharmonic and they send us the plans to build space-ships of our own."

"That hardly sounds like fair trade," Thalia said.

The Special tapped the side of his nose. "Do you know how the Archipelago Company makes its money, miss?" he asked. "Used to be, they'd buy wool and pig iron and timber in the islands and sell it here, in Basia; buy woven cloth and steel tools and whatnot here and sell them in the islands. They still do a bit of that, of course. But about fifty years ago some enterprising Company factor realized it would be cheaper to build mills and factories right there in the islands. Now most of what the Company sells in the islands is made in the islands, in Company mills and Company factories, out of wool from Company herds and iron from Company mines, and what they mostly ship back to Basia is money."

"It's not just plans for space-ships they're proposing to sell us, then," Thalia said. "We wouldn't know what to do with them, any more than an Eastern Desert tribesman would know what to do with the plans for a steam locomotive. It's science, and engineering, and everything we'd need to understand those plans. They could teach us so much. . . ."

"For a price, miss," the Special said. He seemed to think Thalia had missed his point. "For whatever the market will bear."

"I know," Thalia said. "I *have* studied economics, don't forget."

"Not for a moment, miss," said the Special. "But you see where this leads. As the only source of all that knowledge, there's no limit to the price they could set on it. Within a century these people might own half the world, the way the Company owns half the Archipelago."

"Within a century *these* people will probably have sold off their stakes and retired," Thalia said, "but I take your point."

Then she shook her head.

"This is mad," she said. "Even if it's all true, you can't possibly think Dr. Cicero is one of them."

It would explain so much—Cicero's hard-to-place foreignness, his indifference to convention, the way he combined an understanding of the most esoteric things with an ignorance of the most trivial ones. But while it was no trouble for Thalia to imagine Cicero as an alien, the idea of Cicero as an avaricious colonial speculator was laughable.

The Special stood up. He was silent for a moment, pacing, looking out into the corridor.

"The Marginal expedition arrived about three years ago," he began. "They came straight to the Senate and announced themselves; explained where they came from and what they proposed to do for us. The Senate wanted proof, naturally. They showed us plenty of gadgets and trinkets, but the Senate—Senator Oradour-Monatte, actually, the man you see in the picture—wanted more; some taste of all this knowledge they were proposing to sell us. 'Tell me something,' he said. 'Something I don't know.' And do you know what they told him?"

The Special stopped his pacing and turned to face her.

"They told him, miss, that there was another expedition, already here. A different lot of space-people, from some other—some other constellation, I suppose—altogether."

Thalia stared at him for a moment, then nodded, slowly. "You, think Cicero's one of *them*," she said.

"Miss," the Special said, "I'm quite sure of it. That thing I cut out of his ear proves he's not from this world, but even without it, I have plenty of evidence." He pulled out the other chair again and sat down. "Don't waste my time pretending you don't believe me," he said.

Thalia shook her head. Cicero was going to tell me, she thought. He almost did, this morning, when he talked about leaving. He must have thought I wouldn't believe him.

Would I have believed him?

"So what do *they* want?" she said.

In answer, the Special took out another photograph. She couldn't tell where or when it had been taken. It showed Cicero, in the clothes of a common dockworker, in conversation with another man, similarly dressed. He might have been Cicero's brother, though his features were heavier and his hair was not so straight; at any rate, he was from the same part of the world—whatever that world was.

"Have you seen this man before?" the Special said.

"Never," said Thalia.

"He goes by the name of Philip Marius," the Special said. "Nasty piece of work. He's a saboteur and an anarchist, among other things. It's the talkers in the workers' movement, men like Maspero and Coser, that get their names in the newspapers, but it's our boy Marius who gets things done. Sure you haven't seen him?"

"I'm sure," Thalia said.

The Special sighed. "Well, miss," he said, "the gentlemen from Marginal *may* be bent on enslaving us all, in the end, but they're men of business. By the standards of men of business, they've been quite amicable—negotiating directly with the Senate, providing the state with the odd bit of helpful information now and then." He tapped the photograph of Cicero and the anarchist, Marius. "But your professor's lot—they've been much less polite. Ten years and more they've been watching us, without so much as an introduction; five years they've walked among us in secret, stirring up civil unrest, corrupting our poor and our young folk. Infiltrating factories, hospitals, churches . . . and universities."

"Teaching political economy to the children of the upper classes hardly qualifies as *corrupting young folk*," Thalia said. "If it does, the entire University faculty is guilty."

The Special smiled knowingly. "We can leave the professor's private life—and yours—alone for now," he said. "What's been keeping me awake nights—and what I wanted to know from you—isn't that; it's the thought that your professor, and his friend Marius, and the rest of their friends, might have been working *with* Mr. Macleane and his lot. Playing both ends against the middle, you see—against us."

"And have they?" Thalia said.

"I wish I knew, miss." The Special shook his head. "But I don't think so. I find your witness to Dr. Cicero's character oddly persuasive. He may be a liar, a murderer"—he drew the word slowly out, and Thalia flinched—"an anarchist sympathizer and an alien spy, but he's not a capitalist. And besides—"

A tentative knock came at the door.

"Come in," the Special said sharply.

A uniformed prison guard entered.

"The van's ready, sir," he said.

"Right," said the Special. "I'll be along in just a moment."

"Yes, sir." The door closed.

The Special gathered up the photographs and put them back in the folder. He put the folder back in his bag and stood up.

"'And besides'?" Thalia prompted.

"What?" the Special said.

"Besides what?" Thalia said. "What's the other reason you don't think Cicero's friends and this Marginal Corporation are working together?"

"Ah, that." The Special knocked on the door, and the guard opened it. "Well, miss, between arresting your young man and a few of his friends, arranging a little riot outside Marginal's offices in the City, and a few other pieces of misdirection. . . .

Assuming they're not just staging it for our benefit, it looks as though we've had the two sides shooting at each other for the past hour and a half."

He tipped his hat to Thalia.

"Ta, miss," he said, and she heard the click of the lock behind him.

The guards maneuvered Cicero—with some difficulty, because of the manacles and leg irons—through the narrow corridors, and down several flights of stairs. He tried to count the number of flights, and to remember how tall the Alicata Prison was, how many stories, but he couldn't keep the figures in his head. He kept seeing the gables of Trilisser House, counting the steps of the spiral staircase up to his rooms. His ear was bleeding again, but with his hands bound there was no way for him to do anything about it.

They came out into a covered carriageway, so long and dark that it seemed to be underground. Both ends of the arched passage were sheets of rainwater, and what daylight made it through was gray-green and cheerless.

A van was waiting, windowless and unmarked. The Special took a seat up front, beside the driver. The guards bundled Cicero into the back, and climbed in behind him. He was not entirely surprised to find the compartment's opposite bench already occupied, and the slumped figure of Marius wedged there between two other guards. Marius was in a bad way. Unlike Cicero, who was still in the academic robes he'd been wearing when he was arrested, Marius was dressed in green prison coveralls, patched and stained, and some of the stains were fresh. Bloody bandages covered his right eye and right ear; his right side was bloody as well, and there was dried blood and vomit down the front of his chest. Cicero couldn't tell whether he was even conscious.

The engine started, and the van lurched into motion. There was a brief rattle of rain on the roof, and the van stopped again; the doors were opened, and Cicero had a quick glimpse of a wide courtyard, enclosed by high walls and overlooked by towers. Then his view was blocked by the Special again, and two more guards, draped in rain capes and carrying carbines. One of the guards had a tablet and a pen.

"Prisoner number 91264, alias Philip Marius," that one said. The Special gestured to Marius, and the guard looked up, making a note on the tablet. "Prisoner 91186, alias Alexander Cicero." The guard on Cicero's right took Cicero's manacled hands and raised them. The guard with the tablet made another note.

"To be taken from the Alicata Prison to the Imaz Prison," the Special said.

"That's what it says here," the guard with the tablet said. He tore off a sheet and handed it to the Special. "There you go."

"Ta," said the Special.

They closed the doors again, and the van started moving. The storm was blowing in earnest now. Cicero could hear it, the wind shrieking across the roof of the van, throwing rain against the sides like handfuls of gravel. Between the wind and the state of the road, evident in the jouncing of the seat and the noises of complaint from the suspension, he half expected the van to tip over at any moment. It was hot and close, and he found it hard to breathe.

The Imaz. The Alicata was an ordinary prison, for ordinary criminals. The Imaz was where they took the dangerous prisoners, the ones who had tried to escape, and the sort of political prisoners whose allies or followers might be expected to attempt a rescue. He fell into all three categories, he supposed.

How did they get people out to the Imaz, anyway? It was on an island, he knew that, the prison built within the walls of an old medieval seafort. Storm-season waves in the inland sea, funneled by the narrow, cliff-steep shores, regularly topped fifty meters. No boat could survive those waters, and only a brave fool would trust himself to Salomé's rickety, experimental dirigibles—certainly the police, even the Specials, had none.

The van's journey seemed to be tending up, into the hills, not down to the port. Maybe they weren't being taken to the Imaz at all; at least not directly.

The van came to a stop, and, from the cab, Cicero heard muffled conversation. There was the metallic clang of a gate being opened, then the van jerked into motion again, but only for a little while. The wind died down, and the rain on the roof ceased, as they came into a tunnel, or a garage. Where were they?

The door opened on a dark, clanking space that smelled of machinery and of the storm. The guards hauled Marius out, and one of them told Cicero: "Out you go, then."

The van was parked beneath a wide sheet-metal awning supported by steel girders. They were at the top of the kilometer-high cliffs that made up most of the inland sea's southern shore, looking out into the storm. Far out to sea, across the white-topped, gray-green waves, the sharp rock of the Imaz emerged from the dark, wind-whipped clouds like the prow of a warship in the fog.

Four cobweb-thin cables, two above and two below, stretched toward them. On the far end they faded into the rain, invisible, but closer by Cicero could see that they were in fact thick as a man's wrist, and steel. Next to the van beneath the awning was a mass of machinery, man-high wheels and pulleys and a clattering steam engine, and Cicero saw that it was drawing in the upper pair of cables, and paying out the lower. He looked out into the storm again and saw a car, suspended between the cables, slowly making its way toward them. Cicero was suddenly overwhelmed with vertigo.

The Special caught his eye and smiled.

"All right with heights, are we, professor?"

Cicero didn't answer.

The car was the size of a railway carriage and crudely streamlined, its corners smoothed and sides rounded by bolted sheets of rust-streaked metal. Despite that, it swayed alarmingly as it approached the cliffs, pulling the cables back and forth, and Cicero could hear the wind shrieking across the car's metal skin. The noise abated as the car came under the awning and thumped to a stop. A hatch opened downward, becoming a short flight of steps, and two guards came out, both of them wearing rain capes and carrying heavy machine pistols.

The Special presented his paperwork, and after a quick examination of it the guards stood respectfully aside.

"After you, professor," the Special said.

The Alicata guards pushed Cicero up the steps and into the car. The interior was lit by a line of incandescent bulbs in wire cages, bolted to the roof. There were four more guards inside, and a number of bare steel benches. The windows of the car were heavily barred.

Marius was brought in on a stretcher, and taken to the other end of the car. Cicero was handed over to the Imaz guards and made to sit, while they fastened his manacles and leg irons to eyebolts beneath the bench.

The Special climbed in, followed by the two Imaz guards, who pulled the door up and dogged it shut. With a lurch, the car began to move, and the wind quickly rose to a screech.

"Time was," the Special said, taking the bench across from Cicero, "the Imaz was cut off from the mainland ten weeks out of the year. The old kings used to hole up there, during their wars; took the Senate four years to winkle them out of there, during the Reunion. This thing—" he tapped the bench "—was put up thirty years ago, after some rioting prisoners managed to set fire to the grain store during storm season. Most of the guards made it through, holed up in the citadel with their own stores. But there wasn't one prisoner in twenty left alive by winter when the boats made it across." He gave Cicero a ghoulish smile and added: "Nor many bodies left, neither."

Cicero turned his head away and closed his eyes. The car was dropping swiftly—there was quite a bit of slack in the cables—and it pitched and swayed as the storm winds pushed and lifted it. Cicero's stomach heaved in sympathy, and he realized suddenly why the seats were all bare metal: for ease of cleaning. He opened his eyes again, which was a slight improvement. The Special, Cicero was annoyed to see, looked quite cheerful; he might have been sitting in a parkside café on a sunny day in spring.

The uniformed guards, though, looked more than a little green around the gills. Cicero tried to estimate his chance of disarming one of them and turning his weapon on the others, and thought that without the manacles and leg irons it might be as high as one in three; but the bolts that held the chains were quite secure.

The Special met his eye, and smiled, and Cicero had the uncomfortable feeling that his mind was being read.

Then the car gave a great lurch, sending the Special and all six guards sprawling, and only the prisoners' chains prevented them from being thrown from their seats as well. The lights went out, and the pitch of the wind rose to a scream.

"Fucking hell," growled the Special as he picked himself up. "That happen often?"

"No, sir," one of the Imaz guards said.

"We've stopped moving," said another, looking out the window.

It was true. Not only had they stopped moving out toward the island, but the seasick pitching of the car had died as well.

"Get the emergency lamp," the Special ordered. "Signal the station and find out what the hell's happened."

One of the guards opened a locker beneath one of the benches and took out a battery-operated signal lamp. He went to the end of the car, looking back toward the cliff, and flashed the lamp into the rain.

"It's awful thick out there, sir," he said doubtfully. He turned around. "I don't know if—"

The window behind him imploded, knocking him flat and sending shards of glass and fragments of metal through the car. At the same moment, something—several somethings—hit the sides of the car, and the door blew outward off its hinges.

The Special yelled something, his words impossible to hear over the sudden roar of wind and water, and the car was lit by a white flash as he fired his pistol over the head of the fallen guard. The bullet struck something that Cicero could not quite see, and ricocheted away, shattering another window.

"GET DOWN!" bellowed a woman's amplified voice, a Community voice.

Cicero did his best, leaning forward over his manacled hands. He heard the cracks of electrostatic stunners, and then one of the Imaz guards opened up with his machine pistol; in the muzzle flashes Cicero glimpsed the glassy shape of a suited Outreach missionary, the figure's optical camouflage not quite able to keep up with the rapidly changing light inside the car. The figure went down in a shower of bullets, but more were coming in through the door and the blown-out windows. In moments all the guards were down, and the missionaries—four of them, men and women—were shutting off their camouflage, the suits turning to bright solid colors.

The missionary who had been knocked down, his suit now spring green, came over and knelt in front of Cicero. He took out a tool, and in a moment the bolts that secured Cicero's chains began to smoke and glow red.

The missionary lifted his mask to reveal a dark, bearded face.

"Lucius," said Cicero.

"You all right, then?" the man said. Not waiting for an answer, he took out a medical scanner and ran it quickly over Cicero from head to toe.

"I'm fine," Cicero said. "See to Marius."

Lucius smiled. "You're not fine," he said. "But you'll do." He moved back to examine Marius.

A bright yellow suit proved to be Livia, a very unhappy Livia.

"Led us a chase, didn't you?" she said.

"Pressure of circumstance," said Cicero. "Are the others all right?"

"Everyone in Thyatira and the Archipelago got out," Livia said. "We picked Megaera off a hospital roof and Cassia out of the harbor. But Solon's dead; killed resisting arrest. I don't know about Mus and the others in the southeast; one of the other landers was supposed to go after them."

Cicero tried to remember Solon's face, and found that he couldn't, for all that they, and all the on-world missionaries, had trained together for the better part of five subjective years. A small man, Solon, with a highly refined sense of outrage that had served him well in his cover as a muckraking journalist; that was all Cicero could remember.

Livia glanced down, at a display on the inside of her wrist.

"Come on," she said. "*Equity*'s coming for us; we've got twenty minutes, no more." She turned away. To someone unseen, she said: "Drop the rescue lines."

I can't let them take me away, Cicero thought.

As much as he wanted to relax, to let himself be bundled aboard *Equity* like a tired child carried home from a dinner party, he couldn't do that. He realized that, terrible as the idea was to contemplate, on his way to the interrogation rooms of the

Imaz he had actually been better off. From there, he at least would have had some chance to turn the Travallese state around, to help Salomé resist the dealers; some chance to see Thalia again.

He stood up quickly.

"Livia," he said. "I have to get back to the city."

Livia turned back.

"You're joking," she said. "*Solidarity*'s been *blown*, Cicero. We've lost track of the dealers' ship; they've deployed about half a thousand decoys and automated fighters over our heads, and *Equity*'s running the gauntlet of them right now, trying to get into position to pick us up. We're leaving this system, Cicero; Outreach is leaving." She glanced at her display again. "Eighteen minutes, now." Raising her voice, she said: "Lucius—can we move him?"

Marius answered for himself.

"I can walk," he said. "Just—let's get away from here."

"Right." Livia moved to the door and looked up into the rain.

"Livia—" Cicero said.

"Argue with me on the lander," she said. A safety line dropped down from above; Livia caught it and clipped it to her suit. The pupal form of a rescue harness followed, and she secured it to one of the handrails.

"Here," she said, stepping aside.

Cicero heard the lander's fans surge and whine as they fought to keep the lander airborne and to compensate for the violent winds. He made his way carefully to the door, the wind-driven rain stinging his face. The hull of the lander was a smooth gray curve overhead, its open hatch bright and welcoming, surrounded by white emergency lights.

He looked down. Below—far below—the storm-waves were a dark gray, darker than the lander's hull, gray topped with greenish foam. On one side, the rock of the Imaz rose above them, much taller, and much closer than Cicero would have thought. On the other, the cliff was a long shadow, and when Cicero tried to follow its line down to where the curve of the great bay should have begun, where he should have been able to make out some trace of the city, the storm dissolved everything.

"Marius," he said suddenly. "You first."

Marius limped up to the door.

"Sure?" he said.

Cicero nodded to the rescue harness. "Go on," he said. "I'm . . ." not leaving, he started to say, but his voice failed:

Marius put a hand on Cicero's shoulder, and Cicero saw that he knew.

"Good luck," he said.

"Go *on*," said Cicero.

Marius smiled. He started to step into the rescue harness. Then he glanced at something over Cicero's shoulder, and the smile left his face.

"Down!" he yelled, shoving Cicero aside.

Cicero stumbled and fell back into the tram car. There was a shot, somehow louder than any of the barrage that had filled the car a few minutes earlier; and when Cicero looked up he saw the Special up on one knee, pistol held steady in both hands. The Special's eyes met Cicero's, and the pistol moved, and Cicero saw his death there, in a small circle of blackness.

Cicero froze.

Then stun bolts hit the Special from three sides, and the pistol fell from nerveless fingers.

It took Cicero a moment to get to his feet; his muscles didn't want to work.

He turned to thank Marius, but there was no one there.

And when he moved to the door and looked out, there was no one there either.

Only the lander's futile lights, and the storm-waves, and the rain.

Thalia didn't know how long she waited. She slept for a while, head down on the table; the chair wasn't comfortable, but it was more comfortable than the cold concrete of the floor.

At one point the lights flickered, and there were raised voices in the hall, but she was unable to make out the words. At another point a guard in a green uniform brought in a tray with a bowl of oily fish soup and a cup of bad tea. The guard didn't answer any of Thalia's questions, or even look her in the eye.

When the door of her cell opened, Thalia expected the Special. Instead there were two armed guards, and another man. The man was on the late side of middle age, and despite his height—he was rather short—walked with a stoop. His hair, where it was not gray, was an odd shade of yellow, like dry leaves. He was wearing a matte gray coat that was not quite like anything Thalia had ever seen before, and he looked as tired as she herself felt.

It was some moments before she recognized him as the man from the Special's photograph of the library steps.

The guards went out, and closed the door behind them.

"Sorry about this," the man said. The words were clear, but his accent was as strange as his coat. "My name's Allen Macleane. I'm with Marginal LLC." He made a strange gesture, holding out his right hand with the fingers together and the palm perpendicular to the floor.

"Yes," Thalia said. "I know. Does this mean you've won?"

Macleane's face reddened, and his hand dropped. He shook his head. "Do you mind if I sit down?" he said.

Wordlessly, Thalia gestured toward the other chair, and Macleane took it.

"Thanks," he said. He looked down for a moment; his fingers traced designs on the table. "I understand your friend Cicero was rescued," he said, looking up. "I thought you'd want to know that. His people hit the tram that was taking him out to the Imaz."

Thalia's heart leapt.

"Does that mean—" she began.

"Does that mean *they* won?" Macleane said. "Not exactly. We destroyed one of their ships; the other one's running. Past the orbit of Herodias now, and still accelerating at two Gs. They won't be back any time soon." He sighed. "But that doesn't mean *we* won, either. Our ship, our only ship, is crippled, maybe destroyed; we're trapped here. Without the ship, we've got no way to contact our own people, and anyhow they're too far away to help. All we've got left in orbit is machines we can't control. Everyone who was on the ship is dead; my own brother is dead."

"I'm sorry," Thalia said. But she was barely listening; she was thinking about the distances between the stars, and about the Semard professor's new theory of light and time.

Oh, Cicero, she thought. Oh, my heart.

He might as well be dead, she thought, that's what this means; he'll never be back.

But then she thought: No, that's not what it means at all. It means he's alive, out there somewhere; and if they keep going, he'll be alive still, when I'm an old woman and can no longer remember his face, he'll still be young, preserved in slow time like amber, out there between the stars, chasing the light.

And that was a reason to be thankful. That was a reason to go on.

She realized that tears were running down her cheeks.

I have to pull myself together, she thought. This man will think I'm crying for his brother.

But she looked up into Allen Macleane's lined face and saw that he was wiser than that.

"We both lost," Macleane said gently. "*You've* won, don't you see? The people of Salomé have won."

"What do you mean?" Thalia said.

"We came here thinking you were a bunch of barbarians," Macleane said. "Primitives. I'm sure Outreach—your friend Cicero's people—thought the same way. We didn't take you seriously, you see. When you, I mean the Travallese government, moved against us, we figured that Outreach was behind it, just like they figured we were behind the government's moves against them." He smiled. "Both of us were watching each other so carefully, we forgot there was a third party at the table—*you*. You played us off against each other beautifully, and we never knew you were doing it."

"Mr. Macleane," Thalia said. "I'm not a player in your game. I'm not even a pawn. I'm a spectator. I have only the slightest idea what you're talking about."

"I'm sorry," Macleane said. "I didn't mean you, personally. But your people have got us right where they want us. There are only about twenty of us left. If we're going to survive here it's going to be on their charity."

"Not my people, Mr. Macleane." Thalia lifted her manacled hands. "Charity isn't what the Senate of Travalle is noted for."

"I know," Macleane said. "They'll milk us for everything we've got. History, stellar geography, basic science. Technology; weapons, especially, and spacecraft, so they can deal with the next alien arrival on their own terms." He shook his head. "They don't understand what they're up against."

"I'm not one of you, Mr. Macleane," she said. "I'm not Travallese, either. If Cicero was against you, then so am I. What does this have to do with me?"

"They tell me you're good at mathematics," Macleane said.

"I'm *amazing* at mathematics," said Thalia.

Macleane smiled.

"Would you like a job?"

They'd had to sedate Cicero to get him aboard the lander. Livia wasn't happy about that, and trouble would undoubtedly come of it later. But clearly, he'd been raving, demanding to be left aboard the wrecked tram car, even after the locals had shot Marius.

Livia checked her displays. The other landers, with their own cargoes of evacuees, were keeping pace. Behind them, as the dealers' automated fighter fleet and the Outreach mission's rear guard finished annihilating each other, the mad fireworks display of fusion bombs and antimatter explosions was finally dying out, after turning Salomé's night into day.

There was no telling which side, if either, had gained the upper hand back there, but it didn't matter; neither Livia nor Galen wanted to take any more chances, and they were committed, now.

Lucius came forward from checking on Cicero, moving slowly and cautiously under three gravities of acceleration.

"He'll be fine," Livia said.

Lucius shook his head. "But will he be fine when he wakes up?" he said.

Livia didn't answer, though what she thought was: Damned if I was going to come back without *either* of them.

On the forward display, the violet flare of *Equity*'s drive died, as the starship briefly collapsed its ram field and cut its torch to allow the landers to catch up. Faster than seemed possible, the dark bulk of the ship swept up on them; they floated free for a moment as the lander's autopilot cut their own thrust, and there was a jerk and a metallic thump as the grapples caught.

Then the thrust built as the starship's torch came to life again, and they ran for the safety of the deep.

The Voluntary State

CHRISTOPHER ROWE

The weird and wonderful adventure that follows gives us an overview of a society in the process of being swallowed and transformed by a strange and potent Singularity—and the story of what happens to those few who get stuck in its throat on the way *down* . . .

New writer Christopher Rowe was born in Kentucky and lives there still. With Gwenda Bond, he operates a small press and edits the critically acclaimed magazine *Say*. His stories have appeared in *SCI FICTION*, *Realms of Fantasy*, *Electric Velocipede*, *Idomancer*, *Swan Sister*, *Trampoline*, *The Infinite Matrix*, *The Journal of Pulse-Pounding Narratives*, and elsewhere, and have recently been collected in *Bittersweet Creek*.

Soma had parked his car in the trailhead lot above Governor's Beach. A safe place, usually, checked regularly by the Tennessee Highway Patrol and surrounded on three sides by the limestone cliffs that plunged down into the Gulf of Mexico.

But today, after his struggle up the trail from the beach, he saw that his car had been attacked. The driver's side window had been kicked in.

Soma dropped his pack and rushed to his car's side. The car shied away from him, backed to the limit of its tether before it recognized him and turned, let out a low, pitiful moan.

"Oh, car," said Soma, stroking the roof and opening the passenger door, "Oh, car, you're hurt." Then Soma was rummaging through the emergency kit, tossing aside flares and bandages, finally, *finally* finding the glass salve. Only after he'd spread the ointment over the shattered window and brushed the glass shards out onto the gravel, only after he'd sprayed the whole door down with analgesic aero, only then did he close his eyes, access call signs, drop shields. He opened his head and used it to call the police.

In the scant minutes before he saw the cadre of blue and white bicycles angling in from sunward, their bubblewings pumping furiously, he gazed down the beach at Nashville. The cranes the Governor had ordered grown to dredge the harbor would go dormant for the winter soon—already their acres-broad leaves were tinged with orange and gold.

"Soma-With-The-Paintbox-In-Printer's-Alley," said voices from above. Soma turned to watch the policemen land. They all spoke simultaneously in the sing-song chant of law enforcement. "Your car will be healed at taxpayers' expense." Then the ritual words, "And the wicked will be brought to justice."

Efficiency and order took over the afternoon as the threatened rain began to fall. One of the 144 Detectives manifested, Soma and the policemen all looking about as they felt the weight of the Governor's servant inside their heads. It brushed aside the thoughts of one of the Highway Patrolmen and rode him, the man's movements becoming slightly less fluid as he was mounted and steered. The Detective filmed Soma's statement.

"I came to sketch the children in the surf," said Soma. He opened his daypack for the soapbubble lens, laid out the charcoal and pencils, the sketchbook of boughten paper bound between the rusting metal plates he'd scavenged along the midden-mouth of the Cumberland River.

"Show us, show us," sang the Detective.

Soma flipped through the sketches. In black and gray, he'd drawn the floating lures that crowded the shallows this time of year. Tiny, naked babies most of them, but also some little girls in one-piece bathing suits and even one fat prepubescent boy clinging desperately to a deflating beach ball and turning horrified, pleading eyes on the viewer.

"Tssk, tssk," sang the Detective, percussive. "Draw filaments on those babies, Soma Painter. Show the lines at their heels."

Soma was tempted to show the Detective the artistic licenses tattooed around his wrists in delicate salmon inks, to remind the intelligence which authorities had purview over which aspects of civic life, but bit his tongue, fearful of a For-the-Safety-of-the-Public proscription. As if there were a living soul in all of Tennessee who didn't know that the children who splashed in the surf were nothing but extremities, nothing but lures growing from the snouts of alligators crouching on the sandy bottoms.

The Detective summarized. "You were here at your work, you parked legally, you paid the appropriate fee to the meter, you saw nothing, you informed the authorities in a timely fashion. Soma-With-The-Paintbox-In-Printer's-Alley, the Tennessee Highway Patrol applauds your citizenship."

The policemen had spread around the parking lot, casting cluenets and staring back through time. But they all heard their cue, stopped what they were doing, and broke into a raucous cheer for Soma. He accepted their adulation graciously.

Then the Detective popped the soapbubble camera and plucked the film from the air before it could fall. It rolled up the film, chewed it up thoughtfully, then dismounted the policeman, who shuddered and fell against Soma. So Soma did not at first hear what the others had begun to chant, didn't decipher it until he saw what they were encircling. Something was caught on the wispy thorns of a nodding thistle growing at the edge of the lot.

"Crow's feather," the policemen chanted. "Crow's feather Crow's feather Crow's feather."

And even Soma, licensed for art instead of justice, knew what the fluttering bit of black signified. His car had been assaulted by Kentuckians.

Soma had never, so far as he recalled, painted a self-portrait. But his disposition was melancholy, so he might have taken a few visual notes of his trudge back to Nashville if he'd thought he could have shielded the paper from the rain.

Soma Between the Sea and the City, he could call a painting like that. Or, if he'd decided to choose that one clear moment when the sun had shown through the towering slate clouds, *Soma Between Storms*.

Either image would have shown a tall young man in a broad-brimmed hat, black pants cut off at the calf, yellow jersey unsealed to show a thin chest. A young man, sure, but not a young man used to long walks. No helping that; his car would stay in the trailhead lot for at least three days.

The mechanic had arrived as the policemen were leaving, galloping up the gravel road on a white mare marked with red crosses. She'd swung from the saddle and made sympathetic clucking noises at the car even before she greeted Soma, endearing herself to auto and owner simultaneously.

Scratching the car at the base of its aerial, sussing out the very spot the car best liked attention, she'd introduced herself. "I am Jenny-With-Grease-Beneath-Her-Fingernails," she'd said, but didn't seem to be worried about it because she ran her free hand through unfashionably short cropped blond hair as she spoke.

She'd whistled for her horse and began unpacking the saddlebags. "I have to build a larger garage than normal for your car, Soma Painter, for it must house me and my horse during the convalescence. But don't worry, my licenses are in good order. I'm bonded by the city and the state. This is all at taxpayers' expense."

Which was a very great relief to Soma, poor as he was. With friends even poorer, none of them with cars, and so no one to hail out of the Alley to his rescue, and now this long, wet trudge back to the city.

Soma and his friends did not live uncomfortable lives, of course. They had dry spaces to sleep above their studios, warm or cool in response to the season and even clean if that was the proclivity of the individual artist, as was the case with Soma. A clean, warm or cool, dry space to sleep. A good space to work and a more than ample opportunity to sell his paintings and drawings, the Alley being one of the *other* things the provincials did when they visited Nashville. Before they went to the great vaulted Opera House or after.

All that and even a car, sure, freedom of the road. Even if it wasn't so free because the car was not *really* his, gift of his family, product of their ranch. Both of them, car and artist, product of that ranching life Soma did his best to forget.

If he'd been a little closer in time to that ranching youth, his legs might not have ached so. He might not have been quite so miserable to be lurching down the gravel road toward the city, might have been sharp-eyed enough to still see a city so lost in the fog, maybe sharp-eared enough to have heard the low hoots and caws that his assailants used to organize themselves before they sprang from all around him—down from tree branches, up from ditches, out from the undergrowth.

And there was a Crow raiding party, the sight stunning Soma motionless. "This only happens on television," he said.

The caves and hills these Kentuckians haunted unopposed were a hundred miles and more north and east, across the shifting skirmish line of a border. Kentuckians couldn't be here, so far from the frontier stockades at Fort Clarksville and Barren Green.

But here they definitely were, hopping and calling, scratching the gravel with their clawed boots, blinking away the rain when it trickled down behind their masks and into their eyes.

A Crow clicked his tongue twice and suddenly Soma was the center of much activity. Muddy hands forced his mouth open and a paste that first stung then numbed was swabbed around his mouth and nose. His wrists were bound before him with rough hemp twine. Even frightened as he was, Soma couldn't contain his astonishment. "Smoke rope!" he said.

The squad leader grimaced, shook his head in disgust and disbelief. "Rope and cigarettes come from two completely different varieties of plants," he said, his accent barely decipherable. "Vols are so fucking stupid."

Then Soma was struggling through the undergrowth himself, alternately dragged and pushed and even half-carried by a succession of Crow Brothers. The boys were running hard, and if he was a burden to them, then their normal speed must have been terrifying. Someone finally called a halt, and Soma collapsed.

The leader approached, pulling his mask up and wiping his face. Deep red lines angled down from his temples, across his cheekbones, ending at his snub nose. Soma would have guessed the man was forty if he'd seen him in the Alley dressed like a normal person in jersey and shorts.

Even so exhausted, Soma wished he could dig his notebook and a bit of charcoal out of the daypack he still wore, so that he could capture some of the savage countenances around him.

The leader was just staring at Soma, not speaking, so Soma broke the silence. "Those scars"—the painter brought up his bound hands, traced angles down either side of his own face—"are they ceremonial? Do they indicate your rank?"

The Kentuckians close enough to hear snorted and laughed. The man before Soma went through a quick, exaggerated pantomime of disgust. He spread his hands, why-me-lording, then took the beaked mask off the top of his head and showed Soma its back. Two leather bands crisscrossed its interior, supporting the elaborate superstructure of the mask and preventing the full weight of it, Soma saw, from bearing down on the wearer's nose. He looked at the leader again, saw him rubbing at the fading marks.

"Sorry," said the painter.

"It's okay," said the Crow. "It's the fate of the noble savage to be misunderstood by effete city dwellers."

Soma stared at the man for a minute. He said, "You guys must watch a lot of the same TV programs as me."

The leader was looking around, counting his boys. He lowered his mask and pulled Soma to his feet. "That could be. We need to go."

It developed that the leader's name was Japheth Sapp. At least that's what the other Crow Brothers called out to him from where they loped along ahead or behind, circled farther out in the brush, scrambled from limb to branch to trunk high above.

Soma descended into a reverie space, sing-songing subvocally and supervocally (and being hushed down by Japheth hard then). He guessed in a lucid moment that the paste the Kentuckians had dosed him with must have some sort of will-sapping effect. He didn't feel like he could open his head and call for help; he didn't even want to. But *"I will take care of you,"* Athena was always promising. He held onto that and believed that he wasn't panicking because of the Crows' drugs, sure, but also because he would be rescued by the police soon. *"I will take care of you."* After all, wasn't that one of the Governor's slogans, clarifying out of the advertising flocks in the skies over Nashville during Campaign?

It was good to think of these things. It was good to think of the sane capital and forget that he was being kidnapped by aliens, by Indians, by toughs in the employ of a rival Veronese merchant family.

But then the warchief of the marauding band was throwing him into a gully, whistling and gesturing, calling in all his boys to dive into the wash, to gather close and throw their cloaks up and over their huddle.

"What's up, boss?" asked the blue-eyed boy Soma had noticed earlier, crouched in the mud with one elbow somehow dug into Soma's ribs.

Japheth Sapp didn't answer but another of the younger Crow Brothers hissed, "THP even got a bear in the air!"

Soma wondered if a bear meant rescue from this improbable aside. Not that parts of the experience weren't enjoyable. It didn't occur to Soma to fear for his health, even when Japheth knocked him down with a light kick to the back of the knees after the painter stood and brushed aside feathered cloaks for a glimpse of the sky.

There *was* a bear up there. And yes, it was wearing the blue and white.

"I want to see the bear, Japheth," said a young Crow. Japheth shook his head, said, "I'll take you to Willow Ridge and show you the black bears that live above the Green River when we get back home, Lowell. That bear up there is just a robot made out of balloons and possessed by a demon, not worth looking at unless you're close enough to cut her."

With all his captors concentrating on their leader or on the sky, Soma wondered if he might be able to open his head. As soon as he thought it, Japheth Sapp wheeled on him, stared him down.

Not looking at any one of them, Japheth addressed his whole merry band. "Give this one some more paste. But be careful with him; we'll still need this vol's head to get across the Cumberland, even after we bribe the bundle bugs."

Soma spoke around the viscous stuff the owl-feathered endomorph was spackling over the lower half of his face. "Bundle bugs work for the city and are above reproach. Your plans are ill-laid if they depend on corrupting the servants of the Governor."

More hoots, more hushings, then Japheth said, "If bundle bugs had mothers, they'd sell them to me for half a cask of Kentucky bourbon. And we brought more than half a cask."

Soma knew Japheth was lying—this was a known tactic of neoanarchist agitator hero figures. "I know you're lying," said Soma. "It's a known tactic of—"

"Hush hush, Soma Painter. I like you—this you—but we've all read the Governor's curricula. You'll see that we're too sophisticated for your models." Japheth gestured and the group broke huddle. Outrunners ran out and the main body shook off cramps. "And I'm not an anarchist agitator. I'm a lot of things, but not that."

"Singer!" said a young Crow, scampering past.

"I play out some weekends, he means; I don't have a record contract or anything," Japheth said, pushing Soma along himself now.

"Welder!" said another man.

"Union-certified," said Japheth. "That's my day job, working at the border."

More lies, knew Soma. "I suppose Kentuckians built the Girding Wall, then?"

Everything he said amused these people greatly. "Not just Kentuckians, vol, the whole rest of the world. Only we call it the containment field."

"Agitator, singer, welder," said the painter, the numbness spreading deeper than it had before, affecting the way he said words and the way he chose them.

"Assassin," rumbled the Owl, the first thing Soma had heard the burly man say.

Japheth was scrambling up a bank before Soma. He stopped and twisted. His foot corkscrewed through the leaf mat and released a humid smell. He looked at the Owl, then hard at Soma, reading him.

"You're doped up good now, Soma Painter. No way to open that head until we open it for you. So, sure, here's some truth for you. We're not just here to steal her things. We're here to break into her mansion. We're here to kill Athena Parthenus, Queen of Logic and Governor of the Voluntary State of Tennessee."

Jenny-With-Grease-Beneath-Her-Fingernails spread fronds across the parking lot, letting the high green fern leaves dry out before she used the mass to make her bed. Her horse watched from above the half-door of its stall. Inside the main body of the garage, Soma's car slept, lightly anesthetized.

"Just enough for a soft cot, horse," said Jenny. "All of us we'll sleep well after this hard day."

Then she saw that little flutter. One of the fronds had a bit of feather caught between some leaves, and yes, it was coal black, midnight blue, reeking of the north. Jenny sighed, because her citizenship was less faultless than Soma's, and policemen disturbed her. But she opened her head and stared at the feather.

A telephone leapt off a tulip poplar a little ways down the road to Nashville. It squawked through its brief flight and landed with inelegant weight in front of Jenny. It turned its beady eyes on her.

"Ring," said the telephone.

"Hello," said Jenny.

Jenny's Operator sounded just like Jenny, something else that secretly disturbed her. Other people's Operators sounded like television stars or famous Legislators or like happy cartoon characters, but Jenny was in that minority of people whose Operators and Teachers always sounded like themselves. Jenny remembered a slogan from Campaign, "My voice is yours."

"The Tennessee Highway Patrol has plucked one already, Jenny Healer." The voice from the telephone thickened around Jenny and began pouring through her ears like cold syrup. "But we want a sample of this one as well. Hold that feather, Jenny, and open your head a little wider."

Now, here's the secret of those feathers. The one Jenny gave to the police and the one the cluenets had caught already. The secret of those feathers, and the feathers strung like look-here flags along the trails down from the Girding Wall, and even of the Owl feathers that had pushed through that fence and let the outside in. All of them were oily with intrigue. Each had been dipped in potent *math*, the autonomous software developed by the Owls of the Bluegrass.

Those feathers were hacks. They were lures and false attacks. Those feathers marked the way the Kentuckians didn't go.

The math kept quiet and still as it floated through Jenny's head, through the ignorable defenses of the telephone and the more considerable, but still avoidable, rings of barbed wire around Jenny's Operator. The math went looking for a Detective or even a Legislator if one were to be found not braying in a pack of its brethren, an unlikely event.

The math stayed well clear of the Commodores in the Great Salt Lick ringing the Parthenon. It was sly math. Its goals were limited, realizable. It marked the way they didn't go.

The Crows made Soma carry things. "You're stronger than you think," one said and loaded him up with a sloshing keg made from white oak staves. A lot of the Crows carried such, Soma saw, and others carried damp, muddy burlap bags flecked with old root matter and smelling of poor people's meals.

Japheth Sapp carried only a piece of paper. He referred to it as he huddled with the Owl and the blue-eyed boy, crouched in a dry stream bed a few yards from where the rest of the crew were hauling out their goods.

Soma had no idea where they were at this point, though he had a vague idea that they'd described an arc above the northern suburbs and the conversations indicated that they were now heading toward the capital, unlikely as that sounded. His head was still numb and soft inside, not an unpleasant situation, but not one that helped his already shaky geographical sense.

He knew what time it was, though, when the green fall of light speckling the hollow they rested in shifted toward pink. Dull as his mind was, he recognized that and smiled.

The clouds sounded the pitch note, then suddenly a great deal was happening around him. For the first time that day, the Crows' reaction to what they perceived to be a crisis didn't involve Soma being poked somewhere or shoved under something. So he was free to sing the anthem while the Crows went mad with activity.

The instant the rising bell tone fell out of the sky, Japheth flung his mask to the ground, glared at a rangy redheaded man, and bellowed, "Where's my timekeeper? You were supposed to remind us!"

The man didn't have time to answer though, because like all of them he was digging through his pack, wrapping an elaborate crenellated set of earmuffs around his head.

The music struck up, and Soma began.

"Tonight we'll remake Tennessee, every night we remake Tennessee . . ."

It was powerfully odd that the Kentuckians didn't join in the singing, and that none of them were moving into the roundel lines that a group this size would normally be forming during the anthem.

Still, it might have been stranger if they had joined in.

"Tonight we'll remake Tennessee, every night we remake Tennessee . . ."

There was a thicket of trumpet flowers tucked amongst a stand of willow trees across the dry creek, so the brass was louder than Soma was used to. Maybe they were farther from the city than he thought. Aficionados of different musical sections tended to find places like this and frequent them during anthem.

"Tonight we'll remake Tennessee, every night we remake Tennessee . . ."

Soma was happily shuffling through a solo dance, keeping one eye on a fat raccoon that was bobbing its head in time with the music as it turned over stones in the stream bed, when he saw that the young Crow who wanted to see a bear had started keeping time as well, raising and lowering a clawed boot. The Owl was the first of the outlanders who spied the tapping foot.

"Tonight we'll remake Tennessee, every night we remake Tennessee . . ."

Soma didn't feel the real connection with the citizenry that anthem usually provided on a daily basis, didn't feel his confidence and vigor improve, but he blamed that on the drugs the Kentuckians had given him. He wondered if those were the same drugs they were using on the Crow who now feebly twitched beneath the weight of the Owl, who had wrestled him to the ground. Others pinned down the dancing Crow's arms and legs and Japheth brought out a needle and injected the poor soul with a vast syringe full of some milky brown substance that had the consistency of honey. Soma remembered that he knew the dancing Crow's name. Japheth Sapp had called the boy Lowell.

"Tonight we'll remake Tennessee, every night we remake Tennessee . . ."

The pink light faded. The raccoon waddled into the woods. The trumpet flowers fell quiet and Soma completed the execution of a pirouette.

The redheaded man stood before Japheth wearing a stricken and haunted look. He kept glancing to one side, where the Owl stood over the Crow who had danced. "Japheth, I just lost track," he said. "It's so hard here, to keep track of things."

Japheth's face flashed from anger through disappointment to something approaching forgiveness. "It is. It's hard to keep track. Everybody fucks up sometime. And I think we got the dampeners in him in time."

Then the Owl said, "Second shift now, Japheth. Have to wait for the second round of garbage drops to catch our bundle bug."

Japheth grimaced, but nodded. "We can't move anyway, not until we know what's going to happen with Lowell," he said, glancing at the unconscious boy. "Get the whiskey and the food back into the cache. Set up the netting. We're staying here for the night."

Japheth stalked over to Soma, fists clenched white.

"Things are getting clearer and clearer to you, Soma Painter, even if you think things are getting harder and harder to understand. Our motivations will open up things inside you."

He took Soma's chin in his left hand and tilted Soma's face up. He waved his hand to indicate Lowell.

"There's one of mine. There's one of my motivations for all of this."

Slowly, but with loud lactic cracks, Japheth spread his fingers wide.

"I fight her, Soma, in the hope that she'll not clench up another mind. I fight her so that minds already bound might come unbound."

In the morning, the dancing Crow boy was dead.

Jenny woke near dark, damp and cold, curled up in the gravel of the parking lot. Her horse nickered. She was dimly aware that the horse had been neighing and otherwise emanating concern for some time now, and it was this that had brought her up to consciousness.

She rolled over and climbed to her feet, spitting to rid her mouth of the metal Operator taste. A dried froth of blood coated her nostrils and upper lip, and she could feel the flaky stuff in her ears as well. She looked toward the garage and saw that she wasn't the only one rousing.

"Now, you get back to bed," she told the car.

Soma's car had risen up on its back wheels and was peering out the open window, its weight resting against the force-grown wall, bulging it outward.

Jenny made a clucking noise, hoping to reassure her horse, and walked up to the car. She was touched by its confusion and concern.

She reached for the aerial. "You should sleep some more," she said, "and not worry about me. The Operators can tell when you're being uncooperative is all, even when *you* didn't know you were being uncooperative. Then they have to root about a bit more than's comfortable to find the answers they want."

Jenny coaxed the car down from the window, wincing a little at the sharp echo pains that flashed in her head and ears. "Don't tell your owner, but this isn't the first time I've been called to question. Now, to bed."

The car looked doubtful, but obediently rolled back to the repair bed that grew from the garage floor. It settled in, grumbled a bit, then switched off its headlights.

Jenny walked around to the door and entered. She found that the water sacs were full and chilled and drew a long drink. The water tasted faintly of salt. She took another swallow, then dampened a rag with a bit more of the tangy stuff to wipe away the dried blood. Then she went to work.

The bundle bugs crawled out of the city, crossed Distinguished Opposition Bridge beneath the watching eye of bears floating overhead, then described a right-angle turn along the levy to their dumping grounds. Soma and the Kentuckians lay hidden in the brushy wasteland at the edge of the grounds, waiting.

The Owl placed a hand on Japheth's shoulder, pointing at a bundle bug just entering the grounds. Then the Owl rose to his knees and began worming his way between the bushes and dead appliances.

"Soma Painter," whispered Japheth. "I'm going to have to break your jaw in a few minutes and cut out as many of her tentacles as we can get at, but we'll knit it back up as soon as we cross the river."

Soma was too far gone in the paste to hold both of the threats in his mind at the same time. A broken jaw, Crows in the capital. He concentrated on the second.

"The bears will scoop you up and drop you in the Salt Lick," Soma said. "Children will climb on you during Campaign and Legislators will stand on your shoulders to make their stump speeches."

"The bears will not see us, Soma."

"The bears watch the river and the bridges, 'and' —"

"—'And their eyes never close,'" finished Japheth.

"Yes, we've seen the commercials."

A bundle bug, a large one at forty meters in length, reared up over them, precariously balanced on its rearmost set of legs. Soma said, "They're very good commercials," and the bug crashed down over them all.

Athena's data realm mirrored her physical realm. One-to-one constructs mimicked the buildings and the citizenry, showed who was riding and who was being ridden.

In that numerical space, the Kentuckians' math found the bridge. The harsh light of the bears floated above. Any bear represented a statistically significant portion of the Governor herself, and from the point of view of the math, the pair above Distinguished Opposition Bridge looked like miniature suns, casting probing rays at the marching bundle bugs, the barges floating along the Cumberland, and even into the waters of the river itself, illuminating the numerical analogs of the dangerous things that lived in the muddy bottom.

Bundle bugs came out of the city, their capacious abdomens distended with the waste they'd ingested along their routes. The math could see that the bug crossing through the bears' probes right now had a lot of restaurants on its itinerary. The beams pierced the dun-colored carapace and showed a riot of uneaten jellies, crumpled cups, soiled napkins.

The bugs marching in the opposite direction, emptied and ready for reloading, were scanned even more carefully than their outward-bound kin. The beam scans were withering, complete, and exceedingly precise.

The math knew that precision and accuracy are not the same thing.

"Lowell's death has set us back further than we thought," said Japheth, talking to the four Crows, the Owl, and, Soma guessed, to the bundle bug they inhabited. Japheth had detailed off the rest of the raiding party to carry the dead boy back north, so there was plenty of room where they crouched.

The interior of the bug's abdomen was larger than Soma's apartment by a factor of two and smelled of flowers instead of paint thinner. Soma's apartment, however, was not an alcoholic.

"This is good, though, good good." The bug's voice rang from every direction at once. "I'm scheduled down for a rest shift. You-uns was late and missed my last run, and now we can all rest and drink good whiskey. Good good."

But none of the Kentuckians drank any of the whiskey from the casks they'd cracked once they'd crawled down the bug's gullet. Instead, every half hour or so, they poured another gallon into one of the damp fissures that ran all through the interior. Bundle bugs abdomens weren't designed for digestion, just evacuation, and it was the circulatory system that was doing the work of carrying the bourbon to the bug's brain.

Soma dipped a finger into an open cask and touched finger to tongue. "Bourbon burns!" he said, pulling his finger from his mouth.

"Burns good!" said the bug. "Good good."

"We knew that not all of us were going to be able to actually enter the city—we don't have enough outfits, for one thing—but six is a bare minimum. And since we're running behind, we'll have to wait out tonight's anthem in our host's apartment."

"Printer's Alley is two miles from the Parthenon," said the Owl, nodding at Soma.

Japheth nodded. "I know. And I know that those might be the two longest miles in the world. But we expected hard walking."

He banged the curving gray wall he leaned against with his elbow. "Hey! Bundle bug! How long until you start your shift?"

A vast and disappointed sigh shuddered through the abdomen. "Two more hours, bourbon man," said the bug.

"Get out your gear, cousin," Japheth said to the Owl. He stood and stretched, motioned for the rest of the Crows to do the same. He turned toward Soma. "The rest of us will hold him down."

Jenny had gone out midmorning, when the last of the fog was still burning off the bluffs, searching for low moisture organics to feed the garage. She'd run its reserves very low, working on one thing and another until quite late in the night.

As she suspected from the salty taste of the water supply, the filters in the housings between the tap roots and the garage's plumbing array were clogged with silt. She'd blown them out with pressurized air—no need to replace what you can fix—and reinstalled them one, two, three. But while she was blowing out the filters, she'd heard a whine she didn't like in the air compressor, and when she'd gone to check it she found it panting with effort, tongue hanging out onto the workbench top where it sat.

And then things went as these things go, and she moved happily from minor maintenance problem to minor maintenance problem—wiping away the air compressor's crocodile tears while she stoned the motor brushes in its A/C motor, then replacing the fusible link in the garage itself. "Links are so easily fusible," she joked to her horse when she rubbed it down with handfuls of the sweet-smelling fern fronds she'd intended for her own bed.

And all the while, of course, she watched the little car, monitoring the temperatures at its core points and doing what she could to coax the broken window to reknit in a smooth, steady fashion. Once, when the car awoke in the middle of the night making colicky noises, Jenny had to pop the hood, where she found that the points needed to be pulled and regapped. They were fouled with the viscous residue of the analgesic aero the owner had spread about so liberally.

She tsked. The directions on the labels clearly stated that the nozzle was to be pointed *away* from the engine compartment. Still, hard to fault Soma Painter's goodhearted efforts. It was an easy fix, and she would have pulled the plugs during the tune-up she had planned for the morning anyway.

So, repairings and healings, lights burning and tools turning, and when she awoke to the morning tide sounds the garage immediately began flashing amber lights at her wherever she turned. The belly-grumble noises it floated from the speakers worried the horse, so she set out looking for something to put in the hoppers of the hungry garage.

When she came back, bearing a string-tied bundle of dried wood and a half bucket of old walnuts some gatherer had wedged beneath an overhang and forgotten at least a double handful of autumns past, the car was gone.

Jenny hurried to the edge of the parking lot and looked down the road, though she couldn't see much. This time of year the morning fog turned directly into the midday haze. She could see the city, and bits of road between trees and bluff line, but no sign of the car.

The garage pinged at her, and she shoved its breakfast into the closest intake. She didn't open her head to call the police—she hadn't yet fully recovered from yesterday afternoon's interview. She was even hesitant to open her head the little bit she needed to access her own garage's security tapes. But she'd built the garage, and either built or rebuilt everything in it, so she risked it.

She stood at her workbench, rubbing her temple, as a see-through Jenny and a see-through car built themselves up out of twisted light. Light Jenny put on a light rucksack, scratched the light car absently on the roof as she walked by, and headed out the door. Light Jenny did not tether the car. Light Jenny did not lock the door.

"Silly light Jenny," said Jenny.

As soon as light Jenny was gone, the little light car rolled over to the big open windows. It popped a funny little wheelie and caught itself on the sash, the way it had yesterday when it had watched real Jenny swim up out of her government dream.

The light car kept one headlight just above the sash for a few minutes, then lowered itself back to the floor with a bounce (real Jenny had aired up the tires first thing, even before she grew the garage).

The light car revved its motor excitedly. Then, just a gentle tap on the door, and it was out in the parking lot. It drove over to the steps leading down to the beach, hunching its grill down to the ground. It circled the lot a bit, snuffling here and there, until it found whatever it was looking for. Before it zipped down the road toward Nashville, it circled back round and stopped outside the horse's stall. The light car opened its passenger door and waggled it back and forth a time or two. The real horse neighed and tossed its head at the light car in a friendly fashion.

Jenny-With-Grease-Beneath-Her-Fingernails visited her horse with the meanest look that a mechanic can give a horse. The horse snickered. "You laugh, horse," she said, opening the tack locker, "but we still have to go after it."

Inside the bundle bug, there was some unpleasantness with a large glass-and-pewter contraption of the Owl's. The Crow Brothers held Soma as motionless as they could, and Japheth seemed genuinely sorry when he forced the painter's mouth open much wider than Soma had previously thought possible. "You should have drunk more of the whiskey," said Japheth. There was a loud, wet, popping sound, and Soma shuddered, stiffened, fainted.

"Well, that'll work best for all of us," said Japheth. He looked up at the Owl, who was peering through a lens polished out of a semiprecious gemstone, staring down into the painter's gullet.

"Have you got access?"

The Owl nodded.

"Talk to your math," said the Crow.

The math had been circling beneath the bridge, occasionally dragging a curiosity-begat string of numbers into the water. Always low-test numbers, because invariably whatever lived beneath the water snatched at the lines and sucked them down.

The input the math was waiting for finally arrived in the form of a low hooting sound rising up from the dumping grounds. It was important that the math not know which bundle bug the sound emanated from. There were certain techniques the bears had developed for teasing information out of recalcitrant math.

No matter. The math knew the processes. It had the input. It spread itself out over the long line of imagery the bundle bugs yielded up to the bears. It affected its changes. It lent clarity.

Above, the bears did their work with great precision.

Below, the Kentuckians slipped into Nashville undetected.

Soma woke to find the Kentuckians doing something terrible. When he tried to speak, he found that his face was immobilized by a mask of something that smelled of the docks but felt soft and gauzy.

The four younger Crows were dressed in a gamut of jerseys and shorts colored in the hotter hues of the spectrum. Japheth was struggling into a long, jangly coat hung with seashells and old capacitors. But it was the Owl that frightened Soma the most. The broad-chested man was dappled with opal stones from collar bones to ankles and wore nothing else save a breech cloth cut from an old newspaper. Soma moaned, trying to attract their attention again.

The blue-eyed boy said, "Your painter stirs, Japheth."

But it was the Owl who leaned over Soma, placed his hand on Soma's chin and turned his head back and forth with surprising gentleness. The Owl nodded, to himself, Soma guessed, for none of the Crows reacted, then peeled the bandages off Soma's face.

Soma took a deep breath, then said, "Nobody's worn opals for months! And those shorts," he gestured at the others, "Too much orange! Too much orange!"

Japheth laughed. "Well, we'll be tourists in from the provinces, then, not princes of Printer's Alley. Do *I* offend?" He wriggled his shoulders, set the shells and circuits to clacking.

Soma pursed his lips, shook his head. "Seashells and capacitors are timeless," he said.

Japheth nodded. "That's what it said on the box." Then, "Hey! Bug! Are we to market yet?"

"It's hard to say, whiskey man," came the reply. "My eyes are funny."

"Close enough. Open up."

The rear of the beast's abdomen cracked, and yawned wide. Japheth turned to his charges. "You boys ready to play like vols?"

The younger Crows started gathering burlap bundles. The Owl hoisted a heavy rucksack, adjusted the flowers in his hat, and said, "Wacka wacka ho."

In a low place, horizon bounded by trees in every direction, Jenny and her horse came on the sobbing car. From the ruts it had churned up in the mud, Jenny guessed it had been there for some time, driving back and forth along the northern verge.

"Now what have you done to yourself?" she asked, dismounting. The car turned to her and shuddered. Its front left fender was badly dented, and its hood and windshield were a mess of leaves and small branches.

"Trying to get into the woods? Cars are for roads, car." She brushed some muck off the damaged fender.

"Well, that's not too bad, though. This is all cosmetic. Why would a car try to go where trees are? See what happens?"

The horse called. It had wandered a little way into the woods and was standing at the base of a vast poplar. Jenny reached in through the passenger's window of the car, avoiding the glassy knitting blanket on the other side, and set the parking brake. "You wait here."

She trotted out to join her horse. It was pawing at a small patch of ground. Jenny was a mechanic and had no woodscraft, but she could see the outline of a cleft-toed sandal. Who would be in the woods with such impractical footwear?

"The owner's an artist. An artist looking for a shortcut to the Alley, I reckon," said Jenny. "Wearing funny artist shoes."

She walked back to the car, considering. The car was pining. Not unheard of, but not common. It made her think better of Soma Painter that his car missed him so.

"Say, horse. Melancholy slows car repair. I think this car will convalesce better in its own parking space."

The car revved.

"But there's the garage still back at the beach," said Jenny.

She turned things over and over. "Horse," she said, "you're due three more personal days this month. If I release you for them now, will you go fold up the garage and bring it to me in the city?"

The horse tossed its head enthusiastically.

"Good. I'll drive with this car back to the Alley, then—" But the horse was already rubbing its flanks against her.

"Okay, okay." She drew a tin of salve from her tool belt, dipped her fingers in it, then ran her hands across the horse's back. The red crosses came away in her hands, wriggling. "The cases for these are in my cabinet," she said, and then inspiration came.

"Here, car," she said, and laid the crosses on its hood. They wriggled around until they were at statute-specified points along the doors and roof. "Now you're an ambulance! Not a hundred percent legal, maybe, but this way you can drive fast and whistle sirenlike."

The car spun its rear wheels but couldn't overcome the parking brake. Jenny laughed. "Just a minute more. I need you to give me a ride into town."

She turned to speak to the horse, only to see it already galloping along the coast road. "Don't forget to drain the water tanks before you fold it up!" she shouted.

The bundles that were flecked with root matter, Soma discovered, were filled with roots. Carrots and turnips, a half dozen varieties of potatoes, beets. The Kentuckians spread out through the Farmer's Market, trading them by the armload for the juices and gels that the rock monkeys brought in from their gardens.

"This is our secondary objective," said Japheth. "We do this all the time, trading doped potatoes for that shit y'all eat."

"You're poisoning us?" Soma was climbing out of the paste a little, or something. His thoughts were shifting around some.

"Doped with nutrients, friend. Forty ain't old outside Tennessee. Athena doesn't seem to know any more about human nutrition than she does human psychology. Hey, we're trying to *help* you people."

Then they were in the very center of the market, and the roar of the crowds drowned out any reply Soma might make.

Japheth kept a grip on Soma's arm as he spoke to a gray old monkey. "Ten pounds, right?" The monkey was weighing a bundle of carrots on a scale.

"Okay," grunted the monkey. "Okay, man. Ten pounds I give you . . . four blue jellies."

Soma was incredulous. He'd never developed a taste for them himself, but he knew that carrots were popular. Four blue jellies was an insulting trade. But Japheth said, "Fair enough," and pocketed the plastic tubes the monkey handed over.

"You're no trader," said Soma, or started to, but heard the words slur out of him in an unintelligible mess of vowels. *One spring semester, when he'd already been a* TA *for a year, he was tapped to work on the interface. No more need for scholarships.*

"Painter!" shouted Japheth.

Soma looked up. There was a Crow dressed in Alley haute couture standing in front of him. He tried to open his head to call the Tennessee Highway Patrol. He couldn't find his head.

"Give him one of these yellow ones," said a monkey. "They're good for fugues."

"Painter!" shouted Japheth again. The grip on Soma's shoulder was like a vise.

Soma struggled to stand under his own power. "I'm forgetting something."

"Hah!" said Japheth, "You're remembering. Too soon for my needs, though. Listen to me. Rock monkeys are full voluntary citizens of Tennessee."

The outlandishness of the statement shocked Soma out of his reverie and brought the vendor up short.

"Fuck you, man!" said the monkey.

"No, no," said Soma, then said by rote, "Tennessee is a fully realized postcolonial state. The land of the rock monkeys is an autonomous partner-principality within our borders, and while the monkeys are our staunch allies, their allegiance is not to our Governor, but to their king."

"Yah," said the monkey. "Long as we get our licenses and pay the tax machine. Plus, who the jelly cubes going to listen to besides the monkey king, huh?"

Soma marched Japheth to the next stall. "Lot left in there to wash out yet," Japheth said.

"I wash every day," said Soma, then fell against a sloshing tray of juice containers. *The earliest results were remarkable.*

A squat man covered with black gems came up to them. The man who'd insulted the monkey said, "You might have killed too much of it; he's getting kind of wonky."

The squat man looked into Soma's eyes. "We can stabilize him easy enough. There are televisions in the food court."

Then Soma and Japheth were drinking hot rum punches and watching a newsfeed. There was a battle out over the Gulf somewhere, Commodores mounted on bears darted through the clouds, lancing Cuban zeppelins.

"The Cubans will never achieve air superiority," said Soma, and it felt right saying it.

Japheth eyed him wearily. "I need you to keep thinking that for now, Soma Painter," he said quietly. "But I hope sometime soon you'll know that Cubans don't live in a place called the Appalachian Archipelago, and that the salty reach out there isn't the Gulf of Mexico."

The bicycle race results were on then, and Soma scanned the lists, hoping to see his favorites' names near the top of the general classifications.

"That's the Tennessee River, dammed up by your Governor's hubris."

Soma saw that his drink was nearly empty and heard that his friend Japheth was still talking. "What?" he asked, smiling.

"I asked if you're ready to go to the Alley," said Japheth.

"Good good," said Soma.

The math was moving along minor avenues, siphoning data from secondary and tertiary ports when it sensed her looming up. It researched ten thousand escapes but rejected them all when it perceived that it had been subverted, that it was inside her now, becoming part of her, that it *is primitive in materials but clever clever in architecture and there have been blindings times not seen places to root out root out all of it check again check one thousand more times all told all told eat it all up all the little bluegrass math is absorbed*

"The Alley at night!" shouted Soma. "Not like where you're from, eh, boys?"

A lamplighter's stalk legs eased through the little group. Soma saw that his friends were staring up at the civil servant's welding mask head, gaping openmouthed as it turned a spigot at the top of a tree and lit the gas with a flick of its tongue.

"Let's go to my place!" said Soma. "When it's time for anthem we can watch the parade from my balcony. I live in one of the lofts above the Tyranny of the Anecdote."

"Above what?" asked Japheth.

"It's a tavern. They're my landlords," said Soma. "Vols are so fucking stupid."

But that wasn't right.

Japheth's Owl friend fell to his knees and vomited right in the street. Soma stared at the jiggling spheres in the gutter as the man choked some words out. "She's taken the feathers. She's looking for us now."

Too much rum punch, thought Soma, thought it about the Owl man and himself and about all of Japheth's crazy friends.

"Soma, how far now?" asked Japheth.

Soma remembered his manners. "Not far," he said.

And it wasn't, just a few more struggling yards, Soma leading the way and Japheth's friends half-carrying, half-dragging their drunken friend down the Alley. Nothing unusual there. Every night in the Alley was Carnival.

Then a wave at the bouncer outside the Anecdote, then up the steps, then sing "Let me in, let me in!" to the door, and finally all of them packed into the cramped space.

"There," said the sick man, pointing at the industrial sink Soma had installed himself to make brush cleaning easier. *Brushes . . . where were his brushes, his pencils, his notes for the complexity seminar?*

"Towels, Soma?"

"What? Oh, here let me get them." Soma bustled around, finding towels, pulling out stools for the now silent men who filled his room.

He handed the towels to Japheth. "Was it something he ate?" Soma asked.

Japheth shrugged. "Ate a long time ago, you could say. Owls are as much numbers as they are meat. He's divesting himself. Those are ones and zeroes washing down your drain."

The broad man—hadn't he been broad?—the scrawny man with opals falling off him said, "We can only take a few minutes. There are unmounted Detectives swarming the whole city now. What I've left in me is too deep for their little minds, but the whole sphere is roused and things will only get tighter. Just let me—" He turned and retched into the sink again. "Just a few minutes more until the singing."

Japheth moved to block Soma's view of the Owl. He nodded at the drawings on the wall. "Yours?"

The blue-eyed boy moved over to the sink, helped the Owl ease to the floor. Soma looked at the pictures. "Yes, mostly. I traded for a few."

Japheth was studying one charcoal piece carefully, a portrait. "What's this one?"

The drawing showed a tall, thin young man dressed in a period costume, leaning against a mechanical of some kind, staring intently out at the viewer. Soma didn't remember drawing it, specifically, but knew what it must be.

"That's a caricature. I do them during Campaign for the provincials who come into the city to vote. Someone must have asked me to draw him and then never come back to claim it."

And he remembered trying to remember. He remembered asking his hand to remember when his head wouldn't.

"I'm . . . what did you put in me?" Soma asked. There was moisture on his cheeks, and he hoped it was tears.

The Owl was struggling up to his feet. A bell tone sounded from the sky and he said, "Now, Japheth. There's no time."

"Just a minute more," snapped the Crow. "What did *we* put in you? You . . ." Japheth spat. "While you're remembering, try and remember this. You *chose* this! All of you chose it!"

The angry man wouldn't have heard any reply Soma might have made, because it was then that all of the Kentuckians clamped their ears shut with their odd muffs. To his surprise, they forced a pair onto Soma as well.

Jenny finally convinced the car to stop wailing out its hee-haw pitch when they entered the maze of streets leading to Printer's Alley. The drive back had been long, the car taking every northern side road, backtracking, looping, even trying to enter the dumping grounds at one point before the bundle bugs growled them away. During anthem, while Jenny drummed her fingers and forced out the words, the car still kept up its search, not even pretending to dance.

So Jenny had grown more and more fascinated by the car's behavior. She had known cars that were slavishly attached to their owners before, and she had known cars that were smart—almost as smart as bundle bugs, some of them—but the two traits never seemed to go together. "Cars are dogs or cars are cats," her Teacher had said to explain the phenomenon, another of the long roll of enigmatic statements that constituted formal education in the Voluntary State.

But here, now, here was a bundle bug that didn't seem to live up to those creatures' reputations for craftiness. The car had been following the bug for a few blocks—Jenny only realized that after the car, for the first time since they entered the city proper, made a turn *away* from the address painted on its name tag.

The bug was a big one, and was describing a gentle career down Commerce Street, drifting from side to side and clearly ignoring the traffic signals that flocked around its head in an agitated cloud.

"Car, we'd better get off this street. Rogue bugs are too much for the THP. If it doesn't self-correct, a Commodore is likely to be rousted out from the Parthenon." Jenny sometimes had nightmares about Commodores.

The car didn't listen—though it was normally an excellent listener—but accelerated toward the bug. The bug, Jenny now saw, had stopped in front of a restaurant and cracked its abdomen. Dumpster feelers had started creeping out of the interstices between thorax and head when the restaurateur charged out, beating at the feelers with a broom. "Go now!" the man shouted, face as red as his vest and leggings, "I told you twice already! You pick up here Chaseday! Go! I already called your supervisor, bug!"

The bug's voice echoed along the street. "No load? Good good." Its sigh was pure contentment, but Jenny had no time to appreciate it. The car sped up, and Jenny covered her eyes, anticipating a collision. But the car slid to a halt with bare inches to spare, peered into the empty cavern of the bug's belly, then sighed, this one not content at all.

"Come on, car," Jenny coaxed. "He must be at home by now. Let's just try your house, okay?"

The car beeped and executed a precise three-point turn. As they turned off Commerce and climbed the viaduct that arced above the Farmer's Market, Jenny caught a hint of motion in the darkening sky. "THP bicycles, for sure," she said. "Tracking your bug friend."

At the highest point on the bridge, Jenny leaned out and looked down into the controlled riot of the Market. Several stalls were doing brisk business, and when Jenny saw why, she asked the car to stop, then let out a whistle.

"Oi! Monkey!" she shouted. "Some beets up here!"

Jenny loved beets.

signals from the city center subsidiaries routing reports and recommendations increase percentages dedicated to observation and prediction dispatch commodore downcycle biological construct extraparametrical lower authority

"It's funny that I don't know what it means, though, don't you think, friends?" Soma was saying this for perhaps the fifth time since they began their walk. "*Church* Street. *Church*. Have you ever heard that word anywhere else?"

"No," said the blue-eyed boy.

The Kentuckians were less and less talkative the farther the little group advanced west down Church Street. It was a long, broad avenue, but rated for pedestrians and emergency vehicles only. Less a street, really, than a linear park, for there were neither businesses nor apartments on either side, just low gray government buildings, slate-colored in the sunset.

The sunset. That was why the boulevard was crowded, as it was every night. As the sun dropped down, down, down it dropped behind the Parthenon. At the very instant the disc disappeared behind the sand-colored edifice, the Great Salt Lick self-illuminated and the flat acres of white surrounding the Parthenon shone with a vast, icy light.

The Lick itself was rich with the minerals that fueled the Legislators and Bears, but the white light emanating from it was sterile. Soma noticed that the Crows faces grew paler and paler as they all got closer to its source. *His work was fascinating, and grew more so as more and more disciplines began finding ways to integrate their fields of study into a meta-architecture of science. His department chair coauthored a paper with an expert in animal husbandry, of all things.*

The Owl held Soma's head as the painter vomited up the last of whatever was in his stomach.

Japheth and the others were making reassuring noises to passersby. "Too much monkey wine!" they said, and, "We're in from the provinces, he's not used to such rich food!" and, "He's overcome by the sight of the Parthenon!"

Japheth leaned over next to the Owl. "Why's it hitting him so much harder than the others?"

The Owl said, "Well, we've always taken them back north of the border. This poor fool we're dragging ever closer to the glory of his owner. I couldn't even guess what's trying to fill up the empty spaces I left in him—but I'm pretty sure whatever's rushing in isn't all from her."

Japheth cocked an eyebrow at his lieutenant. "I think that's the most words I've ever heard you say all together at once."

The Owl smiled, another first, if that sad little half grin counted as a smile. "Not a lot of time left for talking. Get up now, friend painter."

The Owl and Japheth pulled Soma to his feet. "What did you mean," Soma asked, wiping his mouth with the back of his hand, "'the glory of his owner?'"

"Governor," said Japheth. "He said, 'the glory of his Governor,'" and Japheth swept his arm across, and yes, there it was, the glory of the Governor.

Church Street had a slight downward grade in its last few hundred yards. From where they stood, they could see that the street ended at the spectacularly defined border of the Great Salt Lick, which served as legislative chambers in the Voluntary State. At the center of the lick stood the Parthenon, and while no normal citizens walked the salt just then, there was plenty of motion and color.

Two bears were laying face down in the Lick, bobbing their heads as they took in sustenance from the ground. A dozen or more Legislators slowly unambulated, their great slimy bodies leaving trails of gold or silver depending on their party affiliation. One was engulfing one of the many salt-white statues that dotted the grounds, gaining a few feet of height to warble its slogan songs from. And, unmoving at the corners of the rectangular palace in the center of it all, four Commodores stood.

They were tangled giants of rust, alike in their towering height and in the oily bathyspheres encasing the scant meat of them deep in their torsos, but otherwise each a different silhouette of sensor suites and blades, each with a different complement of articulated limbs or wings or wheels.

"Can you tell which ones they are?" Japheth asked the blue-eyed boy, who had begun murmuring to himself under his breath, eyes darting from Commodore to Commodore.

> *"Ruby-eyed Sutcliffe, stomper, smasher,*
> *Tempting Nguyen, whispering, lying,*
> *Burroughs burrows, up from the underground . . ."*

The boy hesitated, shaking his head. "Northeast corner looks kind of like Praxis Dale, but she's supposed to be away West, fighting the Federals. Saint Sandalwood's physical presence had the same profile as Dale's, but we believe he's gone, consumed by Athena after their last sortie against the containment field cost her so much."

"I'll never understand why she plays at politics with her subordinates when she *is* her subordinates," said Japheth.

The Owl said, "That's not as true with the Commodores as with a lot of the . . . inhabitants. I think it *is* Saint Sandalwood; she must have reconstituted him, or part of him. And remember his mnemonic?"

"*Sandalwood staring*," sang the blue-eyed boy.

"*Inside and outside*," finished Japheth, looking the Owl in the eye. "Time then?"

"Once we're on the Lick I'd do anything she told me, even empty as I am," said the Owl. "Bind me."

Then the blue-eyed boy took Soma by the arm, kept encouraging him to take in the sights of the Parthenon, turning his head away from where the Crows were wrapping the Owl in grapevines. They took the Owl's helmet from a rucksack and seated it, cinching the cork seals at the neck maybe tighter than Soma would have thought was comfortable.

Two of the Crows hoisted the Owl between them, his feet stumbling some. Soma saw that the eyeholes of the mask had been blocked with highly reflective tape.

Japheth spoke to the others. "The bears won't be in this; they'll take too long to stand up from their meal. Avoid the Legislators, even their trails. The THP will be on the ground, but won't give you any trouble. You boys know why you're here."

The two Crows holding the Owl led him over to Japheth, who took him by the hand. The blue-eyed boy said, "We know why we're here, Japheth. We know why we were born."

And suddenly as that, the four younger Crows were gone, fleeing in every direction except back up Church Street.

"Soma Painter," said Japheth. "Will you help me lead this man on?"

Soma was taken aback. While he knew of no regulation specifically prohibiting it, traditionally no one actually trod the Lick except during Campaign.

"We're going into the Salt Lick?" Soma asked.

"We're going into the Parthenon," Japheth answered.

As they crossed Church Street from the south, the car suddenly stopped.

"Now what, car?" said Jenny. Church Street was her least favorite thoroughfare in the capital.

The car snuffled around on the ground for a moment, then, without warning, took a hard left and accelerated, siren screeching. Tourists and sunset gazers scattered to either side as the car and Jenny roared toward the glowing white horizon.

The Owl only managed a few yards under his own power. He slowed, then stumbled, and then the Crow and the painter were carrying him.

"What's wrong with him?" asked Soma.

They crossed the verge onto the salt. They'd left the bravest sightseers a half-block back.

"He's gone inside himself," said Japheth.

"Why?" asked Soma.

Japheth half laughed. "You'd know better than me, friend."

It was then that the Commodore closest to them took a single step forward with its right foot, dragged the left a dozen yards in the same direction, and then, twisting, fell to the ground with a thunderous crash.

"Whoo!" shouted Japheth. "The harder they fall! We'd better start running now, Soma!"

Soma was disappointed, but unsurprised, to see that Japheth did not mean run *away*.

There was only one bear near the slightly curved route that Japheth picked for them through the harsh glare. Even light as he was, purged of his math, the Owl was still a burden and Soma couldn't take much time to marvel at the swirling colors in the bear's plastic hide.

"Keep up, Soma!" shouted the Crow. Ahead of them, two of the Commodores had suddenly turned on one another and were landing terrible blows. Soma saw a tiny figure clinging to one of the giants' shoulders, saw it lose its grip, fall, and disappear beneath an ironshod boot the size of a bundle bug.

Then Soma slipped and fell himself, sending all three of them to the glowing ground and sending a cloud of the biting crystal salt into the air. One of his sandaled feet, he saw, was coated in gold slime. They'd been trying to outflank one Legislator only to stumble on the trail of another.

Japheth picked up the Owl, now limp as a rag doll, and with a grunt heaved the man across his shoulders. "Soma, you should come on. We might make it." *It's not a hard decision to make at all.*

How can you not make it? At first he'd needed convincing, but then he'd been one of those who'd gone out into the world to convince others. It's not just history; it's after history.

"Soma!"

Japheth ran directly at the unmoving painter, the deadweight of the Owl across his shoulders slowing him. He barreled into Soma, knocking him to the ground again, all of them just missing the unknowing Legislator as it slid slowly past.

"Up, up!" said Japheth. "Stay behind it, so long as it's moving in the right direction. I think my boys missed a Commodore." His voice was very sad.

The Legislator stopped and let out a bellowing noise. Fetid steam began rising from it. Japheth took Soma by the hand and pulled him along, through chaos. One of the Commodores, the first to fall, was motionless on the ground, two or three Legislators making their way along its length. The two who'd fought lay locked in one another's grasp, barely moving and glowing hotter and hotter. The only standing Commodore, eyes like red suns, seemed to be staring just behind them.

As it began to sweep its gaze closer, Soma heard Japheth say, "We got closer than I would have bet."

Then Soma's car, mysteriously covered with red crosses and wailing at the top of its voice, came to a sliding, crunching stop in the salt in front of them.

Soma didn't hesitate, but threw open the closest rear door and pulled Japheth in behind him. When the three of them—painter, Crow, Owl—were stuffed into the rear door, Soma shouted, "Up those stairs, car!"

In the front seat, there was a woman whose eyes seemed as large as saucers.

---

commodores faulting headless people in the lick protocols compel reeling in, strengthening, temporarily abandoning telepresence locate an asset with a head asset with a head located

Jenny-With-Grease-Beneath-Her-Fingernails was trying not to go crazy. Something was pounding at her head, even though she hadn't tried to open it herself. Yesterday, she had been working a remote repair job on the beach, fixing a smashed window. Tonight, she was hurtling across the Great Salt Lick, Legislators and bears and *Commodores* acting in ways she'd never seen or heard of.

Jenny herself acting in ways she'd never heard of. Why didn't she just pull the emergency brake, roll out of the car, wait for the THP? Why did she just hold on tighter and pull down the sunscreen so she could use the mirror to look into the backseat?

It *was* three men. She hadn't been sure at first. One appeared to be unconscious and was dressed in some strange getup, a helmet of some kind completely encasing his head. She didn't know the man in the capacitor jacket, who was craning his head out the window, trying to see something above them. The other one though, she recognized.

"Soma Painter," she said. "Your car is much better, though it has missed you terribly."

The owner just looked at her glaze-eyed. The other one pulled himself back in through the window, a wild glee on his face. He rapped the helmet of the prone man and shouted, "Did you hear that? The unpredictable you prophesied! And it fell in our favor!"

Soma worried about his car's suspension, not to mention the tires, when it slalomed through the legs of the last standing Commodore and bounced up the steeply cut steps of the Parthenon. *He hadn't had a direct hand in the subsystems design—by the time he'd begun to develop the cars, Athena was already beginning to take over a lot of the details. Not all of them, though; he couldn't blame her for the guilt he felt over twisting his animal subjects into something like onboard components.*

But the car made it onto the platform inside the outer set of columns, seemingly no worse for wear. The man next to him—Japheth, his name was Japheth and he was from Kentucky—jumped out of the car and ran to the vast, closed counterweighted bronze doors.

"It's because of the crosses. We're in an emergency vehicle according to their protocols." That was the mechanic, Jenny, sitting in the front seat and trying to staunch a nosebleed with a greasy rag. "I can hear the Governor," she said.

Soma could hear Japheth raging and cursing. He stretched the Owl out along the back seat and climbed out of the car. Japheth was pounding on the doors in futility, beating his fists bloody, spinning, spitting. He caught sight of Soma.

"*These* weren't here before!" he said, pointing to two silver columns that angled up from the platform's floor, ending in flanges on the doors themselves. "The doors aren't locked, they're just sealed by these fucking cylinders!" Japheth was shaking. "Caw!" he cried. "Caw!"

"What's he trying to do?" asked the woman in the car.

Soma brushed his fingers against his temple, trying to remember.

"I think he's trying to remake Tennessee," he said.

The weight of a thousand cars on her skull, the hoofbeats of a thousand horses throbbing inside her eyes, Jenny was incapable of making any rational decision. So, irrationally, she left the car. She stumbled over to the base of one of the silver columns. When she tried to catch herself on it, her hand slid off.

"Oil," she said. "These are just hydraulic cylinders." She looked around the metal sheeting where the cylinder disappeared into the platform, saw the access plate. She pulled a screwdriver from her belt and used it to removed the plate.

The owner was whispering to his car, but the crazy man had come over to her. "What are you doing?" he asked.

"I don't know," she said, but she meant it only in the largest sense. Immediately, she was thrusting her wrists into the access plate, playing the licenses and government bonds at her wrists under a spray of light, murmuring a quick apology to the machinery. Then she opened a long vertical cut down as much of the length of the hydraulic hose as she could with her utility blade.

Fluid exploded out of the hole, coating Jenny in the slick, dirty green stuff. The cylinders collapsed.

The man next to Jenny looked at her. He turned and looked at Soma-With-The-Paintbox-In-Printer's Alley and at Soma's car.

"We must have had a pretty bad plan," he said, then rushed over to pull the helmeted figure from the backseat.

breached come home all you commodores come home cancel emergency designation on identified vehicle and downcycle now jump in jump in jump in

Jenny could not help Soma and his friend drag their burden through the doors of the temple, but she staggered through the doors. She had only seen Athena in tiny parts, in the mannequin shrines that contained tiny fractions of the Governor.

Here was the true and awesome thing, here was the forty-foot-tall sculpture—armed and armored—attended by the broken remains of her frozen marble enemies. Jenny managed to lift her head and look past sandaled feet, up cold golden raiment, past tart painted cheeks to the lapis lazuli eyes.

Athena looked back at her. Athena leapt.

Inside Jenny's head, inside so small an architecture, there was no more room for Jenny-With-Grease-Beneath-Her-Fingernails. Jenny fled.

Soma saw the mechanic, the woman who'd been so kind to his car, fall to her knees, blood gushing from her nose and ears. He saw Japheth laying out the Owl like a sacrifice before the Governor. *He'd been among the detractors, scoffing at the idea of housing the main armature in such a symbol-potent place*.

Behind him, his car beeped. The noise was barely audible above the screaming metal sounds out in the Lick. The standing Commodore was swiveling its torso, turning its upper half toward the Parthenon. Superheated salt melted in a line slowly tracking toward the steps.

Soma trotted back to his car. He leaned in and *remembered the back door, the Easter egg he hadn't documented*. A twist on the ignition housing, then press in, and the key sank into the column. The car shivered.

"Run home as fast you can, car. Back to the ranch with your kin. Be fast, car, be clever."

The car woke up. It shook off Soma's ownership and closed its little head. It let out a surprised beep and then fled with blazing speed, leaping down the steps, over the molten salt, and through the storm, bubblewinged bicycles descending all around. The Commodore began another slow turn, trying to track it.

Soma turned back to the relative calm inside the Parthenon. Athena's gaze was baleful, but he couldn't feel it. The Owl had ripped the ability from him. The Owl lying before Japheth, defenseless against the knife Japheth held high.

"Why?" shouted Soma.

But Japheth didn't answer him, instead diving over the Owl in a somersault roll, narrowly avoiding the flurry of kicks and roundhouse blows being thrown by Jenny. Her eyes bugged and bled. More blood flowed from her ears and nostrils, but still she attacked Japheth with relentless fury.

Japheth came up in a crouch. The answer to Soma's question came in a slurred voice from Jenny. Not Jenny, though. Soma knew the voice, remembered it from somewhere, and it wasn't Jenny's.

"*there is a bomb in that meat soma-friend a knife a threat an eraser*"

Japheth shouted at Soma. "You get to decide again! Cut the truth out of him!" He gestured at the Owl with his knife.

Soma took in a shuddery breath. "So free with lives. One of the reasons we climbed up."

Jenny's body lurched at Japheth, but the Crow dropped onto the polished floor. Jenny's body slipped when it landed, the soles of its shoes coated with the same oil as its jumpsuit.

"My Owl cousin died of asphyxiation at least ten minutes ago, Soma," said Japheth. "Died imperfect and uncontrolled." Then, dancing backward before the scratching thing in front of him, Japheth tossed the blade in a gentle underhanded arc. It clattered to the floor at Soma's feet.

All of the same arguments.

All of the same arguments.

Soma picked up the knife and looked down at the Owl. The fight before him, between a dead woman versus a man certain to die soon, spun on. Japheth said no more, only looked at Soma with pleading eyes.

Jenny's body's eyes followed the gaze, saw the knife in Soma's hand.

"you are due upgrade soma-friend swell the ranks of commodores you were 96th percentile now 99th soma-with-the-paintbox-in-printer's-alley the voluntary state of tennessee applauds your citizenship"

But it wasn't the early slight, the denial of entry to the circle of highest minds. Memories of before *and* after, decisions made by him and for him, sentiences and upgrades decided by fewer and fewer and then one; one who'd been a *product*, not a builder.

Soma plunged the knife into the Owl's unmoving chest and sawed downward through the belly with what strength he could muster. The skin and fat fell away along a seam straighter than he could ever cut. The bomb—the knife, the eraser, the threat—looked like a tiny white balloon. He pierced it with the killing tip of the Kentuckian's blade.

A nova erupted at the center of the space where math and Detectives live. A wave of scouring numbers washed outward, spreading all across Nashville, all across the Voluntary State to fill all the space within the containment field.

The 144 Detectives evaporated. The King of the Rock Monkeys, nothing but twisted light, fell into shadow. The Commodores fell immobile, the ruined biology seated in their chests went blind, then deaf, then died.

And singing Nashville fell quiet. Ten thousand thousand heads slammed shut and ten thousand thousand souls fell insensate, unsupported, in need of revival.

North of the Girding Wall, alarms began to sound.

At the Parthenon, Japheth Sapp gently placed the tips of his index and ring fingers on Jenny's eyelids and pulled them closed.

Then the ragged Crow pushed past Soma and hurried out into the night. The Great Salt Lick glowed no more, and even the lights of the city were dimmed, so Soma quickly lost sight of the man. But then the cawing voice rang out once more. "We only hurt the car because we had to."

Soma thought for a moment, then said, "So did I."

But the Crow was gone, and then Soma had nothing to do but wait. He had made the only decision he had left in him. He idly watched as burning bears floated down into the sea. A striking image, but he had somewhere misplaced his paints.

shiva in shadow

NANCY KRESS

Here's the story of an intensely dangerous journey into deep space, where the travelers learn that no matter how far away you go, it's not far enough to get away from *yourself* . . .

Nancy Kress began selling her elegant and incisive stories in the mid-seventies, and has since become a frequent contributor to *Asimov's Science Fiction, The Magazine of Fantasy & Science Fiction, Omni,* and elsewhere. Her books include the novels *The Prince of Morning Bells, The Golden Grove, The White Pipes, An Alien Light, Brain Rose, Oaths and Miracles, Stinger, Maximum Light,* the novel version of her Hugo and Nebula-winning story, *Beggars in Spain,* a sequel, *Beggars and Choosers,* and a popular recent sequence of novels, *Probability Moon, Probability Sun,* and *Probability Space.* Her short work has been collected in *Trinity And Other Stories, The Aliens of Earth,* and *Beaker's Dozen.* Her most recent books are two new novels, *Crossfire* and *Nothing Human.* Upcoming is a new novel, *Crucible.* She has also won Nebula Awards for her stories "Out of All Them Bright Stars" and "The Flowers of Aulit Prison." She has had stories in our Second, Third, Sixth through Fifteenth, and Eighteenth through Twenty-first Annual Collections.

1. SHIP

I watched the probe launch from the *Kepler*'s top-deck observatory, where the entire Schaad hull is clear to the stars. I stood between Ajit and Kane. The observatory, which is also the ship's garden, bloomed wildly with my exotics, bursting into flower in such exuberant profusion that even to see the probe go, we had to squeeze between a seven-foot-high bed of comoralias and the hull.

"God, Tirzah, can't you prune these things?" Kane said. He pressed his nose to the nearly invisible hull, like a small child. Something streaked briefly across the sky. "There it goes. Not that there's much to see."

I turned to stare at him. Not much to see! Beyond the *Kepler* lay the most violent and dramatic part of the galaxy, in all its murderous glory. True, the *Kepler* had stopped one hundred light-years from the core, for human safety, and dust-and-gas clouds muffled the view somewhat. But, on the other hand, we were far enough away for a panoramic view.

The supermassive black hole Sagittarius A*, the lethal heart of the galaxy, shone gauzily with the heated gases it was sucking downward into oblivion. Around Sag A* circled Sagittarius West, a three-armed spiral of hot plasma ten light-years across, radiating furiously as it cooled. Around *that*, Sagittarius East, a huge shell left over from some catastrophic explosion within the last hundred thousand years, expanded outward. I saw thousands of stars, including the blazing blue-hot stars of IRS16, hovering dangerously close to the hole, and giving off a stellar wind fierce enough to blow a long fiery tail off the nearby red giant star. Everything was racing, radiating, colliding, ripping apart, screaming across the entire electromagnetic spectrum. All set against the sweet, light scent of my brief-lived flowers.

Nothing going on. But Kane had never been interested in spectacle.

Ajit said in his musical accent, "No, not much to see. But much to pray for. There go *we*."

Kane snapped, "I don't pray."

"I did not mean 'pray' in the religious sense," Ajit said calmly. He is always calm. "I mean hope. It is a miraculous thing, yes? There go we."

He was right, of course. The probe contained the Ajit-analogue, the Kane-analogue, the Tirzah-analogue, all uploaded into a crystal computer no bigger than a comoralia bloom. "We" would go into that stellar violence at the core, where our fragile human bodies could not go. "We" would observe, and measure, and try to find answers to scientific questions in that roiling heart of galactic spacetime. Ninety percent of the probe's mass was shielding for the computer. Ninety percent of the rest was shielding for the three minicapsules that the probe would fire back to us with recorded and analyzed data. There was no way besides the minicaps to get information out of that bath of frenzied radiation.

Just as there was no way to know exactly what questions Ajit and Kane would need to ask until they were close to Sag A*. The analogues would know. They knew everything Ajit and Kane and I knew, right up until the moment we were uploaded.

"Shiva, dancing," Ajit said.

"What?" Kane said.

"Nothing. You would not appreciate the reference. Come with me, Tirzah. I want to show you something."

I stopped straining to see the probe, unzoomed my eyes, and smiled at Ajit. "Of course."

This is why I am here.

Ajit's skin is softer than Kane's, less muscled. Kane works out every day in ship's gym, scowling like a demon. Ajit rolled off me and laid his hand on my glowing, satisfied crotch.

"You are so beautiful, Tirzah."

I laughed. "We are all beautiful. Why would anyone effect a genetic alteration that wasn't?"

"People will do strange things sometimes."

"So I just noticed," I teased him.

"Sometimes I think so much of what Kane and I do is strange to you. I see you sitting at the table, listening to us, and I know you cannot follow our physics. It makes me sad for you."

I laid my hand on top of his, pushing down my irritation with the skill of long practice. It does irritate me, this calm sensitivity of Ajit's. It's lovely in bed—he is gentler and more considerate, always, than Kane—but then there comes the other side, this faint condescension. "*I feel sad for you*." Sad for me! Because I'm not also a scientist! I am the captain of this expedition, with master status in ship control and a first-class license as a Nurturer. On the *Kepler*, my word is law, with virtually no limits. I have over fifty standard-years' experience, specializing in the nurture of scientists. I have never lost an expedition, and I need no one's pity.

Naturally, I showed none of this to Ajit. I massaged his hand with mine, which meant that his hand massaged my crotch, and purred softly. "I'm glad you decided to show me this."

"Actually, that is not what I wanted to show you."

"No?"

"No. Wait here, Tirzah."

He got up and padded, naked, to his personal locker. Beautiful, beautiful body, brown and smooth, like a slim polished tree. I could see him clearly; Ajit always makes love with the bunk lights on full, as if in sunlight. We lay in his bunk, not mine. I never take either him or Kane to my bunk. My bunk contained various concealed items that they don't, and won't, know about, from duplicate surveillance equipment to rarely used subdermal trackers. Precautions, only. I am a captain.

From his small storage locker, Ajit pulled a statue and turned shyly, even proudly, to show it to me. I sat up, surprised.

The statue was big, big enough so that it must have taken up practically his entire allotment of personal space. Heavy, too, from the way Ajit balanced it before his naked body. It was some sort of god with four arms, enclosed in a circle of flames, made of what looked like very old bronze.

"This is Nataraja," Ajit said. "Shiva dancing."

"Ajit—"

"No, I am not a god worshipper," he smiled. "You know me better than that, Tirzah. Hinduism has many gods—thousands—but they are, except to the ignorant, no more than embodiments of different aspects of reality. Shiva is the dance of creation and destruction, the constant flow of energy in the cosmos. Birth and death and rebirth. It seemed fitting to bring him to the galactic core, where so much goes on of all three."

This explanation sounded weak to me—a holo of Shiva would have accomplished the same thing, without using up nearly all of Ajit's weight allotment. Before I could say this, Ajit said, "This statue has been in my family for four hundred years. I must bring it home, along with the answers to my scientific questions."

I don't understand Ajit's scientific concerns very well—or Kane's—but I know down to my bones how much they matter to him. It is my job to know. Ajit carries within his beautiful body a terrible coursing ambition, a river fed by the longings of a poor family who have sacrificed what little they had gained on New Bombay for this favored son. Ajit is the receptacle into which they have poured so much hope, so much sacrifice, so much selfishness. The strain on that vessel is what makes Ajit's lovemaking so gentle. He cannot afford to crack.

"You'll bring the Shiva statue back to New Bombay," I said softly, "and your answers, too."

In his hands, with the bright lighting, the bronze statue cast a dancing shadow on his naked body.

I found Kane at his terminal, so deep in thought that he didn't know I was there until I squeezed his shoulder. Then he jumped, cursed, and dragged his eyes from his displays.

"How does it progress, Kane?"

"It doesn't. How could it? I need more data!"

"It will come. Be patient," I said.

He rubbed his left ear, a constant habit when he's irritated, which is much of the time. When he's happily excited, Kane runs his left hand through his coarse red hair until it stands up like flames. Now he smiled ruefully. "I'm not much known for patience."

"No, you're not."

"But you're right, Tirzah. The data will come. It's just hard waiting for the first minicap. I wish to hell we could have more than three. Goddamn cheap bureaucrats! At an acceleration of—"

"Don't give me the figures again," I said. I wound my fingers in his hair and pulled playfully. "Kane, I came to ask you a favor."

"All right," he said instantly. Kane never counts costs ahead of time. Ajit would have turned gently cautious. "What is it?"

"I want you to learn to play *go* with Ajit."

He scowled. "Why?"

With Kane, you must have your logic ready. He would do any favor I asked, but unless he can see why, compliance would be grudging at best. "First, because *go* will help you pass the time until the first minicap arrives, in doing something other than chewing the same data over and over again until you've masticated it into tastlessness. Second, because the game is complex enough that I think you'll enjoy it. Third, because I'm not too bad at it myself but Ajit is better, and I think you will be, too, so I can learn from both of you."

And fourth, I didn't say aloud, because Ajit is a master, he will beat you most of the time, and he needs the boost in confidence.

Ajit is not the scientist that Kane is. Practically no one in the settled worlds is the scientist that Kane is. All three of us know this, but none of us have ever mentioned it, not even once. There are geniuses who are easy for the inferior to work with, who are generous enough to slow down their mental strides to the smaller steps of the merely gifted. Kane is not one of them.

"*Go*," Kane says thoughtfully. "I have friends who play that."

This was a misstatement. Kane does not have friends, in the usual sense. He has colleagues, he has science, and he has me.

He smiled at me, a rare touch of sweet gratitude on his handsome face. "Thanks, Tirzah. I'll play with Ajit. You're right, it *will* pass the time until the probe sends back the prelim data. And if I'm occupied, maybe I'll be less of a monster to you."

"You're fine to me," I say, giving his hair another tug, grinning with the casual flippancy he prefers. "Or if you're not, I don't care."

Kane laughs. In moments like this, I am especially careful that my own feelings don't show. To either of them.

2. PROBE

We automatically woke after the hyperjump. For reasons I don't understand, a hyperjump isn't instantaneous, perhaps because it's not really a "jump" but a Calabi-Yau dimension tunnel. Several days' ship-time had passed, and the probe now drifted less than five light-years from the galactic core. The probe, power off, checked out perfectly; the shielding had held even better than expected. And so had we. My eyes widened as I studied the wardroom displays.

On the *Kepler*, dust clouds had softened and obscured the view. Here, nothing did. We drifted just outside a star that had begun its deadly spiral inward toward Sag A*. Visuals showed the full deadly glory around the hole: the hot blue cluster of IRS16. The giant red star IRS7 with its long tail distended by stellar winds. The stars already past the point of no return, pulled by the gravity of Sag A* inexorably toward its event horizon. The radio, gamma-ray, and infrared displays revealed even more, brilliant with the radiation pouring from every single gorgeous, lethal object in the bright sky.

And there, too, shone one of the mysteries Kane and Ajit had come to study: the massive young stars that were not being yanked toward Sag A*, and which in this place should have been neither massive nor relatively stable. Such stars should not exist this close to the hole. One star, Kane had told me, was as close to the hole as twice Pluto's orbit from Sol. How had it gotten there?

"It's beautiful, in a hellish way," I said to Ajit and Kane. "I want to go up to the observatory and see it direct."

"The observatory!" Kane said scornfully. "I need to get to work!" He sat down at his terminal.

None of this is true, of course. There is no observatory on the probe, and I can't climb the ladder "up" to it. Nor is there a wardroom with terminals, chairs, table, displays, a computer. We *are* the computer, or rather we are inside it. But the programs running along with us make it all seem as real as the fleshy versions of ourselves on the *Kepler*. This, it was determined by previous disastrous experience in space exploration, is necessary to keep us sane and stable. Human uploads need this illusion, this shadow reality, and we accept it easily. Why not? It's the default setting for our minds.

So Kane "sat" "at" his "terminal" to look at the preliminary data from the sensors. So did Ajit, and I "went" "upstairs" to the observatory, where I gazed outward for a long time.

I—the other "I," the one on the *Kepler*—grew up on a station in the Oort Cloud,

Sol System. Space is my natural home. I don't really understand how mud-dwellers live on planets, or why they would want to, at the bottom of a murky and dirty shroud of uncontrollable air. I have learned to simulate understanding planetary love, because it is my job. Both Kane and Ajit come from rocks, Ajit from New Bombay, and Kane from Terra herself. They are space scientists, but not real spacers.

No mud-dweller ever really sees the stars. And no human being had ever seen what I saw now, the frantic heart of the human universe.

Eventually I went back downstairs, rechecked ship's data, and then sat at the wardroom table and took up my embroidery. The ancient, irrelevant cloth-ornamenting is very soothing, almost as much so as gardening, although of course that's not why I do it. All first-class Nurturers practice some humble handicraft. It allows you to closely observe people while appearing absorbed and harmless.

Kane, of course, was oblivious to me. I could have glared at him through a magnifying glass and he wouldn't have noticed, not if he was working. Back on the *Kepler*, he had explained in simple terms—or at least as simple as Kane's explanations ever get—why there should not be any young stars this close to the core, as well as three possible explanations for why there are. He told me all this, in typical Kane fashion, in bed. Postcoital intimacy.

"The stars' spectra show they're young, Tirzah. And *close*—SO-2 comes to within eighty AU's of Sag A*! It's *wrong*—the core is incredibly inhospitable to star formation! Also, these close-in stars have very peculiar orbits."

"You're taking it personally," I observed, smiling.

"Of course I am!" This was said totally without irony. "Those young stars have no business there. The tidal forces of the hole should rip any hot dust clouds to shreds long before any stars could form. And if they formed farther out, say one hundred light-years out, they should have died before they got this close in. These supermassive stars only last a few million years."

"But there they are."

"Yes. Why do you still have this lacy thing on? It's irritating."

"Because you were so eager that I didn't have time to get it off."

"Well, take it off now."

I did, and he wrapped my body close to his, and went on fretting over star formation in the core.

"There are three theories. One is that a dust cloud ringing the core, about six light-years out, keeps forming stars, which are then blown outwards again by galactic winds, and then drawn in, and repeat. Another theory is that there's a second, intermediate medium-sized black hole orbiting Sag A* and exerting a counterpull on the stars. But if so, why aren't we detecting its radio waves? Another idea is that the stars aren't really young at all, they're composites of remnants of elderly stars that merged to form a body that only looks bright and young."

I said, "Which theory do you like?"

"None of them." And then, in one of those lightning changes he was capable of, he focused all his attention on me. "Are you all right, Tirzah? I know this has got to be a boring voyage for you. Running ship can't take much of your time, and neither can baby-sitting me."

I laughed aloud and Kane, having no idea why, frowned slightly. It was such a typically Kane speech. A sudden burst of intense concern, which would prove equally transitory. No mention of Ajit at all, as if only Kane existed for me. And his total ignorance of how often I interceded between him and Ajit, smoothed over tensions between them, spent time calming and centering separately each of these men who were more like the stars outside the ship than either of them were capable of recognizing. Brilliant, heated, intense, inherently unstable.

"I'm fine, Kane. I'm enjoying myself."

"Well, good," he said, and I saw that he then forgot me, back to brooding about his theories.

Neither Kane nor Ajit knows that I love Kane. I don't love Ajit. Whatever calls up love in our hidden hearts, it is unfathomable. Kane arouses in me a happiness, a desire, a completeness that puts a glow on the world because he—difficult, questing, vital—is in it. Ajit, through no fault of his own, does not.

Neither of them will ever know this. I would berate myself if they did. My personal feelings don't matter here. I am a captain.

"Damn and double damn!" Kane said, admiringly. "Look at that!"

Ajit reacted as if Kane had spoken to him, but of course Kane had not. He was just thinking aloud. I put down my embroidery and went to stand behind them at their terminals.

Ajit said, "Those readings must be wrong. The sensors were damaged after all, either in hypertransit or by radiation."

Kane didn't reply; I doubt he'd heard. I said, "What is it?"

It was Ajit who answered. "The mass readings are wrong. They're showing high mass density for several areas of empty space."

I said, "Maybe that's where the new young stars are forming?"

Not even Ajit answered this, which told me it was a stupid statement. It doesn't matter; I don't pretend to be a scientist. I merely wanted to keep them talking, to gauge their states of mind.

Ajit said, "It would be remarkable if all equipment had emerged undamaged from the jump into this radiation."

"Kane?" I said.

"It's not the equipment," he muttered. So he had been listening, at least peripherally. "Supersymmetry."

Ajit immediately objected to this, in terms I didn't understand. They were off into a discussion I had no chance of following. I let it go on for a while, then even longer, since it sounded the way scientific discussions are supposed to sound: intense but not acrimonious, not personal.

When they wound down a bit, I said, "Did the minicapsule go off to the *Kepler*? They're waiting for the prelim data, and the minicap takes days to jump. Did either of you remember to record and send?"

They both looked at me, as if trying to remember who I was and what I was doing there. In that moment, for the first time, they looked alike.

"I remembered," Ajit said. "The prelim data went off to the *Kepler*. Kane—"

They were off again.

3. SHIP

The *go* games were not a success.

The problem, I could see, was with Ajit. He was a far better player than Kane, both intuitively and through experience. This didn't bother Kane at all; he thrived on challenge. But his own clear superiority subtly affected Ajit.

"Game won," he said for the third time in the evening, and at the slight smirk in his voice I looked up from my embroidery.

"Damn and double damn," Kane said, without rancor. "Set them up again."

"No, I think I will go celebrate my victories with Tirzah."

This was Kane's night, but the two of them had never insisted on precedence. This was because I had never let it come to that; it's part of my job to give the illusion that I am always available to both, on whatever occasion they wish. Of course, I control, through a hundred subtle signals and without either realizing it, which occasions they happen to wish. Where I make love depends on whom I need to observe. This direct claim by Ajit, connecting me to his *go* victories, was new.

Kane, of course, didn't notice. "All right. God, I wish the minicap would come. I want that data!"

Now that the game had released his attention, he was restless again. He rose and paced around the wardroom, which doesn't admit too much pacing. "I think I'll go up to the observatory. Anybody coming?"

He had already forgotten that I was leaving with Ajit. I saw Ajit go still. Such a small thing—Ajit was affronted that Kane was not affected by Ajit's game victory, or by his bearing me off like some earned prize. Another man would have felt a moment of pique and then forgotten it. Ajit was not another man. Neither was Kane. Stable men don't volunteer for missions like this.

It's different for me; I was bred to space. The scientists were not.

I put down my embroidery, took Ajit's hand, and snuggled close to him. Kane, for the moment, was fine. His restless desire for his data wouldn't do him any harm. It was Ajit I needed to work with.

I was the one who had suggested the *go* games. Good captains are not supposed to make mistakes like that. It was up to me to set things right.

By the time the minicap arrived, everything was worse.

They would not, either of them, stop the *go* games. They played obsessively, six or seven times a day, then nine or ten, and finally every waking minute. Ajit continued to win the large majority of the games, but not all of them. Kane focused his formidable intelligence on devising strategies, and he had the advantage of caring but not too much. Yes, he was obsessed, but I could see that once he had something more significant to do, he would leave the *go* games without a backward glance.

Ajit grew more focused, too. Even more intent on winning, even as he began to lose a few games. More slyly gleeful when he did win. He flicked his winning piece onto the board with a turn of the wrist in which I read both contempt and fear.

I tried everything I could to intervene, every trick from a century of experience.

Nothing worked. Sex only made it worse. Ajit regarded sex as an earned prize, Kane as a temporary refreshment so he could return to the games.

One night Ajit brought out the statue of Shiva and put it defiantly on the wardroom table. It took up two-thirds of the space, a wide metal circle enclosing the four-armed dancer.

"What's that?" Kane said, looking up from the game board. "Oh, God, it's a god."

I said quickly, "It's an intellectual concept. The flow of cosmic energy in the universe."

Kane laughed, not maliciously, but I saw Ajit's eyes light up. Ajit said, "I want it here."

Kane shrugged. "Fine by me. Your turn, Ajit."

Wrong, wrong. Ajit had hoped to disturb Kane, to push him into some open objection to the statue. Ajit wanted a small confrontation, some outlet to emphasize his gloating. Some outlet for his growing unease as Kane's game improved. And some outlet for his underlying rage, always just under the surface, at Kane, the better scientist. The statue was supposed to be an assertion, even a slap in the face: *I am here and I take up a lot of your space. Notice that!*

Instead, Kane had shrugged and dismissed it.

I said, "Tell me again, Ajit, about Nataraja. What's the significance of the flames on the great circle?"

Ajit said quietly, "They represent the fire that destroys the world."

Kane said, "Your *turn*, Ajit."

Such a small incident. But deep in my mind, where I was aware of it but not yet overtly affected, fear stirred.

I was losing control here.

Then the first minicap of data arrived.

4. PROBE

Mind uploads are still minds. They are not computer programs in the sense that other programs are. Although freed of biological constraints such as enzymes that create sleep, hunger, and lust, uploads are not free of habit. In fact, it is habit that creates enough structure to keep all of us from frenzied feedback loops. On the probe, my job was to keep habit strong. It was the best safeguard for those brilliant minds.

"Time to sleep, gentlemen," I said lightly. We had been gathered in the wardroom for sixteen hours straight, Kane and Ajit at their terminals, me sitting quietly, watching them. I have powers of concentration equal in degree, though not in kind, to their own. They do not suspect this. It has been hours since I put down my embroidery, but neither noticed.

"Tirzah, not sleep now!" Kane snapped.

"Now."

He looked up at me like a sulky child. But Kane is not a child; I don't make that mistake. He knows an upload has to shut down for the cleansing program to run, a necessity to catch operating errors before they grow large enough to impair function. With all the radiation bathing the probe, the program is more necessary than ever. It takes a few hours to run through. I control the run cues.

Ajit looked at me expectantly. It was his night. This, too, was part of habit, as well as being an actual aid to their work. More than one scientist in my care has had that critical flash of intuition on some scientific problem while in my arms. Upload sex, like its fleshy analogue, both stimulates and relaxes.

"All right, all right," Kane muttered. "Good night."

I shut him down and turned to Ajit.

We went to his bunk. Ajit was tense, stretched taut with data and with sixteen hours with Kane. But I was pleased to see how completely he responded to me. Afterward, I asked him to explain the prelim data to me.

"And keep it simple, please. Remember who you're talking to!"

"To an intelligent and sweet lady," he said, and I gave him the obligatory smile. But he saw that I really did want to know about the data.

"The massive young stars are there when they should not be . . . Kane has explained all this to you, I know."

I nodded.

"They are indeed young, not mashed-together old stars. We have verified that. We are trying now to gather and run data to examine the other two best theories: a fluctuating ring of matter spawning stars, or other black holes."

"How are you examining the theories?"

He hesitated, and I knew he was trying to find explanations I could understand. "We are running various programs, equations, and sims. We are also trying to determine where to jump the probe next—you know about that."

Of course I did. No one moves this ship without my consent. It has two more jumps left in its power pack, and I must approve them both.

"We need to choose a spot from which we can fire beams of various radiation to assess the results. The heavier beams won't last long here, you know—the gravity of the superhole distorts them." He frowned.

"What is it, Ajit? What about gravity?"

"Kane was right," he said, "the mass detectors aren't damaged. They're showing mass nearby, not large but detectable, that isn't manifesting anything but gravity. No radiation of any kind."

"A black hole," I suggested.

"Too small. Small black holes radiate away, Hawking showed that long ago. The internal temperature is too high. There are no black holes smaller than three solar masses. The mass detectors are showing something much smaller than that."

"What?"

"We don't know."

"Were all the weird mass-detector readings in the prelim data you sent back to the *Kepler?*"

"Of course," he said, a slight edge in his voice.

I pulled him closer. "I can always rely on you," I said, and I felt his body relax.

I shut us down, as we lay in each other's arms.

It was Ajit who, the next day, noticed the second anomaly. And I who noticed the third.

"These gas orbits aren't right," Ajit said to Kane. "And they're getting less right all the time."

Kane moved to Ajit's terminal. "Tell me."

"The infalling gases from the circumnuclear disk . . . see . . . they curve here, by the western arm of Sag A West . . ."

"It's wind from the IRS16 cluster," Kane said instantly. "I got updated readings for those yesterday."

"No, I already corrected for that," Ajit said.

"Then maybe magnetization from IRS7, or—"

They were off again. I followed enough to grasp the general problem. Gases streamed at enormous speeds from clouds beyond the circumnuclear disk which surrounded the entire core like a huge doughnut. These streaming gases were funneled by various forces into fairly narrow, conelike paths. The gases would eventually end up circling the black hole, spiraling inward and compressing to temperatures of billions of degrees before they were absorbed by the maw of the hole. The processes were understood.

But the paths weren't as predicted. Gases were streaming down wrong, approaching the hole wrong for predictions made from all the forces acting on them.

Ajit finally said to Kane, "I want to move the probe earlier than we planned."

"Wait a moment," I said instantly. Ship's movements were *my* decision. "It's not yet the scheduled time."

"Of course I'm including you in my request, Tirzah," Ajit said, with all his usual courtesy. There was something beneath the courtesy, however, a kind of glow. I recognized it. Scientists look like that when they have the germ of an important idea.

I thought Kane would object or ridicule, but something in their technical discussion must have moved him, too. His red hair stood up all over his head. He glanced briefly at his own displays, back at Ajit's, then at the younger man. He said, "You want to put the probe on the other side of Sagittarius A West."

"Yes."

I said, "Show me."

Ajit brought up the simplified graphic he had created weeks ago for me to gain an overview of this mission. It showed the black hole at the center of the galaxy, and the major structures around it: the cluster of hot blue stars, the massive young stars that should not have existed so close to the hole, the red giant star IRS16, with its long fiery tail. All this, plus our probe, lay on one side of the huge, three-armed spiraling plasma remnant, Sagittarius A West. Ajit touched the computer and a new dot appeared on the other side of Sag A West, farther away from the hole than we were now.

"We want to go there, Tirzah," he said. Kane nodded.

I said, deliberately sounding naïve, "I thought there wasn't as much going on over there. And besides, you said that Sag A West would greatly obscure our vision in all wavelengths, with its own radiation."

"It will."

"Then—"

"There's something going on over there now," Kane said. "Ajit's right. That region is the source of whatever pull is distorting the gas infall. We need to go there."

We.

Ajit's right.

The younger man didn't change expression. But the glow was still there, ignited by Ajit's idea and fanned, I now realized, by Kane's approval. I heated it up a bit more. "But, Kane, your work on the massive young stars? I can only move the probe so many times, you know. Our fuel supply—"

"I have a lot of data on the stars now," Kane said, "and this matters more."

I hid my own pleasure. "All right. I'll move the probe."

But when I interfaced with ship's program, I found the probe had already been moved.

5. SHIP

Kane and Ajit fell on the minicap of prelim data like starving wolves. There were no more games of *go*. There was no more anything but work, unless I insisted.

At first I thought that was good. I thought that without the senseless, mounting competition over *go*, the two scientists would cooperate on the intense issues that mattered so much to both of them.

"Damn and double damn!" Kane said, admiringly. "Look at that!"

Ajit reacted as if Kane had spoken to him, but of course Kane had not. He was just thinking aloud. I put down my embroidery and went to stand behind them at their terminals.

Ajit said, with the new arrogance of the *go* wins in his voice, "Those readings must be wrong. The sensors were damaged after all, either in hypertransit or by radiation."

Kane, for a change, caught Ajit's tone. He met it with a sneer he must have used regularly on presumptuous postgrads. "'Must be wrong'? That's just the kind of puerile leaping to conclusions that gets people nowhere."

I said quickly, "What readings?"

It was Ajit who answered me, and although the words were innocuous, even polite, I heard the anger underlying them. "The mass readings are wrong. They're showing high mass density for several areas of empty space."

I said, "Maybe that's where the new young stars are forming?"

Not even Ajit answered this, which told me it was a stupid statement. It doesn't matter; I don't pretend to be a scientist. I merely wanted to keep them talking, to gauge their states of mind.

Ajit said, too evenly, "It would be remarkable if *all* probe equipment had emerged undamaged from the jump into core radiation."

"Kane?" I said.

"It's *not* the equipment." And then, "Supersymmetry."

Ajit immediately objected to this, in terms I didn't understand. They were off into a discussion I had no chance of following. What I could follow was the increasing pressure of Ajit's anger as Kane dismissed and belittled his ideas. I could almost see that anger, a hot plasma. As Kane ridiculed and belittled, the plasma collapsed into greater and greater density.

Abruptly they broke off their argument, went to their separate terminals, and worked like machines for twenty hours straight. I had to make them each eat something. They were obsessed, as only those seized by science or art can obsess. Neither of them would come to bed with me that night. I could have issued an executive order, but I chose not to exert that much trust-destroying force until I had to, although I did eventually announce that I was shutting down terminal access.

"For God's sake, Tirzah!" Kane snarled. "This is a once-in-a-species opportunity! I've got work to do!"

I said evenly, "You're going to rest. The terminals are down for seven hours."

"Five."

"All right." After five hours, Kane would still be snoring away.

He stood, stiff from the long hours of sitting. Kane is well over a hundred; rejuves can only do so much, so long. His cramped muscles, used to much more exercise, misfired briefly. He staggered, laughed, caught himself easily.

But not before he'd bumped the wardroom table. Ajit's statue of Shiva slid off and fell to the floor. The statue was old—four hundred years old, Ajit had said. Metal shows fatigue, too, although later than men. The statue hit the deck at just the right angle and broke.

"Oh . . . sorry, Ajit."

Kane's apology was a beat too late. I knew—with every nerve in my body, I knew this—that the delay happened because Kane's mind was still racing along his data, and it took an effort for him to refocus. It didn't matter. Ajit stiffened, and something in the nature of his anger changed, ionized by Kane's careless, preoccupied tone.

I said quickly, "Ship can weld the statue."

"No, thank you," Ajit said. "I will leave it as it is. Good night."

"Ajit—" I reached for his hand. He pulled it away.

"Good night, Tirzah."

Kane said, "The gamma-ray variations within Sag A West aren't quite what was predicted." He blinked twice. "You're right, I am exhausted."

Kane stumbled off to his bunk. Ajit had already gone. After a long while I picked up the pieces of Ajit's statue and held them, staring at the broken figure of the dancing god.

The preliminary data, Kane had declared when it arrived, contained enough information to keep them both busy until the second minicap arrived. But by the next day, Kane was impatiently demanding more.

"These gas orbits aren't right," he said aloud, although not to either me or Ajit. Kane did that, worked in silence for long stretches until words exploded out of him to no particular audience except his own whirling thoughts. His ear was raw with rubbing.

I said, "What's not right about them?" When he didn't answer, or probably even hear me, I repeated the question, much louder.

Kane came out of his private world and scowled at me. "The infalling gases from beyond the circumnuclear disk aren't showing the right paths to Sag A*."

I said, repeating something he'd taught me, "Could it be wind from the IRS16 cluster?"

"No. I checked those updated readings yesterday and corrected for them."

I had reached the end of what I knew to ask. Kane burst out, "I need more data!"

"Well, it'll get here eventually."

"I want it now," he said, and laughed sourly at himself, and went back to work.

Ajit said nothing, acting as if neither of us had spoken.

I waited until Ajit stood, stretched, and looked around vaguely. Then I said, "Lunch in a minute. But first come look at something with me." Immediately I started up the ladder to the observatory, so that he either had to follow or go through the trouble of arguing. He followed.

I had put the welded statue of Shiva on the bench near clear hull. It was the wrong side of the hull for the spectacular view of the core, but the exotics didn't press so close to the hull here, and thousands of stars shone in a sky more illuminated than Sol had seen since its birth. Shiva danced in his mended circle of flames against a background of cosmic glory.

Ajit said flatly, "I told you I wanted to leave it broken."

With Kane, frank opposition is fine; he's strong enough to take it and, in fact, doesn't respect much else. But Ajit is different. I lowered my eyes and reached for his hand. "I know. I took the liberty of fixing it anyway because, well, I thought you might want to see it whole again and because I like the statue so much. It has so much meaning beyond the obvious, especially here. In this place and this time. Please forgive me."

Ajit was silent for a moment, then he raised my hand to his lips. "You do see that."

"Yes," I said, and it was the truth. Shiva, the endless dance, the endless flow of energy changing form and state—how could anyone not see it in the gas clouds forming stars, the black hole destroying them, the violence and creation outside this very hull? Yet, at the same time, it was a profound insight into the very obvious, and I kept my eyes lowered so no glimpse of my faint contempt reached Ajit.

He kissed me. "You are so spiritual, Tirzah. And so sweet-natured."

I was neither. The only deceptions Ajit could see were the paranoid ones he assumed of others.

But his body had relaxed in my arms, and I knew that some part of his mind had been reassured. He and I could see spiritual beauties that Kane could not. Therefore he was in some sense superior to Kane. He followed me back down the ladder to lunch, and I heard him hum a snatch of some jaunty tune. Pleased with myself, I made for the galley.

Kane stood up so abruptly from his terminal that his eyes glowed. "Oh, my shitting stars. Oh, yes. Tirzah, I've got it."

I stopped cold. I had never seen anyone, even Kane, look quite like that. "Got what?"

"All of it." Suddenly he seized me and swung me into exuberant, clumsy dance. "All of it! I've got all of it! The young stars, the gas orbits, the missing mass in the universe! All shitting fucking *all* of it!"

"Wwwhhhaaatttt . . ." He was whirling me around so fast that my teeth rattled. "Kane, stop!"

He did, and enveloped me in a rib-cracking hug, then abruptly released me and dragged my bruised body to his terminal. "Look, sweetheart, I've got it. Now sit right there and I'm going to explain it in terms even you can understand. You'll love it. It'll love you. Now look here, at this region of space—"

I turned briefly to look at Ajit. For Kane, he didn't even exist.

6. PROBE

"The probe has moved," I said to Ajit and Kane. "It's way beyond the calculated drift. By a factor of ten."

Kane's eyes, red with work, nonetheless sharpened. "Let me see the trajectory."

"I transferred it to both your terminals." Ordinarily ship's data is kept separate, for my eyes only.

Kane brought up the display and whistled.

The probe is under the stresses, gravitational and radiational, that will eventually destroy it. We all know that. Our fleshy counterparts weren't even sure the probe would survive to send one minicap of data, and I'm sure they were jubilant when we did. Probably they treated the minicap like a holy gift, and I can easily imagine how eager they are for more. Back on the ship, I—the other "I"—had been counting on data, like oil, to grease the frictions and tensions between Ajit and Kane. I hoped it had.

We uploads had fuel enough to move the probe twice. After that, and since our last move will be no more than one-fiftieth of a light-year from the black hole at the galactic core, the probe will eventually spiral down into Sag A*. Before that, however, it will have been ripped apart by the immense tidal forces of the hole. However, long before that final death plunge, we analogues will be gone.

The probe's current drift, however, considerably farther away from the hole, was nonetheless much faster than projected. It was also slightly off course. We were being pulled in the general direction of Sag A*, but not on the gravitational trajectory that would bring us into its orbit at the time and place the computer had calculated. In fact, at our current rate of acceleration, there was a chance we'd miss the event horizon completely.

What was going on?

Kane said, "Maybe we better hold off moving the probe to the other side of Sag A West until we find out what's pulling us."

Ajit was studying the data over Kane's shoulder. He said hesitantly, "No . . . wait . . . I think we should move."

"Why?" Kane challenged.

"I don't know. I just have . . . call it an intuition. We should move now."

I held my breath. The only intuition Kane usually acknowledged was his own. But earlier things had subtly shifted. Kane had said, "*Ajit's right. That region is the source of whatever pull is distorting the gas infall.*" Ajit had not changed expression, but I'd felt his pleasure, real as heat. That had given him the courage to now offer this unformed—"half-baked" was Kane's usual term—intuition.

Kane said thoughtfully, "Maybe you're right. Maybe the—" Suddenly his eyes widened. "Oh my god."

"What?" I said, despite myself. "What?"

Kane ignored me. "Ajit—run the sims for the gas orbits in correlation with the probe drift. I'll do the young stars!"

"Why do—" Ajit began, and then he saw whatever had seized Kane's mind. Ajit said something in Hindi; it might have been a curse, or a prayer. I didn't know. Nor did I know anything about their idea, or about what was happening with the gas orbits and young stars outside the probe. However, I could see clearly what was happening within.

Ajit and Kane fell into frenzied work. They threw comments and orders to each other, transferred data, backed up sims and equation runs. They tilted their chairs toward each other and spouted incomprehensible jargon. Once Kane cried, "We need more data!" and Ajit laughed, freely and easily, then immediately plunged back into whatever he was doing. I watched them for a long time, then stole quietly up to the observation deck for a minute alone.

The show outside was more spectacular than ever, perhaps because we'd been pulled closer to it than planned. Clouds of whirling gases wrapped and oddly softened that heart of darkness, Sag A*. The fiery tail of the giant red star lit up that part of the sky. Stars glowed in a profusion unimaginable on my native Station J, stuck off in a remote arm of the galaxy. Directly in front of me glowed the glorious blue stars of the cluster IRS16.

I must have stayed on the observation deck longer than I'd planned, because Kane came looking for me. "Tirzah! Come on down! We want to show you where we're moving and why!"

We.

I said severely, gladness bursting in my heart, "You don't show me where we're going, Kane, you ask me. I captain this ship."

"Yeah, yeah, I know, you're a dragon lady. Come on!" He grabbed my hand and pulled me toward the ladder.

They both explained it, interrupting each other, fiercely correcting each other, having a wonderful time. I concentrated as hard as I could, trying to cut through the technicalities they couldn't do without, any more than they could do without air. Eventually I thought I glimpsed the core of their excitement.

"Shadow matter," I said, tasting the words on my tongue. It sounded too bizarre to take seriously, but Kane was insistent.

"The theory's been around for centuries, but deGroot pretty much discredited it in 2086," Kane said. "He—"

"If it's been discredited, then why—" I began.

"I said 'pretty much,'" Kane said. "There were always some mathematical anomalies with deGroot's work. And we can see now where he was *wrong*. He—"

Kane and Ajit started to explain why deGroot was wrong, but I interrupted. "No, don't digress so much! Let me just tell you what I think I understood from what you said."

I was silent a moment, gathering words. Both men waited impatiently, Kane running his hand through his hair, Ajit smiling widely. I said, "You said there's a theory that just after the Big Bang, gravity somehow decoupled from the other forces in the universe, just as matter decoupled from radiation. At the same time, you scientists have known for two centuries that there doesn't seem to be enough matter in the universe to make all your equations work. So scientists posited a lot of 'dark matter' and a lot of black holes, but none of the figures added up right anyway.

"And right now, neither do the orbits of the infalling gas, or the probe's drift, or the fact that massive young stars were forming that close to the black hole without being ripped apart by tidal forces. The forces acting on the huge clouds that have to condense to form stars that big."

I took a breath, quick enough so that neither had time to break in and distract me with technicalities.

"But now you think that if gravity *did* decouple right after the Big Bang—"

"About 10^{-43} seconds after," Ajit said helpfully. I ignored him.

"—then two types of matter were created, normal matter and 'shadow matter.' It's sort of like matter and antimatter, only normal matter and shadow matter can't interact except by gravity. No interaction through any other force, not radiation or strong or weak forces. Only gravity. That's the only effect shadow matter has on *our* universe. Gravity.

"And a big chunk of this stuff is there on the other side of Sag A West. It's exerting enough gravity to affect the path of the infalling gas. And to affect the probe's drift. And even to affect the young stars because the shadow matter-thing's exerting a counterpull on the massive star clouds, and that's keeping them from being ripped apart by the hole as soon as they otherwise would be. So they have time to collapse into young stars."

"Well, that's sort of it, but you've left out some things that alter and validate the whole," Kane said impatiently, scowling.

"Yes, Tirzah, dear heart, you don't see the—you can't just say that 'counterpull'—let me try once more."

They were off again, but this time I didn't listen. So maybe I hadn't seen the theory whole, but only glimpsed its shadow. It was enough.

They had a viable theory. I had a viable expedition, with a goal, and cooperatively productive scientists, and a probability of success.

It was enough.

Kane and Ajit prepared the second minicap for the big ship, and I prepared to move the probe. Our mood was jubilant. There was much laughing and joking, interrupted by intense bursts of incomprehensible jabbering between Ajit and Kane.

But before I finished my programming, Ajit's head disappeared.

7. SHIP

Kane worked all day on his shadow-matter theory. He worked ferociously, hunched over his terminal like a hungry dog with a particularly meaty bone, barely glancing up and saying little. Ajit worked, too, but the quality of his working was different. The terminals both connect to the same computer, of course; whatever Kane had, Ajit had, too. Ajit could follow whatever Kane did.

But that's what Ajit was doing: following. I could tell it from the timing of his accesses, from the whole set of his body. He was a decent scientist, but he was not Kane. Given the data and enough time, Ajit might have been able to go where Kane raced ahead now. Maybe. Or, he might have been able to make valuable additions to Kane's thinking. But Kane gave him no time; Kane was always there first, and he asked no help. He had shut Ajit out completely. For Kane, nothing existed right now but his work.

Toward evening he looked up abruptly and said to me, "They'll move the probe. The uploads—they'll move it."

I said, "How do you know? It's not time yet, according to the schedule."

"No. But they'll move it. If I figured out the shadow matter here, I will there, too. I'll decide that more data is needed from the other side of Sag A West, where the main shadow mass is."

I looked at him. He looked demented, like some sort of Roman warrior who has just wrestled with a lion. All that was missing was the blood. Wild, filthy hair—when had he last showered? Clothes spotted with the food I'd made him gulp down at noon. Age lines beginning, under strain and fatigue and despite the rejuve, to drag down the muscles of his face. And his eyes shining like Sag A West itself.

God, I loved him.

I said, with careful emphasis, "You're right. The *Tirzah upload* will move the ship for better measurements."

"Then we'll get more data in a few days," Ajit said. "But the radiation on the other side of Sag A West is still intense. We must hope nothing gets damaged in the probe programs, or in the uploads themselves, before we get the new data."

"We better hope nothing gets damaged long before that in my upload," Kane said, "or they won't even know what data to collect." He turned back to his screen.

The brutal words hung in the air.

I saw Ajit turn his face away from me. Then he rose and walked into the galley.

If I followed him too soon, he would see it as pity. His shame would mount even more.

"Kane," I said in a low, furious voice, "you are despicable."

He turned to me in genuine surprise. "What?"

"You know what." But he didn't. Kane wasn't even conscious of what he'd said. To him, it was a simple, evident truth. Without the Kane upload, no one on the probe would know how to do first-class science.

"I want to see you upstairs on the observation deck," I said to him. "Not now, but in ten minutes. And *you* announce that you want *me* to see something up there." The time lag, plus Kane's suggesting the trip, would keep Ajit from knowing I was protecting him.

But now I had put up Kane's back. He was tired, he was stressed, he was inevitably coming down from the unsustainable high of his discovery. Neither body nor mind can keep at that near-hysterical pitch for too long. I had misjudged, out of my own anger at him.

He snapped, "I'll see you on the observation deck when *I* want to see you there, and not otherwise. Don't push me around, Tirzah. Not even as captain." He turned back to his display.

Ajit emerged from the galley with three glasses on a tray. "A celebratory drink. A major discovery deserves that. At a minimum."

Relief was so intense I nearly showed it on my face. It was all right. I had misread Ajit, underestimated him. He ranked the magnitude of Kane's discovery higher than his own lack of participation in it, after all. Ajit was, first, a scientist.

He handed a glass to me, one to Kane, one for himself. Kane took a hasty, perfunctory gulp and returned to his display. But I cradled mine, smiling at Ajit, trying with warmth to convey the admiration I felt for his rising above the personal.

"Where did you get the wine? It wasn't on the ship manifest!"

"It was in my personal allotment," Ajit said, smiling.

Personal allotments are not listed nor examined. A bottle of wine, the statue of Shiva . . . Ajit had brought some interesting choices for a galactic core. I sipped the red liquid. It tasted different from the Terran or Martian wines I had grown up with: rougher, more full-bodied, not as sweet.

"Wonderful, Ajit."

"I thought you would like it. It is made in my native New Bombay, from genemod grapes brought from Terra."

He didn't go back to his terminal. For the next half hour, he entertained me with stories of New Bombay. He was a good storyteller, sharp and funny. Kane worked steadily, ignoring us. The ten-minute deadline I had set for him to call me up to the observation deck came and went.

After half an hour, Kane stood and staggered. Once before, when he'd broken Ajit's statue, stiffness after long sitting had made Kane unsteady. That time he'd caught himself after simply bumping the wardroom table. This time he crashed heavily to the floor.

"Kane!"

"Nothing, nothing . . . don't make a fuss, Tirzah! You just won't leave me alone!"

This was so unfair that I wanted to slap him. I didn't. Kane rose by himself, shook his head like some great beast, and said, "I'm just exhausted. I'm going to bed."

I didn't try to stop him from going to his bunk. I had planned on sleeping with Ajit, anyway. It seemed that some slight false note had crept into his storytelling in the last five minutes, some forced exaggeration.

But he smiled at me, and I decided I'd been wrong. I was very tired, too. All at once I wished I could sleep alone this night.

But I couldn't. Ajit, no matter how well he'd recovered from Kane's unconscious brutality, nonetheless had to feel bruised at some level. It was my job to find out where, and how much, and to set it to rights. It was my job to keep the expedition as productive as possible, to counteract Kane's dismissing and belittling behavior toward Ajit. It was my job.

I smiled back at him.

8. PROBE

When Ajit's head disappeared, no one panicked. We'd expected this, of course; in fact, we'd expected it sooner. The probe drifted in a sea of the most intense radiation in the galaxy, much of it at lethal wavelengths: gamma rays from Sagittarius East, X-rays, powerful winds of ionized particles, things I couldn't name. That the probe's shielding had held this long was a minor miracle. It couldn't hold forever. Some particle or particles had penetrated it and reached the computer, contaminating a piece of the upload-maintenance program.

It was a minor glitch. The backup kicked in a moment later and Ajit's head reappeared. But we all knew this was only the beginning. It would happen again, and again, and eventually programming would be hit that couldn't be restored by automatic backup, because the backup would go, too, in a large enough hit—or because uploads are not like other computer programs. We are more than that, and less. An upload has backups to maintain the shadows we see of each other and the ship, the shadows that keep our captured minds sane. But an upload cannot house backups of itself. Even one copy smudges too much, and the copy contaminates the original. It has been tried, with painful results.

Moreover, we uploads run only partly on the main computer. An upload is neither a biological entity nor a long stream of code, but something more than both. Some of the substratum, the hardware, is wired like actual neurons, although constructed of sturdier stuff: thousands of miles of nano-constructed organic polymers. This is why analogues think at the rate of the human brain, not the much faster rate of computers. It's also why we feel as our originals do.

After Ajit's maintenance glitch our mood, which had been exuberant, sobered. But it didn't sour. We worked steadily, with focus and hope, deciding where exactly to position the probe and then entering the coordinates for the jump.

"See you soon," we said to each other. I kissed both Kane and Ajit lightly on the lips. Then we all shut down and the probe jumped.

Days later, we emerged on the other side of Sag A West, all three of us still intact. If it were in my nature, I would have said a prayer of thanksgiving. Instead I said to Ajit, "Still have a head, I see."

"And a good thing he does," Kane said absently, already plunging for the chair in front of his terminal. "We'll need it. And—Ajit, the mass detectors . . . great shitting gods!"

It seems we were to have thanksgiving after all, if only perversely. I said, "What is it? What's there?" The displays showed nothing at all.

"Nothing at all," Ajit said. "And everything."

"Speak English!"

Ajit—I doubt Kane had even heard me, in his absorption—said, "The mass detectors are showing a huge mass less than a quarter light-year away. The radiation detectors—all of them—are showing nothing at all. We're—"

"We're accelerating fast." I studied ship's data; the rate of acceleration made me blink. "We're going to hit whatever it is. Not soon, but the tidal forces—"

The probe was small, but the tidal forces of something this big would still rip it apart when it got close enough.

Something this big. But there was, to all other sensors, nothing there.

Nothing but shadows.

A strange sensation ran over me. Not fear, but something more complicated, much more eerie.

My voice sounded strange in my ears. "What if we hit it? I know you said radiation of all types will go right through shadow matter just as if it isn't there"—*because it isn't, not in our universe*—"but what about the probe? What if we hit it before we take the final event-horizon measurements on Sag A*?"

"We won't hit it," Ajit said. "We'll move before then, Tirzah, back to the hole. Kane—"

They forget me again. I went up to the observation deck. Looking out through the clear hull, I stared at the myriad of stars on the side of the night sky away from Sag A West. Then I turned to look toward that vast three-armed cloud of turning plasma, radiating as it cools. Nothing blocked my view of Sag A West. Yet between us lay a huge, massive body of shadow matter, unseen, pulling on everything else my dazed senses could actually see.

To my left, all the exotic plants in the observatory disappeared.

Ajit and Kane worked feverishly, until once more I made them shut down for "sleep." The radiation here was nearly as great as it had been in our first location. We were right inside Sagittarius A East, the huge expanding shell of an unimaginable explosion sometime during the last hundred thousand years. Most of Sag A East wasn't visible at the wavelengths I could see, but the gamma-ray detectors were going crazy.

"We can't stop for five hours!" Kane cried. "Don't you realize how much damage the radiation could do in that time? We need to get all the data we can, work on it, and send off the second minicap!"

"We're going to send off the second minicap right now," I said. "And we'll only shut down for three hours. But, Kane, we are going to do that. I mean it. Uploads run even more damage from not running maintenance than we do from external radiation. You know that."

He did. He scowled at me, and cursed, and fussed with the mini-cap, but then he fired the minicap off and shut down.

Ajit said, "Just one more minute, Tirzah. I want to show you something."

"Ajit—"

"No, it's not mathematical. I promise. It's something I brought onto the *Kepler*. The object was not included in the probe program, but I can show you a holo."

Somewhere in the recesses of the computer, Ajit's upload created a program and a two-dimensional holo appeared on an empty display screen. I blinked at it, surprised.

It was a statue of some sort of god with four arms, enclosed in a circle of flames, made of what looked like very old bronze.

"This is Nataraja," Ajit said. "Shiva dancing."

"Ajit—"

"No, I am not a god worshipper," he smiled. "You know me better than that, Tirzah. Hinduism has many gods—thousands—but they are, except to the ignorant, no more than embodiments of different aspects of reality. Shiva is the dance of creation and destruction, the constant flow of energy in the cosmos. Birth and death and rebirth. It seemed fitting to bring him to the galactic core, where so much goes on of all three. This statue has been in my family for four hundred years. I must bring it home, along with the answers to our experiments."

"You will bring Shiva back to New Bombay," I said softly, "and your answers, too."

"Yes, I have begun to think so." He smiled at me, a smile with all the need of his quicksilver personality in it, but also all the courtesy and hope. "Now I will sleep."

9. SHIP

The next morning, after a deep sleep one part sheer exhaustion and one part sex, I woke to find Ajit already out of bed and seated in front of his terminal. He rose the moment I entered the wardroom and turned to me with a grave face. "Tirzah. The minicap arrived. I already put the data into the system."

"What's wrong? Where's Kane?"

"Still asleep, I imagine."

I went to Kane's bunk. He lay on his back, still in the clothes he'd worn for three days, smelling sour and snoring softly. I thought of waking him, then decided to wait a bit. Kane could certainly use the sleep, and I could use the time with Ajit. I went back to the wardroom, tightening the belt on my robe.

"What's wrong?" I repeated.

"I put the data from the minicap into the system. It's all corrections to the last minicap's data. Kane says the first set was wrong."

"Kane?" I said stupidly.

"The Kane-analogue," Ajit explained patiently. "He says radiation hit the probe's sensors for the first batch, before any of them realized it. They fired off the preliminary data right after the jump, you know, because they had no idea how long the probe could last. Now they've had time to discover where the radiation hit, to restore the sensor programs, and to retake the measurements. The Kane analogue says these new ones are accurate, the others weren't."

I tried to take it all in. "So Kane's shadow-matter theory—none of that is true?"

"I don't know," Ajit said. "How can anybody know until we see if the data supports it? The minicap only just arrived."

"Then I might not have moved the probe," I said, meaning "the other I." My analogue. I didn't know what I was saying. The shock was too great. All that theorizing, all Kane's sharp triumph, all that tension . . .

I looked more closely at Ajit. He looked very pale, and as fatigued as a genemod man of his youth can look. I said, "You didn't sleep much."

"No. Yesterday was . . . difficult."

"Yes," I agreed, noting the characteristically polite understatement. "Yes."

"Should I wake Kane?" Ajit said, almost diffidently.

"I'll do it."

Kane was hard to wake. I had to shake him several times before he struggled up to consciousness.

"Tirzah?"

"Who else? Kane, you must get up. Something's happened."

"Wh-what?" He yawned hugely and slumped against the bulkhead. His whole body reeked.

I braced myself. "The second minicap arrived. Your analogue sent a recording. He says the prelim data was compromised, due to radiation-caused sensor malfunction."

That woke him. He stared at me as if I were an executioner. "The data's compromised? *All* of it?"

"I don't know."

Kane pushed out of his bunk and ran into the wardroom. Ajit said, "I put the mini-cap data into the system already, but I—" Kane wasn't listening. He tore into the data, and after a few minutes he actually bellowed.

"No!"

I flattened myself against the bulkhead, not from fear but from surprise. I had never heard a grown man make a noise like that.

But there were no other noises. Kane worked silently, ferociously. Ajit sat at his own terminal and worked, too, not yesterday's tentative copying but the real thing. I put hot coffee beside them both. Kane gulped his steaming, Ajit ignored his.

After half an hour, Kane turned to me. Defeat pulled like gravity at everything on his face, eyes and lips and jaw muscles. Only his filthy hair sprang upward. He said simply, with the naked straightforwardness of despair, "The new data invalidates the idea of shadow matter."

I heard myself say, "Kane, go take a shower."

To my surprise, he went, shambling from the room. Ajit worked a few minutes longer, then climbed the ladder to the observation deck. Over his shoulder he said, "Tirzah, I want to be alone, please. Don't come."

I didn't. I sat at the tiny wardroom table, looked at my own undrunk coffee, and thought of nothing.

10. PROBE

The data from the probe's new position looked good, Kane said. That was his word: "good." Then he returned to his terminal.

"Ajit?" I was coming to rely on him more and more for translation. He was just as busy as Kane, but kinder. This made sense. If, to Kane, Ajit was a secondary but still necessary party to the intellectual action, that's what I was to both of them. Ajit had settled into this position, secure that he was valued. I could feel myself doing the same. The cessation of struggle turned us both kinder.

Kane, never insecure, worked away.

Ajit said, "The new readings confirm a large gravitational mass affecting the paths of both the infalling gas and the probe. The young stars so close to Sag A* are a much knottier problem. We've got to modify the whole theory of star formation to account for the curvatures of spacetime caused by the hole *and* by the shadow mass. It's very complex. Kane's got the computer working on that, and I'm going to take readings on Sag A West, in its different parts, and on stars on the other side of the mass and look at those."

"What about the mass detectors? What do they say?"

"They say we're being pulled toward a mass of about a half million suns."

A half million suns. And we couldn't see it: not with our eyes, nor radio sensors, nor X-ray detectors, nor anything.

"I have a question. Does it have an event horizon? Is it swallowing light, like a black hole does? Isn't it the gravity of a black hole that swallows light?"

"Yes. But radiation, including light, goes right through this shadow matter, Tirzah. Don't you understand? It doesn't interact with normal radiation at all."

"But it has gravity. Why doesn't its gravity trap the light?"

"I don't know." He hesitated. "Kane thinks maybe it doesn't interact with radiation as particles, which respond to gravity. Only as waves."

"How can it do that?"

Ajit took my shoulders and shook them playfully. "I told you—*we don't know.* This is brand-new, dear heart. We know as much about what it will and will not do as primitive hominids knew about fire."

"Well, don't make a god of it," I said, and it was a test. Ajit passed. He didn't stiffen as if I'd made some inappropriate reference to the drawing of Shiva he'd shown me last night. Instead, he laughed and went back to work.

"Tirzah! Tirzah!"

The automatic wake-up brought me out of shutdown. Ajit must have been brought back online a few moments before me, because he was already calling my name. Alarm bells clanged.

"It's Kane! He's been hit!"

I raced into Kane's bunk. He lay still amid the bedclothes. It wasn't the maintenance program that had taken the hit, because every part of his body was intact; so were the bedclothes. But Kane lay stiff and unresponsive.

"Run the full diagnostics," I said to Ajit.

"I already started them."

"Kane," I said, shaking him gently, then harder. He moved a little, groaned. So his upload wasn't dead.

I sat on the edge of the bunk, fighting fear, and took his hand. "Kane, love, can you hear me?"

He squeezed my fingers. The expression on his face didn't change. After a silence in which time itself seemed to stop, Ajit said, "The diagnostics are complete. About a third of brain function is gone."

I got into the bunk beside Kane and put my arms around him.

Ajit and I did what we could. Our uploads patched and copied, using material from both of us. Yes, the copying would lead to corruption, but we were beyond that.

Because an upload runs on such a complex combination of computer and nano-constructed polymer networks, we cannot simply be replaced by a backup program cube. The unique software/hardware retes are also why a corrupted analogue is not exactly the same as a stroke- or tumor-impaired human brain.

The analogue brain does not have to pump blood or control breathing. It does not have to move muscles or secrete hormones. Although closely tied to the "purer" programs that maintain our illusion of moving and living as three-dimensional beings in a three-dimensional ship, the analogue brain is tied to the computer in much more complex ways than any fleshy human using a terminal. The resources of the computer were at our disposal, but they could only accomplish limited aims.

When Ajit and I had finished putting together as much of Kane, or a pseudo-Kane, as we could, he walked into the wardroom and sat down. He looked, moved, smiled the same. That part is easy to repair, as easy as had been replacing Ajit's head or the exotics on the observation deck. But the man staring blankly at the terminal was not really Kane.

"What was I working on?" he said.

I got out, "Shadow matter."

"Shadow matter? What's that?"

Ajit said softly, "I have all your work, Kane. Our work. I think I can finish it, now that you've started us in the right direction."

He nodded, looking confused. "Thank you, Ajit." Then, with a flash of his old magnificent combativeness, "But you better get it right!"

"With your help," Ajit said gaily, and in that moment I came close to truly loving him.

They worked out a new division of labor. Kane was able to take the sensor readings and run them through the pre-set algorithms. Actually, Ajit probably could have trained me to do that. But Kane seemed content, frowning earnestly at his displays.

Ajit took over the actual science. I said to him, when we had a moment alone, "Can you do it?"

"I think so," he said, without either anger or arrogance. "I have the foundation that Kane laid. And we worked out some of the preliminaries together."

"We have only one more jump left."

"I know, Tirzah."

"With the risk of radiation killing us all— "

"Not yet. Give me a little more time."

I rested a moment against his shoulder. "All right. A little more time."

He put his arm around me, not in passion but in comradeship. None of us, we both knew, had all that much time left.

11. SHIP

Kane was only temporarily defeated by the contamination of the probe data. Within half a day, he had aborted his shadow-matter theory, archived his work on it, and gone back to his original theories about the mysteriously massive young stars near the hole. He used the probe's new data, which were all logical amplifications of the prelim readings. "I've got some ideas," he told me. "We'll see."

He wasn't as cheerful as usual, let alone as manically exuberant as during the shadow-matter "discovery," but he was working steadily. A mountain, Kane. It would take a lot to actually erode him, certainly more than a failed theory. That rocky insensitivity had its strengths.

Ajit, on the other hand, was not really working. I couldn't follow the displays on his terminal, but I could read the body language. He was restless, inattentive. But what worried me was something else, his attitude toward Kane.

All Ajit's anger was gone.

I watched carefully, while seemingly bent over ship's log or embroidery. Anger is the least subtle of the body's signals. Even when a person is successfully concealing most of it, the signs are there if you know where to look: the tight neck muscles, the turned-away posture, the tinge in the voice. Ajit displayed none of this. Instead, when he faced Kane, as he did during the lunch I insisted we all eat together at the wardroom table, I saw something else. A sly superiority, a secret triumph.

I could be wrong, I thought. I have been wrong before. By now I disliked Ajit so much that I didn't trust my own intuitions.

"Ajit," I said as we finished the simple meal I'd put together, "will you please—"

Ship's alarms went off with a deafening clang. *Breach, breach, breach.*

I whirled toward ship's display, which automatically illuminated. The breach was in the starboard hold, and it was full penetration by a mass of about a hundred grams. Within a minute, the nanos had put on a temporary patch. The alarm stopped and the computer began hectoring me.

"Breach sealed with temporary nano patch. Seal must be reinforced within two hours with permanent hull patch, type 6-A. For location of breach and patch supply, consult ship's log. If unavailability of—" I shut it off.

"Could be worse," Kane said.

"Well, of course it could be worse," I snapped, and immediately regretted it. I was not allowed to snap. That I had done so was an indication of how much the whole situation on the *Kepler* was affecting me. That wasn't allowed, either; it was unprofessional.

Kane wasn't offended. "Could have hit the engines or the living pod instead of just a hold. Actually, I'm surprised it hasn't happened before. There's a lot of drifting debris in this area."

Ajit said, "Are you going into the hold, Tirzah?"

Of course I was going into the hold. But this time I didn't snap; I smiled at him and said, "Yes, I'm going to suit up now."

"I'm coming, too," Kane said.

I blinked. I'd been about to ask if Ajit wanted to go with me. It would be a good way to observe him away from Kane, maybe ask some discreet questions. I said to Kane, "Don't you have to work?"

"The work isn't going anywhere. And I want to retrieve the particle. It didn't exit the ship, and at a hundred grams, there's going to be some of it left after the breach."

Ajit had stiffened at being preempted, yet again, by Kane. Ajit would have wanted to retrieve the particle, too; there is nothing more interesting to space scientists than dead rocks. Essentially, I'd often thought, Sag A* was no more than a very hot, very large dead rock. I knew better than to say this aloud.

I could have ordered Ajit to accompany me, and ordered Kane to stay behind. But that, I sensed, would only make things worse. Ajit, in his present mood of deadly sensitivity, would not take well to orders from anyone, even me. I wasn't going to give him the chance to retreat more into whatever nasty state of mind he currently inhabited.

"Well, then, let's go," I said ungraciously to Kane, who only grinned at me and went to get our suits.

The holds, three of them for redundancy safety, are full of supplies of all types. Every few days I combine a thorough ship inspection with lugging enough food forward to sustain us. We aren't uploads; we need bodily nurturing as well as the kind I was supposed to be providing.

All three holds can be pressurized if necessary, but usually they aren't. Air generation and refreshment doesn't cost much power, but it costs some. Kane and I went into the starboard hold in heated s-suits and helmets.

"I'm going to look around," Kane said. He'd brought a handheld, and I saw him calculating the probable trajectory of the particle from the ship's data and the angle of the breach, as far as he could deduce it. Then he disappeared behind a pallet of crates marked SOYSYNTH.

The breach was larger than I'd expected; that hundred-gram particle had hit at a bad angle. But the nanos had done their usual fine job, and the permanent patch went on without trouble. I began the careful inspection of the rest of the hull, using my handheld instruments.

Kane cursed volubly.

"Kane? What is it?"

"Nothing. Bumped into boxes."

"Well, don't. The last thing I want is you messing up my hold." For a physically fit man, Kane is clumsy in motion. I would bet my ship that he can't dance, and bet my life that he never tries.

"I can't see anything. Can't you brighten the light?"

I did, and he bumped around some more. Whenever he brushed something, he cursed. I did an inspection even more carefully than usual, but found nothing alarming. We met each other back by the hold door.

"It's not here," Kane said. "The particle. It's not here."

"You mean you didn't find it."

"No, I mean it's not here. Don't you think I could find a still hot particle in a hold otherwise filled only with large immobile crates?"

I keyed in the door code. "So it evaporated on impact. Ice and ions and dust."

"To penetrate a Schaad hull? No." He reconsidered. "Well, maybe. What did you find?"

"Not much. Pitting and scarring on the outside, nothing unexpected. But no structural stress to worry about."

"The debris here is undoubtedly orbiting the core, but we're so far out it's not moving all that fast. Still, we should had some warning. But I'm more worried about the probe—when is the third minicap due?"

Kane knew as well as I did when the third minicap was due. His asking was the first sign he was as tense as the rest of us.

"Three more days," I said. "Be patient."

"I'm not patient."

"As if that's new data."

"I'm also afraid the probe will be hit by rapidly orbiting debris, and that will be that. Did you know that the stars close in to Sag A* orbit at several thousand clicks per second?"

I knew. He'd told me often enough. The probe was always a speculative proposition, and before now, Kane had been jubilant that we'd gotten any data at all from it.

I'd never heard Kane admit to being "afraid" of anything. Even allowing for the casualness of the phrase.

I wanted to distract him, and, if Kane was really in a resigned and reflective mood, it also seemed a good time to do my job. "Kane, about Ajit—"

"I don't want to talk about that sniveling slacker," Kane said, with neither interest not rancor. "I picked badly for an assistant, that's all."

It hadn't actually been his "pick"; his input had been one of many. I didn't say this. Kane looked around the hold one more time. "I guess you're right. The particle sublimed. Ah, well."

I put the glove of my hand on the arm of his suit—not exactly an intimate caress, but the best I could do in this circumstance. "Kane, how is the young-star mystery going?"

"Not very well. But that's science." The hold door stood open and he lumbered out.

I gave one last look around the hold before turning off the light, but there was nothing more to see.

The mended statue of Shiva was back on the wardroom table, smack in the center, when Kane and I returned from the hold. I don't think Kane, heading straight for his terminal, even noticed. I smiled at Ajit, although I wasn't sure why he had brought the statue back. He'd told me he never wanted to see it again.

"Tirzah, would you perhaps like to play *go?*"

I couldn't conceal my surprise. "*Go?*"

"Yes. Will you play with me?" Accompanied by his most winning smile.

"All right."

He brought out the board and, bizarrely, set it up balanced on his knees. When he saw my face, he said, "We'll play here. I don't want to disturb the Cosmic Dancer."

"All right." I wasn't sure what to think. I drew my chair close to his, facing him, and bent over the board.

We both knew that Ajit was a better player than I. That's why both of us played: he to win, me to lose. I would learn more from the losing position. Very competitive people—and I thought now that I had never known one as competitive as Ajit—relax only when not threatened.

So I made myself nonthreatening in every way I knew, and Ajit and I talked and laughed, and Kane worked doggedly on his theories that weren't going anywhere. The statue of the dancing god leered at me from the table, and I knew with every passing moment how completely I was failing this already failing mission.

12. PROBE

Kane was gentler since the radiation corruption. Who can say how these things happen? Personality, too, is encoded in the human brain, whether flesh or analogue. He was still Kane, but we saw only his gentler, sweeter side. Previously that part of him had been dominated by his combative intellect, which had been a force of nature all its own, like a high wind. Now the intellect had failed, the wind calmed. The landscape beneath lay serene.

"Here, Ajit," Kane said. "These are the equations you wanted run." He sent them to Ajit's terminal, stood, and stretched. The stretch put him slightly off balance, something damaged in the upload that Ajit and I hadn't been able to fix, or find. A brain is such a complex thing. Kane tottered, and Ajit rose swiftly to catch him.

"Careful, Kane. Here, sit down."

Ajit eased Kane into a chair at the wardroom table. I put down my work. Kane said, "Tirzah, I feel funny."

"Funny how?" Alarm ran through me.

"I don't know. Can we play *go*?"

I had taught him the ancient strategy game, and he enjoyed it. He wasn't very good, not nearly as good as I was, but he liked it and didn't seem to mind losing. I got out the board. Ajit, who was a master at *go*, went back to Kane's shadow-matter theory. He was making good progress, I knew, although he said frankly that all the basic ideas were Kane's.

Halfway through our second game of *go*, the entire wardroom disappeared.

A moment of blind panic seized me. I was adrift in the void, nothing to see or feel or hold onto, a vertigo so terrible it blocked any rational thought. It was the equivalent of a long anguished scream, originating in the most primitive part of my now blind brain: *lost, lost, lost, and alone* . . .

The automatic maintenance program kicked in and the wardroom reappeared. Kane gripped the table edge and stared at me, white-faced. I went to him, wrapped my arms around him reassuringly, and gazed at Ajit. Kane clung to me. A part of my mind noted that some aspects of the wardroom were wrong: the galley door was too low to walk through upright, and one chair had disappeared, along with the *go* board. Maintenance code too damaged to restore.

Ajit said softly, "We have to decide, Tirzah. We could take a final radiation hit at any time."

"I know."

I took my arms away from Kane. "Are you all right?"

He smiled. "Yes. Just for a minute I was . . ." He seemed to lose his thought.

Ajit brought his terminal chair to the table, to replace the vanished one. He sat leaning forward, looking from me to Kane and back. "This is a decision all three of us have to make. We have one minicap left to send back to the *Kepler*, and one more jump for ourselves. At any time we could lose . . . everything. You all know that. What do you think we should do? Kane? Tirzah?"

All my life I'd heard that even very flawed people can rise to leadership under the right circumstances. I'd never believed it, not of someone with Ajit's basic personality structure: competitive, paranoid, angry at such a deep level he didn't even know it. I'd been wrong. I believed now.

Kane said, "I feel funny, and that probably means I've taken another minor hit and the program isn't there to repair it. I think . . . I think . . ."

"Kane?" I took his hand.

He had trouble getting words out. "I think we better send the minicap now."

"I agree," Ajit said. "But that means we send it without the data from our next jump, to just outside the event horizon of Sag A*. So the *Kepler* won't get those readings. They'll get the work on shadow matter, but most of the best things on that already went in the second minicap. Still, it's better than nothing, and I'm afraid if we wait to send until after the jump, nothing is what the *Kepler* will get. It will be too late."

Both men looked at me. As captain, the jump decision was mine. I nodded. "I agree, too. Send off the minicap with whatever you've got, and then we'll jump. But not to the event horizon."

"Why not?" Kane burst out, sounding more like himself than at any time since the accident.

"Because there's no point. We can't send any more data back, so the event horizon readings die with us. And we can survive longer if I jump us completely away from the core. Several hundred light-years out, where the radiation is minimal."

Together, as if rehearsed, they both said, "No."

"*No?*"

"No," Ajit said, with utter calm, utter persuasiveness. "We're not going to go out like that, Tirzah."

"But we don't have to go out at all! Not for decades! Maybe centuries! Not until the probe's life-maintenance power is used up—" Or until the probe is hit by space debris. Or until radiation takes us out. Nowhere in space is really safe.

Kane said, "And what would we do for centuries? I'd go mad. I want to work."

"Me, too," Ajit said. "I want to take the readings by the event horizon and make of them what I can, while I can. Even though the *Kepler* will never see them."

They were scientists.

And I? Could even I, station bred, have lived for centuries in this tiny ship, without a goal beyond survival, trapped with these two men? An Ajit compassionate and calm, now that he was on top. A damaged Kane, gentle and intellectually gutted. And a Tirzah, captaining a pointless expedition with nowhere to go and nothing to do.

I would have ended up hating all three of us.

Ajit took my left hand. My right one still held Kane's, so we made a broken circle in the radiation-damaged wardroom.

"All right," I said. "We'll send off the minicap and then jump to the event horizon."

"Yes," Kane said.

Ajit said, "I'm going to go back to work. Tirzah, if you and Kane want to go up to the observation deck, or anywhere, I'll prepare and launch the minicap." Carefully he turned his back and sat at his terminal.

I led Kane to my bunk. This was a first; I always went to the scientists' bunks. My own, as captain, had features for my eyes only. But now it didn't matter.

We made love, and afterward, holding his superb, aging body in my arms, I whispered against his cheek, "I love you, Kane."

"I love you, too," he said simply, and I had no way of knowing if he meant it, or if it was an automatic response dredged up from some half-remembered ritual from another time. It didn't matter. There are a lot more types of love in the universe than I once suspected.

We were silent a long time, and then Kane said, "I'm trying to remember *pi*. I know 3.1, but I can't remember after that."

I said, through the tightness in my throat, "3.141. That's all I remember."

"Three point one four one," Kane said dutifully. I left him repeating it over and over, when I went to jump the probe to the event horizon of Sag A*.

13. SHIP

The second breach of the hull was more serious than the first.

The third minicap had not arrived from the probe. "The analogues are probably all dead," Kane said dully. "They were supposed to jump to one-twenty-fifth of a light-year from the event horizon. Our calculations were always problematic for where exactly that *is*. It's possible they landed inside, and the probe will just spiral around Sag A* forever. Or they got hit with major radiation and fried."

"It's possible," I said. "How is the massive-young-star problem coming?"

"It's not. Mathematical dead end."

He looked terrible, drawn and, again, unwashed. I was more impatient with the latter than I should be. But how hard is it, as a courtesy to your shipmates if nothing else, to get your body into the shower? How long does it take? Kane had stopped exercising, as well.

"Kane," I began, as quietly but firmly as I could manage, "will you—"

The alarms went off, clanging again at 115 decibels. *Breach, breach, breach . . .*

I scanned the displays. "Oh, God—"

"Breach sealed with temporary nano patch," the computer said. "Seal must be reinforced within one half hour with permanent hull patch, type 1-B, supplemented with equipment repair, if possible. For location of breach and patch supply, consult—" I turned it off.

The intruder had hit the backup engine. It was a much larger particle than the first one, although since it had hit us and then gone on its merry way, rather than penetrating the ship, there was no way to recover it for examination. But the outside mass detectors registered a particle of at least two kilos, and it had probably been moving much faster than the first one. If it had hit us directly, we would all be dead. Instead it had given the ship a glancing blow, damaging the backup engine.

"I'll come with you again," Kane said.

"There won't be any particle to collect this time." Or not collect.

"I know. But I'm not getting anywhere here."

Kane and I, s-suited, went into the backup engine compartment. As soon as I saw it, I knew there was nothing I could do. There is damage you can repair, and there is damage you cannot. The back end of the compartment had been sheared off, and part of the engine with it. No wonder the computer had recommended a 1-B patch, which is essentially the equivalent of "Throw a tarp over it and forget it."

While I patched, Kane poked around the edges of the breach, then at the useless engine. He left before I did, and I found him studying ship's display of the hit on my wardroom screen. He wasn't trying to do anything with ship's log, which was not his place and he knew it, but he stood in front of the data, moving his hand when he wanted another screen, frowning horribly.

"What is it, Kane?" I said. I didn't really want to know; the patch had taken hours and I was exhausted. I didn't see Ajit. Sleeping, or up on the observation deck, or, less likely, in the gym.

"Nothing. Whatever that hit was made of, it wasn't radiating. So it wasn't going very fast, or the external sensors would have picked up at least ionization. Either the mass was cold, or the sensors aren't functioning properly."

"I'll run the diagnostics," I said wearily. "Anything else?"

"Yes. I want to move the ship."

I stared at him, my suit half peeled from my body, my helmet defiantly set on the table, pushing the statue of Shiva to one side. *"Move the ship?"*

Ajit appeared in the doorway from his bunk.

"Yes," Kane said. "Move the ship."

"But these are the coordinates the minicap will return to!"

"It's not coming," Kane said. "Don't you listen to anything I say, Tirzah? The uploads didn't make it. The third minicap is days late; if it were coming, it would be here. The probe is gone, the uploads are gone, and we've got all the data we're going to get from them. If we want more, we're going to have to go after it ourselves."

"Go after it?" I repeated, stupidly. "How?"

"I already told you! Move the ship closer into the core so we can take the readings the probe should have taken. Some of them, anyway."

Ajit said, "Moving the ship is completely Tirzah's decision."

His championship of me when I needed no champion, and especially not in that pointlessly assertive voice, angered me more than Kane's suggestion. "Thank you, Ajit, I can handle this!"

Mistake, mistake.

Kane, undeterred, plowed on. "I don't mean we'd go near the event horizon, of course, or even to the probe's first position near the star cluster. But we could move much closer in. Maybe ten light-years from the core, positioned between the northern and western arms of Sag A West."

Ajit said, "Which would put us right in the circumnuclear disk! Where the radiation is much worse than here!"

Kane turned on him, acknowledging Ajit's presence for the first time in days, with an outpouring of all Kane's accumulated frustration and disappointment. "We've been hit twice with particles that damaged the ship. Clearly we're in the path of some equivalent of an asteroid belt orbiting the core at this immense distance. It can't be any less safe in the circumnuclear disk, which, I might remind you, is only shocked molecular gases, with its major radiation profile unknown. Any first-year astronomy student should know that. Or is it just that you're a coward?"

Ajit's skin mottled, then paled. His features did not change expression at all. But I felt the heat coming from him, the primal rage, greater for being contained. He went into his bunk and closed the door.

"Kane!" I said furiously, too exhausted and frustrated and disappointed in myself to watch my tone. "You can't—"

"I can't stand any more of this," Kane said. He slammed down the corridor to the gym, and I heard the exercise bike whirr in rage.

I went to my own bunk, locked the door, and squeezed my eyes shut, fighting for control. But even behind my closed eyelids I saw our furious shadows.

After a few hours I called them both together in the wardroom. When Kane refused, I ordered him. I lifted Ajit's statue of Shiva off the table and handed it to him, making its location his problem, as long as it wasn't on the table. Wordlessly he carried it into his bunk and then returned.

"This can't go on," I said calmly. "We all know that. We're in this small space together to accomplish something important, and our mission overrides all our personal feelings. You are both rational men, scientists, or you wouldn't be here."

"Don't patronize us with flattery," Ajit said.

"I'm sorry. I didn't intend to do that. It's true you're both scientists, and it's true you've both been certified rational enough for space travel."

They couldn't argue with that. I didn't mention how often certification boards had misjudged, or been bribed, or just been too dazzled by well-earned reputations to look below the work to the worker. If Kane or Ajit knew all that, they kept it to themselves.

"I blame myself for any difficulties we've had here," I said, in the best Nurturer fashion. Although it was also true. "It's my job to keep a ship running in productive harmony, and this one, I think we can all agree, is not."

No dissension. I saw that both of them dreaded some long, drawn-out discussion on group dynamics, never a topic that goes down well with astrophysicists. Kane said abruptly, "I still want to move the ship."

I had prepared myself for this. "No, Kane. We're not jumping closer in."

He caught at my loophole. "Then can we jump to another location at the same distance from the core? Maybe measurements from another base point would help."

"We're not jumping anywhere until I'm sure the third minicap isn't coming."

"How long will that be?" I could see the formidable intelligence under the childish tantrums already racing ahead, planning measurements, weighing options.

"We'll give it another three days."

"All right." Suddenly he smiled, his first in days. "Thanks, Tirzah."

I turned to Ajit. "Ajit, what can we do for your work? What do you need?"

"I ask for nothing," he said, with such a strange, intense, unreadable expression that for a moment I felt irrational fear. Then he stood and went into his bunk. I heard the door lock.

I had failed again.

No alarm went off in the middle of the night. There was nothing overt to wake me. But I woke anyway, and I heard someone moving quietly around the wardroom. The muscles of my right arm tensed to open my bunk, and I forced them to still.

Something wasn't right. Intuition, that mysterious shadow of rational thought, told me to lie motionless. To not open my bunk, to not even reach out and access the ship's data on my bunk screen. To not move at all.

Why?

I didn't know.

The smell of coffee wafted from the wardroom. So one of the men couldn't sleep, made some coffee, turned on his terminal. So what?

Don't move, said that pre-reasoning part of my mind, from the shadows.

The coffee smell grew stronger. A chair scraped. Ordinary, mundane sounds.

Don't move.

I didn't have to move. This afternoon I had omitted to mention to Kane and Ajit those times that certification boards had misjudged, or been bribed, or just been too dazzled by well-earned reputations to look below the work to the worker. Those times in which the cramped conditions of space, coupled with swollen egos and frenzied work, had led to disaster for a mission Nurturer. But we had learned. My bunk had equipment the scientists did not know about.

Carefully I slid my gaze to a spot directly above me on the bunk ceiling. Only my eyes moved. I pattern-blinked: two quick, three beats closed, two quick, a long steady stare. The screen brightened.

This was duplicate ship data. Not a backup; it was entirely separate, made simultaneously from the same sensors as the main log but routed into separate, freestanding storage that could not be reached from the main computer. Scientists are all sophisticated users. There is no way to keep data from any who wish to alter it except by discreet, unknown, untraceable storage. I pattern-blinked, not moving so much as a finger or a toe in the bed, to activate various screens of ship data.

It was easy to find.

Yesterday, at 1850 hours, the minicap bay had opened and received a minicap. Signal had failed to transmit to the main computer. Today at 300 hours, which was fifteen minutes ago, the minicap bay had been opened manually and the payload removed. Again signal had failed to the main computer.

The infrared signature in the wardroom, seated at his terminal, was Ajit.

It was possible the signal failures were coincidental, and Ajit was even now transferring data from the third minicap into the computer, enjoying a cup of hot coffee while he did so, gloating in getting a perfectly legitimate jump on Kane. But I didn't think so.

What did I think?

I didn't have to think; I just knew. I could see it unfolding, clear as a holovid. All of it. Ajit had stolen the second minicap, too. That had been the morning after Kane and I had slept so soundly, the morning after Ajit had given us wine to celebrate Kane's shadow-matter theory. What had been in that wine? We'd slept soundly, and Ajit told us that the minicap had come before we were awake. Ajit said he'd already put it into the computer. It carried Kane's upload's apology that the prelim data, the data from which Kane had constructed his shadow-matter thesis, was wrong, contaminated by a radiation strike.

Ajit had fabricated that apology and that replacement data. The actual second minicap would justify Kane's work, not undo it. Ajit was saving all three minicaps to use for himself, to claim the shadow matter discovery for his own. He'd used the second minicap to discredit the first; he would claim the third had never arrived, had never been sent from the dying probe.

The real Kane, my Kane, hadn't found the particle from the first ship's breach because it had, indeed, been made of shadow matter. That, and not slow speed, had been why the particle showed no radiation. The particle had exerted gravity on our world, but nothing else. The second breach, too, had been shadow matter. I knew that as surely as if Kane had shown me the pages of equations to prove it.

I knew something else, too. If I went into the shower and searched my body very carefully, every inch of it, I would find in some inconspicuous place the small, regular hole into which a subdermal tracker had gone the night of the drugged wine. So would Kane. Trackers would apprise Ajit of every move we made, not only large-muscle moves like a step or a hug, but small ones like accessing my bunk display of ship's data. That was what my intuition had been warning me of. Ajit did not want to be discovered during his minicap thefts.

I had the same trackers in my own repertoire. Only I had not thought this mission deteriorated enough to need them. I had not wanted to think that. I'd been wrong.

But how would Ajit make use of Kane's stolen work with Kane there to claim it for himself?

I already knew the answer, of course. I had known it from the moment I pattern-blinked at the ceiling, which was the moment I finally admitted to myself how monstrous this mission had turned.

I pushed open the bunk door and called cheerfully, "Hello? Do I smell coffee? Who's out there?"

"I am," Ajit said genially. "I cannot sleep. Come have some coffee."

"Coming, Ajit."

I put on my robe, tied it at my waist, and slipped the gun from its secret mattress compartment into my palm.

14. PROBE

The probe jumped successfully. We survived.

This close to the core, the view wasn't as spectacular as it was farther out. Sag A*, which captured us in orbit immediately, now appeared as a fuzzy region dominating starboard. The fuzziness, Ajit said, was a combination of Hawking radiation and superheated gases being swallowed by the black hole. To port, the intense blue cluster of IRS16 was muffled by the clouds of ionized plasma around the probe. We experienced some tidal forces, but the probe was so small that the gravitational tides didn't yet cause much damage.

Ajit has found a way to successfully apply Kane's shadow-matter theory to the paths of the infalling gases, as well as to the orbits of the young stars near Sag A*. He says there may well be a really lot of shadow matter near the core, and maybe even farther out. It may even provide enough mass to "balance" the universe, keeping it from either flying apart forever or collapsing in on itself. Shadow matter, left over from the very beginning of creation, may preserve creation.

Kane nods happily as Ajit explains. Kane holds my hand. I stroke his palm gently with my thumb, making circles like tiny orbits.

15. SHIP

Ajit sat, fully dressed and with steaming coffee at his side, in front of his terminal. I didn't give him time to get the best of me. I walked into the wardroom and fired.

The sedative dart dropped him almost instantly. It was effective, for his body weight, for an hour. Kane didn't hear the thud as Ajit fell off his chair and onto the deck; Kane's bunk door stayed closed. I went into Ajit's bunk and searched every cubic meter of it, overriding the lock on his personal storage space. Most of that was taken up with the bronze statue of Shiva. The minicaps were not there, nor anywhere else in his bunk.

I tried the galley next, and came up empty.

Same for the shower, the gym, the supply closets.

Ajit could have hidden the cubes in the engine compartments or the fuel bays or any of a dozen other ship's compartments, but they weren't pressurized and he would have had to either suit up or pressurize them. Either one would have shown up in my private ship data, and they hadn't. Ajit probably hadn't wanted to take the risk of too much covert motion around the ship. He'd only had enough drugs to put Kane and me out once. Otherwise, he wouldn't have risked subdermal trackers.

I guessed he'd hidden the cubes in the observatory.

Looking there involved digging. By the time I'd finished, the exotics lay yanked up in dying heaps around the room. The stones of the fountain had been flung about. I was filthy and sweating, my robe smeared with soil. But I'd found them, the two crystal cubes from the second and third minicaps, removed from their heavy shielding. Their smooth surfaces shed the dirt easily.

Forty-five minutes had passed.

I went downstairs to wake Kane. The expedition would have to jump immediately; there is no room on a three-man ship to confine a prisoner for long. Even if I could protect Kane and me from Ajit, I didn't think I could protect Ajit from Kane. These minicaps held the validation of Kane's shadow-matter work, and in another man, joy over that would have eclipsed the theft. I didn't think it would be that way with Kane.

Ajit still lay where I'd dropped him. The tranquilizer is reliable. I shot Ajit with a second dose and went into Kane's bunk. He wasn't there.

I stood too still for too long, then frantically scrambled into my s-suit.

I had already searched everywhere in the pressurized sections of the ship. Oh, let him be taking a second, fruitless look at the starboard hold, hoping to find some trace of the first particle that had hit us! Let him be in the damaged backup engine compartment, afire with some stupid, brilliant idea to save the engine! Let him be—

"Kane! *Kane!*"

He lay in the starboard hold, on his side, his suit breached. He lay below a jagged piece of plastic from a half-open supply box. Ajit had made it look as if Kane had tried to open a box marked SENSOR REPLACEMENTS, had torn his suit, and the suit sealer nanos had failed. It was an altogether clumsy attempt, but one that, in the absence of any other evidence and a heretofore spotless reputation, would probably have worked.

The thing inside the suit was not Kane. Not anymore.

I knelt beside him. I put my arms around him and begged, cried, pleaded with him to come back. I pounded my gloves on the deck until I, too, risked suit breach. I think, in that abandoned and monstrous moment, I would not have cared.

Then I went into the wardroom, exchanged my tranquilizer gun for a knife, and slit Ajit's throat. I only regretted that he wasn't awake when I did it, and I only regretted that much, much later.

I prepared the ship for the long jump back to the Orion Arm. After the jump would come the acceleration-deceleration to Skillian, the closest settled world, which will take about a month standard. Space physics which I don't understand make this necessary; a ship cannot jump too close to a large body of matter like a planet. Shadow matter, apparently, does not count.

Both Ajit and Kane's bodies rest in the cold of the nonpressurized port hold. Kane's initial work on shadow matter rests in my bunk. Every night I fondle the two cubes which will make him famous—more famous—on the settled Worlds. Every day I look at the data, the equations, the rest of his work on his terminal. I don't understand it, but sometimes I think I can see Kane, his essential self, in these intelligent symbols, these unlockings of the secrets of cosmic energy.

It was our shadow selves, not our essential ones, that destroyed my mission, the shadows in the core of each human being. Ajit's ambition and rivalry. Kane's stunted vision of other people and their limits. My pride, which led me to think I was in control of murderous rage long after it had reached a point of no return. In all of us.

I left one thing behind at the center of the galaxy. Just before the *Kepler* jumped, I jettisoned Ajit's statue of a Shiva dancing, in the direction of Sag A*. I don't know for sure, but I imagine it will travel toward the black hole at the galaxy's core, be caught eventually by its gravity, and spiral in, to someday disappear over the event horizon into some unimaginable singularity. That's what I want to happen to the statue. I hate it.

As to what will happen to me, I don't have the energy to hate it. I'll tell the authorities everything. My license as a Nurturer will surely be revoked, but I won't stand trial for the murder of Ajit. A captain is supreme law on her ship. I had the legal authority to kill Ajit. However, it's unlikely that any scientific expedition will hire me as captain ever again. My useful life is over, and any piece of it left is no more than one of the ashy, burned-out stars Kane says orbit Sag A*, uselessly circling the core until its final death, giving no light.

A shadow.

16. PROBE

We remain near the galactic core, Kane and Ajit and I. The event horizon of Sag A* is about one-fiftieth of a light-year below us. As we spiral closer, our speed is increasing dramatically. The point of no return is one-twentieth of a light-year. The lethal radiation, oddly enough, is less here than when we were drifting near the shadow matter on the other side of Sag A West, but it is enough.

I think at least part of my brain has been affected, along with the repair program to fix it. It's hard to be sure, but I can't seem to remember much before we came aboard the probe, or details of why we're here. Sometimes I almost remember, but then it slips away. I know that Kane and Ajit and I are shadows of something, but I don't remember what.

Ajit and Kane work on their science. I have forgotten what it's about, but I like to sit and watch them together. Ajit works on ideas and Kane assists in minor ways, as once Kane worked on ideas and Ajit assisted in minor ways. We all know the science will go down into Sag A* with us. The scientists do it anyway, for no other gain than pure love of the work. This is, in fact, the purest science in the universe.

Our mission is a success. Ajit and Kane have answers. I have kept them working harmoniously, have satisfied all their needs while they did it, and have captained my ship safely into the very heart of the galaxy. I am content.

Not that there aren't difficulties, of course. It's disconcerting to go up on the observation deck. Most of the exotics remain, blooming in wild profusion, but a good chunk of the hull has disappeared. The effect is that anything up there—flowers, bench, people—is drifting through naked space, held together only by the gravity we exert on each other. I don't understand how we can breathe up there; surely the air is gone. There are a lot of things I don't understand now, but I accept them.

The wardroom is mostly intact, except that you have to stoop to go through the door to the galley, which is only about two feet tall, and Ajit's bunk has disappeared. We manage fine with two bunks, since I sleep every night with Ajit or Kane. The terminals are intact. One of them won't display anymore, though. Ajit has used it to hold a holo he programmed on a functioning part of the computer and superimposed over where the defunct display stood. The holo is a rendition of a image he showed me once before, of an Indian god, Shiva.

Shiva is dancing. He dances, four-armed and graceful, in a circle decorated with flames. Everything about him is dynamic, waving arms and kicking uplifted leg and mobile expression. Even the flames in the circle dance. Only Shiva's face is calm, detached, serene. Kane, especially, will watch the holo for hours.

The god, Ajit tells us, represents the flow of cosmic energy in the universe. Shiva creates, destroys, creates again. All matter and all energy participate in this rhythmic dance, patterns made and unmade throughout all of time.

Shadow matter—that's what Kane and Ajit are working on. I remember now. Something decoupled from the rest of the universe right after its creation. But shadow matter, too, is part of the dance. It exerted gravitational pull on our ship. We cannot see it, but it is there, changing the orbits of stars, the trajectories of lives, in the great shadow play of Shiva's dancing.

I don't think Kane, Ajit, and I have very much longer. But it doesn't matter, not really. We have each attained what we came for, and since we, too, are part of the cosmic pattern, we cannot really be lost. When the probe goes down into the black hole at the core, if we last that long, it will be as a part of the inevitable, endless, glorious flow of cosmic energy, the divine dance.

I am ready.

the people of sand and slag

PAOLO BACIGALUPI

Here's a visit to a grim future about which the *good* news is, humans have survived. The bad news is, not much *else* has . . .

New writer Paolo Bacigalupi made his first sale in 1998, to *The Magazine of Fantasy & Science Fiction,* took a break from the genre for several years, and has returned to it in the new century, with new sales to *F&SF* and *Asimov's*. He had a story in our Twenty-first Annual Collection. Bacigalupi lives with his family in western Colorado, where he works for an environmental newspaper.

"Hostile movement! Well inside the perimeter! Well inside!"

I stripped off my Immersive Response goggles as adrenaline surged through me. The virtual cityscape I'd been about to raze disappeared, replaced by our monitoring room's many views of SesCo's mining operations. On one screen, the red phosphorescent tracery of an intruder skated across a terrain map, a hot blip like blood spattering its way toward Pit 8.

Jaak was already out of the monitoring room. I ran for my gear.

I caught up with Jaak in the equipment room as he grabbed a TS-101 and slashbangs and dragged his impact exoskeleton over his tattooed body. He draped bandoleers of surgepacks over his massive shoulders and ran for the outer locks. I strapped on my own exoskeleton, pulled my 101 from its rack, checked its charge, and followed.

Lisa was already in the HEV, its turbofans screaming like banshees when the hatch dilated. Sentry centaurs leveled their 101's at me, then relaxed as friend/foe data spilled into their heads-up displays. I bolted across the tarmac, my skin pricking under blasts of icy Montana wind and the jet wash of Hentasa Mark V engines. Overhead, the clouds glowed orange with light from SesCo's mining bots.

"Come on, Chen! Move! Move! Move!"

I dove into the hunter. The ship leaped into the sky. It banked, throwing me against a bulkhead, then the Hentasas cycled wide and the hunter punched forward. The HEV's hatch slid shut. The wind howl muted.

I struggled forward to the flight cocoon and peered over Jaak's and Lisa's shoulders to the landscape beyond.

"Have a good game?" Lisa asked.

I scowled. "I was about to win. I made it to Paris."

We cut through the mists over the catchment lakes, skimming inches above the water, and then we hit the far shore. The hunter lurched as its anti-collision software jerked us away from the roughening terrain. Lisa overrode the computers and forced the ship back down against the soil, driving us so low I could have reached out and dragged my hands through the broken scree as we screamed over it.

Alarms yowled. Jaak shut them off as Lisa pushed the hunter lower. Ahead, a tailings ridge loomed. We ripped up its face and dropped sickeningly into the next valley. The Hentasas shuddered as Lisa forced them to the edge of their design buffer. We hurtled up and over another ridge. Ahead, the ragged cutscape of mined mountains stretched to the horizon. We dipped again into mist and skimmed low over another catchment lake, leaving choppy wake in the thick golden waters.

Jaak studied the hunter's scanners. "I've got it." He grinned. "It's moving, but slow."

"Contact in one minute," Lisa said. "He hasn't launched any countermeasures."

I watched the intruder on the tracking screens as they displayed realtime data fed to us from SesCo's satellites. "It's not even a masked target. We could have dropped a mini on it from base if we'd known he wasn't going to play hide-and-seek."

"Could have finished your game," Lisa said.

"We could still nuke him." Jaak suggested.

I shook my head. "No, let's take a look. Vaporizing him won't leave us anything and Bunbaum will want to know what we used the hunter for."

"Thirty seconds."

"He wouldn't care if someone hadn't taken the hunter on a joyride to Cancun."

Lisa shrugged. "I wanted to swim. It was either that, or rip off your kneecaps."

The hunter lunged over another series of ridges.

Jaak studied his monitor. "Target's moving away. He's still slow. We'll get him."

"Fifteen seconds to drop," Lisa said. She unstrapped and switched the hunter to software. We all ran for the hatch as the HEV yanked itself skyward, its auto pilot desperate to tear away from the screaming hazard of the rocks beneath its belly.

We plunged out the hatch, one, two, three, falling like Icarus. We slammed into the ground at hundreds of kilometers per hour. Our exoskeletons shattered like glass, flinging leaves into the sky. The shards fluttered down around us, black metallic petals absorbing our enemy's radar and heat detection while we rolled to jarred vulnerable stops in muddy scree.

The hunter blew over the ridge, Hentasas shrieking, a blazing target. I dragged myself upright and ran for the ridge, my feet churning through yellow tailings mud and rags of jaundiced snow. Behind me, Jaak was down with smashed arms. The leaves of his exoskeleton marked his roll path, a long trail of black shimmering metal. Lisa lay a hundred yards away, her femur rammed through her thigh like a bright white exclamation mark.

I reached the top of the ridge and stared down into the valley.

Nothing.

I dialed up the magnification of my helmet. The monotonous slopes of more tailings rubble spread out below me. Boulders, some as large as our HEV, some cracked and shattered by high explosives, shared the slopes with the unstable yellow shale and fine grit of waste materials from SesCo's operations.

Jaak slipped up beside me, followed a moment later by Lisa, her flight suit's leg torn and bloodied. She wiped yellow mud off her face and ate it as she studied the valley below. "Anything?"

I shook my head. "Nothing yet. You okay?"

"Clean break."

Jaak pointed. "There!"

Down in the valley, something was running, flushed by the hunter. It slipped along a shallow creek, viscous with tailings acid. The ship herded it toward us. Nothing. No missile fire. No slag. Just the running creature. A mass of tangled hair. Quadrupedal. Splattered with mud.

"Some kind of bio-job?" I wondered.

"It doesn't have any hands," Lisa murmured.

"No equipment either."

Jaak muttered. "What kind of sick bastard makes a bio-job without hands?"

I searched the nearby ridgelines. "Decoy, maybe?"

Jaak checked his scanner data, piped in from the hunter's more aggressive instruments. "I don't think so. Can we put the hunter up higher? I want to look around."

At Lisa's command, the hunter rose, allowing its sensors a fuller reach. The howl of its turbofans became muted as it gained altitude.

Jaak waited as more data spat into his heads-up display. "Nope, nothing. And no new alerts from any of the perimeter stations, either. We're alone."

Lisa shook her head. "We should have just dropped a mini on it from base."

Down in the valley, the bio-job's headlong run slowed to a trot. It seemed unaware of us. Closer now, we could make out its shape: A shaggy quadruped with a tail. Dreadlocked hair dangled from its shanks like ornaments, tagged with tailings mud clods. It was stained around its legs from the acids of the catchment ponds, as though it had forded streams of urine.

"That's one ugly bio-job," I said.

Lisa shouldered her 101. "Bio-melt when I'm done with it."

"Wait!" Jaak said. "Don't slag it!"

Lisa glanced over at him, irritated. "What now?"

"That's not a bio-job at all." Jaak whispered. "That's a dog."

He stood suddenly and jumped over the hillside, running headlong down the scree toward the animal.

"Wait!" Lisa called, but Jaak was already fully exposed and blurring to his top speed.

The animal took one look at Jaak, whooping and hollering as he came roaring down the slope, then turned and ran. It was no match for Jaak. Half a minute later he overtook the animal.

Lisa and I exchanged glances. "Well," she said, "it's awfully slow if it's a bio-job. I've seen centaurs walk faster."

By the time we caught up with Jaak and the animal, Jaak had it cornered in a dull gully. The animal stood in the center of a trickling ditch of sludgy water, shaking and growling and baring its teeth at us as we surrounded it. It tried to break around us, but Jaak kept it corralled easily.

Up close, the animal seemed even more pathetic than from a distance, a good thirty kilos of snarling mange. Its paws were slashed and bloody and patches of fur were torn away, revealing festering chemical burns underneath.

"I'll be damned," I breathed, staring at the animal. "It really looks like a dog."

Jaak grinned. "It's like finding a goddamn dinosaur."

"How could it live out here?" Lisa's arm swept the horizon. "There's nothing to live on. It's got to be modified." She studied it closely, then glanced at Jaak. "Are you sure nothing's coming in on the perimeter? This isn't some kind of decoy?"

Jaak shook his head. "Nothing. Not even a peep."

I leaned in toward the creature. It bared its teeth in a rictus of hatred. "It's pretty beat up. Maybe it's the real thing."

Jaak said, "Oh yeah, it's the real thing all right. I saw a dog in a zoo once. I'm telling you, this is a dog."

Lisa shook her head. "It can't be. It would be dead, if it were a real dog."

Jaak just grinned and shook his head. "No way. Look at it." He reached out to push the hair out of the animal's face so that we could see its muzzle.

The animal lunged and its teeth sank into Jaak's arm. It shook his arm violently, growling as Jaak stared down at the creature latched onto his flesh. It yanked its head back and forth, trying to tear Jaak's arm off. Blood spurted around its muzzle as its teeth found Jaak's arteries.

Jaak laughed. His bleeding stopped. "Damn. Check that out." He lifted his arm until the animal dangled fully out of the stream, dripping. "I got me a pet."

The dog swung from the thick bough of Jaak's arm. It tried to shake his arm once again, but its movements were ineffectual now that it hung off the ground. Even Lisa smiled.

"Must be a bummer to wake up and find out you're at the end of your evolutionary curve."

The dog growled, determined to hang on.

Jaak laughed and drew his monomol knife. "Here you go, doggy." He sliced his arm off, leaving it in the bewildered animal's mouth.

Lisa cocked her head. "You think we could make some kind of money on it?"

Jaak watched as the dog devoured his severed arm. "I read somewhere that they used to eat dogs. I wonder what they taste like."

I checked the time in my heads-up display. We'd already killed an hour on an exercise that wasn't giving any bonuses. "Get your dog, Jaak, and get it on the hunter. We aren't going to eat it before we call Bunbaum."

"He'll probably call it company property," Jaak groused.

"Yeah, that's the way it always goes. But we still have to report. Might as well keep the evidence, since we didn't nuke it."

We ate sand for dinner. Outside the security bunker, the mining robots rumbled back and forth, ripping deeper into the earth, turning it into a mush of tailings and rock acid that they left in exposed ponds when they hit the water table, or piled into thousand-foot mountainscapes of waste soil. It was comforting to hear those machines cruising back and forth all day. Just you and the bots and the profits, and if nothing got bombed while you were on duty, there was always a nice bonus.

After dinner we sat around and sharpened Lisa's skin, implanting blades along her limbs so that she was like a razor from all directions. She'd considered monomol blades, but it was too easy to take a limb off accidentally, and we lost enough body parts as it was without adding to the mayhem. That kind of garbage was for people who didn't have to work: aesthetes from New York City and California.

Lisa had a DermDecora kit for the sharpening. She'd bought it last time we'd gone on vacation and spent extra to get it, instead of getting one of the cheap knock-offs that were cropping up. We worked on cutting her skin down to the bone and setting the blades. A friend of ours in L.A said that he just held DermDecora parties so everyone could do their modifications and help out with the hard-to-reach places.

Lisa had done my glowspine, a sweet tracery of lime landing lights that ran from my tailbone to the base of my skull, so I didn't mind helping her out, but Jaak, who did all of his modification with an old-time scar and tattoo shop in Hawaii, wasn't so pleased. It was a little frustrating because her flesh kept trying to close before we had the blades set, but eventually we got the hang of it, and an hour later, she started looking good.

Once we finished with Lisa's front settings, we sat around and fed her. I had a bowl of tailings mud that I drizzled into her mouth to speed her integration process. When we were weren't feeding her, we watched the dog. Jaak had shoved it into a makeshift cage in one corner of our common room. It lay there like it was dead.

Lisa said, "I ran its DNA. It really is a dog."

"Bunbaum believe you?"

She gave me a dirty look. "What do you think?"

I laughed. At SesCo, tactical defense responders were expected to be fast, flexible, and deadly, but the reality was our SOP was always the same: drop nukes on intruders, slag the leftovers to melt so they couldn't regrow, hit the beaches for vacation. We were independent and trusted as far as tactical decisions went, but there was no way SesCo was going to believe its slag soldiers had found a dog in their tailings mountains.

Lisa nodded. "He wanted to know how the hell a dog could live out here. Then he wanted to know why we didn't catch it sooner. Wanted to know what he pays us for." She pushed her short blond hair off her face and eyed the animal. "I should have slagged it."

"What's he want us to do?"

"It's not in the manual. He's calling back."

I studied the limp animal. "I want to know how it was surviving. Dogs are meat eaters, right?"

"Maybe some of the engineers were giving it meat. Like Jaak did."

Jaak shook his head. "I don't think so. The sucker threw up my arm almost right after he ate it." He wiggled his new stump where it was rapidly regrowing. "I don't think we're compatible for it."

I asked, "But we could eat it, right?"

Lisa laughed and took a spoonful of tailings. "We can eat anything. We're the top of the food chain."

"Weird how it can't eat us."

"You've probably got more mercury and lead running through your blood than any pre-weeviltech animal ever could have had."

"That's bad?"

"Used to be poison."

"Weird."

Jaak said, "I think I might have broken it when I put it in the cage." He studied it seriously. "It's not moving like it was before. And I heard something snap when I stuffed it in."

"So?"

Jaak shrugged. "I don't think it's healing."

The dog did look kind of beat up. It just lay there, its sides going up and down like a bellows. Its eyes were half-open, but didn't seem to be focused on any of us. When Jaak made a sudden movement, it twitched for a second, but it didn't get up. It didn't even growl.

Jaak said, "I never thought an animal could be so fragile."

"You're fragile, too. That's not such a big surprise."

"Yeah, but I only broke a couple bones on it, and now look at it. It just lies there and pants."

Lisa frowned thoughtfully. "It doesn't heal." She climbed awkwardly to her feet and went to peer into the cage. Her voice was excited. "It really is a dog. Just like we used to be. It could take weeks for it to heal. One broken bone, and it's done for."

She reached a razored hand into the cage and sliced a thin wound into its shank. Blood oozed out, and kept oozing. It took minutes for it to begin clotting. The dog lay still and panted, clearly wasted.

She laughed. "It's hard to believe we ever lived long enough to evolve out of that. If you chop off its legs, they won't regrow." She cocked her head, fascinated. "It's as delicate as rock. You break it, and it never comes back together." She reached out to stroke the matted fur of the animal. "It's as easy to kill as the hunter."

The comm buzzed. Jaak went to answer.

Lisa and I stared at the dog, our own little window into prehistory.

Jaak came back into the room. "Bunbaum's flying out a biologist to take a look at it."

"You mean a bioengineer," I corrected him.

"Nope. Biologist. Bunbaum said they study animals."

Lisa sat down. I checked her blades to see if she'd knocked anything loose. "There's a dead-end job."

"I guess they grow them out of DNA. Study what they do. Behavior, shit like that."

"Who hires them?"

Jaak shrugged. "Pau Foundation has three of them on staff. Origin of life guys. That's who's sending out this one. Mushi-something. Didn't get his name."

"Origin of life?"

"Sure, you know, what makes us tick. What makes us alive. Stuff like that."

I poured a handful of tailings mud into Lisa's mouth. She gobbled it gratefully. "Mud makes us tick," I said.

Jaak nodded at the dog. "It doesn't make that dog tick."
We all looked at the dog. "It's hard to tell what makes it tick."

Lin Musharraf was a short guy with black hair and a hooked nose that dominated his face. He had carved his skin with swirling patterns of glow implants, so he stood out as cobalt spirals in the darkness as he jumped down from his chartered HEV.

The centaurs went wild about the unauthorized visitor and corralled him right up against his ship. They were all over him and his DNA kit, sniffing him, running their scanners over his case, pointing their 101's into his glowing face and snarling at him.

I let him sweat for a minute before calling them away. The centaurs backed off, swearing and circling, but didn't slag him. Musharraf looked shaken. I couldn't blame him. They're scary monsters: bigger and faster than a man. Their behavior patches make them vicious, their sentience upgrades give them the intelligence to operate military equipment, and their basic fight/flight response is so impaired that they only know how to attack when they're threatened. I've seen a half-slagged centaur tear a man to pieces barehanded and then join an assault on enemy ridge fortifications, dragging its whole melted carcass forward with just its arms. They're great critters to have at your back when the slag starts flying.

I guided Musharraf out of the scrum. He had a whole pack of memory addendums blinking off the back of his skull: a fat pipe of data retrieval, channeled direct to the brain, and no smash protection. The centaurs could have shut him down with one hard tap to the back of the head. His cortex might have grown back, but he wouldn't have been the same. Looking at those blinking triple fins of intelligence draping down the back of his head, you could tell he was a typical lab rat. All brains, no survival instincts. I wouldn't have stuck mem-adds into my head even for a triple bonus.

"You've got a dog?" Musharraf asked when we were out of reach of the centaurs.

"We think so." I led him down into the bunker, past our weapons racks and weight rooms to the common room where we'd stored the dog. The dog looked up at us as we came in, the most movement it had made since Jaak put it in the cage.

Musharraf stopped short and stared. "Remarkable."

He knelt in front of the animal's cage and unlocked the door. He held out a handful of pellets. The dog dragged itself upright. Musharraf backed away, giving it room, and the dog followed stiff and wary, snuffling after the pellets. It buried its muzzle in his brown hand, snorting and gobbling at the pellets.

Musharraf looked up. "And you found it in your tailings pits?"

"That's right."

"Remarkable."

The dog finished the pellets and snuffled his palm for more. Musharraf laughed and stood. "No more for you. Not right now." He opened his DNA kit, pulled out a sampler needle and stuck the dog. The sampler's chamber filled with blood.

Lisa watched. "You talk to it?"

Musharraf shrugged. "It's a habit."

"But it's not sentient."

"Well, no, but it likes to hear voices." The chamber finished filling. He withdrew the needle, disconnected the collection chamber and fitted it into the kit. The analysis software blinked alive and the blood disappeared into the heart of the kit with a soft vacuum hiss.

"How do you know?"

Musharraf shrugged. "It's a dog. Dogs are that way."

We all frowned. Musharraf started running tests on the blood, humming tunelessly to himself as he worked. His DNA kit peeped and squawked. Lisa watched him run his tests, clearly pissed off that SesCo had sent out a lab rat to retest what she had already done. It was easy to understand her irritation. A centaur could have run those DNA tests.

"I'm astounded that you found a dog in your pits," Musharraf muttered.

Lisa said, "We were going to slag it, but Bunbaum wouldn't let us."

Musharraf eyed her. "How restrained of you."

Lisa shrugged. "Orders."

"Still, I'm sure your thermal surge weapon presented a powerful temptation. How good of you not to slag a starving animal."

Lisa frowned suspiciously. I started to worry that she might take Musharraf apart. She was crazy enough without people talking down to her. The memory addendums on the back of his head were an awfully tempting target: one slap, down goes the lab rat. I wondered if we sank him in a catchment lake if anyone would notice him missing. A biologist, for Christ's sake.

Musharraf turned back to his DNA kit, apparently unaware of his hazard. "Did you know that in the past, people believed that we should have compassion for all things on Earth? Not just for ourselves, but for all living things?"

"So?"

"I would hope you will have compassion for one foolish scientist and not dismember me today."

Lisa laughed. I relaxed. Encouraged, Musharraf said, "It truly is remarkable that you found such a specimen amongst your mining operations. I haven't heard of a living specimen in ten or fifteen years."

"I saw one in a zoo, once," Jaak said.

"Yes, well, a zoo is the only place for them. And laboratories, of course. They still provide useful genetic data." He was studying the results of the tests, nodding to himself as information scrolled across the kit's screen.

Jaak grinned. "Who needs animals if you can eat stone?"

Musharraf began packing up his DNA kit. "Weeviltech. Precisely. We transcended the animal kingdom." He latched his kit closed and nodded to us all. "Well, it's been quite enlightening. Thank you for letting me see your specimen."

"You're not going to take it with you?"

Musharraf paused, surprised. "Oh no. I don't think so."

"It's not a dog, then?"

"Oh no, it's quite certainly a real dog. But what on Earth would I do with it?" He held up a vial of blood. "We have the DNA. A live one is hardly worth keeping around. Very expensive to maintain, you know. Manufacturing a basic organism's food is quite complex. Clean rooms, air filters, special lights. Recreating the web of life isn't easy. Far more simple to release oneself from it completely than to attempt to recreate it." He glanced at the dog. "Unfortunately, our furry friend over there would never survive weeviltech. The worms would eat him as quickly as they eat everything else. No, you would have to manufacture the animal from scratch. And really, what would be the point of that? A bio-job without hands?" He laughed and headed for his HEV.

We all looked at each other. I jogged after the doctor and caught up with him at the hatch to the tarmac. He had paused on the verge of opening it. "Your centaurs know me now?" he asked.

"Yeah, you're fine."

"Good." He dilated the hatch and strode out into the cold.

I trailed after him. "Wait! What are we supposed to do with it?"

"The dog?" The doctor climbed into the HEV and began strapping in. Wind whipped around us, carrying stinging grit from the tailings piles. "Turn it back to your pits. Or you could eat it, I suppose. I understand that it was a real delicacy. There are recipes for cooking animals. They take time, but they can give quite extraordinary results."

Musharraf's pilot started cycling up his turbofans.

"Are you kidding?"

Musharraf shrugged and shouted over the increasing scream of the engines. "You should try it! Just another part of our heritage that's atrophied since weeviltech!"

He yanked down the flight cocoon's door, sealing himself inside. The turbofans cycled higher and the pilot motioned me back from their wash as the HEV slowly lifted into the air.

Lisa and Jaak couldn't agree on what we should do with the dog. We had protocols for working out conflict. As a tribe of killers, we needed them. Normally, consensus worked for us, but every once in a while, we just got tangled up and stuck to our positions, and after that, not much could get done without someone getting slaughtered. Lisa and Jaak dug in, and after a couple days of wrangling, with Lisa threatening to cook the thing in the middle of the night while Jaak wasn't watching, and Jaak threatening to cook her if she did, we finally went with a majority vote. I got to be the tie-breaker.

"I say we eat it," Lisa said.

We were sitting in the monitoring room, watching satellite shots of the tailings mountains and the infrared blobs of the mining bots while they ripped around in the earth. In one corner, the object of our discussion lay in its cage, dragged there by Jaak in an attempt to sway the result. He spun his observation chair, turning his attention away from the theater maps. "I think we should keep it. It's cool. Old-timey, you know? I mean, who the hell do you know who has a real dog?"

"Who the hell wants the hassle?" Lisa responded. "I say we try real meat." She cut a line in her forearm with her razors. She ran her finger along the resulting blood beads and tasted them as the wound sealed.

They both looked at me. I looked at the ceiling. "Are you sure you can't decide this without me?"

Lisa grinned. "Come on, Chen, you decide. It was a group find. Jaak won't pout, will you?"

Jaak gave her a dirty look.

I looked at Jaak. "I don't want its food costs to come out of group bonuses. We agreed we'd use part of it for the new Immersive Response. I'm sick of the old one."

Jaak shrugged. "Fine with me. I can pay for it out of my own. I just won't get any more tats."

I leaned back in my chair, surprised, then looked at Lisa. "Well, if Jaak wants to pay for it, I think we should keep it."

Lisa stared at me, incredulous. "But we could cook it!"

I glanced at the dog where it lay panting in its cage. "It's like having a zoo of our own. I kind of like it."

Musharraf and the Pau Foundation hooked us up with a supply of food pellets for the dog and Jaak looked up an old database on how to splint its busted bones. He bought water filtration so that it could drink.

I thought I'd made a good decision, putting the costs on Jaak, but I didn't really foresee the complications that came with having an unmodified organism in the bunker. The thing shit all over the floor, and sometimes it wouldn't eat, and it would get sick for no reason, and it was slow to heal so we all ended up playing nursemaid to the thing while it lay in its cage. I kept expecting Lisa to break its neck in the middle of the night, but even though she grumbled, she didn't assassinate it.

Jaak tried to act like Musharraf. He talked to the dog. He logged onto the libraries and read all about old-time dogs. How they ran in packs. How people used to breed them.

We tried to figure out what kind of dog it was, but we couldn't narrow it down much, and then Jaak discovered that all the dogs could interbreed, so all you could do was guess that it was some kind of big sheep dog, with maybe a head from a Rottweiler, along with maybe some other kind of dog, like a wolf or coyote or something.

Jaak thought it had coyote in it because they were supposed to have been big adapters, and whatever our dog was, it must have been a big adapter to hang out in the tailings pits. It didn't have the boosters we had, and it had still lived in the rock acids. Even Lisa was impressed by that.

I was carpet bombing Antarctic Recessionists, swooping low, driving the suckers further and further along the ice floe. If I got lucky, I'd drive the whole village out onto a vestigial shelf and sink them all before they knew what was happening. I dove again, strafing and then spinning away from their return slag.

It was fun, but mostly just a way to kill time between real bombing runs. The new IR was supposed to be as good as the arcades, full immersion and feedback, and portable to boot. People got so lost they had to take intravenous feedings or they withered away while they were inside.

I was about to sink a whole load of refugees when Jaak shouted. "Get out here! You've got to see this!"

I stripped off my goggles and ran for the monitoring room, adrenaline amping up. When I got there, Jaak was just standing in the center of the room with the dog, grinning.

Lisa came tearing in a second later. "What? What is it?" Her eyes scanned the theater maps, ready for bloodshed.

Jaak grinned. "Look at this." He turned to the dog and held out his hand. "Shake."

The dog sat back on its haunches and gravely offered him its paw. Jaak grinned and shook the paw, then tossed it a food pellet. He turned to us and bowed.

Lisa frowned. "Do it again."

Jaak shrugged and went through the performance a second time.

"It thinks?" she asked.

Jaak shrugged. "Got me. You can get it to do things. The libraries are full of stuff on them. They're trainable. Not like a centaur or anything, but you can make them do little tricks, and if they're certain breeds, they can learn special stuff, too."

"Like what?"

"Some of them were trained to attack. Or to find explosives."

Lisa looked impressed. "Like nukes and stuff?"

Jaak shrugged. "I guess."

"Can I try?" I asked.

Jaak nodded. "Go for it."

I went over to the dog and stuck out my hand. "Shake."

It stuck out its paw. My hackles went up. It was like sending signals to aliens. I mean, you expect a bio-job or a robot to do what you want it to. Centaur, go get blown up. Find the op-force. Call reinforcements. The HEV was like that, too. It would do anything. But it was designed.

"Feed it," Jaak said, handing me a food pellet. "You have to feed it when it does it right."

I held out the food pellet. The dog's long pink tongue swabbed my palm.

I held out my hand again. "Shake." I said. It held out its paw. We shook hands. Its amber eyes stared up at me, solemn.

"That's some weird shit," Lisa said. I shivered, nodding and backed away. The dog watched me go.

That night in my bunk, I lay awake, reading. I'd turned out the lights and only the book's surface glowed, illuminating the bunkroom in a soft green aura. Some of Lisa's art buys glimmered dimly from the walls: a bronze hanging of a phoenix breaking into flight, stylized flames glowing around it, a Japanese woodblock print of Mount Fuji and another of a village weighed down under thick snows; a photo of the three of us in Siberia after the Peninsula campaign, grinning and alive amongst the slag.

Lisa came into the room. Her razors glinted in my book's dim light, flashes of green sparks that outlined her limbs as she moved.

"What are you reading?" She stripped and squeezed into bed with me.

I held up the book and read out loud.

Cut me I won't bleed. Gas me I won't breathe.
Stab me, shoot me, slash me, smash me
I have swallowed science
I am God.
Alone.

I closed the book and its glow died. In the darkness, Lisa rustled under the covers. My eyes adjusted. She was staring at me. " 'Dead Man,' right?"

"Because of the dog," I said.

"Dark reading." She touched my shoulder, her hand warm, the blades embedded, biting lightly into my skin.

"We used to be like that dog," I said.

"Pathetic."

"Scary."

We were quiet for a little while. Finally I asked, "Do you ever wonder what would happen to us if we didn't have our science? If we didn't have our big brains and our weeviltech and our cellstims and—"

"And everything that makes our life good?" She laughed. "No." She rubbed my stomach. "I like all those little worms that live in your belly." She started to tickle me.

Wormy, squirmy in your belly,
wormy squirmy feeds you Nelly.
Microweevils eat the bad,
and give you something good instead.

I fought her off, laughing. "That's no Yearly."

"Third Grade. Basic bio-logic. Mrs. Alvarez. She was really big on weeviltech."

She tried to tickle me again but I fought her off. "Yeah, well Yearly only wrote about immortality. He wouldn't take it."

Lisa gave up on the tickling and flopped down beside me again. "Blah, blah, blah. He wouldn't take any gene modifications. No c-cell inhibitors. He was dying of cancer and he wouldn't take the drugs that would have saved him. Our last mortal poet. Cry me a river. So what?"

"You ever think about why he wouldn't?"

"Yeah. He wanted to be famous. Suicide's good for attention."

"Seriously, though. He thought being human meant having animals. The whole web of life thing. I've been reading about him. It's weird shit. He didn't want to live without them."

"Mrs. Alvarez hated him. She had some rhymes about him, too. Anyway, what were we supposed to do? Work out weeviltech and DNA patches for every stupid species? Do you know what that would have cost?" She nuzzled close to me. "If you want animals around you, go to a zoo. Or get some building blocks and make something, if it makes you happy. Something with hands, for god's sake, not like that dog." She stared at the underside of the bunk above. "I'd cook that dog in a second."

I shook my head. "I don't know. That dog's different from a bio-job. It looks at us, and there's something there, and it's not us. I mean, take any bio-job out there, and it's basically us, poured into another shape, but not that dog. . . ." I trailed off, thinking.

Lisa laughed. "It shook hands with you, Chen. You don't worry about a centaur when it salutes." She climbed on top of me. "Forget the dog. Concentrate on something that matters." Her smile and her razor blades glinted in the dimness.

I woke up to something licking my face. At first I thought it was Lisa, but she'd climbed into her own bunk. I opened my eyes and found the dog.

It was a funny thing to have this animal licking me, like it wanted to talk, or say hello or something. It licked me again, and I thought that it had come a long way from when it had tried to take off Jaak's arm. It put its paws up on my bed, and then in a single heavy movement, it was up on the bunk with me, its bulk curled against me.

It slept there all night. It was weird having something other than Lisa lying next to me, but it was warm and there was something friendly about it. I couldn't help smiling as I drifted back to sleep.

We flew to Hawaii for a swimming vacation and we brought the dog with us. It was good to get out of the northern cold and into the gentle Pacific. Good to stand on the beach, and look out to a limitless horizon. Good to walk along the beach holding hands while black waves crashed on the sand.

Lisa was a good swimmer. She flashed through the ocean's metallic sheen like an eel out of history and when she surfaced, her naked body glistened with hundreds of iridescent petroleum jewels.

When the Sun started to set, Jaak lit the ocean on fire with his 101. We all sat and watched as the Sun's great red ball sank through veils of smoke, its light shading deeper crimson with every minute. Waves rushed flaming onto the beach. Jaak got out his harmonica and played while Lisa and I made love on the sand.

We'd intended to amputate her for the weekend, to let her try what she had done to me the vacation before. It was a new thing in L.A., an experiment in vulnerability.

She was beautiful, lying there on the beach, slick and excited with all of our play in the water. I licked oil opals off her skin as I sliced off her limbs, leaving her more dependent than a baby. Jaak played his harmonica and watched the Sun set, and watched as I rendered Lisa down to her core.

After our sex, we lay on the sand. The last of the Sun was dropping below the water. Its rays glinted redly across the smoldering waves. The sky, thick with particulates and smoke, shaded darker.

Lisa sighed contentedly. "We should vacation here more often."

I tugged on a length of barbed wire buried in the sand. It tore free and I wrapped it around my upper arm, a tight band that bit into my skin. I showed it to Lisa. "I used to do this all the time when I was a kid." I smiled. "I thought I was so bad-ass."

Lisa smiled. "You are."

"Thanks to science." I glanced over at the dog. It was lying on the sand a short distance away. It seemed sullen and unsure in its new environment, torn away from the safety of the acid pits and tailings mountains of its homeland. Jaak sat beside the dog and played. Its ears twitched to the music. He was a good player. The mournful sound of the harmonica carried easily over the beach to where we lay.

Lisa turned her head, trying to see the dog. "Roll me."

I did what she asked. Already, her limbs were regrowing. Small stumps, which would build into larger limbs. By morning, she would be whole, and ravenous. She studied the dog. "This is as close as I'll ever get to it," she said.

"Sorry?"

"It's vulnerable to everything. It can't swim in the ocean. It can't eat anything. We have to fly its food to it. We have to scrub its water. Dead end of an evolutionary chain. Without science, we'd be as vulnerable as it." She looked up at me. "As vulnerable as I am now." She grinned. "This is as close to death as I've ever been. At least, not in combat."

"Wild, isn't it?"

"For a day. I liked it better when I did it to you. I'm already starving."

I fed her a handful of oily sand and watched the dog, standing uncertainly on the beach, sniffing suspiciously at some rusting scrap iron that stuck out of the beach like a giant memory fin. It pawed up a chunk of red plastic rubbed shiny by the ocean and chewed on it briefly, before dropping it. It started licking around its mouth. I wondered if it had poisoned itself again.

"It sure can make you think," I muttered. I fed Lisa another handful of sand. "If someone came from the past, to meet us here and now, what do you think they'd say about us? Would they even call us human?"

Lisa looked at me seriously. "No, they'd call us gods."

Jaak got up and wandered into the surf, standing knee-deep in the black smoldering waters. The dog, driven by some unknown instinct, followed him, gingerly picking its way across the sand and rubble.

The dog got tangled in a cluster of wire our last day on the beach. Really ripped the hell out of it: slashes through its fur, broken legs, practically strangled. It had gnawed one of its own paws half off trying to get free. By the time we found it, it was a bloody mess of ragged fur and exposed meat.

Lisa stared down at the dog. "Christ, Jaak, you were supposed to be watching it."

"I went swimming. You can't keep an eye on the thing all the time."

"It's going to take forever to fix this," she fumed.

"We should warm up the hunter," I said. "It'll be easier to work on it back home." Lisa and I knelt down to start cutting the dog free. It whimpered and its tail wagged feebly as we started to work.

Jaak was silent.

Lisa slapped him on his leg. "Come on, Jaak, get down here. It'll bleed out if you don't hurry up. You know how fragile it is."

Jaak said, "I think we should eat it."

Lisa glanced up, surprised. "You do?"

He shrugged. "Sure."

I looked up from where I was tearing away tangled wires from around the dog's torso. "I thought you wanted it to be your pet. Like in the zoo."

Jaak shook his head. "Those food pellets are expensive. I'm spending half my salary on food and water filtration, and now this bullshit." He waved his hand at the tangled dog. "You have to watch the sucker all the time. It's not worth it."

"But still, it's your friend. It shook hands with you."

Jaak laughed. "You're my friend." He looked down at the dog, his face wrinkled with thought. "It's, it's . . . an animal."

Even though we had all idly discussed what it would be like to eat the dog, it was a surprise to hear him so determined to kill it. "Maybe you should sleep on it." I said. "We can get it back to the bunker, fix it up, and then you can decide when you aren't so pissed off about it."

"No." He pulled out his harmonica and played a few notes, a quick jazzy scale. He took the harmonica out of his mouth. "If you want to put up the money for his feed, I'll keep it, I guess, but otherwise . . ." He shrugged.

"I don't think you should cook it."

"You don't?" Lisa glanced at me. "We could roast it, right here, on the beach."

I looked down at the dog, a mass of panting, trusting animal. "I still don't think we should do it."

Jaak looked at me seriously. "You want to pay for the feed?"

I sighed. "I'm saving for the new Immersive Response."

"Yeah, well, I've got things I want to buy too, you know." He flexed his muscles, showing off his tattoos. "I mean, what the fuck good does it do?"

"It makes you smile."

"Immersive Response makes you smile. And you don't have to clean up after its crap. Come on, Chen. Admit it. You don't want to take care of it either. It's a pain in the ass."

We all looked at each other, then down at the dog.

Lisa roasted the dog on a spit, over burning plastics and petroleum skimmed from the ocean. It tasted okay, but in the end it was hard to understand the big deal. I've eaten slagged centaur that tasted better.

Afterward, we walked along the shoreline. Opalescent waves crashed and roared up the sand, leaving jewel slicks as they receded and the Sun sank red in the distance.

Without the dog, we could really enjoy the beach. We didn't have to worry about whether it was going to step in acid, or tangle in barbed wire half-buried in the sand, or eat something that would keep it up vomiting half the night.

Still, I remember when the dog licked my face and hauled its shaggy bulk onto my bed, and I remember its warm breathing beside me, and sometimes, I miss it.

The Clapping Hands of God

MICHAEL F. FLYNN

Here's a trip through a dimensional gateway to another universe altogether—but, as the intrepid travellers discover, no matter how far from home you go, some of the problems you encounter may be all too familiar . . .

Born in Easton, Pennsylvania, Michael F. Flynn has a BA in math from La Salle College and an MS for work in topology from Marquette University, and he works as an industrial quality engineer and statistician. Since his first sale there in 1984, Flynn has become a mainstay of *Analog,* and one of their most frequent contributors. He has also made sales to *The Magazine of Fantasy & Science Fiction, Asimov's Science Fiction, Weird Tales, New Destinies, Alternate Generals*, and elsewhere, and is thought of as one of the best new "hard science" writers to enter the field in several decades. His books include *In the Country of the Blind, Fallen Angels,* a novel written in collaboration with Larry Niven and Jerry Pournelle, *Firestar, Rogue Star, Lodestar*, and *Falling Star,* and his stories have been collected in *The Forest of Time and Other Stories* and *The Nanotech Chronicles*. His most recent book is a new novel, *The Wreck of the River of Stars*. His stories have appeared in our Fifth and Twelfth Annual Collections. He now lives in Edison, New Jersey.

To a world unnamed by humans, humans came. The gate swung open on a pleasant mountain glade, where the weather could be cool without being cold, and which lay cupped in a high valley below the tree line and far from the gray smudges of the cities on the plains below. This isolation was by happy chance and not by wise choice. Gates swung where God willed, and man could but submit. Once, one had opened in the midst of a grim fortress full of armed and hostile *things* and what befell the team that crossed no man knows, for the gatekeeper sealed it forever.

Here, the humans erected a fine pavilion of gay cloth among mighty growths that might be called trees and colorful splays that might be called flowers, although they were neither trees nor flowers exactly. The motley of the fabric clashed with the surrounding vegetation. The colors were off. They aped the complexion of a different world and seemed here a little out of place. But that was acceptable. The humans were themselves a little out of place and a bit of the familiar ought to surround them in the midst of all the strangeness.

They decked the pavilion with bright cushions and divans and roped the sides up so the gentle and persistent eastern breeze could pass through. They stoked their larder with melons and dates and other toothsome delights and laid their carpets out for prayer. Though no one knew which direction served—the stars, when the night sky came, provided no clue—the gate itself would do for *mihrab*.

The humans spent a night and a day acclimating themselves to the strange sun and testing the air and the water and the eccentric plants and such of the motiles as they could snare. They named these creatures after those they knew—rabbit, goat, swallow, cedar—and some of the names were fair. They stretched their twenty-four hours like taffy to fill up a slightly longer day. By the second night-fall they had shed their environmental suits and felt the wind and the sun on their skin and in their hair. It was good to breathe the world's largesse, and many an outlandish aroma teased them.

Exploring their valley, they found a great falls and spent another night and day at its foot, spellbound. A stream poured into the valley from high above, where the snows always fell and the snows always melted. It tumbled from the sky with a roar like the voice of God, throwing up a mist from which they named the mountain and within which a kaleidoscope of rainbows played. Its ageless assault had worn a pool unknowably deep in the rock below. Where and how the waters drained from the pool God withheld. There was not another like it in all the Known Worlds.

Afterwards, they clustered in their pavilion and reviewed their plans and inspected their equipment, and assembled those items that required assembly. Then they told off one of their number to ward the gate they had passed through and settled themselves to study the strange folk on the wide plains below.

Hassan Maklouf was their leader, a man who had walked on seventeen worlds and bore in consequence seventeen wounds. To ten of those worlds, he had followed another; to seven, others had followed him. From four, he had escaped with his life. With two, he had fallen in love. He came to the lip of the little bowl valley and from a gendarme of rock studied the plains through a pair of enhanced binoculars. Which are you, he asked the planet spread below him, assassin or lover? The answer, like the waters of the pool, remained hidden.

"This is a fine place," Bashir al-Jamal declared beside him, as broadly approving as if he himself had fashioned the glade. Bashir was Hassan's cousin and this was his first outing. A young man, freshly graduated from the House of Gates, he bubbled with innocence and enthusiasm. Hassan had promised their grandfather that Bashir would come back. *With a scar*, the old man had said severely. *The trek is not worth the going if one bears no scars back*. But then, grandfather was *Bedu* and such folk had hard ways.

"The water is pure; the air clean," Bashir continued. "Never have I camped in a more beautiful place."

Hassan continued to scan the lowlands. "I have seen men killed by beautiful things."

"But the biochemistry here must be so different, none of the beasts would find us tasty."

Hassan lowered his binoculars and looked at his cousin. "Before or after they have taken a bite?"

"Ah," Bashir bowed to the older man's advice. "You are the fountain of wisdom."

"I live still," Hassan told him raising the binoculars again. "Call that wisdom, if you wish."

"At least, we may study this world unseen," Bashir said. Deprived of one good fortune, he would seize another. "There is no evidence that the locals have ever been up here."

"Perhaps it is one of their holy places," Hassan suggested, "and we have violated it. God has granted to each folk one place that is holy above all others."

Bashir was not impressed. "If He has this well may be it; but I think it is too remote."

Hassan grunted and lowered the binoculars. "I want a guard posted here and a sensor array, so that nothing may approach from this direction."

"Up a sheer cliff-face?"

"Perhaps the worldlings have climbing pads on their hands and feet. Perhaps they have wings. Perhaps they have nothing more than cleverness and perseverance." He capped his binoculars and returned them to their case. "I would fear that last more than all the others."

This is how they came to be there, in that enchanted glade upon the Misty Mountain.

Behind this world lies a shadow world. It is called the Other 'Brane, and it lies not so very far away, save that it is in *the wrong direction*. It is behind us, beneath us, within us. It is as close as two hands clapping, and as far. Once before, they clapped, this 'brane and the other, and from the echoes and the ripples of that Big Clap, came matter and energy and galaxies and stars and planets and flowers and laughing children. Should they clap again, that will end it all, and many wise men fret their lives on the question of whether the two be approaching or no. But to know this they must learn to measure *the wrong direction* and that is a hard thing to do.

Hassan thinks of the two 'branes as the Hands of God, for this would make literal one of the hidden Recitations of the Prophet, peace be upon him. But he sees no reason to worry over whether they are to clap or not, since all will be as God wills. What, after all, could be done? To where would one run? "The mountains are as fleeting as the clouds." So reads the fiqh of the 'Ashari 'aqida, and the other schools have assented with greater or lesser joy.

What *can* be done is to travel through the Other 'Brane. That skill, men have learned. The Other 'Brane is spanned like ours by three space-like dimensions and one time-like dimension; but it contains no planets, no vast spaces—only an endless, undulating plain, cut through by featureless chasms and buttes. Or maybe it is nothing of the sort, and the landscape is only an illusion that the mind has imposed on a vista incomprehensible to human senses.

Crossing the Other 'Brane is a hard road, for the journey from gate beacon to gate beacon must be swift and without hesitation. There is an asymmetry, a breaking of parity, hidden somewhere in the depths of that time which was before Time itself. To linger is to perish. Some materials, some energy fields, last longer, but in the end they are alien things in an alien land, and the land will have them. What man would endure such peril, were not the prize the whole great universe itself? For the metric of space lies smaller on the Other 'Brane, and a few strides there leap light-years here at home.

How many light years, no man knew. Hassan explained that to Bashir on the second night when, studying the alien sky, his cousin asked which star was the Earth's, for no answer was likely. Was this planet even in a galaxy known from Earth? How many light years had their lumbering *other*-buses oversprung, and in which direction? And even if Earth's sun lay in this planet's sky, it would not be the sun they knew. Light speed does not bind the universe; but it binds man's knowing of it, for in a peculiar way *place* is *time*, and all man's wisdom and knowing is but a circle of candle light in an everspreading dark. No one may see farther or faster than the light by which one sees. Hence, one perceives only a time-bound sphere within a quasar halo. Now they had stepped into the sphere of another campfire, somewhere else in the endless desert of night.

"The stars we see from Earth," Hassan explained, "are the stars as they were when their light departed, and the deeper into the sky we peer, the deeper into the past we see. Here, we see the stars from a different place, and therefore at a different time."

"I don't understand," Bashir said. He had been taught the facts, and he had learned them well enough for the examinations, but he did not yet *know* them.

"Imagine a star that is one million light-years from the Earth," Hassan said, "and imagine that this world we are on lies half-way between the two. On Earth, they see the star as it was a million years ago. Here, we see it as it was a mere five hundred thousand years ago, as we might see a grown man after having once glimpsed the child. In the mean time, the star will have moved. Perhaps it will have changed color or luminosity. So we do not see the same star, nor do we see it in the same place. Ah, cousin, each time we emerge from our gate heads, we find not only a different world, but a different universe."

Bashir shivered, although that may have been only the evening breeze. "It's as if we are cut off and alone. I don't like it."

Hassan smiled to himself. "No one asked that you do." He turned toward the pavilion, where the others buzzed with discussion, but Bashir lingered a moment longer with face upturned to the sky. "I feel so alone," he said softly, but not so softly that Hassan failed to hear.

They studied the world in every way they could: the physics, the chemistry and biology, the society and technology. The presence of sentients—and sentients of considerable attainment—complicated the matter, for they must understand the folk first as they were and not as they would become; and that meant to see without being seen, for the act of knowing changes forever both knower and known. But to study even a small world was no small thing. A single flower is unfathomable.

They sought the metes and bounds of the planet. What was its size? Its density? Where upon its face had the gate swung open? How far did it lie from its star? Soong marked the risings and the settings of sun and moons and stars and groped toward answers.

They sampled the flora and the fauna in their mountain valley, scanned their viscera, and looked into the very architecture of their cells. Mizir discovered molecules that were like DNA, but not quite. They imagined phyla and classes upon the creatures, but did not dare guess at anything more precise.

Ladawan and Yance launched small, stealthy birds, ultralight and sun powered, to watch and listen where men themselves could not. On their bellies these drones displayed a vision of the sky above, captured by microcameras on their backs, in that way achieving an operational sort of invisibility, and allowing the tele-pilots to hover and record unseen.

"No radio," Soong complained and Hassan laughed a little at that, for always Soong preferred the easy way. "We will have to plant bugs," Hassan told the team when they met after the first flight for debriefing, "to study their tongue, for we cannot hear them otherwise."

"They don't have tongues," Mizir said, though with him it was less complaint than fascination. "They make sounds, and they communicate with these sounds, but I don't know how they make them."

"See if you can locate a body," Hassan told the tele-pilots. "Perhaps there are morgues in the city," pointing to the dark, smoky buildings that nestled distant against the bay of a cold, blue ocean. "Mizir needs to know how those people are put together."

"Tissue samples would be nice," Mizir added, but he knew that was lagniappe.

"An elementary school might have simple displays of their written language," Bashir suggested. It was a standard checklist item for the assay of inhabited worlds, studied and carefully memorized in his training, but Hassan was pleased that the boy had remembered it.

"Coal smoke," Klaus Altenbach announced the next day after a drone had lasered the emissions of a building they believed to be a factory. "Or something carbonaceous. Peat? Not petroleum—those bunkers are with something solid filled. Technology is mid-nineteenth century equivalent," he said, adding after a moment, "by the Common Era. I expect soon the steamships to come to those docks." When Ladawan asked him from where these ships would come, he shrugged and told her, "There cannot be a horizon to no good purpose."

"It is a strange-looking city," Mizir said, "although I cannot say why."

Yance Darby scratched his head. "Don't look all that strange to me. 'Cept for the folk in it."

"They really are graceful," Iman said of the indigenes, "once you grow accustomed to their strangeness. They are curlicues, filigrees of being. They must have art of some sort. Their buildings are intaglio—plain boxes, towers, but they have incised their every surface. Look for painting, look for sculpture." And she set about to build a mannequin of the folk.

"There's so much to learn!" cried Bashir, overwhelmed by it all. Being young, he was easily overwhelmed; but a world is not something to be nibbled at. If one is to taste it at all, it must be swallowed whole; and yet that is impossible.

"As well sip the Nile," Mizir grumbled. "We could spend the rest of our lives here and not learn the first thing."

"Oh, we'd learn the first thing," said Hassan. What worried him, and kept him awake into the night, was not the first thing they might learn, but the last.

And so it went. The drones flew. Digital photographs downloaded into a mosaic map of landforms and soil types and vegetation. (Soong longed for a satellite in low orbit.) They sprinkled small ears about the city one night and harvested from them a Babel of sounds for the Intelligence to sort into phonemes and other patterns. (The Intelligence concluded that two languages were in use, and set itself to ponder the matter.) Mizir had for the time to content himself with creatures he could collect nearby. ("Alpine species," he grumbled. "How representative are they of the coastal plains, the estuaries?") Klaus discovered a railroad coming into the city on the far side. ("They had somehow to bring that coal in," he joked, "and muleback I thought unlikely.") The engines were steam-powered, with spherical boilers.

Bashir wanted to name the world.

Long-timers like Hassan and Soong and Mizir seldom bothered with such things. In time, the planet would speak and its name would be revealed. Until then, Hassan would simply call it *the world*. Still, when the team debriefed on the seventh day and Bashir broached the issue, Hassan did not stop the others from discussing it.

They lounged on the cushions and ate dates and cheeses. Yance Darby, like Bashir recently graduated from the House of Gates, tossed pieces of food at the curious animals, causing them to scamper away, until Iman scolded him for it. That the crumbs were indigestible would not stop animals from swallowing, and who knew what would come of that? Soong sat a little apart, on high furniture at a table spread with printout maps, while he and Klaus and Ladawan traced geography and the road network on maps made of light. A phantom sphere floated in the air above the projector: all black, all unknown, save the little spot where they encamped—and they were not yet certain they had placed it properly.

Hassan stood apart, outside the pavilion, under stars strange and distant. He held a cup of nectar in his hands and studied the MRI holograms of the local fauna that had been arranged on a display board, and he traced with a fingertip the clade lines that Mizir had guessed at. *How strange*, he thought, *and yet how familiar, too*. God was a potter and Nature was His knife. Everywhere life took form, He shaped it toward the same ends. And so there were things like mice, and things like hawks, although they were quite different in their details. The mouse had six legs, for one thing—its gait absorbing thereby many hours of Mizir's close attention—and the hawk had claws on wingtip and feet and concealed, too, beneath its covert.

Iman had constructed a mannequin of the sapients and had placed it by the entrance to the pavilion. Man or woman, no one knew, or even if such categories had meaning here. It stood shorter than a human and, at rest, assumed a curious sinusoid posture, like a cobra risen. In form, bilaterally symmetric, but possessed of four arms and two legs. Large lifting arms grew from mid-torso; smaller manipulators farther up. Claws tipped the one set, tentacles the other. The feet ended in claws, too, though these were stubbier. Mizir thought that the ancestral form had been six-legged, too, like so many of the scuttling things in the meadow, and the clawed lifting arms had evolved from the midlegs. "They are rodents," he had said, arranging their image under that clade, "or what things like rodents might become."

"Yet the 'rodents' here are territorial," Iman then told him, "which is very unrodentlike."

"Everything is the same the universe over," Mizir had answered philosophically, "except that everything is different, too."

Atop the torso sat a structure shaped like an American "football" positioned for a kick-off. The skin was smooth, without hair or feathers, but with small plates, as if the creature had been tiled by a master mason. The creature's coloring was a high cerulean, like the clear sky over the desert, though with darker patches on its back. But Mizir had spotted others in the throngs of the city—taller, slimmer, tending toward cobalt—which he thought might hail from the world's tropics.

It was a rich world. Diverse. There were many races, many tongues. There were alpine meadows and high prairies and coastal estuaries. How many eons deep was it? What lay over the curve of the horizon? How could they hope to grasp more than a meager slice? They would never know its history. They could hardly know its culture. Was that city below them—blackened with soot, lively with activity—the pinnacle of this world's civilization? Or was it a cultural and technological backwater? Later, they would send the drones out on longer recon flights, but even that would only scratch at the surface. *Men will come here for years,* Hassan thought, *perhaps for generations. And maybe then we will know a little.*

The creature in the model had no face.

There were filaments that Mizir thought scent receptors; there were gelatin pools that were likely eyes. There was a cavity into which they had watched indigenes spoon food. But none of these features were arranged into a face. Indeed, its mouth was in its torso. The filaments waved above the football like ferns. The gelatin-filled pits were distributed asymmetrically around the headball, as were other pits, apparently empty, and a large parabolic cavity perversely set where a human mouth would be, although it was not a mouth at all.

"They really are beautiful," Iman said. She had come to stand by Hassan while the others chattered on about possible names for the planet. Hassan nodded, though in acknowledgement rather than agreement. He thought the indigenes looked scarred, pockmarked, twisted out of true. But that was because his mind sought a greater symmetry of features than was offered.

"Beautiful, perhaps; though they differ somewhat from the life forms Mizir has found up here," he said. "I think they are interlopers. I think they have come from somewhere else, these people of yours. Perhaps from across that ocean."

"Perhaps," she allowed the possibility. "Soong says that the entire coastal plain came from somewhere else, and its collision with this continent raised the Misty Mountains."

"I keep seeing a face," he said to her. "I know there isn't one, but my brain insists on nostrils and ears. It seems to be smiling at me."

"Recognition template," Iman said. "People have seen 'Isa, praise be upon him, in a potato; or Shaitan in a billow of smoke."

"It bothers me. We need to see these people the way they are, not the way we think they are."

"It was easier on Concannon's World," she told him. "The indigenes there looked like flowers."

"Did they?"

"A little. They flew."

"Ah."

"Vapors jetted out their stems. They could only travel in short hops. But one doesn't look for faces in a flower."

"And here I have always mistaken you for a lily."

Iman turned from him and made a show of watching the debate of the others. "Will you call this place Maklouf's World? As team leader, it is your privilege."

Hassan shook his head. "I met Concannon once. He had an ego big enough for a world, but I'm not so vain as he. What do *you* think we should call this place?"

Iman pursed her lips and adjusted the *hijab* under her chin. Her face was only a pale circle wrapped in a checkered cloth of red and white squares after the fashion of the Jordan Valley. "We should learn what the indigenes call it in their own tongue."

Hassan laughed. "They will call it 'the world,' and likely in hundreds of tongues, most of which we will never hear."

"Shangri-la!" said Bashir, loud enough that Hassan heard and turned toward him. Yance clapped his hands. "Perfect!" he agreed. "This place is sure enough a paradise." Klaus nodded slowly, as did Ladawan and Khalid, the gate warden. Soong said nothing and glanced at Hassan.

"No." Hassan stepped inside the pavilion. "That is a dangerous name for a world, and dangerous because it sounds so safe. Every time we spoke it we would think this place safer yet."

"Well, isn't it?" asked Iman.

Hassan looked back over his shoulder and saw her run a hand along the muscled lifting arm of her statue. "I don't know," he said. "I haven't seen the surprise yet."

"Surprise?" asked Bashir. "What surprise is that?"

Soong chuckled, but Hassan didn't bother to answer. He continued to watch Iman stroke the statue.

"Well, what would *you* call it?" Yance asked, making it sound a challenge.

"It *is* your privilege, Hassan," said Mizir.

"If you must have a name for this world," and Hassan looked again outside the tent, at the strange constellations above, at the expressionless, immobile "face" on the statue. "If you must have a name for this world, call it al-Batin."

Mizir stiffened, Bashir and Khalid exchanged glances. Iman smiled faintly. "It means, 'The Hidden,'" she whispered to the others.

"Not exactly," Hassan added.

"It is one of the Names of God," Mizir protested. "That isn't proper for a planet."

"It is fit," Hassan said, "for as long as God hides its nature from us. After that . . . after that, we will see."

They called the city "East Haven" because of its position on a broad and deep estuary. A channel led from the Eastern Sea well into the mouth of a swift river—to embrace piers, docks, warehouses. This much they learned from high altitude sonar pictures from their drones. Why no ships nestled at those docks, the drones could not say.

South and west of the city lay flatlands thick with greening crops, by which they guessed at a season much like late spring. The crops were broad and flat, like clover, but whether intended for the Batinites or for their livestock was unclear. Harrows and cultivators were drawn by teams of six-legged creatures the claws of whose mid- and hindlegs had nearly vanished into a hoof-like structure. Its forelegs stubbornly divided the hoof. Inevitably the team named them "horses," although something in their demeanor suggested "oxen," as well.

One field was more manicured, covered by a fine ground-hugging carpet of waxy, fat-leafed, yellow-green plants, broken here and there with colorful flowers and shrubs arranged in decorative patterns. A sample of the "grass," when crushed, gave forth a pleasant odor—somewhat like frankincense. The park—for such they assumed it was—spread across the top of a swell of ground and from it one gained a fine vista of the city, its port, and the Eastern Sea beyond. As the weather grew warmer, groups of Batinites ventured forth from the city to spend afternoons or sunsets there, spooning baskets of food into their gaping stomachs and watching their younglings leap and somersault through the chartreuse oil-grass.

A road they called the Grand Trunk Road ran southwest from the city. The portions nearest the city had been paved with broad, flat stones, across which rattled a motley array of vehicles: carriages resembling landaus and hansoms, open wagons that Yance called "buck boards," and freight wagons heavy with goods and strapped with canvas covers, whose drivers goaded their teams of oxen six-horses with enormously long whips.

The Batinites themselves dressed in garb that ranged from pale dun to rainbow plumage, as task or mood dictated. They had a taste for beauty, Iman told the others, though for a different sort of beauty than Earth then knew, and she spent some of her free time adapting local fashion to the limbs and stature of humans—for there was a fad for matters alien in the cities of the Earth.

One fork of the Grand Trunk Road branched northwestward toward a pass in the coastal range of which the Misty Mountain was a part. The road simplified itself as it receded, like a countryman shedding his urban clothes piecemeal as he fled the city: it became first hard-driven gravel then earth damped with a waxy oil, finally, as it began the long switchback up to the pass, rutted dirt. The drone they sent through the pass returned with images of a second, more distant city, smaller than East Haven and nestled in a rich farming valley. Beyond, at the limits of resolution, lay drier and more barren country and the hint of something approaching desert.

"There is something energetic about those people," Hassan observed. "They have a commotion to them, a busyness that is very like Americans. They are forever *doing* something."

"*That* is why the city seems so odd!" Iman exclaimed, a cry so triumphant that, following as it did so many weeks of study, seemed tardy in its proclamation, as if the sociologist had been paying scant attention 'til now.

"Don't you see?" she told them. "They *are* Americans! Look at the streets, how linear they are. How planned. Only by the docks do they twist and wander. That city did not *grow* here; it was *planted*. Yes, Mizir, you were right: They came from across the Eastern Sea."

A lively people, indeed. One of a pair of younglings capering in the park caromed off a six-cedar tree and lay stunned while its parents rushed to comfort it. Three parents, Iman noted, and wondered at their roles. "Or is the third only an uncle or aunt or older sibling?" Yet the posture of consolation is much the same on one world as another and tentacles could stroke most wondrous delicate.

"They care for one another," Iman told Hassan that evening in the pavilion.

"Who does not?" he answered, rising from the divan and walking out into the night toward the vantage point from which they watched the city. East Haven was a dull orange glow. Oil from the chartreuse grass burned slowly in a hundred thousand lamps. Iman joined him and opened her mouth to speak, but Hassan silenced her with a touch to the arm and pointed to the shadow form of Bashir, who sat cross-legged on a great pillow and watched with night-vision binoculars. Silently, they withdrew into Hassan's pavilion, where Hassan sat on an ottoman while Iman, standing behind him, kneaded his shoulder muscles.

"You've been carrying something heavy on these," she said, "they are so hard and knotted up."

"Oh, nothing much. A world."

"Listen to Atlas." She squeezed hard and Hassan winced. "Nothing you can do will affect this world. All you do is watch."

"People will come here for the wonderfall, for the oil-grass perfume, for the fashion and cut of their clothing. In the end, that cannot go unnoticed."

"What of it? To our benefit and theirs. One day we will greet them, trade with them, listen to their music and they to ours. It is only the when and the how that matter. I think you carry a weight much less than a world."

"All right. The eight of you. That is heavy enough."

"What, are Soong and Mizir children that you must change their diapers? Or I?"

That conjured disturbing thoughts. He reached back over his shoulder and stilled her ministrations. "Perhaps you had better stop now."

"Am I so heavy, then?"

"It's not that. You scare me. I don't know who you are."

"I am as plain as typeset. Children read me for a primer."

"That's not what I meant."

"Do you wonder what is beneath the *hijab*? I could take it off."

The fire ran through him like a molten sword. He turned on his pillow and Iman took an abrupt step back, clasping her hands before her. "We've never been teamed before, you and I," he told her. "What do you know about me?"

"I know that Bashir is not so heavy as you think."

Hassan was silent for a while. "He grows no lighter for all your assurances."

"What can happen to him here?"

"Very little, I think," he admitted reluctantly. "And that is dangerous, for his next world may not be so safe."

"I think he likes the Batinites."

"They are easy folk to like."

"There are more such folk than you might think."

"I think you are bald. Beneath the *hijab*, I mean. Bald, and maybe with ears like conch shells."

"Oh, you are a past master of flattery! You and I may never team again. You will go through a gate and I will go though another, and maybe one of us will not come back."

"I am no Shi'a. I do not practice *muta'a*."

Iman's face set into unreadable lines. "Is that what you think? A marriage with an expiration date? Then perhaps you do not know me, after all." She went to the flap of his pavilion and paused a moment slightly bent over before passing without. "It's black," she said, turning a bit to cast the words back. "Black and very long, and my mother compared it to silk. As for the ears, that price is higher than you've paid so far."

With that, she was gone. Hassan thought they had quarreled. *I have seniority*, he told himself. *She will join Soong and Mizir and me when we next go out*. He could arrange that. There were people in the House of Gates who owed him favors.

The next day, Hassan sent Bashir back to Earth for supplies and because he was so young, sent Mizir to accompany him and Khalid to drive the other-bus. They took discs full of information and cases of specimens for the scholars to study "Check calibration on clock," Soong reminded them as they buttoned down. "Time run differently in Other 'Brane."

"Thank you, O grandfather," said Khalid, who had driven many such runs before, "I did not know that."

"Insolence," Soong complained to Hassan afterward. "Reminder never hurt."

"Makes me nervous having only the one buggy left," Yance said. "Y'know what I mean? We can't get all of us and all our gear into one, if'n we have to bug out in a hurry."

"Bug out?" Soong thought the word related to "buggy."

"Y'never know," Yance said, feigning wisdom by saying nothing, so that Soong was no more enlightened.

That evening, Klaus came to Hassan with a puzzle. "These are for today the surveillance flights over 'Six-foot City'."

"Don't call the natives 'six-foots.' What's on the videos?"

"I hope that you will tell me."

Klaus was usually more forthcoming. He had the German's attitude toward facts. He ate them raw, without seasoning, and served them up the same way. There was something brutal about this, for facts could be hard and possess sharp edges, making them hard to swallow. Better to soften them a little first by chewing them over.

Klaus' video had been shot at night and had the peculiar, greenish luminescence of night vision. The time stamp in the lower right named the local equivalent of three in the morning. The drone had been conducting a biosurvey over the tidal flats north of the city—Mizir had spotted some peculiar burrowing creatures there on an earlier flyover—and during the return flight, motion in the city below had activated the drone's sensors.

"It is most peculiar," Klaus said. "Most peculiar."

How peculiar, Hassan did not know. Perhaps it was customary for large groups of the Batinites to wake from their sleep and come outdoors in the small hours of the morning, although they had never done so before. Yet, here they were in their multitudes: on balconies, on rooftops, at their windowsills, in small knots gathered before the doorways of their buildings. All turned skyward with a patient stillness that Hassan could only call expectation. The drone had lingered in circles, its small Intelligence sensing an anomaly of some sort in the sudden mass behavior. And then, first one worldling, then another pointed skyward and they began to behave in an agitated manner, turning and touching and waving their tentacled upper arms.

"Have they seen the drone?" Hassan asked. It was hard to imagine, stealthed as it was and at night in the bargain. "Perhaps they sense the engine's heat signature?" Mizir had floated the hypothesis that some of the gelatin pits on the headball were sensitive to infrared.

"No," said Klaus, "observe the direction in which they stare. It is to the east, and not directly above."

"How do you know which way they stare, when they have no faces?" In truth, it was difficult to judge in the unearthly light of night-vision. Everything was just a little soft at the edges, and features did not stand out.

"Look how they hold their bodies. I assume that their vision is in the direction in which they walk. It makes reason, not so?"

"Reason," said Hassan. "I wonder what reason brought them all out in the middle of the night?"

"Something in the sky. Ask Soong. Such a mystery will please him."

Hassan made a note to talk to Soong, but as he turned away, something in the panning video caught his eye, and that something was this:

When all men fall prostrate in prayer, the one who kneels upright stands out like bas-relief. When all men run, the one remaining still is noted. And when all men look off to the east, the one with face upturned seemed to be staring directly at Hassan himself.

Which was to say, directly at the drone. "This one," said Hassan, striking the freeze-frame. "What do you make of him?"

"So . . . I had not noticed him before." Klaus peered more closely at the screen. "A heretic, perhaps." But his chuckle stuck in his throat. "I meant no offense."

Hassan, much puzzled, took none. Only later would Mizir remind him that to a European, Mecca lies proverbially east.

"Planet," Soong announced with grave satisfaction after evening had fallen. "Most systems, many planets. This rising significant to sixlegs."

"Don't call them sixlegs. Why would it have special significance?"

Soong made a gesture signifying patient ignorance. "Perhaps beginning of festival. Ramadan. Fasching. Carnival."

"Ramadan is not a festival."

"So hard, keep Western notions straight," Soong answered. Hassan was never certain when Soong was being droll. "Is brightest object now in sky," the geophysicist continued, "save inner moon. Maybe next planet starward. Blue tint, so maybe water there. Maybe second living world in system!"

The next day, the worldlings went about their city bearing arms.

There had been little sign of a military hitherto, but now Havenites drilled and marched on the parkland south of the city. They ran. They jumped. They practiced ramming shot down the long barrels of their weapons. They marched in rank and file and executed intricate ballets to the rhythmic clapping of their lower arms. Formations evolved from marching column to line of battle and back again. The floral arrangements that had checkerboarded the park were soon trampled and their colors stamped into a universal sepia. It bothered Hassan when behaviors suddenly changed. It meant that the team had missed something basic. "Why?" he asked, watching through the binoculars, expecting no answer.

But he received one of sorts that evening: When the Blue Planet rose, some of the worldlings fired their weapons in its direction and raised a staccato tattoo that rose and fell and rippled across the city like the chop on a bothered sea.

"Fools," muttered Soong, but Hassan recognized defiance when he saw it.

"Of *planet?*" the Chinese scoffed. "Of *omen?*"

Iman was saddened by the guns. "I had hoped them beyond such matters."

"What people," Hassan said, "have ever been beyond such matters?"

Klaus grunted. "It will be like Bismarck's wars, I think. No radio, but they must have telegraphy. No airplanes, but a balloon would not surprise me."

Iman turned on him. "How can you talk of war with such detachment?"

But Klaus only shrugged. "What other way is there?" he asked. "All we can do is watch." Ladawan and Yance and the others said nothing.

The day after that, the second other-bus returned with fresh supplies and equipment. Mizir off-loaded a wealth of reagents, a sounding laser, and a scanning electron microscope. "It's only a field model," he said of the microscope, "but at last I can *see!*" Soong regarded the aerosondes and high-altitude balloons and judged them passable. "View from height, maybe informative," he conceded, then he turned to Mizir and grinned, "So I, too, look at very small things." A team of mechanics had come back with Bashir and Khalid and they set about assembling the ultralight under Yance's impatient eyes.

"They wanted to know if you'll let the other teams through yet," Bashir told Hassan.

"No."

"But . . . I told them—"

"It was not for you to tell them anything!" Hassan shouted, which caused heads to turn and Bashir to flinch. Hassan immediately regretted the outburst, but remained stern. "Something has developed in the city," he said brusquely, and explained about the rising of the Blue Planet, al-Azraq, and the sudden martial activity.

"The new star marks their season for *jihad*," Bashir guessed.

"Who ever had such seasons?" Hassan scolded him. "It is the struggle with our own heart that is the true *jihad*."

"Maybe so," said Yance, who had overheard, "but when folks are in a mood for a ruckus, any reason'll do." He studied the ultralight thoughtfully. "I just hope they don't have anti-aircraft guns."

Iman learned to recognize Batinites.

"They only look alike," she said, "because they are so strange, and the common strangeness overwhelms the individual differences."

"Yes," said Soong. "Like Arab curlicues. All letters look same."

"The Batinites do not have faces, exactly," Iman reminded them, "but the features on their headball are not random. There are always the same number of pits and ferns and they always appear in the same approximate locations . . ."

"No surprise there," said Mizir. "How many humans are born with three eyes, or with noses where their ears should be?"

". . . But the sizes of these features and the distances between them vary just as they do among humans. How else do we recognize one another, but by the length of the nose, the distance between the eyes, the width of the mouth . . ."

"Some mouths," Yance whispered to Bashir, "being wider than others."

". . . I have identified seventy-three eigenface dimensions for the Batinite headball. The diameters of the pits; reflectivity of the gelatin in them; the lengths of the fronds and the number and size of their 'leaves'; the hue of the skin-plates . . ."

"You don't have to name them all," Hassan said.

". . . And so on. All too strange to register in our own perception, but the Intelligence can measure an image and identify specific individuals."

"Are there systematic differences between the two races?" Mizir asked. "I think you will find the cobaltics have more and broader 'leaves' than the ceruleans."

"Why so they have! On the dorsal fronds."

Mizir nodded in slow satisfaction. "I believe those function as heat radiators, though I cannot be certain until I explore their anatomies. If the cobaltics are a tropical folk, they may need to spill their heat more rapidly. None of the mountain species here in our valley have those particular fronds—or any related feature. At this altitude, spilling excess heat is not a great problem."

"More evidence," Bashir suggested, "that the Havenites have come from somewhere else."

The Intelligence had been teasing threads of meaning from the great ball of yarn that was the Batinites' spoken tongues. The task was complicated by the presence of two such tongues, which the Intelligence declared to be unrelated at the fifth degree, and by the inferred presence of scores of specialized jargons and argots. "The folk at the docks," Klaus pointed out, "must have their own language. And the thieves that we sometimes hear whisper in the night."

"They don't whisper," Iman told him. "They hum and pop and click."

"Those pits on the headball," Mizir mused, "are drums. Wonderfully adapted. They no more evolved for speaking than did human lips and tongue. They were recruited; and yet they serve."

"If they cannot speak from both sides of the mouth," Klaus observed, "they may sometimes say two things at once."

"The advantage of having more than one orifice adapted to making sounds."

Klaus made a further comment and laughed; but because he made it in German no one else got the joke, although it concerned making sounds from more than one orifice.

They input the murmuring of the crowd from the night when al-Azraq first appeared and the Intelligence responded with . . . murmuring, and the occasional cry of [the Blue Planet! It rises/appears!] and [expression of possible dismay and/or fear]. It was not a translation, but it was progress toward a translation.

There may have been another language, a third one, which made no use of sounds, for at times they observed two Batinites together, silent but in evident communication.

"It's the fern-like structures," said Mizir. "They are scent receptors. At close range, they communicate by odors."

"Inefficient," scoffed Klaus.

"Inefficiency is a sign of natural selection," Mizir assured him. "And some messages may be very simple. Run! Come!"

"It's not the scents," said Iman. "Or not the scents alone. Observe how they touch, how they stroke one another's fronds. They communicate by touching one another." She challenged the others with an upthrust chin and no one dared gainsay her, for she herself often communicated by touch. "What else is a handshake, a clap on the shoulder," she insisted, "or a kiss?"

They decided that the frond-stroking amounted to kissing. Some was done perfunctorily. "Like a peck on the cheek," Yance said. Some was done with great show. Some, indeed with lingering stillness. Whatever it meant, the Havenites did it a lot. "They are an affectionate people," Bashir said. Iman said nothing, but tousled the young man's hair.

Bashir had tele-piloting duty the night when a drone followed a soldier out into the park. This soldier wore an ill-fitting uniform of pale yellow on his high cerulean form, one unmarked by any of the signifiers of rank or status that the Intelligence had deduced. It rode a sixleg horse past neglected fields and up the gravel road that led to the once-manicured hilltop. It rode unarmed.

When it reached the level ground where the Haven folk had sported at games before taking up more deadly rehearsals, the soldier dismounted and spoke soft drumbeats, as of a distant and muffled *darbuka*.

Other drumbeats answered and a second Batinite, a tall slim cobaltic, emerged from the grove of six-cedar and poplar. The two approached and stood together for a while, intertwining their tentacled upper arms. Then the second spoke in two voices. One voice said [Show/demonstrate/make apparent—(to) me/this-one—you/present-one agency—immediate time] and the other said [Fear/dread/flight-or-fight—I/this-one agency—now-and-from-now]. At least so the Intelligence thought it said. Yet what manner of ears must they have, Bashir marveled, to parse a duet!

The soldier answered in like harmony, [Appears/shows—it/that-one agency—not-yet] and [this-one (pl?)—defiance resolution/resignation (?)—now-and-from-now.]

The cobaltic had brought a basket and opened it to reveal covered dishes of the puree of grains and legumes that the Batinites favored on their picnic outings and which the Earthlings called batin-hummus. [Eat/take in—this item/thing—you/present-one agency—immediate time] and [Cook/prepare—I/this-one agency—past-time.]

The soldier had brought food as well: a thick, yellow-green liquid in pear-shaped bottles from which he pried the caps with a small instrument. The two removed their upper garments—a complex procedure in that four arms must withdraw from four sleeves—and exposed thereby the mouths in their torsos.

"I wonder if humans can eat those foods of theirs," Iman said. She had come up behind Bashir and had been watching over his shoulder. "A new, exotic flavor to excite the jades . . ." Ever since *al NahTHa*, the appetite for such things had grown and grown. The Rebirth, the Rediscovery. Art. Literature. Song. Science. Everything old was new again, and the new was gulped down whole.

"I've distilled a fluid from the oil-grass," Mizir told them. He sat at the high table drinking coffee with Ladawan and Klaus. "But whether I have obtained a drink or a fuel I cannot say. Yance will not let me put it in the ultralight's gas tank; but he will not drink it for me, either." The others laughed and Klaus indicated Mizir's small, exquisite mug, whose contents had been brewed in the Turkish fashion. "My friend, how would you know the difference?"

"Coffee," said Mizir with mock dignity, "is more than hot water in which a few beans have passed an idle moment." He took his cup and left the table to stand with Iman and Bashir. "Hassan?" he asked her through lips poised to sip. Iman shook her head and Mizir said, "He is always cautious when encountering a new world." He turned his attention to the screen just as the soldier ran its tentacles across the fronds of the taller one's headball and then . . . inserted those tentacles into its own mouth. "What is this?" Mizir said, setting his cup on its saucer and bending closer.

"A new behavior," Iman said delighted and pulled her datapad from her belt pouch. "Bashir, what is the file number on the bird's download? I want to view this later." She entered the identifier the boy gave her and with her stylus scratched quick curlicues across the touch-screen. "Into the oral cavity . . ." she mused.

"What does it mean?" Bashir asked, and no one could tell him.

Usually the Batinites fed themselves by gripping spoons or tines with an upper hand, most often with the left. Sometimes, though rarely, they held food directly using one of their middle hands, typically the right. ("Complementary handedness," Mizir had called it.) Yet the two Batinites on this double-mooned evening abandoned their spoons to their awkward middle hands, while their delicate and tentacled uppers entwined each other's like restless snakes.

Then the cobaltic reached directly into the cerulean's mouth orifice. The soldier grew very taut and still and laid its bowl of batin-hummus slowly aside. With its own tentacles it stroked the other's scent receptors or touched briefly certain of the pits on the cobaltic's headball. Mizir, entranced by the ritual, made careful note of which pits were touched on a sketch of the headball. Iman made notes as well, though with different purpose.

Using its large middle hands, the soldier took the cobaltic by the torso and pushed gently until the other had disengaged and the two pulled away from each other. "Look! What is that?" Bashir asked. "Inside the soldier's mouth!"

"A 'tongue' perhaps," Mizir said. "See how it glistens! Perhaps a mucous coating. A catalyst for digestion?"

Iman looked at him a moment. "Do you think so?" Then she turned her attention to the screen and watched with an awful intensity. She placed a hand on Bashir's shoulder and leaned a little on him. When the two Batinites brought their mouths together, her grip grew hard. Bashir said, "Why, they're kissing!"

Mizir said doubtfully, "We've seen no such kisses before among them. Only the brief frond stroke."

"This is more serious than the frond stroke, I think," Iman said.

"It's a rather long kiss," said Bashir.

"The mouth and tongue are the most sensitive organs of touch that humans possess," she told him, "aside from one other."

Hassan, drawn by the interest of the three clustered before the telescreen, had come up behind them. Now he said, "Turn that screen off!" with a particular firmness.

It was at that moment that Bashir realized. "They weren't kissing! They were . . . I mean . . ." He blacked the screen, then turned to Iman. "You knew!" But Iman had turned round to face Hassan.

"You're right," she said. "They deserve their privacy."

Klaus and Ladawan had joined them. "What is befallen?" the technologist asked.

Iman answered him without turning away from Hassan. "There is a struggle coming, a *jihad* of some sort, and two who may never see each other again have stolen a precious night for their own."

Klaus said, "I don't understand."

Ladawan told him. "A lover is bidding her soldier-boy good-bye."

Mizir was doubtful. "We don't know which one is 'he' or 'she.' They may be either, or neither, or it may be a seasonal thing. Among the fungi—"

"Oh, to Gehenna with your fungi!" said Iman, who then turned from the still-silent Hassan and stalked to her own tent. Mizir watched, puzzled, then turned to Hassan and continued, "I really must study the process. That 'tongue' must have been a . . ."

"Have the Intelligence study it, or do it in private," Hassan ordered. "Grant these people their dignity."

Klaus tugged Mizir on the sleeve as the biologist was leaving. "The soldier is probably the male. At this level of technology, no society can afford to sacrifice its females in combat."

Oddly, it was Ladawan, who was usually very quiet, who had the last word. "Sometimes," she said, "I do not understand you people." She told Soong about it later and Soong spoke certain words in Mandarin, of which tongue Ladawan also knew a little. What he said was, "Treasure that which you do not understand."

Two things happened the next day, or maybe more than two. The first was quite dramatic, but not very important. The second was not so dramatic.

Yance Darby brought forewarning. He had taken the ultralight out in the morning and had flown a wide circuit around the backside of the Misty Mountain to avoid being seen from East Haven. The ultralight was stealthed in the same manner as the drones and its propeller was hushed by MEMS; but it was larger and hence more likely to be detected, so he needed a flight path that would gain him sufficient altitude before passing over habitations. Yance had followed a river across the Great Western Valley to where it plunged through a purple gorge in the mountain range and so onto the coastal plain.

There was a small town at the gorge and another a little farther downstream on the coastal side of the mountains, but the mouth of this river was a morass of swamps and bayous and there was no city there as there was at East Haven. Yance reported, "Cajuns in the delta," but no one at the base camp understood what he meant at first: namely, trappers and fishers living in small, isolated cabins.

"Two of 'em looked up when I flew past," he mentioned.

That troubled Mizir. "I think the indigenes sense into the infrared. The waste heat of our engines is minimal, but . . ." The team had occasionally noted locals glancing toward passing drones, much as a human might glance toward a half-seen flicker of light. Hassan made a note to schedule fewer night flights, when the contrast of the engine exhaust against the deep sky was greater.

A large covered wagon accompanied by five horsemen set out from East Haven on the Grand Trunk Road, but the humans paid it no mind, as there was often heavy traffic in that direction.

Yance followed the line of the mountains out to sea. Soong thought that there might be islands in that direction, a seamount continuation of the mountain range, and Mizir lusted to study insular species to see how they might differ from those they had found on the coastal plain, the river valley on the western slope, and their own alpine meadow. To this end, Yance carried several drones slaved to the ultralight to act as outriders.

What they found was a ship.

"You should see the sunuvabitch!" he told them over the radio link. "It's like an old pirate ship, sails all a-billow, gun-ports down the sides, cutting through the water like a plough. Different shape hull, though I couldn't tell you just how. Wider maybe, or shorter. And the sails—the rigging—aren't the same, either. There's a sunburst on the main sail."

"They don't use a sunburst emblem in the city," Klaus said. "The six-eagle seems to be the local totem." He meant the ferocious bird with claws on its wings and feet and covert.

"It's not a totem," Hassan said. "It's an emblem. Didn't your people use an eagle once?"

"The Doppeladler," Klaus nodded. "But it *was* a totem," he added, "and we sacrificed a great many to it."

"Maybe it's an invasion force," Bashir said. "Maybe this is why the Haven folk have been preparing for war."

"A single ship?" said Hassan.

"A *first* ship," Bashir said, and Hassan acknowledged the possibility.

"I would hate to see these people attacked," Bashir continued. "I like them. They're kind and they're clever and they're industrious."

Hassan, who had bent over the visual feed from Yance's drone, straightened to look at him. "Do you know of Philippe Habib?"

"Only what I was taught in school."

"He was clever and industrious, and they say that he was kind—at least to his friends, though he had not many of those."

"He was a great man."

"He was. But history has a surfeit of great men. We could do with fewer. The *Légion Étrangère* was never supposed to enter France. But what I tried to tell you is that we do not know the reasons for this coming struggle. The 'clever and industrious' folk we have been observing may be the innocent victims of a coming attack—or an oppressive power about to be overthrown. When the Safavid fought the Ak Kolunyu, which side had justice?"

"Cousin, I do not even know who they are!"

"Nor do you know these folk on the plains. Yance, conduct a search pattern. See if there is a flotilla or only this one vessel."

But it was only the one vessel and it furled its sails and entered East Haven under steam to a tumultuous but wary welcome. There was much parading and many displays and the sailors and marines aboard the ship—who wore uniforms of crimson and gold decked with different braid and signifiers—had their backs slapped and their fronds stroked by strangers in the city and not a few had their orifices entertained in the evening that followed.

("Sailors," observed Klaus, "are much the same everywhere.")

A ceremony was held in the park. Flags were exchanged—a ritual apparently of some moment, for the ruffles and paradiddles of drum-like chatter rose to a crescendo. Ugly and entirely functional sabers were exchanged by the ship's captain and a high-ranking Haven soldier.

"I believe they are making peace," Iman said. "These are two old foes who have come together."

"That is a seductive belief," Hassan said. "We love it because it is our belief. How often in Earth's past have ancient enemies clasped hands and stood shoulder to shoulder?"

"I like the Havenites better than the Sunburst folk," Bashir stated.

Hassan turned to him. "Have you chosen sides, then—at a *peace* ceremony?"

"Remember," said Iman, "that Haven uses a bird of prey as its sigil. A golden sun is entirely less threatening an emblem."

"It's not that. It's their uniforms."

"You prefer yellow to crimson?"

"No. The Havenite uniforms fit more poorly, and their insignia are less splendid. This is a folk who make no parade of fighting."

Hassan, who had begun to turn away, turned back and looked at his young cousin with new respect. "You are right. They are no peacocks about war, like these fancy folk from over the sea. And that is well, for it is no peacock matter. But ask yourself this: *Why* do old enemies come together?"

Mizir chortled over the images he and Iman were collecting of the newcomers. "Definite morphological differences. The fronds on their headballs show a different distribution of colors. There are more of the greenish sort than we have seen in the city. And the Sunbursters are shorter on the average."

Ladawan told them that the Intelligence had found close matches between the phonemes used by the sailors and those used by the city folk. "They are distinct tongues—or perhaps I should say distinct 'drums'—but of the same family. That which the cobaltics here sometimes speak is quite different."

After the ceremony in the park, there was raucous celebration. Music was created—by plucking and beating and bowing. "They know the cymbal and the xylophone and the fiddle," said Iman, "but not the trumpet or the reed."

"One needs a mouth connected to a pair of lungs for that sort of thing," Mizir told her.

"But, oh, what four hands can do with a *tunbur*!" And indeed, their stringed instruments were marvels of complexity beside which *tunbur*, guitar, *sitar*, violin were awkward and simple. Clawtips did for plectrums and tentacles fretted and even bowed most wondrously.

There was dancing, too, though not as humans understood the dance. They gyrated in triplets, Sunbursters and Havenites together, clapping with their lifting arms while they did. Mizir could not tell if the triplets were single or mixed gender. "You have to reach into the thorax opening and call forth the organ," he said. "Otherwise, who can tell?"

"Not I," Iman answered. "I wonder if they can. A people whose gender is known only through discovery will have . . . interesting depths." She glanced first at Hassan, then at Mizir, who winked. The sound of the clapping in the parkland evolved from raindrop randomness to marching cadence and back again, providing a peculiar ground to the intricate, contrapuntal melodies.

The team gave up trying to make sense of the great babble and settled for recording everything that transpired. But dance is contagious, and soon Khalid and Bashir had coaxed the other men into a line that strutted back and forth while Iman clapped a rhythm and Soong and Ladawan looked on with amused detachment. Caught up, Hassan broke from the line into a *mesri*, and Iman with him. They bent and swiveled and they twisted their arms like serpents in challenge and response, while Khalid and Bashir clapped 11/4-time and Mizir mimed throwing coins at them until, finally exhausted, they came to a panting halt, face to face.

It was only a moment they stood that way, but it was a very long moment and whole worlds might have whirled about like Sufis while they caught their breath. Then Iman straightened her *hijab*, which the dance had tugged askew. Hassan thought he saw a dark curl of escaped hair on her shiny forehead. She gave him a high look, cocking her head just so, and departed for her tent. Hassan was left standing there, wondering if he was supposed to follow or not, while Soong and Mizir looked to each other.

He did pass by her tent on his way to sleep and, standing by the closed flap—he did not dare to lift it—said, "When we return to Earth, we will speak, you and I." He waited a moment in case there was a reply, but there was none, unless the tinkling of wind chimes was her laughter.

The morning dawned with mist. A fog had rolled in from the Eastern Sea and lay, a soft blanket, over everything. Hilltops emerged like islands from a sea of smoke. A few of the tallest buildings in Haven thrust above the fog, suggesting the masts of a sunken shipwreck. Frustrated, the drones crisscrossed the shrouded landscape, seeking what could be found on frequencies non-visual. Yance took the ultralight out again, and from a great height spied a speckling of islands on the horizon. Delighted, Soong placed them on the map and, with droll humor added, "Here there be dragons" to the blank expanse beyond. The Intelligence dutifully created a virtual globe and dappled it in greens and browns and blues. Yet it remained for the most part a disheartening black, like a lump of coal daubed with a few specks of paint.

"The Havenites came here from somewhere near where the Sunbursters live," Iman declared, tracing with an uncertain finger curlicues within the darkened part of the globe. "If only we knew where. The cobaltic folk may be indigenes, but I think they come from still a third place, and are strangers on these shores as well."

But fog is a morning sort of thing and the sun slowly winnowed it. The park, lying as it did on a swell of land, emerged early, as if from a receding flood and, as in any such ebb, was dotted with bits of debris left behind.

"There are five," Hassan told the others when he pulled his binoculars off. "Two of the bodies lie together, but the other three lie solitary. One is a marine off the foreign ship."

"Suicide?" wondered Iman. "But why?"

Soong said, "Not so strange. Hopelessness often follow unreasonable hope."

"Why was their hope unreasonable?" Bashir challenged him; but Soong only spread his hands in a helpless gesture, and Bashir cursed him as an unbeliever.

Hassan cased the binoculars. "People will do things behind a curtain that they otherwise entertain only in their hearts. There is something disheartening and solitary about fog. I suspect there are other bodies in the bushes."

"But, so many?" Mizir asked with mixed horror and fascination; for the Prophet, praise be upon him, had forbidden suicide to the Faithful.

Hassan turned to the tele-pilots. "Khalid, Bashir, Ladawan. Quickly. Send your drones to the park and retrieve tissue samples from the corpses. Seed the bodies with micromachines, so Mizir can explore their inner structures." Glancing at Mizir, he added, "That should please you. You've longed for a glimpse of their anatomy ever since we arrived."

Mizir shook his head. "But not this way. Not this way."

Bashir cried in distress. "Must you, cousin?"

Yet they did as they were told, and the drones swooped like buzzards onto the bodies of the dead. Clever devices no larger than dust motes entered through wounds and orifices, where they scurried up glands and channels and sinuses and took the metes and bounds of the bodies. "Quickly," Hassan told them. "Before the folk from the city arrive to carry them off."

"The folk in the city may have other concerns," Iman said. When Hassan gave her a question in a glance, she added, "Other bodies."

"I don't understand," said Bashir. "They seemed so happy yesterday, at the peace ceremony."

"How can you know what they felt?" Hassan asked him. "We may have no name for what they felt."

Yance said, "Maybe it was a sham, and the Sunbursters pulled a massacre during the night." But as a practical matter, Hassan doubted that. The ship had not borne enough marines to carry out such a task so quickly and with so little alarm.

Before the fog had entirely dissipated Hassan ordered the drones home, and thither they flew engorged with the data they had sucked from the bodies, ready to feed it to the waiting Intelligence. On the scrublands south of the park, a covered wagon had left the road and stood now near the base of the Misty Mountain exposed in the morning sun and bracketed by three tents and a picket line of six-horses. Sensors warding the cliffside approach revealed five Batinites in various attitudes: tending the campfires, feeding the horses, and when the drones passed above, two of them turned their headballs to follow the heat track and one sprang to a tripod and adjusted its position.

"A surveyor's tripod," Klaus said when Hassan showed him the image. "They survey a new road, perhaps to those fishing villages in the southern Delta."

"I think these folk have seen our drones," Hassan decided.

"But our drones are stealthed," Bashir objected.

"Yes. And hushed and cooled, but they still leave a heat footprint, and against the ocean chill of this morning's mist they must stand out like a silhouette on the skyline."

"Still . . ."

"Among humans," said Iman, "there are those who may hear the softest whisper. Or see the shimmering air above the sands of *Ar Rub al-Khali*. Is it so strange if some of our Batinites have glimpsed strange streaks of sourceless heat in the sky?"

Hassan continued to study the last, backward-glancing image captured by the drones as they passed over the surveying party. A short-statured Batinite crouched behind the tripod, his tentacles adjusting verniers on an instrument of some sort. "If so, they may have taken a bearing on what they perceived."

"If they have," said Bashir, "what can they do? The cliff is sheer."

Hassan ordered that all drones be grounded for the time being and that no one stand in sight of the cliff's edge. "We can watch the city with the peepers we have already emplaced." Yance was especially saddened by the order and said that he could still fly over the western slope of the mountains, but Hassan pointed out that to gain the altitude he needed he must first circle over the very scrublands across which the surveying party trekked. "It will be for only a little while," he told his team. "Once they have laid out the road and have returned to the City, we will resume the flights." The one thing he had not considered was that the party might not be blazing a road. This did not occur to him until after Iman brought him the strange report from the Intelligence.

"There is no doubt?" he asked her, for even when she had placed the two images side by side, Hassan could not be sure. Not so the Intelligence, which, considering only data, was not distracted by strangeness.

"None at all. The images are identical down to the last eigenface. The surveyor in your road party is the same individual who followed the flight of the drone on the night the Blue Planet rose."

Soong, listening, said, "Remarkable! First Batinite twice seen."

Hassan picked up the first image and saw again the headball turned against the grain of that agitated crowd. "I do not trust coincidence," he said. "I think he has been taking vectors on each sighting of a heat trail, and has set out to find their source."

Iman sensed his troubled mind. "Should we prepare to evacuate?"

"No!" said Bashir.

"When you are more seasoned, young cousin," Hassan told him, "you may give the orders." To Iman: "Not yet. But all may depend on what is under the tarp on his wagon."

Which was, as they learned a few days later, a hot-air balloon. Klaus was delighted. "Ja! Very like Bismarck's age. Railroads, telegraphs, sailing ships with steam, and now balloons. The technological congruence! Think what it implies!"

Hassan did not wait to hear what it implied but walked off by himself, away from the tele-pilot booths and the tent flaps snapping in the dry mountain breeze. Iman followed at a distance. He paused at the shimmering gate and passed a few words with Khalid that Iman did not hear. Then he continued through the meadow, his legs kicking up the sparkling colored pollen from the knee-high flowers, until he reached the place where the wonderfall plummeted from very the top of the world. There he stood in silence gazing into the hidden depths of the pool. Mist filled the air, saturated it, until it seemed only a more tenuous extension of the pool itself. After watching him for a while, Iman approached and stood by his side.

Still he said nothing. When a few moments had gone past, Iman took his hand in hers; not in any forward way, but as one person may comfort another.

"I wonder where it goes?" he said at last, his voice distant beneath the steady roar. "All the way into the heart of the world, I think. But no one will ever know. Who could enter that pool without being crushed under by the force of the water? Who could ever return against that press to tell us?"

"Will you order evacuation?" She had to bend close to his ear to make herself heard.

"Do you think we should?"

"I think we should meet these people."

Hassan turned to regard her, which brought them very close together. *The better to hear over the roar,* he told himself.

"We are not forbidden contact," Iman insisted. "Circumstances vary from world to world. When to make contact is a judgment each captain must make."

"Though few are called upon to make it. I never have. Concannon never did. Life is rare. Sentient life rarer still. Sentient life robust enough to endure contact, a jewel. Your flying flowers were not sentient."

"No. They were only beautiful."

He laughed. "You are as hidden as this world."

"Shall I remove the *hijab?*" Fingers twitched toward her head-scarf.

He reached out and held her wrists, keeping her hands still. "It is not the *hijab* that hides you. You could remove all of your clothing and reveal nothing. Are the Batinites beautiful, too? You told us that once."

"Yes. Yes they are, in their own way. But they prepare for war and cry defiance; and dance when enemies make friends; and sometimes, in the dark, they kill themselves. How can we go and never know who they are?"

Hassan released her and, stooping, picked up a fallen branch of six-elder wood. Like all such vegetation in that place, it was punkish in its texture, breaking easily into corded strings and fibers. "It doesn't matter." Then, seeing as she had not heard him over the roar of the falls, he came very close to her face. "Our curious friend will have his balloon aloft before we could gather up this scatter of equipment and pack it away. And we cannot hide ourselves in this meadow, if he can see our heat. So the decision to initiate contact is his, not mine, whether he knows it or not." He threw the branch into the churning waters of the pool, and the maelstrom took it and it was gone. Hassan stared after it for a while, then turned to go. Iman placed her hand in the crook of his arm and walked with him.

She said when they were away from the wonderfall and voices could be voices once again and neither shouts nor whispers, "One other thing, you could do."

"What?"

"We have the laser pistols in the bus lockers. You could burn a hole in his balloon before he even rises from the ground."

"Yes. A hole mysteriously burned through the fabric. A fine way to conceal our presence."

"As you said, we can not conceal ourselves in any case. To burn his balloon would buy us the time to leave unobserved."

"Yes . . . but that's not what you want."

"No, I want to meet them; but you need to consider all your options."

"Can the Intelligence translate adequately for a meeting?"

"Who can know that until we try?"

Hassan laughed. "You are becoming like me."

"Is that so bad?"

"It is terrible. One Hassan is more than enough. One Iman will barely suffice."

The others had gathered at the pavilion, some at the ropes, as if awaiting the command to strike camp. The ultralight technicians were gathered in a group at one end of the camp. Whichever the decision, they would be leaving on the next supply run.

Bashir caught Hassan's eye and there was a pleading in his face. Only Soong remained engrossed in his instruments. The world could end. God could clap his hands and mountains dissipate like the clouds, and Soong would only monitor the opacity and the density of their vapors.

To the technicians, Hassan gave a comp-pad containing his interim report and told them to carry it straight to the director's office on their return. "I've called for a contact follow-up team." Bashir and some of the others let out a cheer, which Hassan silenced with a glare. "I think our Batinite balloonist has shown sufficient enterprise that he deserves the fruit of it. But this decision has come on us too quickly and I dislike being rushed."

Passing Mizir on the way to his own pavilion, Hassan clapped his old colleague on the shoulder. "Once we have established contact, you will no longer need wonder about this world's ecology. Their own scholars will give you all the information you want."

Mizir shook his head sadly. "It won't be the same."

Later, Hassan noticed that Soong had not moved from his monitors. Through long acquaintance, Hassan knew that this was not entirely unworldliness on the man's part. So he joined the other at the astronomy board, though for several moments he did not interrupt Soong's concentration, allowing his presence to do for a question.

After a while, Soong said as if to the air, "At first, I think: *moonlet*. Strange skies, these, and we not know all out there. But orbit very low. Ninety-minute orbit." He pointed to a tiny speck of light that crossed the screen. "Every ninety minute he come back. Yesterday five. Today, ten, maybe twelve."

"What are they?" Hassan asked. "You said moonlets?"

"Only see when catch sunlight. Maybe many more, not see."

"Perhaps al-Batin has a ring of small moons . . ." But Soong was shaking his head.

"Two big moons sweep low-orbit free."

"Then what . . . ?"

"Men go to moon, long time past. Go to Mars. I think now we see . . ."

"Rocket ships?" Hassan stood up, away from the screen where last night's telescope data replayed and looked into the pale, cloud-shrouded sky. "Rocket ships," he whispered.

"I think," said Soong, "from Blue Planet."

Soong's discovery added another layer of urgency to the team's activities. "A second sapient, and in the same system!" said Iman. "Unprecedented," said Mizir. "We should leave, now," said Klaus; and Yance agreed: "We can stay hid from the folks here, but maybe not from these newcomers."

"We have to stay!" Bashir cried. Soong himself said nothing more than that this would complicate matters, and it seemed as if the complications bothered him quite more than other possibilities. Hassan retreated to his tent to escape the din and there he pondered matters.

But not too long. There was the balloonist to consider. Balloons and space ships, and here the Earthlings sat with a Nagy hypergate and vehicles that could travel in *the wrong direction*—and it was the Earthlings who were considering flight. There was something very funny about that. When Hassan emerged from his tent, everyone else stopped what he or she was doing and turned toward him in expectation. "Prepare for D&D," was all he said and turned back into his tent. He heard someone enter behind him and knew before turning that it was Iman.

Iman said, "Destruction and demolition? But . . ."

"But what?" Hassan said. "We cannot get everything into the buses quickly enough. We must destroy what we cannot take."

"But you had said we would stay!"

"The equation has been altered. The risks now outweigh the opportunities."

"What risks?"

"You heard Klaus. Folk with spaceships have other capabilities. We have grown careless observing the Batinites. These . . . these Azraqi will know radar, radio, laser, powered flight. Perhaps they know stealth and micromachines. I would rather they did not know of other-buses."

"But the chance to observe First Contact *from a third-party perspective!*"

"We will stay and observe as long as possible, but with one hand on the latch-handles of our other-buses. Soong counted at least twelve ships in orbit, and the Batinites began re-arming some while ago. I do not think we will observe a First Contact."

The team powered down nonessentials, transferred vital samples and data to the other-buses, and policed the meadow of their artifacts. Mizir drafted the ultralight technicians, who had been acting detached about the whole affair. They reported to a different Section Chief than did the Survey Team, but the old man leered at them. "There are no idlers on-planet," he told them. Hassan spent the evening redrafting his report.

The next morning, Soong told him that the ships had begun to land. "One ship fire retro-burn while in telescope view. Intelligence extrapolate landing in antipodes. Other ships not appear on schedule, so maybe also deorbit."

Hassan passed the word for everyone to stay alert and imposed radio silence on the team. "We are no longer so remote here on our mountain as we once were. We must be cautious with our drones, with radar pings. With anything that these newcomers might be able to detect."

He did not suppose that there was anything especially remarkable about their alpine meadow that the orbiting ships would have studied it from aloft, but he had the tents struck—they clashed with the colors—and moved the primary monitors beneath a stand of six-cedar. He ordered Khalid and Ladawan to bring the other-buses to idle, so that they would be a little out of phase with the Right 'Brane and, in theory, impossible to detect by any but *other* instruments. When they had all gathered under the trees, Hassan did a head count and discovered that Bashir was missing.

With many curses, he set out to look for him and found him by the edge of the cliff that overlooked the plains. Bashir lay prone with a pair of enhanced binoculars pressed to his eyes. Hassan, too, dropped prone upon the grass beside him—strange grass, too-yellow grass, velvety and oily and odd to the touch. Hassan remembered that he was on a distant and alien world and was surprised to realize that for a time he had forgotten.

Bashir said, "Do you think he knows? About the ships in orbit, I mean."

Hassan knew his cousin was speaking of the balloonist. "He knew they were coming. They all knew. When al-Asraq came into opposition, the ships would come. Someone must have worked out the orbital mechanics."

"He's coming to us to ask for help."

"Against the Asraqi."

"Yes. They are brave folk. Regimented companies in squares, firing one-shot rifles. Field cannon like Mehmet Ali had. And against what? *People in space ships!* What chance do they have, Hassan, unless we help them? 'Surrender to God and do good deeds.' Is that not what God said through his Messenger, praise be upon him?"

"Bashir, there are nine of us, plus the technicians for the ultralight. We have no arms but the four lasers in the weapons lockers. Only Klaus has any knowledge of military theory—and it is *only* theory. What can we possibly do?"

The attack was swift and brutal and came without warning. The shuttlecraft flew in low from the west, screaming over the crests of the mountains, shedding velocity over the ocean as they banked and turned. There were three of them, shaped like lozenges, their heat shields still glowing dully on their undersides. "Scramjets," said Klaus into his headset and the Intelligence heard and compiled the observation with the visuals. "Bring the cameras to bear," said Hassan. "Bring the cameras to bear. One is landing on the park. The second on the far side of the city. It may land in the swamp and be mired. Ladawan, we'll take the chance. Send a drone over that way. On a narrow beam. Yance, if the invaders put anything between us and the drone, destroy the drone immediately. Where did the third shuttle go? Where is it? Klaus, your assessment!"

"Mid-twenty-first-century equivalent," the German said. "Scramjet SSTOs. Look for smart bombs, laser targeting, hopper-hunters. High-density flechette rifles with submunitions. Oh, those poor bastards. Oh, those poor bastards!" Black flowers blossomed in the sky. "The Havenites have their field guns to maximum elevation. Low-energy shells bursting in the air . . . but too low to matter. Ach, for an AA battery!"

"You are choosing sides, Klaus."

The technologist lowered his binoculars. "Yes, naturally," he snapped, and the binoculars rose again.

"It is not our quarrel," Hassan said, but the Roumi was not listening to him.

"The second shuttle is in the swamp," Ladawan reported. "I do not think the Havenites expected that. They have few defenses on that side."

"I do not think the Asraqi expected so, either," Klaus said. "These shuttles have only the limited maneuverability. More than the first American shuttles, but not much more. They may have little choice in where they land."

"Where did the third one go?" Hassan asked.

Bashir raised an ululation. "It was hit! It was hit! It flew into a shell burst. It's down in the surf."

"A lucky shot," said Klaus, but he too raised a fist and shook it at the sky.

"Listen to them cheer in the City," said Iman, who was monitoring the ears that they had planted during their long observation and study.

The other two shuttles released missiles, which flew into the City, and two of the tallest buildings coughed and shrugged and slid into ruin. Smoke and flame rose above the skyline. Hassan turned to Iman. "Did the cheering stop?" he asked, and Iman turned away from him.

"No, show me," Klaus said to Soong, bending over the screen where the drone's feed was displayed. The Chinese pointed. Here. Here. Here. Klaus turned to Hassan.

"I was wrong. The third shuttle made by intent the ocean landing. They have triangulated the City. Park. Swamp. Ocean. Look at it out there. See? It floats. They must be for both the water or ground landing designed."

Soong said, "Ah! I find radio traffic. Feeding data stream to Intelligence." He put the stream on audio and everyone in the team paused to listen for a moment. There was something liquid, something squishy, about the sounds. Frogs croaking, iguanas barking. Not computer signals, but voices. The sounds had an analog feel to them.

Bashir said, "The balloon is up."

Hassan turned to stare at him. "Are you certain? The man must be mad. To go up in *this?* Iman, Bashir, Khalid. Go to the cliff. I will come shortly." Hassan could not take his eyes from the dying city. Upping the magnification on his binoculars, he saw troops emerge from the first shuttle, the one that had landed in the park. "Close images!" he cried. "I want close images of those people."

"There are not very many of them," Mizir ventured.

"There do not need to be very many of them," Klaus told him. "These will be light airborne infantry. They are to hold a landing zone for the mother ship."

"You're guessing," Hassan said.

"*Ganz natürlich.*"

The landing force scattered into teams of three and fanned across the park. The Asraqi were bipedal, shorter than the Batinites, stockier. They wore flat black uniforms of a leathery material. Helmets with masks covered their faces—if anything like faces lurked under those masks. Skin, where it showed, was scaled and shiny. "Reptiloids," said Mizir, half-delighted to have a new race to study but not, under the circumstances, fully so. "The works of God are wonderfully diverse, but he uses precious few templates."

"Speculate," Hassan said. "What am I seeing?"

"The helmets are heads-up displays," Klaus said. "The mother ship has in Low Orbit satellites placed and the Lizards receive on the battle space, the information."

"If they are reptiloid," said Mizir, "they would likely come from a dry place."

Klaus pursed his lips. "But Earth has many aquatic reptiles, not so? And al-Asraq is watery."

"So it does!" cried Mizir, "but there are yet deserts. Besides, those may be *fish* scales. Amphibians. What do you expect from me from the glimpse of a single bare arm!"

"Mizir!" Hassan cautioned him, and the exobiologist took a deep calming breath and turned away.

"Hassan." It was Bashir's voice on the radio. "The balloonist is halfway up, but the winds are contrary, keeping him away from the cliff."

Hassan cursed and broke his own rule long enough to bark, "Radio silence!" He turned. "What is it, for the love of God? Khalid, I told you to go to the cliff and wait for the balloonist."

Khalid glanced at the progress of the battle on the large plasma screen. "Not a fair fight, is it. Here, sir. You may need this."

Hassan looked down at his hand and saw that the gate warden had given him a laser pistol.

"There are only four laser pistols," Khalid explained, "two in each bus. Ladawan and I keep one each. We are trained marksmen. I give one to you, because you are team captain. Who gets the fourth?"

"Warden, if the Asraqi attack us here, four laser pistols will do no good. Against a cruise missile?"

"Sir, they will do more good than if we were utterly disarmed."

Hassan tucked the pistol into his waistband. "Klaus?"

The German lowered his binoculars, saw what the gate warden had, and shook his head. "Military strategy is to me small squares on a map-screen. I have never fired a handgun. Give it to Yance. Americans make the *Fickerei* to pistols."

Soong reached up from his console seat. "I take."

Khalid hesitated. "Do you know how to use one?"

"I show you by burning rabbit." He pointed to a six-legged rodent on the far side of the meadow.

Khalid did not ask for the proof, but handed over the pistol. Soong laid it on his console.

"Do you shoot so well?" Hassan asked him after Khalid had gone to the cliffside.

"No, but now he does not give pistol to Yance. Too young, like your cousin. Too excitable. Better pistol with me. I not know use. But I *know* I not know use."

"The Batinites must have expected a landing in the park," Klaus announced. "They have a regiment in the woods concealed. Now they charge while the Asraqi they are scattered!"

Hassan paused in the act of leaving and watched while ranks and files decked in yellow marched from the woods to the drum-claps of their tympanums and their lower arms. He saw the corporals bawl orders. He saw the ranks dress themselves and two banners—the six-eagle and some device that was probably the regiment's own—rose aloft. The first rank knelt and both it and the second rank fired in volley, then they sidestepped to allow the next two ranks to pass through and repeat the process while they reloaded.

They managed the evolution twice before the invaders tore them apart. High velocity rounds from scattered, mobile kill squads firing from shelter shredded the pretty uniforms and the fine banners and splattered the six-cedars and iron-wood and the chartreuse oil-grass with glistening pools of yellow-green ichor. A few cannon shots from the shuttle completed the slaughter. Nothing was left of the regiment but twitching corpses and body parts. Hassan wondered whether the young soldier they had once watched make love to his sweetheart lay among them.

"O, *les braves gens*," Klaus whispered, echoing a long-dead King of Prussia at a long-forgotten battle.

Hassan could bear to see no more. "Record everything," he barked. "The rest of you, get those buses packed. Power down any equipment whose source might be traced by those . . . lizards. Klaus . . . Klaus! Estimate the invaders' capabilities. What can we operate safely? At the moment, the Asraqi are . . . preoccupied; but sooner or later they'll bring down aircraft—or a satellite will chance to look down on this meadow. Leave nothing behind that those folk may find useful—and they might find anything useful!" He turned to walk to the cliffside, where the balloonist was attempting his ascent. Klaus said, "But, I thought we might . . ." Hassan silenced him with a glare.

When he reached the edge of the six-cedar grove that grew close to the cliffside, Hassan saw Iman monitoring the balloon through her goggles. She seemed an alien creature herself, with her head wrapped in a scarf and her face concealed by the glasses.

"He's using a grappling line," Bashir announced as Hassan joined them. "He whirls it around, then throws it toward the cliff."

"Has he seen you?"

"No." It was Iman, who answered without taking her eyes off the balloonist. "A dangerous maneuver," she added. "He could foul his mooring rope, or rake the balloon above him."

"We've been watching the battle," Bashir said, "on our hand comms."

Iman lowered her glasses and turned around. Hassan glanced at Khalid, who squatted on his heels a little behind the others in the brush; but the warden's face held no expression. Hassan rubbed his fist and did not look at any of them. "It's not a battle. It's a massacre. I think the Batinites have killed two Asraqi. Maybe. The invaders evacuated their wounded into their shuttle, so who can say?"

"We have to *do* something!" Bashir cried.

Hassan whirled on him. "Do *we?* What would you have us do, cousin? We have no weapons, but the four handguns. Soong is clever, and perhaps he could create a super-weapon from the components of our equipment, but I do not think Soong is quite that clever. Yance could fly out in the ultralight and perhaps drop the gas chromatograph on someone's head—but he could never do that twice."

Iman turned 'round again. "Stop that! Stop mocking him! He wants to help. We all do."

"I want him to face reality. We can do nothing—but watch and record."

"We could send one of the buses back to Earth," Bashir entreated him, "and show them what's happening here. They'll send help. They'll send the Legion, or the American Marines, and we'll see how those *lizards* like being on the other side of the boot!"

"What makes you think that the Union, or the Americans, or *anyone* would send so much as a policeman? What interests do they have here?"

Bashir opened his mouth and closed it and opened it a second time. "They'd, they'd have to. These people need help!"

"And if they did send the Legion," Hassan continued remorselessly, "every last trooper would have to come through the gate. The Asraqi may be brutal, but they can not be stupid. One cruise missile to take out the gate and the whole expeditionary force would be trapped, cut off from home forever. Or the Asraqi would simply pick off whoever came through, seize the buses, and . . . what general would be mad enough to propose such a plan? What politician fool enough to approve it? What legionnaire suicidal enough to obey?"

Khalid spoke up. "And you haven't yet asked how we would move a force large enough to matter down a sheer cliff onto the plains."

"Thank you, warden," Hassan said, "but I think my cousin begins to understand. But there is one thing we can do," he added quietly.

Bashir seized on hope. "What? What can we do?"

"Little enough. We can give information—if the Intelligence has mastered enough of their speech. We can tell our balloonist friend about asymmetric warfare. About the Spanish *guerrilla* that tormented Napoleon. About Tito's partisans."

"Will that help?"

Hassan wanted to tell him no, that few irregular forces had ever triumphed without a secure refuge or a regimented army to back them. The *guerrilla* had had Wellington; Tito's partisans, the Red Army. "Yes," he told Bashir. Khalid, who may have known better, said nothing.

"He's latched hold," said Iman.

"What?"

"The balloonist," she told him. "His grapple. He's pulling the balloon toward the edge of the cliff to moor it."

"Ah. Well. Time to welcome the poor bastard."

"Why," asked Khalid of no one in particular, "with all that is happening to his city, does he insist on reaching this peak?"

"I think," said Hassan, "because he has nothing else left to reach for."

The Batinite headball cannot show expression, at least no expression that humans can read. Yet it was not hard to discern the emotions of the balloonist when, after he had clambered from the balloon's basket onto solid ground and secured it by a rope to the stump of a tree, the waiting humans rose from concealment. The Batinite reared nearly vertical, waving his tentacled upper arms in the air, and staggered backward. One step. Then another.

"No!" said Iman. "The cliff!" And she moved toward him.

Groping behind into the basket, the balloonist pulled out a musket and, before Hassan could even react to the sight, fired a load of shot that ripped Iman across the throat and chest. Hassan heard a pellet pass him by like an angry bee and heard, too, Bashir cry out in pain.

Grapeshot is not a high-velocity round; it did not throw Iman back. She stood in place, swaying, while her *hijab* turned slowly from checkerboard to black crimson. She began to turn toward Hassan with a puzzled look on her face, and Hassan thought she meant to ask him what had happened, but the act unbalanced her, and, sighing, she twisted to the ground.

Hassan caught her and lowered her gently the rest of the way. Speaking her name, he yanked the sodden *hijab* away and held her head to his breast. Her hair was black, he noted. Black, and wound tightly in a coiled braid.

The Batinite was meanwhile methodically reloading his musket, ramming a load down the muzzle, preparing for a second murder. With a cry, Hassan rose to his feet, tugged the pistol from his waistband, and aimed it at the thing that had come in the balloon. The red targeting spot wavered across the alien's headball. The laser would slice the leathery carapace open, spilling—not brains, but something like a ganglion that served to process sense impressions before sending them to the belly. Hassan shifted his aim to the belly, to the orifice from which might emerge slimy, unclean organs, behind the diaphragm of which Mizir had named the creature's life and thought.

He almost fired. He had placed his thumb on the activation trigger, but Khalid shoved his hand down and fired his own laser four times with cruel precision, burning the hands of the beast, so that it dropped the musket and emitted sounds like a mad percussionist. With a fifth and more sustained burn, Khalid ran a gash along the body of the balloon hovering in the sky beyond. The colorful fabric sighed—much like Iman had sighed—and crumpled in much the same way, too, hanging for a while on the rocky escarpment while the wind teased its folds.

Hassan dropped his pistol to the dirt unfired. He turned and walked into the alien cedars.

Khalid indicated the thrumming prisoner. "Wait! What are we to do with him?"

Hassan did not look back. "Throw it over the cliff."

Soong found Hassan at last in the place where he ought to have looked first, by the endless falls and bottomless pool at the far end of the mountain valley. There the team leader knelt on a prayer rug that he had rolled out on the damp earth and rock and prostrated himself again and again. Soong watched for a time. He himself honored his ancestors and followed, when the mood struck, an Eight-Fold Path. Perhaps there was a god behind it all, perhaps not. His ancestors were not forthcoming on the subject. Soot from the burning city had begun to settle on the plateau. Explosions boomed like distant thunder. If that were the work of a god, it was one beyond Soong's comprehending.

Hassan sat back on his haunches. "Why did she have to die?" he cried, loudly enough that even the roar of the falls was overcome.

Soong wondered momentarily whether Hassan had addressed him or his god before he answered. "Because pellets sever carotid artery."

Hassan hesitated, then turned around. "What sort of reason is that?"

"No reason," Soong said. "Westerners think *reason*, always *reason*. But, no reason. 'Shit happens.' Life is wheel. Someday you escape."

"Do not presume to question God."

"Gods not answer, however often asked. Maybe they not know, either."

"I can't even blame that poor bastard in the balloon." Hassan covered his face with his hands. "His planet has been invaded, his people massacred, the proudest achievements of his civilization exposed as less than nothing. What were we to him but more invaders? Tell me Khalid did not throw him over the cliff."

"He know not lawful order. But survival up here, more cruel. Without balloon, how he descend? With hands burned so, how he fend?"

"It was my fault, Soong. What sort of captain am I? I let al-Batin lull me. I should never have allowed Iman to approach him like that, without taking time to calm his fears."

"Not matter," said Soong. "He no fear. He hate."

"What do you mean? How can you know that?"

Soong spread his hands. "Maybe Intelligence not translate well. But say headball drum hate and loathing. We question him. Mizir, Khalid, me. This not first visit from Blue Planet. Asraqi come once before. Come in peace. Trade, discovery, I think. And Batinites kill all—for defiling holy soil of Batin."

"Without provocation?"

"Arrival provocation enough, balloonist say. Asraqi ship damaged, but some escape, come to Haven. Warn of terrible revenge, next approach, *but Batinites not care*. No logic, just fury. Kill survivors too. Balloonist one of them. *Proud* to defend al-Batin. Remember, Hassan, he bring balloon here *before* Asraqi land, and bring gun already loaded. Not know *who* up here or *why*, only *someone* up here. Come to kill, not to greet."

"Xenophobes . . ." Hassan could not reconcile that with the gentle, carefree folk he had been observing for so long. And yet, the one never did preclude the other.

Soong shook his head. "Balloonist not hate Asraqi; only hate that they come."

"Does the difference matter? And is the Asraqi punishment not worse than the original crime?" Hassan did not expect an answer. He did not think that there ever would be an answer. He rolled his prayer rug and slung it over his shoulder. "Are the buses ready to go?"

Soong nodded. "Waiting for captain."

"Is . . . is Iman on board?"

"In specimen locker."

Hassan winced. "I'm ordering Khalid to seal the gate. No one comes back here. Ever."

"Too dangerous," Soong agreed.

"Not in the way you think."

From a world named The Hidden by humans, humans departed. The gate closed on a pleasant mountain glade, far above the flaming cities on the plains below. Gates swung where God willed, and man could only submit. Perhaps they opened where they did for a reason, but it was not man's place to question God's reasons.

Hassan Maklouf was their leader, a man who had walked on eighteen worlds and bore in consequence eighteen wounds. To ten of those worlds, he had followed another; to eight, others had followed him. From four, he had escaped with his life. With two, he had fallen in love. On one, he had lost his soul.

TOURISM

M. JOHN HARRISON

M. John Harrison is not a prolific writer, and, until recently, was little-known to the American SF readership at large. In Britain, however, he has been an influential figure behind the scenes since the days of Michael Moorcock's *New Worlds* in the late sixties, and has had a disproportionate effect with a relatively small body of work; in fact, recently he was given the Richard Evans Memorial Award, a new award designed to honor just that sort of career and reputation. Harrison made his first sale, to *New Worlds*, in 1975, and in the decades that followed, has also sold to *Interzone, The Magazine of Fantasy & Science Fiction, Other Edens, Little Deaths, Sisters of the Night, MetaHorror, Elsewhere, New Terrors, Tarot Tales, The Shimmering Door, Prime Evil, The New Improved Sun*, and other markets, stories that have been collected in *The Machine in Shaft Ten and Other Stories, The Ice Monkey, Travel Arrangements: Short Stories*, and, most recently, *Things That Never Happen*. It was the stories and novels about the enigmatic city of Viriconium, though, work on the shifting and amorphous borderland of science fiction and fantasy, that would prove to be among his most influential work in the genre. The Viriconium cycle has recently been reissued in an omnibus volume, *Viriconium*, consisting of the novels *The Pastel City, A Storm of Wings, In Viriconium*, and the collection *Viriconium Nights*.

In the nineties, Harrison would turn away from genre work to produce a sequence of ostensibly "mainstream" novels (although many of them contain subtle fantastic elements) such as *Climbers* and *Signs of Life*, but recently he has returned to core science fiction with a stylish and intricate Space Opera, *Light*, which is attracting enough attention that it may gain him the wide American audiences that have eluded him up till now. Harrison's other books include the novels *The Committed Men* and *The Centauri Device*. Coming up is a new novel, *The Course of the Heart*. He had a story in our Seventeenth Annual Collection.

In the atmospheric and inventive story that follows, he takes us to a tourist destination you won't find in any of today's guidebooks . . .

Jack Serotonin sat in a bar on Strait Street, just inside the aureole of the Raintown event, in conversation with a fat man from another planet who called himself Antoyne. They had been playing dice all night. It was just before dawn, and a brown light, polished but dim at the same time, crept out the streetlights to fill the place.

"I was never in there," the fat man admitted, meaning the event zone, "but what I think—"

"If this is going to be bullshit, Antoyne," Serotonin advised him, "don't even start."

The fat man looked hurt.

"Have another drink," Jack said.

The bar was about halfway down Strait, a cluttered, narrowish street of two-storey buildings, along which two out of three had their windows boarded up. Like all the streets in that part of Raintown, Strait was full of cats, especially at dawn and dusk, when they went in and out of the event site. As if in acknowledgement, the bar was called Black Cat White Cat. It featured a zinc counter slightly too high for comfort. A row of bottles that contained liquids of unlikely colours. A few tables. The long window steamed up easily, no one but Antoyne cared. In the morning the bar smelled of last night's garlic. Some mornings it smelled of mould too, as if something had crept out of the event aureole in the dark and, after a few attempts to breathe the air in the bar, died underneath a corner table. Shadow operators hung high up in the join between the walls and the ceiling, like cobwebs. There wasn't much for them to do.

Jack was in the bar most days. He ate there. He ran his business out of it. He used it as a mail drop, and as a place to check out his clients: but really it was what they called a jump-off joint, positioned well, not too far back from the event site, not so close as to suffer effects. Another advantage it had: Jack was on good terms with the owner, a woman called Liv Hula who never put in a manager but ran it herself day and night. People thought she was the barkeep; that suited her. She wasn't known to complain. She was one of those women who draw in on themselves after their fortieth year, short, thin, with brush-cut grey hair, a couple of smart tattoos on her muscular forearms, an expression as if she was always thinking of something else. She had music in the bar. Her taste ran to the outcaste beats and saltwater dub you heard a few years back. That aged her as far as Jack Serotonin was concerned. Which is to say they'd been round a time or two.

"Hey," she told Jack now, "leave the fat man alone. Everyone's entitled to an opinion."

Serotonin stared at her. "I won't even answer that."

"Bad night, Jack?"

"You should know. You were there."

She poured him a shot of Black Heart rum, along with whatever the fat man was having. "I would say you were out there on your own, Jack," she said. "Much of the time." They both laughed. Then she looked over his shoulder at the open door of the bar and said—

"Maybe you got a customer here."

The woman who stood there was a little too tall to wear the high heels in fashion then. She had long thin hands, and that way of looking both anxious and tranquil a lot of those tourist women have. There was a tentativeness about her. She was elegant and awkard at the same time. If she knew how to wear clothes, perhaps that was a learned thing, or perhaps it was a talent she had never fully brought out in herself. You thought instantly she had lost her way. When she came into the bar that morning, she was wearing a black two-piece with a little fitted jacket and calf-length kick-pleat skirt, under a long, honey-colored fur coat. She stood there uncertainly in the doorway, with the cold morning light from Strait Street behind her, and the unflattering light from the window falling across one side of her face, and the first words anyone heard her say were, "Excuse me, I—"

At the sound of her voice, the shadow operators unfolded themselves and streamed toward her from every corner of the room, to whirl about her head like ghosts, bats, scrap paper, smoke, or old women clasping antique lockets of hair. They recognised privilege when they saw it.

"My dear," they whispered. "What beautiful hands."

"Is there anything we can do—"

"—Can we do anything, dear?"

"What lovely, lovely hands!"

Liv Hula looked amused. "They never did that for me," she admitted to the woman in the fur coat. Then she had a sudden vision of her own life as hard-won, dug out raw from nothing much even the few times it seemed to swoop or soar.

"You came for Jack, he's over there," she said.

She always pointed him out. After that she washed her hands of whatever happened next. This time Jack was waiting. He was low on work, it was a slow year though you wouldn't guess that from the number of ships clustered in the tourist port. Jack accounted himself intelligent and determined; women, on the other hand, saw him as weak, conflicted, attractive, reading this as a failed attempt to feminize himself. He had been caning it for weeks with fat Antoyne and Liv Hula, but he still looked younger than his age. He stood there with his hands in his pockets, and the woman leaned toward him as if he was the only way she could get her bearings in the room. The closer she approached him the more uncertain she seemed. Like most of them, she wasn't sure how to broach things.

"I want you to take me in there," she said eventually.

Jack laid his finger on his lips. He could have wished for some statement less bald. "Not so loud," he suggested.

"I'm sorry."

He shrugged and said, "No problem."

"We're all friends here," Liv Hula said.

Jack gave Liv a look, which he then turned into a smile.

The woman smiled too. "Into the event site," she said, as if there might be any doubt about it. Her face was smooth and tight across longings Jack didn't quite understand. She looked away from him as she spoke. He should have thought more about that. Instead he ushered her to a table, where they talked for five minutes in low voices. Nothing was easier, he told her, than what she wanted. Though the risk had to be understood, and you underrated at your peril the seriousness of things in there. He would be a fool not to make that clear. He would be irresponsible, he said. Money changed hands. After a time they got up and left the bar.

"Just another sucker on the vine," Liv Hula said, loud enough to pause him in the doorway.

Antoyne claimed to have flown dipships with Ed Chianese. He passed the days with his elbows on the bar staring out through the window at the contrails of descending K-ships in the sky above the houses on the other side of Strait Street. To most people it seemed unlikely he flew with anyone, but he could take a message and keep his mouth shut. The only other thing he ever said about himself was:

"No one gives a shit about a fat man called Antoyne."

"You got that right," Liv Hula often told him.

When Jack had gone, there was a silence in the bar. The shadow operators calmed down and packed themselves back into the ceiling corners so the corners looked familiar again—that is, as if they had never been cleaned. Antoyne stared at the table in front of him then across at Liv Hula. It seemed as if they'd speak about Jack or the woman but in the end neither of them could think of anything to say. The fat man was angry that Liv Hula had defended him to Jack Serotonin. He drove his chair back suddenly, it made a kind of complaining sound against the wooden floor. He got up and went over to the window, where he wiped the condensation off with the palm of his hand.

"Still dark," he said.

Liv Hula had to admit that was true.

"Hey," he said. "Here's Joe Leone."

Over the street from Black Cat White Cat it was the usual frontages, busted and askew, buildings that had lost confidence in their structural integrity and that now housed shoestring tailor operations specializing in cosmetics or one-shot cultivars. You couldn't call them "parlors." The work they did was too cheap for that. They got a trickle of stuff from the Uncle Zip and Nueva Cut franchises dowtown; also they took work from the Shadow Boys, work like Joe Leone. Just now Joe was pulling himself down Strait using the fences and walls to hold himself up. His energy ebbed and flowed. He would fall down, wait for a minute, then struggle up again. It looked like hard work. You could see he was holding something in down there with one hand while he leaned on the fence with the other. The closer he got the more puzzled he looked.

Antoyne made a tube out of his two damp fists and said through it in the voice of a sports commentator at Radio Retro:

". . . and will he make it this time?"

"Be sure to let us know when you join the human race, Antoyne," Liv Hula said. The fat man shrugged and turned away from the window. "It's no bet," he said in his normal voice. "He never failed yet."

Joe kept dragging himself down Strait. As he approached you could see the tailors had done something to his face so it had a crude lionlike cast. It was white and sweated up, but it didn't move properly. They had given it a one-piece look as if it was sculpture, even the long hair swept back and out from his big forehead and cheekbones. Eventually he fell down outside one of the chopshops and stopped moving, and after a couple of minutes two men almost as big as him came out to drag him inside.

Joe started to fight when he was seven.

"Never strike out at the other, son," his father would explain in a patient way. "Because the other is yourself."

Joe Leone didn't follow that, even at seven years old which everyone agreed was his most intelligent time. He liked to fight. By twelve it was his trade, nothing more or less. He had signed with the Shadow Boys. From that time on he lived in one-shot cultivars. He liked the tusks, the sentient tattoos, and the side-lace trousers. Joe had no body of his own. It cost him so much to run those cultivars he would never save up enough to buy himself back. Every day he was in the ring, doing that same old thing. He was getting pretty well messed up. "I lost count the times I seen my own insides. Hey, what's that? Lose your insides ain't so hard. Losing a fight, that's hard." And he would laugh and buy you another drink.

Every day they dragged the fucked-up cultivar out the ring, and the next day Joe Leone had been to the tailor on Strait and come out fresh and new and ready to do it all again. It was a tiring life but it was the life he loved. Liv Hula never charged him for a drink. She had a soft spot for him, it was widely acknowledged.

"Those fights, they're cruel and stupid," she told the fat man now.

He was too smart to contradict that. After a moment, looking for something else to quarrel over, he said: "You ever do anything before you kept bar?"

She brought out a lifeless smile for him to consider.

"One or two things," she said.

"Then how come I never heard about them?"

"Got me there, Antoyne."

She waited for him to respond, but now something new on Strait had caught his attention. He wiped the window glass again. He pressed his face up against it. "Irene's a little late today," he said.

Liv Hula busied herself suddenly behind the bar.

"Oh yes?"

"A minute or two," he said.

"What's a minute or two to Irene?"

The fights were a dumb career, that was Liv Hula's opinion. They were a dumb life. Joe Leone's whole ambition was as dumb as his self-presentation until he met Irene: then it got worse. Irene was a Mona who had a good track record working the noncorporate spaceport. She was what you call petite, five-three in transparent urethane heels and full of appeal with her flossy blonde hair. Like all those Uncle Zip products she had something organic about her, something real. She watched Joe Leone at the fights and after she smelled his blood she couldn't leave him alone. Every morning when he came home to the tailor's, Irene was there too. Between them they summed up New Venusport, the sex industry and the fight industry. When Joe and Irene were together you couldn't be sure which industry was which. They were a new form of entertainment in themselves.

Irene commenced to hammer at the chopshop door.

"How long you think they'll let her shout before they open up?" fat Antoyne asked. Liv Hula had found a map-shaped stain on the zinc bartop, which she stared at with interest.

"I don't know why you're asking me," she said.

"She's got feelings for him," said Antoyne, to press his advantage. "That's undeniable. No one questions that . . . Jesus," he added to himself, "look at those tits."

He tried to imagine Joe Leone, dead and liquefied while his bones and organs reassembled themselves and Irene gave him the Mona side of her mouth. The joke was, Irene's opinion was no different than Liv Hula's. Every morning she made them fetch her an old wooden chair and put it at the head of Joe's tank, with his faded publicity slogan on it, *Hold the painkillers*. There she sat, ignoring the pink flashing LEDs, which were for show anyway, while the tank proteome slushed around like warm spit, cascades of autocatalysis through a substrate of forty thousand molecular species, flushing every twenty minutes to take off what unwanted product the chemistry couldn't eliminate. She hated the sucking noises it made.

One day you won't get back, she would tell the Lion. One more fight and you're fucked with me. But Joe was an algorithm by now, somewhere off in operator space. He was choosing new tusks from the catalogue, he was getting tuning to his glycolytic systems. He couldn't hear a word.

Oh Joe, I really mean it, she'd say. One more fight.

Liv Hula sometimes watched the rockets too.

Near dawn, you got her and the fat man standing by the window together as two tubby brass-looking freighters lifted from the corporate yard. Then a K-ship exited the military pits on the hard white line from its fRAM engine. In the backwash of light a warmer expression came on her face than you would expect. By then the Kefahuchi Tract had begun to fade from the sky, which was tilted like a lid to show one thin eastern arc of pale green, false dawn. Offshore winds would come up soon and, forced along the narrow pipe of Strait Street, churn the low-lying fogs of the event site. That would be the signal for all sorts of people to start the day. Live Hula and Antoyne the fat man watched the K-ship cut the sky like scissors.

"You ever fly one of those, Antoyne?" she remarked.

He blinked and turned his head away. "There's no need for that," he said. "There's no need for sarcasm like that."

Just then, Jack Serotonin came back in the bar, walking quickly and looking behind him. He had the air of someone whose morning was already off its proper track. His face was white, with a graze on one cheek leaking beads of blood. He had waded through oily water not long ago it seemed; and his zip-up gabardine jacket had one sleeve half off at the shoulder—as if someone had held on to it while they fell, Liv Hula thought immediately, although she did not know why.

"Jesus, Jack," she said.

"Get me a drink," Jack Serotonin said.

He walked halfway across the room as if he was going to drink it at the counter, then changed his mind and sat down suddenly at the nearest table. Once there he didn't seem to know what to do. A few shadow operators detached themselves from the ceiling to examine him; he stared through them. "Shit," he kept saying in a quiet, surprised way. After a while his breathing calmed down.

The fat man forgot his hurt feelings as soon as Jack came in. He pulled up a chair and began to tell Jack some story, leaning into it in his enthusiasm so his soft body enveloped the table edge. His voice was quiet and urgent, but you could hear the odd word, "entradista"; "hard X-rays"; "Ed Chianese." Jack stared through him too, then said, "Shut up or I'll shoot you where you sit." The fat man looked hopelessly away. He said all he wanted in this bar was a chance, Jack should give him a chance. He was trying not to cry. "I'm sorry," Jack said, but he was already thinking about something else, and when Liv Hula brought him his drink, and sat down and said, "Black Heart, Jack, just the way you like it," he barely seemed to recognise her.

"Shit," he said again.

"Where's the woman, Jack?"

"I don't know," he said.

"Only I don't want to hear you left her there."

"She cracked and ran. She's in the aureole somewhere. Antoyne, go to the door, tell me if anyone's in the street."

"All I want is a chance to fit in," the fat man said.

"For fuck's sake, Antoyne."

Antoyne said, "No one understands that."

Serotonin opened his mouth to say more, then he seemed to forget Antoyne altogether. "I never saw panic like it," he said. He shook his head. "You couldn't even say we'd got inside. It's bad this morning, but it's not that bad." He finished his drink and held out the glass. Instead of taking it, Liv Hula caught his wrist.

"So how bad is it?" she said. She wouldn't let go until he told her.

"Things are moving about," he admitted. "I've seen worse, but usually further in."

"Where is she, Jack?"

He laughed. It was a laugh he had practised too often. "I told you," he said tiredly, "she's somewhere in the aureole. We never got any further. She runs off between the buildings, I see silk stockings and that fucking fur coat, then I see nothing. She was still calling from somewhere when I gave up," he said. "Get me another drink, Liv, or I don't know what I'll do."

Liv Hula said: "You didn't go after her, Jack."

He stared.

"You stayed where it was safe, and shouted a couple times, and then you came home."

"Jack would never do that," the fat man said in a blustering way. No one was going to say Jack would do that. "Hey, Jack. Tell her. You would never do that!" He got up out of his chair. "I'm going in the street and keep an eye open now, just the way you wanted. You got a wrong idea about Jack Serotonin," he said to Liv Hula, "if you think he'd do that." As soon as he had gone, she went to the bar and poured Jack another Black Heart rum, while Jack rubbed his face with his hands like someone who was very tired and couldn't see his way through life any more. His face had an older look than it had when he left. It was sullen and heavy, and his blue eyes took on a temporary pleading quality which one day would be permanent.

"You don't know what it's like in there," he told her.

"Of course I don't," she said. "Only Jack Serotonin knows that."

"Streets transposed on one another, everything laid down out of sync one minute to the next. Geography that doesn't work. There isn't a single piece of dependable architecture in the shit of it. You leave the route you know, you're finished. Lost dogs barking day and night. Everything struggling to keep afloat."

She wasn't disposed to let him get away with that.

"You're the professional, Jack," she reminded him. "They're the customers. Here's your other drink if you want it." She leaned her elbows on the bar. "You're the one has to hold himself together."

This seemed to amuse him. He took the rum down in one swallow, the color came back into his face, and they looked at one another in a more friendly way. He wasn't finished with her though. "Hey Liv," he said softly after a moment or two, "what's the difference between what you've seen and what you are? You want to know what it's like in there? The fact is, you spend all those years trying to make something of it. Then guess what, it starts making something of you."

He got up and went to the door.

"What are you fucking about at, Antoyne?" he called. "I said 'look'. I said 'take a look'."

The fat man, who had trotted up Strait a little into the predawn wind to clear his head, also to see if he could get a glimpse of Irene the Mona through a chink in the boarded windows of the chopshop, came in grinning and shivering with the cold. "Antoyne here can tell us all about it," Jack Serotonin said. "Everything he knows."

"Leave Antoyne alone."

"You ever been in there when everything fell apart, Antoyne?"

"I was never in there, Jack," Antoyne said hastily. "I never claimed I was."

"Everything was just taken away, and you had no idea what established itself in exchange? The air's like uncooked pastry. It's not a smell in there, it's a substrate. In every corner there's a broken telephone nailed to the wall. They're all labelled Speak but there's no line out. They ring but no one's ever there."

Liv Hula gave him a look, then shrugged. To the fat man she explained, "Jack just so hates to lose a client."

"Fuck you," Jack Serotonin said. "Fuck the two of you."

He pushed his glass across the counter and walked out.

After Jack Serotonin left silence returned to the bar. It crowded in on itself, so that Liv Hula and the fat man, though they wanted to speak, were hemmed in with their own thoughts. The onshore wind decreased while the light increased, until they could no longer deny it was dawn. The woman washed and dried the glass Jack Serotonin had used, then put it carefully in its place behind the bar. Then she went upstairs to the room above, where she thought about changing her clothes but in the end only stared in a kind of mounting panic at the disordered bed, the blanket chest and the bare white walls.

I ought to move on, she thought. I ought to leave here now.

When she came down again, Antoyne had resumed his place by the window and with his hands on the sill stood watching the payloads lift one after another from the corporate port. He half-turned as if to speak but, receiving no encouragement, turned back again.

Across the street someone opened the chopshop door.

After a brief quiet struggle, Irene the Mona stumbled out. She took an uncertain step or two forward, peering blindly up and down Strait like a drunk assessing heavy traffic, then sat down suddenly on the edge of the sidewalk. The door slammed shut behind her. Her skirt rode up. Antoyne pressed his face closer to the glass. "Hey," he whispered to himself. Irene, meanwhile, set her little shiny red urethane vanity case down beside her and began to claw through its contents with one hand. She was still sitting there two or three minutes later, showing all she had, sniffing and wiping her eyes, when the cats came out of the Raintown event site in an alert silent rush.

Who knew how many of those cats there were? Another thing, you never found so much as a tabby among them, every one was either black or white. When they poured out of the zone it was like a model of some chaotic mixing flow in which, though every condition is determined, the outcome can never be predicted. Soon they filled Strait in both directions, bringing with them the warmth of their bodies, also a close, dusty but not unpleasant smell. Irene struggled upright, but the cats took no more notice than if she had been one of the street lamps.

Irene was born on a planet called Perkin's Rent. She left there tall and bony, with an awkward walk and big feet. When she smiled her gums showed, and she did her hair in lacquered copper waves so tight and complex they could receive the mains hum, the basic transmissions of the universe. She had a sweet way of laughing. When she boarded the rocket to leave, she was seventeen. Her suitcase contained a yellow cotton dress with a kind of faux-Deco feel, tampons, and four pairs of high heel shoes. "I love shoes," she would explain to you when she was drunk. "I love shoes." You got the best of her in those days. She would follow you anywhere for two weeks then follow someone else. She loved a rocket jockey.

Now she stood with tears streaming down her face, watching the Raintown cats flow around her, until Liv Hula waded fastidiously into the stream and fetched her back to the bar, where she sat her down and said:

"What can I get you, honey?"

"He's dead this time," Irene said in a rush.

"I can't believe that," Liv Hula said. Immediately she was tidying up inside, planning to stay back inside herself away from the fact of it. But Irene kept repeating in her disorganised way, "He's dead this time, that's all," which made it hard to dissociate. Irene took Liv Hula's hand and pressed it to her cheek. It was her opinion, she said, that something makes men unfit for most of life; to which Liv Hula replied, "I always thought so, too." Then Irene broke into snuffling again and had to fetch out her vanity mirror. "Especially the best parts," she said indistinctly.

Later, when Antoyne came and tried to make conversation with her, she gave him the full benefit of her looks. He bought her a drink that settled out the same colors as her skirt, pink and yellow, and which he said they drank on some dumb planet he knew fifty lights down the line.

"I been there, Fat Antoyne," she told him with a sad smile.

That original Irene, she thought, wasn't good at being on her own. She would sit on the bed one place or another, listening to the rain and trying to hold herself together. On the other hand, she never lacked ambition. The stars of the Halo were like one big neon sign to her. The sign said: ALL THE SHOES YOU CAN EAT. When she bought the Mona package, the tailor promised her hair would always smell of peppermint shampoo. She had gone through the catalogues, and that was what she wanted, and the tailor designed it in. On the Raintown streets it was her big selling point.

"I been there," she told Antoyne, letting him get the peppermint smell, "and just now I'm glad to meet someone else who's been there, too."

Antoyne was as encouraged by this as any man. He sat on after she finished the drink, trying to engage her with stories of the places he had seen back when he rode the rockets. But Irene had been to all those places too—and more, Liv Hula thought—and fat Antoyne had all he was going to get for one cheap cocktail drink. Liv watched them from a distance, her own thoughts so churned she didn't care how it ended. Eventually even Antoyne could see the way things were. He scraped his chair back and retreated to his place by the window. What time was it? How had the things happened that ended him up here? He looked out on to Strait. "It's day," he said. "Hey," he grumbled, "I actually respected the guy. You know?" Meanwhile the stream of cats flowed on like a problem in statistical mechanics, without any apparent slackening or falling away of numbers, until suddenly it turned itself off and Strait was empty again. Across the road at the tailor's they were flushing Joe Leone's proteins down the drain.

At the civilian port, the cruise ships, half-hidden in the mist, towered above the buildings; while along the tall narrow streets a traffic of rickshaw girls and tattoo boys had begun, ferrying the tourists from the New Cafe Al Aktar to Moneytown, from the Church on the Rock to the Rock Church, while around them their shreds and veils of shadow operators whispered, "A sight everyone will be sure to see, a discourse of oppositions." Fur coats were all over Raintown by eight, dyed the color of honey or horse chestnut, cut to flow like some much lighter fabric. What sort of money was this? Where did it come from? It was off-planet money. It was corporate money. However cruel the trade that produced them, you could hardly deny the beauty of those coats and their luxurious surfaces.

Shortly after the last cat had vanished into the city, Jack's client returned to the bar.

Where Jack had come back filthy, she came back clean. You wouldn't notice anything new about her, except her shoulders were a little hunched and her face was still. Her hands she thrust into the pockets of her coat. Nothing had been taken away from her, but she held her head more carefully than before, always looking forward as if her neck hurt, or as if she was trying not to notice something happening in the side of her eye. It was hard to read body language like that. She placed herself with care at a table near the window, crossed one leg over the other, and asked in a low voice for a drink. After a little while she said, "I wonder if someone could give that other man the rest of his fee."

Antoyne sat forward eagerly.

"I can do that," he offered.

"No you can't," Liv Hula warned him. To the woman in the fur coat she said: "Jack's cheap, he left you for dead. You owe him nothing."

"Still," the woman said. "I feel he should have the rest of his money. It's here. And I was fine, really." She stared ahead of herself. "A little puzzled, I suppose, at how unpleasant it is."

Liv Hula threw up her hands.

"Why do they come here?" she asked fat Antoyne in a loud voice. Before he could say anything, she added: "They leave the nice safe tour and they end up in this bar here. They always find our Jack."

"Hey, Jack's okay," the fat man said.

"Jack's a joke, Antoyne, and so are you."

Antoyne struggled to his feet and looked as if he was going to challenge that, but in the end he only shrugged. Jack's client gave him a faint, encouraging smile, but then seemed to look past him. Silence drew out a moment or two; then a chair scraped back and Irene the Mona came over to the table where these events were happening. Her little urethane shoes clattered on the wooden floor. She had wiped her tears and done her lipstick. She was over Joe the Lion now. What had she been on, to invest her considerable life-energy that way? Irene had a future in front of her, everyone agreed, and it was a good, light-hearted one. She had her plans, and they were good ones, too. Though it was true she would keep Joe in her heart pocket many years because that was the kind of girl she knew herself to be.

"That sure is a beautiful coat," she said. She held out her hand.

For a moment, the woman looked nonplussed. Then she shook Irene's hand and said, "Thank you. It is, isn't it?"

"Very beautiful, and I admire it so," Irene agreed. She gave a little bob, seemed about to add something, then suddenly went and sat down again and toyed with her glass. "Don't be hard on him, honey," she called across to Liv Hula. "He's nothing but a man after all." It was hard to tell which man she meant.

"I feel he should have his money," appealed the woman in the fur coat. When no one answered she set the cash on the table in front of her, in high denomination notes. "Anyway, it's here for him," she said.

"Jesus," was Liv Hula's comment. "Antoyne," she said, "you want another drink?"

But the fat man had lost patience with the way they treated him in there. He was just a man trying to fit in, someone who had seen as much as anyone else, more than some. It made him angry they didn't listen. He thought about when he rode the dynaflow ships, and all the planets he saw then, and the things he saw on them. Gay Lung, Ambo Danse and Fourth Part, Waitrose Two and the Thousand Suns: he had scattered himself like money across the Beach stars and down into Radio Bay. He had gone deep in those days. Surfed the Alcubiere warp with Ed Chianese. Owned a rocket, he called her the Kino Chicken. Failed at being solitary. On Santa Muerte inhaled something that deviated both his septum and his sense of where things were. That was it for being a sky pilot.

What the hell, he thought. Nothing's ever yours to keep.

At least he was out of that place now, into the morning somewhere he could breathe, heading for Moneytown and the strip mall wonderland running south of Strait, down past the spaceports to the sea. He was narrowing his eyes in the strong light glittering up off the distant water. He was going to look for work. He was going to look for people who meant it when they smiled.

After he had gone Liv Hula's bar was silent. One by one, the shadow operators detached themselves furtively from the ceiling and went to the woman in the fur coat, who acknowledged them absently. Smells crept out of the kitchen and out of the pipes. The three women appeared preoccupied with their own thoughts. Every so often one or the other of them would go to the door and peer up Strait Street toward the event zone, wreathed—silent, heaving, and questionable—in its daytime chemical fogs, while the others watched her expectantly.

SCOUT'S HONOR

TERRY BISSON

Terry Bisson is the author of a number of critically acclaimed novels such as *Fire on the Mountain*, *Wyrldmaker*, the popular *Talking Man* (which was a finalist for the World Fantasy Award in 1986), *Voyage to the Red Planet*, *Pirates of the Universe*, *The Pickup Artist*, and, in a posthumous collaboration with Walter M. Miller, Jr., a sequel to Miller's *A Canticle for Leibowitz* called *Saint Leibowitz and the Wild Horse Woman*. He is a frequent contributor to such markets as *SCI FICTION*, *Asimov's Science Fiction*, *Omni*, *Playboy*, and *The Magazine of Fantasy & Science Fiction*, His famous story "Bears Discover Fire" won the Hugo Award, the Nebula Award, the Theodore Sturgeon Memorial Award, *and* the Asimov's Reader's Award in 1991, the only story ever to sweep them all. In 2000, he won another Nebula Award for his story "macs." His short work has been assembled in the collections *Bears Discover Fire and Other Stories* and *In the Upper Room and Other Likely Stories*. His most recent book is a chapbook, *Dear Abbey*. His stories have appeared in our Eighth, Tenth, Twelfth, Thirteenth, and Twenty-first Annual Collections. He lives with his family in Oakland, California.

In last year's *Dear Abbey*, he sent us ahead to the distant future. Here he sends us back to the equally distant past, for a poignant lesson in what it means to be human.

On the morning of July 12, 20__ I got the following message on my lab computer, the only one I have:

MONDAY

Made it. Just as planned. It's real. Here I am in the south of France, or what people think of now (now?) as the south of France. It seems to the north of everywhere. If the cleft is at forty-two hundred feet, it means the ice is low. I can see the tongue of a glacier only about five hundred feet above me. No bones here yet, of course. It's a clear shot down a narrow valley to the NT site, about one-half mile away. I can see smoke; I didn't expect that. Wouldn't they be more cautious? Maybe they aren't threatened by HS yet and I'm too early. Hope not. Even though it's not part of the protocol, I would love to learn more about our first encounter (and last?) with another human (hominid?) species. I do like to see the smoke, though. I never thought I would feel loneliness but here I do. Time is space and space is distance (Einstein). Heading down for the NT site. More later.

The subject line was all noise and so was the header. I was still puzzling what it was all about, for excepting the Foundation's newsgroup, I get no messages at all, when another came through the very next morning. The dates are mine.

TUESDAY

It's them all right. I am watching about twenty NTs, gathered in the site around a big smoky fire. Even through binoculars, from fifty yards away, they look like big moving shadows. It's hard to count them. They cluster together then break apart in groups of two or three, but never alone. I can't tell the males from the females, but there are four or five children, who also stay together in a clump. Wish I could see faces, but it's dim here. Perpetual overcast. I have been watching almost four hours by the clock on my com, and none have left the site. Separating one out may prove a problem. But I have almost five days (–122) to worry about that. Tomorrow I'll observe from a different position where I can get a little closer and the light may be better; above, not closer. I know the protocols. I helped write them. But somehow I want to get closer.

I began to suspect a prank, to which I enjoy a certain deliberate and long-standing immunity. But I do have a friend—Ron—and naturally I suspected him (who else?) after the next and longer text came through, on the very day we were to meet.

WEDNESDAY

Totally unexpected change in plans. I am sitting here in the cleft with "my own" NT. He's the perfect candidate for the snatch, if I can keep him here for four days (–98). They are nothing like we thought. The reconstructions are far too anthropomorphic. This is NOT a human, though certainly a hominid. What we thought was a broad nose is more of a snout. He's white as a ghost, which I guess is appropriate. Or am I the ghost? He is sitting across the fire staring at me, or through me. He seems oddly unconscious much of the time, thoughtless, like a cat. What happened was this: I was heading down to observe the site this morning when I dislodged a boulder that fell on my left leg. I thought for sure it was broken (it isn't), but I was trapped. The rock had my leg wedged from the knee downward, out of sight in a narrow crevice. I couldn't help thinking of that turn-of-the-century Utah dude who sawed off his own arm with a Swiss army knife. I was wondering when I would be ready to do that, for I was in a worse spot than him: unless I made it back to the cleft in less than a hundred hours, I was trapped here, and by more than a stone. By Time itself. The numbness scared me worse than pain. It was starting to snow and I was worried about freezing. I must have fallen asleep, for the next thing I remember, "my" NT was squatting there looking at me—or through me. Quiet as a cat. Oddly, I was as little surprised as he was. It was like a dream. I pointed at my leg, and he rolled the stone away. It was as simple as that. Either he was immensely strong or had a better angle, or both. I was free, and my leg was now throbbing painfully and bleeding but not broken. I could even stand on it. I hobbl

Ron is a sci-fi writer who teaches a course at the New School. We meet every Wednesday and Friday, right before his class at 6. This is not by his plan or mine. It's a promise he made to my mother, I happen to know, right before she died, but that's okay with me. No friends at all would be too few, and more than one, too many.

"What is this?" he asked, when he finished reading the printout.

You oughta know, I said, raising my eyebrows in what I hoped was a suggestive manner. In accord with my own promise to my mother, I practice these displays in front of the mirror, and for once it seems to have paid off.

"You think I wrote this?"

I nodded, knowingly I hoped, and listed my reasons: who else knew that I was studying Neanderthal bones? Who but he and I had savored the story of the Utah dude so long ago? Who else wrote sci-fi?

"Science fiction," he said grumpily (having made that correction before). While we waited for his burger and my buttered roll, he listed his objections.

"Maybe it's a mistake, not intended for you. Lots of people knew about the Utah dude; it was a national story. And I am a little insulted that you think that I wrote this."

Huh?

"It's crude," Ron said. "He, or maybe she, uses 'oddly' twice in one paragraph; that would never get by me. And the time line is all wrong. The escape comes before the danger, which deflates the suspense."

You didn't send this, then?

"No way. Scout's Honor."

And that was that. We talked, or rather he talked, mostly of his girlfriend Melani and her new job, while the people walked by on Sixth Avenue, only inches away. They were hot, and we were cold. It was like two separate worlds, separated by the window glass.

Thursday morning I went in eagerly, anxious to get back to my bones. I scanned the Foundation's newsgroup first (rumors about a top secret new project) before opening the latest message.

THURSDAY

Sorry about that. I stopped transmitting yesterday because "my" NT woke up, and I didn't want to alarm him. Since my last truncated message, we've been snowed in. He watched me build a fire with a sort of quiet amazement. God knows what he would think of this thing I'm talking into. Or of the talk itself. He only makes three or four sounds. I wait until he's asleep to use the com. After the NT freed me, he followed me up the hill. It was clear that he didn't intend to harm me, although it would have been pretty easy. He is about six feet tall if he stood straight up, which he never does. Maybe 250 lbs. It's hard to judge his weight since he's pretty hairy, except for his face and hands. I was in a big hurry to dress my leg, which was bleeding (okay after all). We found the cleft very different from the way I had left it. Something had gotten into my food. A bear? The follow box was smashed and half the KRs were gone. Luckily the space blanket had been left behind. I spread it out, and he laid his stuff beside it: a crude hand axe, a heavy, stiff and incredibly smelly skin robe, and a little sack made of gut, with five stones in it: creek stones, white. He showed them to me as if they were something I should understand. And I do: but of that later. He's starting to stir.

On Fridays I skip lunch so I will have an appetite in the restaurant. I wasn't surprised to find yet another message, and I printed both Thurs. and Fri. to show to Ron. At the least, it would give him something to talk about. I think (know) my silences are awkward for him.

FRIDAY

It's snowing. The stones are his way of counting. I watched him throw one away this morning. There are three left: like me, he's on some kind of schedule. We've been eating grubs. Seems the NTs hide rotten meat under logs and stones and return for the grubs. It's a kind of farming. They're not so bad. I try to think of them as little vegetables. Grub "talks" a lot with his hands. I try to reply in kind. When we are not talking, when I do not get his attention, he is as dead, but when I touch his hands or slap his face, he comes alive. It's as if he's half asleep the rest of the time. And really asleep the other half; the NT sleep a *lot*. His hands are very human, and bone white like his face. The rest of him is brown, under thick blond fur. I call him Grub. He doesn't call me anything. He doesn't seem to wonder who I am or where I came from. The snatch point is still 2 days away (–46), which means that I get him to myself until then. An unexpected bonus. Meanwhile, the weather, which was already fierce, is getting fiercer, and I worry about the com batteries, with no sun to charge them. More later.

Ron and I always meet at the same place, which is the booth by the window in the Burger Beret on Sixth Ave at Tenth St. Ron shook his head as he read the messages. That can mean lots of different things.

He said, "You astonish me."

Huh?

"Don't huh me. You wrote it. It's very clever, considering."

I couldn't say huh again, so I was just very still.

"The vegetarian business is what tipped me off. And no one else knows that much about Neanderthals. Their counting, the limited speech. It's what you told me."

That was common theory, I said. There was nothing new in it. Besides, I don't make stories. I write reports.

Even I could see that he was disappointed. "Scout's Honor?"

Scout's honor, I said. Ron and I went to Philmont Scout Ranch together. That was years ago, before he had entered the world and I had decided to keep it at arm's length. But the vows still hold.

"Well, okay. Then it must be one of your colleagues playing a joke. I'm not the only one who knows you do research. Just the only one you deign to talk to."

Then he told me that he and Melani were getting married. The conversation sort of speeded up and slowed down at the same time, and when I looked up, he was gone. I felt a moment's panic, but after I paid the bill and went up to my apartment, it gradually dissipated, like a gas in an open space. For me a closed space is like an open space.

The newsgroup was silent for the weekend, but the scrambled-header messages kept coming through, one a day, like the vitamins I promised my mother I would take.

SATURDAY

The KRs are gone, but Grub drags me with him to look under logs for grubs. He won't go alone. Third day snowed in. One more to go. I have to conserve our wood, so we stay huddled together against the back wall of the cleft, wrapped in my space blanket and Grub's smelly robe. We sit and watch the snow and listen to the booming of the icefall—and we talk. Sort of. He gestures with his hands and takes mine in his. He plucks at the hair on my forearms and pulls at my fingers and sometimes even slaps my face. I'm sure he doesn't understand that I am from the far future; how could he even have a concept of that? But I can understand that he is in exile. There was a dispute, over what, who knows, and he was sent away. The stones are his sentence, that I know: Grub *feels* that about them. Every morning he gets rid of one, tossing it out the door of the cleft into the snow. His sense of number is pretty crude. Five is many, and two—the number left this morning—is few. I assume that when they are gone, he gets to go "home," but he's just as desolate with two as he was with five. Perhaps he can't think ahead, only back. Even though I'm cold as hell, I wish the snatch point wasn't so near. I'm learning his language. Things don't have names, but the feelings about them do.

Saturday and Sunday I spend at the lab, alone. What else would I do? When else could I be alone with my bones? I am the only one who has access to the Arleville Find, which is two skeletons, an NT and an HS found side by side, which proves there was actual contact. The grubs confirmed my study of the NT teeth. Of course, this was just a story, according to Ron. Or was it? Sunday I found this:

SUNDAY

Change in plans: I want to alter the snatch point, put it back one cycle. I know this is against the protocols, but I have my reasons. Grub is desperate to get rid of the stones and return to the site and his band. These creatures are much more social than we. It's as if they hardly exist, alone. I'm getting better at communicating. There is much handwork involved, gesture and touch, and I understand more and more. Not by thinking but by feel. It's like looking at something out of the corner of my eye; if I look directly, it's gone. But if I don't, there it is. It's almost like a dream, and maybe it is, since I am in and out of sleep a lot. My leg is healing okay. Grub is down to one stone, and he's happy, almost. I am feeling the reverse: the horror he would feel at being separated from his band forever. Are we going to create an Ishi? What desolation. I am convinced we will wind up with a severely damaged NT. So we start our count at 144 again. Some peril here, since the com is getting low. But I have a plan—

Monday is my least favorite day, when I have to share the lab (but not the bones) with others. Not that they don't leave me alone. I scrolled down past the newsgroup, looking for the daily message and found it like an old acquaintance:

MONDAY

Made it. I am speaking this amid a circle of hominids, not humans, squatting (rather than sitting: they either stand, lie, or squat but never sit) around a big smoky fire. I quit worrying about what they would think of the com; they don't seem curious. Since I arrived with Grub, they have accepted me without question or interest. Maybe it's because I have picked up Grub's smell. They lay or squat silently a lot of the time, and then when one awakens, they all awaken, or most, anyway. There are twenty-two altogether, including Grub: eight adult males, seven females, and five children, two of them still nursing; plus two "Old Ones" of indeterminate sex. The Old Ones are not very mobile. The NTs grab hands and "talk" with a few sounds and a lot of pushing and pulling, plus gestures. Their facial expressions are as simple and crude as their speech. They look either bored or excited, with nothing in between. Lots of grubs and rotten meat get eaten. They put rotten meat under logs and rocks, and then come back for the grubs and maggots. It's a kind of farming, I guess, but it has all but spoiled my appetite. Perhaps any kind of farming does, seen up close.

All of this was interesting, but none of it was new. Any of it could *have been written by my colleagues at the lab, but I knew it wasn't. They're in another world, like the people on Sixth Avenue on the other side of the glass. Most of them didn't even know my name.*

TUESDAY

Something is happening tomorrow. A hunt? I sense fear and danger, and lots of work and lots of food. All these imprecise communications I got from the group as a whole. This afternoon they burned a bush of dry leaves and inhaled the smoke, passing it around. It's some kind of herb that seems to help in NT communication. Certainly it helps me. Between the "burning bush" and the grunts and pulling of hands, I got a picture (not visual but emotional) of a large beast dying. It's hard to describe. I'm learning not to try and pin things down. It's as if I were open to the feelings of the event itself instead of the participants. Death, defeat, and victory; terror and hope. A braided feeling, like the smoke. All this was accompanied, I might even say amplified, by one of the Old Ones (more mobile than I thought!) spinning around by the fire, brandishing a burning stick. Later I amused the little ones (more easily amused than their elders) by cooking some grubs on a stick. Like cooking marshmallows. They wouldn't eat them though, except for one small boy I call "Oliver" who kept smacking his lips and grinning at me as if it were me he wanted to eat. Even the little NTs have a fierce look that belies their gentle nature. The men (Grub, too) have been sharpening sticks and hardening the points in the fire. Now they are asleep in a big pile between the fire and the wall, and I am staying apart, which doesn't bother them. I can take the smell of Grub, but not of the whole pile; that is, band.

Wednesday was a long day. I printed out the last four (including Wednesday) to show Ron. For some reason, I was eager for a little "conversation." Maybe mother was right, and I need to maintain at least one friend. Mother was a doctor, after all.

WEDNESDAY

This morning we were awakened by the children pulling at the space blanket. Grub had joined me during the night. Is it me or the space blanket he likes? No matter; I am glad of his company and used to his smell. He was part of the hunt and dragged me along. He understood that I wanted to go. The others ignore me, except for the children. The party consisted of seven men and two women. No leader that I could tell. They carried sharpened sticks and hand axes, but no food or water. I don't think they know how to carry water. We left the children behind with the Old Ones and the nursing mothers and spent most of the morning climbing up a long slope of scree and over a ridge into a narrow valley where a glacial stream was surrounded by tall grass. There I saw my first mammoth, already dead. It lay beside a pile of brush and leaves, and I "got" that they had baited it into this narrow defile. But something else had killed it. It lay on its side, and for the first time I saw what I thought might be sign of HS, for the beast had already been butchered, very neatly. Even the skull had been split for the brain. Only the skin and entrails were left, with a few shreds of stringy meat. The NTs approached fearfully, sniffing the air and holding hands (mine included). I could feel their alarm. Was it the remnants of the smoke or my own imagination that gave me a terrified sense of the "dark ones" that had killed this beast? Then it was gone before I could be sure. The NTs went to work with their sticks, driving away three hyenalike dogs that were circling the carcass. Their fear was soon forgotten with this victory, and they started carving on the carcass, eating as they went. The kill was new, but pretty smelly. The NTs piled entrails and meat in a huge skin, which we had brought with us. By late afternoon we had a skin full, which we carried and dragged over the ridge and down the long scree slope. We were within a half mile of the site when the sun set, but the NTs hate and fear the dark. So here we are holed up under a rock ledge, in a pile. A long, cold, and smelly night ahead. No fire, of course. They whimper in their sleep. They don't like being away from their fire. Me neither. I am beginning to worry about the com, which is showing a low power (LP) signal every time I log on. Not as much sunlight here as anticipated. None at all, in fact.

"Scout's Honor?" Ron asked again after he had read the printouts, and I nodded. "It must be one of your colleagues, then. Who else knows this Neanderthal stuff, or calls them NTs. Did they really eat grubs?"

I shrugged. How would I know?

"Cave men are full of surprises, I guess. And I have a surprise of my own. Friday's my last day of class. We're moving to California. Melani has an assistantship at Cal State. We're getting married in Vegas, on the way. Otherwise I would invite you to the wedding. Even though I know you wouldn't come."

I stayed home sick Thursday. And so I didn't check my e-mails until Friday morning, when I had two, after a lot of Foundation Newsgroup gossip about a new project, which I skipped. It was mostly rumors, and I don't like rumors. That's why I became a scientist.

THURSDAY

Dawn finally came, sunless. Something was wrong. I could feel it as we went down the hill, holding hands. The cave was filled with shadows, as before, but these were different in the way they stood and the way they moved. Then NTs saw them too, and fell to their knees, clutching one another with little cries. I was forgotten, even by Grub. The Dark Ones had come. The fire was less smoky, and the shadows moved like humans, like us, and chattering. Quarrelling, too. Many blows exchanged. They were butchering something. I drew closer before realizing, to my horror, that I was alone. The NTs had all fled. Before I had time to look around and see where they were gone, I was noticed by the dogs. The NTs don't keep dogs, but the HS do. Perhaps they smelled the meat the NTs had dropped when they fled. They were barking all around me, nasty little creatures. Food or pets? Two of the HS came out of the cave toward me. They started to shout, and I shouted back, imitating their sounds, hoping they would perceive that I was one of them. No such luck. They moved closer, shaking their spears, which were tipped with vicious stone points. Shake-spear: they were acting, I realized. They were only interested in scaring me away. I took a step toward them, and they shook their spears harder. They are completely, unmistakably human. Their faces are very expressive. Their skins are hairless and very black. I think they thought I was an NT because I was so white, at least compared to them. Nothing else in my gait or face or speech seemed to matter. I saw over their shoulders what the others were butchering. It was the boy who had dared to eat the cooked grubs, Oliver. His head was laid off to one side, opened for the brains. NTs have big brains, even the kids. I was almost sad, but didn't have the luxury. The two HS were shaking their spears, coming toward me one step at a time. I stepped back, still trying to talk, hoping that they would recognize me as one of their own, when something grabbed me by the ankle. It was Grub. He had come back for me. Come! Run! I scrambled after him, through the bushes, up the scree, toward the rocks and snow. The humans didn't follow us.

FRIDAY

Snowing again, harder than ever. We're in the cleft, Grub and I. I'm trying to save the batteries for the snatch connection (–21). No sun. Haven't seen the sun for a week. After my last (too long) com, we circled up into the high country, careful to avoid the HS—me as well as Grub. It's ironic that even here, at the beginning of human history, skin color trumps everything. Logical, I suppose, since it is the largest and most evident of the organs. The band has gone over the glacier; we found the tracks leading up onto the ice. Grub wanted to follow them, but I can't get too far from the cleft and the snatch. Luckily, he won't go anywhere without me. I maneuvered him back to the cleft, which was mercifully empty, and built a fire which seemed to comfort him—the building of it as much as the fire itself. I sat down beside him, and he quit shivering, and we slept under the space blanket, plus the skin. All we have to do is hole up here for another day and we will both be gone. Grub doesn't know that, of course. He is shivering and whimpering in my arms. His desolation floods me as if it were my own. And his fear. The Dark Ones! The Dark Ones! What would he think if he knew I were one of them?

"I really don't need to read any more," Ron said, tossing the printout aside. "Didn't you say that Homo sapiens had originally come up from Africa?"

I nodded and shrugged. Nods and shrugs are "piece of cake" for me.

"So there they are, your dark ones. There will be a fight, and the Neanderthals, the NTs, will lose. It is clearly an amateur time-travel story. If you ask me, and I suppose you have no

one else to ask, I think it just bounced in off some anomaly in the Web. The Web has released all sorts of wannabe writers, sending stuff to one another and to little amateur sites. This is a piece of a sci-fi story that got misaddressed in cyberspace."

SF, I said, but he didn't get the joke. There are ways to indicate that you're joking but I have never mastered them. Why me? I asked.

"I'll bet it's because you're on the Foundation server," Ron said. "The one in New Mexico. Doesn't it use that new quantum computer, the one that received a message a few milliseconds before it was sent? I read the story in Science News. *Some kind of loop thing. But hey, it makes it the perfect receiver for a time travel yarn. Speaking of time—"*

He looked at his watch, then stood up and shook my hand. For the first time I understood his relief in saying good-bye. I tried to hold on, but he pulled his hand away.

"I'll stay in touch," he said.

The people on the street were hurrying by. Sixth Avenue is one-way for cars but two-way for people. I didn't mind them through the glass. Scout's Honor? I asked.

"Scout's Honor."

I tried to take his hand again, just to be sure, but he was gone. My mother had finally set him free.

SATURDAY

Disaster. We missed the snatch, both Grub and me. We've been run off from the cleft. We were awakened—or rather, I was awakened by Grub. I was dragged out of the cleft and onto my feet, past the three HS with long spears at the cave door.

Grub had smelled them before he had seen or heard them. They seized our supplies and the fire, and of course, the cleft, as we scurried up the rocks toward the ice above. They had no interest in following or harming us, just scaring us away. I can now see what happened in the Encounter: the HS didn't kill off the NTs: they only grabbed their sites, their food, their fires, and ran them off; and ate those of their children who fell into their hands. That was enough. Meanwhile, it is getting dark, and Grub is counting on me to build a fire. I will make it a small one, to be sure.

I used to love Saturdays, I think, but now they felt sad, even at the lab. I wondered where Ron was, in the air somewhere. He likes to fly. Of course it was none of my business, not anymore. I almost wished my mother were still alive. I would have somebody to call. There are lots of phones at the lab. Sunday was the same.

SUNDAY

There was no snatch. Nothing happened. The HS who ran us off are still in the cleft, two of them. If I had left the com behind, you would at least have them. To their surprise. It was all I could do to drag Grub close enough to see. He's terrified. Me, too. We're 144 hours from a new snatch, if it can be accomplished. I am going to try and keep these coms down to keep the batteries functioning as long as possible. Haven't seen the sun since I got here.

On Monday I had a personal eyes-only message from the Foundation. Attached was an e-ticket for a flight to New Mexico to discuss the new project. Don't they know I never fly? I scrolled on down and there it was, my next-to-last message, from the distant past and near future:

MONDAY

This morning Grub and I found four of his band, fireless and frozen in a small cave high on the ridgeline, above the ice. We buried them with great effort. No sign of the others, no more than five or six. I have a dreadful feeling that they are in fact the last band, childless now. When the HS took their fire, they signed their death warrant, unless the NTs luck upon a lightning strike or a live volcano. Perhaps such events are not as rare "then" as they are "now." We'll see.

On Tuesday I went to the Bagel Beret alone for the first time. It felt weird. Don't think I'll go back. Today's message, my last, cleared it all up. I now know who the messages are from. I also know that I will fly to New Mexico. I will have to "suck it up" and go. It is only one stop on a longer journey.

TUESDAY

This may be my last, since even the LP light on the com is dying. Giving up the ghost, I think is the term. We have other worries anyway. More HS have arrived in the site below. We see them in twos and threes, out hunting. Us? We aren't about to find out. Tomorrow we are going to cross the ridge and see if we can pick up tracks. Grub sleeps now, but it was hours before he stopped shivering. His hands wouldn't leave hold of mine. Please don't leave me, he said with that NT mix of gesture and touch and speech, and I said I wouldn't, but I could tell he didn't believe me, and who could blame him? He was alone in the world, more alone, I suspected, than he knew. If his band is alive (and I doubt it) they are somewhere above us, childless, fireless, slowly dying of heartbreak and cold. I shiver to think of it. You won't leave me? he asked again, tentatively, all fingertips, right before he went to sleep. I put his fingertips on my lips so he would understand what I was saying and know that it was for him, Grub.

Scout's Honor, I said.

Men Are Trouble

JAMES PATRICK KELLY

James Patrick Kelly made his first sale in 1975, and since has gone on to become one of the most respected and popular writers to enter the field in the last twenty years. Although Kelly has had some success with novels, especially with *Wildlife*, he has perhaps had more impact to date as a writer of short fiction, with stories such as "Solstice," "The Prisoner of Chillon," "Glass Cloud," "Mr. Boy," "Pogrom," "Home Front," "Undone," and "Bernardo's House," and is often ranked among the best short story writers in the business. His story "Think Like a Dinosaur" won him a Hugo Award in 1996, as did his story, "10^{16} to 1," in 2000. Kelly's first solo novel, the mostly ignored *Planet of Whispers*, came out in 1984. It was followed by *Freedom Beach*, a mosaic novel written in collaboration with John Kessel, and then by another solo novel, *Look Into the Sun*. His short work has been collected in *Think Like a Dinosaur*, and, most recently, in a new collection, *Strange But Not a Stranger*. A collaboration between Kelly and Kessel appeared in our First Annual Collection, and solo Kelly stories have appeared in our Third, Fourth, Fifth, Sixth, Eighth, Ninth, Fourteenth, Fifteenth, Seventeenth, and Nineteenth Annual Collections. Born in Minneola, New York, Kelly now lives with his family in Nottingham, New Hampshire. He has a Web site at www.JimKelly.net, and reviews Internet-related matters for *Asimov's Science Fiction*.

Private Eyes have traditionally had to venture all alone down Mean Streets, and here Kelly walks us down some very *strange* Mean Streets in a bizarre future dominated by some enigmatic, unpredictable, and totally ruthless aliens, a world where human existence as we now know it has been turned completely on its head by alien whim, and where a PI reluctantly investigating a politically touchy case bites off far more than she can chew . . .

1

I stared at my sidekick, willing it to chirp. I'd already tried watching the door, but no one had even breathed on it. I could've been writing up the Rashmi Jones case, but then I could've been dusting the office. It needed dusting. Or having a consult with Johnnie Walker, who had just that morning opened an office in the bottom drawer of my desk. Instead, I decided to open the window. Maybe a new case would arrive by carrier pigeon. Or wrapped around a brick.

Three stories below me, Market Street was as empty as the rest of the city. Just a couple of plain janes in walking shoes and a granny in a blanket and sandals. She was sitting on the curb in front of a dead Starbucks, strumming street guitar for pocket change, hoping to find a philanthropist in hell. Her singing was faint but sweet as peach ice cream. *My guy, talking 'bout my guy*. Poor old bitch, I thought. There are no guys—not yours, not anyone's. She stopped singing as a devil flapped over us, swooping for a landing on the next block. It had been a beautiful June morning until then, the moist promise of spring not yet broken by summer in our withered city. The granny struggled up, leaning on her guitar. She wrapped the blanket tight around her and trudged downtown.

My sidekick did chirp then, but it was Sharifa, my about-to-be ex-lover. She must have been calling from the hospital; she was wearing her light blue scrubs. Even on the little screen, I could see that she had been crying. "Hi, Fay."

I bit my lip.

"Come home tonight," she said. "Please."

"I don't know where home is."

"I'm sorry about what I said." She folded her arms tight across her chest. "It's your body. Your life."

I loved her. I was sick about being seeded, the abortion, everything that had happened between us in the last week. I said nothing.

Her voice was sandpaper on glass. "Have you had it done yet?" That made me angry all over again. She was wound so tight she couldn't even say the word.

"Let me guess, Doctor," I said, " 'Are we talking about me getting scrubbed?"

Her face twisted. "Don't."

"If you want the dirt," I said, "you could always hire me to shadow myself. I need the work."

"Make it a joke, why don't you?"

"Okey-doke, Doc," I said and clicked off. So my life was cocked—not exactly main menu news. Still, even with the window open, Sharifa's call had sucked all the air out of my office. I told myself that all I needed was coffee, although what I really wanted was a rich aunt, a vacation in Fiji, and a new girlfriend. I locked the door behind me, slogged down the hall and was about to press the down button when the elevator chimed. The doors slid open to reveal George, the bot in charge of our building, and a devil—no doubt the same one that had just flown by. I told myself this had nothing to do with me. The devil was probably seeing crazy Martha down the hall about a tax rebate or taking piano lessons from Abby upstairs. Sure, and drunks go to bars for the peanuts.

"Hello, Fay," said George. "This one had true hopes of finding you in your office."

I goggled, slack-jawed and stupefied, at the devil. Of course, I'd seen them on vids and in the sky and once I watched one waddle into City Hall but I'd never been close enough to slap one before. I hated the devils. The elevator doors shivered and began to close. George stuck an arm out to stop them.

"May this one borrow some of your time?" George said.

The devil was just over a meter tall. Its face was the color of an old bloodstain and its maw seemed to kiss the air as it breathed with a wet, sucking sound. The wings were wrapped tight around it; the membranes had a rusty translucence that only hinted at the sleek bullet of a body beneath. I could see my reflection in its flat compound eyes. I looked like I had just been hit in the head with a lighthouse.

"Something is regrettable, Fay?" said George.

That was my cue for a wisecrack to show them that no invincible mass-murdering alien was going to intimidate Fay Hardaway.

"No," I said. "This way."

If they could've sat in chairs, there would've been plenty of room for us in my office. But George announced that the devil needed to make itself comfortable before we began. I nodded as I settled behind my desk, grateful to have something between the two of them and me. George dragged both chairs out into the little reception room. The devil spread its wings and swooped up onto my file cabinet, ruffling the hardcopy on my desk. It filled the back wall of my office as it perched there, a span of almost twenty feet. George wedged himself into a corner and absorbed his legs and arms until he was just a head and a slab of gleaming blue bot stuff. The devil gazed at me as if it were wondering what kind of rug I would make. I brought up three new icons on my desktop. *New Case. Searchlet. Panic button.*

"Indulge this one to speak for Seeren?" said George. "Seeren has a bright desire to task you to an investigation."

The devils never spoke to us, never explained what they were doing. No one knew exactly how they communicated with the army of bots they had built to prop us up.

I opened the *New Case* folder and the green light blinked. "I'm recording this. If I decide to accept your case, I will record my entire investigation."

"A thoughtful gesture, Fay. This one needs to remark on your client Rashmi Jones."

"She's not my client." It took everything I had not to fall off my chair. "What about her?"

"Seeren conveys vast regret. All deaths diminish all."

I didn't like it that this devil knew anything at all about Rashmi, but especially that she was dead. I'll found the body in Room 103 of the Comfort Inn just twelve hours ago. "The cops already have the case." I didn't mind that there was a snarl in my voice. "Or what's left of it. There's nothing I can do for you."

"A permission, Fay?"

The icon was already flashing on my desktop. I opened it and saw a pix of Rashmi in the sleeveless taupe dress that she had died in. She had the blue ribbon in her hair. She was smiling, as carefree as a kid on the last day of school. The last thing she was thinking about was sucking on an inhaler filled with hydrogen cyanide. Holding her hand was some brunette dressed in a mannish chalk-stripe suit and a matching pillbox hat with a veil as fine as smoke. The couple preened under a garden arch that dripped with pink roses. They faced right, in the direction of the hand of some third party standing just off camera. It was an elegant hand, a hand that had never been in dishwater or changed a diaper. There was a wide silver ring on the fourth finger, engraved with a pattern or maybe some kind of fancy writing. I zoomed on the ring and briefly tormented pixels but couldn't get the pattern resolved.

I looked up at the devil and then at George. "So?"

"This one notices especially the digimark," said George. "Date-stamped June 12, 2:52."

"You're saying it was taken yesterday afternoon?"

That didn't fit—except that it did. I had Rashmi downtown shopping for shoes late yesterday morning. At 11:46 she bought a thirteen-dollar pair of this season's Donya Durands and, now missing. At 1:23 she charged eighty-nine cents for a Waldorf salad and an iced tea at Maison Diana. She checked into the Comfort Inn at 6:40. She didn't have a reservation, so maybe this was a spur of the moment decision. The desk clerk remembered her as distraught. That was the word she used. A precise word, although a bit high-brow for the Comfort Inn. Who buys expensive shoes the day she intends to kill herself? Somebody who is distraught. I glanced again at my desktop. Distraught was precisely what Rashmi Jones was not in this pix. Then I noticed the shoes: ice and taupe Donya Durands.

"Where did you get this?" I said to the devil.

It stared through me like I was a dirty window.

I tried the bot. I wouldn't say that I liked George exactly, but he'd always been straight with me. "What's this about, George? Finding the tommy?"

"The tommy?"

"The woman holding Rashmi's hand."

"Seeren has made this one well aware of Kate Vermeil," said George. "Such Kate Vermeil takes work at 44 East Washington Avenue and takes home at 465 12th Avenue, Second Floor Left."

I liked that, I liked it a lot. Rashmi's mom had told me that her daughter had a Christer friend called Kate, but I didn't even have a last name, much less an address. I turned to the devil again. "You know this how?"

All that got me was another empty stare.

"Seeren," I said, pushing back out of my chair, "I'm afraid George has led you astray. I'm the private investigator." I stood to show them out. "The mind reader's office is across the street."

This time George didn't ask permission. My desktop chirped. I waved open a new icon. A certified bank transfer in the amount of a thousand dollars dragged me back onto my chair.

"A cordial inducement," said George. "With a like amount offered after the success of your investigation."

I thought of a thousand dinners in restaurants with linen tablecloths. "Tell me already." A thousand bottles of smoky scotch.

"This one draws attention to the hand of the unseen person," said the bot. "Seeren has the brightest desire to meeting such person for fruitful business discussions."

The job smelled like the dumpster at Fran's Fish Fry. Precious little money changed hands in the pretend economy. The bots kept everything running, but they did nothing to create wealth. That was supposed to be up to us, I guess, only we'd been sort of discouraged. In some parts of town, that kind of change could hire a Felony 1, with a handful of Misdemeanors thrown in for good luck.

"That's more than I'm worth," I said. "A hundred times more. If Seeren expects me to break the arm attached to that hand, it's talking to the wrong jane."

"Violence is to be deplored," said George. "However, Seeren tasks Fay to discretion throughout. Never police, never news, never even rumor if possible."

"Oh, discretion." I accepted the transfer. "For two large, I can be as discreet as the Queen's butler."

2

I could've taken a cab, but they're almost all driven by bots now, and bots keep nobody's secrets. Besides, even though I had a thousand dollars in the bank, I thought I'd let it settle in for a while. Make itself at home. So I bicycled over to 12th Avenue. I started having doubts as I hit the 400 block. This part of the city had been kicked in the head and left bleeding on the sidewalk. Dark bars leaned against pawnshops. Board-ups turned their blank plywood faces to the street. There would be more bots than women in this neighborhood and more rats than bots.

The Adagio Spa squatted at 465 12th Avenue. It was a brick building with a reinforced luxar display window that was so scratched it looked like a thin slice of rainstorm. There were dusty plants behind it. The second floor windows were bricked over. I chained my bike to a dead car, set my sidekick to record and went in.

The rear wall of the little reception area was bright with pix of some Mediterranean seaside town. A clump of bad pixels made the empty beach flicker. A bot stepped through the door that led to the spa and took up a position at the front desk. "Good afternoon, Madam," he said. "It's most gratifying to welcome you. This one is called . . ."

"I'm looking for Kate Vermeil." I don't waste time on chitchat with bots. "Is she in?"

"It's regrettable that she no longer takes work here."

"She worked here?" I said. "I was told she lived here."

"You was told wrong." A granny filled the door, and then hobbled through, leaning on a metal cane. She was wearing a yellow flowered dress that was not quite as big as a circus tent and over it a blue smock with *Noreen* embroidered over the left breast. Her face was wide and pale as a hardboiled egg, her hair a ferment of tight gray curls. She had the biggest hands I had ever seen. "I'll take care of this, Barry. Go see to Helen Ritzi. She gets another needle at twelve, then turn down the heat to 101."

The bot bowed politely and left us.

"What's this about then?" The cane wobbled and she put a hand on the desk to steady herself.

I dug the sidekick out of my slacks, opened the PI license folder and showed it to her. She read it slowly, sniffed and handed it back. "Young fluffs working at play jobs. Do something useful, why don't you?"

"Like what?" I said. "Giving perms? Face peels?"

She was the woman of steel; sarcasm bounced off her. "If nobody does a real job, pretty soon the damn bots will replace us all."

"Might be an improvement." It was something to say, but as soon as I said it I wished I hadn't. My generation was doing better than the grannies ever had. Maybe someday our kids wouldn't need bots to survive.

Our kids. I swallowed a mouthful of ashes and called the pix Seeren had given me onto the sidekick's screen. "I'm looking for Kate Vermeil." I aimed it at her.

She peered at the pix and then at me. "You need a manicure."

"The hell I do."

"I work for a living, fluff. And my hip hurts if I stand up too long." She pointed her cane at the doorway behind the desk. "What did you say your name was?"

The battered manicure table was in an alcove decorated with fake grapevines that didn't quite hide the water stains in the drop ceiling. Dust covered the leaves, turning the plastic fruit from purple to gray.

Noreen rubbed a thumb over the tips of my fingers. "You bite your nails, or do you just cut them with a chainsaw?"

She wanted a laugh so I gave her one.

"So, nails square, round, or oval?" Her skin was dry and mottled with liver spots.

"Haven't a clue." I shrugged. "This was your idea."

Noreen perched on an adjustable stool that was cranked low so that her face was only a foot above my hands. There were a stack of stainless steel bowls, a jar of Vaseline, a round box of salt, a bowl filled with packets of sugar stolen from McDonald's, and a liquid soap dispenser on the table beside her. She started filing each nail from the corner to the center, going from left to right and then back. At first she worked in silence. I decided not to push her.

"Kate was my masseuse up until last week," she said finally. "Gave her notice all of a sudden and left me in the lurch. I've had to pick up all her appointments and me with the bum hip. Some days I can't hardly get out of bed. Something happen to her?"

"Not as far as I know."

"But she's missing."

I shook my head. "I don't know where she is, but that doesn't mean she's missing."

Noreen poured hot water from an electric kettle into one of the stainless steel bowls, added cool water from a pitcher, squirted soap and swirled the mixture around. "You soak for five minutes." She gestured for me to dip my hands into the bowl. "I'll be back. I got to make sure that Barry doesn't burn Helen Ritzi's face off." She stood with a grunt.

"Wait," I said. "Did she say why she was quitting?"

Noreen reached for her cane. "Couldn't stop talking about it. You'd think she was the first ever."

"The first to what?"

The granny laughed. "You're one hell of a detective, fluff. She was supposed to get married yesterday. Tell me that pix you're flashing ain't her doing the deed."

She shuffled off, her white nursemate shoes scuffing against dirty linoleum. From deeper in the spa, I heard her kettle drum voice and then the bot's snare. I was itching to take my sidekick out of my pocket, but I kept my hands in the soak. Besides, I'd looked at the pix enough times to know that she was right. A wedding. The hand with the ring would probably belong to a Christer priest. There would have been a witness and then the photographer, although maybe the photographer was the witness. Of course, I had tumbled to none of this in the two days I'd worked Rashmi Jones's disappearance. I was one hell of a detective, all right. And Rashmi's mom must not have known either. It didn't make sense that she would hire me to find her daughter and hold something like that back.

"I swear," said Noreen, leaning heavily on the cane as she creaked back to me, "that bot is scary. I sent down to City Hall for it just last week and already it knows my business left, right, up, and down. The thing is, if they're so smart, how come they talk funny?"

"The devils designed them to drive us crazy."

"They didn't need no bots to do that, fluff."

She settled back onto her stool, tore open five sugar packets and emptied their contents onto her palm. Then she reached for the salt box and poured salt onto the sugar. She squirted soap onto the pile and then rubbed her hands together. "I could buy some fancy exfoliating cream but this works just as good." She pointed with her chin at my hands. "Give them a shake and bring them here."

I wanted to ask her about Kate's marriage plans, but when she took my hands in hers, I forgot the question. I'd never felt anything quite like it; the irritating scratch of the grit was offset by the sensual slide of our soapy fingers. Pleasure with just the right touch of pain—something I'd certainly be telling Sharifa about, if Sharifa and I were talking. My hands tingled for almost an hour afterward.

Noreen poured another bowl of water and I rinsed. "Why would getting married make Kate want to quit?" I asked.

"I don't know. Something to do with her church?" Noreen patted me dry with a threadbare towel. "She went over to the Christers last year. Maybe Jesus don't like married women giving backrubs. Or maybe she got seeded." She gave a bitter laugh. "Everybody does eventually."

I let that pass. "Tell me about Kate. What was she like to work with?"

"Average for the kind of help you get these sorry days." Noreen pushed at my cuticles with an orangewood stick. "Showed up on time mostly; I could only afford to bring her in two days a week. No go-getter, but she could follow directions. Problem was she never really got close to the customers, always acting like this was just a pitstop. Kept to herself mostly, which was how I could tell she was excited about getting married. It wasn't like her to babble."

"And the bride?"

"Some Indian fluff—Rashy or something."

"Rashmi Jones."

She nodded. "Her I never met."

"Did she go to school?"

"Must have done high school, but damned if I know where. Didn't make much of an impression, I'd say. College, no way." She opened a drawer where a flock of colored vials was nesting. "You want polish or clear coat on the nails?"

"No color. It's bad for business."

She leered at me. "Business is good?"

"You say she did massage for you?" I said. "Where did she pick that up?"

"Hold still now." Noreen uncapped the vial; the milky liquid that clung to the brush smelled like super glue's evil twin. "This is fast dry." She painted the stuff onto my nails with short, confident strokes. "Kate claimed her mom taught her. Said she used to work at the health club at the Radisson before it closed down."

"Did the mom have a name?"

"Yeah." Noreen chewed her lower lip as she worked. "Mom. Give the other hand."

I extended my arm. "So if Kate didn't live here, where she did live?"

"Someplace. Was on her application." She kept her head down until she'd finished. "You're done. Wave them around a little—that's it."

After a moment, I let my arms drop to my side. We stared at each other. Then Noreen heaved herself off the stool and led me back out to the reception room.

"That'll be eighty cents for the manicure, fluff." She waved her desktop on. "You planning on leaving a tip?"

I pulled out the sidekick and beamed two dollars at the desk. Noreen opened the payment icon, grunted her approval and then opened another folder. "Says here she lives at 44 East Washington Avenue."

I groaned.

"Something wrong?"

"I already have that address."

"Got her call too? Kate@Washington.03284."

"No, that's good. Thanks." I went to the door and paused. I don't know why I needed to say anything else to her, but I did. "I help people, Noreen. Or at least I try. It's a real job, something bots can't do."

She just stood there, kneading the bad hip with a big, dry hand.

I unchained my bike, pedaled around the block, and then pulled over. I read Kate Vermeil's call into my sidekick. Her sidekick picked up on the sixth chirp. There was no pix.

"You haven't reached Kate yet, but your luck might change if you leave a message at the beep." She put on the kind of low, smoky voice that doesn't come out to play until dark. It was a nice act.

"Hi Kate," I said. "My name is Fay Hardaway and I'm a friend of Rashmi Jones. She asked me to give you a message about yesterday so please give me a call at Fay@Market.03284." I wasn't really expecting her to respond, but it didn't hurt to try.

I was on my way to 44 East Washington Avenue when my sidekick chirped in the pocket of my slacks. I picked up. Rashmi Jones's mom, Najma, stared at me from the screen with eyes as deep as wells.

"The police came," she said. "They said you were supposed to notify them first. They want to speak to you again."

They would. So I'd called the law after I called the mom—they'd get over it. You don't tell a mother that her daughter is dead and then ask her to act surprised when the cops come knocking. "I was working for you, not them."

"I want to see you."

"I understand."

"I hired you to find my daughter."

"I did," I said. "Twice." I was sorry as soon as I said it.

She glanced away; I could hear squeaky voices in the background. "I want to know everything," she said. "I want to know how close you came."

"I've started a report. Let me finish it and I'll bring it by later . . ."

"Now," she said. "I'm at school. My lunch starts at eleven-fifty and I have recess duty at twelve-fifteen." She clicked off.

I had nothing to feel guilty about, so why was I tempted to wriggle down a storm drain and find the deepest sewer in town? Because a mom believed that I hadn't worked fast enough or smart enough to save her daughter? Someone needed to remind these people that I didn't fix lost things, I just found them. But that someone wouldn't be me. My play now was simply to stroll into her school and let her beat me about the head with her grief. I could take it. I ate old Bogart movies for breakfast and spit out bullets. And at the end of this cocked day, I could just forget about Najma Jones, because there would be no Sharifa reminding me how much it cost me to do my job. I took out my sidekick, linked to my desktop and downloaded everything I had in the Jones file. Then I swung back onto my bike.

The mom had left a message three days ago, asking that I come out to her place on Ashbury. She and her daughter rattled around in an old Victorian with gingerbread gables and a front porch the size of Cuba. The place had been in the family for four generations. Theirs had been a big family—once. The mom said that Rashmi hadn't come home the previous night. She hadn't called and didn't answer messages. The mom had contacted the cops, but they weren't all that interested. Not enough time would have passed for them. Too much time had passed for the mom.

The mom taught fifth grade at Reagan Elementary. Rashmi was a twenty-six year-old-grad student, six credits away from an MFA in Creative Writing. The mom trusted her to draw money from the family account, so at first I thought I might be able to find her by chasing debits. But there was no activity in the account we could attribute to the missing girl. When I suggested that she might be hiding out with friends, the mom went prickly on me. Turned out that Rashmi's choice of friends was a cause of contention between them. Rashmi had dropped her old pals in the last few months and taken up with a new, religious crowd. Alix, Gratiana, Elaine, and Kate—the mom didn't know their last names—were members of the Church of Christ the Man. I'd had trouble with Christers before and wasn't all that eager to go up against them again, so instead I biked over to campus to see Rashmi's advisor. Zelda Manotti was a dithering old granny who would have loved to help except she had all the focus of paint spatter. She did let me copy Rashmi's novel-in-progress. And she did let me tag along to her advanced writing seminar, in case Rashmi showed up for it. She didn't. I talked to the three other students after class, but they either didn't know where she was or wouldn't say. None of them was Gratiana, Alix, or Elaine.

That night I skimmed *The Lost Heart*, Rashmi's novel. It was a nostalgic and sentimental weeper set back before the devils disappeared all the men. Young Brigit

Bird was searching for her father, a famous architect who had been kidnapped by Colombian drug lords. If I was just a fluff doing a fantasy job in the pretend economy, then old Noreen would have crowned Rashmi Jones queen of fluffs.

I'd started day two back at the Joneses' home. The mom watched as I went through Rashmi's room. I think she was as worried about what I might find as she was that I would find nothing. Rashmi listened to the Creeps, had three different pairs of Kat sandals, owned everything Denise Pepper had ever written, preferred underwire bras and subscribed to *News for the Confused*. She had kicked about a week's worth of dirty clothes under her bed. Her wallpaper mix cycled through koalas, the World's Greatest Beaches, ruined castles, and *Playgirl* Centerfolds 2000–2010. She'd kept a handwritten diary starting in the sixth grade and ending in the eighth in which she often complained that her mother was strict and that school was boring. The only thing I found that rattled the mom was a Christer Bible tucked into the back of the bottom drawer of the nightstand. When I pulled it out, she flushed and stalked out of the room.

I found my lead on the Joneses' home network. Rashmi was not particularly diligent about backing up her sidekick files, and the last one I found was almost six months old, which was just about when she'd gotten religion. She'd used simple encryption, which wouldn't withstand a serious hack, but which would discourage the mom from snooping. I doglegged a key and opened the file. She had multiple calls. Her mother had been trying her at Rashmi@Ashbury.03284. But she also had an alternate: Brigitbird@Vincent.03284. I did a reverse lookup and that turned an address: The Church of Christ the Man, 348 Vincent Avenue. I wasn't keen for a personal visit to the church, so I tried her call.

"Hello," said a voice.

"Is this Rashmi Jones?"

The voice hesitated. "My name is Brigit. Leave me alone."

"Your mother is worried about you, Rashmi. She hired me to find you."

"I don't want to be found."

"I'm reading your novel, Rashmi." It was just something to say; I wanted to keep her on the line. "I was wondering, does she find her father at the end?"

"No." I could hear her breath caressing the microphone. "The devils come. That's the whole point."

Someone said something to her and she muted the speaker. But I knew she could still hear me. "That's sad, Rashmi. But I guess that's the way it had to be."

Then she hung up.

The mom was relieved that Rashmi was all right, furious that she was with Christers. So what? I'd found the girl: case closed. Only Najma Jones begged me to help her connect with her daughter. She was already into me for twenty bucks plus expenses, but for another five I said I'd try to get her away from the church long enough for them to talk. I was on my way over when the searchlet I'd attached to the Jones account turned up the hit at Grayle's Shoes. I was grateful for the reprieve, even more pleased when the salesbot identified Rashmi from her pix. As did the waitress at Maison Diana.

And the clerk at the Comfort Inn.

3

Ronald Reagan Elementary had been recently renovated, no doubt by a squad of janitor bots. The brick facade had been cleaned and repointed; the long row of windows gleamed like teeth. The asphalt playground had been ripped up and resurfaced with safe-t-mat, the metal swingsets swapped for gaudy towers and crawl tubes and slides and balance beams and decks. The chain link fences had been replaced by redwood lattice through which twined honeysuckle and clematis. There was a boxwood maze next to the swimming pool that shimmered, blue as a dream. Nothing was too good for the little girls—our hope for the future.

There was no room in the rack jammed with bikes and scooters and goboards, so I leaned my bike against a nearby cherry tree. The very youngest girls had come out for first recess. I paused behind the tree for a moment to let their whoops and shrieks and laughter bubble over me. My business didn't take me to schools very often; I couldn't remember when I had last seen so many girls in one place. They were black and white and yellow and brown, mostly dressed like janes you might see anywhere. But there were more than a few whose clothes proclaimed their mothers' lifestyles. Tommys in hunter camo and chaste Christers, twists in chains and spray-on, clumps of sisters wearing the uniforms of a group marriage, a couple of furries and one girl wearing a body suit that looked just like bot skin. As I lingered there, I felt a chill that had nothing to do with the shade of a tree. I had no idea who these tiny creatures were. They went to this well-kept school, led more or less normal lives. I grew up in the wild times, when everything was falling apart. At that moment, I realized that they were as far removed from me as I was from the grannies. I would always watch them from a distance.

Just inside the fence, two sisters in green-striped shirtwaists and green knee socks were turning a rope for a ponytailed jumper who was executing nimble criss-crosses. The turners chanted,

> "*Down in the valley where the green grass grows,*
> *there sits Stacy pretty as a rose! She sings, she sings, she sings so sweet,*
> *Then along comes Chantall to kiss her on the cheek!*"

Another jumper joined her in the middle, matching her step for step, her dark hair flying. The chant continued,

"How many kisses does she get?

One, two, three, four, five . . ."

The two jumpers pecked at each other in the air to the count of ten without missing a beat. Then Ponytail skipped out and the turners began the chant over again for the dark-haired girl. Ponytail bent over for a moment to catch her breath; when she straightened, she noticed me.

"Hey you, behind the tree." She shaded her eyes with a hand. "You hiding?"

I stepped into the open. "No."

"This is our school, you know." The girl set one foot behind the other and then spun a hundred and eighty degrees to point at the door to the school. "You supposed to sign in at the office."

"I'd better take care of that then."

As I passed through the gate into the playground, a few of the girls stopped playing and stared. This was all the audience Ponytail needed. "You someone's mom?"

"No."

"Don't you have a job?" She fell into step beside me.

"I do."

"What is it?"

"I can't tell you."

She dashed ahead to block my path. "Probably because it's a pretend job."

Two of her sisters in green-striped shirtwaists scrambled to back her up.

"When we grow up," one of them announced, "we're going to have real jobs."

"Like a doctor," the other said. "Or a lion tamer."

Other girls were joining us. "I want to drive a truck," said a tommy. "Big, big truck." She specified the size of her rig with outstretched arms.

"That's not a real job. Any bot could do that."

"I want to be a teacher," said the dark-haired sister who had been jumping rope.

"Chantall loves school," said a furry. "She'd marry school if she could." Apparently this passed for brilliant wit in the third grade; some girls laughed so hard they had to cover their mouths with the backs of their hands. Me, I was flummoxed. Give me a spurned lover or a mean drunk or a hardcase cop and I could figure out some play, but just then I was trapped by this giggling mob of children.

"So why you here?" Ponytail put her fists on her hips.

A jane in khakis and a baggy plum sweater emerged from behind a blue tunnel that looked like a centipede. She pinned me with that penetrating but not unkind stare that teachers are born with, and began to trudge across the playground toward me. "I've come to see Ms. Jones," I said.

"Oh." A shadow passed over Ponytail's face and she rubbed her hands against the sides of her legs. "You better go then."

Someone called, "Are you the undertaker?"

A voice that squeaked with innocence asked, "What's an undertaker?"

I didn't hear the answer. The teacher in the plum sweater rescued me and we passed through the crowd.

I didn't understand why Najma Jones had come to school. She was either the most dedicated teacher on the planet or she was too numb to accept her daughter's death. I couldn't tell which. She had been reserved when we met the first time; now she was locked down and welded shut. She was a bird of a woman with a narrow face and thin lips. Her gray hair had a few lingering strands of black. She wore a long-sleeved white kameez tunic over shalwar trousers. I leaned against the door of her classroom and told her everything I had done the day before. She sat listening at her desk with a sandwich that she wasn't going to eat and a carton of milk that she wasn't going to drink and a napkin that she didn't need.

When I had finished, she asked me about cyanide inhalers.

"Hydrogen cyanide isn't hard to get in bulk," I said. "They use it for making plastic, engraving, tempering steel. The inhaler came from one of the underground suicide groups, probably Our Choice. The cops could tell you for sure."

She unfolded the napkin and spread it out on top of her desk. "I've heard it's a painful death."

"Not at all," I said. "They used to use hydrogen cyanide gas to execute criminals, back in the bad old days. It all depends on the first breath. Get it deep into your lungs and you're unconscious before you hit the floor. Dead in less than a minute."

"And if you don't get a large enough dose?"

"Ms. Jones . . ."

She cut me off hard. "If you don't?"

"Then it takes longer, but you still die. There are convulsions. The skin flushes and turns purple. Eyes bulge. They say it's something like having a heart attack."

"Rashmi?" She laid her daughter's name down gently, as if she were tucking it into bed. "How did she die?"

Had the cops shown her the crime scene pictures? I decided they hadn't. "I don't think she suffered," I said.

She tore a long strip off the napkin. "You don't think I'm a very good mother, do you?"

I don't know exactly what I expected her to say, but this wasn't it. "Ms. Jones, I don't know much about you and your daughter. But I do know that you cared enough about her to hire me. I'm sorry I let you down."

She shook her head wearily, as if I had just flunked the pop quiz. One third does not equal .033 and Los Angeles has never been the capital of California. "Is there anything else I should know?" she said.

"There is." I had to tell her what I'd found out that morning, but I wasn't going to tell her that I was working for a devil. "You mentioned before that Rashmi had a friend named Kate."

"The Christer?" She tore another strip off the napkin.

I nodded. "Her name is Kate Vermeil. I don't know this for sure yet, but there's reason to believe that Rashmi and Kate were married yesterday. Does that make any sense to you?"

"Maybe yesterday it might have." Her voice was flat. "It doesn't anymore."

I could hear stirring in the next classroom. Chairs scraped against linoleum. Girls were jabbering at each other.

"I know Rashmi became a Christer," she said. "It's a broken religion. But then everything is broken, isn't it? My daughter and I . . . I don't think we ever understood each other. We were strangers at the end." The napkin was in shreds. "How old were you when it happened?"

"I wasn't born yet." She didn't have to explain what *it* was. "I'm not as old as I look."

"I was nineteen. I remember men, my father, my uncles. And the boys. I actually slept with one." She gave me a bleak smile. "Does that shock you, Ms. Hardaway?"

I hated it when grannies talked about having sex, but I just shook my head.

"I didn't love Sunil, but I said I'd marry him just so I could get out of my mother's house. Maybe that was what was happening with Rashmi and this Kate person?"

"I wouldn't know."

The school bell rang.

"I'm wearing white today, Ms. Hardaway, to honor my darling daughter." She gathered up the strips of napkin and the sandwich and the carton of milk and dropped them in the trashcan. "White is the Hindu color of mourning. But it's also the color of knowledge. The goddess of learning, Saraswati, is always shown wearing a white dress, sitting on a white lotus. There is something here I must learn." She fingered the gold embroidery at the neckline of her kameez. "But it's time for recess."

We walked to the door. "What will you do now?" She opened it. The fifth grade swarmed the hall, girls rummaging through their lockers.

"Find Kate Vermeil," I said.

She nodded. "Tell her I'm sorry."

4

I tried Kate's call again, but when all I got was the sidekick I biked across town to 44 East Washington Avenue. The Poison Society turned out to be a jump joint; the sign said it opened at nine P.M. There was no bell on the front door, but I knocked hard enough to wake Marilyn Monroe. No answer. I went around to the back and tried again. If Kate was in there, she wasn't entertaining visitors.

A sidekick search turned up an open McDonald's on Wallingford, a ten-minute ride. The only other customers were a couple of twists with bound breasts and identical acid-green vinyl masks. One of them crouched on the floor beside the other, begging for chicken nuggets. A bot took my order for the twenty-nine-cent combo meal—it was all bots behind the counter. By law, there was supposed to be a human running the place, but if she was on the premises, she was nowhere to be seen. I thought about calling City Hall to complain, but the egg rolls arrived crispy and the McLatte was nicely scalded. Besides, I didn't need to watch the cops haul the poor jane in charge out of whatever hole she had fallen into.

A couple of hardcase tommys in army surplus fatigues had strutted in just after me. They ate with their heads bowed over their plastic trays so the fries didn't have too far to travel. Their collapsible titanium nightsticks lay on the table in plain sight. One of them was not quite as wide as a bus. The other was nothing special, except that when I glanced up from my sidekick, she was giving me a freeze-dried stare. I waggled my shiny fingernails at her and screwed my cutest smile onto my face. She scowled, said something to her partner and went back to the trough.

My sidekick chirped. It was my pal Julie Epstein, who worked Self-Endangerment/Missing Persons out of the second precinct.

"You busy, Fay?"

"Yeah, the Queen of Cleveland just lost her glass slipper and I'm on the case."

"Well, I'm about to roll through your neighborhood. Want to do lunch?"

I aimed the sidekick at the empties on my table. "Just finishing."

"Where are you?"

"McD's on Wallingford."

"Yeah? How are the ribs?"

"Couldn't say. But the egg rolls are triple dee."

"That the place where the owner is a junkliner? We've had complaints. Bots run everything?"

"No, I can see her now. She's shortchanging some beat cop."

She gave me the laugh. "Got the coroner's on the Rashmi Jones. Cyanide induced hypoxia."

"You didn't by any chance show the mom pix of the scene?"

"Hell no. Talk about cruel and unusual." She frowned. "Why?"

"I was just with her. She seemed like maybe she suspected her kid wrestled with the reaper."

"We didn't tell her. By the way, we don't really care if you call your client, but next time how about trying us first?"

"That's cop law. Me, I follow PI law."

"Where did you steal that line from, *Chinatown*?"

"It's got better dialogue than *Dragnet*." I swirled the last of my latte in the cup. "You calling a motive on the Rashmi Jones?"

"Not yet. What do you like?" She ticked off the fingers of her left hand. "Family? School? Money? Broke a fingernail? Cloudy day?"

"Pregnancy? Just a hunch."

"You think she was seeded? We'll check that. But that's no reason to kill yourself."

"They've all got reasons. Only none of them makes sense."

She frowned. "Hey, don't get all invested on me here."

"Tell me, Julie, do you think I'm doing a pretend job?"

"Whoa, Fay." Her chuckle had a sharp edge. "Maybe it's time you and Sharifa took a vacation."

"Yeah." I let that pass. "It's just that some granny called me a fluff."

"Grannies." She snorted in disgust. "Well, you're no cop, that's for sure. But we do appreciate the help. Yeah, I'd say what you do is real. As real as anything in this cocked world."

"Thanks, flatfoot. Now that you've made things all better, I'll just click off. My latte is getting cold and you're missing so damn many persons."

"Think about that vacation, shamus. Bye."

As I put my sidekick away, I realized that the tommys were waiting for me. They'd been rattling ice in their cups and folding McWrappers for the past ten minutes. I probably didn't need their brand of trouble. The smart move would be to bolt for the door and leave my bike for now; I could lose them on foot. But then I hadn't made a smart move since April. The big one was talking into her sidekick when I sauntered over to them.

"What can I do for you ladies?" I said.

The big one pocketed the sidekick. Her partner started to come out of her seat but the big one stretched an arm like a telephone pole to restrain her.

"Do we know you?" The partner had close-set eyes and a beak nose; her black hair was short and stiff as a brush. She was wearing a black tee under her fatigue jacket and black leather combat boots. Probably had steel toes. "No," she continued, "I don't think we do."

"Then let's get introductions out of the way," I said. "I'm Fay Hardaway. And you are . . . ?"

They gave me less than nothing.

I sat down. "Thanks," I said. "Don't mind if I do."

The big one leaned back in her chair and eyed me as if I was dessert. "Sure you're not making a mistake, missy?"

"Why, because you're rough, tough, and take no guff?"

"You're funny." She smirked. "I like that. People who meet us are usually so very sad. My name is Alix." She held out her hand and we shook. "Pleased to know you."

The customary way to shake hands is to hold on for four, maybe five seconds, squeeze good-bye, then loosen the grip. Maybe big Alix wasn't familiar with our customs—she wasn't letting go.

I wasn't going to let a little thing like a missing hand intimidate me. "Oh, then I do know you," I said. We were in the McDonald's on Wallingford Street—a public place. I'd just been talking to my pal the cop. I was so damn sure that I was safe, I decided to take my shot. "That would make the girlfriend here Elaine. Or is it Gratiana?"

"Alix." The beak panicked. "Now we've got to take her."

Alix sighed, then yanked on my arm. She might have been pulling a tissue from a box for all the effort she expended. I slid halfway across the table as the beak whipped her nightstick to full extension. I lunged away from her and she caught me just a glancing blow above the ear but then Alix stuck a popper into my face and spattered me with knockout spray. I saw a billion stars and breathed the vacuum of deep space for maybe two seconds before everything went black.

Big Ben chimed between my ears. I could feel it deep in my molars, in the jelly of my eyes. It was the first thing I had felt since World War II. Wait a minute, was I alive during World War II? No, but I had seen the movie. When I wiggled my toes, Big Ben chimed again. I realized that the reason it hurt so much was that the human head didn't really contain enough space to hang a bell of that size. As I took inventory of body parts, the chiming became less intense. By the time I knew I was all there, it was just the sting of blood in my veins.

I was laid out on a surface that was hard but not cold. Wood. A bench. The place I was in was huge and dim but not dark. The high ceiling was in shadow. There was a hint of smoke in the air. Lights flickered. Candles. That was a clue, but I was still too groggy to understand what the mystery was. I knew I needed to remember something, but there was a hole where the memory was supposed to be. I reached back and touched just above my ear. The tip of my finger came away dark and sticky.

A voice solved the mystery for me. "I'm sorry that my people overreacted. If you want to press charges, I've instructed Gratiana and Alix to surrender to the police."

It came back to me then. It always does. McDonald's. Big Alix. A long handshake. That would make this a church. I sat up. When the world stopped spinning, I saw a vast marble altar awash in light with a crucifix the size of a Cessna hanging behind it.

"I hope you're not in too much pain, Miss Hardaway." The voice came from the pew behind me. A fortyish woman in a black suit and a Roman collar was on the kneeler. She was wearing a large silver ring on the fourth finger of her left hand.

"I've felt worse."

"That's too bad. Do you make a habit of getting into trouble?" She looked concerned that I might be making some bad life choices. She had soft eyes and a kindly face. Her short hair was the color of ashes. She was someone I could tell my guilty secrets to, so I could sleep at night. She would speak to Christ the Man himself on my behalf, book me into the penthouse suite in heaven.

"Am I in trouble?"

She nodded gravely. "We all are. The devils are destroying us, Miss Hardaway. They plant their seed not only in our bodies, but our minds and our souls."

"Please, call me Fay. I'm sure we're going to be just the very best of friends." I leaned toward her. "I'm sorry, I can't read your name tag."

"I'm not wearing one." She smiled. "I'm Father Elaine Horváth."

We looked at each other.

"Have you ever considered suicide, Fay?" said Father Elaine.

"Not really. It's usually a bad career move."

"Very good. But you must know that since the devils came and changed everything, almost a billion women have despaired and taken their lives."

"You know, I think I did hear something about that. Come on, lady, what's this about?"

"It is the tragedy of our times that there are any number of good reasons to kill oneself. It takes courage to go on living with the world the way it is. Rashmi Jones was a troubled young woman. She lacked that courage. That doesn't make her a bad person, just a dead one."

I patted my pocket, looking for my sidekick. Still there. I pulled it out and pressed *record*. I didn't ask for permission. "So I should mind my own business?"

"That would be a bad career move in your profession. How old are you, Fay?"

"Thirty-three."

"Then you were born of a virgin." She leaned back, slid off the kneeler and onto the pew. "Seeded by the devils. I'm old enough to have had a father, Fay. I actually remember him a little. A very little."

"Don't start." I spun out of the pew into the aisle. I hated cock nostalgia. This granny had me chewing aluminum foil; I would have spat it at Christ himself if he had dared come down off his cross. "You want to know one reason why my generation jumps out of windows and sucks on cyanide? It's because twists like you make us feel guilty about how we came to be. You want to call me devil's spawn, go ahead. Enjoy yourself. Live it up. Because we're just waiting for you old bitches to die off. Someday this foolish church is going to dry up and blow away and you know what? We'll go dancing that night, because we'll be a hell of a lot happier without you to remind us of what you lost and who we can never be."

She seemed perversely pleased by my show of emotion. "You're an angry woman, Fay."

"Yeah," I said, "but I'm kind to children and small animals."

"What is that anger doing to your soul? Many young people find solace in Christ."

"Like Alix and Gratiana?"

She folded her hands; the silver ring shone dully. "As I said, they have offered to turn themselves . . ."

"Keep them. I'm done with them." I was cooling off fast. I paused, considering my next move. Then I sat down on the pew next to Father Elaine, showed her my sidekick and made sure she saw me pause the recording. Our eyes met. We understood each other. "Did you marry Kate Vermeil and Rashmi Jones yesterday?"

She didn't hesitate. "I performed the ceremony. I never filed the documents."

"Do you know why Rashmi killed herself?"

"Not exactly." She held my gaze. "I understand she left a note."

"Yeah, the note. I found it on her sidekick. She wrote, 'Life is too hard to handle and I can't handle it so I've got to go now. I love you Mom, sorry.' A little generic for a would-be writer, wouldn't you say? And the thing is there's nothing in the note about Kate. I didn't even know she existed until this morning. Now I have a problem with that. The cops would have the same problem if I gave it to them."

"But you haven't."

"Not yet."

She thought about that for a while.

"My understanding," said Father Elaine at last, "is that Kate and Rashmi had a disagreement shortly after the ceremony." She was tiptoeing around words as if one of them might wake up and start screaming. "I don't know exactly what it was about. Rashmi left, Kate stayed here. Someone was with her all yesterday afternoon and all last night."

"Because you thought she might need an alibi?"

She let that pass. "Kate was upset when she heard the news. She blames herself, although I am certain she is without blame."

"She's here now?"

"No." Father Elaine shrugged. "I sent her away when I learned you were looking for her."

"And you want me to stop."

"You are being needlessly cruel, you know. The poor girl is grieving."

"Another poor girl is dead." I reached into my pocket for my penlight. "Can I see your ring?"

That puzzled her. She extended her left hand and I shone the light on it. Her skin was freckled but soft, the nails flawless. She would not be getting them done at a dump like the Adagio Spa.

"What do these letters mean?" I asked. "IHS?"

"*In hoc signo vinces.* 'In this sign you will conquer.' The emperor Constantine had a vision of a cross in the sky with those words written in fire on it. This was just before a major battle. He had his soldiers paint the cross on their shields and then he won the day against a superior force."

"Cute." I snapped the light off. "What's it mean to you?"

"The Bride of God herself gave this to me." Her face lit up, as if she were listening to an angelic chorus chant her name. "In recognition of my special vocation. You see, Fay, our Church has no intention of drying up and blowing away. Long after my generation is gone, believers will continue to gather in Christ's name. And someday they'll finish the work we have begun. Someday they will exorcise the devils."

If she knew how loopy that sounded, she didn't show it. "Okay, here's the way it is," I said. "Forget Kate Vermeil. I only wanted to find her so she could lead me to you. A devil named Seeren hired me to look for a certain party wearing a ring like yours. It wants a meeting."

"With me?" Father Elaine went pale. "What for?"

"I just find them." I enjoyed watching her squirm. "I don't ask why."

She folded her hands as if to pray, then leaned her head against them and closed her eyes. She sat like that for almost a minute. I decided to let her brood, not that I had much choice. The fiery pit of hell could've opened up and she wouldn't have noticed.

Finally, she shivered and sat up. "I have to find out how much they know." She gazed up at the enormous crucifix. "I'll see this devil, but on one condition: you guarantee my safety."

"Sure." I couldn't help myself; I laughed. The sound echoed, profaning the silence. "Just how am I supposed to do that? They disappeared half the population of Earth without breaking a sweat."

"You have their confidence," she said. "And mine."

A vast and absurd peace had settled over her; she was seeing the world through the gauze of faith. She was a fool if she thought I could go up against the devils. Maybe she believed Christ the Man would swoop down from heaven to protect her, but then he hadn't been seen around the old neighborhood much of late. Or maybe she had projected herself into the mind of the martyrs who would embrace the sword, kiss the ax that would take their heads. I reminded myself that her delusions were none of my business.

Besides, I needed the money. And suddenly I just had to get out of that big, empty church.

"My office is at 35 Market," I said. "Third floor. I'll try to set something up for six tonight." I stood. "Look, if they want to take you, you're probably gone. But I'll record everything and squawk as loud as I can."

"I believe you will," she said, her face aglow.

5

I didn't go to my office after I locked my bike to the rack on Market Street. Instead I went to find George. He was stripping varnish from the beadboard wainscoting in Donna Belasco's old office on the fifth floor. Donna's office had been vacant since last fall, when she had closed her law practice and gone south to count waves at Daytona Beach. At least, that's what I hoped she was doing; the last I'd heard from her was a Christmas card. I missed Donna; she was one of the few grannies who tried to understand what it was like to grow up the way we did. And she had been generous about steering work my way.

"Hey George," I said. "You can tell your boss that I found the ring."

"This one offers the congratulations." The arm holding the brush froze over the can of stripper as he swiveled his head to face me. "You have proved true superiority, Fay." George had done a good job maintaining our building since coming to us a year ago, although he had something against wood grain. We had to stop him from painting over the mahogany paneling in the foyer.

I hated to close the doorbut this conversation needed some privacy. "So I've set up a meeting." The stink of the varnish stripper was barbed wire up my nose. "Father Elaine Horváth will be here at six."

George said nothing. Trying to read a bot is like trying to read a refrigerator. I assumed that he was relaying this information to Seeren. Would the devil be displeased that I had booked its meeting into my office?

"Seeren is impressed by your speedy accomplishment," George said at last. "Credit has been allotted to this one for suggesting it task you."

"Great, take ten bucks a month off my rent. Just so you know, I promised Father Elaine she'd be safe here. Seeren is not going to make a liar out of me, is it?"

"Seeren rejects violence. It's a regrettable technique."

"Yeah, but if Seeren disappears her to wherever, does that count?"

George's head swiveled back toward the wainscoting. "Father Elaine Horváth will be invited to leave freely, if such is her intention." The brush dipped into the can. "Was Kate Vermeil also found?"

"No," I said. "I looked, but then Father Elaine found me. By the way, she didn't live at 465 12th Avenue."

"Seeren had otherwise information." The old varnish bubbled and sagged where George had applied stripper. "Such error makes a curiosity."

It was a little thing, but it pricked at me as I walked down to the third floor. Was I pleased to discover that the devils were neither omnipotent nor infallible? Not particularly. For all their crimes against humanity, the devils and their bots were pretty much running our world now. It had been a small if bitter comfort to imagine that they knew exactly what they were doing.

I passed crazy Martha's door, which was open, on the way to my office. "Yaga combany wading," she called.

I backtracked. My neighbor was at her desk, wearing her Technopro gas mask, which she claimed protected her from chlorine, hydrogen sulfide, sulfur dioxide, ammonia, bacteria, viruses, dust, pollen, cat dander, mold spores, nuclear fallout, and sexual harassment. Unfortunately, it also made her almost unintelligible.

"Try that again," I said.

"You've. Got. Company. Waiting."

"Who is it?"

She shook the mask and shrugged. The light of her desktop was reflected in the faceplate. I could see numbers swarming like black ants across the rows and columns of a spreadsheet.

"What's with the mask?"

"We. Had. A. Devil. In. The. Building."

"Really?" I said. "When?"

"Morning."

There was no reason why a devil shouldn't come into our building, no law against having one for a client. But there was an accusation in Martha's look that I couldn't deny. Had I betrayed us all by taking the case? She said, "Hate. Devils."

"Yeah," I said. "Me too."

I opened my door and saw that it was Sharifa who was waiting for me. She was trying on a smile that didn't fit. "Hi Fay," she said. She looked as elegant as always and as weary as I had ever seen her. She was wearing a peppered black linen dress and black dress sandals with thin crossover straps. Those weren't doctor shoes—they were pull down the shades and turn up the music shoes. They made me very sad.

As I turned to close the door, she must have spotted the patch of blood that had dried in my hair. "You're hurt!" I had almost forgotten about it—there was no percentage in remembering that I was in pain. She shot out of her chair. "What happened?"

"I slipped in the shower," I said.

"Let me look."

I tilted my head toward her and she probed the lump gently. "You could have a concussion."

"PI's don't get concussions. Says so right on the license."

"Sit," she said. "Let me clean this up. I'll just run to the bathroom for some water."

I sat and watched her go. I thought about locking the door behind her but I deserved whatever I had coming. I opened the bottom drawer of the desk, slipped two plastic cups off the stack and brought Johnnie Walker in for a consultation.

Sharifa bustled through the doorway with a cup of water in one hand and a fistful of paper towels in the other but caught herself when she saw the bottle. "When did this start?"

"Just now." I picked up my cup and slugged two fingers of Black Label Scotch. "Want some?"

"I don't know," she said. "Are we having fun or are we self-medicating?"

I let that pass. She dabbed at the lump with a damp paper towel. I could smell her perfume, lemon blossoms on a summer breeze and just the smallest bead of sweat. Her scent got along nicely with the liquid smoke of the scotch. She brushed against me and I could feel her body beneath her dress. At that moment I wanted her more than I wanted to breathe.

"Sit down," I said.

"I'm not done yet," she said.

I pointed at a chair. "Sit, damn it."

She dropped the paper towel in my trash as she went by.

"You asked me a question this morning," I said. "I should've given you the answer. I had the abortion last week."

She studied her hands. I don't know why; they weren't doing anything. They were just sitting in her lap, minding their own business.

"I told you when we first got together, that's what I'd do when I got seeded," I said.

"I know."

"I just didn't see any good choices," I said. "I know the world needs children, but I have a life to lead. Maybe it's a rude, pointless, dirty life but it's what I have. Being a mother . . . that's someone else's life."

"I understand," said Sharifa. Her voice was so small it could have crawled under a thimble. "It's just . . . it was all so sudden. You told me and then we were fighting and I didn't have time to think things through."

"I got tested in the morning. I told you that afternoon. I wasn't keeping anything a secret."

She folded her arms against her chest as if she were cold. "And when I get seeded, what then?"

"You'll do what's best for you."

She sighed. "Pour me some medication, would you?"

I poured scotch into both cups, came around the desk, and handed Sharifa hers. She drank, held the whiskey in her mouth for a moment and then swallowed.

"Fay, I . . ." The corners of her mouth were twitchy and she bit her lip. "Your mother told me once that when she realized she was pregnant with you, she was so happy. So happy. It was when everything was crashing around everyone. She said you were the gift she needed to . . . not to . . ."

"I got the gift lecture, Sharifa. Too many times. She made the devils sound like Santa Claus. Or the stork."

She glanced down as if surprised to discover that she was still holding the cup. She drained it at a gulp and set it on my desk. "I'm a doctor. I know they do this to us; I just wish I knew how. But it isn't a bad thing. Having you in the world can't be a bad thing."

I wasn't sure about that, but I kept my opinion to myself.

"Sometimes I feel like I'm trying to carry water in my hands but it's all leaking out and there's nothing I can do to stop it." She started rubbing her right hand up and down her left forearm. "People keep killing themselves. Maybe it's not as bad as it used to be, but still. The birth rate is barely at replacement levels. Maybe we're doomed. Did you ever think that? That we might go extinct?"

"No."

Sharifa was silent for a long time. She kept rubbing her arm. "It should've been me doing your abortion," she said at last. "Then we'd both have to live with it."

I was one tough PI. I kept a bottle of scotch in the bottom drawer and had a devil for a client. Tommys whacked me with nightsticks and pumped knockout spray into my face. But even I had a breaking point, and Dr. Sharifa Ramirez was pushing me up against it hard. I wanted to pull her into my arms and kiss her forehead, her cheeks, her graceful neck. But I couldn't give in to her that way—not now anyway. Maybe never again. I had a case, and I needed to hold the best part of myself in reserve until it was finished. "I'll be in charge of the guilt, Sharifa," I said. "You be in charge of saving lives." I came around the desk. "I've got work to do, so you go home now, sweetheart." I kissed her on the forehead. "I'll see you there."

Easier to say than to believe.

6

Sharifa was long gone by the time Father Elaine arrived at ten minutes to six. She brought muscle with her; Gratiana loitered in the hallway surveying my office with sullen calculation, as if estimating how long it would take to break down the door, leap over the desk, and wring somebody's neck. I shouldn't have been surprised that Father Elaine's faith in me had wavered—hell, I didn't have much faith in me either. However, I thought she showed poor judgment in bringing this particular thug along. I invited Gratiana to remove herself from my building. Perhaps she might perform an autoerotic act in front of a speeding bus? Father Elaine dismissed her, and she slunk off.

Father Elaine appeared calm, but I could tell that she was as nervous as two mice and a gerbil. I hadn't really had a good look at her in the dim church, but now I studied her in case I had to write her up for the Missing Persons Index. She was a tallish woman with round shoulders and a bit of a stoop. Her eyes were the brown of wet sand; her cheeks were bloodless. Her smile was not quite as convincing in good light as it had been in gloom. She made some trifling small talk, which I did nothing to help with. Then she stood at the window, watching. A wingtip loafer tapped against bare floor.

It was about ten after when my desktop chirped. I waved open the icon and accepted the transfer of a thousand dollars. Seeren had a hell of a calling card. "I think they're coming," I said. I opened the door and stepped into the hall to wait for them.

"It gives Seeren the bright pleasure to meet you, Father Elaine Horváth," said George as they shuffled into the office.

She focused everything she had on the devil. "Just Father, if you don't mind." The bot was nothing but furniture to her.

"It's kind of crowded in here," I said. "If you want, I can wait outside. . . ."

Father Elaine's facade cracked for an instant, but she patched it up nicely. "I'm sure we can manage," she said.

"This one implores Fay to remain," said George.

We sorted ourselves out. Seeren assumed its perch on top of the file cabinet and George came around and compacted himself next to me. Father Elaine pushed her chair next to the door. I think she was content to be stationed nearest the exit. George looked at Father Elaine. She looked at Seeren. Seeren looked out the window. I watched them all.

"Seeren offers sorrow over the regrettable death of Rashmi Jones," said George. "Such Rashmi was of your church?"

"She was a member, yes."

"According to Fay Hardaway, a fact is that Father married Kate Vermeil and Rashmi Jones."

I didn't like that. I didn't like it at all.

Father Elaine hesitated only a beat. "Yes."

"Would Father permit Seeren to locate Kate Vermeil?"

"I know where she is, Seeren," said Father Elaine. "I don't think she needs to be brought into this."

"Indulge this one and reconsider, Father. Is such person pregnant?"

Her manner had been cool, but now it dropped forty degrees. "Why would you say that?"

"Perhaps such person is soon to become pregnant?"

"How would I know? If she is, it would be your doing, Seeren."

"Father well understands *in vitro* fertilization?"

"I've heard of it, yes." Father Elaine's shrug was far too elaborate. "I can't say I understand it."

"Father has heard then of transvaginal oocyte retrieval?"

She thrust our her chin. "No."

"Haploidisation of somatic cells?"

She froze.

"Has Father considered then growing artificial sperm from embryonic stem cells?"

"I'm a priest, Seeren." Only her lips moved. "Not a biologist."

"Does the Christer Church make further intentions to induce pregnancies in certain members? Such as Kate Vermeil?"

Father Elaine rose painfully from the chair. I thought she might try to run, but now martyr's fire burned through the shell of ice that had encased her. "We're doing Christ's work, Seeren. We reject your obscene seeding. We are saving ourselves from you and you can't stop us."

Seeren beat its wings, once, twice, and crowed. It was a dense, jarring sound, like steel scraping steel. I hadn't known that devils could make any sound at all, but hearing that hellish scream made me want to dive under my desk and curl up in a ball. I took it though, and so did Father Elaine. I gave her credit for that.

"Seeren makes no argument with the Christer Church," said George. "Seeren upholds only the brightest encouragement for such pregnancies."

Father Elaine's face twitched in disbelief and then a flicker of disappointment passed over her. Maybe she was upset to have been cheated of her glorious death. She was a granny after all, of the generation that had embraced the suicide culture. For the first time, she turned to the bot. "What?"

"Seeren tasks Father to help numerous Christers become pregnant. Christers who do such choosing will then give birth."

She sank back onto her chair.

"Too many humans now refuse the seeding," said the bot. "Not all then give birth. This was not foreseen. It is regrettable."

Without my noticing, my hands had become fists. My knuckles were white.

"Seeren will announce its true satisfaction with the accomplishment of the Christer Church. It offers a single caution. Christers must assure all to make no XY chromosome."

Father Elaine was impassive. "Will you continue to seed all nonbelievers?"

"It is prudent for the survival of humans."

She nodded and faced Seeren. "How will you know if we do try to bring men back into the world?"

The bot said nothing. The silence thickened as we waited. Maybe the devil thought it didn't need to make threats.

"Well, then." Father Elaine rose once again. Some of the stoop had gone out of her shoulders. She was trying to play it calm, but I knew she'd be skipping by the time she hit the sidewalk. Probably she thought she had won a great victory. In any event, she was done with this little party.

But it was my little party, and I wasn't about to let it break up with the devils holding hands with the Christers. "Wait," I said. "Father, you better get Gratiana up here. And if you've got any other muscle in the neighborhood, call them right now. You need backup fast."

Seeren glanced away from the window and at me.

"Why?" Father Elaine already had her sidekick out. "What is this?"

"There's a problem."

"Fay Hardaway," said George sharply. "Indulge this one and recall your task. Your employment has been accomplished."

"Then I'm on my own time now, George." I thought maybe Seeren would try to leave, but it remained on its perch. Maybe the devil didn't care what I did. Or else it found me amusing. I could be an amusing girl, in my own obtuse way.

Gratiana tore the door open. She held her nightstick high, as if expecting to dive into a bloodbath. When she saw our cool tableau, she let it drop to her side.

"Scooch over, Father," I said, "and let her in. Gratiana, you can leave the door open but keep that toothpick handy. I'm pretty sure you're going to be using it before long."

"The others are right behind me, Father," said Gratiana as she crowded into the room. "Two, maybe three minutes."

"Just enough time." I let my hand fall to the middle drawer of my desk. "I have a question for you, Father." I slid the drawer open. "How did Seeren know all that stuff about haploid this and *in vitro* that?"

"It's a devil." She watched me thoughtfully. "They come from two hundred light years away. How do they know anything?"

"Fair enough. But they also knew that you married Kate and Rashmi. George here just said that I told them, except I never did. That was a mistake. It made me wonder whether they knew who you were all along. It's funny, I used to be convinced that the devils were infallible, but now I'm thinking that they can screw up any day of the week, just like the rest of us. They're almost human that way."

"A regrettable misstatement was made." The bot's neck extended until his head was level with mine. "Indulge this one and refrain from further humiliation."

"I've refrained for too long, George. I've had a bellyful of refraining." I was pretty sure that George could see the open drawer, which meant that the devil would know what was in it as well. I wondered how far they'd let me go. "The question is, Father, if the devils already knew who you were, why would Seeren hire me to find you?"

"Go on," she said.

My chest was tight. Nobody tried to stop me, so I went ahead and stuck my head into the lion's mouth. Like that little girl at school, I'd always wanted to have a real job when I grew up. "You've got a leak, Father. Your problem isn't devil super-science. It's the good old-fashioned Judas kiss. Seeren has an inside source, a mole among your congregation. When it decided the time had come to meet with you, it wanted to be sure that none of you would suspect where its information was actually coming from. It decided that the way to give the mole cover was to hire some gullible PI to pretend to find stuff out. I may be a little slow and a lot greedy but I do have a few shreds of pride. I can't let myself be played for an idiot." I thought I heard footsteps on the stairs, but maybe it was just my own blood pounding. "You see, Father, I don't think that Seeren really trusts you. I sure didn't hear you promise just now not to be making little boys. And yes, if they find out about the boy babies, the devils could just disappear them, but you and the Bride of God and all your batty friends would find ways to make that very public, very messy. I'm guessing that's part of your plan, isn't it? To remind us who the devils are, what they did? Maybe get people into the streets again. Since the devils still need to know what you're up to, the mole had to be protected."

Father Elaine flushed with anger. "Do you know who she is?"

"No," I said. "But you could probably narrow it down to a very few. You said you married Rashmi and Kate, but that you never filed the documents. But you needed someone to witness the ceremony. Someone who was taking pix and would send one to Seeren. . . ."

Actually, my timing was a little off. Gratiana launched herself at me just as big Alix hurtled through the doorway. I had the air taser out of the drawer, but my plan had been for the Christers to clean up their own mess. I came out of my chair and raised the taser but even fifty thousand volts wasn't going to keep that snarling bitch off me.

I heard a huge wet pop, not so much an explosion as an implosion. There was a rush of air through the doorway but the room was preternaturally quiet, as if someone had just stopped screaming. We humans gaped at the void that had formerly been occupied by Gratiana. The familiar surroundings of my office seemed to warp and stretch to accommodate that vacancy. If she could vanish so completely, then maybe chairs could waltz on the ceiling and trashcans could sing *Carmen*. For the first time in my life I had a rough sense of what the grannies had felt when the devils disappeared their men. It would be one thing if Gratiana were merely dead, if there were blood, and bone and flesh left behind. A body to be buried. But this was an offense against reality itself. It undermined our common belief that the world is indeed a fact, that we exist at all. I could understand how it could unhinge a billion minds. I was standing next to Father Elaine beside the open door to my office holding the taser and I couldn't remember how I had gotten there.

Seeren hopped down off the bookcase as if nothing important had happened and wrapped its translucent wings around its body. The devil didn't seem surprised at all that a woman had just disappeared. Maybe there was no surprising a devil.

And then it occurred to me that this probably wasn't the first time since they had taken all the men that the devils had disappeared someone. Maybe they did it all the time. I thought of all the missing persons whom I had never found. I could see the files in Julie Epstein's office bulging with unsolved cases. Had Seeren done this thing to teach us the fragility of being? Or had it just been a clumsy attempt to cover up its regrettable mistakes?

As the devil waddled toward the door, Alix made a move as if to block its exit. After what had just happened, I thought that was probably the most boneheaded, brave move I had ever seen.

"Let them go." Father Elaine's voice quavered. Her eyes were like wounds.

Alix stepped aside and the devil and the bot left us. We listened to the devil scrabble down the hall. I heard the elevator doors open and then close.

Then Father Elaine staggered and put a hand on my shoulder. She looked like a granny now.

"There are no boy babies," she said. "Not yet. You have to believe me."

"You know what?" I shook free of her. "I don't care." I wanted them gone. I wanted to sit alone at my desk and watch the room fill with night.

"You don't understand."

"And I don't want to." I had to set the taser on the desk or I might have used it on her.

"Kate Vermeil is pregnant with one of our babies," said Father Elaine. "It's a little girl, I swear it."

"So you've made Seeren proud. What's the problem?"

Alix spoke for the first time. "Gratiana was in charge of Kate."

7

The Poison Society was lit brightly enough to give a camel a headache. If you forgot your sunglasses, there was a rack of freebies at the door. Set into the walls were terrariums where diamondback rattlers coiled in the sand, black neck cobras dangled from dead branches and brown scorpions basked on ceramic rocks. The hemlock was in bloom; clusters of small, white flowers opened like umbrellas. Upright stems of monkshood were interplanted with death cap mushrooms in wine casks cut out in half. Curare vines climbed the pergola over the alcohol bar.

I counted maybe fifty customers in the main room, which was probably a good crowd for a Wednesday night. I had no idea yet how many might be lurking in the specialty shops that opened off this space, where a nice girl might arrange for a guaranteed-safe session of sexual asphyxia either by hanging or drowning, or else get her cerebrum toasted by various brain lightning generators. I was hoping Kate was out in the open with the relatively sane folks. I didn't really want to poke around in the shops, but I would if I had to. I thought I owed it to Rashmi Jones.

I strolled around, pretending to look at various animals and plants, carrying a tumbler filled with a little Johnnie Walker Black Label and a lot of water. I knew Kate would be disguised but if I could narrow the field of marks down to three or four, I might actually snoop her. Of course, she might be on the other side of town, but this was my only play. My guess was that she'd switch styles, so I wasn't necessarily looking for a tommy. Her hair wouldn't be brunette, and her skin would probably be darker, and contacts could give her cat's eyes or zebra eyes or American flags, if she wanted. But even with padding and lifts she couldn't change her body type enough to fool a good scan. And I had her data from the Christer medical files loaded into my sidekick.

Father Elaine had tried Kate's call, but she wouldn't pick up. That made perfect sense since just about anyone could put their hands on software that could replicate voices. There were bots that could sing enough like Velma Stone to fool her own mother. Kate and Gratiana would have agreed on a safe word. Our problem was that Gratiana had taken it with her to hell, or wherever the devil had consigned her.

The first mark my sidekick picked out was a redhead in silk pajamas and lime green bunny slippers. A scan matched her to Kate's numbers to within 5 percent. I bumped into her just enough to plant the snoop, a sticky homing device the size of a baby tooth.

"'Scuse me, sorry." I said. "S-so sorry." I slopped some of my drink onto the floor.

She gave me a glare that would have withered a cactus and I noodled off. As soon as I was out of her sight, I hit the button on my sidekick to which I'd assigned Kate's call. When Kate picked up, the snoop would know if the call had come from me and signal my sidekick that I had found her. The redhead wasn't Kate. Neither was the bald jane in distressed leather.

The problem with trying to locate her this way was that if I kept calling her, she'd get suspicious and lose the sidekick.

I lingered by a pufferfish aquarium. Next to it was a safe, and in front of that a tootsie fiddled with the combination lock. I scanned her and got a match to within 2 percent. She was wearing a spangle wig and a stretch lace dress with a ruffle front. When she opened the door of the safe, I saw that it was made of clear luxar. She reached in, then slammed the door and trotted off as if she were late for the last train of the night.

I peeked through the door of the safe. Inside was a stack of squat blue inhalers like the one Rashmi had used to kill herself. On the wall above the safe, the management of The Poison Society had spray-painted a mock graffiti. *21L 4R 11L.* There was no time to plant a snoop. I pressed the call button as I tailed her.

With a strangled cry, the tootsie yanked a sidekick from her clutch purse, dropped it to the floor, and stamped on it. She was wearing Donya Durand ice and taupe flat slingbacks.

As I moved toward her, Kate Vermeil saw me and ducked into one of the shops. She dodged past fifty-five gallon drums of carbon tetrachloride and dimethyl sulfate and burst through the rear door of the shop into an alley. I saw her fumbling with the cap of the inhaler. I hurled myself at her and caught at her legs. Her right shoe came off in my hand, but I grabbed her left ankle and she went down. She still had the inhaler and was trying to bring it to her mouth. I leapt on top of her and wrenched it away.

"Do you really want to kill yourself?" I aimed the inhaler at her face and screamed at her. "Do you, Kate? Do you?" The air in the alley was thick with despair and I was choking on it. "Come on, Kate. Let's do it!"

"No." Her head thrashed back and forth. "No, please. Stop."

Her terror fed mine. "Then what the hell are you doing with this thing?" I was shaking so badly that when I tried to pitch the inhaler into the dumpster, it hit the pavement only six feet away. I had come so close to screwing up. I climbed off her and rolled on my back and soaked myself in the night sky. When I screwed up, people died. "Cyanide is awful bad for the baby," I said.

"How do you know about my baby?" Her face was rigid with fear. "Who are you?"

I could breathe again, although I wasn't sure I wanted to. "Fay Hardaway." I gasped. "I'm a PI; I left you a message this morning. Najma Jones hired me to find her daughter."

"Rashmi is dead."

"I know," I said. "So is Gratiana." I sat up and looked at her. "Father Elaine will be glad to see you."

Kate's eyes were wide, but I don't think she was seeing the alley. "Gratiana said the devils would come after me." She was still seeing the business end of the inhaler. "She said that if I didn't hear from her by tomorrow then we had lost everything and I should . . . do it. You know, to protect the church. And just now my sidekick picked up three times in ten minutes only there was nobody there and so I knew it was time."

"That was me, Kate. Sorry." I retrieved the Donya Durand slingback I'd stripped off her foot and gave it back to her. "Tell me where you got this?"

"It was Rashmi's. We bought them together at Grayles. Actually I picked them out. That was before . . . I loved her, you know, but she was crazy. I can see that now, although it's kind of too late. I mean, she was okay when she was taking her meds, but she would stop every so often. She called it taking a vacation from herself. Only it was no vacation for anyone else, especially not for me. She decided to go off on the day we got married and didn't tell me and all of a sudden after the ceremony we got into this huge fight about the baby and who loved who more and she stared throwing things at me—these shoes—and then ran out of the church barefoot. I don't think she ever really understood about . . . you know, what we were trying to do. I mean, I've talked to the Bride of God herself . . . but Rashmi." Kate rubbed her eye and her hand came away wet.

I sat her up and put my arm around her. "That's all right. Not really your fault. I think poor Rashmi must have been hanging by a thread. We all are. The whole human race, or what's left of it."

We sat there for a moment.

"I saw her mom this morning," I said. "She said to tell you she was sorry."

Kate sniffed. "Sorry? What for?"

I shrugged.

"I know she didn't have much use for me," said Kate. "At least that's what Rashmi always said. But as far as I'm concerned the woman was a saint to put up with Rashmi and her mood swings and all the acting out. She was always there for her. And the thing is, Rashmi hated her for it."

I got to my knees, then to my feet. I helped Kate up. The alley was dark, but that wasn't really the problem. Even in the light of day, I hadn't seen anything.

8

I had no trouble finding space at the bike rack in front of Ronald Reagan Elementary. The building seemed to be drowsing in the heavy morning air, its brick wings enfolding the empty playground. A janitor bot was vacuuming the swimming pool, another was plucking spent blossoms from the clematis fence. The bots were headache yellow; the letters RRE in puffy orange slanted across their torsos. The gardening bot informed me that school wouldn't start for an hour. That was fine with me. This was just a courtesy call, part of the total service commitment I made to all the clients whom I had failed. I asked if I could see Najma Jones and he said he doubted that any of the teachers were in quite this early but he walked me to the office. He paged her; I signed the visitors' log. When her voice crackled over the intercom, I told the bot that I knew the way to her classroom.

I paused at the open door. Rashmi's mom had her back to me. She was wearing a sleeveless navy dress with cream-colored dupatta scarf draped over her shoulders. She passed down a row of empty desks, perching origami animals at the center of each. There were three kinds of elephants, ducks and ducklings, a blue giraffe, a pink cat that might have been a lion.

"Please come in, Ms. Hardaway," she said without turning around. She had teacher radar; she could see behind her back and around a corner.

"I stopped by your house." I slouched into the room like a kid who had lost her civics homework. "I thought I might catch you before you left for school." I leaned against a desk in the front row and picked up the purple crocodile on it. "You fold these yourself?"

"I couldn't sleep last night," she said, "so finally I gave up and went for a walk. I ended up here. I like coming to school early, especially when no one else is around. There is so much time." She had one origami swan left over that she set on her own desk. "Staying after is different. If you're always the last one out at night, you're admitting that you haven't got anything to rush home to. It's pathetic, actually." She settled behind her desk and began opening windows on her desktop. "I've been teaching the girls to fold the ducks. They seem to like it. It's a challenging grade, the fifth. They come to me as bright and happy children and I am supposed to teach them fractions and pack them off to middle school. I shudder to think what happens to them there."

"How old are they?"

"Ten when they start. Most of them have turned eleven already. They graduate next week." She peered at the files she had opened. "Some of them."

"I take it on faith that I was eleven once," I said, "but I just don't remember."

"Your generation grew up in unhappy times." Her face glowed in the phosphors. "You haven't had a daughter yet, have you, Ms. Hardaway?"

"No."

We contemplated my childlessness for a moment.

"Did Rashmi like origami?" I didn't mean anything by it. I just didn't want to listen to the silence anymore.

"Rashmi?" She frowned, as if her daughter were a not-very-interesting kid she had taught years ago. "No. Rashmi was a difficult child."

"I found Kate Vermeil last night," I said. "I told her what you said, that you were sorry. She wanted to know what for."

"What for?"

"She said that Rashmi was crazy. And that she hated you for having her."

"She never hated me," said Najma quickly. "Yes, Rashmi was a sad girl. Anxious. What is this about, Ms. Hardaway?"

"I think you were at the Comfort Inn that night. If you want to talk about that, I would like to hear what you have to say. If not, I'll leave now."

She stared at me for a moment, her expression unreadable. "You know, I actually wanted to have many children." She got up from the desk, crossed the room and shut the door as if it were made of hand-blown glass. "When the seeding first began, I went down to City Hall and volunteered. That just wasn't done. Most women were horrified to find themselves pregnant. I talked to a bot, who took my name and address and then told me to go home and wait. If I wanted more children after my first, I was certainly encouraged to make a request. It felt like I was joining one of those mail order music clubs." She smiled and tugged at her dupatta. "But when Rashmi was born, everything changed. Sometimes she was such a needy baby, fussing to be picked up, but then she would lie in her crib for hours, listless and withdrawn. She started anti-depressants when she was five and they helped. And the Department of Youth Services issued me a full-time bot helper when I started teaching. But Rashmi was always a handful. And since I was all by myself, I didn't feel like I had enough to give to another child."

"You never married?" I asked. "Found a partner?"

"Married who?" Her voice rose sharply. "Another woman?" Her cheeks colored. "No. I wasn't interested in that."

Najma returned to her desk but did not sit down. "The girls will be coming soon." She leaned toward me, fists on the desktop. "What is it that you want to hear, Ms. Hardaway?"

"You found Rashmi before I did. How?"

"She called me. She said that she had had a fight with her girlfriend who was involved in some secret experiment that she couldn't tell me about and they were splitting up and everything was shit, the world was shit. She was off her meds, crying, not making a whole lot of sense. But that was nothing new. She always called me when she broke up with someone. I'm her mother."

"And when you got there?"

"She was sitting on the bed." Najma's eyes focused on something I couldn't see. "She put the inhaler to her mouth when I opened the door." Najma was looking into Room 103 of the Comfort Inn. "And I thought to myself, what does this poor girl want? Does she want me to witness her death or stop it? I tried to talk to her, you know. She seemed to listen. But when I asked her to put the inhaler down, she wouldn't. I moved toward her, slowly. Slowly. I told her that she didn't have to do anything. That we could just go home. And then I was this close." She reached a hand across the desk. "And I couldn't help myself. I tried to swat it out of her mouth. Either she pressed the button or I set it off." She sat down abruptly and put her head in her hands. "She didn't get the full dose. It took forever before it was over. She was in agony."

"I think she'd made up her mind, Ms. Jones." I was only trying to comfort her. "She wrote the note."

"I wrote the note." She glared at me. "I did."

There was nothing I could say. All the words in all the languages that had ever been spoken wouldn't come close to expressing this mother's grief. I thought the weight of it must surely crush her.

Through the open windows, I heard the snort of the first bus pulling into the turnaround in front of the school. Najma Jones glanced out at it, gathered herself and smiled. "Do you know what Rashmi means in Sanskrit?"

"No, ma'am."

"Ray of sunlight," she said. "The girls are here, Ms. Hardaway." She picked up the origami on her desk. "We have to be ready for them." She held it out to me. "Would you like a swan?"

By the time I came through the door of the school, the turnaround was filled with busses. Girls poured off them and swirled onto the playground: giggling girls, whispering girls, skipping girls, girls holding hands. And in the warm June sun, I could almost believe they were happy girls.

They paid no attention to me.

I tried Sharifa's call. "Hello?" Her voice was husky with sleep.

"Sorry I didn't make it home last night, sweetheart," I said. "Just wanted to let you know that I'm on my way."

Mother Aegypt

KAGE BAKER

One of the most prolific new writers to appear in the late nineties, Kage Baker made her first sale in 1997, to *Asimov's Science Fiction*, and has since become one of that magazine's most frequent and popular contributors with her sly and compelling stories of the adventures and misadventures of the time-travelling agents of the Company; of late, she's started two other linked sequences of stories there as well, one of them set in as lush and eccentric a High Fantasy milieu as any we've ever seen. Her stories have also appeared in *Realms of Fantasy*, *SCI FICTION*, *Amazing*, and elsewhere. Her first novel, *In the Garden of Iden*, was also published in 1997 and immediately became one of the most acclaimed and widely reviewed first novels of the year. Her second novel, *Sky Coyote*, was published in 1999, followed by a third and a fourth, *Mendoza in Hollywood* and *The Graveyard Game*, both published in 2001. In 2002, she published her first collection, *Black Projects, White Knights*. Her most recent books are a novel set in her unique fantasy milieu, *The Anvil of the World*, a chapbook novella, *The Empress of Mars*, and a new collection, *Mother Aegypt and Other Stories*. Coming up are a new Company novel, *The Life of the World to Come*. Her stories have appeared in our Seventeenth and Twentieth Annual Collections. In addition to her writing, Baker has been an artist, actor, and director at the Living History Center, and has taught Elizabethan English as a second language. She lives in Pismo Beach, California.

Here, in a hugely entertaining tale that seems at first like a fantasy but that experienced Baker fans will recognize as a stealth Company story, she takes us back to an impoverished pre-modern Europe for the saga of an opportunistic rogue and con man, someone who always has his eye out for the main chance, who ends up blundering into a sweet new confidence game that *might* turn out to be just a little more than he can handle . . .

Speak sweetly to the Devil, until you're both over the bridge.

—*Transylvanian proverb*

In a country of mad forests and night, there was an open plain, and pitiless sunlight.

A man dressed as a clown was running for his life across the plain.

A baked-clay track, the only road for miles, reflected the sun's heat and made the man sweat as he ran along it. He was staggering a little as he ran, for he had been running a long while and he was fat, and the silken drawers of his clown costume had begun to work their way down his thighs. It was a particularly humiliating costume, too. It made him look like a gigantic dairymaid.

His tears, of terror and despair, ran down with his sweat and streaked the clown-white, graying his big moustache; the lurid crimson circles on his cheeks had already run, trickling pink down his neck. His straw-stuffed bosom had begun to slip, too, working its way down his dirndl, and now it dropped from beneath his petticoat like a stillbirth. Gasping, he halted to snatch it up, and peered fearfully over his shoulder.

No sign of his pursuers yet; but they were mounted and must catch up with him soon, on this long straight empty plain. There was no cover anywhere, not so much as a single tree. He ran on, stuffing his bosom back in place, whimpering. Gnats whined in his ears.

Then, coming over a gentle swell of earth, he beheld a crossroads. There was his salvation!

A team of slow horses drew two wagons, like the vardas of the Romanies but higher, and narrower, nor were they gaily painted in any way. They were black as the robe of scythe-bearing Death. Only: low, small and ominous, in white paint in curious antiquated letters, they bore the words: MOTHER AEGYPT.

The man wouldn't have cared if Death himself held the reins. He aimed himself at the hindmost wagon, drawing on all his remaining strength, and pelted on until he caught up with it.

For a moment he ran desperate alongside, until he was able to gain the front and haul himself up, over the hitch that joined the two wagons. A moment he poised there, ponderous, watching drops of his sweat fall on hot iron. Then he crawled up to the door of the rear wagon, unbolted it, and fell inside.

The driver of the wagons, hooded under that glaring sky, was absorbed in a waking dream of a place lost for millennia. Therefore she did not notice that she had taken on a passenger.

The man lay flat on his back, puffing and blowing, too exhausted to take much note of his surroundings. At last he levered himself up on his elbows, looking about. After a moment he scooted into a sitting position and pulled off the ridiculous lace milkmaid's cap, with its braids of yellow yarn. Wiping his face with it, he muttered a curse.

In a perfect world, he reflected, there would have been a chest of clothing in this wagon, through which he might rummage to steal some less conspicuous apparel. There would, at least, have been a pantry with food and drink. But the fates had denied him yet again; this was nobody's cozy living quarters on wheels. This wagon was clearly used for storage, holding nothing but boxes and bulky objects wrapped in sacking.

Disgusted, the man dug in the front of his dress and pulled out his bosom. He shook it by his ear and smiled as he heard the *clink-clink*. The gold rings were still there, some of the loot with which he'd been able to escape.

The heat within the closed black box was stifling, so he took off all his costume but for the silken drawers. Methodically he began to search through the wagon, opening the boxes and unwrapping the parcels. He began to chuckle.

He knew stolen goods when he saw them.

Some of it had clearly been lifted from Turkish merchants and bureaucrats: rolled and tied carpets, tea services edged in gold. But there were painted ikons here too, and family portraits of Russians on wooden panels. Austrian crystal bowls. Chased silver ewers and platters. Painted urns. A whole umbrella stand of cavalry sabers, some with ornate decoration, some plain and ancient, evident heirlooms. Nothing was small enough to slip into a pocket, even if he had had one, and nothing convenient to convert into ready cash.

Muttering, he lifted out a saber and drew it from its scabbard.

As he did so, he heard the sound of galloping hooves. The saber dropped from his suddenly nerveless fingers. He flattened himself against the door, pointlessly, as the hoofbeats drew near and passed. He heard the shouted questions. He almost—not quite—heard the reply, in a woman's voice pitched very low. His eyes rolled, searching the room for any possible hiding place. None at all; unless he were to wrap his bulk in a carpet, like Cleopatra.

Yet the riders passed on, galloped ahead and away. When he realized that he was, for the moment, safe, he collapsed into a sitting position on the floor.

After a moment of listening to his heart thunder, he picked up the saber again.

It was night before the wagon halted at last, rumbling over rough ground as it left the road. He was still crouched within, cold and cramped now. Evidently the horses were unhitched, and led down to drink at a stream; he could hear splashing. Dry sticks were broken, a fire was lit. He thought of warmth and food. A light footfall approached, followed by the sound of someone climbing up on the hitch. The man tensed.

The door opened.

There, silhouetted against the light of the moon, was a small pale spindly-looking person with a large head. A wizened child? It peered into the wagon, uncertainty in its big rabbitlike eyes. There was a roll of something—another carpet?—under its arm.

"Hah!" The man lunged, caught the other by the wrist, hauling him in across the wagon's threshold. Promptly the other began to scream, and he screamed like a rabbit too, shrill and unhuman. He did not struggle, though; in fact, the man had the unsettling feeling he'd grabbed a ventriloquist's dummy, limp and insubstantial within its mildewed clothes.

"Shut your mouth!" the man said, in the most terrifying voice he could muster. "I want two things!"

But his captive appeared to have fainted. As the man registered this, he also became aware that a woman was standing outside the wagon, seeming to have materialized from nowhere, and she was staring at him.

"Don't kill him," she said, in a flat quiet voice.

"Uh—I want two things!" the man repeated, holding the saber to his captive's throat. "Or I'll kill him, you understand?"

"Yes," said the woman. "What do you want?"

The man blinked, licked his lips. Something about the woman's matter-of-fact voice disturbed him.

"I want food, and a suit of clothes!"

The woman's gaze did not shift. She was tall, and dark as a shadow, even standing in the full light of the moon, and simply dressed in black.

"I'll give you food," she replied. "But I haven't any clothing that would fit you."

"Then you'd better get me some, hadn't you?" said the man. He made jabbing motions with the saber. "Or I'll kill your little . . . your little . . ." He tried to imagine what possible relationship the creature under his arm might have with the woman. Husband? Child?

"Slave," said the woman. "I can buy you a suit in the next village, but you'll have to wait until morning. Don't kill my slave, or I'll make you sorry you were ever born."

"Oh, you will, will you?" said the man, waving the saber again. "Do you think I believe in Gypsy spells? You're not dealing with a village simpleton, here!"

"No," said the woman, in the same quiet voice. "But I know the police are hunting you. Cut Emil's throat, and you'll see how quickly I can make them appear."

The man realized it might be a good idea to change strategies. He put his head on one side, grinning at her in what he hoped was a charmingly roguish way.

"Now, now, no need for things to get nasty," he said. "After all, we're in the same trade, aren't we? I had a good look around in here." He indicated the interior of the wagon with a jerk of his head. "Nice racket you've got, fencing the big stuff. You don't want me to tell the police about it, while I'm being led away, do you?"

"No," said the woman.

"No, of course not. Let's be friends!" The man edged forward, dragging his captive—Emil, had she called him?—along. "Barbu Golescu, at your service. And you'd be Madam . . . ?"

"Amaunet," she said.

"Charmed," said Golescu. "Sure your husband hasn't a spare pair of trousers he can loan me, Madam Amaunet?"

"I have no husband," she replied.

"Astonishing!" Golescu said, smirking. "Well then, dear madam, what about loaning a blanket until we can find me a suit? I'd hate to offend your modesty."

"I'll get one," she said, and walked away.

He stared after her, momentarily disconcerted, and then put down the saber and flexed his hand. Emil remained motionless under his other arm.

"Don't you get any ideas, little turnip-head," muttered Golescu. "Hey! Don't get any ideas, I said. Are you deaf, eh?"

He hauled Emil up by his collar and looked at him critically. Emil whimpered and turned his face away. It was a weak face. His head had been shaved at one time, and the hair grown back in scanty and irregular clumps.

"Maybe you *are* deaf," conceded Golescu. "But your black mummy loves you, eh? What a useful thing for me." He groped about and found a piece of cord that had bound one of the carpets. "Hold still or I'll wring your wry neck, understand?"

"You smell bad," said Emil, in a tiny voice.

"Bah! You stink like carpet mold, yourself," said Golescu, looping the cord about Emil's wrist. He looped the other end about his own wrist and pulled it snug. "There, so you can't go running away. We're going to be friends, you see? You'll get used to me soon enough."

He ventured out on the hitch and dropped to the ground. His legs were unsteady and he attempted to lean on Emil's shoulder, but the little man collapsed under him like so much cardboard.

"She doesn't use you for cutting wood or drawing water much, does she?" muttered Golescu, hitching at his drawers. Amaunet came around the side of the wagon and handed him the blanket, without comment.

"He's a flimsy one, your slave," Golescu told her. "What you need is a man to help with the business, if you'll pardon my saying so." He wrapped his vast nakedness in the blanket and grinned at her.

Amaunet turned and walked away from him.

"There's bread and tomatoes by the fire," she said, over her shoulder.

Clutching the blanket around him with one hand and dragging Emil with the other, Golescu made his way to the fire. Amaunet was sitting perfectly still, watching the flames dance, and only glanced up at them as they approached.

"That's better," said Golescu, settling himself down and reaching for the loaf of bread. He tore off a hunk, sopped it in the saucepan of stewed tomatoes and ate ravenously. Emil, still bound to his wrist and pulled back and forth when he moved, had gone as limp and unresponsive as a straw figure.

"So," said Golescu, through a full mouth, "No husband. Are you sure you don't need help? I'm not talking of bedroom matters, madame, you understand; perish the thought. I'm talking about security. So many thieves and murderers in this wicked old world! Now, by an astounding coincidence, *I* need a way to get as far as I can from the Danube, and *you* are headed north. Let's be partners for the time being, what do you say?"

Amaunet's lip curled. Contempt? But it might have been a smile.

"Since you mention it," she said, "Emil's no good at speaking to people. I don't care to deal with them, much, myself. The police said you were with a circus; do you know how to get exhibition permits from petty clerks?"

"Of course I do," said Golescu, with a dismissive gesture. "The term you're looking for is *advance man*. Rely on me."

"Good." Amaunet turned her gaze back to the fire. "I can't pay you, but I'll lie for you. You'll have room and board."

"And a suit of clothes," he reminded her.

She shrugged, in an affirmative kind of way.

"It's settled, then," said Golescu, leaning back. "What business are we in? Officially, I mean?"

"I tell people their futures," said Amaunet.

"Ah! But you don't look like a Gypsy."

"I'm not a Gypsy," she said, perhaps a little wearily. "I'm from Egypt."

"Just so," he said, laying his finger beside his nose. "The mystic wisdom of the mysterious East, eh? Handed down to you from the ancient pharaohs. Very good, madame, that's the way to impress the peasants."

"You know a lot of big words, for a clown," said Amaunet. Golescu winced, and discreetly lifted a corner of the blanket to scrub at his greasepaint.

"I am obviously not a real clown, madame," he protested. "I am a victim of circumstances, calumny, and political intrigue. If I could tell you my full story, you'd weep for me."

She grinned, a brief white grin so startling in her dark still face that he nearly screamed.

"I doubt it," was all she said.

He kept Emil bound to him that night, reasoning that he couldn't completely trust Amaunet until he had a pair of trousers. Golescu made himself comfortable on the hard floor of the wagon by using the little man as a sort of bolster, and though Emil made plaintive noises now and then and did in fact smell quite a lot like moldy carpet, it was nothing that couldn't be ignored by a determined sleeper.

Only once Golescu woke in the darkness. Someone was singing, out there in the night; a woman was singing, full-throated under the white moon. There was such throbbing melancholy in her voice Golescu felt tears stinging his eyes; yet there was an indefinable menace too, in the harsh and unknown syllables of her lament. It might have been a lioness out there, on the prowl. He thought briefly of opening the door to see if she wanted comforting, but the idea sent inexplicable chills down his spine. He snorted, rolled on his back, and slept again.

Golescu woke when the wagons lurched back into motion, and stared around through the dissipating fog of vaguely lewd dreams. Sunlight was streaming in through cracks in the plank walls. Though his dreams receded, certain sensations remained. He sat upright with a grunt of outrage and looked over his own shoulder at Emil, who had plastered himself against Golescu's backside.

"Hey!" Golescu hauled Emil out. "What are you, a filthy sodomite? You think because I wear silk, I'm some kind of Turkish fancy boy?"

Emil whimpered and hid his face in his hands. "The sun," he whispered.

"Yes, it's daylight! You're scared of the sun?" demanded Golescu.

"Sun hurts," said Emil.

"Don't be stupid, it can't hurt you," said Golescu. "See?" He thrust Emil's hand into the nearest wavering stripe of sunlight. Emil made rabbity noises again, turning his face away and squeezing his eyes shut, as though he expected his hand to blister and smoke.

"See?" Golescu repeated. But Emil refused to open his eyes, and Golescu released his hand in disgust. Taking up the saber, he sliced through the cord that bound them. Emil promptly curled into himself like an angleworm and lay still, covering his eyes once more. Golescu considered him, setting aside the saber and rubbing his own wrist.

"If you're a *vampyr*, you're the most pathetic one I've ever heard of," he said. "What's she keep you around for, eh?"

Emil did not reply.

Some time after midday, the wagons stopped; about an hour later, the door opened and Amaunet stood there with a bundle of clothing.

"Here," she said, thrusting it at Golescu. Her dead stare fell on Emil, who cringed and shrank even further into himself from the flood of daylight. She removed one of her shawls and threw it over him, covering him completely. Golescu, pulling on the trousers, watched her in amusement.

"I was just wondering, madame, whether I should maybe get myself a crucifix to wear around our little friend, here," he said. "Or some bulbs of garlic?"

"He likes the dark," she replied. "You owe me three piastres for that suit."

"It's not what I'm accustomed to, you know," he said, shrugging into the shirt. "Coarse-woven stuff. Where are we?"

"Twenty kilometers farther north than we were yesterday," she replied.

Not nearly far enough, Golescu considered uneasily. Amaunet had turned her back on him while he dressed. He found himself studying her body as he buttoned himself up. With her grim face turned away, it was possible to concede that the rest of her was lovely. Only in the very young could bodily mass defy gravity in such a pert and springy-looking manner. How old *was* she?

When he had finished pulling on his boots, he stood straight, twirled the ends of his moustaches and sucked in his gut. He drew one of the gold rings from his former bosom.

"Here. Accept this, my flower of the Nile," said Golescu, taking Amaunet's hand and slipping the ring on her finger. She pulled her hand away at once and turned so swiftly the air seemed to blur. For a moment there was fire in her eyes, and if it was more loathing than passion, still, he had gotten a reaction out of her.

"Don't touch me," she said.

"I'm merely paying my debt!" Golescu protested, pleased with himself. "Charming lady, that ring's worth far more than what you paid for the suit."

"It stinks," she said in disgust, snatching the ring off.

"Gold can afford to smell bad," he replied. His spirits were rising like a balloon.

Uninvited, he climbed up on the driver's seat beside her and the wagons rolled on, following a narrow river road through its winding gorge.

"You won't regret your kindness to me, dear madam," said Golescu. "A pillar of strength and a fountain of good advice, that's me. I won't ask about your other business in the wagon back there, as Discretion is my middle name, but tell me: what's your fortunetelling racket like? Do you earn as much as you could wish?"

"I cover my operating expenses," Amaunet replied.

"Pft!" Golescu waved his hand. "Then you're clearly not making what you deserve to make. What do you do? Cards? Crystal ball? Love potions?"

"I read palms," said Amaunet.

"Not much overhead in palm reading," said Golescu, "But on the other hand, not much to impress the customers either. Unless you paint them scintillating word-pictures of scarlet and crimson tomorrows, or warn them of terrifying calamity only *you* can help them avoid, yes? And, you'll excuse me, but you seem to be a woman of few words. Where's your glitter? Where's your flash?"

"I tell them the truth," said Amaunet.

"Ha! The old, 'I-am-under-an-ancient-curse-and-can-only-speak-the-truth' line? No, no, dear madam, that's been done to death. I propose a whole new approach!" said Golescu.

Amaunet just gave him a sidelong look, unreadable as a snake.

"Such as?"

"Such as I would need to observe your customary clientele before I could elaborate on," said Golescu.

"I see," she said.

"Though *Mother Aegypt* is a good name for your act," Golescu conceded. "Has a certain majesty. But it implies warmth. You might work on that. Where's your warmth, eh?"

"I haven't got any," said Amaunet. "And you're annoying me, now."

"Then, *taceo*, dear madame. That's Latin for 'I shall be quiet,' you know."

She curled her lip again.

Silent, he attempted to study her face, as they jolted along. She must be a young woman; her skin was smooth, there wasn't a trace of gray in her hair or a whisker on her lip. One could say of any ugly woman, *Her nose is hooked*, or *Her lips are thin*, or *Her eyes are too close together*. None of this could be said of Amaunet. It was indeed impossible to say anything much; for when Golescu looked closely at her he saw only shadow, and a certain sense of discord.

They came, by night, to a dismal little town whose slumped and rounded houses huddled with backs to the river, facing the dark forest. After threading a maze of crooked streets, they found the temporary camp for market fair vendors: two bare acres of open ground that had been a cattle pen most recently. It was still redolent of manure. Here other wagons were drawn up, and fires burned in iron baskets. The people who made their livings offering rides on painted ponies or challenging all comers to games of skill stood about the fires, drinking from bottles, exchanging news in weary voices.

Yet when Amaunet's wagons rolled by they looked up only briefly, and swiftly looked away. Some few made gestures to ward off evil.

"You've got quite a reputation, eh?" observed Golescu. Amaunet did not reply. She seemed to have barely noticed.

Golescu spent another chilly night on the floor in the rear wagon—alone this time, for Emil slept in a cupboard under Amaunet's narrow bunk when he was not being held hostage, and Amaunet steadfastly ignored all Golescu's hints and pleasantries about the value of shared body warmth. As a consequence, he was stiff and out of sorts by the time he emerged next morning.

Overnight, the fair had assumed half-existence. A blind man, muscled like a giant, cranked steadily at the carousel, and thin pale children rode round and round. A man with a barrel-organ cranked steadily too, and his little monkey sat on his shoulder and watched the children with a diffident eye. But many of the tents were still flat, in a welter of ropes and poles. A long line of bored vendors stood attendance before a town clerk, who had set up his permit office under a black parasol.

Golescu was staring at all this when Amaunet, who had come up behind him, silent as a shadow, said:

"Here's your chance to be useful. Get in line for me."

"Holy Saints!" Golescu whirled around. "Do you want to frighten me into heart failure? Give a man some warning."

She gave him a leather envelope and a small purse instead. "Here are my papers. Pay the bureaucrat and get my permit. You won't eat tonight, otherwise."

"You wouldn't order me around like this if you knew my true identity," Golescu grumbled, but he got into line obediently.

The town clerk was reasonably honest, so the line took no more than an hour to wind its way through. At last the man ahead of Golescu got his permit to sell little red-blue-and-yellow paper flags, and Golescu stepped up to the table.

"Papers," said the clerk, yawning.

"Behold." Golescu opened them with a flourish. The clerk squinted at them.

"Amaunet Kematef," he recited. "Doing business as 'Mother Aegypt.'" A Russian? And this says you're a woman."

"They're not my papers, they're—they're my wife's papers," said Golescu, summoning an outraged expression. "And she isn't Russian, my friend, she *is* a hot-blooded Egyptian, a former harem dancer if you must know, before an unfortunate accident that marred her exotic beauty. I found her starving in the gutters of Cairo, and succored her out of Christian charity. Shortly, however, I discovered her remarkable talent for predicting the future based on an ancient system of—"

"A fortune-teller? Two marks," said the clerk. Golescu paid, and as the clerk wrote out the permit he went on:

"The truth of the matter is that she was the only daughter of a Coptic nobleman, kidnapped at an early age by ferocious—"

"Three marks extra if this story goes on any longer," said the clerk, stamping the permit forcefully.

"You have my humble gratitude," said Golescu, bowing deeply. Pleased with himself, he took the permit and strutted away.

"Behold," he said, producing the permit for Amaunet with a flourish. She took it without comment and examined it. Seen in the strong morning light, the indefinable grimness of her features was much more pronounced. Golescu suppressed a shudder and inquired, "How else may a virile male be of use, my sweet?"

Amaunet turned her back on him, for which he was grateful. "Stay out of trouble until tonight. Then you can mind Emil. He wakes up after sundown."

She returned to the foremost black wagon. Golescu watched as she climbed up, and was struck once more by the drastically different effect her backside produced on the interested spectator.

"Don't you want me to beat a drum for you? Or rattle a tambourine or something? I can draw crowds for you like a sugarloaf draws flies!"

She looked at him, with her white grimace that might have been amusement. "I'm sure you can draw flies," she said. "But I don't need an advertiser for what I do."

Muttering, Golescu wandered away through the fair. He cheered up no end, however, when he discovered that he still had Amaunet's purse.

Tents were popping up now, bright banners were being unfurled, though they hung down spiritless in the heat and glare of the day. Golescu bought himself a cheap hat and stood around a while, squinting as he sized up the food vendors. Finally he bought a glass of tea and a fried pastry, stuffed with plums, cased in glazed sugar that tasted vaguely poisonous. He ate it contentedly and, licking the sugar off his fingers, wandered off the fairground to a clump of trees near the river's edge. There he stretched out in the shade and, tilting his hat over his face, went to sleep. If one had to baby-sit a *vampyr* one needed to get plenty of rest by day.

By night the fair was a different place. The children were gone, home in their beds, and the carousel raced round nearly empty but for spectral riders; the young men had come out instead. They roared with laughter and shoved one another, or stood gaping before the little plank stages where the exhibitions were cried by mountebanks. Within this tent were remarkable freaks of nature; within this one, an exotic dancer plied her trade; within another was a man who could handle hot iron without gloves. The lights were bright and fought with shadows. The air was full of music and raucous cries.

Golescu was unimpressed.

"What do you mean, it's too tough?" he demanded. "That cost fifteen groschen!"

"I can't eat it," whispered Emil, cringing away from the glare of the lanterns.

"Look." Golescu grabbed up the ear of roasted corn and bit into it. "Mm! Tender! Eat it, you little whiner."

"It has paprika on it. Too hot." Emil wrung his hands.

"Ridiculous," said Golescu through a full mouth, munching away. "It's the food of the gods. What the hell *will* you eat, eh? I know! You're a *vampyr*, so you want blood, right? Well, we're in a slightly public place at the moment, so you'll just have to make do with something else. Taffy apple, eh? Deep fried sarmale? Pierogi? Pommes frites?"

Emil wept silently, tears coursing from his big rabbit eyes, and Golescu sighed and tossed the corn cob away. "Come on," he said, and dragged the little man off by one hand.

They made a circuit of all the booths serving food before Emil finally consented to try a Vienna sausage impaled on a stick, dipped in corn batter and deep-fried. To Golescu's relief he seemed to like it, for he nibbled at it uncomplainingly as Golescu towed him along. Golescu glanced over at Amaunet's wagon, and noted a customer emerging, pale and shaken.

"Look over there," Golescu said in disgust. "One light. No banners, nobody calling attention to her, nobody enticing the crowds. And one miserable customer waiting, look! That's what she gets. Where's the sense of mystery? She's *Mother Aegypt*! Her other line of work must pay pretty well, eh?"

Emil made no reply, deeply preoccupied by his sausage-on-a-spike.

"Or maybe it doesn't, if she can't do any better for a servant than you. Where's all the money go?" Golescu wondered, pulling at his moustache. "Why's she so sour, your mistress? A broken heart or something?"

Emil gave a tiny shrug and kept eating.

"I could make her forget whoever it was in ten minutes, if I could just get her to take me seriously," said Golescu, gazing across at the wagon. "And the best way to do that, of course, is to impress her with money. We need a scheme, turnip-head."

"Four thousand and seventeen," said Emil.

"Huh?" Golescu turned to stare down at him. Emil said nothing else, but in his silence the cry of the nearest hawker came through loud and clear:

"Come on and take a chance, clever ones! Games of chance, guess the cards, throw the dice, spin the wheel! Or guess the number of millet grains in the jar and win a cash prize! Only ten groschen a guess! *You* might be the winner! You, sir, with the little boy!"

Golescu realized the hawker was addressing him. He looked around indignantly. "He is not my little boy!"

"So he's your uncle, what does it matter? Take a guess, why don't you?" bawled the hawker. "What have you got to lose?"

"Ten groschen," retorted Golescu, and then reflected that it was Amaunet's money. "What the hell."

He approached the gaming booth, pulling Emil after him. "What's the cash prize?"

"Twenty thousand lei," said the hawker. Golescu rolled his eyes.

"Oh, yes, I'd be able to retire on *that*, all right," he said, but dug in his pocket for ten groschen. He cast a grudging eye on the glass jar at the back of the counter, on its shelf festooned with the new national flag and swags of bunting. "You've undoubtedly got rocks hidden in there, to throw the volume off. Hm, hm, all right . . . how many grains of millet in there? I'd say . . ."

"Four thousand and seventeen," Emil repeated. The hawker's jaw dropped. Golescu looked from one to the other of them. His face lit up.

"That's the right answer, isn't it?" he said. "Holy saints and patriarchs!"

"No, it isn't," said the hawker, recovering himself with difficulty.

"It is so," said Golescu. "I can see it in your eyes!"

"No, it isn't," the hawker insisted.

"It is so! Shall we tip out the jar and count what's in there?"

"No, and anyway you hadn't paid me yet—and anyway it was your little boy, not you, so it wouldn't count anyway—and—"

"Cheat! Shall I scream it aloud? I've got very good lungs. Shall I tell the world how you've refused to give this poor child his prize, even when he guessed correctly? Do you really want—'

"Shut up! Shut up, I'll pay the damned twenty thousand lei!" The hawker leaned forward and clapped his hand over Golescu's mouth. Golescu smiled at him, the points of his moustaches rising like a cockroach's antennae.

Wandering back to Amaunet's wagon, Golescu jingled the purse at Emil.

"Not a bad night's work, eh? I defy her to look at this and fail to be impressed."

Emil did not respond, sucking meditatively on the stick, which was all that was left of his sausage.

"Of course, we're going to downplay your role in the comedy, for strategic reasons," Golescu continued, peering around a tent and scowling at the wagon. There was a line of customers waiting now, and while some were clearly lonely women who wanted their fortunes told, a few were rather nasty-looking men, in fact rather criminal-looking men, and Golescu had the uneasy feeling he might have met one or two of them in a professional context at some point in his past. As he was leaning back, he glanced down at Emil.

"I think we won't interrupt her while she's working just yet. Gives us more time to concoct a suitably heroic and clever origin for this fine fat purse, eh? Anyway, she'd never believe that *you*—" Golescu halted, staring at Emil. He slapped his forehead in a gesture of epiphany.

"Wait a minute, wait a minute! She *knows* about this talent of yours! That's why she keeps you around, is it? Ha!"

He was silent for a moment, but the intensity of his regard was such that it penetrated even Emil's self-absorption. Emil looked up timidly and beheld Golescu's countenance twisted into a smile of such ferocious benignity that the little man screamed, dropped his stick, and covered his head with both hands.

"My dear shrinking genius!" bellowed Golescu, seizing Emil up and clasping him in his arms. "Puny friend, petite brother, sweetest of *vampyrs!* Come, my darling, will you have another sausage? No? Polenta? Milk punch? Hot chocolate? Golescu will see you have anything you want, pretty one. Let us go through the fair together."

The purse of twenty thousand lei was considerably lighter by the time Golescu retreated to the shadows under the rear wagon, pulling Emil after him. Emil was too stuffed with sausage and candy floss to be very alert, and he had a cheap doll and a pinwheel to occupy what could be mustered of his attention. Nonetheless, Golescu drew a new pack of cards from his pocket, broke the seal, and shuffled them, looking at Emil with lovingly predatory eyes.

"I have heard of this, my limp miracle," crooned Golescu, making the cards snap and riffle through his fat fingers. "Fellows quite giftless as regards social graces, oh yes, in some cases so unworldly they must be fed and diapered like babies. And yet, they have a brilliance! An unbelievable grasp of systems and details! Let us see if you are one such prodigy, eh?"

An hour's worth of experimentation was enough to prove to Golescu's satisfaction that Emil was more than able to count cards accurately; if a deck was even fanned before his face for a second, he could correctly identify all the cards he had glimpsed.

"And now, dear boy, only one question remains," said Golescu, tossing the deck over his shoulder into the night. The cards scattered like dead leaves. "Why hasn't Madame Amaunet taken advantage of your fantastic abilities to grow rich beyond the dreams of avarice?"

Emil did not reply.

"Such a perfect setup. I can't understand it," persisted Golescu, leaning down to peer at the line stretching to the door of the forward wagon. A woman had just emerged, wringing her hands and sobbing. Though the fairground had begun to empty out now, there were still a few distinct thugs waiting their turn to . . . have their fortunes told? It seemed unlikely. Three of them seemed to be concealing bulky parcels about their persons.

"With a lucky mannekin like you, she could queen it at gambling houses from Monte Carlo to St. Petersburg," mused Golescu. "In fact, with a body like hers, she could be the richest whore in Rome, Vienna, or Budapest. If she wore a mask, that is. Why, then, does she keep late hours fencing stolen spoons and watches for petty cutthroats? Where's the money in that? What does she want, Emil, my friend?"

"The Black Cup," said Emil.

When the last of the thugs had gone his way, Amaunet emerged from the wagon and looked straight at Golescu, where he lounged in the shadows. He had been intending to make an impressive entrance, but with the element of surprise gone he merely waved at her sheepishly.

"Where's Emil?" demanded Amaunet.

"Safe and sound, my queen," Golescu replied, producing Emil and holding him up by the scruff of his neck. Emil, startled by the light, yelled feebly and covered his eyes. "We had a lovely evening, thank you."

"Get to bed," Amaunet told Emil. He writhed from Golescu's grip and darted into the wagon. "Did you feed him?" she asked Golescu.

"Royally," said Golescu. "And how did I find the wherewithal to do that, you ask? Why, with *this*." He held up the purse of somewhat less than twenty thousand lei and clinked it at her with his most seductive expression. To his intense annoyance, her eyes did not brighten in the least.

"Fetch the horses and hitch them in place. We're moving on tonight," she said.

Golescu was taken aback. "Don't you want to know where I got all this lovely money?"

"You stole it?" said Amaunet, taking down the lantern from its hook by the door and extinguishing it.

"I never!" cried Golescu, genuinely indignant. "I won it for you, if you must know. Guessing how many grains of millet were in a jar."

He had imagined her reaction to his gift several times that evening, with several variations on her range of emotion. He was nonetheless unprepared for her actual response of turning, swift as a snake, and grabbing him by the throat.

"How did you guess the right number?" she asked him, in a very low voice.

"I'm extraordinarily talented?" he croaked, his eyes standing out of his head.

Amaunet tightened her grip. "It was Emil's guess, wasn't it?"

Golescu merely nodded, unable to draw enough breath to speak.

"Were you enough of a fool to take him to the games of chance?"

Golescu shook his head. She pulled his face close to her own.

"If I ever catch you taking Emil to card parlors or casinos, I'll kill you. Do you understand?"

She released him, hurling him back against the side of the wagon. Golescu straightened, gasped in air, pushed his hat up from his face and said:

"All right, so I discovered his secret. Does Madame have any objections to my asking why the hell she isn't using our little friend to grow stinking rich?"

"Because Emil doesn't have a secret," Amaunet hissed. "He *is* a secret."

"Oh, that explains everything," said Golescu, rubbing his throat.

"It had better," said Amaunet. "Now, bring the horses."

Golescu did as he was told, boiling with indignation and curiosity, and also with something he was barely able to admit to himself. It could not be said, by any stretch of the imagination, that Amaunet was beautiful in her wrath, and yet . . .

Something about the pressure of her fingers on his skin, and the amazing strength of her hands . . . and the scent of her breath up close like that, like some unnamable spice . . .

"What strange infatuation enslaves my foolish heart?" he inquired of the lead horse, as he hitched it to the wagon-tongue.

They traveled all the rest of the moonless night, along the dark river, and many times heard the howling of wolves, far off in the dark forest.

Golescu wove their cries into a fantasy of heroism, wherein he was possessed of an immense gun and discharged copious amounts of shot into a pack of ferocious wolves threatening Amaunet, who was so grateful for the timely rescue she . . . she threw off her disguise, and most of her clothing too, and it turned out that she'd been wearing a fearsome mask all along. She was actually beautiful, though he couldn't quite see how beautiful, because every time he tried to fling himself into her arms he kept tangling his feet in something, which seemed to be pink candy-floss someone had dropped on the fairground . . .

And then the pink strands became a spiderweb and Emil was a fly caught there, screaming and screaming in his high voice, which seemed odd considering Emil was a *vampyr.* "Aren't they usually the ones who do the biting?" he asked Amaunet, but she was sprinting away toward the dark river, which was the Nile, and he sprinted after her, pulling his clothing off as he went too, but the sun was rising behind the pyramids.

Golescu sat up with a snort, and shielded his eyes against the morning glare.

"We've stopped," he announced.

"Yes," said Amaunet, who was unhitching the horses. They seemed to have left the road in the night; they were now in a forest clearing, thickly screened on all sides by brush.

"You're camping here," Amaunet said. "I have an appointment to keep. You'll stay with the lead wagon and watch Emil. I should be gone no more than three days."

"But of course," said Golescu, stupid with sleep. He sat there rubbing his unshaven chin, watching her lead the horses out of sight through the bushes. He could hear water trickling somewhere near at hand. Perhaps Amaunet was going to bathe in a picturesque forest pool, as well as water the horses?

He clambered down from the seat and hurried after her, moving as silently as he could, but all that rewarded his stealthy approach was the sight of Amaunet standing by the horses with her arms crossed, watching them drink from a stream. Golescu shuddered. Strong morning light was really not her friend.

Sauntering close, he said:

"So what does the little darling eat, other than sausages and candy?"

"Root vegetables," said Amaunet, not bothering to look at him. "Potatoes and turnips, parsnips, carrots. He won't eat them unless they're boiled and mashed, no butter, no salt, no pepper. He'll eat any kind of bread if the crusts are cut off. Polenta, but again, no butter, no salt. He'll drink water."

"How obliging of him," said Golescu, making a face. "Where'd you find our tiny friend, anyway?"

Amaunet hesitated a moment before replying. "An asylum," she said.

"Ah! And they had no idea what he was, did they?" said Golescu. She turned on him, with a look that nearly made him wet himself.

"And *you* know what he is?" she demanded.

"Just—just a little idiot savant, isn't it so?" said Golescu. "Clever at doing sums. Why you're not using his big white brain to get rich, I can't imagine; but there it is. Is there anything else Nursie ought to know about his care and feeding?"

"Only that I'll hunt you down and kill you if you kidnap him while I'm gone," said Amaunet, without raising her voice in the slightest yet managing to convince Golescu that she was perfectly sincere. It gave him another vaguely disturbing thrill.

"I seek only to be worthy of your trust, my precious one," he said. "Where are you going, anyway?"

"That's none of your business."

"To be sure," he agreed, bowing and scraping. "And you're taking the rear wagon, are you? One can't help wondering, my black dove of the mysteries, whether this has anything to do with all the loot hidden back there. Perhaps you have a rendezvous with someone who'll take it off your hands, eh?"

Her look of contempt went through him like a knife, but he knew he'd guessed correctly.

The first thing Golescu did, when he was alone, was to go into Amaunet's wagon and explore.

Though his primary object was money, it has to be admitted he went first to what he supposed to be her underwear drawer. This disappointed him, for it contained instead what seemed to be alchemist's equipment: jars of powdered minerals and metals, bowls, alembics and retorts. All was so spotlessly clean it might never have been used. When he found her underwear at last, in a trunk, he was further disappointed. It was plain utilitarian stuff; evidently Amaunet didn't go in for frills. Nevertheless, he slipped a pair of her drawers into his breast pocket, like a handkerchief, and continued his search.

No money at all, nor any personal things that might give him any clue to her history. There were a few decorative items, obviously meant to give an Egyptian impression to her customers: a half-size mummy case of papier-mâché. A hanging scroll, hieroglyphs printed on cloth, of French manufacture.

No perfumes or cosmetics by the washbasin; merely a bar of yellow soap. Golescu sniffed it and recoiled; no fragrance but lye. Whence, then, that intoxicating whiff of not-quite-cinnamon on her skin?

No writing desk, no papers. There was something that might have been intended for writing, a polished box whose front opened out flat to reveal a dull mirror of green glass at its rear. It was empty. Golescu gave it no more than a cursory glance. After he'd closed it, he rubbed the fingertips of his hand together, for they tingled slightly.

Not much in the larder: dry bread, an onion, a few potatoes. Several cooking pots and a washing copper. Golescu looked at it thoughtfully, rubbing his chin.

"But no money," he said aloud.

He sat heavily on her bed, snorting in frustration. Hearing a faint squeak of protest, he rose to his feet again and looked down. "Yes, of course!" he said, and opened the drawer under the bed. Emil whimpered and rolled away from the light, covering his face with his hands.

"Hello, don't mind me," said Golescu, scooping him out. He got down on his hands and knees, ignoring Emil's cries, and peered into the space. "Where does your mistress keep her gold, my darling? Not in here, eh? Hell and Damnation."

He sat back. Emil attempted to scramble past him, back into the shadows, but he caught the little man by one leg.

"Emil, my jewel, you'll never amount to much in this world if you can't walk around in the daytime," he said. "And you won't be much use to me, either. What's your quarrel with the sun, anyway?"

"It burns my eyes," Emil wept.

"Does it?" Golescu dragged him close, prized down his hands and looked into his wet eyes. "Perhaps there's something we can do about that, eh? And once we've solved that problem . . ." His voice trailed off, as he began to smile. Emil wriggled free and vanished back into the drawer. Golescu slid it shut with his foot.

"Sleep, potato boy," he said, hauling himself to his feet. "Don't go anyplace, and dear Uncle Barbu will be back with presents this afternoon."

Humming to himself, he mopped his face with Amaunet's drawers, replaced them in his pocket, and left the wagon. Pausing only to lock its door, he set off for the nearest road.

It took him a while to find a town, however, and what with one thing and another it was nearly sundown before Golescu came back to the wagon.

He set down his burdens—one large box and a full sack—and unlocked the door.

"Come out, little Emil," he said, and on receiving no reply he clambered in and pulled the drawer open. "Come out of there!"

"I'm hungry," said Emil, sounding accusatory, but he did not move.

"Come out and I'll boil you a nice potato, eh? It's safe; the sun's gone down. Don't you want to see what I got you, ungrateful thing?"

Emil came unwillingly, as Golescu backed out before him. He stepped down from the door, looking around, his tiny weak mouth pursed in suspicion. Catching sight of the low red sun, he let out a shrill cry and clapped his hands over his eyes.

"Yes, I lied," Golescu told him. "but just try *these*—" He drew from his pocket a pair of blue spectacles and, wrenching Emil's hands away, settled them on the bridge of his nose. They promptly fell off, as Emil's nose was far too small and thin to keep them up, and they only had one earpiece anyway.

Golescu dug hastily in the sack he had brought and drew out a long woolen scarf. He cut a pair of slits in it, as Emil wailed and jigged in front of him. Clapping the spectacles back on Emil's face and holding them in place a moment with his thumb, he tied the scarf about his head like a blindfold and widened the slits so the glass optics poked through.

"Look! Goggles!" he said. "So you're protected, see? Open your damned eyes, you baby!"

Emil must have obeyed, for he stood still suddenly, dropping his hands to his sides. His mouth hung open in an expression of feeble astonishment.

"But, wait!" said Golescu. "There's more!" He reached into the sack again and brought out a canvas coachman's duster, draping it around Emil's shoulders. It had been made for someone twice Emil's size, so it reached past his knees, indeed it trailed on the ground; and Golescu had a difficult three minutes' labor working Emil's limp arms through the sleeves and rolling the cuffs up. But, once it had been painstakingly buttoned, Emil stood as though in a tent.

"And the crowning touch—" Golescu brought from the sack a wide-brimmed felt hat and set it on Emil's head. Golescu sat back to admire the result.

"Now, don't you look nice?" he said. Emil in fact looked rather like a mushroom, but his mouth had closed. "You see? You're protected from the sun. The *vampyr* may walk abroad by day. Thanks are in order to good old Uncle Barbu, eh?

"I want my potato," said Emil.

"Pah! All right, let's feast. We've got a lot of work to do tonight," said Golescu, taking up the sack and shaking it meaningfully.

Fairly quickly he built a fire and set water to boil for Emil's potato. He fried himself a feast indeed from what he had brought: rabbit, bacon and onions, and a jug of wine red as bull's blood to wash it down. The wine outlasted the food by a comfortable margin. He set it aside and lit a fine big cigar as Emil dutifully carried the pans down to the stream to wash them.

"*Good* slave," said Golescu happily, and blew a smoke ring. "A man could get used to this kind of life. When you're done with those, bring out the laundry-copper. I'll help you fill it. And get some more wood for the fire!"

When Emil brought the copper forth they took it to the stream and filled it; then carried it back to the fire, staggering and slopping, and set it to heat. Golescu drew from the sack another of his purchases, a three-kilo paper bag with a chemist's seal on it. Emil had been gazing at the bright fire, his vacant face rendered more vacant by the goggles; but he turned his head to stare at the paper bag.

"Are we making the Black Cup?" he asked.

"No, my darling, we're making a golden cup," said Golescu. He opened the bag and dumped its contents into the copper, which had just begun to steam. "Good strong yellow dye, see? We'll let it boil good, and when it's mixed—" he reached behind him, dragging close the box he had brought. He opened it, and the firelight winked in the glass necks of one hundred and forty-four little bottles. "And when it's cooled, we'll funnel it into these. Then we'll sell them to the poultry farmers in the valley down there."

"Why?" said Emil.

"As medicine," Golescu explained. "We'll tell them it'll grow giant chickens, eh? That'll fill the purse of twenty thousand lei back up again in no time. This never fails, believe me. The dye makes the yolks more yellow, and the farmers think that means the eggs are richer. Ha! As long as you move on once you've sold all your bottles, you can pull this one anywhere."

"Medicine," said Emil.

"That's right," said Golescu. He took a final drag on his cigar, tossed it into the fire, and reached for the wine jug.

"What a lovely evening," he said, taking a drink. "What stars, eh? They make a man reflect, indeed they do. At times like this, I look back on my career and ponder the ironies of fate. I was not always a vagabond, you see.

"No, in fact, I had a splendid start in life. Born to a fine aristocratic family, you know. We had a castle. Armorial devices on our stained glass windows. Servants just to walk the dog. None of that came to me, of course; I was a younger son. But I went to University, graduated with full honors, was brilliant in finance.

"I quickly became Manager of a big important bank in Bucharest. I had a fine gold watch on a chain, and a desk three meters long, and it was kept well polished, too. Every morning when I arrived at the bank, all the clerks would line up and prostrate themselves as I walked by, swinging my cane. My cane had a diamond set in its end, a diamond that shone in glory like the rising sun.

"But they say that abundance, like poverty, wrecks you; and so it was with me. My nature was too trusting, too innocent. Alas, how swiftly my downfall came! Would you like to hear the circumstances that reduced me to the present pitiable state in which you see me?"

"What?" said Emil. Golescu had another long drink of wine.

"Well," he said, "My bank had a depositor named Ali Pasha. He had amassed a tremendous fortune. Millions. Millions in whatever kind of currency you could imagine. Pearls, rubies, emeralds too. You should have seen it just sitting there in the vault, winking like a dancing girl's . . . winky parts. Just the biggest fortune a corrupt bureaucrat could put together.

"And then, quite suddenly, he had to go abroad to avoid a scandal. And, bam! He was killed in a tragic accident when his coal-black stallion, startled by a pie wagon, threw him from its back and trampled him under its hooves.

"Being an honest man, I of course began searching for his next of kin, as soon as I heard the news of his demise. And you would think, wouldn't you, that he'd have a next of kin? The way those lustful fellows carry on with all their wives and concubines? But it was revealed that the late Ali Pasha had had an equally tragic accident in his youth, when he'd attracted the attention of the Grand Turk because of his sweet singing voice, and, well . . . he was enabled to keep that lovely soprano until the time of his completely unexpected death.

"So no wives, no children, a yawning void of interested posterity.

"And this meant, you see, that the millions that lay in our vault would, after the expiration of a certain date, become the property of the Ottoman Empire.

"What could I do? The more I reflected on the tyranny under which our great nation suffered for so long, the more my patriotic blood began to boil. I determined on a daring course of action.

"I consulted with my colleagues in the international banking community, and obtained the name of an investor who was known far and wide for his integrity. He was a Prussian, as it happened, with a handsome personal fortune. I contacted him, apologized for my presumption, explained the facts of the case, and laid before him a proposition. If he were willing to pose as the brother of the late Ali Pasha, I could facilitate his claim to the millions sitting there on deposit. He would receive forty per cent for his part in the ruse; the remaining sixty per cent I would, of course, donate to the Church.

"To make a long story short, he agreed to the plan. Indeed, he went so far as to express his enthusiastic and principled support for Romanian self-rule.

"Of course, it was a complicated matter. We had to bribe the law clerks and several petty officials, in order that they might vouch for Smedlitz (the Prussian) being a long-lost brother of Ali Pasha, his mother having been kidnapped by Barbary Coast pirates with her infant child and sold into a harem, though fortunately there had been a birthmark by which the unfortunate Ali Pasha could be posthumously identified by his sorrowing relation.

"And Smedlitz was obliged to provide a substantial deposit in order to open an account in a bank in Switzerland, into which the funds could be transferred once we had obtained their release. But he agreed to the expenditure readily—too readily, as I ought to have seen!" Golescu shook his head, drank again, wiped his moustache with the back of his hand and continued:

"How I trusted that Prussian! Alas, you stars, look down and see how an honest and credulous soul is victimized."

He drank again and went on:

"The fortune was transferred, and when I went to claim the agreed-upon sixty per cent for charity—imagine my horror on discovering that Smedlitz had withdrawn the entire amount, closed the account, and absconded! As I sought him, it soon became apparent that Smedlitz was more than a thief—he was an impostor, a lackey of the international banking community, who now closed ranks against me.

"To make matters worse, who should step forward but a new claimant! It developed that Ali Pasha had, in fact, a real brother who had only just learned of his death, having been rescued from a remote island where he had been stranded for seven years, a victim of shipwreck.

"My ruin was complete. I was obliged to flee by night, shaming my illustrious family, doomed to the life of an unjustly persecuted fugitive." Golescu wiped tears from his face and had another long drink. "Never again to sit behind a polished desk, like a gentleman! Never again to flourish my walking stick over the heads of my clerks! And what has become of its diamond, that shone like the moon?" He sobbed for breath. "Adversity makes a man wise, not rich, as the saying goes; and wisdom is all I own now. Sometimes I think of self-destruction; but I have not yet sunk so low."

He drank again, belched, and said, in a completely altered voice:

"Ah, now it's beginning to boil! Fetch a long stick and give it a stir, Emil darling."

Golescu woke in broad daylight, grimacing as he lifted his face from the depths of his hat. Emil was still sitting where he had been when Golescu had drifted off to sleep, after some hours of hazily remembered conversation. The empty jug sat where Golescu had left it; but the hundred and forty-four little glass bottles were now full.

"What'd you . . ." Golescu sat up, staring at them. He couldn't recall filling the bottles with concentrated yellow dye, but there they were, all tidily sealed.

"The medicine is ready," said Emil.

Golescu rose unsteadily. The empty copper gleamed, clean as though it were new.

"No wonder she keeps you around," he remarked. "You must be part kitchen fairy, eh? Poke up the fire, then, and we'll boil you another potato. Maybe a parsnip too, since you've been such a good boy. And then, we'll have an adventure."

He picked up the sack and trudged off to attend to his toilet.

Two hours later they were making their way slowly along a country lane, heading for a barred gate Golescu had spotted. He was sweating in the heat, dressed in the finest ensemble the rag shop had had to offer: a rusty black swallowtail coat, striped trousers, a black silk hat with a strong odor of corpse. On his left breast he had assembled an impressive-looking array of medals, mostly religious ones dressed up with bits of colored ribbon, and a couple of foil stickers off a packet of Genoa biscuits. In one hand he carried a heavy-looking satchel.

Emil wore his duster, goggles, and hat, and was having to be led by the hand because he couldn't see very well.

When they came within a hundred yards of the gate, two immense dogs charged and collided with it, barking at them through the bars.

"Take the bag," said Golescu, handing it off to Emil.

"It's heavy," Emil complained.

"Shut up. Good morning to you, my dear sir!" He raised his voice to address the farmer who came out to investigate the commotion.

"I'm too hot."

"Shut up, I said. May I have a moment of your time, sir?"

"Who the hell are you?" asked the farmer, seizing the dogs by their collars.

Golescu tipped his hat and bowed. "Dr. Milon Cretulescu, assistant minister of agriculture to Prince Alexandru, may all the holy saints and angels grant him long life. And you are?"

"Buzdugan, Iuliu," muttered the farmer.

"Charmed. You no doubt have heard of the new edict?"

"Of course I have," said Farmer Buzdugan, looking slightly uneasy. "Which one?"

Golescu smiled at him. "Why, the one about increasing poultry production on the farms in this region. His highness is very concerned that our nation become one of the foremost chicken-raising centers of the world! Perhaps you ought to chain up your dogs, dear sir."

When the dogs had been confined and the gate unbarred, Golescu strode through, summoning Emil after him with a surreptitious shove as he passed. Emil paced forward blindly, with tiny careful steps, dragging the satchel. Golescu ignored him, putting a friendly hand on Buzdugan's shoulder.

"First, I'll need to inspect your poultry yard. I'm certain you passed the last inspection without any difficulties, but, you know, standards are being raised nowadays."

"To be sure," agreed Buzdugan, sweating slightly. In fact, there had never been any inspection of which he was aware. But he led Golescu back to the bare open poultry yard, an acre fenced around by high palings, visible through a wire-screen grate.

It was not a place that invited lingering. Poultry yards seldom are. The sun beat down on it mercilessly, so that Golescu felt the hard-packed earth burning through the thin soles of his shoes. A hundred chickens stood about listlessly, quite unbothered by the reek of their defecation or the smell of the predators impaled on the higher spikes of the fence: two foxes and something so shrunken and sun-dried its species was impossible to identify.

"*Hmmm,*" said Golescu, and drew from his pocket a small book and a pencil stub. He pretended to make notes, shaking his head.

"What's the matter?" asked Buzdugan.

"Well, I don't want to discourage you too much," said Golescu, looking up with a comradely wink. "Good pest control, I'll say that much for you. Make an example of them, eh? That's the only way foxes will ever learn. But, my friend! How spiritless your birds are! Not exactly fighting cocks, are they? Why aren't they strutting about and crowing? Clearly they are enervated and weak, the victims of diet."

"They get nothing but the best feed!" protested Buzdugan. Smiling, Golescu waved a finger under his nose.

"I'm certain they do, but is that enough? Undernourished fowl produce inferior eggs, which produce feeble offspring. Not only that, vapid and tasteless eggs can ruin your reputation as a first-class market supplier. No, no; inattention to proper poultry nutrition has been your downfall."

"But—"

"Fortunately, I can help you," said Golescu, tucking away the book and pencil stub.

"How much will I have to pay?" asked Buzdugan, sagging.

"Sir! Are you implying that a representative of his highness the prince can be bribed? That may have been how things were done in the past, but we're in a new age, after all! I was referring to Science," Golescu admonished.

"Science?"

"Boy!" Golescu waved peremptorily at Emil, who had just caught up with them. "This loyal subject requires a bottle of Golden Formula Q."

Emil did nothing, so Golescu grabbed the satchel from him. Opening it, he drew forth a bottle of the yellow dye. He held it up, cradling it between his two hands.

"This, dear sir, is a diet supplement produced by the Ministry of Agriculture. Our prince appointed none but university-trained men, ordering them to set their minds to the problem of improving poultry health. Utilizing the latest scientific discoveries, they have created a tonic of amazing efficacy! *Golden Formula Q*. Used regularly, it produces astonishing results."

Buzdugan peered at the bottle. "What does it do?"

"Do? Why, it provides the missing nourishment your birds so desperately crave," said Golescu. "Come, let me give you a demonstration. Have you a platter or dish?"

When a tin pan had been produced, Golescu adroitly let himself into the chicken yard, closely followed by Buzdugan. Within the yard it was, if possible, even hotter. "Now, observe the behavior of your birds, sir," said Golescu, uncorking the bottle and pouring its contents into the pan. "The poor things perceive instantly the restorative nature of Golden Formula Q. They hunger for it! Behold."

He set the pan down on the blistering earth. The nearest chicken to notice turned its head. Within its tiny brain flashed the concept: THIRST. It ran at once to the pan and drank greedily. One by one, other chickens had the same revelation, and came scrambling to partake of lukewarm yellow dye as though it were chilled champagne.

"You see?" said Golescu, shifting from one foot to the other. "Poor starved creatures. Within hours, you will begin to see the difference. No longer will your egg yolks be pallid and unwholesome, but rich and golden! All thanks to Golden Formula Q. Only two marks a bottle."

"They *are* drinking it up," said Buzdugan, watching in some surprise. "I suppose I could try a couple of bottles."

"Ah! Well, my friend, I regret to say that Golden Formula Q is in such limited supply, and in such extreme demand, that I must limit you to one bottle only," said Golescu.

"What? But you've got a whole satchel full," said Buzdugan. "I saw, when you opened it."

"That's true, but we must give your competitors a chance, after all," said Golescu. "It wouldn't be fair if you were the only man in the region with prize-winning birds, would it?"

The farmer looked at him with narrowed eyes. "Two marks a bottle? I'll give you twenty-five marks for the whole satchel full, what do you say to that?"

"Twenty-five marks?" Golescu stepped back, looking shocked. "But what will the other poultry producers do?"

Buzdugan told him what the other poultry producers could do, as he dug a greasy bag of coin from his waistband.

They trudged homeward that evening, having distributed several satchels' worth of Golden Formula Q across the valley. Golescu had a pleasant sense of self-satisfaction and pockets heavy with wildly assorted currency.

"You see, dear little friend?" he said to Emil. "This is the way to make something of yourself. Human nature flows along like a river, never changes; a wise man builds his mill on the banks of that river, lets foibles and vanities drive his wheel. Fear, greed, and envy have never failed me."

Emil, panting with exhaustion, made what might have been a noise of agreement.

"Yes, and hasn't it been a red-letter day for you? You've braved the sunlight at last, and it's not so bad, is it? Mind the path," Golescu added, as Emil walked into a tree. He collared Emil and set his feet back on the trail. "Not far now. Yes, Emil, how lucky it was for you that I came into your life. We will continue our journey of discovery tomorrow, will we not?"

And so they did, ranging over to the other side of the valley, where a strong ammoniac breeze suggested the presence of more chicken farms. They had just turned from the road down a short drive, and the furious assault of a mastiff on the carved gate had just drawn the attention of a scowling farmer, when Emil murmured: "Horse."

"No, it's just a big dog," said Golescu, raising his hat to the farmer. "Good morning, dear sir! Allow me to introduce—"

That was when he heard the hoofbeats. He began to sweat, but merely smiled more widely and went on: "—myself Dr. Milon Cretulescu, of the Ministry of Agriculture, and I—"

The hoofbeats came galloping up the road and past the drive, but just as Golescu's heart had resumed its normal rhythm, they clattered to a halt and started back.

"—have been sent at the express wish of Prince Alexandru himself to—"

"Hey!"

"Excuse me a moment, won't you?" said Golescu, turning to face the road. He beheld Farmer Buzdugan urging his horse forward, under the drooping branches that cast the drive into gloom.

"Dr. Cretulescu!" he said. "Do you have any more of that stuff?"

"I beg your pardon?"

"You know, the—" Buzdugan glanced over at the other farmer, lowered his voice. "That stuff that makes the golden eggs!"

"Ah!" Golescu half turned, so the other farmer could see him, and raised his voice. "You mean, *Golden Formula Q*? The miracle elixir developed by his highness's own Ministry of Agriculture, to promote better poultry production?"

"Shush! Yes, that! Look, I'll pay—"

"*Golden eggs*, you say?" Golescu cried.

"What's that?" The other farmer leaned over his gate.

"None of your damn business!" said Buzdugan.

"But, dear sir, *Golden Formula Q* was intended to benefit everyone," said Golescu, uncertain just what had happened but determined to play his card. "If this good gentleman wishes to take advantage of its astonishing qualities, I cannot deny him—"

"A hundred marks for what you've got in that bag!" shouted Buzdugan.

"What's he got in the bag?" demanded the other farmer, opening his gate and stepping through.

"Golden Formula Q!" said Golescu, grabbing the satchel from Emil's nerveless hand and opening it. He drew out a bottle and thrust it up into the morning light. "Behold!"

"What was that about golden eggs?" said the other farmer, advancing on them.

"Nothing!" Buzdugan said. "Two hundred, doctor. I'm not joking. Please."

"The worthy sir was merely indulging in hyperbole," said Golescu to the other farmer. "Golden eggs? Why, I would never make that claim for Golden Formula Q. You would take me for a mountebank! But it is, quite simply, the most amazing dietary supplement for poultry you will ever use."

"Then, I want a bottle," said the other farmer.

Buzdugan gnashed his teeth. "I'll buy the rest," he said, dismounting.

"Not so fast!" said the other farmer. "This must be pretty good medicine, eh? If you want it all to yourself? Maybe I'll just buy two bottles."

"Now, gentlemen, there's no need to quarrel," said Golescu. "I have plenty of Golden Formula Q here. Pray, good Farmer Buzdugan, as a satisfied customer, would you say that you observed instant and spectacular results with Golden Formula Q?"

"Yes," said Buzdugan, with reluctance. "Huge eggs, yellow as gold. And all the roosters who drank it went mad with lust, and this morning all the hens are sitting on clutches like little mountains of gold. Two hundred and fifty for the bag, Doctor, what do you say, now?"

Golescu carried the satchel on the way back to the clearing, for it weighed more than it had when they had set out that morning. Heavy as it was, he walked with an unaccustomed speed, fairly dragging Emil after him. When they got to the wagon, he thrust Emil inside, climbed in himself, and closed the door after them. Immediately he began to undress, pausing only to look once into the satchel, as though to reassure himself. The fact that it was filled to the top with bright coin somehow failed to bring a smile to his face.

"What's going on, eh?" he demanded, shrugging out of his swallowtail coat. "I sold that man bottles of yellow dye and water. Not a *real* miracle elixir!"

Emil just stood there, blank behind his goggles, until Golescu leaned over and yanked them off.

"I said, we sold him fake medicine!" he said. "Didn't we?"

Emil blinked at him. "No," he said. "Medicine to make giant chickens."

"No, you silly ass, that's only what we *told* them it was!" said Golescu, pulling off his striped trousers. He wadded them up with the coat and set them aside. "We were lying, don't you understand?"

"No," said Emil.

Something in the toneless tone of his voice made Golescu, in the act of pulling up his plain trousers, freeze. He looked keenly at Emil.

"You don't understand lying?" he said. "Maybe you don't. And you're a horrible genius, aren't you? And I went to sleep while the stuff in the copper was cooking. Hmmm, hm hm." He fastened his trousers and put on his other coat, saying nothing for a long moment, though his gaze never left Emil's slack face.

"Tell me, my pretty child," he said at last. "Did you put other things in the brew, after I was asleep?"

"Yes," said Emil.

"What?"

In reply, Emil began to rattle off a string of names of ingredients, chemicals for the most part, or so Golescu assumed. He held up his hand at last.

"Enough, enough! The nearest chemist's is three hours' walk away. How'd you get all those things?"

"There," said Emil, pointing at the papier-mâché mummy case. "And some I got from the dirt. And some came out of leaves."

Golescu went at once to the mummy case and opened it. It appeared to be empty; but he detected the false bottom. Prizing back the lining he saw rows of compartments, packed with small jars and bags of various substances. A faint scent of spice rose from them.

"Aha," he said, closing it up. He set it aside and looked at Emil with narrowed eyes. He paced back and forth a couple of times, finally sitting down on the bed.

"How did you know," he said, in a voice some decibels below his customary bellow, "what goes into a medicine to make giant chickens?"

Emil looked back at him. Golescu beheld a strange expression in the rabbity eyes. Was that . . . scorn?

"I just know," said Emil, and there might have been scorn in his flat voice too.

"Like you just know how many beans are in a jar?"

"Yes."

Golescu rubbed his hands together, slowly. "Oh, my golden baby," he said. "Oh, my pearl, my plum, my good-luck token." A thought struck him. "Tell me something, precious," he said. "On several occasions, now, you have mentioned a Black Cup. What would that be, can you tell your Uncle Barbu?"

"I make the Black Cup for her every month," said Emil.

"You do, eh?" said Golescu. "Something to keep the babies away? But no, she's not interested in love. Yet. What happens when she drinks from the Black Cup, darling?"

"She doesn't die," said Emil, with just a trace of sadness.

Golescu leaned back, as though physically pushed. "Holy saints and angels in Heaven," he said. For a long moment ideas buzzed in his head like a hive of excited bees. At last he calmed himself to ask;

"How old is Madame Amaunet?"

"She is old," said Emil.

"Very old?"

"Yes."

"How old are you?"

"I don't know."

"I see." Golescu did not move, staring at Emil. "So that's why she doesn't want any attention drawn to you. You're her philosophers' stone, her source of the water of life. Yes? But if that's the case . . ." He shivered all over, drew himself up. "No, that's crazy. You've been in show business too long, Golescu. She must be sick with something, that's it, and she takes the medicine to preserve her health. Ugh! Let us hope she doesn't have anything catching. Is she sick, little Emil?"

"No," said Emil.

"No? Well. Golescu, my friend, don't forget that you're having a conversation with an idiot, here."

His imagination raced, though, all the while he was tidying away the evidence of the chicken game, and all that afternoon as the slow hours passed. Several times he heard the sound of hoofbeats on the road, someone riding fast—searching, perhaps, for Dr. Cretulescu?

As the first shades of night fell, Golescu crept out and lit a campfire. He was sitting beside it when he heard the approach of a wagon on the road, and a moment later the crashing of branches that meant the wagon had turned off toward the clearing. Golescu composed an expression that he hoped would convey innocence, doglike fidelity and patience, and gave a quick turn to the skillet of bread and sausages he was frying.

"Welcome back, my queen," he called, as he caught sight of Amaunet. "You see? Not only have I not run off with Emil to a gambling den, I've fixed you a nice supper. Come and eat. I'll see to the horses."

Amaunet regarded him warily, but she climbed down from the wagon and approached the fire. "Where is Emil?"

"Why, safe in his little cupboard, just as he ought to be," said Golescu, rising to offer his seat. Seeing her again up close, he felt a shiver of disappointment; Amaunet looked tired and bad-tempered, not at all like an immortal being who had supped of some arcane nectar. He left her by the fire as he led the horses off to drink. Not until he had come back and settled down across from her did he feel the stirring of mundane lust.

"I trust all that unsightly clutter in the wagon has been unloaded on some discreet fence?" he inquired pleasantly.

"That's one way of putting it," said Amaunet, with a humorless laugh. "You'll have all the room you need back there, for a while."

"And did we get a good price?"

Amaunet just shrugged.

Golescu smiled to himself, noting that she carried no purse. He kept up a disarming flow of small talk until Amaunet told him that she was retiring. Bidding her a cheery good night without so much as one suggestive remark, he watched as she climbed into the wagon—her back view was as enthralling as ever—and waited a few more minutes before lighting a candle-lantern and hurrying off to the other wagon.

On climbing inside, Golescu held the lamp high and looked around.

"Beautifully empty," he remarked in satisfaction. Not a carpet, not a painting, not so much as a silver spoon anywhere to be seen. As it should be. But—

"Where is the money?" he wondered aloud. "Come out, little iron-bound strongbox. Come out, little exceptionally heavy purse. She must have made a fortune from the fence. So . . ."

Golescu proceeded to rummage in the cupboards and cabinets, hastily at first and then with greater care, rapping for hollow panels, testing for hidden drawers. At the end of half an hour he was baffled, panting with exasperation.

"It must be here somewhere!" he declared. "Unless she made so little off the bargain she was able to hide her miserable share of the loot in her cleavage!"

Muttering to himself, he went out and banked the fire. Then he retrieved his satchel of money and the new clothes he had bought, including Emil's daylight ensemble, from the bush where he had stashed them. Having resecured them in a cupboard in the wagon, he stretched out on the floor and thought very hard.

"I've seen that dull and sullen look before," he announced to the darkness. "Hopeless. Apathetic. Ill-used. She might be sick, but also that's the way a whore looks, when she has a nasty brute of a pimp who works her hard and takes all her earnings away. I wonder . . .

"Perhaps she's the hapless victim of some big operator? Say, a criminal mastermind, with a network of thieves and fences and middlemen all funneling profits toward him? So that he sits alone on a pyramid of gold, receiving tribute from petty crooks everywhere?

"What a lovely idea!" Golescu sat up and clasped his hands.

He was wakened again that night by her singing. Amaunet's voice was like slow coals glowing in a dying fire, or like the undulation of smoke rising when the last glow has died. It was heartbreaking, but there was something horrible about it.

They rolled on. The mountains were always ahead of them, and to Golescu's relief the valley of his labors was far behind them. No one was ever hanged for selling a weak solution of yellow dye, but people have been hanged for being too successful; and in any case he preferred to keep a good distance between himself and any outcomes he couldn't predict.

The mountains came close at last and were easily crossed, by an obscure road Amaunet seemed to know well. Noon of the second day they came to a fair-sized city in the foothills, with grand houses and a domed church.

Here a fair was setting up, in a wide public square through which the wind gusted, driving yellow leaves before it over the cobbles. Golescu made his usual helpful suggestions for improving Amaunet's business and was ignored. Resigned, he stood in the permit line with other fair vendors, whom he was beginning to know by sight. They also ignored his attempts at small talk. The permit clerk was rude and obtuse.

By the time evening fell, when the fair came to life in a blaze of gaslight and calliope music, Golescu was not in the best of moods.

"Come on, pallid one," he said, dragging Emil forth from the wagon. "What are you shrinking from?"

"It's too bright," whimpered Emil, squeezing his eyes shut and trying to hide under Golescu's coat.

"We're in a big modern city, my boy," said Golescu, striding through the crowd and towing him along relentless. "Gaslight, the wonder of the civilized world. Soon we won't have Night at all, if we don't want it. Imagine that, eh? You'd have to live in a cellar. You'd probably like that, I expect."

"I want a sausage on a stick," said Emil.

"Patience," said Golescu, looking around for the food stalls. "Eating and scratching only want a beginning, eh? So scratch, and soon you'll be eating too. Where the hell is the sausage booth?"

He spotted a vendor he recognized and pushed through the crowd to the counter.

"Hey! Vienna sausage, please." He put down a coin.

"We're out of Vienna sausage," said the cashier. "We have *sarmale* on polenta, or *tochitura* on polenta. Take your pick."

Golescu's mouth watered. "The sarmale, and plenty of polenta."

He carried the paper cone to a relatively quiet corner and seated himself on a hay bale. "Come and eat. Emil dear. Polenta for you and nice spicy sarmale for me, eh?"

Emil opened his eyes long enough to look at it.

"I can't eat that. It has sauce on it."

"Just a little!" Golescu dug his thumb in amongst the meatballs and pulled up a glob of polenta. "See? Nice!"

Emil began to sob. "I don't want that. I want a sausage."

"Well, this is like sausage, only it's in grape leaves instead of pig guts, eh?" Golescu held up a nugget of sarmale. "Mmmm, tasty!"

But Emil wouldn't touch it. Golescu sighed, wolfed down the sarmale and polenta, and wiped his fingers on Emil's coat. He dragged Emil after him and searched the fairground from end to end, but nobody was selling Vienna sausage. The only thing he found that Emil would consent to eat was candy floss, so he bought him five big wads of it. Emil crouched furtively under a wagon and ate it all, as Golescu looked on and tried to slap some warmth into himself. The cold wind pierced straight through his coat, taking away all the nice residual warmth of the peppery sarmale.

"This is no life for a red-blooded man," he grumbled. "Wine, women and dance are what I need, and am I getting any? It is to laugh. Wet-nursing a miserable picky dwarf while the temptress of my dreams barely knows I exist. If I had any self-respect, I'd burst into that wagon and show her what I'm made of."

The last pink streamer of candy floss vanished into Emil's mouth. He belched.

"Then, of course, she'd hurt me," Golescu concluded. "Pretty badly, I think. Her fingers are like steel. And that excites me, Emil, isn't that a terrible thing? Yet another step downward in my long debasement."

Emil belched again.

The chilly hours passed. Emil rolled over on his side and began to wail to himself. As the fair grew quieter, as the lights went out one by one and the carousel slowed through its last revolution, Emil's whining grew louder. Amaunet's last customer departed; a moment later her door flew open and she emerged, turning her head this way and that, searching for the sound. Her gaze fell on Emil, prostrate under the wagon, and she bared her teeth at Golescu.

"What did you do to him?"

"Nothing!" said Golescu, backing up a pace or two. "His highness the turnip wouldn't eat anything but candy, and now he seems to be regretting it."

"Fool," said Amaunet. She pulled Emil out from the litter of paper cones and straw. He vomited pink syrup and said, "I want a potato."

Amaunet gave Golescu a look that made his heart skip a beat, but in a reasonable voice he said: "I could take us all to dinner. What about it? My treat."

"It's nearly midnight, you ass," said Amaunet.

"That café is still open," said Golescu, pointing to a garishly lit place at the edge of the square. Amaunet stared at it. Finally she shrugged. "Bring him," she said.

Golescu picked up Emil by the scruff of his neck and stood him on his feet. "Your potato is calling, fastidious one. Let us answer it." Emil took his hand and they trudged off together across the square, with Amaunet slinking after.

They got a table by the door. For all that the hour was late, the café was densely crowded with people in evening dress, quite glittering and cosmopolitan in appearance. The air was full of their chatter, oddly echoing, with a shrill metallic quality. Amaunet gave the crowd one surly look, and paid them no attention thereafter. But she took off her black shawl and dropped it over Emil's head. He sat like an unprotesting ghost, shrouded in black, apparently quite content.

"And you're veiling him because . . . ?" said Golescu.

"Better if he isn't seen," said Amaunet.

"What may we get for the little family?" inquired a waiter, appearing at Golescu's elbow with a speed and silence that suggested he had popped up through a trap door. Golescu started in his chair, unnerved. The waiter had wide glass-bright eyes, and a fixed smile under a straight bar of moustache like a strip of black fur.

"Are you still serving food?" Golescu asked. The waiter's smile never faltered; he produced a menu from thin air and presented it with a flourish.

"Your *carte de nuit*. We particularly recommend the black puddings. Something to drink?"

"Bring us the best you have," said Golescu grandly. The waiter bowed and vanished again.

"It says the *Czernina Soup* is divine," announced Golescu, reading from the menu. "Hey, he thought we were a family. Charming, eh? You're Mother Aegypt and I'm . . ."

"The Father of Lies," said Amaunet, yawning.

"I shall take that as a compliment," said Golescu. "Fancy French cuisine here, too: *Boudin Noir*. And, for the hearty diner, *Blutwurst*. So, who do you think will recognize our tiny prodigy, Madame? He wouldn't happen to be a royal heir you stole in infancy, would he?"

Amaunet gave him a sharp look. Golescu sat up, startled.

"You can't be serious!" he said. "Heaven knows, he's inbred enough to have the very bluest blood—"

The waiter materialized beside them, deftly uncorking a dusty bottle. "This is very old wine," he said, displaying the label.

"'Egri Bikaver,'" read Golescu. "Yes, all right. Have you got any Vienna sausage? We have a little prince here who'll hardly eat anything else."

"I want a potato." Emil's voice floated from beneath the black drape.

"We will see what can be done," said the waiter, unblinking, but his smile widened under his dreadful moustache. "And for Madame?"

Amaunet said something in a language with which Golescu was unfamiliar. The waiter chuckled, a disturbing sound, and jotted briefly on a notepad that appeared from nowhere in particular. "Very wise. And for Sir?"

"Blutwurst. I'm a hearty diner," said Golescu.

"To be sure," said the waiter, and vanished. Golescu leaned forward and hissed, "Hey, you can't mean you actually stole him from some—"

"Look, it's a gypsy!" cried a young woman, one of a pair of young lovers out for a late stroll. Her young man leaned in from the sidewalk and demanded, "What's our fortune, eh, gypsy? Will we love each other the rest of our lives?"

"You'll be dead in three days," said Amaunet. The girl squeaked, the boy went pale and muttered a curse. They fled into the night.

"What did you go and tell them that for?" demanded Golescu. Amaunet shrugged and poured herself a glass of wine.

"Why should I lie? Three days, three hours, three decades. Death always comes, for them. It's what I tell them all. Why not?"

"No wonder you don't do better business!" said Golescu. "You're supposed to tell them *good* fortunes!"

"Why should I lie?" repeated Amaunet.

Baffled, Golescu pulled at his moustaches. "What makes you say such things?" he said at last. "Why do you pretend to feel nothing? But you love little Emil, eh?"

She looked at him in flat astonishment. Then she smiled. It was a poisonous smile.

"Love *Emil?*" she said. "Who could love that thing? I could as soon love you."

As though to underscore her contempt, a woman at the bar shrieked with laughter.

Golescu turned his face away. Immediately he set about soothing his lacerated ego, revising what she'd said, changing her expression and intonation, and he had nearly rewritten the scene into an almost declaration of tender feeling for himself when the waiter reappeared, bearing a tray.

"See what we have for the little man?" he said, whisking the cover off a dish. "Viennese on a stake!"

The dish held an artful arrangement of Vienna sausages on wooden skewers, stuck upright in a mound of mashed potato.

"Well, isn't that cute?" said Golescu. "Thank the nice man, Emil."

Emil said nothing, but reached for the plate. "He says Thank You," said Golescu, as smacking noises came from under the veil. The waiter set before Amaunet a dish containing skewered animal parts, flame-blackened to anonymity.

"Madame. And for Sir," said the waiter, setting a platter before Golescu. Golescu blinked and shuddered; for a moment he had the strongest conviction that the Blutwurst was pulsing and shivering, on its bed of grilled onions and eggplant that seethed like maggots. Resolutely, he told himself it was a trick of the greenish light and the late hour.

"Be sure to save room for cake," said the waiter.

"You'll be dead in three days, too," Amaunet told the waiter. The waiter laughed heartily.

They journeyed on to the next crossroads fair. Two days out they came to the outskirts of another town, where Amaunet pulled off the road onto waste ground. Drawing a small purse from her bosom, she handed it to Golescu.

"Go and buy groceries," she said. "We'll wait here."

Golescu scowled at the pouch, clinked it beside his ear. "Not a lot of money," he said. "But never mind, dearest. You have a man to provide for you now, you know."

"Get potatoes," Amaunet told him.

"Of course, my jewel," he replied, smiling as he climbed down. He went dutifully off to the main street.

"She is not heartless," he told himself. "She just needs to be wooed, that's all. Who can ever have been kind to her? It's time to drop the bucket into your well of charm, Golescu."

The first thing he did was look for a bathhouse. Having located one and paid the morose Turk at the door, he went in, disrobed, and submitted to being plunged, steamed, scraped, pummeled, and finally shaved. He declined the offer of orange flower water, however, preferring to retain a certain manly musk, and merely asked to be directed to the market square.

When he left it, an hour later, he was indeed carrying a sack of potatoes. He had also onions, flour, oil, sausages, a bottle of champagne, a box of Austrian chocolates, and a bouquet of asters.

He had the satisfaction of seeing Amaunet's eyes widen as he approached her.

"What's this?" she asked.

"For you," he said, thrusting the flowers into her arms. Golescu had never seen her taken aback before. She held them out in a gingerly sort of way, with a queer look of embarrassment.

"What am I supposed to do with these?" she said.

"Put them in water?" he said, grinning at her as he hefted his other purchases.

That night, when they had made their camp in a clearing less cobwebbed and haunted than usual, when the white trail of stars made its way down the sky, Golescu went into the wagon to retrieve his treats. The asters had drooped to death, despite having been crammed in a jar of water, but the champagne and chocolates had survived being at the bottom of his sack. Humming to himself, he carried them, together with a pair of chipped enamel mugs, out to the fireside.

Amaunet was gazing into the flames, apparently lost in gloomy reverie. She ignored the popping of the champagne cork, though Emil, beside her, twitched and started. When Golescu opened the chocolates, however, she looked sharply round.

"Where did you get that?" she demanded.

"A little fairy brought it, flying on golden wings," said Golescu. "Out of his purse of twenty thousand lei, I might add, so don't scowl at me like that. Will you have a sweetmeat, my queen? A cherry cream? A bit of enrobed ginger peel?"

Amaunet stared fixedly at the box a long moment, and then reached for it. "What harm can it do?" she said, in a quiet voice. "Why not?"

"That's the spirit," said Golescu, pouring the champagne. "A little pleasure now and again is good for you, wouldn't you agree? Especially when one has the money."

Amaunet didn't answer, busy with prizing open the box. When he handed her a mug full of champagne, she took it without looking up, drained it as though it were so much water, and handed it back.

"Well quaffed!" said Golescu, as a tiny flutter of hope woke in his flesh. He poured Amaunet another. She meanwhile had got the box open at last, and bowed her head over the chocolates, breathing in their scent as though they were the perfumes of Arabia.

"Oh," she groaned, and groped in the box. Bringing out three chocolate creams, she held them up a moment in dim-eyed contemplation; then closed her fist on them, crushing them as though they were grapes. Closing her eyes, she licked the sweet mess from her hand, slowly, making ecstatic sounds.

Golescu stared, and in his inattention poured champagne in his lap. Amaunet did not notice.

"I had no idea you liked chocolates so much," said Golescu.

"Why should you?" said Amaunet through a full mouth. She lifted the box and inhaled again, then dipped in with her tongue and scooped a nut cluster straight out of its little paper cup.

"Good point," said Golescu. He edged a little closer on the fallen log that was their mutual seat, and offered her the champagne once more. She didn't seem to notice, absorbed as she was in crunching nuts. "Come, drink up; this stuff won't keep. Like youth and dreams, eh?"

To his astonishment, Amaunet threw back her head and laughed. It was not the dry and humorless syllable that had previously expressed her scorn. It was full-throated, rolling, deep, and so frightful a noise that Emil shrieked and put his hands over his head, and even the fire seemed to shrink down and cower. It echoed in the night forest, which suddenly was darker, more full of menace.

Golescu's heart beat faster. When Amaunet seized the mug from him and gulped down its contents once more, he moistened his lips and ventured to say:

"Just let all those cares wash away in the sparkling tide, eh? Let's be good to each other, dear lady. You need a man to lessen the burden on those poor frail shoulders. Golescu is here!"

That provoked another burst of laughter from Amaunet, ending in a growl as she threw down the mug, grabbed another handful of chocolates from the box, and crammed them into her mouth, paper cups and all.

Scarcely able to believe his luck (*one drink and she's a shameless bacchante!*) Golescu edged his bottom a little closer to Amaunet's. "Come," he said, breathing heavily, "Tell me about yourself, my Nile lily."

Amaunet just chuckled, looking at him sidelong as she munched chocolates. Her eyes had taken on a queer glow, more reflective of the flames perhaps than they had been. It terrified Golescu, and yet . . .

At last she swallowed, took the champagne bottle from his hand and had a drink.

"Hah!" She spat into the fire, which blazed up. "You want to hear my story? Listen, then, fat man."

"A thousand thousand years ago, there was a narrow green land by a river. At our backs was the desert, full of jackals and demons. But the man and the woman always told me that if I stayed inside at night, like a good little girl, nothing could hurt me. And if I was a very good little girl always, I would never die. I'd go down to the river, and a man would come in a reed boat and take me away to the Sun, and I'd live forever.

"One day, the Lean People came out of the desert. They had starved in the desert so long, they thought that was what the gods *meant* for people to do. So, when they saw our green fields, they said we were Abomination. They rode in and killed as many as they could. We were stronger people and we killed them all, threw their bodies in the river—no boats came for *them!* And that was when I looked on Him, and was afraid."

"Who was He, precious?" said Golescu.

"Death," said Amaunet, as the firelight played on her face. "The great Lord with long rows of ivory teeth. His scales shone under the moon. He walked without a shadow. I had never seen any boat taking good children to Heaven; but I saw His power. So I took clay from the riverbank and I made a little Death, and I worshipped it, and fed it with mice, with birds, anything I could catch and kill. *Take all these,* I said, *and not me; for You are very great.*

"Next season, more riders came out of the desert. More war, more food for Him, and I knew He truly ruled the world.

"Our people said: *We can't stay here. Not safe to farm these fields.* And many gave up and walked north. But the man and woman waited too long. They tried to take everything we owned, every bowl and dish in our house, and the woman found my little image of Him. She beat me and said I was wicked. She broke the image.

"And He punished her for it. As we ran along the path by the river, no Sun Lord came to our aid; only the desert people, and they rode down the man and the woman.

"I didn't help them. I ran, and ran beside the river, and I prayed for Him to save me." Amaunet's voice had dropped to a whisper. She sounded young, nearly human.

Golescu was disconcerted. It wasn't at all the mysterious past he had imagined for her; only sad. Some miserable tribal struggle, in some backwater village somewhere? No dusky princess, exiled daughter of pharaohs. Only a refugee, like any one of the hatchet-faced women he had seen along the roads, pushing barrows full of what they could salvage from the ashes of war.

"But at least, this was in Egypt, yes? How did you escape?" Golescu inquired, venturing to put his arm around her. His voice seemed to break some kind of spell; Amaunet turned to look at him, and smiled with all her teeth in black amusement. The smile made Golescu feel small and vulnerable.

"Why, a bright boat came up the river," she said. "There was the Sun Lord, putting out his hand to take me to safety. He didn't come for the man and woman, who had been good; He came for *me,* that had never believed in him. So I knew the world was all lies, even as I went with him and listened to his stories about how wonderful Heaven would be.

"And it turned out that I was right to suspect the Sun, fat man. The price I paid for eternal life was to become a slave in Heaven. For my cowardice in running from Death, they punished me by letting the sacred asps bite me. I was bitten every day, and by the end of fifteen years, I was so full of poison that nothing could ever hurt me. And by the end of a thousand years, I was so weary of my slavery that I prayed to Him again.

"I went out beside the river, under the light of the moon, and I tore my clothes and bared my breasts for Him, knelt down and begged Him to come for me. I wailed and pressed my lips to the mud. How I longed for His ivory teeth!

"But He will not come for me.

"And the Sun Lord has set me to traveling the world, doing business with thieves and murderers, telling foolish mortals their fortunes." Amaunet had another drink of champagne. "Because the Sun, as it turns out, is actually the Devil. He hasn't got horns or a tail, oh, no; he looks like a handsome priest. But he's the master of all lies.

"And I am so tired, fat man, so tired of working for him. Nothing matters; nothing changes. The sun rises each day, and I open my eyes and hate the sun for rising, and hate the wheels that turn and the beasts that pull me on my way. And Him I hate most of all, who takes the whole world but withholds His embrace from me."

She fell silent, looking beyond the fire into the night.

Golescu took a moment to register that her story was at an end, being still preoccupied with the mental image of Amaunet running bare-breasted beside the Nile. But he shook himself, now, and gathered his wits; filed the whole story under *Elaborate Metaphor* and sought to get back to business in the real world.

"About this Devil, my sweet," he said, as she crammed another fistful of chocolates into her mouth, "and these thieves and murderers. The ones who bring you all the stolen goods. You take their loot to the Devil?"

Amaunet didn't answer, chewing mechanically, watching the flames.

"What would happen if you didn't take the loot to him?" Golescu persisted. "Suppose you just took it somewhere and sold it yourself?"

"Why should I do that?" said Amaunet.

"So as to be rich!" said Golescu, beginning to regret that he'd gotten her so intoxicated. "So as not to live in wretchedness and misery!"

Amaunet laughed again, with a noise like ice splintering.

"Money won't change that," she said. "For me or you!"

"Where's he live, this metaphorical Devil of yours?" said Golescu. "Bucharest? Kronstadt? I could talk to him on your behalf, eh? Threaten him slightly? Renegotiate your contract? I'm good at that, my darling. Why don't I talk to him, man to man?"

That sent her into such gales of ugly laughter she dropped the chocolate box.

"Or, what about getting some real use out of dear Emil?" said Golescu. "What about a mentalist act? And perhaps we could do a sideline in love philtres, cures for baldness. A little bird tells me we could make our fortunes," he added craftily.

Amaunet's laugh stopped. Her lip curled back from her teeth.

"I told you," she said, "No. Emil's a secret."

"And from whom are we hiding him, madame?" Golescu inquired.

Amaunet just shook her head. She groped in the dust, found the chocolate box and picked out the last few cordials.

"*He'd* find out," she murmured, as though to herself. "And then he'd take him away from me. Not fair. *I* found him. Pompous fool; looking under hills. Waiting by fairy rings. As though the folk tales were real! When all along, he should have been looking in the lunatic asylums. The ward keeper said: here, madame, we have a little genius who thinks he's a *vampyr*. And I saw him and I knew, the big eyes, the big head, I knew what blood ran in his veins. Aegeus's holy grail, but *I* found one. Why should I give him up? If anybody could find a way, he could . . ."

More damned metaphors, thought Golescu. "Who's Aegeus?" he asked. "Is that the Devil's real name?"

"Ha! He wishes he were. The lesser of two devils . . ." Amaunet's voice trailed away into nonsense sounds. Or were they? Golescu, listening, made out syllables that slid and hissed, the pattern of words.

If I wait any longer, she'll pass out, he realized.

"Come, my sweet, the hour is late," he said, in the most seductive voice he could summon. "Why don't we go to bed?" He reached out to pull her close, fumbling for a way through her clothes.

Abruptly he was lying flat on his back, staring up at an apparition. Eyes and teeth of flame, a black shadow like cloak or wings, claws raised to strike. He heard a high-pitched shriek before the blow came, and sparks flew up out of velvet blackness.

Golescu opened his eyes to the gloom before dawn, a neutral blue from which the stars had already fled. He sat up, squinting in pain. He was soaked with dew, his head pounded, and he couldn't seem to focus his eyes.

Beside him, a thin plume of smoke streamed upward from the ashes of the fire. Across the firepit, Emil still sat where he had been the night before. He was watching the east with an expression of dread, whimpering faintly.

"God and all His little angels," groaned Golescu, touching the lump on his forehead. "What happened last night, eh?"

Emil did not respond. Golescu sorted muzzily through his memory, which (given his concussion) was not at its best. He thought that the attempt at seduction had been going rather well. The goose egg above his eyes was clear indication *something* hadn't gone as planned, and yet . . .

Emil began to weep, wringing his hands.

"What the hell's the matter with you, anyway?" said Golescu, rolling over to get to his hands and knees.

"The sun," said Emil, not taking his eyes from the glow on the horizon.

"And you haven't got your shade-suit on, have you?" Golescu retorted, rising ponderously to his feet. He grimaced and clutched at his head. "Tell me, petite undead creature, was I so fortunate as to get laid last night? Any idea where black madame has gotten to?"

Emil just sobbed and covered his eyes.

"Oh, all right, let's get you back in your cozy warm coffin," said Golescu, brushing dust from his clothing. "Come on!"

Emil scuttled to his side. He opened the wagon door and Emil vaulted in, vanishing into the cupboard under Amaunet's bed. Emil pulled the cupboard door shut after himself with a bang. A bundle of rags on the bed stirred. Amaunet sat bolt upright, staring at Golescu.

Their eyes met. *She doesn't know what happened either!* thought Golescu, with such a rush of glee, his brain throbbed like a heart.

"If you please, madam," he said, just a shade reproachfully, "I was only putting poor Emil to bed. You left him out all night."

He reached up to doff his hat, but it wasn't on his head.

"Get out," said Amaunet.

"At once, madame," said Golescu, and backed away with all the dignity he could muster. He closed the door, spotting his hat in a thorn bush all of ten feet away from where he had been lying.

"What a time we must have had," he said to himself, beginning to grin. "Barbu, you seductive devil!"

And though his head felt as though it were splitting, he smiled to himself all the while he gathered wood and rebuilt the fire.

On the feast days of certain saints and at crossroad harvest fairs, they lined up their black wagons beside the brightly-painted ones. Amaunet told fortunes. The rear wagon began to fill once more with stolen things, so that Golescu slept on rolls of carpet and tapestry, and holy saints gazed down from their painted panels to watch him sleep. They looked horrified.

Amaunet did not speak of that night by the fire. Still, Golescu fancied there was a change in her demeanor toward him, which fueled his self-esteem: an oddly unsettled look in her eyes, a hesitance, what in anybody less dour would have been *embarrassment*.

"She's dreaming of me," he told Emil one night, as he poked the fire. "What do you want to bet? She desires me, and yet her pride won't let her yield."

Emil said nothing, vacantly watching the water boil for his evening potato.

Amaunet emerged from the wagon. She approached Golescu and thrust a scrap of paper at him.

"We'll get to Kronstadt tomorrow," she said. "You'll go in. Buy what's on this list."

"Where am I to find this stuff?" Golescu complained, reading the list. "An alchemist's? I don't know what half of it is. Except for . . ." He looked up at her, trying not to smile. "Chocolate, eh? What'll you have, cream bonbons? Caramels? Nuts?"

"No," said Amaunet, turning her back. "I want a brick of the pure stuff. See if you can get a confectioner to sell you some of his stock."

"Heh heh heh," said Golescu meaningfully, but she ignored him.

Though Kronstadt was a big town, bursting its medieval walls, it took Golescu three trips, to three separate chemists' shops, to obtain all the items on the list but the chocolate. It took him the best part of an hour to get the chocolate, too, using all his guile and patience to convince the confectioner's assistant to sell him a block of raw material.

"You'd have thought I was trying to buy state secrets," Golescu said to himself, trudging away with a scant half-pound block wrapped in waxed paper. "Pfui! Such drudge work, Golescu, is a waste of your talents. What are you, a mere donkey to send on errands?"

And when he returned to the camp outside town, he got nothing like the welcome he felt he deserved. Amaunet seized the carry-sack from him and went through it hurriedly, as he stood before her with aching feet. She pulled out the block of chocolate and stared at it. She trembled slightly, her nostrils flared. Golescu thought it made her look uncommonly like a horse.

"I don't suppose you've cooked any supper for me?" he inquired.

Amaunet started, and turned to him as though he had just asked for a roasted baby in caper sauce.

"No! Go back into Kronstadt. Buy yourself something at a tavern. In fact, take a room. I don't want to see you back here for two days, understand? Come back at dawn on the third day."

"I see," said Golescu, affronted. "In that case I'll just go collect my purse and an overnight bag, shall I? Not that I don't trust you, of course."

Amaunet's reply was to turn her back and vanish into the wagon, bearing the sack clutched to her bosom.

Carrying his satchel, Golescu cheered up a little as he walked away. Cash, a change of clothes, and no authorities in pursuit!

He was not especially concerned that Amaunet would use his absence to move on. The people of the road had a limited number of places they could ply their diverse trades, and he had been one of their number long enough to know the network of market fairs and circuses that made up their itinerary. He had only to follow the route of the vardas, and sooner or later he must find Amaunet again. Unless, of course, she left the road and settled down; then she would be harder to locate than an egg in a snowstorm. Or an ink bottle in a coal cellar. Or . . . he amused himself for at least a mile composing unlikely similes.

Having returned to Kronstadt just as dusk fell, Golescu paused outside a low dark door. There was no sign to tell him a tavern lay within, but the fume of wine and brandy breathing out spoke eloquently to him. He went in, ducking his head, and as soon as his eyes had adjusted to the dark he made out the bar, the barrels, the tables in dark corners he had expected to see.

"A glass of schnapps, please," he said to the sad-faced publican. There were silent drinkers at the tables, some watching him with a certain amount of suspicion, some ignoring him. One or two appeared to be dead, collapsed over their drinks. Only a pair of cattle herders standing near the bar were engaged in conversation. Golescu smiled Cheerily at one and all, slapped down his coin, and withdrew with his glass to an empty table.

"Hunting for him everywhere," one of the drovers was saying. "He was selling this stuff that was supposed to make chickens lay better eggs."

"Has anybody been killed?" said the other drover.

"I didn't hear enough to know, but they managed to shoot most of them—"

Golescu, quietly as he could, half rose and turned his chair so he was facing away from the bar. Raising his glass to his lips, he looked over its rim and met the eyes of someone propped in a dark corner.

"To your very good health," he said, and drank.

"What's that you've got in the satchel?" said the person in the corner.

"Please, sir, my mummy sent me to the market to buy bread," said Golescu, smirking. The stranger arose and came near. Golescu drew back involuntarily. The stranger ignored his reaction and sat down at Golescu's table.

He was an old man in rusty black, thin to gauntness, his shabby coat buttoned high and tight. He was bald, with drawn and waxen features, and he smelled a bit; but the stare of his eyes was intimidating. They shone like pearls, milky as though he were blind.

"You travel with Mother Aegypt, eh?" said the old man.

"And who would that be?" inquired Golescu, setting his drink down. The old man looked scornful.

"I know her," he said. "Madame Amaunet. I travel, too. I saw you at the market fair in Arges, loafing outside her wagon. You do the talking for her, don't you, and run her errands? I've been following you."

"You must have me confused with some other handsome fellow," said Golescu.

"Pfft." The old man waved his hand dismissively. "I used to work for her, too. She's never without a slave to do her bidding."

"Friend, I don't do anyone's bidding," said Golescu, but he felt a curious pang of jealousy. "And she's only a poor weak woman, isn't she?"

The old man laughed. He creaked when he laughed.

"Tell me, is she still collecting trash for the Devil?"

"What Devil is that?" said Golescu, leaning back and trying to look amused.

"Her master. I saw him, once." The old man reached up absently and swatted a fly that had landed on his cheek. "Soldiers had looted a mosque, they stole a big golden lamp. She paid them cash for it. It wasn't so heavy, but it was, you know, awkward. And when we drove up to the Teufelberg to unload all the goods, she made me help her bring out the lamp, so as not to break off the fancy work. I saw him there, the Devil. Waiting beside his long wagons. He looked like a prosperous Saxon."

"Sorry, my friend, I don't know what you're talking about," said Golescu. He drew a deep breath and plunged on: "Though I *have* heard of a lord of thieves who is, perhaps, known in certain circles as the Devil. Am I correct? Just the sort of powerful fellow who has but to pull a string and corrupt officials rush to do his bidding? And he accumulates riches without lifting a finger?"

The old man creaked again.

"You think you've figured it out," he said. "And you think he has a place for a fast-talking fellow in his gang, don't you?"

Taken aback, Golescu just stared at him. He raised his drink again.

"Mind reader, are you?"

"I was a fool, too," said the old man, smacking the table for emphasis, though his hand made no more sound than an empty glove. "Thought I'd make a fortune. Use her to work my way up the ladder. I hadn't the slightest idea what she really was."

"What is she, grandfather?" said Golescu, winking broadly at the publican. The publican shuddered and looked away. The old man, ignoring or not noticing, leaned forward and said in a lowered voice:

"There are *stregoi* who walk this world. You don't believe it, you laugh, but it's true. They aren't interested in your soul. They crave beautiful things. Whenever there is a war, they hover around its edges like flies, stealing what they can when the armies loot. If a house is going to catch fire and burn to the ground, they know; you can see them lurking in the street beforehand, and how their eyes gleam! They're only waiting for night, when they can slip in and take away paintings, carvings, books, whatever is choice and rare, before the flames come. Sometimes they take children, too.

"*She's* one of them. But she's tired, she's lazy. She buys from thieves, instead of doing the work herself. The Devil doesn't care. He just takes what she brings him. Back she goes on her rounds, then, from fair to fair, and even the murderers cross themselves when her shadow falls on them, but still they bring her pretty things. Isn't it so?"

"What do you want, grandfather?" said Golescu.

"I want her secret," said the old man. "I'll tell you about it, and then you can steal it and bring it back here, and we'll share. How would you like eternal youth, eh?"

"I'd love it," said Golescu patiently. "But there's no such thing."

"Then you don't know Mother Aegypt very well!" said the old man, grinning like a skull. "I used to watch through the door when she'd mix her Black Cup. Does she still have the little mummy case, with the powders inside?"

"Yes," said Golescu, startled into truthfulness.

"That's how she does it!" said the old man. "She'd put in a little of this—little of that—she'd grind the powders together, and though I watched for years I could never see all that went in the cup, or what the right amounts were. Spirits of wine, yes, and some strange things—arsenic, and paint! And she'd drink it down, and weep, and scream as though she was dying. But instead, she'd live. My time slipped away, peering through that door, watching her live. I could have run away from her many times, but I stayed, I wasted my life, because I thought I could learn her secrets.

"And one night she caught me watching her, and she cursed me. I ran away. I hid for years. She's forgotten me, now. But when I saw her at Arges, and you with her, I thought—he can help me.

"So! You find out what's in that Black Cup of hers, and bring it back to me. I'll share it with you. We'll live forever and become rich as kings."

"Will I betray the woman I love?" said Golescu. "And I should believe such a story, because—?"

The old man, who had worked himself into a dry trembling passion, took a moment to register what Golescu had said. He looked at him with contempt.

"Love? *Mother Aegypt?* I see I have been wasting my breath on an idiot."

The old man rose to his feet. Golescu put out a conciliatory hand. "Now, now, grandfather, I didn't say I didn't believe you, but you'll have to admit that's quite a story. Where's your proof?"

"Up your ass," said the old man, sidling away from the table.

"How long were you with her?" said Golescu, half rising to follow him.

"She bought me from the orphan asylum in Ţimisoara," said the old man, turning with a baleful smile. "I was ten years old."

Golescu sat down abruptly, staring as the old man scuttled out into the night.

After a moment's rapid thought, he gulped the rest of his schnapps and rose to follow. When he got out into the street, he stared in both directions. A round moon had just lifted above the housetops, and by its light the streets were as visible as by day, though the shadows were black and fathomless. Somewhere, far off, a dog howled. At least, it sounded like a dog. There was no sign of the old man, as far as Golescu could see.

Golescu shivered, and went in search of a cheap hotel.

Cheapness notwithstanding, it gave Golescu a pleasant sense of status to sleep once again in a bed. Lingering over coffee and sweet rolls the next morning, he pretended he was a millionaire on holiday. It had long been his habit not to dwell on life's mysteries, even fairly big and ugly ones, and in broad daylight he found it easy to dismiss the old man as a raving lunatic. Amaunet clearly had a bad reputation amongst the people of the road, but why should he care?

He went forth from the hotel jingling coins in his pocket, and walked the streets of Kronstadt as though he owned it.

In the Council Square his attention was drawn by a platform that had been set up, crowded with racks, boxes and bins of the most unlikely looking objects. Some twenty citizens were pawing through them in a leisurely way. Several armed policemen stood guard over the lot, and over two miserable wretches in manacles.

Catching the not unpleasant scent of somebody else's disaster, Golescu hurried to investigate.

"Am I correct in assuming this is a debtors' sale, sir?" he asked a police sergeant.

"That's right," said the sergeant. "A traveling opera company. These two bankrupts are the former managers. Isn't that so?" He prodded one of them with his stick.

"Unfortunately so," agreed the other gloomily. "Please go in, sir, and see if anything catches your fancy. Reduce our debt and be warned by our example. Remember, the Devil has a stake in hell especially reserved for defaulting treasurers of touring companies."

"I weep for you," said Golescu, and stepped up on the platform with an eager expression.

The first thing he saw was a rack of costumes, bright with tinsel and marabou. He spent several minutes searching for anything elegant that might fit him, but the only ensemble in his size was a doublet and pair of trunk hose made of red velvet. Scowling, he pulled them out, and noticed the pointy-toed shoes of red leather, tied to the hanger by their laces. Here was a tag, on which was scrawled FAUST 1-2.

"The Devil, eh?" said Golescu. His eyes brightened as an idea began to come to him. He draped the red suit over his arm and looked further. This production of *Faust* had apparently employed a cast of lesser demons; there were three or four child-sized ensembles in black, leotards, tights and eared hoods. Golescu helped himself to the one least motheaten.

In a bin he located the red tights and skullcap that went with the Mephistopheles costume. Groping through less savory articles and papier-mâché masks, he found a lyre strung with yarn. He added it to his pile. Finally, he spotted a stage coffin, propped on its side between two flats of scenery. Giggling to himself, he pulled it out, loaded his purchases into it, and shoved the whole thing across the platform to the cashier.

"I'll take these, dear sir," he said.

By the time Golescu had carried the coffin back to his hotel room, whistling a cheery tune as he went, the Act had begun to glow in his mind. He laid out his several purchases and studied them. He tried on the Mephistopheles costume (it fit admirably, except for the pointy shoes, which were a little tight) and preened before the room's one shaving mirror, though he had to back all the way to the far wall to be able to see his full length in it.

"She can't object to this," he said aloud. "Such splendor! Such classical erudition! Why, it would play in Vienna! And even if she does object . . . you can persuade her, Golescu, you handsome fellow."

Pleased with himself, he ordered extravagantly when he went down to dinner. Over cucumber salad, flekken and wine he composed speeches of such elegance that he was misty eyed by the bottom of the second bottle. He rose at last, somewhat unsteady, and floated up the stairs from the dining room just as a party of men came in through the street door.

"In here! Sit down, poor fellow, you need a glass of brandy. Has the bleeding stopped?"

"Almost. Careful of my leg!"

"Did you kill them both?"

"We got one for certain. Three silver bullets, it took! The head's in the back of the wagon. You should have seen . . ."

Golescu heard no more, rounding the first turn of the stair at that point, and too intent on visions of the Act to pay attention in any case.

So confident was Golescu in his dream that he visited a printer's next day, and commissioned a stack of handbills. The results, cranked out while he loafed in a tavern across the street in the company of a bottle of slivovitz, were not as impressive as he'd hoped; but they were decorated with a great many exclamation points, and that cheered him.

The Act was all complete in his head by the time he left Kronstadt, just before dawn on the third day. Yawning mightily, he set down the coffin and his bag and pulled out his purse to settle with the tavern keeper.

"And a gratuity for your staff, kind sir," said Golescu, tossing down a handful of mixed brass and copper in small denominations. "The service was superb."

"May all the holy saints pray for you," said the tavern keeper, without enthusiasm. "Any forwarding address in case of messages?"

"Why, yes; if my friend the Archduke stops in, let him know that I've gone on to Paris," said Golescu. "I'm in show business, you know."

"In that case, may I hire a carriage for you?" inquired the tavern keeper. "One with golden wheels, perhaps?"

"I think not," Golescu replied. "I'm just walking on to Predeal. Meeting a friend with a private carriage, you know."

"Walking, are you?" The tavern keeper's sneer was replaced with a look of genuine interest. "You want to be careful, you know. They say there's a new monster roaming the countryside!"

"A monster? Really, my friend," Golescu waggled a reproving finger at him. "Would I ever have got where I am in life if I'd believed such stories?"

He shouldered the coffin once more, picked up his bag and walked out.

Though the morning was cool, he was sweating by the time he reached the outskirts of Kronstadt, and by the time he stepped off to the campsite track Golescu's airy mood had descended a little. Nonetheless, he grinned to see the wagons still there, the horses cropping placidly where they were tethered. He bellowed heartily as he pounded on Amaunet's door:

"Uncle Barbu's home, darlings!"

Not a sound.

"Hello?"

Perhaps a high thin whining noise?

"It's meeee," he said, trying the door. It wasn't locked. Setting down the coffin, he opened the door cautiously.

A strong, strong smell: spice and sweetness, and blood perhaps. Golescu pulled out a handkerchief and clapped it over his nose. He leaned forward, peering into the gloom within the wagon.

Amaunet lay stretched out on her bed, fully dressed. Her arms were crossed on her bosom, like a corpse's. Her skin was the color of ashes and her eyes were closed. She looked so radiantly happy that Golescu was unsure, at first, who lay there. He edged in sideways, bent to peer down at her.

"Madame?" He reached down to take her hand. It was ice-cold. "Oh!"

She just lay there, transfigured by her condition, beautiful at last.

Golescu staggered backward, and something fell from the bed. A cup rolled at his feet, a chalice cut of black stone. It appeared at first to be empty; but as it rolled, a slow black drop oozed forth to the lip.

"The Black Cup," stated Golescu, feeling the impact of a metaphorical cream pie. He blinked rapidly, overwhelmed by conflicting emotions. It was a moment before he was able to realize that the whining noise was coming from the cabinet under Amaunet's bed. Sighing, he bent and hauled Emil forth.

"Come out, poor little maggot," he said.

"I'm hungry," said Emil.

"Is that all you have to say?" Golescu demanded. "The Queen of Sorrow is dead, and you're concerned for a lousy potato?"

Emil said nothing in reply.

"Did she kill herself?"

"The cup killed her," Emil said.

"Poison in the cup, yes, I can see that, you ninny! I meant—*why?*"

"She wanted to die," said Emil. "She was too old, but she couldn't die. She said, 'Make me a poison to take my life away'. I mixed the cup every month, but it never worked. Then she said, 'What if you tried Theobromine?'. I tried it. It worked. She laughed."

Golescu stood there staring down at him a long moment, and finally collapsed backward onto a stool.

"Holy God, Holy mother of God," he murmured, with tears in his eyes. "It was true. She was an immortal thing."

"I'm hungry," Emil repeated.

"But how could anyone get tired of being alive? So many good things! Fresh bread with butter. Sleep. Making people believe you. Interesting possibilities," said Golescu. "She had good luck handed to her, how could she want to throw it away?"

"They don't have luck," said Emil.

"And what are *you*, exactly?" said Golescu, staring at him. "You, with all your magic potions? Hey, can you make the one that gives eternal life, too?"

"No," said Emil.

"You can't? You're sure?"

"Yes."

"But then, what do you know?" Golescu rubbed his chin. "You're an idiot. But then again . . ." He looked at Amaunet, whose fixed smile seemed more unsettling every time he saw it. "Maybe she did cut a deal with the Devil after all. Maybe eternal life isn't all it's cracked up to be, if she wanted so badly to be rid of it. What's that in her hand?"

Leaning forward, he opened her closed fist. Something black protruded there: the snout of a tiny figure, crudely sculpted in clay. A crocodile.

"I want a potato," said Emil.

Golescu shuddered.

"We have to dig a grave first," he said.

In the end he dug it himself, because Emil, when goggled and swathed against daylight, was incapable of using a shovel.

"Rest in peace, my fair unknown," grunted Golescu, crouching to lower Amaunet's shrouded body into the grave. "I'd have given you the coffin, but I have other uses for it, and the winding sheet's very flattering, really. Not that I suppose you care."

He stood up and removed his hat. Raising his eyes to heaven, he added: "Holy angels, if this poor creature really sold her soul to the Devil, then please pay no attention to my humble interruption. But if there were by chance any loopholes she might take advantage of to avoid damnation, I hope you guide her soul through them to eternal rest. And, by the way, I'm going to live a much more virtuous life from now on. Amen."

He replaced his hat, picked up the shovel once more and filled in the grave.

That night Golescu wept a little for Amaunet, or at least for lost opportunity, and he dreamed of her when he slept. By the time the sun rose pale through the smoke of Kronstadt's chimneys, though, he had begun to smile.

"I possess four fine horses and two wagons now," he told Emil, as he poked up the fire under the potato kettle. "Nothing to turn up one's nose at, eh? And I have you, you poor child of misfortune. Too long has your light been hidden from the world."

Emil just sat there, staring through his goggles at the kettle. Golescu smeared plum jam on a slab of bread and took an enormous bite.

"Bucharest," he said explosively, through a full mouth. "Constantinople, Vienna, Prague, Berlin. We will walk down streets of gold in all the great cities of the world! All the potatoes your tiny heart could wish for, served up on nice restaurant china. And for me . . ." Golescu swallowed. "The life I was meant to live. Fame and universal respect. Beautiful women. Financial embarrassment only a memory!

"We'll give the teeming masses what they desire, my friend. What scourges people through life, after all? Fear of old age. Fear of inadequacy. Loneliness and sterility, what terrible things! How well will people pay to be cured of them, eh? Ah, Emil, what a lot of work you have to do."

Emil turned his blank face.

"Work," he said.

"Yes," said Golescu, grinning at him. "With your pots and pans and chemicals, you genius. Chickens be damned! We will accomplish great things, you and I. Future generations will regard us as heroes. Like, er, the fellow who stole fire from heaven. Procrustes, that was his name.

"But I have every consideration for *your* modest and retiring nature. I will mercifully shield you from the limelight, and take the full force of public acclaim myself. For I shall now become . . ." Golescu dropped his voice an octave, "Professor Hades!"

It was on Market Day, a full week later, that the vardas rolled through Kronstadt. At the hour when the streets were most crowded, Golescu drove like a majestic snail. Those edged to the side of the road had plenty of time to regard the new paint job. The vardas were now decorated with suns, moons and stars, what perhaps might have been alchemical symbols, gold and scarlet on black, and the words:

PROFESSOR HADES
MASTER OF THE MISERIES

Some idle folk followed, and watched as Golescu drew the wagons up in a vacant field just outside the Merchants' Gate. They stared, but did not offer to help, as Golescu unhitched the horses and bustled about with planks and barrels, setting up a stage. They watched with interest as a policeman advanced on Golescu, but were disappointed when Golescu presented him with all necessary permits and a handsome bribe. He left, tipping his helmet; Golescu climbed into the lead wagon and shut the door. Nothing else of interest happened, so the idlers wandered away after a while.

But when school let out, children came to stare. By that time, scarlet curtains had been set up, masking the stage itself on three sides, and handbills had been tacked along the edge of the stage planking. A shopkeeper's son ventured close and bent to read.

"'FREE ENTERTAINMENT,'" he recited aloud, for the benefit of his friends. "Health and Potency can be Yours!! Professor Hades Knows All!!! See the Myrmidion Genius!!!!"

"'*Myrmidion?*'" said the schoolmaster's son.

"'Amazing Feats of Instant Calculation,'" continued the shopkeeper's son. "'Whether Rice, Peas, Beans, Millet or Barley, The Myrmidion Genius will Instantly Name the CORRECT Number in YOUR JAR. A Grand Prize will be Presented to Any Person who can Baffle the Myrmidion Genius!'"

"What's a Myrmidion?" wondered the blacksmith's son.

"What's a Feat of Instant Calculation?" wondered the barber's son. "Guessing the number of beans in a jar?"

"That's a cheat," said the policeman's son.

"No, it isn't!" a disembodied voice boomed from behind the curtain. "You will see, little boys. Run home and tell your friends about the free show, here, tonight. You'll see wonders, I promise you. Bring beans!"

The boys ran off, so eager to do the bidding of an unseen stranger that down in Hell the Devil smiled, and jotted down their names for future reference. Dutifully they spread the word. By the time they came trooping back at twilight, lugging jars and pots of beans, a great number of adults followed them. A crowd gathered before the wagons, expectant.

Torches were flaring at either side of the stage now, in a cold sweeping wind that made the stars flare too. The scarlet curtain flapped and swayed like the flames. As it moved, those closest to the stage glimpsed feet moving beneath, accompanied by a lot of grunting and thumping.

The barber cleared his throat and called, "Hey! We're freezing to death out here!"

"Then you shall be warmed!" cried a great voice, and the front curtain was flung aside. The wind promptly blew it back, but not before the crowd had glimpsed Golescu resplendent in his Mephistopheles costume. He caught the curtain again and stepped out in front of it. "Good people of Kronstadt, how lucky you are!"

There was some murmuring from the crowd. Golescu had applied makeup to give himself a sinister and mysterious appearance, or at least that had been his intention, but the result was that he looked rather like a fat raccoon in a red suit. Nevertheless, it could not be denied that he was frightening to behold.

"Professor Hades, at your service," he said, leering and twirling the ends of his moustache. "World traveler and delver-into of forbidden mysteries!"

"We brought the beans," shouted the barber's son.

"Good. Hear, now, the story of my remarkable—"

"What are you supposed to be, the Devil?" demanded someone in the audience.

"No indeed! Though you are surely wise enough to know that the Devil is not so black as he is painted, eh?" Golescu cried. "No, in fact I bring you happiness, my friends, and blessings for all mankind! Let me tell you how it was."

From under his cloak he drew the lyre, and pretended to twang its strings.

"It is true that in the days of my youth I studied the Dark Arts, at a curious school run by the famed Master Paracelsus. Imagine my horror, however, when I discovered that every seven years he offered up one of his seven students as a sacrifice to Hell! And I, I myself was seventh in my class! I therefore fled, as you would surely do. I used my great wealth to buy a ship, wherewith I meant to escape to Egypt, home of all the mysteries.

"Long I sailed, by devious routes, for I lived in terror that Master Paracelsus would discover my presence by arcane means. And so it happened that I grew desperately short of water, and was obliged to thread dangerous reefs and rocks to land on an island with a fair spring.

"Now, this was no ordinary island, friends! For on it was the holy shrine of the great Egyptian god Osiris, once guarded by the fierce race of ant-men, the Myrmidions!"

"Don't you mean the *Myrmidons?*" called the schoolmaster. "They were—"

"No, that was somebody else!" said Golescu. "These people I am talking about were terrors, understand? Giant, six-limbed men with fearsome jaws and superhuman strength, whom Osiris placed there to guard the secrets of his temple! Fangs dripping venom! Certain death for any who dared to set foot near the sacred precinct! All right?

"Fortunately for me, their race had almost completely died out over the thousands of years that had passed. In fact, as I approached the mysterious temple, who should feebly stagger forth to challenge me but the very last of the ant-men? And he himself such a degraded and degenerate specimen, that he was easily overcome by my least effort. In fact, as I stood there in the grandeur of the ancient moonlight, with my triumphant foot upon his neck, I found it in my heart to pity the poor defeated creature."

"Where do the beans come in?" called the policeman's son.

"I'm coming to that! Have patience, young sir. So I didn't kill him, which I might easily have done. Instead, I stepped over his pathetic form and entered the forbidden shrine of Osiris.

"Holding my lantern high, what should I see but a towering image of the fearsome god himself, but this was not the greatest wonder! No, on the walls of the shrine, floor to ceiling, wall to wall, were inscribed words! Yes, words in Ancient Egyptian, queer little pictures of birds and snakes and things. Fortunately I, with my great knowledge, was able to read them. Were they prayers? No. Were they ancient spells? No, good people. They were nothing more nor less than recipes for medicine! For, as you may know, Osiris was the Egyptians' principal god of healing. Here were the secret formulas to remedy every ill that might befall unhappy mankind!

"So, what did I do? I quickly pulled out my notebook and began to copy them down, intending to bring this blessing back for the good of all.

"Faster I wrote, and faster, but just as I had cast my eye on the last of the recipes—which, had I been able to copy it, would have banished the awful specter of Death himself—I heard an ominous rumbling. My lamp began to flicker. When I looked up, I beheld the idol of Osiris trembling on its very foundation. Unbeknownst to me, my unhallowed feet crossing the portal of the shrine had set off a dreadful curse. The shrine was about to destroy itself in a convulsive cataclysm!

"I fled, thoughtfully tucking my notebook into my pocket, and paused only to seize up the last of the Myrmidions where he lay groveling. With my great strength, I easily carried him to my ship, and cast off just before the shrine of Osiris collapsed upon itself, with a rumble like a hundred thousand milk wagons!

"And, not only that, the island itself broke into a hundred thousand pieces and sank forever beneath the engulfing waves!"

Golescu stepped back to gauge his effect on the audience. Satisfied that he had them enthralled, and delighted to see that more townfolk were hurrying to swell the crowd every minute, he twirled his moustache.

"And now, little children, you will find out about the beans. As we journeyed to a place of refuge, I turned my efforts to taming the last of the Myrmidions. With my superior education, it proved no difficulty. I discovered that, although he was weak and puny compared with his terrible ancestors, he nevertheless had kept some of the singular traits of the ant!

"Yes, especially their amazing ability to count beans and peas!"

"Wait a minute," shouted the schoolmaster. "Ants can't count."

"Dear sir, you're mistaken," said Golescu. "Who doesn't remember the story of

Cupid and Psyche, eh? Any educated man would remember that the princess was punished for her nosiness by being locked in a room with a huge pile of beans and millet, and was supposed to count them all, right? And who came to her assistance? Why, the ants! Because she'd been thoughtful and avoided stepping on an anthill or something. So the little creatures sorted and tided the whole stack for her, and counted them too. And that's in classical literature, my friend. Aristotle wrote about it, and who are we to dispute him?"

"But—" said the schoolmaster.

"And *now*," said Golescu, hurrying to the back of the platform and pushing forward the coffin, which had been nailed into a frame that stood it nearly upright, "Here he is! Feast your astonished eyes on—*the last of the Myrmidions*!"

With a flourish, he threw back the lid.

Emil, dressed in the black imp costume that had been modified with an extra pair of straw-stuffed arms, and in a black hood to which two long antenna of wire had been attached, looked into the glare of the lights. He screamed in terror.

"Er—yes!" Golescu slammed the lid, in the process trapping one of the antennae outside. "Though you can only see him in his natural state in, er, the briefest of glimpses, because—because, even though weak, he still has the power of setting things on fire with the power of his gaze! Fortunately, I have devised a way to protect you all. One moment, please."

As the crowd murmured, Golescu drew the curtain back across the stage. Those in the front row could see his feet moving to and fro for a moment. They heard a brief mysterious thumping and a faint cry. The curtain was opened again.

"*Now*," said Golescu. "Behold the last of the Myrmidions!"

He opened the lid once more. Emil, safely goggled, did not scream. After a moment of silence, various members of the audience began to snicker.

"Ah, you think he's weak? You think he looks harmless?" said Golescu, affecting an amused sneer. "Yet, consider his astonishing powers of calculation! You, boy, there." He lunged forward and caught the nearest youngster who was clutching a jar, and lifted him bodily to the stage. "Yes, you! Do you know—don't tell me, now!—do you know exactly how many beans are in your jar?"

"Yes," said the boy, blinking in the torchlight.

"Ah! Now tell me, good people, is this child one of your own?"

"That's my son!" cried the barber.

"Very good! Now, is there a policeman here?"

"I am," said the Captain of Police, stepping forward and grinning at Golescu in a fairly unpleasant way.

"Wonderful! Now, dear child, will you be so kind as to whisper to the good constable—whisper, I say—the correct number of beans in this jar?"

Obediently, the barber's son stepped to the edge of the planking and whispered into the Police Captain's ear.

"Excellent! And now, brave Policeman, will you be so good as to write down the number you have just been given?" said Golescu, sweating slightly.

"Delighted to," said the Police Captain, and pulling out a notebook he jotted it down. He winked at the audience, in a particularly cold and reptilian kind of way.

"Exquisite!" said Golescu. "And now, if you will permit—?" He took the jar of beans from the barber's son and held it up in the torchlight. Then he held it before Emil's face. "Oh, last of the Myrmidions! Behold this jar! *How many beans?*"

"Five hundred and six," said Emil, faint but clear in the breathless silence.

"*How many?*"

"Five hundred and six."

"And, sir, what is the figure you have written down?" demanded Golescu, whirling about to face the Police Captain.

"Five hundred and six," the Police Captain responded, narrowing his eyes.

"And so it is!" said Golescu, thrusting the jar back into the hands of the barber's son and more or less booting him off the stage. "Let's have more proof! Who's got another jar?"

Now a half dozen jars were held up, and children cried shrilly to be the next on stage. Grunting with effort, Golescu hoisted another boy to the platform.

"And you are?" he said.

"That's *my* son!" said the Police Captain.

"Good! How many beans? Tell your papa!" cried Golescu, and as the boy was whispering in his father's ear, "Please write it down!"

He seized the jar from the boy and once more held it before Emil. "Oh last of the Myrmidions, *how many beans?*"

"Three hundred seventeen," said Emil.

"Are you certain? It's a much bigger jar!"

"Three hundred seventeen," said Emil.

"And the number you just wrote down, dear sir?"

"Three hundred seventeen," admitted the Police Captain.

"I hid an onion in the middle," said his son proudly, and was promptly cuffed by the Police Captain when Golescu had dropped him back into the crowd.

Now grown men began to push through the crowd, waving jars of varied legumes as well as barley and millet. Emil guessed correctly on each try, even the jar of rice that contained a pair of wadded socks! At last Golescu, beaming, held up his hands.

"So, you have seen one proof of my adventure with your own eyes," he cried. "But this has been a mere parlor entertainment, gentle audience. Now, you will be truly amazed! For we come to the true purpose of my visit here. *Behold the Gifts of Osiris!*"

He whisked a piece of sacking from the stacked boxes it had concealed. The necks of many medicine bottles winked in the torchlight.

"Yes! Compounded by me, according to the ancient secret formulas! Here, my friends, are remedies to cure human misery! A crown a bottle doesn't even cover the cost of its rare ingredients—I'm offering them to you practically as a charity!"

A flat silence fell at that, and then the Police Captain could be heard distinctly saying, "I thought it would come to this."

"A crown a bottle?" said somebody else, sounding outraged.

"You require persuasion," said Golescu. "*Free* persuasion. Very good! You, sir, step up here into the light. Yes, you, the one who doesn't want to part with his money."

The man in question climbed up on the planks and stood there looking defiant, as Golescu addressed the audience.

"Human misery!" he shouted. "What causes it, good people? Age. Inadequacy. Inability. Loneliness. All that does not kill you, but makes life not worth living! Isn't it so? Now you, good sir!" He turned to the man beside him. "Remove your hat, if you please. I see you suffer from baldness!"

The man turned red and looked as though he'd like to punch Golescu, but the audience laughed.

"Don't be ashamed!" Golescu told him. "How'd you like a full growth of luxurious hair, eh?"

"Well—"

"Behold," said Golescu, drawing a bottle from the stack. "The Potion of Ptolemy! See its amazing results."

He uncorked the bottle and tilted it carefully, so as to spill only a few drops on the man's scalp. Having done this, he grabbed the tail of his cloak and spread the potion around on the man's scalp.

"What are you doing to me?" cried the man. "It burns like Hell!"

"Courage! Nothing is got without a little pain. Count to sixty, now!"

The audience obliged, but long before they had got to forty they broke off in exclamations: for thick black hair had begun to grow on the man's scalp, everywhere the potion had been spread.

"Oh!" The man clutched his scalp, unbelieving.

"Yes!" said Golescu, turning to the audience. "You see? Immediately, this lucky fellow is restored to his previous appearance of youth and virility. And speaking of virility!" He smacked the man's back hard enough to send him flying off the platform. "What greater source of misery can there be than disappointing the fair ones? Who among you lacks that certain something he had as a young buck, eh?

"Nobody here, I'm sure, but just think: someday, you *may* find yourself attempting to pick a lock with a dead fish. When that day comes, do you truly want to be caught without a bracing bottle of the Pharaoh's Physic? One crown a bottle, gentlemen! I'm sure you can understand why no free demonstrations are available for this one."

There was a silence of perhaps five seconds before a veritable tidal wave of men rushed forward, waving fistfuls of coin.

"Here! One to a customer, sirs, one only. That's right! I only do this as a public service, you know, I love to make others happy. Drink it in good health, sir, but I'd suggest you eat your oysters first. Pray don't trample the children, there, even if you can always make more. And speaking of making more!" Golescu stuffed the last clutch of coins down his tights and retreated from the front of the stage, for he had sold all his bottles of Pharaoh's Physic and Potion of Ptolemy.

"What's the use of magnificent potency when your maiden is cold as ice, I ask you? Disinterest! Disdain! Diffidence! Is there any more terrible source of misery than the unloving spouse? Now, you may have heard of love philtres; you may have bought charms and spells from mere gypsies. But what your little doves require, my friends, is none other than the *Elixir of Isis*! Guaranteed to turn those chilly frowns to smiles of welcome!"

A second surge made its way to the front of the platform, slightly less desperate than the first but moneyed withal. Golescu doled out bottles of Elixir of Isis, dropped coins down his tights, and calculated. He had one case of bottles left. Lifting it to the top of the stack, he faced his audience and smiled.

"And now, good people, ask yourselves a question: what is it that makes long life a curse? Why, the answer is transparent: it is *pain*. Rending, searing, horrible agony! Dull aches that never go away! The throb of a rotten tooth! Misery, misery, misery, God have mercy on us! But! With a liberal application of Balm Bast, you will gain instant relief from unspeakable torment."

There was a general movement toward the stage, though not such a flood as Golescu had expected; some distraction was in the crowd, though he couldn't tell what it was. Ah! Surely, this was it: an injured man, with bandaged head and eye, was being helped forward on his crutches.

"Give way! Let this poor devil through!"

"Here, Professor Hades, here's one who could use your medicine!"

"What about a free sample for *him?*"

"What's this, a veteran of the wars?" said Golescu, in his most jovial voice. "Certainly he'll get a free sample! Here, for yo—" He ended on a high-pitched little squeak, for on leaning down he found himself gazing straight into Farmer Buzdugan's single remaining eye. Mutual recognition flashed.

"Yo—" began Farmer Buzdugan, but Golescu had uncorked the bottle and shoved it into his mouth quick as thought. He held the bottle there, as Buzdugan choked on indignation and Balm Bast.

"*Ah, yes, I recognize this poor fellow*!" said Golescu, struggling to keep the bottle in place. "He's delusional as well! His family brought him to me to be cured of his madness, but unfortunately—"

Unfortunately the distraction in the crowd was on a larger scale than Golescu had supposed. It had started with a general restlessness, owing to the fact that all those who had purchased bottles of Pharaoh's Physic had opened the bottles and gulped their contents straight down. This had produced general and widespread priapism, at about the time Golescu had begun his spiel on the Elixir of Isis.

This was as nothing, however, to what was experienced by those who had purchased the Potion of Ptolemy and, most unwisely, decided to try it out before waiting to get it home. Several horrified individuals were now finding luxuriant hair growing, not only on their scalps but everywhere the potion had splashed or trickled in the course of its application, such as ears, eyelids, noses and wives. More appalled still were those who had elected to rub the potion well in with their bare hands.

Their case was as nothing, however, compared to the unfortunate who had decided that all medicines worked better if taken internally. He was now prostrate and shrieking, if somewhat muffledly, as a crowd of horrified onlookers stood well back from him.

Buzdugan threw himself back and managed to spit out the bottle.

"Son of a whore!" he said. "This is him! This is the one who sold us the—"

"*Mad, what did I tell you*?" said Golescu.

"He sold us the stuff that created those—" Buzdugan said, before the Balm Bast worked and he abruptly lost all feeling in his body. Nerveless he fell from his crutches into the dark forest of feet and legs.

But he was scarcely noticed in the excitement caused by the man who had purchased both Pharaoh's Physic and Elixir of Isis, with the intention of maximizing domestic felicity, and in the darkness had opened and drunk off the contents of the wrong bottle. Overcome by a wave of heat, and then inexplicable and untoward passion, and then by a complete loss of higher cerebral function; he had dropped his trousers and was now offering himself to all comers, screaming like a chimpanzee. Several of those afflicted by the Pharaoh's Potion, unable to resist, were on the very point of availing themselves of his charms when—

"Holy saints defend us!" cried someone on the edge of the crowd. "Run for your lives! *It's another demon cock!*"

This confused all who heard it, understandably, but only until the demon in question strode into sight.

Golescu, who had been edging to the back of the platform with tiny little steps, smiling and sweating, saw it most clearly: a rooster, but no ordinary bird. Eight feet tall at the shoulder, tail like a fountain of fire, golden spurs, feathers like beaten gold, comb like blood-red coral, and a beak like a meat cleaver made of brass! Its eyes shone in the light of the torches with ferocious brilliance, but they were blank and mindless as any chicken's. It beat its wings with a sound like thunder. People fled in all directions, save those who were so crazed with lust they could not be distracted from what they were doing.

"Oh why, oh why do these things happen?" Golescu implored no one in particular. "I have *such* good intentions."

The great bird noticed the children crowded together at the front of the platform. Up until this point, they had been giggling at the behavior of their elders. Having caught sight of the monster, however, they dove under the platform and huddled there like so many mice. The bird saw them nonetheless, and advanced, turning its head to regard them with one eye and then the other. Terrified, they hurled jars of beans at it, which exploded like canisters of shot. Yet it came on, raking the ground as it came.

And Golescu became aware that there was another dreadful noise below the cries of the children, below Buzdugan's frenzied cursing where he lay, below the ever more distant yells of the retreating audience. Below, for it was low-pitched, the sort of noise that makes the teeth vibrate, deep as an earthquake, no less frightening.

Something, somewhere, was growling. And it was getting louder.

Golescu raised his head, and in a moment that would return to him in nightmares the rest of his life saw a pair of glowing eyes advancing through the night, eyes like coals above white, white teeth. The nearer they came, floating through the darkness toward the wagon, the louder grew the sound of growling. Nearer now, into the light of the torches, and Golescu saw clearly the outstretched arms, the clawing fingers caked with earth, the murderous expression, the trailing shroud.

"Good heavens, it's Amaunet," he observed, before reality hit him and he wet himself. The Black Cup had failed her again after all, and so—

"*Rrrrrrrkillyou!*" she roared, lunging for the platform. Golescu, sobbing, ran to and fro only a moment; then fear lent him wings and he made one heroic leap, launching himself from the platform to the back of the chicken of gold. Digging his knees in its fiery plumage, he smote it as though it were a horse.

With a squawk that shattered the night, his steed leaped in the air and came down running. Golescu clung for dear life, looking over his shoulder. He beheld Emil, antennae wobbling, scrambling frantically from the coffin.

"Uncle Barbu!" wailed Emil. But Amaunet had Emil by the ankle now. She pulled him close. He vanished into the folds of her shroud, still struggling. Golescu's last glimpse was of Amaunet lifting Emil into her bosom, clutching him possessively, horrific Madonna and limp Child.

Golescu hugged the neck of his golden steed and urged it on, on through the night and the forest. He wept for lost love, wept for sour misfortune, wept for beauty, and so he rode in terrible glory through water and fire and pitiless starlight. When bright day came he was riding still. Who knows where he ended up?

Though there is a remote village beyond the forests, so mazed about with bogs and streams no roads lead there, and every man has been obliged to marry his cousin. They have a legend that the Devil once appeared to them, riding on a golden cock, a fearful apparition before which they threw themselves flat. They offered to make him their prince, if only he would spare their lives.

And they say that the Devil stayed with them a while, and made a tolerably good prince, as princes go in that part of the world. But he looked always over his shoulder, for fear that his wife might be pursuing him. He said she was the Mother of Darkness. His terror was so great that at last it got the better of him and he rode on, rather than let her catch him.

The men of the village found this comforting, in an obscure kind of way. *Even the Devil fears his wife,* they said to one another. They said it so often that a man came from the Ministry of Culture at last, and wrote it down in a book of proverbs.

But if you travel to that country and look in that great book, you will look in vain; for unfortunately some vandal has torn out the relevant page.

synthetic serendipity

VERNOR VINGE

Here's a look at a computer-dominated, high-tech, high-bit-rate future that may be coming along a lot *sooner* than you think that it could, making members of older generations obsolete and unable to compete in society with the tech-savvy Whiz Kids surrounding them. Even in this wired-up future, though, Boys Will Still Be Boys—unfortunately.

Born in Waukesha, Wisconsin, Vernor Vinge now lives in San Diego, California, where he is an associate professor of math sciences at San Diego State University. He sold his first story, "Apartness," to *New Worlds* in 1965; it immediately attracted a good deal of attention, was picked up for Donald A. Wollheim and Terry Carr's collaborative *World's Best Science Fiction* anthology the following year, and still strikes me as one of the strongest stories of that entire period. Since this impressive debut, he has become a frequent contributor to *Analog*; he has also sold to *Orbit, Far Frontiers, If, Stellar*, and other markets. His novella "True Names," which is famous in Internet circles and among computer enthusiasts well outside of the usual limits of the genre, and is cited by some as having been the *real* progenitor of cyberpunk rather than William Gibson's *Neuromancer*, was a finalist for both the Nebula and Hugo awards in 1981. His novel *A Fire Upon the Deep*, one of the most epic and sweeping of modern Space Operas, won him a Hugo Award in 1993; its sequel, *A Deepness in the Sky*, won him another Hugo Award in 2000. The last two years have seen him win two more Hugos, in two consecutive years—for his novella "Fast Times at Fairmont High" in 2003, and his novella "The Cookie Monster" in 2004 . . . and these days Vinge is regarded as one of the best of the American "hard science" writers, along with people such as Greg Bear and Gregory Benford. His other books include the novels *Tatia Grimm's World, The Witling, The Peace War* and *Marooned in Realtime* (which have been released in an omnibus volume as *Across Realtime*), and the collections *True Names and Other Dangers* and *Threats and Other Promises.* His most recent book is the massive collection *The Collected Stories of Vernor Vinge.*

Years ago, games and movies were for indoors, for couch potatoes and kids with overtrained trigger fingers. Now they were on the outside. They were the world. That was the main reason Miguel Villas liked to walk to school with the Radner twins. Fred and Jerry were a Bad influence, but they were the best gamers Mike knew in person.

"We got a new scam, Mike," said Fred.

"Yeah," said Jerry, smiling the way he did when something extreme was in the works.

The three followed the usual path along the flood control channel. The trough was dry and gray, winding its way through the canyon behind Las Mesitas subdivision. The hills above them were covered with iceplant and manzanita; ahead, there was a patch of scrub oaks. What do you expect of San Diego north county in early May?

At least in the real world.

The canyon was not a deadzone. Not at all. County Flood Control kept the whole area improved, and the public layer was just as fine as on city streets. As they walked along, Mike gave a shrug and a twitch just so. That was enough cue for his Epiphany wearable. Its overlay imaging shifted into classic manga/animé: The manzanita branches morphed into scaly tentacles. Now the houses that edged the canyon were heavily timbered, with pennants flying. High ahead was a castle, the home of Grand Duke Hwa Feen—in fact, the local kid who did the most to maintain this belief circle. Mike tricked out the twins in Manga costume, and spikey hair, and classic big-eyed, small-mouthed features.

"Hey, Jerry, look." Mike radiated, and waited for the twins to slide into consensus with his view. He'd been practicing all week to get these visuals.

Fred looked up, accepting the imagery that Mike had conjured.

"Thats old stuff, Miguel, my man." He glanced at the castle on the hill. "Besides, Howie Fein is a nitwit."

"Oh." Mike released the vision in an untidy cascade. The real world took back its own, first the sky, then the landscape, then the creatures and costumes. "But you liked it last week." Back when, Mike now remembered, Fred and Jerry had been maneuvering to oust the Grand Duke.

The twins looked at each other. Mike could tell they were silent messaging. "We told you today would be different. We're onto something special." They were partway through the scrub oaks now. From here you could see ocean haze; on a clear day—or if you bought into clear vision—you could see all the way to the ocean. On the south were more subdivisions, and a patch of green that was Fairmont High School. On the north was the most interesting place in Mike Villas' neighborhood:

Pyramid Hill Park dominated the little valley that surrounded it. Once upon a time the hill had been an avocado orchard. You could still see it that way if you used the park's logo view. To the naked eye, there were other kinds of trees. There were also lawns, and real mansions, and a looping structure that flew a parabolic arc hundreds of feet above the top of the hill. That was the longest freefall ride in California.

The twins were grinning at him. Jerry waved at the hill. "How would you like to play *Cretaceous Returns*, but with real feeling?"

Pyramid Hill had free entrances, but they were just for visuals.

"That's too expensive."

"Sure it is. If you pay."

"And, um, don't you have a project to set up before class?" The twins had shop class first thing in the morning.

"That's still in Vancouver," said Jerry.

"But don't worry about us." Fred looked upward, somehow prayerful and smug at the same time. " 'FedEx will provide, and just in time.' "

"Well, okay. Just so we don't get into trouble." Getting into trouble was the major downside of hanging with the Radners.

"Don't worry about it." The three left the edge of the flood channel and climbed a narrow trail along the east edge of Pyramid Hill. This was far from any entrance, but the twins' uncle worked for County Flood Control and they had access to CFC utilities—which just now they shared with Mike. The dirt beneath their feet became faintly translucent. Fifteen feet down, Mike could see graphics representing a ten-inch runoff tunnel. Here and there were pointers to local maintenance records. Jerry and Fred had used the CFC view before and not been caught. Today they blended it with a map of the local nodes. The overlay was faintly violet against the sunlit day, showing comm shadows and active high-rate links.

The two stopped at the edge of a clearing. Fred looked at Jerry. "Tsk. Flood Control should be ashamed. There's not a localizer node within thirty feet."

"Yeah, Jer. Almost anything could happen here." Without a complete localizer mesh, nodes could not know precisely where they were. High-rate laser comm could not be established, and low-rate sensor output was smeared across the landscape. The outside world knew only mushy vagueness about this area.

They walked into the clearing. They were deep in comm shade, but from here they had a naked-eye view up the hillside. If they continued that way, Pyramid Hill would start charging them.

The twins were not looking at the Hill. Jerry walked to a small tree and squinted up. "See? They tried to patch the coverage with an airball." He pointed into the branches and pinged. The utility view showed only a faint return, an error message. "It's almost purely net guano at this point."

Mike shrugged. "The gap will be fixed by tonight." Around twilight, when maintenance UAVs flitted like bats around the canyons, popping out nodes here and there.

"Heh. Well, why don't we help the County by patching things right now?" Jerry held up a thumb-sized greenish object. He handed it to Mike.

Three antenna fins sprouted from the top, a typical ad hoc node.

The dead ones were more trouble than bird poop. "You've perv'd this thing?" The node had Breakins-R-Us written all over it, but perverting networks was harder in real life than in games. "Where did you get the access codes?"

"Uncle Don gets careless." Jerry pointed at the device. "All the permissions are loaded. Unfortunately, the bottleneck node is still alive." He pointed upwards, into the sapling's branches. "You're small enough to climb this, Mike. Just go up and knock down the node."

"Hmm."

"Hey, don't worry. Homeland Security won't notice."

In fact, the Department of Homeland Security would almost certainly notice, at least after the localizer mesh was patched. But just as certainly they wouldn't care. DHS logic was deeply embedded in all hardware. "See All, Know All," was their motto, but what they knew and saw was for their own mission. They were notorious for not sharing with law enforcement. Mike stepped out of the comm shade and took a look at the crime trackers view. The area around Pyramid Hill had its share of arrests, mostly for enhancement drugs . . . but there had been nothing hereabouts for months.

"Okay." Mike came back to the tree and shinnied up to where the branches spread out. The old node was hanging from rotted velcro. He knocked it loose and the twins caused it to have an accident with a rock. Mike scrambled down and hey watched the diagnostics for a moment. Violet mists sharpened into bright spots as the nodes figured out where they and their perv'd sibling were, and coordinated up toward full function. Now point-to-point, laser routing was available; they could see the property labels all along the boundary of Pyramid Hill.

"Ha," said Fred. The twins started uphill, past the property line. "C'mon, Mike. We're marked as county employees. We'll be fine if we don't stay too long."

Pyramid Hill had all the latest touchie-feelie effects. These were not just phantoms painted by your contact lenses on the back of your eyeballs. On Pyramid Hill, there were games where you could kick lizard butt and steal raptor eggs—or games with warm furry creatures that danced playfully around, begging to be picked up and cuddled. If you turned off all the game views, you could see other players wandering through the woods in their own worlds. Somehow the Hill kept them from crashing into each other.

In *Cretaceous Returns* the plants were towering gingko trees, with lots of barriers and hidey holes. Mike played the purely visual *Cret Ret* a lot these days, in person with the twins and all over the world with others. It had not been an uplifting experience. He had been "killed and eaten" three times so far this week. It was a tough game, one where you had to contribute or maybe you got eaten. Mike was trying. He had designed a species—quick, small things that didn't attract the fiercest of the critics. The twins had not been impressed, though they had no alternatives of their own.

As he walked through the gingko forest, he kept his eye out for critters with jaws lurking in the lower branches. That's what had gotten him on Monday. On Tuesday it had been some kind of paleo disease.

So far things seemed safe enough, but there was no sign of his own contribution. They had been fast breeding and scalable, so where were the little monsters? Maybe someone had exported them. They might be big in Kazakhstan. He had had success there before. Here today . . . nada.

Mike stumped across the Hill, a little discouraged, but still uneaten. The twins had taken the form of game-standard velociraptors.

They were having a grand time. Their chicken-sized prey were Pyramid Hill haptics.

The Jerry-raptor looked over its shoulder at Mike. "Where's your critter?"

Mike had not assumed any animal form. "I'm a time traveler," he said. That was a valid type, introduced with the initial game release.

Fred flashed a face full of teeth. "I mean where are the critters you invented last week?"

"I don't know."

"Most likely they got eaten by the critics," said Jerry. The brothers did a joint reptilian chortle. "Give up on making creator points, Miguel. Kick back and use the good stuff." He illustrated with a soccer kick that connected with something running fast across their path. That got some classic points and a few thrilling moments of haptic carnage. Fred joined in and red splattered everywhere.

There was something familiar about this prey. It was young and clever looking . . . a newborn from Mike's own design! And that meant its Mommy would be nearby. Mike said, "You know, I don't think—"

"The Problem Is, None Of You Think Nearly Enough." The sound was like sticking your head inside an old-time boom box. Too late, they saw that the tree trunks behind them grew from yard-long claws.

Mommy. Drool fell in ten-inch blobs from high above.

This was Mike's design scaled to the max.

"Sh—" said Fred. It was his last hiss as a velociraptor. The head and teeth behind the slobber descended from the gingko canopy and swallowed Fred down to the tips of his hind talons. The monster crunched and munched for a moment. The clearing was filled with the sound of splintering bones.

"Ahh!" the monster opened its mouth and vomited horror. It was scarey good. Mike flicker-viewed on reality: Fred was standing in the steaming remains of his raptor. His shirt was pulled out of his pants, and he was drenched in slime—real, smelly slime. The kind you paid money for.

The monster itself was one of Hill's largest robots, tricked out as a member of Mike's new species.

The three of them looked up into its jaws.

"Was that touchie-feelie enough for you?" the creature said, its breath a hot breeze of rotting meat. Fred stepped backwards and almost slipped on the goo.

"The late Fred Radner just lost a cartload of points,"—the monster waved its truck-sized snout at them—"and I'm still hungry. I suggest you move off the Hill with all dispatch."

They backed away, their gaze still caught on all those teeth.

The twins turned and ran. As usual, Mike was an instant behind him.

Something like a big hand grabbed him. "You, I have further business with." The words were a burred roar through clenched fangs. "Sit down."

Jeez. I have the worst luck. Then he remembered that it was Mike Villas who had climbed a tree to perv the Hill entrance logic.

Stupid Mike Villas didn't need bad luck; he was already the perfect chump. And now the twins were out of sight.

But when the "jaws" set him down and he turned around, the monster was still there—not some Pyramid Hill rentacop. Maybe this really was a *Cret Ret* player! He edged sideways, trying to get out from under the pendulous gaze. This was just a game. He could walk away from this four-storey saurian. Of course, that would trash his credit with *Cretaceous Returns*, maybe drench him in smelly goo. And if Big Lizard took things seriously, it might cause him trouble in other games. *Okay*. He sat down with his back against the nearest gingko. So he would be late another day; that couldn't make his school situation any worse.

The saurian settled back, pushing the steaming corpse of Fred Radner's raptor to one side. It brought its head close to the ground, to look at Mike straight on. The eyes and head and color were exactly Mike's design, and this player had the moves to make it truly impressive. He could see from its scars that it had fought in several *Cretaceous* hotspots.

Mike forced a cheerful smile. "So, you like my design?"

It picked at its teeth with eight-inch foreclaws. "I've been worse." It shifted game parameters, bringing up critic-layer details.

This was a heavy player, maybe even a cracker! On the ground between them was a dead and dissected example of Mike's creation. Big Lizard nudged it with a foreclaw. "The skin texture is pure Goldman. Your color scheme is a trivial emergent thing, a generic cliché."

Mike drew his knees in toward his chin. This was the same crap he had to put up with at school. "I borrow from the best."

The saurian's chuckle was a buzzing roar. "That might work with your teachers. They have to eat whatever garbage you feed them—till you graduate and can be dumped on the street. Your design is so-so. There have been some adoptions, mainly because it scales well. But if we're talking real quality, you just don't measure up." The creature flexed its battle scars.

"I can do other things."

"Yes, and if you never deliver, you'll fail with them, too."

That was a point that occupied far too much of Mike Villas' worry time. He glared back at the slitted yellow eyes, and suddenly it occurred to him that—unlike teachers—this guy was not being paid to be nasty. And it was wasting too much time for this to be some humiliating joke. *It actually wants something, from me!* Mike sharpened his glare. "And you have some suggestions, Oh Mighty Virtual Lizard?"

"Maybe. I have other projects besides *Cret Ret*. How would you like to take an affiliate status on one of them?"

Except for local games, no one had ever asked Mike to affiliate on anything. His mouth twisted in bogus contempt. "Affiliate? A percent of a percent of . . . what? How far down the value chain are you?"

The saurian shrugged and there was the sound of gingkos swaying to the thump of its shoulders. "My guess is I'm way, way down. On the other hand, this is not a dredge project. I can pay real money for each answer I pipe upwards." The creature named a number; it was enough to play the Hill once a week for a year. A payoff certificate floated in the air between them.

"I get twice that or no deal."

"Done!" said the creature, and somehow Mike was sure it was grinning.

"Okay, so what do you want?"

"You go to Fairmont High, right?"

"Yeah."

"It's a strange place, isn't it?" When Mike did not reply, the critter said, "Trust me, it is strange. Most schools don't put Adult Education students in with the children."

"Yeah, Senior High. The old farts don't like it. We don't like it."

"Well, the affiliate task is to snoop around, mainly among the old people. Make friends with them."

Yecch. But Mike glanced at the payoff certificate again. It tested valid. The payoff adjudication was more complicated than he wanted to read, but it was backed by eBay. "Who in particular?"

"So far, my upstream affiliate has only told me its broad interests: basically, some of these senior citizens used to be bigshots."

"If they were so big, how come they're in our classes now?" It was just the question the kids asked at school.

"Lots of reasons, Miguel. Some of them are just lonely. Some of them are up to their ears in debt, and have to figure how to make a living in the current economy. And some of them have lost half their marbles and aren't good for much but a strong body and lots of old memories. . . . Ever hear of Pick's Syndrome?"

"Um," Mike googled up the definition: serious social dysfunction. "How do I make friends with someone like that?"

"If you want the money, you figure out a way. Don't worry. There's only one on the list, and he's in remission. Anyway, here are the search criteria." The Big Lizard shipped him a document. Mike browsed through the top layer.

"This covers a lot of ground." Retired politicians, military officers, bioscientists, parents of persons currently in such job categories. "Um, this really could be deep water. We might be setting people up for blackmail."

"Heh. I wondered if you'd notice that."

"I'm not an idiot."

"If it gets too deep, you can always bail."

"I'll take the job. I'll go affiliate with you."

"I wouldn't want you doing anything you feel un—"

"I *said*, I'll *take* the job!"

"Okay! Well then, this should get you started. There's contact information in the document." The creature lumbered to its feet, and its voice came from high above. "Just as well we don't meet on Pyramid Hill again."

"Suits me." Mike made a point of slapping the creature's mighty tail as he walked off down hill.

The twins were way ahead of him, standing by the soccer field on the far side of campus. As Mike came up the driveway, he grabbed a viewpoint in the bleachers and gave them a ping. Fred waved back, but his shirt was still too gooey for real comm. Jerry was looking upwards, at the FedEx shipment falling toward his outstretched hands. Just in time, for sure. The twins were popping the mailer open even as they walked indoors.

Unfortunately, Mike's first class was in the far wing. He ran across the lawn, keeping his vision tied to unimproved reality: The buildings were mostly three storeys today. Their gray walls were like playing cards balanced in a rickety array.

Indoors, the choice of view was not entirely his own. Mornings, the school administration required that the Fairmont School News appear all over the interior walls. Three kids at Hoover High had won IBM fellowships. Applause, applause, even if Hoover was Fairmont's unfairly advantaged rival, a charter school run by the Math Department at SDSU. The three young geniuses would have their college education paid for, right through grad school, even if they never worked at IBM.

Big deal, Mike thought. Somewhere down the line, some percentage of their fortunes would be siphoned sideways into IBM's treasury.

He followed the little green nav arrows with half his attention . . . and abruptly realized he had climbed two flights of stairs. School admin had rearranged everything since yesterday. Of course, they had updated his nav arrows, too. It was a good thing he hadn't been paying attention.

He slipped into his classroom and sat down.

Ms. Chumlig had already started.

Search and Analysis was Chumlig's thing. She used to teach a fast-track version of this at Hoover High, but well-documented rumor held that she just couldn't keep up. So the Department of Education had moved her to the same-named course here at Fairmont. Actually, Mike kind of liked her. She was a failure, too.

"There are many different skills," she was saying. "Sometimes it's best to coordinate with lots of other people." The students nodded. Be a coordinator. That's where the fame and money were. But they also knew where Chumlig was going with this. She looked around the classroom, nodding that she knew they knew. "Alas, you all intend to be top agents, don't you?"

"It's what some of us will be." That was one of the Aduit Ed students. Ralston Blount was old enough to be Mike's great-grandfather. When Blount had a bad day he liked to liven things up by harassing Ms. Chumlig.

The Search and Analysis instructor smiled back. "The pure 'coordinating agent' is a rare type, Professor Blount."

"Some of us must be the administrators."

"Yes." Chumlig looked kind of sad for a moment, like she was figuring out how to pass on bad news. "Administration has changed a lot, Professor Blount."

Ralston Blount shrugged. "Okay. So we have to learn some new tricks."

"Yes." Ms. Chumlig looked out over the class. "That's my point. In this class, we study search and analysis. Searching may seem simple, but the analysis involves understanding results. In the end, you've got to know something about something."

"Meaning all those courses we got Cs in, right?" That was a voice from the peanut gallery, probably someone who was physically truant.

Chumlig sighed. "Yes. Don't let those skills die. Use them. Improve on them. You can do it with a special form of preanalysis that I call 'study'."

One of the students held up a hand. She was that old.

"Yes, Dr. Xu?"

"I know you're correct. But—" The woman glanced around the room. She looked about Chumlig's age, not nearly as old as Ralston Blount. But there was kind of a frightened look in her eyes. "But some people are just better at this sort of thing than others. I'm not as sharp as I once was. Or maybe others are just sharper. . . . What happens if we try our hardest, and it just isn't good enough?"

Chumlig hesitated. "That's a problem that affects everyone, Dr. Xu. Providence gives each of us our hand to play. In your case, you've got a new deal and a new start on life." Her look took in the rest of the class. "Some of you think your hand in life is all deuces and treys." There were some really dedicated kids in the front rows. They were wearing, but they had no clothes sense and had never learned ensemble coding. As Chumlig spoke, you could see their fingers tapping, searching on "deuces" and "treys."

"But I have a theory of life," said Chumlig. "and it is straight out of gaming: *There is always an angle*. You, each of you, have some special talents. Find out what makes you different and better. Build on that. And once you do, you'll be able to contribute answers to others and they'll be willing to contribute back to you. In short, synthetic serendipity doesn't just happen. *You* must create it."

She hesitated, staring at invisible class notes, and her voice dropped down from oratory. "So much for the big picture. Today, we'll learn about morphing answer board results. As usual, we're looking to ask the right questions."

Miguel like to sit by the outer wall, especially when the classroom was on an upper floor. You could feel a regular swaying back and forth, the limit cycle of the walls keeping their balance. It made his mom real nervous. "One second of system failure and everything will fall apart!" she had complained at a PTA meeting. On the other hand, house-of-cards construction was cheap—and it could handle a big earthquake almost as easy as it did the morning breeze.

He leaned away from the wall and listened to Chumlig. That was why the school made you show up in person for most classes; you had to pay a little bit of attention just because you were trapped in a real room with a real instructor. Chumlig's lecture graphics floated in the air above them. She had the class's attention; there was a minimum of insolent graffiti nibbling at the edges of her imaging.

And for a while, Mike paid attention, too. Answer boards could generate solid results, usually for zero cost. There was no affiliation, just kindred minds batting problems around. But what if you weren't a kindred mind? Say you were on a genetics board. If you didn't know a ribosome from a rippereme, then all the modern interfaces couldn't help you.

So Mike tuned her out and wandered from viewpoint to viewpoint around the room. Some were from students who'd set their viewpoints public. Most were just random cams. He browsed Big Lizard's task document as he paused between hops. In fact, the Lizard was interested in more than just the old farts. Some ordinary students made the list, too. This affiliation tree must be as deep as the California Lottery.

But kids are somebody's children. He started some background checks. Like most students, Mike kept lots of stuff saved on his wearable. He could run a search like this very close to his vest. He didn't route to the outside world except when he could use a site that Chumlig was talking about. She was real good at nailing the mentally truant. But Mike was good at ensemble coding, driving his wearable with little gesture cues and eye-pointer menus. As her gaze passed over him, he nodded brightly and he replayed the last few seconds of her talk.

As for the old students . . . competent retreads would never be here; they'd be rich and famous, the people who owned most of the real world. The ones in Adult

Education were the hasbeens. These people trickled into Fairmont all through the semester. The oldfolks' hospitals refused to batch them up for the beginning of classes. They claimed that senior citizens were "socially mature," able to handle the jumble of a midsemester entrance.

Mike went from face to face, matching against public records: Ralston Blount. The guy was a saggy mess. Retread medicine was such a crapshoot. Some things it could cure, others it couldn't. And what worked was different from person to person. Ralston had not been a total winner.

Just now the old guy was squinting in concentration, trying to follow Chumlig's answer-board example. He had been with the class most of the semester. Mike couldn't see his med records, but he guessed the guy's mind was mostly okay; he was as sharp as some of the kids in class. And once-upon-a-time he had been important at UCSD.

Once-upon-a-time.

Okay, put him on the "of interest" list. Who else? Doris Nguyen. Former homemaker. Mike eyed the youngish face. She looked almost his mom's age, even though she was forty-years older. He searched on the name, shed collisions and obvious myths; the Friends of Privacy piled the lies so deep that sometimes it was hard to find the truth. But Doris Nguyen had no special connections in her past. On the other hand . . . she had a son at Camp Pendleton. Okay, Doris stayed on the list.

Chumlig was still going on about how to morph results into new questions, oblivious to Mike's truancy.

And then there was Xiaowen Xu. PhD physics, PhD electrical engineering. 2005 Winner of Intel's Grove Prize. Dr. Xu sat hunched over, looking at the table in front of her. She was trying to keep up on a *laptop*! Poor lady. But for sure she would have connections.

Politicians, military, scientists . . . and parents or children of such. Yeah. This affiliance could get him into a lot of trouble. Maybe he could climb the affiliate tree a ways, get a hint if Bad Guys were involved. Mike sent out a couple hundred queries, mainly pounding on certificate authorities. Even if the certs were solid, people and programs often used them in stupid ways. Answers came trickling back.

If this weren't Friends of Privacy chaff, there might be some real clues here. He sent out followup queries—and suddenly a message hung in letters of silent flame all across his vision:

Chumlig → Villas:_You've got all day to play games, Miguel! If you won't pay attention here, you can darn well take this course *over*.

Villas → Chumlig: *Sorry. Sorry*! Most times, Chumlig just asked embarrassing questions; this was the first she'd messaged him with a threat.

And the amazing thing was, she'd done it in a short pause, where everyone else thought she was just reading her notes. Mike eyed her with new respect.

Shop class. It was Mike Villas' favorite class, and not just because it was his last of the day. Shop was like a premium game; there were real gadgets to touch and connect. That was the sort of thing you paid money for on Pyramid Hill. And Mr. Williams was no Louise Chumlig. He let you follow your own inclinations, but he never came around afterwards and complained because you hadn't accomplished anything. It was almost impossible not to get an A in Ron Williams' classes; he was wonderfully old-fashioned.

Shop class was also Mike's best opportunity to chat up the old people and the do-not-call privacy freaks. He wandered around the shop class looking like an utter idiot. This affiliance required way too much people skill. Mike had never been any good at diplomacy games.

And now he was schmoozing the oldsters. Trying to.

Ralston Blount just sat staring off into the space above his table. The guy was wearing, but he didn't respond to messages. Mike waited until Williams went off for one of his coffee breaks. Then he sidled over and sat beside Blount. Jeez, the guy might be healthy but he really *looked* old. Mike spent a few moments trying to tune in on the man's perceptions. Mike had noticed that when Blount didn't like a class, he just blew it off. He didn't care about grades. After a few moments, Mike realized that he didn't care about socializing either.

So talk to him! It's just another kind of monster whacking.

Mike morphed a buffoon image onto the guy, and suddenly it wasn't so hard to cold start the encounter. "So, Professor Blount, how do you like shop class?"

Ancient eyes turned to look at him. "I couldn't care less, Mr. Villas."

O-*kay*! Hmm. There was lots about Ralston Blount that was public record, even some legacy newsgroup correspondence. That was always good for shaking up your parents and other grownups . . .

But the old man continued talking on his own. "I'm not like some people here. I've never been senile. By rights, my career should be on track with the best of my generation."

"By rights?"

"I was Provost of Eighth College in 2006. I should have been UCSD Chancellor in the years following. Instead I was pushed into academic retirement."

Mike knew all that. "But you never learned to wear."

Blount's eyes narrowed. "I made it a point never to wear. I thought wearing was demeaning, like an executive doing his own typing." He shrugged. "I was wrong. I paid a heavy price for that. But things have changed." His eyes glittered with deliberate iridescence.

"I've taken four semesters of this 'Adult Education.' Now my resumé is out there in the ether."

"You must know a lot of important people."

"Indeed. It's just a matter of time."

"Y-you know, Professor, I may be able to help. No wait—I don't mean by myself. I have an affiliance."

"Oh?"

At least he knew what affiliance was. Mike explained Big Lizard's deal. "So there could be some real money in this."

Blount squinted his eyes, trying to parse the certificates. "Money isn't everything, especially in my situation."

"But anybody with these certs is important. Maybe you could get help-in-kind."

"True."

The old man wasn't ready to bite, but he said he'd talk to some of the others on Mike's list. Helping them with their projects counted as a small plus in the affiliance. Maybe the Lizard thought that would flush out more connections.

Meantime, it was getting noisy. Marie Dorsey's team had designed some kind of crawler. Their prototypes were flopping around everwhere.

They got so close you couldn't really talk out loud.

Villas→ Blount: *Can you read me*?

"Of course I can," replied the old man.

So despite Blount's claims of withittude, maybe he couldn't manage silent messaging, not even the finger-tapping most grownups used.

Xiaowen Xu just sat at the equipment bench and read from her laptop. It took even more courage to talk to her than Ralston Blount.

She seemed so sad and still. She had the parts list formatted like a hardcopy catalog. "Once I knew about these things," she said. "See that." She pointed at a picture in the museum section. "I designed that chip."

"You're world class, Dr. Xu."

She didn't look up. "That was a long time ago. I retired from Intel in 2005. And during the war, I couldn't even get consulting jobs. My skills have just rusted away."

"Alzheimer's?" He knew she was *much* older than she looked, even older than Ralston Blount.

Xu hesitated, and for a moment Mike was afraid she was really angry. But then she gave a sad little laugh. "No Alzheimer's. You—people nowadays don't know what it was like to be old."

"I do so! I have a great grandpa in Phoenix. G'granma, she does have dementia—you know, a kind they still can't fix. And the others are all dead." Which was about as old as you can get.

Dr. Xu shook her head. "Even in my day, not everyone over eighty was senile. I just got behind in my skills. My girlfriend died. After a while I just didn't care very much. I didn't have the energy to care." She looked at her laptop. "Now, I have the energy I had when I was sixty. Maybe I have the same native intelligence." She slapped the table softly. "But I can't even understand a current tech paper." It looked like she was going to start crying, right in the middle of shop class. Mike scanned around; no one seemed to be watching. He reached out to touch Xu's hand. He didn't have the answer. Ms. Chumlig would say he didn't have the right question.

He thought a moment. "What's your shop project going to be?"

"I don't know." She hesitated. "I don't even understand this parts catalog."

Mike waved at her laptop, but the images sat still as carved stone. "Can I show you what I see?"

"Please."

He slaved her display to his vision of the parts list. The view weaved and dived, a bad approximation to what Mike could see when he looked around with his headup view. Nevertheless, Xu leaned forward and nodded as Mike tried to explain the list.

"Wait. Those look like little wings."

"Yeah, there are lots of small fliers. They can be fun."

She gave a wan smile. "They don't look very stable."

Mike had noticed that, but not in the view she could see. *How did she know?* "That's true, but hardly anything is passively stable. I could take care of that, if you want to match a power supply."

She studied the stupid display. "Ah, I see." The power supplies were visible there, along with obvious pointers to interface manuals.

"You really could manage the stability?" Another smile, broader this time. "Okay, let's try."

The wings were just tissue flappers. Mike slid a few dozen onto the table top, and started some simulations using the usual stuff from ReynoldsNumbers-R-Us. Xiaowen Xu alternated between querying her laptop and poking her small fingers into the still tinier wings.

Somehow, with virtually no help from anywhere, she had a power train figured out. In a few more minutes, they had five design possibilities. Mike showed her how to program the fab board so that they could try a couple dozen variations all at once.

They tossed handsful of the tiny contraptions into the air. They swirled around the room—and in seconds, all were on the floor, failing in one way or another.

From the far end of the table, Marie Dorsey and her friends were not impressed. "We're making fliers, too, only ours won't be brain damaged!" Huh? And he'd thought she was making crawlers!

Dr. Xu looked at the Dorsey team's floppers. "I don't think you've got enough power, Miss."

Marie blushed. "I—yeah." Her group was silent, but there was heavy messaging. "Can we use your solution?" She rushed on: "With official credit, of course."

"Sure."

Marie's gadgets were making small hops by the time the class bell rang.

End of class, end of school day. But Xiaowen Xu didn't seem to notice. She and Mike collected their midges and merged improvements.

Three generations later, all their tiny flappers were flying. Xu was smiling from ear to ear.

"So now we put mininodes on them," said Mike. "You did pretty well with the power configuration." Without any online computation at all.

"Yeah!" She gave him a strange look. "But you got the stability in less than an hour. It would have taken me days to set up the simulations."

"It's easy with the right tools."

She looked disbelieving.

"Hey, I'm near failing at bonehead math. Look Dr. Xu, if you learn to search and use the right packages, you could do all this." He was beginning to sound like Chumlig. *And this fits with the affiliance*! "I-I could show you. There are all sorts of joint projects we could do!" Maybe she would always be one of those deep resource people, but if she found her place, that would be more than he could ever be.

He wasn't sure if Dr. Xu really understood what all he was talking about. But she was smiling. "Okay."

Mike was late walking home, but that was okay. Ralston Blount had signed onto the affiliance. He was working with Doris Nguyen on her project. Xiaowen Xu had also signed on. She was living at Rainbow's End rest home, but she had plenty of money. She could buy the best beginner's wearable that Epiphany made.

Big Lizard would be pleased, and maybe some money would come Mike's way.

And maybe that didn't matter so much. He suddenly realized he was whistling as he walked. What did matter . . . was a wonderful surprise. He had coordinated something today. *He* had been the person who helped other people. It was nothing like being a real top agent—but it was something.

The Radner twins were almost home, but they showed up to chat.

"You've been scarce, Mike." They were both grinning. "Hey, we got an A from Williams!"

"For the Vancouver project?"

"Yup. He didn't even check where we got it," said Jerry.

"He didn't even ask us to explain it. *That* would have been a problem!" said Fred.

They walked a bit in companionable silence.

"The hole we put in the Pyramid Hill fence is already repaired."

"No surprise. I don't think we should try that again anytime soon."

"Yeah," Fred said emphatically. His image wavered. The slime was still messing his clothes.

Jerry continued, "And we collected some interesting gossip about Chumlig." The students maintained their own files on faculty. Mostly it was good for laughs. Sometimes it had more practical uses.

"What's that?"

"Okay, this is from Ron Williams. He says he got it firsthand, no possibility of Friends of Privacy lies." That's how most FoP lies were prefaced, but Mike just nodded.

"Ms. Chumlig was never fired from Hoover High. She's moonlighting there. Maybe other places, too."

"Oh. Do the school boards know?" Ms. Chumlig was such a straight arrow, it was hard to imagine she was cheating.

"We don't know. Yet. We can't figure why Hoover would let this happen. You know those IBM Fellows they were bragging about? All three were in Chumlig's classes! But she kinda drifted out of sight when the publicity hit. Our theory is there's some scandal that keeps her from taking credit . . . Mike?"

Mike had stopped in the middle of the path. He shrugged up his record of this morning, and matched Big Lizard's English usage with Chumlig's.

He looked back at the twins. "Sorry. You . . . surprised me."

"It surprised us too. Anyway, we figure this could be useful if Jerry and I have serious grade problems in her class."

"Yeah, I guess it could," said Mike, but he wasn't really paying attention anymore. It suddenly occurred to him that there could be something beyond top agents. There could be people who helped others on a time scale of years. Something called teachers.

skin deep

MARY ROSENBLUM

One of the most popular and prolific of the new writers of the nineties, Mary Rosenblum made her first sale, to *Asimov's Science Fiction*, in 1990, and has since become a mainstay of that magazine, and one of its most frequent contributors, with almost thirty sales there to her credit. She has also sold to *The Magazine of Fantasy & Science Fiction, Science Fiction Age, Pulphouse, New Legends*, and elsewhere.

Rosenblum produced some of the most colorful, exciting, and emotionally powerful stories of the nineties, earning her a large and devoted following of readers. Her linked series of "Drylands" stories have proved to be one of *Asimov's* most popular series, but she has also published memorable stories such as "The Stone Garden," "Synthesis," "Flight," "California Dreamer," "Casting At Pegasus," "Entrada," "Rat," "The Centaur Garden," "Skin Deep," "Songs the Sirens Sing," and many, many others. Her novella "Gas Fish" won the *Asimov's* Readers Award Poll in 1996, and was a Finalist for that year's Nebula Award. Her first novel, *The Drylands*, appeared in 1993 to wide critical acclaim, winning the prestigious Compton Crook Award for Best First Novel of the year; it was followed in short order by her second novel, *Chimera*, and her third, *The Stone Garden*. Her first short-story collection, *Synthesis and Other Stories*, was widely hailed by critics as one of the best collections of 1996. Her most recent books are a trilogy of mystery novels written under the name Mary Freeman, and she is at now at work at more science fiction novels. A graduate of Clarion West, Mary Rosenblum lives in Portland, Oregon.

In the moving story that follows, she shows us that although beauty may be skin deep, once you get below the surface, you may find quite a bit *more* that you weren't expecting to find . . .

I never thought they'd be looking for me when the media crew came through the restaurant door. I didn't even look up from the pot-sink. I mean, why should I? The crowded little floor out there, with its fifteen tables, was the hot new review in the *Times* these days, so there was always somebody with a name out there. I was never sure if it was Antonio's pricey wild-harvest-only menu, or if it was just that there were so few tables. It was a bad night anyway. The new salad girl was trying hard not to look at my face when she had to come back to my station. And Presidio and the crew kept sending her back here. It was kind of an initiation thing. I never got the joke. It wasn't like I didn't already know what any woman's reaction was, looking at me.

So I was up to my elbows in saffron-colored dishwater and paella pans when all of a sudden there's light and more noise and bodies than usual in the crowded barely legal little kitchen. And I turn around, dripping greasy yellow suds, and there's this woman with a mic and a couple of walking-camera guys all rigged out in the relay-goggles, getting the "human eye" view. And the woman is pointing the mic at me and babbling something in a loud, bright, talking-head voice. Something about technology and Doctor somebody, and how do I feel?

I feel like crap. I don't own a mirror, not even to shave. I don't need one. Any time I want to see my face, I just have to look at somebody. I get a nice clear reflection of the minimum rebuild work that National Health did on me. Not pretty. Be glad you never ran into me on a dark night. And I'm used to it; I mean, I can't even remember what I looked like before the fire, but . . . well, I guess it still bugs me. And I'm looking at the camera goggles and thinking I won't even be able to surf the news streams for at least twenty-four hours.

"So, Eric, tell us how you feel about having a normal face again! Are you excited? Has Doctor Olson-Bernard given you an idea of how long it will take?"

Olson-Bernard. The news-head's words finally make it through the fog. He's the dude over at the University Hospital. I filled out the usual forms for some kind of new artificial skin graft—an experimental cloning thing, or something. And there were thirty other people there, too, and a couple were as bad as me, and I guess I just put it out of my head. I've applied for this kind of thing before, but they always tell me that the damage went too deep and you just can't rebuild. But I still go.

"Doctor . . ." I say and I know I sound like it wasn't just my face that got cooked.

The news-head turns with a bright, perfect Euro phenotype smile to the cameras' eyes and starts this spew about the doctor and poor, pitiful me, and how the good doctor is going to give me back my life and all that. I stop hearing her, because there's this hum in my ears and I can feel the pressure of all the eyes, Rinco, Hairy, Spider, and all these guys who look at me every night, but now they're staring like they never saw me before, and the chefs, too, even Domino, the one who groped me that once, and the waitresses, and even a couple of customers looking over their shoulders from the dining room.

"So how do you feel?" News-head jabs her mic at me like it's a police prod.

"I . . . wouldn't know."

She is disappointed.

Antonio finally tells me, kind of testy, to just go home so he can get back to serving dinner. Which is okay with me, because my face feels hard as plastic from all the stares. I tell Presidio, loudly, that I'm going to take a leak, then hop the service elevator to the back entrance and out into the alley, just in case the media's still hanging around. It's raining and the lights are bleeding red and green and yellow into the puddles, and everybody has umbrellas or hats pulled down low, and the taxis and bicycle rickshaws are all over the place, and the cold New York–smelling rain softens my plastic face as I head for the train. I don't even get a second glance from the bored security behind the scanners as I reach the platform, and the car is almost empty for once.

In my walk-up, my online is shimmering with my "urgent mail" screen—a storm hammering the Hawaiian coast, all gray waves, foam, and shredding palm trees. It's daturk, I bet, and sure enough, when I sit down in front and touch in, her words start scrolling across the screen doubletime.

ure all over the newstreams sweetie guess its a slow week, and miniature fireworks explode on the screen, which is daturk laughing. Then she runs a chunk of stream at me, and before I can blank it, I get to see myself backed up against the pot sink, looking about as cornered as an alley dog. I haven't looked at my face for a long time and the camera light or the angle makes it look bigger than real, flat and a glossy sickly white, like melting candle wax, with stubs for ears, no hair, holes where the nose ought to be, and a twisted grimace. I feel every bite of the chicken curry that Antonio fed the staff tonight.

ges that bigtime doc gonna fix your face good as new.

There's a pause and my screen shows me swirling gray clouds above a mirror-still lake, which is daturk being thoughtful.

he's for real i checked go for it

And daturk is gone leaving a scatter of pink blossoms that drift across the dark screen and settle like snow at the bottom. I don't know what the hell that means and I blank my screen, pissed because I need to be pissed more than that I'm really mad at daturk, who is a major presence on the web and an info broker. I'm guessing, and not a real legal one at that. But the urgent mail screen comes right back up, so I guess it wasn't daturk at all, and it wasn't. It's a formal letter from the hospital where I did the interview, and I have to do a retina scan before I can read it.

In that careful, cover your butt, hard-to-read crap that the legal guys use, the letter tells me that I have been selected to be a participant . . . and all that stuff. There's a taxi password for a free ride, and I'm directed to download a key. I stick a mini CD into the drive and the key burns in. Nine AM, the letter tells me. Show up at the hospital lobby.

It's for real.

I'm . . . scared.

And that's silly, because what the hell have I got to lose? There are a bunch more pages and I'm supposed to retina each one after I read it. They're full of words and numbers and paragraphs I've seen before that mean "you can't sue me" and I snap a retina on each of them without reading a word and send it back. Then I touch up a couple of daturk's links, but she doesn't answer, so maybe she picked up that I was pissed or maybe she's doing whatever she does. It's early, but I don't feel like downloading a book, so I call up some music from one of the fringe sites and listen to somebody mixing oud and clarinet and a hot rhythm section with a Latin flavor, no less. It's not great, but it's better than dodging the newstreams on the web.

The password lets me take one of the sleek new auto cabs, so I don't have to put up with a rickshaw driver looking at me in his mirror, and at the hospital door, I drop the CD in the tray and my retina lets me right through the security lock. Soon as the inner door closes behind me, a yellow arrow lights up on the black matte floor at my feet. Follow the yellow brick road, okay, I'm game. It takes me down a wide hallway, past other zombies shuffling along with their eyes on their own arrows, purple, or green, or blue. Darts, finally, under a wide door made out of some kind of wood-looking material that doesn't feel like wood when I lay my palm on it.

Funny. That's one of the few things I remember from before . . . sitting with this old guy as he carved at this piece of wood. And he hands it to me, and I feel it like silk, all warm and somehow . . . alive. It was curvy, I guess, but all I remember is his smile, hair like tufts of white cotton, and that wood like felt like an animal's flank beneath my hand. Or a woman's maybe. I wouldn't know.

"Mr. Halsey." The receptionist who buzzed me in smiles, and she's good because it barely falters. Or maybe she sees a lot like me. "You got our letter. The doctor is with a patient, would you take a seat?"

Doctors are always with a patient when you show up, but her voice is warm, and that little flinch I got when I first came in has gone away and I can almost feel her smile. So I smile back . . . I can sort of do that . . . and pick up one of the nice handhelds racked by the comfy chairs. It offers a bunch of magazines, some stories by Name authors and even a couple of quick thrillers, heavy on the graphics. Not your National Health selection. I touch through them, but the Names I've read and the thrillers don't thrill me. About the time I touch it off, the door opens and the doctor comes out. He's not the one who interviewed me. This guy is tall, so that I have to look up when I get to my feet. He's pretty much your average Euro mongrel type, brown hair, long face, ho hum nose. I always notice faces. Funny. And he doesn't flinch. He smiles. And he *looks* at me. *Really* looks. People don't do that. Their glances skid off my face like leather soles on ice. Meanwhile he's shaking my hand, and before I can turn the thinking part of my brain back on, we're in his office, which is all carpet and grasspaper on the walls, and a real wood desk about as big as my bed. I want to run my hands over it and I don't.

"You got my letter." His smile broadens just a hair. "You're a fast reader."

I shrug. "It could turn out worse?"

Now he shrugs. *My* letter. No doctorial "our" for him. He gets points for that.

"Are you willing to undergo the procedure? You understand that it's still experimental, and although we've repaired more localized damage that is similar in depth of cellular destruction, we haven't actually . . ." He falters for the merest instant.

"Fixed anyone like me," I offer. Helpfully. Belligerently. Okay, I'll admit it.

"Yes." And his eyes are on me, and they're grave, not offended by my petty snap. I feel suddenly . . . small.

"I'm sorry." I look down. Something I don't do much anymore. "Whatever you want to do, *do*." And I am . . . yes, afraid. I hate the feeling. Flinch as the doc puts his hand on my shoulder, want to slap him off.

When was the last time somebody did that? Put his hand on me for no reason? Well, Domino, but that wasn't for no reason and Domino isn't picky.

"Let me show you something." He nods toward the desk top. It has a holoprojector set into the top and a bright blur materializes above it, coalescing slowly into a human head. It's a kid with a bright smile, the kind you see kids give when Mom or Dad points the camera. He has wispy brown hair and blue eyes and a really cute face, and I'm looking and this hand closes around my insides and squeezes, and all of a sudden I can't breathe anymore.

Because it's *me*. I know it, and I don't know why I know it, but I do.

He's . . . pretty. Way off in the distance, I feel the doc's fingers squeezing my shoulder and hear him telling me to sit down, and something bumps the back of my knees and I sort of fall onto a seat, but I can't take my eyes off that kid's face.

"Children's Services had a photo in their file. I've used a modeling program to age that original to the present." The doc squeezes my shoulder again, and the boy's face starts to change and I want to yell stop, but nothing works, so I just sit there frozen and watch him get older. He face lengthens and firms up and his hair goes from wispy to a contemporary buzz and the program even adds a diamond stud to one ear lobe. And his eyes change, too. Oh, they're still a blue that's almost gray, but the expression changes from that happy-kid smile to a look that seems . . . sad. And I wonder if the programmer meant to do that, or if I'm just reading stuff into it that isn't really there. But that's just a trickle of thought, because most of me is . . . numb.

That's how I would look?

"It's going to work." His voice is low, gentle, and his hand is still on my shoulder. "I can't give you proof, because you're the first case where the damage is this extensive, but I *know* it. If I didn't know for sure, I would never have asked you."

He means it. Oh, God, I hear it in his voice, and that face in front of me is so damn beautiful . . . I'm going to start shaking, or crying, or just explode, burst into a scatter of dust in a minute, and it's as if he knows, because he gives my shoulder a final squeeze and steps back. "You'll check into the hospital tomorrow," he tells me. "We've already contacted your employer and he's giving you the time off, with a job return guarantee."

"How . . ." I swallow, try again. "How can you . . . add all that." All the face that isn't there . . . the ears, nose, lips, eyebrows that I see in that holo.

"We're using cloned and modified cell strains," he says. "Using our computer model of how you should look, we'll build a scaffold, layer by layer. That's a three dimensional structure built of microthin layers of a complex mix of biodegradable polyesters loaded with the right enzymes and hormones that trigger cell growth. The scaffold dissolves as the cells grow. We do this kind of thing already, in a big Petrie dish, to make sheets of graft skin . . . you know about that. But in a three-D scaffold, created in place, the cells differentiate to form the appropriate type of tissues and they form in place. No surgery. No implanting. Your face will simply . . . grow back."

I hear passion in his voice and it helps. It cracks some of this numbness that coats me like ice. He *believes* in this. Like it's God, and he's almost touched it.

He turns that look on me, and for once, I don't see my real face in his eyes. I see that face in the holo. And his belief is hot as summer sun.

"I will see you tomorrow," he tells me. "And we'll get started."

I leave. Fast. Go outside, onto concrete and turn left. Start walking. I walk, and it's all concrete with buildings and people and I don't really see any of it. If anybody looked at my face, I missed it. But after awhile, the city looks pretty much normal again, new and old, fancy and cheap, all layered on top of each other, and some woman with fancy braids does a bad double-take and nearly falls off the curb. I figure out where I am, catch the subway, and go back to the walk-up. I figure I'll download a book, a new one by one of those hot Arab writers, you know, one of those guys that grew up in the forever war zone and knows things that I sure hope I don't ever have to learn, and they're not popular because they mostly don't like anyone who's not Arab, but sometimes, you know, all that anger and hatred makes me jealous. They have someone to hate.

Me, I just have a why-did-this-happen wreck, mom and kid, gas tank catches fire . . . Act of God? Maybe if I believed in a God I could hate him. Or her. Why am I *thinking* this tonight?

Because I'm scared. And I don't know why. Because what I told the doc was true, what have I got to lose? But I feel like I'm standing on this cliff, and once I jump off, I can't ever get back here. I don't download the book after all. It's Support Night. The reminder pops up on my screen. It's this weekly thing I have to do to keep my Disability. Proves I'm working on living with my face. That I'm not planning on gunning down tourists in Times Square. I have to go. So I do.

It's almost as good as taking drugs. We all sit around in cheap plastic chairs, and various people get up to share their bad week, rude fast-foodie, nasty in-laws, un-loving lover, and we all make supportive noises. There's a core that's really into this, emoting and swaying like they're worshiping this god of disfigurement, and I bet they could get an Oscar. The rest of us . . . we're just there. But there's one kid I really like. Kitten. That's what she calls herself. She's about fourteen, got caught in a gang firebomb thing, isn't as bad as me, but hey, she's a girl, and it's got to feel worse. She remembers when she was beautiful.

I don't. Didn't. Not before today.

We say hi. Her eyes are lavender and she always says she worries about me, and I think sometimes that she means it.

After, I go home and check to see if daturk is around. She isn't, but there's a screen full of rose petals sprinkled over trampled plants with thorns. I don't know. Ask her.

I show up at the hospital and my key still works. This time, the arrow is orange and it leads me to this desk where a chunky North African type hurries me off to a private waiting room with one chair and a sofa. About ten minutes later, this guy in blue scrubs comes in, doesn't look at me, but smiles so hard I worry about his mouth muscles as he hurries me through the labyrinth of corridors, through doors that swing ominously open into air locks ceilinged with the soft lavender glow of microbe killing ultra-UV. He leaves me in a plastic-walled cubicle, hands me the usual disposable hospital open-back, and tells me to strip. A nurse shows up—a she this time—who doesn't look at me either, but at least doesn't smile. She whacks my inner arm with a sprayjector and tells me it'll be just a little while. It's a heavy sedative. I start to buckle about thirty seconds after she leaves. Then there's a gurney, kids in green who also don't look at me, and before they've pushed me five minutes, the ceiling tiles are swimming across my field of vision. I don't think I'm going to be there when they plug me into the anesthesia machine.

I want to be there.

I'm staring at white and someone is moaning, and I can feel someone wiping my mouth with something rough and scratchy and I can feel my drool, and I realize—sort of—that it's me moaning, only I can't access that *me* to stop it.

I wake up slowly, clutching at this really cool dream of a big field with flowers in it, and I'm walking and just . . . feeling good. It's a long dream. Too long, I think blurrily. I was talking to daturk, but I can't remember what she was saying. She likes flowers. Time to go to work soon. Hope I'm not late . . . I try to scratch my nose and my arm won't work.

I wake up for real, adrenalin pumping through me because I can't move, all I can see is white light, and *where the hell am I?* And I hear hurrying footsteps, the white light is a ceiling, and I remember where I am.

Hospital. Strapped down. Tubes. My face is bandaged. It's so damn familiar.

The nurse or aide or whatever babbles at me, but I don't listen. Just wait. There's nothing to do but wait.

I'm still sort of drifting in and out when the doc comes in, but it's pretty soon, and he says something sharp to the nurse at the door, and then he's leaning over so I can see his face, and that hand grabs my guts again because he's smiling and his eyes are bright.

It worked.

"You're coming along just fine." He steps aside as two nurses in green scrubs, masks, and gloves move in to bustle around, unplugging drip lines and catheter, doing this and that, the things they do. Finally one reaches for my face and I clench up, because I still remember the pain way back then when they changed the dressings and none of the drugs really stopped it.

But there's no pain, not really, just a little prickly discomfort, and they're not bandages on my face, but more like a gauze mask the shape of a face. The air feels icy cold on my skin, and it's real tender. I think I can feel air molecules bumping against it.

"Can I see?" The words come out a croak, and my throat is raw, so they must have had a tube down me.

The doc hesitates. "It's not finished," he says slowly. "You have to understand that the process of growing many layers of tissue doesn't happen in a few hours. This is just a break to let the new cellular grown stabilize and give you some time to regain a bit of muscle tone before the final session. You have an epidermal layer, but it's temporary. We still have a ways to go."

One of the nurses holds a straw to my lips, I suck automatically and the taste of the bottled apples on my tongue brings back all the memories of the first time, but it's sweet and soothes my raw throat. "I want to see," I say when I've finished, and I sit up.

Well, I try to.

The room twirls around me and my stomach heaves and next thing I know hands are laying me back on the bed again and I'm clammy and cold and shaking.

"Take it slow," the doctor says, frowning at the bank of monitors next to my bed. Nothing is beeping anyway. I learned a long time ago that's a good sign. "You're going to have to get used to moving again. Don't forget, you've been out for ten days."

"Ten days?"

"It was in that document I sent you." He raises an eyebrow at me, satisfied with whatever the monitors are telling him. "The one you read and retina-stamped? The first session is the longest. The second will finish up the regeneration, and then there will be only a few plastic modifications."

I wonder what else I didn't read? No wonder the dream seemed to go on so long. And I'm gathering the strength to ask again, but he sticks a hand mirror in front of my face, a cheap import thing with a plastic rim and handle, like you might see in any dollar store in the neighborhood, and I look.

I know it's not done, but disappointment still stabs me right in the gut. But I make myself look. It's a lot better. I've got ears now, sort of. And a nose. My face looks like . . . well, a face anyway. Not very pretty, but you won't scream and faint if I run into you in a dark alley. No hair anywhere and the skin is real pink, like I've got sunburn or something. I let my breath out in a long sigh, trying to breathe all that disappointment out with it, because if he quit now, I'd still be a whole lot better off.

I don't want him to quit.

"I want to give you a week to recover." Doc is looking at me thoughtfully. "You should be able to be released by tomorrow morning." He hesitates and he's frowning a little. "Do you have somebody staying with you? Somebody who can look after you while you get your strength back?"

I shake my head and I could swear that he relaxes a bit.

"Tell you what." He smiles. "Why don't you be my guest? I've got plenty of room in my condo. That way I can keep a first-hand eye on my handiwork. And the building is secure, so we can keep the media from bothering you."

I start to say no, and it's so automatic that it stops me and I swallow it. Why am I so quick? I study him for a minute, but I can't put my finger on anything. He's no Domino. I'm pretty sure of that. Maybe it's just that . . . nobody *does* that. Just offers. No strings. He's waiting, and I can see that he's getting a little impatient, maybe offended because I didn't jump at his offer. What the hell?

"I'm . . . sorry." I don't have to pretend to be confused because I am. "That's really . . . that's nice of you." I'm groping for the words I'm supposed to say, but hey, I've never really been in this situation before. "Thank you," I finally say, feeling like a boob. But he smiles, his eyes happy.

"That's fine then. You rest, and I'll come by to get you when I get ready to leave. I shouldn't be here too late." He looks at the nurse now, and I watch all the warmth vanish from his face. He gives her some instructions and I guess I'm supposed to go walk around later, but not too much, and there's some med codes, too.

He goes off and she goes off, but comes back in a little bit to bring me a cup full of pills and a lunch tray with hospital blah on it, Jell-O that looks like green plastic, some of that fake chicken soup, custard. It hasn't changed since I was here the first time, and that was twenty years ago, when I was four. The first taste of custard brings it all back and I lay the spoon back on the tray and lean back, hoping that one of those pills is going to make me sleep. Without dreams.

But it doesn't. So I pull the bedside screen over and get online, and as soon as I get there, I get a screen full of bright flowers, like someone dropped about six bunches from a downtown flower stall on the floor. Bright red script written in a pointed slanty hand spells out the words, *how u doin—sweet so far*. It's daturk's online handwriting. I recognize it, wonder if she's good enough that she's really been hacking my med records or if she's just guessing. I trace the words *Doing sweet. Not done yet* on the screen, watch the words take shape in black shaky script. It's an effort to write that much and I want to let my hand fall. But I make the effort, and trace a few more letters: *Doc invited me to stay with him. I said yes.* And I'm not sure why I told her that, but all of a sudden it seems real important to know what she thinks about it. And it's pointless to stare at the screen, because she may not get back to me for days. But right away, a crimson line starts to curve to life on the screen. I wait expectantly, but there are no words, just a fiery question mark glowing among all the spilled flowers and scattered petals.

I shrug, and I don't know why it bothers me. But I write "it's okay" on the screen and then I really do have to lie flat for a minute or two. And when the ceiling stops moving and I look back up at the screen, all the writing is gone. There are just the flowers, scattered all over.

I kind of feel comforted and I'm not sure why. I guess because daturk seems to be able to get in anywhere, so I guess sometimes I've sort of pretended that she's always there. Just checking in, you know? So I don't worry about it anymore, I'll see what happens when I go home with the doc. I can always catch a cab back to the walk-up if I have to.

So I pull down a new book, some guy who walked across Canada, and it's okay, but the author's trying too hard, and the nurse is happy when I sit up, and even happier when I wobble down the hall and back without her nagging me too much. Hey, I know the drill. I spent a lot of time here, learned that if you do what they ask and don't bug them, they're nice to you, and if you're a pain, they get even, sooner or later.

And about the time they bring in another meal tray that's loaded with food that carries way too much baggage from the past, the doc shows up again. This time, he's not wearing the white doctor suit, just a classic jacket and shirt, no tie, no virus mask, every bit the doc, but smiling and relaxed, like we're old friends meeting for a golf game or something. And the nurse brings me a release to sign and retina and a wheelchair, because they never let you walk out of the building, guess they're afraid you'll sue if you fall down and break a leg. And it's not too bad walking to the car that the attendant brings up. A car. Well, I guess if you're a doc, you can afford the registration fees and maybe he has to hurry into the hospital for emergencies.

I think it's the first time I've ridden in a car that wasn't a taxi since that day. And it's still real bright out, because it's summer, and the streets are full of after-work crowds out shopping and eating and making eyes, squatting with wireless access screens on the pedestals of statues, on curbs, leaning against storefronts. No reason to be inside except to sleep. We pass them and they don't even look.

The condo is in one of the new towers, with a garage underneath with a gate and a guard with hard eyes. It's fluorescent bright, and the elevator that whisks us upstairs is covered with really clean green carpet, walls, floor, everywhere. No mirrors. I get a little dizzy from the rush . . . I'm still feeling pretty rocky.

We get off into this little space that's supposed to look like a courtyard, I guess, with a brick path and gravel and a pool, and even the light feels like sunlight, and as the elevator doors close, something *plops* into the pool. A frog? A real one? I want to look, but the doc has his hand on my elbow now and he isn't going to let me stop, I can feel it.

Uh oh. Domino after all?

The door that the brick path leads to opens all by itself, and I only see one other door on the other side of the courtyard space, so this is a pretty fancy place. I'm really shaky now, and I don't much care if the doc is a Domino or not, I just want to sit down somewhere before I pass out, and everything sort of has this too bright, too clear look, like you get just before the black closes in. The room inside is huge, so big I can't really sort it out, it's all windows and light, and I can see blue sky, so we have to be way high, and green leaves and flowers and the sound of water, and the doc is pushing me and I sort of fall down into this chair.

It takes a little bit for the room to come into focus again, and when it does, the doc is holding out a glass, and he's looking a little worried, but not enough to scare me.

"I'm sorry." He pushes the glass a centimeter in my direction. "Take a drink of water."

And I do, and it helps, and I can look around. It's one big room, with a marble-topped kitchen island at one end and a fireplace with fake logs at the other, and chairs and small sofas covered in leather-looking stuff, grouped together, all tasteful soft browns and grays with a few real bright splashes of color. The glass is a greenhouse wall with plants and bright splashy flowers and a little waterfall and rocks. It looks like one of those upscale ads you get hit with online.

"You should get your strength back in a day or two." Doc bustles in the kitchen area. "Juice?" he asks. "I've got just about anything you might want."

"Thanks. Anything is fine."

He brings me a tall glass, like the glass that had the water in it. It's too heavy to be glass, cut into sharp geometric designs. Crystal? The juice is pink and I don't recognize the flavor, maybe something tropical. It helps. I didn't really eat the hospital stuff and all of a sudden I'm hungry. Doc has shed his jacket and poured a glass of dark red wine, and he's bustling around in the kitchen, not chattering, which I like, but getting out pans and mushrooms and a thick slab of salmon, cooking quickly and efficiently enough that Antonio would only curl his lip and not really sneer. And in a pretty short time, he serves up salmon sautéed in olive oil with some tiny perfect vegetables and fresh pasta and we eat at the small wooden table at the edge of the kitchen space. There's a single flower in a vase on the table and the food is good . . . really good, I mean, as good as what Antonio feeds the family at the restaurant. And I'm starving.

Doc pours me a glass of wine to go with the salmon, a lighter red then he was drinking before, and it's nice, light with a hint of fruit. A merlot? Domino has been teaching me wine, saving the stuff that the customers don't finish, making me pay attention. He may be handsy, but he's an okay guy and he really knows his wine.

"I'll be gone early in the morning." Doc swirls his wine in his glass, his eyes on the darkening city beyond the glass. "Make yourself at home here. Do you mind staying in the condo?" He raises his eyebrows. "I haven't reprogrammed my security, and once you go outside, you can't get back in."

"That's fine." I shrug. "I don't really have any place to go." Then I frown at my own glass, the wine tugging at me. "How come you picked me?" I blurt the words out, and there's this twinge of fear, like he might suddenly realize that he made a mistake. "I mean . . . why *me*?"

He smiles at me then, just a little. Folds his napkin up and lays it beside his plate. "I was wondering how long it would take you to ask." He leans his elbows on the table. "I looked at a lot of applicants." He's speaking slowly, thoughtfully. "You weren't the only one with this kind of extensive damage." His lips tighten briefly. "I'm not sure exactly what made me choose you in particular. Maybe because the cause was so . . . trivial. Not war, not an act of terrorism . . . just an accident."

He's lying. I feel a small thin sliver of ice in my gut. Oh, yeah, I can always tell. I don't know why. Maybe because I watch people a lot and they most of the time try not to notice me. So they act like I'm not there. But I'm just about never wrong.

And he's lying.

"Look, you really got rushed into this." He picks up his glass of wine. "I don't know who leaked the project to the media, but they really went for the story." He makes a face. "I wanted to get you safely into the hospital before someone interfered. Someone always has a reason. I'm not surprised that you feel a bit overwhelmed."

I run my thumb across the grain of the table, remembering that old man again. "How did you get . . . my picture." My voice is a little shaky in spite of myself.

"I contacted Children's Services." He clears his throat. "I assume they got permission to collect personal effects after your mother . . . after the accident. There was no other family. I'm letting you get too tired. Why don't you come sit?" He nods toward the living room area. "The city is lovely after dark. Or would you rather go straight to bed?"

I don't want to go to bed. If I don't sleep, I'm going to start thinking about this and . . . I don't want to think about this. So I get up and go over to one of the big leather chairs and I don't wobble too much. The view from here really *is* lovely. It's not quite full dark, but the sky is a deep royal blue and the lights spangle the towers and streets with gold and green and red, and the new aerial trams slide like glowing beads across invisible wires, and I've never been this high up in my life. And the doc talks for awhile, real easy, as if we've been friends for a long time. He tells me about medical school and wanting to do this twenty years ago, back when it was just an experimental concept and stem cell research was getting outlawed everywhere, and it looked like this kind of thing—regrowing tissues—would never happen. And his eyes glow when he talks about it, and I think of the old guy with the gaunt face who preaches about his angry god down at the little square near my walk-up, and that's how *his* eyes shine.

I finally start nodding off and I lose track of what he's saying. So he shows me to bed, and it's a room about the size of my walk-up with its own bathroom and a spa tub and a separate shower and windows that look out at a bridge. And from this angle and height, I'm not even sure which bridge it is. And there are two twin beds and a chest, and there's a robe and a new set of pajamas on one of the beds.

"You didn't bring a lot with you," Doc says with a smile. "There are some clothes in the chest and basic stuff in the bathroom. Let me know if you need anything."

"I will," I say, and he says good night and closes the door.

I sit on the edge of the bed, my feet bare, the carpet thick as a mattress under my bare feet. I'm kind of dizzy from the wine and the day and probably all the time I was out while my face was growing back. I finally get up and I go into the bathroom, and I make myself look in the mirror. Yeah. Better. Closer to human. Not there yet, but closer. And there is toothpaste and that kind of stuff, but I just go straight to bed. And it's weird. As I pull the cover up over me, already half asleep, it comes to me that this is somebody's room. Not a guest room. Somebody sleeps here. And I'm not sure why I think that, because there's no other clothes or stuff lying around. But I'm sure of it.

I wake up late, and for a minute, I can't remember where I am, and then it all comes back to me. And I can't help it. I go into the bathroom, first thing, and I look at my face. And the doc is gone and I prowl around. I don't know why I thought this was somebody's room. There's nothing to show. Clothes in the drawers all new, all my size. Expensive stuff, like I was a doc, too. It kind of creeps me out that they're there, but I put them on because my crummy pants seem wrong in this fancy place, like they might rub off somehow, stain the furniture. And I really feel . . . different now. Like I'm changing and not just my face. I jumped off that cliff, that's for sure. There's a screen in the bedroom and I try it, but a polite woman's voice tells me that I don't have the password to get online, but there's a separate library link and I can download books without a password. And I want to talk to daturk, but I settle for that book I started in the hospital, and by the time the doc arrives, I've finished it.

The evening is strange, nice and somehow creepy at the same time. Doc fixes another really fine dinner, and there's wine, and he asks me about what I've read and we talk—and you know, I've never talked about what I read to anybody but daturk. He's smart. Well, I guess you got to be, to be a doc, huh? And he asks me about school and gets all thoughtful when I tell him about doing all the online courses I could get from the state. Then he starts talking about the benefit of in the flesh classes, and how maybe I want to do that when I'm done with the medical stuff and that would be fine.

But he forgets how I live.

That takes real money.

And when I ask him about online, he sort of waves the question away, saying something about security and changing it is a pain. And just as I'm getting ready to go to bed, I remember and I ask him who used to sleep in the bedroom. He gets quiet, and I know right then I said the wrong thing. Then he says nobody.

He's lying again.

It goes on like this, and it's nice. Like the support group . . . only he really talks.

Most of them don't, except for Kitten. I go back to the hospital, and this time the session is short, and I'm not so whacked when I wake up. I come back to the condo after the second treatment. Doc doesn't even ask me. He just shows up, and I'm not so shaky this time. I guess this session didn't take as long. I didn't dream as much, but I saw the old man again, and this time he held my hand around the blade of his knife and I felt such *pride* as the first pale sliver of wood curled back over my knuckles. There are no scars on those hands. They're all smooth. So it's from before, but I knew that. I wonder who the old guy is. My grandfather? I stretch for some kind of memory, but all I get is a picture of those small smooth hands and that pride and the curl of blonde wood.

"I brought this home." Doc pulls a mini CD out of his pocket after dinner one night. "I thought you might want to see what I'm doing."

It's creepy, watching it. I sit in one of the chairs with my knees up under my chin and watch the cold arch of the machine crawl back and forth across my face. That's all you can see—my face—the rest is all green sheets and hot light. Tubes and wires connect the silver arch of the machine to something I can't see, and it runs on a kind of track, like a train, you know? And I guess he edited it some, because this is days and days, right? Weeks. But the machine zips back and forth and it maybe takes a half hour to watch . . . my face grow. On one pass, the machine squirts out this pale stuff . . . the scaffold, Doc calls it. Then it goes back again and sprays pinker stuff over . . . the cells. And they grow and then the machine sprays on more scaffold. . . .

It keeps crawling back and forth and my face . . . grows. There's a little hump where most people have a nose and then it's more of a hump and it gets bigger and arches and I've got cheeks and lips and . . .

"After you were anaesthetized this time, we used an enzyme to dissolve the temporary dermal layer that was in place." Doc is leaning forward, staring at the screen. "So that the new layers of tissue could bond seamlessly."

I think about lying there on that table unconscious, my skin melting away. I've never dreamed about the fire, but now I shiver, and for a moment I think I'm going to be sick.

On the screen, the silver, tube-trailing machine crawls back and forth, and my nose looks like . . . a nose.

I touch it. It juts out of my face. I can't quite get my mind around that feeling. On the screen, the silvery arch slides back and forth and back again, growing my face, one layer of cells at a time.

Living with the doc is kind of strange. It's like a dream that I can't quite wake up from. I think I've figured out what this is all about by now. It's starting to feel okay to be there in that room that was somebody's. It's kind of like jail, too, I guess, because I still can't get online and I can't leave. I can, but we both know that if I do, it wrecks something. And I feel like a part of me I can't really get inside of is having a conversation with Doc, and *I'm* not part of it, and this sounds really nuts, I know. But it's okay.

I want to talk to daturk about it.

And one night, I dream that my face is talking to me and it scares the crap out of me, because if my face is out there talking to me, what is on the front of my skull? And I wake up yelling, and the doc is there, putting his arms around me, holding me, and just sitting there until I fall asleep again. And this time, I dream about this woman and she's looking down at me and crying and she has red hair, and I wake up knowing that this is my mother, and I've never dreamed about her before. Not once.

Why is she crying? I try to remember and I can't.

My face is wrong. I don't know how I know. But I do. When I tell Doc, he tells me it's normal. The feeling will go away after awhile.

He's not lying this time.

Two more sessions to go. I look like a painting that's not quite finished yet. And when I look in the mirror, this stranger looks back at me. I don't think he likes me.

I dream about the old man a lot. I'm pretty sure he's my grandfather. He lets me carve a piece of wood, holding my hands in his and mine are very small. I dream about my mother, too. And I dream about her crying again, and sometimes, there is all this white light and stuff that means . . . hospital. How could she be in the hospital? She died in the car, before I went there.

Didn't she?

Didn't she?

The doc talks about my staying here with him after, about going to college. He talks about having no kids, and money, and why have it if you don't use it? There's a story about this, real old . . . a man who carved this statue and then it came to life and was his perfect lover. I guess that's what Doc's doing, with all his talk about college and my staying with him. Like Domino after all . . . but you know? It's an okay trade. Really. It is. But I still feel like I'm living in a dream and my face still looks at me like I'm a stranger. And there's no reason to say no, so I don't know why I don't say yes right then. But I can't. Not out loud.

Doc thinks that means yes, I guess. I don't know.

And I ask him if my mother might still be alive and he looks at me real strange. "No," he says. And he's not lying.

And then daturk finds me.

I'm downloading a book and the screen lights up with a storm of wind and yellow leaves swirling around in what looks like a miniature tornado. *gd security but not gd enough* Green words swirl with the wind and then the screen is full of fireworks—daturk laughing. *u ok?*

"Yeah," I can say the words out loud because this is a sweet system and does voice. I wonder what the wind and leaves mean. "I couldn't get out. Doc's paranoid about security."

The gray clouds and mirror lake appear. She's being thoughtful. *u gonna b pretty?* she finally asks.

"Yeah. But . . . I don't think he's got the face right." The words just blurt out. I haven't even said them in my head. Not really. "It doesn't look right. And he says that's normal—even the plastic patients feel that way—but I don't know. It's like I'm looking at someone else. Maybe he . . . got the wrong picture." But the kid I saw . . . that smiling one. I remember how it twisted my insides. Nah. He didn't get the wrong picture.

On the screen, clouds and lake. No words.

"Something doesn't feel right." And when I say that, it really smacks me. Because it doesn't. And I've been telling myself that it's just me and everything is really all right, because it *is*.

And I don't want to talk anymore, but I missed daturk a lot and I don't want to lose her either. "Can you get in again?" I say, and I get a handful of sunflowers tumbling across the screen. That's a yes. Then she's gone. She's always really good at reading me. I don't know how you do that in digital, but she does. And I feel better . . . and realize all of a sudden that I've been feeling bad.

And Doc is gone, and I'm supposed to go in tomorrow for the final session, and when it's all over . . . it's a long one again, I guess . . . I'll . . . be done. I walk through the condo, out to the little jungle that grows under the glass wall, kind of framing the city. It looks so beautiful up here. You can't see the ugly stuff down there. I wonder what it's like to live for years and years up above all the people who wash the dishes and panhandle and rob. I mean, I've been up here for a couple of weeks now, but it's not like I live here. It's more like I'm walking around in a dream, and any day I'm going to wake up and it'll be time to go eat the spicy curries that Antonio feeds us and wash the paella pans and taste wine with Domino. I hold my hands out and look at them. Doc says he'll fix them, too, but they work and . . . I don't know. I think I don't want him to. I run my thumb over some of the shiny white skin and it feels hard like plastic. I don't want to be perfect. And I think about the old man again and the little-boy hands and that pride. Twenty years ago. No family, Doc said, so I guess he's dead. Like my mother?

I turn my back on the city . . . I don't know it from up here . . . and I go down the short wide hall, and I go into Doc's room. I haven't been in here before, just looked in. It's dim, because silk drapes that match the silk quilt on the big bed kind of shut out the light, and the quiet furniture makes me think of my grandfather stroking that satiny wood and showing me how to hold a knife, I can smell Doc—a rich musky odor of flesh and some kind of scent, like he's really here, maybe hiding in the closet, and the back of my neck prickles.

I've never snooped in here. Honest. I could have. Looked to see what he hides in his sock drawer. But I haven't.

I'm not sure why I'm doing it now. I should just turn off the brain and go download a book, and wait for the final session, I guess. But I'm walking over to the dresser and I don't think I could stop myself, it's like I'm two people, and right now the other one is running the muscles. I don't find anything in the drawers, or the drawers of the night stand. There's a remote for the wall vid and music system. Clothes. Some pills with no labels. Tissues. That kind of thing.

It's in the closet, flat against the wall up on a shelf, stuffed behind a stack of silky folded sheets or blankets or something. A picture. It's not a holo base, but a flat frame with a digital photo printed out on real old fashioned glossy paper, as if it came from an antique camera. But maybe it really did. The Doc is fifty at least, probably more, if his plastic buddies have worked on him.

My hand is shaking. As if the part of me pulling the muscle-strings has already figured it out. But I guess *I* haven't. Because when I take the picture over to the window and pull aside the drapes, my mind is empty. I just stand there, staring at the face in the picture, not thinking anything. Just staring.

Years ago . . . in another life . . . I sat in a chair and watched that laughing kid face that stabbed me in the gut lengthen and firm up and grow older. He stares up at me right now from the slick surface of the picture, his hair in a military buzz with a diamond stud in one ear lobe, and his eyes are a blue that's almost gray, and he seems . . . sad.

It's some kind of formal thing, like graduation but not military 'cause there's no uniform, just a blue shirt with a collar. There's another picture under this one. I can just see the edge and I kind of pry the frame apart and slide it out. It's the same kid. Younger, or maybe just grubbier. He's in a canoe that looks like it's made from real wood. It's floating on this gorgeous lake, kind of like daturk's thoughtful lake.

Doc's in the canoe with him. The kid's smiling for the camera and Doc's smiling at the kid.

I was wrong. About what Doc is doing.

It's his son.

You can see it in his face.

I wonder what happened.

I slide that picture back where I found it and I feel . . . slimy. Like I've been hiding, watching him have sex. I feel . . .

. . . I'm not sure how I feel.

But now I know.

I go into the bathroom in the room I've been sleeping in. *His* room. That's who I've been feeling. I stand in front of the mirror. I haven't looked at my face yet. Oh, I've *looked*. I watched the vids with Doc. I saw it *happen*. But I've just sort of inventoried it before this . . . I kind of skid over seeing the whole thing. It's like my face in the mirror is ice, and I can't get my footing.

But now, I *look*. I stand in front of the mirror and I don't let my shoulders turn, my face duck, my eyes slide. Nah, I look. Like I'm meeting me on the street, on the way to Antonio's to scrub the paella pans. Interesting guy. What do you think of him? What's his past? I want to shake, and I kind of slap myself inside my head, you know? Hey. Look at him. He's walking down the street, so *look* at him. And I do.

He's ugly. That's all. Just *ugly*. I mean, his face is kind of too bold, too bald. Not really formed quite right, you know? It should be . . . dunno . . . more *defined*. Maybe his mom ate something wrong or drank the wrong water when she was pregnant or something. And I remember one year way back, when I was in this kind of homey place for kids, like a real house. It wasn't just us burn kids, it was some others, too, and their faces weren't damaged. . . . They just weren't quite faces yet. And they had other problems, too. But that's what I see. I'm not normal, but you know. . . .

I'm just some guy that doesn't look normal.

Not a monster. Not somebody where all you can think is *ohmygod-whathappenedtohim?*

I end up on my knees on the floor and I'm goddam crying, my tears are leaking all over my jeans and . . . it's nuts . . . I've never cried. Well, in the hospital, yeah, when it hurt. But not after.

What was the point?

I'm crying now.

Doc is going to be home pretty soon. My knees hurt when I get up off the floor. I kind of focus on the pain as I stumble into the bedroom. He's going to be home soon, and I don't know how to get hold of daturk.

But she's waiting for me. When I touch up the online, the screen is full of shriveled leaves, but they vanish as soon as I touch the screen. All of a sudden, it's a snow of white petals against black. I guess she's there.

I gotta go. I type the words in slowly 'cause I don't think I can say them out loud. *I can't go through with this.*

That same crimson question mark I saw that first day in the hospital curves onto the screen, burning into me.

I'm just finished, I type. *I just need to get away from here. Nothing twisted. Not really.* Well maybe that's not true, maybe love is always twisted. *Nobody serious is gonna come looking for me,* I tell her.

The screen is frozen, question mark, white petals, I'm here all by myself.

I just need to go.

I type the words in, but she's gone. Elsewhere. And I should just get up, go back to the walk-up, because I haven't broken any law and the worst that can happen is that the media follows me and makes a fuss and I have to stay away from the news streams for awhile. But I just sit there, frozen as the screen.

And then all of a sudden it goes blank and blue. Scary. White letters and numbers suddenly blink into life. No flowers, no visuals at all. Just an address. Some street address in Baltimore, of all places.

Thanks, I type.

The screen goes blank. She really is gone, this time.

I go find paper and pen in Doc's bedroom, figuring he probably has some for fancy notes to friends or something. This isn't something to type online and e-mail or print. I write the address down from memory, just in case I forget. Then . . . I lay a clean sheet on the desk beside the keyboard. I wonder what kind of wood the desk is made of, if the old man would know. Probably. The pen feels weird and clumsy in my fingers. I'll take money from my account in cash, pay the surcharge for using it to buy a ticket. That should throw the media off. And Doc. Antonio isn't going to care that I'm gone. And I wonder what I'm going to find at that address.

daturk?

Maybe. It occurs to me that I don't really know even that she's a she. I've just sort of . . . guessed. It doesn't really matter.

Maybe . . . just maybe . . . my mother is alive and it's my memories that are right and not the state database. I mean . . . it had to cost a million bucks to fix me. And if she walked away . . . well, National Health did it. Maybe that was the reason? You can find out anything if you're willing to pay. Antonio doesn't pay much, but what did I have to spend my money on, before? I think maybe . . . if she's really alive . . . all I want to do is go look at her. Just once, you know?

Nah. I don't know.

I touch the pen to the paper, make a tiny blue dot, perfectly round and the color of the sky that first night here, when I watched the city lights all come on. *Doc,* I write. The words form slowly, letters looping out across the sand colored paper. *I found the picture. Of your son. I haven't snooped before, I'm sorry, and I don't know what happened to him or to you both. I just don't know, and I want you to know that you did such a great job and I really really mean it. And I'm sorry I'm not staying, but I just can't. I don't know really why, maybe just because I've never been me, you know? I mean, I guess I was, a long time ago, but after the crash, I was the kid in bed four, and then I was the burn kid, and then the monster who made people look away, and the paella pan washer and now I don't know. . . .*

I guess I just want to try being me. I don't know if I can even do that, isn't that a joke? But I need to try. And there's this girl and she'd be a whole lot easier than me to do, and she's blonde and you can see she was real pretty and the media would love her and it would be like Cinderella or something. Her name is Kitten and you can find her at the support group I used to belong to, the Tuesday one, and it's gotta be in my file. And I need to say more to him, but the words won't come. I think maybe I don't know yet what it is that I need to say. It might take awhile to know and maybe then I can come back and say it. I don't know.

But it's a possibility, and I'm not sure that I've had *possibilities* before. Just stuff that happened to me.

So I just write, *thanks Doc* and I leave the note on the table and I go out the door. First time I've done it by myself, but no alarms go off. The frog plops into the little pool in the pretty courtyard, and I take the elevator down to the lobby, and I've never been through there. And this woman is coming in all dressed in this nice business suit and boots, and I can see her eyes coming up to my face and I'm going to do the thing I do on the street, look past her, not see.

Only I make myself not do that.

And she looks and I'm ugly, you can see that in her eyes.

But she looks.

And then she goes past me and gets into the elevator.

That's it.

Thanks, Doc. And I'm sorry. I wish I could have been what you needed.

I'm scared.

I go out the door, onto the street, and I head for Baltimore.

Delhi

VANDANA SINGH

New writer Vandana Singh was born and raised in India, and currently resides with her family in the United States, where she teaches physics and writes. Her stories have appeared in several volumes of *Polyphony*, as well as in *Strange Horizons*, *Trampoline*, and *So Long Been Dreaming*. Her first book for children, *Younguncle Comes to Town*, has just been published in India.

In the compelling story that follows, she shows us a man who's being haunted not just by *one* ghost, or even by a houseful of them, but by an entire *city* . . .

Tonight he is intensely aware of the city: its ancient stones, the flat-roofed brick houses, threads of clotheslines, wet, bright colors waving like pennants, neem-tree lined roads choked with traffic. There's a bus going over the bridge under which he has chosen to sleep. The night smells of jasmine and stale urine, and the dust of the cricket field on the other side of the road. A man is lighting a bidi near him: face lean, half in shadow, and he thinks he sees himself. He goes over to the man, who looks like another layabout. "My name is Aseem," he says.

The man, reeking of tobacco, glares at him, coughs, and spits, "Kya chahiye?"

Aseem steps back in a hurry. No, that man is not Aseem's older self; anyway, Aseem can't imagine he would take up smoking bidis at any point in his life. He leaves the dubious shelter of the bridge, the quiet lane that runs under it, and makes his way through the litter and anemic street lamps to the neon-bright highway. The new city is less confusing, he thinks; the colors are more solid, the lights dazzling, so he can't see the apparitions as clearly. But once he saw a milkman going past him on Shahjahan road, complete with humped white cow and tinkling bell. Under the stately, ancient trees that partly shaded the street lamps, the milkman stopped to speak to his cow and faded into the dimness of twilight.

When he was younger, he thought the apparitions he saw were ghosts of the dead, but now he knows that is not true. Now he has a theory that his visions are tricks of time, tangles produced when one part of the time-stream rubs up against another and the two cross for a moment. He has decided (after years of struggle) that he is not insane after all; his brain is wired differently from others, enabling him to discern these temporal coincidences. He knows he is not the only one with this ability, because some of the people he sees also see him, and shrink back in terror. The thought that he is a ghost to people long dead or still to come in this world both amuses and terrifies him.

He's seen more apparitions in the older parts of the city than anywhere else, and he's not sure why. There is plenty of history in Delhi, no doubt about that—the city's past goes back into myth, when the Pandava brothers of the epic Mahabharata first founded their fabled capital, Indraprastha, some 3,000 years ago. In medieval times alone there were seven cities of Delhi, he remembers, from a well-thumbed history textbook—and the eighth city was established by the British during the days of the Raj. The city of the present day, the ninth, is the largest. Only for Aseem are the old cities of Delhi still alive, glimpsed like mysterious islands from a passing ship, but real nevertheless. He wishes he could discuss his temporal visions with someone who would take him seriously and help him understand the nature and limits of his peculiar malady, but ironically, the only sympathetic person he's met who shares his condition happened to live in 1100 AD or thereabouts, the time of Prithviraj Chauhan, the last Hindu ruler of Delhi.

He was walking past the faded white colonnades of some building in Connaught Place when he saw her: an old woman in a long skirt and shawl, making her way sedately across the car park, her body rising above the road and falling below its surface parallel to some invisible topography. She came face to face with Aseem—and saw him. They both stopped. Clinging to her like grey ribbons were glimpses of her environs—he saw mist, the darkness of trees behind her. Suddenly, in the middle of summer, he could smell fresh rain. She put a wondering arm out toward him but didn't touch him. She said: "What age are you from?" in an unfamiliar dialect of Hindi. He did not know how to answer the question, or how to contain within him that sharp shock of joy. She, too, had looked across the barriers of time and glimpsed other people, other ages. She named Prithviraj Chauhan as her king. Aseem told her he lived some 900 years after Chauhan. They exchanged stories of other visions—she had seen armies, spears flashing, and pale men with yellow beards, and a woman in a metal carriage, crying. He was able to interpret some of this for her before she began to fade away. He started toward her as though to step into her world, and ran right into a pillar. As he picked himself off the ground he heard derisive laughter. Under the arches a shoeshine boy and a man chewing betel leaf were staring at him, enjoying the show.

Once he met the mad emperor, Mohammad Shah. He was walking through Red Fort one late afternoon, avoiding clumps of tourists and their clicking cameras, and feeling particularly restless. There was a smoky tang in the air because some gardener in the grounds was burning dry leaves. As the sun set, the red sandstone fort walls glowed, then darkened. Night came, blanketing the tall ramparts, the lawns through which he strolled, the shimmering beauty of the Pearl Mosque, the languorous curves of the now distant Yamuna that had once flowed under this marble terrace. He saw a man standing, leaning over the railing, dressed in a red silk sherwani, jewels at his throat, a gem studded in his turban. The man smelled of wine and rose attar, and was singing a song about a night of separation from the Beloved, slurring the words together.

Bairan bhayii raat sakhiya. . . .
Mammad Shah piya sada Rangila. . . .

Mohammad Shah Rangila, early 1700s, Aseem recalled. The Emperor who loved music, poetry, and wine more than anything, who ignored warnings that the Persian king was marching to Delhi with a vast army. . . . "Listen, King," Aseem whispered urgently, wondering if he could change the course of history, "you must prepare for battle. Else Nadir Shah will overrun the city. Thousands will be butchered by his army. . . ."

The king lifted wine-darkened eyes. "Begone, wraith!"

Sometimes he stops at the India Gate lawns in the heart of modern Delhi and buys ice-cream from a vendor and eats it sitting by one of the fountains that Lutyens built. Watching the play of light on the shimmering water, he thinks about the British invaders, who brought one of the richest and oldest civilizations on earth to abject poverty in only two hundred years. They built these great edifices, gracious buildings, and fountains, but even they had to leave it all behind. Kings came and went, the goras came and went, but the city lives on. Sometimes he sees apparitions of the goras, the palefaces, walking by him or riding on horses. Each time he yells out to them: "Your people are doomed. You will leave here. Your Empire will crumble." Once in a while they glance at him, startled, before they fade away.

In his more fanciful moments, he wonders if he hasn't, in some way, *caused* history to happen the way it does. Planted a seed of doubt in a British officer's mind about the permanency of the Empire. Despite his best intentions, convinced Mohammad Shah that the impending invasion is not a real danger but a ploy wrought against him by evil spirits. But he knows that apart from the Emperor, nobody he has communicated with is of any real importance in the course of history, and that he is simply deluding himself about his own significance.

Still, he makes compulsive notes of his more interesting encounters. He carries with him at all times a thick, somewhat shabby notebook, one-half of which is devoted to recording these temporal adventures. But because the apparitions he sees are so clear, he is sometimes not certain whether the face he glimpses in the crowd, or the man wrapped in shawls passing him by on a cold night, belong to this time or some other. Only some incongruity—spatial or temporal—distinguishes the apparitions from the rest.

Sometimes he sees landscapes too, but rarely—a skyline dotted with palaces and temple spires, a forest in the middle of a busy thoroughfare—and, strangest of all, once an array of tall, jewelled towers reaching into the clouds. Each such vision seems to be charged with a peculiar energy, like a scene lit up by lightning. And although the apparitions are apparently random and not often repeated, there are certain places where he sees (he thinks) the same people again and again. For instance, while travelling on the Metro, he almost always sees people in the subway tunnels, floating through the train and the passengers on the platforms, dressed in tatters, their faces pale and unhealthy as though they have never beheld the sun. The first time he saw them, he shuddered. "The Metro is quite new," he thought to himself, "and the first underground train system in Delhi. So what I saw must be in the future. . . ."

One day, he tells himself, he will write a history of the future.

The street is Nai Sarak, a name he has always thought absurd. New Road, it means, but this road has not been new in a very long time. He could cross the street in two jumps if it wasn't so crowded with people, shoulder to shoulder. The houses are like that too, hunched together with windows like dull eyes, and narrow, dusty stairways and even narrower alleys in between. The ground floors are taken up by tiny, musty shops containing piles of books that smell fresh and pungent, a wake-up smell like coffee. It is a hot day, and there is no shade. The girl he is following is just another Delhi University student looking for a bargain, trying not to get jostled or groped in the crowd, much less have her purse stolen. There are small, barefoot boys running around with wire-carriers of lemon-water in chipped glasses, and fat old men in their undershirts behind the counters, bargaining fiercely with pale, defenseless college students over the hum of electric fans, rubbing clammy hands across their hairy bellies while they slurp their ice drinks, signaling to some waif when the transaction is complete, so that the desired volume can be deposited into the feverish hands of the student. Some of the shopkeepers like to add a little lecture along the lines of, "Now, my son, study hard, make your parents proud. . . ." Aseem hasn't been here in a long time (since his own college days, in fact); he is not prepared for any of this: the brightness of the day, the white dome of the mosque rising up behind him, the old stone walls of the city engirdling him, enclosing him in people and sweat and dust. He's dazzled by the white kurtas of the men, the neat beards and the prayer caps; this is, of course, the Muslim part of the city, Old Delhi, but not as romantic as his grandmother used to make it sound. He has a rare flash of memory into a past where he was a small boy listening to the old woman's tales. His grandmother was one of the Hindus who never went back to old Delhi, not after the madness of Partition in 1947, the Hindu-Muslim riots that killed thousands, but he still remembers how she spoke of the places of her girlhood: parathe-walon-ki-gali, the lane of the paratha-makers, where all the shops sell freshly cooked flatbreads of every possible kind, stuffed with spiced potatoes or minced lamb, or fenugreek leaves, or crushed cauliflower and fiery red chillies; and Dariba Kalan, where after hundreds of years they still sell the best and purest silver in the world, delicate chains and anklets and bracelets. Among the crowds that throng these places he has seen the apparitions of courtesans and young men, and the blood and thunder of invasions, and the bodies of princes hanged by British soldiers. To him the old city, surrounded by high, crumbling stone walls, is like the heart of a crone who dreams perpetually of her youth.

The girl who's caught his attention walks on. Aseem hasn't been able to get a proper look at her—all he's noticed are the dark eyes, and the death in them. After all these years in the city he's learned to recognize a certain preoccupation in the eyes of some of his fellow citizens: the desire for the final anonymity that death brings. Sometimes, as in this case, he knows it before they do.

The girl goes into a shop. The proprietor, a young man built like a wrestler, is dressed only in cotton shorts. The massage-man is working his back, kneading and sculpting the slick, gold muscles. The young man says: "Advanced Biochemistry? Watkins? One copy, only one copy left." He shouts into the dark, cavernous interior, and the requisite small boy comes up, bearing the volume as though it were a rare book. The girl's face shows too much relief; she's doomed even before the bargaining begins. She parts with her money with a resigned air, steps out into the noisy brightness, and is caught up with the crowd in the street like a piece of wood tossed in a river. She pushes and elbows her way through it, fending off anonymous hands that reach toward her breasts or back. He loses sight of her for a moment, but there she is, walking past the mosque to the bus stop on the main road. At the bus stop she catches Aseem's glance and gives him the pre-emptive cold look. Now there's a bus coming, filled with people, young men hanging out of the doorways as though on the prow of a sailboat. He sees her struggling through the crowd toward the bus, and at the last minute she's right in its path. The bus is not stopping but (in the tantalizing manner of Delhi buses) barely slowing, as though to play catch with the crowd. It is an immense green and yellow metal monstrosity bearing down on her as she stands rooted, clutching her bag of books. This is Aseem's moment. He lunges at the girl, pushing her out of the way, grabbing her before she can fall to the ground. There is a roaring in his ears, the shriek of brakes, and the conductor yelling. Her books are scattered on the ground. He helps pick them up. She's trembling with shock. In her eyes he sees himself for a moment: a drifter, his face unshaven, his hair unkempt. He tells her: don't do it, don't ever do it. Life is never so bereft of hope. You have a purpose you must fulfill. He repeats it like a mantra, and she looks bewildered, as though she doesn't understand that she was trying to kill herself. He can see that he puzzles her: his grammatical Hindi and his fair English labels him middle class and educated, like herself, but his appearance says otherwise. Although he knows she's not the woman he is seeking, he pulls out the computer printout just to be sure. No, she's not the one. Cheeks too thin, chin not sharp enough. He pushes one of the business cards into her hand and walks away. From a distance, he sees that she's looking at the card in her hand and frowning. Will she throw it away? At the last minute, she shoves it into her bag with the books. He remembers all too clearly the first time someone gave him one of the cards. "Worried About Your Future? Consult Pandit Vidyanath. Computerized and Air-Conditioned Office. Discover Your True Purpose in Life." There is a logo of a beehive and an address in South Delhi.

Later he will write up this encounter in the second half of his notebook. In three years, he has filled this part almost to capacity. He's stopped young men from flinging themselves off the bridges that span the Yamuna. He's prevented women from jumping off tall buildings, from dousing themselves with kerosene, from murderous encounters with city traffic. All this by way of seeking *her*, whose story will be the last in his book.

But the very first story in this part of his notebook is his own. . . .

Three years ago. He is standing on a bridge over the Yamuna. There is a heavy, odorous fog in the air, the kind that mars winter mornings in Delhi. He is shivering because of the chill, and because he is tired, tired of the apparitions that have always plagued him, tired of the endless rounds of medications and appointments with doctors and psychologists. He has just written a letter to his fiancée, severing their already fragile relationship. Two months ago, he stopped attending his college classes. His mother and father have been dead a year and two years respectively, and there will be no one to mourn him, except for relatives in other towns who know him only by reputation as a person with problems. Last night he tried, as a last resort, to leave Delhi, hoping that perhaps the visions would stop. He got as far as the railway station. He stood in the line before the ticket counter, jostled by young men carrying hold-alls and aggressive matrons in bright saris. "Name?" said the man behind the window, but Aseem couldn't remember it. Around him, in the cavernous interior of the station, shouting, red-clad porters rushed past, balancing tiers of suitcases on their turbaned heads, and vast waves of passengers swarmed the stairs that led up across the platforms. People were nudging him, telling him to hurry up, but all he could think of were the still trains between the platforms, steaming in the cold air, hissing softly like warm snakes, waiting to take him away. The thought of leaving filled him with a sudden terror. He turned and walked out of the station. Outside, in the cold, glittering night, he breathed deep, fierce breaths of relief, as though he had walked away from his own death.

So here he is, the morning after his attempted escape, standing on the bridge, shivering in the fog. He notices a crack in the concrete railing, which he traces with his finger to the seedling of a pipal tree, growing on the outside of the rail. He remembers his mother pulling pipal seedlings out of walls and the paved courtyard of their house, over his protests. He remembers how difficult it was for him to see, in each fragile sapling, the giant full-grown tree. Leaning over the bridge, he finds himself wondering which will fall first—the pipal tree or the bridge. Just then he hears a bicycle on the road behind him, one that needs oiling, evidently, and before he knows it some rude fellow with a straggly beard has come out of the fog, pulled him off the railing and on to the road. "Don't be a fool, don't do it," says the stranger, breathing hard. His bicycle is lying on the roadside, one wheel still spinning. "Here, take this," the man says, pushing a small card into Aseem's unresisting hand. "Go see them. If they can't give you a reason to live, your own mother wouldn't be able to."

The address on the card proves to be in a small marketplace near Sarojini Nagar. Around a dusty square of withered grass where ubiquitous pariah dogs sleep fitfully in the pale sun, there is a row of shops. The place he seeks is a corner shop next to a vast jamun tree. Under the tree, three humped white cows are chewing cud, watching him with bovine indifference. Aseem makes his way through a jangle of bicycles, motor-rickshaws, and people, and finds himself before a closed door with a small sign saying only, "Pandit Vidyanath, Consultations." He goes in.

The Pandit is not in, but his assistant, a thin, earnest-faced young man, waves Aseem to a chair. The assistant is sitting behind a desk with a PC, a printer, and a plaque bearing his name: Om Prakash, BSc Physics (Failed), Delhi University. There is a window with the promised air-conditioner (apparently defunct) occupying its lower half. On the other side of the window is a beehive in the process of completion. Aseem feels he has come to the wrong place, and regrets already the whim that brought him here, but the beehive fascinates him, how it is still and in motion all at once, and the way the bees seem to be in concert with one another, as though performing a complicated dance. Two of the bees are crawling on the computer and there is one on the assistant's arm. Om Prakash seems completely unperturbed; he assures Aseem that the bees are harmless, and tries to interest him in array of bottles of honey on the shelf behind him. Apparently the bees belong to Pandit Vidyanath, a man of many facets, who keeps very busy because he also works for the city. (Aseem has a suspicion that perhaps the great man is no more than a petty clerk in a municipal office.) Honey is ten rupees a bottle. Aseem shakes his head, and Om Prakash gets down to business with a noisy clearing of his throat, asking questions and entering the answers into the computer. By now Aseem feels like a fool.

"How does your computer know the future?" Aseem asks.

Om Prakash has a lanky, giraffe-like grace, although he is not tall. He makes a deprecating gesture with his long, thin hands that travels all the way up to his mobile shoulders.

"A computer is like a beehive. Many bits and parts, none is by itself intelligent. Combine together, and you have something that can think. This computer is not an ordinary one. Built by Pandit Vidyanath himself."

Om Prakash grins as the printer begins to whir.

"All persons who come here seek meaning. Each person has their own dharma, their own unique purpose. We don't tell future, because future is beyond us, Sahib. We tell them why they need to live."

He hands a printout to Aseem. When he first sees it, the page makes no sense. It consists of xs arranged in an apparently random pattern over the page. He holds it at a distance and sees—indistinctly—the face of a woman.

"Who is she?"

"It is for you to interpret what this picture means," says Om Prakash. "You must live because you need to meet this woman, perhaps to save her or be saved. It may mean that you could be at the right place and time to save her from some terrible fate. She could be your sister or daughter, a wife or stranger."

There are dark smudges for eyes, the hint of a high cheekbone, and swirl of hair across the cheek, half-obscuring the mouth. The face is broad and heart-shaped, narrowing to a small chin.

"But this is not very clear. . . . It could be almost anyone. How will I know. . . ."

"You will know when you meet her," Om Prakash says with finality. "There is no charge. Thank you, sir, and here are cards for you to give other unfortunate souls."

Aseem takes the pack of business cards and leaves. He distrusts the entire business, especially the bit about no charge. No charge? In a city like Delhi?

But despite his doubts he finds himself intrigued. He had expected the usual platitudes about life and death, the fatalistic pronouncements peculiar to charlatan fortune tellers, but this fellow Vidyanath obviously is an original. That Aseem must live simply so he might be there for someone at the right moment: what an amusing, humbling idea! As the days pass it grows on him, and he comes to believe it, if for nothing else than to have something in which to believe. He scans the faces of the people in the crowds, on the dusty sidewalks, the overladen buses, the Metro, and he looks for her. He lives so that he will cross her path some day. For three years, he has convinced himself that she is real, that she waits for him. He's made something of a life for himself, working at a photocopy shop in Lajpat Nagar, where he can sleep on winter nights, or making deliveries for shopkeepers in Defence Colony, who pay enough to keep him in food and clothing. For three years, he has handed out hundreds of the little business cards, and visited the address in South Delhi dozens of times. He's become used to the bees, the defunct air-conditioner, and even to Om Prakash. Although there is too much distance between them to allow friendship (a distance of temperament, really), Aseem has told Om Prakash about the apparitions he sees. Om Prakash receives these confidences with his rather foolish grin and much waggling of the head in wonder, and says he will tell Pandit Vidyanath. Only, each time Aseem visits there is no sign of Pandit Vidyanath, so now Aseem suspects that there is no such person, that Om Prakash himself is the unlikely mind behind the whole business.

But sometimes he is scared of finding the woman. He imagines himself saving her from death or a fate worse than death, realizing at last his purpose. But after that, what awaits him? The oily embrace of the Yamuna?

Or will she save him in turn?

One of the things he likes about the city is how it breaks all rules. Delhi is a place of contradictions—it transcends thesis and antithesis. Here he has seen both the hovels of the poor and the opulent monstrosities of the rich. At major intersections, where the rich wait impatiently in their air-conditioned cars for the light to change, he's seen bone-thin waifs running from car to car, peddling glossy magazines like *Vogue* and *Cosmopolitan*. Amid the glitzy new high-rises are troupes of wandering cows and pariah dogs; rhesus monkeys mate with abandon in the trees around Parliament House.

He hasn't slept well—last night the police raided the Aurobindo Marg sidewalk where he was sleeping. Some foreign VIP was expected in the morning so the riffraff on the roadsides were driven off by stick-wielding policemen. This has happened many times before, but today Aseem is smarting with rage and humiliation: he has a bruise on his back where a policeman's stick hit him, and it burns in the relentless heat. Death lurks behind the walled eyes of the populace—but for once he is sick of his proximity to death. So he goes to the only place where he can leave behind the city without actually leaving its borders—another anomaly in a city of surprises. Amid the endless sprawl of brick houses and crowded roads, within Delhi's borders, there lies an entire forest: the Delhi Ridge, a green lung. The coolness of the forest beckons to him.

Only a little way from the main road, the forest is still, except for the subdued chirping of birds. He is in a warm, green womb. Under the acacia trees, he finds an old ruin, one of the many nameless remains of Delhi's medieval era. After checking for snakes or scorpions, he curls up under a crumbling wall and dozes off.

Some time later, when the sun is lower in the sky and the heat not as intense, he hears a tapping sound, soft and regular, like slow rain on a tin roof. He sees a woman—a young girl—on the paved path in front of him, holding a cane before her. She's blind, obviously, and lost. This is no place for a woman alone. He clears his throat and she starts.

"Is someone there?"

She's wearing a long blue shirt over a salwaar of the same color, and there is a shawl around her shoulders. The thin material of her dupatta drapes her head, half covering her face, blurring her features. He looks at her and sees the face in the printout. Or thinks he does.

"You are lost," he says, his voice trembling with excitement. He fumbles in his pockets for the printout. Surely he must still be asleep and dreaming. Hasn't he dreamed about her many, many times already? "Where do you wish to go?"

She clutches her stick. Her shoulders slump.

"Naya Diwas Lane, good sir. I am traveling from Jaipur. I came to meet my sister, who lives here, but I lost my papers. They say you must have papers. Or they'll send me to Neechi-Dilli with all the poor and the criminals. I don't want to go there! My sister has money. Please, sir, tell me how to find Naya Diwas."

He's never heard of Naya Diwas Lane, or Neechi Dilli. New Day Lane? Lower Delhi? What strange names. He wipes the sweat off his forehead.

"There aren't any such places. Somebody has misled you. Go back to the main road, turn right, there is a marketplace there. I will come with you. Nobody will harm you. We can make enquiries there."

She thanks him, her voice catching with relief. She tells him she's heard many stories about the fabled city and its tall, gem-studded minars that reach the sky, and the perfect gardens. And the ships, the silver udankhatolas, that fly across worlds. She's very excited to be here at last in the Immaculate City.

His eyes widen. He gets up abruptly, but she's already fading away into the trees. The computer printout is in his hand, but before he can get another look at her, she's gone.

What has he told her? Where is she going, in what future age, buoyed by the hope he has given her, which (he fears now) may be false?

He stumbles around the ruin, disturbing ground squirrels and a sleepy flock of jungle babblers, but he knows there is no hope of finding her again except by chance. Temporal coincidences have their own unfathomable rules. He's looked ahead to this moment so many times, imagined both joy and despair as a result of it, but never this apprehension, this uncertainty. He looks at the computer printout again. Is it mere coincidence that the apparition he saw looked like the image? What if Pandit Vidyanath's computer generated something quite random, and that his quest, his life for the past few years, has been completely pointless? That Om Prakash or Vidyanath (if he exists) is enjoying an intricate joke at his expense? That he has allowed himself to be duped by his own hopes and fears?

But beyond all this, he's worried about this young woman. There's only one thing to do—go to Om Prakash and get the truth out of him. After all, if Vidyanath's computer generated her image, and if Vidyanath isn't a complete fraud, he would know something about her, about that time. It is a forlorn hope, but it's all he has.

He takes the Metro on his way back. The train snakes its way under the city through the still-new tunnels, past brightly lit stations where crowds surge in and out and small boys peddle chai and soft drinks. At one of these stops, he sees the apparitions of people, their faces clammy and pale, clad in rags; he smells the stench of unwashed bodies too long out of the sun. They are coming out of the cement floor of the platform, as though from the bowels of the earth. He's seen them many times before; he knows they are from some future he'd rather not think about. But now it occurs to him with the suddenness of a blow that they are from the blind girl's future. Lower Delhi—Neechi Dilli—that is what this must be: a city of the poor, the outcast, the criminal, in the still-to-be-carved tunnels underneath the Delhi that he knows. He thinks of the Metro, fallen into disuse in that distant future, its tunnels abandoned to the dispossessed, and the city above a delight of gardens and gracious buildings, and tall spires reaching through the clouds. He has seen that once, he remembers. The Immaculate City, the blind girl called it.

By the time he gets to Vidyanath's shop, it is late afternoon, and the little square is filling with long shadows. At the bus stop where he disembarks, there is a young woman sitting, reading something. She looks vaguely familiar; she glances quickly at him but he notices her only peripherally.

He bursts into the room. Om Prakash is reading a magazine, which he sets down in surprise. A bee crawls out of his ear and flies up in a wide circle to the hive on the window. Aseem hardly notices.

"Where's that fellow, Vidyanath?"

Om Prakash looks mildly alarmed.

"My employer is not here, sir."

"Look, Om Prakash, something has happened, something serious. I met the young woman of the printout. But she's from the future. I need to go back and find her. You must get Vidyanath for me. If his computer made the image of her, he must know how I can reach her."

Om Prakash shakes his head sadly.

"Panditji speaks only through the computer." He looks at the beehive, then at Aseem. "Panditji cannot control the future, you know that. He can only tell you your purpose. Why you are important."

"But I made a mistake! I didn't realize she was from another time. I told her something and she disappeared before I could do anything. She could be in danger! It is a terrible future, Om Prakash. There is a city below the city where the poor live. And above the ground there is clean air and tall minars and udan khatolas that fly between worlds. No dirt or beggars or poor people. Like when the foreign VIPS come to town and the policemen chase people like me out of the main roads. But Neechi Dilli is like a prison, I'm sure of it. They can't see the sun."

Om Prakash throws his hands in the air.

"What can I say, Sahib?"

Aseem goes around the table and takes Om Prakash by the shoulders.

"Tell me, Om Prakash, am I nothing but a strand in a web? Do I have a choice in what I do, or am I simply repeating lines written by someone else?"

"You can choose to break my bones, sir, and nobody can stop you. You can choose to jump into the Yamuna. Whatever you do affects the world in some small way. Sometimes the effect remains small, sometimes it grows and grows like a pipal tree. Causality as we call it is only a first-order effect. Second-order causal loops jump from time to time, as in your visions, sir. The future, Panditji says, is neither determined nor undetermined."

Aseem releases the fellow. His head hurts and he is very tired, and Om Prakash makes no more sense than usual. He feels emptied of hope. As he leaves he turns to ask Om Prakash one more question.

"Tell me, Om Prakash, this Pandit Vidyanath, if he exists—what is his agenda? What is he trying to accomplish? Who is he working for?"

"Pandit Vidyanath works for the city, as you know. Otherwise he works only for himself."

He goes out into the warm evening. He walks toward the bus stop. Over the chatter of people and the car horns on the street and the barking of pariah dogs, he can hear the distant buzzing of bees.

At the bus stop, the half-familiar young woman is still sitting, studying a computer printout in the inadequate light of the street lamp. She looks at him quickly, as though she wants to talk, but thinks better of it. He sits on the cement bench in a daze. Three years of anticipation, all for nothing. He should write down the last story and throw away his notebook.

Mechanically, he takes the notebook out and begins to write.

She clears her throat. Evidently she is not used to speaking to strange men. Her clothes and manner tell him she's from a respectable middle-class family. And then he remembers the girl he pushed away from a bus near Nai Sarak.

She's holding the page out to him.

"Can you make any sense of that?"

The printout is even more indistinct than his. He turns the paper around, frowns at it, and hands it back to her.

"Sorry, I don't see anything."

She says: "You could interpret the image as a crystal of unusual structure, or a city skyline with tall towers. Who knows? Considering that I'm studying biochemistry and my father really wants me to be an architect with his firm, it isn't surprising that I see those things in it. Amusing, really."

She laughs. He makes what he hopes is a polite noise.

"I don't know. I think the charming and foolish Om Prakash is a bit of a fraud. And you were wrong about me, by the way. I wasn't trying to . . . to kill myself that day."

She's sounding defensive now. He knows he was not mistaken about what he saw in her eyes. If it wasn't then, it would have been some other time—and she knows this.

"Still, I came here on an impulse," she says in a rush, "and I've been staring at this thing and thinking about my life. I've already made a few decisions about my future."

A bus comes lurching to a stop. She looks at it, then at him, and hesitates. He knows she wants to talk, but he keeps scratching away in his notebook. At the last moment before the bus pulls away, she swings her bag over her shoulder, waves at him, and climbs aboard. The look he had first noticed in her eyes has gone, for the moment. Today, she's a different person.

He finishes writing in his notebook, and with a sense of inevitability that feels strangely right, he catches a bus that will take him across one of the bridges that span the Yamuna.

At the bridge, he leans against the concrete wall looking into the dark water. This is one of his familiar haunts; how many people has he saved on this bridge? The pipal tree sapling still grows in a crack in the cement—the municipality keeps uprooting it, but it is buried too deep to die completely. Behind him there are cars and lights and the sound of horns, the jangle of bicycle bells. He sets his notebook down on top of the wall, wishing he had given it to someone, like that girl at the bus stop. He can't make himself throw it away. A peculiar lassitude, a detachment, has taken hold of him and he can think and act only in slow motion.

He's preparing to climb on to the wall of the bridge, his hands clammy and slipping on the concrete, when he hears somebody behind him say, "Wait!" He turns. It is like looking into a distorting mirror. The man is hollow-cheeked, with a few days' stubble on his chin, and the untidy thatch of hair has thinned and is streaked with silver. He holds a bunch of cards in his hand. A welt mars one cheek, and his left sleeve is torn and stained with something rust-coloured. His eyes are leopard's eyes, burning with a dreadful urgency. "Aseem," says the stranger who is not a stranger, panting as though he has been running, his voice breaking a little. "Don't . . ." He is already starting to fade. Aseem reaches out a hand and meets nothing but air. A million questions rise in his head, but before he can speak the image is gone.

Aseem's first impulse is a defiant one. What if he were to jump into the river now—what would that do to the future, to causality? It would be his way of bowing out of the game that the city's been playing with him, of saying: I've had enough of your tricks. But the impulse dies. He thinks instead about Om Prakash's second-order causal loops, of sunset over the Red Fort, and the twisting alleyways of the old city, and death sleeping under the eyelids of the citizenry. He sits down slowly on the dusty sidewalk. He covers his face with his hands; his shoulders shake.

After a long while he stands up. The road before him can take him anywhere, to the faded colonnades and bright bustle of Connaught Place, to the hush of public parks, with their abandoned cricket balls and silent swings, to old government housing settlements where, amid sleeping bungalows, ancient trees hold court before somnolent congresses of cows. The dusty bylanes and broad avenues and crumbling monuments of Delhi lie before him, the noisy, lurid marketplaces, the high-tech glass towers, the glitzy enclaves with their citadels of the rich, the boot-boys and beggars at street corners. . . . He has just to take a step and the city will swallow him up, receive him the way a river receives the dead. He is a corpuscle in its veins, blessed or cursed to live and die within it, seeing his purpose now and then, but never fully.

Staring unseeingly into the bright clamor of the highway, he has a wild idea that, he realizes, has been bubbling under the surface of his consciousness for a while. He recalls a picture he saw once in a book when he was a boy: a satellite image of Asia at night. On the dark bulge of the globe there were knots of light; like luminous fungi, he had thought at the time, stretching tentacles into the dark. He wonders whether complexity and vastness are sufficient conditions for a slow awakening, a coming-to-consciousness. He thinks about Om Prakash, his foolish grin and waggling head, and his strange intimacy with the bees. Will Om Prakash tell him who Pandit Vishwanath really is, and what it means to "work for the city?" He thinks not. What he must do, he sees at last, is what he has been doing all along: look out for his own kind, the poor and the desperate, and those who walk with death in their eyes. The city's needs are alien, unfathomable. It is an entity in its own right, expanding every day, swallowing the surrounding countryside, crossing the Yamuna which was once its boundary, spawning satellite children, infant towns that it will ultimately devour. Now it is burrowing into the earth, and even later it will reach long fingers towards the stars.

What he needs most at this time is someone he can talk to about all this, someone who will take his crazy ideas seriously. There was the girl at the bus stop, the one he had rescued in Nai Sarak. Om Prakash will have her address. She wanted to talk; perhaps she will listen as well. He remembers the printout she had shown him and wonders if her future has something to do with the Delhi-to-come, the city that intrigues and terrifies him: the Delhi of udan-khatolas, the "ships that fly between worlds," of starved and forgotten people in the catacombs underneath. He wishes he could have asked his future self more questions. He is afraid because it is likely (but not certain, it is never that simple) that some kind of violence awaits him, not just the violence of privation, but a struggle that looms indistinctly ahead, that will cut his cheek and injure his arm, and do untold things to his soul. But for now there is nothing he can do, caught as he is in his own timestream. He picks up his notebook. It feels strangely heavy in his hands. Rubbing sticky tears out of his eyes, he staggers slowly into the night.

The Tribes of Bela

ALBERT E. COWDREY

Albert E. Cowdrey quit a government job to try his hand at writing. So far, he's appeared almost exclusively in *The Magazine of Fantasy & Science Fiction*, where he's published a handful of well-received stories over the last few years, most of them supernatural horror, many of them taking place in a New Orleans haunted by demons and dark magic. In 2000, he took a sudden unexpected turn away from horror and into science fiction, producing two of the year's best science fiction novellas, "Crux" (which appeared in our Eighteenth Annual Collection) and its sequel "Mosh," which were expanded in 2004 into a novel called *Crux*. Although most of Cowdrey's output remains fantasy, he continues to turn his hand occasionally to science fiction as well, with results that make readers wish he'd do it more often, as in the tense and exciting tale that follows, a pure-quill old-fashioned science fiction adventure story that takes us to a troubled alien world where the natives are considerably *more* than restless . . .

Cowdrey lives in New Orleans, although whether *his* New Orleans is as scary as the one in his fantasy stories is probably something that it's better not to ask.

D*ocuments Assembled by the Honorable Committee Investigating the Tragedy on Planet Bela, and JUDGMENT Thereupon.*

ITEM (1)
Extracts from the Notebook of
Kohn, Robert Rogers, Colonel, Security Forces

I feel like I'm diving, not landing.

Bucking headwinds, the freighter's shuttle fights wind and rain until we drop out of the overcast over a blue-black sea. We're heading for a small rocky headland that juts out of a dim coastline.

The green duroplast shuttleport looks like a large fake emerald set in a broken ring of foam. The retros sear the pad, and clouds of steam boil up. As the sole passenger, I'm allowed to exit the ship before its rusty handling bots begin loading. An army of shiny ingots—gold, titanium, metals I don't have a name for—stands to attention, scoured by rain, awaiting the outward journey.

Two moronic guards (male and female) named Vizbee and Smelt retrieve my luggage under the baleful eye of Julia Mack, Captain, Security. My local counterpart salutes and I say falsely that I'm glad to be here. Smelt comments, "You may be glad now, but you won't be for long."

Vizbee adds, "Oughta give this goddamn swamp back to the Arkies."

"*Quiet!*" trumpets Captain Mack, and without further comment, the guards stow my things in a little flyer waiting in a hangar with airfoils retracted. Climbing in, I feel the four or five extra kilos I weigh here—also taste a fizzy, champagne-like something in the air. Maybe the extra oxygen will help me carry the extra weight. Or maybe just make me drunk.

Welcome to Planet Bela, old man.

We're barreling toward Main Base over fog-shrouded cliffs, through a squall blowing in from the ocean. Mack thinks it's all beautiful.

"Born here," she proclaims, her voice overfilling the cabin. "Only human that ever was. Against company policy, of course; Mama was on the pill, but something went wrong. Folks died in a mining accident and the colony raised me. Now, with these murders, they're talking about closing down the mines. People say we're going home—but for me, this *is* home."

"If I can help you catch the killer," I tell her, "the mines will stay open."

The smell of disbelief mingles with the odor of mildew from her uniform and lacquer from her regulation black wig. Christ, what a huge woman—must weigh close to ninety kilos. Yet not flabby. Her haunch pressed against me is solid as a buffalo's.

We turn west—or is it north?—above the estuary of a wide river where it swirls into the sea, spreading crescents of foam. A pod of enormous sea creatures rises all together, like dancers, and submerges again. I spot the gleam of tusks. Then we're skating in toward a cliff covered with a cluster of domes, semiplast storehouses, and connecting corridors like chicken-runs.

Whoa . . . what the hell?

Beneath the clutter lie huge blocks of stone shaped and fitted together like a puzzle. Did I come four-point-something light years to find the Incas have been here before me?

"Welcome to Zamók, Colonel," says Captain Mack, expertly bringing us in to a landing on the gray circle of a rain-slick pad.

As a boy I loved listening to the adventures of old Navigator Mayakovsky—the Explorer of a Thousand Worlds, as one of my textbooks used to say in the clear neutral voice I still hear in dreams.

He named this one Bela, meaning white. When I saw it from space, I thought the reason was the clouds of water vapor that make it glow almost like Venus. But I was wrong.

"Some information for you," says Mack, handing me a memory cube as we stand at the Entries and Departures desk. I plug it into my notebook and listen idly while an autoclerk enters my essential data into the colony's mainframe.

The cube tells me much I already knew. About Bela's wildly eccentric orbit. About the 241 standard years it takes to make its awesome trek. About its endless seasons, whose radical heat and cold result from the orbital path, not the tilt of its axis, which is only about two degrees. Earthlike features: It rotates west to east and its day is 22.7 hours, which ought to be easy to adapt to, even for somebody like me (I have trouble with circadian rhythms).

Then the cube recites the text of Mayakovsky's original report. The great Russian arrived in late winter, finding the skies ice-blue and clear, the surface a white wilderness—hence the name. His scanners spotted an artificial shape and he investigated and found an abandoned city.

"Who could have built this huge stone platform and the lovely temples that bedeck it?" he demanded. "This world is dead. Beings like ourselves, alien wanderers, must have built this place. But why, in this endless Antarctic?"

He named it *Zamók*, the castle, and the unknown builders *arkhitektori*. Hence the slang term Arkies.

Exploring the castle led to a nasty encounter with carnivores laired in the temples. At first the species seemed merely interesting, a rough parallel to the Earth's polar bears—and what Russian doesn't like bears? So that was the name he gave them, *medvedi*.

"Their long fur changes from dark to white as they move from shadow to sunlight," murmurs the cube. "Tusks and claws are formidable."

Then a blizzard blew in. With complete white-out at seventy below and all bioscanners inoperative due to cold, the beasts ambushed an exploring party. "Two crewmen dead. Skulls crushed. Another vanished, probably eaten. A dangerous degree of cunning and intelligence in these animals."

That of course was a mere incident. The ores his deep metal-scanners found brought the mining cartel. The miners bulldozed off the lovely temples and built the current trashy hovels instead. Meantime winter had ended, and Bela turned out to be anything but dead. Thousands of species swarmed out of hiding and billions of seeds and spores sprouted, to thrive until summer arrived and turned the surface into a howling desert.

A banal thought: How fragile life is, and how tough. Once it gets started, seemingly it can survive anything.

At this point I have to turn off the cube. The local doc's arrived, a tiny energetic Chinese woman named Anna Li.

She puts me through the usual mediscan. Odd business she's in, meeting so many naked strangers—probably wondering later on, when she sees them clothed: Is this the guy with the birthmark on his butt?

I tell her I'm not bringing in any dreadful diseases, unless being over-the-hill is a disease. She smiles automatically, pays no attention.

"You're okay," she says, studying the printout, "but stay off sweets." Then dashes away.

When I'm dressed, Captain Mack takes charge again, leading me through bilious green corridors crowded with people in gray coveralls. Name tags echo all the tribes of Earth: Jiang, Grinzshpan, Basho, Mbasa, Jones.

To my surprise, my quarters are in the executive suite. A comfortable bedroom, an opulent private bath. On a broad terrace outside, the Inca-like stonework lies bare and gleaming in the rain. The view over the river valley to the distant mountains would be spectacular, except for a heavy steel screen that obstructs it. What look like maggots are inching their way around in the wet.

"Somebody'll bring your luggage," Mack tells me. "Security Central's right next door if you need anything. Like your suite, it has two doors, corridor and terrace. The Controller will see you in the morning after you've rested."

She turns to go. But I've got a question: "What's the screen out there for?"

Mack frowns. "Mr. Krebs used to sleep in here, until somebody fired a missile at him. Fortunately he was in the Security office chatting with me, and he wasn't hurt."

"A missile?"

"Just a shoulder-fired job," she says defensively, as if a small missile makes you less dead than a big one. "Some disgruntled employee. That's when we put the screens up. There's one in front of the Security office, too."

"Was the missile stolen from your armory?"

Mack glares and says, "Yes."

"And where does the Controller sleep now?"

"Someplace else."

She closes the door firmly, leaving me to rest as well as I can—in the middle of a bull's-eye.

Supper's in the dining hall. Mack guides me to the head table in a private room. I'm hoping to see Mr. Krebs. But the Controller dines alone.

Instead I meet a dozen or so executives and engineers. English is everybody's second language, and I listen to a babel of accents expressing fervent hope that I can find the killer. His current score is nineteen dead—almost 2 percent of the population of 1,042. Dr. Li again bustles in, wearing a laboratory smock, and tells me she has holograms of the bodies and all the autopsy data. I can see them after dinner.

"Hope you've got a strong stomach," says the senior engineer, a guy named Antonelli. Making a face.

"Actually, there's not much mess," says Li. "Always one blow through the top of the skull with a sharp instrument. Odd way to kill someone, but it's silent and effective."

"Any particular sort of victims?" I ask. "Men or women, old or young, homs or hets?"

"No. If somebody was trying to wipe out a statistical cross-section of the colony, you couldn't get much more variety. True, they're nearly all young people. But that's just demographics."

Right. Mining colonies are like that: a few seniors to run the show, many young vigorous people to do what's often hard and dangerous work.

"There is one pattern. The crimes all happen here," puts in Captain Mack, who up to this point has sat silent, stuffing her face. "Never at the mining camp. For the first time, people are volunteering for extra duty at the mines."

A grim chuckle goes around the table.

When the meal's over, I ask Doctor Li to introduce me to the younger people. I stroll through the main dining room, shaking hands and gazing into a kaleidoscope of faces having nothing in common but underthirtyish freshness. These youngsters probably all think of themselves as larval executives, here to punch their tickets, then home to climb the promotion ladder. I wonder how many will make it.

A few minutes later, I'm walking with Anna—we've quickly gotten on first-name terms—down a chicken-run leading to her clinic. When we're halfway through, she stops and says, "The first killing took place right here."

"Here?"

We're standing in the middle of a perfectly blank, empty corridor about twenty meters long—windowless, well lit and devoid of the slightest concealment. I ask about the victim.

"A woman named Cabrera. Athlete—good runner; life's so dull here that anybody who doesn't take to drink takes to athletics. She could've escaped, I'm sure of it, if she'd seen him coming."

"What was she hit with?"

"Probably a mountaineer's pickaxe—short handle, easily concealed. The point penetrated the longitudinal fissure of the cranium and sank about seven centimeters into the midbrain. Cabrera lived a few hours in a comatose state, then died."

"Does the killer have to be a man?"

"Not with all the girls who take martial arts classes. We're outnumbered by the men and there'd be a rape a week if we couldn't defend ourselves."

"You're implying that not all miners are gentlemen?"

"They're gentlemen in about the same proportion that cops are."

A woman of spirit, I see.

ITEM (2)
From the Written Report of Anna Li, D.Sc., M.D.

This person met Robert—Colonel Kohn—on the evening of his first day on Bela.

I remembered nothing from doing his mediscan except that he was uncircumcised. At dinner I noted that he was a large man with prematurely white hair.

Our initial talk was useful, I think, in helping him understand the situation here on Bela. He seemed interested in the data I was able to show him. Whether he was intelligent I could not at first decide, though he spoke like a cultured man. I admit that intellectual arrogance is one of my grave flaws. We professionals always look down a bit at policemen, whatever we may claim to the contrary.

When he left, I locked the laboratory door. I had begun investigating a common worm or larva, hoping that unraveling the structure of its genome might provide a model for later work on Bela's more complex and interesting creatures.

Wishing the colonel well in my thoughts, I settled down to quiet, enthralling work that took my mind far away from corpses and those who make them.

ITEM (3)
From the Notebook of Colonel Kohn

The cool voices of clocks are announcing midnight, but of course it doesn't feel like midnight. I'm ready for bed but not, it would seem, for sleep. The old brain keeps cycling in the dry tedium of fatigue.

I'm glad I had this chip implanted in my larynx so I don't have to speak out loud to record my thoughts. You never know who's listening. The technique is somewhat like ventriloquism, and not hard to learn. All the rubbish from my stream of consciousness winds up in my notebook, buried deep in a coded memory.

Anna's pictures are moderately gruesome and not very helpful. Mack's notes on the murders are much the same. The killer's efficient. The MO's bizarre. The victims are anybody.

The crimes began in the corridors, shifted briefly to the hydroponics nurseries, then everywhere. Joggers were struck down on running trails, late workers in machine shops and offices.

Even after Mack issued orders that people were not to go anywhere without a companion, the killings went on. A woman was using a toilet stall while another stood guard outside. When she tried to open the door, it hit an obstruction that proved to be her friend's body.

Customary methods of investigation have failed. Tests for occult bloodstains, hair, and fibers turned up nothing. The colony lacks the equipment for sophisticated psych tests. Mack's methods have been rough-hewn; after the first crime she grilled everybody, eliminated those with solid alibis, then arrested three people who lacked them.

The results were not happy. After two more murders, the suspects had to be set free.

Now *everybody* has an alibi for at least one, and usually for several, of the crimes. No trace of the weapon has been found. Despite the prevalence of mining engineers, it wasn't standard issue; somebody whose hobby was mountain climbing might have brought it in their personal baggage. Mack's computers have searched personal-baggage invoices as far back as they go, but found no record of such an implement.

The stone platform under our feet is seamed with narrow passages. When stories sprang up about alien killers, the Controller first ridiculed the notion, then ordered Mack to explore. Almost any adult human would be too big to go down there, so she used a bot.

The memory cube contains a few images of wall paintings it found down below—the first ever seen of Zamók's Arkies, little hunchbacked brownish bipeds with three-toed feet and gourd-shaped heads and serious dental problems. But no sign of any recent presence except the scat and bones of small animals.

None of this surprised Anna. From the circumstances of the crime, she'd already concluded that the killer, like the victims, must be human. . . .

Oh, hell. I'm still trying to sleep, but no luck. Just too tired, and the old brain keeps churning.

Seeking air, I put on a robe and open a thick transplant door onto the terrace and edge around the screen. A tremulous roar rises from the river. A few chilly raindrops are falling. Thunder grumbles among distant hills.

The air tastes good up here—phytoplankton in the sea and greenstuff in the jungle are hard at work excreting the poison gas we love to breathe. I can feel my heart beat a bit faster. I suppose when you're down in the jungle among all the rotting stuff, it stinks. Most jungles do.

My bare feet are cold—forgot to pack slippers. The blocks of stone are smooth and slick. Little worms squish nastily underfoot. I cross the terrace to a low parapet and look down. Lightning flickers on a dense black jungle lining the riverbank below. Then I smell something like the lion cage at a zoo—

Aghh!

Phew. Rude shock.

Let me catch up. Light was emanating from the Security office and I'd turned that way and was padding along toward it when somebody flung open the door, pointed an impact pistol at me and yelled, "*À bas!*"

I hit the wet stones just as a shot whanged by. I twisted around in time to see something big that had been coming over the parapet tumble back and vanish.

Feeling better now. I'm in Security and a young guy in uniform is offering me a towel, which I need.

"Sir," he says politely, "I don't think you ought to be outside at night. Wild ahnee-mahls sometimes climb the walls."

A skinny little watchspring of a guy with a blue chin and dancing black eyes. His English is fluent but sometimes original. He's Security Officer Lt. Michel Verray.

All around us monitors are blinking and humming to themselves. A voyeur's dream of heaven. In one bedroom, a tumultuous pile of bedclothes suggests a couple trying for a little privacy as they make love. One of the least interesting scenes—an empty bedroom—is my own.

Michel is Captain Mack's only full-time assistant at Main Base. He calls her, with ironic inflection, Maman.

"Here, Colonel," he says. "Let me give you a key to the security office. I'm sure Maman wants you to have one. And I'll sign you out with a pistol."

We chat while completing this transaction. I heft the pistol, check the load, press the recognition stud until it memorizes the pattern of capillaries in my hand. Hi, pistol. Hi, Colonel.

We chat some more. "I presume she's not really your mother?"

He makes a comical face. "Non. But I think she would like to be."

If he's right about that, it's the first sign of human feeling I've noticed in Mack. Michel shows me around, explaining that the monitors were installed after the early killings.

"We try to persuade people to keep to areas under surveillance. I wish we had more equipment. We don't have enough cameras and anybody could be prowling the dark areas, looking for a chance to attack."

"Do people complain that you're spying on them?"

"They did at first. Not so much now they are scared. Anyway, we spy on ourselves, too. There's my room, with my roommates. And in that one you will be thrilled to observe Maman reading in bed."

Mack has her wig off and her hair is close cropped. She looks like Picasso's portrait of Gertrude Stein. I ask if the dozen or so weapons in the rack are the only ones in the colony. No, of course not. The Security people—Mack and Michel and Vizbee and Smelt—all carry guns. So does Mr. Krebs and Senior Engineer Antonelli and one or two other top dogs. In fact, everybody wants one, but Mack's resisting and so far Krebs has backed her up.

Damn right, too. Armed civilians can be more dangerous than the murderer.

"How about the missiles?" I ask.

Michel grins, knowing what I'm thinking. "All five that remain are here locked up, and only Maman has the key."

"I suppose the attack on the controller made her look bad."

"The whole situation makes her look bad. She gets grimmer every day it goes on. She may look like Mont Blanc but actually she suffers from the stress. And refuses to take the medications Dr. Li offers her."

Michel fetches a bottle of cognac and two plastic cups from a supply room. The drink lights a welcome fire in my gut. We chat and soon get chummy. It turns out that Michel did the exploration of the subsurface passages.

"You built the bot?"

"Non. Miners already had them to explore places too narrow or dangereuse for people. Call them Spiders [he said speed-airs]—little guys, walk on three legs, carry a digicam and an HI-light. I guided it through the passages, made Maman a memory cube and sneaked a copy for myself."

He shrugs, rolling his eyes upward in comic alarm. "Boy, she'd be pissed if she knew that."

"Why?"

"Like many mamans, she's difficult. She thinks knowledge is power. Okay, she's right. She wants to know everything that goes on here. Okay, that's her job. But she also wants to monopolize information, store it up to use against her enemies."

"She has enemies, then."

"Mais oui," says my new friend cheerfully, tossing off the last of his drink. "Everybody but me and Krebs hates her comme la peste."

Like the plague, eh? Well, I never imagined she'd be wildly popular. Michel's becoming franker (and also Frencher) as he absorbs alcohol. While he refills our glasses, I ask, "What do you want the cube for, Michel?"

"When I get home, I want to get a degree in Alien Civ and start teaching. I've started going over the cube frame by frame, and I think I can get my whole tay-seize [thesis?] from it. Le bon Dieu didn't mean me to be a cop," he added, then blushes, thinking I may take this as an insult to my profession.

"I agree with God," I assure him solemnly, and say good night. Now armed, I cross the terrace without incident.

Good kid, I think, turning in. He's saved me a lot—my life, plus a ton of postmortem embarrassment. Wouldn't that have been a fine terminal note in my personnel file? *On the first day of his last assignment, KOHN, Robert R., COL, SN 52.452.928, contrived to get himself eaten.*

Good night, all. And pleasant dreams.

Morning comes with rain, thunder, lightning, and a nasty shock.

Early on I'm summoned to Krebs's office. Captain Mack pounds on the door and, when I stagger out with eyelids still stuck together, leads me in grim silence through a labyrinth of corridors.

We're somewhere deep inside Main Base when we reach the new executive suite—so deep that the noise of the storm has faded into silence. Clearly, Mr. Krebs does not intend his quarters to be hit by any more missiles if he can help it.

His office is large, blank, and ugly, and so is the occupant thereof. Mack withdraws without a word and a spongy, grim-faced man leans forward in a tall executive chair and gives me two weak-feeling fingers to shake.

The chief feature of his face is a jaw like an excavator. His lower right canine sticks up outside. His gut billows over the edge of the desk, but his arms are thin and look unused. I typecast him as the perfect executive, a fat guy with a stone behind, good for nothing but giving orders to people smarter and stronger than he is.

"You'll be going in half an hour," is his greeting.

"Going where?"

"Why, to check the body," he growls, relapsing against the back of the chair. "Take Li with you. Third-rate doctor, but she's all we've got."

"There's been another killing?"

"Mack didn't tell you? Goddammit, I got to do everything around here. Yeah, it's at Mining Camp Alfa."

"The first at a mining camp."

"Right. Now these cowardly shits I got working for me won't want to go to the field at all. They all think they're here to eat company food and punch their tickets and do as little work as possible."

I begin to see why somebody might fire a missile at Mr. Krebs. He seems to have a similarly unkind view of me. He sits there glaring for a few seconds, then demands suddenly, "Are you piggybacking on my budget?"

Sticking his jaw out even further.

"No. HQ pays me and the mining cartel reimburses them."

"Well, thank God for small favors," says Mr. Krebs. "The dead guy was nobody special. Another small favor."

That ends the interview.

I collect my notebook, put in a new battery and meet Anna outside her clinic. She has an overnight bag full of specimen bottles and a medical chest, which I carry for her.

"I met your boss," I tell her as we hasten to the pad.

"To know him is to hate him," she says. "Hurry up, only one flyer's working and this is it."

Ten minutes later we're taking off into the very teeth of the storm.

What a flight. It lasts one hour or one eternity, however you choose to look at it. The damn black box piloting us has been programmed to take the most direct route—misplaced notion of fuel economy, I suppose—and that involves crossing a wide bay full of churning black water. A squall is barreling toward the shore, and we fly directly into it.

I feel sure the lightning's going to fry the black box and send us careening down into the sea. Haven't had breakfast, so there's nothing to come up except, of course, my stomach itself.

Anna takes all the pounding and shaking stoically, or seems to. Still, I notice she too heaves a sigh of relief when at last we leave the bay behind and bounce down onto another rain-scoured concrete circle near another clutter of domes and sheds.

"Well, here's Alfa," she says.

People come running with umbrellas—yes, real Earth-type umbrellas—but of course we get soaked anyway. Two dozen people are stationed here, but three guys are away fixing a slurry pump, whatever that is. So I get introduced to twenty live people and one corpse.

The latter is a young man named Thoms. He's lying facedown on the poured-stone floor of the machine shop. At first glance the only difference in MO was the fact that he'd been hit on the base of the skull instead of the top.

"Weapon appears to have penetrated the posterior median sulcus of the medulla," Anna tells her notebook.

But then she puts on a headset with a xenon lamp and high-power 3D magnifier, lowers the lenses over her eyes, and kneels down, her nose almost touching the dead man's blood-stiff hair.

When I help her up, she's frowning. "The wounds at Zamók were punched through," she mutters. "But this time . . . the wound's not nearly so neat. As if the weapon flattened on impact. I'll have to check when I've got the body back at the lab. Help me turn him over."

Somehow, handling a dead body has a calming effect on me. When I first see a corpse I'm always shocked, even after so many years of looking at violent death. But when I handle the body and feel that special weight, especially—as now—with rigor setting in, I know I'm dealing with earth and stone, not a person, and I can treat it like any other forensic exhibit.

Superficial examination shows that except for being dead Thoms' body is not, as Anna puts it, remarkable in any way. After taking a bunch of holograms, we bag it and the miners help us put it in their freezer.

The rest of the day I spend in a small, bare office with a single monitor bleeping on a chipped duroplast desk. I'm sipping coffee, noshing on bad sandwiches covered with some kind of ghastly synthetic mayo, and interviewing survivors.

Nobody saw or heard anything. Thoms was well liked, with no known enemies, and every single person at Alfa was under observation by others at the most probable hour of death, which Anna puts between 6.30 and 8.00. I reach the last name on my list before Madam Justice lifts her blindfold and peeks at me.

The witness—named Ted Szczech, pronounced Sheck—is a pale, twitchy, skinny kid who looks about sixteen and wears coveralls that could serve him for a tent. He shuffles into the room carrying an envelope.

"I've uh, uh, uh, got something for you, sir," he stutters.

"Oh yeah? What?" Bad food plus no progress has put me in a foul humor.

Ted spends the next five minutes tripping over his own tongue. The story gradually emerges that he worked with Thoms in the machine shop and so was the first to spot the body. Before sounding the alarm he ran for his digicam, rightly anticipating that everybody in Alfa soon would swarm in and obliterate every clue.

"Why didn't you bring me the pictures at once?" I demand in my growliest voice. Actually, I'm impressed by his initiative.

"I w-w-was w-w-w-waiting my turn," Ted explains. "And uh, uh, uh—"

"What?" I say, beginning to pull the printouts from the envelope.

"Well, you can see the f-f-f-footprints pretty clear."

"*Footprints?*"

"Yeah. They showed up when I used the infrared flash. Standard light don't show n-n-nothing. I never even knew they were there until I p-p-p-printed out."

I stare at dim little three-toed marks around a corpse so fresh that under black light it still glows with the warmth of life. In the early morning the stone floor was cold and the killer's body heat created just enough transient warming for the cam to register.

"It probably ran away when you started to open the door," I comment. That seems to scare Ted.

"You think so?" he asks, eyes bugging out. "You really think so?" Not a single stutter.

When I show the pictures to Anna, she looks ready to tear out her graying hair. "Oh, great Tao. We got it *settled*. The killer has to be *human*," she moans.

"Okay, a human did it. And then Threetoes walks in, trots over to body, trots away again and disappears into the jungle, and—"

My voice dies in midpassage. Anna looks at me. I look at Anna. We're both remembering where we've seen three-toed feet before.

"We'd better get back to Zamók," she says. "Now."

The storm's abated and the trip back is a bit tedious, which certainly was not a problem on the trip out. Lying behind us wrapped in translucent plastic the corpse reminds me unpleasantly of a giant fetus swathed in its placenta.

Back at the Castle we hump our gear across broad puddles and down gray corridors into Anna's lab. I retrieve my infopack and we check the pictures the Spider took underground. And yes, the Arkies have three-toed feet that resemble Ted's blurry images.

While I make tea on a hotspot under a vacuum hood, Anna calls Mack and asks for the memory cube containing the full exploration of the subsurface passages.

"You're not authorized to see it," that ungracious woman growls.

"What do you mean?" snaps Anna. "I've got top clearance. I need it for the work I do."

"You're a penis machinist, not a security officer. You don't have a security-type clearance."

At this point I step forward. "I'm cleared for everything you are, Captain, and a lot more. Send that goddamn cube and send it now."

That makes me feel pretty good. Pulling rank may not be nice, but it's effective.

We relax until Michel appears with a sealed container, for which Anna and I both have to sign. He gives me a wink, then heads back to his job. A couple of minutes later, she and I are head to head, staring into the image box of her computer.

The solid-looking forms jounce, steady, fuzz out, clarify. We're entering a narrow slot between two of Zamók's cyclopean stone blocks. We descend steep narrow steps. The high-intensity light swivels back and forth, its movement complicated by the robot's walk. Anna's forever freezing a frame here and there so we can get a fairly clear picture.

Along walls of smooth stone marches a painted procession of Arkies wearing fantastic outfits of skins and feathers. Projecting teeth give their heads a spiky appearance. At the foot of the steps a narrow corridor splits left and right and the robot begins to explore. Passages divide and subdivide and it pokes into small rooms covered with garish paintings that make me think of Mayan art at Tikal and Dzibilchaltun.

It's all quite fascinating and, as far as our current problems are concerned, absolutely useless. When the show's over, our tea has gotten cold. "So what's your conclusion, Colonel Sir?" asks Anna with ungentle irony.

"An alien—" I begin.

"The Arkies are natives," she corrects me. "We're the aliens."

"Okay, okay. First of all, you were right. An Arkie couldn't have done the killings at Zamók. You turn around in a corridor and see a strange creature, you run, you scream, you fight back, you do something the victims didn't do. The killings here were done by a human. So we have an anomaly."

We sit staring at each other. Feeling around helplessly in my empty head, I ask, "What do we know about the Arkies?"

She gestures. "What you've seen."

"I mean—" I don't know what I mean. "How'd they survive in this world? It's so bizarre, radical cold, radical heat, seasons that last for decades . . . how'd they get along?"

She sighs. "Nobody knows. We're like a pimple on the body of the planet. We came here with typical engineer's tunnel vision, to dig and smelt and ship the ingots home and follow them when the mines play out."

She spends a while reheating the tea, then goes on: "I'm as bad as the rest of them. Spend my days doing routine physicals and treating orthopedic injuries from the mines. That's where the crack about me being a penis machinist comes from. And there's truth in it. I try to do some real science after hours."

"Anything helpful?"

"For solving the murders? No. On the contrary—it's as far as possible from anything to do with them. I'm trying to get a start on understanding the molecular biology of—"

"Oh," I say. "Okay."

"Anyway, you asked me how the natives fit into their world. Answer: I don't know how anything really functions on Bela. We're all so busy being practical that we don't have time to be intelligent."

So we give up; I send Michel the info we gathered at Alfa, and then we go to dinner.

Replay of last night—Mack feeding her face, the engineers eyeing me, wondering if I know something they don't about the latest atrocity. To avoid questions I don't want to (meaning: can't) answer, I avoid socializing, say good night to Anna and as soon as possible drag my aging butt off to bed.

Through the door to the terrace I see that another storm's moving in. The cube says the "spring rains" are scheduled to last about forty standard years. What would Noah say to that?

Hit the hay but again can't sleep, this time because the lightning keeps waking me up. Cursing, I get up and start searching for a way to darken the window.

Lightning flashes. Inside the screen a monster stares at me.

Lightning flashes. I stare back. Oh come on, it's only an animal.

But it's impressive. Standing upright, bowlegged, body covered with rough fur of indefinite color. It's a boar, by God—a huge two-legged boar. The hairy ears, the little red eyes with startling piggish intelligence in them—and the tusks, two down and two up, dirty orange but rubbed white where they cross each other—and especially the flat snout, quivering, with the hairy nostrils spread . . .

And then, of course, I see it's not a boar or anything else I've ever known. Long claws instead of trotters. Muscled forelimbs adept for walking or climbing. Imagine a big bear crossed with a swine, crossed with . . . what? Something.

In the dark this triumph of natural genetic manipulation claws at the thick transplast with twenty-centimeter talons that make a nerve-jangling skreek. Lightning flashes. It exposes the full length of its twelve-centimeter tusks and turns away, frustrated.

Lightning flashes. The animal's gone.

Somewhat shaken, I continue my search, find a switch on the wall and touch it. Yes, praise whatever gods may be, the window darkens. I go to bed again and try to fall asleep.

Processions of feathered creatures march through my head, tracked by two-legged pigs and by Mayakovsky's *medvedi*, the bearlike animals that ambushed his people seventy years ago when it was wintertime on Bela . . .

Why do all these strange critters seem vaguely alike?

ITEM (4)
From the Written Report of
Li, Anna M., M.D.

I spent that evening in my laboratory, meaning to work on my project. But my mind kept drifting to the body in my freezer.

At length I gave up, dragged poor Mr. Thoms onto an examining table, and began to explore his wound. Almost at once I found something odd.

Perhaps I should have called the Colonel at once, but I decided he was probably asleep. So I promised myself to speak to him at breakfast, not realizing that tired as I was after our adventures of the day, I might oversleep and miss him in the morning. And that is exactly what happened.

ITEM (5)
From Colonel Kohn's Notebook

"So," says Mr. Krebs, champing his jaws, "what've you learned so far?"

His windowless office gives me a feeling of premature burial. The man himself, with his piranha profile and billowing stomach and weak little hands, manages to look dangerous and helpless at the same time.

"Who do you think tried to hit you with a missile?" I respond conversationally. This is a question I (literally) dreamed up last night, when the old subconscious finally did something useful.

"I want answers, not questions."

"Well, I don't have any, yet. But you haven't just had twenty murders here. You've had that plus an attempted assassination of the colony's executive head. I'm curious as to whether there might be a connection."

He growls. Literally—grrrrr. Like a dog.

"Talk to Captain Mack," he says. "That's her department."

"I'm surprised you've kept her in such an important position after all the things that've gone wrong here," I say frankly.

"I trust her absolutely."

I take this as an admission that anybody appointed in her place might use Security's armory to try to kill him—again.

"Now, if you don't mind answering my original question, what've you found out about *the murders*?"

I open my notebook and set it humming. Briefly I outline the events of the day before. At the end I summarize, "The Arkies have joined the fun."

"But they're all *dead!*" he almost yells.

"No more than Mayans or Egyptians or Celts or Cambodians or any of the other builders of abandoned cities on the Earth are dead. They just moved away. Their descendants live on. Spring brought the Arkies out of hiding, and what did they find? Their Acropolis, their temple mount, had been desecrated by aliens—us. That pissed them off, and they've just killed their first human."

I think that's kind of a neat theory—much too neat to be true.

"You're saying none of our people killed anybody?"

Patiently I explain the difficulties in trying to blame the first nineteen killings on the natives.

"So you're telling me we've got two killers, in two different places, killing people in the same bizarre way, and one's a human and other's a whatchacallit. That's the dumb-assedest notion I ever heard."

"Sir, you've summed up the problem," I tell him. "The evidence is unreasonable. *But it's still evidence.*"

The rest of the interview's a total waste of time. We just yell at each other, accomplishing nothing. A supply ship's due pretty soon and I guess he'll send me home, as he's authorized to do. That will make both of us happy.

Needing time to cool off a bit after the shouting match, I set out to find Anna's lab and promptly get lost.

I don't know if I've made this clear, but Main Base is a hopeless maze. The buildings were put up at different times for different purposes out of whatever materials were at hand. Meanwhile the population increased to a high of two thousand or so and then declined as mines were worked out and abandoned. Now a dozen buildings are permanently vacant, and a tangle of corridors lead here and there with no rhyme or reason, often ending in blank walls where an abandoned structure's been sealed off.

Adding to the general confusion, about half the people are absent at any one time. Some at mining camp Alfa—the only site that's presently active—the rest at the smelter, or exploring for new sites. Then they come back to work at administration or housekeeping. The idea is to train the youngsters in all phases of running a colony.

But that also means they rotate in and out, causing ceaseless turbulence. I've got a near-photographic memory for faces, and yet I've never seen many of the people I encounter.

Two I do recognize are Vizbee and Smelt, the guards from the shuttleport, who must have rotated back. Vizbee's as near insolent as he dares to be. "Enjoying Bela, *Sir?*" he asks with a nasty smile.

At least he's learned the word sir since I saw him last.

"You're looking a bit lost, *Sir,*" Smelt chimes in, with a washed-out smile. Someday I will deal with this pair.

Actually, getting lost turns out to be one of the more useful things I've done. I've been dealing with facts, which are fine as far as they go. Now I'm getting the feel of the situation, too. The killer's been hunting his victims in a kind of indoor jungle. Add the fact that he doesn't seem to care who gets bashed as long as somebody does, and the bloody orgy becomes comprehensible.

I spend a couple of hours wandering, asking directions, finding the directions don't work, and getting lost again. Periodically I come across a sealed window and look out on the river valley. Or a landside enclosure with high fences and shrouded machinery on duroplast skids. Or a big cube sprouting thick cables—the main generator, a primitive fission-type reactor. Bela, I perceive, is run on the economy plan.

But I can't get out, and soon I'm wandering the maze again like a baffled rat.

Finally admitting I'm lost for the nth time, I ask directions from a pretty dark-haired engineer named Eloise. We chat, and she invites me to visit her room, explaining that she and her boyfriend are "on off-rotation"—awkward phrase—from the mines.

The boyfriend's named Jamal, and he's solidly built and dark and bitter as a cup of Turkish coffee. He and Eloise share a very cramped room, which they consider themselves lucky to get. I ask why space is so tight when, with all the empty buildings, it should be just the opposite.

"Mack says it's for security," growls Jamal. "Stay where the cameras can watch your every move, including when you shower and make love. I can just see her and Krebs lying in bed—incredible as it seems, a lot of people think they sleep together—and peeping at us like the swine they are."

My own impression is that Mack and Krebs are both asexual beings, but I don't argue the point. Instead I remark that morale in the colony is close to rock-bottom.

"It's dying," says Jamal, now sounding weary rather than bitter. "Everybody hates the leadership and everybody's scared to death."

I'm sitting with Eloise on the edge of their bed. Jamal is sitting on the floor.

"See, you haven't been here the last two years," he goes on. "You look at the number of victims and think, 'Oh, well, ninety-eight percent of the people are still alive.' But when you live through a campaign of murder, the effect is cumulative. I never leave El without wondering if I'll ever see her again, and she wonders the same thing about me."

She strokes his coarse black hair and nods. She has an inner stillness that he completely lacks, yet she backs him up.

"It's been hard," she says simply. "I'm sure nobody will want to come here again, and everybody who's here already is counting the days until they can leave. Bela will have to be abandoned."

She's less bitter than he is and makes an effort to be fair, even to Mack, whom everybody else blames for their miseries.

"She's in a terrible situation. If she's afraid of anything, it's having to leave Bela. I'm sure she's doing her best to find the killer, and I'm not sure anybody else could do any better. I mean, how do you catch somebody who doesn't care who dies as long as somebody does?"

"Some goddamn maniac," Jamal mutters.

"I don't think so," says Eloise thoughtfully. "The killing's random, yet at the same time it's calculated and deliberate. It's . . . cold. Somebody's aiming at something, and it can only be to drive us all away."

"Why would a human want to drive humans away?" asks Jamal, and neither of us has an answer.

There is, of course, the big exception—Thoms' murder. My hosts haven't heard about that yet. But the conversation starts me brooding about it once again.

Feeling a strong urge to revisit Alfa, I thank the young folks and ask them to show me an exit to the pad. They do so, and my luck's in, because on the pad the flyer's revving up. It's a dull trip, and everything seems normal until we arrive.

Then I ask for Ted Szczech, and learn that he won't be taking any more pictures. Ever.

No, he didn't die by the customary head-bashing.

Less than an hour before, something resembling a two-legged boar grabbed him when he was outside working on a stuck valve of a slurry pipe, and dragged him away—presumably to eat.

They're getting up a search party to try and recover his remains. I ask to go along and they say sure.

As I'm suiting up, a call comes in from Anna. She's been hunting me, called

Michel in the security office and asked if I was on any of his monitors. He told her he'd seen me with Eloise and Jamal, so she called them and they told her they'd seen me catch the flyer. Then Michel called her back and said he needed to see me, too.

Funny, all you have to do to get popular is to go away.

Anna's full of her latest discovery. "Last night I found bronze fragments embedded in Thoms's skull. I'm not set up to do metallurgical analysis, so I asked one of our engineers to check the fragments out."

"Why?"

"I think the bronze was smelted by some very crude, primitive process. The alloy's soft and that's why the skull did almost as much damage to the weapon as it did to the skull. Or maybe it was meant for use on a softer, thinner cranium."

"In short, it was made by an Arkie to smack other Arkies and the hardness of the human head took its wielder by surprise."

"Something like that. When are you coming back?"

"They're sending out a party to search for Ted Szczech, and I'm going along. A wild animal got him."

"Great Tao. What kind of animal?"

I describe it.

"Oh, that's *Ursasus terribilis*," she says.

"Meaning?"

"Terrible bearpig. I started doing taxonomy on the local fauna, giving Latin names and so on. Then stopped, because it seemed so futile. Oh, poor Ted."

"We may find him yet."

Somebody's yelling for me. Michel will have to wait.

We put on transparent rain gear, the kind that breathes so you don't drown in your own sweat, and water-repellent goggles. We're all armed to the teeth. The flyer takes off to circle over the search area. Nobody's expecting it to find anything; the jungle's too full of big organic molecules that confuse the bioscanner.

Down below, it's exciting at first—walking in the deep wet woods of Bela. Up to now its green/blue/purple colors seen through misty rain didn't look especially strange. Close up it's a crawly place. Everything drips; every step squishes. Vines are in motion, like the hands of an antique clock; you can't see them move, but if you look away and look back, yes, they've changed.

The trees form short, twisty lattices of rope-like growths with trunks not much thicker than limbs. No large trees—there's been no time for them to grow yet. Leaves of all shapes stretch up and out toward the little light that's available, ruthlessly shading each other out so that the understory is choked with masses of dead and rotting vegetation.

No flowers. Everything in monotone. Things buzz around that look like flying crayfish. In glimpses of the sky, we see dashing small shadows that somebody on my intercom calls daybats. Hunting the crayfish, I suppose. Now and then I catch sight of an elaborately feathered creature crawling through the branches with its beak and talons, like a parrot. The usual little white worms are crawling around the wet ground, millions of them. My feet squash them at every step. I begin to feel like I'm walking through the innards of a dead, decaying beast. Even through the filters in my breathing apparatus I catch whiffs of decay, not quite like decay on Earth; a sharp touch of ammonia, stench of methane, a gagging bubble of—what? Chlorine? Plus that smell like a lion cage I sniffed before on the terrace at Zamók.

Lasers hiss in the murky air and slashed limbs fall smoking to the ground where the wet extinguishes them. The ground's like a spongy mattress and I sink knee-deep at every step. Soon my legs ache and my knees are quivering. We circle the whole camp, finding nothing.

Ted's just gone. Period.

Back at Alfa, I'm bushed. Fall on somebody's cot and snooze for about two hours. When I awaken, one of the guys tells me Zamók's been buzzing me.

"Why didn't you wake me up?"

"Easier said than done, old-timer. You were *out*."

First time anybody's called me old-timer to my face.

I stagger to the nearest monitor and press the return-call button. Michel's image says he'd like to see me as soon as possible. I call his code but get only his image again, promising to return my call at the earliest possible moment.

I have ersatz coffee and another plastic-mayo sandwich and think it over. If Michel wants to see me, why hasn't he called again and why doesn't he answer my call?

I call Captain Mack and ask if she knows where he is. She's looking, if possible, grimmer than usual. No, he's off duty until tomorrow. Where's he sleep? Impatiently she gives me the code for the room he shares with two girls and another guy. I call and his roommates are there, but he isn't. I call Anna and ask her to look for him.

"I'm waiting for the analysis of the bronze."

"Look for Michel, please."

I go to Alfa's commandant and ask to borrow the flyer. No, he says, it's on a regular schedule.

When will it be going back to Zamók? Tomorrow noon, he says. Thank you, I say.

I walk out onto the pad and find a tech just finishing his service routine. I tell him Hi, and when he goes back inside, I climb in and tell the black box to take me to Zamók.

"Hearing and obeying," says the gadget.

"Accept no calls from any source until we arrive," I add.

"Hearing and obeying," says the gadget.

I settle back in the seat and wonder how I can explain snatching this machine if, after all, Michel meets me alive and well.

I needn't have worried.

By the time I arrive he's been found, and Main Base is in the state of an overturned anthill.

As startling as the murder itself is the way it was done: Michel Verray has been shot in the back in the same chicken-run where Cabrera's body was found almost two standard years ago.

There was no approach, no hands-on attack. An impact slug was fired from the far end of the corridor. His beltpouch has been roughly opened, breaking the catch, suggesting robbery. His pistol's missing. Was he killed with his own weapon?

A scenario flits through my mind: Michel confronts the killer, draws his weapon, has it knocked out of his hand—maybe by somebody who's been taking those martial-arts classes Anna talked about. He turns and runs away, and the killer picks it up and coolly takes aim and shoots him . . .

But I'm not even sure he was running when he was shot. Mack thinks so, but the holograms she took of the body seem ambiguous to me. A runner hit from the rear in midstride on a smooth surface slams down and slides. I think the abrasions on his face are insufficient for that. I'd say he was hurrying but not running, and Anna's inclined to agree.

In her clinic she starts crying, the first time I've seen her do so. She has Michel's body on her examining table, and it's a horrible mess. As usual with that type of ammo, the entry wound near the spine is the size of my little finger and the exit wound through the chest is the size of my head. The slug, of course, disintegrated as it's supposed to do, leaving no evidence.

"Even Mack's shaken up," she tells me when she's cried on my shoulder. "I saw her when they brought the body in, and she looked paralyzed. She kept saying, 'Oh no. Not him. Oh no.' He was kind of a substitute son, you know. Now she's really alone."

Well, murder gets to the toughest of us, sooner or later.

Anna washes her face at a laboratory sink and says dolefully, "I have to do the autopsy."

"Not now, you don't. Tomorrow's fine. Michel won't run away. Come on, I'll help you put him on ice."

I hate to touch the body, but as soon as I do, it's okay. Michel is gone; the good mind, the lively wit, the Gallic accent, the future he had sketched out for himself—none of that exists anymore. The corpse is merely evidence.

We wrap it up and put it in the freezer next to Thoms. We're getting quite a collection of dead youth.

Anna needs company, so I take her to my suite and, after I check my weapon—in case of bearpigs—we step out on the terrace.

Rain's falling in the distance, but a gap has opened in the clouds and pale sunset colors, lemon and rose, are showing. It's the first sunshine I've seen on the surface of Bela. I begin to see what this world will be like in those magical decades—between spring and summer, again between autumn and winter—when it's neither savagely cold, nor unbearably hot, nor a sodden mess. It'll be gorgeous.

For a while we stand there like a young couple holding hands. Anna needs distraction, so I begin telling her about the wet wild woods around Alfa, about the strange creatures and the restless trees. Her mood lightens a little.

"I want to do some real science here," she says. "I just won't let myself keep getting sucked into the routine. I've been doing a little work on these larvae."

She gestures at the worms crawling on the terrace. "They're all over the place and they're genuinely weird. A human has maybe forty thousand genes, but they've got five times as many."

"What, those little worms? Why?"

"I don't know. They're about as simple creatures as you could imagine—a kind of motile gut. And think about all the chances for genetic errors, for destructive variations—it's too much information."

She added, "Rather like the murders. Where we've also got too much information and can't make any sense out of it, either."

She's back on that subject now, and with a sigh I admit to myself there's no avoiding it. Now she's mourning Michel, who evidently had a gift for making older women want to take care of him.

"Such a nice young man. A little while and he'd have been headed home. It's terrible, all these young people dying."

She starts to cry again. I put my arms around her, and she's so small that for all the gray in her hair it's like holding a child. I'm just about to embark on some serious comforting when intuition—as usual—seizes an inconvenient moment to strike.

"Anna, listen. Tell me this: Why was Michel hurrying down that particular corridor?"

She looks up at me, eyes bleary, mind as usual clear. "Oh. Sure, it leads to my lab. You mean he couldn't find you, so he was coming to see me."

We stare at each other for a few seconds.

"Come on," I say.

"Where?"

"I just saw a ray of light. This time internal. I think I know what the killer was looking for in Michel's beltpouch. Let's go talk to his roommates."

Vengeance is on my mind.

Anna's an unusual woman. Asks no questions, just leads the way through the maze of shoddy construction. I stumble a few times because my mind's elsewhere, thinking of a lot of things that at last, dimly, seem to be making some kind of sense.

Michel's room is in an outlying building: large, clean, well-lighted; semiplast partitions between four bunks; a bouquet of artificial flowers lying on Michel's pillow.

His roommates are all drinking something with the sour smell of home brew and talking together in low voices. I ask to see Michel's belongings.

"Captain Mack took them all," says a young Eurasian woman named Jospin, who seems to be the spokesperson for the group. "She and those two characters Vizbee and Whatever practically turned the place upside down."

"She *said*," adds the guy, "that she was looking for evidence."

That starts an argument between those who say Mack was just doing her duty and those who say she was harsh and unfeeling. I short-circuit this argument.

"Listen. You all know who I am and what I'm doing on Bela. Now I need something and one of you may have it. I hope you do."

I explain what I think Michel has been killed for, and how much I need to see it if it still exists. Jospin looks steadily at me, then reaches into her beltpouch and takes out a pillbox.

"For PMS," she explains with a faint smile. She shakes out, not a pill, but a memory cube and hands it over.

"He asked me to hide it," she explains. "He said not to give it to anybody. He didn't say why."

"I don't know why either," I tell her. "But I hope to find out. Many thanks, and" (speaking as impressively as I can) "don't . . . say . . . *anything* about this."

In Anna's lab we play the cube and, yes, it's the copy Michel made for himself of the Spider's exploration of the subsurface passages of Zamók.

"We've seen this already," says Anna, disappointed.

"But perhaps not all of it."

As before, we settle down head-to-head to watch. Once again the little robot descends a slot half a meter wide. Once again pictures of garish creatures in bizarre attire wobble past. We enter familiar rooms, leave them, walk three-leggedly down corridors, enter other rooms.

I'm beginning to get worried. The trouble with intuition is that until you test it, an error looks just as convincing as the truth.

"I don't see anything n—" Anna's beginning when I yell something, maybe "Shit!"

We both stare breathlessly at the screen.

The Spider is entering a room we've never seen before. Slowly it pans the walls and ceiling with its HI-light. We're looking at a sacrifice. As with medieval paintings or comic strips, a series of scenes tells a story.

Unlike our Aztecs, the Arkies had metal weapons, the favorite being an implement with a long handle ending in a curved blade on one side and a spike on the other. With one of these gadgets a priest ceremoniously sacrifices one of his own kind to whatever gods he believes in.

The method is familiar; a fatal blow delivered with the spike against the back or top of the head. Only he does a follow-up, splitting the skull with the axe, after which the believers gather to eat the brain.

The victims don't seem to be resisting; light streams from their faces and rainbows encircle them with full-spectrum haloes. Above them god figures hover, radiating light; in the last scene, they welcome the sacrificial victim to Valhalla.

"Looks like a retirement dinner," I remark unfeelingly.

"No," says Anna. "They're not cannibalizing for food. It's magic. They're acquiring wisdom. They aren't murdering anybody, not in their own minds. They've sacrificed somebody they respect, made him a god, and now the tribe is sharing his knowledge and strength—oh!"

For the second time in a few minutes she's been interrupted, this time by herself. As for me, I am, as they say, struck dumb. Whatever I expected to see in the underground, it isn't this.

The Spider has emerged from the room with the images of sacrifice. In the corridor just beyond, a human child is lying against the wall—a tiny, an improbably tiny girl with golden hair.

For a moment I think I'm going mad. Then Anna says, "It's a doll," breaking the spell.

And with that, of course, the whole case opens before my mind.

Anna and I are outside in the rain. We stroll to the power station with its comforting roar of turbines and its EM fields to mess up listening devices.

We lean our heads together and whisper, reviewing the evidence.

A child can get down the steps into the underground, can take her doll and a flashlight, can see the paintings.

Perhaps, surrounded by busy adults who fundamentally don't give a damn about her, she spends a lot of time down there. She meets other small beings her own size. She plays with and loses her toy.

Mack grew up on Bela, the only human who ever did.

Mack is physically powerful. She's nobody's friend, yet she represents security. Somebody, turning and seeing her coming up from behind, would feel only relief—whew, I'm safe—but nobody would stop to chat with her.

They'd turn and walk on. And feel only one stunning blow before the darkness.

Anna talks about Michel, what a terrible thing it must have been even for a mass murderess to realize that for safety's sake she had to kill the nearest approach she knew to human affection.

I'm more concerned with how she caught on to him. "I bet the kid got careless, made a copy of his cube and left the images in a backup memory, where she found them."

"Mack's insane," whispers Anna.

"No," I say. "She's a native. Like the Arkies. She's helping them reclaim their world. When we go, she'll stay here with them. That's what she really wants—to be rid of us, and stay here forever."

The rain patters around us. It's getting dark, or darker. The power station roars and shakes. My imagination's doing acrobatics.

Suddenly I'm seeing in a whole new light that missile attack on Krebs, the one that conspicuously missed, while scaring the shit out of its target.

What if the whole episode was intended to make him feel surrounded by enemies, make him more dependent on her? And whose missile was it, anyway?

She said she was "chatting" with him in Security when it hit. She wouldn't lie about something like that—too easy to check. And I'm sure Michel wouldn't have fired it. Suddenly I'm remembering her other subordinates, Corporal Vizbee and Private Smelt.

Voilà! I think, in honor of Michel.

At last breathing all that oxygen is paying off—I'm in ecstasy, making connections, when Anna interrupts with a practical question. "What are you going to do?"

"Confront her, accuse her, arrest her. And I'm going to grab those two grungy enlisted people of Mack's. There's something I want to ask them."

"You won't get Vizbee and Smelt," she says. "They were just in to pick up supplies. Right after they helped her shake the place down, she sent them back to the shuttleport."

"Then it's Mack alone."

I'm a happy man. I'm about to crack my case and go the hell home and my ego's purring. When I get back to Earth, I'm thinking, I'll take a long vacation—preferably in Death Valley.

"You're really confident, aren't you?" she asks with an odd inflection. I peer at her, curious.

"Spit it out, Anna," I say. "This is no time to be feminine."

"Well, I think you're underestimating her. And this world. You don't seem to realize that she's not just a lone criminal. We've already had Thoms and Szczech attacked at an outstation. And think of *Ursasus terribilis*—what if the Arkies control the local carnivores? What if they've already used them twice to try to kill you?"

Goddamn women anyway. They have a gift for imagining worst-case scenarios. "If you're right, I'll have to move fast."

"When will you arrest her?"

"Now. Right this minute. Want to come along?"

As we hurry back into the maze, she's muttering, "There's something else. I know there's something we haven't thought of."

But I'm not really listening. First I use a public machine to call Jamal and Eloise.

"Do you feel energetic?" I ask.

Jamal looks baffled. "I guess so. Why?"

"I may need a little assistance. In my room. For something important and possibly a mite dangerous."

He looks at me with narrowed eyes, suspicious of anyone in authority. Eloise comes up behind him.

"We'll be there," she says over his shoulder. I break the connection.

"Don't hurry, just in case we're being watched," I tell Anna, and we move with what, I believe, is legally termed deliberate speed through the usual throng, anonymous in spite of their name tags: Ellenbogen, Menshnikoff, Nguyen, Rice-Davies.

In my bedroom we check the terrace outside, then exit and head for Security. I try the electronic key Michel gave me and it doesn't work.

"Shit," I profoundly comment. "She's changed the settings on the lock. Stand back."

The impact slug knocks out the lock and I kick the door open. The gun rack is empty. At the same moment my eyes fall on the monitor that shows Michel's room.

Oh, Christ.

So while I was busy solving my case, so goddamn sure of myself, she was watching us, changing the lock, removing the weapons.

Did she take the missiles, too? I check hastily. One's gone; the other four are still locked in. But she's removed the detonators so I can't arm them. Who's serving this match?

All things considered, Anna's voice is remarkably calm as she says, "Look outside."

My friend the bearpig—or his cousin—is coming over the parapet. He uses his claws like grappling hooks, climbs easily despite his weight of maybe three hundred kilos. As he moves into the light pouring from my quarters I see sticking through his coarse yellowish fur a million black spines, like a hedgehog's. The guy's armored as well as armed.

He rears up, freeing his forepaws for action. Then he moves bowleggedly yet with disturbing speed around the screen and a scream tells me that Eloise and Jamal have arrived there.

I fling open Security's door and run outside, Anna following. But before I can fire, the beast takes what looks like a tremendous punch from an invisible fist, right on the snout. He rears up, flops over and lies twisting on the Incan stonework.

The great skull is ruined. One eye stares at Anna and me with helpless rage before it films over. The body smells like the lion cage at a zoo—an acrid, sulfurous, somehow fiery odor.

I look into my room and Jamal's standing there in the approved shooter's crouch, holding a pistol in both hands, index finger on the firing stud.

"Where'd you get that?" I ask after we've all greeted each other.

"Swiped it from my boss's locker. I didn't see any good reason why the senior guys should have protection and El and I shouldn't."

"Good for you. Look, we have something of a situation here." I explain.

The four of us huddle. We've got two weapons. Each has fired once, leaving fifteen shots each. Mack's got a dozen weapons and all the spare ammo. She knows Main Base backward and forward, and however she calls her friends—those in the jungle, and those in the passages down below—she's undoubtedly doing it now.

Touching my forehead in salute, I tell Anna, "You were right. This *is* the worst-case scenario."

She's standing there as if in a trance, looking like a statue of Guanyin, the Goddess of Mercy.

"There's more," she murmurs.

So much for mercy.

"I've just realized," she goes on. "The larvae. Two hundred thousand genes."

I don't understand, even though I know what she's referring to. Eloise and Jamal are, of course, looking absolutely blank. But Anna now speaks with calm professional assurance, as if she's telling somebody they need to get their triglycerides down.

"The larvae must be the basic form. They must hatch from some kind of spore with a really tough capsule to survive the extreme heat and cold. Something triggers development into different forms—partly it must be temperature, but I'm sure it's more complicated than that. The Arkies are one form and Mayakovsky's *medvedi* are another and the carnivore Jamal shot is another. And there may be more.

"They're all cousins, so to speak. That's how they dominate their environment and survive the fantastic changes that happen here on Bela . . ."

Silence follows. Then the quiet voice insists, "Don't you see?"

"Unfortunately," I say, "yes."

We try to put out a warning.

Eloise has just settled down at the huge console in Security and spoken a first word of command when a sound of distant thunder comes through the shattered terrace door and the machine and the monitors and the lights all go out.

I step to the other door, the one leading into the corridor, and fling it open. It's dark inside Main Base, almost as dark as on the wet and dusky terrace outside. Battery-fed emergency lights are flickering on and beginning to glow redly. People are standing around, looking baffled, their faces purplish as if they had lupus. I turn back with my latest bad news.

"Mack just used her missile on the power station. Zamók's been shut down. All of it."

We head into the corridor and try to spread the alarm by word of mouth. It's not easy. The maze is more confusing than ever. Everywhere people are milling around, bitching about the power failure. Many were headed for the dining hall; complaining they'll have to eat cold rations tonight.

We try shouting, telling them an attack is about to begin, telling them if they've got weapons to join us, if not go to the dining hall and lock the doors. People crowd around us, trying to decide if we're crazy.

Some of them have never seen me before. Anna they know, but so what? She's just the doc. Jamal and Eloise are too young to count.

Where are their leaders? they want to know. Where's Krebs, where are the senior engineers—above all, where's Captain Mack?

"What does Captain Mack say?" a young guy demands. "I mean, she's in charge of security, right?"

"Captain Mack has already killed twenty people and is about to kill a lot more," I inform him, biting off my words.

The fact that I'm getting pissed off doesn't make this unpalatable news any more believable. Yet some people take alarm and start to hasten away. Even if we're nuts, the lights are out; something's clearly wrong.

Others stand around arguing. Some are belligerent—what the hell are we saying? Who the hell do we think we are? Are we trying to start a panic just because there's an equipment failure? Somebody will fix it. That's what engineers do, right?

Then comes a shout. "Doc Li! Come quick! The Controller's been shot!"

And that does it. Suddenly the *toute ensemble* gets to them. The shadows, the dim red lights, the air growing stuffy, the palpable anxiety, Jamal and me waving weapons and talking about an attack, warning them against Captain Mack—and now somebody's yelling that the Controller's shot.

So they hated him, and they hated her, so what, they're the symbols of command and control, right? If they're hostile or wounded or dead, everything's coming apart, right?

Suddenly they panic. And they bolt. They're like cattle scared by lightning. I see shadowy people caroming into one another, knocking one another down. Running into half-dark corridors, headed for I don't know where. Some for the dining hall, some bolting for cover in their rooms.

The guy who yelled for Anna fights his way to us where we stand together, waiting for the hall to clear. He's Senior Engineer Antonelli, and I met him for the first and only time on the day I arrived here. He's armed, and I'm glad to see him.

Anna asks, "Is it true Krebs has been shot?"

"Yes. I found him in his office and—"

He never gets to finish. Somewhere in the maze, people start screaming. There are roars and howls. People start running out of the corridors they ran into not five minutes ago. A chunky young woman trots up.

"Arkies are coming up through the floors," she gasps. "And there's some kind of big animal loose."

We hurry to the dining hall. About twenty people have gathered there, two with guns. They're using furniture to barricade the doors, of which there are four. The only light comes from the emergency system.

"Stay here," I tell everybody. I tap Antonelli. "You're in charge."

"I know that," he snaps.

"Where are you going?" asks Anna.

"To snatch a flyer if I can. The only reserves we have are at Alfa, and we're going to need them."

"I'm going with you."

"No, you're not. These people may need a doctor."

"You couldn't find your way with the lights on. How about with them off?"

Eloise steps up and says quietly, "I'll go with him."

To this Jamal objects so violently that I lose patience and, while he's ordering Eloise not to move a muscle, I give him a short left to the point of his dark stubbly chin. He drops like a stone.

I tell Antonelli, "When he wakes up, tell him we'll be back with reinforcements."

In the dark corridor, Eloise says, "I suppose you had to do that."

After we've walked a few meters, she adds, "He's such a dickhead, I've often wanted to punch him out myself."

Of course Anna was right. If I'd tried to find my way out of the maze I'd have gotten hopelessly lost.

Eloise, on the other hand, turns out to be one of those irritating people who always know exactly where they are and the precise azimuth to follow to get anywhere else. When I compliment her, she says, "I'm part homing pigeon."

There's a body in the way, the back of the head caved in. It's nobody I know, but Eloise gives a little muted cry before we hurry on.

"Know him?"

"Oh, yes. Before I . . . met Jamal."

Something roars up ahead. I'm smelling an odor like lions. I pull her into a dark doorway and we wait. Something big lurches past, making the floor creak, thick coarse fur and spines rasping the wall with a sound like a wire brush. Then a patter of footsteps, a chink of metal and a rapid warbling as varied as a mockingbird's song, only deeper.

Everything fades into the distance. A woman screams. There's a little popping sound—an impact weapon. A roar.

Eloise whispers, "You notice something? The Cousins—that's what Anna called them, wasn't it?—all smell kind of alike. The big ones and the little ones. Maybe that's how they recognize their own kind."

Right, they all have the lion smell, as penetrating as burning sulfur, and why not? They all must have the same basic body chemistry. An idiot rhyme runs through my head: If you stink alike, you think alike.

The birdlike voice of the Arkies fascinates Eloise. "Maybe there's only one 'word' in their language," she whispers, "that long sweet whistle, and the rising and falling tones make the differences in meaning."

"It would be nice," I say repressively, "to speculate about that if we had nothing else to do."

We venture into the darkness, turn down this corridor and that one. Under a red light the semiplast flooring's been burst out from below. I have no trouble recognizing the narrow slot in the stonework beneath, the steps leading down. I even catch a brief glimpse of painted walls.

"You know," Eloise tells me as we edge past and hurry on, "if circumstances were just a bit different, my sympathies would be with the Cousins. It's their world . . . turn here."

Suddenly we're slamming through a door onto the pad and the shuttle is sitting there, completely empty except for the black box that runs it. Standing in a hangar nearby are two others: one half-dismantled, one that looks service-ready. That fact may be important. Then we're inside the waiting flyer and I'm locking the door and shouting an order to take off. The black box is perfectly calm. "Hearing and obeying," it says.

Abruptly we're soaring into light rain, and as we tilt and turn, Main Base except for a few security lights is plunged in darkness as deep as the jungle below it.

Now we're over the bay, nothing to be seen below but faint crescents of white foam as another in the endless succession of squalls blows in from the ocean. Why do I have these repetitive nightmares, and why do they all turn out to be real?

Emerging from wind-driven rain, we see Alfa's lights still on. A valve is stuck open somewhere and the slurry from the mine—pollution, humanity's signature—is gushing downslope in an oily torrent toward the bay. Eloise makes a faint sound and points.

A guy and a young woman are sitting on top of Alfa's brightly lit power station. He's armed, and they wave at us. There's a dead bearpig lying below. As we bank and turn on our spotlight, something flickers, an arrow maybe, and the two flatten themselves as it flies over.

I doubt that our black box has been programmed for the current circumstances, so I wedge myself into the pilot's seat, hit the manual cutoff and take control of the flyer myself. It's a cranky little machine, and I have some trouble getting it under control. Meanwhile Eloise grabs the pistol and opens the right-side door. As I start swinging back over the power station she fires twice. There's a commotion in the shadows.

"Get something?"

"I don't know. I think there was a bunch of—of whatever, getting ready to attack."

I finally figure out how to bring us to a low hover. The attitude control's stiff—probably a long time since the machine's been on manual. We tip this way and that, then steady and move closer to the shed.

Over the whine of the engine I yell, "What about the others?"

Can the answer really be, "All dead."?

ITEM (6)
From Doctor Li's Report

This person regrets intruding herself again.

However, I have a positive contribution to make, for Colonel Kohn's absence left him without knowledge of events at Main Base during many crucial hours.

I may state at the outset that locking the doors of the dining hall proved to be impossible. Regrettably, all the locks were electronic and failed when the power went down. How we longed for an antique mechanical bolt or two!

Fortunately the doors opened inward, and piling furniture against them provided a partial defense. Almost at once the doors began to move, pushing back the chairs, tables, etc. Our enemies had no machines but an abundance of muscle, and we were hard put to it to hold them out.

Then noises were heard from the kitchens. Antonelli led a small group of us to the source. When the tiles composing the floor began to shift and then to be knocked out from below, he was waiting.

An Arkie appeared wielding a bronze axe, and Antonelli's shot went through his body and killed also the warrior behind him, who was armed with a sort of barbed hook. Wild scurrying and scampering followed, leaving the mouth of the tunnel empty save for the bodies.

This gave me an idea. After the corpses had been dragged out, I found that I could just fit into the passage, being quite a small person. I asked to borrow Antonelli's weapon. Instead of waiting for a new attack, I proposed to drive back our enemies. And he agreed.

So for the first time I entered the subterranean world of which we had all heard so much and seen so little. I confess that my motive was far more curiosity than any desire to kill Arkies. I believed that the passages provided them protection from heat and cold, all-weather connections between the buildings that used to stand on the surface of Zamók, as well as storerooms and robing rooms where priests prepared themselves for public ceremonies. All this proved to be true as far as it went—which was not very far!

I carried a battery-powered lamp detached from the wall. It was dim and red, and I kept watching uneasily for side chambers, where anything might be hiding. But for twenty meters the passage ran straight and unbroken. It was profoundly silent, and I guessed that our enemies had abandoned any hope of getting at us by this approach.

Then I heard noises ahead, birdsong voices that sounded strangely in these caverns. I switched off the lamp, and stood for a time in profound darkness. Then I began to see very dimly, the way one does on a clouded night—peripherally, while the center of the retina registers only a blur.

This seemed strange to me, for of course the eyes do not work where no light at all exists. There was light, then, although very little, and I soon realized that microscopic fungi lived on the walls, emitting a dim greenish bioluminescence. Thus the lamp I carried had never been essential; but when we were looking down from the kitchen, the tunnel had appeared perfectly dark.

I placed the extinguished lamp on the floor, stepped over it with some difficulty, and moved on. The pistol was heavy, and I now held it with both hands, ready for action.

My next discovery was that my shoulders no longer brushed against the walls, though I still had to bow my head. The passage was widening, and I could see an opening ahead with something moving just inside it.

I stopped at once. When the obscure movement ceased, I advanced very, very cautiously, well aware that as the space opened around me I would be subject to attack. The tunnel widened into a broad room, where long slabs of stone stretched away into the dimness in mathematically straight lines.

On each slab lay terra-cotta trays a few centimeters deep, and in each the familiar larvae were swarming.

This was an impressive sight. Clearly, the Arkies no longer depended on the natural development of their kind in the forest. I heard whistling and movement toward the other end of this strange nursery, saw an Arkie emerge from the dimness and post itself beside a tray. Something began to trickle, and I realized that the adult was urinating into the trays, a few drops to each, and I caught the penetrating "smell of lions," as the Colonel called it.

No doubt, I thought, the urine contains hormones which speed the development of the larvae into the Arkies' form: a most fascinating achievement for a species that, so far as we know, has nothing that can properly be called science!

Well, and why not? I asked myself. Folk medicine gave us humans quinine for malaria and inoculation for smallpox. I was full of these thoughts when suddenly the Arkie spotted me and broke into a frenzy of birdsong.

ITEM (7)
From Colonel Kohn's Notebook

We have them aboard now, the two Alfans, and yes, everybody else in the mining camp is dead.

The technique reminded me a bit of Ted Szczech's abduction. Something broke the slurry pipe, that set off alarms, and when a repair crew went out to fix it the Cousins ambushed them. The Arkies used poisoned arrows as well as bronze hand weapons, and with the bearpigs to aid them soon forced their way inside.

The Alfans say two species fight together like humans with war dogs or war horses or war elephants. Only here there's a family connection much more direct than ours with our symbionts. They recognize each other by smell, and seem to feel a kind of tribal loyalty. There may even be a telepathic bond—the Arkies seem to give orders at a distance. They're the most intellectual members of the clan, but even the ones we think of as beasts are—as Mayakovsky noted so long ago—disturbingly intelligent. In fighting, the bearpigs display initiative and cunning as well as savagery.

Down below, they're dragging the bodies out into the open, into the glaring lights. The bearpigs begin to feed and the scene is garish, horrible, a kind of Grand Guignol theater. The Arkies look on, but don't share the meal. Clearly, humans are not eligible for the company of their gods in Valhalla.

Watching the butchery, I know we've lost the war. Period. We have to assume that the four of us in this flyer and the people holding out at Main Base and *maybe* the guards at the shuttleport are the only survivors. So back we go.

ITEM (8)
From Dr. Li's Report

As I retreated down the tunnel, I could hear and sense rather than see them following me, and I fired the pistol.

The place was so narrow that I did not have to aim. Of course, neither did they. Something came sliding and scraping along the floor and touched my shoe, and it proved to be a short throwing or thrusting spear with a leaf-shaped bronze point.

I fired again. There was no use trying to evade the necessity to kill or be killed. My heel struck an obstacle and I almost fell over backward, saved only by the narrowness of the tunnel. It was the lamp. I stepped over it and continued my fighting retreat.

The sounds at the end of the tunnel indicated that bodies were being pulled out of the way. I fired again, producing much agitated noise. My heel encountered another obstacle: the first step.

It is no easy task to retreat up a staircase that is both narrow and steep, at the same time keeping one's head down and one's guard up. With a metallic ping an arrow struck the riser of a step I had just vacated and the wooden shaft broke. Then friendly hands were pulling me out of the slot, into what seemed at first the blinding light of the kitchen.

I had hardly begun to tell the others of the mysterious world beneath our feet when a deafening impact rocked us all. We stumbled over one another rushing into the dining hall, now adrift in dust and shattered fragments.

The wounded, still shocked, had not yet begun to scream. One of the piles of furniture had been blown to bits and the door to the hall was a gaping hole.

Captain Mack had used another missile, and used it well. Our enemies were upon us.

ITEM (9)
From Colonel Kohn's Notebook

I think the Cousins are awestruck—it's the only word I can think of. Stunned by Mack's demonstration of godlike power.

I left the Alfans at the pad with orders to rev up the other workable flyer to aid the evacuation. Then Eloise guided me to this scene of ruin.

In the dim red glow of the hallway outside the mess hall our enemies stand, small and great shadows under a forest of glinting spearpoints and axes with curved blades. Clouds of smoke and dust are billowing around them, masking shapes and distorting outlines. I bet their ears are deafened and ringing, just like mine.

For some of the animals it's too much. Frightened, they begin to lumber away, colliding with one another and the Arkies and the walls. The moment of confusion is perfect.

I can see Mack, wigless, with the missile launcher still on her shoulder. I take careful aim at her, fire, and hit a bearpig that lurches between us at the critical moment.

Then Jamal and Anna run out of the mess hall, both armed, firing too, and panic hits our foes. The coughing of the impact weapons is almost inaudible, and creatures large and small start falling over. Some scream, just like wounded humans.

Then they're running, fading into the darkness of the corridors, maybe some retreating into the underground passages until they can figure out what's going on. Mack's gone too—at any rate, I can't see her distinctive figure anywhere.

We stumble over bodies, shouting. Jamal hugs Eloise, glares at me. That left hook I gave him seems to have made me an enemy. Then Anna mistakes me for something hostile and almost shoots me before I yell at her.

The mess hall's in ruins, some people dead, some wounded, some stunned. We don't have a minute to lose, we grab the living and run. It's a total rout. We're like Spaniards fleeing Mexico City on the *noche triste*. Or like Americans fleeing conquered Saigon.

Eloise and Anna are leading the way through the corridors with their smears of red light, and I'm hearing our enemies roar and sing and reassemble for a new attack.

The walking wounded have to take care of themselves; the helpless ones are hauled and dragged by the shoulders or even by the feet. We've got four weapons but only about a dozen shots left, as near as I can figure.

Then we're out onto the pad. In the rainy dark the lights of the two functional flyers cast frenzied shadows everywhere. Those of us who are armed prepare to resist while the others are jamming people aboard. Two who died on the retreat from the mess hall get thrown aside like rubbish.

Anna has given her weapon back to Antonelli. She's in medical mode, doing a sort of instant triage. She orders the bad cases stacked like cordwood in one flyer so she can ride with them and try to treat them.

Meantime figures are gathering just inside the doors and arrows begin to flicker and ping. A young woman I don't know turns a frightened face toward the door of Main Base and takes an arrow soundlessly in her throat. It's short, about thirty centimeters, and it only pricks her, yet suddenly she's flopping helplessly on the ground, her face cyanosing.

We abandon her, too.

I don't really notice the last moments. All at once I'm hanging half out of the door of a flyer, there's no room inside for all of me because I'm too goddamn big, and arrows with little barbed brazen points are sticking in the skin of the machine.

I hear the black box—so calm, so cool, a voice from another world—as it says, "Hearing and obeying," and we're lifting away from Main Base.

So slowly, so slowly. And I'm riding like that, arm crooked around a stanchion, and some friendly hand's holding on to my belt as we wobble and yaw out over the estuary and the white-crested black waves of the sea.

ITEM (10)
From Dr. Li's Report

We were packed together like rice in sushi. At first I couldn't do anything for my patients, because I couldn't move.

Two of them died right there, and with great difficulty we extracted the corpses and threw them into the sea, making a little more room so that Colonel Kohn at last found a place to sit inside.

I discovered that eleven of us were on that little flyer, which was built to handle four plus luggage. That it stayed aloft at all was quite wonderful. I feared, however, that the excess fuel consumption might drop us into the sea before we reached the shuttleport.

It was the darkest part of the night, and I shall not soon forget the trip. Sometimes a soft moan, the rank marshy smell of human bodies that have been sweating with fear. The odor of blood. Fortunately, the wounded were in shock from their injuries and burns, and lay quiet.

Exhaustion was our great friend, and I suddenly opened my eyes to find that I had been sleeping, and that a pale gray misty dawn had begun to filter through the clouds.

Soon every eye was trying to pierce the veils of rain for our first sight of the promontory and the egg-shaped green dome. What we would find there no one knew—whether it had been attacked, whether its two guards survived—and I was thinking also of the months that must elapse before the next supply ship came.

It is no light thing to be at war with a whole world.

And then I saw something—I saw something—I saw a smooth geometrical shape rising out of the clouds and mist, and it was still there, the portal by which humans enter and leave Bela. I thought: Oh, that we may yet leave it alive!

ITEM (11)
Extract from the Bela Shuttleport Log

7.56. Have spoted 2 flyers approtching. Linda and me didnt hardly have time to jump out the sack and put our draws on when they come boncing down on to the pad and a bunch of people come spiling out. Memo: file complant with Krebs re (1) unskeduled flyte and (2) overloded flyers. (Singed) Cpl Vizbee, Securty.

ITEM (12)
From Colonel Kohn's Notebook

Vizbee and Smelt are looking pretty sour and disheveled, and give us minimum help carrying the wounded. They keep saying they take orders only from Mack and I have to get a bit rough to convince them they now take orders from me.

We number twenty-two, of whom nine are too seriously injured to work or fight.

Brief tour of inspection shows a freezer stocked with foodstuffs for the guards and the loading parties who used to bring in the ingots. I ask Antonelli to check it out. He says that if all the wounded recover, we'll starve before the supply ship gets here.

Medicines: the shuttleport has a small dispensary, but Anna looks grim when she inventories the drug locker. I suspect Vizbee and Smelt have been into it for recreational purposes, though of course they deny it.

The port contains about three hundred square meters of floor space. Walls and floor are thick translucent duroplast—solid stuff, nothing will break in. Power source: another antique reactor housed in its own dome and accessible by a protected corridor.

Escape possibilities: We now have three flyers, but the two we brought with us are almost out of fuel—that overloaded last trip, among other things. The flyer V&B came down in is usable, with enough fuel for a return flight to Zamók, where, of course, we don't dare go. One dismantled flyer remains there—I hope beyond repair.

Outside it is, surprise, raining. The pad is wet and shining. There's a bare space, maybe half a hectare in all, where everything except a kind of lichen has been killed off by the retros of incoming and departing shuttles.

Beyond are gray rocks and clumps of stunted trees. A neck of barren land connects us to the shore and the usual gray-green-purple wall of jungle.

Situation summary: We're in good shape, with ample space, bedded down warm and dry, with lights on and medical care and nothing to do but wait for the supply ship. It's due in about sixty-seven days—local days, that is. If it's late (and it often is) we'll be living on air and water. *Lots* of water.

The first need is to increase food supplies somehow.

I call on Jamal and Antonelli to help me search the peninsula. Jamal wears his patented scowl but obeys scrupulously, which is all I ask for. We take our weapons, just in case.

We complete our circuit in under an hour. It's not much of a place. I doubt it's more than a couple of square kilometers of volcanic slag. You can hear the sound of surf everywhere. The beaches are gray shingle or black sand.

We walk out on the rocky neck that connects us to the shore. The water's shallow on one side where the sand has built up, but deep on the other. Could be a fine fishing spot. I'm sure we can fabricate some tackle.

I've surf-fished on coasts like this, and for a moment it all seems halfway familiar—the sea air and the smell of the deep and the sting of salt in the flying drops of spray.

Jamal turns back toward the shuttleport, but I walk a few steps on with Antonelli. He begins to tell me something, shouting to be heard over the crash of the waves.

"Sometimes I dream about retiring to an island. Just me, a good library, a wine cellar, a bot or two to do the dirty work—"

Aagh!

The deep erupts and something huge and black falls with a weight that shakes the rocks.

It's big, big as an orca, and it has broad flippers in front and four huge splayed tusks. It takes Antonelli's whole head in its mouth and thrusts with the flippers and slides back into the water, dragging him under. The wind flings a geyser of foam into my face. I wipe my eyes and the last thing I see are the man's legs thrashing deep down like the arms of a squid.

Antonelli's gone. Just like that. The kelplike odor of the deep mingles for an instant with the fiery smell of lions. Then there's only wind and salt and Jamal is dragging me away.

Behind us something big roils the surface of the sea and there's a great bellowing roar, *Aa! Aa! Aa! Aa!*

ITEM (13)
From Dr. Li's Report

Nothing of this tragedy was audible inside the dome.

I'd done what I could for my patients and was trying to comfort a young woman named Mbasa, concealing my fear that she might be permanently blind.

To treat this one injury properly, we needed a set of replacement eyes, fetal-monkey stem cells to regrow the damaged optic nerves, and the services of a skilled neurotransplant surgeon. We had none of the above. And there were other cases even more serious than this one.

Then Colonel Kohn appeared in the doorway, white-faced and soaking wet. He gestured for me to follow him. I gave him a blanket, made fresh hot tea and met him in the station's departure lounge. In one corner Eloise and Jamal were hugging each other as if they never intended to let go. The colonel sat hunched over, wrapped in his blanket like a beggar, and sucked greedily at the steaming tea.

"The Cousins have a cousin we knew nothing about," he said, and told me of Antonelli's death. "The trouble with the worst-case scenario is there's usually a worser one. How are your patients?"

I replied that at least four and possibly as many as seven would not survive.

"That's good," he said.

I looked at him and saw a man who was both familiar and strange. Despite his professional toughness, he had always seemed to me a humane man. Now I was seeing another side of him. Though he still trembled with the cold, his face was bleak and hard as the rocks of this nameless island.

"It's a good thing," he muttered, "that we have a big freezer. We're going to run out of food, Anna, and we're under siege and can't get any more. Once our supplies are gone, we'll have no choice but to eat our dead."

We sat quietly together, sipping tea, while the profound depth of our dehumanization sank in. Suddenly I knew that I could not face the coming ordeal alone.

I brought him another cup, plus fifty milligrams of Serenac, which he obviously needed. There was nothing else I could do for him, except go to bed with him and hold him and keep him warm. At that moment I resolved to do so, if he would have me.

ITEM (14)
From Colonel Kohn's Notebook

I see it's been several weeks since I made an entry, so let me try to catch up. Much has happened, also little. Anna and I have become lovers—a development that was a surprise, at least to me.

By default we've also become the rulers of our tiny besieged colony. As Anna predicted, four people have died of their wounds and two more are moribund. With Antonelli gone, that leaves seventeen of us, soon to be fifteen.

In all we've suffered almost 99 percent casualties. Even if some people at Main Base or the mining camp or the smelter have escaped into the jungle, they won't survive there long. They'll be killed, or they'll simply starve.

All the senior engineers being dead, I appointed Jamal as technical officer. His business is to keep the place working. I know he has long-term plans for revenge. I humiliated him in front of Eloise with that long-ago punch, and he's one of those people who never, never, never forget. Well, I need his brains, courage, and knowhow, and in return he can have his revenge.

Anna has the job of keeping the survivors alive. Eloise works under her and is rapidly turning into a capable physician's assistant. In bright people, on-the-job training produces quick results. I see to defense and discipline, make out and enforce the duty rosters, preside over the distribution of rations (about eighteen hundred calories for the healthy, twenty-one hundred for the sick) and act generally prickish. Like Mr. Krebs in his time, I am not beloved, nor do I expect to be.

The only serious violation of rules has been, inevitably, by Vizbee and Smelt. Ordered to turn over keys to all doors, cabinets and cupboards, they did so, but kept a duplicate set. When Anna told me that six vials of something called M2—a synthetic morphine substitute—had disappeared from the medicine cabinet, I staged a raid and found them in Vizbee's laundry bag.

The matter was serious, because we're low on painkillers and have a lot of pain to kill. In a container of Smelt's vaginal cream I also found the duplicate keys.

My first impulse was to shoot both of them. However, Anna spoke up for mercy and the general feeling in our community seemed to be that they were too stupid to be fully accountable.

So I held a private session with each of them, offering them life in exchange for some answers.

Both babbled freely. Each blamed the other for firing that missile at Krebs's quarters. Both affirmed that Captain Mack gave them the weapon and the order, which as good soldiers they had to obey, whatever their personal feelings.

"I'm sure you understand, Sir," says Smelt with her soapy smile.

"Only too well."

I had them sign confessions, and then I tied both of them up and put them in the freezer beside the corpses. Half an hour later I took them out. They emerged wrapped in spiderwebs of ice, and when revived seemed to have gotten the message. The next time they're going in for good, although the thought of having to eat Vizbee stew or Smelt croquettes eventually is pretty repugnant.

Aside from that, the time has been routine. We haven't been attacked. Those of us who hadn't already paired off are doing so now—most with the other sex, a few with their own. Everybody needs a companion here.

Recreation: Hidden away in cabinets we've found some chess sets, tennis racquets but no balls, a game called *Conquer the Galaxy*—excuse me, I'd rather not—poker and blackjack and Airborne Polo programs, and old sets of greasy playing cards, some of which are marked.

Daytimes we clean the place and tend the injured and service the machinery; at night we mark our calendars, make love and play games and gossip and feel hungry and bitch. And, as much as possible, sleep.

Between Anna and me there's a surprising amount of ardor, considering our mature age and marginal diet. Also a lot of caution. The conjunction of two loners of settled habits is dicey at best. And there are some physical problems, because she's so small and I'm so large. But—in sex as in life—where there's a will, there's usually a way. We've found privacy in what used to be a storeroom. I've locked the door with a confiscated key. At the moment, Anna and I are lying starkers on a pile of discarded shuttlecraft cushions, warmed by proximity and by some clean mechanics' coveralls she found in a bin and turned into bedspreads.

Now she turns to me with a smile and lets her tiny but very capable hand settle on my arm, like a dragonfly. I think this will be all my note-taking for tonight.

ITEM (15)
Extract from a Letter of Eloise Alcerra to Her Mother

Dearest Mama, So many things have happened to us that I hardly know where to begin. First of all, there's been a war . . .

So that's the story to date. Now I'm working in the hospital in the shuttleport here on Bela. We only have three patients left—the others have died or have recovered as much as they're going to here.

I'm doubly happy when Anna (Dr. Li) declares somebody well. I'm glad that I've been able to help them get better, but I'm also glad that they'll be going on the same eighteen hundred calories as the rest of us. That way we'll all last a bit longer.

I'm tired all the time. Yet when I lie down I usually can't sleep, and when I do I dream mainly about big dinners. Jamal's the same way. He works hard, much harder than I do. Maybe as a result he's less demanding about sex. I don't know whether I like that or not.

I dread the thought of our first cannibal feast. Yet it can't be far off. Will I be able to eat human stew? Yes, of course. When you're hungry enough, you'll eat anything.

Jamal makes ghastly little jokes about it. "You heard about the cannibal who passed his brother in the forest?" he asks, leering. Or pats my still ample backside and says, "Lunch. Hey, take that back. Lunch and dinner."

How, and above all why, have I put up with him so long?

At least once a day I sneak away and walk outside. I need to be alone for a while, away from the intolerably repetitive faces of my fellow prisoners. Needless to say, I stay off the beaches!

I don't feel so tired outside, I guess because of the enriched air, and I love the smell of the sea. Yesterday a sunbeam worked its way through the clouds and the seawind seemed to glitter with salt.

Yet today even my walk left me feeling down. I climbed, muscles quivering, up a pile of black rock and stood for a while looking out to where the horizon line ought to be. Only it wasn't, because the usual squalls were all around and as I turned, first the ocean and then the drenched jungle faded into the sky without a break.

The dome isn't our prison. This world is our prison, and I ask myself again and again if any of us will ever escape it.

Even if we don't, I'm sure people will come here again looking for us, and I hope they find this. Meantime I hold to the thought of you and the Earth and its sunlight and blue skies as my lifeline.

ITEM (16)
From Colonel Kohn's Notebook

The time until the supply ship arrives is getting short. If it's late, ciao, good-bye, sayonara. We're running out of food.

So today we eat human. Two of us do the butchering, I suppose to spread the guilt around. We rotate cooking by roster, and just as I won't name the other butcher, I won't name the cook, other than to state that (s)he doesn't turn a hair over the grisly task.

In fact, once the meat is separated from the frame, it looks just like anything else. We keep the head for decent burial on Earth, assuming we ever get back there. I won't give the name of the entree, other than to say it was someone I knew and liked. But once life has departed, we're all just meat and might as well feed our friends. Think of it as giving the ultimate dinner party.

The smell of cooking permeates the dome. People go about their usual duties, but they keep sniffing. Little groups talk together and I hear some high-pitched laughter. That worries me a bit. No hysterics needed here.

Then we sit down to eat. There are two schools of thought about our protein supplement: It tastes like veal; it tastes like pork. I belong to the pork school. After the meal, everybody's a bit frantic. Next day: We have leftovers. Nobody bats an eye, and two guys ask for seconds, which I have to refuse them. Cannibalism turns out to be like any other rite of passage. The first time's hard, the second time's a lot easier, and after that you don't think much about it anymore.

However, there's one thing we'll all soon have to think about, and I have to admit it's getting me down.

ITEM (17)
From Dr. Li's Report

The problem facing us was this: When we had eaten the dead, what then?

I began to hear jokes about "drawing straws." But was it a joke? Surely, I thought, if the supply ship doesn't appear soon, we'll have to be killed one at a time, so that hopefully a few of us—or two of us—or even one of us can return to Earth to tell our story.

At dinner I saw Robert looking over our people with a curiously bleak face, empty of expression. I realized that he was mentally drawing up a new roster. He was arranging our people in order, from those who could be spared most easily to those without whom the whole colony would perish.

Others understood also. I began to miss Vizbee and Smelt, and realized that they were hiding from Robert's lethal gaze. How stupid! Surely the path of wisdom was for them to look as busy and useful as possible. But the poor wretches were just intelligent enough to realize whose names must head the list of expendables (I almost said "perishables"). And they remembered the freezer, and the shrouded bodies lying beside them.

ITEM (18)
From Colonel Kohn's Notebook

I'm weighing the remaining rations for the umpteenth time when Eloise puts her head in the storeroom door. She's white as our last kilo of sugar.

Would I step outside with her? Well, sure. I don't ask why, because I know there'll be a good reason.

"Do you come out here alone?" I ask as we crunch through the lichen. "You shouldn't."

"I have to," she says. "I'd go nuts being inside all the time. Now stop being commander in chief for a minute, because I've got something to show you."

She leads the way up a black pile of—what do they call it—scoria? Broken lava chunks the sea will turn into black sand, and—

I only need a glance. "Go back and tell Jamal and Anna to join us."

"If Jamal's busy he'll want to know why."

"The reason is I want him now."

"Yes, sir," she says, and goes.

When the others arrive, I don't even have to point. There's only one thing to see.

A pod of the sea creatures is approaching, maybe twenty, maybe more. They're gray, and close enough now that we can see irregular crusty white patches on their backs and tails—I guess the local version of barnacles. They're a ballet of monsters, rhythmically rising and sinking like the waves, all together.

"They can't come ashore, can they?" asks Eloise, hopefully.

Jamal and I look at each other. We're remembering the one that got Antonelli. The way it rose up on its flippers, the way it tossed its head back, the barking noise. Remembering the inevitable smell of lions. Sea lions. These things are pinnipeds that feed in the sea but drag themselves up on beaches to rest and fight and mate.

"Look," says Anna, pointing in another direction. "It took her a while, but she got it running. Clever lady."

Way, way off, a gray dot in the gray clouds darkens, takes shape, and turns into the last flyer, repaired and functional and heading our way.

ITEM (19)
From Dr. Li's Report

Since we had no option but to resist or die, it was unnecessary to encourage the troops—we could rely on our enemies to do that.

As for myself, I put my hardcopy notes in order, wrapped them in plastic and hid them under loose ice in the freezer. Even if we are all killed, I thought, people sooner or later will come here looking for us, and with luck they may find this record. The last corpse that remained uneaten seemed to be watching me, and I came out shivering for more reasons than the cold.

Yet I continued speaking into my notebook, hoping to transcribe the rest of the story later.

Robert had deployed eight people, which was the number of weapons we had. Adding the shuttleport stock to our own slim armory, we had one hundred and eighty rounds, which was enough to do much damage, though not to drive off all our enemies.

I set up an aid station at the foot of the heap of scoria we had taken to calling the Black Hill, and filled a medical kit with M2, tourniquets, a few antibiotics, etc.

Then I climbed the hill to see exactly what was happening. The sea lions (as Robert called them) had vanished under the waves, meaning that they could reappear anyplace. The flyer had turned and was circling, perhaps a kilometer out. It passed over the shoreline, swung back. Wisely, Robert ordered his people to hold their fire.

I noticed that Eloise was standing beside Jamal. I called her over to help me at the aid station, and she had begun to approach with slow steps when in the corner of my eye I caught a flash from the flyer.

I shouted, "Down!" and she dropped to the ground just as the missile struck the Black Hill and exploded. The sound was loud enough to leave my head ringing. Then the sound *Aa! Aa! Aa!* from behind us warned that the sea lions were coming ashore. At the same moment the flyer veered and from an amplifier came a burst of birdsong so loud that it might have been the giant mythical Roc calling to its mate. At that, the margin of the jungle trembled and something roared in reply.

ITEM (20)
From Colonel Kohn's Notebook

I can't say I ever liked Julia Mack. But I always respected her, never more so than now. She's got a very weird army, but she's doing first-rate command and control.

She's got an Arkie sitting beside her with an amplifier and she's got her goddamn launcher. Must be awkward—leaning out the pilot's port to fire it, so the backflash doesn't fry her. But she manages. A managing gal.

Okay, here come the lions from the sea.

Okay, here come the bearpigs from the jungle. There's more birdsong, this time from the line of trees, so Arkies are in the jungle as well, leading the troops.

The Cousins are closing in. If we make every single shot count, they'll still win. If panicking was any use, I'd panic.

Since it isn't, I'll have to try something else.

I cross over to Jamal and hand him my notebook. "Take care of this."

He raises black arched eyebrows.

"I have something to do. You're in command till I get back. If we live through today, you can sock me good and hard on the jaw."

That's sort of a good-bye.

ITEM (21)
From Colonel Kohn's Notebook
(continued by Jamal al-Sba'a)

Kohn leaves the field of battle. Much as I dislike him, I don't think he is running away. He is a brave Jew.

May the Ever-Living One preserve him, for I hope to collect on his offer at the end of this day.

It's strange, I've never seen him talk into this notebook, yet he always has it with him. The idiot light goes on when I speak, so I suppose it's picking my voice up. I have no notebook of my own—all my stuff except my weapon was lost in the flight from Main Base.

All right, we have only eight weapons. We will soon be assailed from two sides. Do we fight out here in the open, or withdraw to the dome and try to defend it? This is the kind of decision a commander must make, and if he's wrong, everyone is lost. I've always longed for power, now I feel its crushing weight.

I decide that we'll retreat, for two reasons: first, Captain Mack and her goddamn missiles. She can kill many of us and we can't afford losses. Second, the Cousins can afford losses, so the damage we do to them is beside the point. The only strategy is to resist as long as possible and then accept our fate. I call Doctor Li and instruct her to move the aid station inside the dome. Eloise gathers up the medical kit and heads back, while Li waits to see if we take any casualties on the retreat. The Chinese woman appears perfectly calm.

Mack is coming round again in her flyer. The noise of the engine is lost in the volume of sound rising on all sides—the roaring, the warbling, the barking of the creatures from the sea.

And—*Inshallah!*—another flyer is rising to meet her! So this is why Kohn left us!

ITEM (22)
From Doctor Li's Report

All my life I had struggled to attain the Buddhist ideal of nonattachment—maybe out of cowardice, because I feared the pain of loss.

Maybe this is why I fled from life into the laboratory—from the knowledge of passion to a passion for knowledge. Why, until Robert came to Bela, I was so much alone.

When I saw our one fully functional flyer take off, I felt as if I'd been stabbed in the heart with an icicle. Then I told myself that if Robert intended to crash into the other flyer, he would have said good-bye to me first.

So I comforted myself, thinking that, yes, he intended a dangerous game—to distract and alarm Mack, make her fire and waste her remaining missiles. He went, I decided, to court danger, not to seek death. Yet the flyer shot straight at her, moving far too fast for safety, and she must have been startled, for her craft yawed and for a wonderful moment I thought it would spin out of control and crash. But then she mastered the controls and the two aircraft began a twisting, turning ballet that I can only compare to the mating dance of mayflies.

Then our craft turned and fled, with Mack in pursuit.

I found myself again atop the Black Hill without any sense of how I got there. Looking down for a moment, I saw an incredible sight, the creatures of two worlds paralyzed by shared amazement and staring upward.

A sea lion had crashed through a barrier of stunted trees, and it rested propped on immense flippers with its tusked face in the air. Without the support of the sea its own weight oppressed it, and its great scarred sides heaved with the effort of breathing.

On the landward side, bearpigs standing on their hind legs moved their heads from side to side, following the action above like entranced listeners following the music at a concert. Arkies were pointing with their bronze weapons and exchanging wild and strangely sweet snatches of song.

I saw the launcher emerge from the pilot's port of Mack's ship, and an instant later came the blinding backflash. The missile burned a long twisting trail, and my heart stopped because I realized that it was homing in, that it was too swift for its target to escape, and then it struck our flyer, which exploded in a great orb of flame like an opening peony. Dark fragments floated downward like gull's feathers into the sea. From our enemies came a crescendo of sound that I can never describe—one world triumphant over another, howling its victory.

Next I felt a grip on my arm; it was Jamal and he said, "Come on, we're retreating to the dome. Save yourself."

I answered, "Why?" wishing only for my life to be over.

ITEM (23)
From a Letter of Eloise Alcerra to Her Mother

We're all inside the dome together. There was one real shocker when it turned out the door to the hangar had been left open.

Something forced its way in, I didn't see what, but I heard an impact weapon cough and then a couple of guys slammed the door, I think pushing a body out. End of Crisis One.

I was looking for Doctor Li. I'd brought in the medical kit, but to be any good it had to be married to the one person who knew how to use it.

I found her looking awful and I said in alarm, "Are you wounded?" She said, "No, only dead," which I took to be some kind of weird joke—meaning, like, aren't we all?

Jamal was yelling orders, and I said to him, "Colonel Kohn won't like you taking his job away from him."

To my amazement, Jamal said, "Kohn's dead."

"No, he's not."

He ran off, saying he had to check the rest of the doors, especially the loading doors onto the pad, because they were big enough to let in an army if they'd been left open too.

Paying, of course, no attention to me whatever.

I went back to Anna Li, and she was preparing our hospital for new casualties. Her movements were strange, jerky like a marionette, and she hardly seemed to see what she was doing.

I said, "Anna, what's wrong? I mean, aside from the fact that we're all going to be killed, what's the matter?"

She said, "Robert's dead."

Second one in five minutes. Patiently I told her, "No, he's not, he's up on one of the catwalks under the dome, checking the air intakes."

She stopped and looked at me steadily. "I saw him die," she said.

"Well, he must've died very recently, because I saw him climbing a ladder when I was bringing in the medical kit."

"Inside the dome?"

"Of course inside the dome. He'd have to be nuts to be climbing an exterior ladder."

At that her face turned to parchment and she fainted. I caught her going down and laid her on an empty cot. The blind woman, Mbasa, was demanding to know what was going on, so I led her over and sat her down and gave her Anna's hand to hold.

Then I went looking for Colonel Kohn. As I pushed through the people milling around in the main lobby area, most of them were talking about his death. Apparently everybody had seen him die, and only I had seen him alive.

I suppose I should say I doubted my own sanity, but I didn't. What I doubted was everybody else's.

I found a metal ladder with its supports embedded in the duroplast and started climbing. I really don't like heights, but pretty soon I was twenty meters in the air and running along a metal catwalk, wondering where the damp warm air was coming from until I realized it was everybody's breath, rising and collecting up there.

I spotted him standing at the main air intake. He'd pulled off the housing and shoved back the big flexible duct and he was aiming his pistol between the metal louvers. He fired the way real marksmen do, touching the stud so gently that I could hardly see his fingertip move. The pistol coughed and something outside roared.

"One less," he muttered, and I didn't know whether he meant one less round or one less enemy, or both. "What are you doing here, Eloise?"

I told him that everybody had seen him die, including Anna, and he'd better show himself alive before she died of grief and before Jamal had time to make everybody hate him.

"You underestimate them both," he said. "Oh, oh. Step back and open your mouth and cover your ears."

I did and the catwalk jumped and I felt like I'd had an iron bell over my head and somebody had hit it with a sledgehammer.

"Oh my God," I was muttering. "Oh my God." He yelled something at me but I was almost deaf.

He walked me away from the spot. My ears were still ringing, but after a little while I could understand him. He talked like a lecturer.

"If that last missile had hit the grille we'd have a big hole in the dome. And it's accessible to an exterior ladder. But it just occurred to me that we ought to let them come in this way, because they'll be squeezed together on this goddamn catwalk and we can shoot them like rabbits. Or maybe just pry the catwalk loose and let them fall."

He told me to go see Jamal and have him order two people with guns up here. "And tell Anna not to wet her pants. I'm alive as I ever was. As soon as my two shooters get here, I'll be down."

Before going I asked, "Why does everybody think you're dead?"

"It's the flyer. I was going to take it up and harass Mack and see if I could get her to waste her last missiles. But somebody else got there first."

"Who?"

"Vizbee and Smelt, of course. I guess they figured they were on the menu and the battle gave them a good chance to escape. Though where they hoped to escape to, I don't know. Idiots. Now, scram."

ITEM (24)
From Colonel Kohn's Notebook
(Kohn speaking)

Jamal tells me he's deferred the punch on the jaw until either the Cousins break in, or else we get away. That way if he knocks out a few teeth I can either have dental care or else not need it.

I've had some of the guys loosen the retaining bolts on the upper catwalk. A bearpig tore out the grille and louvers but nothing's tried to get through yet. I suppose they've figured out that it's like climbing into a bull's eye.

I wish I knew if Mack's got any missiles left. Let's see, there were six in the armory to start with. One fired into Krebs' quarters. One to blast the power station. One to open up the mess hall. Three fired here. Does that mean she's out?

I bet not. I bet she had a couple stored away in some secret place, maybe underground. This lady is daring but also careful. If she has more, they'll soon be hitting a door. Preferably two doors, one on each side. Then the big beasts will break down what's left, and they'll be inside.

We'll kill a lot of them but it won't make any difference, because, as Anna said, you can't fight a whole world.

WHAM!

Hear that? Just in case anybody gets to listen to this record. I wish I wasn't so goddamn right all the time. I wish I was dumber, so I couldn't see things coming. I wish Anna and I were anyplace but here.

It's the door into the hangar again. It's bent and bulging inward but still standing.

Lots of pressure against the outside. Nerve-shattering squeals of metal grinding on metal. It moves slowly, but it does move. *E pur si muove*—what Galileo told the Inquisition—but it does move. Meaning the Earth, which probably we'll never see again.

That noise like a very loud shot was a hinge breaking. If only these things were nuclear steel, but they're not; they're strong, but we need something indestructible.

I order four shooters to the threatened door. Order one guy to stand behind each shooter and grab his weapon if he's killed or wounded. Yell for the shooters on the catwalk to come down. Order one to join Jamal, the other to blow off the loosened retaining bolts if something comes through the intake, as of course something will. Order everybody to stay away from the area underneath. Order Jamal to watch the double doors that open onto the shuttlepad. If the Cousins break in there, we're seriously screwed.

Finally stop giving orders. I've done the best I can, now we'll fight it out and they'll win, as possibly they deserve to do. As Eloise said, it *is* their world.

On the way to her hospital, Anna gives me a blissful smile. She's actually happy to be dying with me—compared to living without me. In all my long life, nobody ever looked at me that way before.

ITEM (25)
From the Letter of Eloise Alcerra to Her Mother

I feel like such an idiot, talking, talking to you across the light years at a time like this. But what else can I do?

It'll hurt you to know exactly how I died, but not as much as not knowing. And I want you to know my last thoughts are with you.

The expected blast just hit the double doors to the pad right in the middle and the metal snapped and bent. Then steady, unrelenting pressure.

All the usual sounds from outside. Warbling, roaring, barking. I hardly hear them, I'm listening to the outcry of the metal as it bends. A lot of muscle out there. An arm reaches through, one of the bearpigs, long claws scratching at the metal. Jamal yells *Hold your fire!*

And of course he's right, that would've been a waste of ammo. There's scrabbling around outside, more singing, more roaring, and then the pressure suddenly gets much, much worse. You can see the strong metal bulge, something snaps, something else snaps. Whatever's pushing is breathing in huge gasps.

We have to wait until the doors collapse, then shoot whatever's on the other side. Its body will block the opening, but not for long.

Mama, when I close my eyes for an instant I see your face.

ITEM (26)
From Colonel Kohn's Notebook

The double doors to the pad burst open. One of the sea lions that's been leaning against them takes two shots and screams, screams like a wounded animal anywhere, only thirty times as loud.

Then with a huge metallic crash the catwalk comes down, carrying half a dozen bearpigs with it. I step up and shoot the one that's still moving.

Turn back and see that the body of the sea lion is blocking the double doors. It's like the hull of a boat, black and slick except for many white scars of past battles for mates and the two small entry holes left by the impact weapons.

Bearpigs are trying to pull him out of the way, and an Arkie scrambles over him, takes one look at what's waiting for him and scrambles back. But the body's moving now, and it's last-stand time in the old Beladome.

ITEM (27)
From Dr. Li's Report

And then came a thunderous roar and such a collective scream as I never thought to hear even in hell.

ITEM (28)
From the Letter of Eloise Alcerra
(as dictated to Dr. Li)

Jamal spun on his heel and picked me up and threw me out of the way before jumping himself.

I landed against the curved wall of the dome just as a long plume of fire licked into the doorway and the body of the sea lion burst into flame, all the layers of fat under its hide igniting like wax, melting, spattering here and there, burning gobbets flying. A guy who was caught in the blast was turning black and falling apart like a doll hit by a blowtorch.

If the Cousins hadn't been there to block the opening partly, we'd all have been fried. As it was, Jamal's clothes caught on fire and I threw myself on him and rolled, feeling the flame and not feeling it, until it was out.

And then people were grabbing me by the wrists and pulling me into the hospital, and somebody had Jamal too, and about the same moment the roaring stopped and I realized that the supply ship's shuttle was down and the retros had finally been turned off.

ITEM (29)
From the Report of Doctor Li

I have never been busier than during the loading of the shuttle.

The surviving Cousins had fled for the moment, but of course they would be back. So time was of the essence, and we had serious burn cases. Robert had suffered compound fractures of the radius and ulna of his left arm. He had either been blown down or had fallen hard trying to escape the blast.

Fortunately, the shuttle was bringing in medical supplies among many other things, and we tore the boxes apart to find what we needed.

Jamal had severe second-degree burns on the torso and some charring on the hands. Eloise had painful but superficial burns on her hands, belly, and right breast. A young man serving with Jamal had been burned beyond recognition, and died as we were loading him.

The shuttle pilot, a Lieutenant Mannheim, talked to me as I worked. He was still amazed by what he had found. He said the overcast had been unusually dense, even for Bela, and he was almost on top of the port before he saw that it was under attack.

Since the shuttle is unarmed, he did the only thing he could by landing in the usual way, using the retros as weapons. Robert praised and commended him, as indeed was only just, for this young officer—though suddenly confronted with an unimaginable situation—had saved all our lives.

At the earliest possible moment, we lifted off. I did not feel entirely safe until we rose above the clouds, into eternal sunlight blazing against the blackness of space.

ITEM (30)
From Colonel Kohn's Second Notebook

Naturally, Anna wants to knock me out and put me in sickbay for the next six months. I tell her to give me a nerve block and splint the broken wing.

I also get a rest, which I need. Anna bathes me. I'm fed and allowed to sleep under sedation for twelve standard hours. When I wake up, I visit Jamal and find him encased in a kind of body suit that protects his burns from infection and promotes healing. Anna says he'll need a lot of grafting when we get home.

His hands are in no condition for punching me, but I renew my offer for whenever they are. He's wearing a blissfully silly smile, and I think is still too far under the M2 to hear me or care much, one way or the other. He's alive and loved and floating on a morphine cushion, and that's as close to paradise as any of us are likely to get.

Sitting beside him, Eloise is bright and talkative. She's wearing bandages soaked in a topical anesthetic, and when I ask how she's doing, says, "My right tit will look like hell for a while." She holds up her thickly wrapped hands and intones, "And never, never will I play the harp again." Funny lady.

Then I brief the supply ship's Captain Cetewayo (pronounced approximately Chetch-why-oh, with a click to start). He's a big guy with a polished bald head like a bronze ingot, which nods as I brief him. Fortunately he wears a uniform too, and I don't have to spell out the facts of life for him.

The loss of a whole mining colony is going to cause a stupendous stink back home. I expect to spend several years as a professional witness, being grilled by all sorts of people. I want everything done by the book before we leave Bela for good.

He agrees, collects my notebook and a number of other pieces of evidence and seals them in his safe. Issues me this new notebook. Orders Mannheim to start collecting statements from the survivors—all ten of us.

Since bureaucrats believe nothing until it's written down and all the signature blocks properly filled in with names and ranks, these statements will be collated and an after-action report prepared, signed and sealed.

Admittedly, this is a cover-your-ass operation. But there's one more thing. It's essential that we check the mining camp and Main Base from the air, to insure that there are no human survivors. If we had troopers with us, we'd have to physically go inside and inspect, whatever the danger. Since we haven't the people or weapons to do that, we must do what we can—or risk our careers.

That sounds cold, but I am metaphysically certain that everybody except ourselves is dead. We gotta do what we gotta do, but we will not save anybody by doing it. Cetewayo agrees and gives the necessary orders.

Then I join Mannheim in the shuttle. We strap in and drop off the underbelly of the ship, and all at once it's déjà vu all over again, as some ancient philosopher put it.

We're diving into the endless roiling clouds, rain hits us like surf and a huge crooked bolt of lightning flashes from cloud to cloud. I think how silly it would be, after all I've been through, if I get killed by a commonplace thunderbolt while performing a routine and essentially meaningless duty.

Instead we drop through the last and darkest layer of the eternal overcast, and we're flashing over the familiar blue-black sea. With a navigator disk in hand I'm directing Mannheim to Alfa. Soon we're viewing the familiar sheds and domes and chicken runs of the mining camp, and I ask Mannheim to drop down lower.

The jungle's closing in, preparing to erase every track humans ever made here. Only our machines are still alive, the power station chugging away, the brown stream of slurry gushing down the hill like a giant case of dysentery. The lights are long burned out, of course, and—

Something moving—

No! Somebody!

A little figure that's not an Arkie!

Standing in a doorway, waving!

We dip down for an instant, I haul him in with my workable right arm and we're soaring again. I look at him in awe, trying to imagine how he survived in an alien jungle this long—all alone!

He's even skinnier than I remember him, he's wearing rags, his pants are held up with a vine, he's got long angry scars on face and hands, and whatever isn't scarred is covered with some kind of insect bites. He smells like the whole rotten understory of Bela's jungle. He's beautiful.

"Ted," I tell him, "I'm sorry I missed you the last time."

"Well, here I am," he says, and starts to tell his story—without a single stutter.

How he wriggled out of the bearpig's grasp, leaving his oversized coveralls behind; how the beast wasted time trying to eat the coveralls, allowing him time to slide into the thickets; how he ran and hid; how he made himself a cape of leaves to keep warm and shed the rain. How he watched a wingless feathered creature like a parrot, and began cautiously eating what it ate. How in time he worked his way back to Alfa, found it deserted, scavenged some torn clothing and lived off the contents of a couple of sealed supply cartons until he heard the flyer.

"You weren't worried we'd go off and leave you?"

"No," he says serenely. "I know you're not like that," at which I have the grace to blush.

While listening to Ted Szczech, we've crossed the roiling bay and now arrive at the estuary of that river whose name I never learned—not that human names mean anything on Bela anymore. I suppose the Arkies have a musical phrase for it, as they have for everything else.

Zamók is rising before us, and I see that things have changed. It's no longer Main Base; the Arkies have already cleared some of the human hovels off their Incan stonework. Reconstruction of lovely temples to follow, I'm sure.

There's a crowd of them gathered in the cleared area, standing in circles, and they turn their heads when they see us. Some of them shake weapons, but most merely look once and then turn back to what they're doing. We don't count any longer, but a rite is a rite.

In the center of the crowd stands Julia Mack. I tell Mannheim to bring us to a low hover so we can watch. She completely ignores us, looking straight ahead, and she's wearing a gorgeous robe of some sort, and no wig, and she looks more than ever like Picasso's portrait of Gertrude Stein, or how Gertrude would have looked if she'd been wrapped in a Persian carpet.

Suddenly Ted's stutter comes back, and he starts sputtering, "Wh-wh-wh-wh-wh-wh-"

"I'll explain later," I murmur.

Now an Arkie steps up behind her and he's carrying—not the usual bronze implement—no, by God, it's white metal, it's the titanium mountaineer's pickaxe that Mack's parents must have brought to Bela so long ago. Only it's been fitted with a longer handle, so the little Arkie can reach her.

He swings it, and Mannheim exclaims something, I don't know what, and Ted gives a strange cry as Mack falls heavily with the point in her brain. Another priest comes forward, carrying the usual curved axeblade to complete the ritual.

Mannheim says, "We've got to stop this," and I say, "No, we don't."

This is her reward for all she's done for them—to become a god of the Arkies, to join their pantheon and live here forever. At last she's joined her true species, and she's no longer alone.

When it's over—all but the ritual meal—I have to jiggle Mannheim's arm to get his attention.

"It's their church," I tell him, "and it's their communion. We don't belong here. We never did. So let's go."

CONCLUSION AND JUDGMENT

KOHN, Robert Rogers, cannot be held legally culpable for the disaster on Planet Bela. However, as the only surviving senior official he must be held administratively responsible, since there is no one else left to blame. He is therefore involuntarily retired from the Security Forces with official reprimand and reduced pension.

PROTEST of judgment filed by Citizens Alcerra, al-Sba'a, and Szczech is hereby REJECTED.

PETITION of KOHN, Robert Rogers, and spouse to be allowed to live in retirement in an oasis of the Great American Desert is hereby GRANTED.

BY ORDER OF THE HONORABLE COMMITTEE

sitka

WILLIAM SANDERS

William Sanders lives in Tahlequah, Oklahoma. A former powwow dancer and sometime Cherokee gospel singer, he appeared on the SF scene in the early eighties with a couple of alternate-history comedies, *Journey to Fusang* (a finalist for the John W. Campbell Award) and *The Wild Blue and the Gray*. Sanders then turned to mystery and suspense, producing a number of critically acclaimed titles under a pseudonym. He credits his old friend Roger Zelazny with persuading him to return to SF, this time via the short story form; his stories have appeared in *Asimov's Science Fiction*, *The Magazine of Fantasy & Science Fiction*, and numerous anthologies, earning himself a well-deserved reputation as one of the best short-fiction writers of the last decade, winning a Sideways Award for Best Alternate History story. He has also returned to novel writing, with books such as *The Ballad of Billy Badass and the Rose of Turkestan* and *The Bernadette Operations*, a new SF novel, *J.*, and a mystery novel, *Smoke*. Some of his acclaimed short stories have been collected in *Are We Having Fun Yet? American Indian Fantasy Stories*. His most recent book is a historical study, *Conquest: Hernando de Soto and the Indians: 1539–1543*. (Most of his books, including reissues of his earlier novels, are available from Wildside Press, or on Amazon.com.) His stories have appeared in our Twelfth, Thirteenth, Fifteenth, and Nineteenth Annual Collections.

In the sharp little story that follows, he escorts us around the town of Sitka, which proves to be a very cold place, even in the summertime.

Late in the afternoon, a little before sundown, the fog moved in off the ocean and settled in over the islands and peninsulas of the coast. It wasn't much of a fog, by the standards of Russian America in late summer; just enough to mask the surface of the sea and soften the rough outlines of the land.

On the waterfront in the town of New Arkhangelsk, on the western side of the big island that the Russians called Baranof and the natives called Sitka, two men stood looking out over the harbor. "Perfect," one of them said. "If it'll stay like this."

The other man looked at him. "Perfect, Jack? How so?"

The first man flung out a hand. "Hell, just look. See how it's hanging low over the water?"

The other man turned back toward the harbor, following his gesture. He stood silently for a moment, seeing how the fog curled around the hulls of the anchored ships while leaving their upper works exposed. The nearest, a big deepwater steamer, was all but invisible down near the waterline, yet her masts and funnels showed clear and black against the hills beyond the harbor, and the flag of the Confederate States of America was clearly recognizable at her stern.

"Perfect," the man called Jack said again. "Just enough to hide a small boat, but not enough to hide a ship. Less chance of a mistake."

He was a powerfully built young man with curly blond hair and a tanned, handsome face. His teeth flashed white in the fading light. "After all," he said, "we don't want to get the wrong one, do we, Vladimir?"

The man called Vladimir, whose last name was Ulyanov and who sometimes called himself Lenin, closed his eyes and shuddered slightly. "No, that would be very bad." His English was excellent but strongly accented. "Don't even joke about it."

"Don't worry," the younger man said. "We'll get her for you."

"Not for me. You know better than that."

"Yeah, all right. For the cause." Jack slapped him lightly on the upper arm, making him wince. "Hey, I'm a good socialist too. You know that."

"So you have assured me," Lenin said dryly. "Otherwise I might suspect—"

He stopped suddenly as a pair of long-bearded Orthodox monks walked past. Jack said, "What," and then, "Oh, hell, Vladimir, don't you ever relax? I bet they don't even speak English."

Lenin looked after the two black-robed figures and shook his head. "Two years away from the twentieth century," he murmured, "and still the largest country in the world is ruled by medieval superstition. . . ."

He turned to the younger man. "We shouldn't be standing here like this. It looks suspicious. And believe me," he said as Jack started to speak, "to the people we are dealing with, *everything* looks suspicious. Trust me on this."

He jerked his head in the direction of a nearby saloon. "Come," he said. "Let us have a drink, Comrade London."

As the two men started down the board sidewalk, a trio of dark-faced women suddenly appeared from the shadows and fell in alongside, smiling and laughing. One of them grabbed Jack's arm and said something in a language that was neither English nor Russian. "For God's sake," Jack said, and started to pull free. "Just what we need, a bunch of Siwash whores."

"Wait." Lenin held up a hand. "Let them join us for now. With them along, no one will wonder what we are doing here."

"Huh. Yeah, all right. Good idea." Jack looked at the three women. They weren't bad-looking in a shabby sort of way. The one holding his arm had red ribbons in her long black hair. He laughed. "Too bad I'm going to be kind of busy this evening. Give them a bath, they might be good for some fun."

Lenin's nose twitched slightly. "You're not serious."

"Hell, no. I may be down on my luck but I'm still a white man."

Lenin winced. "Jack, I've got to talk to you some time about your—"

The saloon door swung open and a couple of drunken Cossacks staggered out, leaning on the unpainted timber wall for support. When they were past, Lenin led the way through the narrow doorway and into a long, low-ceilinged, poorly lit room full of rough wooden tables and benches where men, and a few women, sat drinking and talking and playing cards. An old man rested on a tall stool near the door, playing a slow minor-key tune on an accordion. The air was dense with smoke from cheap *mahorka* tobacco.

"There," Lenin said. "In the back, by the wall, where we can watch the door."

He strode up to the bar, pushing past a group of sailors in the white summer uniform of the Imperial German navy, and came back a moment later carrying a bottle and a couple of glasses. "One minute," he said, setting the glasses down and pouring, while Jack dragged up a bench and sat down. "I've got an idea."

Stepping over to the next table, Lenin beckoned to the three women. They looked blank. "Come," he said, in Russian and then in English, and at last they giggled in unison and moved over to join him. "Here." He set the bottle in the center of the table, making exaggerated sit-down motions with his free hand. "*Sadityes*'. You sit here," he said, speaking very slowly. He touched the bottle. "You can have this. *Ponimaitye?*"

As they seated themselves, with another flurry of giggles, Lenin came back and sat down across from Jack. "There," he said. "That's the only table in the place close enough for anyone to overhear us. Better to have it occupied by harmless idiots."

Jack snorted. "For God's sake, Vladimir!"

"Laugh if you like," Lenin said. "I don't take risks. Already I have been arrested—"

"Me too."

"Pardon me." Lenin's voice was very flat. "You have been arrested by stupid American policemen, who beat you and threw you in a cell for a few days and then made you leave town and forgot about you. You have been detained briefly, at a military outpost, for prospecting for gold without a permit. You have no idea what a Cheka interrogation is like. Or," he said, "what it is like to live under the eyes of a vigilant and well-organized secret police force and their network of informers."

He lifted his glass. "What is that American idiom? 'The walls have ears,' yes? In the Russian Empire they have both ears and eyes—and feet, to run and tell the men with the big boots what you say and do. Until you have been stepped on by those boots, you have no business to laugh at the caution of those who have."

At the next table the woman with the red ribbons in her hair said, "I'm looking at him and I still don't believe it."

She said it in a language that was not spoken anywhere in that world.

The woman beside her pushed back her own hair, which was done up in thick braids that hung down to the swell of her bosom under her trade-blanket coat. She said in the same language, "Well, he *was* one of the great figures of history, for better or worse."

"Not Lenin," the woman with the red ribbons said impatiently. "Jack London. He's gorgeous. The pictures didn't even come close."

Across the table, the third woman was doing something with one of the seashell ornaments that dangled from her ears. She looked over at the men's table for a moment and then smiled and nodded without speaking.

"Hand me that bottle," the one with the red ribbons said. "I think I'm in love."

"Of course," Lenin said, "for me things did perhaps work out for the best. Siberia wasn't pleasant, but it gave me time to think, to organize my ideas. And then the authorities decided to send some of the Siberian exiles even farther away, to this remote American outpost of the empire, and in time this presented . . . possibilities."

Jack gave a meaningless grunt and reached for his own glass, staring off across the room. The German sailors were clustered around the accordion player, who was trying to accompany them on "Du, Du Liegst Mir Am Herzen." Some of the Russians were giving them dirty looks but they didn't seem to notice.

"That's right," Jack muttered. "Sing, have yourselves a good time. Get drunk, find some whores, get skinned in a rigged card game. Just for God's sake don't go back to the ship tonight."

The woman with the red ribbons said, "He looks a lot younger. Than Lenin, I mean."

"Only six years' difference in their ages," the woman with the braids said. "But you're right. Or rather Lenin looks older—"

"Sh." The other woman raised a finger, still fiddling with her seashell ear pendants. "Quiet. I've almost—there. There." She dropped her hands to her lap and sat back. "Locked on and recording."

"All right," the woman with the red ribbons said. She reached up and pushed back her hair with a casual-looking motion, her hand barely brushing the area of her own ear. A moment later the woman beside her did something similar.

"Oh," the one with the red ribbons said. "Yes. Nice and clear. All this background noise, too, I'm impressed."

The one with the braids said, "Speaking of background noise, we need to generate some. We're being too quiet. We're supposed to be cheap whores drinking free vodka. Time to laugh it up again."

Lenin glanced over at the next table as the three women broke into another fit of noisy giggles. "They seem to be making inroads on that bottle," Lenin said. "If you want any more, you'd better go get it before they finish it off."

"They're welcome to it," Jack said. He looked at his own glass and grimaced. "Damn vodka tastes like something you'd rub on a horse. How the hell do you people stand it?"

"Practice."

"Yeah, well, better you than me. What I'd give for a taste of good old honest John Barleycorn."

"It's available," Lenin said. "Though probably not in a place like this. It's just very expensive, like everything else not made in Russia, thanks to the exorbitant import duties. Another blessing from our beloved official bureaucracy."

"Tell me about it," Jack said. "Came up here figuring to dig some gold, make a little something for myself instead of always being broke on my ass. Found out foreigners have to have a special permit to prospect or even to travel in the interior, no way to get it without paying off a bunch of crooks behind government desks. So I said the hell with it."

"And you were caught."

"Yep. Damn near went to jail, too, but by then I'd hit just enough pay dirt to be able to grease a certain Cossack officer. And here I am, broke on my ass again and a long way from home. I'm telling you, Vladimir," he said, "if you wanted somebody to blow up that bunch of greedy sons of bitches who run things here, I'd be your man and I wouldn't charge a nickel to do it."

He rubbed his face and sighed. "Instead I'm about to go blow the bottom out of a German battleship and kill a bunch of people who never did me any harm, all for the sake of the great workers' revolution. How about that?"

The three women exchanged looks. The one with the red ribbons said, "No." She squeezed her eyes shut. "*No.*"

"So it's true." The woman with the seashell ear pendants shook her head. "Incredible."

"Watch it," the one with the braids said, breaking into a broad sloppy smile. "Lenin's already nervous—see, he's looking around again. Act drunk, damn it."

"That's easy," the woman with the red ribbons said, reaching for the vodka bottle. "After hearing that, I *need* a drink."

"In fact," Lenin said, "you are doing it for the price of a ticket back to your own country. Not that I question your socialist convictions, but right now you would blow up your own mother—"

Jack's hand shot across the table and clamped down on Lenin's forearm. "Don't you ever speak to me about my mother," he said thickly. "You got that?"

Lenin sat very still. His face had gone pale and there were pain lines at the corners of his mouth. "Yes," he said in a carefully even voice. "Yes, I apologize."

"Okay, then." Jack let go and gulped at his drink. "Just watch it."

Lenin rubbed his forearm. After a moment he said, "Go easy on that vodka. You're going to need a clear head and steady hands tonight."

Jack gave a short harsh laugh. "Save your breath. Even I'm not fool enough to tie one on when I'm going to be handling dynamite in the dark. Make a mistake with that much giant, it'd be raining Jack London for a week. Mixed up with a couple of Aleut paddlers, too, they'd never get the pieces sorted out."

He sipped his drink again, more cautiously. "Not that it's all that tricky a job," he added. "Nothing to it, really. Come alongside the *Brandenburg*, just forward of her aft turret, so we're next to the powder magazine. Arm the mine, start the timer—neat piece of work there, your pal Iosif knows what he's doing—and ease the whole thing up against the hull till the magnets take hold, being careful not to let it clang. Take the forked stick and slide the mine down under the waterline, below the armor belt, and then tell the boys to high-tail it. Hell, anybody could do it."

He grinned crookedly. "When you get right down to it, you only need me to make sure we get the right ship. Those Aleuts are the best paddlers in the world, but they wouldn't know the *Brandenburg* from the *City of New Orleans*."

The woman with the braids said, "You know, I never believed it. I got into some pretty hot arguments, in fact. 'Ridiculous' was one of the milder words I used."

The one with the seashell ear pendants said, "Well, you were hardly alone. All the authorities agree that Jack London's involvement in the *Brandenburg* affair is merely a romantic legend, circulated by a few revisionist crackpots. I don't know any responsible scholar who takes it seriously."

She chuckled softly. "And oh, is the shit going to fly in certain circles when we get back! I can hardly wait."

"Not quite true," Lenin said. "I also need you to make sure that our aboriginal hirelings don't change their minds and run away home with their advance money. If they haven't already done so."

"Oh, they wouldn't do that. See," Jack said, "they think it's a Russian ship we're after."

Lenin's eyebrows went up. "You told them that?"

"Hell, I had to tell them something. So they'll be there. The way they hate Russians, they wouldn't pass up a chance like this. Christ," Jack said, "I know we did some rotten things to the Indians in the States, but compared to what your people did to those poor devils . . ."

"Oh, yes. The exploitation of native peoples, here and in Asia, has been one of the worst crimes of the Tsarist state."

"Yeah, well," Jack said, "all I'm saying, the boys will do their job and I'll do mine. Quit worrying about it."

"Hey," the woman with the braids said. "Go easy on that stuff. You're going to make yourself sick."

"I'm already sick," the woman with the red ribbons said. "Just thinking about it, sitting here listening to them talk about it, seeing it about to happen, I'm as sick as I've ever been in my life. Aren't you?"

"Now what happens after that," Jack said, "whether things turn out the way you want, I can't guarantee. I'll sink the ship for you, but if it doesn't get you your war, don't come to me wanting a refund."

Lenin's lips twitched in what was very nearly a smile. "That," he said, "is perhaps the surest part of the entire business. Believe me, nothing is more predictable than the reaction of the Kaiser to the sinking of one of his precious warships in a Russian port."

"Really? I don't know as much as I should about things like that," Jack admitted. "Foreign rulers and all, I need to read up . . . but I can see how it would make him pretty mad. Mad enough to go to war, though?"

"Wilhelm will be furious," Lenin said. "But also secretly delighted. At last he will have a pretext for the war he has wanted for so long."

Jack frowned. "He's crazy?"

"Not mad, no. Merely a weakling—a cripple and, according to rumor, a homosexual—determined to prove his manhood by playing the great warrior."

"Ah." Jack nodded slowly. "A punk trying to pick a fight to show he's not a punk. Yeah, I know the kind. Saw a good many of them when I was riding the rails."

"Even so. Wilhelm has been looking for a fight ever since ascending the throne. Since no one has so far obliged him, he contents himself with playing the bully."

Lenin nodded in the direction of the German sailors, who were now roaring out "Ach, Du Lieber Augustin" in somewhat approximate harmony. "As for example this little 'good-will cruise,'" he said. "This series of visits to various ports by a *Hochseeflotte* battleship. Nothing but a crude show of force to impress the world."

"Showing everybody who's the boss?"

"Exactly. And therefore its destruction will be taken as a response to a challenge."

"Hm. Okay, you know more about it than I do." Jack shrugged. "Still seems pretty strange, though, starting a war hoping your own country will get whipped."

"I don't like it," Lenin said. "I am Russian, after all, and this isn't easy for me. But there is no better breeding ground for revolution than a major military defeat. Look at France."

"The Communards lost, didn't they?"

"True. They made mistakes, from which we have learned."

"If he says anything about omelettes and eggs," the woman with the red ribbons said through her teeth, "I'm going to go over there and beat his brains out with this bottle. Screw the mission and screw noninterference and screw temporal paradox. I don't care. I'll kill him."

Jack said, "You know, the joke's really going to be on you if Russia wins."

"Not much chance of that. Russia's armed forces are a joke, fit only to keep the Tatars in line and occasionally massacre a village of Jews. The officers are mostly incompetent buffoons, owing their rank to family connections rather than ability. The troops are badly trained, and their equipment is decades out of date. The German military, on the other hand, are very nearly as good as they think they are."

"Russia's a big country, though."

"Yes. A big country with too much territory to protect. A German offensive in the west, a Japanese attack in the east—it will be too much. You'll see."

"You're awfully sure the Japs are going to come into it."

"Comrade London," Lenin said softly, "where do you think our funds come from? Who do you think is paying for this business tonight?"

The three women stared at one another. "Now that," the one with the braids said after a moment, "is going to knock *everyone* on their butts."

"The Japs are bankrolling us?" Jack said incredulously. "For God's sake, why?"

"They have territorial ambitions in Asia. Russia has become an obstacle. A war in Europe would create opportunities."

"Damn." Jack looked unhappy. "I don't know if I like that part. Working for Orientals against white—all right, all right," he said quickly, seeing Lenin's expression. "I didn't say I wouldn't do it. All I want is to get back home. I don't really care if I have to go to work for the Devil."

He looked at Lenin over the rim of his glass. "If I haven't already. . . ."

"Oh, dear," the woman with the braids said. "He does have some unfortunate racial attitudes, doesn't he?"

"So did Ernest Hemingway," the one with the red ribbons said without looking up from the bottle. "And I thought we were going to have to peel you off him with a steam hose."

"The interesting question," Lenin said, "is whether the other European countries will become involved. The French may well decide that this is an opportunity to settle old scores with Germany. The others, who knows? This could turn into a general conflict, like nothing since Napoleon."

"What the hell. As long as the United States doesn't get involved," Jack said. "And that's not going to happen. We've just barely *got* an army, and they're still busy with the Indians. The Confederates, now, they just might be crazy enough to get in on it."

"If the war spreads, so much the better," Lenin said. "Because if it spreads, so will the revolution."

He took out a heavy silver pocket watch and snapped it open. "And now I think we should be going. It is still several hours, but we both have things we must do."

He started to push himself back from the table. Jack said, "Wait. Just one more thing."

Lenin sank back onto the bench. Jack said, "See, I've been thinking. Suppose somebody were to hire somebody to do something against the law. And maybe the man doing the hiring was the cautious type, and wanted to make sure the other bastard didn't get talkative afterward. Maybe the law might catch him and beat the story out of him, maybe he might just get drunk and shoot his mouth off. I mean, you never know, do you?"

Jack's voice was casual, his expression bland; he might have been asking about a good place to eat.

"But when the job involves a bomb," he said, "then there's one sure way to make sure the man *never* talks, isn't there? With the little added bonus that you don't have to pay him. Not," he added quickly, "that I'm suggesting anything. I don't really think you'd do something like that. Not to a good old revolutionary comrade."

He leaned forward, staring into Lenin's eyes. "But just in case I'm wrong, you might be interested to know that a few things have been written down and left in safe hands, and if I don't make it back tonight there are some people who will be reading them with deep interest by this time tomorrow."

Lenin sat unmoving, returning the younger man's stare, for perhaps five seconds. Then he laughed out loud. "*Nu, molodyets!*" He slapped the table with his palm. "Congratulations, Comrade London. At last you are learning to think like a Russian."

"Looks like they're leaving," the woman with the braids said. "Do we follow them, or—"

The woman with the red ribbons said, "I can't stand this."

Suddenly she was on her feet, moving very fast, brushing past Lenin and grabbing Jack by the arms, pushing him back against the wall. "Listen," she said, speaking quickly but with great care, "listen, you mustn't do this. You're about to start the most terrible war in your world's history. Millions of people will die and nothing will come of it but suffering and destruction. Listen," she said again, her voice rising. "You have a great talent—"

Jack stood looking down at her, open-mouthed, as her voice grew higher and louder. "Damn!" he said finally. "Vladimir, did you ever hear the like? Sorry, honey." He reached up and pulled her hands away, not roughly. "Me no speak Tlingit, or whatever the hell that is."

He grinned and slapped her bottom. "Run along, now. Big white brothers got heap business."

And to Lenin, "Give her a few kopecks, would you, or she'll follow me like a hound pup. And then let's get out of here."

The woman with the red ribbons said, "But I *heard* myself speaking English!"

They were climbing slowly up a hillside above the town of New Arkhangelsk. It was dark now, but the stars gave a good deal of light and the fog didn't reach this high.

The woman with the shell ear pendants, walking in the lead, said without looking around, "That's how it works. Don't ask me why. Some quirk of the conditioning program."

"It was covered in training," the third woman said. "Don't tell me you forgot something that basic. But then as much vodka as you put away, it's a wonder you can remember where you left your own ass . . . you didn't take the anti-intoxicants, did you?"

"They make my skin itch."

"Gods." The woman with the braids raised her hands in a helpless flapping motion. "You're a menace, you know? One of these days we're going to stop covering for you."

"No, we won't," the woman in the lead said. "We'll cover for her this time—going to be a job doctoring the recording, but I can do it—and we'll keep on covering for her. For the same reason she's helped cover for us, when we lost it or just blew it. The same reason everyone covers for their partners. Because when you're out on the timelines there's no one else you can depend on and when you're back home there's no one else who really knows what it was like."

She stopped. "Hold on. It's getting a little tricky."

She took out a pair of oddly shaped goggles and slipped them on. "All right," she said. "Stay close behind me. It shouldn't be much farther."

The Aleuts were waiting in the shadow of a clump of cedars as Jack came walking down the beach. "*Zdras'tye*," one of them said, stepping out and raising a hand. "We ready. Go now?"

"*Da*. Go now." Jack's gold-field Russian was even worse than their pidgin. "Uh, *gdye baidarka?*"

"*Von tam.*" The man gestured and Jack saw it now, a long low black shape pulled up on the shore.

"*Harasho.*" Jack made a come-on gesture and the two men followed him down to the water's edge. His boots made soft crunching sounds in the damp sand. Theirs made none at all.

Together they lifted the big three-man sea kayak and eased it out until it floated free. Jack slid the heavy pack off his back, while the two Aleuts began the elaborate process of cleaning their feet and clothing, getting rid of any sand that might damage the boat's sealskin covering.

The forward paddler said cheerfully, "We go kill Russians, *da?*"

"Oh, yes," Jack said in English. "More than you know, you poor ignorant bastard. More than you'll ever know."

The woman with the red ribbons said, "I'm sorry. I let it get to me and I'm sorry." She turned her head to look at the other two. "It's just the stupid stinking *waste* of it all."

They were well up on the hillside now, sitting on the trunk of a fallen tree, facing out over the dark fog-blanketed harbor. It was the last hour before midnight.

The woman with the seashell ear pendants said, "It was a dreadful war, all right. One of the worst in all the lines—"

"Not that. All right, that too, but I meant him. Jack London," the woman with the red ribbons said. "You know what happens to him after this. He's going to ruin himself with drink and then shoot himself in another five years, and never write anything in a class with his best work from the other lines. And now we know why, don't we?"

"Guilt? Yes," the woman with the seashell ear pendants said. "Probably. But that's just it. He *is* going to do those things, just as he *is* going to sink the *Brandenburg* tonight, because he's already *done* them and there's nothing you can do about it."

She raised a hand and stroked the red-ribboned hair. “And that’s what gets to you, isn’t it? The inevitability. That’s what gets to all of us. That’s why we burn out so soon.”

The woman with the braids said, “How many known timelines are there, now, that have been mapped back this far?”

“I don’t know.” The woman with the seashell ear pendants shrugged. “Well over a hundred, the last I heard.”

“And so far not a single one where it didn’t happen. One way or another, a huge and bloody world war always breaks out, invariably over something utterly stupid, sometime within the same twenty-year bracket. Talk about inevitability.”

“I know all that,” the woman with the red ribbons said. “But this is the first time I’ve had to watch it happening. With someone I cared about getting destroyed by it.”

She put an arm around the woman beside her and laid her head on her shoulder, making the seashell ear pendants clack softly. “How much longer?” she said.

“Not long. Any time now.”

They sat looking out into the darkness, watching for the tall flame that would mark the end of yet another world.

Leviathan Wept

DANIEL ABRAHAM

New writer Daniel Abraham lives with his wife in Albuquerque, New Mexico, where he is director of technical support at a local Internet service provider. He's made sales to *Asimov's Science Fiction, SCI FICTION, The Magazine of Fantasy & Science Fiction, Realms of Fantasy, The Infinite Matrix, Vanishing Acts, The Silver Web, Bones of the World, The Dark, Wild Cards*, and elsewhere. Not one to do things by halves, he's just sold his first *three* novels, a fantasy trilogy, which will be appearing over the next couple of years.

In the unsettling story that follows, he shows us that it's really true that all of us are connected on some level—and that that might not be a *good* thing.

"Good crowd," Pauel said, from Paris.

"Things are weird," Renz said, passing his gaze over that auditorium so that Pauel could see it better. "People are scared."

When Renz had first trained with the link—when he began what Anna called his split-screen life—he had wanted the display windows to show the other people in his cell instead of what they were seeing; to make him feel they were speaking face to face. It had taken months for him to become comfortable with the voices of people he couldn't see and the small screens in his own visual field that showed what they were seeing. Now it lent their conversations a kind of intimacy; it was as if they were a part of him. Pauel and Marquez, Paasikivi and Thorn.

The auditorium was full, agents of CATC—Coordinated Antiterrorist Command—in almost every seat and so many others linked in that the feed was choppy from bandwidth saturation. The air was thick with the heat and scent of living bodies.

Of the other members of his cell, only Marquez was physically present, sitting beside him and tapping the armrest impatiently. Pauel, Paasikivi, and Thorn were linked in from elsewhere. Pauel was in his apartment, lying back on his old couch so that the rest of them were looking up at his dirty skylight and the white-blue Parisian sky. Paasikivi and Thorn were sharing a booth at a Denver coffee shop so that Renz could see each of them from the other's perspective—Thorn small and dark as an Arab, Paasikivi with her barely graying hair cut short. Renz wondered how long they would all be able to pretend those two weren't lovers, then placed all the window in his peripheral vision so he wouldn't be distracted from the man on the stage.

"Renz. I heard Anna was back in the hospital," Paasikivi said. Her tone of voice made it a question.

"It's just follow-up," Renz said. "She's fine."

The man at the front tilted his head, said something into a private link, and stepped up to the edge of the stage. In Denver, Thorn stirred his coffee too hard, rattling the spoon against the cup the way he did when he was uncomfortable. Renz lowered the volume from the link.

"Good afternoon," the man said. "I'd like to welcome you all here. And I have to say I wish we had this kind of turnout for the budget meetings."

A wave of nervous laughter swept over the crowd. Without meaning to, Renz found himself chuckling along with the rest. He stopped.

"For those of you who don't know me, my name's Alan Andrews. I'm a tactical liaison for the Global Security Council's theoretical branch. Think of me as the translator for the folks in the ivory tower."

"Condescending little pigfuck, isn't he?" Pauel said.

"By now I'm sure you've all heard about the anomalies," the speaker said. "OG 47's experience with the girls in New York, OG 80 and the old woman in Bali, the disruptions at the CATC root databases. I'm here to give you an idea what the theoretical branch has made of them."

"Yes, Pauli," Marquez muttered. "But are you sure about the pig? He looks more a chimp man to me."

"Would you two shut up," Renz said. "I want to hear this."

"The first thing I want to make clear," the man said, holding his hands out to the crowd, palms out, placating, "is that there are no direct ties between these incidents and any known terrorist network. Something's going on, and we all know that, but it's not a conspiracy. It's something else."

The man dropped his hands.

"That's the good news. The bad news is it's probably something worse."

Looking back, the first anomaly had been so small, Renz had hardly noticed it. It had presented as a series of small sounds at a moment when his attention had been a thousand other places. He had heard it and forgotten until later.

The town they had been in at the time was nothing remarkable; the Persian Interest Zone was peppered with places like it. Concrete apartment buildings and ruined mosques mixed with sad, prefab Western strip malls. The asphalt roads had been chewed by tank treads sometime a decade before and never repaired. But intelligence said that an office building in the run-down central district was still running network servers for the al-Nakba.

Organizational Group 47—Renz, Marquez, Pauel, Thorn, Paasikivi—were in an old van parked on a side street, waiting. Thorn and Pauel—the only two who could pass for local—sat in the front playing the radio and smoking cigarettes. Paasikivi and Marquez squatted in the belly of the machine, using the three-foot-tall degaussed steel case of the EMP coil as a table for Marquez's chess set. Renz kept watch out the tiny tinted windows in the back. Waiting was the hardest part.

The operation was organized in a small-world network, the cells like theirs connected loosely with fifty or a hundred like it around the world and designed to behave organically, adjusting to contingency without need for a central authority.

It gave them, Renz supposed, the kind of flexibility that a war between networks required. But it cost them a solid timetable. They might be called up in the next thirty seconds; they might be waiting for an hour. It might be that allowing the target to survive would be a viable strategy, and they'd all pull quietly out without anyone knowing they'd been there.

Paasikivi sighed, tipped her king with a wooden click, and moved forward in the van, leaving Marquez to chuckle and put the pieces away.

"You're thinking about Anna," Marquez said.

Renz glanced back, shook his head, and turned to the windows again.

"No, I'm winding myself up about the mission."

"Should be thinking about Anna, then. Nothing we can do about the mission right now."

"Nothing I can do about Anna either."

"You going to spend some time with her when this is over?"

"Yeah," Renz said.

"Really, this time?"

It wasn't the sort of question Renz would have taken from anyone but Marquez. He shifted forward, staring out at the sun-drenched street.

"Really, this time," he said.

An out-cell window flashed open. The blond man appearing in it looked harried as an air-traffic controller. Renz supposed the jobs weren't so different.

"OG 47, this is CG 60. Please begin approach to subject. Your target is fifteen minutes."

"Acknowledged," Paasikivi said for them all. Pauel flicked his still-burning cigarette onto the sidewalk and started the van. Renz didn't shift his position at the rear, but as he watched the street flow away behind them, the old electric feeling of adrenaline and anticipation grew in his belly.

There were four stages to the operation: penetration, reconnaissance, delivery, and withdrawal. Or, more plainly, get in, look around, do the thing, and leave. They had all rehearsed it together, and everyone knew what to do.

The van turned the corner two minutes later, angled into a ramp down to underground parking. A security guard at the entrance frowned at Pauel and barked something that wasn't Arabic but might have been Armenian. Pauel replied in Farsi, managing to sound bored and put upon. The guard waved them through. Renz watched the guard turn his back to them.

"Twelve minutes to target," Paasikivi said.

Pauel drove past the stairway leading up to the building proper, around a cinderblock corner, and parked across three parking spaces. The first stage was over; they were in. Without a word, Pauel and Marquez got out and started walking. Renz increased the size of their windows. Marquez, whistling, moved around a corner and deeper into the parking structure. Pauel went up the way they had come, toward the guard and the stairs.

"Pauel, you have something at your ten o'clock."

The window with Pauel's viewpoint shifted. Beside an old white Toyota, a woman in a birka was chiding a wiry man. The man, ignoring her, began walking toward the stairway.

"Civilians," Pauel murmured, hardly loud enough for the link to pick it up.

"Are you sure?" Paasikivi asked.

"Of course not," he said.

"Nine minutes," Thorn said. Hearing the words through the link and in the van simultaneously made them seem to reverberate, carrying a sense of doom and threat they didn't deserve. He felt Thorn tap his shoulder, and, still watching Pauel and Marquez, Renz shifted back, his hands resting on the cool metal carrying handles of the EMP coil, but not gripping them yet.

Marquez's window showed Arabic graffiti, oil-stained concrete, a few cars. More than half the lights were out.

"Looks good here," Marquez said.

In Pauel's window, the guard glanced back, frowning. Renz watched Pauel's hand rise in greeting.

"I'm going to go chat this bastard up, keep him busy," Pauel said. "Apart from him, I think we're clear."

The second stage was complete. Paasikivi slid to the front, into the driver's seat. Renz looked across the steel case to Thorn. Thorn nodded, and Renz leaned forward and pushed the rear door open.

"All right," Thorn said. "Renz and I are coming out. If you see anyone about to kill us, speak up." Renz thought his voice sounded bored. It was only a few steps to the wall, but the coil was heavy. His wrists strained as they snugged the metal against the cinderblock wall.

Renz stepped back as Thorn slid adhesive packs around the base of the coil, and then between the side of the metal case and the wall. He checked the time. Six minutes to target.

There were five small, very similar sounds, quickly but evenly spaced. The guard with Pauel scraped open a pack of cigarettes, the radio in the van beside Paasikivi popped as she put the key in the ignition, Thorn's adhesive packs went off with a hiss, a bit of gravel scraped under Renz's heel, and something like a cough came from deeper in the garage behind Marquez. Each sound seemed to pick up the next. A little musical coincidence that sounded like nothing so much as a man clearing his throat. Renz noticed it, and then was immediately distracted.

"Someone's back here," Marquez said. Renz caught a movement in Marquez's window. Someone ducking behind a car. "I think we may have a problem."

Everything happened at once, improvised and contingent but with the perfect harmony of a team acting together, so practiced it was like a single mind. Renz drew his sidearm and moved forward, prepared to lay down suppressing fire. Pauel, at the front, shot the security guard twice in the chest, once in the head. Paasikivi started the van. Marquez, seeing that Renz was coming, moved quickly backward, still scanning the darkness for movement.

Within seconds, Renz was around the corner, Marquez fifteen or twenty feet ahead of him, a pistol in his hand. Behind them and around the corner, where they couldn't have seen without the link, Thorn had the rear doors of the van opened and waiting, and Paasikivi was turning it around to face the exit. Pauel, at the base of the ramp, was dragging the guard out of the roadway.

Something moved to Marquez's left. Renz shifted and fired while Marquez pulled back past him to the corner. When Renz saw his own back in Marquez's window and Marquez braced to fire in Thorn's, he broke off, turned, and ran as Marquez opened up on the darkness. From listening, it would have been impossible to say when one had stopped shooting and the other started.

On the out-cell link, the blond man from OC 60 was saying that OG 47 had been compromised and Paasikivi was shouting at him that they had not. The coil was in place. They were withdrawing.

Marquez broke off as Renz reached the van, turned, and sprinted toward them, white tombstone teeth bared in what might have been effort or glee. Renz and Thorn both knelt inside the van, guns trained on the corner, ready to kill anyone who came around it.

"Okay," Pauel said from the ramp as Marquez reached the relative safety of the group. "Can you come get me now?"

The van surged forward, tires squealing as they rounded the corner—the van coming into view in Pauel's window, Pauel silhouetted against the blaring light of the street in Paasikivi's.

"Pauel! The stairs!" Renz said almost before he realized he'd seen something. There in Paasikivi's window, coming down from the building. He watched as Pauel shot the girl—five years old? six?

Time slowed. If they had been compromised, Renz thought, the girl could be wired—a walking bomb. There wasn't enough room in the parking structure to avoid her. If she went off, they were all going to die. Fear flushed his mouth with the taste of metal.

He heard Thorn exhale sharply, and the van sped past the stairway. The dead girl failed to explode. A dud.

"Jesus," Marquez said, relief in the sound of the word. "Oh, sweet Jesus."

Paasikivi stopped for less than a second, and Pauel was in the passenger's seat. Renz pulled the rear doors closed and latched them as they went up the ramp and out to the brightness of the street.

They were half a mile from the building when the trigger signal attenuated and the coil sparked out. With a shock like a headache, Renz's link dropped for a half second, leaving the disorienting sensation of only being inside his own head again. It felt like waking from a dream. And then the display windows were back, each showing slightly different views out the front while he alone looked back at a plume of white smoke rising from the town behind them.

By the time they reached the base in Hamburg, the news was on all the major sites. CATC under the orders of the Global Security Council had launched simultaneous attacks on the al-Nakba network, including three opium processing plants, two armories, and a training camp. Also the al-Nakba communications grid and network had suffered heavy damage.

The opposition sites added that a preschool near one of the armories had also been firebombed and that the training camp was a humanitarian medical endeavor. Eighteen innocent bystanders had died, including ten children from the preschool and two teachers.

There was also a girl shot in a minor raid in the Persian Interest Zone. Her name was Samara Hamze. Renz looked at the picture of her on the newsnets—shoulder-length black hair that rounded in at her neck, dark, unseeing eyes, skin fair enough she could have passed in the most racist quarters of Europe if she'd been given the chance. If she'd wanted to.

By the time they'd dropped Pauel off in Paris and found seats in a transatlantic carrier, the news cycle had moved on, and the girl—the dud—was forgotten.

Renz had never expected to see her again.

"That's the good news. The bad news is it's probably something worse," said the man on the stage. "Now, this is going to seem a little off-topic, but we may be in some strange territory before we're done here, so I hope you'll all indulge me. Ask yourselves this: Why aren't we all brilliant neurochemists? I don't mean why didn't we choose to go to med school—there are lots of reasons for that. I mean doesn't it seem like if you're able to *do* something, you must know about it? Aaron Ka can play great football because he knows a lot about football.

"But here we are, all juggling incredibly complex neurochemical exchanges all the time, and we're all absolutely unaware of it. I mean, no one says 'Oops, better watch those calcium channels or I might start getting my amygdala all fired up.' We just take ten deep breaths and try to calm down. The cellular layer just isn't something we're conscious of.

"And you can turn that around. Our neurons aren't any more aware of us than we are of them. If you ask a neuron why it fired or muscle tissue why it flexed, it wouldn't say 'Because it was my turn to run' or 'The bitch had it coming.' Those are the sorts of answers *we'd* give. If our cells could say anything, they'd say something about ion channels and charges across lipid membranes. And on that level—on the cellular level—that would be a fine explanation.

"The levels don't talk to each other. Your neurons don't know you, and you aren't aware of them. And, to torture a phrase, as above, so presumably below."

Renz felt Marquez shift in his seat. It wasn't impatience. Marquez was frowning, his gaze intent on the stage. Renz touched his arm and nodded a question.

"I don't like where this is going," Marquez said.

When Renz got back from the mission, Anna was sitting at the kitchen table—cheap laminate on peeling-chrome legs—scrolling through another Web page on her disease. Outside the dirty windows, the streetlights of Franklin Base glowed bright enough to block out the stars. Renz closed the door behind him, went over, and kissed his wife on the crown of her head. She smelled of the same cheap shampoo that she'd used since he met her. The sudden memory of her body when it was young and powerful and not quite his yet sent a rush of lust through him. It was embarrassing. He turned away, to the refrigerator, for some soda.

Anna turned off her screen and shifted. Her movements were awkward, disjointed. Her face was pinched and oddly expressionless. He smiled and lifted a bottle of soda. She shook her head—the movement took a second to get going, and it took a second to stop.

"Douglas Harper had Hulme's Palsy too," she said.

"The serial killer?"

"Yup," she said. "Apparently it's old news. Everyone in the support group knew about it. I'm still green compared to all of them. He wasn't symptomatic. They didn't diagnose it until after he'd been executed."

Renz pulled out a chair and sat, his heels on the kitchen table. The air conditioner kicked on with a decrepit hum.

"Do they think what . . . I mean, was killing people related?"

Anna laughed. Her eyes wide, she made an overhand stabbing motion like something out of a murder flick. Renz laughed, surprised to find his amusement was genuine.

"They just think if it had progressed faster, some of those girls might have lived," she said.

Renz took a sip of his soda. It was too sweet, and the fizz was already gone, but it was cold. There wasn't more he could ask than cold. Anna dropped her hands to the table.

"I was going to make dinner for you," she said. "But . . . well, I didn't."

"No trouble. I can make something," he said. Then, "Bad week?"

She sighed. She was too thin. He could see her collarbone, the pale skin stretched tight over it.

"The new immunosuppressants gave me the shits," she said, "and I think I'm getting another fucking cold. Other than that, just another thrilling week of broadcast entertainment and small town gossip."

"Any good gossip, then?"

"Someone's screwing someone else even though they're both married. I didn't really pay attention to the details. You? The news feeds made things look pretty good."

Anna's eyes were blue and so light that they made him think of icicles when they caught the light from the side. He'd fallen in love with her eyes as much as her tits and the taste of her mouth. He pushed the sorrow away before she could see it.

"We killed a kid. But things went pretty well otherwise."

"Only one kid? That thing with the preschool . . ."

"Yeah, them too. I mean *we* killed a kid. My guys."

Anna nodded, then reached awkwardly across the table. Her fingertips touched his wrist. He didn't look up, but he let the tears come. He could pretend they were for the dud.

"So, not such a good week for you either, huh?"

"Had its rough parts," he said.

"You're too good for this," she said. "You've got to stop it."

"I can't," he said.

"Why not?"

He spoke before he thought. Truth came that way; sudden, unexpected. Like illness. "We'd lose the medical coverage."

Her fingertips pulled back. Renz watched them retreat across the table, watched them fold into her flat, crippled fist. The air conditioner hummed, white noise as good as silence. Renz swung his legs down.

"I wouldn't change anything," he said.

"*I* fucking would." There was pain in her voice, and it pressed down on him like a hand.

"You know, boss, I'm not really hungry," he said. "Let's go to bed. We can eat a big breakfast in the morning."

Once she was asleep—her breath slow and deep and even—he got gently out of bed, pulled on his robe, and took himself out the front door to sit on the rotting concrete steps. The lawn was bare grass, the street empty. Renz ran his hands over his close-cropped hair and stared up at the moon, blue-white and pale in the sky. After a while, he turned up his link, seeing if there was anyone online.

Paasikivi and Thorn were both disconnected.

Pauel's link was open with the video feed turned off, but it had been idle for three and a half hours—he was probably asleep. Only Marquez was awake and connected. Renz excluded the other three feeds, considering the world from Marquez's point of view. It looked like he was in a bar. Renz turned up the volume and thin country-pop filled his ears.

"Hey, Marquez," he said.

The video feed jumped and then settled.

"Ah! Renz. I thought you were actually here. Is that your street?"

He looked up and down the empty asphalt strip—block houses and thin, water-starved trees. Buffalo grass lawns that never needed mowing. His street.

"I guess so," he said, then more slowly, "I guess so."

"Looks like the same shit as last time."

"It's hotter. There's more bugs."

Marquez chuckled, and Renz wasn't really on the step outside his shitty base housing, Anna dying by inches behind him. Marquez wasn't entirely in the cheap bar. They were on the link together, in the unreal, private space it made, and it removed the distance between them.

"How's Anna?" Marquez asked.

"She's all right. I mean her immune system's still eating her nerves, but apart from that."

"You sound bitter. You're not cutting out on her, are you?"

"No. I said I'd stay, and this time I will. It just sucks. It all just sucks."

"Yeah. I'm sorry. It's hard when your woman's down."

"Not just that. It *all* sucks. That girl we killed. We call her a dud like she wasn't a kid. What's that about?"

"It's about how a lot of those kids have mommies who strap them up with cheap dynamite. You know that."

"Are we soldiers, Marquez? Are we cops? What the fuck are we doing out there?"

"We're doing whatever needs to get done. That's not what's chewing you, and you know it."

It was true, so he ignored it.

"I've been doing this for too many years," Renz said. "I'm getting burned out. When I started, every operation was like an adventure from start to stop. Half the time I didn't even know how what I was doing fit in, you know? I just knew it did. Now I wonder why we do it."

"We do it because they do it."

"So why do they do it?"

"Because of us," Marquez said, and Renz could hear the smile. "This is the way it is. It's the way it's always been. You put people out in the world, and they kill each other. It's the nature of the game. Your problem, man, you never read Hobbes."

"The pissing cartoon kid?"

"Five hundred years ago, this guy named Hobbes wrote a book about how the only way to get peace was to give up all your rights to the state—do what the king said, whether it was crazy or not. Fuck justice. Fuck whether it made sense. Just do what you're told."

"And you read this thing."

"Shit no. There was this lecture I saw on a philosophy site. The guy said you build a government so motherfucking huge, it can *make* peace. Grind peace into people with a fucking hammer. Crush everyone, all the time. He called it Leviathan. He thought it was the only way to stop war."

"Sounds like hell."

"Maybe. But you got a better idea?"

"So we're making them be part of our government. And when we get them all in on it, this'll stop."

Marquez's window panned slowly back and forth—the man shaking his head. "This shit isn't going to stop until Jesus comes back."

"And if he doesn't?"

"Come on, man. You know all this. I said it before; it's not what's really on your mind."

"And what do *you* know about *my* mind?"

"I spend a lot of time there is all."

Renz sighed and scratched at the welt on his arm growing where a mosquito had drunk from him. The moon sailed slowly above him, the same as it always had, seen or unseen. He swallowed until his throat wasn't so tight.

"She still turns me on," he said at last. "It makes me feel like I'm . . . she's crippled. She's dying and I can't fix it, and all I want to do when I see her is fuck."

"So why don't you?"

"Don't be gross."

"She might want to, you know. It's not like she stopped being a woman. Knowing you still want her like that . . . might be the kind of thing she needs."

"You're out of your mind."

"There is no sorrow so great it cannot be conquered by physical pleasure," Marquez said.

"That Hobbes?"

"Nah. French girl named Colette. Just the one name. Wrote some stuff was supposed to be pretty racy at the time. It was a long time ago, though. Doesn't do much compared to net porn."

"You read the weirdest shit."

"I don't have anyone to come home to. Makes for a lot of spare time," Marquez said, his voice serious. Then, "Go inside, Renz. Sleep next to your wife. In the morning, make her a good breakfast and screw her eyes blue."

"Her eyes are blue," he said.

"Then keep up the good work."

"Fuck off," Renz said, but he was smiling.

"Good night, man."

"Yeah," Renz said. "Hey, Marquez. Thanks."

"De nada."

Renz dropped the link but sat still in the night for a while, trailing his fingers over flakes of concrete and listening to the crickets. Before he went to bed again, he ate a bowl of cereal standing up in the kitchen and then used her toothbrush to scrape the milk taste off his tongue. Anna had shifted in her sleep, taking up the whole bed. He kissed her shoulder as he rolled her back to her side. To his surprise, he slept.

At 6:30 in the morning, central time, a school bus packed with diesel-soaked fertilizer exploded in California, killing eighteen people and taking out civilian network access for half of the state. At 6:32, a fifteen-year-old girl detonated herself twenty feet away from the CEO of the EU's biggest bank while he was finishing his breakfast at a restaurant in midtown Manhattan. At 6:35, simultaneous brushfires started outside ten major power transmission stations along the Eastern Seaboard. At 7:30, Renz was on a plane to New York. At ten minutes before ten, a ground car met him at the airport, and by noon, he was at the site of the attack.

The street should have been beautiful. The buildings soared up around them; nothing in Manhattan was built on less than a cathedral scale—it was the personality of the city. From the corner, he could just catch sight of the Chrysler Building. The café had been elegant once, not very long before. Two blackened, melted cars squatted at the curbside. The bodies had been taken away long before Renz and the others arrived, but the outlines were there, not in chalk but bright pink duct tape.

"Hey, Renz," Paasikivi said as they took in the carnage. "Sorry about this. I know you wanted to see Anna."

"Don't let it eat you," he said. "This is what they pay me for, right?"

Inside, the window of the café had blown in. Chunks of bulletproof glass three fingers thick lay on the starched linen, the wooden floors polished to a glow. The air still smelled like match heads.

The briefing had been short. OG 47 had done this kind of duty before. Renz pulled up an off-cell window on the right margin of his visual field so the forensics experts could demonstrate what they wanted. The feeds from his cell were stacked on the left. OGs 34 and 102 were security, keeping the area clear while they worked, but he didn't open links to them; things were cluttered enough as it was.

Renz and his cell were the eyes and hands of the deep forensics team—men and women too valuable to risk in the field. A second attack designed to take out agents at the scene was a common tactic. Pauel, still in Paris, joined in not because he was useful, but because he was a part of the cell and so part of the operation. He was good to talk with during the quiet times.

The next few hours were painfully dull. Paasikivi and Thorn, Marquez and himself—the expendables—all took simple instructions from the experts, measuring what they were told to, collecting samples of scorched metal and stained linen, glass and shrapnel in self-sealing bags, and waiting for the chatter of off-cell voices to agree on the next task to be done.

Renz and his cell were the eyes and hands, not the brain. He found he could follow the directions he was given without paying much attention. They drove his body; he waited.

They finished just after 8 P.M. local. There were flights out that night, but Paasikivi argued for a night in the city. Renz could feel Marquez's attention on him like the sensation of being watched as Paasikivi and Thorn changed reservations for the whole cell. Renz almost stopped them, almost said he needed to go home and be with his wife. When he didn't, Marquez didn't mention it. With the forensics team gone, Renz arranged the other in-cell windows at the four corners of his visual field. An hour later, they were scattered over the island.

Marquez was on the edge of Central Park, his window showing Renz vistas of thick trees, their leaves black in the gloom of night. Paasikivi was sitting in a coffee shop at the top of a five-story bookstore, watching the lights of the city as much as the people in the café. Thorn sat in a sidewalk restaurant. Renz himself was walking through a subway station, heading south to SoHo because Pauel told him he'd like it. And Pauel, in the small hours of Paris morning, had taken himself out to an all-night café just to be in the spirit of things.

"I've always wanted to walk through Central Park," Marquez said. "It's probably safe enough, don't you think?"

"Wait until morning," Pauel said. "It's too dangerous at night."

Renz could hear the longing in Marquez's sigh, imagined the way he would stuff his hands into his pockets to hide the disappointment, and found to his amusement that he'd done the same. Marquez's gesture seemed to fit nicely on his own evening. The first breeze of the incoming train started to wash the subway platform, fluttering the fabric of his pants.

"I hate days like this," Thorn said, cutting into a steak. In that window, Renz watched the blood well up around the knife and wondered what it smelled like. "The nights, however, go a long way toward making up for it."

Marquez had turned and was walking now, people on the streets around him that would have been a crowd anywhere else. Paasikivi pushed her coffee cup away, stood and glanced back into the bookstore. In Paris, Pauel's waitress—a young woman with unlikely red hair—brought him his eggs Benedict and poured him a cup of coffee. Thorn lifted a fork of bleeding steak to his mouth. The train slid up to the platform, the doors opening with a hiss and a smell of fumes and ozone.

"All I really want . . ." Renz began, and then let the sentence die.

The girl came out of the bathroom in Pauel's Parisian diner at the same moment Renz saw her sitting in the back of his half-full subway car. Paasikivi caught sight of her near the music department, looking over the shoulder of a man who was carrying her—he might have been her father. Thorn, looking out the restaurant window saw her on the street. Marquez saw her staring at him from the back seat of a taxi.

In all four windows and before him in the flesh, the same girl or near enough, was staring at him. Pale skin, dark eyes, shoulder-length hair that rounded in at the neck. Samara Hamze. The dead girl. The dud.

As one, the five girls raised a hand and waved. Renz's throat closed with fear.

Thorn's voice, deceptively calm, said, "Well that's odd."

"Pull back," Paasikivi snapped, "all of you get out of there."

"I'm on a moving train," Renz said.

"Then get to a different car."

The others were already in motion. Walking quietly, quickly, efficiently away from the visitations toward what they each hoped might be safety. He heard Paasikivi talking to an off-cell link, calling in the alert. Renz moved to the shaking doors at the front of the car, but paused and turned, his eyes on the girl at the back. There were differences. This girl had a longer face, eyes that made him think of Asia. The woman beside her—the girl's mother, he guessed—saw him staring and glared back, pulling the girl close to her.

"Renz!" Paasikivi said, and he realized it hadn't been the first time she'd said it.

"Sorry. I'm here. What?"

"The transit police will be waiting for you at the next station. We're evacuating the train, but before we start that, I want you out of there."

"This isn't an attack," Renz said, unsure how he knew it. The mother's glare, the protective curve of her body around her child. "I don't know what it is, but it's not an attack."

"Renz," Marquez said. "Don't get heroic."

"No, guys, really," he said. "It's all right."

He stood and walked down the trembling car. Mother and child watched him approach. The mother's expression changed from fierce to frightened and then back to a different, more sincere fierceness. Renz smiled, trying to seem friendly, and squatted in front of them. He took out his CATC agent's ID and handed it to the mother. The darkness outside the windows gave way to the sudden blurred pillars of a station.

"Ma'am," he said. "I'm afraid you and your girl are going to have to come with me."

The doors hissed open. The police rushed in.

"I don't like where this is going," Marquez said.

"Some of you may have heard of the singularity," the man on the stage said. "It's one of those things that people keep saying is just about to happen, but then seems like it never does. The singularity was supposed to be when technology became so complex and so networked, that it woke up. Became conscious. It was supposed to happen in the 1990s and then about once every five years since then. There's a bunch of really bad movies about it.

"But remember what I said before. *Levels can't communicate*. So, what if something did wake up—some network with humans as part of it and computers as part of it. Planes, trains, and automobiles as part of it. This girl is like an individual human cell—a neuron, a heart cell. That man over there is another one. This community is like an organ or a tissue; even before we were linked, there've been constant communications and interactions between people. What if conscious structures rose out of that. Maybe they got a boost when we started massive networking, or maybe they were always there. Call them hive minds. We might never know, just like our cells aren't aware that they're part of us.

"And these hive minds may have been going along at their own level, completely unaware of us for . . . well, who knows? How long did we go along before we understood neurochemistry?

"I know we're all used to thinking of ourselves as the top. Molecules make up cells, cells make up tissues, tissues make up organs, organs make up people, but people don't make up anything bigger. Complexity stops with us. Well, ladies and gentlemen, it appears that ain't the case."

"Do any of you understand what the hell this guy's talking about?" Pauel asked. From the murmur of voices in the room, the question was being asked across more links than theirs. The speaker, as if expecting this, stepped back and put his hands in his pockets, waiting with an expression like sympathy, or else like pity.

"He's saying there's a war in heaven," Marquez said.

"No, he isn't," Renz said. "This isn't about angels. It's minds. He's talking about minds."

The man stepped forward again, holding up his hands, palm out. The voice of the crowd quieted, calmed. The man nodded, smiling as if he was pleased with them all.

"Here's the thing," he said. "Some of you have already seen the hole in the model. I said levels of complexity can't talk to each other. That's not quite true. You do it every time you drink a glass of wine or go on antidepressants. We understand neurons. Not perfectly, maybe, but well enough to affect them.

"Well, the only theory that fits the kind of coordinated coincidences we've been seeing is this: something up there—one level of complexity up from us—is starting to figure out how to affect *us*."

When Paasikivi interrupted the debriefing and told him, Renz didn't immediately understand. He kept having visions of bombs going off in the doctor's office, of men with guns. It was the only sense he could make of the words *Anna's in the hospital. She's had an attack.*

Her room stank of disinfectant. The hum and rattle of the air purifier was almost loud enough to keep the noise of the place at bay. White noise, like the ocean. She managed a smile when she saw him.

"Hey," she said. "Did you see? Salmon are extinct again."

"You spend too much time on the net," he said, keeping his voice gentle and teasing.

"Yeah, well. It's not like you take me dancing anymore."

He tried to smile at it. He wanted to. He saw the tears in her eyes, her stick-thin arms rising unsteadily to him. Bending down, he held her, smelled her hair, and wept. She hushed him and stoked the back of his neck, her shaking fingers against his skin.

"I'm sorry," he said, when he could say anything. "I'm supposed to be here fluffing your pillows and stuff, not . . ."

"Not having any feelings of your own? Sweetie, don't be stupid."

He was able to laugh again, a little. He set her down and wiped his eyes with his shirtsleeve.

"What do the doctors say?" he asked.

"They think it's under control again for now. We won't know how much of the damage is permanent for another week or two. It was a mild one, sweet. It's no big deal."

He knew from the way she said it, from the look in her eyes, that *It's no big deal* meant *There's worse than this coming*. He took a deep breath and nodded.

"And what about you?" she asked. "I saw there was some kind of attack that got stopped in New York. Did they try a follow-up to the restaurant?"

"No, it wasn't an attack," he said. "It was something else. It's really weird. They've got all the girls who were involved, but as far as anyone can tell there's no connection between them at all. It was some kind of coincidence."

"Girls?"

"Little ones. Maybe five, six years old."

"Were they wired?"

"No, they were all duds. And they weren't linked to any networks. They were just . . . people," Renz said, looking at his hands. "I hate this, Anna. I really hate this. All of it."

"Even the parts you like?"

The memory of exhilaration passed through him, of setting the coil, of fear and excitement and success. The feeling of being part of something bigger and more important than himself. The warmth of Anna's body against him as they danced, or as they fucked.

"Especially the parts I like," he said. "Those are godawful."

"Poor sweetie," she said. "I'm sorry, you know. I wouldn't have it like this if I could help it. I keep telling my body to just calm down about it, but . . ."

She managed a shrug. It was painful to watch. Renz nodded.

"Well, I wouldn't want to be in depths of hell with anyone else," he said.

"Now *that* was sweet," she said. Then, tentatively, "Have you thought about going to the support group? A lot of the people in my group have husbands and wives in it. It seems like it helps them."

"I'm not around enough. It wouldn't do any good."

"They've got counselors. You should at least talk to them."

"Okay. I'll talk to them. I've got leave coming up soon. I can soldier through until then."

She laughed, looked away. The light caught her eyes just right—icicles.

"What?" he asked.

"Soldiering through. It's just funny. You've got your war, honey, and I've got mine."

"Except you're the enemy too."

"Yeah, it does have that war-between-the-states feel to it," she said, and grinned. "There's a guy in my group named Eric. You'd like him. He says it's like having two people in the same body, one of them trying to live, the other one trying to kill the first one even if it means dying right along with."

"The good him and the bad him," he said.

"That's a matter of perspective. I mean, his immune system thinks it's being pretty heroic. Little white cells swimming around high-fiving each other. Hard to convince those guys to stop doing their jobs."

Renz shook his head. Anna's fingers found his, knitting with them. The air purifier let out a pop and then fell back to its normal grinding.

"Is everyone in your group that grim?"

"They haven't gotten to a place where they divide children into wireds and duds, but yes, there's a grimmish streak to them."

"Sounds like Marquez's kind of people."

"And how is the group mind?" Anna asked.

"Pretty freaked about the New York thing."

"So what exactly happened?"

He wasn't supposed to tell her. He did.

"Something up there—one level of complexity up from us—is starting to figure out how affect *us*," the man said. "The question is what we're going to do about it. And the answer is nothing. What we have to do is *nothing*. Go on with our work, the same as we always have. Let me explain why that's critically important.

"So far, the anomalies all have the same structure. They're essentially propaganda. We see the enemy approaching us in a friendly, maybe conciliatory manner. We start thinking of them as cute little girls and nice old women. Or else we're flooded with death reports that remind us that people we care about may die. That we might.

"And maybe we take that into the field with us. In a struggle between two hive minds, that kind of weakening of the opposition would be a very good move. Imagine how easy it would be to win a fistfight if you could convince the other guy's muscles that they really liked you. The whole thing would be over like that," the man said, snapping.

"We all need to be aware. We all need to keep in mind what's going on, but if we change our behavior, it wins. Let the other side get soft, that's fine, but we can't afford to. If this thing up there fails, it may give up the strategy. If we let it get a toehold—if what it's doing works—there's no reason to think it'll ever stop.

"Now, there is some good news. Some of you already know this. There are chatter reports that these incidents are happening to terrorist brigades too, so maybe one of these things is on our side. If that's the case, we just need to make sure the bad guys get soft before we do."

Renz shook his head. His mind felt heavy, stuffed with cotton. Marquez touched his arm.

"You okay?"

"Why does he think there's two?"

"What?"

The man was going on, saying something else. Renz leaned in to Marquez, whispering urgently.

"Two. Why does he think there are two of these things? If there's only one, then it's not a war. If this is . . . why would it be a fight and not a disease? Why couldn't it be telling us that this isn't supposed to be the way things are? Maybe the world's like Anna."

"What's the difference?" Marquez asked.

"With a disease you try to get better," Renz said. "With a war, you just want to win."

"Now before we go on," the man on the stage said, "there are a couple of things I want to make clear."

He raised his hand, index finger raised to make his point, but the words—whatever they were—died before he spoke them. Renz's link dropped, Pauel and Paasikivi and Thorn vanishing, Marquez only a body beside him and not someone in his mind. There was a half-second of dead silence as each agent in the room individually realized what was happening. In the breathless pause, Renz wondered if Anna was on the net and how quickly she would hear what had happened. He heard Marquez mutter *shit* before the first explosions.

Concussion pressed the breath out of him. The dull feeling that comes just after a car wreck filled him, and the world turned into a chaos of running people, shouted orders, the bright, acidic smell of explosives. Renz stumbled toward the exits at the side of the hall, but stopped before he reached them. It was where they'd expect people to go—where many of the agents were going. Marquez had vanished into the throng, and Renz reflexively tried to open the link to him. Smoke roiled at the high ceiling like storm cloud. Another more distant explosion came.

The auditorium was nearly empty now. A series of bombs had detonated on the right side of the hall—rows of seats were gone. The speaker lay quietly dead where he'd stood, body ripped by shrapnel. Fire spread as Renz watched. He wondered if the others were all right—Paasikivi and Thorn and Pauel. Maybe they'd been attacked too.

There were bodies in the wreckage. He went through quickly, the air was thickening. Dead. Dead. Dead. The first living person was man a little older than he was, lying on the stairs. Salt-and-pepper hair, dark skin, wide hands covered in blood.

"We have to get out," Renz said. "Can you walk?"

The man looked at him, gaze unfocussed.

"There's a fire," Renz said. "It's an attack. We have to get out."

Something seemed to penetrate. The man nodded, and Renz took his arm, lifted him up. Together they staggered out. Someone behind them was yelling, calling for help.

"I'll be back," Renz called over his shoulder. "I'll get this guy out and I'll be right back."

He didn't know if it was true. Outside, the street looked like an anthill that a giant child had kicked over. Emergency vehicles, police, agents. Renz got his ward to an ambulance. The medic stopped him when he turned to go back.

"You stay here," the medic said.

"There's still people in there," Renz said. "I have to go back. I'm fine, but I have to go back."

"You're not fine," the medic said, and pulled him gently down. Renz shook his head, confused, until the medic pointed at his arm. A length of metal round as a dime and long as a pencil stuck out of his flesh. Blood had soaked his shirt.

"Oh," Renz said. "I . . . I hadn't noticed."

The medic bent down, peering into his eyes.

"You're in shock," he said. "Stay here."

Renz did as he was told. The shapes moving in the street seemed to lose their individuality—a great seething mass of flesh and metal, bricks and fire, moving first one way and then another. He saw it as a single organism, and then as people, working together. Both interpretations made sense.

Firemen appeared, their hoses blasting, and the air smelled suddenly of water. He tried to link to Marquez, but nothing came up. Someone bound his arm, and he let them. It was starting to hurt now, a dull, distant throbbing.

He caught sight of a girl as she slipped into a doorway. So far, no one else seemed to have noticed her. Renz pushed himself up with his good arm and walked to her.

But she wasn't the same—not another ghost of Samara. This child was older, though only by a year or two. Her skin was deep olive, her hair and eyes black. Flames glittered in her eyes. Her coat was thick and bulky even though it was nearly summer. She looked at him and smiled. Her expression was beatific.

"We have to stop this," he said. "It's not war, it's a sickness. It's a fever. We're all part of the same thing, and it's dying. How are we going to make this *stop*?"

He was embarrassed to be crying in front of a stranger, much less a child. He couldn't stop it. And it was stupid. Even in his shock, he knew that if there was something up there, some hive mind sick and dying in its bed, he could no more reach it by speaking to this girl than by shouting at the sky. Could no more talk it out of what was happening than he could save Anna by speaking to her blood.

Renz saw the girl before him shift inside her coat, and understood. An Arab girl in New York in a bulky coat. A second attack to take out the emergency services answering the first one.

"Please. We have to stop this," Renz said. "You and me, we have to stop." The girl shook her head in response. *No, we don't.*

"God is great," she said, happily. Like she was sharing a secret.

The Defenders

COLIN P. DAVIES

New British writer Colin P. Davies is a building surveyor from Liverpool, England. His stories have appeared in *Spectrum SF, Asimov's Science Fiction, 3SF, Paradox, Elysian Fiction*, and *Andromeda Spaceways Inflight Magazine*, and he is at work on his first novel.

In the incisive and elegant little story that follows, one packed with enough ideas to fuel many another author's eight-hundred-page novel, he shows us the price that sometimes has to be paid to maintain the *status quo* . . .

Finally, Grandfather slowed the dinghy, and the retinue of iridescent wakefish skated away under a punishing noon sun.

Elisa leaned over the side and watched another wavering giant carcass pass below while Grandfather whistled a tune far older than Elisa's thirteen years.

"That's enough!" she said—then softer, "I've seen enough."

"And do you still consider me wicked?" Grandfather pushed back his white cap and wiped a crumpled handkerchief across his brow. He stopped the engine. The gentle splashing faded along with the murmur of the power unit.

"I never did think you were wicked."

Elisa scanned the horizon. From this far out in the Spherical Ocean, none of the archipelago was visible.

New Sicily was two hours to the west. She'd never traveled so far from Homeport, from people, before. The knowledge of isolation was like a hand squeezing her lungs—just her and Grandfather and an ocean a world wide.

She gazed again into the clear shallow water of the plateau, at the graveyard of great white bones. "How big is the battlefield?"

Grandfather held his arms wide so that his white shirt caught the breeze. "Vast. I watched from a prudent distance."

"I can't see the bodies of any demons. You said they're as big as the defenders."

"The winged demons are there—trust me. Look again . . . you may see their bronze spears."

"I see only my children." Elisa took off her brimmed grassweave hat and pulled her red hair back from her face. She touched a fingertip to her cheek, hoping for a tear, but found none. The sun burned on her scalp and she replaced the hat.

Grandfather shifted uncomfortably on his seat. "I think you stretch the point a little too far." He crouched forward and rummaged in a canvas bag, coming up with a pair of binoculars.

"Okay—maybe not children."

"You're a resource, Elisa, and I'm a creator. I don't have feelings of guilt."

"And yet you brought me out here."

"You're my granddaughter . . . I was coming here . . . and you *asked*." With the binoculars, he examined the sky to the east. "Besides . . . I thought you might learn something."

Elisa trailed her fingers in the water. The coolness surprised her, yet it seemed fitting for this place of the dead. She had come here looking for emotion, for a connection . . . or at least a reaction. But she was unmoved. Her heart was as cold as the ocean.

The monsters on the sea bed—those flying behemoths that had defended Homeport from the demons' attack, that had battled in a sky dark with wings and flesh, with blood falling like rain—were a *part* of her, created *from* her. The house-sized skull, the ribs like rafters, cells of her cells. What had she expected to feel?

"Grandfather . . . you're certain none survived?" She dried her fingers on her shorts.

He lowered the glasses. "When the spotters called, we sent out your litter. The demons fled, and no defenders returned to the labyrinth. Now only harvester fish inhabit the nest."

"What if the demons return?"

"They *will* return, in time. But we will always have another litter."

"But not mine."

"You've done your duty. No one will ask you again."

"I'm curious. . . . How does it feel to create life only for it to be destroyed? To create with that very aim? Doesn't it bother you?"

Grandfather sighed. "It has become a necessity. How else could we hold the demons back? It must be hard for you to understand."

"No, it's not hard." Understanding came easily—it was *emotion* that was hard. Elisa searched for melancholy, or grief. All she could find was discomfort in the harsh heat of the sun. "I'd like to believe that mine died heroically, that somehow a bit of my personality lived in them."

"Defenders have no choice. They fight, they return to the nest. They're *designed* to have no choice—is that heroic?"

"You're a cold-hearted old soldier, Grandfather. They're not machines. You told me that they can feel."

He nodded. "Of *course* they feel. They feel love for us. Why else would they die for us?"

Grandfather returned the binoculars to the bag by his feet; when he straightened up, he was holding a small radio or communicator. He extended an aerial and tapped a fingertip on the keys. "Sometimes I wonder who the real defenders are," he said.

"What do you mean? You made them. You should know."

"And who are the real demons. . . ."

"Whoever they are, one day you'll find them and destroy them—right?"

He smiled at her. "This is their world. *Humans* are the intruders here."

"What are you doing?" she said, pointing a finger at the radio in his hand.

"Fishing."

The sun burned down upon Elisa's brown shoulders; her pink vest offered little protection. She didn't want to be here anymore.

"I've seen enough, Grandfather. I want to go back."

"Just a little while . . . I'm almost done."

"What if the defenders loved themselves more than they loved us?"

"You're a strange one, Elisa. Full of questions. No one has asked me such questions before."

"Maybe I'm not like everyone else."

"They *have* to love us more than life. Our survival here depends on it. But I'm no fool. I have planned for surprises."

"I think I don't have it in me to be a martyr."

"You'll have time to . . ."

His words fell away as the sea heaved and the boat rocked as something passed beneath them. Elisa peered into the water, but only glimpsed a darkness through the flashes of reflected sun. A moment of quiet and trepidation, and then a huge shape burst from the water three hundred meters distant. Out of a fountain of spray, a monstrous creature took to the air. It turned in their direction as a wave rushed toward the boat.

"A defender!" Elisa screamed as the dinghy tossed and threw her about. She clamped her fingers to the seat.

The creature climbed above them on black reptilian wings, then swooped and circled low, its scythelike claws slicing the wave tops. The massive head retained human characteristics, but exaggerated and drawn forward into a spike-tipped snout. The chitin-plated neck seemed unfeasibly slender, but allowed for maneuverability in the air and for slashing strokes with the serrated tusks. A magnificent beast that had proved the equal of the self-destructive recklessness of the brown-furred demons.

"It's one of mine!" Elisa cried. "It must be!"

The defender rose and blocked out the sun for a moment, sweeping the air back to gain height, then banked and returned to dive toward them.

"Yes, it's one of mine," she said. "And it must be smarter than the rest. It found out how to hide and survive."

The defender was calling—a howl as mournful as a lost child's—as it swept so low over them that Elisa's hair was blown about her face. She caught the creature's seaweed scent. "It's because of *me*, isn't it, Grandfather? My defender is different. It has my spirit. It made its own choices. It's stronger, brighter. . . . It could become a leader."

The defender came around again and glided overhead, and there came a crack and a thud and a large smouldering blue-sky hole appeared in the creature's body . . . and it screamed and reeled and plunged from the sky . . . crashed into the water some distance away.

Elisa cried and grasped the side of the rocking boat. "Grandfather . . ." She saw him push down the aerial. "You killed it! It was *you*. Why? Why did you kill it?"

She watched as the great body was sucked beneath the surface. First whirlpools, then cold boiling, then calmness. This was terrible. A tragedy. She could have had the best defender ever!

"Grandfather?"

He dropped the transmitter into the bag and stared down at the water. She could not see his face. Though she spoke to him, again and again, he would not reply. Slowly, the boat ceased its agitated motion.

The sun crawled across the sky.

Finally, Grandfather started the engine and directed the dinghy toward Homeport.

Mayflower II

STEPHEN BAXTER

Like many of his colleagues here at the beginning of a new century, British writer Stephen Baxter has been engaged for more than a decade now with the task of revitalizing and reinventing the "hard-science" story for a new generation of readers, producing work on the cutting edge of science that bristles with weird new ideas and often takes place against vistas of almost outrageously cosmic scope.

Baxter made his first sale to *Interzone* in 1987, and since then has become one of that magazine's most frequent contributors, as well as making sales to *Asimov's Science Fiction, Science Fiction Age, Analog, Zenith, New Worlds*, and elsewhere. He's one of the most prolific new writers in science fiction, and is rapidly becoming one of the most popular and acclaimed of them as well. In 2001, he appeared on the Final Hugo Ballot twice, and won both *Asimov's* Readers Award and *Analog*'s Analytical Laboratory Award, one of the few writers ever to win both awards in the same year. Baxter's first novel, *Raft*, was released in 1991 to wide and enthusiastic response, and was rapidly followed by other well-received novels such as *Timelike Infinity, Anti-Ice, Flux*, and the H. G. Wells pastiche—a sequel to *The Time Machine—The Time Ships,* which won both the John W. Campbell Memorial Award and the Philip K. Dick Award. His other books include the novels, *Voyage, Titan, Moonseed, Mammoth, Book One: Silverhair, Manifold: Time, Manifold: Space, Evolution, Coalescent*, and (in collaboration with Arthur C. Clarke) *The Light of Other Days*, as well as the collections *Vacuum Diagrams: Stories of the Xeelee Sequence, Traces*, and *Hunters of Pangaea.* His most recent books are a chapbook novella, *Mayflower II*, and a new novel, *Exultant*. Coming up is another novel written in collaboration with Arthur C. Clarke, *Time's Eye, a Time Odyssey*.

Here he gives us ringside seats for the painful birth of a new civilization—one destined to spend the next few thousand years confined within four walls.

Author's Note:

My proceeds from this work will be donated to the Asian Elephant Survival Appeal, of which I am a patron.

Once elephants could be found throughout Asia, India, Africa, and North America. Their remains, with tusks like sculptures and teeth like carbstones, are still dug out of the ground in Los Angeles and London. Today all the elephants are gone, save only three species. But now human population pressure is endangering one of these: the Asian (or Indian) elephants. It is highly likely they will be gone in decades.

The North of England Zoological Society, a nonprofit conservation organization, is spearheading an international program to sustain the Asian elephant in its native ranges, as well as to establish a reserve breeding population in European zoos. Preserving the elephant will bring the additional benefit of preserving the wider ecosystem it inhabits, while respecting the economic and cultural interests of neighboring human populations.

For more details or to make a donation please contact:

Asian Elephant Survival Appeal
Chester Zoo
FREEPOST
Chester CH2 1LH
UK

or visit www.chesterzoo.co.uk.

Twenty days before the end of his world, Rusel heard that he was to be saved.

"Rusel. Rusel . . ." The whispered voice was insistent. Rusel rolled over, trying to shake off the effects of his usual mild sedative. His pillow was soaked with sweat. The room responded to his movement, and soft light coalesced around him.

His brother's face was hovering in the air at the side of his bed. Diluc was grinning widely.

"Lethe," Rusel said hoarsely. "You ugly bastard."

"You're just jealous," Diluc said. The Virtual made his face look even wider than usual, his nose more prominent. "I'm sorry to wake you. But I just heard—you need to know—"

"Know what?"

"Blen showed up in the infirmary." Blen was the nanochemist assigned to Ship Three. "Get this: he has a heart murmur." Diluc's grin returned.

Rusel frowned. "For that you woke me up? Poor Blen."

"It's not that serious. But, Rus—it's congenital."

The sedative dulled Rusel's thinking, and it took him a moment to figure it out.

The five Ships were to evacuate the last, brightest hopes of Port Sol from the path of the incoming peril. But they were slower-than-light transports, and would take many centuries to reach their destinations. Only the healthiest, in body and genome, could be allowed aboard a generation starship. And if Blen had a hereditary heart condition—

"He's off the Ship," Rusel breathed.

"And that means you're aboard, brother. You're the second-best nanochemist on this lump of ice. You won't be here when the Coalition arrives. You're going to live!"

Rusel lay back on his crushed pillow. He felt numb.

Diluc kept talking. "Did you know that families are *illegal* under the Coalition? Their citizens are born in tanks. Just the fact of our relationship would doom us, Rus! I'm trying to fix a transfer from Five to Three. If we're together, that's something, isn't it? I know it's going to be hard, Rus. But we can help each other. We can get through this . . ."

All Rusel could think about was Lora, whom he would have to leave behind.

The next morning Rusel arranged to meet Lora in the Forest of Ancestors. He took a bubble-wheel surface transport, and set out early.

Port Sol was a ball of friable ice and rock a couple of hundred kilometers across. It was actually a planetesimal, an unfinished remnant of the formation of Sol system. Inhabited for millennia, its surface was heavily worked, quarried and pitted, and littered by abandoned towns. But throughout Port Sol's long human usage some areas had been kept undamaged, and as he drove Rusel kept to the marked track, to avoid crushing the delicate sculptures of frost that had coalesced here over four billion years.

This was the very edge of Sol system. The sky was a dome of stars, with the ragged glow of the Galaxy hurled casually across its equator. Set in that diffuse glow was the sun, the brightest star, bright enough to cast shadows, but so remote it was a mere pinpoint. Around the sun Rusel could make out a tiny puddle of light: That was the inner system, the disc of worlds, moons, asteroids, dust and other debris that had been the arena of all human history before the first interplanetary voyages some three thousand years earlier, and still the home of all but an invisible fraction of the human race. This was a time of turmoil, and today humans were fighting and dying, their triumphs and terror invisible. Even now, from out of that pale glow, a punitive fleet was ploughing toward Port Sol.

And visible beyond the close horizon of the ice moon was a squat cylinder, a misty sketch in the faint rectilinear sunlight. That was Ship Three, preparing for its leap into the greater dark.

The whole situation was an unwelcome consequence of the liberation of Earth from the alien Qax.

The Coalition of Interim Governance was the new, ideologically pure and viciously determined authority that had emerged from the chaos of a newly freed Earth. Relentless, intolerant, unforgiving, the Coalition was already burning its way out through the worlds and moons of Sol system. When the Coalition ships came, the best you could hope for was that your community would be broken up, your equipment impounded, and that you would be hauled back to a prison camp on Earth or its Moon for "reconditioning."

But if you were found to be harboring anyone who had collaborated with the hated Qax, the penalties were much more extreme. The word Rusel had heard was "resurfacing."

Now the Coalition had turned its attention to Port Sol. This ice moon was governed by five Pharaohs, who had indeed collaborated with the Qax—though they described it as "mediating the effects of the occupation for the benefit of mankind"—and they had received antiageing treatments as a reward. So Port Sol was a "nest of illegal immortals and collaborators," the Coalition said, which its troops had been dispatched to "clean out." They seemed indifferent to the fact that in addition to the Pharaohs, some fifty thousand people called Port Sol home.

The Pharaohs had a deep network of spies on Earth, and they had had some warning. As the colonists had only the lightest battery of antiquated weaponry—indeed the whole moon, a refuge from the occupation, was somewhat low-tech—nobody expected to be able to resist. But there was a way out.

Five mighty Ships were hastily thrown together. On each Ship, captained by a Pharaoh, a couple of hundred people, selected for their health and skill sets, would be taken away: a total of a thousand, perhaps, out of a population of fifty thousand, saved from the incoming disaster. There was no faster-than-light technology on Port Sol; these would be generation starships. But perhaps that was well: between the stars there would be room to hide.

All of these mighty historical forces had now focused down on Rusel's life, and they threatened to tear him away from his lover.

Rusel was an able nanochemist, he was the right age, and his health and pedigree were immaculate. But unlike his brother he hadn't been good enough to win the one-in-fifty lottery and make the cut to get a place on the Ships. He was twenty-eight years old: not a good age to die. But he had accepted his fate, so he believed—for Lora, his lover, had no hope of a place. At twenty she was a student, a promising Virtual idealist but without the mature skills to have a chance of competing. So at least he would die with her, which seemed to him some consolation. He was honest with himself; he had never been sure if this serenity would have survived the appearance of the Coalition ships in Port Sol's dark sky—and now, it seemed, he was never going to find out.

Lora was waiting for him at the Forest of Ancestors. They met on the surface, embracing stiffly through their skinsuits. Then they set up a dome-tent and crawled through its collapsible airlock.

In the Forest's long shadows, Rusel and Lora made love: at first urgently, and then again, more slowly, thoughtfully. In the habs, inertial generators kept the gravity at one-sixth standard, about the same as Earth's Moon. But there was no gravity control out here in the Forest, and as they clung to each other they drifted in the tent's cool air, light as dreams.

Rusel told Lora his news.

Lora was slim, delicate. The population of this low-gravity moon tended to tallness and thin bones, but Lora seemed to him more elfin than most, and she had large, dark eyes that always seemed a little unfocussed, as if her attention were somewhere else. It was that sense of other-world fragility that had first attracted Rusel to her, and now he watched her fearfully.

With blankets bundled over her legs, she took his hand and smiled. "Don't be afraid."

"I'm the one who's going to live. Why should I be afraid?"

"You'd accepted dying. Now you've got to get used to the idea of living." She sighed. "It's just as hard."

"And living without you." He squeezed her hand. "Maybe that's what scares me most. I'm frightened of losing you."

"I'm not going anywhere."

He gazed out at the silent, watchful shapes of the Ancestors. These "trees," some three or four meters high, were stumps with "roots" that dug into the icy ground. They were living things, the most advanced members of Port Sol's low-temperature aboriginal ecology. This was their sessile stage. In their youth, these creatures, called 'Toolmakers," were mobile, and were actually intelligent. They would haul themselves across Port Sol's broken ground, seeking a suitable crater slope or ridge face. There they would set down their roots and allow their nervous systems, and their minds, to dissolve, their purposes fulfilled. Rusel wondered what icy dreams might be coursing slowly through their residual minds. They were beyond decisions now; in a way he envied them.

"Maybe the Coalition will spare the Ancestors."

She snorted. "I doubt it. The Coalition only care about humans—and their sort of humans at that."

"My family have lived here a long time," he said. "There's a story that says we rode out with the first colonizing wave." It was a legendary time, when the great engineer Michael Poole had come barnstorming all the way to Port Sol to build his great starships.

She smiled. "Most families have stories like that. After thousands of years, who can tell?"

"This is my home," he blurted. "This isn't just the destruction of us, but of our culture, our heritage. Everything we've worked for."

"But that's why you're so important." She sat up, letting the blanket fall away, and wrapped her arms around his neck. In Sol's dim light her eyes were pools of liquid darkness. "You're the future. The Pharaohs say that in the long run the Coalition will be the death of mankind, not just of *us*. Somebody has to save our knowledge, our values, for the future."

"But you—" *You will be alone, when the Coalition ships descend.* Decision sparked. "I'm not going anywhere."

She pulled back. "What?"

"I've decided. I'll tell Andres . . . and my brother. I can't leave here, not without you."

"You must," she said firmly. "You're the best for the job; believe me, if not the Pharaohs wouldn't have selected you. So you have to go. It's your duty."

"What human being would run out on those he loved?"

Her face was set, and she sounded much older than her twenty years. "It would be easier to die. But you must live, live on and on, live on like a machine, until the job is done, and the race is saved."

Before her he felt weak, immature. He clung to her, burying his face in the soft warmth of her neck.

Nineteen days, he thought. *We still have nineteen days.* He determined to cherish every minute.

But as it turned out, they had much less time than that.

Once again he was awakened in the dark. But this time his room lights were snapped full on, dazzling him. And it was the face of Pharaoh Andres that hovered in the air beside his bed. He sat up, baffled, his system heavy with sedative.

"—thirty minutes. You have thirty minutes to get to Ship Three. Wear your skinsuit. Bring nothing else. If you aren't there we leave without you."

At first he couldn't take in what she said. He found himself staring at her face. Her head was hairless, her scalp bald, her eyebrows and even her eyelashes gone. Her skin was oddly smooth, her features small; she didn't look young, but as if her face had sublimated with time, like Port Sol's ice landscapes, leaving this palimpsest. She was rumoured to be two hundred years old.

Suddenly her words snapped into focus. "Don't acknowledge this message, just move. We lift in twenty-nine minutes. If you are Ship Three crew, you have twenty-nine minutes to get to—"

She had made a mistake: that was his first thought. Had she forgotten that there were still sixteen days to go before the Coalition ships were due? But he could see from her face there was no mistake.

Twenty-nine minutes. He reached down to his bedside cabinet, pulled out a nano pill, and gulped it down dry. Reality bleached, becoming cold and stark.

He dragged on his skinsuit and sealed it roughly. He glanced around his room, at his bed, his few pieces of furniture, the Virtual unit on the dresser with its images of Lora. *Bring nothing.* Andres wasn't a woman you disobeyed in the slightest particular.

Without looking back he left the room.

The corridor outside was bedlam. A thousand people shared this under-the-ice habitat, and all of them seemed to be out tonight. They ran this way and that, many in skinsuits, some hauling bundles of gear. He pushed his way through the throng. The sense of panic was tangible—and, carried on the recycled air, he thought he could smell burning.

His heart sank. It was obviously a scramble to escape—but the only way off the moon was the Ships, which could take no more than a thousand.

He couldn't believe what he was seeing. Had the sudden curtailing of the time left triggered this panic? But these were citizens of Port Sol, and this was its ultimate emergency. Had they lost all their values, all their sense of community? What could they hope to achieve by hurling themselves at Ships that had no room for them, but to bring everybody down with them? *But what would I do?* He could afford the luxury of nobility; he was getting out of here.

Twenty minutes.

He reached the perimeter concourse. Here, surface transports nuzzled against a row of simple airlocks. Some of the locks were already open, and people were crowding in, pushing children, bundles of luggage.

His own car was still here, he saw with relief. He pulled open his skinsuit glove and hastily pressed his palm to the wall. The door hissed open. But before he could pass through, somebody grabbed his arm.

A man faced him, a stranger, short, burly, aged perhaps forty. Behind him a woman clutched a small child and an infant. The adults had blanket-wrapped bundles on their backs. The man wore an electric-blue skinsuit, but his family were in hab clothes.

The man said desperately, "Buddy, you have room in that thing?"

"No," Rusel said.

The man's eyes hardened. "Listen. The Pharaohs' spies got it wrong. Suddenly the Coalition is only seven days out. Look, friend, you can see how I'm fixed. The Coalition breaks up families, doesn't it? All I'm asking is for a chance."

But there won't be room for you. Don't you understand? And even if there were— There were to be no children on the Ships at launch: that was the Pharaohs' harsh rule. In the first years of the long voyage, everybody aboard had to be maximally productive. The time for breeding would come later.

The man's fist bunched. "Listen, buddy—"

Rusel shoved the man in the chest. He fell backwards, stumbling against his children. His blanket bundle broke open, and goods spilled on the floor: clothes, diapers, children's toys.

"Please—" The woman approached him, stepping over her husband. She held out a baby. "Don't let the Coalition take him away. Please."

The baby was warm, soft, smiling. Rusel automatically reached out. But he stopped himself cold. Then he turned away.

The woman continued to call after him, but he didn't let himself think about it. *How could I do that? I'm no longer human,* he thought. He pushed into his car, slammed shut the door, and stabbed a preset routine into the control panel.

The car ripped itself away from the airlock interface, ignoring all safety protocols, and began to haul itself on its bubble wheels up the ramp from the under-the-ice habitat to the surface. Shaking, Rusel opened his visor. He might be able to see the doomed family at the airlock port. He didn't look back.

It wasn't supposed to be like this.

Andres' Virtual head coalesced before him. "Sixteen minutes to get to Ship Three. If you're not there we go without you. Fifteen forty-five. Fifteen forty . . ."

The surface was almost as chaotic as the corridors of the hab, as transports of all types and ages rolled, crawled, or jumped. There was no sign of the Guardians, the Pharaohs' police force, and he was apprehensive about being held up.

He made it through the crowd, and headed for the track that would lead through the Forest of Ancestors to Ship Three. Out here there was a lot of traffic, but it was more or less orderly, everyone heading out the way he was. He pushed the car up to its safety-regulated maximum speed. Even so, he was continually overtaken. Anxiety tore at his stomach.

The Forest, with the placid profiles of the Ancestors glimmering in Sol's low light, looked unchanged from when he had last seen it, only days ago, on his way to meet Lora. He felt an unreasonable resentment that he had suddenly lost so much time, that his careful plan for an extended farewell to Lora had been torn up. He wondered where she was now. Perhaps he could call her.

Thirteen minutes. No time, no time.

The traffic ahead was slowing. The vehicles at the back of the queue weaved, trying to find gaps, and bunched into a solid pack.

Rusel punched his control panel and brought up a Virtual overhead image. Ahead of the tangle of vehicles, a ditch had been cut roughly across the road. People swarmed, hundreds of them. Roadblock.

Eleven minutes. For a moment his brain seemed as frozen as the Port Sol ice; frantic, bewildered, filled with guilt, he couldn't think.

Then a heavy-duty long-distance truck broke out of the pack behind him. Veering off the road to the left, it began to smash its way through the Forest. The elegant eightfold forms of the Ancestors were nothing but ice sculptures, and they shattered before the truck's momentum. It was ugly, and Rusel knew that each impact wiped out a life that might have lasted centuries more. But the truck was clearing a path.

Rusel hauled at his controls, and dragged his car off the road. Only a few vehicles were ahead of him in the truck's destructive wake. The truck was moving fast, and he was able to push his speed higher.

They were already approaching the roadblock, he saw. A few suit lights moved off the road and into the Forest; the blockers must be enraged to see their targets evade them so easily. Rusel kept his speed high. Only a few more seconds and he would be past the worst.

But there was a figure standing directly in front of him, helmet lamp bright, dressed in an electric-blue skinsuit, arms raised. As the car's sensors picked up the figure, its safety routines cut in, and he felt it hesitate. *Nine minutes*. He slammed his palm to the control panel, overriding the safeties.

He closed his eyes as the car hit the protester.

He remembered the blue skinsuit. He had just mown down the man from the airlock, who had been so desperate to save his family. He had no right to criticize the courage or the morals or the loyalty of others, he saw. *We are all just animals, fighting to survive. My seat on Ship Three doesn't make me any better*. He hadn't even had the guts to watch.

Eight minutes. He disabled the safety governors and let the car race down the empty road, its speed ever increasing.

He had to pass through another block before he reached Ship Three—but this one was manned by Guardians. At least they were still loyal. They were an orderly line across the road, dressed in their bright yellow skinsuit-uniforms. Evidently they had pulled back to tight perimeters around the five Ships.

The queuing was agonizing. With only five minutes before Andres's deadline, a Guardian pressed a nozzle to the car's window, flashed laser light into Rusel's face, and waved him through.

Ship Three was directly ahead of him. It was a drum, a squat cylinder about a kilometer across and half as tall. It sat at the bottom of its own crater, for Port Sol ice had been gouged out and plastered roughly over the surface of its hull. It looked less like a ship than a building, he thought, a building coated by thick ice, as if long abandoned. But it was indeed a starship, a ship designed for a journey of not less than centuries, and fountains of crystals already sparkled around its base in neat parabolic arcs: steam from the Ship's rockets, freezing immediately to ice. People milled at its base, running clumsily in the low gravity, and scurried up ramps that tongued down from its hull to the ground.

Rusel abandoned the car, tumbled out onto the ice, and ran toward the nearest ramp. There was another stomach-churning wait as a Guardian in glowing yellow checked each identity. At last, after another dazzling flash of laser light in his eyes, he was through.

He hurried into an airlock. As it cycled it struck him that as he boarded this Ship, he was never going to leave it again: whatever became of him, this Ship was his whole world, for the rest of his life.

The lock opened. He ripped open his helmet. The light was emergency red, and klaxons sounded throughout the ship; the air was cold, and smelled of fear. Lethe, he was aboard! But there could only be a minute left. He ran along a cold, ice-lined corridor towards a brighter interior.

He reached an amphitheater, roughly circular, carpeted by acceleration couches. People swarmed, looking for spare couches. The scene seemed absurd to Rusel, like a children's game. Andres's voice boomed from the air. "Get into a couch. Any couch. It doesn't matter. Forty seconds. Strap yourself in. Nobody is going to do it for you. Your safety is your own responsibility. Twenty-five seconds."

"Rus! Rusel!" Through the throng, Rusel made out a waving hand. It was Diluc, his brother, wearing his characteristic orange skinsuit. "Lethe, I'm glad to see you. I kept you a couch. Come on!"

Rusel pushed that way. Ten seconds. He threw himself down on the couch. The straps were awkward to pull around the bulk of his suit.

As he fumbled, he stared up at a Virtual display that hovered over his head. It was a view as seen from the Ship's blunt prow, looking down. Those tongue ramps were still in place, radiating down to the ice. But now a dark mass boiled around the base of the curving hull: people, on foot and in vehicles, a mob of them closing in. In amongst the mass were specks of bright yellow. Some of the Guardians had turned on their commanders, then. But others stood firm, and in that last second Rusel saw the bright sparks of weapon fire, all around the base of the Ship.

A sheet of brilliant white gushed out from the Ship's base. It was Port Sol ice, superheated to steam at tens of thousands of degrees. The image shuddered, and Rusel felt a quivering, deep in his gut. The Ship was rising, right on time, its tremendous mass raised on a bank of rockets.

When that great splash of steam cleared, Rusel saw small dark forms lying motionless on the ice: the bodies of the loyal and disloyal alike, their lives ended in a fraction of a second. A massive shame descended on Rusel, a synthesis of all the emotions that had churned through him since that fateful call of Diluc's. He had abandoned his lover to die; he had probably killed himself; and now he sat here in safety as others died on the ice below. What human being would behave that way? He felt the shame would never lift, never leave him.

Already the plain of ice was receding, and weight began to push at his chest.

Soon the other Ships were lost against the stars, and it was as if Ship Three was alone in the universe.

In this opening phase of its millennial voyage Ship Three was nothing more than a steam rocket, as its engines steadily sublimated its plating of ice and hurled it out of immense nozzles. But those engines drew on energies that had once powered the expansion of the universe itself. Later the Ship would spin up for artificial gravity and switch to an exotic ramjet for its propulsion, and its true journey would begin.

The heaviest acceleration of the whole voyage had come in the first hours, as the Ship hurled itself away from Port Sol. After that the acceleration was cut to about a third standard—twice lunar gravity, twice what the colonists of Port Sol had been used to. For the time being, the acceleration couches were left in place in that big base amphitheater, and in the night watches everybody slept there, all two hundred of them massed together in a single vast dormitory, their muscles groaning against the ache of the twice-normal gravity.

The plan was that for twenty-one days the Ships would run in toward the puddle of light that was Sol system. They would penetrate as far as the orbit of Jupiter, where they would use the giant planet's gravity field to slingshot them on to their final destinations. It seemed paradoxical to begin the exodus by hurling oneself deep into the inner system, the Coalition's home territory. But space was big, the Ships' courses had been plotted to avoid the likely trajectory of the incoming Coalition convoy, and they were to run silently, not even communicating with each other. The chances of them being detected were negligible.

Despite the wearying gravity the first days after launch were busy for everybody. The Ship's interior had to be rebuilt from its launch configuration to withstand this high-acceleration cruise phase. And the daily routines of the long voyage began.

The Ship was a closed environment and its interior had plenty of smooth surfaces where biofilms, slick detergent-proof cities of bugs, would quickly build up. Not only that, the fallout of the Ship's human cargo—flakes of skin, hair, mucus—were all seed beds for bacterial growth. All of this had to be eliminated; Captain Andres declared she wanted the Ship to be as clean as a hospital.

The most effective way to achieve that—and the most "future-proof," in Andres' persistent jargon—was through the old-fashioned application of human muscle. Everybody had to pitch in, even the Captain herself. Rusel put in his statutory half-hour per day, scrubbing vigorously at the walls and floors and ceilings around the nanofood banks that were his primary responsibility. He welcomed the mindlessness of the work; he continued to seek ways in which to distract himself from the burden of thought.

He was briefly ill. In the first couple of weeks, everybody caught colds from everybody else. But the viruses quickly ran their course through the Ship's small population, and Rusel felt obscurely reassured that he would likely never catch another cold in his life.

A few days after launch Diluc came to find him. Rusel was up to his elbows in slurry, trying to find a fault in a nanofood bank's waste vent. Rusel, working nonstop, had seen little of his brother. He was surprised by how cheerful Diluc appeared, and how energetically he threw himself into his own work on the air cycling systems. He spoke brightly of his "babies," fans and pumps, humidifiers and dehumidifiers, filters and scrubbers and oxygenators.

The crew seemed to be dividing into two rough camps, Rusel thought. There were those who were behaving as if the outside universe didn't exist; they were bright, brash, too loud, their laughter forced. The other camp, to which Rusel felt he belonged, retreated the other way, into an inner darkness, full of complicated shadows.

But today Diluc's mood seemed complex. "Brother, have you been counting the days?"

"Since launch? No." He hadn't wanted to think about it.

"It's day seven. There's a place to watch. One of the observation lounges. Captain Andres says it's not compulsory, but if . . ."

It took Rusel a moment to think that through. *Day seven*: the day the Coalition convoy was due to reach Port Sol. Rusel flinched from the thought. But one of his worst moments of that chaotic launch day was when he had run down that desperate father and driven on, without even having the courage to watch what he was doing. Perhaps this would atone. "Let's do it," he said.

Ship Three, like its four siblings, was a fat torus. To reach the observation lounge the brothers had to ride elevators up through several decks to a point in the Ship's flattened prow, close to the rim. The lounge, crammed with Virtual generation gear, was already configured for the spin-up phase, and most of its furniture was plastered to the walls, which would become the floor. It was big enough for maybe fifty people, and it was nearly full; Rusel and Diluc had to crowd in.

Pharaoh Andres—now Captain Andres, Rusel reminded himself—was here, sitting in a deep, heavy-looking chair, front and center before an immense, shining Virtual.

A ball of ice spun grandly before their eyes. It was Port Sol, of course; Rusel immediately recognized its icy geography of ancient craters, overlaid by a human patterning of quarries and mines, habitats and townships, landing ports. In the inhabited buildings lights shone, defiantly bright in outer-system gloom. It was a sculpture in white and silver, and it showed no sign of the chaotic panic that must be churning in its corridors.

The sight took Rusel's breath away. Somewhere down there was Lora; it was an almost unbearable thought, and he wished with all his heart he had stayed with her.

The Coalition convoy closed in.

Its ships materialized from the edge of the three-dimensional image, as if sliding in from another reality. The fleet was dominated by five, six, seven Spline warships, living ships each a kilometer or more wide. Confiscated from the expelled Qax, they were fleshy spheres, their hulls studded with weapons and sensors and crudely scrawled with the green tetrahedron that was the sigil of a free humanity.

Rusel's stomach filled with dread. "It's a heavy force," he said.

"They've come for the Pharaohs," Diluc said grimly. "The Coalition is showing its power. Images like this are no doubt being beamed throughout the system."

Then it began. The first touch of the energy beams, cherry-red, was almost gentle, and Port Sol ice exploded into cascades of glittering shards that drifted back to the surface, or escaped into space. Then more beams ploughed up the ice, and structures began to implode, melting, or to fly apart. A spreading cloud of crystals that began to swathe Port Sol in a temporary, pearly atmosphere. It was silent, almost beautiful, too large-scale to make out individual deaths, a choreography of energy and destruction.

"We'll get through this," Diluc muttered. "We'll get through this."

Rusel felt numbed, no grief, only shame at his own inadequacy. This was the destruction of his home, of a world, and it was beyond his imagination. He tried to focus on one person, on Lora, to imagine what she must be doing—if she was still alive—perhaps fleeing through collapsing tunnels, or crowding into deep shelters. But, in the ticking calm of this lounge, with its fresh smell of new equipment, he couldn't even picture that.

As the assault continued, numbers flickered across the status display, an almost blasphemous tallying of the estimated dead.

Even after the trauma of Port Sol, work had to continue on booting up the vital systems that would keep them all alive.

Rusel's own job, as he suddenly found himself the senior nanochemist on the Ship, was to set up the nanofood banks that would play a crucial part in recycling waste into food and other consumables like clothing. The work was demanding from the start. The banks were based on an alien technology, nanodevices purloined from the occupying Qax. Only partially understood, they were temperamental and difficult.

It didn't help that of the two assistants he had been promised a share of—most people were generalists in this small, skill-starved new community—only one had made it onto the Ship. It turned out that in the final scramble about 10 percent of the crew hadn't made it aboard; conversely, about 10 percent of those who actually were aboard shouldn't have been here at all. A few shame-faced "passengers" were yellow-uniformed Guardians who in the last moments had abandoned their posts and fled to the sanctuary of the Ship's interior.

The work had to get done anyhow. And it was urgent; until the nanofood was available the Ship's temporary rations were steadily depleting. The pressure on Rusel was intense. But Rusel was glad of the work, so hard mentally and physically in the high gravity he had no time to think, and when he hit his couch at night he slept easily.

On the fifteenth day Rusel achieved a small personal triumph as the first slab of edible food rolled out of his nanobanks.

Captain Andres had a policy of celebrating small achievements, and she was here as Rusel ceremoniously swallowed the first mouthful of his food, and she took the second. There was much clapping and back-slapping. Diluc grinned in his usual huge way. But Rusel, still numbed inside, didn't feel much like celebrating. Half the crew, it was estimated, were in some kind of shock; people understood. He got away from the crush as quickly as he could.

On the twenty-first day the Ship was to encounter Jupiter.

Captain Andres called the crew together in the acceleration-couch amphitheater, all two hundred of them, and she set up a Virtual display in the air above them. The sun was just a pinpoint, though much brighter than seen from Port Sol, and Jupiter was a flattened ball of cloud, mottled with grey-brown bruises—the result, it was said, of an ancient battle. Few of the crew had travelled away from Port Sol before; they craned to see.

The most intriguing sight of all was four sparks of light that slid across the background of stars. They were the other Ships, numbers One, Two, Four and Five; the little fleet would come together at Jupiter for the first time since leaving Port Sol, and the last.

Andres walked though the crowd on their couches, declaiming loudly enough for all to hear, her authority easy and unforced. "We Pharaohs have been discussing destinations," she said. "Obviously the targets had to be chosen before we reached Jupiter; we needed to plan for our angles of emergence from Jupiter's gravity well. The Coalition is vindictive and determined, and it has faster-than-light ships. It will soon overtake us—but space is big, and five silent-running generation starships will be hard to spot. Even so, it's obviously best to separate, to give them five targets to chase, not just one.

"So we have five destinations. And ours," she said, smiling, "is the most unique of all."

She listed the other Ships' targets, star systems scattered through the disc of the Galaxy—none closer than five hundred light-years. "All well within the Ships' design parameters," she said, "and perhaps far enough to be safe. But *we* are going farther."

She overlaid the image of the shining Ships with a ruddy, shapeless mass of mist. "This is the Canis Major Dwarf Galaxy," she said. "Twenty-four thousand light-years from Sol. It is the closest of the satellite galaxies—*but it is beyond the main Galaxy itself*, surely far outside the Coalition's grasp for the foreseeable future."

Rusel heard gasps throughout the amphitheater. To sail beyond the Galaxy?

Andres held her hands up to quell the muttering. "Of course, such a journey is far in excess of what we planned. No generation starship has ever challenged such distances before, let alone achieved them." She stared around at them, fists on hips. "But if we can manage a thousand years of flight, we can manage ten, or fifty—why not? We are strong, we are just as determined as the Coalition and its drones—more so, for we know we are in the right."

Rusel wasn't used to questioning the Pharaohs' decisions, but he found himself wondering at the arrogance of the handful of Pharaohs to make such decisions on behalf of their crew—not to mention the generations yet unborn.

But Diluc muttered, "Can't say it makes much difference. A thousand years or ten thousand, I'll be dead in a century, and *I* won't see the end . . ."

Andres restored the images of the ships. Jupiter was expanding rapidly now, and the other Ships were swarming closer.

Andres said, "We have discussed names for our vessels. On such an epic voyage numbers won't do. Every ship must have a name! We have named our Ship-homes for great thinkers, great vessels of the past." She stabbed her finger around the Virtual image. "*Tsiolkovsky. Great Northern. Aldiss. Vanguard.*" She looked at her crew. "And as for us, only one name is possible. Like a band of earlier pilgrims, we are fleeing intolerance and tyranny; we sail into the dark and the unknown, carrying the hopes of an age. We are *Mayflower.*"

You didn't study history on Port Sol. Nobody knew what she was talking about.

At the moment of closest approach Jupiter's golden brown cloudscape bellied over the upturned faces of the watching crew, and the Ships poured through Jupiter's gravity well. Even now the rule of silence wasn't violated, and the five Ships parted without so much as a farewell message.

From now on, wherever this invisible road in the sky took her, the second *Mayflower* was alone.

As the days stretched to weeks, and the weeks to months, Rusel continued to throw himself into work—and there was plenty of it for everybody.

The challenges of running a generation starship were familiar to some extent, as the colonists of Port Sol had long experience in ecosynthesis, in constructing and sustaining closed artificial environments. But on Port Sol they had had the ice, rock, and organic-chemistry resources of the ice moon itself to draw on. The Ship was now cut off from the outside universe.

So the cycles of air, water, and solids would have to be maintained with something close to 100 percent efficiency. The control of trace contaminants and pests would have to be ferociously tight: swarms of nanobots were sent scurrying in pursuit of flakes of hair and skin. And the sealing of the Ship against leakages was vital—more nanomachines labored to knit together the hull.

Not only that, the Ship's design had been hastily thrown together, and the vessel wasn't even completed on launch. The construction had been a hurried project anyhow, and the shaving off of those final ten or twelve days of preparation time, as the Coalition fleet sneaked up in the dark, had made a significant difference. The crew labored to complete the Ship's systems in flight.

The most significant difficulty, Rusel believed, was the sudden upping of the design targets. A thousand-year cruise, the nominal design envelope, was one thing. Now it was estimated that, cruising at about half lightspeed, it would take Ship Three *fifty times* as long to reach Canis Major. Even relativistic time dilation would only make a difference of a few percent to the subjective duration. As a consequence the tolerances on the Ship's systems were tightened by orders of magnitude.

There was yet another goal in all this rebuilding. The Ship's essential systems were to be simplified and automated as far as possible, to reduce the skill level required to maintain them. They were trying to "future-proof" the project, in Andres's jargon: to reduce the crew to the status of nonproductive payload. But a key lesson of ecosynthesis was that the smaller the biosphere, the more conscious control it would require. The Ship was a much smaller environment than a Port Sol habitat, and that presented problems of stability; the ecological system was poorly buffered and would always be prone to collapse. It was clear that this small, tight biosphere would always have to be consciously managed if it were to survive.

As Diluc put it with grim humor, "We can't allow civilization to fall in here."

Despite the horror of Port Sol, and the daunting timescale Andres had set—which Rusel suspected nobody believed anyhow—the rhythms of human life continued. It was as if they were all slowly healing, Rusel thought.

Diluc found a new partner, a plump, cheerful woman of about thirty called Tila. Diluc and Tila had both left lovers behind on Port Sol—and Tila had been forced to abandon a child. Now they seemed to be finding comfort with each other. Diluc was somewhat put out when they were both hauled into Andres's small private office to be quizzed about their relationship, but Andres, after much consulting of genetic maps, approved their continuing liaison.

Rusel was pleased for his brother, but he found Tila a puzzle. Most of the selected crew had been without offspring, back on Port Sol; few people with children, knowing they would have to leave them behind, had even offered themselves for selection. But *Tila had abandoned a child.* He saw no sign of this loss in her face, her manner; perhaps her new relationship with Diluc, and even the prospect of more children with him in the future, was enough to comfort her. He wondered what was going on inside her head, though.

As for Rusel, his social contacts were restricted to work. He found himself being subtly favored by Captain Andres, along with a number of others of the Ship's senior technicians. There was no formal hierarchy on the Ship—no command structure below Andres herself. But this group of a dozen or so, a meritocracy selected purely by proven achievement, began to coalesce into a kind of governing council of the Ship.

That was about as much social life as Rusel wanted. Otherwise he just worked himself to the point of exhaustion, and slept. The complex mass of emotions lodged inside him—agony over the loss of Lora, the shock of seeing his home destroyed, the shame of living on—showed no signs of breaking up. None of this affected his contributions to the Ship, he believed. He was split in two, split between inside and out, and he doubted he would ever heal.

In fact he didn't really want to heal. One day he would die, as so many others had, as Lora probably had; one day he would atone for his sin of survival in death.

Meanwhile there was always the Ship. He slowly widened the scope of his work, and began to develop a feel for the Ship as a whole. As the systems embedded, it was as if the Ship were slowly coming alive, and he learned to listen to the rhythm of its pumps, feel the sighing of its circulating air.

Though Andres continued to use the fanciful name she had given it, Rusel and everybody else thought of it as they always had: as Ship Three—or, increasingly, just the Ship.

Almost a year after Jupiter, Andres called her "council" together in the amphitheater at the base of the Ship. This big chamber had been stripped of its acceleration couches, and the dozen or so of them sat on temporary chairs in the middle of an empty grey-white floor.

Andres told them she wanted to discuss a little anthropology.

In her characteristic manner she marched around the room, looming over her crew. "We've had a good year, for which I thank you. Our work on the Ship isn't completed—in a sense it never will be completed—but I'm now satisfied that *Mayflower* will survive the voyage. If we fail in our mission, it won't be the technology that betrays us, but the people. And that's what we've got to start thinking about now."

Mayflower was a generation starship, she said. By now mankind had millennia of experience of launching such ships. "And as far as we know, every last one of them has failed. And why? Because of the people.

"The most basic factor is population control. You'd think that would be simple enough! The Ship is an environment of a fixed size. As long as every parent sires one kid, on average, the population ought to stay stable. But by far the most common causes of failure are population crashes, in which the number of crew falls below the level of a viable gene pool and then shuffles off to extinction—or, more spectacularly, explosions in which people eat their way to the hull of their ship and then destroy each other in the resulting wars."

Diluc said dryly, "Maybe all that proves it's just a dumb idea. The scale is just too big for us poor saps to manage."

Andres gazed at him challengingly. "A bit late to say that now, Diluc!"

"Of course it's not just numbers but our population's genetic health that we have to think about," pointed out Ruul. This lanky, serious man was the Ship's senior geneticist. "We've already started, of course. All of us went through genetic screening before we were selected. There are only two hundred of us, but we're as genetically diverse a sample of Port Sol's population as possible. We should avoid the founder effect—none of us has a genetically transmitted disease to be spread through the population—and, provided we exert some kind of control over breeding partnerships, we should be able to avoid genetic drift, where defective copies of a gene cluster."

Diluc looked faintly disgusted. " 'Control over breeding partnerships?' What kind of language is that?"

Andres snapped, "The kind of language we're going to have to embrace if we're to survive. We must take control of reproductive strategies. Remember, on this Ship the purpose of having children is not for the joy of it and similar primate rewards, but to maintain the crew's population levels and genetic health, and thereby to see through our mission." She eyed Diluc. "Oh, I'm not against comfort. I was human once! But we are going to have to separate companionship needs from breeding requirements." She glanced around. "I'm sure you are all smart enough to have figured that out for yourselves. But even this isn't enough, if the mission is to be ensured."

Diluc said, "It isn't?"

"Of course not. This is a desperately small universe. We will always rely on the ship's systems, and mistakes or deviances will be punished by catastrophe—for as long as the mission lasts. Nonmodified human lifespans average out at around a century; we just haven't evolved to think further. But a century is but a moment for our mission. *We must future-proof*; I've said it over and over. And to do that we will need a continuity of memory, purpose, and control far beyond the century-long horizons of our transients."

Transients: it was the first time Rusel had heard her use that word.

He thought he saw where all this was leading. He said carefully, "Port Sol was not a normal human society. With respect. Because it had you Pharaohs at its heart."

"Yes," she said approvingly, her small face expressionless. "And *that* is the key." She lifted her hand before her face and inspected it. "Two centuries ago the Qax Governor made me ageless. Well, I served the Qax—but my deeper purpose was always to serve mankind. I fled to Port Sol, with others, to escape the Qax; and now I have had to flee Sol system itself to escape my fellow human beings. But I continue to serve mankind. And it is the continuity I provide, a continuity that transcends human timescales, which will enable this mission to succeed, where even Michael Poole failed."

Diluc pulled a face. "What do you want from us—to worship you as a god?"

There were gasps; you didn't speak to a Pharaoh like that. But Andres seemed unfazed. "A god? No—although a little awe from you wouldn't come amiss, Diluc. And anyhow, it probably won't be *me*. Remember, it wasn't a human agency that gave me my antiageing treatments, but the Qax . . ."

The Qax's own body architecture had nothing in common with humanity's. They were technically advanced, but their medicinal manipulation of their human subjects was always crude.

"The success rate was only ever some forty percent," Andres said. She inspected her hand, pulling at slack skin. "Oh, I would dearly love to live through this mission, all fifty millennia of it, and see it through to its conclusion. But I fear that's unlikely to happen." She gazed around at them. "I can't do this alone; that's the bottom line. I will need help."

Diluc suddenly saw it, and his mouth dropped open. "You aren't serious."

"I'm afraid so. It is necessary for the good of the mission that *some of the people in this room do not die*."

Ruul the geneticist unfolded his tall frame from his chair. "We believe it's possible. We have the Qax technology." Without drama, he held up a yellow pill.

There was a long silence.

Andres smiled coldly. "We can't afford to die. We must remember, while everybody else forgets.

"And we must manage. We must achieve *total* social control—total over every significant aspect of our crew's lives—and we must govern their children's lives just as tightly, as far as we can see ahead. Society has to be as rigid as the bulkheads which contain it. Oh, we can give the crew freedom within limits! But we need to enforce social arrangements in which conflict is reduced to negligible, appropriate skill levels kept up—and, most importantly, a duty of maintenance of the Ship is hammered home into every individual at birth."

Rusel said, "And what about the rights of those you call the transients? We Pharaohs would be taking away all meaningful choice from them—and their children, and their children's children."

"Rights? Rights?" She loomed over him. "Rusel, a transient's only purpose is to live, reproduce, and die in an orderly fashion, thus preserving her genes to the far future. There is no room on this Ship for democracy, no space for love! A transient is just a conduit for her genes. She has no rights, any more than a bit of pipe that carries water from source to sink. Surely you thought this through. When we get to Canis Major, when we find a world to live on, when again we have an environment of surplus—then we can talk about rights. But in the meantime we will control." Her expression was complex. "But you must see that we will control through love."

Diluc gaped. "*Love*?"

"The Qax technology was based on a genetic manipulation, you know. We Pharaohs were promised that our gift would be passed on to our children. And we had those children! But we Pharaohs never bred true. I once had a child myself. She did not survive." She hesitated, just for a second. Then she went on, "But by now there are genes for immortality, or at least longevity, scattered through the human population—even among *you*. Do you see now why we had to build these arks—why we couldn't flee and abandon you, or just take frozen zygotes or eggs?" She spread her hands wide. "Because you are my children, and I love you."

Nobody moved. Rusel thought he could see tears in her stony eyes. *She is grotesque*, he thought.

Diluc said carefully, "Pharaoh, would I be able to bring Tila with me? And our children, if we have them?"

"I'm sorry," she said gently. "Tila doesn't qualify. Besides, the social structure simply wouldn't be sustainable if"—

"Then count me out." Diluc stood up.

She nodded. "I'm sure you won't be the only one. Believe me, this is no privilege I'm offering you."

Diluc turned to Rusel. "Brother, are you coming with me?"

Rusel closed his eyes. The thought of his eventual death had actually been a comfort to him—a healing of his inner wounds, a lifting of the guilt he knew he would carry throughout his life. Now even the prospect of death was being taken away, to be replaced by nothing but an indefinite extension of duty.

But he had to take it on, he saw. As Lora herself had told him, he had to live on, like a machine, and fulfil his function. That was why he was here; only that way could he atone.

He looked up at Diluc. "I'm sorry," he said.

Complex emotions crossed his brother's face: anger, despair, perhaps a kind of thwarted love. He turned and left the room.

Andres behaved as if Diluc had never existed.

"We will always have to combat cultural drift," she said. "It is the blight of the generation starship. Already we have some pregnancies; soon we will have the first children, who will live and die knowing nothing but this Ship. And in a few generations—well, you can guess the rest. First you forget where you're going. Then you forget you're going anywhere. Then you forget you're on a damn ship, and start to think the vessel is the whole universe. And so forth! Soon nothing is left but a rotten apple full of worms, falling through the void. Even the great engineer Michael Poole suffered this; a fifteen-hundred-year generation starship he designed—the first *Great Northern*—barely limped home. Oh, every so often you might have a glorious moment as some cannibalistic savage climbs the decks and peers out in awe at the stars, but that's no consolation for the loss of the mission.

"Well, not this time. You engineers will know we're almost at the end of our GUTdrive cruise phase; the propellant ice is almost exhausted. And that means the

Ship's hull is exposed." She clapped her hands—and, to more gasps from the crew, the amphitheater's floor suddenly turned transparent.

Rusel was seated over a floor of stars; something inside him cringed.

Andres smiled at their reaction. "Soon we will leave the plane of the Galaxy, and what a sight *that* will be. In a transparent hull our crew will never be able to forget they are on a Ship. There will be no conceptual breakthroughs on *my* watch!"

With the ice exhausted, the Ship's banks of engines were shut down. From now on a dark matter ramjet would provide a comparatively gentle but enduring thrust.

Dark matter constituted most of the universe's store of mass, with "light matter"—the stuff of bodies and ships and stars—a mere trace. The key advantage of dark matter for the Ship's mission planners was that it was found in thick quantities far beyond the visible disc of the Galaxy, and would be plentiful throughout the voyage. But dark matter interacted with the light only through gravity. So now invisible wings of gravitational force unfolded ahead of the Ship. Spanning thousands of kilometers, these acted as a scoop to draw dark matter into the hollow center of the torus-shaped Ship. There, concentrated, much of it was annihilated and induced to give up its mass-energy, which in turn drove a residuum out of the Ship as reaction mass.

Thus the Ship ploughed on into the dark.

Once again the Ship was rebuilt. The acceleration provided by the dark matter ramjet was much lower than the ice rockets, and so the Ship was spun about its axis, to provide artificial gravity through centrifugal force. It was an ancient solution and a crude one—but it worked, and ought to require little maintenance in the future.

The spin-up was itself a spectacular milestone, a great swivelling as floors became walls and walls became ceilings. The transparent floor of the acceleration-couch amphitheater became a wall full of stars, whose cool emptiness Rusel rather liked.

Meanwhile the new "Elders," the ten of them who had accepted Andres' challenge, began their course of treatment. The procedure was administered by geneticist Ruul and a woman called Selur, the Ship's senior doctor. The medics took it slowly enough to catch any adverse reactions, or so they hoped.

For Rusel it was painless enough, just injections and tablets, and he tried not to think about the alien nanoprobes embedding themselves in his system, cleaning out ageing toxins, repairing cellular damage, rewiring his very genome.

His work continued to be absorbing, and when he had spare time he immersed himself in studies. All the crew were generalists to some degree, but the ten new Elders were expected to be a repository of memory and wisdom far beyond a human lifespan. So they all studied everything, and they learned from each other.

Rusel began with the disciplines he imagined would be most essential in the future. He studied medicine; anthropology, sociology and ethics; ecosynthesis and all aspects of the Ship's life support machinery; the workings of the Ship's propulsion systems; techniques of colonization; and the geography of the Galaxy and its satellites. He also buttonholed Andres herself and soaked up her knowledge of human history. Qax-derived nanosystems were so prevalent throughout the Ship that Rusel's own expertise was much in demand.

His major goal continued to be to use up as much of his conscious time as possible with work. The studying was infinitely expandable, and very satisfying to his naturally acquisitive mind. He found he was able to immerse himself in esoteric aspects of one discipline or another for days on end, as if he was an abstract intellect, almost forgetting who he was.

His days passed in a dream, as if time itself flowed differently for him now.

The Elders' placid lives were not without disturbance, however. The Qax biotechnology was far from perfect. In the first year of treatment one man suffered kidney failure; he survived, but had to be taken out of the program.

And it was a great shock to all the Elders when Ruul himself succumbed to a ferocious cancer, as the technological rebuilding of his cells went awry.

The day after Ruul's death, as the Elders adjusted to the loss of his competence and dry humour, Rusel decided he needed a break. He walked out of the Elders' Cloister and into the body of the Ship, heading for the area where his brother had set up his own home with Tila.

On all the Ship's cylindrical decks, the interior geography had been filled by corridors and cabins, clustered in concentric circles around little open plazas—"village squares." Rusel knew the theory, but he quickly got lost; the layout of walls and floors and false ceilings was changed again and again as the crew sorted out their environment.

At last he came to the right doorway on the right corridor. He was about to knock when a boy, aged about five with a shock of thick black hair, rocketed out of the open door and ran between Rusel's legs. The kid wore a bland Ship's-issue coverall, long overdue for recycling judging by its grime.

This must be Tomi, Rusel thought, Diluc's eldest. Child and Elder silently appraised each other. Then the kid stuck out his tongue and ran back into the cabin.

In a moment Diluc came bustling out of the door, wiping his hands on a towel. "Look, what in Lethe's going on—Rusel! It's you. Welcome, welcome!"

Rusel embraced his brother. Diluc smelt of baby sick, cooking, and sweat, and Rusel was shocked to see a streak of grey in his brother's hair. Perhaps he had been locked away longer than he had realized.

Diluc led Rusel into his home. It was a complex of five small interconnected cabins, including a kitchen and bathroom. Somebody had been weaving tapestries; gaudy, space-filling abstract patterns filled one wall.

Rusel sat on a sofa adapted from an acceleration couch, and accepted a slug of some kind of liquor. He said, "I'm sorry I frightened Tomi. I suppose I've let myself become a stranger."

Diluc raised an eyebrow. "Two things about that. Not so much *stranger* as *strange*." He brushed his hand over his scalp.

Rusel involuntarily copied the gesture, and felt bare skin. He had long forgotten that the first side effect of the Pharaoh treatment had been the loss of his hair; his head was as bald as Andres's. Surrounded all day by the other Elders, Rusel had got used to it, he supposed. He said dryly, "Next time I'll wear a wig. What's the second thing I got wrong?"

"That isn't Tomi. Tomi was our first. He's eight now. That was little Rus, as we call him. He's five."

"*Five?*" But Rusel had attended the baby Rusel's naming ceremony. It seemed like yesterday.

"And now we're due for another naming. We've missed you, Rus."

Rusel felt as if his life was slipping away. "I'm sorry."

Tila came bustling in, with an awestruck little Rus in tow, and an infant in her arms. She too seemed suddenly to have aged; she had put on weight, and her face was lined by fine wrinkles. She said that Tomi was preparing a meal—of course uncle Rusel would stay to eat, wouldn't he?—and she sat down with the men and accepted a drink.

They talked of inconsequentials, and of their lives.

Diluc, having stormed out of Andres's informal council, had become something of a leader in his own new community. Andres had ordered that the two-hundred-strong crew should be dispersed to live in close-knit "tribes" of twenty or so, each lodged in a "village" of corridors and cabins. There were to be looser links between the tribes, used for such purposes as finding partners. Thus the Ship was united in a single "clan." Andres said this social structure was the most common form encountered among humans "in the wild," as she put it, all the way back to pretechnological days on Earth. Whether or not that was true, things had stayed stable so far.

Andres had also specified the kind of government each tribe should aspire to. In such a small world each individual should be cherished for her unique skills, and for the value of the education invested in her. People were interdependent, said Andres, and the way they governed themselves should reflect that. Even democracy wouldn't do, as in a society of valued individuals the subjection of a minority to the will of a majority must be a bad thing. So Diluc's tribe ran by consensus.

"We talk and talk," Diluc said with a rueful grin, "until we all agree. Takes hours, sometimes. Once, the whole of the night watch—"

Tila snorted. "Don't tell me you don't like it that way. You always did like the sound of your own voice!"

The most important and difficult decisions the tribe had to make concerned reproduction. Most adults settled down into more-or-less monogamous marriages. But there had to be a separation between marriages for companionship and liaisons for reproduction; the gene pool was too small to allow matings for such trivial reasons as love.

Diluc showed Rusel a draft of a "social contract" he was preparing to capture all this. "First, on reaching adulthood you submit yourself to the needs of the group as a whole. For instance, your choice of career depends on what we need as much as what you want to do. Second, you agree to have kids only as the need allows. If we're short of the optimum, you might have three or four or five, whether you want them or not, to bring up the numbers; if we're over, you might have none at all and die childless. Third, you agree to postpone parenthood as long as possible, and to keep working as long as possible. That way you maximize the investment the tribe has made in educating you. Fourth, you can select your own breeding-spouse, who *may* be the same as your companionship-spouse—"

"We were lucky," Tila said fervently.

"But she can't be closer than a second cousin. And you have to submit to having your choice approved by the Elders. That's you," he grinned at Rusel. "Your match will be screened for genetic desirability, to maximize the freshness of the gene pool—all of that. And finally, if despite everything you're unlucky enough to have been born with some inheritable defect that might, if propagated, damage the Ship's chances of completing its mission, you agree not to breed at all. Your genetic line stops with you."

Rusel frowned. "That's eugenics."

Diluc shrugged. "What else can we do?"

Diluc hadn't studied Earth history, and without that perspective, Rusel realized, that word carried none of the horrific connotations it had once borne. As Diluc had implied, they had little choice anyhow given the situation they were in. And anyhow, eugenics was lower-tech than genetic engineering: more future-proofing.

Rusel studied the draft. "And what happens if I break the rules?"

Diluc was uncomfortable; suddenly Rusel was aware that he was an Elder, as well as this man's brother. "We'll cross that bridge when we come to it," Diluc said. "Look, Rus, we don't have police here, and we haven't room for jails. Besides, everybody really is essential to the community as a whole. We can't coerce. We work by persuasion; we hope that such situations will be easily resolved."

Diluc talked of personal things too: of the progress of his boys at school, how Tomi had always hated the hour's wall-cleaning he had to put in each day, while little Rus loved it for the friends he was making.

"They are good kids," Rusel said.

"Yes. And you need to see more of them," Diluc said pointedly. "But, you know, Rus, they're not like us. They are the first Shipborn generation. They are *different*. To them, all our stories of Port Sol and Canis Major are so many legends of places they will never see. This Ship is *their* world, not ours: we, born elsewhere, are aliens here. You know, I keep thinking we've bitten off more than we can chew, for all Andres's planning. Already things are drifting. No wonder generation starships always fail!"

Rusel tried to respond to their openness by giving them something of himself. But he found he had little to say. His mind was full of studying, but there was very little *human* incident in his life. It was if he hadn't been alive at all, he thought with dismay.

Diluc was appalled to hear of Ruul's death. "That pompous geneticist—I suppose in a way it's fitting he should be the first to go. But don't let it take you, brother." Impulsively he crossed to Rusel and rested his hand on his brother's shoulder. "You know, all this is enough for me: Tila, the kids, the home we're building together. It's good to know that our lives serve a higher goal, but *this* is all I need to make me happy. Maybe I don't have much imagination, you think?"

Or maybe you're more human than I am, Rusel thought. "We must all make our choices," he said.

Diluc said carefully, "But you can still make a different choice."

"What do you mean?"

He leaned forward. "Why don't you give it up, Rus? This crappy old Qax nanomedicine, this dreadful anti-ageing—you're still young; you could come out of there, flush the shit out of your system, grow your hair back, find some nice woman to make you happy again . . ."

Rusel tried to keep his face expressionless, but he failed.

Diluc backed off. "Sorry. You still remember Lora."

"I always will. I can't help it."

"We've all been through an extraordinary experience," Tila said. "I suppose we all react differently."

"Yes." Tila, he remembered, had left behind a child.

Diluc looked into his eyes. "You never will come out of that Cloister, will you? Because you'll never be able to cast off that big sack of guilt on your back."

Rusel smiled. "Is it that obvious?"

Tila was a gracious hostess. She perceived his discomfort, and they began to talk of old times, of the days on Port Sol. But Rusel was relieved when Tomi, unreasonably tall, came in to announce that the meal was ready, relieved to hurry through the food and get away, relieved to shut himself away once more in the bloodless monastic calm of the Cloister.

He would remember that difficult visit again, much later, when a boy came to find him.

As time passed, the Elders withdrew from the crew. They requisitioned their own sealed-off living area. It was close to the Ship's axis where the artificial gravity was a little lower than farther out, a sop to muscles and bones expected to weaken with the centuries. Ruul humorously called this refuge the "Cloister." And the Elders were spared the routine chores, even the cleaning, to which the rest of the crew were subject. Soon it was hard to avoid the feeling that the crew were only there to serve the Elders.

Of course it was all part of Andres' grand social design that there should eventually be an "awe gap," as she put it, between Elders and transients. But Rusel wondered if a certain distancing was inevitable anyhow. The differential ageing of transients and Elders became apparent surprisingly quickly. When an Elder met a transient she saw a face that would soon crumble with age and vanish, while the transient saw a mysteriously unchanging figure who would see events that transpired long after the transient was dead. Rusel watched as friendships dissolved, even love affairs evaporated, under this stress.

However the increasingly isolated Elders, thrown on each other's company, were no chummy club. They were all bright, ambitious people; they wouldn't have been filtered out for Andres' inner circle otherwise, and there was always a certain tension and bickering. Doctor Selur remarked sourly that it was like being stuck with a bunch of jealous academics, *forever*.

But the Elders were also cautious of each other, Rusel thought. Always at the back of his mind was the thought that he would have to live with these people for a *long* time. So he strove not to make any enemies—and conversely not to get too close to anyone. Eternity with a lover was one thing, but with an *ex*-lover it would be hellish. Better that things were insipid, but tolerable.

Life settled down. In the calm of the Cloister, time passed smoothly, painlessly.

One day a boy came knocking timorously on the Cloister's door, asking for Rusel. He was aged about sixteen.

Rusel thought he recognised him. He had spent a long time on his own, and his social skills were rusty, but he tried to focus and greet the boy warmly. "Tomi! It's so long since I saw you."

The boy's eyes were round. "My name is Poro, sir."

Rusel frowned. "But that day I came to visit—you made us all a meal, me and Diluc and Tila, while little Rus played . . ." But that was long ago, he told himself, he wasn't sure *how* long, and he fell silent.

The boy seemed to have been prepared for this. "My name is Poro," he said firmly. "Tomi was—"

"Your father."

"My *grand*father."

So this was Diluc's great-grandson. *Lethe, how long have I spent inside this box?*

The boy was looking around the Cloister. His eyes were unblinking, his mouth pulled back in a kind of nervous grin. None of the Elders was hot on empathy, especially with transients, but suddenly Rusel felt as if he saw this place through this child's eyes.

The Cloister was like a library, perhaps. Or a hospital room. The Elders sat in their chairs or walked slowly through the silence of the room, their every step calculated to reduce the risk of harm to their fragile, precious bodies. It had been this way since long before Poro had been born, these musty creatures pursuing their cold interests. *And I, who once loved Lora when she wasn't much older than this child, am part of this dusty stillness.*

"What do you want, Poro?"

"Diluc is ill. He is asking for you."

"Diluc? . . ."

"Your brother."

It turned out that Diluc was more than ill; he was dying.

So Rusel went with the boy, stepping outside the confines of the Cloister for the first time in years.

He wasn't at home out here any more. The transients among the original crew had died off steadily, following a demographic curve not terribly different to that they would have endured had they been able to remain on Port Sol. Rusel grew used to seeing faces he had known since childhood crumple with age and disappear before him. Still, it had been a shock when that first generation reached old age—and, since many of them had been around the same age at launch, the deaths came in a flood.

Meanwhile, everything about the new sort was *different*, the way they rebuilt the Ship's internal architecture, their manner with each other, the way they wore their hair—even their language, which was full of a guttural slang.

The basic infrastructure of the Ship itself, of course, remained unchanged. In a way he came to identify with that level of reality much more than with the flickering, fast-paced changes wrought by the transients. Though his senses were slowly dulling—the Qax treatment had slowed his ageing but not stopped it entirely—he felt he was becoming more attuned to the Ship's subtle vibrations and noises, its mechanical moods and joys. Transients came and went, and the other Elders were awkward old cusses, but the Ship itself was his constant friend, demanding only his care.

But the transients knew him, of course. They stared at him with curiosity, or irreverence—or, worst of all, awe.

As they walked he saw that the boy had a bruise on his forehead. "What happened to you?"

"Punishment." Poro averted his eyes, ashamed. One of his teachers had whacked him with a ruler for "impudence," which turned out to mean asking too-deep questions.

There was a paradox in the philosophy of education aboard the Ship. The students had to be bright enough to be able to understand and maintain the Ship's systems. But there was no room for expansion or innovation. There was unusually only one way to do things: you learned it that way, and you did *not* tinker. It had been quickly found that education needed to be restrictive, and that curiosity couldn't be allowed to go unchecked; you learned only what you needed to know, and were taught not to ask any more, not to explore.

It was necessary, Rusel knew. But he didn't like the idea of battering students into submission. Perhaps he would have a word with Andres about it, get a new policy formulated.

They reached Diluc's corridor-village and came to a familiar doorway.

Tila was still alive, though she was bent, her hair exploded to white, and her face crushed to a wrinkled mask. "Thank you for coming," she whispered, and she took Rusel's hands in her own. "There are so few of us left, you know, so few not Ship-born. And he did keep asking for you."

Rusel pressed her hand, reserved, awkward. He felt out of practice with people, with emotions; before this broken-hearted woman he felt utterly inadequate.

Before he could see his brother he had to be met by a series of tribe worthies. Burly men and women in drab Ship's-issue clothing, they gathered with solemn expressions. The greetings were lengthy and complicated. The transients were evolving elaborate rituals to be used on every social occasion: meeting, parting, taking meals. Rusel could see the value of such rituals, which used up time, and reduced social friction. But it was hard to keep up with the ever-changing rules. The only constant was that these politeness games always got more elaborate—and it was very easy to get something wrong and give offense.

The worthies looked concerned at the prospective loss of Diluc, as well they might.

Andres's imposition of "rule-by-consensus" had been less than effective. In some of the Ship's dozen or so tribes, there was endless jaw-jaw that paralyzed decision-making. Elsewhere strong individuals had begun to grasp power, more or less overtly. Andres wasn't too concerned as long as the job got done, the basic rules obeyed: whoever was in command had to get the approval of the Elders, and so Andres and her team were still able to exert a moderating influence.

The situation in Diluc's tribe had been more subtle, though. As the brother of an Elder he had a unique charisma, and he had used that power subtly to push his peers to conclusions they might not otherwise have reached. He had been a leader, but of the best sort, Rusel thought, leading from the back, invisibly. Now he was about to be taken away, and his people knew they would miss him.

With the worthies out of the way, the Elder was presented to Diluc's children, grandchildren, great-grandchildren. All of them went through more elaborate transient-to-Elder rituals, even the smallest children, with an unsmiling intensity Rusel found disturbing.

At last, with reluctance, he entered Diluc's apartment.

The rooms were much as he remembered them, though the tapestries on the wall had changed. Diluc lay on a bed, covered by a worn blanket. Rusel was shocked by how his brother had imploded with age. And he could see, even through the blanket, the swelling of the stomach tumor that was killing him.

He had thought Diluc was sleeping. But his brother opened one eye. "Hello, Rusel," he said, his voice a croak. "You bastard."

"I'm sorry—"

"You haven't been here in fifty years."

"Not that long."

"Fifty years! *Fifty years!* It's not as if—" He broke up in coughing. "As if it's that big a Ship . . ."

They talked, as they had talked before. Diluc told rambling anecdotes about his grandchildren and great-grandchildren, all properly genetically selected, all wonderful kids.

Rusel spoke of a cull of the Elders.

Diluc grimaced. "So even immortals die." He reached out his hand. Rusel took it; the bones were frail, the flesh almost vanished. "Look after them," Diluc said.

"Who?"

"Everybody. *You* know. And look after yourself." He looked up at his brother, and Rusel saw pity in his brother's eyes—pity for *him*, from a withered, dying man.

He could bear to stay only a few minutes more.

The cull of Elders had had a variety of causes, according to Doctor Selur, but Andres had sniffed at that. "I've seen it before. Call it a death wish," she had said. "You reach an age where your body knows it's time to die. You accept it. Maybe it's some kind of neural programming, a comfort as we face the inevitable." She cackled; she was ageing too, and was now toothless. "The Qax treatments don't do anything about it. And it carries away more would-be immortals than you'd imagine. Strange, isn't it? That longevity should turn out to be a matter of the mind as much as the body."

Rusel had spent some years in faint trepidation, wondering if and when his own dark-seeking mental programming might kick in. But it never did, and he wondered if he had some unsuspected strength—or, perhaps, a deficiency.

Rusel tried to talk over his feelings about Diluc's death. But Andres was dismissive. "Diluc was a coward who shunned his duty," she said. "Anyhow, better when the first crew have all gone. *They* always saw us as peers, to some extent. So they resisted our ideas, our leadership; it was natural. We're totally alien to the new sort, and that will make them more malleable.

"And the new lot never suffered the trauma of seeing Port Sol trashed before their eyes. The psychological trauma ran deep, Rusel; you aren't the only one. . . . This new batch are healthy, adjusted to the environment of the Ship, because they've known nothing else. When there's only them left, we'll be able to get things shaken down properly around here at last. You'll see."

With relief Rusel returned to his studies, away from the complications of humanity. Once more time flowed smoothly past him, and that difficult day receded down the dimming corridors of his memory.

No more relatives came to see him, ever again.

". . . Rusel. Rusel!" The voice was harsh—Andres' voice.

Sleep was deep these days, and it took him an age to emerge. And as he struggled into the light he swam up through layers of dream and memory, until he became confused about what was real and what wasn't. He always knew *where* he was, of course, even in his deepest sleep. He was on the Ship, his drifting tomb. But he could never remember *when* he was.

He tried to sit up. The Couch responded to his feeble movements, and its back smoothly lifted him upright. He peered around in the dim, golden light of the Cloister. There were three Couches, great bulky mechanical devices half bed and half medical support system: only three, because only three of the Elders stayed alive.

Somebody was moving around him. It was a transient, of course, a young woman. She kept her eyes averted, and her hands fluttered through an elaborate greetings-with-apology ritual. He dismissed her with a curt gesture; you could eat up your entire day with such flim-flam.

Andres was watching him, her eyes sharp in her ruin of a face. She looked like a huge bug in her cocoon of blankets.

"Well?" he snapped.

"You are drooling," she said mildly. "Not in front of the transients, Rusel."

Irritated, he wiped his chin with his sleeve.

"Oh," she said, her tone unchanged, "and Selur died."

That news, so casually delivered, was like a punch in the throat. He turned clumsily, weighed down by blankets and life-sustaining equipment. The doctor's Couch was surrounded by transients who were removing her mummylike body. They worked in silence, cautiously, reverently. They were trembling, he saw dimly.

"I never did like her much," Rusel said.

"You've said that before. Many times."

"I'll miss her, though."

"Yes. And then there were two. Rusel, we need to talk. We need a new strategy to deal with the transients. We're supposed to be figures of awe. Look at us. Look at poor Selur! We can't let them see us like this again."

He glanced cautiously at the transients.

"Don't worry," Andres said. "They can't understand. Linguistic drift."

"We have to deal with them. We're the top of their pyramid of authority—that's what you've always said."

"So we are, and it has to stay that way. But I don't think we should allow transients in here any more. The machines can sustain us. Lethe knows there are enough spare parts, now we have so many empty Couches! What I suggest is—"

"Stow it," he said crossly. "You're always the same, you old witch. You always want to jam a solution down my throat before I even know what the problem is. Let me gather my thoughts."

"Stow it, stow it," she parroted, grotesquely.

"Shut up." He closed his eyes to exclude her, and lay back in his couch.

Through the implant in the back of his skull he allowed data from his body, the Ship, and the universe beyond filter into his sensorium.

His body first, of course, the slowly failing biomachinery that had become his prison. The good news was that, more than two centuries after his brother's death, his slow ageing had bottomed out. Since he had last checked—Lethe, all of a month ago, it seemed like yesterday, how long had he slept this time?—nothing had got significantly worse. But he was stuck in the body of a ninety-year-old man, and a frail old man at that. He slept almost all the time, his intervals of lucidity ever more widely separated, while the Couch fed him, removed his waste, gently turned him to and fro and manipulated his stick-thin limbs. Oh, and every few weeks he received a blood transfusion, an offering to the Elders from the grateful transients outside the Cloister. He may as well have been a coma victim, he thought grumpily.

His age was meaningless, his condition boring. Briskly he moved on.

His Virtual viewpoint roamed through the Ship. Despite the passage of centuries, the physical layout of the corridor-village that had been Diluc's was the same, save for detail, the same knots of corridors around the "village square." But the people had changed, as they always did, youth blossoming, old age crumbling.

The Autarch he remembered from his last inspection was still in place. He was a big bruiser who called himself Ruul, in subtle defiance of various inhibitions against taking the name of an Elder, even one long dead. He at least didn't look to have aged much. Flanked by two of his wives, Ruul received a queue of supplicants, all seeking the Autarch's "wisdom" concerning some petty problem or other. Ruul was brisk and efficient, and as Rusel listened—though the time-drifted language was hard to decipher—he couldn't spot any immediate errors of doctrine in the Autarch's summary harshness.

He allowed his point of view to drift on.

He watched the villagers go about their business. Four of them were scrubbing the walls clean of dirt, as they took turns to do every day. Two plump-looking worthies were discussing a matter of etiquette, their mannerisms complex and time-consuming. There were some new bits of artwork on the walls, many of them fool-the-eye depth-perspective paintings, designed to make the Ship's corridors look bigger than they were. One woman was tending a "garden" of bits of waste polymer, combing elaborate formations into it with a small metal rake. These transients, Shipborn for generations, had never heard of Zen gardens; they had rediscovered this small-world art form for themselves.

A little group of children was being taught to disassemble and maintain an air-duct fan; they chanted the names of its parts, learning by rote. They would be taught nothing more, Rusel knew. There was no element of *principle* here: nothing about how the fan as a machine worked, or how it fitted into the greater systems of the Ship itself. You only learned what you needed to know.

Everybody was busy, intent on their affairs. Some even seemed happy. But it all looked drab to Rusel, all the villagers dressed in colorless Ship's-issue clothing, their lives bounded by the polished-smooth bulkheads of the Ship. Even their language was dull, and becoming duller. The transients had no words for *horizon* or *sky*—but as if in compensation they had over forty words describing degrees of love.

As he surveyed the village, statistics rolled past his vision in a shining column. Everything was nominal, if you took a wider perspective. Maintenance routines were being kept up satisfactorily. Reproduction rules, enforced by the Autarch and his peers in the other villages, were largely being adhered to, and there was a reasonable genetic mix.

The situation was stable. But in Diluc's village, only the Autarch was free.

Andres's uncharacteristically naïve dream of respectful communities governing themselves by consensus had barely outlasted the death of Diluc. In the villages strong characters had quickly taken control, and in most cases had installed themselves and their families as hereditary rulers. Andres had grumbled at that, but it was an obviously stable social system, and in the end the Elders, in subtle ways, lent the Autarchs their own mystical authority.

The Autarchs were slowly drifting away from their subject populations, though.

Some "transients" had always proven to be rather longer lived than others. It seemed that the Qax's tampering with the genomes of their Pharaohs had indeed been passed on to subsequent generations, if imperfectly, and that gene complex, a tendency for longevity, was expressing itself. Indeed the Autarchs actively sought out breeding partners for themselves who came from families that showed such tendencies.

So, with time, the Autarchs and their offspring were ageing more slowly than their transient subjects.

It was just natural selection, argued Andres. People had always acquired power so that their genes could be favored. Traditionally you would do your best to outbreed your subjects. But if you were an Autarch, in the confines of the Ship, what were you to do? There was obviously no room here for a swarm of princes, bastards or otherwise. Besides, the Elders' genetic-health rules wouldn't allow any such thing. So the Autarchs were seeking to dominate their populations with their own long lives, not numbers of offspring.

Andres seemed to find all this merely intellectually interesting. Rusel wondered what would happen if this went on.

He allowed his consciousness to drift back to his own body. When he surfaced, he found Andres watching him, as she so often did.

"So you think we have to change things," he said.

"We need to deal with the Autarchs. Some of them are tough customers, Rusel, and they imagine they're even tougher. If they start to believe we're weak—for instance, if we sleep for three days before delivering the answer to the simplest question—"

"I understand. We can't let the transients see us." He sighed, irritated. "But what else can we do? Delivering edicts through disembodied voices isn't going to wash. If they don't see us they will soon forget who we are." *Soon*, in the language of the Elders, meaning in another generation or two.

"Right," she snapped. "So we have to personalise our authority. What do you think of this?" She gestured feebly, and a Virtual coalesced in the air over her head.

It showed Rusel. Here he was as a young man, up to his elbows in nanofood banks, laboring to make the Ship sound for its long journey. Here he was as a youngish Elder, bald as ice, administering advice to grateful transients. There were even images of him from the vanishingly remote days before the launch, images of him with a smiling Lora.

"Where did you get this stuff?"

She sniffed. "The Ship's log. Your own archive. Come on, Rusel, we hardly have any secrets from each other after all this time! Pretty girl, though."

"Yes. What are you intending to do with this?"

"We'll show it to the transients. We'll show you at your best, Rusel, you at the peak of your powers, you walking the same corridors they walk now—you as a human being, yet *more* than human. That's what we want: engagement with their petty lives, empathy, yet awe. We'll put a face to your voice."

He closed his eyes. It made sense of course; Andres's logic was grim, but always valid. "But why me? It would be better if both of us—"

"That wouldn't be wise," she said. "I wouldn't want them to see me die."

It took him a while to work out that Andres, the first of the Pharaohs, was failing. Rusel found this impossible to take in: her death would be to have a buttress of the universe knocked away. "But you won't see the destination," he said peevishly, as if she were making a bad choice.

"No," she said hoarsely. "But the *Mayflower* will get there! Look around, Rusel. The Ship is functioning flawlessly. Our designed society is stable and doing its job of preserving the bloodlines. And *you*, you were always the brightest of all. You will see it through. That's enough for me."

It was true, Rusel supposed. Her design was fulfilled; the Ship and its crew were working now just as Andres had always dreamed they should. But only two hundred and fifty years had worn away, only *half of one percent* of the awesome desert of time he must cross to reach Canis Major—and now, it seemed, he was going to have to make the rest of that journey alone.

"No, not alone," said Andres. "You'll always have the Ship . . ."

Yes, the Ship, his constant companion. Suddenly he longed to escape from the endless complications of humanity and immerse himself in its huge technological calm. He lay back in his Couch and allowed his mind to roam out through the crowded torus of the hull, and the pulsing ramjet engines, and the wispy gravitational wings behind which the Ship sailed.

He looked back. The Ship had covered only a fraction of its epic journey, but already it was climbing out of the galactic plane, and the Core, the crowded heart of the Galaxy, rose like a sun from the dust-strewn lanes of the spiral arms. It was a stunning, comforting sight.

By the time he came back from his intergalactic dreaming, Andres was gone, her Couch disassembled for spare parts, her body removed to the cycling tanks.

Rusel was awakened from his long slumber by the face of a boy, a face twisted with anger—an anger directed at *him.*

In retrospect Rusel should have seen the rebellion coming. All the indicators had been there: the drift of the transients' social structures, the gathering tensions. It was bound to happen.

But it was so hard for him to pay attention to the brief lives of these transients, their incomprehensible language and customs, their petty concerns and squabbling. After all, Hilin was a boy of the forty-fifth generation since launch: *forty-five generations,* Lethe, nearly a thousand years . . .

The exploits of Hilin, though, forced themselves on his attention.

Hilin was sixteen years old when it all began. He had been born in Diluc's corridor-village.

By now the Autarchs of the different villages had intermarried to form a seamless web of power. They lived on average twice as long as their subjects, and had established a monopoly on the Ship's water supply. A water empire ruled by gerontocrats: their control was total.

Hilin was not one of the local Autarch's brood; his family were poor and powerless, like all the Autarch's subjects. But they seemed to accept their lot. As he played in corridors whose polymer floors were rutted by generations of passing feet, Hilin emerged as a bright, happy child. He seemed compliant when he was young, cheerfully joining in swabbing the bulkheads when it was his turn, and accepting the cuffs of his teachers when he asked impudent questions.

He had always been oddly fascinated by the figure of Rusel himself—or rather the semimythical presence portrayed to the villagers through the cycling Virtual storyboards. Hilin soaked up the story of the noble Elder who had been forced to choose between a life of unending duty and his beloved Lora, an undying model to those he ruled.

As he had grown, Hilin had flourished educationally. At fourteen he was inducted into an elite caste. As intellectual standards declined, literacy had been abandoned, and these monkish thinkers now committed to memory every significant commandment regarding the workings of the Ship and their own society. You would start on this vital project at fourteen, and wouldn't expect to be done until you were in your fifties, by which time a new generation was ready to take over anyhow.

Rusel dryly called these patient thinkers Druids: he wasn't interested in the transients' own names for themselves, which would change in an eye-blink generation anyhow. He had approved this practice when it emerged. All this endless memorizing was a marvelous way to use up pointless lives—and it established a power base to rival the Autarchs.

Again Hilin had flourished, and he passed one Druidic assessment after another. Even a torrid romance with Sale, a girl from a neighboring village, didn't distract him from his studies.

When the time came, the couple asked their families for leave to form a companionship-marriage, which was granted. They went to the Autarch for permission to have children. To their delight, it turned out their genetic makeups, as mapped in the Druids' capacious memories, were compatible enough to allow this too.

But even so the Druids forbade the union.

Hilin, horrified, learned that this was because of the results of his latest Druidic assessment, a test of his general intelligence and potential. He had failed, not by posting too low a score, but too *high*.

Rusel, brooding, understood. The eugenic elimination of weaknesses had in general been applied wisely. But under the Autarch-Druid duopoly, attempts were made to weed out the overbright, the curious—anybody who might prove rebellious. Rusel would have stamped out this practice, had he even noticed it. If this went on, the transient population would become passive, listless, easily manipulated by the Autarchs and the Druids, but useless for the mission's larger purposes.

It was too late for Hilin. He was banned from ever seeing his Sale again. And he was told by the Autarch's ministers that this was by order of the Elder himself, though Rusel, dreaming his life away, knew nothing about it.

Hilin spent long hours in the shrinelike enclosure where Rusel's Virtuals played out endlessly. He tried to understand. He told himself the Elder's wisdom surpassed his own; this severance must be for the best, no matter what pain it caused him. He even tried to draw comfort from what he saw as parallels between his own doomed romance and Rusel and his lost Lora. But understanding didn't come, and his bewilderment and pain soon blossomed to resentment—and anger.

In his despair, he tried to destroy the shrine.

As punishment, the Autarch locked him in a cell for two days. Hilin emerged from his confinement outwardly subdued, inwardly ready to explode. Again Rusel would later castigate himself for failing to see the dangers in the situation.

But it was so hard to see anything now.

His central nervous system was slowly deteriorating, so the Couch informed him. He could still move his arms and legs—he could still walk, even, with a frame—but he felt no sensation in his feet, nothing but the faintest ache in his fingertips. As pain and pleasure alike receded, he felt he was coming loose from time itself. When he surfaced into the world of lucidity he would be shocked to find a year had passed like a day, as if his sense of time were becoming logarithmic.

And meanwhile, as he became progressively disconnected from the physical world, his mind was undergoing a reconstruction of its own. After a thousand years his memories, especially the deepest, most precious memories of all, were, like the floors of the Ship's corridors, worn with use; he was no longer sure if he *remembered*, or if he only had left memories of memories.

If he came adrift from both present and past, what was he? Was he even human any more? Certainly the latest set of transients meant less than nothing to him: why, each of them was made up of the atoms and molecules of her ancestors, cycled through the Ship's systems forty times or more, shuffled and reshuffled in meaningless combinations. They could not touch his heart in any way.

At least he thought so, until Hilin brought him the girl.

The two of them stood before Rusel's Virtual shrine, where they believed the Elder's consciousness must reside. Trying to match the Elder's own timescales, they stayed there for long hours, all but motionless. Hilin's face was set, pinched with anger and determination. She, though, was composed.

At last Rusel's drifting attention was snagged by familiarity. It was the girl. She was taller than most of the transients, pale, her bones delicate. And her eyes were large, dark, somehow unfocused even as she gazed into unseen imaging systems.

Lora.

It couldn't be, of course! How could it? Lora had had no family on the Ship. And yet Rusel, half-dreaming, immersed in memory, couldn't take his eyes off her image.

As Hilin had planned.

The uprising occurred all over the Ship. In every village the Autarchs and their families were turned out of their palatial cabins. The Autarchs, having commanded their short-lived flocks for centuries, were quite unprepared, and few resisted; they had no conception such an uprising was even possible. The old rulers and their peculiar children were herded together in a richly robed mass in the Ship's largest chamber, the upturned amphitheater where Rusel had long ago endured the launch from Port Sol.

The revolt had been centrally planned, carefully timed, meticulously executed. Despite generations of selective breeding to eliminate initiative and cunning, the transients no longer seemed so sheepish, and in Hilin they had discovered a general. And it was over before the Elder's attention had turned away from the girl, before he had even noticed.

Hilin, king of the corridors, stood before the Elder's shrine. And he pulled at the face of the girl, the Lora lookalike. It had been a mask, just a mask; Rusel realized shamefully that this boy had manipulated the emotions of a being more than a thousand years old.

A bloody club in his hand, Hilin screamed his defiance at his undying god. The Cloister's systems translated the boy's language, after a thousand years quite unlike Rusel's. "You allowed this to happen." Hilin yelled. "You allowed the Autarchs to feed off us like [*untranslatable—body parasites?*]. We wash the decks for them with our blood, while they keep water from our children. And you, you [*untranslatable—an obscenity?*] allowed it to happen. And do you know why?" Hilin stepped closer to the shrine, and his face loomed in Rusel's vision. "Because you don't exist. Nobody has seen you in centuries—if they ever did! You're a lie, cooked up by the Autarchs to keep us in our place, that's what I think. Well, we don't believe in you any more, not in any of that [*untranslatable—feces?*]. And we've thrown out the Autarchs. We are free!"

"Free" they were. Hilin and his followers looted the Autarchs' apartments, and gorged themselves on the food and water the Autarchs had hoarded for themselves, and screwed each other senseless in blithe defiance of the genetic-health prohibitions. And not a single deck panel was swabbed down.

After three days, as the chaos showed no signs of abating, Rusel knew that this was the most serious crisis in the Ship's long history. He had to act. It took him another three days to get ready for his performance, three days mostly taken up with fighting with the inhibiting protocols of his medical equipment.

Then he ordered the Cloister door to open, for the first time in centuries. It actually stuck, dry-welded in place. It finally gave way with a resounding crack, making his entrance even more spectacular than he had planned.

But there was nobody around to witness his incarnation but a small boy, no more than five years old. With his finger planted firmly in one nostril, and his eyes round with surprise, the kid looked heartbreakingly like Tomi, Diluc's boy, long since dead and fed to the recycling banks.

Rusel was standing, supported by servomechanisms, gamely clutching at a walking frame. He tried to smile at the boy, but he couldn't feel his own face, and didn't know if he succeeded. "Bring me the chief Druids," he said, and a translation whispered in the air around him.

The boy yelled and fled.

The Druids actually knelt before him, covering their faces. He walked very cautiously among them, allowing them even to touch his robe. He wanted to be certain they accepted his reality, to smell the dusty tang of centuries on him. Maybe these monkish philosophers had in their hearts, like Hilin, never really believed in the Elder's existence. Well, now their messiah had suddenly reincarnated among them.

But he saw them as if through a flawed lens; he could hear little, feel less, smell or taste nothing. It was like walking around in a skinsuit, he thought.

He was an angry god, though. The rules of Shipboard life had been broken, he thundered. And he didn't just mean the recent mess. There must be no more water empires, and no knowledge empires either: the Druids would have to make sure that *every* child knew the basic rules, of Ship maintenance and genetic-health breeding.

He ordered that the Autarchs should not be returned to their seats of power. Instead, the governing would be done, for this generation, by a Druid—he picked out one terrified-looking woman at random. As long as she ruled wisely and well, she would have the Elder's backing. On her death the people would select a successor, who could not be more closely related to her predecessor than second cousin.

The old Autarchs and their brood, meanwhile, were to be spared. They would be shut away permanently in their amphitheater prison, where there were supplies to keep them alive. Rusel believed they and their strange slow-growing children would die off; within a generation, a tick of time, that problem would go away. He had done his share of killing, he thought.

Then he sighed. The worst of it had still to be faced. "Bring me Hilin," he ordered.

They dragged in the corridor king tied up with strips of cloth. He had been assaulted, Rusel saw; his face was battered and one arm seemed broken. The erstwhile leader was already being punished for his blasphemy by those who sought the favor of the Elder. But Hilin faced Rusel defiantly, strength and intelligence showing in his face.

Rusel's scarred heart ached a little more, for strength and intelligence were the last features you wanted in a transient.

Hilin had to die, of course. His flayed corpse would be displayed before the shrine of the Elder, as a warning to future generations. But Rusel didn't have the courage to watch it done. He remembered the man in the electric-blue skinsuit: he always had been a coward, he thought.

As he returned to his Cloister, he looked back once more. "And clean up this damn mess," he said.

He knew it would take a long time, even on his timescales, before he managed to forget the contemptuous defiance on Hilin's young face. But Hilin had gone into the dark like all his transient ancestors, and soon his siblings and nieces and nephews and everybody who looked remotely like him went too, gone, all gone into the sink of time, and soon only Rusel was left alive to remember the rebellion.

Rusel would never leave the Cloister again.

Some time after that, there was a decimating plague.

It was brought about by a combination of factors: a slow unmonitored buildup of irritants and allergens in the Ship's environment, and then the sudden emergence of a latent virus in a population already weakened. It was a multiple accident, impossible for the Pharaoh designers of the Ship to plan away, for all their ingenuity. But given enough time—more than five thousand years—such events were inevitable.

The surviving population crashed to close to a threshold of viability. For a few decades Rusel was forced to intervene, through booming commands, to ensure that the Ship was maintained at a base level, and that genetic-health protocols were observed and breeding matches planned even more carefully than usually.

The low numbers brought benefits, though. The Ship's systems were now producing a large surplus of supplies, and there was no possibility of any more water empires. Rusel considered, in his glacial way, establishing a final population at a lower level than before.

It intrigued him that the occurrence of the plague mirrored the restructuring of his own mental processes. The day-to-day affairs of the Ship, and the clattering of the transient generations, barely distracted him now. Instead he became aware of slower pulses, deeper rhythms beyond any transients' horizon of awareness. It fascinated him to follow the million-year turning of the Galaxy, whose brilliant face continued to open up behind the fleeing Ship.

And his perception of risk changed. His endless analysis of the Ship's systems uncovered obscure failure modes: certain parameter combinations that could disrupt the governing software, interacting failures among the nanomachines that still labored over the Ship's fabric inside and out. Such failures were highly unlikely; he estimated the Ship might suffer significant damage once every ten thousand years or so. On Earth, whole civilizations had risen and fallen with greater alacrity than that. But *he* had to plan for such things, to prepare the Ship's defenses and recovery strategies. The plague, after all, was just such a low-risk event, but given enough time it had come about.

The transients' behavior, meanwhile, adjusted on its own timescales.

Once every decade or so the inhabitants of Diluc's corridor-village would approach the shrine of the Elder, where the flickering Virtual still showed. One of them would dress up in a long robe and walk behind a frame with exaggerated slowness, while the rest cowered. And then they would fall on a manikin and tear it to pieces. Rusel had watched such displays several times before he had realized what was going on: it was, of course, a ritualized re-enactment of his own last manifestation. Sometimes the bit of theater would culminate in the flaying of a living human, which they must imagine he demanded; when such savage generations arose, Rusel would avert his cold gaze.

Meanwhile, in the village in which Hilin's doomed lover Sale had been born, the local transients were trying another tactic to win his favor. Perhaps it was another outcome of Hilin's clever exploits, or perhaps it had been inherent in the situation all along.

Girls, tall slim girls with dark elusive eyes: as the generations ticked by, he seemed to see more of them running in the corridors, making eyes at muscular wall-scrubbing boys, dandling children on their knees. They were like cartoon versions of Lora: tall Loras and short, thin Loras and fat, happy Loras and sad.

It was selective breeding, if presumably unconscious, people turning themselves into replicas of the images in the Virtual. They were appealing directly to his own cold heart: if the Elder loved this woman so much, then choose a wife that looks like her, if only a little, and hope to have daughters with her elfin looks, and so win favor.

Rusel was simultaneously touched and appalled. They could do what they liked, he told himself, as long as they got their jobs done.

Meanwhile, on the other side of the barricade he had erected, the Autarchs and their long-lived families had not died out as Rusel had hoped. They had lived on. And as they inbred ferociously, their lives were stretched out longer and longer.

Again this made sense in terms of their heredity, he thought. In their cordoned-off compartment there was simply no room to expand their population. So the genes' best bet of propagating themselves into the future, always their only objective, was to stretch out the lives of their carriers. Adults lived for centuries, and for the vanishingly few children born, childhood lasted decades. Rusel found these creatures, with their blank eyes and wizened-faced children, peculiarly creepy. On the other hand, he still couldn't bring himself to kill them off. Perhaps in them he saw a distorted reflection of himself.

There was one constant throughout the Ship. On both sides of the barrier the transients were clearly getting dumber.

As generations passed—and, for fear of repeating Hilin's fate, potential mates were repelled by any signs of higher-than-average intelligence—it was obvious that the transients were breeding themselves into stupidity. If anything the Autarchs' environment was less stimulating than that of their cousins in the rest of the Ship, and despite their slower generational cycle they were shedding their unnecessary intelligence with even more alacrity, perhaps from sheer boredom.

The transients kept the Ship working, however, and in their increasingly brutish liaisons followed the genetic-health mandates scrupulously. This puzzled Rusel: surely by now they could have no real understanding of *why* they were doing these peculiar things.

But he observed that when it came time to attract a mate the most vigorous deck-swabbers and cousin-deniers stood out from the crowd. It made sense: after all, a propensity to please the undeniable reality of the Elder was a survival characteristic, and therefore worth displaying if you had it, and worth preserving in your children's heredity.

He filed away such observations and insights. By now, nothing that happened inside the Ship's hull interested him as much as what happened outside.

He was thoroughly wired into the Ship, its electromagnetic and other equipment taking the place of his own failed biological senses. He cruised with it through the intergalactic gulf, feeling the tingle of dark matter particles as they were swept into the Ship's gut, sensing the subtle caress of magnetic fields. The space between the galaxies was much more interesting than he had ever imagined. It wasn't a void at all. There was structure here, he saw, a complex webbing of the dark stuff that spanned the universe, a webbing in which galaxies were trapped like glowing flies. He learned to follow the currents and reefs of the dark matter which the Ship's gravitational maw greedily devoured.

He was alone with the galaxies, then, and with his own mind.

Once, just once, as he drifted in the dark, he heard a strange signal. It was cold and clear, like the peal of a trumpet, far off in the echoing intergalactic night. It wasn't human at all.

He listened for a thousand years. He never heard it again.

Andres came to him.

"Leave me alone, you nagging old witch," he grumbled.

"Believe me, that would be my choice," said Andres fervently. "But there's a problem, Rusel. And you need to come out of your damn shell and sort it out."

He could see her face clearly, that worn-smooth expressionless skin. The rest of her body was a blur, a suggestion. None of that mattered, of course.

"What kind of problem?"

"With the transients. What else? They are all that matters. You need to take a look."

"I don't want to. It hurts."

"I know it hurts. But it's your duty."

Duty? Had she said that, or had he? Was he awake, or dreaming? With time, everything blurred, every category, every boundary.

He was far beyond biology now, of course. The decay of his central nervous system had proceeded so far that he wasn't sure if it returned any signals at all to the hardening nugget of his brain. It was only technology that kept him alive. With time, the Ship had infiltrated its treatments and systems deeper into the shell of what had been his body. It was as if he had become just another of the Ship's systems, like the air-cycling system or the water purifiers, just as old and balky, and just as much in need of endless tender loving care.

Even the walls of his consciousness were wearing away. He thought of his mind as a dark hall filled with drifting forms, like zero-gravity sculptures. These were his memories—or perhaps memories of memories, recycled, reiterated, edited, and processed.

And *he* was here, a pinpoint awareness that flitted and flew between the drifting reefs of memory. At times, as he sailed through the abstraction of emptiness, free of memory or anticipation, indeed free of any conscious thought save only a primal sense of *self*, he felt oddly free—light, unburdened, even young again. But whenever that innocent point settled into the dark tangle of a memory reef, the guilt came back, a deep muddy shame whose origins he had half forgotten, and whose resolution he could no longer imagine.

He wasn't alone, however, in this cavernous awareness. Sometimes voices called from the dark. Sometimes there were even faces, their features softened, their ages indeterminate. Here was Diluc, his brother, or Andres, or Ruul, or Selur, or one of the others. He knew they were all long dead save for him, who lived on and on. He had vague memories of setting up some of these Virtual personas as therapy for himself, or as ways for the Ship to attract his attention—Lethe, even as company. But by now he wasn't sure what was Virtual and what was a dream, a schizoid fantasy of his rickety mind.

Lora was never there, however.

And Andres, the cold Pharaoh who had become his longest-enduring companion, was his most persistent visitant.

She said, "Nobody ever said this would be easy, Rusel."

"You said that before."

"Yes. And I'll keep on saying it until we get to Canis Major."

"Canis Major? . . ." The destination. He'd forgotten about it again, forgotten that an end to all this even as a theoretical possibility might exist. The trouble was, thinking about such things as a beginning and an end made him aware of time, and that was always a mistake.

How long? The answer came to him like a whisper. *Round numbers? Twenty thousand years gone. Some five thousand left.* Twenty thousand years. It was ridiculous, of course.

"Rusel," Andres snapped. "You need to focus."

"You're not even Andres," he grumbled.

Her mouth was round with mock horror. "Oh, no! What an existential disaster. Just do it, Rus."

So, reluctantly, he gathered his scattered concentration, and sent his viewpoint out into the body of the Ship. He was faintly aware of Andres riding alongside him, a ghost at his shoulder.

He found the place he still thought of as Diluc's village. The framework of corridors and cabins hadn't changed, of course; it was impossible that it should. But even the nonpermanent partitions that had once been built up and torn down by each successive generation of transients had been left unmoved since the last time he was here. Building things wasn't what people did anymore.

He wandered into the little suite of rooms that had once been Diluc's home. There was no furniture. Nests were crammed into each corner of the room, disorderly heaps of cloth and polymer scraps. He had seen the transients take standard-issue clothing from the Ship's recycler systems and immediately start tearing it up with hands or teeth to make their coarse bedding. There was a strong stink of piss and shit, of blood and milk, sweat and sex, the most basic human biology. But the crew remained scrupulously clean. Every few days all this stuff would be swept up and carted off to the recycler bins.

This was the way people lived now.

Outside, the walls and partitions were clean, gleaming and sterile, as was every surface he could see, the floor and ceiling. One partition had been rubbed until it was worn so thin the light shone through it: another couple of generations and it would wear away altogether, he thought. The crew still kept up their basic duties; that had remained, while so much else had vanished.

But these latter transients were not crewing this Ship as his generation had. They were doing it for deeper reasons.

Those selection pressures, as the transients competed in how well they did their chores in order to attract mates, had, given time, sculpted the population. By now, he understood, the transients were maintaining a starship's systems as bees had once danced, stags had locked antlers, and peacocks had spread their useless tails: *they were doing it for sex*, and the chance to procreate. As mind receded, Rusel thought, biology had taken over.

As long as they were doing it in the first place, Rusel didn't care. Besides, it worked. Sexual drivers seemed very effective in locking in behavior with the precision required to keep the Ship's systems functioning: you could fix a ceiling ventilation grill with a show-off flourish or not, but you had to do it *exactly* right to impress the opposite sex, even if you didn't understand what it was for. Even when mind was gone, you had to do it right.

He heard weeping, not far away.

He let his viewpoint follow the weeping, just drifting along the corridor. He turned a corner, and came on the villagers.

There were perhaps twenty-five of them, adults and children. They were all naked, of course; nobody had worn clothes for millennia. Some of them had infants in their arms or on their backs. Squatting in the corridor, they huddled around a central figure, the woman who was doing the weeping. Surrounded by bare backs and folded limbs, she was cradling something, a bloody scrap. The others reached out and stroked her back and scalp; some of them were weeping too, Rusel saw.

Andres said dryly, "Their empathy is obvious."

"Yes. They've lost so much else, but not that—"

Suddenly their heads turned, all of them save the weeping woman, faces swivelling like antennae. Something had disturbed them—perhaps the tiny hovering drone that was Rusel's physical manifestation. Their brows were low, but their faces were still human, with straight noses and delicate chins. It was like a flower bed of faces, Rusel thought, turned up to his light. Their eyes were wide, their mouths pulled back in fear-grins.

And every one of them looked like Lora, more or less, with that delicate, elfin face, even something of her elusive eyes. Of course they did: the blind filter of natural selection, operating for generations on this hapless stock, had long determined that though mind was no longer necessary, to look *this* way might soften the heart of the wizened creature who ruled the world.

The strange tableau of upturned Lora-faces lasted only a moment. Then the transients took flight. They poured away down the corridor, running, knuckle-walking, bounding off the walls and ceiling.

Andres growled, "I'll swear they get more like chimps with every generation."

In a few seconds they had gone, all save the weeping woman.

Rusel allowed his viewpoint to swim toward the woman. He moved cautiously, not wishing to alarm her. She was young—twenty, twenty-one? It was increasingly hard to tell the age of these transients; they seemed to reach puberty later each generation. This girl had clearly passed her menarche—in fact she had given birth, and recently: her belly was slack, her breasts heavy with milk. But her chest was smeared with blood, shocking bright crimson in the drab, worn background of the corridor. And the thing she was cradling was no child.

"Lethe," said Rusel. "*It's a hand*. A child's hand. I think I'm going to throw up."

"You no longer have the equipment. Take a closer look."

A white stump of bone stuck out of a bloody mass of flesh. The hand had been severed at the wrist. And two tiny fingers had been almost stripped of flesh, ligament and muscle, leaving only tiny bones.

"That wrist," Andres said pitilessly, "has been bitten through. By *teeth*, Rusel. And teeth have been at work on those fingers as well. Think about it. With a bit of practice, you could take one of those little morsels between your incisors and just strip off the flesh and muscle—"

"Shut up! Lethe, Andres, I can see for myself. We always avoided cannibalism. I thought we beat that into their shrinking skulls hard enough."

"So we did. But I don't think this is cannibalism—or rather, whatever did this wasn't *her* kind."

Rusel elevated the viewpoint and cast around. He saw a trail of blood leading away from the woman, smeared along the walls and floor, quite unmistakeable, as if something had been dragged away.

Andres said, "I think our transients suddenly have a predator."

"Not so suddenly," Rusel said. A part of his scattered consciousness was checking over the Ship's logs, long ignored. This kind of incident had been going on for a couple of centuries. "It's been rare before, once or twice a generation. Mostly it was the old, or the very young—dispensable, or replaceable. But now they seem to be upping the rate."

"And making a dent in the transients' numbers."

"Yes. You were right to bring me here." This had to be resolved. But to do it, he thought with a deepening dread, he was going to have to confront a horror he had shut out of his awareness for millennia.

"I'm here with you," Andres said gently.

"No, you're not," he snapped. "But I have to deal with this anyhow."

"Yes, you do."

His viewpoint followed the bloody trail as it wound through the corridor-villages of the transients. Broken in places, the trail slinked through shadows or through holes worn in the walls. It was the furtive trail of a hunter, he thought.

At last Rusel came to the bulkhead that cut the Ship in two, marking the limit of his transients' domain. He had long put out of his mind what lay beyond this wall: in fact, if he could have cut away the Ship's aft compartment and let the whole mess float away into space he would long ago have done so.

But there was a hole in the bulkhead, just wide enough to admit a slim body.

The bulkhead was a composite of metal and polymer, extremely tough, and a meter thick; the hole was a neat tunnel, not regular but smooth-walled, drilled right through it. "I can't believe they have tools," he said. "So how did they get through?"

"Teeth," Andres said. "Teeth and nails—and time, of which they have plenty. Remember what you're dealing with. Even if the bulkhead was made of diamond they'd have got through eventually."

"I hoped they were dead."

"Hope! Wishful thinking! That always was your weakness, Rusel. I always said you should have killed them off in the first place. They're just a drain on the Ship's resources."

"I'm no killer."

"Yes, you are—"

"And they are human, no less than the transients."

"No, they're *not*. And now, it seems, they are *eating* our transients."

His viewpoint drifted before the hole in the wall. Andres seemed to sense his dread; she didn't say anything.

He passed through the barrier.

He emerged in the big upended chamber he still thought of as the amphitheater, right at the base of the Ship. This was a big, bare volume, a cylinder set on its side. After the spin-up it had been used to pursue larger-scale reconstruction projects necessary to prepare the Ship for its long intergalactic voyage, and mounted on its floor and walls were the relics of heavy engineering, long abandoned: gantries, platforms of metal, immense low-gravity cranes like vast skeletons. Globe lights hovered everywhere, casting a yellow-white, complex light. It was an oddly magnificent sight, Rusel thought, and its stirred fond memories of brighter, more purposeful days. On the wall of the chamber, which had been its floor, he could even make out the brackets that had held the acceleration couches on launch day.

Now, every exposed surface was corroded. Nothing moved. And that upturned floor, which Andres had turned transparent a mere year after the launch, was caked by what looked like rock. It was a hardened pack of feces and cloth scraps and dirt, a wall of shit to block out the Galaxy.

At first, in this jungle of engineering, he couldn't make out anything living. Then, as he watched and allowed the worn-out ambience of the place to wash over him, he learned to see.

They were like shadows, he thought, slim, upright shadows that flitted through the gantries, furtive, cautious. At times they looked human—clearly upright, bipedal, purposeful—though their limbs were spindly, their bellies distended. But then they would collapse to all fours and lope away with a bent gait, and that impression of humanity vanished. They didn't seem to be wearing clothes, any more than the transients did. But unlike the transients, their bodies were coated with a kind of thick hair, dark brown, a fur.

Here and there hovering drones trailed the shambling creatures, carrying food and water. The creatures ignored these emissaries of the Ship that kept them alive.

Andres said grimly. "I know you haven't wanted to think about these relics, Rusel. But the Ship has watched over them. They are provided with food, of course. Clothing, blankets, and the like—they rip all that up to serve as nesting material, like the transients. They won't go to the supply hoppers as the transients will; drones have to bring them the stuff they need, and take out their waste. But they're really quite passive. They don't mind the drones, even when the drones clean them, or tend to wounds or sicknesses. They are used to being cared for by machines."

"But what do they *do* all day?"

Andres laughed. "Why, nothing. Nothing but eat the food we give them. Climb around the gantries a little, perhaps."

"They must have some spark of curiosity, of awareness. The transients do! They're *people*."

"Their ancestors used to be. Now they're quite mindless. . . . There. Look. They are gathering at one of their feeding places. Perhaps we'll be able to see what they do."

The feeding site was just a shallow depression, worn into a floor of steel. Its base was smeared green and brown. A drone had delivered a cache of food to the center of the pit, a pile of spheres and cylinders and discs, all sized for human hands, all brightly colored.

From around the amphitheater the animals came walking, loping, moving with the slow clumsiness of low gravity—and yet with an exaggerated care, Rusel thought, as if they were very fragile, very old. They gathered around the food pile. But they did not reach for the food; they just slumped down on the ground, as if exhausted.

Now smaller creatures emerged from the forest of gantries. They moved nervously, but just as cautiously as the larger forms. They must be children, Rusel thought, but they moved with no spontaneity or energy. They were like little old people themselves. There were far fewer children than adults, just a handful among perhaps fifty individuals.

It was the children who went to the food pile, broke off pieces of the brightly colored fodder, and carried it to the adults. The adults greeted this service with indifference, or at best a snarl, a light blow on the head or shoulder. Each child servant went doggedly back to the pile for more.

"They're not particularly hygienic," Rusel observed.

"No. But they don't have to be. Compared to the transients they have much tougher immune systems. And the Ship's systems keep the place roughly in order."

Rusel said, "Why don't the adults get the food themselves? It would be quicker."

Andres shrugged. "This is their way. And it is their way to eat another sort of food, too."

At the very center of the depression was a broad scar stained a deep crimson brown, littered with lumpy white shapes.

"That's blood," Rusel said, wondering. "Dried blood. And those white things—"

"Bones," said Andres evenly. Rusel thought she seemed oddly excited, stirred by the degraded spectacle before her. "But there's too much debris here to be accounted for by their occasional raids into transient country."

Rusel shuddered. "So they eat each other too."

"No. Not quite. *The old eat the young*; mothers eat their children. It is their way."

"Oh, Lethe—" Andres was right; Rusel couldn't throw up. But he was briefly aware of his body, cradled by the concerned Ship, thrashing feebly in distress.

Andres said dispassionately, "I don't understand your reaction."

"I didn't know—"

"You should have thought it through—thought through the consequences of your decision to let these creatures live."

"You are a monster, Andres."

She laughed without humor.

Of course he knew what these animals were. They were the Autarchs—or the distant descendants of the long-lived, inbred clan that had once ruled over the transients. Over nearly twenty thousand years selection pressure had worked relentlessly, and the gene complex that had given them their advantage over the transients in the first place—genes for longevity, a propensity injected into the human genome by the Qax—had found full expression. And meanwhile, in the sterile nurture of this place, they had had even less reason to waste precious energy on large brains.

As time had passed they had lived longer and longer, but thought less and less. Now these Autarchs were all but immortal, and all but mindless.

"They're actually rather fascinating," Andres said cheerfully. "I've been trying to understand their ecology, if you will."

"Ecology? Then maybe you can explain how it can benefit a creature to treat its children so. Those young seem to be *farmed*. Life is about the preservation of genes: even in this artificial little world of ours, that remains true. So how does eating your kids help achieve that? . . . Ah." He gazed at the hairy creatures before him. "*But these Autarchs are not mortal.*"

"Exactly. They lost their minds, but they stayed immortal. And when mind had gone, natural selection worked with what it found."

Even for these strange creatures, the interests of the genes were paramount. But now a new strategy had to be worked out. It had been foreshadowed in the lives of the first Autarchs. There was no room to spread the genes by expanding the population—but if individuals could become effectively immortal, the genes could survive through them.

Andres said, "But simple longevity wasn't enough. Even the longest-lived will die through some accident eventually. The genes themselves can be damaged, though radiation exposure for instance. Copying is safer! For their own safety the genes need to see *some* children produced, and for some, the smartest and strongest, to survive.

"But, you see, living space is restricted here. The parents must compete for space against their own children. They don't *care* about the children. They use them as workers—or even, when there's an excess, as a cannibalistic resource. . . . But there are always one or two children who fight their way through to adulthood, enough to keep the stock numbers up. In a way the pressure from the adults is a mechanism to ensure that only the smartest and strongest of the kids survive. From the genes' point of view it's a mixed strategy."

"It's a redundancy mechanism," Rusel said. "That's the way an engineer would put it. The children are just a fail-safe."

"Precisely," Andres said.

It was biology, evolution: the destiny of the *Mayflower* had come down to this.

Rusel had brooded on the fate of his charges. And he had decided it was all a question of timescales.

The conscious purpose of the Ship had sustained its crew's focus for a century or so, until the first couple of generations, and the direct memory of Port Sol, had vanished into the past.

Millennia, though, were the timescale of historical epochs on Earth, over which empires rose and fell. His studies suggested that to sustain a purpose over such periods required the engagement of a deeper level of the human psyche: the idea of Rome, say, or a devotion to Christ. If the first century of the voyage had been an arena for the conscious, over longer periods the unconscious took over. Rusel had seen it himself, as the transients had become devoted to the idea of the Ship and its mission, as embodied by his own Virtual. Even Hilin's rebellion had been an expression of that cult of ideas. Call it mysticism: whatever, it worked for thousands of years.

That far, he believed, Andres and the other Pharaohs had been able to foresee and plan for. But beyond that even they hadn't been able to imagine; Rusel had sailed uncharted waters. And as time heaped up into *tens* of millennia, he had crossed a span of time comparable to the rise and fall, not just of empires, but of whole species.

A continuity of the kind that kept the transients cleaning the walls over such periods could only come about, not through even the deepest layers of mind, but through much more basic biological drivers, like sexual selection: the transients cleaned for sex, not for any reason to do with the Ship's goals, for they could no longer comprehend such abstractions. And meanwhile natural selection had shaped his cradled populations, of transients and Autarchs alike. Of course, if biology were replacing even the deepest layers of mind as the shaping element in the mission's destiny, Rusel's own role became still more important, as the only surviving element of continuity, indeed of consciousness.

Sometimes he felt queasy, perhaps even guilty, at the distorted fate to which generation upon generation had been subjected, all for the sake of a long-dead Pharaoh and her selfish, hubristic dream. But individual transients were soon gone, their tiny motes of joy or pain soon vanishing into the dark. Their very brevity was comforting.

Whatever, there was no going back, for any of them.

Andres was still watching the Autarchs. These frail, cautious animals were like a dark reflection of himself, Rusel thought reluctantly. And how strange it was for the transients to be caged in by the undying: his own attenuated consciousness guiding the Ship from above, while these fallen Autarchs preyed on them from below.

Andres said, "You know, immortality, the defeat of death, is one of mankind's oldest dreams. But immortality doesn't make you a god. *You* have immortality, Rusel, but, save for your crutch the Ship, you have no power. And these—animals—have immortality, but nothing else."

"It's monstrous."

"Of course! Isn't life always? But the genes don't care. And in the Autarchs' mindless capering, you can see the ultimate logic of immortality: for an immortal, to survive, must in the end eat her own children."

But everybody on this Ship was a child of this monstrous mother, Rusel thought, whose hubris and twisted longings had impelled this mission in the first place. "Is that some kind of confession, Pharaoh?"

Andres didn't reply. Perhaps she couldn't. After all, this wasn't Andres but a Virtual, a software-generated crutch for Rusel's fading consciousness, at the limit of its programming. And any guilt he saw in her could only be a reflection of himself.

With an effort of will he dismissed her.

One of the adults, a male, sat up, scratched his chest, and loped to the center of the feeding pit. The young fled at his approach. The male scattered the last bits of primary-color food, and picked up something small and white. It was a skull, Rusel saw, the skull of a child. The adult crushed it, dropped the fragments, and wandered off, aimless, immortal, mindless.

Rusel withdrew, and sealed up the gnawed-through bulkhead. After that he set up a new barrier spanning the Ship parallel to the bulkhead, and opened up the thin slice of the vessel between the walls to intergalactic vacuum. He never again gave any thought to what lay on the other side of that barrier.

Twenty-five thousand years after the end of his world, Rusel heard that he was to be saved.

"Rusel. Rusel . . ."

Rusel wanted the voices to go away. He didn't need voices now—not Diluc's, not even Andres'. He had no body, no belly, no heart; he had no need of people at all. His memories were scattered in emptiness, like the faint smudges that were the remote galaxies all around the Ship. And like the Ship he forged on steadily, pointlessly into the future, his life empty of meaning.

The last thing he wanted was *voices*. But they wouldn't go away. With deep reluctance, he forced his scattered attention to gather.

The voices were coming from Diluc's corridor-village. Vaguely, he saw people there, near a door—the door where he had once been barrelled into by little Rus, he remembered, in a shard of bright warm memory blown from the past—two people, by that same door.

People standing upright. People wearing clothes.

They were not transients. And they were calling his name into the air. With a mighty effort he pulled himself to full awareness.

They stood side by side, a man and a woman—both young, in their twenties, perhaps. They wore smart orange uniforms and boots. The man was clean-shaven, and the woman bore a baby in her arms.

Transients had clustered around them. Naked, pale, eyes wide with curiosity, they squatted on their haunches and reached up with their long arms to the smiling newcomers. Some of them were scrubbing frantically at the floor and walls, teeth bared in rictus grins. They were trying to impress the newcomers with their prowess at cleaning, the only way they knew how.

The woman allowed the transients to stroke her child. But she watched them with hard eyes and a fixed smile. And the man's hand was never far away from the weapon at his belt.

It took Rusel a great deal of effort to find the circuits that would allow him to speak. He said, "*Rusel*. I am Rusel."

As the disembodied voice boomed out of the air the man and woman looked up, startled, and the transients cowered. The newcomers looked at each other with delight. "It's true," said the man. "It really is the *Mayflower*!" A translation whispered to Rusel.

The woman scoffed. "Of course it's the *Mayflower*. What else could it be?"

Rusel said, "Who are you?"

The man's name was Pirius, the woman's Torec.

"Are we at Canis Major?"

"No," Pirius said gently.

These two had come from the home Galaxy—from Sol system itself, they said.

They had come in a faster-than-light ship; it had overtaken the *Mayflower's* painful crawl in a few weeks. "You have come thirteen thousand light-years from Port Sol," Pirius said. "And it took you more than twenty-five thousand years. It is a record for a generation starship! An astonishing feat."

Thirteen thousand light-years? Even now, only half way. It seemed impossible.

Torec cupped the face of a transient girl in her hand—cupped Lora's face. "And," Torec said, "we came to find you."

"Yes," said Pirius, smiling. "And your floating museum!"

Rusel thought that over. "Then mankind lives on?"

Oh, yes, Pirius told him. The mighty Expansion from which the *Mayflower's* crew had fled had burned its way right across the Galaxy. It had been an age of war; trillions had gone into the dark. But mankind had endured.

"And we won!" Pirius said brightly. Pirius and Torec themselves had been involved in some kind of exotic combat to win the center of the Galaxy. "It's a human Galaxy now, Rusel."

"Human? But how are *you* still human?"

They seemed to understand the question. "We were at war," Pirius said. "We couldn't afford to evolve."

"The Coalition—"

"Fallen. Vanished. Gone. They can't harm you now."

"And my crew—"

"We will take them home. There are places where they can be cared for. But, ah—"

Torec said, "But the Ship itself is too big to turn around. I'm not sure we can bring *you*."

Once he had seen himself, a stiff ageless man, through the eyes of Diluc's great-grandson Poro, through the eyes of a child. Now, just for an instant, he saw himself through the eyes of Pirius and Torec. A wizened, charred thing suspended in a webbing of wires and tubes.

That didn't matter, of course. "Have I fulfilled my mission?"

"Yes," Pirius said gently. "You fulfilled it very well."

He wasn't aware of Pirius and Torec shepherding the transients and Autarchs out of the Ship and into their own absurdly small craft. He wasn't aware of Pirius' farewell call as they shot away, back toward the bright lights of the human Galaxy, leaving him alone. He was only aware of the Ship now, the patient, stolid Ship.

The Ship—and one face, revealed to him at last: an elfin face, with distracted eyes. He didn't know if she was a gift of Pirius or even Andres, if she was outside his own head or inside. None of that seemed to matter when at last she smiled for him, and he felt the easing of a tension twenty-five millennia old, the dissolving of a clot of ancient guilt.

The Ship forged on into the endless dark, its corridors as clean and bright and empty as his thoughts.

Riding the White Bull

CAITLIN R. KIERNAN

Caitlin R. Kiernan is the author of four novels, *The Five of Cups, Silk, Threshold,* and *Low Red Moon*. Her short fiction has appeared in *Lethal Kisses, Love in Vein, White of the Moon, High Fantastic, Children of Cthulu, Argosy, Shadows Over Baker Street, Silver Birch, Blood Moon*, and elsewhere, and has been collected in *Tales of Pain and Wonder* and *From Weird and Distant Shores*. She has also scripted *The Dreaming* series for DC Comics/Vertigo. Her most recent book is a chapbook novella, *The Dry Salvages*. She lives in Atlanta, Georgia.

In the harrowing story that follows, she offers us a unique vision of First Contact—which turns out to be nothing like it is on *Star Trek*.

"You've been drinking again, Mr. Paine," Sarah said, and I suppose I must have stopped whatever it was I was doing, probably staring at those damned pics again, the ones of the mess the cops had turned up that morning in a nasty little dump on Columbus—or maybe chewing at my fingernails, or thinking about sex. Whatever. Something or another that suddenly didn't matter anymore because she wasn't asking me a question. Sarah rarely had time for questions. She just wasn't that sort of a girl anymore. She spoke with a directness and authority that would never match her pretty artificial face, and that dissonance, that absolute betrayal of expectation, always made people sit up and listen. If I'd been looking at the photos—I honestly can't remember—I probably laid them down again and looked at her instead.

"There are worse things," I replied, which I suppose I thought was some sort of excuse or defense or something, but she only scowled at me and shook her head.

"Not for you there aren't," she whispered, speaking so low that I almost couldn't make out the words over the faint hum of her metabolic servos and the rumble of traffic down on the street. She blinked and turned away, staring out my hotel window at the dark gray sky hanging low above the Hudson. The snow had finally stopped falling and the clouds had an angry, interrupted intensity to them. Jesus. I can remember the fucking clouds, can even assign them human emotions, but I can't remember what I was doing when Sarah told me I was drinking again. The bits we save, the bits we throw away. Go figure.

"The Agency doesn't need drunks on its payroll, Mr. Paine. The streets of New York are full of drunks and junkies. They're cheaper than rat shit. The Agency needs men with clear minds."

Sarah had a way of enunciating words so that I knew they were capitalized. And she always capitalized Agency. Always. Maybe it was a glitch in one of her language programs, or, then again, maybe she just made me paranoid. Sarah and the booze and the fucking Agency and, while I'm on the subject, February in Manhattan. By that point, I think I'd have given up a couple of fingers and a toe to be on the next flight back to LA.

"We hired you because Fennimore said you were sober. We checked your records with the Department of—"

"Why are you here, Sarah? What do you want? I have work to do," and I jabbed a thumb at the cluttered desk on the other side of my unmade bed. "Work for you and the Agency."

"Work you can't do drunk."

"Yeah, so why don't you fire my worthless intoxicated ass and put me on the next jump back to Los Angeles? After this morning, I honestly couldn't give a shit."

"You understood, when you took this job, Mr. Paine, that there might be exceptional circumstances."

She was still staring out the window towards the sludgy, ice-jammed river and Jersey, an almost expectant expression on her face, the sullen winter light reflecting dull and iridescent off her unaging dermafab skin.

"We were quite explicit on that point."

"Of course you were," I mumbled, half to myself, even less than half to the cyborg who still bothered to call herself Sarah, and then I stepped around the foot of the bed and sat down on a swivel-topped aluminum stool in front of the desk. I made a show of shuffling papers about, hoping that she'd take the hint and leave. I needed a drink and time alone, time to think about what the hell I was going to do next. After the things I'd seen and heard, the things in the photographs I'd taken, the things they wouldn't let me photograph, I was beginning to understand why the Agency had decided not to call an alert on this one, why they were keeping the CDC and BioCon and the WHO in the dark. Why they'd called in a scrubber, instead.

"It'll snow again before morning," Sarah said, not turning away from the window.

"If you can call that crap out there snow," I replied impatiently. "It's not even white. It smells like . . . fuck, I don't know what it smells like, but it doesn't smell like snow."

"You have to learn to let go of the past, Mr. Paine. It's no good to you here. No good at all."

"Is that Agency policy?" I asked and Sarah frowned.

"No, that's not what I meant." She sighed then, and I wondered if it was just habit or if she still needed to breathe, still needed oxygen to drive the patchwork alchemy of her biomechs. I also wondered if she still had sex and, if so, with what. Sarah and I had gone a few rounds, way back in the day, back when she was still one-hundred-percent flesh and blood, water and bone and cartilage. Back when she was still scrubbing freelance, before the Agency gave her a contract and shipped her off to the great frozen dung heap of Manhattan. Back then, if anyone had asked, I'd have said it was her life, her decisions to make, and a girl like Sarah sure as fuck didn't need someone like me getting in her way.

"I was trying to say—here, now—we have to live in the present. That's all we have—"

"Forget it," I told her, glancing up too quickly from the bloody, garish images flickering across the screen of my old Sony-Akamatsu laptop. "Thanks for the ride, though."

"No problem," Sarah whispered. "It's what I do," and she finally turned away from the window, the frost on the plexiglass, the wide interrupted sky.

"If I need anything, I'll give you or Templeton a ring," I said and Sarah pretended to smile, nodded her head, and walked across the tiny room to the door. She opened it but paused there, one foot across the threshold, neither in nor out, the heavy, cold air and flat fluorescent lighting from the hallway leaking in around her, swaddling her like a second-rate halo.

"Try to stay sober," she said. "Please. Mr. Paine. This one . . . it's going to be a squeeze." And her green-brown eyes shimmered faintly, those amazing eight-mill-a-pair spheres of fiberoptic filament and scratch-resistant acrylic, tinted mercury suspension-platinum lenses and the very best circuitry German optimetrics had figured out how to cram into a 6.5 cc socket. I imagined, then or only later on—that's something else I can't remember—that the shimmer stood for something Sarah was too afraid to say aloud, or something the Agency's behavioral inhibitors wouldn't allow her to say, something in her psyche that had been stamped Code Black, Restricted Access.

"Please," she said again.

"Sure. For old time's sake," I replied.

"Whatever it takes, Mr. Paine," and she left, pulling the door softly closed behind her, abandoning me to my dingy room and the dingier afternoon light leaking in through the single soot-streaked window. I listened to her footsteps on the tile, growing fainter as she approached the elevator at the other end of the hall, and when I was sure she wasn't coming back, I reached for the half-empty bottle of scotch tucked into the shadows beneath the edge of the bed.

Back then, I still dreamed about Europa every fucking night. Years later, after I'd finally been retired by the Agency and was only Dietrich Paine again, pensioned civilian has-been rotting away day by day by day in East LA or NoHo or San Diego—I moved around a lot for a drunk—a friend of a friend's croaker hooked me up with some black market head tweaker. And he slipped a tiny silver chip into the base of my skull, right next to my metencephalon, and the bad dreams stopped, just like that. No more night flights, no more cold sweats, no more screaming until the neighbors called the cops.

But that winter in Manhattan, I was still a long, long decade away from the tweaker and his magic silver chip, and whenever the insomnia failed me and I dozed off for ten or fifteen or twenty minutes I was falling again, tumbling silently through the darkness out beyond Ganymede, falling toward that Great Red Spot, that eternal crimson hurricane, my perfect, vortical Hell of phosphorous-stained clouds. Always praying to whatever dark Jovian gods might be watching my descent that this time I'd sail clear of the moons and the anticyclone's eye would swallow me at last, dragging me down, burning me, crushing me in that vast abyss of gas and lightning and infinite pressure.

But I never made it. Not one single goddamn time.

"Do you believe in sin?" Sarah would ask me, when she was still just Sarah, before the implants and augmentations, and I would lie there in her arms, thinking that I was content, and stare up at the ceiling of our apartment and laugh at her.

"I'm serious, Deet."

"You're always serious. You've got serious down to an exact science."

"I think you're trying to avoid the question."

"Yeah, well, it's a pretty silly fucking question."

"Answer it anyway. Do you believe in sin?"

There's no way to know how fast I'm moving as I plummet toward the hungry, welcoming storm, and then Europa snags me. Maybe next time, I think. Maybe next time.

"It's only a question," Sarah would say. "Stop trying to make it anything more than that."

"Most of us get what's coming to us, sooner or later."

"That's not the same thing. That's not what I asked you."

And the phone would ring, or I'd slip my hand between her unshaven legs, or one of our beepers would go off, and the moment would melt away, releasing me from her scrutiny.

It never happened exactly that way, of course, but who's keeping score?

In my dreams, Europa grows larger and larger, sprouting from the darkness exactly like it did in the fucking orientation vids every scrubber had to sit through in those days if he or she wanted a license. Snippets of video from this or that probe borrowed for my own memories. Endless fractured sheets of ice the color of rust and sandstone, rising up so fast, so fast, and I'm only a very small speck of meat and white EMU suit streaking north and east across the ebony skies above Mael Duín, the Echion Linea, Cilix, the southeastern terminus of the Rhadamanthys Linea. I'm only a shooting star hurtling along above that terrible varicose landscape and I can't remember how to close my eyes.

"Man, I was right fucking there when they opened the thing," Ronnie says again and takes another drag off her cigarette. Her hand trembles and ash falls to the formica tabletop. "I'd asked to go to Turkey, right, to cover the goddamn war, but I pulled the IcePIC assignment instead. I was waiting in the pressroom with everyone else, watching the feed from the quarantine unit when the sirens started."

"The Agency denies you were present," I reply as calmly as I can, and she smiles that nervous, brittle smile she always had, laughs one of her dry, humorless laughs, and gray smoke leaks from her nostrils.

"Hell, I know that, Deet. The fuckers keep rewriting history so it always comes out the way they want it to, but I was there, man I saw it, before they shut down the cameras. I saw all that shit that 'never happened,'" and she draws quotation marks in the air with her index fingers.

That was the last time I talked to Ronnie, the last time I visited her out at La Casa

Psychiatric, two or three weeks before she hanged herself with an electrical cord. I went to the funeral, of course. The Agency sent a couple of black-suited spooks with carefully worded condolences for her family and I ducked out before the eulogy was finished.

And here, a few kilometers past the intersection of Tectamus Linea and Harmonia Linea, I see the familiar scatter of black dots laid out helter-skelter on the crosscut plains. "Ice-water volcanism," Sarah whispers inside my helmet; I know damn well she isn't there, hasn't been anywhere near me for years and years and I'm alone and only dreaming her voice to break the deafening weight of silence. I count the convection cells like rosary beads, like I was ever Catholic, like someone who might have once believed in sin. I'm still too far up to see any evidence of the lander, so I don't know which hole is The Hole, Insertion Point 2071A, the open sore that Emmanuel Weatherby-Jones alternately referred to as "the plague gate" and "the mouth of Sakpata" in his book on the Houston incident and its implications for theoretical and applied astrobiology. I had to look that up, because he never explained who or what Sakpata was. I found it in an old book on voodoo and Afro-Caribbean religions. Sakpata is a god of disease.

I'm too far up to guess which hole is Sakpata's mouth and I don't try.

I don't want to know.

A different sort of god is patiently waiting for me on the horizon.

"They started screaming," Ronnie says. "Man, I'll never forget that sound, no matter how many pills these assholes feed me. We all sat there, too fucking stunned to move, and this skinny little guy from CNN—"

"Last time he was from *Newsweek*," I say, interrupting her, and she shakes her head and takes another drag, coughs, and rubs at her bloodshot eyes.

"You think it makes any goddamned difference?"

"No," I reply dishonestly, and she stares at me for a while without saying anything else.

"When's the last time you got a decent night's sleep?" she asks me, finally, and I might laugh, or I might shrug, and "Yeah," she says. "That's what I thought."

She starts rattling on about the hydrobot, then, the towering black smokers, thermal vents, chemosynthesis, those first grainy snatches of video, but I'm not listening. I'm too busy zipping helplessly along above buckled Europan plains and vast stretches of blocky, shattered chaos material; a frozen world caught in the shadow of Big Daddy Jupiter, frozen for ages beyond counting but a long fucking way from dead, and I would wake up screaming or crying or, if I was lucky, too scared to make any sound at all.

"They're ready for you now, Mr. Paine," the cop said, plain old NYPD street blue, and I wondered what the fuck he was doing here, why the Agency was taking chances like that. Probably the same poor bastard who'd found the spooch, I figured. Templeton had told me that someone in the building had complained about the smell and the super buzzed the cops, so this was most likely the guy who answered the call. He might have a partner around somewhere. I nodded at him and he glanced nervously back over his shoulder at the open door to the apartment, the translucent polyurethane iso-seal curtain with its vertical black zipper running right down the middle, all the air hoses snaking in and out of the place, keeping the pressure inside lower than the pressure outside. I doubted he would still be breathing when the sweeper crews were finished with the scene.

"You see this sort of shit very often?" he asked, and it didn't take a particularly sensitive son of a bitch to hear the fear in his voice, the fear and confusion and whatever comes after panic. I didn't respond. I was busy checking the batteries in one of my cameras and, besides, I had the usual orders from Templeton to keep my mouth shut around civvies. And knowing the guy was probably already good as dead, that he'd signed his death warrant just by showing up for work that morning, didn't make me particularly eager to chat.

"Well, I don't mind telling you, I've never seen shit like that thing in there," he said and coughed. "I mean, you see some absolutely fucked-up shit in this city, and I even did my four years in the army—hell, I was in fucking Damascus after the bomb, but holy Christ Almighty—"

"You were in Damascus?" I asked, but didn't look up from my equipment, too busy double-checking the settings on the portable genetigraph clipped to my belt to make eye contact.

"Oh yeah, I was there. I got to help clean up the mess when the fires burned out."

"Then that's something we have in common," I told him and flipped my vidcam's on switch and the gray LED screen showed me five zeros. I was patched into the portable lab down on the street, a black Chevy van with Maryland plates and a yellow ping-pong ball stuck on the antenna. I knew Sarah would be in the van, waiting for my feed, jacked in, riding the amps, hearing everything I heard, seeing everything I saw through her perfectly calibrated eyes.

"You were in Syria?" the cop asked me, glad to have something to talk about besides what he'd seen in the apartment.

"No, I clean up other people's messes."

"Oh," he said, sounding disappointed. "I see."

"Had a good friend in the war, though. But he was stationed in Cyprus, and then the Taurus Mountains."

"You ever talk with him? You know, about the war?"

"Nope. He didn't make it back," I said, finally looking up and I winked at the cop and stepped quickly past him to the tech waiting for me at the door. I could see she was sweating inside her hazmat hood, even though it was freezing in the hallway. Scrubbers don't get hazmat suits. It interferes with the contact, so we settle for a couple of hours in decon afterwards, antibiotics, antitox, purgatives, and hope we don't come up red somewhere down the line.

"This is bad, ain't it?" the cop asked. "I mean, this is something real bad," and I didn't turn around, just shrugged my shoulders as the tech unzipped the plastic curtain for me.

"Is that how it looked to you?" I replied. I could feel the gentle rush of air into the apartment as the slit opened in front of me.

"Jesus, man, all I want's a straight fucking answer," he said. "I think I deserve that much. Don't you?" and since I honestly couldn't say one way or the other, since I didn't even care, I ignored him and stepped through the curtain into this latest excuse for hell.

There's still an exhibit at the American Museum of Natural History, on the fourth floor with the old Hall of Vertebrate Origins and all the dinosaur bones. The Agency didn't shut it down after the first outbreaks, the glory spooches that took out a whole block in Philadelphia and a trailer park somewhere in West Virginia, but it's not as popular as you might think. A dark, dusty alcove crowded with scale models and dioramas, video monitors running clips from the IcePIC's hydrobot, endless black-and-white loops of gray seafloors more than half a billion kilometers from earth. When the exhibit first opened, there were a few specimens on loan from NASA, but those were all removed a long time ago. I never saw them for myself, but an acquaintance on staff at the museum, a geologist, assures me they were there. A blue-black bit of volcanic rock sealed artfully in a lucite pyramid, and two formalin-filled specimen canisters, one containing a pink wormlike organism no more than a few centimeters in length, the other preserving one of the ugly little slugs that the mission scientists dubbed "star minnows."

"Star leeches" would have been more accurate.

On Tuesday afternoon, the day after I'd worked the scene on Columbus, hungover and hoping to avoid another visit from Sarah, I took B line from my hotel to the museum and spent a couple of hours sitting on a bench in that neglected alcove, watching the video clips play over and over again for no one but me. Three monitors running simultaneously—a NASA documentary on the exploration of Europa, beginning with Pioneer 10 in 1973, a flyover of the moon's northern hemisphere recorded shortly before the IcePIC orbiter deployed its probes, and a snippet of film shot beneath the ice. That's the one I'd come to see. I chewed aspirin and watched as the hydrobot's unblinking eyes peered through veils of silt and plankton into the interminable darkness of an alien ocean, the determined glare of the bot's lights never seeming to reach more than a few feet into the gloom. Near the end of the loop, you get to see one of the thermal vents, fringed with towering sulfide chimneys spewing superheated methane- and hydrogen-rich water into the frigid Europan ocean. In places, the sides of the chimneys were completely obscured by a writhing, swaying carpet of creatures. Something like an eel slipped unexpectedly past the camera lens. A few seconds later, the seafloor was replaced by a brief stream of credits and then the NASA logo, before the clip started itself over again.

I tried hard to imagine how amazing these six minutes of video must have seemed, once upon a time, how people must have stood in lines just to see it, back before the shit hit the fan and everyone everywhere stopped wanting to talk about IcePIC and its fucking space minnows. Before the government axed most of NASA's exobiology program, scrapped all future missions to Europa, and cancelled plans to explore Titan. Back before ET became a four-letter word. But no matter how hard I tried, all I could think about was that thing on the bed, the crap growing from the walls of the apartment and dripping from the goddamn ceiling.

Above the monitor, there was a long quote from H. G. Wells printed in red-brown ink on a clear lexan plaque and I read it several times, wishing that I had a cigarette—"We look back through countless millions of years and see the great will to live struggling out of the intertidal slime, struggling from shape to shape and from power to power, crawling and then walking confidently upon the land, struggling generation after generation to master the air, creeping down into the darkness of the deep; we see it turn upon itself in rage and hunger and reshape itself anew, we watch it draw nearer and more akin to us, expanding, elaborating itself, pursuing its relentless inconceivable purpose, until at last it reaches us and its being beats through our brains and arteries."

I've never cared very much for irony. It usually leaves a sick, empty feeling in my gut. I wondered why no one had taken the plaque down.

By the time I got back to my room it was almost dark, even though I'd splurged and taken a taxi. After the video, the thought of being trapped in the crowded, stinking subway, hurtling along through the city's bowels, through those tunnels where the sun never reaches, gave me a righteous fucking case of the heebie-jeebies and, what the hell, the Agency was picking up the tab. All those aspirin had left my stomach aching and sour and hadn't done much of anything about the hangover, but there was an unopened pint waiting for me beneath the edge of the bed.

I was almost asleep when Sarah called.

Here's a better quote. I've been carrying it around with me for the last few years, in my head and on a scrap of paper. It showed up in my e-mail one day, sent by some anonymous someone or another from an account that turned out to be bogus. Scrubbers get a lot of anonymous e-mail. Tips, rumors, bullshit, hearsay, wicked little traps set by the Agency, confessions, nightmares, curses, you name it and it comes rolling our way, and after a while you don't even bother to wonder who sent the shit. But this one, this one kept me awake a few nights:

"But what would a deep-sea fish learn even if a steel plate of a wrecked vessel above him should drop and bump him on the nose?

"Our submergence in a sea of conventionality of almost impenetrable density.

"Sometimes I'm a savage who has found something on the beach of his island. Sometimes I'm a deep-sea fish with a sore nose.

"The greatest of mysteries:

"Why don't they ever come here, or send here, openly?

"Of course there's nothing to that mystery if we don't take so seriously the notion—that we must be interesting. It's probably for moral reasons that they stay away—but even so, there must be some degraded ones among them."

It's that last bit that always sinks its teeth (or claws or whatever the fuck have you) into me and hangs on. Charles Hoyt Fort. *The Book of the Damned*. First published in 1919, a century and a half before IcePIC, and it occurs to me now that I shouldn't be any less disturbed by prescience than I am by irony. But there you go. Sometimes I'm a savage. Sometimes I'm a deep-sea fish. And my life is become the sum of countless degradations.

"You're not going down there alone," Sarah said, telling, not asking, because, like I already noted, Sarah stopped being the kind of girl who asks questions when she signed on with the Agency for life plus whatever else they could milk her biomeched cadaver for. I didn't reply immediately, lay there a minute or three, rubbing my eyes, waiting for the headache to start in on me again, listening to the faint, insistent crackle from the phone. Manhattan's landlines were shit and roses that February, had been that way for years, ever since some Puerto Ricans in Brooklyn had popped a homemade micro-EMP rig to celebrate the Fourth of July. I wondered why Sarah hadn't called me on my thumbline while I looked about for the scotch. Turned out I was lying on the empty bottle, and I rolled over, wishing I'd never been born. I held the phone cradled between my left shoulder and my cheek and stared at the darkness outside the window of my hotel room.

"Do you even know what time it is?" I asked her.

"Templeton said you were talking about going out to Roosevelt. He said you might have gone already."

"I didn't say dick to Templeton about Roosevelt," I said, which was the truth, I hadn't, but also entirely beside the point. It was John Templeton's prerogative to stay a few moves ahead of his employees, especially when those employees were scrubbers, especially freebie scrubbers on the juice. I tossed the empty bottle at a cockroach on the wall across the room. It didn't break, but squashed the roach and left a satisfying dent in the drywall.

"You know Agency protocol for dealing with terrorists."

"They went and stuck something in your head so you don't have to sleep anymore, is that it?"

"You can't go to the island alone," she said. "I'm sending a couple of plainclothes men over. They'll be at your hotel by six A.M. at the latest."

"Yeah, and I'll be fucking asleep at six," I mumbled, more interested in watching the roaches that had emerged to feed on the remains of the one I'd nailed than arguing with her.

"We can't risk losing you, Mr. Paine. It's too late to call in someone else if anything happens. You know that as well as I do."

"Do I?"

"You're a drunk, not an idiot."

"Look, Sarah, if I start scutzing around out there with two of Temp's goons in tow, I'll be lucky if I find a fucking stitch, much less get it to talk to me."

"They're all animals," Sarah said, meaning the stitches and meat-dolls and genetic changelings that had claimed Roosevelt Island a decade or so back. There was more than a hint of loathing in her voice. "It makes me sick, just thinking about them."

"Did you ever stop to consider they probably feel the same way about you?"

"No," Sarah said coldly, firmly, one hundred percent shitsure of herself. "I never have."

"If those fuckers knock on my door at six o'clock, I swear to god, Sarah, I'll shoot them."

"I'll tell them to wait for you in the lobby."

"That's real damn thoughtful of you."

There was another static-littered moment of silence then and I closed my eyes tight. The headache was back and had brought along a few friends for the party. My thoughts were starting to bleed together and I wondered if I'd vomit before or after Sarah finally let me off the phone. I wondered if cyborgs vomited. I wondered exactly what all those agents in the black Chevy van had seen on their consoles and face-screens when I'd walked over and touched a corner of the bed in the apartment on Columbus Avenue.

"I'm going to hang up now, Sarah. I'm going back to sleep."

"You're sober."

"As a judge," I whispered and glanced back at the window, trying to think about anything at all except throwing up. There were bright lights moving across the sky above the river, red and green and white, turning clockwise; one of the big military copters, an old Phoenix 6-98 or one of the newer Japanese whirlybirds, making its circuit around the Rotten Apple.

"You're still a lousy liar," she said.

"I'll have to try harder."

"Don't fuck this up, Mr. Paine. You're a valued asset. The Agency would like to see you remain that way."

"I'm going back to sleep," I said again, disregarding the not-so-subtle threat tucked between her words; it wasn't anything I didn't already know. "And I meant what I said about shooting those assholes. Don't think I didn't. Anyone knocks on this door before eight sharp and that's all she wrote."

"They'll be waiting in the lobby when you're ready."

"Goodnight, Sarah."

"Goodnight, Mr. Paine," she replied and a second or two later there was only the ragged dial tone howling in my ear. The lights outside the window were gone, the copter probably all the way to Harlem by now. I almost made it to the toilet before I was sick.

If I didn't keep getting the feeling that there's someone standing behind me, someone looking over my shoulder as I write this, I'd say more about the dreams. The dreams are always there, tugging at me, insistent, selfish, wanting to be spilled out into the wide, wide world where everyone and his brother can get a good long gander at them. They're not content anymore with the space inside my skull. My skull is a prison for dreams, an enclosed and infinite prison space where the arrows on the number line point toward each other, converging but never, ever, ever meeting and so infinite all the same. But I do keep getting that feeling and there's still the matter of the thing in the apartment.

The thing on the bed.

The thing that the cop who'd been in Damascus after the Israeli's 40-megaton fireworks show died for.

My thirteenth contact. The one that might have been my last, if I'd had the nerve to stop. If the Agency hadn't been so desperate for hired guns.

After I was finished with the makeshift airlock at the door, one of Templeton's field medics, safe and snug inside a blue hazmat suit, led me through the brightly lit apartment. I held one hand cupped over my nose and mouth, but the thick clouds of neon yellow disinfectant seeped easily between my fingers, gagging me. My eyes burned and watered, making it even more difficult to see. I've always thought that shit smelled like licorice, but it seems to smell like different things to different people. Sarah used to say it reminded her of burning tires. I once knew a guy who said it smelled like carnations.

"It's in the bedroom," the medic said, his voice flat and tinny through the suit's audioport. "It doesn't seem to have spread to any of the other rooms. How was the jump from Los Angeles, sir?"

I didn't answer him, too ripped on adrenaline for small talk and pleasantries, and he didn't really seem to care, my silence just another part of the routine. I took shallow breaths and followed the medic through the yellow fog, which was growing much thicker as we approached ground zero. The disinfectant was originally manufactured by Dow for domestic bioterrorism clean-up, but the Agency's clever boys and girls had added a pinch of this, a dash of that, and it always seemed to do the job. We passed a kitchenette, beer cans and dirty dishes, and an open box of corn flakes sitting on the counter, then turned left into a short hallway leading past a bathroom too small for a rat to take a piss in, past a framed photograph of a lighthouse on a rocky shore (the bits we remember, the bits we forget), to the bedroom. Templeton was there, of course, decked out in his orange hazmat threads, one hand resting confidently on the butt of the big Beretta Pulse 38A on his hip, and he pointed at me and then pointed at the bed.

Sometimes I'm a deep-sea fish.

Sometimes I'm a savage.

"We're still running MRS and backtrace on these two," Templeton said, pointing at the bed again, "but I'm pretty sure the crit's a local." His gray eyes peered warily out at me, the lights inside his hood shining bright so I had no trouble at all seeing his face through the haze.

"I figure one of them picked it up from an untagged mobile, probably the woman there, and it's been hitching dormant for the last few weeks. We're guessing the trigger was viral. She might have caught a cold. Corona's always a good catalyst."

I took a deep breath and coughed. Then I gagged again and stared up at the ceiling for a moment.

"Come on, Deet. I need you frosty on this one. You're not drunk, are you? Fennimore said—"

"I'm not drunk," I replied, and I wasn't, not yet. I hadn't had a drink in almost six months, but, hey, the good news was, the drought was almost over.

"That's great," Templeton said. "That's real damn great. That's exactly what I wanted to hear."

I looked back at the bed.

"So, when you gonna tell me what's so goddamn special about this one?" I asked. "The way Sarah sounded, I figured you'd already lost a whole building."

"What's so goddamn special about them, Deet, is that they're still conscious, both of them. Initial EEGs are coming up pretty solid. Clean alpha, beta, and delta. The theta's are weakening, but the brain guys say the waves are still synchronous enough to call coherent."

Temp kept talking, but I tuned him out and forced myself to take a long, hard look at the bed.

Sometimes I'm a deep-sea fish.

The woman's left eye was still intact, open very wide and wet with tears, her blue irises bright as Christmas Day, and I realized she was watching me.

"It's pure," Templeton said, leaning closer to the bed, "more than ninety percent proximal to the Laelaps strain. Beats the fuck outta me why their brains aren't soup by now."

"I'm going to need a needle," I muttered, speaking automatically, some part of me still there to walk the walk and talk the talk, some part of me getting ready to take the plunge because the only way out of this hole was straight ahead. A very small, insensate part of me not lost in that pleading, blue eye. "Twelve and a half max, okay, and not that fife-and-drum Australian shit you gave me in Boston. I don't want to feel anything in there but the critter, you understand?"

"Sure," Templeton said, smiling like a ferret.

"I mean it. Whatever's going through their heads right now, I don't want to hear it, Temp. Not so much as a peep, not even a fucking whisper."

"Hey, you're calling the shots, Deet."

"Bullshit," I said. "Don't suck my dick, just get me the needle."

He motioned to a medic and in a few more minutes the drugs were singing me toward that spiraling ebony pipeline, the Scrubber's Road, Persephone's Staircase, the White Bull, whatever the hell you want to call it, it's all the same to me. I was beginning to sweat and trying to make it through the procedure checklist one last time. Templeton patted me on the back, the way he always did when I was standing there on the brink. I said a silent prayer to anything that might be listening that one day it'd be his carcass rotting away at the center of the Agency's invisible clockwork circus. And then I kneeled down at the edge of the bed and got to work.

Sarah sent the goons over, just like she'd said she would, but I ducked out the back and, luckily, she hadn't seen fit to have any of Temp's people watching all the hotel's exits. Maybe she couldn't pull that many warm bodies off the main gig down on Columbus. Maybe Temp had bigger things on his mind. I caught a cash-and-ride taxi that took me all the way to the ruins along York Avenue. The Vietnamese driver hadn't wanted to get any closer to the Queensboro Bridge than Third, but I slipped him five hundred and he found a little more courage somewhere. He dropped me at the corner of Second and East Sixty-first Street, crossed himself twice, and drove away, bouncing recklessly over the trash and disintegrating blacktop. I watched him go, feeling more alone than I'd expected. Overhead, the Manhattan sky was the color of buttermilk and mud and I wished briefly, pointlessly, that I'd brought a gun. The 9mm Samson-L4 Enforcer I'd bought in a Hollywood pawnshop almost four years before was back at the hotel, hidden in a locked compartment of my suitcase. But I knew it'd be a whole lot worse to be picked up crossing the barricades without a pass if I were carrying an unregistered weapon, one more big red, blinking excuse for the MPs to play a few rounds of Punch and Judy with my face while they waited for my papers and my story about the Agency to check out.

I started walking north, the gray-blue snow crunching loudly beneath my boots, the collar of my coat turned up against the wind whistling raw between the empty, burned-out buildings. I'd heard security was running slack around the Sixty-third Street entrance. I might get lucky. It had happened before.

"Yes, but what exactly did you think you'd find on the island?" Buddhadev Krishnamurthy asked when he interviewed me for his second book on technoshamanism and the Roosevelt posthumanists, the one that won him a Pulitzer.

"Missing pieces, maybe," I replied. "I was just following my nose. The Miyake girl turned up during the contact."

"But, going to the island alone, wasn't that rather above and beyond? I mean, if you hated Templeton and the Agency so much, why stick your neck out like that?"

"Old habits," I said, sipping at my tequila and trying hard to remember how long it had taken me to find a way past the guards and up onto the bridge. "Old habits and bad dreams," I added, and then, "But I never said I was doing it for the Agency." I knew I was telling him more than I'd intended. Not that it mattered. None of my interview made it past the censors and into print.

I kept to the center lanes, except for a couple of times when rusted and fire-blackened tangles of wrecked automobiles and police riot-rollers forced me to the edges of the bridge. The West Channel glimmered dark and iridescent beneath the late February clouds, a million shifting colors dancing lazily across the oily surface of the river. The wind shrieked through the cantilever spans, like angry sirens announcing my trespass to anyone who would listen. I kept waiting for the sound of helicopter rotors or a foot patrol on its way back from Queens, for some sharpshooter's bullet to drop me dead in my tracks. Maybe it was wishful thinking.

Halfway across I found the access stairs leading down to the island, right where my contact in Street and Sanitation had said they would be. I checked my watch. It was five minutes until noon.

"Will you tell me about the dreams, Mr. Paine?" Krishnamurthy asked, after he'd ordered me another beer and another shot of tequila. His voice was like silk and cream, the sort of voice that seduced, that tricked you into lowering your defenses just long enough for him to get a good peek at all the nasty nooks and crannies. "I hear lots of scrubbers had trouble with nightmares back then, before the new neural-drag sieves were available. The suicide rate's dropped almost fifty percent since they became standard issue. Did you know that, Mr. Paine?"

"No," I told him. "Guess I missed the memo. I'm kind of outside the flow these days."

"You're a lucky man," he said. "You should count your blessings. At least you made it out in one piece. At least you made it out sane."

I think I told him to fuck off then. I know I didn't tell him about the dreams.

"What do you see down there, Deet? The sensors are getting a little hinky on me," Sarah said and, in the dreams, back when, in the day, before the tweaker's silver chip, I took another clumsy step toward the edge of the chasm created by hot water welling up from the deep-sea vents along the Great Charon Ridge. A white plume of salty steam rose high into the thin Europan atmosphere, blotting out the western horizon, boiling off into the indifferent blackness of space. I knew I didn't want to look over the edge again. I'd been there enough times already and it was always the same, and I reminded myself that no one had ever walked on Europa, no one human, and it was only a dream. Shit. Listen to me. Only a dream. There's a contradiction to live by.

"Am I coming through?" Sarah asked. "Can you hear me?"

I didn't answer her. My mouth was too dry to speak, bone dry from fear and doubt and the desiccated air circulating through the helmet of my EMU suit.

"I need you to acknowledge, Deet. Can you hear me?"

The mouth of Sakpata, the plague gate, yawning toothless and insatiable before me, almost nine kilometers from one side to the other, more than five miles from the edge of the hole down to the water. I was standing near the center of the vast field of cryo-volcanic lenticulae first photographed by the Gallileo probe in 1998, on its fifteenth trip around Jupiter. Convection currents pushed the crust into gigantic pressure domes that finally cracked and collapsed under their own weight, exposing the ocean below. I took another step, almost slipping on the ice, and wondered how far I was from the spot where IcePIC had made landfall.

"Deet, do you copy?"

"Do you believe in sin, Deet?"

Nor shapes of men nor beasts we ken—
The ice was all between.

Sarah sets her coffee cup down and watches me from the other side of our apartment on Cahuenga. Her eyes are still her eyes, full of impatience and secrets. Sh
reaches for a cigarette and I wish this part wasn't a dream, that I could go back t
here and start again. This sunny LA morning, Sarah wearing nothing but her b
and panties, and me still curled up in the warm spot she left in the sheets. Go b
and change the words. Change every goddamn day that's come between now
then.

"They want my decision by tomorrow morning," she says and lights her cig
The smoke hangs like a caul about her face.

"Tell them you need more time," I reply. "Tell them you have to think a

"This is the fucking Agency," she says and shakes her head. "You don't
for more time. You don't ask them shit."

"I don't know what you want me to say, Sarah."

"It's everything I've always wanted," she says and flicks ash into a
drink can.

Are those her ribs through which the Sun
Did peer, as through a grate?

I took another step nearer the chasm and wished that this woul
wake up. If I could wake up I wouldn't have to see. If I could w
bottle of scotch or bourbon or tequila waiting for me, a drink
the edge off the dryness in my mouth. The sun was rising behi
thing lost among the stars, and the commlink buzzed and cr

"If it's what you want, take it," I say, the same thing I alwa

can never take back. "I'm not going to stand in your way." I could tell it was the last thing that Sarah wanted to hear. The End. The curtain falls and everyone takes a bow. The next day, Wednesday, I'll drive her to LAX-1 and she'll take the 4:15 jump to D.C.

We are more alone than ever.

Ronnie used her own blood to write those six words on the wall of her room at La Casa, the night she killed herself.

My boots left no trace whatsoever on the slick, blue-white ice. A few more steps and I was finally standing at the edge, walking cautiously onto the wide shelf formed by an angular chaos block jutting a few meters out over the pit. The constant steam had long since worn the edges of the block smooth. Eventually, it would melt free, undercut by ages of heat and water vapor, and plunge into the churning abyss far below. I took a deep breath of the dry, stale air inside my helmet and peered into the throat of Sakpata.

"Tell me, what the hell did we expect to find out there, Deet?" Ronnie asked me. "What did we think it would be? Little gray men with the answers to all the mysteries of the universe, free for the asking? A few benign extremophiles clinging stubbornly to the bottom of a lifeless sea? I can't remember anymore. I try, but I can't. I lay awake at night trying to remember."

"I don't think it much matters," I told her and she started crying again.

"It was waiting for us, Deet," she sobbed. "It was waiting for us all along, a million fucking years alone out there in the dark. It knew we'd come, sooner or later."

Sarah was standing on the ice behind me, naked, the wind tearing at her plastic skin.

"Why do you keep coming here?" she asked. "What do you think you'll find?"

"Why do you keep following me?"

"You turned off your comms. I wasn't getting a signal. You didn't leave me much choice."

I turned to face her, turning my back on the hole, but the wind had already pulled her apart and scattered the pieces across the plain.

We are more alone than ever.

And then I'm in the pipe, slipping along the Scrubber's Road, no friction, no re-istance, rushing by high above the frozen moon, waiting for that blinding, twin-ling moment of perfect agony when my mind brushes up against that other mind. hat instant when it tries to hide, tries to withdraw, and I dig in and hang on and ag it screaming into the light. I hear the whir of unseen machineries as the techs the outside try to keep up with me, with it.

I stand alone at the edge of Sakpata's mouth, where no man has ever stood, at the t of the bed on Columbus, in the airport lobby saying goodbye to Sarah. I have ny cameras, my instruments, because I'll need all that later on, when the spin is and I'm drunk and there's nothing left but the footwork.

hen I have nothing left to do but track down the carrier and put a bullet or two or her or its head.

t the cord. Tie off the loose ends.

o you believe in sin, Deet?"

ead of the cross, the Albatross . . .

"It's only a question. Stop trying to make it anything more than that."

"Do you copy?" Sarah asks again. "Global can't get a fix on you." I take another step closer to the hole, and it slips a few feet farther away from me. The sky is steam and stars and infinite night.

I followed East Road north to Main Street, walking as quickly as the snow and black ice and wrecks littering the way would allow. I passed through decaying canyons of brick and steel, broken windows and gray concrete, the tattered ruins of the mess left after the Feds gave Roosevelt Island up for lost, built their high barricades and washed their hands of the place. I kept my eyes on the road at my feet, but I could feel them watching me, following me, asking each other if this one was trouble or just some fool out looking for his funeral. I might have been either. I still wasn't sure myself. There were tracks in the snow and frozen mud, here and there, some of them more human than others.

Near the wild place that had once been Blackwell Park, I heard something call out across the island. It was a lonely, frightened sound, and I walked a little faster.

I wondered if Sarah would try to send an extraction team in after me, if she was in deep sharn with Templeton and the boys for letting me scoot. I wondered if maybe Temp was already counting me among the dead and kicking himself for not putting me under surveillance, trying to figure out how the hell he was going to lay it all out for the bastards in Washington. It took me the better part of an hour to reach the northern tip of the island and the charred and crumbling corpse of Coler Goldwater Hospital. The ragtag militia of genetic anarchists that had converged on Manhattan in the autumn of 'sixty-nine taking orders from a schizo ex-movie star who called herself Circe Nineteen, had claimed the old hospital as their headquarters. When the army decided to start shelling, Coler had taken the worst of the mortars. Circe Nineteen had been killed by a sniper, but there'd been plenty of freaks on hand to fill her shoes, so to speak.

Beneath the sleeting February sky, the hospital looked as dead as the day after Armageddon. I tried not to think about the spooch, all the things I'd seen and heard the day before, the things I'd felt, the desperate stream of threats and promises and prayers the crit had spewed at me when I'd finally come to the end of the shimmering aether pipeline and we'd started the dance.

Inside, the hospital stunk like a zoo, a dying, forgotten zoo, but at least I was out of the wind. My face and hands had gone numb. How would the Agency feel about a scrubber without his fingers? Would they toss me on the scrap heap, or would they just give me a shiny new set made in Osaka, better than the originals? Maybe work a little of the biomech magic they'd worked on Sarah? I followed a long ground-floor hallway past doors and doorways without doors, pitch dark rooms and chiaroscuro rooms ruled by the disorienting interplay of shadow and light, until I came to a row of elevators. All the doors had been jammed more or less open at some point, exposing shafts filled with dust and gears and rusted cables. I stood there a while, as my fingers and lips began to tingle, the slow pins-and-needles thaw, and listened to the building whispering around me.

"They're all animals," Sarah had sneered the day before. But they weren't, of course, no more than she was truly a machine. I knew Sarah was bright enough to see the truth, even before they'd squeezed all that hardware into her skull. Even if she could never admit it to herself or anyone else. The cyborgs and stitches were merely opposing poles in the same rebellion against the flesh—black pawn, white pawn—north and south on the same twisted postevolutionary road. Not that it made much difference to me. It still doesn't. But standing there, my breath fogging and the feeling slowly returning to my hands, her arrogance was pissing me off more than usual. Near as I could tell, the biggest difference between Sarah and whatever was waiting for me in the bombed-out hospital that afternoon—maybe the only difference that actually mattered—was that the men and women in power had found a use for her kind, while the stitches and changelings had never been anything to them but a nuisance. It might have gone a different way. It might yet.

There was a stairwell near the elevators and I climbed it to the third floor. I hadn't thought to bring a flashlight with me, so I stayed close to the wall, feeling my way through the gloom, stumbling more than once when my feet encountered chunks of rubble that had fallen from somewhere overhead.

On the third floor, the child was waiting for me.

"What do you want here?" he barked and blinked at me with the golden eyes of a predatory bird. He was naked, his skin hidden beneath a coat of fine yellow-brown fur.

"Who are you?" I asked him.

"The manticore said you were coming. She saw you on the bridge. What do you want?"

"I'm looking for a girl named Jet."

The child laughed, a strange, hitching laugh, and rolled his eyes. He leaned forward, staring at me intently, expectantly, and the vertical pupils of those big golden eyes dilated slightly.

"Ain't no girls here, Mister," he chuckled. "Not anymore. You skizzled or what?"

"Is there anyone here named Jet? I've come a long way to talk to her."

"You got a gun, maybe?" he asked. "You got a knife?"

"No," I said. "I don't. I just want to talk."

"You come out to Stitchtown without a gun or a knife? Then you must have some bangers, Mister. You must have whennymegs big as my fist," and he held up one clenched fist so I could see exactly what he meant. "Or you don't want to live so much longer, maybe."

"Maybe," I replied.

"Meat's scarce this time of year," the boy chuckled and then licked his thin, ebony lips.

Down at the other end of the hallway, something growled softly and the boy glanced over his shoulder, then back up at me. He was smiling, a hard smile that was neither cruel nor kind, revealing the sharp tips of his long canines and incisors. He looked disappointed.

"All in good time," he said and took my hand. "All in good time," and I let him lead me toward the eager shadows crouched at the other end of the hallway.

Near the end of his book, Emmanuel Weatherby-Jones writes, "The calamities following, and following from, the return of the IcePIC probe may stand as mankind's gravest defeat. For long millennia, we had asked ourselves if we were alone in the cosmos. Indeed, that question has surely formed much of the fundamental matter of the world's religions. But when finally answered, once and for all, we were forced to accept that there had been greater comfort in our former, vanished ignorance."

We are more alone than ever. Ronnie got that part right.

When I'd backed out of the contact and the techs had a solid lockdown on the critter's signal, when the containment waves were pinging crystal mad off the putrescent walls of the bedroom on Columbus and one of the medics had administered a stimulant to clear my head and bring me the rest of the way home, I sat down on the floor and cried.

Nothing unusual about that. I've cried almost every single time. At least I didn't puke.

"Good job," Templeton said and rested a heavy gloved hand on my shoulder.

"Fuck you. I could hear them. I could hear both of them, you asshole."

"We did what we could, Deet. I couldn't have you so tanked on morphine you'd end up flatlining."

"Oh my god. Oh Jesus god," I sobbed like an old woman, gasping, my heart racing itself round smaller and smaller circles, fried to a crisp on the big syringe full of synthetadrine the medic had pumped into my left arm. "Kill it, Temp. You kill it right this fucking instant."

"We have to stick to protocol," he said calmly, staring down at the writhing mass of bone and meat and protoplasm on the bed. A blood-red tendril slithered from the place where the man's mouth had been and began burrowing urgently into the sagging mattress. "Just as soon as we have you debriefed and we're sure stasis is holding, then we'll terminate life signs."

"Fuck it," I said and reached for his Beretta, tearing the pistol from the velcro straps of the holster with enough force that Temp almost fell over on top of me. I shoved him aside and aimed at the thing on the bed.

"Deet, don't you even fucking think about pulling that trigger!"

"You can go straight to hell," I whispered, to Templeton, to the whole goddamn Agency, to the spooch and that single hurting blue eye still watching me. I squeezed the trigger, emptying the whole clip into what little was left of the man and woman's swollen skulls, hoping it would be enough.

Then someone grabbed for the gun and I let them take it from me.

"You stupid motherfucker," Temp growled. "You goddamn stupid bastard. As soon as this job is finished, you are out. Do you fucking understand me, Deet? You are history!"

"Yeah," I replied and sat back down on the floor. In the silence left after the roar of the gun, the containment waves pinged and my ears rang and the yellow fog settled over me like a shroud.

At least, that's the way I like to pretend it all went down. Late at night, when I can't sleep, when the pills and booze aren't enough, I like to imagine there was one moment in my wasted, chicken-shit life when I did what I should have done.

Whatever really happened, I'm sure someone's already written it down somewhere. I don't have to do it again.

In the cluttered little room at the end of the third-floor hallway, the woman with a cat's face and nervous, twitching ears sat near a hole that had been a window before the mortars. There was no light but the dim winter sun. The boy sat at her feet and never took his eyes off me. The woman—if she had a name, I never learned it—only looked at me once, when I first entered the room. The fire in her eyes made short work of whatever resolve I had left and I was glad when she turned back to the hole in the wall and stared north across the river toward the Astoria refineries.

She told me the girl had left a week earlier. She didn't have any idea where Jet Miyake might have gone.

"She brings food and medicine, sometimes," the woman said, confirming what I'd already suspected. Back then, there were a lot of people willing to risk prison or death to get supplies to Roosevelt Island. Maybe there still are. I couldn't say.

"I'm sorry to hear about her parents."

"It was quick," I lied. "They didn't suffer."

"You smell like death, Mr. Paine," the woman said, flaring her nostrils slightly. The boy at her feet laughed and hugged himself, rocking from side to side. "I think it follows you. I believe you herald death."

"Yeah, I think the same thing myself sometimes," I replied.

"You hunt the aliens?" she purred.

"That's one way of looking at it."

"There's a certain irony, don't you think? Our world was dying. We poisoned our world and then went looking for life somewhere else. Do you think we found what we were looking for, Mr. Paine?"

"No," I told her. "I don't think we ever will."

"Go back to the city, Mr. Paine. Go now. You won't be safe after sunset. Some of us are starving. Some of our children are starving."

I thanked her and left the room. The boy followed me as far as the stairs, then he stopped and sat chuckling to himself, his laughter echoing through the stairwell, as I moved slowly, step by blind step, through the uncertain darkness. I retraced my path to the street, following Main to East, past the wild places, through the canyons, and didn't look back until I was standing on the bridge again.

I found Jet Miyake in Chinatown two days later, hiding out in the basement of the Buddhist Society of Wonderful Enlightenment on Madison Street. The Agency had files on a priest there, demonstrating a long history of prostitch sentiment. Jet Miyake ran, because they always run if they can, and I chased her, down Mechanics Alley, across Henry, and finally caught up with her in a fish market on East Broadway, beneath the old Manhattan Bridge. She tried to lose me in the maze of kiosks, the glistening mounds of octopus and squid, eel and tuna and cod laid out on mountains of crushed ice. She headed for a back door and almost made it, but slipped on the wet concrete floor and went sprawling ass over tits into a big display of dried soba and canned chicken broth. I don't actually remember all those details, just the girl and the stink of fish, the clatter of the cans on the cement, the angry, frightened shouts from the merchants and customers. But the details, the octopus and soba noodles, I don't know. I think I'm trying to forget this isn't fiction, that it happened, that I'm not making it up as I go along. That I played any part in it.

Sometimes.

Sometimes I'm a savage.

I held the muzzle of my pistol to her right temple while I ran the scan. She gritted her teeth and stared silently up at me. The machine read her dirty as the gray New York snow, though I didn't need the blinking red light on the genetigraph to tell me that. She was hurting, the way only long-term carriers can hurt. I could see it in her eyes, in the sweat streaming down her face, in the faintly bluish tinge of her lips. She'd probably been contaminated for months. I knew it'd be a miracle if she'd infected no one but her parents. I showed her the display screen on the genetigraph and told her what it meant, and I told her what I had to do next.

"You can't stop it, you know," she said, smiling a bitter, sickly smile. "No matter how many people you kill, it's too late. It's been too late from the start."

"I'm sorry," I said, whether I actually was or not, and squeezed the trigger. The 9mm boomed like thunder in a bottle and suddenly she wasn't my problem anymore. Suddenly she was just another carcass for the sweepers.

I have become an unreliable narrator. Maybe I've been an unreliable narrator all along. Just like I've been a coward and a hypocrite all along. The things we would rather remember, the things we choose to forget. As the old saying goes, it's only a movie.

I didn't kill Jet Miyake.

"You can't stop it, you know," she said. That part's the truth. "No matter how many people you kill, it's too late. It's been too late from the start."

"I'm sorry," I said.

"We brought it here. We invited it in, and it likes what it sees. It means to stay." She did smile, but it was a satisfied, secret smile. I stepped back and lowered the muzzle of the gun. The bore had left a shallow, circular impression on her skin.

"Please step aside, Mr. Paine," Sarah said and when I turned around she was standing just a few feet behind me, pointing a ridiculously small carbon-black Glock at the girl. Sarah fired twice and waited until the body stopped convulsing, then put a third bullet in Jet Miyake's head, just to be sure. Sarah had always been thorough.

"Templeton thought you might get cold feet," she said and stepped past me, kneeling to inspect the body. "You know this means that you'll probably be suspended."

"She was right, wasn't she?" I muttered. "Sooner or later, we're going to lose this thing," and for a moment I considered putting a few rounds into Sarah's skull, pulling the trigger and spraying brains and blood and silicon across the floor of the fish market. It might have been a mercy killing. But I suppose I didn't love her quite as much as I'd always thought. Besides, the Agency would have probably just picked up the pieces and stuck her back together again.

"One day at a time, Mr. Paine," she said. "That's the only way to stay sane. One day at a time."

"No past, no future."

"If that's the way you want to look at it."

She stood up and held out a hand. I popped the clip from my pistol and gave her the gun and the ammo. I removed the genetigraph from my belt and she took that, too.

"We'll send someone to the hotel for the rest of your equipment. Please have everything in order. You have your ticket back to Los Angeles."

"Yes," I said. "I have my ticket back to Los Angeles."

"You lasted a lot longer than I thought you would," she said.

And I left her there, standing over the girl's body, calling in the kill, ordering the sweeper crew. The next day I flew back to LA and found a bar where I was reasonably sure no one would recognize me. I started with tequila, moved on to scotch, and woke up two days later, facedown in the sand at Malibu, sick as a dog. The sun was setting, brewing a firestorm on the horizon, and I watched the stars come out above the sea. A meteor streaked across the sky and was gone. It only took me a moment to find Jupiter, Lord of the Heavens, Gatherer of Clouds, hardly more than a bright pinprick near the moon.

falling star

BRENDAN DUBOIS

We like to compliment ourselves on the bright, tidy rationality of our technological civilization, but the fact is, as the powerful story that follows demonstrates, that technological civilization is fragile, easy to break—and, once broken, the Old Days and the Old Ways, with all of their bigotry, intolerance, and fear are waiting to sweep in again . . . miring and dragging down even those who've always had their eyes on the stars.

Brendan DuBois has twice received the Shamus Award from the Private Eye Writers of America, and has been nominated three times for the Edgar Allan Poe Award given by the Mystery Writers of America. He's made sales to *Playboy, Ellery Queen's Mystery Magazine, Alfred Hitchcock's Mystery Magazine, Space Stations, Civil War Fantastic, Pharaoh Fantastic, Knight Fantastic, The Mutant Files*, and *Alternate Gerrysburgs*, among other markets. His mystery novels include the "Lewis Cole" series, *Dead Sand, Black Tide, Shattered Shell, Killer Waves*, and *Buried Dreams*. His SF novels include *Resurrection Day* and *Six Days*. His most recent novel is the suspense thriller *Betrayed*. He lives in Exeter, New Hampshire, with his family, and maintains a Web site at www.brendandubois.com.

On a late July day in Boston Falls, New Hampshire, Rick Monroe, the oldest resident of the town, sat on a park bench in the town common, waiting for the grocery and mail wagon to appear from Greenwich. The damn thing was supposed to arrive at two PM, but the Congregational Church clock had just chimed three times and the road from Greenwich remained empty. Four horses and a wagon were hitched up to the post in front of the Boston Falls General Store, some bare-chested kids were playing in the dirt road, and flies were buzzing around his face.

He stretched out his legs, saw the dirt stains at the bottom of the old overalls. Mrs. Chandler, his once-a-week house cleaner, was again doing a lousy job with the laundry, and he knew he should say something to her, but he was reluctant to do it. Having a cleaning woman was a luxury and a bad cleaning woman was better than no cleaning woman at all. Even if she was a snoop and sometimes raided his icebox and frowned whenever she reminded him of the weekly church services.

Some of the kids shouted and started running up the dirt road. He sat up, shaded his eyes with a shaking hand. There, coming down slowly, two tired horses pulling the wagon that had high wooden sides and a canvas top. He waited as the wagon pulled into the store, waited still until it was unloaded. There was really no rush, no rush at all. Let the kids have their excitement, crawling in and around the wagon. When the wagon finally pulled out, heading to the next town over, Jericho, he slowly got up, wincing as his hips screamed at him. He went across the cool grass and then the dirt road, and up to the wooden porch. The children moved away from him, except for young Tom Cooper, who stood there, eyes wide open. Glen Roundell, the owner of the General Store and one of the town's three selectmen, came up to him with a paper sack and a small packet of envelopes, tied together with an piece of twine.

"Here you go, Mister Monroe," he said, his voice formal, wearing a starched white shirt, black tie, and white store apron that reached the floor. "Best we can do this week. No beef, but there is some bacon there. Should keep if you get home quick enough."

"Thanks, Glen," he said. "On account, all right?"

Glen nodded. "That's fine."

He turned to step off the porch, when a man appeared out of the shadows. Henry Cooper, Tom's father, wearing a checked flannel shirt and blue jeans, his thick black beard down to midchest. "Would you care for a ride back to your place, Mister Monroe?"

He shifted the bag in his hands, smiled. "Why, that would be grand." And he was glad that Henry had not come into town with his wife, Marcia, for even though she was quite active in the church, she had some very un-Christian thoughts toward her neighbors, especially an old man like Rick Monroe, who kept to himself and wasn't a churchgoer.

Rick followed Henry and his boy outside, and he clambered up on the rear, against a couple of wooden boxes and a barrel. Henry said, "You can sit up front, if you'd like," and Rick said, "No, that's your boy's place. He can stay up there with you."

Henry unhitched his two-horse team, and in a few minutes, they were heading out on the Town Road, also known as New Hampshire Route 12. The rear of the wagon jostled and was bumpy, but he was glad he didn't have to walk it. It sometimes took him nearly an hour to walk from home to the center of town, and he remembered again—like he had done so many times—how once in his life it only took him ninety minutes to travel thousands of miles.

He looked again at the town common, at the stone monuments clustered there, commemorating the war dead from Boston Falls, those who had fallen in the Civil War, Spanish-American War, World Wars I and II, Korea, Vietnam, and even the first and second Gulf Wars. Then, the town common was out of view, as the horse and wagon made its way out of a small New Hampshire village, hanging on in the sixth decade of the twenty-first century.

When the wagon reached his home, Henry and his boy came down to help him, and Henry said, "Can I bring some water out for the horses? It's a dreadfully hot day," and Rick said, "Of course, go right ahead." Henry nodded and said, "Tom, you help Mister Monroe in with his groceries. You do that."

"Yes, sir," the boy said, taking the bag from his hands, and he was embarrassed at how he enjoyed being helped. The inside of the house was cool—but not cool enough, came a younger voice from inside, a voice that said, remember when you could set a switch and have it cold enough to freeze your toes?—and he walked into the dark kitchen, past the coal-burning stove. From the grocery sack he took out a few canned goods—their labels in black and white, glued sloppily on—and the waxed paper with the bacon inside. He went to the icebox, popped it open quickly, and shut it. Tom was there, looking on, gazing around the room, and he knew what the boy was looking at: the framed photos of the time when Rick was younger and stronger, just like the whole damn country.

"Tom?"

"Yessir?"

"Care for a treat?"

Tom scratched at his dirty face with an equally dirty hand. "Momma said I shouldn't take anything from strangers. Not ever."

Rick said, "Well, boy, how can you say I'm a stranger? I live right down the road from you, don't I."

"Unh-hunh."

"Then we're not strangers. You sit right there and don't move."

Tom clambered up on a wooden kitchen chair and Rick went over to the counter, opened up the silverware drawer, took out a spoon. Back to the icebox he went, this time opening up the freezer compartment, and he quickly pulled out a small white coffee cup with a broken handle. He placed the cold coffee cup down on the kitchen table and gave the boy the spoon.

"Here, dig in," he said.

Tom looked curious but took the spoon and scraped against the icelike confection in the bottom of the cup. He took a taste and his face lit up, like a lightbulb behind a dirty piece of parchment. The next time the spoon came up, it was nearly full, and Tom quickly ate everything in the cup, and then licked the spoon and tried to lick the inside of the cup.

"My, that was good!" he said. "What was it, Mister Monroe?"

"Just some lemonade and sugar, frozen up. Not bad, hunh?

"It was great! Um, do you have any more? Sir?"

Rick laughed, thinking of how he had made it this morning, for a dessert after dinner. Not for a boy not even ten, but so what? "No, 'fraid not. But come back tomorrow. I might have some then, if I can think about it."

At the kitchen sink he poured water into the cup, and the voice returned. *Why not,* it said. *Tell the boy what he's missing. Tell him how it was like, back when a kid his age would laugh rather than eat frozen, sugary lemonade. That with the change in his pocket, he could walk outside and meet up with an ice-cream cart that sold luxuries unknown today in the finest restaurants. Tell him that, why don't you?*

He coughed and turned, saw Tom was looking up again at the photos. "Mister Monroe . . ."

"Yes?"

"Mister Monroe, did you really go to the stars? Did you?"

Rick smiled, glad to see the curiosity in the boy's face, and not fear. "Well, I guess I got as close as anyone could, back then. You see—"

The boy's father yelled from outside. "Tom! Time to go! Come on out!"

Rick said, "Guess you have to listen to your dad, son. Tell you what, next time you come back, I'll tell you everything you want to know. Deal?"

The boy nodded and ran out of the kitchen. His hips were still aching and he thought about lying down before going through the mail, but he made his way outside, where Tom was up on the wagon. Henry came up and offered his hand, and Rick shook it, glad that Henry wasn't one to try the strength test with someone as old as he. Henry said, "Have a word with you, Mister Monroe?"

"Sure," he said. "But only if you call me Rick."

From behind the thick beard, he thought he could detect a smile. "All right . . . Rick."

They both sat down on old wicker rocking chairs and Henry said, "I'll get right to it, Rick."

"Okay."

"There's a town meeting tonight. I think you should go."

"Why?"

"Because . . . well, there's some stirrings. That's all. About a special committee being set up. A morals committee, to ensure that only the right people live here in Boston Falls."

"And who decides who are the right people?" he asked, finding it hard to believe this conversation was actually taking place.

Henry seemed embarrassed. "The committee and the selectmen, I guess . . . you see, there's word down south, about some of the towns there, they still got trouble with refugees and transients rolling in from Connecticut and New York. Some of those towns, the natives, they're being overwhelmed, outvoted, and they're not the same anymore. And since you, um—"

"I was born here, Henry. You know that. Just because I lived someplace else for a long time, that's held against me?"

"Well, I'm just sayin' it's not going to help . . . with what you did back then, and the fact you don't go to church, and other things, well . . . it might be worthwhile if you go there. That's all. To defend yourself."

Even with the hot weather, Rick was feeling a cold touch upon his hands. *Now we're really taking a step back, he thought. Like the Nuremberg laws, in Nazi Germany. Ensuring that only the ethnically and racially pure get to vote, to shop, to live . . .*

"And if this committee decides you don't belong? What then? Arrested? Exiled? Burned at the stake?"

Now his neighbor looked embarrassed as he stepped up from the wicker chair. "You should just be there, Mister uh, I mean, Rick. It's at eight o'clock. At the town hall."

"That's a long walk in, when it's getting dark. Any chance I could get a ride?"

Even with his neighbor's back turned to him, Rick could sense the humiliation. "Well, I, well, I don't think so, Rick. I'm sorry. You see, I think Marcia wants to visit her sister after the meeting, and I don't know what time we might get back, and, well, I'm sorry."

Henry climbed up into the wagon, retrieved the reins from his son, and Rick called out. "Henry?"

"Yes?"

"Any chance your wife is on this committee?"

The expression on his neighbor's face was all he needed to know, as the wagon turned around on his brown lawn and headed back up to the road.

Back inside, he grabbed his mail and went upstairs, to the spare bedroom that he had converted into an office during the first year he had made it back to Boston Falls. He went to unlock the door and found that it was already open. Damn his memory, which he knew was starting to show its age, just like his hips. He was certain he had locked it the last time. He sat down at the desk and untied the twine, knowing he would save it. What was that old Yankee saying? Use it up, wear it out, or do without? Heavy thrift, one of the many lessons being relearned these years.

One envelope he set aside to bring into Glen Roundell, the General Store owner. It was his Social Security check, only three months late, and Glen—who was also the town's banker—would take it and apply it against Rick's account. Not much being made for sale nowadays, so whatever tiny amount his Social Security check was this month was usually enough to keep his account in good shape.

There was an advertising flyer for the Grafton County Fair, set to start next week. Another flyer announcing a week-long camp revival at the old Boy Scout camp on Conway Lake, during the same time. Competition, no doubt. And a thin envelope, postmarked Houston, Texas, which he was happy to see. It had only taken a month for the envelope to get here, which he thought was a good sign. Maybe some things were improving in the country.

Maybe.

He slit open the envelope with an old knife, saw the familiar handwriting inside.

Dear Rick,

Hope this sees you doing well in the wilds of New Hampshire.

Down here what passes for recovery continues. Last month, two whole city blocks had their power restored. It only comes on for a couple of hours a day, and no a/c is allowed, but it's still progress, eh?

Enclosed are the latest elements for Our Boy. I'm sorry to say the orbit degradation is continuing. Latest guess is that Our Boy may be good for another five years, maybe six.

Considering what was spent in blood and treasure to put him up there, it breaks my heart.

If you get bored and lonely up there, do consider coming down here. I understand that with Amtrak coming back, it should only take four weeks to get here. The heat is awful but at least you'll be in good company with those of us who still remember.

Your pal,

Brian

With the handwritten sheet was another sheet of paper, with a listing of dates and times, and he shook his head in dismay. Most of the sightings were for early mornings, and he hated getting up in the morning. But tonight—how fortunate!—there was going to be a sighting at just after eight o'clock.

Eight o'clock. Why did that sound familiar?

Now he remembered. The town meeting tonight, where supposedly his fate and those of any other possible sinners was to be decided. He carefully folded up the letter, put it back in the envelope. He decided one more viewing was more important, more important than whatever chatter session was going to happen later. And besides, knowing what he did about the town and its politics, the decision had already been made.

He looked around his small office, with the handmade bookshelves and books, and more framed photos on the cracked plaster wall. One of the photos was of him and his friend, Brian Poole, wearing blue-zippered jumpsuits, standing in front of something large and complex, built ages ago in the swamps of Florida.

"Thanks, guy," he murmured, and he got up and went downstairs, to think of what might be for dinner.

Later that night he was in the big backyard, a pasture that he let his other neighbor, George Thompson, mow for hay a couple of times each summer, for which George gave him some venison and smoked ham over the long winters in exchange. He brought along a folding lawn chair, its bright plastic cracked and faded away, and he sat there, stretching out his legs. It was a quiet night, like every night since he had come here, years ago. He smiled in the darkness. What strange twists of fate and fortune had brought him back here, to his old family farm. He had grown up here, until his dad had moved the family south, to a suburb of Boston, and from there, high school and Air Force ROTC, and then many, many years traveling, thousands upon thousands of miles, hardly ever thinking about the old family farm, now owned by a second or third family. And he would have never come back here, until the troubles started, when—

A noise made him turn his head. Something crackling out there, in the underbrush.

"Who's out there?" he called out, wondering if some of the more hot-blooded young'uns in town had decided not to wait until the meeting was over. "Come out and show yourself."

A shape came out from the wood line, ambled over, small, and then there was a young boy's voice, "Mister Monroe, it's me, Tom Cooper."

"Tom? Oh, yes, Tom. Come on over here."

The young boy came up, sniffling some, and Rick said, "Tom, you gave me a bit of a surprise. What can I do for you?"

Tom stood next to him, and said slowly, "I was just wondering . . . well, that cold stuff you gave me earlier, that tasted really good. I didn't know if you had any more left . . ."

He laughed. "Sorry, guy. Maybe tomorrow. How come you're not with your mom and dad at the meeting?"

Tom said, "My sister Ruth is supposed to be watching us, but I snuck out of my room and came here. I was bored."

"Well, boredom can be good, it means something will happen. Tell you what, Tom, wait a couple of minutes, I'll show you something special."

"What's that?"

"You just wait and I'll show you."

Rick folded his hands together in his lap, looked over at the southeast. Years and years ago, that part of the night sky would be a light yellow glow, the lights from the cities in that part of the state. Now, like every other part of the night sky, there was just blackness and the stars, the night sky now back where it had once been, almost two centuries ago.

There. Right there. A dot of light, moving up and away from the horizon.

"Take a look, Tom. See that moving light?"

"Unh-hunh."

"Good. Just keep your eye on it. Look at it go."

The solid point of light rose up higher and seemed brighter, and he found his hands were tingling and his chest was getting tighter. Oh, God, how beautiful, how beautiful it had been up there, looking down on the great globe, watching the world unfold beneath you, slow and majestic and lovely, knowing that as expensive and ill-designed and overbudget and late in being built, it was there, the first permanent outpost for humanity, the first step in reaching out to the planets and stars that were humanity's destiny . . .

The crickets seemed louder. An owl out in the woods hoo-hoo'ed, and beside him, Tom said, "What is it, Mister Monroe?"

The light seemed to fade some, and then it disappeared behind some tall pines, and Rick found that his eyes had gotten moist. He wiped at them and said, "What do you think it was?"

"I dunno. I sometimes see lights move at night, and Momma tells me that it's the Devil's work, and I shouldn't look at 'em. Is that true?"

He rubbed at his chin, thought for a moment about just letting the boy be, letting him grow up with his illusions and whatever misbegotten faith his mother had put in his head, letting him think about farming and hunting and fishing, to concentrate on what was real, what was necessary, which was getting enough food to eat and a warm place and—

No! the voice inside him shouted. *No, that's not fair, to condemn this boy and the others to a life of peasantry, just because of some wrong things that had been done, years before the child was even born.* He shook his head and said, "Well, I can see why some people would think it's the Devil's work, but the truth is, Tom, that was a building up there. A building made by men and women and put up in the sky, more than a hundred miles up."

Tom sounded skeptical. "Then how come it doesn't fall down?"

Great, the voice said. *Shall we give him a lecture about Newton? What do you suggest?*

He thought for a moment and said, "It's complex, and I don't want to bore you, Tom. But trust me, it's up there. In fact, it's still up there and will be for a while. Even though nobody's living in it right now."

Tom looked up and said, "Where is it now?"

"Oh, I imagine it's over Canada by now. You see, it goes around the whole globe in what's called an orbit. Only takes about ninety minutes or so."

Tom seemed to think about that and said shyly, "My dad. He once said you were something. A spaceman. That you went to the stars. Is that true?"

"True enough. We never made it to the stars, though we sure thought about it a lot."

"He said you flew up in the air. Like a bird. And the places you went, high enough, you had to carry your own air with you. Is that true, too?"

"Yes, it is."

"Jeez. You know, my momma, well . . ."

"Your momma, she doesn't quite like me, does she?"

"Unh-hunh. She says you're not good. You're unholy. And some other stuff."

Rick thought about telling the boy the truth about his mother, decided it could wait until the child got older. God willing, the boy would learn soon enough about his mother. Aloud Rick said, "I'm going back to my house. Would you like to get something?"

"Another cold treat?" came the hopeful voice.

"No, not tonight. Maybe tomorrow. Tonight, well, tonight I want to give you something that'll last longer than any treat."

A few minutes later they were up in his office, Tom talking all the while about the fishing he had done so far this summer, the sleep-outs in the back pasture, and about his cousin Lloyd, who lived in the next town over, Hancock, and who died of something called polio. Rick shivered at the matter-of-fact way Tom had mentioned his cousin's death. A generation ago, a death like that never would have happened. Hell, a generation ago, if somebody of Tom's age had died, the poor kid would have been shoved into counseling sessions and group therapies, trying to get closure about the damn thing. And now? Just part of growing up.

In his office Tom oohed and aaahed over the photos on his wall, and Rick explained as best he could what they were about. "Well, that's the dot of light we just saw. It's actually called a space station. Over there, that's what you used to fly up to the space station. It's called a space shuttle. Or a rocket, if you prefer. This . . . this is a picture of me, up in the space station."

"Really?" Tom asked. "You were really there?"

He found he had to sit down, so he did, his damn hips aching something fierce.

"Yes, I was really up there. One of the last people up there, to tell you the truth, Tom. Just before, well . . . just before everything changed."

Tom stood before a beautiful photo of a full moon, the craters and mountains and flat seas looking as sharp as if they were made yesterday. He said, "Momma said that it was God who punished the world back then, because men were evil, because they ignored God. Is that true, Mister Monroe? What really happened back then?"

His fists suddenly clenched, as if powered by memory. Where to begin, young man, he thought. Where to begin. Let's talk about a time when computers were in everything, from your car to your toaster to your department store cash register. Everything linked up and interconnected. And when the systems got more and more complex, the childish ones, the vandals, the destructive hackers, they had to prove that they had the knowledge and skills and wherewithal to take down a system. Oh, the defenses grew stronger and stronger, as did the viruses, and the evil ones redoubled their efforts, like the true Vandals coming into Rome, burning and destroying something that somebody else created. The defenses grew more in-depth, the attacks more determined until one bright soul—if such a creature could be determined to have a soul—came up with ultimate computer virus. No, not one that wormed its way into software through backdoors or anything fancy like that. No sir. This virus was one that attacked the hardware, the platforms, that spread God knows how—theories ranged from human touch to actual impulses over fiber optics—and destroyed the chips. That's all. Just ate the chips and left burned-out crumbs behind, so that in days, almost every thing in the world that used a computer was silent, dark, and dead.

Oh, he was a smart one—for the worst of the hackers were always male—whoever he was, and Rick often wished that the designer of the ultimate virus (called the Final Virus, for a very good reason) had been on an aircraft or an operating room table when it had struck. For when the computers sputtered out and died, the chaos that was unleashed upon the world . . . cars, buses, trains, trucks. Dead, not moving. Hundreds of thousands of people, stranded far from home. Aircraft falling out of the skies. Ships at sea, slowly drifting, unable to maneuver. Stock markets, banks, corporations, everything and anything that stored the wealth of a nation in electronic impulses, silent. All the interconnections that fed and clothed and fueled and protected and sheltered most of the world's billions had snapped apart, like brittle rubber bands. Within days the cities had become uninhabitable, as millions streamed into the countryside. Governments wavered and collapsed. Communications were sparse, for networks and radio stations and the cable stations were off the air as well. Rumors and fear spread like a plague itself, and the Four Horsemen of the Apocalypse—called out from retirement at last—swept through almost the entire world.

There were a few places that remained untouched: Antarctica and a few remote islands. But for the rest of the world . . . sometimes the only light on the nightside of the planet were the funeral pyres, where the bodies were being burned.

He grew nauseous, remembering what had happened to him and how it took him months to walk back here, to his childhood home, and he repressed the memory of eating something a farmer had offered him—it hadn't looked exactly like dog, but God, he had been so hungry—and he looked over to young Tom. How could he even begin to tell such a story to such an innocent lad?

He wouldn't. He composed himself and said, "No, God didn't punish us back then. We did. It was a wonderful world, Tom, a wonderful place. It wasn't perfect and many people did ignore God, did ignore many good things . . . but we did things. We fed people and cured them and some of us, well, some of us planned to go to the stars."

He went up to the wall, took down the picture of the International Space Station, the Big Boy himself, and pointed it out to Tom. "Men and women built that on the ground, Tom, and brought it up into space. They did it for good, to learn things, to start a way for us to go back to the Moon and to Mars. To explore. There was no evil there. None."

Tom looked at the picture and said, "And that's the dot of light we saw? Far up in the sky?"

"Yes."

"And what's going to happen to it?"

He looked at the framed photo, noticed his hands shaking some. He put the photo back up on the wall. "One of these days, it's going to get lower and lower. It just happens. Things up in orbit can't stay up there forever. Unless somebody can go up there and do something . . . it'll come crashing down."

He sat down in the chair, winced again at the shooting pains in his hips. There was a time when he could have had new hips, new knees, or—if need be—new kidneys, but it was going to take a long time for those days to ever come back. From his infrequent letters from Brian, he knew that work was still continuing in some isolated and protected labs, to find an answer to the Final Virus. But with people starving and cities still unlit, most of the whole damn country had fallen back to the late 1800s, when power was provided by muscles, horses, or steam. Computers would just have to wait.

Tom said, "I hope it doesn't happen, Mister Monroe. It sounds really cool."

Rick said, "Well, maybe when you grow up, if you're really smart, you can go up there and fix it. And think about me when you're doing it. Does that sound like fun?"

The boy nodded and Rick remembered why he had brought the poor kid up here. He got out of his chair, went over to his bookshelf, started moving around the thick volumes and such, until he found a slim book, a book he had bought once for a future child, for one day he had promised Kathy Meserve that once he left the astronaut corps, he would marry her. . . . Poor Kathy, in London on a business trip, whom he had never seen or heard from ever again after the Final Virus had broken out.

He came over to Tom and gave him the book. It was old but the cover was still bright, and it said, *My First Book on Space Travel*. Rick said, "You can read, can't you?"

"Unh-hunh, I sure can."

"Okay." He rubbed at the boy's head, not wanting to think of Kathy Meserve or the children he never had. "You take this home and read it. You can learn a lot about the stars and planets and what it was like, to explore space and build the first space station. Maybe you can get back up there, Tom." Or your children's children, he thought, but why bring that depressing thought up. "Maybe you can be what I was, a long time ago."

Tom's voice was solemn. "A star man?"

Rick shook his head. "No, nothing fancy like that. An astronaut. That's all. Look, it's getting late. Why don't you head home."

And the young boy ran from his office, holding the old book in his hands, as if scared Rick was going to change his mind and take it away from him.

It was the sound of the horses that woke him, neighing and moving about in his yard, early in the morning. He got out of bed, cursed his stiff joints, and slowly got dressed. At the foot of the bed was a knapsack, for he knew a suitcase would not work. He picked up the knapsack—which he had put together last night—and walked downstairs, walked slowly, as he noticed the woodwork and craftsmanship that a long forgotten great-great-great grandfather had put into building this house, which he was now leaving.

He went out on the front porch, shaded his eyes from the hot morning sun. There were six or seven horses in his front yard, three horse-drawn wagons, and a knot of people in front. Some children were clustered out under the maple tree by the road, their parents no doubt telling them to stay away. He recognized all of the faces in the crowd, but was pleased to see that Glen Roundell, the store owner and one of the three selectmen, was not there, nor was Henry Cooper. Henry's wife Marcia was there, thin-lipped and perpetually angry, and she strode forward, holding something at her side. She wore a long cotton skirt and long-sleeve shirt—and that insistent voice inside his head wondered why again, with technology having tumbled two hundred years, why did fashion have to follow suit?—and she announced loudly, "Rick Monroe, you know why we're here, don't you."

"Mrs. Cooper, I'm sure I have some idea, but why don't you inform me, in case I'm mistaken. I know that of your many fine attributes, correcting the mistakes of others is your finest."

She looked around the crowd, as if seeking their support, and she pressed on, even though there was a smile or two at his comment. "At a special town meeting last night, it was decided by a majority of the town to suspend your residency here, in Boston Falls, due to your past crimes and present immorality."

"Crimes?" In the crowd he noticed a man in a faded and patched uniform, and he said, "Chief Godin. You know me. What crimes have I committed?"

Chief Sam Godin looked embarrassed. A kid of about twenty-two or thereabouts, he was the Chief because he had strong hands and was a good shot. The uniform shirt he wore was twice as old as he was, but he wore it proudly, since it represented his office.

Today, though, he looked like he would rather be wearing anything else. He seemed to blush and said, "Gee, Mister Monroe . . . no crimes here, since you've moved back. But there's been talk of what you did, back then before . . . before the change. You were a scientist or something. Worked with computers. Maybe had something to do with the change, that's the kind of crimes that we were thinking about."

Rick sighed. "Very good. That's the crime I've been accused of, of being educated. That I can accept. But immoral? Where's your proof?"

"Right here," Marcia Cooper said triumphantly. "See? This old magazine, with depraved photos and lustful woman . . . kept in your house, to show any youngster that came by. Do you deny having this in your possession?"

And despite it all, he felt like laughing, for Mrs. Cooper was holding up—and holding up tight so nothing inside would be shown, of course—an ancient copy of *Playboy* magazine. The damn thing had been in his office, and sometimes he would just glance though the slick pages and sigh at a world—and a type of woman—long gone. Then something came to him and he saw another woman in the crowd, arms folded tight, staring in distaste toward him. It all clicked.

"No, I don't deny it," Rick said, "and I also don't deny that Mrs. Chandler, for once in her life, did a good job cleaning my house. Find anything else in there, Mrs. Chandler, you'd like to pass on to your neighbors?"

She just glared, said nothing. He looked up at the sun. It was going to be another hot day.

The chief stepped forward and said, "We don't want any trouble, Mister Monroe. But it's now the law. You have to leave."

He picked up his knapsack, shrugged his arms through the frayed straps, almost gasped at the heavy weight back there. "I know."

The Chief said, "If you want, I can get you a ride to one of the next towns over, save you—"

"No," he said, not surprised at how harshly he responded. "No, I'm not taking any of your damn charity. By God, I walked into this town alone years ago, and I'll walk out of this town alone as well."

Which is what he started to do, coming down the creaky steps, across the unwatered lawn. The crowd in front of him slowly gave way, like they were afraid he was infected or some damn thing. He looked at their dirty faces, the ignorant looks, the harsh stares, and he couldn't help himself. He stopped and said, "You know, I pity you. If it hadn't been for some unknown clown, decades ago, you wouldn't be here. You'd be on a powerboat in a lake. You'd be in an airconditioned mall, shopping. You'd be talking to each other over frozen drinks about where to fly to vacation this winter. That's what you'd be doing."

Marcia Cooper said, "It was God's will. That's all."

Rick shook his head. "No, it was some idiot's will, and because of that, you've grown up to be peasants. God save you and your children."

They stayed silent, but he noticed that some of the younger men were looking fidgety, and were glancing to the chief, like they were wondering if the chief would intervene if they decided to stone him or some damn thing. Time to get going, and he tried not to think of the long miles that were waiting for him. Just one step after another, that's all. Maybe, if his knees and hips held together, he could get to the train station in Concord. Maybe. Take Brian up on his offer. He made it out to the dirt road, decided to head left, up to Greenwich, for he didn't want to walk through town. Why tempt fate?

He turned and looked one last time at his house, and then looked over to the old maple tree, where some of the children, bored by what had been going on, were now scurrying around the tree trunk.

But not all of the children.

One of them was by himself, at the road's edge. He looked nervous, and he raised his shirt, and even at this distance, he could make out young Tom Cooper, standing there, his gift of a book hidden away in the waistband of his jeans. Tom lowered his shirt and then waved, and Rick, surprised, smiled and waved back.

And then he turned his back on his home and his town, and started walking away.

The Dragons of Summer Gulch

ROBERT REED

"There were giants in the Earth in those days," the Bible tells us, but in the Alternate World that Robert Reed is about to take you to, those giants in the Earth were even stranger, and more powerful, and more *dangerous*, than the dinosaurs who left their bones in the Earth in *our* reality . . .

Robert Reed sold his first story in 1986, and quickly established himself as a frequent contributor to *The Magazine of Fantasy & Science Fiction* and *Asimov's Science Fiction*, as well as selling many stories to *Science Fiction Age, Universe, New Destinies, Tomorrow, Synergy, Starlight*, and elsewhere. Reed may be one of the most prolific of today's young writers, particularly at short-fiction lengths, seriously rivaled for that position only by authors such as Stephen Baxter and Brian Stableford. And—also like Baxter and Stableford—he manages to keep up a very high standard of quality *while* being prolific, something that is not at all easy to do. Reed stories such as "Sister Alice," "Brother Perfect," "Decency," "Savior," "The Remoras," "Chrysalis," "Whiptail," "The Utility Man," "Marrow," "Birth Day," "Blind," "The Toad of Heaven," "Stride," "The Shape of Everything," "Guest of Honor," "Waging Good," and "Killing the Morrow," among at least a half-dozen others equally as strong, count as among some of the best short work produced by anyone in the eighties and nineties; many of his best stories were assembled in his first collection, *The Dragons of Springplace*. Nor is he nonprolific as a novelist, having turned out eight novels since the end of the eighties, including *The Lee Shore, The Hormone Jungle, Black Milk, The Remarkables, Down the Bright Way, Beyond the Veil of Stars, An Exaltation of Larks, Beneath the Gated Sky, Marrow*, and *Sister Alice*. His most recent book is a novella chapbook, *Mere*. Coming up is a new novel, *The Well of Stars*. Reed lives with his family in Lincoln, Nebraska.

1

A hard winter can lift rocks as well as old bones, shoving all that is loose up through the most stubborn earth. Then snowmelt and flash floods will sweep across the ground, wiping away the gravel and clay. And later, when a man with good vision and exceptional luck rides past, all of the world might suddenly change.

"Would you look at that," the man said to himself in a firm, deep voice. "A claw, isn't it? From a mature dragon, isn't it? Good Lord, Mr. Barrow. And there's two more claws set beside that treasure!"

Barrow was a giant fellow with a narrow face and a heavy cap of black hair that grew from his scalp and the back of his neck and between the blades of his strong shoulders. Born on one of the Northern Isles, he had left his homeland as a young man to escape one war, coming to this new country just in time to be thrown into a massive and prolonged civil conflict. Ten thousand miseries had abused him over the next years. But he survived the fighting, and upon his discharge from the Army of the Center, a grateful nation had given him both his citizenship and a bonus of gold coins. Barrow purchased a one-way ticket on the Western railroad, aiming to find his fortune in the wilderness. His journey ended in one of the new prairie towns—a place famous for hyrax herds and dragon bones. There he had purchased a pair of quality camels, ample supplies for six months of solitude, and with shovels enough to move a hillside, he had set out into the washlands.

Sliding off the lead camel, he said, "Hold."

The beast gave a low snort, adjusting its hooves to find the most comfortable pose.

Barrow knelt, carefully touching the dragon's middle claw. Ancient as this artifact was, he knew from painful experience that even the most weathered claw was sharp enough to slash. Just as the fossil teeth could puncture the thickest leather gloves, and the edges of the great scales were nastier than any saw blade sharpened on the hardest whetstone.

The claw was a vivid deep purple color—a sure sign of good preservation. With his favorite little pick, Barrow worked loose the mudstone beneath it, exposing its full length and the place where it joined into the front paw. He wasn't an educated man, but Barrow knew his trade: this had been a flying dragon, one of the monsters that once patrolled the skies above a vanished seacoast. The giant paw was meant for gripping. Presumably the dragons used their four feet much as a coon-rascal does, holding their prey and for other simple manipulations. These finger claws were always valuable, but the thick thumb claw—the Claw of God—would be worth even more to buyers. As night fell, Barrow dug by the smoky light of a little fire, picking away at the mudstone until the paw was revealed—a palm-down hand large enough to stand upon and, after ages of being entombed, still displaying the dull red color made by the interlocking scales.

The man didn't sleep ten blinks. Then with first light he followed a hunch, walking half a dozen long strides up the gully and thrusting a shovel into what looked like a mound of ordinary clay.

The shovel was good steel, but a dull *thunk* announced that something beneath was harder by a long ways.

Barrow used the shovel and a big pickax, working fast and sloppy, investing the morning to uncover a long piece of the dragon's back—several daggerlike spines rising from perhaps thirty big plates of ruddy armor.

Exhaustion forced him to take a break, eating his fill and drinking the last of his water. Then, because they were hungry and a little thirsty, he led both of his loyal camels down the gully, finding a flat plain where sagebrush grew and seepage too foul for a man to drink stood in a shallow alkaline pond.

The happy camels drank and grazed, wandering as far as their long leashes allowed.

Barrow returned to his treasure. Twice he dug into fresh ground, and twice he guessed wrong, finding nothing. The monster's head was almost surely missing. Heads almost always were. But he tried a third time, and his luck held. Not only was the skull entombed along with the rest of the carcass, it was still attached to the body, the long muscular neck having twisted hard to the left as the creature passed from the living.

It had been a quick death, he was certain.

There were larger specimens, but the head was magnificent. What Barrow could see was as long as he was tall, narrow and elegant, a little reminiscent of a pelican's head, but prettier, the giant mouth bristling with a forest of teeth, each tooth bigger than his thumb. The giant dragon eyes had vanished, but the large sockets remained, filled with mudstone and aimed forward like a hawk's eyes. And behind the eyes lay a braincase several times bigger than any man's.

"How did you die?" he asked his new friend.

Back in town, an educated fellow had explained to Barrow what science knew today and what it was guessing. Sometimes the dragons had been buried in mud, on land, or underwater, and the mud protected the corpse from its hungry cousins and gnawing rats. If there were no oxygen, then there couldn't be any rot. And that was the best of circumstances. Without rot, and buried inside a stable deep grave, an entire dragon could be kept intact, waiting for the blessed man to ride by on his happy camel.

Barrow was thirsty enough to moan, but he couldn't afford to stop now.

Following the advice of other prospectors, he found the base of the dragon's twin wings—the wings still sporting the leathery flesh strung between the long, long finger bones—and he fashioned a charge with dynamite, setting it against the armored plates of the back and covering his work with a pile of tamped earth to help force the blast downward. Then, with a long fuse, he set off the charge. There was a dull thud followed by a steady rain of dirt and pulverized stone, and he ran to look at what he had accomplished, pulling back the shattered plates—each worth half a good camel when intact—and then using a heavy pick to pull free the shattered insides of the great beast.

If another dragon had made this corpse, attacking this treasure from below, there would be nothing left to find. Many millions of years ago, the precious guts would have been eaten, and lost.

"But still," Barrow told himself. "These claws and scales are enough to pay for my year. If it comes to that."

But it didn't have to come to that.

Inside the fossil lay the reason for all of his suffering and boredom: behind the stone-infected heart was an intricate organ as long as he was tall—a spongelike thing set above the peculiar dragon lungs. The organ was composed of gold and lustrous platinum wrapped around countless voids: In an instant, Barrow had become as wealthy as his dreams had promised he would be. He let out an enormous yell, dancing back and forth across the back of the dead dragon. Then he collapsed beside his treasure, crying out of joy, and when he wiped back the tears one final time, he saw something else.

Eons ago, a fine black mud had infiltrated the dead body, filling the cavities while keeping away the free oxygen.

Without oxygen, there was almost no decay.

Floating in the old mudstone were at least three round bodies, each as large as the largest naval cannon balls. They were not organs, but they belonged inside the dragon. Barrow had heard stories about such things, and the educated man in town had even shown him a shard of something similar. But where the shard was dirty gray, these three balls were white as bone. That was their color in life, he realized, and this was their color now.

With a trembling hand, Barrow touched the nearest egg, and he held his palm against it for a very long while, leaving it a little bit warm.

2

At one point, the whore asked, "Where did you learn all this crap?"

Manmark laughed quietly for a moment. Then he closed the big book and said, "My credentials. Is that what you wish to have?"

"After your money, sure. Your credentials. Yes."

"As a boy, I had tutors. As a young man, I attended several universities. I studied all the sciences and enjoyed the brilliance of a dozen great minds. And then my father died, and I took my inheritance, deciding to apply my wealth and genius in the pursuit of great things."

She was the prettiest woman of her sort in this town, and she was not stupid. Manmark could tell just by staring at her eyes that she had a good, strong mind. But she was just an aboriginal girl, tiny like all of the members of her race, sold by her father for opium or liquor. Her history had to be impoverished and painful. Which was why it didn't bother him too much when she laughed at him, remarking, "With most men, listening is easier than screwing. But with you, I think it's the other way around."

Manmark opened the book again, ignoring any implied insult.

Quietly, he asked the woman, "Can you read?"

"I know which coin is which," she replied. "And my name, when I see it. If it's written out with a simple hand."

"Look at this picture," he told her. "What does it show you?"

"A dragon," she said matter-of-factly.

"Which species of dragon?" Manmark pressed.

She looked at the drawing, blowing air into her cheeks. Then she exhaled, admitting, "I don't know. Is it the flying kind?"

"Hardly."

"Yeah, I guess it isn't. I don't see wings."

He nodded, explaining, "This is a small early dragon. One of the six-legged precursor species, as it happens. It was unearthed on this continent, resting inside some of the oldest rocks from the Age of Dragons." Manmark was a handsome fellow with dreamy golden eyes that stared off into one of the walls of the room. "If you believe in natural selection and in the great depths of time," he continued, "then this might well be the ancestor to the hundred species that we know about, and the thousands we have yet to uncover."

She said, "Huh," and sat back against the piled-up pillows.

"Can I look at the book?" she asked.

"Carefully," he warned, as if speaking to a moody child. "I don't have another copy with me, and it is the best available guide—"

"Just hand it over," she interrupted. "I promise. I won't be rough."

Slowly, and then quickly, the woman flipped through the pages. Meanwhile, her client continued to speak about things she could never understand: on this very land, there once stood dragons the size of great buildings—placid and heavily armored vegetarians that consumed entire trees, judging by the fossilized meals discovered in their cavernous bellies. Plus there had been smaller beasts roaming in sprawling herds, much as the black hyraxes grazed on the High Plains. The predatory dragons came in two basic types—the quadrupeds with their saber teeth and the Claws of God on their mighty hands; and later, the winged giants with the same teeth and Claws but also grasping limbs and a brain that might well have been equal to a woman's.

If the girl noticed his insult, she knew better than show it, her face down and nodding while the pages turned. At the back of the book were new kinds of bones and odd sketches. "What is this tiny creature?" she inquired.

Manmark asked, "What does it resemble?"

"Some kind of fowl," she admitted.

"But with teeth," he pointed out. "And where are its wings?"

She looked up, almost smiling. "Didn't it have wings? Or haven't you found them yet?"

"I never work with these little creatures," Manmark reported with a prickly tone. "But no, it and its kind never grew particularly large, and they were never genuinely important. Some in my profession believe they became today's birds. But when their bones were first uncovered, the creatures were mistakenly thought to be a variety of running lizard. Which is why those early fossil hunters dubbed them 'monstrous lizards.' "

She turned the page, paused, and then smiled at a particular drawing. "I know this creature," she said, pushing the book across the rumpled sheets. "I've seen a few shrews in my day."

The tiny mammal huddled beneath a fern frond. Manmark tapped the image with his finger, agreeing, "It does resemble our shrew. As it should, since this long-dead midget is the precursor to them and to us and to every fur-bearing animal in between."

"Really?" she said.

"Without question."

"Without question," she repeated, nodding as if she understood the oceans of time and the slow, remorseless pressures of natural selection.

"Our ancestors, like the ancestors of every bird, were exceptionally tiny," Manmark continued. "The dragons ruled the land and seas, and then they ruled the skies too, while these little creatures scurried about in the shadows, waiting patiently for their turn."

"Their turn?" She closed the book with authority, as if she would never need it again. Then, with a distant gaze, she said, "Now and again, I have wondered. Why did the dragons vanish from this world?"

Manmark reminded himself that this was an aboriginal girl. Every primitive culture had its stories. Who knew what wild legends and foolish myths she had heard since birth?

"Nobody knows what happened to them," was his first, best answer.

Then, taking back the book, he added, "But we can surmise there was some sort of cataclysm. An abrupt change in climate, a catastrophe from the sky. Something enormous made every large animal extinct, emptying the world for the likes of you and me."

She seemed impressed by the glimpse of the apocalypse. Smiling at him, she set her mouth to say a word or two, perhaps inviting him back over to her side of the great down-filled bed. But then a sudden hard knock shook the room's only door.

Manmark called out, "Who is it?"

"Name's Barrow," said a rough male voice.

Barrow? Did he know that name?

"We spoke some weeks back," the stranger reported, speaking through the heavy oak. "I told you I was going out into the wash country, and you told me to be on the lookout—"

"Yes."

"For something special."

Half-dressed and nearly panicked, Manmark leaped up, unlocking the door while muttering, "Quiet, quiet."

Barrow stood in the hallway, a tall man who hadn't bathed in weeks or perhaps years. He was grimy and tired and poorly fed and mildly embarrassed when he saw the nearly naked woman sitting calmly on the edge of another man's bed. But then he seemed to recall what had brought him here. "You mentioned money," he said to Manmark. "A great deal of money, if a hunter found for you—"

"Yes."

"One or more of them—"

"Quiet," Manmark snapped.

"Eggs," whispered the unwashed fossil hunter.

And with that, Manmark pulled the dullard into the room, clamping a hand over his mouth before he could utter another careless word.

3

Once again, the world was dying.

Zephyr enjoyed that bleak thought while strolling beside the railroad station, passing downwind from the tall stacks of rancid hyrax skins. The skins were waiting for empty cars heading east—the remains of thousands of beasts killed by hunters and then cleaned with a sloppy professional haste. It was a brutal business, and doomed. In just this one year, the nearby herds had been decimated, and soon the northern and southern herds would feel the onslaught of long rifles and malevolent greed. The waste was appalling, what with most of the meat being left behind for the bear-dogs or to rot in the brutal summer sun. But like all great wastes, it would remake the world again. Into this emptiness, new creatures and peoples would come, filling the country overnight, and that new order would persist for a day or a million years before it too would collapse into ruin and despair.

Such were the lessons taught by history.

And science, in its own graceful fashion, reiterated those grand truths.

"Master Zephyr?"

An assistant had emerged from the railroad station, bearing important papers and an expression of weary tension. "Is it arranged?" Zephyr asked. Then, before the man could respond, he added, "I require a suitable car. For a shipment of this importance, my treasures deserve better than to be shoved beneath these bloody skins."

"I have done my best," the assistant promised.

"What is your best?"

"It will arrive in three days," the man replied, pulling a new paper to the top of the stack. "An armored car used to move payroll coins to the Westlands. As you requested, there's room for guards and your dragon scales, and your private car will ride behind it."

"And the dragons' teeth," Zephyr added. "And several dozen Claws of God."

"Yes, sir."

"And four dragon spleens."

"Of course, sir. Yes."

Each of those metallic organs was worth a fortune, even though none were in good condition. Each had already been purchased. Two were owned by important concerns in the Eastlands. The other two were bound for the Great Continent, purchased by wealthy men who lived along the Dragon River: the same crowded green country where, sixty years ago, Zephyr began his life.

The spleens were full of magic, some professed. Others looked on the relics as oddities, beautiful and precious. But a growing number considered them to be worthy of scientific study—which was why one of the Eastland universities was paying Zephyr a considerable sum for a half-crushed spleen, wanting their chance to study its metabolic purpose and its possible uses in the modern world.

Like his father and his grandfather, Zephyr was a trader who dealt exclusively in the remains of dragons. For generations, perhaps since the beginning of civilized life, the occasional scale and rare claws were much in demand, both as objects of veneration as well as tools of war. Even today, modern munitions couldn't punch their way through a quality scale pulled from the back of a large dragon. In the recent wars, soldiers were given suits built of dragon armor—fantastically expensive uniforms intended only for the most elite units—while their enemies had used dragon teeth and claws fired by special guns, trying to kill the dragon men who were marching across the wastelands toward them.

Modern armies were much wealthier than the ancient civilizations. As a consequence, this humble son of a simple trader, by selling to both sides during the long civil war, had made himself into a financial force.

The fighting was finished, at least for today. But every government in the world continued to dream of war, and their stockpiles continued to grow, and as young scientists learned more about these lost times, the intrigue surrounding these beasts could only increase.

"This is good enough," Zephyr told his assistant, handing back the railroad's contract.

"I'll confirm the other details," the man promised, backing away in a pose of total submission. "By telegraph, I'll check on the car's progress, and I will interview the local men, looking for worthy guards."

And Zephyr would do the same. But surreptitiously, just to reassure an old man that every detail was seen to.

Because a successful enterprise had details at its heart, the old man reminded himself. Just as different details, if left unnoticed, would surely bring defeat to the sloppy and the unfortunate.

Zephyr occupied a spacious house built on the edge of the workers' camp—the finest home in this exceptionally young town but relegated to this less desirable ground because, much as everyone who lived in the camp, its owner belonged to a questionable race. Passing through the front door, the white-haired gentleman paused a moment to enjoy the door's etched glass, and in particular the ornate dragons captured in the midst of life, all sporting wings and fanciful breaths of fire. With a light touch, the trader felt the whitish eye of one dragon. Then, with a tense, disapproving voice, the waiting manservant announced, "Sir, you have a visitor."

Zephyr glanced into the parlor, seeing no one.

"I made her wait in the root cellar," the servant replied. "I didn't know where else to place her."

"Who is she?" the old man inquired. And when he heard the name, he said, "Bring her to me. Now."

"A woman like that?" the man muttered in disbelief.

"As your last duty to me, yes. Bring her to the parlor, collect two more weeks of wages, and then pack your belongings and leave my company." With an angry finger, he added, "Your morals should have been left packed and out of sight. Consider this fair warning should you ever find employment again."

Zephyr could sound frightfully angry, if it suited him.

He walked into the parlor, sat on an overstuffed chair, and waited. A few moments later, the young aboriginal woman strolled into the parlor, investing a moment to look at the furnishings and ivory statues. Then she said, "I learned something."

"I assumed as much."

"Like you guessed, it's the barbarian with all the money." She smiled, perhaps thinking of the money. "He's promised huge payoffs to the dragon hunters, and maybe that's why this one hunter brought him word of a big discovery."

"Where is this discovery? Did you hear?"

"No."

"Does this hunter have a name?"

"Barrow."

Unless Barrow was an idiot or a genius, he would have already applied for dig rights, and they would be included in any public record. It would be a simple matter to bribe the clerk—

"There's eggs," she blurted.

Zephyr was not a man easily startled. But it took him a moment to repeat the word, "Eggs." Then he asked, "More than one egg, you mean?"

"Three, and maybe more."

"What sort of dragon is it?"

"Winged."

"A Sky-Demon?" he said with considerable hope.

"From what they said in front of me, I'm sure of it. He has uncovered the complete body of a Sky-Demon, and she died in the final stages of pregnancy." The girl smiled as she spoke, pleased with everything that had happened. "He didn't realize I understood the importance of things, or even that I was listening. That Manmark fellow . . . he is such a boring, self-important prick— "

"One last question," Zephyr interrupted. "What color were these eggs? Was that mentioned?"

The girl nodded and looked about the room again. Then, picking up a game cube carved from the whitest hyrax ivory, she said, "Like this, they were. They are. Perfectly, perfectly preserved."

4

Manmark was an endless talker, and most of his talk was senseless noise. Barrow treated the noise as just another kind of wind, taking no pleasure from it, nor feeling any insult. To be mannerly, he would nod on occasion and make some tiny comment that could mean anything, and, bolstered by this gesture, Manmark would press on, explaining how it was to grow up wealthy in the Old World, or why bear-dogs were the most foul creatures, or why the world danced around the sun, or how it felt to be a genius on that same world—a grand, deep, wondrous mind surrounded by millions of fools.

It was amazing what a man would endure, particularly if he had been promised a heavy pile of platinum coins.

There were five other men working with them. Four were youngsters—students of some type brought along to do the delicate digging. While the fifth fellow served as their protector, armed with a sleek modern rifle and enough ammunition to kill a thousand men. Some months ago, before he left for the wilderness, Manmark had hired the man to be their protector, keeping him on salary for a day such as this. He was said to be some species of professional killer, which was a bit of a surprise. A few times in conversation, Barrow had wormed honest answers out of the fellow. His credentials were less spectacular than he made them out to be, and even more alarming, the man was extraordinarily scared of things that would never present a problem. Bear-dogs were a source of much consternation, even though Barrow never had trouble with the beasts. And then there were the aborigines; those normally peaceful people brought nightmares of their own. "What if they come on us while we sleep?" the protector would ask, his voice low and haunted. "I am just one person. I have to sleep. What if I wake to find one of those miserable bastards slicing open my throat?"

"They wouldn't," Barrow assured him. Then he laughed, adding, "They'll cut into your chest first, since they'll want to eat your heart."

That was a pure fiction—a grotesque rumor made real by a thousand cheap novels. But their protector seemed to know nothing about this country, his experience born from the novels and small-minded tales told in the slums and high-class restaurants left behind on the distant, unreachable coast.

In his own fashion, Manmark was just as innocent and naïve. But there were moments when what he knew proved to be not only interesting but also quite valuable.

During their second night camped beside the dragon, Manmark topped off his tall glass of fancy pink liquor, and then he glanced at the exposed head of the great beast, remarking, "Life was so different in those old times."

There was nothing interesting in that. But Barrow nodded, as expected, muttering a few bland agreements.

"The dragons were nothing like us," the man continued.

What could be more obvious? Barrow thought to himself.

"The biology of these monsters," said Manmark. Then he looked at Barrow, a wide grin flashing. "Do you know how they breathed?"

It was just the two of them sitting before the fire. The students, exhausted by their day's work, were tucked into their bedrolls, while the camp protector stood on a nearby ridge, scared of every darkness. "I know their lungs were peculiar affairs," Barrow allowed. "Just like their hearts, and their spleens—"

"Not just peculiar," Manmark interrupted. "Unique."

Barrow leaned closer.

"Like us, yes, they had a backbone. But it was not our backbone. There are important differences between the architectures—profound and telling differences. It is as if two separate spines had evolved along two separate but nearly parallel lineages."

The words made sense, to a point.

"North of here," said Manmark. "I have colleagues who have found ancient fossils set within a bed of fine black shale. Unlike most beds of that kind, the soft parts of the dead have been preserved along with their hard shells and teeth. Have you heard of this place? No? Well, its creatures expired long before the first dragon was born. The world was almost new, it was so long ago . . . and inside that beautiful black shale is a tiny wormlike creature that has the barest beginnings of a notochord. A spine. The first vertebrate, say some."

"Like us," Barrow realized.

"And lying beside that specimen is another. Very much the same, in its fashion. Wormlike and obscure. But in other ways, it is full of subtle, very beautiful differences."

"Different how?"

"Well, for instance . . . there is a minuscule speck of metal located in the center of its simple body."

"Like a dragon's spleen?"

"But simpler, and made of ordinary metals. Iron and copper and such." Manmark finished his drink and gazed into the fire. "This dragon's lungs were very different, of course. Instead of sucking in a breath and then exhaling it out the same way, she took the air through her nostrils, into the lungs and out through a rectal orifice. We don't know enough to be certain yet. But it seems reasonable to assume that our dragon did a much better job of wringing the oxygen out of her endless deep breath."

Barrow nodded, very much interested now.

"And then there's the famous spleen," Manmark continued. "Have you ever wondered why these beasts needed to collect precious metals? What possible advantage could they have lent to the beasts?"

"I've thought about it some," he confessed.

"Gold and platinum and sometimes silver," said Manmark. "They are precious to us because they are rare, yes. But also because they barely rust in the presence of oxygen, which is why they retain their lovely sheen. And for the newest industries of our world, these elements are increasingly valuable. Were you aware? They can serve as enzymatic surfaces for all kinds of impressive chemical reactions. Perhaps our lady dragon would mix her breath and blood inside the spleen's cavities, producing all kinds of spectacular products. Even fire, perhaps."

Barrow nodded as if he understood every word.

"One day, we'll decipher what happened inside these creatures. And I suspect that knowledge, when it arrives, will revolutionize our world."

"Someday, maybe," Barrow conceded.

"In the distant future, you think?" Manmark grinned and took a long drink from his mostly drained glass. "But not in our lives, surely. Is that what you are thinking?"

"Isn't that the truth?"

"The truth." The self-described genius stared into the campfire, his gold eyes full of greed and a wild hope. "This isn't well known. Outside of scientific circles, that is. But a few years ago, an immature egg was dug from the belly of a giant tree-eating dragon. Dead for perhaps a hundred million years, yet its color was still white. The oxygen that had fueled its parent had been kept away from the egg in death, and some kind of deep coma state had been achieved. Which is not too surprising. We know dragon eggs are exceptionally durable. It's perhaps a relic trait from those days when their ancestors laid their eggs in sloppy piles and buried them under dirt and then left the nest, sometimes for decades, waiting for the proper conditions. Since these creatures had a very different biochemistry from ours I . . . a much superior physiology . . . they could afford to do such things—"

"What are you saying?" Barrow interrupted. "I'm sorry, I don't understand half your words."

"I'm saying that the dragons were exceptionally durable."

The dragon hunter glanced at the long, lovely skull and its cavernous eye sockets. "I have never heard this before. Is there some chance that those eggs over there . . . in that ground, after all of these years . . . ?"

"Remember the immature egg that I mentioned?" Manmark was whispering, his voice a little sloppy and terribly pleased. "The egg from the tree-eater? Well, I have read the paper written about its dissection. A hundred times, I have read it. Diamond blades were used to cut through the shell, and despite everything that common and uncommon sense would tell you . . . yes, there was still fluid inside the egg, and a six-legged embryo that was dead but intact . . . dead, but that looked as if it had died only yesterday, its burial lasting just a little too long . . ."

5

Three eggs became four, and then five, and quite suddenly there were seven of the treasures set on a bed of clean straw, enjoying the temporary shade of a brown canvas tarp. It was a sight that dwarfed Manmark's great dreams, marvelous and lovely as they had been. Each egg was perfectly round, and each was the same size, their diameter equal to his forearm and extended hand. They were heavier than any bird egg would be, if a bird could lay such an enormous egg. But that was reasonable, since the thick white shell was woven partly from metal and strange compounds that were barely understood today—ceramics and odd proteins laid out in a painfully delicate pattern. The shell material itself contained enough mystery to make a great man famous. But Manmark could always imagine greater honors and even wilder successes, as he did now, touching the warm surface of the nearest egg, whispering to it, "Hello, you."

The students were standing together, waiting for orders. And behind them stood a freight wagon, its team of heavy camels ready to pull their precious cargo to town and the railhead.

Barrow was perched on the wagon's front end, leather reins held tight in both hands.

Manmark took notice of him, and for a moment he wondered why the man was staring off into the distance. What did he see from that vantage point? Looking in the same general direction, Manmark saw nothing. There was a slope of gray clay punctuated with a few clusters of yucca, and the crest of the little ridge formed a neat line dividing the rain-washed earth from the intense blue of the sky.

The dragon hunter was staring at nothing.

How peculiar.

Manmark felt a little uneasy, but for no clear reason. He turned to the students now, ready to order the wagon loaded. And then, too late by a long ways, he remembered that their very expensive security man had been walking that barren ridge, his long gun cradled in both arms, haunted eyes watching for trouble.

So where is my protector? Manmark asked himself.

An instant later, the clean crack of a bullet cut through the air, and one of the large camels decided to drop its head and then its massive body, settling with a strange urgency onto the hard pan of clay.

Manmark knelt down between the great eggs. Otherwise, he was too startled to react.

The students dropped low and stared at the sky.

Barrow remained on the wagon, yanking at the reins and braking with his left foot, telling the surviving three camels, "Hold. Stay. Hold now. Stay."

Something about that voice steadied Manmark. Something in the man's calmness allowed him to look up, shouting to Barrow, "What is this? What is happening?"

Next came the sound of hooves striking dirt—many hooves in common motion—and he turned the other way, seeing six . . . no, eight camels calmly walking down the long draw, each built to race, each wearing a small saddle as well as a man dressed in shapeless clothes and heavy masks.

Manmark's first thought was to deny that this was happening. Hadn't he taken a thousand precautions? Nobody should know the significance of this dig, which meant that this had to be some random bit of awful luck. These were raiders of some kind—simple thieves easily tricked. A few coins of debased gold would probably satisfy them. He started to calculate the proper figure, filling his head with nonsense until that moment when the lead rider lowered his fat rifle and fired.

A fountain of pulverized earth slapped Manmark in the face.

He backed away, stumbled and dropped onto his rump. Then in his panic, he began digging into his pockets, searching for the tiny pistol that he had carried from the Old World and never fired once.

"Don't," said a strong, calming voice.

Barrow's voice.

"Give them what they want," said the dragon hunter, speaking to him as he would to a nervous camel.

"I won't," Manmark sputtered. "They are mine!"

"No," Barrow said from high on the wagon. "They aren't yours anymore, if they ever were . . ."

The riders didn't speak, save to wave their weapons in the air, ordering him to back away from the eggs. Then each claimed a single white sphere, dismounting long enough to secure their prize inside a silk sling apparently woven for this single task.

The final pair of riders was dressed as the others, yet they were different. One was small in build, while the other moved like a healthy but definitely older man. Manmark stared at both of them, and with an expertise garnered from years of imagining flesh upon ancient bone, he made two good guesses about who was beneath all those clothes.

"Zephyr," he muttered.

How many candidates were there? In one little town, or even at this end of the territory, how many other men were there who could possibly appreciate the significance of this find?

"And you," he said to the whore, his voice tight and injured.

She hesitated, if only for a moment.

Through the slits about the eyes, Zephyr stared at his opponent, and then he made some decision, lifting a hand and glancing back at the lead rider. For what purpose? To order him shot, perhaps?

The next blast of a gun startled everyone. The riders. Zephyr. And Manmark too. The concussion cut through the air, and while the roar was still ringing in their ears, Barrow said, "If we want to start killing, I'll start with you. Whoever you are. Understand me, old man? Before they aim my way, I'll hit your head and then your heart."

Barrow was standing on the back of the wagon now, holding his own rifle against his shoulder.

"Hear me, stranger? The eggs are yours. Take them. And I'll give you your life in the deal. Is that good enough?"

"It is adequate," said the accented voice.

Under his breath, Manmark muttered grim curses. But he stood motionless while Zephyr claimed the last of his eggs, and he swallowed his rage while the riders turned and started back up the long draw, the final man riding backward in his saddle, ready to fire at anyone with a breath of courage.

Manmark had none.

When the thieves vanished, he collapsed, panting and sobbing in a shameless display.

Barrow leaped off the wagon and walked toward him.

The students were standing again, chattering among themselves. One and then another asked no one in particular, "Will we still get paid?"

All was lost, Manmark believed.

Then the dragon hunter knelt beside him, and with an almost amused voice, he said, "All right. Let's discuss my terms."

"Your what?"

"Terms," he repeated. Then he outright laughed, adding, "When I get these eggs back to you, what will you pay me?"

"But how can you recover them?"

"I don't know yet. But give me the right promises, and maybe I'll think of something."

Manmark was utterly confused. "What do you mean? If there are six of them, and if they defeated my security man . . . what hope do you have?"

"I fought in the war," Barrow replied.

"A lot of men fought."

"Not many did the kind of fighting that I did," the dragon hunter replied. "And few of them fought half as well either."

Manmark stared at the hard dark eyes. Then, because he had no choice, none whatsoever, he blurted, "Yes. Whatever it costs. Yes!"

6

Here stood the best locomotive available on short notice—a soot-caked machine built of iron and fire, wet steam, and rhythmic noises not unlike the breathing of a great old beast. Since details mattered, Zephyr had hired workmen to paint dragon eyes on the front end and little red wings on its sides, and when the job wasn't done with the proper accuracy, he commissioned others to fix what was wrong. Two engineers stoked the fire, while a third sat on top of the tender, ready to spell whomever tired first. Behind the locomotive was the armored car hired to move spleens and scales—a wheeled fortress encased in steel and nearly empty, carrying nothing but seven white eggs and six mercenaries armed with enough munitions to hold off a regiment. And trailing behind was Zephyr's private car, luxurious and open in appearance, except for the small windowless room at the rear that served as a bath.

The original plan for the dragons' spleens was to travel east. But the eggs were too precious to risk losing among the barbarians. Which was why Zephyr ordered his little train to head for the mountains and the Westlands beyond. A telegraph message dressed in code had been sent ahead. By the time he arrived at the Great Bay, a steamer would be waiting, ready to carry him back to the land of fables and childhood memories.

"I haven't been home for years," he confessed to his companion.

The young woman smiled at him, and once again, she said, "Thank you for taking me."

"It was the very least I could do," Zephyr allowed. "You were wise to ask, in fact. If Manmark realized you were responsible—"

"And for this," she interrupted, letting her fat coin purse jingle in an agreeable fashion.

"You have earned every mark. For what you have done to help me, madam, I will always be in your gratitude . . ."

There was only one set of tracks, with the occasional sidings and rules of conduct between oncoming trains. But Zephyr had sprinkled the world before them with bribes, and for the time being, there might as well be no other train in the world. As they picked up speed—as the engine quickened its breathing and its pace—he looked through the thick window glass, watching a hand-painted sign pass on their right. "You are leaving Summer Gulch," he read. "The fastest growing city between here and there."

What an odd, interesting thing to write. Zephyr laughed for a moment, and again mentioned, "I haven't been home since I was a young man."

"I'd love to see the Great Continent," the aboriginal girl reported.

What would become of this creature? Zephyr was of several minds on the subject, but his happy mood steered him to the more benevolent courses.

She slipped her purse out of sight.

"Do you know why we call it the Dragon River?" he asked.

"I don't," she replied.

Somehow he doubted that. But a prostitute makes her living by listening as much as anything, and this old man could do little else but talk with her, at least for the moment. "Of course there are some substantial beds of fossils along the river's course, yes. Dragon bones and claws and the great scales are part of my people's history. And we are an ancient nation, you know. The oldest in the world, perhaps. From the beginning, our gods have been dragons and our emperors have been their earthly sons and daughters."

The woman had bright, jade-colored eyes and a pleasant, luring smile.

"My favorite story, true or not, is about a young emperor from the Fifth Dynasty." Zephyr allowed his eyes to gaze off to the north, looking at the broken, rain-ripped country. "He found a flying dragon, it is said. The bones and scales were intact, as was her heart and spleen. And behind her spleen were eggs. At least two eggs, it is said. Some accounts mention as many as six, but only two of her offspring were viable. After three weeks of sitting above the ground, in the warming sun—and I should add, because the emperor was a very good man—the eggs finally hatched. Two baby dragons slithered into the world. Brothers, they were, and they belonged to him.

"The emperor had always been cared for by others. But he made a wise decision. He refused to let others care for his new friends, raising them himself, with his own hands. A mistake took one of those hands from him, but that was a minor loss. He refused to let his guards kill the offending dragon. And for his kindness, the dragon and its brother loved the emperor for all of his days."

Zephyr paused for a moment, considering his next words.

"It was a weak time for my great nation," he reported. "Barbarians were roaming the steppe and mountains, and peoples from the sea were raiding the coasts. But it is said—by many voices, not just those of my people—that a one-handed emperor appeared in the skies, riding the winged monsters. They were huge beasts, swift and strange. They breathed a strange fire, and they were powerful, and they had to eat a thousand enemy soldiers every day just to feed their endless hunger. An unlikely, mythic detail, I always believed. Except now, when I read scientific papers about the biology of dragons, I can see where they must have had prodigious appetites."

The woman nodded, listening to every word.

"As a skeptical boy, I doubted the story about the emperor's warrior dragons. Great men didn't need monsters to save their nation, I believed. But I was wrong. I realized my error some time ago. Two monsters could save my people then, and think what seven dragons could do today . . . particularly if several of them are female, and fertile, and agreeable to mating with their brothers. . . ."

The young woman gave a little shrug, saying nothing for a long moment.

The train continued to churn toward the west, the locomotive sounding steady and unstoppable.

"We have a story," she muttered. "My people do, I mean."

"About the dragons? Yes, I suppose you do."

"Since I was old enough to listen, I heard how the world holds thousands of dragons in its chest, and from time to time, for reasons known only to the gods, one of them is released. Which makes sense, I suppose. If what everyone tells me is true, and their eggs can sleep for an eternity in the ground."

Even from a single fertile female, only one egg at a time would be exposed by erosion. Yes, it was a reasonable explanation.

"The freed dragons die of loneliness, always." She spoke those words with sadness, as if she knew something about that particular pain. "They kill and burn because of their longing for others like themselves, and then they fly too high in order to end their own miserable lives, and that is why the dragons cannot come back into this world."

"This is a very common story," Zephyr assured her. "Maybe every place in the world tells fables much like that."

"But there is more to my story," she said, her tone defensive.

"Is there?"

"Much more," she promised.

Neither of them spoke for a long moment. The young woman didn't want to say anything else, and Zephyr wasn't in the mood to let another people's legends distract him. He looked out another window, toward the empty south, and then from somewhere up ahead came a dull *whump* as a heavy block of dynamite detonated. Instantly, the brakes were applied, and the little train started to shake and shiver, fighting its momentum to remain on the suddenly unstable tracks.

The young woman was thrown from her seat, as was Zephyr.

He stood first and heard the early shots coming from inside the armored car. Again he looked to the south, seeing nothing, and then he hunkered down and looked in the other direction. A solitary figure was approaching on foot, armed with a rifle that he hadn't bothered to fire. He was marching steadily across the stunted grasses, allowing the mercenaries to fire at him. And while most of their bullets struck, each impact made only sparks and a high-pitched snap that seemed to accomplish nothing. Because the attacker was wearing a suit made from overlapping dragon scales, Zephyr realized. And with an impressive eye for detail, the man had gone to the trouble of stretching cloth between his arms and chest, as if he had wings, while on his masked face were painted the large, malevolent eyes of an exceptionally angry dragon.

7

This was what Barrow did during the war. With a platoon of picked soldiers, he would squeeze into his costume and pick up a gun that was always too heavy to carry more than a few steps, and after swallowing his fears as well as his common sense, he and his brethren would walk straight at the enemy, letting them shoot at will, waiting to reach a point where he could murder every idiot who hadn't yet found reason enough to run away.

This was the war all over again, and he hated it.

His suit wasn't as good as the one he wore in the war. Manmark's students were experts at arranging the scales and fixing them to his clothes—a consequence of spending weeks and years assembling old bones—but there hadn't been enough time to do a proper, permanent job. The scales were tilted in order to guide the bullets to one side or the other, but they weren't always tilted enough. Every impact caused a bruise. One and then another blow to the chest seemed to break a rib or two, and Barrow found himself staggering now, the weight of his clothes and his own fatigue making him wish for an end to his suffering.

That old platoon had been a mostly invincible bunch, but by the war's end, those who hadn't died from lucky shots and cannon fire were pretty much crazy with fear. Barrow was one of the few exceptions—a consequence of getting hit less often and doing a better job of killing those who wanted him dead.

Through the narrow slits of his mask, he stared at the firing ports built into the armored car. Then he paused, knelt, and with a care enforced by hours of practice, he leveled his weapon and put a fat slug of lead into one man's face.

Two more rounds hit Barrow, square in the chest and on the scalp.

He staggered, breathed hard enough to make himself lightheaded, and then aimed and fired again, killing no one but leaving someone behind the steel screaming in misery.

The surviving men finally got smart. One would cry out, and all would fire together, in a single volley.

Barrow was shoved back off his feet.

Again, there was a shout followed by the blow of a great hammer.

They would break every bone inside his bruised body if this continued. Barrow saw his doom and still could not make his body rise off the dusty earth. How had he come to this awful place? He couldn't remember. He sat upright, waiting for the next misery to find him . . . but a new voice was shouting, followed by the odd, high-pitched report of a very different gun.

The dirt before him rose up in a fountain and drifted away, and left lying between his legs was a single purple Claw of God.

Damn, somebody had a dragon-buster gun.

If he remained here, he would die. Reflexes and simple panic pushed Barrow up onto his feet, and on exhausted legs he ran, trying to count the seconds while he imagined somebody working with the breech of that huge, awful gun, inserting another expensive charge before sealing it up and aiming at him again.

When Barrow thought it was time, he abruptly changed direction.

The next claw screamed through the air, peeling off to the right.

Three engineers were cowering on the dragon-eyed locomotive. Plainly, they hadn't come here expecting to fight. Barrow pointed his rifle at each of their faces, just for a moment, and then they leaped down together and started running back toward town.

The men inside the armored car fired again. But Barrow kept close to the tender, giving them no easy shots. A few steps short of them, he reached behind his back, removing a satchel that he had carried from the beginning, out of sight, and he unwrapped the fuse and laid it on the ground, shooting it at pointblank range to set it on fire. Then he bent low and threw the satchel with his free arm, skipping it under the car before he stepped back a little ways, letting the guards see him standing in front of them with barely a care.

"There's enough dynamite under you now to throw that car up high and break it into twenty pieces," he promised. Then he added, "It's a long fuse. But I wouldn't spend too much time thinking before you decide to do what's smart."

An instant later, the main door was unlocked and unlatched. Five men came tumbling out into the open, one of them bleeding from the shoulder and none of them armed.

"Run," Barrow advised.

The mercenaries started chasing the train crew down the iron rails.

The fuse continued to burn, reaching the canvas satchel and sputtering for a few moments before it died away.

Barrow stared into the windowless car. The seven eggs were set inside seven oak crates, and he didn't look at any of them. He was staring at the man whom he had shot through the face, his mind thinking one way about it, then another.

A breech closed somewhere nearby, and a big hammer was cocked.

Barrow turned too late, eyes focusing first on the cavernous barrel of the gun and then on the old foreign man who was fighting to hold it up. At this range, with any kind of dragon-round, death was certain. But Barrow's sense of things told him that if he didn't lift his own weapon, the man would hesitate. And another moment or two of life seemed like reason enough to do nothing.

"I am a creature of foresight," Zephyr remarked.

"You're smarter than me," agreed Barrow.

"Details," the old man muttered, two fingers wrapped around the long brass trigger. "The world is built upon tiny but critical details."

Behind him stood one detail—a rather pretty detail, just as Barrow had recalled—and using a purse full of heavy gold, she struck Zephyr on the top of his skull, and the long barrel dropped as the gun discharged, and a Claw of God came spinning out, burying itself once again inside the ancient Earth.

8

Manmark had the freight wagon brought out of the draw, and he used a whip on the surviving camels, forcing them into a quick trot toward the motionless train. But there was a generous distance to be covered; open country afforded few safe places to hide. There was time to watch Barrow and the aboriginal girl with his binoculars, a little dose of worry nipping at him, and then Zephyr was awake again, sitting up and speaking at some length to the dragon hunter. All the while, Manmark's students were happily discussing their golden futures and what each planned to do with his little share of the fame. They spoke about the dragons soon to be born, and they discussed what kinds of cages would be required to hold the great beasts, and what would be a fair price for the public to see them, and what kinds of science could be done with these travelers from another age.

What was Zephyr saying to the dragon hunter?

Of course, the crafty old trader was trying to top Manmark's offers of wealth. And if he was successful? If Barrow abruptly changed sides . . . ?

"Look at that cloud," one student mentioned.

Somewhere to the south, hooves were slapping at the ground, lifting the dust into a wind that was blowing north, obscuring what was most probably a small herd of hard-running hyraxes.

Manmark found the little pistol in his pocket, considering his options for a long moment.

If it came to it, would he have the courage?

Probably not, no. If these last days had taught Manmark anything, it was that he had no stomach for mayhem and murder.

He put the pistol back out of sight and again used the binoculars, the jumpy images showing that Zephyr had fallen silent for now and Barrow was gazing off to the south and all of the talking was being done by the prostitute who stood between the two men, arms swirling in the air as she spoke on and on.

The worry that he felt now was nebulous and terrible.

Again, Manmark struck the big camels with his whip, and he screamed at everyone, telling them, "We need to hurry. Hurry!"

But the wagon was massive and one camel short, and there was still a long, empty distance to cover. The curtain of dust was nearly upon the motionless train, and inside it were dozens, or perhaps hundreds of aboriginal men riding on the backs of the half-wild ponies that they preferred to ride—an entire tribe galloping toward the treasures that Manmark would never see again.

9

She spoke quietly, with force.

"My favorite fable of all promises that the dragons will come again to this world. They will rise up out of the Earth to claim what has always been theirs, and only those men and women who help them will be spared. All the other people of the world will be fought and killed and eaten. Only the chosen few will be allowed to live as they wish, protected beneath the great wings of the reawakened gods."

Zephyr rubbed his sore head, trying to focus his mind. But really, no amount of cleverness or any promise of money would help now. Even with a splitting headache, he understood that inescapable lesson.

Speaking to the man wearing dragon scales, she said, "Your ugly people came into my country and stole everything of worth. You gave us disease and drink, and you are murdering our herds. But now I intend to destroy everything you have built here, and my children will take back all the lands between the seas."

She was a clever, brutal girl, Zephyr decided. And she had done a masterful job of fooling everyone, including him.

Barrow turned and stared at the oncoming riders. He had pulled off his armored mask, but he was still breathing hard, winded by his fight and terrified. He might defeat half a dozen mercenaries, if he was lucky. But not a nation of wild men and women armed with rifles and a communal rage.

"You need me," he muttered.

The young woman didn't respond. It was Zephyr who said, "What do you mean? Who needs you?"

"She does," Barrow announced. Then he pointed at the riders, adding, "If they want to help themselves, they should accept my help."

The woman laughed and asked, "Why?"

"When I was a boy," said Barrow, "I kept baby birds. And I learned that my little friends would take my food and my love best if I wore a sock on my hand, painting it to resemble their lost mothers and fathers."

The rumbling of hooves grew louder, nearer.

"I'm a big man in this big costume," he remarked. "This costume is bigger than anything any of your people can wear, I would think. And I'm brave enough to do stupid things. And you will have seven dragons to care for now . . . to feed and protect, and to train, if you can . . . and wouldn't you like to take along somebody who's willing to risk everything on a daily basis . . . ?"

Zephyr laughed quietly now.

Clearly, this Barrow fellow was at least as surprising as the young woman, and maybe twice as bold.

The woman stared at the man dressed as a dragon, a look of interest slowly breaking across her face.

Zephyr had to laugh louder now.

Dust drifted across the scene, thick and soft, muting the sound of their voices. And then the woman turned to her people, shouting to be heard.

"I have dragons to give you!" she called out.

"Eight, as it happens! Eight dragons to build a new world . . ."

The Ocean of the Blind

JAMES L. CAMBIAS

Here's a short, sharp look at how unexamined cultural assumptions can sometimes come back to bite you in the ass—sometimes *literally* . . .

James S. Cambias was a finalist for the 2001 James Tiptree Jr. Memorial Award for his short story "A Diagram of Rapture"; he was also a finalist for the 2001 John W. Campbell Award for Best New Writer. He's become a frequent contributor to *The Magazine of Fantasy & Science Fiction*, and has also sold to *Crossroads: Tales of the Southern Literary Fantastic* and other markets. A native of New Orleans, he currently lives in Deerfield, Massachusetts, with his wife and children.

By the end of his second month at Hitode Station, Rob Freeman had already come up with eighty-five ways to murder Henri Kerlerec. That put him third in the station's rankings—Josef Palashnik was first with one hundred forty-three, followed by Nadia Kyle with ninety-seven. In general, the number and sheer viciousness of the suggested methods was in proportion to the amount of time each spent with Henri.

Josef, as the primary submarine pilot, had to spend upward of thirty hours each week in close quarters with Henri, so his list concentrated on swift and brutal techniques suitable for a small cockpit. Nadia shared lab space with Henri—which in practice meant she did her dissections in the kitchen or on the floor of her bedroom—and her techniques were mostly obscure poisons and subtle deathtraps.

Rob's specialty was underwater photography and drone operation. All through training he had been led to expect he would be filming the exotic life forms of Ilmatar, exploring the unique environment of the remote icy world and helping the science team understand the alien biology and ecology. Within a week of arrival he found himself somehow locked into the role of Henri Kerlerec's personal cameraman, gofer, and captive audience. His list of murder methods began with "strangling HK with that stupid ankh necklace" and progressed through cutting the air hose on Henri's drysuit, jamming him into a thermal vent, abandoning him in midocean with no inertial compass, and feeding him to an *Aenocampus*. Some of the others on the station who routinely read the hidden "Death to HK" board had protested that last one as being too cruel to the *Aenocampus*.

Rob's first exposure to killing Henri came at a party given by Nadia and her husband Pierre Adler in their room, just after the support vehicle left orbit for the six-month voyage back to Earth. With four guests there was barely enough room, and to avoid overloading the ventilators they had to leave the door open. For refreshment they served melons from the hydroponic garden filled with some of Palashnik's home-brew potato vodka. One drank melon-flavored vodka until the hollow interior was empty, then cut vodka-flavored melon slices.

"I've got a new one," said Nadia after her third melon slice. "Put a piece of paper next to Le Nuke for a few months until it's radioactive, then write him a fan letter and slip it under his door. He'd keep the letter for his collection and die of gradual exposure."

"Too long," said Josef. "Even if he kept it in his pocket it would take years to kill him."

"But you'd have the fun of watching him lose his hair," said Nadia.

"I would rather just lock him in the reactor shed and leave him there," said Josef.

"Who are they talking about?" Rob asked.

"Henri Kerlerec," whispered the person squeezed onto the bed next to him.

"Irradiate his hair gel," said Pierre. "That way he'd put more on every day and it would be right next to his brain."

"Ha! That part has been dead for years!"

"Replace the argon in his breathing unit with chlorine," said someone Rob couldn't see, and then the room went quiet.

Henri was standing in the doorway. As usual, he was grinning. "Planning to murder somebody? Our esteemed station director, I hope." He glanced behind him to make sure Dr. Sen wasn't in earshot. "I have thought of an infallible technique: I would strike him over the head with a large ham or gigot or something of that kind, and then when the police come, I would serve it to them to destroy the evidence. They would never suspect!"

"Roald Dahl," murmured Nadia. "And it was a *frozen* leg of lamb."

Henri didn't hear her. "You see the beauty of it? The police eat the murder weapon. Perhaps I shall write a detective novel about it when I get back to Earth. Well, goodnight everyone!" He gave a little wave and went off toward Hab Three.

This particular morning Rob was trying to think of an especially sadistic fate for Henri. Kerlerec had awakened him at 0500—three hours early!—and summoned him to the dive room with a great show of secrecy.

The dive room occupied the bottom of Hab One. It was a big circular room with suits and breathing gear stowed on the walls, benches for getting into one's gear, and a moon pool in the center where the Terran explorers could pass into Ilmatar's dark ocean. It was usually the coldest room in the entire station, chilled by the subzero seawater.

Henri was there, waiting at the base of the access ladder. As soon as Rob climbed down he slammed the hatch shut. "Now we can talk privately together. I have an important job for you."

"What?"

"Tonight at 0100 we are going out on a dive. Tell nobody. Do not write anything in the dive log."

"What? Why tonight? And why did you have to get me up at five in the goddamned morning to have this conversation?"

"It must be kept absolutely secret."

"Henri, I'm not doing anything until you tell me exactly what is going on. Enough cloak and dagger stuff."

"Come and see." Henri led him to the hatch into Hab Three, opened it a crack to peek through, then gestured for Rob to follow as he led the way to the lab space he shared with Nadia Kyle. It was a little room about twice the size of a sleeping cabin, littered with native artifacts, unlabeled disks, and tanks holding live specimens. Standing in the middle was a large gray plastic container as tall as a man. It was covered with stenciled markings in Cyrillic and a sky blue UNICA shipping label.

Henri touched his thumb to a lock pad and the door swung open to reveal a bulky diving suit. It was entirely black, even the faceplate, and had a sleek, seamless look.

"Nice suit. What's so secret about it?"

"This is not a common sort of diving suit," said Henri. "I arranged specially for it to be sent to me. Nobody else has anything like it. It is a Russian Navy stealth suit, for deactivating underwater smart mines or sonar pods. The surface is completely anechoic. Invisible to any kind of sonar imaging. Even the fins are low-noise."

"How does it work?" Rob's inner geek prompted him to ask.

Henri gave a shrug. "That is for technical people to worry about. All I care is that it does work. It must—it cost me six million Euros to get it here."

"Okay, so you've got the coolest diving suit on Ilmatar. Why are you keeping it locked up? I'm sure the bio people would love to be able to get close to native life without being heard."

"Pah. When I am done they can watch all the shrimps and worms they wish to. But first, I am going to use this suit to observe the Ilmatarans up close. Imagine it, Robert! I can swim among their houses, perhaps even go right inside! Stand close enough to touch them! They will never notice I am there!"

"What about the contact rules?" The most frustrating part of the whole Ilmatar project was the ban on contacting the sentient natives of the planet. The UN committee in charge kept insisting more study was needed. Rob suspected maybe the UN was trying to appease the groups back on Earth that wanted to close down Hitode Station and pull back from Ilmatar.

"Contact? What contact? Didn't you hear—the Ilmatarans will not notice me! I will stand among them, filming at close range, but with this suit I will be invisible to them!"

"Doctor Sen's going to shit a brick when he finds out."

"By the time he finds out it will be done. What can he do to me? Send me home? I will go back to Earth on the next ship in triumph!"

"The space agencies aren't going to like it either."

"Robert, before I left Earth I did some checking. Do you know how many people regularly access space agency sites or subscribe to their news feeds? About fifty million people, worldwide. Do you know how many people watched the film of my Titan expedition? Ninety-six million! I have twice as many viewers, and that makes me twice as important. The agencies all love me."

Rob suspected Henri's numbers were made up on the spur of the moment, the way most of his numbers were, but it was probably true enough that Henri Kerlerec, the famous scientist-explorer and shameless media whore, got more eyeballs than the rest of the entire interstellar program.

He could feel himself being sucked into the mighty whirlpool of Henri's ego, and tried to struggle against it. "I don't want to get in any trouble."

"You have nothing to worry about. Now, listen: here is what we will do. You come down here quietly at about 0030 and get everything ready. Bring the cameras and two of the quiet impeller units. Also a drone or two. I will get this suit on myself in here, and then at 0100 we go out. With the impellers we can get as far as the Maury 3 vent. There is a little Ilmataran settlement there."

"That's a long way to go by impeller. Maury 3's what, sixty kilometers from here?"

"Three hours out, three hours back, and perhaps two hours at the site. We will get back at about 0900, while the others are still eating breakfast. They may not even notice we have gone."

"And if they do?"

"Then we just say we have been doing some filming around the habitat outside." Henri began locking up the stealth suit's container. "I tell you, they will never suspect a thing. Leave all the talking to me. Now: not another word! We have too much to do! I am going to sleep this afternoon to be fresh for our dive tonight. You must do the same. And do not speak of this to anyone!"

Broadtail is nervous. He cannot pay attention to the speaker, and constantly checks the reel holding his text. He is to speak next, his first address to the Bitterwater Company of Scholars. It is an audition of sorts—Broadtail hopes the members find his work interesting enough to invite him to join them.

Smoothshell 24 Midden finishes her address on high-altitude creatures and takes a few questions from the audience. They aren't easy questions, either, and Broadtail worries about making a fool of himself before all these respected scholars. When she finishes, Longpincer 16 Bitterwater clacks his pincers for quiet.

"Welcome now to Broadtail 38 Sandyslope, who comes to us from a great distance to speak about ancient languages. Broadtail?"

Broadtail nearly drops his reel, but catches it in time and scuttles to the end of the room. It is a wonderful chamber for speaking, with a sloped floor so that everyone can hear directly, and walls of quiet pumice stone. He finds the end of his reel and begins, running it carefully between his feeding-tendrils as he speaks aloud. His tendrils feel the knots in the string as it passes by them. The patterns of knots indicate numbers, and the numbers match words. He remembers being careful to space his knots and tie them tightly, as this copy is for the Bitterwater library. The reel is a single unbroken cord, expensive to buy and horribly complicated to work with—very different from the original draft, a tangle of short notes tied together all anyhow.

Once he begins, Broadtail's fear dissipates. His own fascination with his topic asserts itself, and he feels himself speeding up as his excitement grows. When he pauses, he can hear his audience rustling and scrabbling, and he supposes that is a good sign. At least they aren't all going torpid.

The anchor of his speech is the description of the echo-carvings from the ruined city near his home vent of Continuous Abundance. By correlating the images of the echo-carvings with the number markings below them, Broadtail believes he can create a lexicon for the ancient city builders. He reads the Company some of his translations of other markings in the ruins.

Upon finishing, he faces a torrent of questions. Huge old Roundhead 19 Downcurrent has several tough ones—he is generally recognized as the expert on ancient cities and their builders, and he means to make sure some provincial upstart doesn't encroach on his territory.

Roundhead and some others quickly home in on the weak parts of Broadtail's argument. A couple of them make reference to the writings of the dead scholar Thickfeelers 19 Swiftcurrent, and Broadtail feels a pang of jealousy because he can't afford to buy copies of such rare works. As the questions continue, Broadtail feels himself getting angry in defense of his work, and struggles to retain his temper. The presentation may be a disaster, but he must remain polite.

At last it is over, and he rolls up his reel and heads for a seat at the rear of the room. He'd like to keep going, just slink outside and swim for home, but it would be rude.

A scholar Broadtail doesn't recognize scuttles to the lectern and begins struggling with a tangled reel. Longpincer sits next to Broadtail and speaks privately with shell-taps. "That was very well done. I think you describe some extremely important discoveries."

"You do? I was just thinking of using the reel to mend nets."

"Because of all the questions? Don't worry. That's a good sign. If the hearers ask questions it means they're thinking, and that's the whole purpose of this Company. I don't see any reason not to make you a member. I'm sure the others agree."

All kinds of emotions flood through Broadtail—relief, excitement, and sheer happiness. He can barely keep from speaking aloud. His shell-taps are rapid. "I'm very grateful. I plan to revise the reel to address some of Roundhead's questions."

"Of course. I imagine some of the others want copies, too. Ah, he's starting."

The scholar at the lectern begins to read a reel about a new system for measuring the heat of springs, but Broadtail is too happy to pay much attention.

At midnight, Rob was lying on his bunk trying to come up with some excuse not to go with Henri. Say he was sick, maybe? The trouble was that he was a rotten liar. He tried to make himself feel sick—maybe an upset stomach from ingesting seawater? His body unhelpfully continued to feel okay.

Maybe he just wouldn't go. Stay in bed and lock the door. Henri could hardly complain to Dr. Sen about him not going on an unauthorized dive. But Henri could and undoubtedly would make his life miserable with nagging and blustering until he finally gave in.

And of course the truth was that Rob did want to go. He really wanted to be the one in the stealth suit, getting within arm's reach of the Ilmatarans and filming them up close, instead of getting a few murky long-distance drone pictures. Probably everyone else at Hitode Station felt the same way. Putting them here, actually on the sea bottom of Ilmatar, yet forbidding them to get close to the natives, was like telling a pack of horny teenagers they could get naked in bed together, but not touch.

He checked his watch. It was 0020. He got up and slung his camera bag over his shoulder. Damn Henri anyway.

Rob made it to the dive room without encountering anyone. The station wasn't like a space vehicle with round-the-clock shifts. Everyone slept from about 2400 to 0800, and only one poor soul had to stay in the control room in case of emergency. Tonight it was Dickie Graves on duty, and Rob suspected that Henri had managed to square him somehow so that the exterior hydrophones wouldn't pick up their little jaunt.

He took one of the drones off the rack and ran a quick check. It was a flexible robot fish about a meter long, more Navy surplus—American, this time. It wasn't especially stealthy, but instead was designed to mimic a mackerel's sonar signature. Presumably the Ilmatarans would figure it was some native organism and ignore it. His computer linked up with the drone brain by laser. All powered up and ready to go. He told it to hold position and await further instructions, then dropped it into the water. Just to be on the safe side, Rob fired up a second drone and tossed it into the moon pool.

Next the impellers. They were simple enough—a motor, a battery, and a pair of counter-rotating propellors. You controlled your speed with a thumb switch on the handle. They were supposedly quiet, though in Rob's experience they weren't any more stealthy than the ones you could rent at any dive shop back on Earth. Some contractor in Japan had made a bundle on them. Rob found two with full batteries and hooked them on the edge of the pool for easy access.

Now for the hard part: suiting up without any help. Rob took off his frayed and slightly smelly insulated jumpsuit and stripped to the skin. First the diaper—he and Henri were going to be out for eight hours, and getting the inside of his suit wet would invite death from hypothermia. Then a set of thick fleece longjohns, like a child's pajamas. The water outside was well below freezing; only the pressure and salinity kept it liquid. He'd need all the insulation he could get.

Then the drysuit, double-layered and also insulated. In the chilly air of the changing room he was getting red-faced and hot with all this protection on. The hood was next, a snug fleece balaclava with built-in earphones. Then the helmet, a plastic fishbowl more like a space helmet than most diving gear, which zipped onto the suit to make a watertight seal. The back of the helmet was packed with electronics—biomonitors, microphones, sonar unit, and an elaborate heads-up display that could project text and data on the inside of the faceplate. There was also a freshwater tube, from which he sipped before going on to the next stage.

Panting with the exertion, Rob struggled into the heavy APOS backpack, carefully started it up *before* attaching the hoses to his helmet, and took a few breaths to make sure it was really working. The APOS gear made the whole Ilmatar expedition possible. It made oxygen out of seawater by electrolysis, supplying it at ambient pressure. Little sensors and a sophisticated computer adjusted the supply to the wearer's demand. The oxygen mixed with a closed-loop argon supply; at the colossal pressures of Ilmatar's ocean bottom, the proper air mix was about one thousand parts argon to one part oxygen. Hitode Station and the subs each had bigger versions, which was how humans could live under six kilometers of water and ice.

The price, of course, was that it took six days to go up to the surface. The pressure difference between the three hundred atmospheres at the bottom of the sea and the half standard at the surface station meant a human wouldn't just get the bends if he went up quickly—he'd literally explode. There were other dangers, too. All the crew at Hitode took a regimen of drugs to ward off the scary side effects of high pressure.

With his APOS running (though for now its little computer was sensible enough to simply feed him air from the room outside), Rob pulled on his three layers of gloves, buckled on his fins, put on his weight belt, switched on his shoulder lamp, and then crouched on the edge of the moon pool to let himself tumble backward into the water. It felt pleasantly cool, rather than lethally cold, and he bled a little extra gas into his suit to keep him afloat until Henri could join him.

He gave the drones instructions to follow at a distance of four meters, and created a little window on his faceplate to let him watch through their eyes. He checked over the camera clamped to his shoulder to make sure it was working. Everything nominal. It was 0120 now. Where was Henri?

Kerlerec lumbered into view ten minutes later. In the bulky stealth suit he looked like a big black toad. The foam cover of his faceplate was hanging down over his chest, and Rob could see that he was red and sweating. Henri waddled to the edge of the pool and fell back into the water with an enormous splash. After a moment he bobbed up next to Rob.

"God, it is hot in this thing. You would not believe how hot it is. For once I am glad to be in the water. Do you have everything?"

"Yep. So how are you going to use the camera in that thing? Won't it spoil the whole stealth effect?"

"I will not use the big camera. That is for you to take pictures of me at long range. I have a couple of little cameras inside my helmet. One points forward to see what I see, the other is for my face. Link up."

They got the laser link established and Rob opened two new windows at the bottom of his faceplate. One showed him as Henri saw him—a pale, stubbly face inside a bubble helmet—and the other showed Henri in extreme close-up. The huge green-lit face beaded with sweat looked a bit like the Great and Powerful Oz after a three-day drunk.

"Now we will get away from the station and try out your sonar on my suit. You will not be able to detect me at all."

Personally Rob doubted it. Some Russian had made a cool couple of million Euros selling Henri and his sponsors at ScienceMonde a failed prototype or just a fake.

The two of them descended until they were underneath Hab One, only a couple of meters above the seafloor. The light shining down from the moon pool made a pale cone in the silty water, with solid blackness beyond.

Henri led the way away from the station, swimming with his headlamp and his safety strobe on until they were a few hundred meters out. "This is good," he said. "Start recording."

Rob got the camera locked in on Henri's image. "You're on."

Henri's voice instantly became the calm, friendly but all-knowing voice of Henri Kerlerec, scientific media star. "I am here in the dark ocean of Ilmatar, preparing to test the high-tech stealth diving suit which will enable me to get close to the Ilmatarans without being detected. I am covering up the faceplate with the special stealth coating now. My cameraman will try to locate me by sonar. Because the Ilmatarans live in a completely dark environment, they are entirely blind to visible light, so I will leave my safety strobe and headlamp on."

Rob opened up a window to display sonar images and began recording. First on passive—his computer could build up a vague image of the surroundings just from ambient noise and interference patterns. No sign of Henri, even though Rob could see his bobbing headlamp as he swam back and forth ten meters away.

Not bad, Rob had to admit. Those Russians know a few things about sonar baffling. He tried the active sonar. The seabottom and the rocks flickered into clear relief, an eerie false-color landscape where green meant soft and yellow meant hard surfaces. The ocean itself was completely black on active. Henri was a green-black shadow against a black background. Even with the computer synthesizing both the active and passive signals, he was almost impossible to see.

"Wonderful!" said Henri when Rob sent him the images. "I told you: completely invisible! We will edit this part down, of course—just the sonar images with me explaining it in voiceover. Now come along. We have a long trip ahead of us."

The Bitterwater Company are waking up. Longpincer's servants scuttle along the halls of his house, listening carefully at the entrance to each guest chamber and informing the ones already awake that a meal is ready in the main hall.

Broadtail savors the elegance of having someone to come wake him when the food is ready. At his own house, all would starve if he waited for his apprentices to prepare the meals. He wonders briefly how they are getting along without him. The three of them are reasonably competent, and can certainly tend his pipes and crops without him. Broadtail does worry about how well they can handle an emergency—what if a pipe breaks or one of his nets is snagged? He imagines returning home to find chaos and ruin.

But it is so very nice here at Longpincer's house. Mansion, really. The Bitterwater vent isn't nearly as large as Continuous Abundance or the other town vents, but Longpincer controls the entire flow. Everything for ten cables in any direction belongs to him. He has a staff of servants and hired workers. Even his apprentices scarcely need to lift a pincer themselves.

Broadtail doesn't want to miss the meal. Longpincer's larder is as opulent as everything else at Bitterwater. As he crawls to the main hall he marvels again at the thick growths on the walls and floor. Some of his own farm pipes don't support this much life. Is it just that Longpincer's large household generates enough waste to support lush indoor growth? Or is he rich enough to pipe some excess vent water through the house itself? Either way it's far more than Broadtail's chilly property and tepid flow rights can achieve.

As he approaches the main hall Broadtail can taste a tremendous and varied feast laid out. It sounds as if half a dozen of the Company are already there; it says much for Longpincer's kitchen that the only sounds Broadtail can hear are those of eating.

He finds a place between Smoothshell and a quiet individual whose name Broadtail can't recall. He runs his feelers over the food before him and feels more admiration mixed with jealousy for Longpincer. There are cakes of pressed sourleaf, whole towfin eggs, fresh jellyfronds, and some little bottom-crawling creatures Broadtail isn't familiar with, neatly impaled on thorns and still wiggling.

Broadtail can't recall having a feast like this since he inherited the Northslope property and gave the funeral banquet for old Flatbody. He is just reaching for a third jellyfrond when Longpincer clicks loudly for attention from the end of the hall.

"I suggest a small excursion for the Company," he says. "About ten cables beyond my boundary stones up current is a small vent, too tepid and bitter to be worth piping. I forbid my workers to drag nets there, and I recall finding several interesting creatures feeding at the vent. I propose swimming there to look for specimens."

"May I suggest applying Sharpfrill's technique for temperature measurement to those waters?" says Smoothshell.

"Excellent idea!" cries Longpincer. Sharpfrill mutters something about not having his proper equipment, but the others bring him around. They all finish eating (Broadtail notices several of the company stowing delicacies in pouches, and grabs the last towfin egg to fill his own), and set out for the edge of Longpincer's property.

Swimming is quicker than walking, so the party of scholars cruise at just above net height. At that height Broadtail can only get a general impression of the land below, but it all seems neat and orderly—a well-planned network of stone pipes radiating out from the main vent, carrying the hot, nutrient-rich water to nourish thousands of plants and bacteria colonies. Leaks from the pipes and the waste from the crops and Longpincer's household feed clouds of tiny swimmers, which in turn attract larger creatures from the cold waters around. Broadtail notes with approval the placement of Longpincer's nets, in staggered rows along the prevailing current. With a little envy he estimates that Longpincer's nets probably produce as much wealth as his own entire property.

Beyond the boundary stones the scholars instinctively gather into a more compact group. There is less conversation and more careful listening and pinging. Longpincer assures them that he allows no bandits or scavengers around his vent, but even he pings behind them once or twice, just to make sure. But all anyone can hear are a few wild children, who flee quickly at the approach of adults.

Henri and Ron didn't talk much on the way to the vent community. Both of them were paying close attention to the navigation displays inside their helmets. Getting around on Ilmatar was deceptively easy: take a bearing by inertial compass, point the impeller in the right direction, and off you go. But occasionally Ron found himself thinking about just how hard it would be to navigate without electronic help. The stars were hidden by a kilometer of ice overhead, and Ilmatar had no magnetic field worth speaking of. It was barely possible to tell up from down—if you had your searchlights on and could see the bottom and weren't enveloped in a cloud of silt—

but maintaining a constant depth depended entirely on watching the sonar display and the pressure gauge. A human without navigation equipment on Ilmatar would be blind, deaf, and completely lost.

At 0500 they were nearing the site. "Passive sonar only," said Henri. "And we must be as quiet as possible. Can you film from a hundred meters away?"

"It'll need enhancement and cleaning up afterward, but yes."

"Good. You take up a position there—" Henri gestured vaguely into the darkness.

"Where?"

"That big clump of rocks at, let me see, bearing one hundred degrees, about fifty meters out."

"Okay."

"Stay there and do not make any noise. I will go on ahead toward the vent. Keep one of the drones with me."

"Right. What are you going to do?"

"I will walk right into the settlement."

Shaking his head, Rob found a relatively comfortable spot among the stones. While he waited for the silt to settle, he noticed that this wasn't a natural outcrop—these were cut stones, the remains of a structure of some kind. Some of the surfaces were even carved into patterns of lines. He made sure to take pictures of everything. The other xeno people back at Hitode would kill him if he didn't.

Henri went marching past in a cloud of silt. The big camera was going to be useless with him churning up the bottom like that, so Rob relied entirely on the drones. One followed Henri about ten meters back, the second was above him looking down. The laser link through the water was a little noisy from suspended particulates, but he didn't need a whole lot of detail. The drone cameras could store everything internally, so Rob was satisfied with just enough sight to steer them. Since he was comfortably seated and could use his hands, he called up a virtual joystick instead of relying on voice commands or the really irritating eye-tracking menu device.

"Look at that!" Henri called suddenly.

"What? Where?"

Henri's forward camera swung up to show eight Ilmatarans swimming along in formation, about ten meters up. They were all adults, wearing belts and harnesses stuffed with gear. A couple carried spears. Ever since the first drone pictures of Ilmatarans, they had been described as looking like giant lobsters, but watching them swim overhead, Rob had to disagree. They were more like beluga whales in armor, with their big flukes and blunt heads. Adults ranged from three to four meters long. Each had a dozen limbs folded neatly against the undersides of their shells: walking legs in back, four manipulators in front, and the big praying-mantis pincers on the front pair. They also had raspy feeding tendrils and long sensory feelers under the head. The head itself was a smooth featureless dome, flaring out over the neck like a coal-scuttle helmet—the origin of the Ilmatarans' scientific name *Salletocephalus structor*. Henri's passive microphones picked up the clicks and pops of the Ilmatarans' sonar, with an occasional loud ping like a harpsichord note.

The two humans watched as the group soared over Henri's head. "What do you think they're doing?" asked Rob when they had passed.

"I am not sure. Perhaps a hunting party. I will follow them."

Rob wanted to argue, but knew it was pointless. "Don't go too far."

Henri kicked up from the bottom and began to follow the Ilmatarans. It was hard for a human to keep up with them, even when wearing fins. Henri was sweaty and breathing hard after just a couple of minutes, sounding relieved.

The Ilmatarans were dropping down to a small vent formation, which Rob's computer identified as Maury 3b. Through the drone cameras Rob watched as Henri crept closer to the Ilmatarans. At first he moved with clumsy stealth, then he abandoned all pretense and simply waded in among them. Rob waited for a reaction, but the Ilmatarans seemed intent on their own business.

A rock is missing. Broadtail remembers a big chunk of old shells welded together by ventwater minerals and mud, just five armspans away across-current. But now it's gone. Is his memory faulty? He pings again. There it is, just where it should be. Odd. He goes back to gathering shells.

"—you hear me? Broadtail!" It is Longpincer. He appears out of nowhere just in front of Broadtail, sounding alarmed.

"I'm here. What's wrong?"

"Nothing," says Longpincer. "My own mistake."

"Wait. Tell me."

"It's very odd. I remember hearing you clattering over the rocks, then silence. I recall pinging and sensing nothing."

"I remember a similar experience—a rock seeming to disappear and then appear again."

Smoothshell comes up. "What's the problem?" After they explain she asks, "Could there be a reflective layer here? Cold water meeting hot does that."

"I don't feel any change in the water temperature," says Longpincer. "The current here is strong enough to keep everything mixed."

"Let's listen," says Broadtail. The three of them stand silently, tails together, heads outward Broadtail relaxes, letting the sounds and interference patterns of his surroundings create a model in his mind. The vent is there, rumbling and hissing. Someone is scrabbling up the side—probably Sharpfrill with his jars of temperature-sensitive plants. Roundhead and the quiet person are talking together half a cable away, or rather Roundhead is talking and his companion is making occasional polite clicks. Two others are swishing nets through the water upcurrent.

But there is something else. Something moving nearby. He can't quite hear it, but it blocks other sounds and changes the interference patterns. He reaches over to Smoothshell and taps on her leg. "There is a strange effect in the water in front of me, moving slowly from left to right."

She turns and listens that way while Broadtail taps the same message on Longpincer's shell. "I think I hear what you mean," she says. "It's like a big lump of very soft mud, or pumice stone."

"Yes," Broadtail agrees. "Except that it's moving. I'm going to ping it now." He tenses his resonator muscle and pings as hard as he can, loud enough to stun a few small swimmers near his head. All the other Company members about the vent stop what they are doing.

He hears the entire landscape in front of him—quiet mud, sharp echoes from rocks, muffled and chaotic patterns from patches of plants. And right in the center, only a few armspans in front of him, is a hole in the water. It's big, whatever it is: almost the size of a young adult, standing upright like a boundary marker.

Henri was completely gonzo. He was rattling off narration for the audience completely off the top of his head. Occasionally he would forget to use his media star voice and give way to an outburst of pure cackling glee. Rob was pretty excited, too, watching through the cameras as Henri got within arm's reach of the Ilmatarans.

"Here we see a group of Ilmatarans gathering food around one of the seabottom vents. Some are using hand-made nets to catch fish, while these three close to me appear to be scraping algae off the rocks."

"Henri, you're using Earth life names again. Those aren't fish, or algae either."

"Never mind that now. I will dub in the proper words later if I must. The audience will understand better if I use words they understand. This is wonderful, don't you think? I can pat them on the backs if I want to!"

"Remember, no contact."

"Yes, yes." Back into his narrator voice. "The exact nature of Ilmataran social organization is still not well understood. We know they live in communities of up to a hundred individuals, sharing the work of food production, craft work, and defense. The harvest these bring back to their community will be divided among all."

"Henri, you can't just make stuff up like that. Some of the audience are going to want links to more info about Ilmataran society. We don't know how they allocate resources."

"Then there is nothing to say that this is untrue. Robert, people do not want to hear that aliens are just like us. They want wise angels and noble savages. Besides, I am certain I am right. The Ilmatarans behave exactly like early human societies. Remember I am an archaeologist by training. I recognize the signs." He shifted back into media mode. "Life is difficult in these icy seas. The Ilmatarans must make use of every available source of food to ward off starvation. I am going to get closer to these individuals so that we can watch them at their work."

"Don't get too close. They might be able to smell you or something."

"I am being careful. How is the picture quality?"

"Well, the water's pretty cloudy. I've got the drone providing an overhead view of you, but the helmet camera's the only thing giving us any detail."

"I will bend down to get a better view, then. How is that?"

"Better. This is great stuff." Rob checked the drone image. "Uh, Henri, why are they all facing toward you?"

"We must capture it," says Longpincer. "I don't remember reading about anything like this."

"How to capture something we can barely make out?" asks Broadtail.

"Surround it," suggests Smoothshell. She calls to the others. "Here, quickly! Form a circle!"

With a lot of clicking questions the other members of the Bitterwater Company gather around—except for Sharpfrill, who is far too absorbed in placing his little colonies of temperature indicators on the vent.

"Keep pinging steadily," says Longpincer. "As hard as you can. Who has a net?"

"Here!" says Raggedclaw.

"Good. Can you make it out? Get the net on it!"

The thing starts to swim upward clumsily, churning up lots of sediment and making a faint but audible swishing noise with its tails. Under Longpincer's direction the Company form a box around it, like soldiers escorting a convoy. Raggedclaw gets above it with the net. There is a moment of struggling as the thing tries to dodge aside, then the scientists close in around it.

It cuts at the net with a sharp claw, and kicks with its limbs. Broadtail feels the claw grate along his shell. Longpincer and Roundhead move in with ropes, and soon the thing's limbs are pinned. It sinks to the bottom.

"I suggest we take it to my laboratory," says Longpincer. "I am sure we all wish to study this remarkable creature."

It continues to struggle, but the netting and ropes are strong enough to hold it. Whatever it is, it's too heavy to carry swimming, so the group must walk along the bottom with their catch while Longpincer swims ahead to fetch servants with a litter to help. They all ping about them constantly, fearful that more of the strange silent creatures are lurking about.

"Robert! In the name of God, help me!" The laser link was full of static and skips, what with all the interference from nets, Ilmatarans, and sediment. The video image of Henri degenerated into a series of still shots illustrating panic, terror, and desperation.

"Don't worry!" he called back, although he had no idea what to do. How could he rescue Henri without revealing himself and blowing all the contact protocols to hell? For that matter, even if he did reveal himself, how could he overcome half a dozen full-grown Ilmatarans?

"Ah, bon Dieu!" Henri started what sounded like praying in French. Rob muted the audio to give himself a chance to think, and because it didn't seem right to listen in.

He tried to list his options. Call for help? Too far from the station, and it would take an hour or more for a sub to arrive. Go charging in to the rescue? Rob really didn't want to do that, and not just because it was against the contact regs. On the other hand he didn't like to think of himself as a coward, either. Skip that one and come back to it.

Create a distraction? That might work. He could fire up the hydrophone and make a lot of noise, maybe use the drones as decoys. The Ilmatarans might drop Henri to go investigate, or run away in terror. Worth a shot, anyway.

He sent the two drones in at top speed, and searched through his computer's sound library for something suitable to broadcast. "Ride of the Valkyries"? Tarzan yells? "O Fortuna"? No time to be clever; he selected the first item in the playlist and started blasting Billie Holiday as loud as the drone speakers could go. Rob left his camera gear with Henri's impeller, and used his own to get a little closer to the group of Ilmatarans carrying Henri.

Broadtail hears the weird sounds first, and alerts the others. The noise is coming from a pair of swimming creatures he doesn't recognize, approaching fast from the left. The sounds are unlike anything he remembers—a mix of low tones, whistles, rattles, and buzzes. There is an underlying rhythm, and Broadtail is sure this is some kind of animal call, not just noise.

The swimmers swoop past low overhead, then, amazingly, circle around together for another pass, like trained performing animals. "Do those creatures belong to Longpincer?" Broadtail asks the others.

"I don't think so," says Smoothshell. "I don't remember seeing them in his house."

"Does anyone have a net?"

"Don't be greedy," says Roundhead. "This is a valuable specimen. We shouldn't risk it to chase after others."

Broadtail starts to object, but he realizes Roundhead is right. This thing is obviously more important. Still—"I suggest we return here to search for them after sleeping."

"Agreed."

The swimmers continue diving at them and making noise until Longpincer's servants show up to help carry the specimen.

Rob had hoped the Ilmatarans would scatter in terror when he sent in the drones, but they barely even noticed them—even with the speaker volume maxed out. He couldn't tell if they were too dumb to pay attention, or smart enough to focus on one thing at a time.

He gunned the impeller, closing in on the little group. Enough subtlety. He could see the lights on Henri's suit about fifty meters away, bobbing and wiggling as the Ilmatarans carried him. Rob slowed to a stop about ten meters from the Ilmatarans. The two big floodlights on the impeller showed them clearly.

Enough subtlety and sneaking around. He turned on his suit hydrophone. "Hey!" He had his dive knife in his right hand in case of trouble.

Broadtail is relieved to be rid of the strange beast. He is getting tired and hungry, and wants nothing more than to be back at Longpincer's house snacking on threadfin paste and heat-cured eggs.

Then he hears a new noise. A whine, accompanied by the burble of turbulent water. Off to the left about three lengths there is some large swimmer. It gives a loud call. The captive creature struggles harder.

Broadtail pings the new arrival. It is very odd indeed. It has a hard cylindrical body like a riftcruiser, but at the back it branches out into a bunch of jointed limbs covered with soft skin. The thing gives another cry and waves a couple of limbs.

Broadtail moves toward it, trying to figure out what it is. Two creatures, maybe? And what is it doing? Is this a territorial challenge? He keeps his own pincers folded so as not to alarm it.

"Be careful, Broadtail," Longpincer calls.

"Don't worry." He doesn't approach any closer, but evidently he's already too close. The thing cries out one more time, then charges him. Broadtail doesn't want the other Bitterwater scholars to see him flee, so he splays his legs and braces himself, ready to grapple with this unknown monster.

But just before it hits him, the thing veers off and disappears into the silent distance. Listening carefully lest it return, Broadtail backs toward the rest of the group and they resume their journey to Longpincer's house.

Everyone agrees that this expedition is stranger than anything they remember. Longpincer seems pleased.

Rob stopped his impeller and let the drones catch up. He couldn't think of anything else to do. The Ilmatarans wouldn't be scared off, and there was no way Rob could attack them. Whatever happened to Henri, Rob did not want to be the first human to harm an alien.

The link with Henri was still open. The video showed him looking quite calm, almost serene.

"Henri?" he said. "I tried everything I could think of. I can't get you out. There are too many of them."

"It is all right, Robert," said Henri, sounding surprisingly cheerful. "I do not think they will harm me. Otherwise why go to all the trouble to capture me alive? Listen: I think they have realized I am an intelligent being like themselves. This is our first contact with the Ilmatarans. I will be humanity's ambassador."

"You think so?" For once Rob found himself hoping Henri was right.

"I am certain of it. Keep the link open. The video will show history being made."

Rob sent in one drone to act as a relay as the Ilmatarans carried Henri into a large rambling building near the Maury 3a vent. As he disappeared inside, Henri managed a grin for the camera.

Longpincer approaches the strange creature, laid out on the floor of his study. The others are all gathered around to help and watch. Broadtail has a fresh reel of cord and is making a record of the proceeding. Longpincer begins. "The hide is thick, but flexible, and is a nearly perfect sound absorber. The loudest of pings barely produce any image at all. There are four limbs. The forward pair appear to be for feeding, while the rear limbs apparently function as both walking legs and what one might call a double tail for swimming. Roundhead, do you know of any such creature recorded elsewhere?"

"I certainly do not recall reading of such a thing. It seems absolutely unique."

"Please note as much, Broadtail. My first incision is along the underside. Cutting the hide releases a great many bubbles. The hide peels away very easily; there is no connective tissue at all. I feel what seems to be another layer underneath. The creature's interior is remarkably warm."

"The poor thing," says Raggedclaw. "I do hate causing it pain."

"As do we all, I'm sure," says Longpincer. "I am cutting through the underlayer. It is extremely tough and fibrous. I hear more bubbles. The warmth is extraordinary—like pipe-water a cable or so from the vent."

"How can it survive such heat?" asks Roundhead.

"Can you taste any blood, Longpincer?" adds Sharpfrill.

"No blood that I can taste. Some odd flavors in the water, but I judge that to be from the tissues and space between. I am peeling back the underlayer now. Amazing! Yet another layer beneath it. This one has a very different texture—fleshy rather than fibrous. It is very warm. I can feel a trembling sensation and spasmodic movements."

"Does anyone remember hearing sounds like that before?" says Smoothshell. "It sounds like no creature I know of."

"I recall that other thing making similar sounds," says Broadtail.

"I now cut through this layer. Ah—now we come to viscera. The blood tastes very odd. Come, everyone, and feel how hot this thing is. And feel this! Some kind of rigid structures within the flesh."

"It is not moving," says Roundhead.

"Now let us examine the head. Someone help me pull off the shell here. Just pull. Good. Thank you, Raggedclaw. What a lot of bubbles! I wonder what this structure is?"

The trip back was awful. Rob couldn't keep from replaying Henri's death in his mind. He got back to the station hours late, exhausted and half out of his mind. As a small mercy Rob didn't have to tell anyone what had happened—they could watch the video.

There were consequences, of course. But because the next supply vehicle wasn't due for another twenty months, it all happened in slow motion. Rob knew he'd be going back to Earth, and guessed that he'd never make another interstellar trip again. He didn't go out on dives; instead he took over drone maintenance and general tech work from Sergei, and stayed inside the station.

Nobody blamed him, at least not exactly. At the end of his debriefing, Dr. Sen did look at Rob over his little Gandhi glasses and say, "I think it was rather irresponsible of you both to go off like that. But I am sure you know that already."

Sen also deleted the "Death to HK" list from the station's network, but someone must have saved a copy. The next day it was anonymously relayed to Rob's computer with a final method added: "Let a group of Ilmatarans catch him and slice him up."

Rob didn't think it was funny at all.

The Garden

A *Hwarhath* Science Fictional Romance

ELEANOR ARNASON

Here's something you may have never seen before—a fascinating take on what a science fiction story would be like if it was written by an *alien* rather than by a human . . .

Eleanor Arnason published her first novel, *The Sword Smith*, in 1978, and followed it with novels such as *Daughter of the Bear King* and *To the Resurrection Station*. In 1991, she published her best-known novel, one of the strongest novels of the nineties, the critically acclaimed *A Woman of the Iron People*, a complex and substantial novel that won the prestigious James Tipree Jr. Memorial Award. Her short fiction has appeared in *Asimov's Science Fiction, The Magazine of Fantasy & Science Fiction, Amazing, Orbit, Xanadu*, and elsewhere. Her most recent novel is *Ring of Swords*. Her story "Stellar Harvest" was a Hugo Finalist in 2000. Her stories have appeared in our Seventeenth, Nineteenth, and Twentieth Annual Collections.

There was a boy who belonged to the Atkwa lineage. Like most of his family, he had steel-gray fur. In the case of his relatives the color was solid. But the boy's fur was faintly striped and spotted. In dim light this wasn't visible. In sunlight his pelt looked like one of the old pattern-welded swords that hung in his grandmother's greathouse and were taken outside rarely, usually to be polished, though sometimes for teaching purposes, when adult male relatives were home. Not that anyone used swords in this period, except actors in plays. But children ought to learn the history of their family.

The boy's pelt was due to a recessive gene, emerging after generations, since the Atkwa had not gone to a spotted family for semen in more than two hundred years. This was not due to prejudice. Unlike humans, the *hwarhath* find differences in color more interesting than disturbing. Their prejudices lie in other directions.*

*Most likely the author is referring to regional bias, since this is the kind of prejudice the *hwarhath* are most willing to discuss and condemn. Inhabitants of the home planet's southern hemisphere regard northerners as overcivilized and likely to stray from traditional values. Inhabitants of the northern hemi-

It was circumstance and accident that kept the Atkwa solid grey. They lived in a part of the world where this was the dominant coloration; and—being a small and not especially powerful family—they did not look to distant places when arranging breeding contracts.

As a toddler, the boy was forward and active, but not to an extraordinary degree. At the age of eight or so, he lengthened into a coltish child, full of energy, but also prone to sudden moods of thoughtfulness. These worried his mother, who consulted with her mother, the family matriarch, a gaunt woman, her fur frosted by age, her big hands twisted by joint disease.

"Well," the matriarch said after listening. "Some men are thoughtful. They have to be, if they're going to survive in space, with no women around to do their thinking."

"But so young?" the mother asked. "He spends hours watching fish in a stream or bugs in a patch of weeds."

"Maybe he'll become a scientist." The matriarch gave her daughter a stern look. "He's your only boy. He's been strange and lovely looking from birth. This has led you to pay too much attention and to worry without reason. Straighten up! Be solid! The boy will probably turn out well. If he doesn't, he'll be a problem for our male relatives to handle."

At ten, the boy discovered gardening—by accident, while following a *tli* that had come out of the nearby woods to steal vegetables. The sun was barely up. Dew gleamed on the vegetation around his grandmother's house. The air he drew into his mouth was cool and fragrant.

The *tli*, a large specimen with strongly marked stripes, trundled over his grandmother's lawn, its fat furry belly gathering dew like a rag wiping moisture off something bright. A metal blade maybe, the boy thought. A dark trail appeared behind the animal, and it was this the boy followed at a safe distance. Not that a *tli* is ever dangerous, unless cornered, but he didn't want to frighten it.

The animal skirted the house, entering the garden in back. There the *tli* began to pillage, a messy process with much (it seemed to the boy) unnecessary destruction. He ought to chase it away. But he was hit—suddenly and with great force—by the beauty of the scene in front of him. The perception was like a blade going into his chest. Don't think of this as a figure of speech, exaggerated and difficult to believe. There are emotions so intense that they cause pain, either a dull ache or a sudden sharp twinge. Under the influence of such an emotion, one's heart may seem to stop. One may feel wounded and changed, as one changed by a serious injury.

This happened to the boy when he didn't, as yet, understand much of what he felt. If he'd been older, he might have realized that most emotions go away, if one ignores them. Instead, he was pierced through by beauty. For the rest of his life he remembered how the garden looked: a large rectangular plot, edged with ornamental

---

sphere regard southerners as rubes. In addition, neighboring families often snipe at one another; and most people, north and south, regard cities with suspicion. It's one thing for men to live intermixed in space. They're kept in line by military discipline. But most of the inhabitants of cities are women. Obviously, they aren't in the army, which is entirely male. What's going to keep them in line, now that they live among unkin?

plants, their leaves—red, purple, yellow, and blue—like the banners of a guard in a military ceremony.

Inside this gaudy border were the vegetables, arranged in rows. Some grew on poles or trellises. Others were bushes. Still others rose directly from the soil as shoots, fronds, clusters of leaves. The variety seemed endless. While the garden's border was brightly colored, most of these plants were shades of green or blue. Yet they seemed—if anything—more lovely and succulent, beaded with dew and shining in the low slanting rays of the sun.

So it was, on a cool summer morning, the air barely stirring, that Atkwa Akuin fell in love—not with another boy, as might have been expected, if not this year, then soon, but with his grandmother's garden.

He spent the rest of that summer in the plot, helping the two senior female cousins who did most of the house's gardening. In the fall, he turned soil, covered beds with hay, trimmed what needed trimming and planted chopped-up bits of root. Black and twisted, they looked dead to him. But they'd send up shoots in the spring, his cousins promised.

Akuin's mother watched doubtfully. The boy was settling down to a single activity. That had to be better than his former dreaminess. But she would have been happier if he'd taken up a more boyish hobby: riding *tsina*, fishing in the nearby river, practicing archery, playing at war.

"Give him more time," said Akuin's grandmother. "Boys are difficult, as I know."

She'd raised three. One had died young in an accident. Another had died in space, killed in the war that had recently begun. The enemy—humans, though their name was not yet known—had come out of nowhere in well-armed ships. Almost everything about them remained hidden in darkness as complete as the darkness from which they'd emerged. But no one could doubt their intentions. The first meeting with them had ended in violence. So had every encounter since.

The matriarch's third son was still alive and had reached the rank of advancer one-in-front. This should have given her satisfaction, but the two of them had never gotten along. Akuin's uncle rarely came home for a visit. The matriarch lavished her attention on her one daughter, her nieces, and their children.

Now she said, folding her twisted hands, "Maybe Akuin will become a gardener in a space station. Such people are useful. An army needs more than one kind of soldier."

When he was fifteen, Akuin went to boarding school, as do all boys of that age. In these places they learn to live without women and among males who belong to other lineages. This becomes important later. A boy who can't detach himself from family and country is of little use in space.

In addition, the boys complete their education in the ordinary *hwarhath* arts and sciences, the ones learned by both females and males; and they begin their education in the specifically male art and science of war.

Akuin's school was on the east coast of his continent, in an area of sandy dunes and scrub forest: poor land for gardening. Nonetheless, the school had a garden. Botany is a science, and horticulture is an art.

It was on the landward side of the school complex, sheltered by buildings from the prevailing wind. Akuin found it the day after he arrived. To the west was a row of dunes, with the afternoon sun standing just above them. Long shadows stretched toward the garden. The gardener—a man with a metal leg—moved slowly between the rows of plants, bending, examining, picking off bugs, which he pressed between the fingers of his good hand. His other arm hung at his side, clearly damaged and not recently. It had shrunk till little remained except black fur over bone.

Akuin thought he was unnoticed. But the gardener turned suddenly, straightened, and glared at him with yellow eyes. Akuin waited motionless and silent. He might be a little odd, but there was nothing wrong with his manners.

"You're new," said the man finally. "Where from?"

Akuin told him.

"Inland. Why aren't you on the beach? Or exploring the school? We have a fine museum, full of things which former students have sent back."

"I like gardens," Akuin said.

The man glared at him a second time, then beckoned, using his good hand. The boy came forward into the garden.

The man's name, it turned out, was Tol Chaib. He'd gone to this school years before, gone into space, then come back to teach. He said nothing more about himself in that first encounter. Instead he talked about the difficulty of growing healthy plants in sand. Partly, he said, he worked to change the soil. The school provided him with compost and manure. More than that was needed. "If there's anything certain about boys and *tsina*, it's that they will produce plenty of fertilizer."

Some of the excess went into lawns and ornamental borders. The rest was sold to local farmers.

Mostly, he found plants that fit the local soil and weather. "Nothing else works. This is why it's so difficult to grow our plants on other planets. The light is different, so is the invisible radiation. The soil has the wrong minerals, or minerals in the wrong proportions. A plant always grows best on its home planet, unless—as sometimes happens—it proliferates unnaturally in a strange place."

Akuin had been feeling lonely and afraid. How could he survive five years in school? At the end of his school years stood a fate even worse. Few *hwarhath* men remain on the home planet. From twenty to eighty, their lives are spent in space, exploring and preparing to meet the enemies who will inevitably appear. The universe is a dangerous place, and the *hwarhath* are a careful species. So the men go into space, looking for trouble, while their female relatives stay home, raising children, and practicing the arts of peace.

Sixty years in metal corridors, with only brief visits home. Hah! The prospect was terrible.

Now, listening to Tol Chaib, he felt a little comfort. Maybe he'd be able to survive school. He could certainly learn much from the crippled man.

The school had a curriculum, of course. There were classes, labs, field trips, military exercises. Most of what Akuin did was required. But when he could decide for himself, he went to Tol Chaib's garden or to the greenhouses where Chaib kept flowers growing all winter.

That was a comfort on days when snow lay over the campus and a knife-wind blew off the ocean. The glass walls were covered by condensed moisture, making the world outside invisible. Inside was damp warm air, the smell of dirt and growing things, flowers that blossomed as brightly as a campfire, the gardener's dry harsh voice.

At first he told Akuin about the plants around them, then about the gardening he'd done in space. Gardens up there—Tol Chaib waved at the ceiling—are necessary for five reasons. Men are healthier if they eat fresh fruit and vegetables. The plants help keep air breathable by removing carbon dioxide and providing oxygen. "This can be done by inorganic chemical reactions or by microbes, but a garden is more pleasant and produces air with a better aroma."

In addition, Tol Chaib said, every station and ship is supposed to be self-sufficient. "Ships become lost. A station might be cut off, if the war goes badly. If this happens, the men on board will need ways to provide themselves with air, food, and medicine."

"You've given me three reasons for gardens in space," Akuin said. "Health, clean air, and self-sufficiency. What are the other two?"

"Joy," the gardener said. "Which is not usually produced by vats of microbes or inorganic chemical reactions, and hope that we will finally come home."

Toward the end of winter Akuin learned how Tol Chaib had been injured.

He'd been the foremost gardener in a small station designed for research rather than war. A supply ship arrived, and the pilot made a mistake while docking—several mistakes, since he panicked when he realized the coupling of ship and station was going badly. The station's outer skin had been punctured. There was sudden loss of pressure, and—Tol Chaib grinned. "The air lock system in my section of the station was new and had improvements, which did not work as planned."

When the rescue workers reached the garden, they found most of the plants gone, sucked into space. The garden's equipment was mostly in pieces. Tol Chaib lay under a heap of debris, next to a lock that had finally closed.

"They think—I don't remember—that I was pulled from one end of the garden to the other, through several rooms. Most likely I hit things on the way. I certainly hit the airlock after it closed; and the debris hit me."

What a story! Akuin shivered.

"The pilot of the ship killed himself. The engineer in front of the air lock design team asked to die. But his senior officers decided the problem with the system had not been caused by anything he did, and could not have been foreseen."

"What was the problem?" Akuin asked. "Why did the system malfunction?"

"I never learned. At first, I was in no condition to pay attention. Later, I didn't care."

"Did the pilot have permission to kill himself?"

"That's another thing I don't know," Tol Chaib said.

The pilot had panicked in an emergency. That was the one thing Akuin knew about him. Maybe, after he saw the damage he'd done, the pilot had panicked a second time and made the decision to die on his own. A terrible idea! "If he asked for permission and got it, then what he did was right," Akuin said finally. "And it was right for the engineer to live, after permission had been refused to him, though—hah! He must have wanted to die."

"Maybe," said Tol Chaib.

There was another thought in Akuin's mind, which he did not express.

"You're wondering why I'm still alive," Tol Chaib said. "I gave serious thought to taking the option." He paused, his good hand gently touching the frilly edge of a tropical bloom. "I was a handsome man. Many approached me or watched from a distance, hoping for encouragement. Hah! It was fine to know that I could make another man happy by saying 'yes.'

"Then I woke and discovered my leg was gone. What a surprise! Where was the rest of me?"

Akuin felt uncomfortable. No child wants to know that adults can be unhappy. Heroes in hero plays—yes. They can suffer, and a boy Akuin's age will be inspired. But a man like Tol Chaib, a teacher and crippled, should never reveal pain.

"I had no desire to limp and crawl through life," the teacher said, his dry voice inexorable. "I wanted to be quick and lovely and loved.

"One of my senior male relatives came to visit me while I was in sick bay. I asked him for permission to die. He said, 'Wait.' So I did. My male relatives consulted with each other and with the officers in front of me. This is how such things are done," the dry voice said. "Except in hero plays."

"I know," Akuin said. In a sense he hadn't known. Before this moment, the rules for killing oneself had been unreal, something learned as one learns formulae one is never going to use. How fine that I can use sticks and triangles to determine the height of that tall tree! Do I want to know the tree's height? No.

"In that kind of situation," Tol Chaib added, "the kind that occurs in hero plays, when a man is entirely alone or the people around him are confused and wrong, it makes sense for the man to take his fate into his own hands. What choice does he have? But it's a good idea to be sure that one is a hero and in a heroic situation, before acting in such a way.

"It was decided I ought to live—for various reasons. My skill as a gardener was remarkable; and I'm good at teaching. Also, I'm an only child; and my mother is well-loved in our family. It was thought she might grieve too much, if I killed myself."

Akuin left the greenhouse soon after, trudging back to his dormitory through a new fall of snow. Overhead the sky was full of stars. For once the air was almost still, though stabbingly cold. The boy walked in a cloud of his own breath.

He reached the middle of a playing field and looked around, first at the snow, unmarked except by the trail he was in the process of making, then at the sky. How brilliant! How many-colored! How difficult to measure!

All at once he lost his sense of position and direction. Up and down seemed no longer different. The ground beneath his feet was gone; so was his body's weight; he was falling into the innumerable stars.

It was a terrible sensation. Akuin closed his eyes. For a moment, the sense of falling continued. Then it was gone, as quickly as it had come. When he opened his eyes, everything was ordinary again.

Later, he wondered if this had been a vision. Most likely not. He'd never shown any signs of having a diviner's ability, nor did he want it. Seeing what other people can't see is unsettling. Diviners tend to be odd ungraceful folk, who go through life out of step and off balance, never fitting into any group. No rational boy wants a fate like this.

More likely, Akuin thought, he'd been tired and disturbed by his mentor's story. In any case, the experience was over and did not recur.

He completed school in the usual period of time. Education is not a race for the *hwarhath*. No one finishes before the others. How can they? Every *hwarhath* male goes into the army as soon as he graduates; and no one can enter the army until he has reached the age of adulthood.*

At twenty, Akuin left school, going home for a long visit. As usual, on visits home, he worked in the family garden. His mother watched with her usual concern. He had turned into a lovely young man, slim and graceful; his pale stippled pelt reminded her of sunlight moving over metal, or water moving over stones. But he was too quiet for a youth his age, too thoughtful and too in love with the plants he tended.

With luck, she told herself, he'd be assigned to work as a gardener. The teachers at his school had recommended this. According to her male relatives, the officers in charge of making assignments often paid attention to such recommendations. Though not always, of course.

A little before harvest, Akuin's assignment came. As expected, it was in space, though where in space the message did not say. He packed the one bag permitted him and said goodbye to his family. It wasn't easy to bid his mother farewell. Unlike humans, the *hwarhath* do not express grief by excreting water from the corners of their eyes. Nor do they have the human love of making noise. Given any reason—grief, anger, happiness, a flash of irritation, a momentary surprise—humans will be noisy. An uncomfortable kind of behavior. Maybe it comes from their ancestors, who spent their time (we are told) screaming at the tops of trees. The *hwarhath* must be descended from animals who spent more time on the ground, where they could see one another, and where noise might attract unwelcome attention. In most situations, they are quiet, at least in comparison to humans.

But what man wants to see a look of grim endurance on his mother's face?

It was a relief to get outside. The plants that bordered the garden were waist-high now. Their long sharp leaves seemed (to Akuin) like a fence of swords, inlaid with precious metals and encrusted with jewels, so they shone red, blue, yellow, green. The green especially was a shade so intense and pure that it seemed to pierce him. Hah! He could feel it in his throat and chest!

Bugs with the same rich late-summer colors floated in the hot air. Bending down and peering, Akuin could see ripe fruits and vegetables nestled among the leaves of the plants raised for food. He found a few last pests, pressed them to death between his fingers, then turned toward the waiting car.

One of his female cousins drove him to the nearest rail line. They parted quietly. He went by train to the regional airport, then by plane to one of the rocket islands. From the island he went (by rocket of course) to a keeping-pace-with-the-place-below station.† At each stage of this journey, his environment became more closed-in and artificial, till at last in the station it was a maze of grey metal corridors. No windows opened out on space. If they had, what would he have seen?

*This passage may refer to human education, which strikes the *hwarhath* as strangely like a contest where some players must win and others lose. What kind of society wants to produce young men who have already failed at the age of twenty? What kind of society treats the training of the next generation as if it were a game?

†The human term would be a geosynchronous station.

His unreachable home planet.

Akuin felt his spirit shrink like a plant shriveling in a drought. How was he going to survive? His grandmother's voice, speaking in his mind, gave the answer: through loyalty and discipline. In his imagination he made the gesture of acknowledgement.

An FTL transport carried him (along with other men) to a station in the most remote region of *hwarhath*-explored space. This was not a place where the *hwarhath* would usually have built a station. It was too far out, and the route that led to it was not easy to follow.

But when the *hwarhath* came to this region, they found many stars in close proximity. By itself this would have been interesting. The stars in *hwarhath* space are, for the most part, scattered as thinly as trees on Great Central Plain; and in general they are solitary rather than communal. It's rare to find more than two or three together.

If ordinary stars are like a bottle tree, standing alone on the dusty plain, with at most a couple of offshoots or companions, then this group was like a grove or thicket, gathered around some hidden reason for their gathering: a spring or sunken pool.

Of course the *hwarhath* scientists wanted to study the grove, and they had enough influence to get the station built. But they did not get the resources they wanted. Remember that a war was on. This region was far distant from the *hwarhath* home planet and from the region where humans were a recurring problem. The work done here did not seem important to the men who made decisions. Akuin's new home was inadequately funded.

Imagine a metal cylinder orbiting a dim and dusty, unimpressive star. The cylinder is small and plain, with none of the additions characteristic of the great stations, which unfold over time like flowering plants, producing metal stalks, blossoms, and pods. Around them move attendant bodies: maintenance craft, shuttles, satellites devoted to research or specialized manufacture, so the great station seems enveloped in a cloud of glittering bugs.

Akuin's destination was nothing like this. There was only the cylinder, a simple geometric shape, orbiting its primary, which had no planets. In the distance were other stars, packed closely together, all of them dim and red.

"Like an army camped on a plain," said one of the new arrivals. (Not Akuin.) "How long the night has been! The army's fires have burnt down. Now they are almost out."

"It may look like an army to you," another soldier commented. "To me it looks like a group of stars."*

Scattered through the star-grove (or if you like the image, the army-camp of stars) were other bodies, which the new arrivals could not see. These came in several varieties. Most were burning-into-darkness stars, which had exhausted their fuel, turning into the stellar equivalent of cinders. Others, less numerous, were breaking-into-pieces stars, which had become so dense that gravity had crushed their matter, so it became a kind of *puree* or thick soup. The last group, least numer-

*This interchange may be an example of the *hwarhath* sense of humor.

ous of all, were called falling-into-strangeness; and these were the stars that interested the *hwarhath* scientists.*

Akuin paid little attention to the grove (or camp) of stars. Instead he noticed the interior of the station: a cramped maze of corridors and rooms. There were no windows, of course, and most of the holograms (there were some, though not as large and splendid as the ones in a great station) showed more impressive parts of the galaxy.

At the end of one corridor a huge planet turned, surrounded by moons and braided rings. At the end of another corridor was a human ship, which exploded over and over, hit by *hwarhath* missiles. Hah! It was a thing to see! Dramatic and encouraging!

He was assigned to a room with four other young men, also new arrivals. Each got a bed, a storage locker, and a niche in the wall, where a hologram could be installed. Three of his companions put scenes of home, as did Akuin: his grandmother's garden at midsummer. The last man, a thin lad with the most amazingly ugly markings on his pale grey fur, put nothing in his niche.

The ugly lad was named Gehazi Thev. He seemed remarkably calm and friendly, for a man who looked as if he'd been used to blot up ink. How could any family have kept a child like this one?

"Easy enough to explain," Thev said on the second or third day that Akuin knew him. "My mother is a mathematician, the best in our lineage; and the semen used to produce me came from a family—the Thevar—who are famous scientists. They also have a tendency toward splotchiness, which shows up rarely. It's a defect they have tried to eliminate.

"In any case—" No question that Thev was a talker. "My mother had a terrible pregnancy. Not only did she feel sick, but her ability to think about math vanished almost entirely, either due to her queasiness or to some change in her hormones.

"When I was born, they thought of killing me. Just look!" He ran one hand over an arm disfigured by a great dark blotch. "How could I possibly have a normal life? But my mother had already announced that she would never allow her family to breed her again. These were her good years, when she could do original work. She wasn't going to waste them on motherhood. So—" The calm friendly voice sounded amused. "My relatives could kill me, and lose my mother's genetic material, or they could keep me. There was no reason to believe that I would be stupid."

"It doesn't bother you?" asked Akuin.

"My lack of stupidity? No. The Goddess has made sure that the universe is well provided with stupid people. As far as I can tell from their behavior, humans are as dim as most *hwarhath*. What is this war about, for example? How can we fight people when we can't even talk with them? What has war been about, through our entire history? The taking of land! The acquisition of women and children! But what good are human females to us? If they even have females, as we understand that term. For all we know, humans may have five different sexes, none of them produc-

*Black dwarfs, EDSOs, and clothed singularities. There is no reason to believe the *hwarhath* have discovered such a stellar cluster.

ing children in a way we understand. As for their land, how can we use it? It isn't likely that our plants will grow on their planet. So, what are we fighting for? Women who cannot mother *hwarhath* children, and land which is—for us—infertile. The humans are just as stupid. Unless, of course, they have another reason for killing people." Thev tilted his head, considering the idea of a new reason for war.

"I was talking about your looks," said Akuin. He touched a patch of fur that wasn't blotchy. Instead, it shone like silver. "If you had been like this all over—"

"Hah! I would have been something! There would have been men lined up at our door, and very inconvenient it would have been for the rest of you." Thev paused. He was sprawled on his bed, resting on his elbows, regarding Akuin with resin-yellow eyes. "Yes, it has bothered me at times," he said at last. "When I first realized how very ugly I was, and again when I was in school and the age when boys begin to fall in love. No one would ever love me, I thought. I would have to be content with my hands, and the programs about safe and healthy sexual behavior which the Public Health Corps makes."*

"Has that happened?" Akuin said.

Thev smiled. "I have seen a lot of public health programs. But I have discovered that some men like intelligence. Believe me, I am intelligent!"

They became friends, though the other roommates couldn't understand why. Akuin was lovely and also sad, the kind of youth that older men—some older men—liked to comfort. No one would ever try to comfort Thev. He was too confident and happy. In addition, they were slightly different ages. Thev had stayed on the home world for two extra years, studying at the famous Helig Institute. Instead of being twenty or twenty-one, he was twenty-three, though he didn't seem especially old. His time had been devoted to ideas rather than experience. It was stars he knew, not manners.

They stayed together through the period when new arrivals were oriented to life in space. "Like two burrs," said the other roommates, who began to suspect it was Akuin's beauty that drew the other man. But what drew Akuin to a man whose conversation was so often impossible to understand? All these kinds of stars that fell into themselves, changing (as they did so) the nature given them by the Goddess, and even in some cases (according to Thev) falling out of the universe the Goddess had created. This was unexpected! Who could make sense of it? Who could find it interesting or erotic?

When the orientation period was over, Thev began to spend his time with other physicists. Akuin started his new job, in the station's garden.

A garden, you may think. The lad had been saved. He'd found his natural environment.

The garden occupied a series of rooms, grey metal like everything else in the station. The plants, all useful rather than ornamental, grew in raised beds like metal boxes. Light came from panels in the ceiling. Moisture was provided by a network of tubes, which dripped water directly on the roots. Nothing was wasted. Nothing was present unless it was needed.

*The *hwarhath* believe public health should not be boring. The best of their sex education programs are, according to scholars who have studied this subject, absolutely first-class erotica, to which humans can—and often will—respond.

Akuin discovered that gardening (for him) comprised many things besides the garden itself. He missed sunlight, clouds, rain, bugs, raiding *tli*, the sight of hills rising in the distance, the smell of a nearby forest or ocean. It was home he missed, the home world in its entirety. Most especially he missed his home country: the valleys full of stones and stony rivers, the indomitable granite mountains.

But he could not go home, except for an occasional brief visit, until he was eighty. To think of sixty years in stations like this one! The idea was horrible!

"Don't be morose," Thev said. "You have a gift for gardening. The senior gardener has said that often. In time you'll be transferred to one of the big stations, where there are ornamental plants and bugs, maybe even a hologram of the home world sky. Think of that above you, while you pick suckers off stems! And I, by then, will be a distinguished physicist. They'll bring me in to lecture, and we'll make jokes about the way our lives used to be."

Akuin felt doubtful and said as much.

"And then, finally, when you are a success, I'll confess to you that I've always loved you. And only the Goddess can know why, because you have an awful disposition."

Akuin looked at his friend. "Do you mean that?"

"About your disposition? Absolutely!"

"About loving me?"

"From the first moment I laid eyes on your shining pelt. From the first time I heard you complain."

"Why?"

"I have no idea. Remember that my area of competence is stars, not people."

Akuin kept looking at Thev, who was (as usual) sprawled on his bed, under the empty wall niche. He'd just come from the communal shower. Naked, it was possible to see all the blotches on his front. One covered half his forehead. Another, even larger and just as badly shaped, covered half a thigh.

"Did you ever think of coloring your fur?" Akuin asked.

"My aunts tried dying me when I was young. I hated it, a horrible messy process that stank and had to be done over and over. When it was time, when I smelled the dye cooking, I'd run away and hide, and they would come hunting. They made my cousins join in, until they began to refuse. 'If Thev wants to be ugly, let him be. We don't want to hunt him down like an animal.' My aunts gave up finally."

"You never rethought that decision?"

"What are you telling me, Akuin? You are willing to become my lover if I turn myself black? But not otherwise? Can't you be content to be the lovely one? I am certainly content to be the smart one."

No question the spots were ugly. But the thin body was good enough, and so was the voice, even and friendly and amused. The mind was in front of any mind he'd ever encountered. What would it be like to make love with someone who could peer into the center of stars and see what lies beyond ordinary experience?

Akuin kissed his friend. Thev responded with passion. Ugly he might be, and intellectual, but he was also passionate.

They became lovers. This is always a difficult situation when the couple is young, without much privacy. Either they waited till their roommates were gone, or they used the rooms-for-sex-and-other-intimate-behavior that are associated with gymnasia.

It would be better to do these things, Akuin thought, in the woods of Atkwa or in a secluded part of his grandmother's garden. Even the dunes next to his boarding school would have been better. Love did not belong in the station. Though Thev didn't seem to mind the grey rooms and the air that smelled of machinery.

Would life have been different, Akuin wondered later, if he'd chosen a more appropriate lover? One of the older men, who showed an interest in him? The senior gardener, for example?

The problem now, aside from the uncomfortable places they made love, was Thev's other passion. He was onto something interesting about the star grove.

Maybe if Akuin had loved his work as much, he would have been able to endure Thev's periods of abstraction or his long discussions of the behavior of aging stars. He tried to be as boring, telling Thev about the garden's problems. It is always difficult to keep an incomplete ecology in balance. This particular garden had recurrent infestations of a parasitic organism that was neither a plant nor an animal, but rather alive in its own peculiar way. It was native to the *hwarhath* home world, but had changed after the *hwarhath* had inadvertently carried it into space, a region it liked; or rather it liked the conditions of gardens in space. It thrived under lights that did not have the exact spectrum of the *hwarhath* home star; and soil that wasn't full of the home world's microorganisms seemed like a gift from the Goddess.

Thev listened patiently, but what he heard—more than anything else—was complaining. Obviously, a garden in space was going to be different from a garden on the home planet. Obviously, there were going to be difficulties and problems. But to a man of his temperament, optimistic and determined, problems were something one overcame or suffered cheerfully, the way he suffered his spots.

If Akuin's plants were covered with mold, well then, Akuin would have to find a cure. If a cure could not be found, the garden would have to grow other kinds of plants.

"Does nothing discourage you?" asked Akuin.

"You do, sometimes. Why not enjoy life? Is anything improved by moping? Think of how handsome you are! Think of my devotion! Do you think mold is any worse than my equations, which are not going where I want them to?"

In spite of his excellent heritage, Thev said, he was not a first-rate mathematician. Rather, he had an instinct for how things are. "Where that came from, I don't know. The same place as my spots, maybe. In any case, I don't reason out what the Goddess has done with the universe. It comes to me almost as a vision; and if you think it's easy to see things in more than the usual five dimensions, you are wrong.* That's

*Premodern *hwarhath* math and physics recognized five aspects of objects in space. These were: location, extension, expansion-to-the-side, expansion-up-and-down, and relation. (The human equivalents to these are: point, line, plane, and volume. Relation has no exact equivalent.) Early modern theory required a sixth dimension: duration or time. This made people uneasy, since the *hwarhath* like to count everything in groups of five, and attempts were made to get back to five dimensions. Time could not be eliminated, but maybe something could be done with one of the original aspects of space. Were location and relation both necessary? Did the two kinds of expansion need to be counted separately? But all six aspects seemed to have a kind of reality. There were problems that couldn't be solved without them, just as there were problems that couldn't be solved, until they were simplified by the elimination of one or more aspects. In the end most *hwarhath* accepted the existence of all six, though they continue to speak of "five dimensions" in ordinary speech. More recent theories, such as those explaining FTL travel and why the what the grove is like: a place that requires far more than five dimensions, if I'm going to understand it. There are so many stars here, and they are packed so closely!"

Maybe the problem was a difference in magnitude. Mold seems like a trivial problem, compared to Thev's struggles with his equations. More likely it was a difference in temperament. Thev's energy made everything he did important. When he struggled, it was a real struggle. Akuin's sadness, which was chronic now, diminished his concerns. Nothing he did seemed worth doing, to himself or to those around him.

His first year in space ended. The second began. According to messages from relatives, everyone at home was doing well, though his grandmother's garden didn't thrive as it had when he tended it. Beyond doubt, he had a gift. "How lucky that you can use it where you are," his mother said.

The mold was under control now. He had convinced the senior gardener to introduce a few ornamental plants.

"Just in the corners, lad. The places we aren't using. This isn't a great station. If the officers here want flowers for their lovers, too bad. And no matter how you beg, I'm not going to send for bugs. They aren't in the budget."

At first he put in plants with colored leaves. They shone like jewels at the corners of beds full of green and blue-green vegetation.

"Like fire in the night," said one of the station's senior officers. "Are flowers possible?"

"Talk to the man in front of me. He says we don't have the money."

The officer, a physicist and a good one, according to Thev, ran his hand along a bright red leaf. "Maybe something can be worked out, though he's right that research never gets the funding it deserves." The man glanced at Akuin. "You are Gehazi Thev's friend."

"Yes."

"You've made a good choice. He's going to have a future, in spite of being as ugly as a wall made of mud. Beauty isn't everything." The man touched the leaf a second time. "But it's something."

Money was found for flowers, though not for bugs. The senior officer picked the first bloom that opened. "To give to someone dear."

"I know who that is," Thev said. "A man who gets ahead on charm. He'll go into administration. He hasn't got the mind for research. But he isn't a bad fellow, and he'll make sure the men who can think get the chance to think. Do you think charm can take a person all the way to the front, Akuin?"

"I never got the impression that the Frontmen-in-a-Bundle were charming."*

"Research scientists don't make it to the Bundle," Thev said. "Accountants, yes, and administrators, though I'm not sure they are especially charming administrators. Also experts on warfare. But not experts on how the universe really works."

"Are you ambitious?" Akuin asked.

---

universe exists, have required even more dimensions. How the *hwarhath* have dealt with this problem is not yet clear to humans.

*The *hwarhath* equivalent of the human High Command. The Bundle rules *hwarhath* society in space and *hwarhath* males wherever they may be.

"Yes, but not in that way. What I want, aside from you—" He rolled over and took hold of Akuin, pulling him close. "Is fame that goes on forever and a good teaching position."

At the end of his second year in space, Akuin got leave and went home, like any other young man, to his native country and the house where he'd been raised. He was there for the usual length of time, working in his grandmother's garden and taking hikes in the stony hills. For the most part, he spent his time alone.

Hah! He had grown, his female relatives told him. He was handsomer than ever! They didn't mention his aloofness, which troubled them, or the expression of sadness that appeared too often on his face.

"It may be nothing," his grandmother said in private. "There are men who have trouble adjusting to space, but almost everyone manages in the end. This other young man sounds encouraging. I've done research on the family. They are a small lineage, not rich, but they have made excellent alliances; and their traits seem fine. If this romance works out, and Akuin stays involved with the Gehazi boy, we ought to think of approaching them for semen."

"It's the other side of the planet!" Akuin's mother exclaimed. "And the young man has spots!"

"He'd be a poor choice to father children," the grandmother admitted. "Though he is apparently a genius. But I agree with you. It would be better to go to his male relatives. He has plenty who look normal, and most are bright. As for Gehazi's location, these are modern times. We can't be provincial. Who can say which alliances will prove useful?"

At the end of his leave, Akuin visited his former school. It was almost empty, the students on vacation, but Tol Chaib was there, getting his garden ready for winter. Hah! The air was cold already and smelled, when the wind came off the land, of drying vegetation.

He spent a day working with his mentor, digging into the sandy soil, cutting stalks and branches, gathering fallen leaves. In the evening they drank *halin* and talked, alone together in Tol Chaib's quarters. The rest of the building was unoccupied.

After they were both drunk, Tol Chaib said, "I always wanted to have sex with you. It wasn't possible, until you became a man. But the longing was there. It frightened me. I'm not usually attracted to boys."

What was it, Akuin wondered, about him and ugly men? Maybe they could see the wrongness in him, though it was different from their ugliness. There was nothing wrong with Thev except his spots. In every other way, he was a model young man: loyal, determined, direct, pious. Though not violent. Thev lacked the fifth male virtue. Well, no one was perfect, and Thev's other traits—his intelligence and cheerfulness—ought to count for something.

Tol Chaib was more disturbing. Looking at him, Akuin saw loneliness and grief for things lost: his old beauty, his life in space. The old man was like a mirror, reflecting Akuin's future. He could end like this. Though he didn't think he would ever be attracted to boys. That was a perversion, after all; and his wrongness—whatever it was exactly—seemed unconnected with perversity. He was a gardener, who wanted to garden at home. A shameful ambition! But not the same as wanting to molest children.

In the end, after another cup of *halin*, he went to bed with Tol Chaib, though he was never certain exactly why. The old man wanted this to happen, and he felt he owed his mentor something. That was as good an explanation as any. In the morning they parted, Tol Chaib giving him a tropical flower from the school greenhouse. It was huge and intricate and as blue as the sky, though almost scentless. Akuin carried it until it wilted, then threw it in the ocean. This was on one of the rocket islands. An *ikun* later he boarded a rocket, which carried him into space.

Gehazi Thev greeted him with affection when he got back to their station. "Though it was a good idea to have time away from you. I thought about stellar evolution instead of sex. There is much to be said for both, of course, but my job is stars."

During his absence, Thev had moved into a new dormitory, this one occupied by four young physicists.

"There didn't seem to be any reason to stay in my old room. I have nothing in common with the other men. It was only habit that kept me there. Habit and you, and you were gone."

Their romance continued, though it might have ended. Who can say what ties men (or women) together? They returned to their old habits, exercising in the station's gymnasia, going to its one theatre to see recordings of plays put on in the great stations, places such as Tailin. Both enjoyed soaking in the pools-for-soaking. Both enjoyed sex in the rooms-for-privacy.

These last were small, like everything in the station. There was a low bed, fastened to the floor, and two stools that moved in grooves. The ceiling had a mirror, which could be turned off, though the lovers usually kept it on. The wall opposite the bed could be replaced with a hologram. Thev liked scenes of space: galaxies, nebulae, stars, and planets. Akuin (of course) preferred scenes of home.

During one of their stays in a private room, Thev spoke about the work he was doing. They'd had sex and were lying together on the bed's thin mattress. A trio of stars—red, white and orange—blazed at the room's end. The mirror above them showed their bodies, quiet now, Thev resting on his belly, Akuin on his back.

Later, Akuin remembered the scene, as he remembered the day he first fell in love with his grandmother's garden.

Thev had been working with geometry. "Making models, so I can visualize what is happening in this region of space. Mind you, it isn't easy. We evolved to see five dimensions, and that's the number we insist on seeing, no matter how many there may be.

"But it is possible, especially if one uses a computer. How did our ancestors get anything done, before the existence of computers? Imagine trying to understand the universe by counting on fingers! Or making lines in the dirt! No wonder the universe was small in those days! No wonder it was simple!

"What one does—" Thev rolled over and began to go through his uniform's pockets.* A moment later he was kneeling by the hologram projector. The triple star van-

*The *hwarhath* male uniform is a pair of shorts: knee-length, loose and abundantly provided with pockets. This, plus sandals, is adequate for life in a space station or ship. Their costume when on planets is more varied.

ished. In its place was an irregular object made of glowing white lines. It floated in midair, turning slowly and changing shape as it turned.

"—Is eliminate one of the ordinary visible dimensions and replace it with a dimension that can't be seen. Obvious, you may say to me; and certainly it has been done many times before; and certainly it isn't adequate to show what's happening in this region of space.

"But if one makes a large number of these partial models, each one showing an aspect of reality—"

Now the room was full of floating objects, all made of glowing lines, but not all the same color. Some were red or orange, like the vanished stars. Others were green, blue, yellow. Hah! It was like a garden! Except these flowers were all deformed and deforming. Some expanded like leaves opening in spring. Others folded in and seemed to be swallowing themselves. As one diminished, the one beside it grew, either in size or complexity. Akuin began to feel queasy.

"The problem, of course, is fitting all these partial models together. This is where a computer is essential."

"What is this about?" Akuin asked. "Does this array of ugly objects serve any purpose?"

"Ugly!" said Thev. "Dear one, they are the achievement of my life!" He was back on the bed now, sitting with his arms around his knees, admiring the things. "Of course, I'm young and likely to do better. But this isn't bad, I assure you."

"You have told me," Akuin said, "that you are trying to see what can't be seen, and comprehend what isn't comprehensible. Maybe you can do this. Everyone agrees that you are brilliant. But I'm not going to understand these things swallowing themselves."

"You want another kind of model. Something which has to do with plants and bugs."

"That's what I know," Akuin said.

Thev was silent for a while, watching his things, which continued to grow, change shape, divide, diminish and vanish. A garden out of a bad dream. A sorcerer's garden.

Thev spoke finally. "Think of this region, this grove of stars, as a grove of trees growing in a dry place, so the trees are forced to seek water. We think the ground is dirt and stone; we think it's solid. In reality, a multitude of roots go down and out, forcing their way through dirt and stone, twisting around each other. It's possible the roots are connected."

Akuin had grown up in a part of the home world where many species of trees were communal, their various trunks rising from a single root system. But he had trouble imagining stars connected in the same way. This suggests that he hadn't paid attention to his physics class in school, which is true.

"We know that strange stars can be connected with other strange stars. Usually, the partners are not in close proximity. Here, I think they are. Imagine what this must do to reality. Strangeness loops back on itself. The fabric of space is pierced—again and again—by strangeness.

"What I've said so far is ordinary. Few scientists would disagree, except about the strangeness looping. That's not a generally accepted idea, though I'm not the only person who's come forward with it. But from this point on—" Thev glanced and smiled. "The ideas are mine.

"According to the usual theory, the ground under our grove of trees is stable. Yes, the roots have pushed through it, causing stress—most evident at the surface, where the ground may buckle, forced up from below. In areas settled by people, this pressure-from-below is easily perceived. Sidewalks are lifted. The walls of buildings crack and fall. All done by roots." Thev wiggled his fingers, apparently showing the action of roots.

"But let's imagine that the ground is not stable. Maybe the land is limestone and full of caves. The roots, burrowing down, are cracking stone—a thin layer—which forms the roof of one of these caves. In time the roof will break. The grove will fall into a sinkhole."

This was understandable. There are places in the Great Central Plain where the ground is limestone, and water is usually found in pools at the bottom of sinkholes. Nowadays, windmills bring the water up. In the old days, people cut steps in the stone walls and carried buckets. Akuin knew all this, and knew that sinkholes could appear suddenly. But how could a sinkhole appear in space? After all, a sinkhole was an absence of stone. But space wasn't there in the first place. How could one have an absence of something already absent?

"Let me give you another model," Thev said. "Think of this region of space as a cheese."

"What?" said Akuin.

"A large, round one." Thev spread his arms to show the cheese's size. "Bugs have infested it. It looks solid, but inside is a maze of tunnels. If one bends the cheese a little, or twists it, if any extra strain is put on it—hah! It breaks apart! There's nothing left but crumbs. The bugs have destroyed their home."

"These are disturbing images," Akuin said. "What are you saying with them? That this region of space could break into crumbs? I find it hard to imagine such an occurrence. What is a space crumb like?"

"Maybe the grove is a better model than the cheese, though you wanted plants and bugs, and I have given you both. I think it's possible this region will collapse. More than possible. In time, collapse is certain."

"But what will it become? Not a sinkhole?"

"My guess would be a large area of strangeness. Spherical, of course. Such things always are."

"What would happen to the station?" By this time Akuin was sitting up and looking at Thev with horror. This wasn't a pleasant situation that Thev was describing. But Thev's voice was full of interest and pleasure. What Thev was enjoying, of course, was his own cleverness. In addition, it's possible that he saw the situation as one of the many fine jokes with which the Goddess has filled her universe. A pious man will always enjoy the Great Mother's tricks.

"It depends on the size of the collapse," Thev said. "If it takes the entire region out, the station will be destroyed. But if it's the right size, and happens at the right distance, we'll be able to observe the process."

Akuin was getting a headache, either from the conversation or his lover's ugly things, which still filled the room and continued to change in disturbing ways. He mentioned the headache. Thev stopped the recording. The garden remained, but everything in it was motionless.

Much better! Akuin lay back. The mirror above him reflected his own dark body. On one side of him was a funnel made of bright red lines. It appeared to be dissolving and pouring itself down itself, though nothing moved now; and the center of the funnel was empty.

On the other side of him was a blue sphere, which had apparently stopped in the middle of turning itself into something full of many sharp angles. Both the angles and the sphere's smooth surface were visible. Akuin closed his eyes.

Thev kept talking. More research was needed. He'd written a proposal. "But you know the funding situation. If an idea can't be turned into a weapon at once, the frontmen aren't interested; and I can't see any obvious way to do harm with my ideas. Maybe some day we'll be able to use strangeness as a weapon, but not soon."

Thev must be getting tired. His conversation was beginning to wander. So much was uncertain. So many things might happen. If the station wasn't swallowed, it might still be destroyed by the event. "I don't think this process of collapse will be entirely quiet and peaceful." Or, if the station survived, and the men inside were alive, they might find that they'd lost their Heligian gate.*

"We'd be trapped," Akuin said. No one had ever warned him to beware of sex with physicists. Maybe they should have. It would be easier to have a lover who thought about more trivial problems.

"We could send information home," Thev answered in an encouraging tone. "Only at the speed of light. But that would be sufficient. It would take less than five years for a message to reach the nearest working gate. Surely the frontmen would post a ship there, after our gate vanished."

"What is most likely to happen?" Akuin asked.

"The station will be destroyed."

"Soon?"

"I don't know," Thev said. "Some of the work done here suggests the space in this region is badly strained already; and it's possible that our presence is making things worse."

"How?" Akuin asked.

"Through the coming and going of star ships. They do have an effect, though not one that matters in ordinary situations. And there is at least one experiment which may be acting like roots pushing through a crack in limestone, or maybe like a slight twist of the cheese." Thev smiled briefly. "The experiment is continuing, though I've mentioned that it may cause trouble. The men running it don't believe the risk is significant."

"Aren't you worried?" Akuin asked.

"What can I do, except put my ideas out in front? Maybe I'm wrong. I have sent my theory, and recordings of my models, to the Helig Institute. If I die here, I will become famous. If I don't die here, if this region of space does not collapse, then I'll become famous later for something else. One cannot live in fear of thoughts, Akuin."

*The *hwarhath* name for an FTL transfer point.

That was the end of the conversation. Akuin found he couldn't get Thev's ideas out of his mind. They haunted him: the collapsing grove, the cheese eaten out by bugs, the garden of ugly things.

Bad enough to think of living for years in the station. But to think of dying here! How could he feel the same affection for Thev? A man who came up with such ideas and models!

Gradually the two lovers drew apart. Thev accepted this with his usual calm good sense. Nothing pushed him back for long. He always recovered and went forward. Soon he found a lover among the physicists: not a thinker, but a hands-on builder, who said that Thev's models were likely to prove useful, though he didn't believe the station was in danger.

"You theoreticians love terrifying ideas! The Goddess may be sloppy in her details. We know she is, from looking around. But the basic structure of her universe is solid. Space doesn't fall to pieces like a bridge with bad mortar. It lasts! And will outlast everything!"

As for Akuin, he took a series of sexual partners. All were casual. This didn't especially bother him. Some men must have a true love, a companion for life. He wasn't such a man. Sex was fine. So was friendship. But his real love—the center of his life—was plants.

Another year passed. Once again he traveled home. His grandmother had died suddenly, shortly after his previous trip. Now it was time to put her ashes in the ground and carve her name on the monument for Atkwa women.

When he reached his home country, it was spring. In his grandmother's garden flowers bloomed, attracting early bugs. The house was full of female relatives, busy with details of the coming ceremony.

There was nothing for Akuin to do, so he went hiking. South and west of the house were hills, not high, but made impressive by huge outcroppings of igneous rock. No limestone here, eroding easily! His country had bones of granite! An *ikun* from home, he came to his favorite spot for looking into the distance.* Up he climbed, until he was atop the great bald knob. Now he could see the folded hills, covered with pale blue foliage. They stretched in every direction. Here and there were patches of color: yellow, light orange or lavender, flowering shrubs and trees.

All at once, he realized he had reached the limit of his endurance. He could not bear to leave this place again. He would not return to space.

Why did this happen? How can any man turn away from duty? His grandmother, the most formidable member of his family, was dead. He'd lost his lover. His mentor had turned out to be a pervert, attracted to children. The garden in the station was not an adequate substitute for the country here, extending around him in every direction under a cloudless sky.

Always, in the station, he was aware of the space outside: dark, cold, airless, hostile to life. If Thev was right, the emptiness outside the station was not even reliable. It might collapse at any moment, becoming something worse.

Here he stood on granite.

By the time he returned to his grandmother's house, he was already making

*A *hwarhath* measure of time: one tenth of a standard *hwarhath* day, 2.31 human hours.

plans. His female relatives continued to be busy, his mother especially. She would be the new matriarch. Akuin gathered supplies, sneaking them out of storerooms and hiding them in a forest. Tools. Clothing. A rifle and ammunition. A hunting bow and arrows. Medical supplies. Plenty of seeds. A computer full of information.

By the time his grandmother was underground, he was ready. There was a final ceremony: cutting his grandmother's name in the stone which memorialized the family's dead women. When that was over, his mother bid him farewell. A cousin took him to the train station. He climbed on board, climbing out the far side and ducking behind a bush. The train pulled away. His cousin returned to her car. Akuin took off for the forest and his hidden supplies.

He reached them without trouble. With luck, it would be several days before his family realized that he had vanished: time enough to get into the high mountains, the wilderness. He was strong, determined, and not afraid of anything in his homeland. Pack on back, he set off.

There's no reason to tell his life in detail from this point on. The important thing had happened. Akuin had decided to turn away from loyalty and obligation. Now, he lived for himself rather than his family or his species. This is something humans do, if the stories we hear are true. This is why their home planet is full of violence and has far too many inhabitants, produced not by careful breeding contracts, but random acts of heterosexuality.

He found a valley high in the mountains, away from all trails with a hard-to-find entrance. There he built a hut and established his garden. The first year was difficult. So was the second. But he persisted. At times he was lonely. Not often. He'd always been comfortable with solitude. The things around him—sunlight, rain, wind, his garden, the mountains—were a constant source of joy.

In the third year he built a solid cabin. Having done this, he began to wonder what was happening in the house where he'd grown up. He waited till harvest was over, and his cabin full of food. Then he went home.

He couldn't arrive openly, of course. He was a criminal now, and the women of his family had always been law-abiding and respectful of tradition. Instead, he lurked in the forest shadow and crept close after dark, peering in windows. There his family was, the same as always. Only he had changed. For a while he felt regret. Then he remembered the station, and Gehazi Thev's terrifying ideas. He'd made the right choice.

The next fall he came down again. This time he did a little stealing. There were tools he needed, and he could always use more seeds.

The fifth year of his exile, he decided to visit the library in his grandmother's house, which was held by his mother now. He crept in after midnight, when the house was entirely dark, and made his way without trouble to the room. Some of the houses in Atkwa were old. Their libraries were full of actual books, ancient cherished objects. This house had been built a century before. There were a few books, brought from other places, but most of the glass-fronted cabinets held modern recordings. When his electric torch played over them, they glittered like so many jewels: garnet-red novels, poetry like peridots, topaz-yellow plays. The music was shades of blue. What a fool he'd been to take only nonfiction before! Quickly, he picked the recordings he wanted and copied them into his computer, then replaced the shining bits of silicon and metal in their proper resting places.

When he was almost done, he heard a noise. Akuin turned and saw his mother, standing in the doorway.

Hah! She reached out a hand. The ceiling light went on. Akuin stood ashamed, his hands full of music, like a jewel thief holding sapphires.

His mother stepped into the room, closing the door behind her. "It was you who stole from us last fall."

He tilted his head in agreement.

"I thought so, and I thought, 'He's alive.' That idea brought me joy, Akuin, though it shouldn't have. What's wrong with you? Why was it so difficult for you to live like other men? When you came home the first time, your grandmother and I made plans. If your romance worked out, she wanted to ask the Gehazi for semen. A young man of so much promise! A family worth forming an alliance with! We thought—we hoped—you had overcome your oddness at last."

No words of explanation came to him. Instead, he said, "What?" and stopped. His voice sounded harsh. The tone was wrong. He was no longer used to speaking.

"What am I going to do? Nothing. By now the neighboring families have forgotten about you. If I give you to the male police, it will bring our shame into daylight. People will know for certain that you ran from duty. Before, there was a possibility that something happened—an accident, a murder."

"You could tell me to die," Akuin said in his new strange voice.

"Would you kill yourself, if I asked you to?"

He didn't answer.

"No," his mother said. "I think not. Go back to your mountains. Every family has embarrassing secrets. You will be ours."

He set the music on a table. How it glittered!

"Don't come into the house again," his mother added. "I'll see that things are left in the far barn for you."

He opened his mouth to thank her.

"Go."

Akuin left, carrying his computer.

The next year he came home twice, though not to the greathouse. Instead he found his mother's gifts in the far barn: tools, small boxes containing seeds, recordings of music, favorite pieces from when he was young, a letter full of family news.

After this, there were no changes in his life for many years. Bit by bit, he expanded his garden and made his cabin more comfortable. Slowly he read his way through most of the great male plays, which are—as everyone knows—about honor and the making of difficult choices. The heroes, the men who must choose, usually die, as he should have. Or they sacrifice their happiness to obligation. Another thing he had failed to do.

In addition, he read many of the plays written about women and their lives. These deal with endurance and compromise, which are not male virtues.

Maybe he would have made a better woman, though it didn't seem likely. Nothing about him seemed especially feminine. He certainly didn't have his grandmother's solidity. His mother was the same. Women like the mountains of Atkwa! Nothing ordinary could wear them down!

Akuin's mother died prematurely, when he was only forty. Coming down from the mountains through an early snow, he found the usual kind of supplies in the far barn, also a letter. It was from one of his female cousins, telling him the news. A sudden illness, that should not have killed a woman so healthy, not yet old. But it did! *Life is full of these kinds of surprises,* his cousin wrote in an elegant, flowing script, though Akuin was not thinking about calligraphy at the moment.

He fell to his knees, chest heaving. The groans inside him would not come out. Beyond the barn's open door, snow fell in thick soft flakes.

The gifts would continue, his cousin wrote. She had promised his mother while the woman lay dying. *This is not the kind of promise one breaks. Though I have to say, Akuin, that I do not approve of your behavior.*

"So, so," Akuin said. He got up finally, walking into the snow. No chance the people in the house would see him through this whiteness. He lifted his head and hands, as if to catch something, though he didn't know what. The life he should have had? The snow flakes melted when they touched his palms.

More time passed. This is what the real world is like. Instead of the sudden important decisions that heroes must make in plays, everything solved in less than an *ikun*, real life is gradual.

His cousin kept her promise. He continued to find gifts in the barn. For many years he saw no people, except at a distance. He always managed to avoid them.

One summer morning when he was almost fifty, Akuin stepped out his cabin door and saw a monster in his garden. That was his first impression. The thing stood in brilliant sunlight. Akuin, coming out of his cabin's dimness, could make out nothing except the creature's shape: upright on two legs like a person, but far too thin and tall. A stick-person. A person made of bones. Like bones, the monster was pale.

He stepped back into his cabin, picked up his rifle and waited, hoping the monster had not seen him. Maybe it would go away. He'd never had a problem with monsters before.

The thing remained in the middle of Akuin's vegetables. He saw it more clearly now. It had on clothing, pants and a red checked shirt. A head rose above the shirt. The face was hairless, the features like no *hwarhath* features he had ever seen: everything narrow and pushed together, as if someone had put hands on either side of the creature's head and pressed, forcing the cheeks in, the nose out, the forehead up, the chin into a jutting bulge.

"It's a magnificent garden," the creature said in Akuin's own language.

He'd been spotted. Akuin raised his rifle.

A second voice said, "You are looking at a human. This one is friendly. Put the gun down."

Akuin glanced around, until he made out the second person, standing at the forest edge. He was short with steel-gray fur, dressed in hiking shorts and boots. A *hwarhath* male, beyond any question. But not a relative. Like the monster, he spoke with an accent that wasn't local. In the case of this man, the accent was southern.

"Believe me," added the *hwarhath* in a quiet voice. "Neither one of us will do you any harm. We are here with the permission of the Atkwa, for recreational purposes."

"Hiking in the mountains," said the monster in agreement.

"Enemy," Akuin said in the voice he almost never used. Hah! The word came out like a branch creaking in the wind!

"The war has ended," the *hwarhath* said. "We have peace with the humans."

This didn't seem possible, but the news Akuin got from his cousin was all family news.

"Put the gun down," the *hwarhath* male repeated. "You really must not kill this human. He works for us. His rank is advancer one-in-back."*

Akuin had been a carrier. The monster far outranked him. It was definitely wrong to point a gun at a senior officer. He lowered the rifle.

The *hwarhath* man said, "Good. Now, come out."

Slowly, Akuin moved into the sunlight. The monster remained motionless. So did the man at the edge of the forest.

What next? Akuin stood with his rifle pointing down. He was making out more details now. There was a patch of hair, or possibly feathers, on top of the monster's head. The patch was bone-white, like the hairless face. Even the monster's eyes were white, though a dark spot floated in the middle of each eye. Was this a sign of disease? Could the monster be blind? No. Akuin had a clear sense that the thing was watching. The dark spots moved, flicking from him to the *hwarhath* male, then back again.

"I think it would be easier to talk, if you put the gun down entirely," the *hwarhath* said.

A calm voice, low and even, but Akuin recognized the tone. This was authority speaking. He laid the rifle on the ground and straightened up, trying to remember the way he used to hold himself, back when he was a soldier.

"Much better," said the *hwarhath*. He walked forward and picked up the rifle, handing it to the monster.

For a moment, Akuin was afraid. But the monster held the rifle properly, barrel pointed down. The oddly shaped hands did not reach for the trigger. The backs of the hands were pale and hairless. Was the creature the same all over? White and as hairless as a fish?

The *hwarhath* man looked at Akuin, who glanced down at once. This was a very senior officer. It showed in his tone of voice, the way he moved, the way he treated the monster, expecting obedience, which the monster gave him. Not a man you looked at directly.

If the man had questions, he did not ask them. Instead, he explained their arrival. It had been an accident. They'd gotten off their trail and lost. "Though not by much, I suspect. If your relatives become worried, they will be able to find us."

The night before had been spent at the entrance to Akuin's valley. This morning,

*The equivalent human rank is major. There is no easy (or politically neutral) way to discuss the two characters just introduced. Therefore they will not be discussed, except to note that any ordinary *hwarhath* reader would recognize the pair at once. Much of the humor in the rest of the story lies with Akuin's attempts to figure out things all other *hwarhath* know.

curious, they had hiked in. "I don't think we could find this place again. In fact, we'll need your help to get back to our trail."

"I'll give it in return for news," Akuin said, then felt surprise at what he'd said.

The *hwarhath* man tilted his head in agreement. "That can be done."

Akuin remembered he was the host and got busy making tea. The two visitors wandered through his garden. The human still carried Akuin's rifle. There was another rifle in the cabin. If necessary, Akuin could kill both of them.

But if they vanished, Akuin's relatives would look for them and keep looking till the men were found. Hospitality required as much. So did respect for rank and the connections far-in-front officers always had. The *hwarhath* picked a flower—a yellow midsummer bloom—and handed it to his companion, who took it with a flash of teeth. A smile. Then the two of them strolled back toward the cabin, the *hwarhath* first, the monster following, rifle in one hand, flower in the other.

This was a peculiar situation! And likely to turn out badly. If the men became curious about him, they'd discover that he was AWOL. His family would be shamed in public. He would have to kill himself.

His mother should have turned him in twenty-five years before. The result would have been the same for him: death by suicide or execution. But the Atkwa would have escaped embarrassment. At least his mother wasn't alive to see the result of her affection.

Maybe it would be better to ask no questions, send the men off as quickly as possible, and hope they did not become curious. But his longing for information was intense. In any case, they must suspect that he was a runaway. How could they not? He was alone in the mountains and so ignorant that he didn't know the war with the humans was over.

There was a flat rock near his cabin door. He used it as a table, setting out teapot and cups. His two guests settled down, the monster leaning Akuin's rifle against the cabin where Akuin could not reach it, though the monster could. He kept the flower, twirling its stem between oddly proportioned fingers. "It really is a very fine garden."

"What kind of news do you want to hear?" asked the *hwarhath*.

"The war," Akuin said.

"It turned out to be a mistake. Humans can be reasoned with, though I can't say the process is easy; and we live at such great distances from one another that there isn't much to fight over."

"Some fool, apparently a human fool, fired at the first strange ship he encountered," the monster added. "That's how the war began." He showed his teeth to Akuin, another smile. It wasn't quick and friendly like a *hwarhath* smile, but wide and slow. Disturbing. "It continued because the two sides lacked a way to communicate, unless one calls the firing of weapons a form of communication. In the end, we learned each other's languages."

"That helped," the *hwarhath* said. "Though once a war has gotten going, it's hard to stop. This proved no exception."

Akuin asked about Kushaiin, the station where he and Thev had met and become lovers. The *hwarhath* man was silent.

"It's not an important place," Akuin said. "Maybe you haven't heard of it."

"Why do you want to know about it?" the man asked.

"I had a friend who was assigned there, a man named Gehazi Thev."

"The physicist."

"You know about him," said Akuin. "Is he still alive?"

"He wasn't at the station when it disappeared."

Hah! Akuin thought and refilled the cups. The monster had barely touched his tea, but the *hwarhath* male was obviously a drinker. "Did the region collapse, as he said it would? Was the station swallowed by strangeness?"

The *hwarhath* male was silent for a moment. Finally he spoke. "At first, we knew only that something had happened to the gate next to the station. We could no longer use it, though the scientists couldn't tell us why—or if the gate still existed or where it might be, if it still existed. In any case, we could no longer reach the station or communicate with it, except at the speed of light.

"The nearest gate we could use was light-years from Kushaiin. Obviously we sent people there. Looking from a distance, everything around the station—your station—seemed fine. The star grove shone as it always had. The station's beacon was still on; and its signal indicated no problems. But we were looking into the past, and the information we needed would not reach us for years. We set up an observation post and sent an STL probe, though light from the station would reach our post long before the probe reached its destination. The universe is a large place, if one doesn't have access to the Heligian highway system. Then we waited, and the physicists wove theories. It's an activity they love, as you must have noticed."

"Yes," said Akuin. "Didn't Gehazi tell you his ideas? You said he had survived."

"Yes." The *hwarhath* gave him a proper smile, small and quick, not the least bit threatening. "The other scientists had their doubts about his theory, and there were some fine loud arguments. As far as I could determine, nothing was settled, though the physicists kept knotting and unknotting ideas.

"Finally the star grove vanished. It happened from one moment to the next, almost without warning. By looking closely, the scientists were able to find abnormalities in the star grove's spectrum immediately prior to the vanishing. In addition, there was radiation, which originated in the station's region at the time when the station vanished. But none of this was dramatic. Nothing like a nova. I'm not sure how much we would have noticed, if we hadn't been watching closely. When the probe reached the place where the stars had been, it found only empty space."

"How is that possible?" Akuin asked.

"Gehazi Thev revised his theory. If you know him, you know that nothing pushes him back. His first ideas did not explain what happened, so he brought new ideas to the fore. He now thinks the collapse served to separate the region from our universe."

"What do you mean?" Akuin asked. "What happened to the station? Does it still exist?"

"How can we know?" the man said in answer. "If it has survived, then it's in another universe, along with the stars that vanished. A very small universe, according to Gehazi Thev, who has described the place. There is no way to check his ideas, but it's a fine description.

"At first, according to Gehazi Thev, the new universe would be dark, except for the stars around the station. Imagine how that would look!" The man exhaled. Akuin couldn't tell if the exhalation meant horror or interest. Horror seemed more reasonable. "In time the light produced by the stars will be bent back. Then it will seem that new stars are appearing in the distance, all dim and red, like the stars around the station. If the men in the station had good enough instruments, they'd be able to see themselves. They will certainly be able to see and hear the messages they send."

"The men in the station must be dead," Akuin said.

"Most likely, though Gehazi Thev thinks—or did, the last time I heard him speak—there's a slight possibility they are alive. It depends on what happened to all the strangeness in the region when it collapsed, not to mention the energy which should have been generated by the collapse. If these went into this new universe, then the universe is almost certainly uninhabitable. But if the strangeness and energy were somehow dissipated or used up in the creation of the universe—"

It was, Akuin realized, another one of Thev's terrible ideas. "When did this happen?"

"Twenty-three years ago," the *hwarhath* said.

Akuin would have been there, when the station vanished. He almost certainly knew men who had died or gone into their own universe. Had Thev's lover, the hands-on physicist, been among them? He could no longer remember the fellow's name. Akuin looked toward his garden, but did not see its midsummer brightness. Instead, for a moment, he imagined darkness and isolation, relieved—finally—by dim red stars that were an illusion, light bent back toward its origin. What a fate!

"Most likely the station was destroyed," the *hwarhath* said in a comfortable tone, then excused himself and went off to eliminate tea.

The monster stayed where he was, his cup still full. "I have bad reactions to a number of *hwarhath* foods," he said. "It's better not to experiment."

"How did you end up working for us?" Akuin asked.

"I was offered a job. I took it."

"Was this after the war ended?"

The monster smiled his slow, disturbing smile. "No."

"Is this acceptable behavior among humans?" Akuin asked.

"To change sides in the middle of a war? No."

Obviously Akuin found the monster interesting. This was a person who'd done something worse than running away. "What would happen if your people got hold of you?"

"Nothing now. There is a treaty. I'm a *hwarhath* officer. That should protect me. But the usual penalty for disloyalty is death."

Akuin wanted to ask the monster why he'd changed sides, but there wasn't time.* The *hwarhath* male was returning, moving through Akuin's garden, pausing to pick another flower, this one red. He laid the flower down on Akuin's rock table, then resettled himself on the ground. "Is there anything else you want to know?"

*Most *hwarhath* believe that Nicholas Sanders changed sides because of love. As a group, they are more romantic than humans. This is especially true of *hwarhath* men. Romantic love is the great consolation in lives that are often difficult. It is also a dangerous emotion, which threatens basic loyalties and thus the fabric of *hwarhath* society. The *hwarhath*, men especially, regard it with gratitude and fear.

"What are you going to do about me?" Akuin asked and was surprised by the question. Surely it would have been wiser to keep quiet.

The *hwarhath* tilted his head, considering. "We're both on leave at the moment. Our work, when we are at work, is not for the Corps that keeps track of *hwarhath* men. And we are guests in this country. I assume the Atkwa know about you. Let them deal with you. I don't see that your behavior is our business."

He was not going to die. His relatives were not going to suffer embarrassment. In his relief, he offered them vegetables from his garden.

"We can't carry much," the *hwarhath* said. "And my friend can't eat most of our edible plants. Either they don't nurture him, or they make him ill. So he lives on specially prepared rations. It's a hard fate for a human. Eating is an amusement for them. They expect their food to be as entertaining as a good play. Our human rations are—I have been told—dull."

"This is true," the monster said.

"But I'll accept your offer," his *hwarhath* companion concluded. "I don't know that I've ever seen handsomer looking vegetables. This is something worthy of respect, though I don't have the human attitude toward food."*

That afternoon, Akuin led them back to their trail. After he left them, heading back toward home, he realized that he hadn't learned their names. Nor had they learned his, but he was obviously Atkwa. If they wanted to find his records, they'd be able to do it without difficulty.

He reached his cabin late in the afternoon. Shadows covered the valley's floor and lower slopes, but light still filled the sky and touched the eastern hilltops. A copperleaf tree stood high on one of these, shining as if it were actually made of uncorroded copper. Lovely!

He gathered the teapot and cups, carrying them inside, then came out and picked up the yellow flower, which had been left. The red one had gone with his visitors, tucked under a flap on the *hwarhath* man's pack. He'd seen it go bobbing down the trail, as the *hwarhath* followed his long-legged companion. Easy to see who the athlete in the pair was.

Holding the withered flower, Akuin realized the two were lovers. It was as clear as something seen in a vision, though he was not a diviner and did not have visions. None the less, he knew.

Impossible! was his first reaction. But how could he tell what was possible these days? He'd heard a monster speak his native language and been told the monster was a *hwarhath* officer. If this could happen, and a station vanish out of the universe, who could say what other events might occur?

He laid the flower down, unwilling to discard it yet, and watched as sunlight faded off the copperleaf tree. A disturbing day, though he was glad to hear that Thev was still alive and apparently famous. It was what Thev wanted. The news brought

*The *hwarhath* often comment on humanity's obsession with food and violence. Both food and violence are necessary, but neither requires the huge amount of thought and practice that humans put in. The human interest in food strikes the *hwarhath* as funny. Our interest in violence makes their fur rise.

by the two men made him feel isolated and ignorant, for a moment doubtful about the choice he'd made.

Overhead the sky seemed limitless, not a roof, but an ocean into which he could fall and sink—if not forever, then far enough to drown.

Hah! That was an unpleasant idea! And also untrue. He stood with his feet in the dirt of Atkwa. Below the dirt was granite and the great round planet, which held him as a mother holds a child. There was no way for him to fall into the sky.

As for the choice he'd made—this was what he'd always wanted, as intensely as Thev had wanted fame: the garden in front of him, the copperleaf tree shining on its cliff, evening bugs beginning to call in the shadows. Only a fool mourns for the impossible or asks for everything, as if the Goddess had made the universe for his comfort.

If he had lost through his choice, he had also gained. Surely this valley—the bugs, the scent of his garden carried on a slight cool wind—was better than a lifetime spent in grey metal corridors. It was certainly better than vanishing into a very small universe of dim red stars. Thev and his ideas!

He stayed at the cabin doorway, watching day end. The sky was a roof again. The ground beneath his feet was solid. Gradually his uncertainty—his sense of loss—faded, like sunlight fading off the copperleaf tree. He regretted nothing. This was the right place for him to be.

That evening Ettin Gwarha and Sanders Nicholas made their camp next to the trail. A stream ran in a gully below them, producing a pleasant quiet noise. Ettin Gwarha ate fresh vegetables, while his companion made do with human rations. Then the son of Ettin turned on a map and studied it. "We'll take a different route out than the one we originally planned," he said.

"Why?" asked Sanders Nicholas.

"The original plan had us ending at one of the Atkwa greathouses. I'd just as soon avoid the family."

"Is there a reason?"

"If they realize how close we came to that man's territory, they'll worry, and that will force me to reassure them. As much as possible, I want nothing to do with this situation."

"But you told the man you wouldn't turn him in."

"Every family has its secrets, and we are guests in the country of the Atkwa. Never think that I approve of behavior such as his. There is no acceptable reason to run away from duty." The frontman turned off his map and closed it, then added, "I'm not going to comment on the behavior of the Atkwa women in letting their male relative go wild. Only women can judge women."

Sanders Nicholas considered this for a while. Maybe Ettin Gwarha could read the expression on his pale, hairless face. No ordinary *hwarhath* can. "I have another question," he said finally.

The frontman looked at him.

"Why do you know so much about Gehazi Thev and the station which vanished? Physics has never been one of your areas of competence."

"Negotiation is my great skill, as you know. When the station disappeared, the

Bundle had two questions it wanted answered; and they wanted one question at least to be asked diplomatically, since it was a disturbing question, and they had to go—I had to go—to the Helig Institute for an answer."*

Sanders Nicholas waited.

"The first question was, had some kind of weapon caused our station to disappear? Was it possible that humans—or another alien species—had so much power? Remember that a Heligian gate had been rendered impossible to use. An entire grove of stars had vanished! This was an event! If intelligent beings caused it to happen, then we were in trouble.

"The next question was, could such an event be caused? Was there a way to make a weapon out of whatever had happened?"

Sanders Nicholas gave his lover the wide, slow, unfriendly-seeming smile of humans. "You were hoping you could force the human home system into another universe."

"It was a thought that occurred to several men," Ettin Gwarha admitted. "Surely you can imagine the appeal of the idea, Nicky! The human threat could be eliminated without doing direct harm to humanity. We wouldn't have to go to our female relatives and say, 'We have destroyed women and children.'"

Sanders Nicholas sat quietly, looking at the small fire they had made. It was dying to embers already. Overhead the sky was dark. The Banner of the Goddess stretched across it, a wide swathe of dimly shining light. "I have two objections," he said finally. "How could the Bundle be certain that people would not be harmed? It would be an untested procedure, after all; and I find it hard to believe that any universe, even a small one, comes into existence quietly."

Ettin Gwarha inclined his head, perhaps in agreement. "What is your other objection?"

"Even if it could be done without immediate physical harm, think of the consequences. You would be depriving humanity of this—" He looked up, gesturing toward the starry sky. "Would you like to live in a very small universe, Ettin Gwarha?"

"No."

"I may be showing a bias, but I think this universe would be diminished if it lost humanity, though there's no question we are a difficult species."

"We could have found better neighbors," Ettin Gwarha said in agreement. "But it doesn't seem likely we'll be able to get rid of you. The scientists at the Helig Institute say there's no way to reproduce whatever happened at Kushaiin. Gehazi Thev does not agree. He believes we could cause such an event, but only in a region on the verge of collapse. Such a region would be full of old stars and strangeness. It's not the kind of place one would expect to find intelligent life. At most, in such a place, we might find a research station." Ettin Gwarha smiled briefly, his teeth flashing in the red light of the fire. "Hardly worth destroying in such an elaborate fashion. 'Avoid force in excess of the force needed,' as the old proverb says."

"Well, then," Sanders Nicholas said. "We are stuck with each other and with a very large universe."

*The Helig Institute is on the home planet and thus under the control of the *hwarhath* female government rather than the Bundle. As far as can be determined from a distance, the two halves of *hwarhath* society treat each other as genuine sovereign governments, whose interests are not always identical.

"A disturbing situation," his lover said in agreement. "Though I think we can endure it.

"There is a final aspect which I pointed out to the Bundle. The situation we were considering never seemed likely. Destroying an entire system—or moving it out of our universe—is beyond any science we know; and I don't believe humanity will develop a weapon able to do this. Their technology, at least in the relevant areas, is not impressive; and their economic and political problems are so severe I don't think they can afford the necessary R and D. But if there are two star-faring species in the galaxy, there ought to be three and four and five. Suppose one of these other species is as hostile as humanity and better organized. Could they create a weapon able to destroy an entire area of space?

"That's one thing to consider. The other is, it's comparatively easy to make a single planet uninhabitable. Even humans could do it. Our home world was safe during the war, because humanity didn't know where it was. At some point they are going to learn. It's possible the human government knows already."

"Maybe," said Sanders Nicholas. "I certainly think you ought to assume they know. But they'd have to fight their way here, and I think the *hwarhath* can stop them. In addition, as you ought to remember, there is a peace treaty."

"Some treaties last. Others don't. This one has no breeding clause.* How can we trust an agreement that hasn't been made solid—knotted—through the exchange of genetic material?"

Sanders Nicholas did not answer this question, though the answer is obvious. No treaty can be entirely trusted, if it lacks a breeding clause.

"Humans send women to the stars. Destroying the Solar System would not destroy their species. But our women prefer to stay at home. If something happened to our home planet, we would not be able to reproduce."

"You could borrow human biotechnology," Sanders Nicholas said.

"And produce cloned children who are raised by men?" asked Ettin Gwarha. His voice combined disgust and horror, as it should, of course.

"They wouldn't have to be clones."

"Well, suppose we decided to combine genetic material from men belonging to different lineages. Who would arrange the breeding contract, if our women were all gone? And how could men possibly raise children?"

"That leaves one obvious alternative," Sanders Nicholas said. "The *hwarhath* could do what humans have done: move women out of the home system. You must have thought of this."

"The Bundle has discussed the idea," Ettin Gwarha admitted. "And we have suggested it to the female government. Obviously, unfolding such a plan required far-in-front diplomatic ability. I was sent." He smiled briefly. "The idea was to establish colonies of young women in distant systems, in stations initially, since they are safer than the surface of any inhabitable planet.

"'To live without the advice of their mothers and senior female relatives?' the Weaving said. 'Absolutely not! It's the job of men to keep the home system safe. If

*As every reader ought to know, humans and *hwarhath* can't interbreed.

you can't do it, then we need to talk about your failings and limitations. But we won't send our daughters to the stars.'"

"Did you suggest sending older women as well?"

"The Weaving didn't like the idea; nor was the Bundle entirely happy with it. There are frontmen whose mothers are still living, not to mention other female relatives. Space might become considerably less comfortable, if senior women began to travel."

"This is true," said Sanders Nicholas. "But comfort is not the only important aspect of life. I think the Weaving, and the Bundle, are making a mistake." He glanced at Ettin Gwarha. "There's a human proverb which warns against putting all one's ova in one container. If anything happens to the container—"*

Ettin Gwarha tilted his head in agreement. "Nonetheless, the Bundle is not going to argue with the Weaving over an issue that concerns women, at least not at the moment. Most likely, the home system is safe. As you have mentioned, it's well guarded. Anyone seeking to destroy this world would have to get past many armed and armored ships. But I'd like to see women among the stars. Some of them would enjoy the experience."

Sanders Nicholas made no answer, possibly because he was tired.

Soon after the two of them went to sleep. In the morning they continued their journey, going down out of the mountains to a railroad junction. There, at day's end, they caught a local train. All night they rattled through the Atkwa foothills, riding in a freight car, since there wasn't a passenger car for men.

He'd had worse accommodations, Sanders Nicholas said. At least there were windows, though not much to see: the hills as areas of darkness against a starry sky. Now and then the lights of a station flashed past, revealing nothing except an empty platform.

By sunrise they had reached the plain.†

*Obviously, the author did some research on human culture, though it isn't certain what she thought this proverb means, since the word translated here as "ova" is much more likely to be used in reference to *hwarhath* reproduction than in reference to eggs for eating. The *hwarhath* know that humans have the ability to freeze human eggs and early-stage embryos and can grow foetuses to term outside a human uterus. The *hwarhath* have not developed a comparable technology; it strikes them as wrong to interfere with the female part of reproduction. However, they practice artificial insemination and have frozen their men's sperm from the moment it became possible to do so. Almost all *hwarhath* families have sperm banks. Prudent families have several banks in different locations. Most *hwarhath* think this is excessive caution. It's enough to have a solid building, several refrigeration units and a back-up power supply. The sperm of important men is, of course, kept in more than one refrigerator.

†There is no reason to believe that the Bundle, or any *hwarhath* senior officer, has advocated an idea as radical as putting women into space. It belongs to the author, who is almost certainly female, though the story (like most *hwarhath* fiction) was published anonymously. Apparently, there are *hwarhath* women who want to travel outside the home system, and the real point of the story, what the *hwarhath* would call its center or hearth, seems to be this final argument in favor of travel for women. Why didn't the author argue her point directly, by—for example—writing a story about women actually going to the stars? Maybe because she felt that would be fantasy, at least at present, and she wanted to write science fiction.

FOOTVOTE

PETER F. HAMILTON

There's an old expression: to vote with your feet. The story that follows takes us to a troubled near-future England, and, courtesy of an amazing new invention, gives us a disquieting demonstration of just exactly what that *means* . . .

Prolific British writer Peter F. Hamilton has sold to *Interzone, In Dreams, New Worlds, Fears*, and elsewhere. He sold his first novel, *Mindstar Rising*, in 1993, and quickly followed it up with two sequels, *A Quantum Murder* and *The Nano Flower*. Hamilton's first three books didn't attract a great deal of attention, on this side of the Atlantic, at least, but that changed dramatically with the publication of his *next* novel, *The Reality Dysfunction*, a huge modern Space Opera (it needed to be divided into two volumes for publication in the United States) that was itself only the start of a projected trilogy of staggering size and scope, the Night's Dawn trilogy, with the first volume followed by others of equal heft and ambition (and which also raced up genre best-seller lists), *The Neutronium Alchemist*, and *The Naked God*. The Night's Dawn trilogy put Hamilton on the map as one of the major players in the expanding subgenre of The New Space Opera, along with writers such as Dan Simmons, Iain Banks, Paul McAuley, Gregory Benford, Alastair Reynolds, and others; it was successful enough that a regular SF publisher later issued Hamilton's reference guide to the complex universe of the trilogy, *The Confederation Handbook*, the kind of thing that's usually done as a small-press title, if it's done at all. Hamilton's other books include the novels *Misspent Youth* and *Fallen Dragon*, a collection, *A Second Chance at Eden*, and a novella chapbook, *Watching Trees Grow*. His most recent book is a new novel, *Pandora's Star*. He's had stories in our Fifteenth and Eighteenth Annual Collections.

I *Bradley Ethan Murray pledge that starting from this day the First of January 2003, and extending for a period of two years, I will hold open a wormhole to the planet New Suffolk in order that all decent people from this United Kingdom can freely travel through to build themselves a new life on a fresh world. I do this in the sad knowledge that our old country's leaders and institutions have failed us completely.*

Those who seek release from the oppression and terminal malaise that now afflict the United Kingdom are welcome to do so under the following strictures.

1. *With citizenship comes responsibility.*
2. *The monoculture of New Suffolk will be derived from current English ethnicity.*
3. *Government will be a democratic republic.*
4. *It is the job of Government to provide the following statutory services to the citizenship to be paid for through taxation.*
   a. *The enforcement of Law and Order; consisting of a police force and independent judiciary. All citizens have the right to trial by jury for major crimes.*
   b. *A socialized health service delivered equally to all. No private hospitals or medical clinics will be permitted, with the exception of 'vanity' medicine.*
   c. *Universal education, to be provided from primary to higher levels. No private schools are permitted. Parents of primary and secondary school pupils are to be given a majority stake in governorship of the school, including its finances. All citizens have the right to be educated to their highest capability.*
   d. *Provision and maintenance of a basic civil infrastructure, including road, rail, and domestic utilities.*
5. *It is not the job of Government to interfere with and overregulate the life of the individual citizen. Providing they do no harm to others or the state, citizens are free to do and say whatever they wish.*
6. *Citizens do not have the right to own or use weapons.*

JANNETTE

It was the day Tony Blair was due to give evidence to the Hutton enquiry. The *Today* program on Radio Four was full of eager anticipation, taunting their opponent to come out and face their allegations full on, confident he would screw up. Over in Iraq, what was left of the British Army contingent had suffered more attacks from the population overnight. And I'd forgotten to buy Frosties for Steve.

"Not muesli!" he spat with the true contempt only seven-year-olds can muster. If only the TUC leadership had that kind of determination when facing Gordon Brown's latest abysmal round of budget cuts.

"It's good for you," I said without engaging my brain. After seven years you'd think I'd know not to make that kind of tactical error with my own son.

"Mum! It's just dried pigeon crap," he jeered as I stopped pouring it into the bowel. Olivia, his little sister, started to giggle at the use of the NN word. At least she was spooning up her organic yogurt without a fuss. "Not nice, not nice," she chanted.

"What do you want then?" I asked.

"McDonald's. Big Cheesy One."

"No!" I know he only says it to annoy me, but the reflex is too strong to resist. And I'm the Bad Mother yet again. Maybe I shouldn't preach so hard. But then, that's Colin speaking.

"How about toast?" I asked.

"Okay."

I couldn't believe it was that easy. But he sat down at the table and waited with a smug look on his face. God he does so look like Colin these days. Is that why he's becoming more impossible?

"What's the *prim*?" Olivia asked.

Today had moved on from snipping at their public enemy number one to cover the demonstration at Stanstead.

"Public Responsibility Movement," I said. "Now please finish your breakfast. Daddy will be here soon." *He'd better be.*

I put the toast down in front of Steve, and he squirted too much liquid honey over it. Golden goo oozed down over the table. Both of them were suddenly silent and eating quickly, as if that would speed his arrival.

The flat's back door was open in an attempt to let in some cooler air. The summer was damn hot, and dry. Here in Islington the breeze coursed along the streets like gusts of desert air.

"Pooooeee," Steve said, holding his nose as he munched down more toast. I had to admit, the smell that drifted in wasn't good.

Olivia crumpled her face up in real dismay. "That's horrid, mum. What is it?"

"Someone hasn't tied up their bin bags properly." The pile in the corner of De Beauvoir Square was getting ridiculously big. As more bags were flung on top, so the ones at the bottom split open. The SkyNews and News24 programs always showed them with comparison footage of the '79 Winter of Discontent.

"When are they going to clear it?" Steve asked.

"Once a fortnight." Though I'd heard on the quiet that nearly 10 percent of the army had already deserted, and that was before they had to provide civic utility assistance squads along with fire service cover, prison guard duties, engineering support to power stations, and invading Iraq. We'd be lucky if the pile was cleared every month. I'd seen a rat the size of a cat run across the square the other day. I always thought rodents that big were just urban legend.

"Why can't they take rubbish away like they used to?" Olivia asked.

"Not enough people to do that anymore, darling."

"There's hundreds of people standing round the streets all day. It's scary sometimes. I don't like the park anymore."

She was right in a way. It wasn't the lack of people, of course, it was money, and the frightening way the pound was collapsing. What would happen when the true tax revenue figures came in was anyone's guess. Officially, tax received by the Treasury had only fallen by 10 percent since that little *shit* Murray opened his racist, fascist, arseholing wormhole. Nobody believed that. But naturally, the first thing the Treasury reduced was local government grants, with Brown standing up in Westminster and telling the councils to *cut back on wastage*. What a pitiful joke. Central Government has been saying that for the last fifty years at least—because it's never their fault.

As a way to finally get the UK to sign on for the Euro, it couldn't be beaten. We desperately needed a currency that wasn't so susceptible to our traitors. Except that suddenly, France and Germany were blocking us from joining. The two biggest offenders when it came to breaking the budgetary stability arrangement. Bastards.

For once Colin actually turned up on time. He did his silly little ring tune on the front door, and both kids shot off from the table screeching hellos. Did they do that when I turned up to his place to collect them? I doubted it.

He came into the kitchen wearing a smart new sweatshirt and clean jeans; his curly brown hair neatly trimmed. I hated that old nontruism, that men just get more handsome as they get older. But they did seem to preserve themselves well after thirty. Colin hadn't put on a pound since he had started jogging and visiting the gym on a regular basis again. I supposed that bloody twelve-year-old he was shacked up with didn't appreciate a sagging beer gut. *Damn: why did I always sound like a stereotype bitch?*

He'd scooped Olivia up under one arm and was swinging her around. "Hiya," he called out to me. "Seen my daughter anywhere?"

She was shrieking: "Daddy, Daddy!" as she was twirled about.

"Don't do that. She's just eaten."

"Okey dokey," he dropped her to the floor and collected a happy kiss from her.

"Come on then," he clapped his hands, hustling them along. "Get ready. I'm leaving in five . . . four . . . three . . ."

They both ran downstairs to collect their bags.

"How are you doing?" he asked.

"Never better." I gave the kitchen table and its mess a weary look—beyond it, the work surfaces were covered in junk and the sink was a cliché of unwashed pans. "How about you, still servicing the rich?"

His expression hardened, that way it always did when he had to speak slowly and carefully to explain the bleeding obvious to me. "I have to work at the BUPA hospital now. It's the only way I can earn enough money after your lawyer took me to the cleaners in that sexist divorce court of yours."

I almost opened my jaw in surprise—I was the one that always made the needling comments. He was Mr. Reasonable through everything. "Oh fine, sure," I said. "I thought it would be my fault."

He gave one of those smug little victory smiles that used to annoy the hell out of me.

"What time do you want them back tomorrow?" he asked.

"Um, in the afternoon. Before six?"

"Okey dokey. No problem."

"Thanks. Are you taking them anywhere special?"

"I thought *Pirates of the Caribbean*, tonight. The reviews have all been great."

"As long as you don't take them for burgers."

He rolled his eyes.

I glanced out through the window, seeing his new BMW 4 × 4 parked on the pavement outside. The stupid thing was the size of the tanks the army rolled into Basra with. There wasn't anyone sitting in it. "Is she coming with you today?"

"Who's that, then?"

"Zoe."

"Ah, you remembered her name."

"I think I read it on her school report."

"As a matter of fact, yes, she is coming with us. She took the day off to help out. The kids do like her, you know. And if you ever find yourself someone, I won't mind them going out with him."

Oh well done, Colin, another point scored off your shrew of an ex, especially with that emphasis on 'ever.' Aren't you the clever one.

The kids charged back into the kitchen, hauling their overnight bags along the floor. "Ready!"

"Have a lovely time," I said, *ever* gracious.

Colin's smile faltered. He hesitated, then leant forward and kissed me on the cheek. Nothing special, not a peace offering, just some platonic gesture I didn't understand. "See you," he said.

I was too surprised to answer. Then the door slammed shut. The kids were gone. The flat was silent.

I had fifteen minutes to make the bus. I was going on a protest for the first time in years. Making my voice heard, and my feelings known. Doing exactly what Colin despised and ridiculed. God, it felt wonderful.

33. *There will be no prisons. Convicted criminals will spend their sentence in isolated penal colonies, working for the public good.*
34. *New Suffolk will use the Imperial system of measurement for length, weight, and volume. Use of the metric system is a criminal offense.*
35. *Police are required to uphold the law and apprehend criminals. Police will not waste all their time persecuting motorists.*
36. *Citizens are not entitled to unlimited legal funding. Citizens facing prosecution can only have their defense fees paid for by public funding three times during their lifetime. They may select which cases.*
37. *The intake of alcohol, nicotine, and other mild narcotics is permitted. Citizens found endangering others when intoxicated, e.g., driving under the influence, will face a minimum sentence of four years in a penal colony.*
38. *New Suffolk laws will not be structured to support or encourage any type of compensation culture.*
39. *Any lawyer who has brought three failed cases of litigation judged to be frivolous is automatically sentenced to a minimum five years in a penal colony.*

COLIN

The finance agency's solicitor was waiting on the doorstep, talking to Zoe, when I drove up in front of the house.

"Who's that?" Steve asked as I started to maneuver the BMW up the gravel, backing it up to the horsebox.

"Bloke from the bank," I told him. "Got a few papers to sort out." At least the agency didn't stick a For Sale sign up outside the house. That tended to earn you a brick—or worse—through the window these days.

Zoe smiled and waved as I stopped just short of the horsebox. "Wait in here," I told the kids. I didn't want them to see the empty house. Last night we'd used sleeping bags. Zipped together. Very romantic.

The solicitor shook my hand and produced a file of documents for me to sign. He glanced at the kids, who were pressed up against the BMW's window, but didn't comment. I guess he'd seen it many times before.

Zoe opened the garage door, and picked up the first of the boxes stacked on the concrete floor. She carried it over to the rear of the BMW, and put it in the boot.

The solicitor wanted five signatures from me, and that was it—the house belonged to the agency. A four-bedroom house with garage and a decent-sized garden in Enfield along with all the contents, sold for £320,000. Maybe two thirds of what I could have got last year. But that gave me enough to pay off the mortgage, and leave me with £30,000 in equity, which the agency had advanced me. That's what they specialized in, one of many such businesses to spring up since January. A Franco-Dutch company that sold a little bit of England to people who weren't going to be accepted on the other side of the wormhole.

I'd bought the BMW on finance from the garage. My pension portfolio had been sold to another specialist agency based in Luxembourg—God bless our EU partners—giving me £11,000. That just left the credit cards. I'd applied for another two; more than that and the monitor programs would spot the new loan pattern. But they'd given me an extra £15,000 to spend over the last month.

It had all gone into a community partnership I signed up for at www.newsuffolklife.co.uk. Most of the stuff was being shipped out in a convoy, with all the personal items we'd need crammed into the horsebox. The Web site recommended using them; they could take a lot more weight than a caravan.

The solicitor shook my hand and said: "Good luck." I handed him the keys, and that was it.

Zoe had jammed the last box in the back of the BMW. There were just four suitcases left. I picked up two of them. She was giving the house a forlorn look.

"We're doing the right thing," I told her.

"I know." She produced a brave smile. "I just didn't expect it to be like this. Murray surprised all of us, didn't he?"

"Yeah. You know I grew up with a whole bunch of sci-fi shows and films; it's amazing how their vocabulary and images integrated with modern culture. They all had bloody great ships flying through space; captains sitting in their command chair and making life-and-death decisions, shooting lasers and missiles at bugeyed monsters. Everybody knew that was how it would happen for real. Then Murray found a way to open his wormhole, and the bastard won't tell anyone how he does it. Not that I blame him. He's quite right, we'd only misuse the technology. We always do. It's just that . . . this isn't the noble crossing of the void I expected. It feels almost like a betrayal of my beliefs."

Zoe looked embarrassed. She was nothing like Jannette made out: some piece of underage nurse totty I pulled because she was blinded by the title of Dr. in front of my name; all big boobs, long legs, and no brain. In fact, she was training to be a midwife, which required just as much dedication and intelligence as was needed to become a doctor. And she was small, the top of her head only coming up to my chin. I was bloody lucky she even looked at a life-wreckage like me. The fact that she would take me on with a couple of kids in tow made her extraordinary.

"I meant the way this finally split the country," she said quietly. "Everyone always talked about the North-South divide, and the class war, and the distance between rich and poor. But it was just ideology, politicians lobbing spinning sound bites at each other. Murray went and made it physical."

I put my arms round her. "He gave us the chance politicians always promise and never provide. God, can you believe I actually voted for Blair. Twice!"

She grinned evilly. "Wish you'd voted Tory?"

"Stop putting words in my mouth." I gave her a quick kiss; then we shoved the suitcases in on top of the boxes.

Steve and Olivia looked unusually solemn when we got into the 4 × 4. Zoe gave them a welcoming smile. "Hi, guys."

"Where are we going, daddy?" Olivia asked.

"I'm going to take you to see something. Something I hope you'll like."

"What?"

"Can't explain. You have to see it."

"What's in the horsebox?" Steve asked. "You don't like horses."

"Tent," I said. "Big tent, actually. Food. Solar panels. Four brand-new laptops, one with a widescreen display and multiregion software."

"Cool! Can I use it?"

"Maybe."

"What else?" Olivia asked, excited.

"Some toys. Lots of new clothes. Books."

"What's it all for?" Steve asked.

"You'll see." I put my hand on the ignition key, and gave Zoe an apprehensive glance. This was such a huge step to be taking, and there didn't seem to be any defining moment, just a long sequence of covert events that had deftly led to this point in time. I didn't feel any guilt about bringing the kids with us; in fact I'd have been remiss as a father if I hadn't included them; there was never going to be an opportunity like this again. I wasn't stupid and naive enough to believe New Suffolk was going to be paradise, but it had the *potential* to be something better than what we had in this world. We were never going to evolve or progress here, not with so much history and inertia shackling us to the past.

As for Jannette . . . well, as far as I was concerned she hadn't been a mother to the kids for years.

"Let's go," Zoe said. "We chose a long time ago."

I turned the ignition and pulled out of the drive, the overloaded horsebox rattling along behind.

"What's that ring?" Steve asked suddenly, sharp and observant.

"This?" Zoe held her finger up.

"It's an engagement ring!" Olivia squeaked. "Are you getting married?"

"Yes," I said. It was the first thing we wanted to do on the other side.

"Does mum know?" Steve asked.

"No."

62. In order to prevent the mistakes of the old country being repeated on New Suffolk, no organized religions will be permitted. All citizens must acknowledge that the universe is a natural phenomenon.
63. In order to prevent the mistakes of the old country being repeated on New Suffolk, members of extremist political parties and undesirable organizations are banned from passing through the wormhole, as well as criminals and others I deem injurious to the public good.

Examples of prohibited groups and professions include (but are not limited to) the following:—

a. Labor Party.
b. Conservative Party.
c. Liberal Democrat Party.
d. Communist Party.
e. National Front.
f. Socialist Alliance.
g. Tabloid journalists.
h. European Union bureaucrats.
i. Trade union officials.
j. Traffic wardens.

JANNETTE

Abbey was waiting for me at Liverpool Street station. It was a miracle I ever found her. The concourse was overrun by backpackers. There didn't appear to be one of them over twenty-five, or maybe that's just the way it is when you're looking at young people from the wrong side of thirty-five. And I certainly hadn't seen that much denim in one place since I went to the Reading Festival in the late eighties. Their backpacks were *huge*. I didn't even know they manufactured them that size.

I gawped in astonishment as the youngsters jostled around me. Nearly all of them were couples. And everybody had a Union Jack patch sewn on their clothes or backpack. I don't think one in ten was speaking English, and they certainly weren't all white.

Abbey yelled, and walked toward me, pushing her way aggressively forward. She wasn't a small woman; her progress was causing quite a disturbance amid the smiley happy people. Her expression was locked into contempt as they flashed hurt looks her way. It softened when she hugged me. "Hi comrade darling, our train's on platform three."

I followed meekly behind as she ploughed onward. The badges on her ancient jacket were clinking away, one for every cause she'd ever supported or march she'd been on. The rusty Pearly Queen of the protest nation.

Half the station seemed to want to get on our train. Abbey forced her way into a carriage, queuing being a bourgeois concept to her. We found a couple of empty seats with reserved tickets, which she threw on the floor.

"I don't know where this lot all think they're going," she announced in a too-loud voice as we settled in. "Murray doesn't approve of poor foreign trash. There's no way he's going to let Europe's potheads live in stoner bliss under an alien sun. They'll get bounced right off his hole for middle-class worms."

"His restrictions are self-perpetuating," I said. "He doesn't actually have lists of all the people he doesn't like. And even if he did there's no way of checking everyone who goes through. It's pure psychology. Tell Thatcher's Children that no big bad pinkos will be allowed, and they'll flock there in their hundreds. While the rest of us see who is actually going and we steer the hell clear. Who wants to live in their world?"

"Ha! I bet the security services sold him our names."

You couldn't argue with Abbey when she was in this mood, which admittedly was most of the time.

She pulled a large hip flask out of her jacket and took a slug. "Want some?"

I looked at the battered old flask, ready to refuse. Then I remembered I didn't have the kids tonight. I wasn't stupid enough to take a slug as big as Abbey's. Thankfully. "Jesus, what the hell is that?"

"Proper Russian vodka, comrade," she smiled, and took another. "Nathan went through to join Murray last week," she said sourly.

"Nathan? Your brother Nathan?"

"Only by DNA, and I'm not even certain of that after this. Little prick. Mary and the kids went with him."

"Why?"

"Why do any of them go? War in Iraq, crap public transport, psycho Bush threatening North Korea, the congestion charge, council tax. The real world, in other words, that's what he's running away from. He thinks he's going to be living in some kind of tropical tax haven with fairies doing all the hard work, the dumb shit."

"I'm sorry. What did your mum say? She must be devastated."

Abbey growled, and took another slug. "She says she's glad he's gone; that he and the grandkids deserve a fresh start *somewhere nice*. Can you believe that? Selfish cow, she's gone senile if you ask me. And who's going to be looking after her, hey? She can't walk to the bus stop even these days. Did Nathan ever think of that? Oh no, he just took off and expected me to pick up the pieces, just like everyone else left behind."

"I know, Steve's school is talking about classes of sixty for next term. The Governors have been having emergency meetings all summer, so I know how many staff have left." I hesitated.

"It surprised me. I thought they were more dedicated than that."

"They would be if they were paid properly."

"The principal has to recruit another fifteen teachers before term starts, or they won't be able to open at all."

"Fifteen? He wouldn't have got that many in a normal year."

"He said he's quite confident. There's all sorts of new placement agencies starting up to source overseas professionals for the UK. Life's going to go on pretty much the same as before once the exodus is over."

"Great," Abbey grunted. "Just what we're fighting for."

Our train started to pull out of the station. The backpackers were squashed down the length of the aisle; nobody could move anywhere. There was a big cheer when the PA announced the stop at Bishop's Stortford.

Abbey took another swig, and muttered: "Wankers."

"Don't worry," I said. "If we ever get our own wormhole to a new world, we wouldn't let any of this lot through."

"That's the whole fucking point, isn't it?" Abbey snarled. Her anger was directed at me now, which was kind of scary. She gulped back another mouthful of vodka. "We wouldn't want to have a new world even if we could open a wormhole. It's a stupid waste of talent that could be used to help people down here. We have to solve the problems we've got on this world first, starting with the biggest problem there is, that bloody warmongering Tory: Blair. Colonization is Imperialism. We've got to teach people to have social responsibility instead." She jabbed an unsteady finger at a badge on her lapel. It was one showing an Icelandic whaler being broken in two by a suspiciously Soviet-looking hammer; but above it was a shiny new Public Responsibility Movement badge. "That's what today is all about. Murray isn't building himself a new world; what he's doing is ruining ours. You can't just do that, just open a doorway to somewhere else because you feel like it; it's fucking outrageous. They've got to be stopped."

"It's the scale that's the problem," I said. "You can't stop people leaving, that's Stalinist. What we're not ready for is this mass panic exodus that the wormhole has made possible. Emigration to North America was slow; it lasted for decades. This is fast. Two years, that's all he's giving us. No wonder the UK can't cope with the loss as it happens. But it'll settle down in the long term."

"We can stop them," Abbey said forcefully. "There's enough people taking part in the movement today to block the roads and turn back all those middle-class bastards. Murray didn't think it through; half of the police have pissed off through the wormhole. People power is going to come back with a vengeance today. This is when the working class finds its voice again. And it's going to say: no more. You see."

p. Stockbrokers.
q. Weapons designers and manufacturers.
r. Arts Council executives.
s. Pension fund managers.
t. Cast and production staff of all TV soaps.
u. All sex crime offenders.
v. All violent crime offenders.
w. Call center owners and managers.

COLIN

As ever, the M11 was horrendous, a solid queue of bad-tempered traffic. Nearly two hours from the M25 to the Stanstead junction. Not *strictly* as ever because I was smiling most of the way. It just didn't bother me anymore. I just kept thinking this was the last time I would ever have to drive down one of this country's abysmal, potholed, clogged, nineteen-sixties anachronisms. Never again would I come home ranting about about why we couldn't have Autobahns, or eight-lane freeways like they had in America. From now on my moaning was going to be reserved for sixteen-legged alien dinosaurs wandering over the garden.

The estate car in front had a bumper sticker with a picture of an angry Gordon Brown hammering on the side of the wormhole, with *Tax for the memory* printed underneath. We'd been seeing more and more pro-exodus stickers as we crawled our way North. I reckoned that all the vehicles sharing the off road with us were heading to New Suffolk. After all those months of furtive preparation it was kind of comforting finally being amongst your own kind.

"It's the wormhole, isn't it?" Steve asked cautiously. "That's where we're going."

"Yeah," I said. "We're going to take a look at what's there."

"Are we going *through*?" Olivia asked, all wide eyes and nervous enthusiasm.

"I think so. Don't you? Now we've come all this way, it'll be fun." I saw the sign for assembly park F2, and started indicating.

"But they're bad people on the other side," Steve said. "Mum said."

"Has she been there herself?"

"No way!"

"Then she doesn't really know what it's like on the other side, does she?"

The kids looked at each other. "Suppose not," Steve said.

"Just because you don't agree with someone, doesn't make them bad. We'll take a look round for ourselves and find out what's true and what's not. That's fair isn't it?"

"When are we coming back?" Steve asked.

"Don't know. That depends how nice it is on the new planet. We might want to stay a while."

Zoe was giving me a disapproving look. I shrugged at her. She didn't understand; you've got to acclimatize kids slowly to anything this big and new.

"Is Mummy coming?" Olivia asked.

"If she wants to, she can come with us. Of course she can," I said.

Zoe let out a little hiss of exasperation.

"Will I have to go to school?" Steve asked.

"Everybody goes to school no matter what planet they're on," Zoe said.

"Bummer."

"Not nice," Zoe squealed happily.

I found the entrance to park F2 and pulled in off the road. It was a broad open field hired out to newsuffolklife.co by the farmer. Hundreds of vehicles had spent all summer driving over it, reducing the grass to shredded wisps of straw pressed down into the dry iron-hard soil. Today, twenty-odd lorries were parked up at the far end, including three refrigerated containers and a couple of fuel tankers. Over seventy cars, people carriers, transit vans, and 4 × 4s were clustered around the lorries; most of them contained families, with kids and parents out stretching their legs before the final haul. The fields on either side replicated similar scenes.

I drew up beside a marshal, who was standing just inside the gate, and showed him our card. He looked at it and grinned as he ticked us off his clipboard. "You're the doc, huh?"

"That's me."

"Fine. There's about five more cars to come and we're all set. I'm your community convoy liaison, so I'll be travelling with you all the way to your new home. Any problems, come and see me."

"Sure."

"You want to check over the medical equipment you'll be taking, make sure it's all there? Your new neighbors have been going through the rest of the stuff."

I drove over to the other cars and we all climbed out. Several men were up in the lorries, looking round the crates and pallets that were inside. Given how much we'd spent between us, I was glad to see how thorough they were being checking off the inventory. In theory the equipment and supplies on the lorries was enough to turn us into a self-sufficient community over the next year.

"This shouldn't take long," I told Zoe. "We need to be certain. In the land of the new arrivals, the owner of the machine tool is king."

"We'll go meet people," she said.

I met a few of them myself as I tracked down the two crates of medical supplies and equipment. They seemed all right—decent types. A little over-eager in their greetings, as I suppose I was. But then we were going to spend an awful long time together. The rest of our lives, if everything went smoothly.

Half an hour later the last of the group had arrived, we were satisfied everything we'd bought through newsuffolklife.co was with us, and the marshals were getting the convoy organized for the last section.

"Where's the wormhole?" Steve asked plaintively as we got back into the BMW. "I want to see it."

"Two miles to go," Zoe said. "That's all now."

The lorries were first out of the assembly park and onto one of the new tarmac roads that led to the wormhole, with the rest of us following. There was a wide path on the left of the road. Backpackers marched along it, a constant file of them. I couldn't see the end of the line in either direction. They all had the same eager smile on their faces as they moved ever closer to the wormhole. Zoe and I probably looked the same.

"There!" Olivia suddenly shouted. She was pointing at the trees on the other side of the backpackers. For a moment I was confused, it was like a dawn sun was shining through the trunks. Then we cleared the end of the spinney, and we could see the wormhole directly.

The zero-length gap in space-time was actually a sphere three hundred yards in diameter. Murray had opened it so that the equator was at ground level, leaving a hemisphere protruding into the air. There was nothing solid; it was simply the place one planet ended and another began. You crossed the boundary, and New Suffolk stretched out in front of you. That was the notorious eye-twister that made a lot of people shiver and even flinch away. As you drew near the threshold, you could see an alien landscape dead ahead of you, inside the hemisphere. Yet it opened outward, delivering a panoramic view. When you went through, you emerged on the outside of the corresponding hemisphere. There was no inside.

It was early morning on New Suffolk, where its ginger-tinted sun was rising, sending a rouge glow across the gap to light up the English countryside.

We were half a mile away now. The kids were completely silent, entranced by the wormhole. Zoe and I flashed a quick triumphant smile at each other.

The road curved round to line up on the wormhole, running through a small cutting. Police lined the top of each bank, dressed in full riot gear. They were swaying back and forward as they struggled to hold a crowd of protestors away from the road. I could see banners and placards waving about. The chanting and shouting reached us over the sound of the convoy's engines. Things were flying through the air over the top of the police to rain down on the road. I saw several bottles smash apart on the tarmac. Backpackers were bent double as they scurried along, holding their hands over their heads to ward off the barrage from above.

Something thudded onto the BMW's roof. Both kids yelped. I saw a stone skittering off the side. It didn't matter now. The first of our convoy's lorries had reached the wormhole. I saw it drive through, thundering off over the battered mesh road that cut across the alien landscape, silhouetted by the bright rising sun. We were so close.

Then Olivia was shouting: "Daddy, Daddy, stop!"

87. *Government may not employ more than one manager per twelve front-line workers in any department.* No *Government department may spend more than 10 percent of its budget on administration.*
88. *Government will not fund any unemployment benefit scheme. Anyone without a job is entitled to five acres of arable land, and will be advanced enough crop seed to become self-sufficient.*
89. *There will be no death duties. Dying is not a taxable action. Citizens are entitled to bequeath everything they have worked for to whomever they choose.*

JANNETTE

It took us bloody hours to get from the station to the wormhole. The Public Responsibility Movement was supposed to lay on buses. I only ever saw two of them, and they took forever to drive around the jammed-up circuit between the station and the rally site. As for the PRM stewards, they'd got into fights with the backpackers streaming out of the station, asking directions and wanting to know if they could use our buses. The police were separating the two factions as best they could, but the station car park was a perpetual near riot.

Abbey used the waiting time to stock up at an off-license. By the time we got on the bus she was completely pissed. And she wasn't a quiet drunk.

As we inched our way across the motorway flyover I could look down on the solid stream of motionless vehicles clotting all the lanes below. There were hundreds of them. All of them waiting their turn to drive up the off road. Each one full of people who wanted to go through the wormhole. So *many?* They said it was like this every day.

The bus finally made it to the rally area. A huge 747 flew low overhead as we climbed out, coming in to land at Stanstead just a couple of miles north. I had to press my hands over my ears the engine noise was so loud. I didn't recognize the airline logo; but it was no doubt bringing another batch of eager refugees from abroad who wanted to join in with the exodus.

I tracked it across the sky. And there right ahead of me was the wormhole. It was like some gold-chrome bubble squatting on the horizon. I squinted into the brilliant rosy light it was radiating.

"I didn't realize it was that big," I muttered. The damn thing was intimidating this close up. Now I could finally understand how so many people had vanished into it, swallowed up by Murray's stupid promises.

"Let's get to it," Abbey slurred, and marched off towards the long scrum of protestors ahead of us.

Now I remembered why I'd stopped going to protests. All that romance about bonding with the crowd, sharing a purpose with your fellow travellers; the singing, the camaraderie, the communal contentment. It was all bollocks.

For a start, it wasn't just the PRM supporters who'd turned out to make their voice heard. There were a lot of unaffiliated comrades looking for trouble. Real serious trouble. I got batted about like some cheap football. Everybody wanted to score points by shoving into me. The shouting was loud, in my ear, and unending. I got clobbered by placards several times as their carriers dropped them for a rest.

Then we got real near to the police line, and a beer can landed on my shoulder. I jumped at the shock. Fortunately it was empty. But I could see bottles flying overhead, which made me very nervous.

"Let me through, you arseholes!" Abbey thundered at the police.

The nearest constable gave her a confused look. Then she was banging on his riot shield in fury. "I have a right to get past you can't stop me you fascist bastard this is still a free country why don't you piss off and go and bugger your chief constable let me through." All the while she was pushing up against his shield. I was pressed up behind her. Our helpful comrades behind me were making a real effort to add their strength to the shove. I shouted out in pain from the crushing force but no one heard or took any notice.

Something had to give. For once it was the police line. I was suddenly lurching forward to land on top of Abbey, who had come to rest on top of the policeman. A ragged cheer went up from behind. There were a lot of whistles going off. I heard dogs barking, and whimpered in fright. I hated dogs . . . really scared of them. Policemen were moving fast to plug the gap. Several wrestling matches had developed on either side of me. Protestors were being cuffed and dragged off. Clothes ripped. I saw blood.

Someone tugged the neck of my blouse, lugging me to my feet. I was crying and shaking. My knee was red hot; I could barely stand on it.

A police helmet was thrust into my face. "You all right?" a muffled voice demanded from behind the misted visor.

I just wailed at them. It was pathetic, but I was so miserable and panicky I didn't care.

"Sit there! Wait!" I was pushed onto the top of the bank. Ten feet below me backpackers were cowering as they scrambled along the path. The vehicles heading for the wormhole were swishing past, their drivers grim as they gripped the steering wheels.

I saw a big BMW 4 × 4 towing a horsebox. The driver was peering forward intently. Visual recognition kicked in.

"Get your fucking hands off me dickhead this is assault you know I'll have you in court oh shit get those cuffs of they're too tight you're deliberately torturing me help help," Abbey was yelling behind me.

"It's Colin," I whispered. "Abbey, that's Colin!" my voice was rising.

"What?"

"Colin!" I pointed frantically. There was Olivia sitting in the back seat, face pressed up against the glass to look out at all the mad people. "He's taking them. Oh God, he's taking them through the wormhole."

Abbey gave her arresting officer an almighty shove. "Get them," she screamed at me. "Move." Three policemen made a grab for her. Her shoulder slammed into me. I tumbled down the bank, arms windmilling wildly for balance. My knee was agony. I crashed into a backpacker, and fell onto the tarmac, barely a foot from a transit van that swerved violently.

"Grab them," Abbey cried. "Grab them back. They're yours. It's your right."

The vehicles along the road were all braking. I looked up. Everybody was stuck behind Colin's BMW, which had stopped. The driver's window slid down smoothly and he stuck his head out. We just gazed at each other. A whole flood of emotions washed over his face. Mainly anger, but I could see regret there as well.

"Come on then," he said in a weary voice. The rear door opened.

I looked at the open door. I got to my feet. I looked back up the bank at Abbey's snarling features. I looked back at the BMW. The wormhole was waiting beyond it. Cars were blowing their horns in exasperation, people shouting at me to get a move on.

I started walking toward the BMW with its open door. I knew it was morally wrong. At least, I thought it was. But what else could I do?

sisyphus and the stranger

PAUL DI FILIPPO

Although he has published novels, including two in collaboration with Michael Bishop, Paul Di Filippo shows every sign of being one of those rare writers, like Harlan Ellison and Ray Bradbury, who establish their reputations largely through their short work. His short fiction popped up with regularity almost everywhere in the eighties and nineties and continues to do so into the oughts, a large body of work that has appeared in such markets as *Interzone, SCI FICTION, The Magazine of Fantasy & Science Fiction, Science Fiction Age, Realms of Fantasy, The Twilight Zone Magazine, New Worlds, Amazing, Fantastic,* and *Asimov's Science Fiction*, as well as in many small press magazines and anthologies. His short work has been gathered into critically acclaimed collections such as *The Steampunk Trilogy, Ribofunk, Calling All Brains!, Fractal Paisleys,* and *Strange Trades*. Di Filippo's other books include the novels *Ciphers, Lost Pages, Joe's Liver, A Mouthful of Tongues: Her Totipotent Tropicanalia,* and *Fuzzy Dice*, and, in collaboration with Michael Bishop, *Would It Kill You to Smile?* and *Muskrat Courage*. His most recent books are *Harp, Pipe and Symphony* and *Neutrino Drag*. Coming up is a new book, *Spondulix*. His stories have appeared in our Nineteenth and Twenty-first Annual Collections. Di Filippo is also a well-known critic, working as a columnist for *two* of the leading science fiction magazines simultaneously, with his often wry and quirky critical work appearing regularly in both *Asimov's Science Fiction* and *The Magazine of Fantasy & Science Fiction*—a perhaps unique distinction; in addition, he frequently contributes reviews and other critical work to *Science Fiction Weekly, Locus Online, Tangent Online*, and other Internet venues.

Here he shuttles us sideways in time for a slyly entertaining (if somewhat unlikely) look at how life might have turned out for a famous author in a somewhat *different* universe. . . .

Albert Camus was tired. Tired of his job. Tired of his life. Tired of the vast empire he daily helped, in however small a manner, to sustain.

Yet he had no choice but to continue, he felt, like Sisyphus forever rolling his stone up the mountain. His future was determined, all options of flight or rebirth foreclosed.

Sitting in his office in the Imperial Palace in Algiers, Camus held his weary head in his hands. He had been awake now for thirty-six hours straight, striving to manage all the preparations for the dual anniversary celebrations about to commence. This year of 1954 marked fifty years since the glorious discovery of N-rays, and forty years since the birth of the French Empire out of the insufficient husk of the Third Republic. All around the empire, from the palmy isles of the Caribbean to the verdant coasts of South America, from the steaming jungles of Indochina to the tranquil lagoons of Polynesia, across the tawny veldts and plains of Africa and into the lonely islands of the Indian Ocean, wherever the proud French flag flew, in scores of colonies and protectorates, similar preparations were under way.

Poster-sized images of the stern-faced emperor and of the genius inventor René Blondlot, bald and Vandyked, had to be mounted everywhere under yards of tricolor bunting. The façades of public buildings had to be cleansed with a mild application of N-rays. Ballrooms had to be decorated, caterers consulted, parade routes mapped, permits for vendors stamped, invitations issued. Indigent street Arabs had to be rounded up and shipped to the provinces. The narrow, stepped streets of the Casbah had to be locked down to prevent any awkward demonstrations, however small and meek, against the French and their festivities. (Listening to the complaints of merchants whose trade was preemptively hurt in advance of any unlawful gatherings was infinitely preferable to answering the questions of cynical reporters concerning the corpses of demonstrators charred to cinders by the N-ray cannons of the police.) And perhaps most importantly, security measures for the visit of the emperor had to be checked and double-checked.

And of course, Camus' superior, Governor-General Merseault, was absolutely no help. The fat, pompous toad was excellent at delivering speeches once they were written for him, and at glad-handing businessmen and pocketing their bribes. But for achieving any practical task the unschooled Merseault (an appointee with relatives in high places back in France) relied entirely on his underling, Camus, trained in the demanding foreign-service curriculum of the prestigious Ecole Nationale d'Administration.

Camus lifted his head from the cradle of his hands and smiled grimly, his craggily handsome face beneath a thick shock of oiled black hair seamed with the lines of stress. *Ah, Mother and Father,* he thought, *if only you could see your little boy today, for whom you scraped and saved so that he might get the best education in the ancestral homeland. At a mere forty-one years of age, he has become the power behind a certain small throne, yet finds himself utterly miserable.*

But of course Camus' parents could not witness today his abject state. They had both perished in Algiers in the antipiednoir riots of 1935, roughly twenty years into the existence of the empire, when Camus himself had been safely abroad in Paris. So many had died in that holocaust, both Europeans and Arabs, before the soldiers of the Empire with their fearsome N-ray weapons and N-ray-powered armored vehicles had managed to restore order. Since that harsh exercise of power, however, peace and harmony had reigned in Algeria and across the Empire's many other possessions, several of which had received similar instructional slaughters.

Camus's sardonic smile faded as he contemplated the bloody foundations of the current era of global peace and prosperity emanating from Paris. He reached for a pack of cigarettes lying next to an overflowing ashtray, secured one and lit up. An abominable, necessary habit, smoking, but one that was slightly excusable in these days when lung cancer could be cured by medically fractionated N-rays, as easily as the rays had cured Camus' childhood tuberculosis—at least if the patient was among the elite, of course. Puffing his cigarette, leaning back in his caster-equipped chair, Camus permitted himself a few minutes of blissful inactivity. Two flies buzzed near the high ceiling of his small, unadorned, spartan office. The blinding summer sunlight of Algiers, charged with supernal luminance by reflection off Camus' beloved ancient Mediterranean, slanted in molten bars through the wooden Venetian blinds, rendering the office a cage of radiance and shadow. Yet the space remained cool, as N-ray-powered air conditioners hummed away.

Camus' mind had drifted into a wordless place when the screen of the interoffice televisor on his desk pinged, then lit up with the N-ray-sketched face of his assistant, Simone Hié, an austere woman of Camus' own years.

"M'sieur Camus, the American ambassador is here to see you."

Camus straightened up and stubbed out his cigarette. "Send him in, please."

As the door opened, Camus was already on his feet and moving around his desk to greet the diplomat.

"Ah, Ambassador Rhinebeck," said Camus in his roughly accented English as he shook the American's hand, "a pleasure to see you. I assume your office has received all the necessary ducats for the various celebrations. There will be no admission to events without proper invitations, you understand. Security demands—"

The silver-haired, jut-jawed Rhinebeck waved away the question in a gruff manner. Not for the first time, Camus was simultaneously impressed and appalled by the American's typical bluntness.

"Yes, yes," the ambassador replied, "all that paperwork is being handled by my assistants. I'm here on a more important matter. I need to see the governor-general immediately, to register a formal protest."

One of Camus' many duties was, if at all possible, blocking just such annoying demands on Merseault's limited capacities. "A formal protest? On what matter? Surely such a grave step is not required between two nations with the amiable relations that characterize the bonds between the United States and the Empire. I'm certain I could be of help in resolving any trivial matter that has arisen."

Rhinebeck's blue eyes assumed a steely glint against his sun-darkened skin. Despite the air-conditioning, Camus began to sweat. The two flies that had been hovering far above had now descended and were darting about Camus' head, making an irritating buzz. Camus wanted to swat at them, but refrained, fearing to look foolish.

"This is not a trivial matter," said Rhinebeck. "Your Imperial soldiers have detained a party of innocent American tourists on the southern border with Niger. They are refusing to release them until they have been interrogated by your secret service. There's even talk of transferring them to Paris. These actions are in violation of all treaties, protocols, and international standards. I must see Merseault immediately to demand their release."

Camus considered this news. There was a large military installation on the border with Niger, where N-ray research deemed too hazardous to be permitted in the homeland took place. Was it possible that these "innocent American tourists" were spies, seeking to steal the latest developments in the technology that had granted France uncontested global supremacy? Quite possibly. And if so, then Merseault, in his amateurish, naive, blundering way, might very well cave in to Rhinebeck's demands and grant the American concessions that would prove damaging to the best interests of the Empire. This possibility Camus could not permit. Best to let the military and the omnipresent Direction Generale de la Securité Exterieure handle this affair.

Camus was tired of the Empire, yes. But when all was said and done, he knew nothing else. His course became clear, and any hesitancy vanished.

Time to push the rock uphill once again.

"Ambassador Rhinebeck, I regret that I cannot forward your request for an audience to the governor-general. However, you may rest assured that I will personally monitor the situation and keep you informed as to the fate of your countrymen."

Rhinebeck's resolve and bluster seemed to evaporate in a moment, in the face of Camus' brusqueness. He suddenly looked older than his years. "So, more stonewalling. I had hoped for better from you, Albert, since I thought we were friends. But ultimately I should have expected such a response from someone in your superior position of strength. You realize that America is toothless against the Empire. There's nothing we have to offer in exchange, nothing we can do, no threat we can make, to sway the Empire toward our point of view."

"Oh, come now, Henry, don't take that tack. Surely you exaggerate—"

"Do I? Maybe you know something about my country's international stature that I don't. We face French outposts on all sides of our nation, limiting our actions, forbidding our natural expansion. Quebec, Cuba, Mexico, the Sandwich Islands, all of them under French control and bristling with N-ray armaments. Our trade deficit with France and its possessions grows more burdensome every year. Our allies are equally weak. Spain, Germany, even the formerly majestic United Kingdom have all proven powerless in the face of French conquests. Your Empire has become something totally unprecedented in human history. Let's call it a superpower. No, no—a *hyper*power. There is no nation left to offer a counterweight to your actions. You do exactly as you please, in any situation, and tell the rest of the world to be damned. Yet frustrating as the political situation is, we could contend with fair competition in international matters. But it's your cultural dominion back home that's really killing us. Our young people are aping French fashions, watching French cinema reading French books. Our own domestic arts are dying. We're being colonized mentally by your Empire. And that's the most insidious threat of all."

Camus was about to attempt to refute Rhinebeck's unblinkingly real-politik analysis of global affairs, when he realized that everything the ambassador had said was absolutely true. Disdaining hypocrisy, Camus merely said, "I am sorry, Henry, that the world is as it is. But we must both make the best of the reality presented to us."

"Easy enough to say from where you sit, in the catbird seat," said Rhinebeck. The ambassador turned away sharply then and exited.

The encounter left Camus unsettled. He had to get away from his desk. Consulting his watch, Camus saw that it was past one PM. He would go have lunch at Céleste's restaurant.

Camus activated the televisor. "I will be out of the office for the next hour."

"Yes, M'sieur."

Outside, the heat of the July day and the sheer volume of the sunlight smote Camus brutally, yet with a certain welcome familiarity. Born and raised here, Camus had integrated the North African climate into his soul. He recalled his time in Paris as years of feeling alien and apart, distressed by the city's foreign seasons almost as much as by the natives' hauteur when confronted by a colonial upstart. At graduation he had been most relieved, upon securing his first posting, to discover that he had been assigned to the land of his birth. He had never left in all the years since. The love he shared with Algiers, a place open to the sky like a mouth or a wound, was a secret thing in his life, but also the engine that sustained him through all his angst and anomie.

Walking easily down the broad boulevard of the Rue d'Isly, with its majestic European-style buildings nearly a century old, Camus felt his spirit begin to expand. If only he had time for a swim, his favorite pastime, life would begin to taste sweet again. But he could not permit himself such indulgences, not at least until after the Emperor's visit. Flanked by sycamores, the Rue d'Isly boasted parallel sets of trolley tracks running down its middle. At one point the tracks bellied outward to accommodate a pedestaled statue of Professor Blondlot, holding aloft the first crude N-ray generator.

Camus enjoyed watching the cool-legged women pass, the sight of the sea at the end of every cross street. He purchased a glass of iced lemonade flavored with orange flowers from an Arab vendor (license prominently displayed). Sipping the cool beverage, Camus was attracted to a public works site where other onlookers congregated. From behind the site's fence spilled the edges of a crackling glare. Camus knew the source of the radiance. N-ray construction machinery was busy slicing through the earth to fashion Algiers's first Metro line, running from Aïn Allah through downtown and on to Aïn Naadja. Camus looked through a smoked-glass port at the busy scene for a moment, then continued on his way. He hoped the new Metro would not mean the extinction of the nostalgia-provoking trolley cars, and made a mental note to arrange some subsidies for the older system.

A few blocks further on, Camus arrived at his destination.

In the doorway of the restaurant, his usual place, stood Céleste, with his apron bulging on his paunch, his white mustache well to the fore. Camus was ushered into the establishment with much to-do and seated at his traditional table. He ordered a simple meal of fish and couscous and sat back to await it with a glass of cold white wine. When his lunch came, Camus consumed it with absentminded bodily pleasure. His thoughts were an unfocused kaleidoscope of recent problems, right up to and including Rhinebeck's visit. But eventually, under the influence of a second glass of wine, Camus found his thoughts turning to his dead parents. He recalled specifically his father's frequent anecdotes surrounding the elder man's personal witnessing of the birth of the Empire.

The year was 1914, and the Great War was newly raging in Europe. Camus' father was a soldier defending France. Far from his tropical home, Lucien Camus and his comrades were arrayed along the River Marne, preparing for a titanic battle against the Germans, and fully expecting to die, when the miracle happened that saved all their lives. From the rear lines trundled on their modified horse-drawn carriages came curious weapons, guns without open bores, strange assemblages of batteries and prisms and focal reflectors. Arrayed in an arc against the enemy, the uncanny weapons, upon command from Marshal Joffre himself, unleashed deadly purple rays of immense destructive power, sizzling bolts that evaporated all matter in their path. The German forces were utterly annihilated, without any loss of life on the French side.

After this initial trial of the new guns, the Great War—or, as most people later ironically called it, "The Abortive Great War"—continued for only another few months. Impressive numbers of the futuristic weapons were deployed on all fronts, cindering all forces who dared oppose the French. The Treaty of Versailles was signed before the year was over, and the troops of the Triple Entente occupied Germany, with the French contingent predominant, despite objections from partners England and Russia. (Just four years ago, Camus had watched with interest the results of the very first postwar elections allowed the Germans. Perhaps now the French civil overseers in the defeated land could be begin to be reassigned to other vital parts of the Empire.) The transition from Third Republic to Empire was formalized shortly thereafter, with the ascension of the emperor, the dimwitted, pliable young scion of an ancient lineage.

Of course, the question on all tongues at the time, including Lucien's and his comrades', concerned the origin of the mystery weapons. Soon, the public was treated to the whole glorious story.

Ten years prior to the Battle of the Marne, Professor René Blondlot had been a simple teacher of physics at the University of Nancy when he became intrigued by the newly discovered phenomenon known as X-rays. Seeking to polarize these invisible rays, Blondlot assembled various apparatuses that seemed to produce a subtle new kind of beam, promptly labeled N-rays, in honor of the professor's hometown of Nancy. At the heart of the N-ray generator was an essential nest of prisms and lenses.

In America, a physicist named Robert Wood had tried to duplicate Blondlot's experiments and failed to replicate the French results. He journeyed to Nancy and soon concluded quite erroneously that Blondlot was a fraud. Seeking, in the light of his false judgment, to "expose" the Frenchmen, Wood had made a sleight-of-hand substitution during a key demonstration, inserting a ruby-quartz prism of his own construction in place of Blondlot's original. When, as Wood expected, Blondlot continued to affirm results no one else could see, the American would step forward and reveal that a crucial portion of the apparatus was not even consistent with the original essential design.

Ironically and quite condignly, the ravening burst of disruptive violet energy that emerged from the modified projector when it was activated incinerated Wood entirely, along with half of Blondlot's lab.

Accepting this fortuitous modification, the scorched but unharmed Blondlot was able to swiftly expand upon his initial discovery. Over the next several years, he discovered dozens of distinct forms of N-rays, all with different applications, from destructive to beneficent. Eventually his work came to the attention of the French government. When hostilities commenced in June of 1914, the French military had already secretly been embarked on a program of construction of N-ray weapons for some time. Under the stimulus of war, the first guns were hastily finished and rushed to the Marne by September.

Now, forty years later, N-ray technology, much expanded and embedded in France's vast navies, armies, and aerial forces, remained a French monopoly, the foundation on which the ever-expanding Empire rested, and the envy of all other nations, which waged constant espionage to steal the Empire's secrets, spying so far completely frustrated by the DGSE. Not the Russian czarina nor the British Marxist cadres nor the Chinese emperor nor the Ottoman pashas nor the American president had been able to successfully extract the core technology for their own use. And as France's dominion grew, so did all these aforenamed nations shrink.

So much did every schoolchild of the Empire learn. Although not many of them could claim, as Camus could, that their fathers had been present at the very first unveiling of the world-changing devices.

Camus' ruminations were interrupted by the arrival of Céleste at his table. The plump proprietor coughed politely, then tendered a slip of paper to his patron.

"A gentleman left this earlier for you, M'sieur. Please pardon me for nearly forgetting to deliver it."

Camus took the folded sheet of notepaper and opened it. Inside was a simple message.

Dear Sisyphus,

Meet me tonight at the dancehall at Padovani Beach. I have a proposition that will change your life, and possibly the world.

Camus was dumbstruck. How did some stranger come to address him by his unrevealed sardonic nickname for himself? What unimaginable proposition could possibly involve Camus in world-altering events?

Camus summoned Céleste back to the table.

"What did this fellow look like?"

The restaurant owner stroked his mustache. "He was an odd duck. Completely bald, very thin, with odd smoked lenses concealing his eyes. But most startling was his mode of dress. If he's wearing the same clothes when you see him, you won't be able to mistake him. A queer suit like an acrobat's leotard, made of some shiny material and covering even his feet, poked out of the holes of a shabby Arab robe that seemed like some castoff of the souks. At first I thought him part of the circus. But upon reflection, I believe that no circus is in town."

Camus pondered this description. This stranger was no one he knew.

Camus thanked Céleste, folded the note into his pocket, paid his bill, and returned to the office.

The rest of the afternoon passed in a stuporous fog. Camus consumed numerous cups of coffee while attending in mechanical fashion to the neverending stream of paperwork that flowed across his desk. All the caffeine, however, failed to alleviate the dullness of his thoughts, the dark befuddlement that had arrived with the stranger's note. Merseault called on the televisor once. The governor-general wanted to ensure that his counterpart from the French Congo was bringing all the native women he had promised to deliver during the upcoming festivities. Merseault had a weakness for Nubians. Camus promised to check.

At eight o'clock Camus bade his equally hard-working secretary goodnight, and left the palace. Two streetcar rides later, he arrived at Padovani Beach.

The famous dancehall situated in this location was an enormous wooden structure set amidst a grove of tamarisk trees. Jutting with awnings, the building's entire seaward side was open to the maritime breezes. With the descent of darkness, the place came alive with the violet-tinged N-ray illumination from large glass globes. (Suitably modulated, N-rays could be conducted along copper wires just like electricity.) Couples and single men and women of all classes streamed in, happy and carefree. Notes of music drifted out, gypsy strains recently popular in France. Camus wondered briefly why the intriguing "jazz" he had heard at a reception at the American Embassy had never caught on outside America, but then realized that Rhinebeck's tirade about the unidirectional flow of culture from France outward explained everything.

Inside, Camus went to the bar and ordered a pastis and a dish of olives and chickpeas. Halfheartedly consuming his selections, Camus wondered how he was to meet the writer of the note. If the stranger remained dressed as earlier described, he would be immensely out of place and immediately attract notice. But Camus suspected that the meeting would not occur so publicly.

For an hour, Camus was content simply to admire the dancers. Their profiles whirled obstinately around, like cut-out silhouettes attached to a phonograph's turntable. Every woman, however plain, swaying in the arms of her man, evoked a stab in Camus' heart. No such romantic gamin occupied his life. His needs were met by the anonymous prostitutes of the Marine district, and by the occasional short-term dalliance with fellow civil servants.

Finally Camus' patience began to wear thin. He drained his third pastis and sauntered out to a deck overlooking the double shell of the sea and sky.

The stranger was waiting for him there, sitting on a bench in a twilit corner nominally reserved for lovers, just as Céleste had depicted him.

The stranger's voice was languorous and yet electric. His shrouded eyes disclosed no hints of his emotional state, yet the wrinkles around his lips seemed to hint a wry amusement. "Ah, Albert my friend, I was wondering how long it would take you to grow bored with the trite display inside and visit me."

Camus came close to the stranger, but did not sit beside him. "You know me. How?"

"Oh, your reputation is immense where I come from, Albert. You are an international figure of some repute."

"Do not toy with me, M'sieur. I am a simple civil servant, not an actor or football hero."

"Ah, but did I specify those occupations? I think not. No, you are known for other talents than those."

Camus chose to drop this useless line of inquiry. "Where exactly do you come from?"

"A place both very near, yet very far."

Growing impatient, Camus said, "If you don't wish to answer me sanely, please at least keep your absurd paradoxes to yourself. You summoned me here with the promise of some life-altering program. I will confess that I stand in need of such a remedy for the moribund quandary I find myself in. Therefore state your proposition, and I will consider it."

"So direct! I can see that your reputation for cutting to the heart of the matter was not exaggerated. Very well, my friend, here it is. If you descend to the beach below and walk half a kilometer north, you will encounter a man sleeping in the dunes. He looks like a mere street Arab, but in reality he is a trained Spanish assassin who has made his laborious covert way here from Algeciras and on through Morocco. He intends to kill the emperor during your ruler's visit here. And he stands a good chance of succeeding, for he is very talented in his trade, and has sympathizers in high places within your Empire."

Camus felt as if a long thin blade were transfixing his forehead. "Assuming this is true, what do you expect me to do about this? Do you want me to inform the authorities? Why don't you just go to them yourself?"

The stranger waved a slim hand in elegant disdain. "Oh, that course of action would be so unentertaining. Too pedestrian by half. You see, I am a connoisseur of choice and chance and character. I believe in allowing certain of my fellow men whom I deem worthy the opportunity to remake their own world by their existential behavior. You are such a man, at such a crucial time and place. You should consider yourself privileged."

Camus tried to think calmly and rationally. But the next words out of his mouth were absolute madness. "You are from the future then."

The stranger laughed heartily. "A good guess! But not the case. Let us just say that I live in the same arrondissement of the multiverse as you."

Camus pondered this response for a time, striving to reorder his very conception of the cosmos. At last he asked a broken question. "This multiverse is ruled—?"

"By no one. It is benignly indifferent to us all. Which makes our own actions all the more weighty and delicious, wouldn't you say?"

Camus nodded. "This is something I only now realize I have always felt."

"Of course."

"Can you give me a hint of the alternate outcomes of my actions? Will one decision on my part improve my world, while its opposite devastates it?"

The stranger chuckled. "Do I look like a prophet to you, Albert? All I can say is that change is inescapable in either case."

Camus contemplated this unsatisfying response for a time before asking, "Do you have anything to aid me if I choose to accept this challenge?"

"Naturally."

The stranger reached beneath his robe and removed a curious gun unlike any Camus had ever seen.

"Its operation is extremely simple. Just press this stud here."

Accepting the gun, Camus said, "I need to be alone now."

"Quite understandable. An act like this is prepared within the silence of the heart, like a work of art."

The stranger arose and made as if to leave. But at the last moment, he stopped, turned, and produced a book from somewhere.

"You might as well have this also. Good luck."

Camus accepted the book. The faint violet light reaching him from the dance-hall allowed him to make out the large font of its title, *The Myth of Sisyphus*.

The author's name he somehow already knew.

After the stranger had gone, Camus sat for some time. Then he descended to the sands and began walking north, carrying both the book and the pistol.

Just where the stranger had specified, Camus found the sleeping man. His hands were pillowing his head as he lay on his side. The waves crashed a maddening lull-aby. In the shadows, the sleeper's Iberian profile reminded Camus of his mother, Catherine, who boasted Spanish ancestry herself, a blood passed down to her son.

It occurred to Camus that all he had to do was turn, walk away, and think no more about this entire insane night. His old life would resume its wonted course, and whatever happened in the world at large would happen without Camus' inter-vention. Yet wasn't that nonaction a choice in itself? It crossed his mind that to fire or not to fire might amount to the same thing.

The assassin stirred, yet did not awake. Camus' grip on the pistol tightened. Every nerve in his body was a steel spring.

A second went by. Then another. Then another. And there was no way at all to stop them.

Ten Sigmas

PAUL MELKO

New writer Paul Melko has made sales to *Realms of Fantasy, Live Without a Net, Asimov's Science Fiction, Talebones, Terra Incognita*, and other markets. He had a story in our Twenty-first Annual Collection. In the quirky and surprising story that follows, he shows us that even if a new universe is created every time we make a decision, somehow it still matters just *which* decision we make . . .

At first we do not recognize the face as such.

One eye is swollen shut, the flesh around it livid. The nose is crusted with blood, the lip flecked with black-red, and the mouth taped with duct tape that does not contrast enough with her pale skin.

It does not register at first as a human face. No face should be peeking from behind the driver's seat. No face should look like that.

So at first we do not recognize it, until one of us realizes, and we all look.

For some the truck isn't even there, and we stand frozen at the sight we have seen. The street outside the bookstore is empty of anything but a pedestrian or two. There is no tractor trailer rumbling down Sandusky Street, no diesel gas engine to disturb the languid spring day.

In some worlds, the truck is there, past us, or there, coming down the road. In some it is red, in some it is blue, and in others it is black. In the one where the girl is looking out the window at us, it is metallic maroon with white script on the door that says, "Earl."

There is just one world where the girl lifts her broken, gagged face and locks her one good eye on me. There is just one where Earl reaches behind him and pulls the girl from sight. In that world, Earl looks at me, his thick face and brown eyes expressionless.

The truck begins to slow, and that me disappears from our consciousness, sundered by circumstance.

No, I did not use my tremendous power for the good of mankind. I used it to steal the intellectual property of a person who exists in one world and pass it off as my own in another. I used my incredible ability to steal songs and stories and publish them as my own in a million different worlds. I did not warn police about terrorist attacks or fires or earthquakes. I don't even read the papers.

I lived in a house in a town that is sometimes called Delaware, sometimes Follett, sometimes Mingo, always in a house on the corner of Williams and Ripley. I lived there modestly, in my two-bedroom house, sometimes with a pine in front, sometimes with a dogwood, writing down songs that I hear on the radio in other worlds, telling stories that I've read somewhere else.

In the worlds where the truck has passed us, we look at the license plate on the truck—framed in silver, naked women—and wonder what to do. There is a pay phone nearby, perhaps on this corner, perhaps on that. We can call the police and say . . .

We saw the girl once, and that self is already gone to us. How do we know that there is a girl gagged and bound in any of these trucks? We just saw the one.

A part of us recognizes this rationalization for the cowardice it is. We have played this game before. We know that an infinite number of possibilities exist, but that our combined existence hovers around a huge multidimensional probability distribution. If we saw the girl in one universe, then probably she was there in an infinite number of other universes.

And safe in as many other worlds, I think.

For those of us where the truck has passed us, the majority of us step into the street to go to the bagel shop across the way. Some fraction of us turn to look for a phone, and they are broken from us, their choice shaking them loose from our collective.

I am—we are—omniscient, at least a bit. I can do a parlor trick for any friend, let another of me open the envelope and see what's inside, so we can amaze those around us. Usually we will be right. One of me can flip over the first card and the rest of me will pronounce it for what it is. Ace of Hearts, Four of Clubs, Ten of Clubs. Probably we are right for all fifty-two, at least fifty of them.

We can avoid accidents, angry people, cars, or at least most of us can. Perhaps one of us takes the hit for the rest. One of us is hit first, or sees the punch being thrown, so that the rest of us can ride the probability wave.

For some of us, the truck shifts gears, shuddering as it passes us. Earl, Bill, Tony, Irma look down at us, or not, and the cab is past us. The trailer is metallic aluminum. Always.

I feel our apprehension. More of us have fallen away today than ever before. The choice to make a phone call has reduced us by a sixth. The rest of us wonder what we should do.

More of us memorize the license plate of Earl's truck, turn to find a phone, and disappear.

When we were a child, we had a kitten named Cocoa. In every universe it had the same name. It liked to climb trees, and sometimes it couldn't get back down again. Once it crawled to the very top of the maple tree out front, and we only knew it was up there by its hysterical mewing.

Dad wouldn't climb up. "He'll figure it out, or . . ."

We waited down there until dusk. We knew that if we climbed the tree we would be hurt. Some of us had tried it and failed, disappearing after breaking arms, legs, wrists, even necks.

We waited, not even going in to dinner. We waited with some neighborhood kids, some there because they liked Cocoa and some there because they wanted to see a spectacle. Finally the wind picked up.

We saw one Cocoa fall through the dark green leaves, a few feet away, breaking its neck on the sidewalk. We felt a shock of sorrow, but the rest of us were dodging, our arms outstretched, and we caught the kitten as it plummeted, cushioning it.

"How'd you do that?" someone asked in a million universes.

I realized then that I was different.

We step back on the sidewalk, waiting for the truck to pass, waiting to get the license plate so we can call the police anonymously. The police might be able to stop Earl with a road block. They could stop him up U.S. 23 a few miles. If they believe us.

If Earl didn't kill the girl first. If she wasn't already dead.

My stomach lurches. We can't help thinking of the horror that the girl must have faced, must be facing.

Giving the license plate to the police wouldn't be enough.

We step into the street and wave our hands, flagging Earl down.

We once dated a woman, a beautiful woman with chestnut hair that fell to the middle of her back. We dated for several years, and finally became engaged. In one of the worlds, just one, she started to change, grew angry, then elated, then just empty. The rest of us watched in horror as she took a knife to us, just once, in one universe, while in a million others, she compassionately helped our retching self to the kitchen sink.

She didn't understand why I broke off the engagement. But then she didn't know the things I did.

Earl's cab shudders as he slams on the brakes. His CB mic slips loose and knocks the windshield. He grabs his steering wheel, his shoulders massive with exertion.

We stand there, our shopping bag dropped by the side of road, slowly waving our hands back and forth.

In a handful of worlds, the tractor trailer slams through us, and we are rattled by my death. But we know he will be caught there. For vehicular manslaughter, perhaps, and then they will find the girl. In almost all the worlds, though, Earl's semi comes to a halt a few inches from us, a few feet.

We look up over the chrome grill, past the hood ornament, a woman's head, like on a sea-going vessel of old, and into Earl's eyes.

He reaches up and lets loose with his horn. We clap our hands over our ears and, in some universes, we stumble to the sidewalk, allowing Earl to grind his truck into first and rumble away. But mostly, we stand there, not moving.

It didn't matter who was president, or who won the World Series. In sum, it was the same world for each of us, and so we existed together, on top of each other, like a stack of us, all living together within a deck of cards.

Each decision that created a subtly different universe, created another of us, another of a nearly infinite number of me's, who added just a fraction more to our intellect and understanding.

We were not a god. One of us once thought he was, and soon he was no longer with us. He couldn't have shared our secret. We weren't scared of that. Who would have believed him? And now that he was alone—for there could only be a handful of us who might have such delusions—there could be no harm to the rest of us.

We were worlds away.

Finally the horn stops and we look up, our ears benumbed, to see Earl yelling at us. We can't hear what he says, but we recognize on his lips "mother fucker" and "son of a bitch." That's fine. We need him angry. To incite him, we give him the bird.

He bends down, reaching under his seat. He slaps a metal wrench against his open palm. His door opens and he steps down. We wait where we are.

Earl is a large man, six-four, and weighing at least three hundred pounds. He has a belly, but his chest and neck are massive. Black sideburns adorn his face, or it is cleanly shaven, or he has a mustache. In all worlds, his dead eyes watch us as if we are a cow and he is the butcher.

I am slight, just five-nine, one hundred and sixty pounds, but as he swings the wrench we dodge inside it as if we know where it is going to be. We do, of course, for it has shattered our skull in a hundred worlds, enough for the rest of us to anticipate the move.

He swings and we dodge again, twice more, and each time a few of us are sacrificed. We are suddenly uncomfortable at the losses. We are the consciousness of millions of me's. But every one of us that dies is a real instance, gone forever. Every death diminishes us.

We can not wait for the police now. We must save as much of ourself as we can.

We dodge again, spinning past him, sacrificing selves to dance around him as if he is a dance partner we have worked with for a thousand years. We climb the steps to the cab, slide inside, slam the door, and lock it.

I am a composite of all versions of myself. I can think in a million ways at once. Problems become picking the best choice of all choices I could ever have picked. I can not see the future or the past, but I can see the present with a billion eyes and decide the safest course, the one that keeps the most of me together.

I am a massively parallel human.

In the worlds where the sleeper is empty, we sit quietly for the police to arrive, weaving a story that they might believe while Earl glares at us from the street. These selves fade away from those where the girl is trussed in the back, tied with wire that cuts her wrists, and gagged with duct tape.

She is dead in some, her face livid with bruises and burns. In others she is alive and conscious and watches us with blue, bloodshot eyes. The cab smells of people living there too long, of sex, of blood.

In the universes where Earl has abducted and raped this young woman, he does not stand idly on the sidewalk, but rather smashes his window open with the wrench.

The second blow catches my forehead, as I have no place to dodge, and I think as my mind shudders that I am one of the sacrificed ones, one of those who has failed so that the rest of us might survive. But then I realize that it is most of us who have been hit. Only a small percentage have managed to dodge the blow. The rest of us roll to our back and kick at Earl's hand as it reaches in to unlock the cab door. His wrist rakes the broken safety glass, and he cries out, though still manages to pop the lock.

I crab backward across the seat, flailing my legs at him. There are no options here. All of my selves are fighting for our lives or dying.

A single blow takes half of us. Another takes a third of those that are left. Soon my mind is a cloud. I am perhaps ten thousand, slow-witted. No longer omniscient.

A blow lands and I collapse against the door of the cab. I am just me. There is just one. Empty.

My body refuses to move as Earl loops a wire around my wrists and ankles. He does it perfunctorily—he wants to move, to get out of the middle of Sandusky Street—but it is enough to leave me helpless on the passenger-side floor. I can see a half-eaten Big Mac and a can of Diet Coke. My face grinds against small stones and dirt.

I am alone. There is just me, and I am befuddled. My mind works like cold honey. I've failed. We all did, and now we will die like the poor girl in the back. Alone.

My vision shifts, and I see the cab from behind Earl's head, from the sleeping cab. I realize that I am seeing it from a self who has been beaten and tossed into the back. This self is dying, but I can see through his eyes, as the blood seeps out of him. For a moment our worlds are in sync.

His eyes lower and I spot the knife, a hunting knife with a serrated edge, brown with blood. It has fallen under the passenger's chair in his universe, under the chair I have my back against.

My hands are bound behind me, but I reach as far as I can under the seat. It's not far enough in my awkward position. My self's eyes lock on the knife, not far from where my fingers should be. But I have no guarantee that it's even in my own universe at all. We are no longer at the center of the curve. My choices have brought me far away from the selves now drinking coffee and eating bagels across the street from the bookstore.

Earl looks down at me, curses. He kicks me, and pushes me farther against the passenger seat. Something nicks my finger.

I reach gently around it. It is the knife.

I take moments to maneuver it so that I hold it in my palm, outstretched like the spine of a stegosaurus. I cut myself, and I feel the hilt get slippery. I palm my hand against the gritty carpet and position the knife again.

I wait for Earl to begin a right turn, then I pull my knees in, roll onto my chest, and launch myself, back first with knife extended, at Earl.

In the only universe that I exist in, the knife enters his thigh.

The truck caroms off something in the street, and I am jerked harder against Earl. He is screaming, yelling, pawing at his thigh.

His fist slams against me and I fall to the floor.

As he turns his anger on me, the truck slams hard into something, and Earl is flung against the steering wheel. He remains that way, unconscious, until the woman in the back struggles forward and leans heavily on the knife hilt in his leg, and slices until she finds a vein or artery.

I lie in Earl's blood until the police arrive. I am alone again, the self who had spotted the knife, gone.

The young woman came to see me while I mended in a hospital bed. There was an air of notoriety about me, and nurses and doctors were extremely pleasant. It was not just the events that had unfolded on the streets of their small town, but that I was the noted author of such famous songs as "Love as a Star" and "Romance Ho" and "Muskrat Love." The uncovering of Earl's exploits, including a grim laboratory in his home town of Pittsburgh, added fuel to the fire.

She seemed to have mended a bit better than I, her face now a face, her body and spirit whole again. She was stronger than I, I felt when I saw her smile. My body was healing, the cuts around my wrist and ankle, the shattered bone in my arm. But the sundering of my consciousness had left me dull, broken.

I listened to songs on the radio, other people's songs, and could not help wondering in how many worlds there had been no knife, there had been no escape. Perhaps I was the only one of us who reached the cab to survive. Perhaps I was the only one who had saved the woman.

"Thanks," she said. "Thanks for what you did."

I reached for something to say, something witty, urbane, nonchalant from my mind, but there was nothing there but me.

"Uh . . . you're welcome."

She smiled. "You could have been killed," she said.

I looked away. She didn't realize that I had been.

"Well, sorry for bothering you," she said quickly.

"Listen," I said, drawing her back. "I'm sorry I didn't . . ." I wanted to apologize for not saving more of her. For not ending the lives of more Earls. "I'm sorry I didn't save you sooner." It didn't make any sense, and I felt myself flush.

She smiled and said, "It was enough." She leaned in to kiss me.

I am disoriented as I feel her lips brush my right cheek, and also my left, and a third kiss lightly on my lips. I am looking at her in three views, a triptych slightly askew, and I manage a smile then, three smiles. And then a laugh, three laughs.

We have saved her at least once. That is enough. In one of the three universes we inhabit, a woman is singing a catchy tune on the radio. I start to write the lyrics down with my good hand, then stop. Enough of that, we three decide. There are other things to do now, other choices.

Investments

Walter Jon Williams

Walter Jon Williams was born in Minnesota and now lives in Albuquerque, New Mexico. His short fiction has appeared frequently in *Asimov's Science Fiction*, as well as in *The Magazine of Fantasy & Science Fiction, Wheel of Fortune, Global Dispatches, Alternate Outlaws*, and in other markets, and has been gathered in the collections *Facets* and *Frankensteins and Other Foreign Devils*. His novels include *Ambassador of Progress, Knight Moves, Hardwired, The Crown Jewels, Voice of the Whirlwind, House of Shards, Days of Atonement, Aristoi, Metropolitan, City on Fire*, a huge disaster thriller, *The Rift*, and a *Star Trek* novel, *Destiny's Way*. His most recent books are the first two novels in his acclaimed Modern Space Opera epic, *Dread Empire's Fall: The Praxis* and *Dread Empire's Fall: The Sundering*. He won a long-overdue Nebula Award in 2001 for his story "Daddy's World." His stories have appeared in our Third through Sixth, Ninth, Eleventh, Twelfth, Fourteenth, Seventeenth, Twentieth, and Twenty-first Annual Collections.

Here he delivers a complex and suspenseful new novella whose characters are caught in a deadly web of intrigue, revolution, conspiracy, betrayal, and counterbetrayal—all complicated by a sudden overwhelming problem that even the most far-sighted and Machiavellian of plotters could not have been expected to see coming . . .

The car sped south in the subtropical twilight. The Rio Hondo was on Lieutenant Severin's right, a silver presence that wound in and out of his perceptions. As long as he stayed on the highway the rental car, which knew Laredo better than he did, implemented its own navigation and steering, and Severin had nothing to do but relax, to gaze through the windows at the thick, vine-wrapped trunks of the cavella trees, the brilliant plumage of tropical birds, the occasional sight of a hovercraft on the river, its fans a deep bass rumble as it carried cargo south to the port at Punta Piedra. Overhead, stars began to glow on either side of the great tented glittering arc of Laredo's accelerator ring. The silver river turned scarlet in the light of the setting sun.

The vehicle issued a series of warning tones, and Severin took the controls as the car left the highway. Severin drove through an underpass, then up a long straight alley flanked by live oaks, their twisted black limbs sprawled like the legs of fantastic beasts. Overhead arced a series of formal gateways, all elaborate wrought-iron covered with scrollwork, spikes, and heraldic emblems, and each with a teardrop-shaped light that dangled from the center of the arch and cast pale light on the path. Beyond was a large house, two stories wrapped with verandahs, painted a kind of orange-rust color with white trim. It was covered with lights.

People strolled along the verandahs and on the expansive lawns. They were dressed formally, and Severin began to hope that his uniform was sufficiently well tailored so as not to mark him out. Practically all the other guests, Severin assumed, were Peers, the class that the conquering Shaa had imposed on humanity and other defeated species. It was a class into which Severin had not been born, but rather one to which he'd nearly been annexed.

At the start of the recent war Severin had been a warrant officer in the Exploration Service, normally the highest rank to which a commoner might aspire. As a result of service in the war he'd received a field promotion to lieutenant, and suddenly found himself amid a class that had been as remote from him as the stars that glimmered above Laredo's ring.

He parked in front of the house and stepped from the car as the door rolled up into the roof. Tobacco smoke mingled uneasily in the air with tropical perfume. A pair of servants, one Terran, one Torminel, trotted from the house to join him. The Torminel wore huge darkened glasses over her nocturnal-adapted eyes.

"You are Lieutenant Severin?" the Torminel asked, speaking carefully around her fangs.

"Yes."

"Welcome to Rio Hondo, my lord."

Severin wasn't a lord, but all officers were called that out of courtesy, most of them being Peers anyway. Severin had got used to it.

"Thank you," he said. He stepped away from the car, then hesitated. "My luggage," he said.

"Blist will take care of that, my lord. I'll look after your car. Please go up to the house, unless of course you'd prefer that I announce you."

Severin, who could imagine only a puzzled, awkward silence in the moments following a servant announcing his presence, smiled and said, "That won't be necessary. Thank you."

He adjusted his blue uniform tunic and walked across the brick apron to the stairs. Perhaps, he thought, he should have brought his orderly, but in his years among the enlisted ranks he'd got used to looking after his own gear, and he never really gave his servant enough work to justify his existence.

Instead of taking his orderly with him to Rio Hondo, he'd given the man leave. In the meantime Severin could brush his own uniforms and polish his own shoes, something he rarely left to a servant anyway.

Severin's heels clacked on the polished asteroid material that made up the floor of the verandah. A figure detached itself from a group and approached. Severin took a moment to recognize his host, because he had never actually met Senior Captain Lord Gareth Martinez face-to-face.

"Lieutenant Severin? Is that you?"

"Yes, lord captain."

Martinez smiled and reached out to clasp Severin's hand. "Very good to meet you at last!"

Martinez was tall, with broad shoulders, long arms, and big hands; he had wavy dark hair and thick dark brows. He wore the viridian-green uniform of the Fleet, and at his throat was the disk of the Golden Orb, the empire's highest decoration.

Severin and Martinez had been of use to each other during the war, and Severin suspected that it had been Martinez who had arranged his promotion to the officer class. He and Severin had kept in touch with one another over the years, but all their communication had been through electronic means.

Martinez was a native of Laredo, a son of Lord Martinez, Laredo's principal Peer, and when he'd returned to his home world, he'd learned that Severin was based on Laredo's ring and invited him to the family home for a few days.

"You've missed dinner, I'm afraid," Martinez said. "It went on most of the afternoon. Fortunately you also missed the speeches."

Martinez spoke with a heavy Laredo accent, a mark of his provincial origins that Severin suspected did him little good in the drawing rooms of Zanshaa High City.

"I'm sorry to have missed your speech anyway, my lord," Severin said in his resolutely middle-class voice.

Martinez gave a heavy sigh. "You'll get a chance to hear it again I give the same one over and over." He tilted his chin high and struck a pose. " 'The empire, under the guidance of the Praxis, contains a social order of unlimited potential.' " The pose evaporated. He looked at Severin. "How long are you on the planet?"

"Nearly a month, I think. *Surveyor* will be leaving ahead of *Titan*, while they're still loading antihydrogen."

"Where's *Surveyor* bound, then?"

"Through Chee to Parkhurst. And possibly beyond even that . . . the spectra from Parkhurst indicate there may be two undiscovered wormholes there, and we're going to look for them."

Martinez was impressed. "Good luck. Maybe Laredo will become a hub of commerce instead of a dead end on the interstellar roadway."

It was a good time to be in the Exploration Service. Founded originally to locate wormholes, stabilize them, and travel through them to discover new systems, planets, and species, the Service had dwindled during the last thousand years of Shaa rule as the Great Masters lost their taste for expanding their empire. Since the death of the last Shaa and the war that followed, the Convocation had decided again on a policy of expansion, beginning with Chee and Parkhurst, two systems that could be reached through Laredo, and which had been surveyed hundreds of years earlier without any settlement actually being authorized.

The Service was expanding to fill its mandate, and that meant more money, better ships, and incoming classes of young officers for Severin to be senior to. The Exploration Service now offered the possibility of great discoveries and adventure, and Severin—as an officer who had come out of the war with credit—was in a position to take advantage of such an offer.

A Terran stepped out of the house with a pair of drinks in his hand. He strongly resembled Martinez, and he wore the dark red tunic of the Lords Convocate, the six-hundred-odd member committee that ruled the empire in the absence of the Shaa.

"Here you are," he said, and handed a drink to Martinez. He looked at Severin, hesitated, and then offered him the second glass.

"Delta whisky?" he asked.

"Thank you." Severin took the glass.

"Lieutenant Severin," Martinez said, "allow me to introduce you to my older brother, Roland."

"Lord convocate," Severin said. He juggled the whisky glass to take Roland's hand.

"Pleased you could come," Roland said. "My brother has spoken of you." He turned to Martinez. "Don't forget that you and Terza are pledged to play tingo tonight with Lord Mukerji."

Martinez made a face. "Can't you find someone else?"

"You're the hero," Roland said. "That makes your money better than anyone else's. You and my lord Severin can rehash the war tomorrow, after our special guests have left."

Martinez looked at Severin. "I'm sorry," he said. "There are people here concerned with the Chee development, and it's the polite thing to keep them happy."

Since the Chee development was the settlement of an entire planet, and the special guests were presumably paying for it, Severin sympathized with the necessity of keeping them happy.

"I understand," he said.

Roland's eyes tracked over Severin's shoulder, and he raised his eyebrows. "Here's Terza now."

Severin turned to see a small group on the lawn, an elegant, black-haired woman in a pale gown walking hand-in-hand with a boy of three, smiling and talking with another woman, fair-haired and pregnant.

"Cassilda's looking well," Martinez remarked.

"Fecundity suits her," said Roland.

"Fecundity and a fortune," Martinez said. "What more could a man ask?"

Roland smiled. "Pliability," he said lightly, then stepped forward to help his pregnant wife up the stairs. Martinez waited for the other woman to follow and greeted her with a kiss.

Introductions were made. The black-haired woman was Lady Terza Chen, heir to the high-caste Chen clan and Martinez's wife. The child was Young Gareth. The light-haired woman was Lady Cassilda Zykov, who was apparently not an heir but came with a fortune anyway.

"Pleased to meet you," Severin said.

"Thank you for keeping my husband alive," Terza said. "I hope you won't stop now."

Severin looked at Martinez. "He seems to be doing well enough on his own."

Lady Terza was slim and poised and had a lovely, almond-eyed face. She put a hand on Severin's arm. "Have you eaten?"

"I had a bite coming down in the skyhook."

She drew Severin toward the door. "That was a long time ago. Let me show you the buffet. I'll introduce you to some people and then—" Her eyes turned to Martinez.

"Tingo with Mukerji," Martinez said. "I know."

She looked again at Severin. "You don't play tingo, do you?"

Bankruptcy doesn't suit me, he thought.

"No," he said, "I'm afraid not."

Terza took Martinez's arm in both her own and rested her head on his shoulder. "It was time you came home," she said. "I've never seen you with your own people."

He looked at her. "You're my people, now," he said.

Terza had spent most of her pregnancy on Laredo, but without him: that had been wartime, with the Convocation in flight from the capital and Martinez fighting with the Fleet. After that, with the rebels driven from Zanshaa and the war at an end, the family had reunited in the High City to bask in the cheers of a thankful population. Chee and Parkhurst had been opened to settlement under Martinez patronage Roland had been coopted into the Convocation.

Now, three years later, the cheers of the High City had faded Enmity on the Fleet Control Board kept Martinez from command of a ship or any meaningful assignments. Terza led an active life that combined a post at the Ministry of Right and Dominion with a full schedule of High City diversions: receptions, balls, concerts, exhibitions, and an endless round of parties. Martinez was feeling more and more like his wife's appendage, trailed around from one event to the next.

The choice was stark: either go home or write his memoirs. Sitting down to write the story of his life, like an old man at the end of his days with nothing to offer to the empire but words, was an image he found repellent. He arranged for passage to Laredo on the huge transport *Wihun,* and embarked his family and their servants.

Before he left, Martinez applied to be appointed Lord Inspector of the Fleet for Laredo, Chee, and Parkhurst, thus giving his journey an official pretext. The appointment was approved so quickly that Martinez could only imagine the joy on the Fleet Control Board at the news that Senior Captain Martinez had been willing, for once, to settle for a meaningless task.

The appointment kept him on the active list. It gave him the authority to interfere here and there, if he felt like interfering. Maybe he would interfere just to convince himself that the postwar arrangement hadn't made him irrelevant.

"Captain Martinez! Lady Terza! Are you ready for tingo?"

Martinez decided that he wouldn't submerge into irrelevance just yet, not as long as games of tingo were without a fifth player.

"Certainly, Lord Mukerji," he said.

Lord Mukerji was a short, spare Terran with wiry gray hair, a well-cultivated handlebar mustache, and all the social connections in the worlds. He had been brought in as the president of the Chee Development Company in order to provide the necessary tone. Opening two whole worlds to settlement was beyond the financial capabilities even of the staggeringly rich Lord Martinez, and outside investors had to be brought in. It had to be admitted that the Peers and financiers of the High City preferred to hear about investment opportunities in tones more congenial to their ears than those uttered in a barbaric Laredo accent.

And Lord Mukerji had certainly done his job. Investment had poured into the company's coffers from the moment he'd begun spreading his balm on the moneyed classes. Important Peer clans were signed on to become the official patrons of settlers, of cities, or even of entire industries. Company stock was doing well on the Zanshaa Exchange; and the bonds were doing even better.

Martinez and Terza took their seats as a tall figure loomed above the table. "Do you know Lord Pa?" Mukerji said.

"We've met only briefly, before dinner," Martinez said.

Lord Pa Maq-fan was a Lai-own, a species of flightless birds, and was the chairman of a privately held company that was one of the prime contractors for the Chee development. From his great height he looked at Terza and Martinez with disturbing blood-red eyes and bared the peg teeth in his short muzzle. "All Lai-own know Captain Martinez," he said. "He saved our home world."

"Very kind of you to say so," Martinez said as Lord Pa settled his keel-like breastbone into his special chair.

He was always heartened when people remembered these little details.

"I haven't kept people waiting, I hope." Lady Marcella Zykov hastened into her place at the table. She was a first cousin of Roland's bride, Cassilda, and the chief of operations for the Chee Company, having been put in place to look after the money the Zykov clan was putting into the venture. She was a very short, very busy woman in her thirties, with a pointed face and auburn hair pulled into an untidy knot behind her head, and she absently brushed tobacco ash off her jacket as she took her place.

"Shall we roll the bones, then?" Lord Mukerji said.

All players bet a hundred zeniths. The bones were rolled, and they appointed Marcella the dealer. She ran the tiles through the sorting machine and dealt each player an initial schema.

"Discard," said Terza, who sat on her right, and removed the Three Virtues from her schema.

"Claim," said Lord Mukerji. He took the Three Virtues into his schema and smiled beneath his broad mustaches. He waited for Marcella to be dealt a new tile, then touched a numbered pad on the table. "Another two hundred," he said.

Martinez thought it was a little early in the game to raise, but he paid two hundred for a new tile just to see where the game would go. Two rounds later, when Lord Mukerji doubled, Martinez and Terza both dropped out. The game was won by Lord Pa, who had quietly built a Tower that he promptly dropped onto Lord Mukerji's Bouquet of Probity.

"Roll the bones," said Mukerji.

The bones decided to make Mukerji the dealer. As he ran the tiles through the sorting machine, Marcella looked up from the table.

"Will you be traveling to Chee, Captain Martinez?"

"I'm Lord Inspector for Chee," Martinez said, "so I'll be required to inspect the skyhook, the station, and the other Fleet facilities."

"And Parkhurst as well?"

"There's nothing in the Parkhurst system at the moment but a Fleet survey vessel. I can wait for it to return."

"I can offer you transport on the *Kayenta*," Marcella said, "if you can leave in twenty days or so." She turned to Terza. "That way Lady Terza can accompany you without the discomforts of a Fleet vessel or a transport."

Martinez was pleasantly surprised. He'd been planning on booking a ride on one of the giant transports heading to Chee—they carried immigrants as well as cargo and had adequate facilities for passengers—but *Kayenta* was the Chee Company's executive yacht, with first-class accommodations and a crew that included a masseur and a cosmetician.

He turned to Terza, who seemed delighted by the offer. "Thank you," he said. "We'll definitely consider the option."

"Are you going out to Chee yourself, Lady Marcella?" Mukerji asked.

"Yes. They're beginning the new railhead at Corona, and Lord Pa and I will need to consult with Allodorm."

Martinez caught the surprise that crossed Terza's face, surprise that was swiftly suppressed. Terza took up her tiles.

"Is that Ledo Allodorm?" she asked.

Lord Pa's blood-red eyes gazed at her from across the table. "Yes," he said. "Do you know that gentleman?"

"Not personally," Terza said, as she looked down at her tiles. "His name came up, I don't know where."

Martinez noted with interest that his wife wore the serene smile that experience told him was a sure sign she was telling less than the truth.

"Shall we roll the bones?" asked Lord Mukerji.

Mukerji doubled three times on the first three rounds and drove everyone else out of the game. Martinez realized he'd found his way into a very serious and potentially expensive contest, and began to calculate odds very carefully.

Terza won the following game with the Six Cardinal Directions. Lord Pa won the next. Marcella the game after. Then Lord Pa, then Martinez with a Bouquet of Delights over Lord Mukerji's Crossroads.

"Roll the bones," Lord Mukerji said.

Lord Pa took another game, then Terza, and Marcella won three games in a row. In the next game, the bones rolled six, so the stakes were doubled and the bones rolled again, and this time proclaimed Martinez dealer. He discarded Two Sunsets, only to have Lord Mukerji claim it, which argued that Lord Mukerji was aiming at filling a Bouquet of Sorrows. Mukerji in his turn was dealt, and discarded, a South, which Martinez claimed to add to his East and Up to make three of the Six Cardinal Directions. On subsequent turns, Martinez was dealt a South, needing only a North and a Down for six. Mukerji claimed Four Night Winds, doubled, kept a tile he was dealt, doubled, was dealt and discarded Two Ancestors, and doubled again anyway. Terza and Lord Pa dropped out of the game during the doubling, turning over their tiles to reveal unpromising schemas.

Martinez looked at the total and felt his mouth go dry. He received a generous allowance from his father, but to continue the game would be to abuse his parent severely.

His worried contemplation of the score made him a critical half-second late when Marcella, dropping out of the game, made her final discard, a Down.

"Claim," Mukerji said.

Mukerji had claimed the tile simply to thwart him. Martinez, the word already spilling from his lips, had no choice but to let Mukerji take the tile he badly needed to complete his hand.

"Double," Mukerji said, his eyes gleaming.

Martinez looked at his schema, then scanned the discards and the tiles of the players who had dropped out of the betting. Neither of the two Norths was revealed, and neither was the second Down.

He looked at his own tiles again. Beside the Directions he had Three and Four Ships, a Sunlit Garden, and a Road of Metal. If he got Two or Five Ships, he'd have a Small Flotilla. A Flotilla plus the Cardinal Directions equaled a Migration.

He scanned the discards and reveals again, and saw singletons of Two and Five Ships, which meant other Ships were still in the sorting machine.

Or already in Lord Mukerji's schema.

Martinez decided it was worth the risk.

Without speaking Martinez dealt himself another tile. It was Four Ships, and he discarded it. Lord Mukerji ignored it and took another tile, which he discarded.

Five Ships. Martinez claimed it, discarded his Road of Metal, then dealt himself another tile, which he discarded.

He was suddenly aware that the room had fallen silent, that others stood around him, watching. Roland watched from amid the spectators with a frown on his face, and Cassilda with her hands pressed protectively over her growing abdomen. Lord Pa's red eyes were obscured by nictitating membranes. Marcella was frozen in her seat, but her hands formed little fists and her knuckles were white.

Terza, on his right, had the serene smile that she wore to conceal her thoughts, but he saw the tension crimping the corners of her eyes.

Lord Mukerji was dealt and discarded a tile, and then Martinez dealt himself an Angle, which he discarded.

"Claim," Mukerji said in triumph.

He laid down his completed Bouquet of Sorrows, then added the Angle to his Point and his Coordinate, making a Geometry. His grin broadened beneath the spreading mustache as he pushed the odd Down into the discard pile.

"That's a game for me, then," he said.

"Claim," said Martinez.

He turned over his tiles to reveal the incomplete Migration, which he completed by adding the Down and discarding his Sunlit Garden. From the room he heard a collective exhalation of breath.

He looked at Mukerji, who was suddenly very white around the eyes. "That's a limit schema," Mukerji said.

Honesty compelled Martinez to speak. "And the bones came up six, if you remember, so the limit is doubled. And I'm dealer, so that doubles again."

Lord Mukerji surveyed the table, then slowly leaned backwards into his chair, draping himself on the chair back as if he were a fallen flag.

"What *is* the limit?" Martinez heard someone ask.

"Ten thousand," came the reply.

"Fucking amazing," said the first.

"Well played," said Lord Mukerji. "I do believe you let me have that Cardinal Direction on purpose."

"Of course," Martinez lied.

Mukerji held out his hand. "You must give me an opportunity for revenge," he said.

Martinez took the hand. "Later tonight, if you like."

There was applause from the crowd as the two clasped hands.

"I need to visit the smoking lounge," Marcella said, and stood.

Martinez rose from the table. His head spun, and his knees felt watery. Terza rose with him and took his arm.

"That was terrifying," she murmured.

"Ten thousand doubled twice," Martinez breathed. "For forty we could buy a small palace in the High City."

"We already *have* a small palace."

"I could have lost it tonight." He passed a hand over his forehead.

Roland loomed up at his other elbow. "That was well judged," he said.

"Thank you."

"But you were lucky."

Martinez looked at him. "I *am* lucky," he said. If he weren't, he wouldn't have been a senior captain before he was thirty.

"Just so you don't go counting on it." A mischievous light glowed in Roland's eyes. "You're not taking up tingo as a substitute for the excitement of combat, are you?"

"Combat's easier," Martinez said. He looked at his brother. "That isn't true, by the way."

"I know."

A thought passed through Martinez's mind. "Mukerji wasn't playing with *our* money, was he?"

"You mean the Company's? No. His presidency is ceremonial; he doesn't have access to the accounts. He doesn't even take a salary."

Martinez raised an eyebrow.

"Oh," Roland said, "we gave him lots of *stock*. If the Chee Company does well, so does he."

"He may have to sell some of his stock after tonight."

Roland shook his head. "He can afford a lot of nights like this."

"How many, I wonder," Terza said. She stroked Martinez's arm. "I should make sure Gareth's got to bed. If you're all right?"

"I could use a drink."

"Absolutely not," Roland said. "Not if you're committed to an evening of high play."

Martinez let go a long breath. "You've got a point."

Terza smiled, patted his arm, and went in search of the children. Martinez went to the bar with Roland, ordered an orange juice, and poured it over ice.

Roland ordered champagne. "You don't have to rub it in," Martinez said, and turned to find Severin at his elbow.

"You're finding your way all right?" he asked.

"Yes. There's a Chee band tuning in the ballroom. I'll dance."

"Good."

"I hear you've done something spectacular at tingo. Everyone's talking about it."

Martinez felt a tingle of vanity. "I made a mistake early on," he said, "but I calculated the odds correctly in the end."

He explained the play as he made his way back to the parlor. They came to Mukerji, who was speaking with Lord Pa. "If the geologist's report was in error, then it must be done again, of course," he said. "I'm sure Cassilda will—" He broke off, then looked at Martinez. "Lord captain," he said. "Shall we resume the game?"

"We seem to be without a few players as yet," Martinez said. "May I introduce Lieutenant Severin? He saved the empire at Protipanu, and saved *me* a few months later, during the battle there."

Pa looked down from his great height, nictitating membranes clearing his red eyes as he gazed at Severin with studious intensity. "I don't recall any of that in the histories," he said.

"The wrong people *wrote* the histories," Martinez said. Those same people had decided to keep Severin's contribution to the war a secret. He had used a trick of physics to physically move a wormhole out from under a Naxid squadron, and since the empire depended for its very existence on the wormholes that knit its systems together, the censors had decided not to remind people that such a thing could be done.

"In any case, lord lieutenant, I am pleased to meet you," said Pa to Severin.

"So am I," Mukerji said. His long mustache gave a twitch. "You wouldn't care to join us for a game of tingo?"

"Thank you, my lord," Severin said, "but I don't play."

"Don't play tingo?" Mukerji said, blinking with apparent astonishment. "What *do* you do in those officers' clubs or wardrooms or whatever you call them?"

"Mostly I do paperwork," Severin said.

"Perhaps we should actively search for a fifth player," Martinez said. "I'm not certain that Terza will return from putting Gareth to bed anytime soon."

He spoke quickly. He knew that, as someone promoted from the ranks, Severin was unlikely to possess the large private income normal for most officers. Very possibly the unfortunate man was forced to live on his pay. A game of tingo played for high stakes wasn't simply unwise for a man like Severin, it was impossible.

Best to get him off the hook as quickly as possible.

Pa and Mukerji went in search of a tingo player, and Martinez asked Severin about his last voyage, several months in which *Surveyor* had been in the Chee system, making one rendezvous after another with asteroids, strapping antimatter-fueled thrusters onto the giant rocks, and sending them on looping courses to Wormhole Station One, where they were used to balance the mass coming into the system on the huge freighters. The task was both dull and dangerous, a risky combination, but the voyage had been successful and the wormhole station wouldn't need any more raw material for a year or more.

"Fortunately the mass driver on Chee's moon is taking over the job of supplying the wormhole stations," Severin said, "so we're available for other duties."

"Excellent. Your voyage was uneventful otherwise?"

"Our skipper's good," Severin said. "No one on the trip tore so much as a hangnail."

"Do I know him?" Martinez asked.

"Lord Go Shikimori. An old Service family."

Martinez considered, then shook his head. "The name's not familiar."

Marcella returned from the smoking lounge brushing ash from her jacket. Pa and Mukerji arrived with an elderly, fangless Torminel named Lady Uzdil.

"I seem to be caught up in the game," Martinez told Severin. "My apologies."

"I think I hear music," Severin said.

"Enjoy."

What *did* Severin do with himself in his ship's wardroom? Martinez wondered. He probably couldn't afford most of an officer's amusements.

And judging by his uniform, he couldn't afford much of a tailor, either.

Martinez settled in to play tingo. Lady Uzdil seemed to be shedding: the air was full of graying fur. Martinez played conservatively, which meant that he frequently allowed himself to be driven out of a round by Mukerji's insistent doubling. He held firm when fortune gave him good tiles, though, and managed a modest profit on top of the forty thousand he'd won earlier. Lord Pa did very well, Cassilda well enough, and Lady Uzdil lost a modest amount. It was Mukerji who lost heavily, plunging heavily on one bad venture after another. Though he didn't run afoul of any limit schemas, and he didn't lose another High City palace, Martinez calculated that he lost at least the value of a sumptuous country villa—and not one on Laredo, either, but on Zanshaa.

After two hours Martinez considered that he'd done his duty in giving Mukerji a chance to win his money back, and left the game. Mukerji protested, but Cassilda and Pa were were happy with their winnings and left the game as well.

"I'm glad he doesn't have any financial control in the Chee Company," Martinez told Terza later, when he was abed. "Not if he runs a business the same way he gambles."

"I'm sure he has no idea whatever of how to run a business," Terza said as she approached the bed. "That's what Marcella's for." She wore a blue silk nightgown, and had bound her long black hair with matching blue ribbon into a long tail that she wore over one shoulder. The look gave her a pleasing asymmetry. Martinez reached out one of his big hands and stroked her hip with the back of his knuckles.

Their marriage had been arranged by their families, one of Roland's more elaborate and insistent conspiracies. Martinez felt free to resent Roland's interference, but he had decided long ago not to resent Terza.

"What about Ledo Allodorm?" he asked.

Terza's almond eyes widened faintly. "You noticed?" she asked.

"I saw you react to the name. I doubt the others know you well enough to have seen what I did."

"Move over. I'll tell you what I know."

Martinez made room on the bed. Terza slipped beneath the covers and curled on her side facing Martinez. Her scent floated delicately through his perceptions.

"I found out about Allodorm when I was asked to review some old contracts left over from the war," she said. The Ministry of Right and Dominion, where she was posted, was the civilian agency that encompassed the Fleet, and dealt with issues of contracts, supply, Fleet facilities, budgets, and support.

"Allodorm is a Daimong from Devajjo, in the Hone Reach," she continued. "During the war he received a contract to build four—or was it five?—transport vessels for the Fleet. The war ended before he could deliver the ships, and the contract was canceled."

"So what did he do?" Martinez asked. "Convert the transports to civilian purposes? That would be allowed, wouldn't it, if the government didn't want them anymore?"

Terza frowned. "There was an allegation that he never built the ships at all."

Martinez blinked. "He took the money and did *nothing*?"

"Other than commission some architects, print some stationery, and recruit some staff and some high-priced legal talent, no." She looked thoughtful. "It was possible to make a calculation that the war would be over before he had to deliver. If we won, the contracts would be canceled; and if the Naxids won, they wouldn't care if he'd started work or not."

"Didn't the Investigative Service climb all over Allodorm's operation? Couldn't the ministry at least have asked for its money back?"

Terza offered a mild shrug. "After the war the IS was involved in purging rebels and their sympathizers, and didn't spare a thought for the people who were supposed to be on *our* side. When the file finally came across my desk I recommended an investigation, but the ministry decided against it. I don't know why; it's possible that Allodorm is politically protected."

"So now Allodorm is on Chee, and Marcella and Lord Pa are traveling to consult with him."

"Maybe he's a subcontractor."

"That doesn't speak well for the prospect of the Chee Company's balance sheet."

"The Chee Company may be all right," Terza pointed out. "It's Lord Pa and the Meridian Company that's the prime contractor. If anyone's being gouged, it's probably them."

"Either way, it's my family's money." He shifted closer to Terza's warmth and she rested her head on his shoulder and put an arm across his chest. "*Our* balance sheet has improved anyway. What shall we do with Mukerji's cash?"

He could sense her amusement. "Buy something preposterous, I suppose. You've always talked about taking up yachting."

Martinez felt a twinge of annoyance. "They wouldn't let me into the Seven Stars or the Ion Club," he said. "A provincial can't get past their august doors, no matter how many medals he's won." He kissed Terza's forehead. "Or how many high-placed ministry officials he's married."

"So join a lesser club," Terza said, "and beat the pants off the Seven Stars in every match."

Martinez grinned at the ceiling. "That's not a half-bad idea," he said.

He felt Terza's warm breath on his neck as she spoke. "Is this the room you lived in as a child?"

"Yes, as a matter of fact. Same furniture, too, but the model Fleet ships that I hung from the ceiling are gone. And so are the uniform guides to the various academies that I'd tacked up on the walls."

Her low chuckle came to his ear. "So joining the Fleet was *your* idea, I take it."

"Oh yes. I had a lot of romantic ideas—must have got those from my mother. And my father didn't mind, because in the Fleet at least I'd learn some useful skills."

He remembered, before the war, when speaking with—with a certain person, a woman he preferred not ever to think about, a woman with pale hair and milky skin and blazing green eyes—he'd expressed his frustration at being in a meaningless service, a club not unlike the Seven Stars but less useful, a club devoted to ritual and display and serving the limitless vanity of its commanders.

The war had changed that, at least for a while.

What hadn't changed, apparently, were the politically connected contractors who gouged the government while delivering shoddy, late, or nonexistent work.

That, he supposed, was the government's business. What concerned Martinez was that if Allodorm were stealing money now, he was no longer stealing it just from the government, but the Martinez family.

That, of course, had to stop.

Terza pressed closer to Martinez on the bed. She kissed his cheek. "I wonder," she said, "if when you were a boy in this bed, you ever imagined—"

Martinez sat up, displacing Terza's head and arm. "Comm," he said. "Wall display: on."

The chameleon-weave fabric of the display normally matched the geometric pattern of the wallpaper, but now it brightened into a video screen displaying the Martinez crest. "Comm: search," Martinez said. "Ledo plus Allodorm plus Meridian plus Company. Begin."

In half a second data flashed on the screen. Martinez chose the first listing, and saw a page from the Meridian Company's official prospectus of the Chee development. He absorbed the information.

"Allodorm's chief engineer for the Meridian Company," he said. "He's in charge of all their projects on Chee. *All* of them."

He turned to Terza and saw her pensive expression. "Something wrong?" he said.

A serene smile crossed her face, the one he knew for its falsity.

"Nothing at all," she said.

"Daddy says I'm a genius. Daddy says I'm going to do great things."

"I'm sure you are," said Severin.

"I'm going to smash Naxids." The dark-haired child raised a hand over his head. In his fist was a toy warship. He flung it on the polished asteroid material of the verandah. "*Bang*!"

"Good shot," Severin observed.

He'd grown up in a family with a pair of younger sisters, and knew how to keep a young child entertained. Lord Gareth Chen—who bore his father's first name but the surname of his mother, who was the Chen heir and ranked higher—picked up the warship and flung it again. Wet explosive sounds came from his pursed lips.

"But what if the Naxids come from *this* direction?" Severin asked, and leaned out of his metal whitewashed chair to threaten the boy's flank.

"*Bang!*"

"Or from here?" The other flank.

"Bang!"

"Or here?" Overhead.

"Bang!"

Lord Gareth the Younger was at a stage of life where this could go on for quite a while before he got bored. Having nothing better to do, Severin was content to continue the game, though his thoughts were elsewhere.

He had awakened that morning with a dream clinging to his memory like a shroud. In the dream he had been driving up the oak alley toward the house, beneath the series of iron arches, and somehow one of the arches had transformed itself into a proscenium, and he'd stepped through the proscenium onto a stage that was the house.

The house had been covered with lights, and a party had been under way. The guests glittered in fine clothes and uniforms. Severin knew none of them. Their conversation was strangely oblique, and Severin kept feeling that he could understand them if only he listened a little harder. At some point he discovered that they were not people at all, but automata, smiling and glimmering as they spoke words that had been preprogrammed by someone else.

In the dream Severin hadn't found this discovery horrifying, but intensely interesting. He wandered through the party listening to the conversation and admiring the brilliance of the puppets' design.

When he woke he was still under the spell of the dream. He breakfasted alone on the terrace—apparently his hosts were not yet awake—and he found himself thinking about the strange conversations that he'd heard, and trying to work out the obscure story behind them.

He thought about going back to bed and hoping to pick the dream up where it had left off, but at this point Gareth Junior arrived, and the battle with the Naxids began.

He was rescued in time by Martinez, who came out of the house and lunged at his son, scooping him up in both arms and whirling him overhead as the child shrilled his laughter.

Following Martinez from the house came his older brother, Roland, who carried a cup of coffee in one hand. Both wore civilian clothes, which made Severin more conscious than usual of his shabby uniform.

"I suppose it won't be long before I'm behaving like that," Roland said as he watched Martinez twirling his son.

"I suppose it won't," Severin said.

Roland sipped coffee. Martinez tucked his son under one arm and turned to Severin. "Has the boy prodigy been bothering you?"

"He's been mashing Naxids, mostly."

Martinez grinned. "Exercising tactical genius, eh? Just like his father!" Young Gareth still under his arm, Martinez sprinted into the house as the child waved his fists and laughed aloud.

"Perhaps I *won't* behave like that, after all," Roland decided.

Martinez returned a few moments later, having delivered his offspring to the nursemaid. He combed his disordered hair with his fingers and dropped into the whitewashed metal chair next to Severin.

"I saw you dancing last night," he said. "With a curly-haired girl."

"Lady Consuelo Dalmas," Severin said.

"Consuelo." Martinez blinked. "I thought she looked familiar. I used to see her older sister, when we were all, ah, much younger."

"She's invited me to a garden party tomorrow afternoon."

Martinez smiled. "Have a good time."

"I will." He considered offering a resigned sort of sigh and decided against it. "Of course," he added, "sooner or later either she or her parents will discover that I'm not a Peer, and have no money, and then I won't see her again." Severin clasped his hands between his knees. "But then I'm used to that."

Martinez gave him an unsettled look. "You're not regretting your promotion, I hope."

"No." Severin considered. "But it's made me aware of how many locked doors there are, doors that I once had no idea even existed."

"If there's anything I can do to open them . . ." Martinez ventured.

"Thank you. I'm not certain there's anything that can be done."

"Unless we have another war," Roland said. "Then all bets are off."

Smiling lightly to himself, Roland walked to the verandah rail and looked out into the oak alley, raising his head at the honeyed scent of the o-pii flowers floating on the morning breeze. "Consuelo's not right for you anyway, if you don't mind my saying so," he said. "Too young, too much a part of the fashionable set. What you need is a comely widow, or a young woman married to a dull old husband."

Martinez looked at him. "You don't have anyone in mind, do you?"

"Let me put my mind to it."

Martinez gave Severin an uneasy look. "Better make your wishes plain. Roland has disturbing success as a matchmaker."

There was something in the air, Severin felt, some history between the brothers that made this an uncomfortable moment.

"I'm only here for a month," Severin said.

"Narrow window of opportunity," Roland said. "I'll see what I can do."

"Apropos conspiracy," Martinez said, "do you know anything about Allodorm, Meridian Company's chief engineer?"

"I've met him on Chee Station," Severin said. "Though I haven't conspired with him."

"I haven't met him at all," Roland said. He turned around, eyes mild as he contemplated his brother. "I appreciate your confidence in my omniscience, but what I really do is look after family interests in the Convocation. I'm not really connected to the Chee development business."

"Terza thinks that Allodorm's a swindler," Martinez said. "And if she's right, he's in a perfect place to walk off with a lot of our money."

Roland absorbed this with a distracted frown. "What does Terza know, exactly?"

"During the war, he took the money to build five ships and then didn't build them."

Severin felt a moment of shock. As an officer in government service he was familiar enough with waste and theft, but five whole missing ships seemed extreme.

There was a moment of silence, and then Roland turned to Severin.

"I'd appreciate your discretion," he said.

"Certainly," Severin said.

"There may not be anything in this," Roland said.

"Of course," Severin said.

He found himself fascinated by the interactions in this household, the delicate play between the decorated Fleet officer and his politician brother. Since his promotion he'd had the opportunity to observe several Peer families, and none had been quite like this one.

"I wish I knew who hired Allodorm," Martinez said pensively.

"Lord Pa, presumably," Roland said. "The question is whether Lord Pa knew about the Fleet ships, or cared if he did." He pulled another of the metal chairs toward Severin and sat. "Would you tell us about this Allodorm?"

Severin shrugged. "He's a Daimong. Youngish, I think, though with Daimong it's hard to tell. When *Surveyor* first docked at Chee Station, he was on hand to make sure we got everything we needed. I thought that was very good of him."

"Were you treated well?" Roland asked.

"Yes. Since I'm the exec, the lord captain assigned me to work with Allodorm, and it was first-class all the way. Supplies came aboard within hours of submitting our requests. The victuals were fresh. Allodorm put one of the worker hostels at Port Vipsania at the disposal of our liberty crew, and he hosted a dinner for the officers."

"Nothing odd?" Martinez asked. "Nothing a little off-center in the way the station's run?"

"Other than it being first-class, no," Severin said. "In the Exploration Service we're used to things being more worn and shabby—it's not like we've got the Fleet's prestige or budget—but everything on Chee Station was new and shiny and efficient. The facilities were bigger than they needed, but then there are plans to expand."

The brothers contemplated this. "I don't suppose we should tell our father."

"What would we tell him? We've got dozens of inspectors on Chee anyway—what can he do that they can't?"

Martinez gave a little shrug. "Not get bribed?" he said.

"Father's supposed to open the meeting of the Petitioners' Council in something like fifteen days." Roland gave a tight little smile. "If he abandons his task and goes charging off to Chee on the *Ensenada* to expose the wicked, that's all the warning Allodorm or anyone else is going to need. Everything would be tidied up by the time he gets there."

"And you?"

"I'm not going anywhere until Cassilda has our baby, after which the whole family will leave for Zanshaa so that I can sit in Convocation."

Martinez sighed. "I'm the Lord Inspector, aren't I? I suppose it's up to me to inspect."

Severin thought again about the two brothers. They knew each other well, they worked together deftly, they had a shared history and vocabulary. It occurred to Severin, however, that perhaps they didn't like each other.

"Lady Liao," Roland said suddenly.

Martinez looked at him. "Beg pardon?"

Roland turned to Severin. "Lady Liao, wife of Lord Judge Omohundro. She's perfect for you. Her husband's on the ring tied up in a long series of hearings, and I'm sure she's looking for amusement."

Severin could do nothing but stare. *Can you do that?* he wanted to ask.

Roland looked at him. "Shall I invite her to tea?" he said.

"We are holding at five minutes," said Lord Go Shikimori, captain of the *Surveyor.*

"Holding at five minutes, my lord," said Severin.

Surveyor awaited final permission from Ring Control to launch on its mission through Chee and Parkhurst to the possible wormholes beyond. Encircled by the round metal hoops of his acceleration cage, Severin glanced down at the pilot's board before him—it was he who would steer *Surveyor* from the ring and into the great emptiness beyond, not that the job was particularly difficult.

The lights of the pilot's board glittered on the ring Severin wore on the middle finger of his right hand. Nine small sapphires sparkled around a central opal. The ring had been a parting gift from Lady Liao, one sapphire for each night she and Severin had spent together.

For a moment he was lost in reverie, memories of smooth cool sheets, silken flesh, Lady Liao's subtle scent. Wind chimes that saluted the dawn on the balcony outside her room.

Lord Roland Martinez, he thought, was very, very smart.

"Message from Ring Control, my lord," reported Lord Barry Montcrief, who sat at the comm board—he had the drawling High City accent that Lord Go preferred as the official voice of his ship. "Permission granted to depart the station en route to Chee system."

"Resume countdown," the captain said.

"Countdown resumed," said Warrant Officer Lily Bhagwati, who sat at the engines station.

"Depressurize boarding tube. Warn crew for zero gravity."

"Depressurizing boarding tube." Alarms clattered through the ship. "Zero gravity alarm, my lord."

Severin checked his board, took the joysticks in his hands, rotated them. "Maneuvering thrusters gimbaled," he said. "Pressure at thruster heads nominal."

"Boarding tube depressurized."

"Withdraw boarding tube," said the captain.

"Boarding tube . . ." Waiting for the light to go on. ". . . withdrawn, my lord."

"Electrical connections withdrawn," said Bhagwati. "Outside connectors sealed. Ship is on 100 percent internal power."

"Data connectors withdrawn," said Lord Barry. "Outside data ports sealed."

"Main engines gimbaled," said Bhagwati. "Gimbal test successful."

"Hold at ten seconds," said the captain. "Status, everyone."

All stations reported clean boards.

"Launch in ten," Lord Go said. "Pilot, the ship is yours."

"The ship is mine, my lord." Severin released and clenched his hands on the joysticks.

The digit counter in the corner of his display counted down to zero. Lights flashed.

"Clamps withdrawn," he said. "Magnetic grapples released."

Severin suddenly floated free in his webbing as *Surveyor* was cast free of Laredo's accelerator ring. *Surveyor* had been moored nose-in, and the release of centripetal force from the upper ring, which was spinning at seven times the rate of the planet below, gave the ship a good rate of speed that carried it clear of any potential obstacles.

Severin checked the navigation display anyway, and saw no threats. He thumbed buttons on his joysticks and engaged the maneuvering thrusters. An increase in gravity snugged him against his chest harness. He fired the thrusters several more times to increase the rate at which *Surveyor* was withdrawing from the ring.

It was very illegal to fire *Surveyor*'s main antimatter engines, with their radioactive plumes, anywhere near the inhabited ring. Severin needed to push the ship past the safety zone before *Surveyor* could really begin its journey.

Again Severin checked the navigation displays. He could see the Chee Company yacht *Kayenta* outbound for Wormhole Station Two, carrying Martinez and Lady Terza to the newly opened planet. *Surveyor* would follow in their wake, fourteen days behind. A chain of cargo vessels were inbound from Station One, many of them carrying equipment or settlers for Chee, all of them standing on huge pillars of fire as they decelerated to their rendezvous with the ring. The closest was still seven hours away.

The only obstacle of note was the giant bulk of the *Titan*, which orbited Laredo at a considerable distance for reasons of safety. *Titan* was full of antimatter destined for Chee and Parkhurst, and even though the antimatter was remarkably stable—flakes of antihydrogen suspended by static electricity inside incredibly tiny etched silicon shells, all so tiny they flowed like a thick fluid—nevertheless if things went wrong the explosion would vaporize a chunk of Laredo's ring and bring the rest down on the planet below.

It would be a good thing for *Surveyor* to stay well clear of *Titan*.

Severin looked at the point of light on the display that represented *Titan* and wondered about the conversation he'd had with Martinez and his brother, the one where Allodorm's name had first been raised. *Titan* was a Meridian Company ship leased long-term by the Exploration Service. The growing settlements on Chee required antimatter to generate power, and as yet had no accelerator ring. Chee Station, with its skyhook that ran cargo to the surface, required power as well.

The wormhole stations at both Chee and Parkhurst, with their colossal mass drivers that kept the wormholes stable, required an enormous output of power.

Since Chee could not as yet generate its own antimatter, it had been decided to ramp up antihydrogen production on Laredo's ring, fill *Titan* with the results, and move the whole ship to a distant parking orbit around the newly settled planet, on the far side of Chee's largest moon so that even if the unthinkable happened and *Titan* blew, none of the energetic neutrons and furious gamma rays would reach Chee's population. When one of Chee's installations needed antihydrogen, they'd send a shuttle to *Titan* and collect some. By the time *Titan* had been depleted, an accelerator ring—a small one, not the vast technological wonder that circled all of Laredo—would have been built in Chee orbit.

Severin wondered if it truly made economic sense to use *Titan* that way, or whether it was a complex scheme to fill Allodorm's coffers.

Surveyor finally reached the limit of Laredo's safety zone, and Severin rotated the ship onto a new heading, his couch sliding lightly within the rings of his acceleration cage.

"We are on our new heading, my lord," Severin said. "Two-two-zero by zero-zero-one absolute. Mission plan is in the guidance computer."

"I am in command," Lord Go called.

"The lord captain is in command," Severin agreed. He took his hands off the joysticks.

"Engines, fire engines," the captain said. "Accelerate at two point three gravities."

Severin felt a kick to his spine and his acceleration couch swung within its cage as the gravities began piling on his chest.

"Accelerating at two point three gravities," Bhagwati said. "Course two-two-zero by zero-zero-one absolute."

They would accelerate hard until they'd achieved escape velocity from Laredo, then slacken for most of the journey to a single gravity, going to harder accelerations for an hour out of each watch.

Severin looked at the displays and saw *Kayenta* again, outbound and approaching the wormhole that would take it to Chee. It was a pity that *Surveyor* wouldn't travel to Chee, but merely pass through the system on its way to Parkhurst and the possible new wormholes. A pity not only because Severin wouldn't see Martinez and Terza again, but because he'd probably never find out how the Allodorm thing worked out.

He'd just have to find something else to amuse him for the next few months, and he thought he knew what it was.

He'd been unable to entirely forget the dream he'd had at Rio Hondo, and he'd loaded his personal data foil with articles on puppets, puppeteers, marionettes, automata, shadow puppets, and recordings of performances.

People on long voyages found many ways to occupy their hours. Some gambled, some drank, some drew into themselves. Some concentrated obsessively on their work. Some watched recorded entertainments, some had affairs with other crew members, some played musical instruments. Some worked as hard as they could at making everyone else on the ship miserable.

Perhaps, Severin thought, he would be the first to plan a puppet theater.

Certainly it was a field that seemed to have a lot of room to expand.

"Are you all on virtual?" asked the astronomer Shon-dan. "I'm transmitting the outside cameras on Channel Seventeen."

"Comm: Channel Seventeen." Terza's soft voice came to Martinez's ears from the nearest acceleration couch.

Martinez was already on the correct channel, his head filled with the stars as viewed from the *Kayenta* as it passed the final moments of its twenty-day acceleration out of the Laredo system. The virtual cap he wore to project the image onto his visual centers was lighter than the Fleet issue, which required earphones and microphone pickups, and he sensed other differences as well: the depth of field was subtly different, a bit flatter, perhaps because the civilian rig required less precision.

The stars were thrown like a great wash of diamonds across the midnight backdrop, silent and steady and grand. They were the home stars under which Martinez had spent the first half of his life, and his mind naturally sought the familiar, comforting constellations in their well-known places. Laredo's own star, this far out, was hardly brighter than other bright stars. The software had been instructed to blot out *Kayenta*'s brilliant tail so as to avoid losing the stars by contrast, and the result was a flickering, disturbing negative blot occupying one part of the display, a void of absolute darkness that seemed to pursue the ship.

Martinez and Terza were in *Kayenta*'s main lounge, the softly scented center of the yacht's social life, and were now twenty days out from Laredo. Shon-dan, an astronomer from the Imperial University of Zarafan who had come aboard as Marcella's guest, was about to show the reason why an astronomical observatory had been placed on Chee Station, and why she had spent months journeying here.

"Ten seconds," Shon-dan said. "Eight. Five."

Kayenta was traveling too fast for Martinez to see the wormhole station as the ship flashed past, or the wormhole itself, the inverted-bowl-of-stars that was their destination. The transition itself was instantaneous, and the star field changed at the same instant.

A vast, lush globe of stars suddenly blazed across Martinez's perceptions, occupying at least a third of the sky, the stars so packed together they seemed nearly as dense as glittering grains of sand stretched along an ocean shore. Martinez felt himself take an involuntary breath, and he heard Terza's gasp. The closer Martinez looked, the more stars he saw. There seemed to be vague clouds and structures within the globe, each made up of more and more brilliants, but Martinez couldn't tell whether the clouds actually existed or were the results of his own mind trying to create order in this vast, burning randomness, seeking the familiar just as it had sought out constellations in Laredo's sky.

Gazing into the vast star-globe was like drifting deeper and deeper into a endless sea, past complex, ill-defined shoals that on closer inspection were made up of millions of coral structures, while the structures themselves, looked at with greater care, were found to be composed of tiny limestone shells, and the shells themselves, on examination, each held tiny specks of life, a kind of infinite regression that baffled the senses.

"Now you see why we've built the observatory." Shon-dan's voice, floating into Martinez' perceptions, was quietly triumphant. "Of all the wormholes in the empire, this one leads to a system that's closest to the center of a galaxy. This is our best chance to observe how a galactic core is structured. From here we can directly observe the effects on nearby stars of the supermassive black hole at the galaxy's center."

With an effort of will Martinez shifted his attention away from the glowing globe to the rest of the starry envelope that surrounded *Kayenta*. By comparison with Laredo the entire sky was packed with stars, with an opalescent strip that marked the galaxy's disk spiraling out into endless space. The Chee system was actually within the galactic core, though on its periphery, and stars on all sides were near and burning bright. Chee's own star, Cheemah, shone with a warm yellow light, but other nearby stars equaled its fire.

"The stars here are very dense," Shon-dan said, "though not as dense as they are farther in. The Chee system has seven stars—or maybe eight, we're not sure—and the orbits are very complex."

"Do we actually know which galaxy we're in?" Terza asked.

"No. We're scanning for Cepheids and other yardsticks that might give us an indication, but so far we haven't found enough to make certain of anything. We could be anywhere in the universe, of course, and anywhere within a billion years of where we started."

Martinez heard footfalls enter the room, then the voice of Lord Pa. "Looking at the stars?" he said. "You'll get tired of them soon enough. Between the galactic core and the other six stars in Chee's system, there's no true night on the planet, and we've had to install polarizing windows on all our workers' dormitories just so our people can get some rest. I've just stopped looking at the sky—galactic centers are nasty violent places, and the less we have to do with them, the better."

"Stars are packed pretty closely here, true enough, my lord." Shon-dan's deference to a wealthy Peer did not quite disguise her disagreement. Clearly she was not about to tire of gazing at this sky anytime soon.

"I'm going to sit and play a game of cinhal," Lord Pa said. "Don't let me disturb you."

Martinez returned his attention to the great, glowing galactic core while he heard Lord Pa shuffle to a table, then give it the muted commands to set up a game.

"So far you're only seeing the light in its visible spectrum," Shon-dan said. "I'm going to add some other spectra in a moment. There will be some false colors. I'll try to fix those later." Martinez heard the Lai-own give a few muted commands, and then the galactic core shifted from a pearly color to a muted amber, and the great sphere was suddenly pierced through by an enormous lance of light, shimmering and alive, a giant pillar that seemed to stretched from the foundations of the universe to its uttermost heaven.

Martinez gave an involuntary cry, and he heard Terza's echo.

"Yes." Triumph had again entered Shon-dan's voice. "That's the beam of relativistic particles generated by the galaxy's supermassive black hole. If you look closely, you'll see it has fine structure—we didn't expect that, and we're working on theories of the phenomenon, but so far we don't have an explanation."

In his virtual display Martinez coasted closer to the great burning pillar of energy, and he saw the pillar pulse with light, saw strands of opalescent color weave and shift as they were caught in some vast incomprehensible flow of power, a hypnotic dance of colossal force.

For the next hour Shon-dan showed Martinez and Terza features within the galactic core, including the four giant stars now in a swift death spiral around the central black hole. "The black hole is feeding now," he said. "Sometimes the supermassive black holes are actively involved in devouring neighboring stars and sometimes they aren't. We don't know why or how they shift from one state to another."

"Nasty, as I said," said Lord Pa. "I have to say that I prefer nature a good deal less chaotic and destructive. I like games with rules. I like comfortable chairs, compound interest, and a guaranteed annual profit. I prefer not to think of some cosmic accident about to jump out of hiding and suck all my comforts right out of the universe."

"We're perfectly safe from the black hole, my lord," Shon-dan said. "We're nowhere near the danger zone."

Martinez quietly turned off the virtual display to take a look at Lord Pa. He sat in a Lai-own chair that cradled his breastbone, and was bent over the room's game board. The light from the display shone up on his face, on the short muzzle and deep red eyes.

Behind Pa the yellow chesz wood panels, inset with red enjo in abstract designs, glowed in the recessed lights of the lounge. A heavy crystal goblet sat near one hand, filled with Lai-own protein broth.

Comforts, Martinez thought. *Guaranteed profit*. Right.

"Perhaps we should break for now," Shon-dan said. He had noticed Martinez leaving the virtual display.

"Thank you," Terza said. "That was breathtaking. I hope we can do it again."

"I'd be delighted," Shon-dan said, rising. She was a Lai-own, with golden eyes, and wore a formal academic uniform of dark brown with several medals of scholastic distinction. She was young for all her honors, and the feathery side hairs on her head were still a youthful brown.

"We have another twenty-three days to Chee," she said, "and the stars will be there the entire time."

"Perhaps tomorrow," Martinez said.

He rose from his couch and walked to the bar, where he poured himself a brandy. He idled toward Lord Pa, who was still bent over his game. Martinez scanned the board, spotted at once the move that Lord Pa should make, and began to point it out before he decided not to.

On the twentieth day of the voyage, *Kayenta*'s passengers were beginning to get on each other's nerves a little.

The first part of the trip had been as pleasant and social as possible, given that Martinez suspected one of the party of stealing from his family. Marcella, Lord Pa, Martinez, Terza, and Shon-dan had dined together each day. Tingo and other games had been suggested, but interest in gambling waned after it became clear that Terza and Martinez weren't interested in playing for high stakes, and that Shon-dan's academic salary didn't allow her to play even for what passed for small change amid Peers.

The conversation during and after meals had ranged far and wide, though Terza had cautioned Martinez about raising the kind of questions he burned to ask, detailed questions about the financial arrangements between the Chee and Meridian companies. "It will sound like an interrogation," she said.

Martinez confined himself to a few mild queries per day, beginning with broad questions about the progress of the Chee settlements, then going into more detail as the conversation developed. Marcella and Pa seemed pleased enough to talk about their work, and Martinez found himself genuinely interested in the technical details, though Martinez made a point of breaking off when he saw a slight frown on Terza's face, or felt the soft touch of her hand on his thigh.

Shon-dan talked about astronomical subjects. Martinez told his war stories. Terza avoided the subject of her work at the Ministry, but spoke of High City society, and brought out her harp and played a number of sonatas.

But now, by the twentieth day, the conversations had grown a little listless. Marcella spent much time in her cabin, working on Chee Company business, smoking endless cigarettes, and playing spiky, nerve-jabbing music that rattled her cabin door in its frame. Lord Pa received and sent detailed memoranda to his crews on Chee, and otherwise spent a lot of time puzzling over his game board.

Martinez sent frequent videos to his son—the three months aboard *Wi-hun* with a small and lively child had been challenging enough for all concerned, so Young Gareth had been left on Laredo with his nursemaid and his doting grandparents. The videos that Martinez received in return were full of excitement, for Lord Martinez had introduced his grandson to his collection of vintage automobiles, and had been roaring around on his private track with Young Gareth as a passenger.

"Gareth's favorite is the Lodi Turbine Express," Martinez told Terza. "At his age I liked that one myself, though I liked the Scarlet Messenger better." And then, at her look, said, "My father hasn't had an accident yet, you know."

"I'll try to be reassured," Terza said. She had just come from her dressing room, where she'd prepared for bed: her black hair had been brushed till it glowed and then tied with ribbon, and her face was scrubbed of cosmetics and softly sheened with health. Over her nightgown she wore a bed jacket that crackled with gold brocade.

After Shon-dan's astronomical exhibition they'd retired to their suite, glossy light behl-wood paneling veined in blood-red, a video screen in a lacy Rakthan frame, a bathtub hacked out of a single block of chocolate-brown marble and which—to avoid gooseflesh on entering—was warmed by hidden heating elements of a vaguely sonic nature.

"My father could have worse hobbies," Martinez pointed out. "Racing pai-car chariots, say."

Her eyes narrowed. "I'll try to keep that in mind, too."

Twenty days on the small vessel had, perhaps, begun to unravel slightly the serenity that Terza carried with her, the unearthly tranquility that Martinez had come to admire as her greatest accomplishment. He rose from his chair and stood behind her, his big hands working through the crisp silk of her jacket to loosen her shoulder muscles. She sighed and relaxed against him.

"You miss Gareth, don't you?" he asked.

"Yes. Of course."

"So do I."

They had not spent so much time apart from the boy since he had been born.

"This has got to be dull for you," Martinez said. "Maybe we should have left you on Laredo."

"Dull?" Her tone was amused. "Reviewing contracts in hopes of discovering hidden felonies? Surely not."

He smiled. "Won't it be exciting if you actually find one?"

"But I won't find one. Not in the contracts. Lawyers have been all over the contracts to make sure no hint of impropriety will be found. If there's anything to be found, it will be in interpretation and practice."

He hadn't been able to obtain any of the contracts that the Chee Company had signed with their prime contractor—neither he nor Terza nor Roland were officers of the company. But in his capacity as Lord Inspector he'd acquired the entire file of the dealings the Meridian Company had with the Fleet, for building Fleet installations on Chee and in Chee orbit. But Martinez hadn't enough experience to understand the contracts particularly well, and so Terza had been pressed into the job.

"Escalator clauses are always suspect, and the contracts have plenty of them," Terza said. "On a big job there are always a thousand places to hide illegitimate expenses, and *this* job is literally as big as a planet. Meridian is allowed to revise the estimates if unexpected conditions cause their own costs to rise, and there are *always* unexpected conditions. A little to the right, please."

Martinez obliged. "Surely they can't jack up their expenses forever," he said.

"No. In the case of the Fleet contracts, the local Fleet representative has to agree that the rises are justified."

"According to the records she almost always did," Martinez said. "And now she's received her captaincy and has been posted to the Fourth Fleet, so I won't be able to ask her any questions."

Amusement returned to Terza's voice. "I'm sure that if you saw her, she would of course immediately inform you of any unjustified cost overrides that she'd personally approved. I think you're better off with the new commander. He won't be obliged to defend his predecessor's expenses." She stretched, raising her arms over her head, torquing her spine left and right. Martinez could feel the muscles flex beneath his fingertips.

He left off his massage as she bent forward, flexing her spine again, pressing her palms to the deep pile carpet. She straightened, sighed, turned to face him.

"Thank you," she said. She put her arms around him, pillowed her head on his chest. "This could still be a pleasant vacation, you know."

I've been on vacation for three years, he wanted to say. Digging around in old Fleet construction contracts was the most useful thing he'd done in ages.

But he knew what Terza meant. "I'll try to remember to look at the stars now and again," he said.

Her arms tightened around him. "I had thought we might make good use of the time."

Martinez smiled. "I have no objection."

Terza drew her head back, her dark eyes raised to his. "That's not *entirely* what I meant," she said. "I thought we might give Gareth a brother or sister."

A rush of sensation took his breath away. Martinez's marriage had been arranged, not an uncommon phenomenon among Peers—and in Martinez's case, Roland had arranged the marriage with a crowbar. For all that Martinez had genuinely wanted a child, young Gareth had been arranged as well. Martinez knew perfectly well that Terza had been lowering herself to marry him—Lord Chen required significant financial help from the Martinez clan at the time—and Martinez had always wondered just what Terza had thought of the long-armed provincial officer she'd been constrained, on only a few hours' acquaintance, to marry.

Wondered, but never asked. He never asked questions when he knew the answers might draw him into sadness.

He had watched with increasing pleasure as Terza floated into his life, supported by that quality of serenity that was, perhaps, just a bit too eerily perfect. He had never been completely certain what might happen if Lord Chen, his finances recovered, ordered his daughter to divorce. It was always possible that she would leave her marriage with the same unearthly tranquility with which she'd entered it. He had never known precisely what was going on behind that composed, lovely face.

Until now. A second child was not part of the contract between their families.

He and Terza were writing their own codicil to the contract, right now.

"Of course," Martinez said, when he got his breath back. "Absolutely. At once, if possible."

She smiled. "At once isn't quite an option," she said. "I'll have to get the implant removed first. *Kayenta*'s doctor can do it, or we can wait till we get to Chee." She kissed his cheek. "Though I'd hate to waste the next twenty-three days."

Kayenta's doctor was a sour, elderly Lai-own who had scarcely been seen since the beginning of the journey, when he gave the obligatory lecture about weightlessness, acceleration, and space-sickness. Whatever the quirks of his personality, however, he was presumably competent at basic procedures for interspecies medicine.

"I think you should see the old fellow first thing tomorrow," Martinez said. "But that doesn't mean we should waste tonight."

Her look was direct. "I hadn't intended to," she said.

Hours later, before the forenoon watch, Martinez woke from sleep with a start, with a cry frozen on his lips. Terza, her perfect tranquility maintained, slept on, her head pillowed on his chest.

He hadn't had one of these dreams in at least two months. For a moment, blinking in the darkness of *Kayenta*'s guest suite, he had seen not Terza's black hair spread on his chest, but hair of white gold, framing a pale face with blazing emerald eyes.

His heart thundered in his chest. Martinez could hear his own breath rasping in his throat.

There were other reasons why he hadn't inquired what Terza thought of their marriage.

He had his own secrets. It seemed only fair that he allow Terza to keep hers.

The cable of the elevator descended from geostationary orbit, a line that disappeared into the deep green of the planet's equator like a fishing line fading into the sea. On the approach, what the monitors showed Martinez of the elevator itself was a pale gray tower of shaped asteroid and lunar material, the massive counterweight to the cable. The tower terminated in a series of sculpted peaks that looked like battlements, but which were actually a kind of jigsaw mechanism to lock additional weights into place should they be needed.

Ships docked at the elevator terminus at the base of the tower, in zero gravity. Passengers then traveled down a weightless tube to the hub of the residential and commercial areas of the station, where they could shift laterally to either one of two fat rotating wheels of white laminate that contained living quarters for workers, Fleet personnel, Shon-dan's astronomers, and anyone in transit from Chee to anywhere else.

Martinez thanked Marcella and Lord Pa for the ride on *Kayenta* before they left the ship, since he knew that once he transferred to the station, the awesome role of Lord Inspector would descend on him, and a long series of rigid protocols would take place.

Which in fact they did. As soon as Martinez floated out of the docking tube, one white-gloved hand on the guide rope that had been strung from the tube into the bay, he heard the bellow of petty officers calling the honor guard to attention, and the public address system boomed out "Our Thoughts Are Ever Guided by the Praxis," one of the Fleet's snappier marching tunes.

The honor guard were all Lai-own Military Constabulary in full dress, with the toes of their shoes tucked under an elastic strap that had been stretched along the deck to keep everyone properly lined up in zero gravity. Standing before them, braced at the salute, was Lieutenant Captain Lord Ehl Tir-bal, who commanded the station, and his staff.

Lord Ehl was young, and short for a Lai-own—he and Martinez could almost look level into one another's eyes. Lord Ehl introduced his staff, and then turned to the cadaverous civilian who stood behind the party of officers.

"My lord," he said, "may I introduce Meridian Company's chief engineer, Mister Ledo Allodorm."

"Mister Allodorm," Martinez said, and nodded.

"An honor to meet you, my lord." Allodorm's face, like those of all Daimong, was permanently fixed in the round-eyed, open-mouthed stare that a Terran could read either as surprise or terror or existential anguish. His voice was a lovely tenor that sounded like a pair of trumpets playing in soft harmony, and Martinez could see his soft mouth parts working behind the gray, fixed bony lips as he spoke.

Martinez performed a ritual inspection of the honor guard, after which Martinez, Terza, their servants, and and their baggage were loaded into a long, narrow viridian-green vehicle that would carry them to their lodging. Lord Ehl and Allodorm both joined them, and Ehl pointed out the features of the station as, on little puffs of air, the vehicle rose and began its journey down the docking bay.

The post of Chee's station commander was Lord Ehl's first major assignment, and his delight in his new command showed. He pointed out the features of the station, which was fresh and glossy and, to Martinez's mind, rather overdesigned. Every feature, from the cargo loaders to the computer-operated ductwork on the air vents, was of the largest, brightest, most efficient type available.

"The air-purifying and circulation systems are custom designed," Ehl said. "So is the power plant."

"We didn't just take a thousand-year-old design off the shelf," Allodorm said. "Everything on this station was rethought from basics."

Custom design is very expensive, Martinez thought. "It's very impressive," he said. "I'm not used to seeing new stations."

"The first new station in nine hundred years," Allodorm said. "And now that the Convocation's began opening new systems to expansion, we can expect to see many more."

"You've done all this in a little over two years," Martinez said. "That's fast work."

And awfully fast for such custom work. Perhaps, he thought, it wasn't custom after all.

How would anyone know? No one had built an orbital station in eons. You could take an old standard design and change a few minor specifications and call it custom work.

All he knew was that, even if the circulation system was custom designed, the air smelled the same as it did on every other station he'd ever been on.

The vehicle jetted down the connecting tube to the hub of the two wheels, where it entered a large elevator and began to descend toward the living areas. "You'll be the first occupant of the Senior Officers' Quarters," Ehl said. "There will be a full staff on hand to look after you. Please let one of them—or me—know if anything is unsatisfactory."

Gravity began to tug with greater insistence at Martinez's inner ear. "Thank you, lord elcap," Martinez said. "I'm sure everything will be satisfactory."

One full gravity had been restored by the time the elevator reached the main level of Wheel Number One. The staff of the Senior Officers' Quarters were lined up by the exit, as if for inspection. Ehl gave an order, and the staff scurried to the vehicle to unload the luggage and to help Terza and Martinez from their seats. The luggage was placed on motorized robot carts, and Martinez and Terza walked followed by the carts and Lord Ehl and the staff and Allodorm.

"My lord," Allodorm said, "I hope you and Lady Terza will accept the hospitality of the Meridian Company, two nights from now. The company's executive and engineering staff would be honored to meet you."

"We'd be delighted," Martinez said.

Lord Ehl and the Fleet officers on station were dining with him tomorrow night, and he'd already been sent a rather ambitious schedule involving trips to various Fleet installations. He recognized Ehl's plan well enough, which was to keep him so busy going from place to place, viewing one engineering wonder after another, and receiving toast after toast at banquets, that he would have precious little time to do any actual inspections. There wasn't necessarily anything sinister in this scheme—it was the sort of thing Martinez might do himself, were he in charge of an installation and saw a Lord Inspector bearing down on him.

Ahead was the bright new corridor, curving only slightly upward, walls that looked as if they were made of pale ceramic, lighting recessed into the tented ceiling. Martinez looked down at the polymerized flooring beneath their feet. It was a dark gray and rubbery, giving slightly under his shoes, the standard flooring for an installation of this type.

"There was some confusion with this flooring, as I recall?" Martinez asked. His review of the Fleet contracts had told him that much.

"Yes, Lord Inspector, there was," Allodorm said in his beautiful voice. "A consequence of our *not* rethinking something—we hadn't worried about anything so basic as station flooring. But when we looked at the standard station flooring we'd ordered, we found that it was inadequate to the stresses of a developing station, the vehicle traffic and weights we'd have to move along in these corridors. We'd have to replace it all within ten years, and of course we couldn't afford to shut down the station to do that, not with our deadlines. So we had to special order new flooring from Zarafan, and ship it out by high-gee express."

"That Torminel crew must have knocked years off their lives getting it here," Ehl said, and made a deliberate, shivering motion of his hands—his hollow-boned species abhorred high gravities.

"Well," said Martinez, "at least the problem was corrected."

He tried to sound offhand, and he wondered how he could get underneath the flooring to take a look at it.

The Senior Officers' Quarters were as overdesigned as the rest of the station, with dark wood paneling and polished brass fittings. Aquaria glowed turquoise along the walls, filled with exotic fish from the planet below, and below the tall ceilings hung chandeliers that looked like ice sculptures. Everything smelled new. Ehl and Allodorm retired to allow their visitors to "recover from the rigors of the journey," as if traveling forty-three days by private yacht were as taxing as crossing a mountain range on the back of a mule.

That left Terza and Martinez alone in the entrance hall, standing on the wood parquet that formed a map of the empire, with Chee a small disk of green malachite and Zanshaa, the capital, a blood-red garnet.

They looked at each other. "They've given us separate bedrooms," Terza said.

"I noticed."

"I'll have Fran move my things into your room, if that's all right."

"Please," Martinez said. "That huge room would be lonely without you."

Their palace in Zanshaa High City didn't have bedrooms as large. The Fleet must have paid a pretty penny for these accommodations, but on the other hand the Fleet wasn't exactly known for depriving its officers of their comforts.

There was an hour or so before dinner. Martinez had his orderly, Alikhan, find him some casual civilian clothes, and he changed and left his quarters through the kitchen entrance, surprising the cooks who were preparing his meal.

This was a free hour on his schedule. He might as well make use of it.

He walked to one of the personnel elevators, then went to the unfinished wheel. He found an area still under construction, where Torminel workers straddled polycarbon beams just beyond portable barriers, working on pipes and ducts, and the flooring waited on huge spools taller than a Lai-own. Martinez quietly made some measurements, then ventured across the barriers to the point where the flooring dropped away to reveal an expanse of plastic sheeting, followed by open beams and the workers.

If the Torminel noticed Martinez making his measurements, they gave no sign. Martinez finished his task and returned to his quarters.

"Not custom-made, not at all," Martinez said over dinner. "They're just laying a second layer of the standard flooring over the first." He raised a glass and sipped some of the Fleet's excellent emerald Hy-oso wine. "The Meridian Company's pocketing the money for all that flooring."

"I'd suggest not," Terza said. "I think the flooring exists. That express ship came out here with *something*. I think the flooring's been diverted to another project, one owned one hundred percent by the Meridian Company."

"I wonder how many people *know*," Martinez said.

"Quite a few, probably," Terza said. "Not the work gangs, who I imagine just do what they're told. You can't do corruption on this scale without a good many people figuring it out. But I'm sure the company keeps them happy one way or another."

"Does Lord Ehl know, I wonder?" Martinez asked. "He'd have to be remarkably incurious not to notice what's happening with the flooring, but perhaps he *is* incurious."

Terza gave Martinez a significant look. "I suggest you not ask him," she said.

Martinez looked at his plate and considered his roast fristigo lying in its sauce of onions and kistip berries. The berries and vegetables were fresh, a delight after forty-three days without—the settlements must have got agriculture under way. "I wish we knew who owns the Meridian Company. But it's privately held, and the exchanges don't know because it's not publicly traded . . ." He let the thought fade away. "As Lord Inspector I could demand the information, but I might not get it, and it's an indiscreet way of conducting an investigation."

"Lord Pa must be one of the owners, and very likely the whole Maq-fan clan is involved," Terza said. "But unless we get access to the confidential records of whatever planet the company's chartered on, we're sunk . . ." She looked thoughtful. "You know, I *could* find out."

Martinez turned to her. "How?" he said.

"Meridian does business with the Fleet, and law requires them to give the Ministry a list of their principal owners. The names are supposed to remain confidential, but—" She gazed upward into a distant corner of the room. "I'm trying to think who I could ask."

"Your father," Martinez pointed out. "He's on the Fleet Control Board, he should have the authority to get the information."

Terza shook her head. "He couldn't do it discreetly. An inquiry from the Control Board is like firing an antimatter missile from orbit." She smiled. "Or like a command from a Lord Inspector. People would notice." She gazed up into the corner again for a long moment. "Bernardo, then," she decided. "He's got access and is reasonably discreet. But I'll owe him a *big* favor."

"Ten days for the query to get to Zanshaa," Martinez said. "Another ten days for the answer to return."

The communication would leap from system to system at the speed of light, but Martinez still felt a burning impatience at the delay.

A smile quirked its way across Terza's face. "I've never seen you work before. Half the time you're frantic with impatience, and the rest of the time you're marching around giving orders like a little king. It's actually sort of fascinating."

Martinez raised his eyebrows at this description of himself, but said, "I hope you can manage to sustain the fascination a little longer."

"I think I'll manage."

Martinez reached across the corner of the table to take her hand. Terza leaned toward him to kiss his cheek. Her voice came low to his ear. "My doctor once told me that a woman's at her most fertile in the month following the removal of her implant. I think we've proved him right. For the second time."

He felt his skin prickle with sudden heat as delight flared along his nerves. "Are you sure?" he asked.

"Well, no," Terza said, "I'm not. But I feel the same way I felt last time, and I think experience counts in these things."

"It definitely should," Martinez said.

Fecundity, he thought. What more could a man want?

"The harbor looks a little bare," Martinez said. He sat, awaiting breakfast, beneath an umbrella on the terrace of the Chee Fishing Club, where he had been given an honorary membership, and where he and Terza were staying. No Fleet accommodation on the ground had been judged worthy of a Lord Inspector, and the only deluxe lodgings on the planet were at the club—conveniently owned by Martinez's father, a part of a sport-fishing scheme.

"The commercial fishing boats are out, and the shuttles aren't coming in any longer," the manager said. He was a Terran, with a beard dyed purple and twined in two thin braids. He wore a jacket with padded shoulders and of many different fabrics, all in bright tropical colors, stitched together in a clashing melee of brilliant pigment. Martinez hadn't seen anyone else similarly dressed, and he suspected the manager's style was peculiar to him alone.

Steam rose as the manager freshened Martinez's coffee. "Without the shuttles we've just got a small fishing fleet and just a few sport boats," he said, "though more will come in time. We can build up an enormous fishery here—though we may have to export most of the catch, since everyone here ate nothing but fish for the first year and a half, and they're all sick of it."

Martinez gazed down a lawn-green slope at three bobbing boats dwarfed by the huge gray concrete quay against which they were moored. Two flew Fishing Club ensigns, and another a private flag, probably that of an official in the Meridian or Chee companies. Across the harbor was the town of Port Vipsania, named after one of Martinez's sisters, and beyond that, stretching up into the sky, was the cable that ran to geosynchronous orbit and Chee Station.

Port Vipsania, like all the early settlements, was built on the sea, because before the skyhook had gone into operation the previous year, workers and their gear had been brought to the planet in shuttles powered by chemical rockets, shuttles that had landed on the open water and then taxied to a mooring. Supplies, too, had been dropped into the sea in unmanned containers braked with retro-rockets, then towed to shore by workers in boats. The huge resinous containers, opened, also served as temporary shelters and warehouses.

Once the skyhook could bring people and cargo from orbit at much less expense, the shuttles were largely discontinued, though Port Gareth, in the north and as yet unconnected to the expanding rail network, was still supplied by shuttles and containers dropped down from orbit.

A bare three years after the opening of the planet to exploitation, the Chee settlements were growing with incredible speed, fueled by even more incredible amounts of capital. The investment was vast, and as the work had only begun the inflow of capital would have to continue. Lord Mukerji's work in attracting ceaseless investment was vital, as was the work of many lesser envoys, and of course the work of Lord Martinez himself, raising funds from his own considerable resources.

The resources of a whole planet were more than enough to repay any investment over time, but the scale of the payouts ran in years, and mismanagement and theft were still dangers to the Chee Company. If investor confidence were lost the company could go bankrupt whether it owned a planet or not . . .

"I'd like to see a fleet of boats on that quay," Martinez said.

"So would I," the manager said. "The business would be a lot better." He grinned. "And after all the trouble building that quay, I'd like to see it in use."

"Trouble?" Martinez asked.

"They shipped down the wrong kind of cement for that pier," the manager said. "They need De-loq cement, that sets underwater and is immune to salt-water corrosion. But they sent down the ordinary stuff, and a special shipment had to be made from Laredo."

"What did they do with the other cement?" Martinez asked.

"Condemned," the manager said. "They couldn't use it. Ah—here's your breakfast."

Martinez's breakfast arrived, a grilled fish with needle-sharp teeth, a pair of eyes on each end, and plates of armor expertly peeled back from the flesh. Martinez's eyes rose from the fish to Port Vipsania, to the rows of white concrete apartments that held the Meridian Company's workers.

"Pity they couldn't find a use for it," he said.

Martinez found that he couldn't resist the lure of the town his father had named after him. After ten days on Chee, Martinez escaped the endless round of formal banquets and receptions by taking a Fleet coleopter to Port Gareth, north in the temperate zone.

The coleopter carried him over land that was a uniform green—while the oceans thronged with a staggering variety of fish, life on land was primitive and confined to a few basic types: the only fauna were worms and millipedes, and plants were confined to molds, fungus, and a wide variety of fern, some as tall as a two-storied building.

All of which were going to face stiff competition, as alien plants and animals were being introduced in abundance. Herds of portschen, fristigo, sheep, bison, and cattle had been landed and allowed more or less to run wild. Without any predators to cull their numbers, the herds were growing swiftly.

Vast farms, largely automated, had also been set up in the interior, upriver from the settlements, or along the expanding railroads. Because no one yet knew what would grow, the farms were simply planting *everything*, far more than the population could conceivably need. If things went reasonably well, the planet could become a grain exporter very quickly and start earning a bit of profit for the Chee Corporation.

Within a couple of centuries, it was calculated, the only native plants a person would see would probably be in a museum.

The coleopter bounded over a range of mountains that kept Port Gareth isolated from the rest of the continent, then dropped over a rich plain that showed rivers of gleaming silver curling amid the green fern forest. The coleopter fell toward a green-blue ocean that began to creep over the horizon, and then began to fly over cultivated fields, the sun winking off the clear canopies of the harvesters.

Port Gareth was very possibly outside the mandate of a Lord Inspector, as it contained no Fleet installations, but Martinez had decided that the railroad that would connect the town to the settlements farther south was a matter of state security, and therefore of interest to the Fleet.

The turbine shrouds on the ends of the aircraft's wings rotated, and the craft began to descend. On the edge of the pad was yet another reception committee.

The coleopter's wide cargo door rolled open. Martinez took off his headset, thanked the pilot, and stepped out onto the landing pad. The brisk wind tore at his hair. As Alikhan stepped from the coleopter with Martinez's luggage, the reception committee advanced behind the Lady Mayor, a client of the Martinez family who Martinez vaguely remembered from childhood. She was a Torminel, whose gray and black fur was more suitable to the bracing climate of Port Gareth than to the tropics of Port Vipsania.

In short order Martinez was introduced to the Mayor's Council, and the local representatives of the Meridian and Chee companies, and then a familiar figure stepped forward from the long, teardrop-shaped car.

"Remember me, my lord?" the man leered.

Martinez could hardly forget. Ahmet had been a rigger on *Corona*, Martinez's first command. He had spent a considerable portion of the commission under arrest or doing punishment duty; and the rest of his time had been occupied with running illegal gambling games, brewing illicit liquor, and performing the occasional bit of vandalism.

"Ahmet," Martinez said. "You're out of the Fleet, I see."

This was only good news for the Fleet.

"I'm a foreman here on the railroad project," Ahmet said. "When I heard you were coming, I told everyone I knew you, and asked to be part of the welcoming committee." With one sleeve he buffed the shiny object pinned to his chest. "I still have the *Corona* medal, as you see. I've been assigned as your guide and driver."

To Martinez, their employment of Ahmet in a position of responsibility was proof enough of criminal negligence or worse. But he smiled as stoutly as he could, said "Good to see you," and was then carried off toward his lodging in the Mayor's Palace, after which he would endure yet another banquet. He had a healthy respect for himself that some considered conceit, but even so he was beginning to grow weary of all these meals in his honor.

Still, he was pleased to discover a statue of himself in the main square, looking stern and carrying the Golden Orb. He was less pleased to see a pump jack in the overgrown green park behind the statue, its flywheel spinning brightly in the sun.

"What's that?" he asked. "Petroleum?"

"Yes," the Lady Mayor said. "We found it close to the surface here—lucky, otherwise we couldn't have brought it up with the equipment we've got."

"What do you use it for?"

"Plastics. We'll have a whole industry running here in a few years."

"How is the railroad progressing?"

The railroad would eventually connect Port Gareth to the south: Supersonic trains would speed north from the skyhook, bringing migrants and supplies, and carrying away produce and plastic products for export. The rails were being laid from each end toward a common center, and would meet somewhere in the mountains.

"There were some delays last month," the Lady Mayor said. "But the track's still ahead of schedule."

"Delays?" Martinez said. "There's nothing the Fleet can do to expedite matters, is there?"

"Very kind, but no. It turned turned out that the early geologists' reports were incorrect, or maybe just incomplete. The engineers encountered a much harder layer of rock than they'd expected, and it held up the work for some time."

Martinez decided that though he didn't know much about geology, he was going to learn.

Next morning Martinez rose early, took the cup of coffee that his orderly handed him, and called Ahmet.

"I'd like to get up to the railhead," he said. "Can you do it?"

"Absolutely, my lord."

"I also don't want a fuss. I'm tired of delegations. Can we go, just the two of us, with you as my guide?"

Martinez sensed a degree of personal triumph in Ahmet's reply. "Of course, lord captain! That's easier than anything!"

The ride to the railhead was made on a train bringing out supplies, and Martinez spent the ride in the car reserved for the transport crews. He wore civilian clothes and heavy boots, which he thought disappointed Ahmet, who wanted a fully dressed military hero to show off to his colleagues. As it was, Martinez had to put up with Ahmet's loud reminiscences of the *Corona* and the battle of Hone-bar, which managed to imply that Martinez, under Ahmet's brilliant direction, had managed to polish off the Naxids in time for breakfast.

"That's when we swung onto our new heading and dazzled the Naxids with our engine flares, so they couldn't see our supports," Ahmet said, and then gave Martinez a confidential wink. "Isn't that right, my lord?"

"Yes," Martinez said. And then, peering out the window, "What's up ahead?"

The track for the supersonic train was necessarily nearly straight and quite level. It approached the mountains on huge ramps, built by equally huge machines and pierced with archways for rivers and future roads. Terraces had been gouged into mountains to provide the necessarily wide roadbed, and tunnels bored through solid rock. The gossamer-seeming bridges that spanned distant valleys were, on closer inspection, built of trusses wider than a bus and cables the thickness of Martinez's leg. The trains themselves, floating on magnetic fields above the rails, would be equipped with vanes that canceled out their sonic shockwave, but even so the tunnels had to be lined with baffles and sound suppressors to keep the mountain from being shaken down.

At the railhead Martinez was treated to a view of the giant drilling machine that bored the tunnel, and the other machines that cleared the rubble, braced the tunnel, and laid the track. The machines were sophisticated enough, and their operators experienced enough, that everyone seemed confident that their tunnel would meet the northbound crews, coming from the other side of the mountain, well ahead of schedule.

"So we can earn that big completion bonus from the Chee Company," Ahmet grinned. "Isn't that right, my lord?"

"Good for you," Martinez said. He waited for a moment alone with Ahmet before he asked the next question.

"Wasn't there a big delay a month or so ago? Can we stop there on our way back?"

Ahmet gave Martinez a wink. "Let me talk to the engine driver."

They took a ride back on a small engine that was shuttling rails to the construction site, and the Lai-own driver was amenable to a brief delay. "Marker 593," Ahmet told him, and the engine slowed and braked. Ahmet, an electric lantern in his hand, hopped off into the dark tunnel, and Martinez heard a splash.

"Careful, my lord," Ahmet said. "It's a bit damp here."

Martinez lowered himself to the roadbed and followed the bobbing lantern. Upheaval of the mountain range had tipped the geologic strata nearly vertical here. "They called it a pluton, or a laccolith, or something like that," Ahmet said. "Whatever it is, it's damn hard. The drill couldn't get through it. There it is." He brandished the lantern.

A deep gray stripe lay along the strata, a river of mica flecks gleaming in the lantern like a river of stars. "That's *it*?" Martinez asked. He could span the layer with his two arms. Whatever this was, it wasn't a pluton.

"Yes, my lord. They had to do a redesign of the drill head."

Couldn't they blast it? Martinez bit back the question.

Of course they could have blasted, he thought; but explosives wouldn't have added a hefty enough overcharge. Then Martinez remembered, during the party held in his honor at Rio Hondo, a conversation between Lords Pa and Mukerji. Something about the geologist's report . . .

Suddenly Martinez wondered if Mukerji—the plunging gambler—had been the Chee Company official responsible for approving the cost overruns. He was president of the company, after all; very possibly he could approve such things.

But Mukerji had never been to Chee—the requests would have had to chase him all over the empire as he went off on his quests for funds. Mukerji had never been to Chee, and wouldn't have been available to fill most spending requests.

Unless . . . unless Mukerji was part of the conspiracy. Receiving payments from the conspirators in order to relieve his gambling debts.

"Interesting," Martinez said.

Ahmet's eyes glittered in the lamplight, the admiration of one thief and confidence man for a job well and professionally done. "Fascinating," he said, "isn't it? Geology?"

The question was how to reveal to Eggfont the relationship between Lord Mince and Lady Belledrawers. If Eggfont was told by the valet Cadaver, that would tell Eggfont something about Cadaver that for the present should remain hidden. Yet how else could Eggfont find out in time for the Grand Ball . . . ?

A token, Severin thought. A mysterious token, which Eggfont would understand but which would be opaque to anyone else. But introduced by *who*?

Severin tapped Lady Liao's ring on the arm of his couch in slow accompaniment to his thoughts. He had to admit that his invention was flagging. It was three hours past midnight in *Surveyor's* official twenty-nine-hour day, and Severin was tired. He could call for a cup of coffee from the wardroom, he supposed, but that would mean waking up someone.

Perhaps Severin should put his puppet show aside and find something else to occupy his thoughts. Commanding the ship, for instance.

Surveyor's control room featured the usual stations, for navigation, for controlling the engines, for communications, for the captain and the pilot and the sensor tech. Each station featured a couch balanced carefully in its acceleration cage, and each couch was equipped with a hinged control board that could lock down in front of the occupant.

At the moment the sensor station was occupied by a very bored Warrant Officer Second Class Chamcha, and the screen that occupied his desultory attention wasn't tuned to the spectacular starscapes of Chee's system, but to a game called Mindsprain, which he was losing through inattention. The sensor station had only been crewed because regulations required it, just as regulations required someone at the engine station, at the moment Lily Bhagwati, another at communications—Signaler Trainee Jaye Nkomo—and yet another, qualified to stand watches, in the captain's couch—Severin himself.

Severin's watch had finished the hour out of each watch for hard acceleration, and breakfast was still hours away. Severin's attention drifted vaguely over the smiling pictures of Lord Go's family that the captain had attached to the command board—the captain was lenient that way, and each station in the control room was decorated with personal items belonging to the various crew who served at that station. Pictures of family, notes from loved ones, paper flowers, jokes, poems, pictures of actors and singers and models, someone pretty to dream about when you were three months away from the nearest ring station.

Severin realized that he'd been staring for many minutes at Lord Go's family, the smiling wife and waving children, proud parents, the pet dog, and the stuffed Torminel doll. He raised his head, shook it violently to clear his mind, and scanned the other stations. Nothing seemed to warrant his attention. No alarms sounded, no violent colors flashed on the displays.

He called up Warrant Officer Chamcha's game onto his own display, saw the comprehensive rate at which Chamcha was losing, and sighed. Perhaps when Chamcha conceded, he'd challenge Chamcha to a game of hypertourney, or something. Anything to keep awake.

While waiting for Chamcha's position to collapse he called up the navigation screen. *Surveyor,* heading straight from Wormhole One to Wormhole Two, was well outside of the normal trade routes that ended at Chee.

No navigational hazards threatened.

Severin looked at Chamcha. Hadn't he lost *yet*?

Something flashed on the sensor screens, and Severin looked down at his display, just as the lights and the display itself went off, then on . . .

"Status check!" Severin shouted, as the lights dimmed, then flashed bright again.

Warrant Officer Lily Bhagwati gave a sudden galvanic leap on her acceleration couch. There were shrill panicky highlights in her voice, "Power spike on Main Bus One! Spike on Main Bus Two!"

Severin's fingers flashed to his display, tried to get the ship's system display onto his board.

The lights went off, then returned. The image on Severin's displays twisted, slowed.

How very interesting, he thought distinctly.

"Breaker trip on Main Bus One!" Bhagwati said. "Main engine trip! Emergency power!"

Whatever was happening to the ship was happening too fast for Bhagwati's reports to keep up. Automatic circuits were responding to protect themselves faster than the Terran crew could possibly act. Severin did catch the words "main engine trip" and had time to register their impact before the all-pervading rumble of the engine ceased, and he began to drift free of his couch.

He reached for his webbing to lash himself in and every light and every display in the room went dark, leaving him in pitch blackness save for the afterimage of his displays slowly fading from his retinas.

"Emergency Circuit One breaker trip!" Bhagwati shouted unnecessarily.

In the ensuing silence Severin heard the distant whisper of the ventilation slowly fade, like the last sigh of a dying man.

This never happens, he told himself.

And because it never happened, there were no standard procedures to follow. An absolutely cold startup of all ship systems, including the ones that had been mysteriously damaged?

This also never happens, he thought.

"Everyone stay in your cages!" he said. "I don't want you drifting around in the dark."

He tapped Lady Liao's ring on the arm of his couch while he tried to think what to do next. Little flickers of light, like fireflies, indicated here and there where battery-powered flashlights waited in their chargers. They weren't intended for emergencies, since the emergency lighting wasn't supposed to fail, but rather for getting light into odd corners of the displays that were undergoing repair.

The flickering lights were inviting. Severin thought he should probably get a flashlight.

"I'm going to get a light," he said. "Everyone else stand by."

His fingers released the webbing that he'd never quite fastened down. Then he unlocked his display and pushed it above his head, out of the way, a maneuver that also pushed him more deeply into his couch. Now free, he reached out, found one of the struts of his cage, and tugged gently till his head and torso floated free of the cage.

With careful movements, he jackknifed to pull his legs out of the cage, a movement that rolled the cage slightly. He straightened his body and his feet contacted the floor.

He couldn't push off the floor to approach the flashlights: that would send him the wrong way. Instead he flung the acceleration cage with both hands, a movement that sent the cage spinning on all three axes while he drifted gently to the nearest wall. Severin reached out a hand and snagged the handle on the battery charger.

He became aware that he was breathing hard. Even this little exertion had taxed him.

There was a distant thump. Then another. Severin realized that someone outside the control room was pounding on the heavy shielded door, slowly and with great deliberation.

He released the flashlight from the charger that was designed to hold it at high gee. He turned it on and flashed it over the control room.

Three sets of eyes stared back at him. The others were awaiting his orders.

From outside the command room door, Severin began to hear the muffled sound of screams.

Screams could still be heard faintly through the door.

Severin shone his light on Chamcha long enough for the sensor operator to work his way out of his cage and push across the room toward another flashlight. Then he turned to the problem of the door. He pulled and locked down a handgrip installed for the purpose, then—floating on the end of the handgrip—opened an access panel, removed a light alloy crank, and inserted it into the door mechanism. With one hand on the grip, the flashlight stuck to the wall on an adhesive strip, and a foot braced against the bottom of an instrument panel, Severin began to crank the door open.

The screams had stopped. Severin didn't know whether to be encouraged by that or not.

By the time Severin had cranked open the heavy door he was puffing and throwing off beads of sweat that floated like drops of molten gold in the light. The control room crew clustered around him, hanging by fingertips onto cage struts or instrument displays, and their lights were turned to the outside corridor. Severin heard a series of gasps, and the single cry, "Lord captain!"

Severin looked out and saw Lord Go hanging weightless in the flashlight beams. He was wearing turquoise satin pajamas. His skin had turned bright red, and his eyes were hidden amid scarlet swellings. Large blisters were forming on his face and hands. His expression was slack.

Burns, Severin thought. But he saw no fire and could smell no burning.

"My lord!" Severin called. With one hand still on the grip, he swung himself toward Lord Go, reached out, and took his captain's hand. Another crew member, he saw, was hovering motionlessly a short distance down the corridor, and from the golden hair that floated in the absence of gravity he knew it was Lady Maxine Wellstone, the ship's junior lieutenant.

Severin drew Lord Go toward him by the hand, and his stomach queased at the slippery way the captain's flesh felt under his fingers—it felt *unattached*, as if he could peel the skin from Lord Go's hand like taking off a glove. He tried to brake Lord Go as gently as he could and brought him to a motionless halt just inside the door.

"Bhagwati," he said. "Tether the lord captain to an acceleration cage or something. Try not to touch him."

"Yes, my lord."

"Nkomo, go find the doctor and bring her here."

Surveyor's doctor was no doctor at all, but a Pharmacist First Class. She would have to do.

"Very good, my lord," Nkomo said. He made an agile dive into the corridor over Severin's head, and Severin pushed off to Nkomo's acceleration cage, where Lily Bhagwati was tethering Lord Go to a cage strut with her belt. Severin held himself a short distance from his captain's face, and tried not to look too closely at the scalded, weeping flesh.

"My lord," he said, "do you know what happened?"

Bloody eyes moved beneath the swollen lids. Lord Go sounded as if he were trying to talk past a tongue twice its normal size.

"Don't . . . know," he said.

"Was there a fire?"

"No . . . fire." Lord Go gave a long sigh. "Hurts," he said.

Severin bit his lip. "You're in pain, my lord?"

"Hurts," the captain said again.

"The doctor's on his way."

"Don't know," Lord Go said again, and then fell silent, lids falling on his dull eyes. His breathing was harsh. Severin looked at Bhagwati and saw his own anxiety mirrored in her wide brown eyes.

He had to get the ship working again.

"Right," he said. "Bhagwati, Chamcha, check the main breakers. We've got to get power on." He remembered the flash of blonde hair in the corridor outside. "I'm going to check on Lieutenant Wellstone."

He pushed off the floor with his fingers and drifted into the corridor outside. He tried not to look at Wellstone's burned, tortured face as he touched her neck in search of a pulse.

There was none. When he returned to the control room, he felt a tremor in his hands.

"My lord," Chamcha said as Severin returned to the command cage. "My lord, it's radiation."

Severin's heart turned over. He turned to Chamcha. "You were monitoring the sensors. Did you see the spectra?"

"I saw spikes, but I didn't get a clear idea of what was happening before everything blew out." Chamcha licked his lips. "But it's got to be radiation, my lord, not a fire. It's the only explanation."

Severin felt a cold finger touch his heart. Chamcha was right.

There were several areas on the ship that had heavy radiation shielding. The control room, and also engine control. There were also hardened radiation shelters where the crew could hide in the event of a solar flare, but they were small and crowded, and unless there was a radiation alert the crew never slept there.

"We'll look at the recordings once we get power," Severin said. "Get busy with the breakers."

"Yes, my lord."

Radiation, Severin thought. But what kind? And from what? They were alone in space, in transit from one wormhole to another, bypassing the one inhabited planet in the system. There were no other planets nearby, no stations, no other ships.

The electronic failures could be explained in terms of a solar flare. The fast protons fired out of a solar flare had a deadly habit of actually traveling along electric field lines until they could find something to blow up. But a solar flare so massive that it could knock out all electric systems in a ship the size of *Surveyor*, plus seriously irradiate any unshielded crew, and do it all in a very few seconds, had to be a solar flare larger than any recorded in history.

A solar flare so huge it might be ripping the atmosphere off Chee right now.

Such a flare, however, seemed very unlikely. Normally under a radiation alert the crew had plenty of time to get into their cramped shelters. Plus, *Surveyor* when under way generated an electric field from metallic strips planted along its resinous hull, a field intended to help repel any high-energy charged particles coming their way.

Which left uncharged particles . . .

"My lord!" Bhagwati called. She'd pulled her head out of an access hatch, and her face was angry. "These breakers are slagged. Whatever hit them destroyed them before they could even trip. We can't just reset them; they have to be replaced."

"Get replacements, then," Severin said.

Severin turned as he caught the gleam of a light dancing in the corridor outside. A grey-haired woman floated past the doorway, and reached out one hand to snag the doorsill in passing. The woman halted and drew her body into the control room, and Severin recognized Engineer First Class Mojtahed.

"Reporting, my lord," Mojtahed said. She was a burly, middle-aged, pot-bellied woman with her hair trimmed short and a prominent mole on one cheek. Severin felt relief at the very sight of her: at least one of the two principal engineers had been in the shielded engine control station when *Surveyor* had been hit.

"What's the situation?" Severin asked.

"A power spike tripped the engine," Mojtahed said. "We've reset breakers, and replaced some others, and I've ordered the engine countdown started. We're at something like twenty minutes."

"You've got enough power for that?"

"Emergency batteries are good, so far." She glanced around the darkened control room, and realized that Severin wasn't in any position to be able to command the ship, and wouldn't be for a while.

"We can stop the countdown at any point," she said.

"Hold at one minute, then."

"Yes, my lord."

Severin looked at her. "How many were in engine control with you?"

A hard sadness settled onto her face. "Minimum engine crew on this watch, my lord. Two."

That gave Severin at least seven people he knew of who had been in hardened areas of the ship when the radiation hit.

Seven, out of a crew of thirty-four.

Mojtahed hesitated for a moment, then spoke. "May I speak with you privately, my lord?"

"Yes." Severin turned to Chamcha and Bhagwati, who were still hovering by the access panel. "Bring the breakers," he said.

The two crewmen made their way out. Severin turned to Mojtahed.

"Yes?" he said.

Mojtahed pushed off from the door and brought herself to a stop a short distance from Severin. She glanced at Lord Go, and her face hardened. She turned to Severin and spoke almost angrily.

"Have you considered that we may have just been attacked?"

"No," Severin said, though he was unsurprised by the question. His thoughts hadn't yet stretched to that possibility, but they would have reached it in time.

"Gamma rays and fast neutrons," Mojtahed said. "That's what we'd get with a missile burst."

"We saw no signs of a missile incoming," Severin said. "No missile flares, nothing on radar. And there's no sign of a fireball."

"A missile could have been accelerated to relativistic velocities outside the system, then shot through a wormhole at us."

Severin thought about this. "But *why*?" *Surveyor* wasn't a military ship, or particularly valuable, and it was engaged in crossing a system from one wormhole to another, outside any trade routes. As the target for the opening salvo of a war, *Surveyor* hardly rated.

"Why," Mojtahed repeated, "and who."

Severin's mind raced. "If it's an attack, the first thing we need to do is get a message to Chee Station and to the wormhole relay station for passage outside. We've got to do that before we light the engine, before we maneuver, before *anything*. Because if an enemy detects a sign of life, they may finish us off."

Mojtahed took in a breath, held it for a moment between clenched teeth, then let it out in a big, angry sigh. "If they're attacking the likes of us, I don't hold much hope for Chee Station or the wormhole relay station."

The silence had reached into its third second when Nkomo stuck her head through the door.

"Doctor's dead, my lord. I looked for her assistant and—" Nkomo hesitated. "He's no better off than the captain."

"Thank you," Severin said, but Nkomo wasn't done.

"Lieutenant Wellstone's dead in the corridor just outside, my lord," she said as she came into the control room. "And I checked in Lieutenant Montcrief's cabin, and he's in his rack. He's alive, but I can't wake him."

"Thank you," Severin said again. He turned to Mojtahed. "Get back to engine control and lock yourself in, just in case we're hit again. I'll concentrate on getting communications geared up before anything else."

"Very good, my lord." Mojtahed began to push off, then paused. "Could it have been *Titan*?" she asked. "If *Titan* blew, we'd get a hell of a lot of radiation."

Mojtahed's theory would have explained everything so conveniently that Severin hated to dispose of it.

"Not unless *Titan* was nearby," he said, "and it wasn't. *Titan* isn't even in the system yet."

Mojtahed apparently regretted the loss of her hypothesis as much as Severin. "Too bad, my lord." she said, and then another idea occurred to her. "Could it be something in nature? We're close to the core of this galaxy. Could something have blown up in the galactic center and the radiation just reached us?"

"I don't know," Severin said. "I don't think so, but I don't know."

Mojtahed pushed off the acceleration cage lightly, with her fingers. Even so that was enough to cause the cage to roll, and Lord Go, tethered to it, woke with a gasp.

"*Hurts!*" he cried, and Severin's nerves gave a leap. He pulled himself closer to his captain.

"Medicine's on its way, my lord."

"Hurts!"

Afraid to disturb Lord Go again, Severin let go of the cage and touched the deck with one shoe. He pushed toward a wall, pushed off again, and snagged the doorsill.

"We're going to the pharmacy," Severin told Nkomo. "Then we're going to start looking after the crew."

On Nkomo's face was a look that combined anxiety and relief. "Yes, my lord," she said.

Severin looked at the body of Lieutenant Wellstone. "Let's get her in her cabin," he said, and he and Nkomo carried the body a short distance down the corridor. They put Wellstone in her rack, then raised the netting at the sides to keep her from floating away.

On their way to the pharmacy they encountered Bhagwati and Chamcha returning with boxes of replacement electric parts. Severin told them to try to get the comm station working first, then led aft through a bulkhead. The pharmacy was in a shielded area of the ship: If the pharmacist had only been at her duty station instead of asleep in her rack, she would have survived.

Two crew had come to the pharmacy in their agony, but had been unable to open the locked door. One was unconscious now, and the other curled in a ball, whimpering. Severin used his lieutenant's key to open the pharmacy door and then the medicine locker. He pulled out a med injector, then began looking through the neatly labeled white plastic boxes slotted into the heavy metal frames that guarded the contents against heavy accelerations. He found Phenyldorphin-Zed, pulled out one of the boxes, and handed it to Nkomo. He took another box, opened it, slotted a vial into the injector, and stuffed the rest of the vials into one of the leg pockets of his coveralls.

Severin switched the med injector on. A tone sounded. Colors flickered on the display. A tiny bubble of air rose in the clear vial, and the injector flashed an analysis of the contents and a range of recommended doses.

The software in the injectors was as idiot-proof as the Exploration Service could manage. He dialed a dose.

He floated toward the nearest of the two crew, the one that whimpered with each breath, and he anchored his feet against the frame of the pharmacy door, pulled the woman toward him, and gently tipped her chin back with his fingers. He placed the med injector against her neck, waited for the display to signal that he'd placed the injector correctly, and fired a dose straight into her carotid.

The woman's eyelids fell. The whimpering stopped, and her breathing grew regular. Severin floated to the unconscious recruit and treated him likewise. Then he offered the injector to Nkomo.

"You go to the female recruits' quarters and then take care of the petty officers. I'll look after the male recruits, the warrant officers, the lieutenant, and the captain."

Nkomo looked at the med injector without touching it, her dark eyes wide. "What about doses? What about—?"

"The highest recommended dose," Severin said. "I've already set it on the injector."

Nkomo didn't move. "Isn't that dangerous, my lord? Because these people are so sick, I mean."

Severin felt a sudden blaze of hatred for Nkomo. Nkomo was going to make him voice a thought that he hated himself for thinking, let alone for speaking out loud. The anger showed in his voice, and it made Nkomo start and stare at him.

"Nkomo," he said, "does it look to you as if the quality of life for these people is going to improve anytime soon?"

Nkomo was cautious. "Ah—no, my lord."

"They're *dying*," Severin said. "We can't do anything about it except try to make them more comfortable. If you give someone an accidental overdose, then as far as I'm concerned that's *fine*. It just means that she won't have to spend days dying in agony. But use whatever dose you want, I don't give a damn."

He held out the injector again. Nkomo hesitated, then took it with fingers that trembled.

"Yes, my lord," she said, and left very fast.

Severin floated in the corridor shaking with rage and badly wanting to hit something, but he knew that if he punched the wall in this weightless state he'd just start ricocheting around the corridor. It wasn't Jaye Nkomo's fault that she was eighteen and had been in the service for less than a year. It wasn't her fault that an officer had given her an order, an order fraught with all the weight of authority and the regulations and the awesome power of the Praxis, that told her to give massive doses of narcotics to the dying women she'd until less than an hour ago been laughing with and serving with and sleeping alongside, and that if she killed any of them by accident that was all right. Nothing in Jaye Nkomo's training had ever prepared her for this.

Nothing in Severin's training had prepared him for giving such an order, either, and the knowledge made him furious. He went back to the pharmacy, found another med injector, loaded it, and went to the male crew quarters.

The smell of it was unforgettable. It wasn't quite the smell of burning and wasn't quite the smell of roasting. It was the smell of ten men dying, and it came with moans and cries. The ones who weren't crying were listless with the apathy that was a symptom of a heavy dose of radiation. Severin went from one rack to the next and administered the doses of endorphin-analog, and by the time he'd finished his anger had passed. He only had the energy left for emotions that might be useful. The emotions that would track down the enemy, whoever they were, and somehow—

somehow, given that he was in a crippled, unarmed ship with only seven crew—somehow destroy them.

He went to the warrant officers' cabins, then to that of Lord Barry Montcrief, and then he returned to the control room.

In the control room the emergency lights were on. More than half the displays were glowing softly. Bhagwati sat at the comm board with the lid of the board raised. She was replacing fuses. Chamcha was bent over the sensor board, a puzzled expression on his face. Both were trying to ignore Lord Go, who was curled into a fetal ball and crying.

Severin floated to the captain and placed the injector against his neck and touched the trigger. Lord Go gave a long, ragged sigh, and his clenched body relaxed.

Severin went to the command cage, took the picture of the captain's family, the children and wife and parents and stuffed Torminel, and he returned to the captain and put the picture in Lord Go's hand where he would see it if he ever woke.

"Report, please," Severin said.

"Replaced breakers in Main Busses One and Two," Bhagwati said, "but the engine isn't lit, so we can't get power from anything but the emergency batteries. Battery power should be enough to send a message, though, so I'm trying to get the comm station up."

"I'm looking at the spectra from just before we got fried," Chamcha said. He turned to Severin, his wiry hair floating around his moon face. "There was nothing, and then *wham!*—x-rays."

"X-*rays*?" Severin said. A missile wouldn't produce x-rays. He kicked off and floated gently toward the sensor station.

"They came in pulses." Chamcha's voice was puzzled. "Eight pulses in the first three-quarters of a second, and then the fuses blew and it stopped recording." He looked at Severin anxiously. "Could someone have hit us with an x-ray laser?"

"Pulses," Severin repeated, and his heart sank.

This wasn't an enemy he could fight with a crippled ship and seven crew. Nor was it an enemy he could hope to vanquish were he a senior fleet commander, with a dozen squadrons of warships under his command.

This was an enemy that could wipe out entire civilizations without even noticing them.

"Chamcha," he said, "what exists in nature that sends out twelve massive bursts of x-rays in one second?"

Chamcha's eyes narrowed as he searched his memory. Then the eyes widened, and the color drained from his face.

"Oh, shit," he said.

After replacing a fuse in the navigation station, Severin located the enemy within half an hour. One of the seven, or possibly eight, stars in the large system of which Chee's star was an element had been catalogued, over eight hundred years ago, as a brown dwarf, a large gaseous body that wasn't quite large enough to have properly ignited as a star.

That categorization was now demonstrably incorrect, and so was the estimate of the number of stars in the system as a whole. There were not seven, or possibly eight, but rather eight, or possibly nine.

The alleged brown dwarf wasn't a brown dwarf, but a degenerate star. It had once been much larger, and had a companion star that was larger still, forming between them a binary pair that rotated about each other as they moved in even more complex orbits around the other six, or possibly seven, stars of the greater Chee system.

The companion star, nearing the end of its life, had exploded as a supernova, hurling vast clouds of its outer shell into space. Much of this material had been absorbed by its neighbor, making it larger, still. The companion, dying, collapsed into a neutron star, and began a deadly dance with gravity, spiraling closer to its neighbor with every orbit. Eventually the neutron star had fallen close enough to begin stripping the outer layers of hydrogen gas off its attendant, drawing the infalling matter into a disk. As the material drew closer, the enormous magnetic fields of the neutron star drew the material inward, compressing and heating it, eventually transforming the infalling matter into powerful beams of x-rays that shot from the magnetic poles.

The neutron star spiraled in, closer and closer, until its orbit was nearly within its companion's outer envelope. The period of its orbit was less than three hours. It had so consumed its companion star that the companion was now indistinguishable from a brown dwarf, especially if the star was being observed from far away, hundreds of years ago, by surveyors who were far more interested in habitable planets.

"Right," Severin said. "Now the question is, what *else* is the pulsar going to hit?"

He and Chamcha sat side by side in the sensor cage. Severin called other displays onto his own, piloting and astrography displays, and an estimate of the angle of the x-ray beam when *Surveyor* had been hit, which would provide a figure for the tilt of the pulsar's magnetic pole and a judgment of what other objects the beam might intersect.

The computer simulation of the multisun system, with the pulsar now added, ran briefly, then stopped. A tone sounded.

Chee.

"Well, of course," Severin said. He was surprised by his lack of surprise.

Chee and the eight, or possibly nine, suns of its system weren't all in the same plane. The pulsar's course was to galactic north of Chee, and the beam fired from its southern magnetic pole would intersect the planet for all of three seconds, long enough to kill any unshielded animal life form either in orbit or on the planet's surface.

Severin compiled the information into as terse a message as he could. "Send to Chee Station Command," he said, "with copies to Lord Inspector Martinez and Astronomer Shon-dan at the Imperial Observatory."

"Very good, my lord," said Nkomo. She had returned to the control room without speaking a word, and had taken her place at the comm board. She looked down at the board. "Comm laser three powering up and—we've lost it, my lord."

Severin turned to stare at her. "*Lost* it? Lost *what*?"

Nkomo looked uncertain. "Lost the laser, my lord. It's . . . malfunctioned somehow."

"Use another laser."

The second laser also failed. Severin thought that perhaps the x-ray flux had turned the metal on the ship brittle as glass, and that the metallic semiconductors used to generate the lasers were blowing apart under the strain of excitation.

When a third laser died, Severin decided that his theory was confirmed.

"Try a VHF antenna," Severin said. "Use the emergency channel."

They were going to get their message to Chee, Severin thought, one way or another, if he had to build an antenna himself.

When Martinez returned to his lodgings at the Mayor's Palace, the Lady Mayor herself bustled toward him as he got out of the car.

"I wondered where you had been today, my lord," she said. She looked in surprise at his muddy boots and informal clothing. "There are a stack of invitations that have come in for you."

"Rigger Ahmet was showing me the sights," Martinez said. He turned to Ahmet and winked. "Right, Ahmet?"

Ahmet grinned broadly. "Absolutely, my lord."

The Lady Mayor hesitated. Martinez smiled at her, and then his sleeve comm chimed.

"Pardon me, my lady." He answered.

The chameleon weave on his sleeve shimmered to an image of Lord Ehl. The feathery dark hairs on the sides of his head were standing oddly, as if he'd just suffered an electric shock.

"My lord," Ehl said. "We've just received a transmission from *Surveyor*, and—well—I'd be obliged if you could get back to the station as fast as you can."

As the coleopter began its descent into Port Vipsania, Martinez looked at Shon-dan in the crystal-clear image of his sleeve display and said, "Do you mean to tell me that despite your entire crew of overpaid astronomers at Chee Station, you failed to detect two beams of deadly energy each *over a light-year long*?"

Shon-dan gazed at Martinez with wide golden eyes. "My lord," she said, "we're *cosmologists*. We haven't looked at *anything* within a hundred light-years of this place."

Martinez looked balefully at the image of Shon-dan, and then realized he was grinding his teeth. He unclenched and spoke.

"Tell me what's going to happen, and how long we've got."

"We've got nine and a half days, my lord. Then Chee will move into the path of that beam, and—" Shon-dan clacked her peg teeth nervously. "Anyone without proper shielding will, ah, be very much in jeopardy."

"The atmosphere won't be shield enough?"

"Not for beams of this intensity." Shon-dan tried to look hopeful. "We've worked out the orbital mechanics, by the way, and this should happen to Chee only once every forty-nine thousand years."

Which, Martinez thought, explained the relatively primitive life forms on the surface of the planet as compared with the superabundant life in the sea. Every forty-nine thousand years any complex species on land was wiped out.

Those fern forests were a clue, if anyone had bothered to read it.

"So," he said, "we'll have nearly fifty thousand good years if we manage to survive the next ten days."

The avian's tone was apologetic. "Ah—there will be problems after the ten days, my lord. Electronics may be destroyed. Food crops may not survive. Metals may turn brittle. And—well, I don't know what will happen to the station and the elevator. I'll have to think of that."

"You do that. I need an estimate of how much shielding people are going to need to hide under."

"Ah—yes, my lord."

Martinez ended the transmission. The coleopter was making its final approach to its landing pad. Martinez thought of people rising from shelters to find the world above destroyed—crops burned in the fields, no communication, buildings with metal frames unsafe, transport liable to fall apart, those beautiful bridges on the railroad collapsed because the support cables could no longer carry them.

And possibly Chee Station destroyed. There was plenty of radiation shielding on the station, but it was all on the outer rims of the habitation wheels and in other parts calculated to protect personnel against a solar flare. The x-ray beam would be coming in at an angle, from galactic north, and very little of the station would be protected.

The wheel and other large structures were made of a tough resinous material, and thus wouldn't be subject to metal fatigue, but even so enough critical components were made of metal that the structure might be in jeopardy. If it came apart under stress the elevator cable would drop into the atmosphere, where it would burn up, but if the cable dragged enough of the station with it, Chee could be subjected to a dangerous bombardment of large objects burning their way through the atmosphere to strike the surface.

And crashing with the station would be Chee Company stock, to the ruination of his father and family.

Helpless anger burned in his thoughts as the coleopter settled to a landing.

Terza waited by the landing pad with a big Fleet car and a driver. She was wearing her brown Ministry uniform. Martinez walked across the pad and kissed her. Her lips were soft, her eyes hard.

"You've heard?" he asked. He had to speak over the sound of the coleopter's turbines.

"Marcella told me."

He took her arm and walked with her to the car. "We'll get you on the first ship out."

"I can stay," Terza said. "I'm an administrator, remember, and I'm sure they'll find an adequate shelter for us."

They paused by the car. Martinez put a large hand over Terza's abdomen. "I don't want x-rays getting anywhere near the next generation of Clan Chen."

Terza made a face. "I was so looking forward to seeing you in action," she said.

"But I suppose caution may be indicated, since the doctor confirmed just this morning there *is* a next generation on the way."

Despite the oppressive weight of his thoughts a flame of joy kindled in Martinez's heart, and he kissed her. "What happens next?" he asked. "I'm not quite sure how this pregnancy business works, since I wasn't around the first time."

Terza took him by the hand and drew him into the automobile. "It's going to be very difficult and taxing, I'm afraid." Her tone was businesslike. "I shall require first-class pampering from you for, oh, several years at least."

"Starting now?" he said hopefully.

Terza gave a sigh. "I'm afraid not. You've got a meeting."

"We've got power in most of the ship," Severin said. "Communication between engine control and main control have been restored. Enough of the computers have been brought on line so that we can do what we need to. The injured are being made as comfortable as possible for the deceleration, and we're fighting dehydration with intravenous drips. Since we're uncertain how the ship will respond to a resumption of gee force, we'll start with a tenth of a gravity, then gradually increase power to one gravity."

Severin paused for a reply, and when none came went on.

"When I tried to turn the ship with the maneuvering thrusters, the thruster heads blew out—metal fatigue in the joints won't let them hold pressure. That means we're going to have to maneuver with the main engine, which is of course designed to resist hard radiation, so if you feel some unusual accelerations at first, that's what they'll be."

He paused again, then licked his dry lips. "May I have permission to begin deceleration, my lord?"

There was a long pause before a single word came from the captain's lips, so soft it was almost a sigh.

"Proceed."

"Very good, my lord." Severin checked the captain's intravenous drip, then spun in the air with a flip of his hands and kicked off for the door.

He didn't know how much of his report the captain had understood, but Severin felt better for having delivered it. Lord Go was a good captain and deserved to know what was happening on his ship, and perhaps Lord Go himself felt better for knowing.

The captain had been returned to his bed prior to the commencement of acceleration. Dehydration was a serious problem with radiation burns and Severin and the other six uninjured crewmen had spent the last few hours giving the surviving victims intravenous drips, an arduous process because they had to learn the technique first, practicing on each other by following the steps in a manual.

Severin had debated with himself over whether the step should be taken at all. Prolonging the lives of the victims was only to extend their suffering without a chance of altering the outcome.

But Severin wanted to be able to look at himself in a mirror. He wanted to be able to tell the families of the victims that he'd done everything he could for them. He didn't want to have to say, "I let them die without trying to help them."

He made his way to the control room and worked his way into the command cage, then pulled the display down in front of him and locked it there. Bhagwati, Nkomo, and Chamcha were all strapped into their acceleration couches.

"Engines," he told Bhagwati, "sound the acceleration warning."

"Yes, my lord." The warning clattered through the ship.

"Engines," Severin said, "prepare to maneuver with the main engine."

"Yes, my lord." Bhagwati looked at her board. "Gimbal test successful, my lord. Engine on standby."

"Course one-five-seven by one-five-seven relative."

"Course laid into the computer, my lord."

"Begin maneuvering."

The thrust was gentle, and Severin heard the engine fire only as a distant rumble that seemed to come up his spine. His couch swung lightly in its cage, and a faint whisper of gravity reached Severin's inner ear. The engine faded, then fired again. Severin's cage rattled. His stomach gave a little lurch.

"Come *on*," Bhagwati urged. The main engine really wasn't intended for this kind of maneuvering.

The engine fired again, a more sustained burst. Severin found himself waiting for the sound of something falling.

Nothing fell. The engine fired thrice more, each minor adjustments. There was triumph in Bhagwati's voice when she announced, "One-five-seven by one-five-seven relative."

"Commence acceleration at point one gravities."

The engine lit, a sustained distant rumble, and Severin's cage swung again. A gentle hand pressed him into his couch.

"Systems check," Severin ordered, just to make certain nothing had broken.

Nothing had. Severin had no worries for the hull, which was tough resin stiffened with polycarbon beams, but there was still enough metal in the ship to cause him concern. There were metal shelves, metal hinges, metal fittings, and the sick crew lay on mattresses placed on metal racks. Pipes and conduits were secured by metal strips. Valves with metal parts pierced the hull to bring in water or electricity from stations, or to discharge waste.

All Severin needed right now was a hull breach.

Severin added gravity a tenth of a gee at a time until the ship was decelerating at one full gravity. Only once did he hear a crash, when a shelf gave way in the captain's pantry.

"Systems check," Severin said.

Nothing was destroyed, nothing breached. Severin began to feel proud of *Surveyor*. It was a tougher craft than he'd expected.

He would get *Surveyor* to Laredo, where there would have to be a complete refit. *Surveyor* was twenty-eight days out from Laredo, so it would take twenty-eight days to reverse the momentum that had built, plus another twenty-eight days to return to port.

By that time all the afflicted crew would be dead. Severin would be conducting funerals every day for many days to come, and in addition *Surveyor* would have a front-row seat for what promised to be a planetary catastrophe.

Severin unlocked his display and pushed it up over his head, out of the way. He unwebbed and stepped out of the cage.

"Bhagwati, you have the ship," he said. "Nkomo, Chamcha, it's time to make the rounds of the sick and make sure they're coping under gravity."

Severin would report to Lord Go that *Surveyor* had done well under acceleration. He hoped the captain would be pleased.

"Life is brief, but the Praxis is eternal," Severin read from the burial service. "Let us all take comfort and security in the wisdom that all that is important is known." He looked up at Engineer Mojtahed.

"Proceed," he said.

Mojtahed pressed the override button that blew from the cargo airlock Captain Lord Go Shikimori, Lieutenant Lord Barry Montcrief, and four other crew. Since *Surveyor's* engine was blazing a huge radioactive tail during the deceleration, and since the bodies, once out of the airlock, were no longer decelerating, the captain and his crew would be cremated within seconds.

Severin and the four others—two remained on watch—remained at rigid attention until the airlock display stopped blinking. Mojtahed looked through the window on the inner airlock.

"Airlock's clear, my lord."

"Close the outer door and repressurize." Severin said. He turned to the others. "Detail dismissed." He began to walk away, then stopped "Mojtahed, Chamcha, please join me for dinner."

Though Severin was now the acting captain, he hadn't moved into the captain's quarters, and didn't intend to. He brought Mojtahed and Chamcha to the wardroom, where he sat them at the table normally reserved for lieutenants.

The pulsar had killed all of *Surveyor's* cooks and the meals had become haphazard, mostly stews of things emptied into the pot from cans, and all cooked by microwave because the metal burners on the galley stove were so brittle they failed if anyone turned them on. Severin and his guests were served by today's cook, an apprentice from Mojtahed's engine room department, who fled before any of them had a chance to taste his handiwork. Severin opened a bottle of wine from the wardroom stores. Till now he had tasted the wine only occasionally, because he'd been unable to afford the sort of private stores the other lieutenants were used to, and he didn't want Lord Barry and Lady Maxine to think he was a leech, drinking from the bottles that would have cost him half a month's pay apiece.

But now Lord Barry and Lady Maxine were radioactive dust floating in the general direction of Wormhole Two, and Severin had conducted his second mass funeral in two days and wanted a drink.

He had two goblets of wine while the others sipped theirs and ate a few dutiful bites of stew. Then he spoke.

"We've done a good job of saving the ship," he said. "Now I'd like to try to save Chee."

There was silence at the wardroom table, and then Mojtahed wiped a bit of gravy off her chin and said, "Beg pardon, my lord?"

"I want to save Chee," Severin said. "And to do that we have to turn off the pulsar, and I think I know how that can be done."

There was another moment of silence. Mojtahed and Chamcha exchanged glances.

Mojtahed, the senior surviving petty officer. Chamcha, who was a highly trained sensor operator trained to detect wormholes, and the closest thing *Surveyor* had to an actual scientist.

"Very good, my lord," Mojtahed said.

"Bear with me," Severin said. He called up the wardroom's wall display, and put up a simulation of an x-ray pulsar he'd got from *Anray's Catalogue of Astronomical Objects*.

"The x-ray pulse is driven by matter infalling from the accretion disk," Severin said. "So if we can turn that mechanism off, the x-rays will turn off as well. Unlike an electromagnetic pulsar, an x-ray pulsar can't work in a vacuum."

"My lord," Chamcha ventured, "we're dealing with something the mass of a *star*. A pulsar is one of the most dense objects in the universe, and about the deadliest—how can you hope to stop it with our resources?"

"The pulsar's mass is colossal, yes," Severin said. "But the accretion disk is nothing but hydrogen gas. So what we do is fire an antimatter missile into the accretion disk, and the antimatter *wipes out* the inner band of hydrogen." He grinned at them. "The pulsar's shut down for a few critical hours, Chee is saved, we all get medals. What do you think?"

Chamcha blinked. Mojtahed's response was more practical. "We don't *have* any antimatter missiles."

"We'll use one of the lifeboats. Pack the crew spaces full of antihydrogen if we have to, and sent it out on automatic pilot."

Chamcha hesitantly raised a hand, as if he was in a classroom.

"Yes?" Severin said.

"I see two problems," Chamcha said. "First, I don't think we have nearly enough antimatter . . ."

"So *we'll* jump in the lifeboats and then shoot *Surveyor* at the pulsar," Severin said.

"And the *other* problem," Chamcha said indomitably, "is that when the antihydrogen hits the accretion disk, it doesn't just wipe it from existence, it turns into *radiation*. The radiation directed at the pulsar won't shut it off, it'll *heat the pulsar up*, and the x-ray emissions will *radically increase in power*. And the radiation directed outward, into the accretion disk, will *heat up the accretion disk*, so when *that* falls onto the pulsar, you'll get *another* super-powerful burst of x-rays." Chamcha made a kind of exploding gesture with his hands. "And then Chee gets *really* fried."

Severin felt himself mentally rock back on his heels. When the idea had first occurred to him, shaving in his bath that morning, it had seemed like a brilliant strike of lightning, and subsequent consideration had only made it seem better. He rubbed his chin for a moment as he considered.

Mojtahed, who apparently considered the discussion at an end, took a long, relieved drink of wine.

Severin decided he wasn't done yet. "But *between* the two big bursts," he said, "there's nothing, right? The pulsar will actually turn off."

An stubborn expression came onto Chamcha's moon face. "For a short time, yes," Chamcha said. "But I doubt that it would last more than a few seconds, not even if we threw all of *Surveyor* at it. And if we got the timing wrong, Chee gets cooked."

"And we *don't* get medals," Mojtahed pronounced.

"A few seconds is all Chee needs," Severin said. He turned back to the display on the wall, and called up rows of figures and the Structured Mathematics Display. "Before breakfast I sent a message to Astronomer Shon-dan at the Chee Observatory," he said, "requesting all available information on the pulsar—its mass, its accretion disk, the power of its x-ray beam. The reply just arrived, so let's do the math."

The math, when it was done, was discouraging. Even if *Surveyor* were packed with antihydrogen fuel, it would barely produce a blip in the pulsar's x-ray yield.

"Sorry, my lord," Chamcha said. "It was an ingenious idea, but it just didn't work out."

Mojtahed finished her stew and rattled the spoon in her bowl. "Yes, my lord. Sorry." She had clearly dismissed the idea from her mind.

"*Titan*," Severin said.

The others looked at him.

"*Titan* is a very large ship and it's packed with antimatter and it's just entered the system," Severin said. "And *Titan*'s on lease to the Exploration Service, and Warrant Officer Junot is in command, and I outrank him. So—" He smiled. "Maybe we'd better do the math again."

There were six hundred people on Chee Station, and eight hundred forty thousand on the planet below. Two cargo ships were docked at the station, and if they discharged all their cargo they could take perhaps four thousand people, assuming the people were packed closely enough and a sufficient number of new toilets were installed.

Which left in excess of eight hundred thirty-six thousand people in danger on the planet's surface, and that meant Martinez attended a *lot* of meetings.

Antiradiation shielding was scavenged from the station, and several of the manufacturing plants on the surface thought they could convert in time and produce some more, but most of the people on the planet were going to have to hide from the pulsar the old-fashioned way, in a deep hole, with a lot of dirt piled on the roof.

There was heavy equipment and construction material to provide enough shelter space for everyone, but the population wasn't unanimous in their cooperation.

"The railroad workers want to take their families up the line and into the tunnels," Allodorm told Martinez. "They think they'll be safer with a mountain on top of them."

Martinez glared from the window of his office on the station down at the blue-and-green planet below. His own reflection, heavy-browed and scowling, glowered back at him. Chee rotated slowly in the window frame as the station wheeled on its axis.

"They'll be safer," Martinez said, "until they try to *leave*." He felt his voice rising in frustration. "How are they going to get their families down from the mountain over bridges that are brittle as icicles? On vehicles floating on electromagnets that may explode the second a current runs through them?" He looked at Allodorm and spoke with finality. "The railroad workers go into the bunkers like everyone else."

"Yes, lord inspector." Allodorm's beautiful voice showed no sign of agitation at any point in the crisis. Martinez had to give him credit for that.

And even if he was a thief, Allodorm was working as hard as anyone to shelter Chee's inhabitants. Martinez had to give him credit for that, too.

"I've heard from the Lady Mayor of Port Gareth," Marcella said from around the cigarette she held fiercely between her teeth. "She has a plan to save the shuttles."

The shuttles were designed to ferry cargo from low orbit to the surface, and were unable to achieve escape velocity and get far enough from Chee to avoid the pulsar. They would remain on the ground, with most of the other heavy equipment, and be subjected to x-ray bombardment and probably ruined.

Martinez hoped the Chee Company had good insurance.

He left the window and dropped heavily into the chair behind his desk. Pneumatics gave an outraged hiss.

"Is the Lady Mayor any kind of aeronautical engineer?" Martinez asked. "Has she actually consulted with the shuttle pilots?"

Marcella smiled. "The answer to the first question is no, and as for the second, I doubt it. She wants to put the shuttles in geosynchronous orbit on the side of Chee away from the pulsar."

"That won't work," Martinez said. "The pulsar beam isn't coming in along the plane of the ecliptic, it'll come at an angle from galactic north. Anything in geosynchronous orbit will be fried. In order to get the planet between the shuttles and the beam, they'd have to go into a polar orbit and get the timing exactly right . . ." He paused for a moment. "Wait a minute, that's a *good* idea. Tell the shuttle pilots that they can proceed with the polar orbit, but they're forbidden to take passengers. It's too dangerous."

As the provisional governor had declared a state of emergency, Martinez as the senior Fleet representative had become the absolute ruler of the Chee system. It was as if all the power of the Shaa conquerors had become invested in his person.

If the situation hadn't been so desperate, he would be really enjoying himself.

"By the way," Marcella added, "can you make use of the *Kayenta*? I'm happy to offer it, though it won't hold very many refugees."

"Thank you," Martinez said. "Let me think about it."

At another meeting, with Lord Ehl and the captains of the two merchant vessels, there was a discussion of who was going on the ships and who wasn't.

"We should bring off the representatives of our company," one of the captains said. "And then paying passengers, of course."

"You will bring off gravid females," Martinez said, "and children under the age of fifteen, each of whom will be accompanied by one parent. If there's any room left, we can discuss allowing slightly older children aboard."

There probably *would* be extra room: there weren't many children on Chee, as the workers had been recruited chiefly from the young and unattached, and settler families hadn't really started arriving yet.

"My owners will protest!" the captain said.

"That will be their privilege, after this is over." Martinez turned to Lord Ehl. "You will place members of the Military Constabulary on the ships' airlock doors and hatches," he said. "I don't want unauthorized people sneaking on board."

"Yes, my lord." Martinez thought he heard satisfaction in Ehl's voice.

"No Fleet personnel will leave Chee till this is over," Martinez said to Ehl later, after the captains had left. "It's our job to stand between the citizens and danger, and if that means sucking up x-rays, so be it."

"Er—yes, my lord." Martinez thought he detected rather less satisfaction in Ehl's tone than had been there a few moments before.

"I'm going to be the last person off Chee Station," Martinez said. "You'll be the next to last, so we'll share an elevator."

"Yes, my lord." A question glowed in Ehl's golden eyes. "We're not staying in Station Command? It's shielded."

"There might be a structural failure of the station. If there isn't, we'll be able to get from the ground back to the station easily enough."

Then Martinez recalled Marcella's offer of *Kayenta*. "No, wait," he said. "*You'll* take the last elevator with the control room crew. I'll see you off, then depart in *Kayenta*. That way I'll be able to return to the station once the pulsar's passed and make certain everything's in order before you bring a crew back up the elevator."

The plan pleased him. Last off the station, and first on again. It was a role that was not only proper for the senior officer in a crisis, but would reflect well on him.

It wasn't as if he minded looking good.

It wasn't until he left his office for the walk to the grandeur of the Senior Officers' Quarters that he found out about another problem. A Terran with a wispy blond mustache and a jacket with a gray stripe came up to Martinez as he walked, and introduced himself as Hedgepath, a stockbroker.

"There are brokers on Chee?" Martinez asked.

"Yes," Hedgepath said, "though most of what I do is invest workers' pay elsewhere in the empire. But Port Vipsania has its own little stock market, for locally raised issues. We even have a futures market."

"Congratulations," Martinez said.

"Perhaps congratulations aren't precisely in order." Hedgepath touched his slight mustache. "There has been an, ah, problem with the market. The futures market in particular. In the hours before the announcement of the threat from the pulsar, there was a lot of selling. Agricultural futures in particular, though there was some selling in industrial and fishery futures as well."

Martinez found himself nodding. "After word about the pulsar came out, the futures turned worthless."

"You might understand that my clients have been complaining. And since you now seem to represent the civil authority as well as the military, I thought I'd pass the complaints to you." He touched his mustache again. "I couldn't seem to make an appointment, by the way. I'm sorry I had to stop you on the street."

Martinez considered this. Hedgepath's lack of an appointment wasn't necessarily an element of a deep conspiracy—a *lot* of people were trying to set meetings with him, and the Lai-own secretary that Lord Ehl had assigned him might well have assigned Hedgepath a low priority.

"I'll look into that," Martinez said. "In the meantime, I'd like to give you some names. Ledo Allodorm. Lord Pa Maq-fan. Lady Marcella Zykov."

Hedgepath seemed surprised only by Marcella's name "I can assure your lordship that Lady Marcella hasn't done any selling that I know of," Hedgepath said. "But there were sell orders from other Chee Company officials—Her-ryng and Remusat, for two."

Martinez couldn't put any faces to the names, though he'd very possibly met them at one or another of the banquets in his honor.

"I'd like you to retain all information of the trades," Martinez said. "Things are urgent right now, and I won't be able to deal with this till after the pulsar's passed. Make sure the data is in hard as well as electronic form."

"Yes, my lord."

"Can you give me contact information?"

Hedgepath sent his information to Martinez from his sleeve display, and Martinez told him that he would be in touch.

"By the way," he said. "How's Chee Company stock doing?"

"It's worth about a third of what it was worth two days ago."

Martinez told Terza this over supper. "I'd been starting to think well of Allodorm and Lord Pa," Terza said. "They've been so responsive in the crisis."

"And all the more responsive for knowing their money's safe. And of course they're working to save their own skins, and their company's assets."

There was a low chime from Martinez's sleeve display. He gave a snarl; he'd forgotten to turn it off at dinner.

"Apologies," he said to Terza, and answered.

The orange eyes of his Lai-own secretary gazed back at him from the display. "I beg your pardon, my lord. A communication has arrived from Lieutenant Severin, logged as personal, confidential, urgent, and immediate."

Martinez exchanged glances with Terza. Severin wouldn't use such a bundle of impressive adjectives without reason.

"Send it," Martinez said.

When Martinez's display indicated that the message had been downloaded, he broke the connection to his secretary and played the message.

"This is going to be complex," Severin said, "and I'd be obliged if somewhere along the line you could check my math."

Severin had considered not telling anyone of his plan to use *Titan* to shut off the pulsar. He was afraid that someone, frightened of the super-powerful bursts of x-rays that would both precede and follow the pulsar's brief time of quiet, would refuse him permission to act.

He certainly knew better than to ask his own superiors on Laredo. The Exploration Service was an organization that had been starved of funding for ages: every time the government was reminded that the Service existed, it had only inspired them to trim the budget still further. The entire institutional culture of the Service was based on not calling attention to themselves, and the culture hadn't changed even though the budget had grown. Throwing away a whole ship full of antihydrogen was calling for attention, and with a vengeance: if Severin approached them with his scheme, their first instinct would refuse to do *anything*.

Yet it would be hard to carry out the operation secretly. *Titan* wasn't exactly inconspicuous, and when its crew took to the lifeboats while the giant ship itself burned for the pulsar at an acceleration that would have killed anyone aboard, someone might well take notice.

So Severin had decided to contact Martinez personally, trusting that the relationship that had developed in the war would continue to work. In the meantime he had told *Titan*'s crew to prepare to abandon the ship and to place it under remote control, and also ordered them to keep their orders secret for the present and not to transmit anything but routine messages to Chee or to anywhere else.

Severin didn't want *Titan* asking their superiors for advice, either. He was sleeping in his cabin when Martinez's reply arrived. Severin was dreaming of warships that were also, secretly, submarines, submarines that fought a lonely covert war in the chill seas of watery planets like Hy-Oso, and he slowly became aware that the insistent chiming he heard wasn't the sound of sonar, but his sleeve display.

The comm unit in his cabin was still nonfunctional, which was why the sleeve display had to be used. Severin called for lights, then remembered that fuse hadn't been replaced either, and groped through the dark cabin for the uniform jacket that had been hung over the back of a chair. He triggered the display, heard from Chamcha that Lord Inspector Martinez had send him a message logged personal, urgent, and confidential, and told Chamcha to send it.

"Permission is tentatively granted to proceed with your project," Martinez said. His face appeared upside-down in the display, and Severin craned his neck to get a better view.

"I'm ordering complete secrecy on this matter," Martinez said. "You will censor all communication off *Surveyor* and order censorship on *Titan* as well. Absolutely nothing must get out. I'm going to explain *Titan*'s movements as a maneuver ordered by the Exploration Service high command."

Severin could only stare at the inverted image.

Martinez's eyes took on a more confiding glance. "Let's hope you're right about all this. I'll check the math, and enjoy talking with you when it's all over."

The orange End Transmission symbol flashed into place on Severin's sleeve. Thoughtfully he felt his way across the cabin and turned on the lights manually.

Total secrecy, he thought. Now *that* was interesting.

Clearly he wasn't the only one here with a scheme up his sleeve.

"Total secrecy," Martinez told Shon-dan. "I want this to be strictly between the two of us."

"Yes, my lord." The astronomer clacked her peg teeth in thought, then spoke hesitantly. "May I ask the reason for the secrecy?"

"People might be less than committed to the evacuations and the shelter-building program if they thought the shelters weren't going to be needed. Even if the math checks there's still too much that can go wrong with this scheme, and if the plan blows up, those shelters will be necessary."

Shon-dan hesitated again. "Very good, my lord."

"I want you to check these figures," Martinez said, "and I'll check them as well. And *no one else is to know*. Understand?"

"Yes, my lord."

"Because if anyone else finds out, I'll know who blabbed, and I'll throw you into that x-ray beam with my own hands."

After hearing a series of heartfelt assurances from Shon-dan, Martinez ended the conversation. His dinner lay cold on the table before him. Terza lowered the cup of coffee from her lips and said, "I hope this means I'm not going to have to take that refugee ship."

Martinez considered this. "No," he decided, "you're going aboard."

Her mouth tightened. "Why?" she asked.

"Because you're the Chen heir and mother of the *next* Chen heir," Martinez said. "And so you will go on board the refugee ship and be gracious and accepting and thoughtful and considerate of the other passengers, because that's what people expect of the next Lady Chen."

Terza looked cross. "Damn," she said.

"Just as I'll be last off this station," Martinez said, "and first on, because it's what people expect of a war hero."

Reluctant amusement tugged at Terza's lips. "I haven't noticed that you find being a hero much of a hardship."

Martinez sipped his cold coffee. "Well," he said, "not *yet*. But when I'm old and mumbling in my rocking chair by the fire, and multitudes of citizens come to me begging to be rescued from some cosmic menace or other, I'm probably going to find it all *very inconvenient*."

"No doubt," Terza said.

Martinez signaled to Alikhan to fill his coffee cup.

"You'll have to excuse me for the next few hours," he told Terza. "I have to confirm all of Severin's calculations."

Terza rose from her chair. "I'll start the job of being gracious and accepting, then, and leave you to your task."

Martinez's calculations supported those of Severin, and more importantly Shon-dan's supported them both. Martinez called Ring Command to tell them that *Titan* and *Surveyor* would be engaged in a series of maneuvers, and that the sensor operations should be told to disregard them. "Put a memo on the sensor display," Martinez said. "I don't want to get a call from Command whenever a new sensor operator goes on watch."

Then it was back to the endless series of planning meetings. Shelters were being dug with furious efficiency, roofed, and then covered with dirt. The accommodations were primitive, but few conveniences were required by a population that would be in the shelters for less than an hour.

The first of the two refugee ships was sent off, with four thousand aboard, mostly children. The ship would boost far enough away to be safe from the pulsar, and could then return to Chee or continue on to Laredo, depending on whether Chee Station survived or not.

The second ship left two days later. Martinez kissed Terza goodbye at the airlock door, and watched her drift aboard in an elegant swirl of grace and gallantry. Martinez paused for a moment of admiration, and then turned to go past the long lines of refugees patiently waiting to board, each tethered to a safety line as they floated weightless in the great docking space.

Some unused to weightlessness looked green and ill. Martinez sped past them before the inevitable consequences began to manifest themselves.

He made his way to Command, and encountered Lord Ehl leaving Ehl braced in salute as he drifted past, then recovered in time to snag a handhold on the wall. He made a nervous gesture with his free hand, then stuffed a sheet of paper in a pocket.

"Is something wrong?" Martinez said.

"No," Ehl began. "Well, yes. There have been some arrests, people who got onto the refugee ship that weren't supposed to be there. Officials of the shipping company, apparently." He lifted the paper from his pocket, then returned it. "I have their names, but they'll have to be checked."

"Do you need my help?"

"No, my lord, I thank you."

"Very well. Once you find out for certain who they are, ship them down the skyhook and put them in the deepest dungeon on Chee."

There were no dungeons on Chee, so far as Martinez knew, but perhaps they'd build one.

From Command Martinez followed the saga of the stowaways, who were marched off the ship by the military constabulary. The refugee ship was given permission to depart, and the enormous vessel gently backed from the station until it reached a safe enough distance to light its torch.

Martinez said another silent farewell to Terza as the displays showed her ship building speed, then took a covert look at *Titan*. *Titan* itself was boosting at nearly twenty gravities toward its rendezvous with the pulsar, a speed that would have killed any crew on board. The icon representing *Titan* on the sensor displays had a large text box attached to it, saying the ship was engaged in maneuvers. The two lifeboats containing its crew were on their way to their rendezvous with *Surveyor*, and had been given the cover of a mission to resupply the crippled craft.

If anyone in Command ever bothered to check the ship's heading and acceleration, they would have had a surprise. But the staff had an emergency on its hands, and much to occupy them; their sensor displays were tuned to the awesome might of the x-ray beam spinning ever closer, and a distant ship that did not call attention to itself was something that floated only on the margins of their attention, like a lily floating in the distant reaches of a pond.

No queries regarding *Titan* came to Martinez's attention. One shelter after another was certified, and the population put to rehearsing their evacuation schemes. At the last moment the Lady Mayor of Port Gareth came up with another plan: she wanted to put much of the population of her town into several of the large containers that had brought goods from orbit, and sink them below the surface of the bay for the duration of the emergency. Martinez, torn between irritation and hilarity, told her that it was too late to change the plans, and she should complete all conventional shelters in her town.

Lord Pa and Allodorm were on the ground, coordinating last-minute emergency and evacuation work. Personnel on Chee Station were sent to the surface, leaving a skeleton crew behind. The two huge rotating wheels were braked to a stop, and the antimatter reactor powered down. Even the emergency lighting was turned off in most of the station to keep surges from following power lines. *Kayenta* was readied at the airlock, with Marcella and select Meridian Company personnel aboard, a team that would return to the station with Martinez for a survey before anyone else was allowed to return to the station. One by one the displays and work spaces at Ring Command were shut down, leaving live only the boards that would be needed to begin the restart.

Martinez, Lord Ehl, and the other crew left the darkened, eerily silent Command room and floated along guide cables to the entrance to the great elevator car. Martinez accepted their salute, wished Ehl luck, and watched them file aboard. The car began its descent, diving smoothly along the cable to its vanishing point in the green land mass below, and then Martinez turned for *Kayenta*'s berth.

When *Kayenta* departed from the station, it would go into a polar orbit calculated to place the mass of the planet between itself and the pulsar for the critical few seconds, just as the shuttles were doing. Martinez would be able to return to the station after less than an hour's absence.

With all the ventilators shut down the air was perfumed by the scent of decaying polymers. Empty and without lights the docks were a monumental, indistinct darkness, vast as space itself. The beam of Martinez's hand flash vanished in the blackness. At a great distance Martinez saw the glow that marked *Kayenta*'s docking port, lit not by station power but by the yacht's own power supply. Martinez placed his feet carefully against a wall and kicked off, and was pleased to find that he was straight on course for the airlock.

Two figures bulked large by the door, their feet tucked into handles on the wall, their arms reaching for Martinez. As he drifted closer, he saw they were both Torminel. They wore only shorts and vests over their thick gray and black fur, and their huge eyes, adapted for hunting at night, glittered as they tracked Martinez.

Two of Marcella's survey team, apparently.

Martinez flew into their arms, and they caught him and absorbed his momentum with ease. A furry hand closed on each of his, and placed his hands on handholds by the airlock.

"Thank you," Martinez said. He tried to shift his left hand, but the Torminel on his left kept it pinned.

The other Torminel, he saw, had a med injector in his free hand.

He barely had time to register alarm before he felt the cool touch of the injector against his neck.

And then he had all the time in the world.

There was silence in the control room, broken only by the sound of his breath, by the pulse that beat a quick march in his chest.

Severin watched from his acceleration cage as *Titan* flew toward its objective, its engines firing a last series of powerful burns that would inject it into the pulsar's accretion disk at exactly the right angle.

The colossal gravity of the pulsar would tear the ship to atoms, hurling its cargo of antihydrogen into the spinning disk. A great swath of the disk's hydrogen would be annihilated in a ferocious burst of gamma rays, energetic neutrons, and pi-mesons. A percentage of these particles would fall into the neutron star and pump up its x-ray emissions. Another percentage would fly outward into the accretion disk, heating the hydrogen there to blazing temperatures so that when it fell into the pulsar another fierce megaburst of x-rays would blaze forth.

But in between the two ferocious blasts would come eighteen minutes of silence. The mechanism that produced the life-destroying double lance of the pulsar would be shut down.

Or at least it would if Severin's calculations were correct.

"Fifteen seconds," Chamcha reported unnecessarily. The seconds were ticking down in a corner of Severin's display.

Titan was standing on a vast, blazing tail of annihilated matter. Severin was using the cargo ship as a giant torpedo, aimed straight for a deadly enemy.

"Ten seconds," Chamcha said.

"Oh, shut up," Severin murmured. Chamcha must have had more acute ears than Severin thought, because the sensor tech maintained a resolute silence right up till *Titan* vanished into the larger blip that was the pulsar and its brown companion.

Severin's attention immediately turned to the pulsar's rotating x-ray beam, which his display had colored a lurid green. The reaction was immediate: the beam, rotating twelve times per second, blazed into an emerald fury. If the beam hit Chee now, it would strip the planet down to its mantle.

Severin could only hope that the pulsar would switch off when it was supposed to.

And suddenly he thought: *the statue!*

That's how he'd work it. Frenella, the gamine, would send Eggfont the little statue of Lord Mince, and that would tip Eggfont to Mince's relationship with Lady Belledrawers.

He felt a little shiver of delight as he contemplated the perfection of the device. And, as he waited to see whether his plan for *Titan* would work, he thought about what Eggfont would do next.

There was a faint gray mist that swirled through the air, an insistent electric humming in his ears. His fingers and toes tingled as if he'd rubbed them with sandpaper. A furry animal seemed to have got lodged partway down his throat.

With a convulsive heave of his chest he tried to expel the object in his throat. He made several attempts before he realized that the animal was in fact his tongue. His mouth was absolutely dry and his tongue scraped painfully against the roof of his mouth.

He closed his mouth and tried to summon saliva. He worked his jaw and throat muscles for several long moments before he managed to produce a little moisture.

Having relieved some of his discomfort he then he tried to work out where he was. The gray mist had darkened, and the humming sound had largely faded. He could feel nothing, not even air moving against his skin. It was as if he'd been packed in cotton up to his neck.

He touched himself just to assure himself that he was still there. He felt the familiar uniform tunic, the medal of the Golden Orb at his neck, and he bent—knelt?—to feel his legs in their trousers, with the shoes still on his feet. There was something that bobbed and interfered with his right hand, and he took hold of it and realized it was his hand flash, attached to his wrist with an elastic lanyard.

At this point he came to the realization that he was in free fall. He was in darkness and in free fall and probably he had never left Chee Station: he was floating somewhere in one of its huge overdesigned open spaces.

A jolt of adrenaline hit Martinez then, a sudden hot burning along his nerves as he remembered the pulsar. If he'd never left the station, then he was still vulnerable to the burning x-rays.

He raised his left forearm before his face and whispered, past his painfully dry tongue and through dry lips.

"Display: show time."

Yellow numerals flashed onto Martinez's sleeve, pulsing in time to the speeding of the seconds. Through the gray fog Martinez tried to fit to the numbers to the chronology of the last days, and with a chill of horror he realized that the pulsar's beam should have struck nearly five minutes before.

Without willing it he began patting himself again, as if in search of a wound. Partway through the action he realized its absurdity, but he couldn't make himself stop until he had assured himself, again, that his parts were all where they were supposed to be.

He didn't feel as if he'd been blasted through with x-rays. He felt strange, with the gray fog drifting past his eyes and the deep electric hum a distant presence in his ears, but he didn't feel ill.

He tried to remember what might have happened to put him in this situation. He recalled leaving Command with Lord Ehl and the last of the station crew. He couldn't remember anything that happened after that.

Then, with a song of relief that chorused in his bones, he remembered Severin. Severin must have succeeded in his effort to switch off the pulsar.

Good old Severin! he thought wildly. Severin had come through! It made Martinez want to sing the "Congratulations" round from *Lord Fizz Takes a Holiday*.

Instead he wiped his mouth and tried to summon saliva into his mouth. The yellow seconds ticked by in his sleeve display. He still couldn't remember how he got here.

He wondered if there had been an accident, but he thought not. An accident would have resulted in more damage, not least to him.

Martinez remembered the hand flash hanging off his wrist, and he reached for it and switched it on, pointing it above his head. The beam vanished into the darkness without encountering anything. He panned the beam down, and at a downward angle the beam found a wall painted a dark gray. Martinez tracked the beam along the wall until he encountered a large sliding cargo door, on which were painted in white the numerals 7-03. Which meant Warehouse Three, Docking Bay Seven.

Bay Seven was where *Kayenta* had been docked. Apparently he'd got as far as *Kayenta*'s berth before . . . before what?

Perhaps the yacht had left early and stranded him on the station. But in that case, it seemed odd that Martinez had no memory of it.

The cargo door, Martinez saw, had handholds by it. There wasn't a lot of point in hanging in midair and waiting for something to happen. Perhaps he ought to get to somewhere where he could *make* something happen.

He swam awkwardly in midair until he had his back to the cargo door, then he took off his shoe and hurled it as hard as he could in the opposite direction.

Equal and opposite reaction, though unfortunately the masses were unequal. Martinez began drifting very slowly toward the cargo door while pitching backwards in long, slow circles.

Several seconds later, he heard a clang as the shoe hit something on the other side of the cargo bay.

The act of throwing his shoe left him panting and out of breath. Something was clearly wrong with him physically. It was going to take him a while to reach the cargo door, and while he slowly drifted and tumbled he thought about how he had got here, and why he couldn't remember.

He had been drugged, he thought. He had been drugged and only the fact of his veins being full of narcotics had prevented him from realizing it earlier.

He probably hadn't been shot with an amnesia drug: some drugs could cause amnesia as a side effect. It was one of those odd reactions that couldn't be predicted.

As he tumbled, his hair flying in front of his eyes, he felt a sudden chill as he realized what had happened.

He'd been drugged and left to be killed by the pulsar, but the person who had left him to die hadn't known that *Titan* was going to shut off the pulsar, and Martinez had survived.

Which meant that as soon as the person who had left him to die worked out that the x-ray beam hadn't hit the station, he was going to have to come back and finish the job.

Martinez almost wrenched his neck as his head darted around, staring into the darkness for his attacker. Who could be lurking on the station, and loading his gun or his med injector even now.

The wall rotated closer and Martinez reached out to grab one of the handholds by door 7-03. The drug almost made him miss, but he touched it with his fingertips and that slowed his rotation slightly, so that when he hit the wall and bounced he was able to make another grab for a different handhold and brought himself to a stop.

It occurred to him that his hand flash was very possibly making a target of him, so he turned it off and tried to think where he needed to go next.

The person who had tried to kill him could have hidden easily on the nearly deserted station, and then from hiding to strike as Martinez moved from the elevator to *Kayenta*. Wherever the assassin had hidden, though, there was only place the assassin would be *now*, and that was in shielded Ring Command, where he'd be safe from the pulsar. Martinez should definitely avoid Ring Command.

The problem was that Ring Command had all he'd need to establish contact with the outside world: control of all communications systems, the antennae, and the power supply to start everything up.

Martinez tried to think where else he might find communication gear, and then sudden light dazzled his eyes.

Across the docking bay, the floodlights at one of the ports had just lit. A ship had docked, and was powering up the airlock through its electrical connection.

Kayenta! Martinez felt his heart give a leap. *Kayenta* had come to rescue him!

He gathered his legs under him, feet pressed against the wall, ready to spring to the airlock and greet his rescuers the second they came through the door.

And then he hesitated. There was something about the sight of the distant airlock, surrounded by its glowing lights, that caused him unease.

Why? Why was someone trying to kill him?

He hadn't stopped to think about that before.

He had found out that the Meridian Company had been committing massive fraud. That might be worth killing over, he supposed, though assassination seemed an immoderate response.

It was so uncivilized. They might at least have tried to bribe him first.

Kayenta, in any case, wasn't a Meridian Company ship; it belonged to the Chee Company, owned principally by the Martinez family. Lady Marcella Zykov, a Chee company executive and a near relation of the Martinez clan, was on board and in charge.

But there were Meridian Company personnel on board, to inspect and help restart the station. Some of them might have been given orders concerning Martinez and his health.

Perhaps, Martinez thought, he shouldn't jump straight to *Kayenta*. Perhaps he should first hide, and then see who left the airlock, and if they had large firearms.

He glanced around the huge space and found no place to hide. To his left was a corridor, rather distant, that led to Ring Command—and he didn't want to go that way, in case an assassin was heading in the other direction. To the right was a huge bulkhead door that led to another cargo bay, but that had been closed and it would require station power to open it.

That left one or another of the warehouse spaces. 7-03 was as good as any.

The cargo door would require a power assist, but each warehouse space also had a personnel hatch, and the hatches were extremely well balanced so that weightless people could use them. Martinez pushed toward it and snagged a handhold. The hatch opened in complete silence. Martinez slipped in feet-first, then drew the hatch partly shut, so that he still had a view of *Kayenta*'s airlock.

The air in the warehouse was close and had an aromatic scent, something like cardamom. Martinez looked over the interior with his hand flash and saw it was packed with standardized shipping containers, all in bright primary colors, stacked atop one another and strapped down to keep them from drifting. Because the weightless conditions permitted it, the containers were strapped to all six surfaces, including those he might arbitrarily designate as walls and ceiling. There was very little open space in the room, only a straight square tunnel that stretched to the back and would permit containers to be maneuvered in and out.

No real place to hide, he realized. He should have chosen another storage room.

Martinez was considering a jump to the next warehouse when he heard the airlock doors open and knew it was too late. He peered over the sill of the hatch and strained to see past the glare of the floodlights. There were at least three figures in the airlock, and from their barrel torsos and squat, powerful legs, Martinez knew the first two for Torminel.

An alarm rang in Martinez's mind. He didn't like the sight of those Torminel, and even though he couldn't remember why, he knew very well that he didn't want to show himself now.

"Lord Inspector?" one of the Torminel called, lisping the words past her fangs. "Lord Inspector, are you there?"

The sound echoed and died away in the vast empty dockyard.

The Torminel turned on bright flashlights and began shining them across the big room. Martinez remembered how well their huge eyes could see in the darkness and shrank from the hatch sill.

"Look!" the other Torminel called. "It's his shoe!"

While the Torminel were inspecting the mystery of the shoe that was floating by itself in the vast room, Martinez drew the hatch shut and locked it down. Unfortunately the manual lock mechanism could be worked from the outside, but at least when it began to move it would provide a bit of warning.

What Martinez really needed was a weapon.

He panned along the wall with his hand flash and saw a small locker on the wall. He drifted toward it and opened it.

In the locker were spare light globes, a pad of stick-on labels for shipping containers, a pair of fire extinguishers, pairs of work gloves, large reels of strapping for holding down crates and containers, and tough plastic clamps for tying down the strapping. But what chiefly attracted Martinez's attention were the two shiny aluminum pry bars, each as long as his leg, that were used to wedge the containers into their proper places. They were octagonal in shape until the business end, where they narrowed into flat, slightly curved blades.

Martinez reached for one and drew it from the clips that held it in place. It was lighter than it looked. He held the bar under his arm and drew out a reel of strapping, thinking that perhaps he could use it to tie down the hatch mechanism and keep anyone from opening the door.

He closed the locker and drifted back to the hatch. He studied the closing mechanism and then the reel of tape.

Martinez did his best, tangling the mechanism in a web of tape. The work left him out of breath, and he panted for air while he gripped one of the handholds next to the door. Once he'd caught his breath he moved to one end of the door, so that he wouldn't be caught like a fly in a bottle once the door opened. He tucked his feet into the handgrips at the top of the door—the metal chilled his stockinged foot—

and he took a few experimental swipes with the pry bar. It cut the air with a particularly nasty hiss. With his feet planted firmly he could be confident in doing a heartening amount of damage if he needed to.

And then he turned off his hand flash and waited in the darkness.

Time passed, over twenty minutes according to the flashing yellow numerals on his sleeve display. From time to time he took a swipe with the bar to keep his muscles warm and supple. He was feeling better and thought that the drug had almost worn off.

Martinez had begun to believe that the Torminel had gone elsewhere when he heard a thump on the far side of the wall on which he was standing, followed by a metallic clang on the door. His heart gave a leap and he felt the sizzle of adrenaline along his nerves. He made sure his feet were firmly in the handholds and cocked the pry bar over his right shoulder.

There were another pair of thuds against the door or the warehouse wall. Martinez felt the vibration against his feet. He heard speech but couldn't make out the words. Then the latching mechanism began to creak open.

And jammed. The tangle of strapping was working.

He heard voices from the other side, more urgent this time, and then there was a kind of slamming noise from the mechanism, and the hatch popped open.

Martinez blinked in the light pouring in from one of the big hand lights. He was suddenly aware of sweat patches all damp under his raised arms, and the fact that his mouth was painfully dry again. He couldn't understand why there was so much moisture under his arms when there was none in his mouth.

"It's him," one of the Torminel said in an urgent whisper. "He did that, with the tape. He's in there."

"My lord?" the other called. "Lord Inspector? You can come out. Everything is safe."

There was a moment in which the Torminel waited for an answer, and then he told his partner, "Hold my legs while I go in."

Martinez felt cramps in his feet where they were braced in the handholds. He shifted the pry bar slightly.

The Torminel appeared in the hatch. His back was to Martinez, and he was peering dead ahead, into the long tunnel surrounded on all sides by shipping containers. He had a flash in one hand and a stun baton in the other. A light on the stun baton winked amber.

The blade of the pry bar caught the Torminel in the side of the head and hurled him violently into the hatch coaming. The flash flew from his limp fingers and tumbled, casting wild strobing lights across the expanse of the warehouse. The stun baton tumbled in another direction. A line of irregular crimson blobs flew from the Torminel's head and resolved themselves as they flew into perfect spherical droplets of blood.

Someone pulled the Torminel out of the hatchway, and then there was a sudden *squalling* noise that froze Martinez's blood, and the second Torminel appeared. Her hair stood on end in her rage and her head looked like a giant puffball with huge angry dark eyes and ferocious white fangs. She knew where Martinez was and one hand clutched the sill of the hatch while the other stabbed at Martinez with a stun baton.

Martinez snatched his shod foot out of the hand grip to keep the baton from hitting his leg. He swung the pry bar, but the Torminel managed to cushion the impact with one arm. She flew against the hatch coaming anyway, but bounced back with the stun baton thrust out like a sword blade. Martinez swung again, awkward with only one foot to anchor him.

This time he connected with the Torminel's head, but the impact jerked his stockinged foot out of the hand grip and sent him spinning slowly toward a side wall. The Torminel drifted limp in the hatchway. Her fur had relaxed and become smooth again.

Martinez hit a bright orange shipping container and bounced. Before he got clear he managed to push wildly with one foot and get himself on a trajectory more or less for the hatchway. His breath rasped in his throat. The pry bar felt slippery in his hands.

Somebody pulled the unconscious Torminel out of the hatchway. Martinez's heart sank at the knowledge that there was at least one more assassin.

One of the stun batons floated toward him and he snatched at it with one hand, careful to take it by the safe end. He looked at the read-outs and saw that the baton was charged and set at maximum.

He looked at the hatch again and he saw that he was going to miss it, drifting past without getting close enough to seize one of the hand grips. For a few seconds Martinez was going to be in plain sight of whoever was on the other side, and then he would have to wait till he hit the far wall and push off again.

His fists clenched around his two weapons. His eyes were fixed on the hatchway as it came closer, at the erratic bouncing light that danced through the opening.

He drifted slowly past and narrowed his eyes against the light. On the other side, Lady Marcella Zykov wrestled with the limp form of one of the Torminel, trying to lash him down to a hand grip with his own belt.

Marcella looked at Martinez and with an expression of great annoyance on her face reached into a pocket and came up with a pistol. The pistol was small and made of plastic and red in color.

Martinez threw the stun baton at her. The reaction sent him tumbling slowly backwards. The pistol made a vast noise and Martinez felt the heat of the bullet flying past his chin.

Martinez craned his neck frantically to keep track of what was happening. The recoil of the pistol had pitched Marcella backwards, rotating at much greater speed than Martinez, and as her legs flew up to replace her head the stun baton struck her on the back of the thigh. There was a crackle and a sudden electric snap of ozone. Marcella gave a cry and spasmed into a foetal ball as her stronger flexors won the battle over her extensors.

Martinez lost track of her as he flew past the hatch. He hit a shipping container and jumped off for the hatch. When he arrived at the hatch he checked his motion, lined up on the distant form of Marcella tumbling end over end, and launched himself for her, the pry bar poised over his head like a battle-axe.

A battle-axe wasn't needed. He caught Marcella easily enough and found that she was frozen into her ball and barely conscious. With some effort he levered the pistol out of her clenched fist.

Once he had the pistol he was reasonably certain that he was in possession of the only firearm on Chee Station.

He intended to take full advantage of this position.

"It was panic," Martinez said. "Marcella saw the message and panicked."

"That would be the message addressed to me, from my friend Bernardo in the Ministry," Terza said. The scent of her breakfast coffee floated agreeably on the air. "The message informing me of the principal owners of the Meridian Company, and that in the emergency we had rather forgotten about. Lord Ehl got a look at the contents as it got routed through the communication center at Meridian Command, and he intercepted it." She lifted the corner of a napkin tucked around a pastry in a silver wire basket, and offered it. "This is the last. Would you like it?"

"Thank you," said Severin. He took the pastry and waved away a pair of large purple bees that were hovering over the jam. He spread jam and turned to Martinez. "But why did Lord Ehl intercept the message?"

"Because his name was on it. He owns something like four percent of the company, and his Tir-bal clan owns more. They're clients of Lord Pa's Maq-fan clan, which is heavily invested as well."

Terza sipped her coffee. "Every time Lord Ehl approved an overrun on Chee Station, his net worth grew that much larger."

Severin chewed his pastry as he gazed through the oak alley at the distant Rio Hondo. The rising sun had outlined each leaf in silver. The shadows beneath the oaks were very dark. Tart and sweet flavors exploded on his tongue.

"I suppose Marcella's name was on the list, too," he said. "That's why she panicked."

"Marcella had two percent," Martinez said.

"Two percent hardly seems worth killing someone over," Terza said.

Martinez looked at her. "Marcella's very focused on outcomes," he said. "Processes don't matter as much, they're just a means to an end. If there's a reward, she grabs it; if there's an obstacle, she removes it. We should have taken note of the efficient way she cleaned Lord Mukerji of his money.

"And once she was caught," he added, "once I got her gun and had her tied up with strapping, she began working toward a new outcome, which was a lessening of her sentence. She confessed to everything and blamed it all on Pa and Lord Ehl. So that once I'd restarted the station, and had Lord Ehl and a company of military constables come up from the surface, I was able to put Lord Ehl under arrest as soon as he stepped out of the elevator doors."

"So far," Severin said, "our players have four percent and two percent. Who really owns the Meridian Company?

"Allodorm had ten percent," Terza said. "He got it when the Meridian Company bought out his engineering company. But the largest owner was Cassilda's father, Lord Zykov, followed by other members of the Zykov clan."

Surprise murmured through Severin's veins. "Must be interesting to be robbed by your in-laws," he said.

"Not just robbed," Terza said. "Lord Zykov's plan was to bankrupt the Chee Company, then buy the remnants with its own money."

Severin turned his head at the sound of footsteps coming out of the house. Lord Roland Martinez strolled toward them, a wry smile on his lips. He was dressed casually, in a blousy white cotton shirt and faded red baggy drawstring trousers.

"How's Cassilda?" Terza asked.

"The doctor says she won't deliver for a few hours yet."

Cassilda had gone into labor the previous evening.

Roland leaned over his brother's shoulder to peer into the silver wire breakfast. "Didn't you leave me any breakfast?"

"We didn't know you'd be coming," Terza said. "You can call the kitchen."

"I don't have a comm unit on me," Roland said. "Gare, could you call the kitchens and get me some pastry and a pair of shirred duck eggs?" He sat heavily in one of the whitewashed metal chairs.

Martinez, looking resigned, made the call on his sleeve comm. Severin finished his pastry and freshened his coffee from the silver pot. He looked at Roland.

"Yes?" Roland said.

"Beg pardon?"

"You had a question on your face."

"I—" Severin started, and then decided to take a more tactful approach. "It must be hard for you, with Lady Cassilda about to give birth and her father sitting on a pile of money he's stolen from you."

Roland grinned. "No. That makes it easier, actually." He poured himself a cup of coffee, then looked at Severin.

"It's very simple," he said. "I don't know if Lord Zykov gives a damn about Marcella or not, but if he ever wants to see his daughter again, or see his grandchild ever, he'll do exactly what we tell him."

Severin felt his mouth hanging open, and closed it. "I see," he said.

"You understand," Roland said, "Allodorm and Lord Pa got too greedy—they didn't just cheat *us*, they cheated the *Fleet*. And that's not civil or corporate law, that's a violation of the Praxis, and the penalties are torture and death. Cassilda had some stock in the Meridian Company, and we can make a case against her."

Can you do that? Severin wondered.

Apparently he could.

"Any case is amazingly easy," Roland went on. "There's scads of information—we had inspectors on the ground, and other informers as well, but they all reported to Marcella, and she sat on the information and told the others that adjustments were being made."

"Plus of course the conspirators are all informing on one another," Martinez said.

"So in return for not laying the information before the Legion of Diligence," Roland said, "we're asking for half of Lord Zykov's interest in the company, plus all of Lord Pa's, and Allodorm's, and Marcella's. Lord Pa will pay us a large fine, enough to knock him flat for some time. Marcella and Allodorm will be locked up until we're reasonably certain we've wrung out of them every zenith they possess."

"And the *first* thing I did," Martinez said, "was procure Lord Ehl's resignation from the Fleet."

Roland shrugged, as if this was of no concern. "We'll have his shares, too, of course." He adopted a contemplative look. "I'm thinking of having Lord Zykov pass over his elder daughter and make Cassilda his heir. So everything comes to us in the end."

Martinez looked at his brother with dissatisfaction showing in his narrowed eyes. "Speaking as the one who got shot at," he said, "I'm not sure I'm happy that everyone gets off with just fines and spankings. I wonder what you'd have done if Marcella had actually succeeded in killing me."

Again Severin felt a line of tension between the two brothers, and thought again that the two might not like each other very much.

Roland very coolly raised his coffee to his lips. "I suppose that after Marcella was good and bankrupt," he said, "she might have had an accident."

Martinez looked at Roland for a moment, then shrugged. Terza reached over and patted his hand.

"Thanks to Commander Severin," she said, "we're not concerned with that outcome."

"Not so much me," Severin said, "as—" Then, "Commander?"

A tight little smile played across Roland's lips. "You will not find us ungrateful, my lord. We've spoken to the higher echelon of the Exploration Service here, and explained in some detail our considerable admiration for you, and my understanding is that you'll be promoted and given *Surveyor* once it's out of dock."

Severin goggled at him. *You can do that?* he wondered.

"In addition," Martinez said, "my father is granting you several sections of prime Chee real estate. You should have a very rich estate to retire to when you leave the Service."

"And I believe there will be a substantial cash reward from the Chee Company," Roland said. "Though I understand we'll have to get your superiors' permission."

Severin's mind whirled. "But," he said, "I didn't really do that much."

"Other than save the Chee Company's entire investment?" Roland smiled.

"I shut off the pulsar, yes, but the reason that Captain Martinez hasn't joined the Great Masters is that he insisted that what I did with *Titan* remain secret. I didn't have anything to do with that."

Martinez grinned. "I had to protect my investments," he said.

Severin looked at him. "My lord?"

"I took the money I won from Lord Mukerji and bought every futures contract on Chee from the poor fools Allodorm and Pa sold them to," Martinez said. "Some will be worthless, no doubt, but I believe I'm now a rich man." He leaned back in his chair and smiled out at the world. "I've never actually had money of my own before," he said. "It's all come from Terza or my father. I wonder what I'll do with it?"

"The possibilities are staggering," Terza murmured.

Martinez looked at his brother. "And of course some of the fines from the conspirators will go to reimburse the investors who were cheated."

Roland was annoyed. "They were gambling, really. It's not as if they can complain. It was the *futures* market, for all's sake."

"Roland." The voice was firm.

Roland flapped his hands. "Very well. If you insist. But if you go on this way, you're going to make me wish Marcella were a better shot."

Martinez smiled. "I seek only perfect justice for the entire universe."

"Ah!" Roland said happily. "My shirred eggs!"

A smiling white-haired servant brought Roland his breakfast and another basket of pastry. Terza looked at Severin from over the rim of her coffee cup.

"Will you be seeing Lady Liao while *Surveyor*'s in dock?" she asked.

Severin darted a glance to the opal ring on his finger. *Does* everyone *know?* he wondered.

"I've sent her a message," he said. "But I imagine a lot will depend on her schedule." *And her husband's.*

"Any plans for the meantime?" Terza asked.

"Well," Severin said, "I'm thinking of building a puppet theater."

There was a moment of silence broken only by the calls of morning birds.

"That's original," Martinez murmured.

"Do you think so?" Severin asked. "Let me tell you about it."

And, as the long morning stretched before them, he did.

—*With thanks for technical assistance to*
Michael Rupen, Kristy Dyer, and Bob Norton

honorable mentions: 2004

Daniel Abraham, "Flat Diane," *F&SF*, October/November.
John Aegard, "The Great Old Pumpkin," *Strange Horizons*, October 25.
Brian W. Aldiss, "Tarzan of the Alps," *Postscripts*, Spring.
Barth Anderson, "Live from the Volgograd Blackout," *Abyss & Apex*, March/April.
Colleen Anderson, "Hold Back the Night," *Open Space*.
Kevin J. Anderson, "The Bistro of Alternate Realities," *Analog*, June.
Poul Anderson, "The Bog Sword," *The First Heroes*.
Lou Antonelli, "Circe in Virto," *Astounding Stories*.
———, "I Got You," *Bewildering Stories*, May.
———, "Pen Pal," *RevolutionSF*, July 2.
———, "The Rocket-Powered Cat," *RevolutionSF*, December 24.
Lynette Aspey, "Sleeping Dragons," *Asimov's*, September.
Neal Asher, "Strood," *Asimov's*, December.
———, "The Veteran," *Asimov's*, June.
A. A. Attanasio, "Zero's Twin," *F&SF*, June.
Kate Bachus, "Echo, Sonar," *Strange Horizons*, November 8.
Paolo Bacigalupi, "The Pasho," *Asimov's*, September.
Kage Baker, "The Catch," *Asimov's*, October/November.
———, "Leaving His Cares Behind Him," *Asimov's*, April/May.
———, "Recipes for the Professional Writer," *Mother Aegypt*.
———, "Silent Leonardo," *ReVisions*.
Dale Bailey, "The End of the World as We Know It," *F&SF*, October/November.
Neal Barrett Jr., "Tourists," *Flights*.
William Barton, "The Gods of a Lesser Creation," *Asimov's*, August.
———, "Moments of Inertia," *Asimov's*, April/May.
———, "Though I Sang in My Chains Like the Sea," *Asimov's*, October/November.
Lee Battersby, "Ecdysis," *Andromeda Spaceways*, February/March.
———, "Father Muerte and the Rain," *Aurealis*, 33/34/35.
Stephen Baxter, "Between Worlds," *Between Worlds*.
———, "The Burster," *The Hunters of Pangaea*.
———, "The Mandate of Heaven," *The Hunters of Pangaea*.
———, "Periandry's Quest," *Analog*, June.
———, "The We Who Sing," *Microcosms*.
Peter S. Beagle, "Quarry," *F&SF*, May.
Elizabeth Bear, "This Tragic Glass," *SCI FICTION*, April 7.
Greg Beatty, "Aliens Enter the Conversation," *Fortean Bureau*, March.
———, "Cycle of Predator and Prey," *Full Unit Hookup*, #5.
Chris Beckett, "Tammy Pendant," *Asimov's*, March.
———, "We Could Be Sisters," *Asimov's*, October/November.
Van Begamundré, "Out of Sync," *So Long Been Dreaming*.

Gregory Benford, "Blood's a Rover," *Cosmic Tales*.
———, "The First Commandment," *SCI FICTION*, May 19.
———, "Station Spaces," *Space Stations*.
———, "Twenty Two Centimeters," *Oceans of the Mind*, XIV.
Paul Berger, "Voice of the Hurricane," *Zeppelin Adventure Stories*.
Judith Berman, "The Fear Gun," *Asimov's*, July.
———, "The Poison Well," *Black Gate*, 7.
Ruth Berman, "The Buried Sword," *Asimov's*, June.
Ilsa J. Bick, "The Key," *SCI FICTION*, August 11.
Michael Bishop, "The Angst of God," *F&SF*, October/November.
———, "The Sacerdotal Owl," *Weird Tales*, March/April.
Terry Bisson, "Super 8," *SCI FICTION*, November 24.
Russell Blackford, "Idol," *Oceans of the Mind*, XIII.
———, "The Name of the Beast Is Number," *Microcosms*.
James P. Blaylock, "Hula Ville," *SCI FICTION*, November 3.
Steven Bratman, "Deletion," *Analog*, January/February.
Damien Broderick, "Yggdrasil," *Synergy SF*.
Eric Brown, "A Choice of Eternities," *Postscripts*, Spring.
Tobias S. Buckell, "Aerophillia," *Zeppelin Adventure Stories*.
———, "Her," *Fortean Bureau*, January.
———, "Necahual," *So Long Been Dreaming*.
Emma Bull, "De La Tierra," *The Faery Reel*.
Michael A. Burstein, "Time Ablaze," *Analog*, June.
Richard Butner, "The Wounded," *Crossroads*.
Jack Cady, "Fog," *F&SF*, December.
Orson Scott Card, "Keeper of Lost Dreams," *Flights*.
James L. Cambias, "The Eckener Alternative," *Zeppelin Adventure Stories*.
———, "See My King All Dressed in Red," *Crossroads*.
Jay Caselberg, "Herd Mentality," *ReVisions*.
Robert R. Chase, "Turing Test," *Asimov's*, June.
E. I. Chin, "The Moment of Truth," *On Spec*, Autumn.
Richard Chwedyk, "In Tibor's Cardboard Castle," *F&SF*, October/November.
Matthew Claxton, "The Anatomist's Apprentice," *SCI FICTION*, July 14.
———, "Changing of the Guard," *SCI FICTION*, December 8.
Brenda Clough, "How the Bells Came from Yang to Hu Bei," *The First Heroes*.
Deborah Coates, "Articles of a Personal Nature," *SCI FICTION*, February 4.
James Cobb, "Dancers of the Gate," *Space Stations*.
Brenda Cooper, "Savant Songs," *Analog*, December.
———, "Star Gardens," *Oceans of the Mind*, Spring.
———, "The War of the Flowers," *Strange Horizons*, January 12.
Elizabeth Counihan, "The Star Called Wormwood," *Asimov's*, December.
Albert E. Cowdrey, "A Balance of Terrors," *F&SF*, July.
———, "The Name of the Sphinx," *F&SF*, December.
———, "Rapper," *F&SF*, February.
———, "Silent Echoes," *F&SF*, April.
Ian Creasey, "Best in Show," *Oceans of the Mind*, XIII.
Julie E. Czerneda, "The Franchise," *Space Stations*.
———, "Out of China," *ReVisions*.

Jack Dann, "Bugs," *Postscripts* 2.
———, "Good Deeds," *Concqueror Fantastic*.
Colin P. Davies, "The Girl with the Four-Dimensional Head," *Andromeda Spaceways*, April/May.
Russell Davis, "Countdown," *Space Stations*.
Stephen Dedman, "Changes," *Andromeda Spaceways*, April/May.
———, "Twilight of Idols," *Conqueror Fantastic*.
———, "The Whole of the Law, *Andromeda Spaceways*, June/July.
Charles de Lint, "Riding Shotgun," *Flights*.
A. M. Dellamonica, "The Children of Port Allain," *On Spec*, Summer.
———, "The Dream Eaters," *The Faery Reel*.
———, "Ruby, in the Storm," *SCI FICTION*, October 6.
Bradley Denton, "Sergeant Chip," *F&SF*, September.
Lena DeTar, "Steep Silence," *Asimov's*, June.
Paul Di Filippo, "Observable Things," *Conqueror Fantastic*.
———, "Shadowboxer," *Amazing*, December.
Thomas M. Disch, "The White Man," *Flights*.
Cory Doctorow, "Anda's Game," *Salon*, November 15.
——— & Charles Stross, "Unwirer," *ReVisions*.
Rudi Dorneman, "Embers," *Realms of Fantasy*, October.
Gardner Dozois, George R. R. Martin, & Daniel Abraham, "Shadow Twin," *SCI FICTION*, June 9
L. Timmel Duchamp, "The Gift," *Love's Body, Dancing Through Time*.
———, "The Heloise Archive," *Love's Body, Dancing Through Time*.
Thomas R. Dulski, "To Emily on the Ecliptic," *Analog*, July/August.
Andy Duncan, "Zora and the Zombie," *SCI FICTION*, February 4.
Greg Van Eekhout, "Native Aliens," *So Long Been Dreaming*.
———, "Tales from the City of Seams," *Polyphony* 4.
Scott Edelman, "My Life Is Good," *Crossroads*.
George Alec Effinger, "Walking Gods," *Conqueror Fantastic*.
Suzette Haden Elgin, "Honor Is Golden," *Analog*, May.
———, "We Have Always Spoken Panglish," *SCI FICTION*, October 27.
Carol Emshwiller, "All of Can Almost," *SCI FICTION*, November 17.
———, "The Library," *F&SF*, August.
———, "My General," *Argosy*, May/June.
Esther M. Friesner, "Johnny Beansprout," *F&SF*, July.
Nancy Etchemendy, "Nimitseahpah," *F&SF*, January.
Gregory Feeley, "Arabian Wine," *Asimov's*, April/May.
———, "Giliad," *The First Heroes*.
Keith Ferrell, "A Reunion," *Asimov's*, December.
Sheila Finch, "Confessional," *F&SF*, January.
———, "So Good a Day," *F&SF*, May.
Charles Coleman Finlay, "After the Guad Chrysalis, *F&SF*, June.
———, "The Factwhore Proposition," *Futurismic*.
———, "The Ill-Fated Crusade," *Paradox*, November.
———, "Pervert," *F&SF*, March.
———, "The Seal Hunter," *F&SF*, January.
Eliot Fintushel, "Gwendolyn Is Happy to Serve You," *Asimov's*, July.

———, "Women Are Ugly," *Strange Horizons*, June 21.
Karen Fishler, "Country Life," *Realms of Fantasy*, June.
———, "Misson Memory," *The Third Alternative*, Spring.
———, "Safe Haven," *The Infinite Matrix*, March 12.
———, "Someone Else," *Interzone*, September/October.
Richard Flood, "Jagganath," *Asimov's*, March.
Jeffrey Ford, "A Night in the Tropics," *Argosy*, January/February.
———, "The Annals of Eellin-Ok," *The Faery Reel*.
———, "Jupiter's Skull," *Flights*.
Hugh David Francis, "The Three Hats of Mutt and Jeff," *Albedo*, 28.
Peter Friend, "The Christmas Tree," *Asimov's*, December.
Esther M. Friesner, "Johnny Beansprout," *F&SF*, July.
Gregory Frost, "Tengu Mountain," *The Faery Reel*.
Susan Fry, "Father Gregori's Relic," *The Third Alternative*, Autumn.
Neil Gaiman, "The Problem of Susan," *Flights*.
Stephen Gallagher, "Restraint," *Postscripts*, Spring.
R. Garcia y Robertson, "Long Voyage Home," *Asimov's*, February.
———, "Stuck Inside of Mobile," *F&SF*, July.
Tom Gerencer, "Almost (But Not Quite) Heaven," *Realms of Fantasy*, October.
David Gerrold, "Dancer in the Dark," *F&SF*, April.
Laura Anne Gilman, "In the Aftermath of Something Happening," *Oceans of the Mind*, XII.
———, "Site Fourteen," *ReVisions*.
Lisa Goldstein, "Finding Beauty," *F&SF*, October/November.
Kathleen Ann Goonan, "Dinosaur Songs," *Asimov's*, July.
Theodora Goss, "The Wings of Meister Wilhelm," *Polyphony 4*.
Gavin J. Grant, "Hold Tight," *Strange Horizons*, August 23.
Glenn Grant, "Burning Day," *Island Dreams*.
John Grant, "Has Anyone Here Seen Kristie?," *The Third Alternative*, Summer.
———, "Q," *SCI FICTION*, October 20.
Dominic Green, "Three Lions on the Armband," *Interzone*, Spring.
Daryl Gregory, "The Continuing Adventures of Rocket Boy," *F&SF*, July.
Eileen Gunn, "Coming to Terms," *Stable Strategies and Others*.
——— & Leslie What, "Nirvana High," *Stable Strategies and Others*.
James Gunn, "Elixir," *Analog*, May.
George Gutheridge, "Nine Whispered Opinions Regarding the Alaskan Secession," *F&SF*, July.
Sally Gwylan, "Rapture," *Strange Horizons*, March 15–March 22.
Andrea Hairston, "Griots of the Galaxy," *So Long Been Dreaming*.
Joe Haldeman, "Faces," *F&SF*, June.
Elizabeth Hand, "Wonderwall," *Flights*.
Charles L. Harness, "In the Catacombs," *Weird Tales*, January/February.
———, "Polly," *Synergy SF*.
Guy Hasson, "The Perfect Girl," *Dreams of Aspamia #12*.
John G. Hemry, "Small Moments in Time," *Analog*, December.
Howard V. Hendrix, "Once Out of Nature," *Microcosms*.
Ernest Hogan, "Jailhouse Rock," *Cosmic Tales*.
Sarah A. Hoyt, "Ganymede," *Oceans of the Mind*, XII.
———, "What She Left Behind," *Asimov's*, March.

Tanya Huff, "Finding Marcus," *Sirius, the Dog Star.*
Matthew Hughes, "The Hat Thing," *Asimov's*, September.
———, "Falberoth's Ruin," *F&SF*, September.
———, "Mastermindless," *F&SF*, March.
———, "Relics of the Thim," *F&SF*, August.
Rober J. Howe, "Miscarriage of Justice," *Salon*, March 24.
Alex Irvine, "Down in the Fog-Shrouded City," *Polyphony 4.*
———, "For Now It's Eight O'Clock," *Strange Horizons*, March 1.
———, "Peter Skilling," *F&SF*, September.
———, "Volunteers," *Sci Fiction*, July 28.
L. Blunt Jackson, "Early Adopters," *Challenging Destiny*, June.
Trent Jamison, "Porcelain Salli," *Aurealis*, 33/34/35.
Matt Jarpe, "Chicken Soup for Mars and Venus," *Asimov's*, August.
———, "Language Barrier," *Asimov's*, February.
——— & Jonathan Andrew Sheeen, "The Bad Hamburger," *F&SF*, December.
Michael J. Jasper, "Coal Ash and Sparrows," *Asimov's*, January.
———, "Redemption, Drawing Near," *Interzone*, November/December.
Phillip C. Jennings, "The Saint," *Asimov's*, March.
Jan Lars Jensen, "Bodily Surrender," *Synergy SF.*
Kij Johnson, "Elfrithe's Ghost," *Realms of Fantasy*, August.
———, "The Empress Jingu Fishes," *Conqueror Fantastic.*
Michael Kandel, "Time to Go," *F&SF*, October/November.
Ian Donald Keeling, "The Archer," *Realms of Fantasy*, June.
James Patrick Kelly, "The Dark Side of Town," *Asimov's*, April/May.
———, "Serpent," *F&SF*, May.
———, "The Wreck of the Godspeed," *Between Worlds.*
Kay Kenyon, "Acid Test," *Talebones*, Winter.
———, "The Executioner's Apprentice," *ReVisions.*
John Kessel, "The Baum Plan for Financial Independence," *SCI FICTION*, March 24.
Stephen King, "Lisey and the Madman," *McSweeney's Enchanted Chamber of Astonishing Stories.*
Ellen Klages, "The Green Glass Sea," *Strange Horizons*, September 6.
Fruma Klass, "Two More for Tolstoi," *Synergy SF.*
Judy Klass, "We'll Have Manhattan," *Asimov's*, April/May.
Sean Klein, "Five Guys Named Moe," *SCI FICTION*, February 25.
Eric Kotani, "Orbital Base Fear," *Space Stations.*
Nancy Kress, "My Mother, Dancing," *Asimov's*, June.
Bill Kte'pi, "You Can Walk on the Moon if the Mood's Right," *Strange Horizons*, November 22.
———, "David Bowie's *Mars Triptych*," *Fortean Bureau*, October.
Marc Laidlaw, "Flight Risk," *SCI FICTION*, April 21.
Jay Lake, "The Algebra of Heaven," *Full Unit Hookup*, Spring.
———, "Adagio for Flames and Jealousy," *Fortean Bureau*, June.
———, "Benedice Te," *Challenging Destiny*, June.
———, "Daddy's Caliban," *The Third Alternative*, Autumn.
———, "Dreams of the White City," *Interzone*, September/October.
———, "The Dying Dream of Water," *Flytrap*, November.
———, "The Git, the Dog, the Fish, and the Gray," *Electric Velocipede*, #6.
———, "A Mythic Fear of the Sea," *Aeon One.*

———, "The Rose Egg," *Postscripts*, Spring.
———, "Those Boiled Bones," *Abyss & Apex*, January/February.
———, "The Water Castle," *Realms of Fantasy*, August.
Geoffrey A. Landis, "Perfectible," *Asimov's*, October/November.
———, "The Resonance of Light," *ReVisions*.
Alexis Glynn Latner, "BLU 97-032D," *Analog*, June.
Tanith Lee, "Elvenbrood," *The Faery Reel*.
———, "Israbel," *Realms of Fantasy*, April.
———, "Midnight," *Weird Tales*, March/April.
———, "Moon-Wolf," *Asimov's*, August.
———, "Stalking the Leopard," *Realms of Fantasy*, June.
Tim Lees, "Relics," *The Third Alternative*, Spring.
Stephen Leigh, "Among the Pack Alone," *Sirius, the Dog Star*.
David D. Levine, "Charlie the Purple Giraffe Was Acting Strangely," *Realms of Fantasy*, June.
———, "Love in the Balance," *Zeppelin Adventure Stories*.
———, "Where Is the Line," *Talebones*, Summer.
Marissa K. Lingen, "Another Hollywood Miracle," *Fortean Bureau*, November.
Jane Lindskold, "Keep the Dog Hence," *Sirius, the Dog Star*.
Kelly Link, "The Faery Handbag," *The Faery Reel*.
Ken Liu, "The Algorithms for Love," *Strange Horizons*,
Karin Lowachee, "The Forgotten Ones," *So Long Been Dreaming*.
Elizabeth A. Lynn, "The Silver Dragon," *Flights*.
J. Annie MacLeod, "Gasoline," *F&SF*, September.
John G. McDaid, "The Ashbazu Effect," *ReVisions*.
Jack McDevitt, "Act of God," *Microcosms*.
———, "The Mission," *Crossroads*.
———, "Windows," *Cosmic Tales*.
Ian McDowell, "They Are Girls, Green Girls," *Realms of Fantasy*, October.
———, "Under the Flag of Night," *Asimov's*, March.
Maureen F. McHugh, "Oversite," *Asimov's*, September.
Patricia A. McKillip, "Out of the Woods," *Flights*.
———, "Undine," *The Faery Reel*.
Danith McPherson, "The Forever Cup of Coffee at Bitsy's Café," *RevolutionSF*, July 23.
Gregory Maguire, "The Oakthing," *The Faery Reel*.
devorah major, "Trade Winds," *So Long Been Dreaming*.
Barry N. Malzberg & Bill Pronzini, "Intensifed Transmogrification," *Conqueror Fantastic*.
Louise Marley, "Night Shift," *Talebones*, Winter.
Paul Marlowe, "Krasnaya Luna," *Oceans of the Mind*, XIV.
Holly Wade Matter, "The Russian Winter," *Aeon One*.
John Meaney, "Blood and Verse," *Aeon One*.
Paul Melko, "Carousel Safari," *Fortean Bureau*, October.
———, "Doctor Mighty and the Case of Ennui," *Strange Horizons*, February 16.
———, "Fallow Earth," *Asimov's*, June.
———, "Strength Alone," *Asimov's*, December.
China Miéville, "Reports of Certain Events in London," *McSweeney's Enchanted Chamber of Astonishing Stories*.
Steven Millhauser, "Cat 'n' Mouse," *The New Yorker*, April 19–26.
David Moles, "The Ideas," *Flytrap*, May.

Devon Monk, "Fishing the Edge of the World," *Talebones*, Summer.
David Morrell, "Perchance to Dream," *Flights*.
John Morressy, "The Courtship of Kate O'Farrissey," *F&SF*, October/November.
———, "The Long Run," *F&SF*, May.
James Morrow, "Martyrs of the Upshot Knothole," *Conqueror Fantastic*.
Richard Mueller, "I Am the City," *F&SF*, September.
———, "Jew if by Sea," *F&SF*, May.
Derryl Murphy, "More Painful than the Dreams of Other Boys," *Open Space*.
Chris Nakashima-Brown, "Prisoners of Uqbaristan," *Strange Horizons*, October 18.
Ruth Nestvold, "King Orfeigh," *Realms of Fantasy*, October.
———, "The Tirasias Project," *Futurismic*.
R. Neube, "Following Orders," *Asimov's*, August.
Kim Newman, "Soho Golem," *SCI FICTION*, October 13.
Larry Niven, "Chicxulub," *Asimov's*, April/May.
———, "Storm Front," *Analog*, March.
Garth Nix, "Heart's Desire," *F&SF*, January.
Jerry Oltion, "The Common Cold," *Analog*, March.
Susan Palwick, "Beautiful Stuff," *SCI FICTION*, August 18.
Paul Park, "No Traveller Returns," *PS Publishing*.
Richard Parks, "The Great Big Out," *Fantastic*, Summer.
———, "A Hint of Jasmine," *Asimov's*, July.
———, "The Right God," *Realms of Fantasy*, August.
Severna Park, "The Three Unknowns," *SCI FICTION*, March 3.
Holly Phillips, "In the Palace of Repose," *H. P. Lovecraft's Magazine of Horror*, Spring.
Steven Popkes, "This Old Man," *Asimov's*, January.
———, "The Old Woman and the Moon," *Realms of Fantasy*, October.
Tim Powers, "Pat Moore," *Flights*.
Tim Pratt, "Hart and Boot," *Polyphony 4*.
———, "In a Glass Casket," *Realms of Fantasy*, October.
———, "Terrible Ones," *The Third Alternative*, Spring.
——— & Michael J. Jasper, "Helljack," *H. P. Lovecraft's Magazine of Horror*, Spring.
Tom Purdom, "Palace Resolution," *Microcosms*.
———, "Romance for Augmented Trio," *Asimov's*, February.
Jean Rabe, "Aurica's Streetcar," *Space Stations*.
Irene Radford, "First Contact Café," *Space Stations*.
Kit Reed, "Yard Sale," *Asimov's*, July.
Robert Reed, "A Change of Mind," *Asimov's*, October/November.
———, "A Plague of Life," *Asimov's*, March.
———, "The Condor's Green-Eyed Child," *F&SF*, August.
———, "Daily Reports," *Asimov's*, July.
———, "Designing with Souls," *F&SF*, September.
———, "How It Feels," *F&SF*, May.
———, "Mere," *Golden Gryphon Press*.
———, "Opal Ball," *F&SF*, October/November.
———, "River of the Queen," *F&SF*, February.
———, "Wealth," *Asimov's*, April/May.
Mike Resnick, "A Princess of Earth," *Asimov's*, December.
———, "El Presidente," *Argosy*, May/June.

———, "Keepsakes," *Between Worlds.*
———, "Travels with My Cats," *Asimov's*, February.
——— & Susan R. Matthews, "Swimming Upstream in the Wells of the Desert," *ReVisions.*
——— & Dean Wesley Smith, "A Moment of Your Time," *Microcosms.*
Alastair Reynolds, "Everlasting," *Interzone*, Spring.
M. Rickert, "Cold Fires," *F&SF*, October/November.
———, "Many Voices," *F&SF*, March.
Chris Roberson, "In the Frozen City," *Electric Velocipede*, #7.
———, "Red Hands, Black Hands," *Asimov's*, December.
Michaela Roessner, "Del Norte," *Conqueror Fantastic.*
———, "Inside Ourside," *SCI FICTION*, March 3.
Deborah Roggie, "The Enchanted Trousseau," *Lady Churchill's Rosebud Wristlet*, 14.
Benjamin Rosenbaum, "Biographical Notes to 'A Discourse on the Nature of Causality, with Air-Planes' by Benjamin Rosenbaum," *Zeppelin Adventure Stories.*
———, "Embracing-the-New," *Asimov's*, January.
———, "The Valley of Giants," *Argosy*, January/February.
Mary Rosenblum, "Jumpers," *SCI FICTION*, July 21.
———, "Songs the Sirens Sing," *Asimov's*, January.
———, "Tracker," *Asimov's*, April/May.
Christopher Rowe, "Whether to Go Through," *Electric Velocipede*, #7.
Kristine Kathryn Rusch, "After the Fall," *Sirius, the Dog Star.*
———, "Collateral Damage," *Asimov's*, August.
———, "Forest for the Trees," *Asimov's*, July.
———, "Paparazzi of Dreams," *Analog*, November.
Don Sakers, "The Slow Train," *Analog*, October.
James Sallis, "Under Construction," *Crossroads.*
William Sanders, "At Ten Wolf Lake," *Asimov's*, February.
Pamela Sargent, "Follow the Sky," *Space Stations.*
———, "Spirit Brothers," *Conqueror Fantastic.*
———, "Venus Flowers at Night," *Microcosms.*
Robert J. Sawyer, "Mikeys," *Space Stations.*
Robert Scherrer, "Extra Innings," *Analog*, November.
Lawrence M. Schoen, "The Sky's the Limit," *Zeppelin Adventure Stories.*
Aaron Schutz, "Being with Jimmy," *Asimov's*, December.
Nisi Shawl, "Deep End," *So Long Been Dreaming.*
Michael Shea, "The Growlimb," *F&SF*, January.
Robert Sheckley, "The Forest on the Asteroid," *F&SF*, April.
Charles Sheffield, "McAndrew and the Law," *Cosmic Tales.*
Lucius Shepard, "The Blackpool Asensions," *Polyphony* 4.
———, "Jailbait," *Two Trains Running.*
———, "Viator," *Night Shade Books.*
Mark Shainblum, "Endogamy Blues," *Island Dreams.*
Gary W. Shockley, "Of Imaginary Airships and Miniscule Matter," *SCI FICTION*, November 10.
William Shunn, "Why I think I'll Be Staying Home Tonight," *Electric Velocipede*, #6.
Robert Silverberg, "The Colonel Returns to the Stars," *Between Worlds.*
———, "The Sorcerer's Apprentice," *Flights.*
Meredith Simmons, "The Guardian," *Asimov's*, August.

———, "Brethren," *Asimov's*, September.
Vandana Singh, "Thirst," *The Third Alternative*, Winter.
———, "Three Tales from Sky River: Myths for a Starfaring Age," *Strange Horizons*, January 5.
Jack Skillingstead, "Reunion," *On Spec*, Spring.
———, "Rewind," *Asimov's*, February.
———, "Scatter," *Asimov's*, October/November.
———, "Transplant," *Asimov's*, August.
Bud Sparhawk, "Clay's Pride," *Analog*, July/August.
Hugh A. D. Spencer, "Problem Project," *Interzone*, November/December.
Wes Spencer, "Moon Monkeys," *Cosmic Tales*.
Brian Stableford, "A Chip off the Old Block," *Postscripts 2*.
———, "Nectar," *Asimov's*, January.
Michael A. Stackpole, "Serpent of the Station," *Space Stations*.
Daniel Starr, "Why I Am Not Gorilla Girl," *Strange Horizons*, April 5.
Allen M. Steele, "The Garcia Narrows Bridge," *Asimov's*, January.
———, "High Roller," *Cosmic Tales*.
———, "Home of the Brave," *Asimov's*, December.
———, "Incident at Goat Kill Creek," *Asimov's*, April/May.
———, "Liberation Day," *Asimov's*, October/November.
———, "Moreau^2," *Analog*, July/August.
———, "Shady Grove," *Asimov's*, July.
———, "Thompson's Ferry," *Asimov's*, March.
Bruce Sterling, "The Spider's Amazement," *Amazing Stories*, #603.
James Stevens-Arce, "Smart Bomb," *Fortean Bureau*, January.
James Stoddard, "The Battle of York," *F&SF*, July.
Peter Straub, "Mr. Aickman's Air Rifle," *McSweeney's Enchanted Chamber of Astonishing Stories*.
Charles Stross, "The Concrete Jungle," *The Atrocity Archieve*.
———, "Elector," *Asimov's*, September.
———, "Survivor," *Asimov's*, October/November.
——— & Cory Doctorow, "Appeals Court," *Argosy*, May/June.
Beverly Suarez-Beard, "Lady of the Birds," *Paradox*, November.
Michael Swanwick, "The Last Geek," *Crossroads*.
———, "The Word That Sings the Scythe," *Asimov's*, October/November.
Judith Tarr, "The God of Chariots," *The First Heroes*.
Mark W. Tiedemann, "If Anyone Should Ask," *Andromeda Spaceways*, April/May.
———, "Rain from Another Country," *F&SF*, September.
———, "The Wind at Carthage," *Oceans of the Mind*, XIV.
Lois Tilton, "The Gladiator's War: A Dialog," *Asimov's*, June.
———, "The Matter of the Ahhiyans," *The First Heroes*.
Karen Traviss, "An Open Prison," *On Spec*, Winter.
———, "Views of a Remote Country," *On Spec*, Spring.
Harry Turtledove, "Coming Across," *Flights*.
———, "The Horse of Bronze," *The First Heroes*.
Steven Utley, "A Paleozoic Palimpset," *F&SF*, October/November.
———, "Babel," *Analog*, March.
———, "Invisible Kingdoms," *F&SF*, February.

———, "Little Whalers," *RevolutionSF*, December 17.
Rajnar Vajra, "The Ghost Within," *Analog*, November.
———, "Layna's Mirror," *Analog*, October.
Jeff VanderMeer, "How Ben Jobi Song Came to Rule Phagenia," *Argosy*, May/June.
———, "Three Days in a Border Town," *Polyphony* 4.
———, "Shark God Versus Octopus God," *Postscripts* 2.
James Van Pelt, "A Wow Finish," *Amazing*, November.
———, "Echoing," *Asimov's*, December.
———, "Where and When," *Zeppelin Adventure Stories*.
Katherine Vas, "Your Garnet Eyes," *The Faery Reel*.
Ray Vukcevich, "Human Subjects," *Amazing Stories*, #603.
Howard Waldrop, "The Wolf-man of Alcatraz," *SCI FICTION*, September 22.
Nicholas Waller, "Enta Geweorc," *Interzone*, November/December.
Ian Watson, "An Appeal to Adolf," *Conqueror Fantastic*.
———, "Lambert, Lambert," *Weird Tales*, March/April.
Peter Watts, "A Word for Heathens," *ReVisions*.
Don Webb, "Ool Athag," *Crossroads*.
Janeen Webb, "The Lion Hunt," *Conqueror Fantastic*.
———, "Red City," *Synergy SF*.
K. D. Wentworth, "Blessed Assurance," *RevolutionSF*, May 21.
———, "Evangel," *Oceans of the Mind*, XII.
Michelle West, "Huntbrother," *Sirius, the Dog Star*.
———, "To the Gods Their Due," *Conqueror Fantastic*.
Leslie What, "Love Me," *The Infinite Matrix*, June 8.
———, "Magic Carpets," *Strange Horizons*, July 26.
———, "The Mutable Borders of Love," *Amazing*, November.
———, "Why a Duck," *Zeppelin Adventure Stories*.
Lori Ann White, "Silver Land," *Aeon One*.
Ysabeau S. Wilce, "The Biography of a Bouncing Boy Terror!," *Asimov's*, September.
———, "Metal More Attractive," *F&SF*, February.
Liz Williams, "Century to Starboard," *Strange Horizons*, February 2.
———, "Loosestrife," *Interzone*, Spring.
———, "The Marsella," *Electric Velocipede*, #7.
———, "The Pale," *Strange Horizons*, August 30.
———, "Skindancing," *The Banquet of the Lords of Night*.
———, "The Water Cure," *Andromeda Spaceways*, August/September.
Walter Jon Williams, "Logs," *Aeon One*.
———, "The Tang Dynasty Underwater Pyramid," *SCI FICTION*, August 4.
Jack Williamson, "Black Hole Station," *Space Stations*.
Eric M. Witchey, "The Mud Fork Cottonmouth Expedition," *Polyphony* 4.
———, "The Tao of Flynn," *Realms of Fantasy*, April.
Paul Witcover, "Left of the Dial," *SCI FICTION*, September 1.
Gene Wolfe, "Calamity Warps," *Realms of Fantasy*, April.
———, "Golden City Far," *Flights*.
———, "The Last Pilgrim," *The First Heroes*.
———, "The Little Stranger," *F&SF*, October/November.
———, "Monster," *Amazing Stories*, #603.
———, "Prize Crew," *Postscripts*, Spring.

———, "Pulp Cover," *Asimov's*, March.
Jim Young, "Ultraviolet Night," *F&SF*, March.
Melissa Yuan-Innes, "Growing Up Sam," *Open Space*.
Timothy Zahn, "The Battle of Space Fort Jefferson," *Space Stations*.
———, "Proof," *Amazing Stories*, #603.
George Zebrowski, "Nappy," *Conqueror Fantastic*.